SECOND SETS OMNIBUS

ALY BECK

bitter notes
ALY BECK

When the first note fills the tension-filled room, every woman's panties in a five-hundred-foot radius disintegrate into thin air, and the crowd goes wild.

Poof! Panties be gone! Mine included.

A sigh of admiration rocks through every patron present when the six-foot God towering over the crowd on stage opens his fucking mouth, belting out the first note of the night. Heaven shines down. God himself shows up and blesses us individually. Miracles happen simultaneously. The lead singer's smooth, gravelly voice echoes through the bar, and we all die a happy collective death.

What an excellent way to go.

My mouth falls open. Watching the stage from my chair at the front door, I sit on the edge of my seat in anticipation, letting their sound envelop me entirely like a hug. With my arm resting against the small podium raised in front of me, my admission stamp hovers mid-air over the back of some poor patron's hand, waiting for their approval into the bar.

Four of the hottest guys I've ever seen demand attention on stage, drawing every eye to their performance. Proving to me they aren't the same four guys I knew in high school. And hell, it's not even their performance that draws everyone's attention to them. It's the way they command the stage, like kings ruling over their subjects.

Kieran, the lead singer's mismatched eyes squeeze shut, and his body bows back when a particular high note slips out of his mouth, drawing us in more. His beefy body bulges and veins protrude as his fingers wrap tighter around the microphone. His jet-black hair plasters to his head from the sweat glistening across his tanned skin. He kicks a leg out and then works the stage like a pro, making love to everyone in the room. My ears rejoice in his melodies, and when I shut my eyes, I see the ghost of my past peeking through.

Kieran waltzes toward Asher, the grumpy, dirty-blond guitarist, and leans in. Asher's bushy brows raise into his forehead until a smirk pulls at his lips. His hazel eyes watch Kieran's every move until they sing a line

together, leaning into the same microphone. Asher bobs his head, belting out every note on key and in perfect harmony. Eventually, Kieran's growl echoes through the speakers, curling my damn toes.

Moisture pools in my panties when he struts to the nearly naked drummer, Rad, and ruffles his mullet as he pounds his sticks into the drums. Yeah, his curly, 1980s-era mullet, drenched in sweat. His lean body constantly moves with every pound of the drum, and his dark eyes sparkle with life, something mischievous hiding in their depths when he looks out at the crowd. A dark tattoo crawls up his chest and neck, displaying a design I can't distinguish from here. But I've studied it before on the worst day of my life.

"It'll be okay, I promise. I'll get help," Rad's dark, faint voice echoes in my memories. I can still feel him pulling a coat over my body.

My body shudders, blinking up at the music notes and splotches of black ink dotting his neck and chest. How the fuck? Panic crawls up my throat, and bile burns on its way up.

"I'll take care of you, okay? Do you need a hospital?" he croaks, holding my hair back as I puke on the lawn of someone's home in the middle of the night as music blares in the background.

I shake myself from the awful reminder before it plays back in vivid detail, running my fingers over the knife nestled deep in my pocket. I've shoved that memory into a solid black box in the back of my brain since the night it happened when I was fifteen—four years ago. No reason to think of it now. Except him—Ashton "Rad" Radcliffe. I must have been nutty to think emailing them and inviting them to perform at the bar I currently manage was a clever idea. They're nothing more than a stark reminder of two different points in my life. Taking a deep breath, I focus on the men on stage.

A grin splits Rad's lips, and he doubles over laughing, managing to keep his rhythm when Kieran makes his way to Callum, the last person in the four-member band, strumming his bass with such concentration his tongue pokes out.

Kieran whacks Callum on the ass, jolting him from his concentration pose. His shaggy blond hair flies with his movement, falling into his pure gray eyes. Like the badass he is, he doesn't miss a note and scowls as the song ends, and the crowd formed in front of the small stage at the front of the bar erupts in whistles and cheers.

I smile at their carefree escapades and clap when they go into another song without addressing the drooling crowd. The atmosphere tonight flares when everyone jumps on their toes, throwing their hands in the air, and rocks out to the beautiful sounds of Whispered Words—my newest discovery—and possibly my worst nightmare.

My heart rate picks up, and sweat prickles at the base of my neck. I can't take my eyes off their cocky grins and swaggering steps. Girls swoon. Guys swoon. Everyone in the fucking bar swoons over them.

I've known most of these guys since high school. Well, I didn't know, know them. I knew of them—ego and all. Two years ago, we roamed the halls of Central City High School together, and then they graduated when I was a sophomore. Watching them command the stage for the second time, I can tell they haven't changed much. They've always been the same demanding pricks, making their presence known. They're larger than life. And yet, they have no idea I exist. Hell, they probably don't even know my name—not anymore, at least.

I was just the poor Central City girl showing up to school with ripped, out-of-date jeans and messy hair, not caring what they thought about me. Or anyone, for that matter. They live the good life in Lakeview, on the good side of town, with two-hundred-dollar shoes and expensive clothes, living off their mommy and daddy's money. At least, that was then. And now? I have no idea what their lives are like. But judging by the name-brand shirts and shoes, I'd say they're still doing pretty well for themselves. Even Kieran…

Kieran and I grew up together in the trenches of Central City. Once neighbors, now—he stares at me like we weren't friends hiding under the stars, talking about our tiny lives. We had experienced so much in such a fleeting time and related to one another on many levels. Even when we were little, I thought Kieran was my knight in shining armor—the hero who saved me over and over again from danger.

My heart aches at our shared memories, and I shake my head. I always wondered what had happened to my best friend, who vanished and was nowhere to be found. Every day I looked for him. In the halls of our elementary school. On the streets, we walked. Or on the shared bus we took home. But he was gone, disappeared into thin air.

It wasn't until I got to our only high school, where every student in town attended, that I learned the cold hard truth—he moved on to bigger and better things on the other side of the city, seemingly forgetting I existed. His new reality was the rich side of town, lined with mansions and money, leaving me in the poverty-stricken apartment complex with nothing but his memory.

"Ahem, bitch!" A whiny voice breaks me out of my little pity party, bringing me back to the present.

Right. I'm at work—time to return to reality.

I jerk back, narrowing my eyes on the pearl-wearing, plaid skirt-toting woman standing with an unattractive sneer on her lips. Great. It's her. Tessa. My snobby bully from high school who has never decided to grow up. Ugh. Gross. She taps her fancy-ass heels on the sticky floor and scoffs at me like I'm an idiot.

"You stupid Central girl, stamp my damn hand so I can watch my man perform." A warm smile glides across her face when her crystal-blue eyes land on the boys on stage with hearts floating above her head.

More specifically, she stares at the delicious morsel singing like someone punched his puppy, and he's been crying for hours. Deep anguish lives in the depths of his voice, and I want to fucking hold it in the palm of my hands and bathe in it and keep it for myself. There's something so right about Kieran's deep voice that calls to me. Or maybe it's the nostalgia of a former friend who is now the ghost of who he was. The only thing that never changed was his love of music.

"Let me play this for you, River Blue. Mom's new boyfriend got me this," Kieran's small raspy voice utters, sitting beside me in the grass, over-looking the parking lot of our dismal existence. Setting a small, janky-looking guitar on his lap, he strums the strings, tuning them by ear, and he hums, playing me our favorite country song by Garth Brooks, as my head rests on his shoulder. Laying his head on top of mine, he plays into the night, drowning out the sounds from his apartment that I was way too young to understand.

"Right, that'll be a ten-dollar cover charge," I say, returning to reality and extending my hand while wiggling my fingers expectantly.

Glaring in my direction, her face heats. Did she expect to get into this bar for free when a popular local band was playing? Probably. She's entitled like that. But not today, Tessy-boo. Pay up or leave before I sic my bouncers on you.

"The audacity," she murmurs through clenched teeth, acting like I'm putting her out by asking for money.

Hello, it says cover charge right behind my head, bitch. Can't you read? But I remain as professional as I can when she continues her tirade on the ethics of our bar. The audacity is correct. Fuck.

I want to bang my head against the wall and crack my skull open when she murmurs more angry words under her breath, digging into her tiny purse. Her nose crinkles when she takes out a few hundred dollar bills, looks through them, and finally finds a ten in the stack. And she was complaining? Jesus. She has enough money in her purse to feed Ma and me for six months and pay all our bills. She thrusts it in my hands with a sneer and holds out her hand for me to stamp.

I raise my brow, stamping her hand. "And your ID?" I ask again, earning another huff.

"I'm twenty-one," she says, digging in her purse again. "You should know that," she hisses again, finally acknowledging we also knew each other from high school.

Sure, high school was big, but everyone knows who you are when you're a punching bag for half the school. And she's no different, seeing as she was the ringleader of it all.

"Yeah, well… this is a bar, and there's the sign to enter for the show," I say in a bored tone, pointing to the sign behind me. "You either show your ID or get an underage stamp, so they know not to serve you any booze." I shrug when she scoffs again, throwing her pretty blonde hair over her shoulder.

"Here," she grumbles again, flashing me her ID, and confirming the bitch is twenty-one.

"Thanks a bunch," I say sarcastically with a sugary, sweet grin.

Stay professional. Stay fucking professional.

This earns me a mean scowl when I throw her ID back at her, and it falls to the floor. Her blue eyes connect with mine with disdain; it would kill me if it could—cue eye roll.

Was it a classy move? Hell no. But I'm tired of these grown adults insulting me and giving me attitude because of where I live and work. Grow up, already. This isn't high school anymore.

Besides, it's not my fault my father decided to kick us out and leave us destitute when he found a new woman to put his wandering schlong in. Gross—shudders—I shouldn't think about my father's dick. Like ever. Also, fuck him for leaving us poorer than shit, forcing us to return to my mom's hometown without a penny to our name. What we've made here is all our own. We didn't need his help, and we never will.

I wave her along, getting the same reaction from her friends behind her. And the people behind them. And so on and so forth. Where's the common decency these days, people? The compassion? The respect for humankind? Nowhere.

Why would there be any here in Central City, Illinois? We're the poor people, the people breaking their backs to earn our money. At the same time, they live in huge mansions and turn their pointy noses down at us from the outskirts of the same damn town just because of our financial differences.

My wandering gaze lands on Kieran again, singing his life away into the microphone. A dreamy sigh slips between my parted lips. Sometimes I miss the boy who told me everything would be okay.

I wonder if I ever crossed his mind. Probably not. Now he lives the good life with his new stepdad in a mansion overlooking the lake. What I wouldn't give to have a conversation with him, or you know, a good romp in the backseat of my car. That would suffice, too. Because he may have been my bestie as a kid, but I always harbored an insatiable crush on the tall, dark, and handsome singer.

Ma always said I shouldn't touch poisonous things, but I can't seem to stay away from the bad boys who will bring me nothing but ruin. Getting Kieran Knight in the backseat of my car for a quickie is nothing out of the ordinary for my toxic ass. In fact, it's right on schedule.

It's happened a few times with other bands that passed through. They gave me the best two hours of my life—or, let's be honest, the best night of my life—and then they were on their way out the door with a thank you, ma'am. That's the beauty of it, though. I got mine. They got theirs—multiple times. Threesomes. Foursomes. Hell, even some fivesomes. It didn't fucking matter. Freedom liberated every inch of me. Oh, and the orgasms were nice, too. Nothing beats multiple partners at one time. Some call it being a whore, but I call it sexually freeing. Fuck the labels!

Then the sun would come up, stream through my car window, or hotel room that accommodated us for the night, and they'd move on to the next city. We didn't exchange names or numbers. It was just a simple roll in the hay. And the best part? No expectations of a relationship in the future. I have way too much going on to be in any sort of relationship. Besides, I'd never date a fucking musician. Fuck them? You bet your ass. Relationship? No. The last thing I'd want is a relationship with flighty rock stars who are unreliable. Good in the sack, sure. But on the boyfriend, girlfriend end? Nope. Thank God for birth control and condoms, or I'd be tied to them for life.

If there's one thing my ma taught me, it was to stay away from rock stars. They bring you nothing but heartache.

Now, if only my heart would continue to listen to that sage advice instead of falling head over heels… Thankfully that shit has only happened once. Past best friends don't count.

I smile when my best friend, Odette, comes bouncing into view, wrinkling her button nose at the crowd forming at the front of the small stage. Her beautiful curls bounce with every step she takes, giving her an angelic presence.

Darkness would have taken over my entire existence if I didn't have her in my life. She moved into Kieran's old apartment after he left, and we've been inseparable ever since. Her family is my second family, not by blood, but by our bond. Her mom, Korrine, helped raise me into the woman I am, constantly taking me in when my mom had to work nights. Ode's brother, Leon, is like my brother and treats me as such.

"Girl," she says, as her dark eyes scan the screaming crowd. "What is up with all the… the…" She scrunches her nose, looking back at me with her mouth gaping. "Damn suburban moms and dads in training. Is that girl wearing pearls?" She gapes, pointing to the mean girl from earlier. "By God, it's fucking Tessa, and she's wearing pearls," she murmurs, looking at me with wide eyes.

"You think she clutches them when her boyfriend suggests booty sex?" I snort when she cackles, drawing the attention of the devil herself.

Once again, Tessa's face contorts into a sneer, twisting her gorgeous face into something ugly. Eventually, her eyes drift back to the man candy on stage with a heavy swoon, and dear God, she fucking clutches her pearls as she throws her head back and sings at the top of her lungs, knowing every lyric.

"How's the first day as the head bitch in charge going?" Ode asks, leaning in to talk over the loud music. "HBIC in da house!" she hoots, shoving my shoulder playfully with a proud grin.

A laugh bursts from me, joy filling my being. I've worked long and hard since I was fifteen to get to this point. I've scrubbed toilets, removed trash, washed tables, and cleaned the floors. Slowly, I've worked toward the manager's position over the years, even at a young age. Some consider a nineteen-year-old manager impossible, but I've bled for this place. And Booker, the owner of Dead End, has always had my back like a father. Years before, he dated my mom, and I got to know him that way. Booker was the best boyfriend she ever had. They may have only lasted two years, but he forever cemented himself into my life. By age fifteen, I was begging on his doorstep for a job to start making my own money. Ma did her best, but it was never enough to keep the heat on. So, with reluctance, he started me out small, and here I am today—the manager. And my specialty? Bringing in bands from around the area to draw in more crowds and money for us.

I pull my loud best friend next to the podium, allowing the rest of the patrons to pile in. I give her a thumbs up, waving more people in line forward.

"Well, I'd say good. This is my doing." I wave a proud hand at the band on stage as more of their fans pile through the door with eager eyes.

It might sound cocky to some, but I've worked my ass off to bring Kieran and his merry band of dickbags here and all the people who follow them from venue to venue. I've stalked them on their barely-there social media, begging them to come here and play. I knew if they performed, all these suburban snobs would turn up, too. Cha-ching, money in my damn pocket. Never mind who he is to me. If it's a chance to make extra cash for my future, I'll take it.

Ode whistles, leaning an arm on my shoulder. "How the hell did you get Whispered Words to come here? They're like the hottest little band in Central Illinois right now."

I snort, waving more people along, stamping their hands, and checking their IDs. "Incentive," I say, biting the inside of my cheek when she throws her head back, laughing.

"Like pussy incentive? Because yeah, Riv, I'd say you'd give them a run for their money. Especially Kieran. I remember him from school," she murmurs through a whole-body shudder, eyeing his thick frame with lustful eyes. "He was so damn dark and mysterious. Who knew he'd end up... up there..." she says, waving a hand in his direction.

"Shut up," I say, elbowing her in the gut, causing her to burst into manic laughter. "I'm not putting out. God, what do you take me for?" I grumble at the last part, earning a few stares from the stragglers handing me their money.

"A Central City whore?" Ode chortles, earning another glare from me.

I frown, pushing my wet stamp right onto her arm. "Way to keep the stereotype going, bitch," I mumble. "Us Central girls have to stick together, especially against them." I nod toward the jumping suburban girls bobbing their heads to the music without a care. They hold their hands in the air, hoping to catch the attention of the four men rocking out on stage.

The boys are too enthralled in their music to notice the bouncing blonde elbowing her way to the front of the stage. Their eyes remain closed and focused on the euphoric sounds spilling from their fingers and vocal cords. I could watch them all day.

"I'm joking, girl," she says through a laugh, tossing her arm over my shoulders. "But in all seriousness, woman. They're like the best band on this side of the Mississippi. How the fuck did you convince the preppy assholes from the burbs to play at a place called Dead End?" She raises a brow in my direction, inspecting my face, and then she smiles. "You bitch, you used your name, didn't you?" My stomach drops at the accusation, and I quickly shake my head.

A lie rests on the tip of my tongue, eager to tell her I didn't. Because if there's one thing I'd never want to admit, it's that I used my name to get me anything in life. I resent the asshole who loaned me my last name for the past nineteen years. If I could give it back and tell him to shove it, I would.

I wave a hand at her, continuing to do my job despite her incessant yapping. "Maybe," I say, side-eyeing her when her mouth drops open in shock and flies swarm out.

Or they would if they were around. Ode is so damn shocked I pulled out the only famous piece of me—my last name. In East Point, California, my last name could get me a limo, a million dollars, and four hunky men willing to do anything for me. But here, in the middle of nowhere Illinois, it got me Whispered Words, and I call that a win in my book.

"River Blue West," she shrieks, hitting my shoulder and nearly knocking me off my stool.

I cringe at the sound of my full name and shake my head, sneaking a peek at Kieran. "Bitch, not so loud."

"I'm just surprised, is all," she says, wrapping an arm around my shoulder. "You hate your name. You hate your father and anything that involves him. Which includes your name, babe."

I scoff, rolling my eyes toward the ceiling. "Hate is a strong word when talking about the West legacy. Besides, I'm not the only loser West daddy dumped. So, I use it when it's to my advantage, like getting bands like this in the door. Besides, they never saw my face. It was only my last name. They probably think I'm a dude, anyway. Plus, I worked it out to get a commission for a good turnout." My grin grows when Ode's eyes turn to the size of saucers. "So, for every person that walks through the door and pays me, I get twenty-five percent."

And the sooner I get the money, the sooner I can get out of town and start my life. Money. College. New life. It's on the horizon for me. Freedom is in my future, far from this shitty stereotype I've had stamped on my forehead since I stepped foot in this town when I was two.

I sigh, thinking about all the shit I'd love to do but can't because I don't have enough money. I've been working here and at Dead Records, the only vinyl record shop in town, since I was fifteen, and saving like my life depends on it. I still don't have enough to escape this hell hole I call my hometown. There's nothing here for me in Central City except a shitty stereotype about where I come from and dirty looks. All I'm trying to do is survive and make it from day to day until I can plot my escape. Until then, I'll put up with the Lakeview douchebags from the suburbs, who turn their noses down at us every chance they get.

"Oh my God, you finally got Booker to agree to that? You have that man wrapped around your pinky finger, I swear," she says, shaking her head without judgment.

"What're you doing here, anyway?" I ask, stamping another hand of the elite and watching as they walk to the bar, ordering a drink.

"Leon called. Apparently, the new manager filled the damn house up, so my brother said he needed an extra hand in the kitchen. The man is cooking his life away. But I'm always willing to give, especially since it is cash under the table." She grins at that, rubbing her hands together.

"The best way to keep the government out of our damn pockets," I say in agreement, sighing in relief at the pause from new people coming in.

"Well, tell your brother I said hi, and he's doing good work. I'll be up here until people stop coming in."

"Aye, aye, Miss Manager!" she sings, slapping me on the shoulder, and disappears behind the kitchen door.

We may be a small band venue at night, but Booker runs a bar complete with delicious food and drinks during the day. Ode, my neighbor turned best friend, sometimes comes in to help her brother Leon prepare the food and serve it to our patrons. We've all worked here together for several years—Leon and I, mostly. Ode has been in and out, going to different opportunities, but she always finds her way back. Together, we're a dysfunctional family making ends meet. Even if we still live with our parents on our journey to bigger and better things.

I glance around, taking in the unruly crowd as the music continues taking me out of this world. Building and building, it finally hits the chorus, and the crowd explodes with cheers. Phones light up and lift into the air, swaying back and forth until the chorus falls into the next verse. The beauty behind music never ceases to send goosebumps down my flesh and shivers up my spine. It takes me to another world, letting me leave the one I'm in. Music lives in the soul—hell, it lives in my DNA. Literally.

My pounding heart accelerates through my lungs when my gaze snaps to the one man I've been drooling over since he cockily walked in. His piercing, mismatched blue eyes stare at me from the top of his kingdom on stage, ripping the soul from my body with one devastating look.

But does he recognize me as the girl he used to run to when his mom drank too much and kicked his ass out so she could make a buck?

Deep in the depths of my body, something shifts, leaving me a gasping mess, desperately pulling oxygen into my lungs. It feels like we're two magnetic pieces shifting into place and finding their match—once again. I only experience relief when Kieran's eyes pass over me, running over the crowd of girls shouting his name. The moment he breaks our stare, oxygen floods my body again, and my trembling fingers halt.

Kieran sings the melody of fucking angels, high in the clouds and looming over us. God, he has the voice of a damn siren that makes me want to come in my damn booty shorts before I speak to him face to face. How the fuck can I face him again when the urge to lick him all over becomes overwhelming?

As the song ends and the music dies, he holds up his toned arm, thrusting his fist into the air. Sweat pours from his head, down his chiseled face, and drips off his carved marble jawline. The lights from above shine down, creating a halo around his unsaintly head.

"How's everyone feeling tonight?" His deep, panty-soaking voice breathes through the microphone, and my damn breath leaves my lungs.

"We love you, Kieran!" some girl shouts with desperation, lifting her shirt, and revealing her tits to the world.

Soon more girls join in on the titty show parade, jiggling them as they dance, giggling their lives away. Kieran smirks, holding up a finger as he leans toward the bass player, whispering secrets between them. Callum blushes deeply, staring at their nipples like a deer caught in the headlights. He can't move away until Kieran slaps him on the back with a grin. Callum shudders, averting his eyes to the stage, and avoids the tit show with all his might.

Ah, shit. We can't have titties on display in the bar. Nudity is very frowned upon. Since I'm the damn manager, I have to force the boobs back into hiding, or more will pop out to join the party, and I can't have that.

"Put your tits away!" I shout, cupping my hands around my lips, amplifying my voice through the crowd.

The girls squeal again, shoving their shirts down. Whispering to one another, they collectively throw me dirty looks. Yeah, barbie dolls, I'm the devil for telling you to put your boobs away. Get over it. Call me the boob police or whatever; keep your damn titties in your shirt, and we'll be peachy. Have to keep this a clean operation, after all.

"What a titkill," the drummer says, leaning into his microphone with a manic grin. He hits his cymbal, tapping out the badum-tss tune.

"Booooooo!" the crowd rings, aiming their displeasure at me with dirty looks and down-turned thumbs.

"You've heard the crowd, Door Girl," Kieran says in a low, warning tone, staring right into my eyes again.

But how much can he see from the brightly lit stage? Can he see who I am? Or am I just another nameless girl to him? My heart plummets into my churning gut with indecision. Do I want him to remember the poor girl from the apartments he left behind? I have no idea. I knew I'd face him eventually, but I'll deal with that when it comes.

"We want the titties!" someone chants, making the rest of the crowd chant right along with them.

I groan, throwing my head back. Jesus Christ. Why do the titties have to come out at a concert? Why's that a thing? Can't we leave the titties out of this and not display nudity? No one bends over and exposes their ass cheeks, so why this?

"No fucking titties!" I shout, standing on my chair, raising myself above the rowdy crowd, still chanting. "You get 'em out. Then you're out! No more show! Capiche?" I raise a brow, scanning the group, frowning at me with displeasure.

Frown all you want. I won't change my mind.

"You heard the titkill!" Rad says with a laugh. "Save your pretty titties for later! Now, K, let's fucking do this." The drummer counts them in with the pound of his sticks, and they begin.

Kieran keeps his eyes on me, burning right into my soul. As the music starts, he sways to the beat, watching my every move when I jump down from the chair and stroll into the kitchen. I feel his gaze everywhere, much like a predator eyeing his prey, scurrying back into the field. It's as if he recognized the girl staring back at him with hope in her eyes. The same hope I've held loosely for the past nine years.

"I'll get the front, HBIC!" Ode says, saluting me, heading out of the kitchen with a grin and settling on a stool at the front.

Kieran's heavenly voice blasts through the house speakers again, forming goosebumps across my flesh. Resting my head against the kitchen door, I regain my breath, begging the oxygen to return. Every time that man pierces me with his stare, I swear my knees wobble and weaken under his scrutiny. Kieran has always had that cocky, dark, and mysterious cloud hovering above him, luring me in.

And that's my fucking kryptonite.

Walking silently up the steps toward the dark lifted stage, I nibble my bottom lip, careful not to spook the man leaning down. Left behind by his band members, one lone figure packs away his things with measured ease. I huff a breath, eyeing his every move. This is the closest I've been to him since they all graduated high school and started at the university across town.

Thirty minutes ago, the spotlights dimmed, and the music died. The boys took one last sweaty bow, smiling at the crowd, and said their good-byes, disappearing behind the large black curtain separating the front from the back. Despite the crowd hooting and hollering for an encore, the boys remained backstage, cooling off after a successful show.

Eventually, the crowd gave up begging for an encore by paying their tabs and calling it quits. Everyone except Tessa and the itty-bitty titty brigade, who are currently standing by the edge of the stage, looking more like desperate groupies than anything.

Squeals of delight, giggles, and whispers follow me as I head onto the darkened stage. Looking back, I smirk at Bert, our burly security guard, who disdainfully frowns at the girls. Shaking his head, he murmurs a few choice words and pins me with a look, begging for help. I snort, playfully saluting him in response. No can do, buddy. I have one last thing to do before I go home, and then I'm free.

Peering down at the hefty check made out to Whispered Words, I can't help but smile at tonight's success. I knew the raging crowd from before would be my good luck charm but fuck if I didn't make bank. And with our split, the band made bank too. No other band in the history of Dead End has made this amount on their first night here. They're definitely coming back. I could kiss their damn faces for granting me such a payday.

My eyes close on their own accord when the remnants of their songs repeatedly hum through my veins. Echoes of their fans' excited whoops and hollers play in my mind like I'm standing before them again, eagerly hearing their orgasmic sounds. A buzz encases my body, and I sigh. When I open my eyes and look around, reality crashes into me. The show plucked

its last string and thumped its last snare thirty minutes ago. All that meets my ears is the whooshing static filling my senses after a long night of loud music and screams.

A heavy sigh rocks me when I take a few more steps, watching Kieran as he packs away his equipment with angry mutters and throws his things around haphazardly—reminding me of his small temper as a kid when things didn't go his way.

His dark, messy, sweat-soaked hair falls into his eyes, and he curses at himself through several frustrated growls. It's one thing when he growls into the microphone. But up close and personal? My core heats to molten levels, heating my cheeks, and my damn toes curl in my shoes.

Kieran throws something into his guitar case with force and curls his fingers into fists. Heavy breaths rock through him, heaving his sculpted chest. My eyes fall down his body, taking in the glory of Kieran Knight. My palms sweat in his proximity, forcing me to wipe them down my jean shorts.

"You guys sounded so good tonight. Good show, Kieran," I say with an enthusiastic smile, stepping up to the massive man with his back to me.

Typically, the musicians happily stay behind for a free drink and a two-a.m. snack before they hit the road again. Usually, we chat about nothing and enjoy each other's company. Some rock my fucking world in the back-seat of my car or the back of their small tour vans. And some we just don't mesh well.

And apparently, this guy is the latter.

He grits his teeth, turning toward me with his fists clenched. Those familiar mismatched blue eyes look right through me as if he doesn't know or see me. I frown when he doesn't immediately respond, returning to packing away his stuff, and completely ignoring my existence.

Talk about rude, dickweed. I'm standing right here. I try not to let the hurt infect me and instead try again.

I clear my throat again, hoping to catch his attention without sounding too damn needy. Like, hello, I'm here to pay you, assbag. But it doesn't work. I could dance a jig with tap shoes naked, and this asshole wouldn't look my way. Maybe I should show him my tits like the girls at the show? I peer down at the bottom of my shirt, seriously contemplating showing off the girls for some attention, and shake my head. I have dignity, damn it.

"I said…"

"Yeah, well, I'm not interested. Especially some Central girl," he says in a rumbly voice, perfect for sexy dirty talk.

But this talk isn't the dirty talk I have in mind. I want him to slap my ass, call me a whore, and maybe a good girl. Not a fucking Central Girl. Jeez, this guy, too? You'd think someone formerly from this side of town would have more respect for the group of people he was once part of.

My stomach twists at the audacity of his judgmental words. The fucker didn't even look at me to know who I was or where I came from. Instead, he kneels in front of his pedalboard, inspecting them with his fingertips. He shakes his head and ignores me again by busying himself with more packing and grumbling.

A sharp arrow pierces through my chest and embeds in my heart. Old feelings burst to life inside me, and I instantly resent the fucker for ever stepping foot inside my establishment.

"I'm sorry. What the fuck did you say?" I say through clenched teeth, standing rigid.

Fuck pleasantries. Fuck professionalism.

My panties dry in an instant at his attitude, tamping down my attraction. Maybe he has changed so much, and he's no longer like the sweet boy I once knew. And instead, he has turned into the asshole everyone says he is.

A deep heat races up my neck and onto my face, burning my ears with a fury so intense I could take down the fucking devil. Tears well in my eyes, fueled by my anger.

God, be good, Riv. Be fucking good, don't curse out the fucking talent just yet.

Even though he deserves every ounce of my ire coming his way, I bite my damn tongue. I grind my teeth, fisting the damn paper check in my fist, contemplating tearing it up in his face, so he sees who he's dealing with. Maybe he'll leave, and I'll take the entire cut. Fuck him.

"You heard me," he grits out, shaking his head. Fiddling with his damn pedals, he tosses them into a case and growls, not paying me an ounce of attention. "I'm not interested. We don't want anything you're giving. You're wasting your breath."

What. The. Fuck. Not only was I friends with this asshole as a kid and went to the same school, but we spoke through email, and I used my name. Hello, River. It's written across my damn boob in tiny writing. I blink a few times, swallowing the angry words in my throat before I say anything else stupid.

His jaw twitches when he stands before me, crossing his arms over his buff chest. I swallow the gasp in my throat, the intensity residing in the depths of his eyes. Two blue eyes stare back at me, but one stands out with a brown stain carving its way through the bottom of his right iris. It's mesmerized me since we were kids, pulling me in again.

"Everything will be okay, Blue," he murmurs, putting an arm over my shoulder after setting his used guitar on the grass. "I'll always be your knight." I always grinned when he said things like that, making a little play at his last name. But it was always true at the time. He was my knight, saving me from the clutches of the bullies at elementary school. Kieran strokes the scratch down my face, given to me by some chick in the fifth grade on the playground who said I stole her kickball.

"But your ma," I say, pointing to his darkened apartment with the curtains drawn and the loud music pouring from it.

"She'll come around," he sighs, shaking his head. "She always does." I lean my head on his shoulder as we fall back into the grass, staring at the stars twinkling down at us.

That was one of the last times he held me like a precious jewel and our last encounter. After that night, a strange man kept coming around, sneaking around with Gloria—Kieran's mom. After that night, Kieran and Gloria left the apartment without a goodbye. He didn't even have the decency to knock on my door, hug me, and tell me he'd see me later. He simply vanished under the moonlight, and Ode and her family replaced him in a matter of days.

Swallowing my memories, I meet the boy who broke my heart head-on, refusing to back down and break off our stare-off. He's hot now. Way hotter than before. But his personality could use a little throat punch until he learns how to talk to me appropriately. Or anyone else, for that matter.

"You're still here?" he questions, raising a brow. He may be looking in my direction, but nothing but fury resides in his eyes. It's like he's looking through me and doesn't seem to notice I'm really here. Or human. Looking down, he continues to fiddle with a pick between his fingers, dismissing me. "Jesus," he mumbles, running a hand through his hair. "I thought I told you..."

"Yeah," I scoff, waving a hand. "You told me you don't want anything I have to offer." I hold up the paycheck in front of his face, happily watching the color drain from every inch of him when I tear it in half and then tear it into tiny pieces, throwing it in the air like little pieces of confetti. "I guess you didn't want your paycheck either. You know, the one we bargained for over email? But fuck you and your high and mighty bullshit," I spit through clenched teeth, turning on my heel and storming off the back of the stage without a look back. The heat of his burning gaze stares after me when I march down the stairs, stomping my feet into the old creaky wood.

As I round the stage next to the security guard, he holds his hand in the air. With a smirk, I high-five him, only letting my rage settle for half a second. The girls around him titter and gossip about me, and I laugh internally when Bert finally shoos them away and kicks them out of the bar.

"Way to go, boss," he murmurs with a tiny whoop, barking out a laugh when I nod my head at him. If I speak any more than I have, I'll blow a damn gasket.

My fingernails dig into the palm of my hand, leaving blood-stained crescent moons behind. As I march across the empty bar with my boss's office in mind, a familiar face joins Assface—that's his name now because he doesn't deserve the name, Kieran—on stage with a disapproving frown.

Rad looks at me without an ounce of recognition and then at his bandmate, shaking his head. If I had more time and energy, I'd ogle the lean, shirtless man hovering on stage, giving his friend a disapproving look. But I'm all out of fucks to give. They flew the coop the moment that assface dismissed me with a growl and wrist flick.

In high school, Rad sported the most ridiculous-looking mullet, pairing it with his new mustache. He's grown into his style, becoming a man all on his own. But the remnants of who he once was, has my heart squeezing when more unwanted memories pour through my mind at the sight of him, reliving one of the worst days of my life.

"Dude, what the hell did you do?" Rad says to Kieran with outrage, tinting his tone.

Stopping my retreat, I knock away the awful memories pushing at the forefront of my mind and lock them deep inside. They beg to reemerge and haunt me, but I don't let them. Long ago, I forced them down, and I never want to think about that day again. Not even with him, my hero, standing before me.

Leaning against the solid door leading to the long, private hallway, I pause to see what Assface has to say for himself because it had better be good.

My eyes narrow at the shirtless drummer, absentmindedly twirling a drumstick, pinching his face with concern. Dark eyes take me in from the stage above until he growls, focusing all his attention on the rude as fuck singer.

"Come on, man, you can't *not* be an asshole for like all of five seconds?" His shouts echo off the walls. Satisfaction soars through me at his outrage, and I smirk, watching the other guy sputter for words. "Fix it, Kieran!" he shouts, pointing at me before I slip into the long, abandoned hallway, letting the door shut firmly behind me.

Passing the bathrooms and a storage closet, I make my way down the checkered linoleum hallway before I finally make it to the back office and enter the room. The once cluttered space now sits clean and organized.

Becoming a manager didn't happen overnight. Hell, it took four years of hard, greasy work. I've been watching Booker run this place for years, taking the opportunity to learn the ins and outs of everything from staffing to taxes to buying food and alcohol. Last month, Booker took the training wheels off and let me manage it as a test to see if I could hack it. I may be too young to run a bar, but Booker trusts me with his baby. I've never been more thankful for the opportunities he's granted me. Despite my mother breaking up with him, having him in my life has been a godsend. I don't know where I'd be financially if it weren't for him suggesting this was a possibility.

The silence stretches around me when I walk into my shared office and lean against the once-cluttered desk—gripping the edges to collect myself. In ten seconds, I need to slip back out of this office with a new check and present them with their money.

Even though they're dicks. Okay, huge dicks.

This is business, and I need their business to continue to grow. The bigger their band gets, the more money I get, and the faster I can run away from this town to my dream college a few states away. All I have to do is survive community college and work two jobs. Easy peasy.

I swallow my damn pride and lean over to collect the company checkbook and write a new check out to the band.

To the Whispered Words, you sack of shits, here's the money I owe you —$1,000.00

I sigh, rub my tired eyes, and flip to the next check. As much as they deserve the first one, written with all my rage, I make a new check with their correct name and a much friendlier tone.

Whispered Words, $1,000.00.

As I rip the first check out to throw out, the office door slams open in a rush, shutting with a heavy thud. An embarrassing squeal leaves my lips as I stare into the same eyes that have left me breathless for many years.

Glazed-over eyes take me in, somehow looking slightly less harsh and judgmental. This time, Kieran doesn't look down at me with disdain or disgust. Nope. It vanished from his expression. His eyes linger down my body, taking in the ripped shorts I stuffed my flat ass into and the tight black shirt clinging to my body. He swallows hard, slowly drifting his gaze up my torso and resting them on the words—River and manager resting on my tit.

"I bet you wish you looked at my tits before you dismissed me, huh?" I growl, crossing my arms over my chest, blocking his view.

Snapping his gaze up to mine, a renewed sense of anger ignites in the back of his eyes.

"If you would have just fucking told me you were the goddamned manager," he scoffs again, throwing his hand in the air like this is all my fault.

What an assface. Seriously? All the oxygen leaves my lungs, renewing my rage.

"Like that would have made a fucking difference?" I growl back, pushing his hard chest two times. Much to my satisfaction, I knock Kieran back a few steps, catching him off guard. His eyes bulge at me when I curl my fingers in his shirt, holding him upright. "You didn't even give me the time of day. Maybe you should learn some respect, Knight," I hiss his name like a curse, never wanting to speak it again. It feels foreign on my tongue, having not been uttered for so many years.

My Knight—the boy who swooped in and saved my pitiful ass from the bullies around the apartment complex and at school. He saved me more times than I can count and was my closest ally until he disappeared.

Something sparkles in the depths of his eyes. He gives a knowing glance when he looks down at me again and reads my name before meeting my eyes again, searching for the answers. All the color drains from his face, and he shakes his head with confusion. Swallowing hard, he licks his lips with a mist glazing over his eyes. His breaths hiccup until he finally returns to himself, and the realization settles in. Every inch of gruffness he displayed before disappears, and before me is the Kieran I knew when I was a kid.

"It's you," he whispers softly, easing the rugged plains of his face, almost disbelieving. His eyes scan my face like he's trying to memorize every inch. "Fucking Callum. I wished he had told me who he was emailing," he murmurs, shaking his head. Shadows lift from his eyes, and a lightness breaks through, bringing back the carefree knight I once knew.

"Tell me now," he whispers in a softer tone, leaning down so our noses touch and our lips rest a millimeter apart. I'd beg him to close the distance and fuse our lips if I didn't loathe his existence right now. "Tell me now, River Blue," he says the last part so softly I swear I'm getting whiplash.

Anger? Happy? Horny? Who knows? This guy is a friggin enigma I should run far away from. In fact, I should high-tail it out of this office before I do anything stupid. Like, fuck him. Now that would be a huge mistake. I glare into his beautiful, mismatched eyes, drawing me into his dangerous web. Piece by piece, I fall deeper into his gaze.

Holy disintegrating panties. If I don't remove myself from this situation, bad things will happen. Or good things, depending on how you look at it.

Sweat breaks out on my neck, lifting the hairs. His eyes dilate, almost turning black with desire. My fingers tighten on his shirt, torn between throwing him out of the room and having him bend me over. Right here. Right fucking now.

"I am River West, the manager of Dead End," I rasp, licking my lips. His eyes follow the movement, and he steps even closer. "Here is your damn check. Maybe we can do business again," I say in a breathless voice, loosening my grip on his sweat-soaked shirt and shoving the check into his chest.

Now—this is the moment I should try to back away and fully uncurl my fingers from his shirt instead of standing there eagerly awaiting his next move. I really should go home. Because, you know, he's an asshole, and I shouldn't put up with it. He dismissed me, yet I want to bang him into next week. Just call it scratching an itch and leave it at that.

So, it shouldn't surprise me when he grabs my wrist and clucks his cocky as fuck tongue at me. A smirk lifts the edge of his lip, yanking me forward and pulling my entire front into his. My eyes narrow, dangerously close to stabbing the fucker in the dick for even thinking he can manhandle me. I palm the knife in my pocket, ten seconds away from yanking it out and threatening his manhood. But then he looks at me—really looks at me, taking me in.

My breaths pick up, a strange sensation tingling across my skin. I soften against the rugged plains of his body, soaking in the way he feels against me once again. When he looks down at me, something strange sparks in his eyes, and I can't place the soft expression. His wide eyes drift to where our bodies fuse, where a weird possessiveness vibrates through his chest in the form of a growl, and something stiff pokes into my belly.

My breath shudders and my mind spirals out of control. How can we go from wanting to rip each other's hair out to wanting to tear each other's clothes off? Huh? This whole situation is bat shit crazy, yet my panties cling to my eager pussy, ready to fucking receive him—traitorous hussy.

He bites into his bottom lip and nods approvingly. His meaty grip weaves through my ponytail, ripping my head back with a sharp yank. Embarrassment tints my cheeks when rogue moans leak between my lips, and his rough grip rips my roots out.

Rock stars and their dirty mouths and expert tongues hold me hostage and weaken my damn legs, proving once again to be my fucking kryptonite.

Kieran leisurely holds me by my damn ponytail, gently tugging as he stuffs the check into his jeans pocket. Every inch of my body is apparently attracted to assholes like him. Proving to me I can never get enough. But it's him—Kieran. And that leaves me with conflicting feelings. WHYYYYYY???? Why does it have to feel so damn good and bad and wrong all at the same time?

"Yeah," he groans, getting in my face. "I think we can do business, but not in the future. Right now. We have some fucking business to finish."

The entire world tilts when Assface slams his lips into mine, and fucking seals our fate with his wild tongue diving into my mouth. I loosen my grip on his shirt entirely, dragging my nails through his shaggy black locks. He grunts into my mouth when I scratch his scalp and dig my nails in deeper, loving how his massive body shivers against mine.

His teeth sink into my bottom lip, dragging it out and sucking it. I swear my eyes roll so far into the back of my head I see my damn brain—if I had one, that is. I melt when a metallic taste explodes on my tastebuds, and he thrusts his tongue back into mine, and I moan.

Fuuuckkkk. It's been a hot minute since I've gotten some, and let's just say I'm thirsty, and Kieran is the tall glass of 'What the fuck am I about to do?' I've been craving.

So, I internally make the call. We fuck. We leave. End of fucking story. Just like all the other musicians who have come through. He's a dick. But I'm goddamn horny.

"This doesn't mean anything," I growl out, trying to shove him back to take control, but it does nothing. He's a damn, immovable brick wall keeping me trapped.

Using his grip on my ponytail, he forcefully spins me, pinning me against the edge of my boss's desk. My hips cut painfully into the sharp wood as he jerks my neck to the side, extending it until pain erupts.

I shiver through the delicious sensation exploding through my body when his warm fingers trail up under my shirt, stopping against the ribs near my boob. My heart beats like a damn drum inside my chest, waiting for him to make his next move. Come on, asshole. Do something already.

A small, desperate whimper leaks through my tightly pressed lips when he leans over me, pressing his hard chest into my back. And that's not the only thing that's hard about him. His warm breaths brush against my ear when he chuckles, tightening his grip around my ribs and grinding himself against my ass. His breaths echo in my ear when his wet tongue rolls over my earlobe until he finally latches on and sucks it into his mouth.

"This means everything, River Blue," he murmurs, and my heart cracks in half at the massive emotions soaring through me. It's the name he called me so many years ago.

Sliding his fingers beneath my bra, I gasp when he pinches my nipple between his fingertips and thrusts my ass into his hard dick. "Fuck, River Blue," he grunts, squeezing harder. "Where have you been?" he whispers again, shaking his head. "I can't believe… It didn't even cross my mind that it was you. The girl from my past."

"Where I've always been," I moan when he kneads my entire tit in his hand like dough. "You were the one who left without a word." Hurt leaks into my voice, and he stops, pressing his forehead into my shoulder. "You didn't even say goodbye."

"Let me make it up to you, then," he murmurs against my neck. "Let me show you how much I've missed you."

Kieran doesn't waste a moment when he flicks the button to my shorts and pulls them down my legs to my ankles. He uses his leverage to force me over the desk, and there's not a damn thing I can do about it.

"All soaked for me?" he whispers in my ear, pulling my thong to the side and letting his fingers explore my soaked core. "I want to hear you say it, River Blue." I shiver at the sound of my stupid full name, the one I hate so damn much, falling from his lips.

His fingers go up and down through my slick folds but never plunge in. My back arches in desperation, silently begging him to fuck me before I do it my own damn self.

"Quit playing, Kieran," I moan when his fingers lightly circle my clit in lazy circles. I'm about to bite his damn fingers if he doesn't get me off. "And fuck me like you hate me already!" I cry out in desperation when one finger enters me and swirls around.

"Then admit it," he whispers, nipping at my earlobe. "Admit that you're gushing for me, and only me. Admit it." My pussy clamps around his finger with every word he speaks, begging this asshole to do me in.

"Yeah, I'm wet for you. Now, what the fuck are you going to do about it?" I hiss, jerkily turning my head to the side to stare back at him.

His beautiful eyes dilate, and he looks me square in the eyes. A sly smirk picks up the left side of his lips before he jams his fingers so far inside my pussy that I come on the spot, seeing white stars. I heave a breath, trying to drag oxygen into my sputtering lungs. Sweat trickles down my spine when his fingers continue their delicious assault.

"Good girl. That's what I thought," he murmurs. "You're going to take my cock, River Blue. And you're going to cum all over it again and again." Possession takes over his voice, dipping it into a deep growl.

My eyes roll into the back of my head. Like breathing life into me, every inch of my body comes alive for the first time in months under his rough touch. Goosebumps erupt across my flesh, and my toes curl into the worn-out linoleum. This is what I'm talking about. Now, slap my ass and tell me I'm a good fucking girl, and we'll be peachy.

"Whatever you say, Assface." I pant when the sound of a condom wrapper ripping fills the air, and my damn pussy clenches around nothing.

"I have a fucking name, River," he whispers my name into my ear like a fucking prayer he's preparing to chant for eternity. "And I want you to fucking scream it. Say it with me," he grunts, rolling on the condom with one hand, securing my hair, and keeping me still with the other. He kicks my feet apart, forcing my ass to arch into the air even more. "Say it. Say, Kieran. Say my name, the one you used to. I want to hear it fall from your lips," he says through clenched teeth, rubbing the tip of his dick through my folds, sending a thrill of shivers down my spine. "Say it, for the love of all things holy, River! Say my goddamn name so I can fuck you over this desk."

Everything inside me says to walk away, no matter how good this feels. Kieran is a walking, talking disaster. The moment I say his name out loud, it will solidify what we had so long ago.

The memory of my first kiss floats to mind. Kieran and I played in the apartment pool late in the evening alone. One second, he was splashing me; the next, his lips were on mine. Before I could react, he had pulled away with a blush and quickly ran home. Leaving me there to consider what had happened. The next time I saw him, he acted like it didn't happen, and we were just friends like we always had been.

"My Knight," I rasp through shuddering breaths.

Every muscle in my body contracts when he surges forward, growling like a beast and burying himself so deep inside me that I swear my cervix brushes his tip, and I meet God himself behind my eyelids. White static takes over my vision. Stars burst. The fucking angels sing their hallelujahs! I try to keep my moans at bay but fuck it. That won't happen.

"Holy fuck, Kieran," I say through a shuddering moan, my mouth gaping open.

"That's right, scream it for the entire bar to hear," he grunts, slamming his hips against mine repeatedly until the sound of flesh hitting flesh fills the office above my loud moans. "Let them know who's giving you the best fuck of your life."

I grip the edge of the desk with all my might when it scratches against the floor, leaving indents and scrapes.

"Touch yourself," Kieran begs through a rasp. "Cum on my cock. Do it!" he demands, grabbing my wrist and forcing my fingers to swirl around my aching clit with heavy pressure. "Good fucking girl," he hisses when my pussy contracts around him, and I gasp for air. "Cum," he demands in a single growl, picking up his pace.

With one demand from his gravelly voice, I fucking detonate like a bomb, contracting around him until he stills behind me and moans so loudly with satisfaction that it fills the air. I'm sure everyone and their mom down the block heard precisely what we were up to. Our heavy breaths echo through the room, and his grip on my hair finally loosens.

"Well, Assface," I retort through heavy breaths, returning to the name I initially chose for him. "That was quite satisfactory. I'd give you a six," I say through a lazy grin when his body stiffens against mine.

That's right. You can't waltz back into my life like you're my damn savior again—no way in hell. Maybe I should add the finger guns and a thumbs up to really sell how I'm feeling. My body sags, and every ounce of stress evaporates. This was precisely what I needed to clear my mind.

"A six? I'm worth more than a six," he scoffs into the crease of my neck. His hands wander down my body again, and he pinches my nipples through my bra, sending electricity through my entire body.

"Nah, just a six," I whisper. He kneads my breasts through my bra, drawing more want from my needy body. If I weren't so pissed at him, I'd say fuck it and go another round.

"That performance was way more than a six," a new voice comes from behind us, startling me.

Kieran protectively tightens his grip on me, keeping his body draped over mine and out of view of our newcomers.

"The fuck are you doing in here?" he hisses, and my entire face heats in embarrassment. Great. I just got the best lay of my life in front of an audience.

"Came to find you, K. I had to make sure you didn't kill the poor Central Girl. We see now you didn't. I mean, you beat that pussy up, but God damn," the man rasps, and I recognize him as the asshole who berated Kieran for being a dick to me—Rad.

"Don't ever say beat that pussy up again," someone else mutters through a tired sigh.

"Jesus Christ, you assholes, get out!" I hiss, throwing an arm out, but Kieran holds me tighter. "Get the fuck out!" I screech.

"Aw, how cute," another voice says with a sneer. Instantly, I recognize his preppy ass—Asher Montgomery. The biggest dick that ever walked the halls of Central City High, thinking he was better than everyone else. "We'll be in the car when you decide to think with your damn brain, not your dick. Hope you get yourself tested too."

"Yeah, maybe you guys should learn to lock the door," another voice I recognize now as the bass player, Callum Rose, mumbles, apologizing under his breath.

I blow out my breath when Kieran releases my body and steps back from me so fast that it's like I have a disease. He takes the condom off his flaccid dick and stares at the mess in his hands.

"I can't believe you didn't lock the door, Assface," I say, pulling up my tiny shorts and righting my bra, thong, and shirt. His eyes watch my every damn move with heat resting behind them as he takes every inch of me in.

"You could have, too," he says with a shrug, tossing the condom into the trash like a gentleman. Quickly, he redresses himself but doesn't bother to fix his dark strands standing on end. His eyes heat again when he stares me up and down. "So, you're the River West from the emails?" he questions, taking a step forward.

"Um, that's my name," I say sarcastically, tossing my arms in the air with a shrug.

"You're the same River Blue," he chuckles at that, throwing his head back and staring at the ceiling. "Fuck," he murmurs to himself, blinking several times.

"Yeah, that's me too," I huff, crossing my arms. "Are we done here? Or?"

"We are far from fucking done," he hisses, snapping his gaze to me. "None of this is over," he gestures between us. "I'll be seeing you, River Blue West."

And with that, his toxic ass waltzes out the door, looking back at me with a manic, knowing grin.

What the hell did I just do?

"WHY THE TEARS, RIVER BLUE?" I MURMUR, RAGE BREWING THROUGH MY veins at the sight of her shaking shoulders.

My fingers curl when her big, moss-green eyes look up at me, glistening with tears. We had just met up on the hill behind the apartment complex— our daily meeting spot.

"Stupid Stacey again," she says, clenching her fists tightly together. One day, I'll show my girl how to use those fists against everyone who decides to put their hands on her.

"You want me to take care of Stacey?" I ask in a low voice, as violent images roar through my mind. I'll rip that girl's head off. I don't care if she's in first grade and I'm in third.

"No." Her answer is simple and to the point, like she always is.

I scrub a hand down my face when I waltz out the bar's back door and head down the dark alleyway toward the SUV parked in the back. A faint sense of nostalgia hits me hard as I make my way through the shadows of the night. Being back on this side of town brings so many emotions flooding to the surface, even if I fight them off at every turn. For as long as I can remember, I've lived on the greener side of town, never venturing into the dark stain of Central City—where I grew up. It's a vague memory nestled in the back of my mind. One I had forgotten for many years. After losing a piece of myself here when I had to leave her behind, I shoved the memories into my deepest, darkest part and incinerated them for eternity.

After my mother moved us away from the only place I had ever known, that's when my real nightmare began. Each night I sat and cried, longing for the girl under the stars talking to the man on the moon. But I was stuck, beaten down, and verbally harassed by the new man in my mother's life— my stepfather, Nigel Montgomery.

At ten years old, I could only handle so much. There comes a time when the beatings become too much, and you stop longing for the one person you crave. Instead, locking the happy memories away until they fade into nothing more than a vague idea.

Now, the memories pour through my mind like a dam bursting open and flooding my every waking thought. Flashes of River's long brown hair hanging past her shoulders and flowing down her back. Those moss-green eyes glared at me when I entered her office, and the pinched look she gave me. Her delicate nose. Those dark eyelashes brushed against her freckled cheeks as her eyes hooded from lust. River Blue, the girl from my old life. The one girl I swore I'd never think about again. Or see again. The girl I forced myself to forget. River Blue was always River Blue to me, never River West. Fuck. I should have read the damn emails Callum wrote to the manager of this place. If I had just seen her name, I could have told them who she was to me—and now, to us.

But now, she's all I can think about as I make the walk of shame toward my friends. Shit. Heat burns my cheeks when I open the driver's door and sit without looking around.

"Oh! There he is! The man of the hour!" Rad whoops from the backseat, obnoxiously pounding his fist into the roof of my Tahoe, making it bounce on its wheels.

I grunt, starting up the SUV, and proceed to the mouth of the alley, waiting for the crowded sidewalks to thin out. Leaning back, I stare at the boys and idle the car.

For once, Gloria—the woman who begs me to call her mother—became reasonable when I asked for a larger car. In her eyes, it was a status symbol for the pot of gold at the end of our fucking suburban rainbow.

For me, though? It was a place to store and transport our instruments and the amps we'd bought ourselves over the years. Whatever we got from gigs went straight into our band's bank account so we could afford new instruments, strings, picks, and sticks. We can provide whatever we need without running to someone for a loan. This band will be entirely ours, and I don't want Gloria's money tainting any of it. I've built this with my hands alongside the guys.

"You good?" Callum asks in his usual short words from the backseat, nervously averting his eyes.

Sweat sticks to every inch of the curly blond hair currently plastered to his forehead. His tired eyes watch out the window, taking in the passing patrons lazily walking down the sidewalks at two a.m.

"I read on Spaceface last night that there have been three attacks in the alleyways in the past three weeks, each getting progressively more violent," Callum mutters to the window, worrying his lip until his worry-filled eyes meet mine.

I raise my brow, turning to look at Callum, and shake my head. I'd hate to have a talent like Callum's, where everything he sees, he stores in his head without effort. Some would kill for a photographic memory, but the cons greatly outweigh the pros. Every event—good or bad, stays with him for the rest of his life. Some would call it a gift, but Callum sees it as the ultimate curse. Especially after what he witnessed with his parents. And God, Jenny. He lost them all, and the only ounce he has left of them is the house he lives in and the enormous trust they left in his name, with stipulations that he lives there for two years before even thinking about selling or moving away from the house that brings him nothing but nightmares. Imagine walking through the halls of your family home and seeing the ghosts of your past staring back at you. I know he's been counting down the days until he can cash in and move on—only five more months.

His gaze drifts up and down the bar, calculations running rampant through his genius, photographic mind. Ignoring us, he puts his earbuds back in and closes his eyes, peace washing over him. Whatever he's listening to drowns out his worries and settles his soul, but most of all, it takes away the memories of the worst night of his life. There's something about music that lifts us and connects us—whether we're making it or listening to it.

My fingers tighten on the damn steering wheel again until my knuckles turn white, but I offer him a cocky grin—one I don't feel. River fucking Blue. My River is the person we were after this whole time.

"You should know. You guys stood there the whole time," I quip, glaring at Rad through the rearview mirror. He grins back at me and nods, giving me a look.

My stepbrother, Asher, snorts from the passenger seat. "Yeah, it seems like you had a fun time. But did you find what we were looking for?" He raises his brow, turning to examine my face.

Swiping away some of his unruly brown locks, his eyes zero in on the lump I swallow, showcasing my fucking nerves. My dear, stuck-up stepbrother is all business—all the damn time. He never lets up with his serious scowls, grunts, and whatever the fuck is going through his engorged head. He's intelligent, manipulative, and incorrigible at times—AKA—every fucking second he's awake.

His eyes narrow in at me, and I blow out a breath, jerking the car into drive. There's no simple answer for what he wants.

Did I find answers? Unexpectedly, yes. Do I want to do this song and dance with him? No. Yes? Fuck. All I had to do was ask the manager to speak with the man we were emailing with before to get a glimpse of the person we needed in our pocket—River West.

My River Blue. And now it's gone to shit. Total fucking shit. I'm a mean ass bastard, but I still have a fucking heart—sometimes.

But if I think about it, it's only ever beaten for her. The only person who calmed my rage and swallowed my sadness, all at the same time. Fuck. How did I live my life without her for so long? And how could I have forgotten those big, moss-green eyes?

This could be our opportunity. Her being her, we could use that as our in with West Records or her brothers. She's a goddamn West daughter to the man who could sign us to an epic record deal. Having her in our back pocket could be priceless, especially when our goal is to blow out of this town and become rich and famous. The music industry is all about who you know; that person is River West. Her name could get us into any venue on the West Coast. No questions asked.

"My dad is mean," she murmurs, holding out an envelope.

"Your dad? Where is he?" I ask, lying back in the grass.

"He won't talk to me. I tried, Knight. I sent him a letter, and he sent it back." Water forms in her eyes when she stares at me, and her hope shatters.

"He doesn't deserve you, Blue," I whisper, setting a hand on hers.

No one deserves her except maybe me. That River is mine. She's always had my name stamped on her ass as Kieran's property. I may have lost her for the past eleven years, but now I'm here to reclaim what's mine. And what's mine is her.

"Yeah," I say, pulling out onto the main road. At two a.m., not many cars travel alongside us as we head straight back to our little slice of suburban hell, ten minutes away from the edge of Central City.

"And? Did you find him?" Rad asks with a lazy grin, leaning back into the seat. "You know we need him." He runs a hand through his mullet, massaging his scalp with his fingertips.

I scowl. Whoever told that idiot an 80s mullet was sexy must have been high. But he's been sporting it since I joined him in friggin middle school on the Lakeview side, where his mullet wasn't seen often but never made fun of. They would have been all over him and laughing if he was a Central kid. But not our middle school on the other side of the tracks, a stone's throw away from Central City, but yet so far away.

Hell, his mullet ass was my first best friend, introducing himself to me on my first day at a new fancy school. His grin alone drew me in and helped me feel comfortable after a hard night of shouts and fists in my face. The moment I stepped through Lakeview's doors, I wasn't looking for any friends. Asher tolerated me at best but meeting Rad was a game-changer.

"We have the talent. We don't need him," Callum murmurs, not bothering to remove his earbuds, which must be on low volume. Asher scoffs.

Rad continues his mini rant, blowing out the smoke from the joint resting between his fingers. "I sure as hell didn't see a damn thing except for all the desperate pussy in the crowd. You see Tessa's titties?" He grins at that, looking at Cal, who shakes his head, trying to hide the deep blush reddening his cheeks. "Aw, tiny tots Tessa," Rad barks out a laugh. "As soon as she raised her shirt, I swear little Rad shriveled away." He grunts, patting his junk playfully.

"Yeah, yeah. We had our fun. When will she learn?" I murmur, cringing at the "fun" we had a year back. It's nothing I'll want to revisit mentally or physically. No, my mind only has one prize now.

Callum snorts, not offering anything else as his eyes close, and he settles further into the seat.

Asher rolls his eyes, gritting his teeth so hard I swear I hear them crack. If he doesn't go for a run or fuck some chick soon, he'll implode. I may have suffered under my stepfather's rule over the last eleven years, but Asher has suffered his whole life. Since the moment his mom overdosed and slipped into an early grave, Asher has taken the brunt of Nigel's abuse. Pounding the pavement is the only coping mechanism he's been using to soothe the anger surging through him.

Rad sighs. "You know that was the only reason we agreed to play at that shithole. It was your idea to find him," Rad says with a huge grin. "Although, I kinda liked the vibe. It was emo and..."

"Fucking dirty," Asher mumbles in irritation. "It was disgusting there. Do they call that a bar? It smelled terrible. It looked like..."

"God damn, Asher, my man! You're one buzzkill after another!" Rad barks out, slapping Ash's shoulder and knocking him toward the window. "Lighten up! Do you think if we make it big, we'll be playing in anything nicer along the way? We're going to have to work our way up. Unless..." Rad smiles at me in the rearview mirror with a knowing look.

His brows raise, and he nods his head in understanding. He may look like an 80s burnout, but he is as bright as a fucking light with no filter.

Streetlights pass by, progressively getting fancier and fancier the further we get out of the near central part of town. The buildings get enormous and more ornate, letting me know we've officially made it back to the Lakeview District—our slice of hell. I swallow hard, my heart hardening in the center of my chest.

Tonight, we'll make hard decisions—decisions that will stick with us for the rest of our lives. Every day we don't have a plan in place, our desperation grows wilder by the second, and we're liable to do anything to get the fuck out of this shitty town. For years, our parents have waved off our aspirations as if they were mere pipe dreams impossible to achieve. And here we are, ready to prove to them it can happen.

"I sure as fuck didn't see him. Not like I knew who the fuck we were looking for," Asher mumbles angrily, contorting his stuck-up face. "Didn't see much of anyone but a bunch of Central chicks working the bar and front door."

If he wasn't a competent guitar player and a master with his fingers, I'd have left my stepbrother to rot in the fucking suburbs, wallowing in his self-loathing. But alas, he plays like a fucking angel, even when he's a know-it-all fucking tool. Not that he's a bad guy by any means. Ash is cool when he's not bitching. Or being a stuck-up prick, which he does all the time, especially if shit doesn't go his way. I know, deep down, Asher Montgomery has my damn back like a real brother would. It may have taken us a while to get to this point, but I know he wouldn't lead us down the wrong path or lie to us. We're a damn family, the only family we have.

I sigh, staring through the windshield when we pull into the driveway leading to hell. A light pops on in the living room, and Gloria's pinched face peeks out. Her eyes narrow in on us, and she shakes her head, looking like she's ready to rip us a new one for pulling in so late and disturbing her sleep. Already I hear the slew of words she'll sling in my direction the moment I walk through the door, criticizing me.

Seeing my mom's face is a stark reminder of who I'm loyal to—the assholes in this SUV. They may be loud, inconsiderate, and make me want to punch them, but they're my family. They're the ones I trust with my damn life. Family doesn't have to be blood; family is the people who see you at your lowest and help to raise you, not lower you down. And that's precisely what these dicks do.

River's bewildered face pops into my mind. I cringe, wiping my hand down my face. God, I'm such a prick after a performance. When the high of being on stage fades away, I always need another hit of euphoria. I always crash after the last note plays, and then I need the time to myself. Time to unwind and relax. Fuck! Why did this have to get so fucking complicated? I punch the steering wheel with a huff, throwing myself back into my seat.

I don't know River anymore. Anyone can change after eleven years apart. Before, she was an innocent angel mercilessly picked on. And now? She's a stranger to me. So, to hell with it all. I'll do something I might regret later, even though River is consuming my mind.

There's something about River that reels me in like a fish on a hook, drawing me into her orbit. Maybe it's our tainted history together. Those nights spent under the stars, spilling our guts, race through my mind calling me back to her. She's the girl I was forced to leave behind and forget at the hands of my stepfather. There's no way I can get River out of my mind. Not with her moss-green eyes burning through me when her luscious lips pop open. Or maybe it's her banging, tight body. Her perfect tits, fitting into my hand, draws me to her.

Now, I want her back, no matter the cost. This may be the only way I can have her without getting any grief. I'll make her mine.

I swallow hard. "River West isn't some dude," I say on exhale.

River West is my River Blue. Mine.

We've searched high and low for an entry into the infamous KC Club in East Point, California, where Seger and Zeppelin West, the famous twin sons of Corbin West, and River's brothers, frequent. They're always scouting for new talent to sign to their label. Getting into The KC Club is next to impossible if you don't know the right people, and we don't know anyone in the industry. Not yet at least.

My dick tightens in my damn pants at the thought of her pussy wrapped around me, and her moans echo in my ears. Her sass. Her fucking small curves. Shit, the way her ass bounced against my hips. Fuck. I'm ready to drop these dickbags off and head back to the outskirts of Central City to find River and tie her down. Does she still live in the same apartment from our childhood? Does she still like to eat those disgusting pink peeps dipped in milk? I swallow the obsession bobbing in my throat and threatening to pull me under.

"Come on, boy. You're going onto better things. Leave the trash behind," my new stepdaddy growls, bruising my arm by throwing me into the back of his SUV. "You're onto bigger and better things now."

I swallow hard, pressing my face into the window as the apartment complex becomes a blip and disappears. My heart breaks into a million pieces. River Blue, I need you. I watch until our new neighborhood comes into view, revealing enormous houses and a shiny lake glistening in the sun.

"Welcome home," the man says with a wide, evil-looking grin.

"What's that supposed to mean? We need him, man. He's our one connection. He's our in," Ash says through gritted teeth. "If we don't have West, we can't get in with West Records or the damn exclusive venue. And if we don't make it into West Records, we're fucked. We need River West. Remember our goals? Getting out of this shit fuck town and leaving everyone behind? We need him." Ash closes his eyes, leaning his forehead against the window to calm himself down.

Desperation ebbs from him in waves, and I get it. He's been through hell and back and wants nothing more than to run from this town and start over. Our plan is his saving grace—the one thing that's kept him going. Even if the guilt eats at me daily, I can't disappoint my family. Not now. But what they don't know won't kill them. I have no intention of letting her go. Whatever plan we cook up to get close, I'll keep her closer.

I close my eyes, resting the back of my head against the headrest. "River West isn't a dude, you fucking morons. River West is the fucking manager chick," I say, feeling my heart drop into the depths of my fucking stomach.

"Buzztit!" Rad gasps in mock horror and then mumbles about her forcing the tits into hiding and what a goddamn tragedy it was.

"The chick?" Asher gapes. "That chick is a West?" Once realization settles and the shock wears off, he menacingly rubs his chin.

Wheels turn in the depths of his overused brain, grinding to a halt when he comes to the same conclusion I have. We'll have to befriend her, which means we'll have to be nice. Which shouldn't be too hard for Rad and me, but the other two? They're a different entity altogether.

Callum looks at us with calculating eyes and sits back in his seat, putting away his earbuds. "So, the manager who tore up our check and we watched you bone, is the West chick we need to get to the KC Club?" I nod in response. He sighs, running a hand down his face. "Well, this should be fun then," he mutters.

Something settles inside me, chasing away my demons at the thought of her. I couldn't agree with Callum more. It will be fun, and I'll reclaim what's mine.

"So, K, you got our in? Do you think she'd be down to help? Make the call?" Rad asks, leaning forward with hope glistening deep in his brown eyes.

I run a hand down my face. "You think the chick that ripped up our paycheck because I insulted her will roll over and call her estranged family to get us a gig at the KC Club?" I snark, raising a brow.

"My dad is mean," she whispers again, clutching another sent-back letter. "I just wanted to say hi," she says through a sniffle, wiping away the tears streaming down her face.

"He sent it back again? Why do you keep doing it?" I ask, wrapping my arm around her shoulders and pulling her in. If her mom is too busy sleeping and won't comfort her, I will. River needs me to help her cope with life, just like I need her.

"I won't anymore," she pouts, growling when she tears up the letter. "That's the last time Daddy will ever hear from me." And from that day forward, I never found River Blue crying over the man who didn't want her in the first place.

Pressing my palms into my eyes, I squeeze them shut, reveling in the vivid memories flowing through my mind. Over the years, I've erased every inch of where I came from—partially due to my stepdad refusing to let me call her or find her across town. Hell, I even tried to ride my bike to her once, but he stopped me within the first mile. Within the first month of living with him, I had a new wardrobe and a brand-new life. Ten-year-old me could never get what I wanted, and River slowly drifted into the past, beaten out of me.

"Don't even think about going back to that side of town," he hisses, heaving his fist in the air. Before I can blink, pain sears through my jaw, and blood spurts from my nose. My mother gasps from the corner of the room, held hostage to witness my punishment. The reality is that she wouldn't lift a finger to help me, anyway. She's here for only one thing—the rich lifestyle Nigel has afforded her.

As I lie motionless on the floor, only grunting when his foot collides with my ribs three times, I promise myself I'll forget about her. If this is what happens when I try to ride my bike across town, I'll never try again. I can't take another fist or kick.

The pain sits with me through the night as I toss and turn, whimpering.

"You can't provoke him," my new stepbrother Asher whispers through

the dark. I jolt at his voice, crying out when I sit up. "He'll only hurt you more." Shaking his head, he moves to the side of the bed and sits.

"Yeah?" I whimper, holding my aching ribs.

"Things will go smoother if you just do what he says."

"Is that what you do?" I whisper, earning a scoff.

"I do what I have to do. Now stop making so much noise so I can go to sleep," Ash grumbles, slipping into his bed.

Quiet overtakes the room, the only sound coming from the air conditioning kicking on, blowing across the blinds, knocking them together. Of all the rooms in this house, Nigel insisted we bunk together. Probably to keep a sharper eye on us and lock us together. He didn't count on us forming a deep bond like brothers normally would.

"Kieran?" Asher asks in a soft voice.

"Yeah?" I rasp, wiping away the tears falling down my cheeks.

"You'll be okay. I promise he'll lay off for a few days," Asher whispers, thick with sleep. "Night."

"Night," I mutter, losing all hope I had before.

Seeing River tonight has knocked all the memories loose, and they're running rampant through my mind. I swore I'd forget about her, and I successfully had. Locking her away was the only way I could protect myself from the fury of fists. Eventually, it was like she had never existed, and I moved on with my new life.

The guys all look at one another with questioning gazes, finally landing on the man who apparently has the answers. Ash, ever the man with a fucking plan, grins like the fucking grinch. Too bad there's no way in hell his heart grew three times too big, probably the other way around, shrinking into a damn prune. If Asher has some diabolical plan to enact, it's no doubt evil and crazy.

"We could make her, you know? You already had your way with her. Did she like you?" Ash asks, studying my face with narrowed eyes again.

Fuck. I hate it when he plans like this and gives nothing away with his stony facial expression.

Blowing out a breath, I remember our heated exchange. I bite my bottom lip, imagining what River would look like dangling her pussy above my face and me ready for a damn feast. What would she taste like coating my tongue? Probably fire and vanilla all mixed into one explosion of taste. What I wouldn't give to stick my tongue deep in her pussy and make her cum all over my tastebuds. But shit, River isn't one to be pushed around. She isn't going to drop to her knees and do our bidding without incentive. Not now. River Blue isn't the same girl I left eleven years ago. She's a fiery fucking treat, and I want another bite of what's mine. And this time, I'm playing for keeps.

"I don't think you could make that girl do shit," I sigh, shaking my head. "She's not the type to sit back and take orders. River needs our trust."

Pinching the bridge of his nose, Rad sighs. "We need this, man. I need out of this fucking place. My mom is driving me fucking bonkers begging me to conform to what Dad wants from me. And I'll be fucked over a pulpit before I do that. I'm my own damn man, damn it." His fists clench in his lap as his eyes drift toward the very house of horrors he escaped and rebelled against when he was just eighteen. Taking one last drag of his joint, Rad tosses it out the window.

Being stuck in a place, financially held hostage by the people who are supposed to love you burns me from the inside out. This car? My phone? My college education? Everything I own, my stepfather taints with his existence, dangling it over our heads. We've tried and tried again to get jobs and further our financial situation. But every step of the way, he's there to knock us on our asses and keep us in his grasp—where he wants us. The only sanctuary we're granted is the music that keeps us alive. According to Nigel, music will get us nowhere in life. Therefore, we can enjoy the ride until our time is up and he needs us to clock into his company—one year. We have one year to get this music thing off the ground, and we're growing desperate.

"I feel your fucking pain," I grunt, gesturing to the woman stalking our every move from the living room window.

Her beady eyes take in every fucking thing we do. Down to the spent joint sitting in her driveway. There's no doubt in my mind that I'll hear about that later through her screeching wails and fucking disappointment. So, yeah—I feel his pain. We all have our reasons for wanting to escape this fucking hell.

"Fine then, we coerce her into doing whatever the fuck we want. I think we can manage that. We're all charming as hell. And we want a gig at her brothers' famous bar, where stars are born. Our name will be in fucking lights. We're destined for that shit..." Asher nods, so fucking sure of himself that we can convince her to help us pursue happiness. Right. Yeah. This will totally fucking work. Considering she probably hates me.

"You left without saying goodbye."

Her words are a punch to the gut. Yeah, I left without a word, basically kidnapped by the man I now call dad. If I could have gone back, I would have. I tried. But he was always there to remind me with his fist that there was no going back to the neighborhood I grew up in.

"And how the hell do you expect to coerce her? She's not exactly the type," I grumble. From the looks of it, she's tough as a fucking nut now and won't take our shit lying down. "You can't make a chick like that do anything but what she wants."

Asher grins over at me, slapping me on the side of the cheek. "Exactly! I've got a plan," he says with confidence, rubbing his hands together. "What's the one thing a woman will do for the man she loves?"

I raise a skeptical brow, looking back to Rad, who shrugs a shoulder.

"No idea," I say, looking at Ash, who grins and wiggles his brows. In the low light of the Tahoe, something evil and conniving crosses his face.

"She'll do anything for the man she loves," he says with a sharp nod full of confidence.

"Please don't tell me you're going to say what I think you're going to say," Callum mumbles uncomfortably from the backseat, forcing his earbuds back into his ears, blocking out the world with murmuring music.

"We'll wine and dine her. We'll make River West fall so madly in love with us that she'll call her family and beg them to hear our music. Imagine the reunion they could have all because of us. It'll be a win-win, but mostly for us."

My mouth gapes open, and I'm not the only one utterly shocked. Rad sputters, choking on his spit.

"Us?" Rad asks with a squeak but quickly soothes his expression. From here, I see the wheels turning in his brain. Wait…us?

"You want us to trick her into loving me?" I gape, shaking my head like it's the worst possible idea on the planet. But a thrill runs through me at the thought. Yes. Let her fall in love with me, and then I'll whisk her away, and she'll never have to live in this shitty town again.

"Where would you go if you left?" I whisper, staring at the stars again, having been kicked out over an hour ago so my mom could conduct business. Whatever that is. All I know is a stereo plays so loud, drowning out the weird noises coming from her room.

"I want to touch the ocean," she whispers, leaning into me with a sigh.

"I'll take you when we're older," I whisper, dreaming of the day I can take both of us away from here.

Our dreams will become a reality if I get my way.

"Nope," Ash says, popping the P. "All of us. What better package deal could you get than having her invested in all of us? Our hearts, our everything. We'll all date her, and then, in the end, she can decide who she likes the best."

My gaze snaps in his direction at the thought of any of them touching her.

"I'm sorry, what?" Callum grumbles through the biggest frown ever, still listening to our conversation, not his music. "You want us to seduce her?" His brows furrow, but he looks to Ash for more direction.

"Then it's settled," Ash says, rubbing his hands together with a cocky-as-hell grin. No one could stop him now if they tried. "Operation seduce our meal ticket is underway. Start planning those dates. How long do you think before she caves? A week? Two? Flash some cash, and her panties will fall?" He chuckles, throwing open the passenger's side door with zest. "Hello, Gloria!" he shouts gleefully at two in the fucking morning, waving toward the window.

She scowls again, giving a small wave before stomping away from the window. That's right, and she won't say shit to Asher. But me? I'll get an earful.

Callum mutters solemnly to himself and pushes out the backdoor with a frown, shutting it behind him. He follows Ash around to the back of the Tahoe, talking to him in a low voice. His arms wave and I can tell his conscience is eating away at him at the idea. But ultimately, Asher will win this fight, and we'll be helpless to do whatever he says. He always does.

Rad's face pinches when he leans forward. "Are we doing that?" he asks in a hushed tone. "Dude, I mean, I'm down for talking to her and getting to know her. But love? That seems kinda..." His lips press together in a tight line, and he shakes his head.

"Demented?" I murmur, throwing my head back into the seat.

This plan is so fucking stupid, but it might just work. We've worked our asses off getting into venues around the big city and building a small following. We only have four hundred followers on social media and a group of people who follow us from venue to venue, buying all our tickets. But if we can get to the venue of our dreams, then we're set. No more parents with expectations. Just music, the road, booze, fame, and River by my fucking side at last. And freedom, the one thing we've craved. No matter the cost, we'll get there.

"Exactly," Rad says, pointing at me.

"You know Ash," I say, swiping a hand down my face.

"Fucker takes it too far," Rad agrees with a sharp nod. "Too fucking extreme."

"Help me watch him," I say, turning to Rad with pleading eyes and curling my fists. "We can't let him take it too far." Not that he'll be able to. River won't have a choice in the matter now. She'll pick me and only me at the end of our time together.

"I'll try." He shrugs, hurrying toward the door. "Who knows, though, this could be fun, right? The four of us, one ballsy chick?" He shrugs and gestures toward my pocket. "How much did we make tonight? It better be a shit ton with all the girls we brought in. Imagine the look on Gloria's face when we make a profit." He's right. We've never managed to make a considerable profit, but with Callum negotiating through email correspondence with River. We got ourselves a golden opportunity with a good chunk of change.

I snort, digging into my pocket and pulling out the check. I flatten it along the center console and turn on the overhead light.

Rad scrunches his face. "Errr, what?" I motion at the check, laughing my ass off. "Dude, she wrote 'To the Whispered Words, you sack of shits, here's the money I owe you.' What the fuck is that?" He groans, shoving himself back. "She didn't even sign it!"

I sigh, staring at the perfect cursive, and rub my jaw. "Well, River gave us the perfect excuse to stalk her." I shrug, shoving the check into my pocket. A thrill of excitement shoots through me at the prospect of seeing her again. Maybe she and I could pick up where we left off.

"Right, dude! She still owes us! Sick!" He chuckles, piles out of the car, and heads to the back of the vehicle.

Huddling together, we plan for the next few months, including what we need to do and how we'll reel her like a fish on a hook.

I FROWN, FIXING MY HAIR IN THE LONG MIRROR ATTACHED TO THE CLOSED office door. Since Kieran walked out with that possessive look sparkling on his face, I haven't been able to move. Twenty minutes and counting since the last time I laid eyes on him. My mind reels from our encounter, producing more conflicting emotions in my gut. Do I hate him? Like him? Want to smother him? Shit, I don't know.

Eleven years ago, he left a cavernous hole in my chest when he disappeared without a trace. It took me years to close the gap and return to myself. Even after that night, which changed me. And now? Now, he's reopening the wound one word at a time.

I can't do this again. I can't let Kieran waltz back into my life like I mean something to him, to waltz back out.

It was one fuck, and that's it. It meant nothing.

Closing my eyes, I count to ten and release my breath. Chances are, Kieran got precisely what he wanted, and I'll never see his handsome face again. Hopefully. Maybe. Shit.

"We are far from fucking done," he hisses, snapping his gaze to me. "None of this is over," he gestures between us. "I'll be seeing you, River Blue West."

His words replay over and over. He promised never to leave me at one point in our young lives. And yet, within a month of his words, he was gone. So, what will it be this time?

I shake my head. Screw these thoughts. How can one guy shake up my entire existence in a matter of ten minutes?

I flip myself off in the mirror and fix my screwed-up ponytail. Shivers run down my spine at the phantom feel of his fist locking around my hair and directing me to where he wanted me. Shit. Stop it. No more self-pity. It is what it is. If he comes back, then I'll deal with him.

Trailing a finger up and down the outside of my pocket, I feel for my pocket knife, the last gift he ever gave me.

"Take this," he said, sitting beside me on the grass.

"Knight!" I gasp, holding the colossal pocketknife in my hand. "It's a...

I can't!" I squeak, closing it and throwing it back to him like it has a disease.

Kieran laughs, throwing his head back. "It's okay, River Blue," he reassures me, flicking open the blade. The bright full moon shines on the reflective blade. "If you look hard enough, your name is here. River Blue," he murmurs, running a finger over the wooden grip where my name sits.

I swallow hard, my fingers shaking when he wraps my fingers around the grip.

"I'll teach you how to protect yourself. One day, you'll need it." He nods, sure of himself, and proceeds to teach me how to use it safely.

My trusty pocketknife has had its fair share of uses over the years, protecting me from unwanted touches and my go-to security when walking alone. Despite its origins, I've kept it firmly in my pocket from the moment he handed it over. It holds more than security in my eyes; it's sentimental.

I huff a breath, wiping a hand down my face. Was the boning worth the pain and satisfaction? No. Maybe? Shit!

All the calmness I felt before evaporates into thin air, and all I want to do is drink, take a bubble bath, and go to bed. I need a goddamn shot before I go home and face the loneliness of my empty apartment. My ma left for work hours ago and always worked through the night. So, it'll be just me, my loneliness, and the ache between my legs—a consolation prize for my consequences.

After cleaning up the office and shutting off the light, I make my way back into the bar area with my head held high.

"All good?" Leon raises a dark brow, and my cheeks heat when his mahogany brown eyes take in my messy appearance. Despite fixing my hair and straightening my clothes, he sees right through me.

Fuck.

I grunt, ripping my hair tie out of my hair and throwing it back into a messy bun, sending him a scathing look and daring him to say something. He snorts, shakes his head, and goes back to minding his own damn business. Good boy.

"You were kinda loud," Ode snickers behind her hand, looking at her brother Leon, and they burst out laughing together. Their laughs bounce around the empty bar, filling the room with roaring amusement.

"Ha, ha, ha, laugh it up. But I got laid," I say, pointing proudly to myself through a smirk.

"About damn time, woman!" Leon says, walking around the bar with his hands shoved into his pocket. "I've been saying that you needed it for what?"

"Every day," Ode adds. "He tells me every damn day that you need a little dick to knock the stick out of your ass."

My jaw falls open at the same time Leon curses back at his sister.

"Ode! What the hell? Throw your brother under the bus like that? I never said nothing like that," he says, shaking his head with a grin. Letting me know he has, in fact, said it multiple times.

Some friends I have.

I snort. "It's cool. I needed to get laid after all this promotion business. Plus, I start my first set of classes tomorrow, and I have to work at the record store Monday, too." I blow out a breath, my chest constricting with all the shit I have planned for the next few years.

I have to work two jobs and attend school if I ever want to make it out of this hell-hole city and move on to bigger and better things, like California. I want to see the ocean, smell the saltwater, and push my toes into the cool sand. Most importantly, I want to attend CaliState to complete my Music Business degree. I've had my eyes on the prize since the moment I decided what I wanted to do with my life.

Through CaliState, I can live a full life without worry. After I walk across the stage with my degree, I can go to any record company and live my dream. Managing bands and music has always been my destiny, running through my blood since birth. Even though my father ripped the easy path from my grasp by the time I was two and forced me away. He may be some big musical influencer with more money than God, but give me five years, and I'll prove to him and everyone else who overlooked me that I'm the fucking greatest.

I want what I want, and I can't do that in Central City, where every corner I turn is a constant reminder of who I am here—no one. To everyone walking these streets, I'm the Central City trash living in the slums of income-based apartments with a mom who strips to make ends meet. I want to thrive on my own without assistance backing me up. I can't achieve that here in the middle of Nowhere, Illinois. So, the first opportunity I get, I'm gone. No matter what. By whatever means necessary, even if my mom has to come with me.

"I'm out! See you tomorrow night, college girl!" Leon says with a mock salute, heading out the back door with his keys in hand.

"Everyone else gone?" I ask Ode, and she nods, grabbing her keys too.

"Ya did good, bestie," she says, wrapping her arm around my shoulders and kissing my cheek. "You're the best damn manager I've ever had."

I sigh with a smile, leaning my head on hers. "You think so?" I ask with uncertainty, furrowing my brows.

"Girl, I can only imagine how much your little band brought in. But let's just say I've never served so many damn drinks. So, yeah. Book will see it and give you a bonus for your hard work." She grins, wiggling her brows. "So, how was Richie Rich? Good dick?" I snort, pushing off her, and laugh when she stumbles, righting herself along the tall, wooden bar.

"You're such a bitch," I laugh, leaning over the bar to grab my backpack purse, and set it on the top. "But I don't kiss and tell." I mimic locking my lips and throwing away the key.

Ode gapes, staring at me like I grew another head.

"You won't even tell your bestie?" she asks with a pout and pushes my shoulder. I snort, shaking my head. "Well… those noises you were making gave you away. OH, RICHIE RICH!!" Her hand slams down on the bar, fake moaning with her head thrown back in false passion.

I groan in embarrassment, feeling the heat travel up my neck and burn my ears. Shit. I forgot how thin the walls of this place were. Just last week, Ode took her on again, off again, hook up, into the bathroom to rock his world. Let's just say, we clapped when they walked out of the bathroom, zipping their flies and straightening their shirts.

So, they heard every dirty little word Kieran whispered in my ear as he pounded me hard. My nipples pebble under my shirt, begging for his lips to encase them. Damn it. I need to get the hell out of here and stop thinking about him. Throwing my strap over my shoulders, we head toward the back door and momentarily stop to shut off all the lights.

"Shut up," I groan, shoving her out the door.

She cackles more, straightening her purse. "I'll see ya later, bestie. You think Bessy will start?" She raises her brow when I lock the door and snorts.

"Bessy better start, or I'm trading her ass in." I gesture toward my car, Bessy—who I, in fact, can't afford to trade in or get rid of.

She's my ride or die. Well, more the die part. Poor Bes is resting on her last leg. But, hey—she gets me from point A to point B, usually with no complaints. She's big and bad and eats a lot of gas, but I can't complain about my nine-hundred-dollar car and my pride and joy. There's no better feeling than saving up for something and finally getting it.

"Babes, if that pile ever shits out on you, I can take you home," Leon says, leaning against his car with a cigarette hanging from his frowning lips. Taking it from his mouth, he blows smoke into the air. "We're neighbors, after all," he grumbles, shaking his head in disappointment.

"Thanks, L," I say with a smile and wave him on.

"We could be like the cool kids and carpool," he suggests with a grin, tossing his used cigarette to the ground and squishing it with the tip of his shoe. "Think about it. I'll see ya at home. Be safe, yeah?" he says, piling into his car when I give him a thumbs up and drives off.

"Love ya, bitch," Ode says, coming in to hug and squeezing me tight. "I'm going to stay at Ricky's tonight. But I'll see you tomorrow?"

I snort, squeezing her back. "Quicky Ricky again?" I murmur into her neck, reveling in her familiar hug.

Odette and Leon are far more than just my neighbors and coworkers. They are my brother and sister. We may not be blood but fuck that. They're the closest thing I have to a family in this hell hole, and I'll cling to them for the rest of my life.

"Quicky Ricky," she murmurs, confirming my suspicions.

What started as a one-night stand from an internet hookup app has now turned into a full-blown relationship she's not ready to admit to yet. Ode grins when her phone lights up, and another car pulls into the lot a second later. Ode squeals, waves goodbye, and runs to the passenger's side.

"Heya, Ricky!" I shout, waving to him, receiving a small wave out the window before they pull away from the empty parking lot, leaving me there to watch it all go dark.

I sigh, getting into my car with a prayer running through my mind. Immediately, like my momma taught me, I lock my doors and set my purse on the passenger's side, praying to the car gods that Bessy starts without a fight.

Settling into the warm driver's seat, my entire body tingles when my mind returns to the rough quickie. The phantom feel of his fingers tightly gripping my hips sends goosebumps skittering across my skin. An ache between my legs has me closing my eyes and wishing he'd come back for round two.

Oh, the rocking we could do in Bessy. Fuck. I run my fingers over my swollen lips and sigh at the feel of his demanding mouth overtaking mine in desperation. I must be a glutton for punishment if I'm aching for Kieran to come back and rock my world. Is the heartache worth seeing him again?

Throwing my head back, I let out a silent scream. Fuck. Why do I always do this to myself? Huh? I can't get attached. Not again. He'll chew me up and spit me out before I can say, please another, sir, just like last time. From now on, I'm staying away from the entire band for as long as possible until I can get myself in check. No more bands. No more bad boys. I'm swearing them off from now on. No more, I swear.

I shake my head and attempt to start my car, only to receive a worn-down, grinding noise. I narrow my eyes on the dashboard and shove my foot into the gas pedal, pumping it. Again, I try to start Bessy, but she gives me nothing but fumes and sputters.

"No! No! Bessy, don't do this to me now," I grumble, rubbing a hand over the steering wheel. All I get in return is the sound of her slowly dying and nothing. "Great," I mumble, leaning my head back in defeat.

With no other choice, I shove my one working earbud into my ear and begin my journey home in the mid-August muggy heat on foot. Sure, I could call Leon and beg him to come back and get me, but he's probably already at home and settled into bed. I'd hate to drag him out to fetch little old me. Besides, the middle of the night is the most peaceful time to walk.

Sometimes, I need my music, the open air, and nothing to worry about. Sure, there could be a creeper lurking in the shadows, ready to haul me off to his basement, but from the looks of the abandoned sidewalks, there isn't —hopefully. It's just me and the music playing the soothing melodies in my ear, carrying my worries away.

Ma and I have lived in the same two-bedroom apartment gifted by the government since my dad decided he was done with us and kicked us out, forcing us out of Cali and back to her hometown. It was all she could afford on nothing, and we've never been able to leave. It's been good to us and has let us thrive in a bad situation. Ma works her ass off on nights down at the local strip club dancing, but it's never been entirely enough.

Walking down the cracked and disintegrating sidewalk, I let my music take me over. Goosebumps pour over my skin, and I momentarily shut my eyes, allowing the tunes to infect my soul. Music is the life force keeping me going and alive. I'd fade into nothing with no meaning if I didn't have it. It's the thing that accompanies me everywhere; no one can take it away from me, not even money. My greatest joy is looking up at a stage in the distance and feeling every ounce of emotion dropping from their words and notes. It completes me.

I sigh in relief when I make it back to my apartment building in one piece. Without any drama, well—besides my stupid car not starting. Some nights on my lonely drive home, the streets are empty. Some nights, they're full of neighborhood people doing whatever they're doing in the middle of the night. I'd be a liar if I said I lived in a safe area. But my home has always been good to me. And the people? They're just trying to make it in the crazy thing called life. No matter the means.

As I make my way to my ground-floor apartment, I raise a brow at Leon, who rests against his door with his eyes on me. He nods once, throwing the cigarette down, and shakes his head.

"Bess not make the trip?" he asks, reaching into his pocket for his key.

"Thought it'd be a good night for a walk," I mumble, rubbing my wrinkled forehead. Exhaustion sweeps through me when my eyes land on my apartment door. Just behind that barrier are my bathtub and my bed.

"Goodnight, you stubborn ass woman," Leon says, inserting his key into his mother's apartment.

"Night, Korrine," I shout when the door opens, and I grin as her stern eyes set on me, and she nods.

"Night, child. Have a good first day tomorrow. Come for dinner before you go to that second job of yours and tell me all about it," she says in a tired voice, face drooping from the lack of sleep. But God love her. She always stays up to ensure we all come home safely from the bar and still greets the sun in the morning to cook breakfast for the family. She always looks out for us.

"Yes, ma'am," I say, my throat tightening up from all the love pouring from every fiber of her being.

She is my second mother, who took over when my mom couldn't care for me properly. Since Kieran moved away, Korrine has been living next door, raising her three kids after a car accident that disabled her and took her husband's life.

Like us, this apartment was all she could afford at the time, and she's never left. After my ma started her night jobs, I slept over at Korrine's and became another family member. If it weren't for her all these years, I never would have had big dreams or hope for the future. She pushed her kids and me to succeed when my mother was drowning in grief and financial woes.

She waves me off with a huff and a stern nod, disappearing into the depths of her apartment. With the snick of her lock, the lights turn out, and I head for my own. I suck in a breath, ready for my damn bubble bath and wine, but stop short when a small light shines through the open window. And when I walk inside, my heart fucking drops at the sight of her.

"Ma?" I question, setting my purse down on the kitchen counter. "You okay?" My brows furrow. She usually works until six in the morning and is never home at night.

My mom moves her chestnut brown hair over her shoulder, sighing, bringing a small glass to her trembling lips, and sets the cup down. Large, dark circles sit under her eyes, and my heart drops when her crystal blue eyes meet mine.

"Fell on stage," she murmurs, kicking out her booted foot. "Broke my damn ankle." Her eyes stay on the floor, observing the cast. "I lost my balance, the room spun, and I just…. I fell, River."

"Oh God, Ma. Are you okay? Need meds? Anything?" I take a tentative step forward, cautiously watching the silent tears run down her cheeks. She shakes her head.

"No, baby," she murmurs, running her cold fingers up my arms and stopping at my shoulder. "Barry fired me." When those words leave her lips, my entire body breaks out in a cold sweat.

"F-fired?" I gape. "He can't just fire you because of a broken leg, dammit. You've worked with him for over fifteen years. You're one of his best dancers. You…"

"Yeah, he can. He pays me under the table, Sugar." She squeezes my shoulder with trembling fingers and loses her grip on me. She curses under her breath, reaching for her glass, but it slips between her fingers. Landing back on the counter, thankfully not shattering. Her long fingers run through her curled and primped hair, and a sob leaks from between her lips.

"Ma?" I whisper, swallowing hard. I can tell by her avoidance of eye contact; she's hiding something from me. "What is it?"

She bites into her bottom lip. "I got Multiple Sclerosis, babe."

"M.S.?" I scrunch my face, and she nods when the realization hits me, and dread fills every muscle in my body.

M.S. is something I've seen before in one of our bar patrons. He could walk one day, but then he started to stumble, and by the end, he was in a wheelchair. Last I saw, he had landed in a nursing home because he couldn't take care of himself anymore. He explained to me one day that it was an autoimmune disease that would never have a cure until he dies.

"I got diagnosed," she takes a large breath, fiddling with her fingers on the counter, "seven years ago, and it's only getting worse. I tried so hard to work through the symptoms and the flare-ups. But I can't anymore. I hurt too much, and the club's heat makes it too hard to stand, walk, or think."

I take a step back, gaping at my mother and her admission. Seven fucking years and I never noticed? I run my finger over my clenched jaw, and my chest heaves. All this time, I was so blind to my mother's symptoms because I was a kid caught up in her own life. Shit.

"Why didn't you tell me you had it? I could have helped. I could have done anything to make it easier on you!" I shout, throwing my arm out.

Inside my chest, my heart works overtime, banging against my ribs. My breaths come in short pants as I wrap my head around her confession.

When she looks up at me with her glossy eyes and another sob leaks from her lips, I close in on her, forgetting the anger brewing in my gut. Throwing my arms around her, I pull her into a much-needed hug, and she sags in my grip.

"You have always worked so hard, Riv. I don't know what I did to get such a good kid like you, but you work harder than anyone I know. You got straight A's, worked two jobs, and still managed to be home every night. I didn't want to worry you, Kid. You're my responsibility, and I already failed you once." Every ounce of emotion I know she's buried deep inside her comes to the surface as she sobs into my chest. "I failed you when I couldn't keep your father around. I failed you when I couldn't secure child support from the good-for-nothing Corbin West. I failed you when we had to move back to the middle of nowhere and raise you by myself."

"It'll be all right, Ma. I promise," I murmur, running my fingers through her ratty hair. "We'll get through this. We always do."

Ma pulls back, wiping the tears from her cheeks. "See, Kid? This isn't how it's supposed to be. You're my baby. I'm supposed to rock you and tell you everything will be okay. But I can't anymore." She shakes her head, running a shaky hand through her hair.

"Okay, so Barry fired you. Can you get disability or unemployment? You have to be eligible for something that could help." I breathe, sitting on the stool beside her, trying to think of a solution to our problems.

"No unemployment. It was cash under the table. I never had to claim a cent, so Barry wins this round. But Disability? Maybe," she says, nodding her head. "Korrine will help me make it to the doctor tomorrow and drive me. I'll have more answers tomorrow." She gives me a sad smile and raises her good foot. She hobbles toward her beat-up recliner near the flat screen and sits down with a huff. Our only saving grace through all this is the medical card we've been on since our arrival. If it weren't for that, our medical bills would be through the roof.

"I'll do some research, Ma. There must be something out there for you." I swallow hard, brushing past her toward my bedroom at the end of the hall.

"Night, Kid. Get some rest. You've got a big day tomorrow," she whispers, blowing me a kiss, and I catch it with a small smile. "You're my big college girl now. I'm so damn proud of you."

"Night, Ma," I say, waltzing into my bedroom with a sigh.

Not only do I have to try and come up with double the money we were making between my job and hers, but now I have to contend with a chronically ill mother, who will only get worse and worse. Then I'll have to put her in a home or try to find a day nurse or… shit, I don't know.

I rub a finger along my forehead and groan at the ceiling. So much for a warm bubble bath and some wine before bed. I have five hours before I must get up and open the store across town. Yay for responsibilities. Yay for being an adult. And yay for walking everywhere! Bessy was our only vehicle, and now…

"I'M PROFESSOR WEBBER, AND WELCOME!" I SIGH, SITTING BACK IN MY computer chair, and rubbing my sweaty forehead.

The walk to work this morning was peaceful but fucking hot. I'm sure I have swamp ass and swamp pussy at this point. Who knew the sun would grace us with one-hundred-degree weather at nine in the morning? Next time, I'll look at the bus schedule and catch a ride.

Sleep desperately gnaws at the back of my eyes, begging me to close them and rest just a little longer. Just one more hour. Or maybe five, for good measure. I need more coffee. Like a bucket full or in an IV attached to my arm for the rest of eternity. Maybe a fucking nap. Or, and hear me out, another good romp in the hay. I'm just saying that it could put a rainbow over my day.

I know, I know. You can tell me all day long—River, it's a bad idea to jump in the sack with a guy who will probably disappear soon. And logically, he's a dick. With a good, massive cock, I want to take a three-hour tour of pound town. God. I'm pathetic.

I rub a circle over my temple. Maybe I'm too sleep-deprived to think about this. My body aches in the most delicious ways from his brutal thrusts and dominant ways, and I'm aching for more.

Plus, I need something to keep me sane, right? Because this schedule is going to fucking annihilate me. In the best possible way—I hope. It's all for a good cause. Hurray for furthering my education and expanding my horizons so I can walk off into the sunset with a degree under my belt and far away from here.

Between online classes three days a week, actual classroom time on Wednesdays, and working two jobs split between two shifts daily. I don't know if I'll make it to my next birthday. I might keel over before I turn twenty.

*Here lies the corpse of River West. Gone too soon after trying to work her ass off.*

Yup. That'd do it. Which reminds me... I turn my attention to my computer screen, pretending to listen as he rambles.

The professor, as he insists, we call him, wanders around the front of the classroom with his hands behind his back and a stern look lining his face.

"I'd like to welcome you all. As you know, this is a hybrid class. Half of you are here, and half are taking this class from the confines of your homes or other areas." My nose twitches when his eyes look through the camera, and I swear he's looking directly at me.

Yeah, yeah, old man. I'm learning from work. Some of us don't have the luxury of screwing off while in school. I've got my beat-up old laptop propped up on the tall front counter, running on what seems like Windows 8 and half-working earbuds.

This was the only way to attend college full-time and work both jobs. Thank God for Booker's understanding soul. Usually, I'd be at the bar by now, but on Tuesdays and Thursdays, I now open his used record store so I can attend class in peace. It's not like anyone comes here anymore. Most people use The Dot to stream their music nowadays, instead of records or CDs. Briefly, records came back, and business boomed, but not anymore. We don't get many walk-ins these days, but we get a good number of online orders from around the world through our website. Thankfully, that keeps this place afloat.

I take out my notebook and pen and take notes on everything he says. He's apparently a stickler for punctuality, and assignments must be turned in on time: no special treatment—his words, not mine. Again, I swear he looks at me with a disapproving gaze, like he thinks I'll skip out because I'm at home and not physically there.

Despite his asshole, stuck-up face, I keep going and listen to him go on and on. His voice grates my damn nerves with every word he says, and I kind of want to stab him. But hey, I only have a year of this, and then I'll move on to the following year, where he'll hopefully not be.

The bell above the door rings, echoing through the small store.

"Welcome to Dead Records. Look—" I stop short when I meet a familiar pair of icy eyes, filled to the brim with a cocky attitude, possession, and pure sex appeal.

My breath leaves my lungs. Did my rampant thoughts summon the devil himself and his merry band of fuckwits? Probably. This is the luck I'm graced with every day.

"River Blue," he says in a smooth voice, gliding toward the large wooden counter I'm nestled behind and leaning against it. "How many jobs do you have to hold down in this shit town?" His brows furrow with concern, eyeing me up and down.

I sigh, rubbing my temple, hoping to soothe the damn headache forming. My professor drags on, but the entire band of Whispered Words stands in front of me with an expecting gaze. What did I do to deserve this type of punishment today? Is God punishing me? Again?

"Well, some of us can't live off mommy and daddy's money forever. What are you, Kieran? Twenty-one? Have you ever held down a real job?" I snark, barely containing the bitter words on my tongue. His face falls, and his friends snicker as they browse the old records. "Don't laugh. You assholes are in the same boat." I wrinkle my nose when their gazes land on me with narrowed eyes, and their mouths gape. Yeah, dickbags, I called you out. Someone has to.

Kieran blows out a breath and swipes a hand down his face. "Yeah, got me there," he freely admits, shoving his hands into his pocket. "Listen…" he murmurs in a smooth, panty-dropping voice.

Goosebumps scatter across my flesh, raising the hairs on every inch of my body as he advances with predatory intent. A warm, familiar smile spreads across his lips when he rounds the L-shaped counter and invades every inch of my space.

My breath shudders inside my chest when Kieran looms above my seated frame, hovering there and watching me with a keen eye. His gaze falls on my rapid breaths. Every inhale I take; he counts it in his mind. Every little twitch, he eyes with intent. Every inch of my body is aware of his presence, heating under his watchful gaze. Try as I might, I can't focus on anything but him. Them. All their eyes are on me and invading my bubble.

I stiffen when the faintest touch brushes through the long strands of my brown hair, pushing it to rest over my shoulders and exposing my neck. Shivers run down my spine when his rough fingertips dance across my flesh, taking whatever, he wants, inch by inch.

A large lump lodges in my throat, and reality comes crashing in. A panic-fueled storm rages in my belly, and the bile rises. For so long, I've fought off the hazy memories of the worst night of my life, and it's times like these that make them come back with a vengeance. Kieran's too close —too touchy. Ants dance across my skin when their unwanted words rush through my mind. My eyes drift across the boys, connecting with Callum's as his head tilts. Concern etches on his face, and his lips pop open like he's connecting the dots in his mind. Swallowing hard, I stare at the ground, trying to ground myself and forget the world around me.

"She's too drunk, just fucking…"

"Just take them off."

"Fuck yes…"

Their voices haunt my every waking moment. The feel of their phantom fingers working down my shorts and tossing them and my panties aside, leaving me bare for an entire group of strangers to see. No matter how hard I struggled. No matter how many times I drunkenly said no, these strangers took what they wanted and eliminated my choices when I was only fifteen. My only saving grace was the man with dark eyes and tattoos creeping up his neck.

"Shit! What the hell?" Rad whispers with concern. "Jesus!" he croaks, emotions rising in his throat. "Hey? Hey? Are you okay? Something happened, Sweetness. I think you need to go to the hospital. Hey? Can you hear me?" A light tapping on my cheeks forces my eyes to crack open, and I look around.

The moist grass encases my nearly naked and aching body, and when I peek at the man sitting beside me with tears on his cheeks, I immediately recognize him. Ashton Radcliffe. My classmate and Kieran's—my knight—new best friend.

My ma said I shouldn't have gone to the party after it was all said and done. She said I was too young for that side of town, and I should have known the Lakeview kids would have done that. But she never understood my reasoning because she was never there.

I wanted a chance to see the boy who had left me behind and glimpse the man he had become. Many nights I wished I had stayed home and forgotten about the boy who handed me a weapon to defend myself and taught me about life.

But what I saw was a stark reminder of why I should have given up on that dream because he was a completely different person, lounging by the pool with his new friends, laughing as girls jumped into the pool naked in front of them. That should have been the first clue I was in way over my head, coming to the party with just one friend.

Even when I tried to gain his attention and say hi, he blew me off and pretended not to know me. Hell, as I've gotten older, I don't think he did. Was I so easily forgettable? Or had I changed so much?

In retaliation and with a broken heart, I took my first, second, third, fourth, and fifth drink of alcohol. Something I swore I'd never do. After seeing its effects on Kieran's mom and mine, alcohol was never my go-to. Shit, it still isn't.

I shudder again, trying to tamp the swirling panic roaring in my gut. It's not those strangers. It's not the situation. Regardless of that, the memory plays on a loop. The rest of my patience breaks like a damn rubber band snapping.

Beads of sweat break out in a slight sheen, misting my whole body at the feel of his unwanted hands ghosting through my hair. I learned to set my fucking boundaries long ago, and now it's time to remind them where I stand. Through the years, I've reclaimed my body and pleasure, but on my terms.

I abruptly push from my seat, startling everyone. Before he can move, I'm weaving my fingers through his short, dark strands. Yanking his neck to the side, I snarl, standing on my tippy toes to reach his massive height. If I thought he was enormous on stage, standing in front of him is a whole other story. He towers over me with impressive stature and bulky muscles. Probably put on by lugging amps, guitars, and drum sets around. I huff.

Now is not the time to think about his sexy body. Now is the time to show him what I think of him touching me without permission—or anyone for that matter. If these guys think they can follow me around and touch me whenever they want, they've got another thing coming.

I yank the small pocketknife I never leave home without out of my pocket. Flicking it open, I expose the razor-sharp edge and nudge it straight into his cock through his jeans. His eyes blow wide when the tiny tip of my knife nestles snuggly against his balls in warning.

Yeah. It's ball-nicking time, Assface. Feel my fucking fury.

His hands go up in the defense, and I pull his hair tighter, making him wince. River West and no sleep do not mix. But sprinkle over-privileged, touchy pricks into the pot? Makes for an unpleasant morning. For all of us, now, apparently.

"Just because we had one mediocre fuck doesn't give you the right to touch me ever again. Ya hear?" I ask, pulling the strands of his hair tighter in my grip until he answers like a good fucking boy with a nod. Tears collect in my eyes from the fucking anger and fear flowing through my damn veins. I try to shake them off, refusing to let them fall. I'll be damned if these assholes see me cry, even if it's not from sadness.

"Whoa," Rad, the drummer, murmurs in alarm.

As quiet as a damn church mouse, he moves beside me, putting his hands up in a placating manner. A grimace spreads across his face, darting his eyes from the storm brewing behind my eyes and the knife currently two seconds away from plunging into his BFF's dick. Sometimes I wonder if he remembers the girl he found half naked, discarded behind a shed like a piece of trash or if I'm simply a blemish in his memories. Because I often think of the man who helped dress the disoriented, sobbing girl and thank him daily. Not only did he pick me up at my lowest, but he also took me to the hospital.

I grind my teeth, staring deep into the eyes of my former classmate, Rad. The boy who held me close after…. I shake my head, ridding my brain of those thoughts again.

"Sorry, River," Rad corrects with a small, understanding smile. "He meant nothing by it. Kieran is a little touchy-feely when he's all hopelessly obsessed." Kieran grunts at his friend's remark but doesn't refute it. In fact, when I look into his icy eyes, I see the fire brewing, just for me—his River Blue.

"Obsessed? What're you, my stalker, now?" I say, staring into Kieran's hooded eyes.

"You kept it," he breathes, gesturing to the knife nestled against his balls with his eyes, not daring to move a muscle.

"I… I…" My tongue sticks to the roof of my mouth as I stare at the name etched into the grip. River Blue.

Butterflies burst to life in my belly, doing somersaults inside me, arousing the beast between my legs. The way he stares at me sends conflicting emotions straight through me. I ache for him to bend me over again and screw me into next week. Hell, even the thrill of his friends watching slickens my panties more, which should disgust me. But it doesn't. And it proves to me more and more how fucked up I am.

Kieran is bad for my health. Bad boy. Rich prick. Can't keep his hands to himself. And looking at me like I'm the answer to everything. Lights burst in his eyes when he looks at me, almost begging to grab me tight, kiss the soul from my body, and claim what's his.

Damn it. I'm spiraling toward poor decisions. Again. I've been down a hopeless road, leading to heartbreak and disaster. If I knew what was good for me, I'd cut his balls off and be done with it. But I never know when to quit. It's my toxic fucking trait.

"I kept it," I whisper, furrowing my brows at my answer.

My breath leaves when I see the desire swimming within the depths of his eyes at my confession like he has me right where he wants me.

Liquid lust spears straight to my pussy, clenching around nothing when his raging hard-on pokes into my stomach. Even with a fucking knife pointed at his balls. He licks his lips, giving me a tiny head shake, and fear overtakes him. Confirming to me all I need to know about the boy who I literally have by the balls. He likes this.

"Not-not stalking you," Callum mumbles, stumbling over his words, carefully flipping through the vintage records nestled in their sleeves.

Callum Rose stands with his broad back to me, flexing every time he pulls a sleeve out and reads the back. He hums to himself mostly, bobbing his head. White earbuds poke out from his ears, obscured by blond curls hanging over his ears. A deep blush overtakes his face when he peeks back at me, giving me a soft smile, and returns to his findings with vigor.

"And you just happen to work here," Asher Montgomery sneers in my direction, standing with his arms folded across his chest. His lip twitches, looking around the store, and sticking his nose in the air.

"I came to apologize," Kieran murmurs, drawing my attention back to him with the brush of his finger under my chin.

I raise a brow, pulling harder on his hair. He grunts, rolling his eyes back when his boner throbs against my stomach. Interesting…

"For what?" I say with confusion, ignoring the butterflies fluttering in my guts.

Stupid butterflies. Just shoo now. I don't have time for shitty feelings.

"For being an asshole after the show," he whispers with pleading eyes. "I didn't know… it was you." He attempts to shake his head, but my fingers tighten, restricting his movements.

"He also wanted to say how sorry he was for not giving you the orgasm you deserved," Rad hums in a quiet voice, almost so low I don't hear the desire dripping from his words.

But I do. It's the same gut-turning feeling twisting my insides when I peek at him. My hero. My fucking saint. Stepping closer, he's a breath away. A kiss away. No! A punch away. His warmth brushes across my neck, sending shivers down my spine. Every inch of me heats to lava levels.

Stupid, complicated hormones. We're done with bands! Done with guys like this.

I jerk back, narrowing my eyes thick with suspicion. Gritting my teeth, I curse myself. Why these guys? Huh? Why does it have to be them? Why can't it be like some nice guy down the road with a good family who wants a healthy relationship?

This whole situation screams my ex, Donavon Drake. All over again. Why can't I have some nice fella who treats me right and doesn't look at me like I'm their next sex pet? This whole thing will lead to one big, fucking colossal disaster. And they're the damn bomb exploding in the middle. I close my eyes and take several deep breaths and count to ten. If I could afford therapy, I'd have a therapist on speed dial ready to hear the chaos ruling my brain.

"Rad," Kieran hisses between his teeth, grunting as he pulls against my grip. "Don't make it fucking worse, idiot," He curses under his breath when the man, firmly known as Rad, signs his death warrant.

I narrow my eyes when the warmth of a finger hovers above my cheek.

"You touch me with that finger you want to stroke my face with, and I'll bite it off. I'm like that llama—no touchy-touchy. I don't even know you," I grit out, eyeing the offending finger like a damn Twinkie. Bring it closer, drummer boy, and you won't be playing with your sticks or dicks any time soon.

"We came for the check you owe us," Ash demands, cutting through the invisible rope of sexual tension hovering above me.

Pushing off the wall, Ash marches toward me with an odd sense of determination. His angular face hardens, and his hazel eyes narrow—my nose wrinkles when he catches Callum's attention and nods in my direction. The tigers are on the prowl, ready to pounce on innocent little me. Callum's eyes roll toward the ceiling at Ash's demand. Placing the record back, he heaves a sigh and follows his leader like the baby duck he is, shoving his hands in his pocket. His gray eyes avoid mine, looking anywhere but at me.

"I paid you," I tsk, shaking my head. "And how did you find me? Do I seriously need to change my address and name?" Shit. I need a security guard or something if these douche canoes are going to be hanging around. Or someone to guard me against doing something stupid, like fucking Kieran again.

"We went to the bar. The cook said you'd be here," Ash says with a calculating eye.

Leon is fucking dead to me. Dead! Gone. I'll dig his grave myself. Ugh! He probably cackled to himself after they left. Oh, yeah. Real fun. Send them to River so she can stress even more on her first day of classes.

"We came so I could apologize for being an asshole," Kieran grunts when my fingers tighten to unimaginable levels, pulling him with my movements.

Rad snorts, pulling my attention to him, and pulls out a crinkled paper from his pocket. His nose wrinkles as he straightens out the crumbled paper on the counter's edge and then holds it in the air with pride. A slight smirk pulls at the edge of his lips when his dark eyes meet mine. My brows furrow when he puts it in front of my face, letting me read the messy print, and it all clicks.

My eyes widen when I read the words etched into the check repeatedly. And finally… I fuckin lose it. A laugh sputters from my lips, and I lose my grip on Kieran and spin around toward the cabinet. Through my fit of laughter, I carefully shut my knife and shove it into my pocket. My husky laugh bounces off the walls and fills the space until I'm practically crying.

"It's not really that funny," Ash says from in front of me with a rigid tone, eyes watching my every move.

"It's kind of funny, dude," Rad says through a chuckle, covering his mouth with his black-painted fingernails.

I stand straight up, feeling the tips of Kieran's fingers brush against my bare legs. Damn, what a day to wear ripped short shorts. Goosebumps erupt, making the hairs on the back of my neck stand on end. This time I don't bother telling him not to touch me. He has enormous balls of steel after I held a knife to his nuts and told him to fuck off. I'll give him a little inch. Now let's see if he takes a mile.

"Come by the bar tonight. I can rewrite this for you," I say, snorting and wiping the tears from my eyes.

"Tonight?" Ash asks, scrunching up his face. "Jesus, you're working tonight too?"

I snort again, shoving the stupid check into my shorts pocket, and shrug. "A girl's gotta eat, Ash. So, yeah, definitely working both jobs today. Like most days." I shrug, swallowing hard when Kieran's hand rests on my leg.

"Wait!" Rad yells with an excited clap, bouncing on his toes. I startle, looking at him with a scathing look. But his joy overtakes everything, and he grins so big the sun shines off his pearly whites. "Sorcha is playing tonight! Isn't she?" His eyes widen with glee. Even making Ash's face go slack as they all look to me for confirmation.

"Yes. Sorcha is playing. There's a cover charge, and it's higher than yours." I give a sharp nod, trying to tamp down my excitement.

Sorcha has the hottest touring independent band in the country. And tonight only, she's stopping at our little bar to play for a room full of her

Midwestern fans—me included. It took months and months of back and forth, but I finally snagged a date for her all-woman band to perform. Not only will I see my fucking idol, but she'll bring lots of money to line my pockets.

I stiffen again, coming back to the quiet conversation around me. Kieran's fingers make slow circles on my upper thigh, slipping beneath the fabric of my jean shorts.

"Do you ever sleep, River Blue? Or are you staring into the stars again, asking the man on the moon questions?" Kieran murmurs huskily, causing more goosebumps to pucker at my skin. My breath shudders when I fall into the memories of our past and let myself feel.

"Dear man on the moon. Will Stacey ever stop being mean?" I mumble, angling my head toward the bright stars and full moon.

"Who is the man on the moon?" a voice says from the shadows, startling me from my spot. I should have listened to my ma and stayed inside.

My heart thunders in my chest when a shadowy figure emerges from behind a tree. Blowing out a breath, I narrow my eyes at the neighbor boy waltzing toward me.

"The man on the moon, duh," I say, gesturing to the giant orb, illuminating our quiet space.

"Right," his brows furrow when he sits beside me at a good distance. "I'm Kieran Knight."

"River Blue," I say with a tiny nod, turning back to the moon. "Now, where was I," I whisper, tapping my chin.

"You were asking the moon about Stacey..." Later that week, Stacey mysteriously broke her arm on the playground after a rough round of kickball, and no one knew how. Only Kieran, the Man on the Moon, and Stacey knew the truth.

"What?" I murmur, momentarily stunned by his rough fingertips against my skin.

He chuckles, moving closer. Bold move for someone who just had his nads threatened. But this seems to be his MO. Cocky. Takes what he wants.

"Relax," he murmurs, eyeing the other boys. "I asked if you ever sleep?" I shiver when his fingers roll further up my thigh, almost to my panty line, and then back down again, teasing my exposed skin.

"I can sleep when I'm dead," I whisper, looking back over to my computer screen, trying to ignore the fingers I want to take for a long ride.

My professor still chatters away in my ear, reviewing the syllabus I should listen to. But I can grab it online later and read it over.

The bell over the front door rings again, drawing our eyes toward the two guys casually walking inside. My body stiffens, watching my stupid ex, Van's eyebrows raise at the sight before him. His wide eyes dart between the four boys standing together and me.

"Well, well, well, Whispered Words," he says mockingly, looking each of the boys over with a snide look.

"Donavan Drake," Ash says calmly, crossing his arms over his chest.

"It's Van," he sniffs haughtily.

Van nods his head at each of the guys in greeting, finally meeting mine. Frantic worry sits in the back of his dark eyes, searing into my soul. Internally, I roll my fucking eyes at the audacity of his stupefied expression. Like a damn deer caught in the headlights. He has no right. He kicked me to the curb. But yet, he still follows me like a lost puppy dog.

"You got the new Hartbraker's album in yet?" he asks, clearing his throat.

Rad snorts, stepping just an inch closer to me, gaining Van's attention. His warm body seeps into my side, and he fucking knows it. He grins like a maniac.

"Hartbraker's bro? Zoe Hart? Didn't she disappear for like seven years?"

Van's eyebrows shoot up into his hairline. "Zoe Hart went into Witness Protection, bro. She almost lost her damn life through it all. She's just now been able to come out and use her real name. She's got a hell of a voice and a hell of a story to tell. This is her first album since she went through that shit in California. Real tragic shit, look it up," Van says, shaking his head.

His brown strands swish with his movements until he swoops it out of his eyes and turns his attention back to me. Just this once, he waits in the winds to hear what I have to say. Of course, he has to, and I don't mind. Music is my fucking life, and The Hartbrakers? They're phenomenal, especially since they came back stronger than ever.

I forget the awkwardness between us and go right into my happy place. Music. The band-aid covers my broken soul, healing me one chord at a time.

"We got the shipment last night," I say quietly, pointing toward the back of the store where stairs will lead him up to the second level. "There's a huge display up there with all her records." He offers me a tight smile, looks around again and then nods.

Van waves his brother along, and they trudge up the stairs, but not before he looks back at me one last time with torment on his face. He licks his lips, looking toward the backroom behind the counter, and then shakes his head.

You know, a long time ago, my ma told me to never, and I repeat, NEVER fuck around with rock stars. She said they were tormented souls who'd screw you over for every penny they could get, and I guess she's right.

Exhibit A: my damn father. But we know all about that.

Exhibit B: Van Drake. The walking, talking sex on a stick, emo, punk rock wannabe who performed at Dead End and stole my heart once in high school. He was the best thing ever to happen to me until his parents discovered us in the back of his rocking Mustang. Naked and panting. Thick with sweat. Then he had to look me in the eye the next day and tell me he couldn't be with me anymore. Yeah, how sweet of him, huh?

It turns out, ole mommy and daddy didn't like him hanging out with the trash—me. Can you see why now I want to escape this stupid town and never look back? He comes in here every so often, giving me those big brown eyes, and I fail almost every time. Somehow, we always end up naked and panting, hiding in my boss's office for a quickie.

But not today. And never again.

I'm so tired of being second-rate pussy that he's too embarrassed to be seen in public with. Especially after he tore my damn heart out because mommy and daddy said so. Besides, the person I really want is rubbing his fingers up and down my leg. Even though I threatened him with a knife to the balls, he's still as bold as they come. And I want another piece. You see, I'm not after love or affection because everyone around me leaves me, including Kieran. I'll take good dick, maybe some dinner, but that's it. No love is in the cards for this gal.

"Donavan Drake, huh? So, you're the girl that sent Judge Drake into an uproar?" Ash asks, watching Van pace the second floor.

I scrunch my nose. "Yeah, I'm not discussing that with you," I mumble because I'd rather choke on bleach than open myself up to a room full of bullies I went to high school with.

Rad whistles. "Man, his dad was on a damn rampage a year ago, going on about some Central chick who had trapped his son," he says, moving a piece of hair from my forehead. "That was you, wasn't it?"

I frown, thinking back to the hot and heavy nine months we spent together. Nine months of filthy sex. Passion. And what I thought was love. And then a hole in my heart.

"I don't know how I trapped him," I say, using rabbit ears over the word trapped. "We dated, had a good time, and then he tucked his tail when mommy and daddy said no." My voice lowers when my eyes connect with his from the second level. A paleness takes over his tanned features, and he averts his eyes, looking ill. That's right, buddy, I figured you out. He's in love with me but refuses to acknowledge it.

"Informative," Ash says, rubbing his chin, looking toward the sun beaming through the tall front windows.

"Informative?" I huff back, shaking my head.

"Just like I said," he replies with a smirk, nodding his head to the other boys and gesturing to them at the front door.

"Buzzkill," Rad murmurs with disappointment but quickly produces a smile. "See ya tonight, Pretty Girl! Make sure you make me a nice Pina Colada, my favorite." He winks, hopping over the tall counter easily.

"Give me a second," Kieran says in a soft voice right in my ear as the others walk out.

"You can go with them, Knight," I say dismissively, fiddling with my earbud.

Despite the distractions around me, I made it through my first class. Granted, I was barely listening to his nasally voice. I huff, closing my laptop and pushing it aside. I don't have another one until later, so I'll do the same thing then, too. Work while listening, and hopefully, there won't be any distractions.

"I can make my sorry up to you later," he whispers directly in my ear, fingers brushing up the inside of my thigh, daring to go further. I swallow hard when he stands even closer to me, fingers working beneath the tethered ends of my shorts. "Or now," he murmurs.

I clutch the counter's edge until my knuckles turn white and nod my head in agreement. I'm taking back what I want, and what I want is his fingers inside me.

"I'd much rather you boss me around and tell me you want to ride my face, but this will do for now, yeah?" he murmurs, flicking his tongue over my ear.

"That's it then, huh?" I gasp when he hits my bundle of nerves with his fingertips. I lick my lip when he nods into my neck, and I sigh. "Then what are you waiting for? You have four seconds to get me off before Van comes downstairs with his brother and sees what you're doing."

"Maybe I want him to see what I'm doing?" Kieran says, rubbing his fingers over my clit in a frantic circle, bringing my orgasm closer and closer to the surface. Fire brews hotter in my stomach, spreading out through my veins. My toes curl in my Chucks, and goosebumps erupt everywhere, despite the heat filling every molecule of my body. "You think he'd get jealous? I think he would. Fun fact, Van never got over the girl they forced him to leave. But you don't belong to Van Drake anymore. The truth is you never did. He was a pathetic excuse of a placeholder. Naw, my sweet River Blue, you belong to me. Always have. Always fucking will," he murmurs into the curve of my neck with such possession that it ties my tongue into knots. I want to yell at him. I am my own fucking woman, and I don't need him. Not after he left me. But nothing seems to come off my heavy tongue except heavy breaths.

My mouth hangs open, and my nails dig into the meaty flesh of his forearm, gripping him so hard I rip my index nail in half. "Fuck him," I grunt, moving my hips with his movements. "Make me come, Kieran," I whisper with desperation, giving in to the euphoric feeling taking over and leaning the back of my head against his shoulder. "And do it quickly," I beg when his teeth sink into the flesh of my shoulder, creating such a delicious pain, stars burst behind my eyelids. A silent scream leaves my lips when the feeling finally wrecks through me.

My pussy clamps around his fingers, and I hold back the scream lodged in my throat. As much as I want to yell it out and let Van hear my pleasure, I hold it back. My breaths come down as soon as their footsteps sound on the metal staircase and head our way.

"Better?" he asks, licking along the wound he created.

"Good boy," I murmur, tapping his leg. "You can go now," I say, eyeing Van, talking to his brother in a low voice. He holds two records in his hands and has a smile on his face.

"I think I'll stay for the show," he says with a chuckle, eyeing the two boys.

"Well, you can remove your damn fingers from my pussy," I say through gritted teeth, earning me another chuckle when he does.

"Van," Kieran says, reaching across the counter with the very hand that was knuckle deep inside me.

My eyes widen in horror at his glistening fingers, soaked to the bone with my pussy juices, grasping onto Van's in a weird bro handshake. They shake for a brief second, exchanging a few words.

"Nice to see you, man. I haven't seen you around the circuit anymore. Your band not playing anymore?" Kieran asks, moving my long strands from the side of my neck and drifting them down my back, seeming to have any excuse to touch me. Hell, maybe he is a stalker, and I'm the willing little prey eating up his touch.

"Uh, nah. We kind of gave that up a year ago. College and all that got in the way." Van shrugs with a cocky smirk, quickly dropping away when his eyes zero in on the exposed part of my neck. He swallows hard, huffing a breath. "Parents wouldn't stop nagging me to give it up and focus on the future. So, they gave me a compromise." Van's eyes dart to me with uncertainty.

"Compromise?" Kieran asks, leaning against the counter with a lazy grin. He watches with glee as Van scratches under his nose and furrows his brows, staring at a glistening spot on his hand. "Was it over that chick?"

Great. I'm that chick now.

Van shifts uncomfortably, still staring at the spot on his hand when he shrugs again. "Um, nah. Dad handed me a check and told me to focus on my real future. So, it was money or the band. Ya know?"

Kieran scoffs, curling his lip back. "You chose money over the band?"

Van scowls. "Yeah. And what would you do, huh? It was take the money and go to college. Or he was going to kick my ass out. Money trumped the band. I needed school. I didn't need the music." He shakes his head, scratching under his nose again, and recoils. With furrowed brows, Van discreetly licks along the wet spot on his hand and jerks back, staring daggers in my direction, but remains rooted in place.

"Any true musician knows the music lives in their souls. It's the fuel for life, man. You can't just give that up for some green. That's like throwing something away you love just because your parents say so." Kieran side-eyes me, and I roll my eyes toward the ceiling, counting down the seconds until Van marches out of here and takes Kieran with him. I got off, and now they can fuck off.

When Van takes a deep breath and his nostrils flare, a twinkle sparkles in Kieran's mismatched eyes. Immediately he turns beet red, stopping the conversation when he shoves the records across the counter.

He pulls out two twenties and tosses them at me without care. "Keep the change," he says through gritted teeth, yanking his confused as fuck brother along. Dillon awkwardly waves over his shoulder, cursing his brother when he shoves him out the door. And once again, I'm left alone with my kryptonite.

Kieran hums, watching them go, and then walks back around the L-shaped counter. He stops in front of my bewildered face and bops my nose with his index finger, grinning like a fucking madman. Which I'm coming to realize he is.

"That was fun, River Blue. We should do it again," he rasps, leaning in to kiss my cheek. The warmth of his lips lingers on my cheek, and my damn body shudders from the contact.

"Don't get too eager. Who says I'll ever let you touch me again? This was a one-time thing," I murmur, leaning my elbow into the counter and inadvertently leaning into his kiss.

He snorts, waving his hand. "See you tonight. But don't make any plans for after your shift."

I scoff. "Asshole, I get off at two in the morning, and then I'm going home." He raises a brow, waltzing towards the front door leisurely.

"Don't make any plans," he all but demands with a possessive growl, spearing right through me.

"Fine." I shrug like he didn't make my pussy fucking gush at the sound of his growl. "But you better up your game, Richy." He scowls at the nick-name, shaking his head.

"It's Kieran, not Richy," he mumbles.

"Yeah, I'm River, not your River Blue or whatever other nicknames you can think of. Remember that. In fact, if you are so inclined, get on your damn knees and worship me next time we meet. I'd be highly disappointed if you didn't. How's that for taking charge?" I demand, putting the bills into the register and shoving the change into my pocket.

"You'll always be my River Blue," he says with a smirk. "And I'll make good on that."

And with that, Kieran walks out the door and gets into the passenger seat of the large Tahoe parked on the other side of the road. I watch through the bright windows as they silently sit until Ash's mouth moves, and they start a discussion. I wish I could be a fly on the damn car ceiling to hear whatever they were saying.

My heart aches in my chest at his sudden reemergence. For so long, I told myself to forget about Kieran Knight. Yet here he is in the flesh, laying down some sort of claim on me like he has any damn right. What's so different now than before? Why is he coming at me so hard with everything he has and stamping his name on my forehead?

I'm pulled from my thoughts as the bell rings over the door again. I frown, staring at the last culprit I thought I'd ever see again. Van comes back through the door with determination etched on his face as he marches up to me.

"Don't trust those assholes," he grits his teeth. "Whatever they say to you, they're lying," he says, slamming a fist onto the counter. "Believe me, they'll screw you over faster than you can count to three, Rivey," he pleads, clenching his teeth.

I nod my head, looking at them through the tall window. They stare over this way. Asher's mouth flaps a few times, and the others stare, waiting in the car, inspecting everything we do with a keen eye.

"Yeah? Just like you, Van?" I hum, leaning my elbow on the counter.

"Yeah, Riv," he sighs, running a hand down his face. "Just like that, trust me on this." His voice sounds urgent, and his eyes plead with me to believe him.

I snort. "Right. Trust you? You're joking, right? Well, I'm a big girl, Van. I've got this. Thanks for your concern."

"Damnit, Rivey, you're too stubborn," he mutters, cursing under his breath. "I'm serious. Whatever they're hanging around for, they're going to use you. That's all they do is use people for what they want."

"Huh, sounds familiar," I say, tilting my head toward the back office, and then I frown.

Shit. I must have a knack for fucking in Booker's offices. First, Van at the record store whenever he wants to slum it, and then Kieran at the bar. I need to get laid in bed or somewhere normal next time.

Van swallows hard, looking toward the ground. "I... Riv, I... you know..." I hold up my hand, cutting him off.

"I don't need your excuses, but our time against the desk is done. I don't need to be second to anyone. No hard feelings," I say with a shrug, eyeing his shallow breaths.

Ah, it appears that Van doesn't like that answer. No. He wants to keep using me and then dumping me all over again. I don't need to keep clawing at these raw wounds and tearing them open for a man who will never love me. He wants me to beg him to fuck me again so he can leave and return to his charmed life without a second glance.

"I, yeah, um.... that's cool," he stutters through his words, rubbing the back of his neck. "I'll still be your friend, though," he murmurs, placing his hand on mine.

At one time, Van's touch made butterflies burst inside my stomach.

And for the first time in a long time, I feel absolutely nothing. Not even his big brown eyes could lure me into their spell. It's taken a long time to get over how he made me feel and how he rejected me so severely. But I think I'm finally moving on. And so, sue me, it may be into the arms of another rich dickface. To me, it's significant progress on the River's heartbreak scale.

I'm moving on from my first and last love onto a better dick. And that's it. How's that phrase go? When one dick disappoints, move on to the next one for a better ride? Yeah, something like that.

His fingers curl around mine, and he squeezes once. "I know you're a big girl, way more capable than me. But I'm serious, Riv. They just take with no regard for who they hurt."

"Yeah? And what did they take from you?" I ask, leaning on the counter again.

"Nothing from me, but they'll stop at nothing to get to the top. They want… they want your dad to sign them," he says, swallowing hard. "I've heard them talk about it when we played shows together. He's their rock idol and getting to the KC Club is their ultimate dream."

"Pfft. My dad can have 'em," I say, wrinkling my nose at the thought. But I'm skeptical of whatever he has to say. "So, let's assume what you're trying to say is… these assholes are getting close to me to get to him? Don't they know Corbin West doesn't do shit with his kids unless they're named Seger or Zeppelin?" I scoff at that, envy brewing in my belly.

I vaguely remember my two older brothers from the brief time I lived with them. But the one thing I know about them is that they got Dad's attention their whole life. And my dad wrote me off the moment he threw us out. So, to say I'm a little jealous they got his love, and I didn't, is an understatement. Why them and not me? That's always been the question.

"Fine," he mumbles. "But don't say I didn't warn you." He shakes his head, moving his long hair from his eyes.

"You're good. You warned me that if I get burned, that's on me. I don't trust them as far as I can throw them, for the record," I say with a shrug, earning a sharp nod.

Van waves goodbye as he walks out the door with a solemn look on his constipated face before stepping out into the sun. So, the boys think they're getting into my daddy's record company through me? That's laughable at best. But let's see them try. I won't let my feelings get in the way. All I'm here for is a good time.

I LICK MY FINGERS AS I WALTZ THROUGH THE RECORD STORE'S FRONT DOOR, moaning at her taste. Her essence fills my damn taste buds, going directly to my dick. God damn. She tastes as sweet as she felt on my dick, and I can't wait to have another fucking bite of her. River might be the drug I've craved for years now.

Never in a million years did I think I'd reconnect with the girl I obsessed over as a kid. My best friend. The girl they forced me to repress. River was too young to understand how deeply I felt about her back then. I could tell her all day long that I loved her, and she'd never understood the true meaning of my words.

My entire world caved when my stupid stepfather marched into my life, hauled me off to greener pastures, and forced me to forget the life I had before. He effectively erased everything from my childhood memories down to the girl I wanted to rush back to. Through expensive new clothes and a butt load of new friends, he took her from me. By the time I reached high school, River was a distant memory and nothing more than a stain on my existence. If I had passed her in the halls or seen her in public, I wouldn't have noticed or known who she was. I was too consumed with my rich new life to fucking care.

I lost myself for eleven years, and now, I've found myself once again. I will do anything to have River by my side, even if it means kidnapping her to wherever we end up. I've only just found her, and I won't lose her. Asher will throw a fit, but—fuck him.

The mid-August sun blares heat down on me like a fucking oven as I walk across the street toward the Tahoe sitting opposite the store. Sweat drips down my back, soaking through my shirt. Man. Screw this one-hundred-degree weather. I could use a dip in the lake. Maybe the boys will want to take the boat out and let loose. A couple of beers, loud music, and a quick dip? Sounds like a dream right now. Maybe River would want to come to hang out on the lake sometime?

As much as I try to imagine the cool water flowing over my skin and

cooling me down, my brain wanders. Memories float, surfacing in my mind, of her moans echoing off the walls and her tight pussy contracting around my cock. Reaching down, I adjust myself. I have no fucking shame. They all know exactly what I did, especially by the stupid expressions lining their faces. And if they have something to say about it, well—they can shove it. I'm doing what Asher instructed and bringing her into our little web, except she's mine. We may use her for her father's influence and gain a little fame. But everything about River West is mine.

Next stop, I'll kneel in her office, awaiting her every instruction. She can grip me by the balls and tell me to squawk like a chicken, and I'd do it if she lets me inside her again. And soon, our plan will all click into place. It's all coming together as I'm coming apart.

Fuck. My dick jumps at that, twitching in my pants, waiting for the moment he can explode to her memory. But I won't touch it until I get to her tonight. I'll make good on my promise and kneel in her office until she allows me a taste and fuck.

I grin when I scoot into the passenger seat of Ash's Tahoe, which is identical to mine. A light feeling falls over me, and my shadows fade away.

"What is Van doing?" Callum asks in a soft voice, eyeing the maniac throwing open the door to the record store with determination on his face.

From here, I can see River's tight expression through the window when he stops in front of her. Concern bleeds from his facial expression as he speaks to her. Fuck him! He left her. He has no fucking right to march back in there like he owns her.

I fucking own her. Those marks on her neck are mine for the world to see who she belongs to. White hot jealousy runs through my damn veins, and I want nothing more than to rip every piece of his throat out and maybe break his face. Fuck him for thinking he could waltz back into her life when he was the dick who fucked her over. No, that's my fucking job. Evil parents forced me away, but now I'm back and better than ever. Van needs to be dealt with.

"Daw look, little Van is trying to get back into her good graces," Rad says mockingly, leaning across Callum to get a better view. He plasters his nose against the backseat window, earning a growl from Asher for leaving marks. Callum pats Rad's back with a sigh as he drapes himself over Cal's lap.

"He still wants to fuck her. He could be a problem," Asher says matter-of-factly.

"Not by the look on her face. Oh, snap," Rad cackles, pointing toward them. "He's trying to hold her hand, and she looks like she wants to puke." He snorts at that, howling with laughter at Van's failures.

"I remember hearing about them, just didn't realize it was her until now," Callum says, shaking his head with furrowed brows. Light creeps into his eyes as he stares at her from afar, watching her every move with quiet intentions.

Our buddy may be a blushing virgin, but I always know when he's interested in a chick. A look always passes over his eyes, and an interest forms. He'll watch from the shadows, inspecting his crush from afar, but never seems to make the moves. I know his reasoning and why he's held onto his V-card for so long, but I think he'll give it up someday soon. Especially with the way he blushes and stumbles around River. Two down, two to go. Now, all I have to do is get Rad and Asher interested in our little mark, and my plan will come together. There will be no protests when I haul her into my lap and force her to California when we get our big break.

"Bleh. It's hotter than my balls outside today," Rad curses, rearranging his junk in his shorts, probably dreaming of the hour when he can drop them and be free. "Oh, fuck balls, we got a little guest coming." Rad nods toward the figure marching his angry ass toward our vehicle.

"This should be interesting," Asher says in a no-nonsense tone, rolling down his window. "Oh, Van, fancy seeing you here," he drawls in a fake, respectful tone, lazily looking at the fuming man outside our window.

Van shakes his head, a deep scowl forming across his lips. "I don't know what you assholes are up to, but you're barking up the wrong fucking tree. Leave River alone. She's not like these other Central girls," he growls, leaning into Ash's window.

"And have you sampled many Central Girls?" I ask, sitting back in my seat, enjoying the cool air-conditioning pouring from the vents.

He scowls at me, shaking his head. "You know my answer. Leave River alone," he growls again, exposing his gritted teeth like an actual threat.

Pfft. The only threat Van Drake poses is a road bump. He could warn River all he wanted about us and whatever else he might say, but she'd never believe him. From the moment River was born, so was her stubbornness.

"Tell me exactly why you care so much?" Ash asks in an even voice, leaning back in the driver's seat with a relaxed and open pose. Casually, he raises a brow as Van's face comically gets redder and redder by the minute.

"What's so great about her, Donnie boy?" Rad asks through a manic grin, rubbing his hands together. "Why should we stay away? Maybe we need a new toy to play with, and maybe she already said yes."

It's a lie, of course. River isn't just a toy to me, anyway. But by the way Van's face falls from our admission; we've got him on our hook. That's right, back off and eat our lie, fuckhead. My fingers curl into fists when he opens his mouth to speak again. I'd rather shove my fist down his throat than continue this tired conversation. There's nothing on this planet he can do to keep us away from River.

Van scoffs. "You assholes may have this entire city fooled into believing you all are some sort of good guys. But I've seen the shit you used to pull back in high school. You're nothing but users. And as for River? She won't be able to help you in your quest for fame," he growls his words, clenching his teeth. "You know it, and she knows it. Her daddy doesn't talk to her. I know exactly what you're up to. You've had this plan since fucking high school to get the hell out of here. But I'm here to stop you from using another person on your bullshit quest."

Ah, there it is. Not only did Donnie Boy want to continue his own quest into music, but he wants her all to himself. Fat chance that'll ever happen, pal. Kieran Knight is back in town and isn't giving up his River Blue for anything, especially a piss ant like him.

"Tell me, Donnie," Ash admonishes, clenching and unclenching his fists. "Does it eat you up? You can't be with her still? Do you dream of the nights you had to hide her in the back of your Mustang, stealing her away and fuck her while introducing your parents to Whitley? You know, the girlfriend you have so cleverly hidden in the shadows while you come here and try to convince River to be your fuck toy in the back room?"

Van's paling face completely falls as he looks at Asher in surprise. I'd say my malevolent brother hit the mark.

"What the fuck, man?" he gasps, dropping his arms from the edge of the window. "How..." He peers back at River through the storefront windows, who watches our exchange, kicking back into her chair. I can't make out her expression, but I feel her eyes burning through me. That's right, River Blue—eyes on me, baby.

"I have my ways," Ash says, slowly turning his evil-ass face to look into Van's dark eyes. "At this moment, I have a letter typed up in an email on a timer. If you don't back away now, I will release everything to Whitley promptly. Not that I shouldn't, anyway. What a despicable way to treat the woman you're going to marry."

"What the hell are you, some evil psycho?" Van says, taking another step back.

"Maybe," Ash says with a grin and a shoulder shrug. "You leave River to us. No harm, no foul. We'll both get what we want in the end."

"Yeah? And what the fuck is that?" Van scolds, crossing his arms over his chest.

"We'll get ours, and she'll get hers. Besides, Kieran didn't even need to beg her to fuck him by how loud and responsive she was. It looks like she doesn't need you anymore, Donnie boy. That's all I'm saying…"

"That's right, Donnie Boy," I interrupt, leaning over Asher to get a better view of the laughable rage consuming Van's twisted face. "You see, it isn't your name she screams anymore. It's mine. My fingers were just knuckle deep in her tight pussy as she came all over them. And my teeth mark her skin as fucking mine. You leave my River alone. You have no rights over her. Not anymore. You lost those privileges. She. Is. Mine," I growl, curling my fingers into fists.

Vivid images of pounding his face in as blood pours from his mouth and nose as he begs me to stop hurting him run through my mind. Make no mistake; if Van touched her again without my permission, he's a dead man.

Through his narrow, dark eyes, hate brews toward me, and he snarls, readying his rebuttal, but nothing comes out.

"Now, if you'll excuse us, we're late for a very important meeting." Ash doesn't let Van respond as he closes the window and takes off.

"Meeting, huh?" I ask, blowing at my anger. Now that the danger has passed, my fingers tremble with the leftover adrenaline running through my veins.

"God, you handed him his ass. We left him sputtering and spitting in the middle of the street," Rad cackles more, falling into the backseat. "I bet he'll tuck tail and run back to mommy and daddy with tears in his pathetic eyes."

"He'll keep his hands off what's ours now," Asher declares, narrowing his eyes in the rearview mirror. Shaking his head, he focuses on the long road ahead of us, navigating us back to Lakeview.

The record store disappears from behind us, replaced by the upscale side of Central City. Boutiques and restaurants become blurs of colors, and trees soon line the edges of the road. We may still be in Central City, but you wouldn't know. The Lakeview District has wild hills with trees and tons of wildlife. A large lake sits to my right, expanding over the horizon. Boats putter along, pulling rafts, wake boarders, and skis, looking like a serene paradise. But it is anything but.

"How about a little music therapy?" Callum asks, eagerly leaning forward, tapping his fingers on the center console, aching to strum his bass.

So much better than taking out the boat. Sure, the sun, wind, and water would be a pleasant treat after such a sweltering day. But nothing compares to the music we're about to create as one unit. I feel it in the depths of my gut. It's the intense need to get my hands moving and create memorable tunes. We all feel it by the sharp nod Ash gives when we pull into our driveway. He throws the SUV into park, strumming his fingers along the steering wheel.

"It's working, isn't it?" he asks with a hint of uncertainty, which is so unlike himself. He twitches uncomfortably, eyeing my smirk.

"Smell Kieran's finger and see if that gives you the answer," Rad says, barking out a sharp laugh. The entire car shakes when he throws himself back into his seat, practically crying with laughter.

Asher scowls. "That's not gonna—" Ash's eyes widen as big as fucking saucers when my pussy-coated fingers slip into his mouth, giving him a taste. He'll never tell Callum and Rad that the tip of his tongue poked against my fingers before he spits and sputters, forcing me out.

"You were saying?" I ask, cocking my head to the side with a feral grin.

Nothing makes me happier than riling up my stepbrother. The angrier he gets, the funnier it is.

His teeth grind when he turns his glare directly at me. His nostrils flare wildly, and his fingers clench into a fist until he's punching the steering wheel and grunting curses in my direction.

"I'll be back," he bites out, throwing his shirt off and into my face.

"We'll warm up while you…" Rad says as Ash takes off down the road, jogging toward the only place that calms him down whenever he works himself up like this.

"So dramatic," I mock, throwing his shirt into the passenger seat. "Now, let's get some practice in before he gets back," I say, getting out of the car with the guys on my heels.

"Think he'll be back in time?" Callum asks, rubbing his chin and staring off into the distance. We all wonder the same thing. How long will he run for now? And when will he make it to his destination?

"Give him time," I say, clutching his shoulder and chuckling. "He'll be back. You know him; he always pushes himself to the brink. No matter if it's ten minutes or two hours. He'll be a sweaty fucking mess by the time he gets back."

Asher may like to pretend he doesn't like us, but deep down, he at least enjoys our presence enough to tolerate us regularly.

Walking up to the garage door, I punch in the four-number code with a sigh. This is it. The moment I've been aching for since I woke up this morning. The moment I've been dreaming about through my first classes of the year to finish up my business degree.

As the garage door slowly lifts, our paradise comes into view just as Ash's sweaty form comes back into view. He heaves a breath, leaning his hands on his knees, and shakes the sweat off.

"You good?" I ask, staring down at him when he nods.

"As good as I'll be for now," he mumbles, standing tall. His eyes drift over our setup, and I see the moment the stress of the world rolls off his shoulders. "Just don't fucking stick your pussy fingers in my mouth again," he gripes, pushing my shoulder. "If I wanted a taste, I'd fucking take a taste." And with that, he waltzes into our band space with sweat pouring from every inch of his skin after pushing himself for ten minutes straight. Throwing his guitar strap over his bare shoulder, he begins tuning his strings. Within a few plucks, guided by his natural ability, he's all tuned up and ready to go.

"Why the fuck are you undressing? Again?" Ash asks, turning to Rad, who sits completely naked on his stool behind his drums, minus the combat boots secured to his feet.

"The boys gotta breathe, bro. It's hot, and my balls are cooking inside my jeans," he says, twirling a drumstick in both hands. "Duh." Without another word, he counts us in, and we construct a new song we've felt in the pits of our dark souls for days, flowing out of us with ease.

This is where it's at. Music brings us together, binding us in a friendship that will never fall apart. We may not always like each other. But we're fucking brothers. As long as we have this. The chords. The melodies. And the words, we have it all—even River in the future.

DAY NUMBER TWO OF MY MANAGER JOB AT DEAD END FINDS ME BACK AT the front door admitting patrons into the bar—AKA my favorite place to be.

When I was fifteen—yeah, fifteen, I know. Probably way too young to be hanging around a bar, but I had good reason. I begged Booker to give me a job. I was desperate to make money and support myself since my mom could barely do that on a good day. Plus, I needed something to take my mind off all the awful shit happening around me. I needed a purpose, and this right here gave me just that.

On the first day on the job, he sat me here and explained what I needed to do. Check IDs, stamp hands, and turn people away when I have to. He was my saving grace. The only adult to look at me and see a responsible girl looking to make a better life for herself.

Nestled on my bar stool with my tiny podium in front of me, I watch the crazy line stretching out the door and onto the sidewalk. Again. Seriously, it has to be a mile long by now. It's the longest line I've ever seen coming into this place. And I fucking did it! I brought these people here. Well, okay. Sorcha's band brought them here to my venue. My hard work made this happen, and I can't wait for Booker to see all the success I'm bringing to Dead End.

Soft murmurs and excited whoops permeate the air, and the growing crowd surrounds our meager stage with such excitement; my fucking heart skips a beat. Packed shoulder to shoulder with their arms touching and their heads leaning back as the lights on stage dim low, leaving us all in the dark. For only a moment, at least.

A sudden cheer erupts through the crowd, their arms bursting into the air. They jump up and down as the band makes their way across the stage, taking their places in the pitch-black atmosphere. Their shoe scuffs, and their heels click against the wooden set. And all hell breaks loose when the bright lights flash. Her crazy red curls bounce when she bobs her head, looking back at the three other women playing with her. She grins, turning her pearly whites toward the crowd.

"Hello, Central City! Glad to be here! Let's wake the damn dead!" she screams into the microphone before gracefully singing the first notes of their opening song.

Pure ecstasy saturates my soul in waves. The weight of the world momentarily lifts from my shoulders. All the stress. All the pain. Everything I've endured in my brief life leaves me like a bird in flight, hopefully never to return. One day I'll live without this hovering above me, but for now, I'll revel in the music carrying me away. My eyes close on their own, my body swaying to the beat of the heavy drums leading up to the song's chorus. She screeches her words, hyping everyone in the crowd up.

Taking a deep, refreshing breath, I bathe in the atmosphere. This is why I'm here. This is why I do what I do for this place and bring these bands in. They're like sage to the soul; I'd never have it any other way.

Life flashes before me again, and I bring myself back out of the clouds with a renewed sense of determination. Whatever I plan to do with my life after I get my degree in business, I want it to involve music. Maybe that comes from my dad, or perhaps that comes from my dependency on tunes. Whatever it is, I'm determined to make my dreams come true. No matter what I have to do. I'll leave this town behind with one finger raised in the air and a degree in the other hand.

"Ahem! Bitch," a familiar woman's voice snaps me out of my reprieve.

Right. This must be my torture for the evening. Peering up, I put on my polite face and smile at Tessa. Her ice-blue eyes again glare at me, scoffing and tossing her perfect blonde locks over her shoulder.

"I'm sorry?" I ask, raising a brow at the girl standing before me with her hip cocked out in her short as hell skirt. If she swishes, I think her perfectly sculpted butt cheeks would pop out and show the world what she's got cooking under her hood.

"I need a stamp; here's my cover charge," she hisses loud enough for me to hear the venom in her words, practically shoving the money at me. Her eyes dart around the room, and she strains her neck to look over the bobbing crowd.

"Have you seen them?" She shouts over the music to her friend standing behind her when I stamp her hand, and she moves aside.

"No," Sara giggles, shoving fifteen dollars into my hand, a little nicer than her friend.

"Ugh. Their FlashGram said they'd be here hanging out tonight. It's my one chance. They won't be onstage for once," she murmurs, grabbing her friend's hand, and tries to take off into the sea of people.

"Central Trash," her friend says, tilting her head when I wrinkle my nose at the name.

"I have a name," I state with a tight expression, narrowing my eyes at her. Running a finger along my boob, I show the name printed on my shirt for good measure. "I'm River. The manager." I, once again, run a finger over the word manager etched into my tit, earning me a haughty scoff.

Three years ago, they graduated from high school, yet they act like we're still roaming the halls together. This is their ridiculous way of putting me in my place and showing me I'm nothing more than a Central girl, which is laughable. To them, I'm firmly under their fucking sharp heels, ready for them to squish me to pieces.

"Have you seen them yet?" Her friend curses, trying to pull her along, muttering under her breath.

"Who?" I ask, waving the next person forward.

I take their money and stamp their hand, repeating the process with the following people, and check IDs along the way. At least fifty people, okay, that's an exaggeration, come through the door before these two make up their minds. When I look back at the doorway, it's practically empty, and the line has died down. Thank God. It'll give me a second to finally breathe.

"Whispered Words," the girl snarks, leaning forward.

"God, Sara!" Tessa mutters, stomping her foot.

"What, Tessa? She sees everyone who comes through the doors. It's her job," she scoffs, rolling her eyes toward the ceiling. "So, she'd know if they were here. They just played a few days ago!" Tessa nods, staring at me for confirmation.

A deep heat invades my cheeks and ears, remembering precisely what Kieran and I got up to earlier. His fingers were inside me and swirling over my clit while my ex-boyfriend browsed the shop, none the wiser. Rad promised Kieran would deliver the best orgasm of my life, and he did. He really fucking did. I want a repeat, spend a day getting lost in his dick, pretending the outside world doesn't exist, and enjoy the man he is now because I've obviously broken my vow about swearing off him. So, why not have some fun?

"No," I state with a shrug, keeping my voice as even as possible. There's no way in hell I'd admit to these two groupies. That has to be what they are, if I have seen them or not.

"See," Tessa scoffs, rolling her eyes again. "We'll find them ourselves. Thanks for nothing, Central Slut," she hisses, dragging her friend into the crowd of people, losing themselves to the loud metal music flowing through the speakers.

"Enjoy the show," I mutter, discreetly lifting my middle finger to their backs.

Who are they going to tell on me, too, anyway? I'm the damn boss right now. I should tell them to shove their judgmental names where the sun doesn't shine, but I like to think I'm a little more professional than that. Well—I cringe, lowering my finger—sometimes I'm professional. I can only handle the whole Central whore/slut, name-calling for so long before I blow a gasket and give them what they deserve.

"Well, hello, Pretty Girl," Rad sings above the music, throwing his arms all around. If he wanted to stay small and away from the two groupies asking about them, he's failing miserably by announcing his damn presence. I sneak a peek at the two girls in question and grin when they're caught up in the crowd and unable to make it over. Too bad, so sad for them. Such a shame.

"Well, hello, drummer boy," I singsong back, cocking my head to the side at the sight of him.

God damn. My momma said don't fuck with rock stars, but it's so hard when they look this delectable and lickable. Seriously! Rad's sporting tight jeans, leaving not-so-little Rad's outline on display. Like holy eggplant in the pants, Batman. I swallow hard, my gaze making it up to his exposed arms coming out of his sleeveless tank, giving me a peek of the tattoo expanding over his chest and into his throat. And finally, his ridiculous curly mullet is perfectly styled, not a curl out of place. But the icing on the cake tonight is the septum piercing glowing in the dark space. His pearly whites pop out when he grins at me again, catching the moment my eyes roamed downwards.

He snorts, leans against my little podium, and grins like a madman. "I don't know if I've properly introduced myself to you yet," he murmurs, reaching for the stamp in my hand, stamping Callum's and his hand. "Although drummer boy is pretty hot coming from your lips, I'm…"

"Ashton Radcliffe the Third," Asher says in a mimicking tone, strolling through the front door with a smirk plastered on his lips. Leaning against Rad, he places his elbow on his shoulder.

"It's Rad," he hisses, a soft red blooming across his cheeks, reaching to the tips of his burning ears. "I'm Rad, definitely not Ashton," he says, shaking his head and curling his lip. He looks back at me with pleading dark eyes and points. "It's Rad, not Ashton," he argues again, leaning down onto the podium and putting the stamp back into my fingers.

My heart falls when I stare into his sparkling, dark eyes. Although I'm in no particular mood to relive the night, he saved me from the shadows and took me to the hospital. It's disheartening to hear he doesn't know who I am. I mean, I don't blame them for not recognizing me from high school. So many students from the surrounding area squished into one building that it'd be hard to keep track of everyone. But to look me in the eye and not remember? I shake my head. Maybe he's like me. That night was horrific; if I had come across that sight, I'd have blocked it out, too.

"Okay, definitely not Ashton, who I went to high school with and have talked to before. You've been stamped. Now pay up," I say, holding my free hand out. "It's a fifteen-dollar cover charge per person."

"It's Rad, for fuck's sake," he grumbles to himself, reaching into the depths of his back pocket. "And wait," he says, holding up a finger. "We went to school together?" His brows furrow when he steps around the podium, taking in my short shorts and a tight black T-shirt. "I'd definitely remember you." He rubs his chin, eyeing me with a hunger that makes my stomach knot.

Fuck. If he doesn't stop staring at me like that, I'll invite him into the back room and rock his world with Kieran. No one says I can't have more. Besides, If I'm breaking my vow, I'm going all in.

"There's only one fucking high school in this mediocre town," Asher huffs out, rolling his eyes at our antics like the douchebag he is. I wonder if he ever lightens up or if he's a perpetual grumpy pants?

Sometimes I think that man needs to get laid or yank the giant stick out of his ass. Even in high school, I remember him being a colossal douche to everyone, and he still hasn't changed. Girls used to chase him as a challenge, and he'd wave them off with a scowl, telling them to fuck off. Maybe Tessa and Sara can rock his world and ease the assholishness out of him, or perhaps he can eat eggs and fuck off. Because I'm not touching him with a twenty-foot pole unless he's nicer. Like buying me lots of diamonds, nicer.

"Although Ashton doesn't sound too bad coming from your mouth. I can see how this relationship is going to go," Rad rambles, disregarding Asher's answer with a grin. Pulling out three twenties and depositing them into my free hand, he wiggles his brows.

"I'm Callum-Callum," Callum says, brushing his blond curly, shaggy locks from his gray eyes.

A deep blush rises on his cheeks, and he quickly looks away with a bashful smile and moves into the room, wringing his hands together. Looking back, he smiles again, and his blush deepens further. Only this time, he looks me in the eye and gives me a shaky wave, like it took everything inside him to make that connection. With a wink and a wave, I successfully make him blush so hard he resembles a tomato.

"This is so fucking unnecessary," Asher grumbles, running a hand down his twisted face. But again, no one pays attention to him. They simply smile at me with goo-goo eyes and continue their weird introductions.

"That's great," I say with sarcasm, looking behind them.

I wave a hand, motioning the other two idiots forward as Callum and Rad look off into the rowdy crowd. Rad, of course, grins at Callum, muttering something into his ear and gesturing toward the sea of people.

Kieran steps forward with his face tipped down and his mismatched eyes locked on me. His Adam's apple bobs when he finally stops in front of my podium and pulls his hands from his pockets. When he finally lifts his chin, my heart stops at the desperation swimming in the depths of his mesmerizing eyes. They bore into me, and I feel him in my clenching core, begging me to finish what we had started earlier. But correctly this time, and balls deep.

Shit. I need therapy and dickaholics anonymous or something to keep me away from him. At this point, I don't think I'll be able to deny him any longer, and I'll give into his every whim. Would that be so bad?

Heat spreads throughout my entire body, and I flush. Starting at the tip of my ears, working down my neck, and onto my chest. The idiot smirks, knowing precisely what's going through my damn brain. The tips of his fingertips brush against my hand when I stamp it.

Ash growls with annoyance, pushing Kieran out of the way. He grabs the stamp from me, like the asshole he seems to be, and stamps his hand with greater force than necessary. He throws it back at me, tossing his arms in the air at Kieran, and takes off toward an empty booth by himself, pouting the entire way.

"What crawled up his ass?" I mutter, fiddling with the stamp to keep my hands busy.

Rad smirks, watching the entire exchange with his back turned toward the crowd. He saunters over, lazily looking around, and finally stops beside me.

"That's Asher," Rad says, getting into my bubble.

Again.

You'd think he didn't witness his friend's balls getting threatened several hours earlier. But yet, here we are again. Maybe he has issues with stepping into people's bubbles? His breath passes across my neck, making me squirm in my seat when his fingers work up my sides, squeezing me. Surprisingly, his touch sends pleasant tingles all over my body.

I'm about to remind him what happens to men who can't keep their fingers to themselves.

"Just Ash," Asher barks out of nowhere, folding his arms across his chiseled chest. He snarls at each of them and finally settles his evil-looking eyes on me. I swear he's possessed by a demon or something.

"The power of Christ compels you," I murmur under my breath, flinging fake holy water in his direction.

"Did you just?" Rad murmurs through sputtering laughter, doubling over until he's a wheezing mess and wiping tears from his eyes.

Asher cocks his head, etching a deep scowl on his face like it might permanently stay there. Shaking his head, he glares at Rad, who practically rolls on the floor, howling over the music. "We came for the band and the drinks," he barks out, nodding his head toward the busy bar surrounded by people waiting for their drinks. "And to see you," he grits out like it fucking hurts to say.

I crack a smile. "To see little old me?" I ask, cocking my head to the side playfully. He scoffs, flapping his arms around, and stomps off again.

"See you later, River," Kieran mutters, a slight tilt lifting the edges of his lips like he knows something I don't. "I'll be kneeling for you," he whispers, leaning in to kiss my cheek. "I'll see you after your shift. Don't be late." And with that sentiment, he struts off without a backward glance.

I shiver at the thought, picturing him kneeling for me later. His words come back to me, replaying repeatedly. He'll be waiting for me tonight, after my shift, and there's nothing I can do about it.

And maybe I don't want to.

My eyes roam the edges of the packed bar, finding the four boys I shouldn't want anything to do with. They'll screw me over, Van says. They'll take, take, take, he says. But what the hell could they want from me? Certainly not my father or his connections. The only thing connecting my father and me is the blood running through my veins. According to Van, that's what the boys want. They can't be serious, right?

My father has been a ghost for nineteen years. Corbin West is a man I know nothing about and vaguely remember what he looks like. All I have is the tiny picture of him holding me as a baby, stashed away in my purse. When I feel like torturing myself, I stare at it, wondering what the hell I did to make him discard me like a piece of trash.

There's no way I can give the boys the connections they're desperate for. I tried for years to write to that waste of space, and he never answered. As a child, I didn't understand what I was doing. All I knew is this man, Corbin West, helped give me life and then abandoned me, and I wanted answers. By the time I was thirteen, I had stopped writing to him, realizing he would never reciprocate my feelings. Every single letter I poured my heart into came back in the same envelope I had sealed. Unopened, with a simple phrase written across the top, return to sender. So, I gave up.

Sinking my teeth into my bottom lip, I blow out a breath. From across the room, a certain man's fiery gaze eats me alive from the inside out, heating every inch of me. One look. One simple stare. That's all it takes to lose my breath and beg for oxygen. Almost as if claws reach through my skin and tear up my insides into a convoluted mess of desire and heartache. The last time I trusted him with my heart, he took off with it down the road without a goodbye. Logically, he was so young; he had no choice, but a phone call or a visit would have let me down easier than just disappearing. Only to reappear years later without a recollection of who I was. I ache for him again, wanting to do all the bad things I shouldn't. It's like his fist grips my soul, entangling us together whether or not I want him to.

Searching the crowd, I instantly find those mismatched eyes checking me out like I'm the prey he's about to pounce on. My damn heart skips a

beat when he licks his lips in anticipation. A sultry smirk tugs at his lips, and he nods, saluting me with his beer bottle. Try as I might, I can't force back the smile from my lips.

If I'm going to dip my toes into poisonous water, I had better make it good and fucking hot. I may not honestly believe his intentions are pure, but I'm all about living in the present. Fuck the future. Fuck the past. This is where it's at. He's here. I'm here. And if he breaks my heart into a million pieces, then so be it.

Breaking the intense stare, I huff. If I can't handle a look without wetting my damn panties, then how am I supposed to handle him kneeling in my office? Shit. I shake my head, turn to the bustling bar, and instruct another worker to stand guard at the door.

"All good?" I shout, leaning over the bar toward Ode. My hips dig into the edges of the bar, and my feet dangle off the floor.

Ode grins, slinging two bottled beers at the men standing beside me. Sweat beads on her brow, but she looks happier than ever with a glow on her cheeks.

"All good," she says with a wink, taking their cash. She smirks when they walk away, stuffing her tip down the front of her bra. "It's been a happening night tonight, boss lady!" she says with a genuine grin. "I can't believe the number of tips I'm getting. You did damn good bringing them in!" She nods toward the ladies rocking out on stage.

Some of the weight eases off my shoulders again, and I swear I can breathe for the first time tonight. Since Ma told me about her diagnosis and how her doctor's visit went, I've felt the entire world on my damn back. Not only do I have to carry our household now, but I have to worry about her health, too.

Ode grabs my hand, squeezing my fingers in hers with affection. The woman staring back at me is not my best friend right now; she's playing the part of my dotting sister. Of course, not by blood—by bond. "You're a good manager, Riv. I swear to God, as much as I want you to stay around, you'll get out of here and live your damn dreams. CaliState, here she comes! You better make room for River Blue West!" A small smile pulls at my lips, and I squeeze her hand in return, letting the terrible full name slide by. Just this time. Because, yeah. I might just live my damn dreams, after all.

"I'll bring ya with me, babe!" I shout back with a giggle, and she releases my hand, taking another order.

"Nah, bitch! I'm good here. You go live your California dream. I'll stay here, living my dream," she shouts back with a grin, winking when the other bartender, Marcus, passes by, giving me a thumbs up.

"Thanks so much for the night, Central City!!" I grin, watching the six-foot-tall red-headed woman banshee screech through the microphone. She stirs up the crowd, promising she'll be back for the second half of her set after a thirty-minute break.

I smile when she approaches the bar and comes right toward me with intent. She taps the bar, grinning with a wild look dancing in her green eyes.

"You!" she shrieks, pointing directly at me. "This place is amazing!" she says, looking me up and down until her brows furrow. "You know, for a manager, you're kinda tiny," she quips with a tiny laugh.

I snort, shaking my head. "Yeah, well, thanks, I guess?" Pursing my lips, I inspect my five-six self and shrug. "Maybe you're just kinda tall," I joke back, leaning back until I can look her in the eyes.

She barks out a laugh, throwing her curls over her shoulder. "Touché, little manager!"

Sorcha and I met at a May Field festival at the end of last year. It was the time of my life getting to see so many unsigned bands performing on ten stages in the middle of nowhere. There was nothing but music, food trucks, and tents. Call us hippies or whatever; I never wanted to leave that place. But it brought me something better and the connections I knew I needed. I met with every band as they mingled with fans and took pictures. I got their email addresses and phone numbers, showing them the card I had made up for the event. It was the event that pushed me into the manager's position. It was the same event I saw those four bumbling idiots from Whispered Words playing their songs for the first time. They stumbled through everything, looking like nervous wrecks on stage.

Their music called to me, though. There was something about Kieran's voice that had always drawn me to him. Even under the stars as a kid, he made my insides flip inside and out.

"Hi," his deep voice echoes the large speakers, echoing across the cornfields surrounding us.

The sun beams down on our sweaty bodies, but we don't mind. Vendors line up along the outskirts of the festival, selling drinks and food. People have popped tents up in the fields to the left, hiding from the sun, but still able to hear the various acts performing today.

My breaths shudder in my chest, looking up at the tall stage. I haven't seen any of them since they graduated two years ago and ran off into the sunset together. I had heard they started a band in Kieran's garage, but I never thought I'd see them perform. Let alone here, of all places.

I swallow hard, rooting my feet to the ground. Raising my hand, I block the sun from my eyes, squinting to glimpse the man who was once the stars to my moon—my other half. The boy who played me melodies for the hell of it and calmed my nerves. Here he is in all his rock star glory, waltzing across the tall, curtained stage.

His jet-black hair plasters to his sweaty forehead as the sun beams down. Lifting an arm, he pumps his fist into the air, capturing everyone's attention when he rips his shirt off. Holy mother of pickles on hamburgers —he's ripped as hell.

"We're Whispered Words," Kieran rasps with raw confidence into the microphone. "I'm Kieran." His smirk is visible from a mile away. "This is Asher, Rad..." My heart pumps double time at the hero sitting half-naked behind the drum kit, waving to the crowd with that glorious smirk. "And Callum." Kieran finishes their introductions, twirling back toward the stage. Not once does he fumble over his words, like he's done it a million times before.

"And this is our first ever live performance," Rad interrupts, stealing the microphone from Kieran with a light laugh.

"So, give us a little grace?" Kieran asks, surveying the crowd with a grin.

The crowd cheered, chanting them into their very first bomb of a performance. Kieran had several microphone issues, cutting out his beautiful voice. But they played on, earning whistles and claps after the twenty-minute performance. I knew then they'd become something big.

And that's how they came here. It's how I knew they were playing and garnering attention from the public. And why I secretly used my full name to get them to come. I thought maybe Kieran would see it and recognize it, but he didn't. To him, I was always River Blue—never River West.

"Seriously though, River! You didn't tell me how many people would be here. I swear we've never sold out a show before, and this... this is... beyond my expectations. My guitarist, Libby, swore we shouldn't come here, but I promised her I had met a kick ass representative in you! And see! Libby, you bitch!" Libby meanders forward with a grin, nodding with a chuckle.

"Yeah, yeah, Sore, you really showed me," she says in a sing-song tone, leaning against the bar. "You must be the little manager that convinced this bitch to bring us here. Love this place; it's so unique!" she says, jerking her head to all the décor hung up on the walls and the dark skull wallpaper behind me.

"That is me," I say with a smile, eyeing Asher as he makes his way beside them, examining them up close with the same calculating stare he always wears. "So, what can I get you guys to drink?"

Sorcha bites her lip, grinning when Libby rolls her eyes. "We'll both have a Jack and Coke. It's our on-stage tradition."

"Two Jack and Cokes, you got it," I say, nodding to Marcus as he stands beside me, mixing their drinks before I can even move.

"And for you?" I ask, raising a brow. Asher watches our exchange with indifference. But if there's anything I've come to learn about the elusive frowny-faced jackass is, he's always watching and taking every ounce of information in.

"Three Blue Moons and a fucking Pina Colada and add theirs to our tab while you're at it," he says, staring into my eyes but nods to the two women gaping at him.

The girls' eyes widen, but they thank him anyway and take a sip of their drinks.

"So, what's next for you guys? You have to be hitting big soon, right? You guys are fucking amazing!" I gush, leaning my elbow on the counter with a grin, soaking in their magnetic presence.

Marcus works around me, prepping the boys' drinks and sliding them one by one to Asher.

"Funny you should ask!" Sorcha says, downing the rest of her drink in one gulp. "We haven't really announced it yet. But I figure we can tell you." She grins more, waggling her eyebrows.

"Battle of the Bands," Libby says, taking a little sip.

"In California," Sorcha says with a squeal, jumping in place.

"Battle of the Bands?" I ask, my heart thumping a little in my chest.

Those types of competitions are so damn invigorating. The raw power from every band performing on stage, competing for the title of winner. Sometimes small venues hold the competition. But other times? It's big names calling bands from all across the world to compete for a record deal and a little cash on the side. Each of those bands holds more talent than I have in my pinky. It's stiff competition, but there's no doubt in my mind they'd win. Hands fucking down, Sorcha deserves it.

"Oh yeah! It'll be hot as hell. California and the winner gets a record deal with West Records," Sorcha says, as my heart falls into my ass. "And a million dollars."

"West Records?" I sputter, moving my eyes between the girls as they nod in confirmation.

Thankfully, they don't see me slip up when I choke on my spit. Throughout our correspondence, with me begging them to come here— they saw my last name. I'd never admit it to Ode or anyone else, but I sometimes use it to my advantage. Only when I want to score the best bands in the area.

"How do you get into that?" Asher asks, with a rigid posture.

A scary-ass smile crosses his lips, and he tilts his head, almost baring all his teeth. Half of me expects fangs to descend from his gums and for him to go on some sort of psycho-killing spree. Asher's fingers flex around one of the beer bottles he's clinging to.

"Invitation," Libby says, furrowing her brows, looking Ash up and down. "We didn't sign up or anything."

"Invitation only, huh?" I muse, trying to keep my voice even. "So, you didn't have to put in an application?"

There's no way in hell I'd tell anyone that my brother's owned that place and that they were the current CEOs of West Records. Nope. No way. People far and wide have already tried that route. They always ask if I still talked to that side of the family or if I had seen my dad recently—what a bunch of friggin' users. Thankfully, West is such a common last name it never occurs to strangers that I'm a part of THAT family. Well, sometimes.

"Oh yeah, it'll be at the KC Club this upcoming winter in February. They just announced the invited bands a few hours ago online. It's their first, and it'll be the biggest we've ever been to. We got a personal email from The West's themselves, inviting us to compete after they heard us on The Dot and saw a performance on YouTube. I guess playing all these festivals and events has really helped," Sorcha says with a knowing grin. "And this place, of course," she says with a wink, setting her empty glass down. "Thanks for the drinks, but we have a second half to get to now." She and Libby wave at me, returning to the rest of her band on stage.

"Need anything else?" I ask Asher as he stares off at the girls climbing back on stage.

Sorcha's voice again comes over the speakers, almost louder this time. The crowd goes nuts, loving the intro to one of their most famous songs.

"No," he shouts in an even tone, watching the two girls rock out on stage with appreciation. "Thanks, River." I rear back when he tips his head like a gentleman. "For everything." And then he fucking winks at me. WINKS!

"Uh, you're welcome?" I ask, twisting my face when a grin plays at the edges of his lips.

"I'll see you later." He taps the bar, almost sounding like he is flirting with me. Uh? Was he? No. There's no way. He's been nothing but a mouthy jerk this entire time, and yet my stupid heart flutters at his simple thanks and stupid wink. Mmhmm, you stupid organ. Stop fluttering at the sight of that douchebag's smile.

I sigh, leaning my chin on my palm when he gets lost in the crowd and swallowed whole. My family's legacy is something dreams are made of. If I was a part of it, that is. Zeppelin and Seger West are the most influential figures in the music industry right now, running West Records, a company every rock musician hopes they can sign with, better than their father did before them. They've taken the time to add new acts to their roster and have boosted their worth by millions in only a few short years. Or maybe it's their weird relationship with their wife. Yeah—their—wife. I've seen magazine articles about their poly relationship with her and the two other dudes involved. Who could handle that many guys, anyway?

My eyes drift to the four boys again, huddling together. I wonder what it would be like to have so many guys in one place? And the sex? Jesus, talk about a good time. I've had my fair share of threesomes and added two more dicks into the mix? Yeah, I could totally see that. But a relationship? I wonder how well that would work out. Do they ever get jealous? Enjoy sharing?

I shake my head. There's no time to think about that right now.

THE SURPRISE IN HER EYES WHEN I DIDN'T SNARK BACK AND ACTUALLY thanked her stalls my steps. Peeking over my shoulder, I watch her with rapt attention, surveying her every move. The crowd around me jumps in place to the music, concealing me from her view and hiding my watchful eyes. I'd be a liar if I said the tiny brunette didn't fascinate me. I couldn't force myself around her if she were anything like Tessa or Sara, who are as unbearable as they come.

Her long brown hair sits past her shoulders, revealing her dainty neck, marked by my stupid brother. A big, red splotch sits in plain view, not unnoticed by everyone. Men walk by, eyeing her like a delicious meal— only stopping themselves from engaging when they see the mark. They could think one or two ways about it. Either she's easy, or she's unavailable. As it is, Kieran watches her every fucking move like a possessive boyfriend ready to defend her honor. I'm surprised the boys kept him seated when I promised them drinks. Since she came back into the picture, he's taken this game a little too seriously. Sure, we need River in our corner to aid us with our bright, famous future. But Kieran's become obsessive, possessive, and any other red flag under the sun, and it's concerning.

"Your drinks," I say, slipping into the sticky booth with a grimace.

You'd think this place would get cleaned every once in a while, but it appears no one has touched the filth in years. Not that I'm a clean freak by any means. Logistically, if they wanted patrons to enjoy their time here more, they'd clean more than once a year.

Kieran's eyes drift toward the bar again, and he growls, threatening to get up as a man approaches her, and she smiles. Fucking smiles at the guy, and now my best friend is about to lose his shit. His fingers curl into fists at the sight of them.

"Calm down," I say in a monotone voice, holding back the tension rising in my throat.

River's smile lights up the damn room, disarming every man in a fifty-foot radius. My damn heart thunks against my ribs as she glides behind the bar, taking care of everyone's drink orders.

"I'll calm down when they stop staring at what's mine," he grunts, pouring mouthfuls of beer down his throat.

"Ours," Rad reminds him with a drunken grin. "You think she'll let me join you in the office tonight? I can keep her quiet when you rail her from behind. God, just imagine the gag I could make her." I take a deep breath, trying not to imagine the scene he implanted in my head. But yet, my dick twitches in my jeans, proving he's very interested in the tiny annoyance named River.

"Ours?" Callum asks, shifting in his seat. A deep red invades his cheeks when he looks between us with uncertainty and a frown.

Oh, Callum. You have much to learn. We may have never shared before, but it's not something I'm opposed to, especially with her.

"She may be your perfect match, Cally Boy," Rad barks out, laughing.

Callum licks his lips, staring over in her direction. He takes in every move she makes behind the bar until she disappears into the back. One long breath blows from between his lips, and his brows furrow. The gears in his brain work double time until she emerges from the back again and greets more customers. His body physically relaxes, and a slight grin tugs at his lips. In River's presence, he seems to unwind from his usually tense behavior. River appears to be the balm that is slowly unraveling our dear Callum.

"That was our game, right?" I ask, taking a sip of my beer. "Make her fall for us and then coax her into talking to her father for us?" I raise a brow at the boys around the table, who stare at me like I'm fucking crazy.

I am fucking crazy. But I'm so goddamn desperate to get out from under my father's clutches. It's bad enough he's financially holding us hostage and taunting us with the means to leave him for good.

But fuck. Maybe we aren't doing enough. As I stare at the girl working her ass off behind the bar, the realization sinks like lead in my gut. We haven't resorted to any other measure to get out of our situation. Sure, we could get extra jobs and save up that way. We could pawn our valued belongings—even if my father keeps a sharp eye on all our possessions. We could do so much more than we are. But it seems like every solution we've come up with has failed us on every level.

Two years ago, we made a deal. Since most of us are stuck here— Callum and Rad pledged to make the band any spare money we needed while Kieran and I were forced to get degrees. Even if college anchored us to this place with no escape right now, in the future, we'd be out of here with a better future on the horizon. We still have time to make our great escape. We'll be out of here if only we can last one more miserable year under the same roof as our father. My stomach sinks whenever Nigel Montgomery crosses my mind, bringing me back to the darkest days of my life.

"Emergency services. What is the nature of your call?" asks the woman from the other side.

Every inch of me shakes, jostling the phone against my face. Tears well in my eyes and burn down my cheeks.

"My mommy," I mutter into the phone through a hiccup.

"What's wrong with your mommy?" the woman asks in a softer tone.

"She's not moving. She's just lying in bed there..." I roll my lips together, stepping toward the woman lying in bed. "There's something in her arm," I choke out. "Mommy! Wake up!" I shout, forgetting the phone on the ground. "Mommy!" I cry more, dropping to my knees.

That night the men in white uniforms took her away, and my dad locked me in my bedroom for three days without explanation. I pounded and begged him to come back and set me free, but all I got in return was three meals and water bottles. I wanted my mom more than anything else. I needed to see her and hug her. She had to get okay.

When my dad finally opened my door, it was the day after her funeral.

"You see what happens to bad boys?" he asks, kneeling in front of me with one single rose between his fingers.

"Mommy?" I choke out.

"She's dead, son," he says in a low voice. "You saw what happened?" When I nod, his grin grows across his face, and he nods without further explanation.

The feel of my hair beneath my fingers is the first clue I've zoned out, falling into the terrible tragedies of my youth. Horrific events my father executed under my little nose. Something I had no idea about until I was a teenager. Everything my mother ever owned was burned in the fire pit as he celebrated his win of finally peeling himself away from her. And as for me? I cried myself to sleep every night, earning a beating for every tear I shed. It wasn't until Kieran and his mom moved in that I got a reprieve from his abuse. He only had more bodies to pound his fist into, instead of mine.

I blink when Kieran stares daggers in my direction, burning holes through my head.

"I'm not playing any fucking games. She's mine," Kieran says matter-of-factly with a sharp nod, exposing his teeth like he'll bite me open if I suggest otherwise.

"Share the goods, bro. River is mine too. I want to splash her titties with my cum and..." Rad grunts when Callum puts his hand over his mouth, shaking his head.

The expression lining Callum's face gives his true feelings away. He didn't stop Rad because he was disgusted with his overly expressive words. It's desire sitting in the depths of his eyes when he peeks at her again with interest, not in disgust. Not with the way his blush deepens, if that's even possible.

Eventually, Callum will decide who the perfect girl is to lose his v-card to, and then he can move on from his embarrassment of sex. Or the opposite sex. Never have I seen a grown man fumble over his words as much as Cal. Despite his good looks, he's been more reluctant than ever to reach out to women and talk to them the older he gets. I suppose his past may play a part in his decisions.

"Oh my god!" I cringe when Tessa and Sara squeal beside our booth, trying to squeeze in with us.

"Not tonight," I bark, taking a swig of my beer.

"But, Asher, baby," Tessa purrs in my ear, rubbing her hand over my shoulder.

"I said not tonight," I growl, catching her wrist and peeling her away. "Not in the mood."

"It's that Central slut, isn't it?" she hisses, earning a growl from Kieran.

"We're not interested. And I'd suggest you not call River names if you know what's good for you," I say, narrowing my eyes at her until she grabs Sara and huffs away.

One day, Tessa will understand we're no longer interested in her company and haven't been for a long time. Somehow, she's been too oblivious to understand, but I feel she'll get the picture now that we have our sights set on the woman across the room. Tessa has run through every person on this planet, hoping to get a little extra. It's girls like her who make my teeth clench at night. They're always looking for something extra like marriage, kids, and a bank account to go with it.

"So long, tiny tots!" Rad calls after her over the music.

After another hour of Sorcha's band playing, the other squeaky bartender jumps on stage, taking their place. Looking at my watch, I frown at the late time and shake my head. We've been cooped up in this corner for so long that I almost forgot what Sorcha spoke of at the bar. Battle of the damn bands. Maybe if we make it through that avenue, we won't need River to help us. But peeking at Kieran, Rad, and Callum again—that will not happen.

"Last call!" the bouncy bartender squeals through the microphone on stage. Throwing her mess of curls all over the place with every step, she grins down at the patrons. "Get your last drinks and pay your tab. You don't have to go home, but you sure as shit can't stay here. Say it with me, folks…" she says, pointing toward a sign above the stage.

"Get the fuck out!" the remaining crowd chants as one unit. They lift their glasses in the air and drink the last of their drinks for the night.

I blink at the small stage at the back of the bar. Dark curtains hide the small backstage, where I'm sure Sorcha and her band of women converge, cooling off after a show well done. My heart pounds when I remember the rush I felt jumping on that stage. It's the one place I can let go of my rising tension and need to flee. It's either that or running away from my issues on foot toward the only woman who ever gave a damn about me. I grind my teeth, taking a deep breath. Every worry in my life piles higher and higher on my shoulders.

My calculating eyes drift across the room toward the object of our newfound obsession—our ticket out of here. And the only reason I even agreed to come to this utter shithole tonight. Her. The girl with the perfect last name. The girl with our way out of this town and into the arms of a record deal—hopefully.

When Sorcha mentioned West records, I watched River's nonexistent reaction. Her facial expressions barely moved, but I caught the slight twist of her face and the hate firing behind her mossy green eyes. If I had to wager a guess, River West hates her family with a fiery passion, which doesn't bode well for us and our plan. If we expect to use her connections, then I don't think we're going to succeed. Not that way, at least. There has to be another way.

I can practically taste our future success on the tip of my tongue, and the cravings come back tenfold, churning in my gut. We need to leave and get out as a band of brothers running toward success. All before my father gets some bright idea about me taking over his company when I graduate from college in May. There's no way in hell I'll ever settle into a nine-to-five—but it's what he's depending on and what he's been grooming me for since I was born. I'm his only son, and in turn, I'm the only person for the job. But I'll be fucked if I step foot inside his business. It's not going to happen. The moment my college degree hits my hand after graduation, I'm gone. But it's never a bad idea to have a fallback degree if shit hits the fan with the band. Wherever I'm going in the future, I'll be prepared.

My only solution… is well… her. Some way, somehow, we're going to utilize her in some capacity. Even if Kieran has to propose to River, drag her to California with us, and throw her at West Record's front door. I frown, thinking about our escape plan. We've saved through the years from each of our gigs in an effort to escape this hellhole, but we've never had enough to execute our plan, even with Rad and Callum running a dirt bike track and taking bets. It never seems to be enough to write home about. One day we'll fucking get there. But today is not the day.

With fascination, I watch her from across the room, talking with patrons and laughing with them. One gentleman steps forward, handing her a wad of cash, and she grins, flirting back with the flutter of her eyelashes. Her brown hair hangs past her shoulders now, swaying when she laughs, throwing her head back. From here, I can hear the happy rasp in her voice when she knocks the guy on the shoulder. He nearly falls over from her push but rights himself and grins at her too. I take a drink of my beer, but I'm really drinking in my newest conquest.

"What the fuck?" Kieran hisses again as Rad holds him down. "Let me fucking go. I'm going to murder him. He's touching what isn't his," he gripes, getting wrestled back into his seat.

Now, how do I make the one girl who won't look my way fall for me? Or slip into bed with me? I think about the quirk of her brow and the confusion earlier when I thanked her for the drinks. Honestly, I'm not an insufferable asshole all the time. Just sometimes. I run my fingers across my forehead, mentally groaning. Okay. I'm an asshole, but sometimes I can't help it. It just comes naturally to me whenever I'm not playing or listening to music. Music is my freedom, and being surrounded by it eases the tension in my chest. I can be wary about River but still execute our plan. Right?

I eye Kieran, the hopeless romantic. He'd do anything to have her as his possession. The image of him hand-feeding her strawberries and swirling whipped cream all over her body comes to mind. It's pleasant imagery, and I'll give him that. Somehow, I don't think Kieran will ever give her up. Not without a fight. But for now, his behavior benefits us. She may want to hate him, but she can't keep her eyes off us. And that's what I wanted all along.

I bite my bottom lip, looking at Callum, who sits back in the booth with his eyes closed and earbuds in, ignoring our presence. Every few minutes, he peeks his eyes open, staring at her like a magnet pulling him in.

Tonight, it was like pulling his molars to get him to come out instead of staying on the couch and playing Xbox with Rad. They've had some sort of weird competition going on with some game called Angel Warrior for weeks. But now, I think he's glad he ventured out. He's not the type to hang at bars with crowds of people.

Rad talks a million miles a minute, the rum hitting him harder since starting his fourth damn drink. He grins and laughs, talking to people behind us, around us, and to anyone who will listen to his stupid stories. Rad never stops talking. The only time he seals his lips is when he's macking on some chick and has his tongue down her throat.

And my dear stepbrother can't stop his fascination from festering to the surface by keeping a keen eye on the short and demanding little manager flitting around the bar.

A loud snort pulls me from my musings, and I turn, looking toward the band sitting behind us. Sorcha and her merry band of women converge after a long, kick-ass set. They laugh and drink in celebration of a show well done. They're a well-oiled machine, playing together like one person, and their music proves it. They have merch on a table near the back of the bar. They're on the damn Dot app and have the most crucial person supporting them. A manager. Someone to schedule these things. Someone so organized, he got them a gig here and with West Records. We have Callum. He does most of our gigs. But to have someone else work on it as we make music would benefit us immensely.

I clench my jaw, pulling out my phone. Battle of the Bands. Hosted by West Records. Skimming the instructions, I take it all in.

Invitations have been sent to fifteen select bands from across the country. Submitted entries are being accepted for any unsigned bands starting September 1st–November 1st. We will select only five bands from the entries, and only twenty will compete. A one-million-dollar prize will be awarded, and a three-year record deal. December 15th, the Battle of the Bands will kick off at the KC Club in East Point, California.

Qualifications include: music present on the streaming app The Dot in the form of an EP, performance footage available on YouTube, a healthy following on ClockTok, and a prominent social media following.

I scroll through our meager social media pages and growl at the dwindling number of likes on each of them. How are we supposed to bring those numbers up in just a few months?

My body jolts up when a loud bang draws my attention to the middle of the empty floor, and my brows raise. River scowls at the broken glasses littering the floor and shakes her head. She's two seconds away from telling the drunken idiot off but takes a breath, holding her professional composure. I have to commend her for her tongue-holding abilities.

"Watch where you're going, bitch."

I'm on my feet before I know what I'm doing and marching over there before Kieran can climb over Callum. A yelp and curses happen in the booth I vacated. My eyes narrow on the polo-wearing douche canoe standing before River, looking at her like she's the scum of the earth, when he was the one who knocked drunkenly into her; his body sways on the spot.

"Fucking Central Cunt," he hisses again, slurring his words and rocking back and forth with unfocused eyes.

"The fuck you say?" I growl, scooping the man by the shirt and bringing his face directly into mine. "Did you just say what I think you just fucking said?" I spit, shaking him with every word.

The stench of day-old beer and cigarettes sends bile up my throat and knots in my stomach, but realizing who this douchebag is, knocks me back. Bradley Bradford. Stupid name for a stupid shithead. His father's the lovely mayor of this town, who conveniently keeps his rap sheet buried deep. I continue to hold him by the scruff of his shirt.

"Is that any way to talk to a lady?" I snarl, exposing my teeth.

"Down, Killer," River murmurs from beside me, furrowing her brows. The warmth of her hand lingers on my chest when she holds me back. My breath shudders in my chest when her warm fingers dig into my flesh, and goosebumps erupt. An instant connection puts my hair on end, and a ringing fills my ears. Her glassy green eyes stare at me in warning. "I really need to invest in holy water. Did your demon disappear?"

My eyes pop wide when she suggests.... I've been... "I'm not possessed, you little brat," I hiss, ignoring the tingling on my chest from her touch, igniting something deep in me, but I shake it off. I have a douchebag to obliterate for thinking he could even speak to her like that.

My attention snaps back to the scumbag currently turning fifty shades of red and fuming. Bradley's fist raises shakily in the air until I toss him on his back, rejoicing in the useless air pouring from his lungs.

"The power of Christ compels you," she murmurs, side-eyeing me with furrowed brows. "Christo!" she hisses, leaning close enough to examine my eyes. "You didn't flinch…" She cocks her head, a grin exploding across her lush lips. "Worked for Dean." She shrugs.

I fight the smile threatening to pull at my lips and swallow my laugh by looking away. Me? Evil? Have I been that much of an asshole over the last few days? Fuck. Yeah. I have been. My lips pop open, ready to retort and apologize for my actions. But Kieran swoops in to save the damn day. This could have been my chance to show her I'm not the demonic assbag she thinks I am. I suppose I'll have to rectify that one day at a time.

I'm not an insufferable asshole all the time, just occasionally. It's the facade I put on to deal with the world—especially my father. Show an ounce of weakness, and he picks it apart. His fist alone taught me too many hard lessons to soften to the world. But there's something about River West that softens my resolve and makes me want to throw caution to the wind and unwind. And that's what terrifies me.

"You okay, River Blue?" Kieran asks, wrapping an arm around her shoulders and pulling her into his chest.

I sigh, wishing I was the one comforting her. But what do I have to offer, anyway? Kieran has a rapport with her. Being his long-lost friend, my asshole father brainwashed him into forgetting and all. She'll fall to her damn knees again for him. But for me? She'll light me on fire just to get warm.

"Bradley Bradford," Rad whistles, standing above him with his arms crossed. "And my favorite lady," Rad says through a drunken, dreamy smile, looking at her with envy, nestled in Kieran's arms. "Don't worry, Sugar Tits! We'll kick this piece of shit to the sidewalk." Rad scrunches his nose, grinding his teeth.

Informative. Rad doesn't get angry quickly, but at the sight of this man —he's infuriated. To the naked eye, you wouldn't be able to tell. But to me? Well, his curled fists, rigid muscles, and silent snarl tell a very long story. Bradley Bradford did something wrong in Rad's eyes, and I'll get to the bottom of it.

"Piece of rapist shit," Rad hisses, grabbing Bradley by the shirt, causing him to stumble over his drunken feet, and dragging him toward the front door. He grunts, trying as hard as he can to drag the flailing idiot out. But all two-hundred and fifty pounds of Bradley protests. Rad tosses his hands in the air with frustration. "Help?" Rad says, narrowing his drunken eyes at us. Looking around, I eye the surrounding area looking for the bouncers I know exist, but I find none for help. Some fucking good they are they can't even protect the one person they should. Well, fine, it's our duty now.

"Ugh. I don't need you guys to do this. You!" River snipes, removing Kieran's arm from her shoulder, and points directly at Bradley, who is trying to stand on his wobbly feet. I bite back a smile when a wet spot forms on the front of his jeans. He groans, slumping against the front of the stage. That's right. You utter waste of space. Pee your pants like a child. "Get the fuck out of my bar, man."

Bradley chuckles like he has a chance and stumbles forward directly into my arms. "Get the fuck off me," he slurs, pushing against my chest.

"Not happening," I growl, dragging his thrashing body out the front door and literally tossing him onto the sidewalk.

"And don't come back here," River says, shaking her head. A paleness takes over her face when she pushes past us and waltzes back into the bar without a word of thanks.

"If I ever catch you talking to, touching, or even thinking about her, I'll rip your scrotum in half. Fucking leave before I do it," Kieran hisses, popping his knuckles directly above Bradley, who groans, rolling around on the sidewalk.

Well, that's one way to threaten a guy who touches the girl you're currently obsessed with.

"Fuck, I'm going to see how she is," Kieran grumbles, swiping a hand down his face.

"She's a big girl," I say, raising a brow. "I'm sure she's fine."

"She will be in a minute," Rad says, rubbing his hand together. "I'm about to gag her into next week," he cackles, running back into the bar like a kid marching down the stairs on Christmas Day.

Kieran stares after him, shaking his head with a frown.

"Before you go to pound town," I murmur, pulling my phone from my pocket. "I wanted to share a little tidbit I picked up today. It was just announced at like 2 a.m." I grin, shoving my phone into his waiting hands. I can tell by the sour look on his face that he's not impressed that I'm holding him up. But it blows into a grin when he reads the rules of Battle of the Bands. "To qualify for Battle of the Bands, we need an EP and an entry video, and having our own merch would help our chances." Excitement spears through me at the chance to finally get there.

"Battle of the fucking Bands," he muses, scrolling through my phone, and nods.

"Imagine we get her to help with all this," I murmur, gesturing toward the list of requirements.

Callum nods and licks his lips, abashedly looking toward the bar with a red tint enveloping his cheeks. "We get all that; then we can get the hell away from here."

"And her?" Kieran asks like the knight in shining armor he is.

I raise a brow at his meaning and shrug. "What about her?" I ask calmly, but I know exactly what he's going to say.

We went after her for a reason; we can't abandon ship now. And hell, maybe I don't want to jump into the churning sea without a safety net to catch us in the end. But there's something about River that draws me into her flame, burning me whole.

"If she gets to know us and falls for us, she can help us achieve all this, and then we make it to the Battle of the Bands? What next? What if we get signed? We can..." Kieran trails off, biting into his bottom lip with unease.

He doesn't want to leave her here in the dust. With his obsession growing every second, he wants to take her with us. I can see it in his pleading eyes. And who am I to deny my brother? Even if it's just soothing him until the time comes. From a mile away, I can see the distraction River is going to bring to us in the future. She'll pull my brothers apart as they eat away at her attention, begging for more bones.

"You want to what? Bring her along, then?" I ask, rubbing my chin, placating every worry he has inside of him. Kieran hyper-fixates on things, obsessing until it's all he can think about. And that's what River is—a hyper fixation. "I suppose it could work. Imagine showing up to West Records with an actual West," I chuckle, but if anything, I placate myself.

We can continue this charade with those facts in mind. River West will serve us well either way. Whether on her glorious knees, sucking cock... I shake my head. Fuck. She's infecting me, too, but maybe I want to be full of her poison.

Callum shrugs, trying to look as nonchalant as possible, but he fails. A spark ignites in his gray eyes as he looks back toward the bar again, and a grin spreads across his jovial face.

"She's our ticket out of here," Callum whispers with sincerity. "From what I've observed, she's organized. She works two jobs, goes to school, and completely manages this bar. If we can gain her trust, then she'll want to help us organize on her own." He nods, rolling his lips together with guilt.

My lip twitches when he narrows his eyes on me because he stole the thoughts directly from my mind.

"Exactly," I say, pointing a finger at him. "That's exactly what we can offer her, too. A way out."

"You're staying?" I raise my brow, a red glow lighting up Kieran's cheeks, and he nods.

"You bet your ass I'm staying," he says with a grin, rubbing his hands together. "I made a promise, and I'm going to deliver on it." With that, my brother glides off through the front doors, presumably in the direction of her office again. Only this time, we won't barge in and disrupt their time together.

I wave, taking a deep breath. I can't leave Kieran and Rad here. "You want me to drop you off at home while I wait for them?"

Callum's cheeks tint a darker shade of red, and he shakes his head, clearing his throat. "I have to go to the bathroom," he rasps in a low voice, pointing toward the bar.

"I'll be in the Tahoe then whenever you're done," I murmur when he scurries away into the bar without a second glance.

Funnily enough, I don't think he's going to just use the bathroom.

Turning on my heel, I march to the Tahoe parked across the street and climb in, patiently waiting for my friends to get done with their fuckfest and come home with me. I'll try not to think about Kieran and Rad sharing her. Just the mention of Rad gagging her has my dick hard and pressing against my jeans.

Fuck blue balls, man.

Her voice hums through my mind on repeat, exciting me even more. A deep ache pulsates in my balls, begging me to touch and release the pent-up tension that has been building since yesterday. My dick stands hard and heavy inside my jeans, begging to spring free.

But I don't dare relieve myself. Or move from my position on my knees, digging into the uncomfortable floor.

Closing my eyes, memories flood my mind from the last time I angrily barged my way in here and took all my after-performance frustrations out on her body. Anger fueled my decisions, but desire held me here.

She held me there.

My River Blue.

How could I have forgotten her for so long? It's like Asher's dad swooped into my life and erased everything before the age of ten. Only now, after seeing her again, do I remember my time in the shitty apartment I was raised in as a kid. The time we spent together under the stars as we hid from our moms.

"When is she coming?" Rad whines, interrupting my peace.

Shifting in her office chair with his eyes closed, his forehead leans against the wood desk. All the alcohol he consumed comes back to bite him in the ass.

Secretly, I hope he falls asleep long before she walks into this room. She's mine. All fucking mine. I'll tattoo my name on her ass if that's what it takes. The last thing I want to do is fucking share her with anyone else. But I know Rad. A little too well.

The prospect of having her command my every move has me aching in my jeans. But it excites Rad more. Don't get me wrong; he likes to partici-pate. But watching from a distance and getting himself off will suffice.

After seeing the knife against my junk, I'm sure he locked himself in his room for hours, pleasuring himself to the image. He moaned "Oh, River," more times than I can count. Not that I was listening or anything.

But that's what happens when we all hang out at their house, shooting the shit.

"Hopefully soon and on my face," I mumble, shifting my knees and trying to get comfortable.

It's only been five minutes since she waltzed back into the bar, and we came here.

"Mmm," he hums, "just like she did at the record store. God, that was the hottest thing I've ever seen. I can't wait to take her out in public and make her come around my cock."

My head jerks back at his comment. I'm two seconds from bashing his face in for even thinking about her like that. The imagery of him and her in public tingles my damn balls. She's mine. But maybe not just mine. River will go where I go; I'll make sure of that. I'll leash her if I have to and shove her in my damn trunk, kicking and screaming. Maybe Asher had a point with the whole—make her fall for all of us—thing. If she does, then she'll willingly help us and come with us whenever we can make it out of here.

"Just be careful," I mumble, keeping my eyes on the carpet.

"Always careful," Rad assures me with a sleepy yawn. "Can't scare her off yet. Ash's dumbass obviously has some plans for her."

"Yeah," I huff. "And as much as I don't want to admit it, his plan is pretty solid. But he didn't account for one thing."

"Yeah? And what's that?" Rad asks, stifling a yawn behind his hand.

"Me," I say in a demanding voice, curling my fingers into fists.

Rad chuckles. "Yeah, that's my Kieran," he says softly. "We'll make sure our pretty girl doesn't get heartbroken. She'll come with and give me a shit ton of Radalicious babies."

I snort. "Babies, dude?"

"You heard me," he slurs, tripping over his tongue. "Just imagine her tits." He sighs like he's dreaming about the day he can knock her up, and fuck, it's not a bad idea.

"We're not knocking her up, dickbag. That's just..." I trail off when images of her in my bed with my cum leaking from her pussy, and my fingers pushing it back in. "Fuck," I mumble, palming myself through my jeans.

"See," he says, barking out a laugh. "It's hot as fuck."

I don't raise my eyes when the office door opens and shuts, keeping my eyes on the carpet.

"Heya, Pretty Girl, fancy meeting you here. You ready to get naked?" Rad says with such enthusiasm I can't help a snort. He must be awake now at the sight of her.

"I didn't order an audience," she says through a tired sigh.

"You're tired," I say, keeping my voice soft when her beat-up Chucks come into view. I nearly cum in my pants when her fingers lightly brush through my hair, and shivers run down my back.

"And you're kneeling," she says, testing the waters and giving my hair a yank.

"Are you staying?" she asks Rad, but her voice only gives away the aching exhaustion she must be feeling.

"Oh my, Pretty Girl," he purrs softly with excitement. The chair makes a squeaking sound, and his footsteps come toward us leisurely. I'm sure not to scare her off. "Only if you'll have me," he says in all seriousness. "Only if you want me to watch or touch you or whatever you want." I can hear the grin on his lips and the sincerity in his voice. He'd leave if she wanted him to. He'd do anything she asked, and never without permission.

"Let us take care of you," I mumble, pushing into her fingers. They tease through my hair in soft and gentle strokes, relaxing my entire body.

"Okay," she whispers without hesitation.

Bravely, I sneak a peek through my lashes, watching as Rad overtakes her mouth and shoves his tongue down her throat, claiming what is his. Fury should build in my gut watching them together, but it doesn't. Watching him take what he wants turns me on even more.

River moans, tightening her other hand through his ridiculous mullet, pulling him flush against her body.

"Ah, Pretty Girl," he murmurs against her lips with a pant. "You taste better than I'd ever imagined."

I get harder when his hand drifts toward her tit, and he gently massages it through her shirt, earning small, sexy noises from her throat—the tip of his finger's circles over her achingly hard bud, punishing it between his fingertips. Something I wish I could do right now, but I let her take the lead.

She moans, leaning her forehead against his with heavy breaths. "Fuck," she curses through her swollen lips, tightening her hold on my hair.

"Use us, River," I demand in a deep voice, feeling it the moment her mossy green eyes spear through me with intense heat, boiling my insides to molten levels. "However, you want," I beg, palming myself, trying to keep my dick from showing how desperate I am for her to ride my goddamn face. "Ride my face," I practically moan, wishing she'd take her shorts off and stick her pussy in my face.

She swallows hard as her pupils dilate, nearly blackening her entire eye. "Take off your clothes," she demands with a hunger building in the back of her darkening moss-green eyes.

"And me?" Rad practically begs, palming her tits again with fascination. His dark eyes twinkle with desire, dilating with the need to fuck her senselessly.

Same dude. Same.

"No touching," she says, glancing back at him with authority. Letting us know she's the one in charge and no one else.

He drops his hands and nods with compliance when she says it. Rad would never take a woman against her will or push her limits. He respects everyone. Especially after the girl he helped save years ago, he's been traumatized ever since knowing what she went through and so brutally.

"You only get to watch right now." His Adam's apple bobs, and he nods with understanding, taking a step back.

"You're the queen of this domain, Pretty Girl," he murmurs, taking a step back toward the desk, leaning against it with a cool, relaxed expression. But his eyes hone on her every move.

I lift on my knees, lifting my shirt over my head. "On your feet," she whispers, putting two fingers beneath my chin. I rise to my feet at the command, nearly coming in my pants, when she flicks the button of my jeans open.

My abdomen jumps under her touch as her fingertips play in the dark happy trail leading to my throbbing dick. If she touches it, I'm going to cum in her hand. Jesus. Get a grip, K. You have to last longer than three seconds in her presence. But I guess If there was one woman to take me that far, it'd be River. I'd happily let her destroy my dignity in one stroke. Even in front of Rad. I'd never hear the end of it but fuck it.

"Don't cum," she whispers, staring directly into my eyes as she reaches into the depths of my pants and strokes me with heavy pressure, squeezing when she reaches the tip. Her thumb brushes over my weeping slit, spreading my pre-cum.

Fuck.

Yeah. Don't cum. Easier said than done. A tingle works down my spine, and I swear my balls tighten when her grip tightens around me. An inhuman noise bubbles in my throat. I can't help it when I toss my head back, and it falls from my lips. Fuck. Shit. This isn't good. I'm going to spew into her hand. Think of something else. Anything else but her hand wrapped perfectly around me…

Earlier today, I made her ride my fingers until she came harder than any woman I've ever met. Her pussy squeezed, clamped down, and marked my fingers as hers to use. The moment I got into the SUV and got home, my dick ached with the most extreme pain, begging me to touch him. He wanted to cum in my fist with her memory on my mind. But I refused. I wouldn't cum until I was nestled deep inside her cunt.

I grit my teeth when she cups my balls with her other hand in the tight confines of my jeans. My breaths come in short pants, and I swear my balls tighten toward my body, and pre-cum drips from my tip like a faucet. Fuck. Hell. I'm going to blow.

Using my pre-cum, she spreads it all around as her mouth attaches to my nipple and sucks it between her teeth. The sensitive shit lights me on fire, and I jerk in her hand, desperate for more friction.

"If you don't want me to cum, you're going to have to stop that," I gasp; my hips thrust forward into her hand repeatedly until I'm basically rutting into her warm palm.

Stars burst behind my eyes. The world around me melts away, leaving just the two of us in this compromising position, with her hand around my dick and that mischievous smirk pulling at the edges of her lips. Every muscle tightens in my body with anticipation. Waiting and waiting for her to make her next move. Waiting and waiting for her to give me permission to finally fucking come.

I heave a heavy breath of disappointment when she pulls her hands away. When her warmth leaves me, I'm begging for more like an addict. My lips pop open, a whine on the tip of my tongue about to beg for more of her touch when she mumbles something, pulling my boxers and jeans down my legs, leaving me to work them over my shoes and toss them aside.

She bites her lip and dips her head, running her tongue over my tip. I blink, staring at the water-stained ceiling, and count to one hundred. If I concentrate on the end of her tongue tracing every protruding vein or the way her lips pop over my tip and suck it into her mouth, I'll cum—everywhere.

"Fuck," Rad rasps from behind me, groaning when she takes me deep in her throat.

I grit my teeth harder, probably cracking a damn tooth in the process. Her throat relaxes and tightens around my tip, and she hums her approval. Fuck. Her forehead meets my abdomen when she takes me in the back of her throat, leaving it there as she hums a damn song.

Hold your shit together, Kieran. Don't let that tempting fucking throat ruin the fun you're about to have.

Her mouth detaches from my dick with a pop, and she stands before me with a heavenly smirk. Her chin glistens with saliva and pre-cum, dripping from her swollen lips into the floor and creating a small wet spot. Her tongue darts out, licking it all up, and she swallows hard.

"Lick it up," she whispers, pointing to the spot on the floor with lustful eyes, awaiting my answer.

My body shivers at her command, goosebumps puckering across my flesh. My eyes flash, darting to the small spot on the ground. Without a second thought, I glide my tongue across our mixed essence and suck it up.

"Good boy," she murmurs, rubbing her fingers through my hair and tightening her grip. With force, she yanks my head back. "Get on your knees," she whispers, lust swimming in the depths of her voice, making it husky with need. "And you stay there." She points to Rad, who hasn't moved a muscle.

"Yes, Pretty Girl," he rasps. "Whatever you say."

I sink to my bare knees again, placing my naked ass on the heels of my shoes.

"On second thought," she says, flicking her eyes to Rad. "Undress me." Rad doesn't have to be told twice when he comes into view behind her, running his hands along the edges of her work uniform. She cranes her neck, allowing his lips to graze her flesh when he pulls at the ends of her shirt and lifts it over her head.

"Jesus," he mumbles, running his fingertips from the middle of her lacy bra and tracing them back toward the clasp. He visibly swallows when the clasp releases, brings it down her arms, and tucks it into the pocket of his jeans.

"My shorts," she says, kicking off her Chucks. They land in a heap near the door, but she never takes her eyes off me.

I bite my lip, my dick throbbing even harder, turning red and purple with need.

"Yes, my Pretty Girl," he murmurs against her skin, flicking the button of her tiny booty shorts and pulling them down her legs. He bends with them, brushing his nose against her bare ass, and groans. "I'm keeping this too," he says, pulling her tiny white thong down her legs and stuffing them into his pocket.

"So, fucking gorgeous," I say, brushing a finger up her creamy thigh and around her belly button, deliberately skipping over her dripping pussy. An eye for an eye is what I always say. And in this case, I can't wait to have her begging me to fuck her.

Goosebumps erupt all over her flesh, and she shudders from my touch.

"What do you want to do?" Rad asks against the flesh of her neck, testing the waters when she cranes her neck, allowing him access. Her eyes roll back when he sinks his teeth into her flesh and softly moans. Her hips instantly rock, seeking the pleasure she's about to receive. "You want to fuck him hard? Fuck his face? Hell, fuck my face for all I care. Let us take you to pleasure town."

If I weren't so turned on by the sight of her naked form, I'd roll my eyes at his stupid phrases. Idiot.

"You say the words, and we do it." He emphasizes every word with the squeeze of her tits, fitting perfectly in his calloused hands.

"Kieran," she moans my name like a prayer, and I know this moment will be etched in my memory forever.

"Yeah, River Blue?" I whisper, eager to hear her answer.

"I want to ride your face. Make me cum." And she doesn't have to ask again when I lurch forward, burying my face between her thighs. I groan when the taste of her tangy pussy crosses over my tongue. And if I wasn't an obsessed addict before, I am now. There's no way this woman is ever going anywhere else again. I'll chain her to me and drag her to California. Fuck Ash and his plans. Fuck everything else.

This pussy?

Mine.

This ass?

Mine.

Fuck, she's mine, and I don't even fucking care. My protective, obsessive side flares to life, and a shrine erects, dedicated to her in the back of my mind.

"Kieran," her stifled moan hits me right in the aching dick. I circle my tongue around her throbbing clit and then back to her pussy, plunging it in over and over again. I want to bathe in her juices and fucking own them all at the same time.

"Here," Rad says, tapping my head, and I back away with a scowl, hating how he interrupted my meal. He nods, showing me what he's doing, and I grin when she squeaks. He lifts her into the air by the backs of her thighs, spreading her pussy out for me just like a dessert. "Good?" he asks her when her head lolls against his shoulder, and she nods with a dreamy grin spreading across her face.

"Yes," she whimpers, reaching to grab my hair. She gently forces my face between her thighs again, and I go to fucking town. I lick and suck, taking everything from her until she's a muffled, screaming mess coming on my tongue. I sit there, licking her clean until her breaths shudder, and she pushes me away.

She swallows hard, closes her eyes, and taps Rad's hands. He gently puts her to her wobbling legs, holding onto her shoulders when she takes a deep breath. I watch with rapt attention when she sinks to her knees and sits before me. Her cheeks flush, and her eyes blow wider than before.

"Fuck me," she whispers, reaching for my face. "Fuck me," she demands again, slowly coming forward until our lips meet. I wrap my fingers around her hair, pulling her harder against me, and moan into her mouth.

She tastes herself, diving her tongue in and out.

"Turn around then," I demand this time, looking deep into her eyes. "Turn around and let me fuck your pussy until you cum again, but we have to let Rad watch, yeah?" She swallows hard, nodding at the switch I've given her.

I can be demanding, or I can be submissive. Whichever pleases me, but right now, I need to take control of her. I need to fuck her until she has to use Rad's dick as a gag to stop her from yelling out our names.

She nods to me one last time, letting the exhaustion from the day settle on her face. I see it in her eyes as well, but she still turns around, showing me her perfectly shaped, round ass. I knead them in my palms, only taking them off when I reach into my pocket and pull out a condom.

"This will be fast and hard," I say through gritted teeth, rolling the condom on my length. "I don't know how much more I can hang on. You're a fucking goddess. But don't think this will be the last time my cock sinks into your pussy." I groan when I push myself to the hilt, trying to think of anything but her clamping around me. "Now, are you going to leave him hanging?" I ask, stilling before I thrust again.

Her eyes bounce up toward Rad when he sinks to his knees on the carpet. "I can watch if you want," he says, running a finger down her jaw when she digs her fingers into the floor. "I may be an asshole, but I'd never force you to..."

"I want to," she says with demand. "You're going to have to gag me anyway."

Rad's eyes widen at her demand, but he lets her undo his jeans and pop his throbbing cock out. She gives a few tentative strokes, licking his tip, then shoves forward, taking him into the depths of her throat. I take that as my sign, praying to whoever I don't cum in five seconds, but I'm pretty sure that's where we're headed.

My hips slam into hers hard and fast, just like I promised. There's no mercy here, especially with this burning need scalding down my spine and tightening my balls. With every thrust I give, it forces her forward, spearing Rad's cock down her throat. Rad's eyes roll into the back of his head when he grabs ahold of her hair and fucks her face with all his might. His hips pound against her gagging face, and saliva falls to the ground, pooling on the floor.

White bright stars take over my vision, and my mouth hangs open, frozen in place when I spill into the condom. My hips continue to rock against hers, savoring the feel of her wrapped around me until Rad groans. He throws his head back, stilling with his dick shoved deep in her mouth. No doubt, spilling himself down her beautiful throat, and she takes every bit of it.

He swallows hard, looking deep into my eyes. And I know the moment his mind goes to "We're super fucked if we have to leave her behind" because it glazes over his eyes, and his jaw sets. Our plan is solid. We've lured her in. Almost too well. And we've become the suckers.

I shake my head. We're not leaving her behind. She's always on my damn mind like an obsession I can't escape. Soon I'll be waiting outside her apartment with binoculars, making sure no one fucks with her, watching her undress from afar, and jacking my shit in the trees.

Rad licks his lips, gently pulling his length from her mouth. He swipes his thumb along her bottom lip, leaning down to kiss her plump lips gently.

"You've given me a little taste, and now I want the whole menu," he whispers against her lips as I reluctantly pull out of her pussy. Removing the condom, I throw it into the trash.

"Maybe," comes her breathy reply when her body gives out and she curls up on the ground. "But later," she snarks, waving a tired hand in the air. Her eyes close, and she sighs.

He grins, searches the room for his clothes, and gets dressed.

"I only have like two bras, give that back," she says, pointing a finger to the bra dangling from Rad's pocket.

His brows furrow. "Fuck no, Pretty Girl. These souvenirs are for me now." He snorts, shoving them further into his pocket, and bats away her hand.

She frowns, rolling her eyes, snatching the bra from his pocket. Crossing her arms over her bare chest, she shakes her head at him when he yelps, attempting to tackle her. With a laugh, I put a hand on his chest, shaking my head with a grin.

"Just this once," he says with a lazy grin. "Next time, don't wear one; then, I can feel your pretty titties whenever I want." He hums at the thought and nods like that's the best solution.

"Pretty titties?" she mutters to herself, getting to her wobbly feet, and stumbling a bit. She groans, leaning against the wall.

"River Blue," I murmur, coming to her side.

"Give me just a minute. I, uh, have to go to the bathroom," River says with a huff, marching out the door as quickly as she can like her ass is on fire.

A door slams next to us, shaking the walls. Rad wrinkles his nose, staring at the door with big, puppy dog eyes.

"You, uh… think she's okay?" he asks in a low voice, fiddling with the bottom of his shirt. "I didn't push her too far, did I? Man…" Shaking his head, he runs his trembling fingers through his hair. "I never want to push a girl too far. After that one chick—" He swallows thickly with a solemn expression lining his face.

"River asked you to, dude. And she didn't take it back. I think…" I stare off in the opposite direction of the bathroom, right next to us. "She'll tell us." With a firm nod, I putter around the back office and collect my clothes. Reluctantly, I pull my shirt over my head, find my boxers and jeans, and put them on.

Once fully dressed, I take a deep breath and reflect on what just happened. As it went down, it didn't fully sink in that I had her again. My obsession begs me to grab her up right now, take her home, lock her in my room for days, and not resurface until next Saturday. I run a hand down my face, sighing.

"I bet they're getting antsy. Let's say goodbye to our girl, and yeah—our girl—and head out. Because knowing Ash, he'll leave us here." Grinning, Rad slaps me on the shoulder, shoving me toward the door.

Rad cackles, throwing his head back. "I can't wait to see the look on Asher's face when we…"

"God, River!" A guttural moan roars through the walls.

"What in the fuck?" I growl, marching through the door, and rip open the bathroom door. My heart beats triple time, and my lips pop open at the sight before me.

"Holy shit," Rad laughs. "No way."

Leaning my head against the puke-green stall, I take a deep breath and center myself. Music plays through my earbuds, drowning out the world as I finish my business in the isolation of the bar bathroom.

After drinking a few beers and enjoying the live show, it hit me when we stepped outside to take care of Bradley—the biggest douchebag in town. In high school, he was the absolute worst person, bullying everyone in sight—including me. I was the quiet kid who barely spoke and relied on my friends too much. To him, I was an easy target. How he treated River after crashing into her was more than despicable. No one deserves that amount of hate, no matter what side of town they're on. My fists clench at the memory of his hate-filled eyes looking up and down her body like a meal. No matter what words he used to describe her, in that drunken moment, there was only one thing he wanted to do with her. I should have clocked him in the jaw when I had the chance and filled my memory with something worthwhile to look back on.

I shudder, remembering River's exact face when he crashed into her and uttered those terrible words. Her lips turned down, and her breathing picked up. All the color drained from her face, and her eyes dilated. She claimed she didn't need our help and could have taken care of it herself, but her expression said it all. River was terrified of Bradley. But why? Sure, he was scary at that moment, snarling in her face and calling her names. But why did River's face fall into oblivion, and her lips tremble before him? The others may not have noticed, but I caught every down-turned lip and every quiver of fear.

The entire night, I watched her out of the corner of my eye, checking her movements like a stalker. No one else noticed my newest fascination festering under my skin. I don't know what it is about River that pulls me in and won't let me go. I'm a transfixed moth flying straight into the roaring flame, praying I don't get burned. We all are. There's something addicting about her that reels us in and begs us to stay.

I mutter a curse under my breath when my music unexpectedly cuts out, leaving only the ringing in my ears to accompany me. The silence

stretches out around me, drowning me in the nothingness I can't seem to outrun.

Flushing the toilet, I frown when I yank my earbuds out with a huff. Checking my phone, I note the battery percentage sits at 0%. Thinking back, I forgot to put them on the charger last night when I crawled into my cold bed. Shoving my earbuds into my pocket in defeat, I shake my head at my incompetence. I need the noise to filter out the world. So, I don't fucking remember. I never want to fucking remember.

My teeth grit together when all the noise around me returns, and my brain works double time, filing everything away for later. Water drips. The wind blows outside, shifting something in the building. Voices mutter in the distance. Even dogs bark somewhere near the bar. The noises will forever be cemented in my memories without an erase button.

Some call what I have a gift. Everything I see, taste, hear, and fucking touch—I remember forever. It never goes away and is never forgotten. If you ask me to quote what I did three years ago on a random day, I can reach back into my brain's filing cabinet and perfectly recall it without missing a beat and explain it in vivid detail.

Kids envied me in school, calling me a cheater for my perfect scores. Teachers grew concerned I wasn't being challenged enough and wanted to speed up my learning. Little did they know I had this horrible secret weapon blooming inside me. I wanted nothing to do with the gift bestowed upon me.

And me? I call it a heavy ass burden to carry. Something I didn't ask for. Being able to remember every event in my life is torture on repeat. The good. The bad. And the extremely ugly. No matter what side of life it is, I can't push it from my brain, and it will forever lie in wait, forcing me to remember.

"Callum! Help me!"

"It's so cold, Cally," she whispers, crawling over me. My breaths shudder as warm blood coats my front and seeps into my skin. Helplessly, I cling to her, begging God to spare us from the wrath of death.

"I love you, Jenny," I murmur, stroking a shaky hand through her damp hair.

"Love you too," she whispers in a small, quiet voice—leaving me only two minutes later.

Her tiny voice screams in my head. Those cries for help, begging me to rescue her from a situation I couldn't get us out of. Fuck. I fumble with my phone, needing something to take away the sound of grinding metal, screams, and the feel of warm blood pooling on my chest.

I grunt, slamming a hand into the side of my head twice, trying to knock my brain around. Without the music blasting in my ears, her tiny cries echo on repeat. Make her voice leave. Make it fucking stop haunting me every day. I slam my hand into my head again, silently screaming into the void, pushing saliva out of my mouth, and dripping onto the floor. I lose my fight, slumping on the toilet and leaning my head back against the tile again. Lightly, I knock the back of my head against the wall, begging for the phantom noises to disappear forever. If I could just fucking forget.

Shaking my head, I try to focus on my surroundings and center myself on the here and now. My therapist swears this grounding method will keep me focused on the present, but sometimes I have doubts. A door hangs off the hinges of the stall, which refused to close when I tried. Didn't matter, anyway. No one else is left in the bar except Kieran, Rad, River, and me. Doors close in the distance, offering goodbyes and laughs to River, and she offers them back in return. As her light footsteps walk past the bathroom, I hold my breath, hoping she doesn't peek in and see the mess huddled on the toilet, barely hanging on to reality.

My fists curl at my sides until she walks right past and into the room next to the bathroom. In the same room, I watched Kieran and Rad disappear into the moment we separated, going to two different places.

Murmured voices rise through the walls with such clarity I hear every word they speak, as if I'm standing in the room. Heat encases my cheeks when the first moans roar through the walls, projecting into the small, echoey bathroom. They're breathy and begging, yet she's the one in charge. Every sound she makes comes through, and my imagination takes off into a fantasy world where I'm a suave, smooth talker who never stumbles over my words.

My breaths pick up as her moans grow louder and louder, and I swear my cock stands at attention in three seconds. All the blood whooshes through my ears and goes straight to my dick, making it jerk in my fucking pants.

With shaky fingers, I close my eyes and undo my pants, bringing the zipper entirely down. With just one tug, I could have my cock out. Only stopping for one second when my conscience barrels in and begs me to stop. This is their private time together, and I'm an intruder listening in like a creep. But the sounds she's making drive me fucking insane. No one has ever gotten me this hard before. Sure, I've kissed a few girls, but none gave me the sparks in my belly like River.

River West will either be our ruination or our fucking salvation—I haven't decided which yet.

Looking down, I move the elastic of my boxers and bring my aching cock out. I swear the tip is purple by the time I rub my thumb over it and swipe along my crease, spreading my clear pre-cum. Fuck my conscience. For once, I want to come to the live sounds of a woman getting what she needs from my two best friends. Temporarily, I'm not Callum Rose, the idiot who blushes at every look River throws at me. No. I'm Callum Rose, the guy getting off to the sounds of her orgasm blasting through her. Her screams break off like someone has captured her lips with theirs, thrusting their tongue in her mouth. I shudder at the image of Rad shoving his cock down her throat, gagging her like he said he would.

Fuck. Wrapping my hand around my cock, I stroke up and down, using what little pre-cum I have as lubrication. Eventually, the friction becomes too heated, and I spit in my palm several times, lubing myself up.

A loud groan leaves my lips when I pick up the pace, fucking my hand with the same intensity they're fucking her now. The slap of skin bleeds through the walls. Deep in my mind, I imagine I'm sitting right before them, locking eyes with the girl I'm desperate to touch. I throw my head back, my balls fucking tingling and teetering on the edge when I see the dilation of her moss-green eyes staring heat into mine in my mind. I'm so fucking close to spilling my damn cum all over this bathroom stall. Heat descends my spine, heading straight for my rock-hard cock, twitching in my hand with every stroke. So, fucking close…

My body jumps, and I stop all movement when the door beside me crashes open and slams closed with heavy force. Rad and Kieran murmur in low voices, so low I can't hear them anymore. I hold my breath, not daring to move a muscle until she walks by the door. Please let her walk by. Please don't let her come in here and see that I'm fucking my hand to her.

The men's bathroom door slams open and closes with the same hurried intensity. Only her heavy breaths fill the room. I roll my lips together, fighting the feeling taking me over. I've edged myself so far now that I need to fucking cum, or the pain will overtake me. Fuck.

"Fuck," she murmurs, a light banging happening against the door, which I can only imagine is the back of her head tapping it. "Fuck…"

I swallow the whimper in my throat when I'm forced to stroke myself lightly. The scent of sex wafts off her body, infecting the bathroom with their combined scents. In turn, my heart beats a million miles a minute, filling my ears with persistent thumps. My dick gets impossibly harder, and I suck in a breath, trying to remain as quiet as possible. She'll hear everything in this quiet bathroom if I move a muscle or tuck myself into my pants.

"Who the fuck is in here?" she says in a quiet voice, making my heart drop into the pits of my stomach.

I lick my lips, covering my dick with both my hands. Closing my eyes, I say a brief prayer and do the only thing I can to make her stay away.

"It's me," I whisper, hoping she'll stay by the door and not come any further.

"Yeah? And who is me?" she growls in a harsh tone, but it does little to ease the desire rushing through me.

Fuck, what I wouldn't give to have her on her knees in front of me, begging for me to come on her tits. My lips pop open when familiar heat races up my neck to the tip of my ears. I swear I'm in a perpetual state of blushing.

Clearing my throat, I utter, "Callum." Instead of coming out in a normal tone, it comes out in a deep rasp, alluding to what I've been doing in the back stall of the bathroom.

"Oh," she breathes, her tiny feet stepping closer to my reality.

"I wouldn't," I plead, begging her to go back out the bathroom door and pretend she didn't fucking see me sitting here jacking my shit to the sexy sounds of her.

But it's too late.

As she steps in front of me, I clench my eyes shut, not bothering to hide anymore. I feel her gaze working up and down my body.

"Callum," she whispers in surprise, a tiny gasp escaping her lips. "What're you… were you?"

I blow out a breath; the heat intensifies on my cheeks. I'm sure turning me a dark shade of red. I can't peel my eyes open and face the disgust that will be on her face. Because I know it'll be there. It's always there.

"I'm sorry," I rasp. "I came to use the bathroom, and then…"

"You heard us," she whispers in a soft voice. No judgment sits in her tone, but I still refuse to open my eyes.

"Y-yes. A-and I'm-I'm sorry," I whisper, stumbling over my words with my heavy tongue. Everything tingles on my body, but yet, my dick stays hard and refuses to fucking leave.

Read the room, you prick. She'll definitely shun you after this. I probably just ruined all our chances…

"Did you get off?" My eyes pop open at her question, and I swallow hard.

There standing before me, River cocks her head. Her long brown locks look ratty from overuse, probably Rad shoving his fingers through her hair. Her pink, swollen lips glisten in the shitty bathroom light. A small smile pulls at the edges of her lips when lust fills her eyes and her bare chest heaves. Before me stands a tiny fucking goddess. The fresh, just-fucked look suits her well, and I will forever remember the look in her eyes as she takes me in.

"I… I…" My eyes bug out of my head when she steps closer.

"Start again," she says in a soft tone.

"Wh-what?" I gasp, tightening my fist around my throbbing dick. I shake my head. There's no way I'd be able to perform in front of her.

"You heard me," she barks again, but softly, so as not to alert the two idiots still having a conversation on the other side of the wall. "Stroke yourself, Callum."

I heave a breath, reluctantly removing my left hand, and reveal myself to her completely. Like in my imagination, I lock eyes with her, and she nods with encouragement. Tentatively, I stroke myself, letting myself fall back into the rhythm I had before. Up and down, I stroke my cock. Like she's not standing before me in all her naked glory and watching my every move.

"Good job," she whispers, taking a step closer. "Do you care that I'm this close, Callum?" she whispers, and I shake my head.

"N-no, you're fine... I..."

"Do you want to come on my tits?" she whispers, softly touching my leg. More heat pours across my flesh at the imagery of spilling my seed across her tits and marking her as mine.

I nod, biting into my lower lip. There's no way I'd ever admit that to anyone else.

"Then do it," she says, falling to her knees onto the bathroom floor, waiting for me to finish.

"You-you're serious?" I whisper frantically, stroking myself harder and harder until the need to come rears its beautiful head again, and I'm ten seconds away from blowing all over River's chest.

"I wouldn't have said it if I wasn't. That's all you're comfortable with, right?" I nod because, yeah, as much as I want to jam my cock down her throat and paint her with it, I can't do that yet. My stupid mind holds me back. "Then I want you to cum all over me."

Without another thought, I let myself revel in the feeling of her kneeling in front of me. My balls tighten. Heat descends my spine, straight into my balls. The tip of my dick tingles, and my orgasm hits its peak.

I throw my head back, grunting when the feeling finally overtakes me, and I let go of every fucking thing around me.

"Oh, River!" I shout, spilling everything I have on her awaiting tits.

"What the fuck?" Kieran shouts from the other room, filled with rage.

"You did good," she whispers with encouragement, putting a hand on my knee.

"You really don't care that I did that? What—what about them? I..." I trip over my tongue again, feeling the heat on my neck. But relief comes when I stare into the depth of her bright eyes.

"It's okay," she says with a shrug, staying on her knees until the bathroom door cranks open and shuts with a thud.

Their footsteps pound toward the back stall. This time, without embarrassment, I let it all hang out. Bliss overtakes me, and I don't care what they think or have to say about it. I finally let loose and let myself feel something right in front of me.

"Holy shit," Rad laughs. "No way." Shaking his head, he leans over and examines the mess I left on River. His dark eyes sparkle with pride when he grins at me.

"What're you guys doing in here?" she asks, narrowing her eyes when she climbs to her feet.

Slowly, I tuck my dick back into my pants and zip myself in. Even if the sight of her with my cum dripping down her tits makes my cock stir again. My breaths shudder when I climb to my wobbly feet.

"We came to see what prick shouted your name. Fuck."

Possession seizes Kieran's voice when his eyes find mine. Instead of the ire I thought I'd receive, a smirk pulls at his lips. He nods at me approvingly and turns to grip River by the hair.

"Now, before we go, be a good girl and tell Callum thank you," Kieran demands in a low voice, sending me a knowing look.

I swallow hard, my heart thumping through my damn chest when she turns to me, sporting a smirk. Shivers run down my spine, and my mouth pops open at her glistening in my jizz. Sliding a finger down her cum-soaked chest, she swirls it in my essence, almost playing with it. I track her movements when she swishes it around her erect nipple, painting it like a masterpiece. Fuck. Making eye contact, she sucks her finger into her mouth, hollowing out her cheeks and moaning.

"Thank you, Callum," she rasps, effectively leaving me and the other two idiots dumbfounded and unable to utter words.

My tongue sticks to the roof of my mouth, twisting when she winks, letting me know I did a good job.

Holy fuck. What a woman.

"Uh, we uhh, we came to say goodbye. Asher is probably losing his shit by now," Kieran finally spits out, leaning in to take her lips hostage.

"Fine, goodbye," she mutters breathlessly, shoving at his chest.

"We'll leave you to get cleaned up, Pretty Girl," Rad says with a megawatt grin, lighting up the entire room.

She shrugs with a tired sigh, rubbing at her temples. He gives her a quick peck on the lips and pulls back.

"Give me a minute," I mutter, nodding for them to leave.

Immediately, they take the hint and head toward the door with their shoulders back and smiles on their faces. I haven't seen my friends this happy in a long time, and it's all because of her. Maybe Kieran and his obsession make sense because I'm falling down the same rabbit hole. Asher won't know what hit him when we bring her along when we get into the Battle of the Bands. Because we're getting in, there's no way around that. It's our one and final chance to drive off into the sunset.

"We'll wait by the front door," Kieran says just as they leave the room, leaving River and me alone.

I give her a soft smile as I walk to the sink and start the water. Reaching up, I grab a few brown paper towels and wet them.

"I'll… I'll clean you up," I whisper, stumbling over my damn tongue again. Swallowing hard, I avert my eyes to the ground as anxiety grabs hold.

"You can look at me," she whispers, lifting my chin with her fingers.

Once my eyes meet hers, my breath shudders. Everything seems to click into place, and I nod, gently wiping away my essence from her chest.

"It's hard to make eye contact sometimes," I mutter, throwing the towels into the trash and reaching for more.

"With me, you don't have to worry. I mean, you came on my chest, Cal. I think we're a little past not making eye contact," she says with a small laugh, pulling a chuckle from my chest.

I blush again, instinctively wanting to look away. "I'll work on it," I promise, smiling down at her when I pat her chest dry.

"Now you're just feeling me up," she quips, pointing to my hands as they dab along her tits.

I rip my hand away, looking down at the ground again. "Just trying to make sure you're dry." I quickly throw the towels out and beeline toward the door. I've been brave enough for one day—my heart pounds when I throw the door open, stopping when she calls out my name.

"Callum!" she laughs, strolling forward with a wad of clothes in her hands. "I was just teasing. Now, go with your bros and back to greener pastures." She grins about it, but a deep-seated fear rests in the back of her moss-green eyes.

I lick my lips, stepping up to her. My palms are slick with sweat, and my heart fucking pounds harder than ever. My head swims in anxiety, but I push through it, pressing my lips against her supple cheek. I linger for longer than necessary, soaking in the feeling of her warm flesh beneath my lips.

"We aren't him-him…Van," I whisper against her flesh, taking in her scent. When I pull back, her lips pop open, and her brows furrow. "I'll see you later. Th-thanks for uh…"

"Letting you come on my tits?" she asks, coming out of her stupor with a quip.

Heat retakes my cheeks, and my eyes fall to the floor. "Yeah-yeah, that. See you," I quickly breathe, rushing from the hallway and out the front door.

"There he is!" Rad says with cheer, wrapping an arm around my shoulder. "The man of the damn hour! How'd it feel, bro?"

"Leave him alone," Kieran cuts in with a laugh, shoving Rad off me.

A smile creeps across my face, and I swear I blush more.

"Finally," Asher gripes, starting up the Tahoe with a yawn. "Did you all have a fun circle jerk?" he quips with an eye roll.

"Better than that. You should have sat in the corner… or the bathroom," Rad says, grinning when he eyes me.

I roll my eyes, shaking my head, but don't utter a word. The last thing I need is to spill the beans about River and me to Asher.

"You too?" Asher asks, raising his brow.

My blush deepens, and I look away, focusing on the outside. "I don't kiss and tell," I murmur in a shaky voice.

They can talk about their sexcapades all they want, but my lips are sealed for eternity.

"Well, he didn't kiss he..." I grunt, slamming my hand over Rad's mouth. "What?" Rad gripes, trying to peel my hand away.

"Shh," I grumble, shaking my head.

"Fine," he says into my palm with a huff and folds his arms.

"Such a baby," Kieran mocks, sitting back in the passenger's seat with a smile.

My brows furrow when a familiar figure emerges from the shadows with an earbud dangling from her ear.

"Is she walking?" I ask in outrage, looking toward the clock. "At three in the morning? Here?"

Ash clenches his fists around the steering wheel, eyeing her with narrowed eyes as she walks by without looking in our direction. He lurches the car forward, slowly following right beside her. The whirl of the window goes down, exposing us to the warm, damp air. She doesn't bat an eye.

"Get in the fucking car," Asher growls out the opened window.

She looks at us and rolls her eyes, walking faster down the cracked sidewalk. Ash snarls again, revving the engine, and speeds ahead of her. Our bodies bounce when he hops the curb, pulling right in front of her on the sidewalk, forcing her to stop.

"Get in the car, River," Asher says in a no-nonsense tone, eyeing her like he's about to snatch her off the street.

River sighs. "Listen, Assfaces. Great to see you again, but I'm capable of making it home without interference. Thanks a bunch." Without a second glance, she walks around the back of the SUV and starts walking down the side of the road without a fucking care.

"Where the fuck is her car? Does she have one?" Rad says, looking behind us, and shakes his head.

"Why she gotta be so fucking stubborn?" Asher grunts, slamming the car into reverse and then into drive. Our tires squeal when he hits the gas pedal harder and drives toward her with a sparkle in his eye.

"Jesus, man! Slow down; you're going to run your meal ticket over," Kieran shouts, hanging onto the oh-shit bar with a grimace.

"Do not make me get out of this car, drag your ass in here, and then spank it raw for being so goddamn defiant!" Asher snarls out the window, throwing the Tahoe into park, and opening the door with a growl. "If you make me get out of this car, I will punish you."

River's eyes pop wide when she turns toward him, defiantly putting her hands on her hips. Raising a brow, she stands her ground, not giving in to his demands. She doesn't even flinch when he jumps out of the SUV, Kieran yelling after him to stop being an asshole.

Asher stops right before her, giving her one last chance to comply.

"You are a goddamn psycho. Don't you know no means no, Assbag? I've walked this way before. Thanks a bunch for…." Her words are cut off when she screams bloody murder, slapping Asher when he heaves her over his shoulder. He grunts, hitting her ass hard, and then throws her into Kieran's lap.

Asher's breaths heave in his chest, and he turns his vicious stare to the woman staring him down with murder in her eyes. Kieran quickly holds down her arms, knowing precisely what she was about to go for, and chuckles at her attempt.

"Next time, listen," Asher growls, throwing the car into drive and slamming on the brake. Taking hold of her jaw, he leans in with a vicious glare, declaring one last promise. "Or you'll receive more than an ass slap, baby brat. I'll make you sorry for ever defying me."

"I. Will. Fucking. Stab. You," she growls with such malice my balls shrivel in my pants.

Asher laughs, leaning in more, and examines her hate-filled eyes. "Maybe I'd like that, brat. But for now, I'm taking you home." He lifts a brow when she snarls at him, egging him on more.

With those parting words, he presses the accelerator again, and we take off down the abandoned road.

"I swear my dick just throbbed and shriveled at the same time. Confusing ass woman. But fuck, I think I'm in love," Rad stage whispers to me, eyeing the woman in question who fumes in Kieran's arms.

"I said I was fine," she sighs, pulling her arm from Kieran's grasp, and pinches Asher's nipple through his shirt in punishment.

He flinches, catching her wrist in his hard grasp, grunting through the pain. A familiar smirk twitches the edge of his lips, and he forcefully pulls her face forward with a jerk. In the middle of the road, like a psycho, he pumps the brakes, and we halt. Again. We'll never make it back to her apartment with Asher at the wheel.

"Psychopath," I mumble, pulling myself from the floorboards with a groan. Pain radiates up my tailbone, and I shake my head, locking my seatbelt. "Seatbelts," I reprimand, tugging on my belt.

"You're testing my limits, Little Brat," Asher hisses, rubbing at his chest.

"Settle," Kieran grumbles, pulling her closer.

"Fine," she says, shaking her head.

River huffs, looking out the window, and then watches us out the edge of her eyes. I nod, and her body relaxes into Kieran's as she gives me a warm smile that I commit to memory. When my haunting nightmares surface, I'll look at this moment and seek salvation in her warmth.

"Now, where do you live? I'll do my gentlemanly duties for the night and escort you home. I can't have my future girlfriend dying at the hands of that guy," Asher growls, waving a hand at two men smoking against a building, watching us with a sharp eye.

"You drew attention to yourself when you fucking kidnapped me!" she growls, staring out the window and paling.

It isn't until her entire body tenses up the moment she lays eyes on them, and a tremble works through her body I take note it's Bradley from before. He leans against a building, talking with two more men I've never seen before, smoking cigarettes.

Mentally, I take note, vowing to ensure her safety from here on out. From the corner of my eye, I notice Kieran taking in everything being said and the men outside. Catching his eye, he heaves a breath and nods, knowing exactly what I'm thinking, too.

"And girlfriend? Are you insane?" she gripes again, resting her head against Kieran's shoulder. With a sigh, she points down the road. "Just down the way," she mumbles with less fire, settling into Kieran more. Fuck, how I wish it were me that held her close instead of him. "Central Apartment Complex." She sighs when she says it, leaning her head back, and shuts her eyes.

I exchange a look with Asher, and he licks his lips, knowing precisely what neighborhood we're pulling into and what danger lurks there, especially for pretty girls like her. She shouldn't be on the streets alone, let alone on this one. Central City isn't known for being safe at any time of day. Crime runs rampant in these parts compared to our slice of heaven in Lakeview. It's night and day between the two.

The street blurs by as we drive the eight blocks from the bar to her apartment complex. It's not a long drive—short and sweet. But the walk would have blistered her feet and taken at least forty-five minutes.

Her apartment building stands in the distance with dark brick and barely any streetlights lining the parking lot. Three more units lay in a semi-circle around her building, with their own dimly lit parking lots filled to the brim with an assortment of cars.

"Over there." She points to a unit in the middle of the complex, bringing me out of my thoughts.

Ash directs the Tahoe toward the middle unit, eyes darting around the filled-up parking lot. He pulls up next to a Toyota, which looks like it's seen better days. I look back at River, slumped against Kieran with even breaths. Her eyes flutter open and shut, and if she trusted me more, I'd carry her to her bed. Or force her into mine for the night. I'd tuck her in and never let her leave.

"Thanks for the ride," she mumbles, rubbing her eyes.

"No, no, thank you!" Rad says with enthusiasm, reaching between the seats. He pulls her tired face toward his and kisses her again, shoving his tongue down her unsuspecting throat. She groans, pushing him away, and wipes the spit from her lips, giving him a death glare.

"Asshole," she mumbles, opening the door, and jumps down. She lingers a moment, staring into my eyes, and doesn't shut the door until I give her a nod.

We watch with rapt attention when she walks to the ground-floor apartment and pulls out her keys. Unit 7—I take note, remembering the information for later.

This obsession crashes down on me, and I can only think about her now. Her and our music. I let it settle beneath my skin and take me over. The more of her I have, the fewer nightmares I'll experience.

She opens the door, not sparing us a glance or a thank you, and shuts the door quietly.

"Fuck," Asher sighs, hitting the steering wheel with an open palm, letting all his frustrations leak through. There's no hiding the interest he holds for our little River.

"Yeah, fuck. Fuck me," Rad reiterates, staring at the door as she disappears behind. "Ah, shit," Rad murmurs, holding up a beat-up old iPhone with a split screen.

I frown, grabbing it from his hand, and holding it up to examine it. Ouch. It's definitely seen better days. Maybe I could buy her a new one with a better case using the trust my parents left me. It would more than accommodate a new phone, or maybe I could lend her my old one. It's just collecting dust. I bite my lip, thinking about all the things I could shower her with. Not like she'd want them, anyway.

River is making her way through this world. That much is obvious. But what is a little present here and there? Besides, if she is going to date us or be our girlfriend, she needs a better phone to communicate with us. And… hmm. Yes. That will be perfect. I grin to myself and nod. Ah, yeah, that's it. A giddy butterfly erupts in my gut at the thought of throwing a new phone at her with a little something extra.

"That hers?" Asher asks, raising a brow at the sight of the poor, abused phone.

"Appears so," Rad whistles under his breath and then snatches it from my hand. "Time to find out where my new favorite girl lives." I choke on my spit when he leaps out of the car, stumbling over his drunken feet, and marches toward her door with copious amounts of liquid courage.

"Shit," I yelp, jumping out and taking off after him at full speed and stopping when we come face to face with her weathered door, with the number 7 on it. Kieran breathes heavily when he joins us at the door and frowns.

"You have to be careful, man," he growls, looking around the complex, and his shoulders sag. "You can't just run out here at night. Never know who's waiting around the corner." Kieran swallows hard, eyeing the surrounding buildings with a sharp eye.

Rad grins again, wiggling his brows, completely disregarding Kieran's concerns. Instead, he obviously thinks he's going another round with her between the sheets. Fat chance. Asher would storm the damn castle and yank them out by their dicks.

"For fuck's sake," Asher gripes, running a hand down his face when he finally catches up to us and locks the Tahoe. "Can't have you idiots leaving me in the car again."

The door bursts open with a frightened-looking River standing on the other side, and my hackles rise. I growl, looking her up and down, noticing the tears she's frantically wiping away and trying to hide.

"What's going on?" Kieran asks, stepping protectively up to her. He grabs her shoulders, forcing her to look at us. Terror and pure panic rest in the back of her eyes when she stares back, and my heart drops.

"Help," she murmurs, staring us in the eyes with a bewildered look. "I need your help."

And every instinct in my body tells me to drop everything and help.

DO NOT FALL IN LOVE WITH THESE ASSHOLES. JUST. DON'T. DON'T THINK about their big dicks sliding inside you, giving you a better release than anyone ever has. Don't think about how powerful you felt pushing Kieran to do as you said, as he gave into the demand in your voice. Don't think about how he filled you up; then, his friend did the same to your mouth. Don't think about Callum's face when he finally had the courage to come and how he cared for you afterward.

Just don't do it, River. Definitely don't think about their friends doing the same and rolling around with each of them to find your pleasure. And most definitely, don't think about going on a date with them or cozying up to them or whatever else your twisted little mind can think of.

I'm in such deep shit. They're all I can think about as I saunter through the night air, immediately sweating from the intensity of the heat. Even if the sun went down hours ago, mugginess drifts in the air.

A rogue thought smacks the smitten feeling right out of me, and I frown. This is one hundred percent the definition of a whore. Right? Shit. Am I a whore? I shake my head, answering my own stupid question. Nah. You know what? Fuck the stereotypes. I'm not a whore. I'm a girl with needs who fucked two guys simultaneously and loved every second of being in their grasp. One to fuck me, the second one to gag me, and the third to cum all over me.

By society's standards, I'm one hundred percent a whore. But you know what? Society can suck my dick for all I care. And I know, I know. People love to remind me I don't have a dick, but I'm not talking about the flesh flute hanging between my legs. I'm talking my soul dick. The dick that lives deep inside of me, not literally. So, suck my aura dick, society, and leave the name-calling out of your mouth.

That's just the deep-seated hate women get for enjoying the same sexual experiences men enjoy without the label. I fucked two guys at once and let their other friend cum on my tits. And you know what? I liked it, and I'm damn proud. And I'd do it again.

Use us, River. We'll do whatever you want.

I shiver as Kieran's words roll around in my brain. More vivid memories flash in rapid succession, like a movie on repeat in my mind. Heat envelops me, going straight to my core and begging for more of Kieran, Rad, and Callum. Hell, throw Asher in there, too. A nice hate fuck, where he bosses me around, and I'm the defiant brat, sounds like a good time. God, as fucked as it sounds, I can't wait for the day when Asher punishes me for every minor infraction. He could bend me over his knee, spank my ass raw, and then fuck me in it.

Yup. I'm fucked.

I sink my teeth into my bottom lip as I unlock my front door. Heaving a breath, I feel the echoes of their stares burning through me and holding me prisoner. It doesn't cease until I shut the door and block their view. Finally, I can take a full breath without them breathing down my neck—without them suffocating me with one heated stare.

Pulling fresh oxygen into my lungs, I step further into the darkened apartment and stare at my mother's empty chair. Since she got fired from her job and broke her leg, she's been chair bound.

Nothing has fucked with my mom's depression more than being stuck in her recliner with her leg in the air, unable to do a damn thing. I peek around the apartment and sigh again at the mess filling the sink and the grime on the countertops.

How the hell am I supposed to help her when I have two jobs, schooling, and four weirdos trailing after me? I know Korrine has been checking in on her and sitting with her for lunch, ensuring my mom's fed. But I can't rely on my neighbor forever. She has her own life, and my mom needs me. But I'm so damn busy taking care of myself and this house. I don't know what I'm going to do with her holed up as essentially a child. My mom is the most important person in my life. I don't know how I will cope with all this on my own at nineteen.

"Ma?" I ask, looking around the deserted apartment.

My heart rate spikes when she doesn't respond. Swallowing hard, I move toward the running water sound coming from our tiny bathroom.

"Hey, Ma? You in there? You doing, okay?" I lightly tap on the wood door.

Once again, she doesn't respond. Normally she hums or sings as she prepares for work, drowning herself in long showers. I search for the comfort of her voice, but it's nothing but emptiness. The shower is roaring down on the tiled tub, filling the space with its noise. Placing my ear against the wooden door, I listen further, still getting nothing in return.

"Fuck, Ma! I'm coming in. If you don't answer, you're about to scar me for life," I shout, twisting the knob, and my heart drops way into my ass at the sight before me. "Ma!" I gasp, dropping to my knees.

Blood drips from the gash on her forehead, pooling on the ground and matting in her hair. Sprawled out completely naked on her back, she's unresponsive, not flinching when I shake her. Yelling out to her again in broken sobs, I try to rouse her, but she doesn't stir. Her broken leg is wrapped in plastic, sticking over the side of the tub where the water rains down. Shaking her again, I get the same response. Nothing.

"Shit, shit, shit!" I curse, covering her naked body with a towel, and shutting off the water. What the hell do I do? How do I? "Fuck," I growl, my hands shaking, looking down at her pale body. What the hell do I do? What the hell? Hospital? Ambulance? Chaotic thoughts take over my brain, spinning like a damn tornado. "Shit. I need Korrine," I gasp out in desperation.

She's a former nurse, only quitting to raise her family many years ago. My hands tremble more when I run them through my hair and get to my feet, but not before checking her pulse. It's strong and beating against my fingers. So, I know she's okay there. Just injured. Severely. And—I pale at the blood sticking to her skin. My stomach churns, threatening to send up the contents of my stomach.

My heavy heartbeat pounds against my chest, and oxygen refuses to enter my lungs. A tight rubber band constricts around my chest, hellbent on suffocating me before I can get the help my mom needs.

I run out of the bathroom in a haze, gasping for breath and throwing open the front door. I only stop when Kieran, Callum, Asher, and Rad stand before me with my phone dangling in the air and confusion etching across their faces.

"What's going on?" Kieran asks, stepping protectively up to me and grabbing my shoulders firmly.

For whatever reason, I slump into him like he's the best protector I've ever had and will shield me from the dangers surrounding us. Maybe it's the familiarity he offers and seeing him shoves my panic to the deepest pit. His scent overtakes my senses, confusing every bit of me, but also calms the raging inferno inside me.

Sincerity and concern bleed through his gaze when he stares me up and down, checking for wounds. For some odd reason, I think he cares for me and maybe my well-being. Quickly, I wipe my tears away, refusing to show them my weaknesses.

"Help," I murmur through a gasp, staring at him with pleading eyes. "I need your help." My heart beats out of control when their faces fall into determined looks. Each of them steps up, awaiting my words. Even Asher looks around, evaluating the apartment from the outside and searching for the culprit of my panic.

"What is it?" Kieran pushes past me, waltzing into my apartment.

Callum ushers me in with his arm tightly wrapping around my shoulders and pulls me into the side of his body. His warmth spreads through me when they all stand in my messy apartment. Someone shuts the front door, cutting off the outside world.

"Pretty Girl," Rad whispers, standing before me, and cups my jaw. "Tell us what's going on, okay?" I shiver under his touch, my body trembling more.

Kieran looks around, snarling when he doesn't see the threat sending me into shock, and jerks his gaze toward me. Eyeing me up and down, he repeatedly looks me over like blood should be pouring from every orifice.

My teeth chatter together, filling the room with their constant noise. Static takes over my brain, and my thoughts work through a thick sludge, slowing it down until I can't form words. Shit. Think. Fucking think! I'm a fucking manager, for Christ's sake. I should be able to figure out disasters without falling on my ass. No matter how often I chant that in my head, I'm stuck in a phantom mud.

Asher snarls, throwing Rad out of the way and standing before me, taking my jaw forcefully in his grip, clamping down on me. Pain spears through my jaw and onto my cheeks, forcing my eyes to his angry stare.

"River West, tell us what's going on!" His demand lands like a whip against my ass, kicking the panic out of my brain long enough for clarity to take over.

"My mom!" I force out through my chattering teeth. Asher's brows raise into his hairline when I snatch his hand from my jaw and lead him toward the bathroom. "My mom-my mom, has MS; she fell!" I gasp, standing in front of the bathroom door, unable to get oxygen into my lungs.

"Shit," Rad hisses as footsteps pound behind us.

"River Blue," Kieran says, turning me to face him and cupping my cheeks. "We'll help, okay? What do you need us to do?" His mismatched eyes examine my face, and my mind goes fucking blank.

B-l-a-n-k! The fuck! I'm supposed to know what I'm doing. But I'm frozen by the sight of my mom's fucking blood on the ground and in her hairline. She's motionless, barely breathing on the bathroom floor. And who knows for how long? Is she still alive?

"I need to get her back in her chair…. God, I can't call an ambulance; that would cost too much money. We can't afford that. I…" Tears burn the back of my eyes, and I'm not too proud to admit fear is coursing through me mixed with indecision. Do this? Do that? The fuck do I do first.

"River, why don't you get your mom some clothes?" Asher demands in a calm voice, leaning over my mom's still body. He checks her forehead, finds gauze under the sink, and puts it on her bleeding wound. "You might have to take her to the ER, just in case. This gash is pretty bad." Asher gives me a pointed stare. "Now is not the time to defy me, River. Go get your mother some clothes." Again, he demands, and it snaps like a rubber band against me, immediately sending me into action. If there's one person to tamp my panic with demands and get me moving, it seems to be Asher. I swallow hard and nod at his words. "Good girl," he says, praising me when I take a step back, following his directions.

If the situation weren't so dire, I'd slap him across the head for his praise. And I'd definitely never admit to him that his words do something odd to me, sending goosebumps down my skin and lightness taking me over.

Turning toward her tiny bedroom, I gather some fresh underwear, shorts, and a shirt. Once they're bundled into my arms, I step into the bathroom, sliding my mom's panties up her legs and shorts on as the guys turn around for privacy.

In the back of my mind, I know the emergency room will cost an arm and a leg. We just have to convince our state insurance to cover the bill. But whatever we can do to save her fucking life.

Rad quietly calls 911 for me, explaining the situation to the dispatcher calmly and precisely. I swallow hard when I put my mom's shirt on, careful of her head injury, sliding her arms through the sleeves and pulling it over her stomach. She still doesn't stir when I'm done, and tears leak from my eyes. She looks dead, barely breathing, and has a giant gash on her fucking forehead.

Callum pulls me into his chest again, letting his shirt soak up my stupid tears. He whispers soft words of comfort in my ear, reassuring me she'll be okay. With every word he speaks, my panic slowly drains out, and I slump into him. I wrap my arms around his body, soaking up his warmth and the safety he offers me when the world around me is so chaotic.

Thank God they came back to... well, why did they come back? My brows furrow as my thoughts slowly come back to me at a rapid pace. If they hadn't been at the door while I threw it open, I would have been lost. Sure, Korrine would have jumped at my pleas for help and come over, but I hate to rely on her so much. She's already done so much.

"Hey, Pretty Girl, they're on their way, okay?" I swallow hard when Rad wraps himself around my back, sandwiching me between them. "Everything will be okay. I promise," he whispers, gently kissing the side of my head.

The moment his warmth hits my back, and his words sink into me, I fucking lose it like a baby, uncontrollably sobbing as I've never done before. Usually, no one gets to see this side of me. I hold it all in. No one takes an over-emotional woman seriously because, well—society is fucked.

Fear tightens every inch of me at the thought of losing my mother to this disease, dragging her down. Ever since she told me, she's folded in on herself and barely talked. It's only been a day, but it feels like my mom has all but given up. I've got to do something to help her get out more and help her get healthy. But what can I do? I work two jobs to feed us and keep us warm and cool. I go to college to better our future. When I am trying to better my life to better hers, I can't stay home and watch her. I could quit everything and just become another statistic, but I refuse. In ten years, I don't want to be here. Instead, I want to work for a record company or manage a business dealing with music and take my mother with me. I want to give her the best care she can ever imagine. I have to stick it out.

Another warm body presses into our sides, whispering kind words when he wraps his arms around the three of us. Together, the boys create a solid circle around me, protecting me from anything that comes our way. Kieran kisses the back of my skull, nuzzling into me with such care I know I'm fucked. So, fucking fucked. Because the moment his lips meet my hair, he has me right where he wants me. I'm falling hard and fast, even though my brain screams it's a bad idea. Like, I don't know already.

I've learned this lesson before with Van. But Van never came over here. He never volunteered to drive me home and ensure my safety like they did. Van let me walk home when my car died, or he'd drop me off a block away. I should have seen the giant red flags from a mile away, but I was too blinded by the look in his eyes and how he made me feel. He never came to see me at the bar, only the record store, or hang out. Why does this feel different? But it gives me the same feeling at the same time. I'm so damn conflicted about how I should feel about them and how they just showed up in my life like a hurricane.

After a moment, I pull away from them when someone pounds on the front door, yelling about being EMTs. Wiping my eyes, I avert my gaze toward the ground, giving them a tight smile—a red tint blossoms on my cheeks when I peek at the wetness covering Callum's shirt.

"Thank you for the help," I say through heavy emotions clogging my throat. Walking out of the bathroom at a quick pace, I try to get to the door as quickly as possible. Probably looking like I'm scurrying away like a little mouse, desperate to get away from them.

"Anytime, River Blue," Kieran says, grabbing my shoulder and stopping my retreat. Turning me to face him, he cups my cheeks again. "You can reach out to us at any time, okay? Especially with something like this. If you need help, we're here." He gives me a firm nod, something in his eyes telling me he might somehow relate to this entire situation. Leaning in, he softly kisses my lips, reaffirming his feelings for me.

Behind me, the front door opens, and Rad graciously shows them to my mother. Callum and Asher stand beside Kieran as he continues to hold me through all the movement in my apartment. Eventually, Kieran escorts me to the bathroom, where I explain the situation to them.

They quickly assess her and help rouse her to the land of the living. She comes to slowly with wide eyes, frantically looking around with confusion. Once she's calmed down, they patch her forehead up, run some tests for a concussion, and clear her.

They advise her not to shower alone again and to go to the ER if any more symptoms pop up. I agree to monitor her as they guide her back to her chair and set her down. They go on their way, waving when they walk out the door.

Kieran, Rad, Callum, and Asher stay by my side through the entire ordeal, helping to center me through my panic. Rad clutches my hands and murmurs sweet words of encouragement. Something about his pretty words centers my whole being, and I settle. My mind comes back online just in time for the four boys to stand around me after the EMTs leave.

"Thank you so much for everything you've done tonight," I murmur, running a hand across my forehead. "I kind of panicked." I look away, wincing with embarrassment. A heat takes over my cheeks and runs down my neck.

Yeah, it's cool; River, just go ahead and show these assholes your vulnerabilities and weaknesses. Just tell them your entire life story, why don't ya? Shit. I have to be more careful about what I share with them or anyone else. I have goals, and sure, they're massive amounts of fun. But I can't afford to get stuck here or with them.

"No probs, Pretty Girl. What're friends for, right?" Rad says with a grin, shoving his hands in his pocket.

"You'll be okay with her for the rest of the day?" Kieran asks, furrowing his brows at my mom, who slumps in her chair, watching some channel that sells jewelry.

"Yeah, it'll be fine," I say through a breath.

Yeah, I'd be fine. I'd have to skip school and the bar, but I'd make do. Right? Right? We'll be okay. Shit, I need to talk to Korrine and see if I can set up nurse visits or something to help me.

"What's your number?" Kieran asks, holding out his phone. "If you need anything, call, okay?" I nod, sending them on their way after putting my number in his contacts, and collapse against the door when they're finally out of view.

Outside, the sound of an engine coming to life echoes through the parking lot and then takes off down the road.

"They seem like good boys," Ma says, settling into her recliner with a sleepy look. I'm not sure why it took me so long to put two and two together, but she's been opting to snooze in her chair over lying in bed.

"Yeah," I breathe.

They seem like good boys—too good of guys for me.

After making sure my mom is okay, I head to bed and attempt to sleep for what feels like the first time this week, forgetting my responsibilities. Tomorrow, I'll deal with work. Tomorrow, I'll deal with school. Tomorrow, I'll deal with the fallout of this whole mess.

Quickly texting Booker about my night, he tells me to watch my mom for the day and not worry about work. Thank God he's a night owl, or he'd have a hell of a message to wake up to in the morning. I quickly change into an oversized shirt, sans pants and panties, and crawl into bed with a sigh.

LYING IN THE DARKNESS OF MY ROOM, I STARE AT THE GLOWING STARS I stuck to the ceiling when I was five. Ma hated them, but Booker helped me stick them up there. I smile at the memory of him setting me on his shoulder so I could stick the little stars myself. After that night, I was never afraid of the dark again as long as I had the stars to guide me.

I roll to my side, watching the trees blow through the sliding glass door of my room. Many moons ago, I'd sneak out through that door to avoid the noises coming from my mom's bedroom. She'd try to cover it up with music, but it never worked. Or I'd sneak out when she left for work, leaving me alone in the tiny apartment.

"Dear Man on the Moon," I mumble, finding the brightly lit moon beaming down on the earth, preparing to leave for another night. Soon the sun will shine, and my day will start all over again. "Will you watch over us again? Just this once, I need my life in order and for everything to go right. Just this once. I need a damn miracle." I sigh and nearly jump out of my skin when a small knock from the sliding glass door shakes me from my pity party.

I furrow my brows, throwing the sheet from my body. Who the hell could that be? It's four in the damn morning. I need to sleep, not company. With caution, I peek out the hanging blinds, and my eyes widen at the darkened figure standing just outside the door. His gray eyes take me in, and he offers me a small, inviting wave. A soft smile pulls at his lips, and every worry flees from my body. Without a thought, I open the sliding glass door and lean against the frame, letting the warm night into my room.

"Callum?" I whisper with confusion at him, standing outside my bedroom at almost four in the morning.

"Could I… Could I…" He blows out a breath, shaking his head when he stumbles over his words. "Can I come in? I thought after tonight; you might want some company?" he murmurs with concern taking over his face. He cocks his head to the side like an observant puppy, watching my every move. Here I thought Asher was the observant one, but Callum seems to take it all in, too. Maybe more.

The prospect of having someone hold me until the sun comes up appeases me to the point I never thought. I'm not the cuddling type or the hugging type. I'm the fuck me and then leave me alone type. But my body preens at the thought of him wrapping his long arms around me and holding me until we fall asleep. Something soft and sweet about Callum pulls me into his orbit. He's like the stars shining above us, dazzling me with his presence, giving me no other option because I can't seem to say no to him right now. Not when he graces me with that slight grin and hope in his eyes.

"Yeah," I whisper, swallowing the lump in my throat. "It's not much, but this is my room." I gesture for him to come in, and he nods, waltzing into my room with his hands in his pockets.

A heavenly smile graces his soft face. "I think it's perfect."

I huff a quiet laugh, shut the sliding glass door, and fix the blinds so it won't disturb us when the sun rises. There's nothing perfect about my tiny room, only housing my bed and a small standing dresser with my few pieces of jewelry sitting on top. There's no TV, only my stars—it's just my space I sleep in and nothing more.

"Any plans today?" I ask, raising a brow when he meanders to the opposite side of my queen-sized bed and shakes his head.

"Only this," he whispers, planting his ass on the edge of my bed and removing his socks and shoes. "Do you mind if I take off my shirt and pants? I-I can keep-keep them on if-if you want me to."

I smile as his nerves get the best of him, and his eyes fall to the worn-out carpet, not meeting my stare. Even with the darkness of my room, a red tint takes over his cheeks. Callum's presence, I realize, is disarming in a way. He's taking down the walls I've carefully erected over the years as a defense—brick by brick.

"As long as you don't mind that I'm not wearing panties under this long shirt," I murmur, climbing into my side of the bed.

His gaze jerks to my bare legs, working up them with a shuddering breath until he meets my gaze. Through the dark, I see the dilation of eyes and more red-tinted cheeks.

"Maybe I should keep my clothes on," he quips with trembling fingers, working his shirt up several times before he finally pulls it over his head and throws it aside.

My breath halts at the multitude of tattoos lining his chest and sides, covering what looks like deep scars running across Callum's body. You'd never guess what lies beneath his shirt, especially not this. Without thinking, I run the tips of my fingers across the deep scars that, to the naked eye, would be hidden under the array of colorful tattoos. But I see the wounds like I try to see everything else on him.

Callum doesn't flinch when I trace them toward his chest, only stopping me when I get near his nipple.

"You can ask," he whispers, leaning back on the bed with his jeans intact. A distinct dick imprint pushes at the material, letting me know he's keeping himself in check by keeping the pants on.

"Only if you want to tell it," I say, leaning my head on my hand.

Callum's expression doesn't change, but I see the ghosts haunting him through his glazed-over eyes. "As long-long as you keep touch-touching me." He swallows hard, clamping his eyes shut. His hand squeezes over mine, holding it hostage on his chest.

"Odd request, Cal. But sure, I'll keep touching you," I quip, trying to lighten the mood for him.

I succeed when a soft smile tugs at his lips, but the haunted look remains.

"It was almost two years ago," he whispers, shivering like the memories are coming back in full picture. "I was in a plane crash. My parents and my little sister Jenny… they-they died-died beside me." I swallow hard, lean into him, and hug him with all my might. "The only thing I have left of them is my house, everything inside it, and the trust they left in my name for bills."

"I'm sure you hear this all the time, but I'm so sorry you went through that. I can't imagine the pain…" my words trail off when he nods.

"There was nothing I could do. I severely broke my leg from the impact. My little sister crawled on top of me, told me she loved me, and then passed away in my arms. Ever since… Without music, I can't keep the nightmares from taking over." Realization hits me like a truck, and I note all the times he had his earbuds in, seeming to ignore the world around him. But it wasn't because he was rude. It was to drown out the ghosts trying to haunt him. He looks at me, curling a piece of my long hair behind my ear. "Since the accident, only one thing has kept me sane. Until today, though, I've discovered there are now two things that chase away the monsters haunting my mind and grant me peace."

"Yeah?" I whisper as he leans in close, bumping his nose against mine.

"Yeah," he confirms, brushing his lips against mine and holding my body close. "You," he whispers with a shaky breath, breaking me with his confession. "And music."

My heart drops into my stomach when he swoops in and steals the breath from my lungs with lazy kisses. His tongue prods at the seam of my lips, and I grant him access, moaning into his mouth when he rocks against me. Pulling back, a sparkle reignites in his eyes, and life seems to reinflate inside him.

"Now, can I ask you a question?" he whispers, keeping me close when I pull the sheet up, covering us together. His confession weighs on my mind, but I nod, snuggling into him. Despite what I've felt before, this is the most comfortable I've been with another human being in almost four years. Since…

"Why were you so afraid of the guy at the bar? Bradley?" I quirk a brow at his bold question, searching his eyes when my heart picks up speed.

"How did you…?" I shake my head when he nods in confirmation.

"I tend to notice things others don't. You froze when he called you those awful names and slammed into you. The vein in your neck pumped double time, and your nostrils flared. But the paleness that took over your face really solidified what was wrong." For the first time since interacting with the quietest member of Whispered Words, he keeps eye contact and stays confident with his speech. It's like he's evaluated the entire situation and knows exactly what happened four years ago.

Heat brews beneath my skin, and I shake my head. "It's nothing…."

"It's something," he whispers. "But I won't pry into your personal matters. I respect you, River. And… I kinda like-like you-you." With a deep breath, he closes his eyes. "I don't want you to talk about anything you don't want to."

I close my eyes, leaning my head on his chest. The deep, thunderous pound of his heart echoes in my ear, soothing all the fear inside me. Maybe Callum and I have a weird connection, after all. If I soothe his nightmares and he seems to pacify the anxiety always begging to ruin my life, we're meant for each other in some fucked up way.

"Four years ago, I went to a party when I was fifteen. That night, after seeing someone who I thought would recognize me—"

"It was Kieran?" he asks in his oh-so-observant way, and I nod. "Sorry, I didn't mean to interrupt."

Remorse clings to his voice, and he holds me tighter, giving me the comfort no one has offered me my entire life. Van sure as hell never held me after we had sex or listened to me when I spoke. Again, all the red flags were present; I just didn't see them.

"Kieran used to live here; one day, he was gone. Asher's dad, I'm assuming, started coming around. I… I knew Kieran would be at that party and wanted to see him. He was my best friend, and… Well, let's just say he had no idea. To make a long, boring story short, I drank too much and found myself at the hands of Bradley and his friend."

Callum gulps a breath, kissing my head when I shudder in his arms. Why is it so easy to spill this secret to him? I haven't told anyone since the police waved me off and practically blamed me for the entire situation. I tried to go forward with my life and ignore the injustice I had been served, but seeing Bradley tonight stirred up all those old, foggy memories.

"They took advantage of me, if you can imagine. Then…" I close my eyes as the memory of Rad's soft, dark eyes looking down on me resurfaces. The comforting words he uttered when he picked me up off the ground and put me in his car.

"I'll find those fuckers for you," he said in a soft but demanding voice. "I'll beat their asses. Who was it?" he whispers, starting up his car. But I just shook my head, tears streaming down my face, and I refused to look at the man who saved me. "Please talk to the cops. Let them know everything. I know something bad happened. Someone at that party… took what wasn't theirs, right?" he asks when he pulls up to the hospital, staring at me when I nod in confirmation.

"Rad has always had a soft spot for you, you know? When he found you like that, it fucking broke him. He went to the cops and told them he found you to corroborate your story, but they…"

"Laughed him off like they did me?" I ask with a shaky breath, shaking my head. "I'll always remember how he took care of me."

"Will you ever let him know it's you?" he asks, stroking a hand through my hair, causing my eyes to close.

It feels like the world lifts from my shoulders at his validation. No one has ever told me it wasn't my fault, or that I didn't deserve it. Even my mother looked down at me and rolled her eyes when I called her from the hospital.

I shrug, unable to speak through the lump in my throat. "I think I need to get some sleep. It's been a long ass day," I mutter, burying my face into his chest.

"Avoidance at its best, but that's okay, my Little Star," he murmurs, snuggling into me. My heart fucking soars at the name, and my eyes find the green neon stars shining on the ceiling. "Let's get some rest."

Taking one last, long breath, Callum and I drift off to sleep in each other's arms, sinking into the best dreams I've had in years.

The first thing I notice when I wake up in the morning is the blaring sunshine beating through the sliding glass door, which I swore I had secured the blinds better than that.

The second thing I notice is the second warm body squishing against me, heating my back. Sweat coats every inch of my skin from the ovens surrounding me and…

"What the hell?" I shriek, pushing the second body away from me with my fist to their hard chest as panic takes over.

He grunts, rolling onto the floor with a loud hiss. If we had downstairs neighbors, they'd be pounding on the ceiling out of frustration.

"Wh-what is it?" Callum asks in a raspy, just woken-up voice, rubbing his eyes with urgency.

Peeking over the bed, my heart hammers in my chest when I meet the gaze of the intruder rolling around on the ground. He groans, holding his chest and wincing through the pain. Huh. Apparently, I punched him harder than I thought.

"Pretty Girl, it's not nice to punch people out of bed. You interrupted an amazing dream. You and me and the rest of the guys naked on the beach with sand in places we shouldn't speak of. But you were about to give me a sandy pussy sandwich, and then you pushed me out of bed," he groans through his entire speech, finally rising to a sitting position. His big brown eyes peer at me with mischief.

"First off, I don't even want to know what a sandy pussy sandwich is," I say, shaking my head. "Second off…"

"How'd I get in your room?" he asks with an enormous grin, climbing to his feet. "You all ask the same questions. How'd you get into my room? Why're my panties in your pockets? They're not, by the way. No panties in here," he says, lying through his teeth when he pats his bulging pocket. "But the answer is always the same. You summoned me with your mind." He grins, tapping the side of his head.

"Are you high?" I ask, furrowing my brows. "Wait, don't answer that. It's way too early in the morning."

"It's noon," Rad says, climbing back into bed beside me. He grins, pulls his phone from his pocket, and shows me the screen. "But you two were the best snuggle buddies. We should get rings made. Snuggle Buddies activate!" he howls, thrusting his fist into the air.

I blink a few times, processing what the fuck is going on. I'm too tired and way too grumpy to deal with his optimism—which he should kindly choke on until I get more sleep. But noon? Seriously? I haven't slept this late since… Well, forever. I've been up at the butt crack of dawn since I was fourteen, busting my ass at work.

"Is he serious?" I stage whisper to Callum, who pulls my body into his and huffs into my neck.

"Unfortunately," he grumbles, sounding half asleep.

Rad frowns, bumping his own fist, and sighs. "You all left me hanging. It's rude. So, what are we doing today? Obviously, my girlfriend is not killing herself at work. So… what should we do?"

I sigh, putting an arm over my eyes. "I'm not your girlfriend, Rad."

"You can say that and believe it, but no matter what you say, you're mine. If another man besides my best friends even approaches you, I'm gouging their eyes out and wearing them as trophies," Rad says with a smug expression, leaning in closer to me to boop my nose.

"I am a biter," I remind him, closing my eyes and trying to go back to sleep. "And very sleepy," I mumble.

Rad grumbles under his breath, slinking up to me and pressing his front against mine. "But, Pretty Girl, we could have so much fun today on your day off! I brought my dirt bike! We can go for a ride down at the track. I can show you a thing or two," he says through fits of fucking giggles.

"You are too damn chipper in the morning…"

"It's noon! The sun is shining and..." I put my hand over his mouth and peek an eye open, glaring at him.

"If you're not careful, she's going to kick you out," Callum mutters the warning into my neck.

"He's got a point," I say, raising a brow.

"Pfft. Don't worry, Pretty girl. Me and your mom, Stella, had some breakfast from the donut shop. I fed her coffee, and we watched the news. She's taking a nap, and then she's got a home health nurse for the day." Rad grins like this is common knowledge, and my lips pop open.

"Who are you?" I ask, slumping into the bed with a groan.

Rad snorts. "You were worried last night, babe," he says in a softer tone, running a finger down my jaw. "I wanted to make it better. I didn't realize this guy was here, though." His warm, dark eyes light up when his best friend huffs.

"I was-was worried, too," Callum says through a frustrated sigh. When I peek back, a red tint takes over his cheeks again.

"But I should have guessed where you were headed the moment you walked out the front door. You didn't even tell me goodbye or invite me to the slumber party, which is rude, by the way," Rad whines, fake pouting. "Next time, it'll be at our house!" he says, wiggling his brows again.

I strum his lip and scoff. "Too early," I mumble again, going over his words. "Wait, you said home health nurse?" My eyes pop wide at his words, making my heart skip a beat.

Rad grins from ear to ear, and he nods. "Your mom is super chill. I like her. She requested donuts every morning, so I guess you'll see me around here a lot. I kind of dig this place. Anyway, I called my mom..."

"You called your mom?" Callum asks in disbelief. "But you..." Rad waves him off, shaking his head before Callum can continue.

"Yeah, through the church, she has a lot of connections. So, I asked her for a favor," Rad says, grimacing. "She still calls me occasionally, to see how I'm doing. We don't talk much, not since my dad kicked me out, but it was worth it this time. There's a company that does this sort of thing and can come to take care of your mom five days a week. She'll never be alone, Pretty Girl."

Rad took every worry from my mind and fixed it overnight. Leaning in, I don't think and press my lips to his in appreciation. I groan when he takes advantage, thrusting his tongue in my mouth and overtaking me. I'm breathless by the time we come up for air.

"You don't know how much that means to me. But the cost, Rad?" I whisper, searching his dark eyes that light up with me so close. "You know I can't afford to pay..."

"Don't worry. It's covered," he says, kissing the edge of my lips. "Now, since I granted you a favor…" He waggles his brows as he jumps out of bed, dragging my reluctant body with him.

"Callum, help," I pout, crossing my arms.

I sigh when Callum stands tall, stretching his long arms above his head. Every inch of his body stretches, pulling his muscles taut and extenuating them. I nearly drool at the sight of all his tattoos until he throws his shirt on and covers them. A small smile pulls at his lips when his gray eyes meet mine.

"He's pretty hot, right?" Rad says, throwing his arm over my shoulders. "You'd never guess all those tats were hiding on that virgin body." I stiffen, but Rad continues his rant. "He's had a needle before he's had pussy; it's a tragedy. Will you fix that for him, Pretty Girl? Will you be the first penis fly trap to grab hold of his trouser snake…" I slap my hand over his mouth, shaking my head.

"Do you ever shut up?" I gripe when he grins beneath my hand. "And seriously, a penis fly trap? What in the… Never mind, I realize that with you, I don't even want to know." He waggles his dark, bushy brows, staying silent beneath my palm.

"Damn-damn it, Rad," Callum curses, throwing his socks and shoes on. He groans, rubbing a hand down his face, hiding the redness taking over his cheeks. "And-and no, he never shuts his trap." Callum sighs, avoiding my eyes when he stands. Shoving his hands in his pockets, he takes a deep breath, probably centering himself from all the embarrassing shit Rad just threw out.

"There's nothing wrong with being a virgin. It just means you were saving your experiences for something better," I say, trying to lighten the conversation. "Besides, virginity is an outdated way of saying you just haven't had sex. It's our stupid society that created it." I roll my eyes at the world we live in, hoping it offers Callum a small light at the end of the tunnel. "Nothing to be ashamed of," I add again, and he nods, finally letting my words sink in.

Callum slowly lifts his eyes from the floor, searching me for honesty. Licking his lips, he nods. "Thanks, Little Star," he whispers.

"Little Star?" Rad asks, removing my hand from his lips and locking our fingers together. "I kinda like that. You are a little star, aren't you?"

I sigh. "I need to get dressed and check on my mom. Maybe wait until the nurse…"

"Oh, she's already here. I let her in at nine. She's pretty cool. Your mom took a shower while I did the dishes and… Why're you looking at me like that?" Rad asks, looking between Callum and me with raised brows, taking in our varying expressions.

"You-you did the dishes? And-and organized the nurse?" Callum asks through bewilderment.

Rad scoffs. "You act like I don't do anything domestic! How do you think our dishes get done? The laundry? Who picks up your rock sock and makes sure it's clean for your next round of taming the snake? I mean, come on, dude! I'm not incapable."

"I'm ignoring the rock sock comment," Callum says, giving Rad a scathing look. "And the tame the snake comment."

"Hold up," I say, lifting a finger. "You two live together?" My head jerks back when Rad stares at me like I'm an idiot.

"My house," Callum murmurs, shuffling his feet on the floor.

Rad shrugs, pulling me toward my closet. "Of course, we do. We always live in roommate bliss. All right, Pretty Girl. Time to get on those sexy booty shorts and a tight shirt. We're going to the dirt bike track so I can show you off. And if anyone asks, you are my girlfriend. Slimy fuckers will try to steal you away. I even have a sign that say*s, 'I suck Rad's dick when he wins'* for motivation," he rambles more, rifling through my closet. "Because that would definitely make me smoke those suckers. The last thing they'll see is my ass when I beat them."

"For the last time, I'm not your girlfriend," I mutter, tossing my hands.

"You say that now. But what's mine is mine, and you're fucking mine. You know Kieran suggested putting a tattoo on your ass, and I'm kinda agreeing. It'll say Property of Rad. The other three can fight it out for you." He shakes his head like what I said was ridiculous, and I give up.

"I could think of other places to put that tattoo," Callum whispers, lifting the hairs on the back of my neck.

I shiver, looking back at him when he shyly grins. "So… the track? What the hell is he talking about?" I ask, folding my arms over my chest. "And I'm not holding a sign that says that." I shake my head when he turns, giving me a disarming grin.

"There are three things you should know about me, Pretty Girl. I like you, drumming, and racing my dirt bike. In that order, too," he says with a wink, pulling out a black, lacy shirt from the back of my closet and thrusting it at me. "Now, put that on! We have lunch to eat and races to win."

I blink a few times when he throws himself on my bed, giving me an expectant look.

"Should I be worried?" I ask Callum out of the corner of my mouth.

He snorts. "With him? Always."

"Wonderful."

Nothing gets my blood pumping more than riding my dirt bike up and down the dirt hills at Raccoon Run, nestled deep in the woods, and hidden from the authorities. If they knew what we were up to out here, they'd haul us all in and slam the book in our faces. I'm too pretty to go to jail.

But out here, it's just me, five solid acres of woods, winding dirt paths, and the privacy to compete against the other fools stupid enough to go up against me. Pfft. Like they'd ever win.

Throwing my head back, I cackle despite the heavy helmet weighing on my head and threatening to send me off my rapidly accelerating bike. This is the fucking time to be alive! The wind in my hair. The stiff competition. And the hottest girl in town is waiting for me on the sidelines. Since she wore me as a gag, I haven't gotten her out of my head. She's like this sexy little bug living in my brain, constantly screaming at me to follow her around and be her damn boyfriend.

Adrenaline pours through my veins when I peek behind me, hearing the telltale sign of the other assholes gaining. Their engines whine and rev up, steadily coming around the last turn I came around three seconds ago. Whenever I think I've taken the lead and relax, they catch up. Someone's upping their game, and we can't have that. I'm the reigning champion and intend to keep it that way. They've been a pain in my ass for the last three laps, and now it's time to smoke their asses.

"Eat my tires, assmunchers!" I shout, holding the clutch; I lightly use my left foot and change gears, darting further away from the competition.

Looking back, I grin. Suckers. They always think they can take on the great Rad, but they never can. I haven't lost a race in two years and don't plan on losing today. Especially not in front of my Pretty Girl—my girlfriend.

As ridiculous as it seems, I have to remind her a lot that she's mine. Fuck. I guess ours. Right? I mean, we made a deal to share her affection and gain her interest. I don't know how I will pound it into her head more…maybe pound her pussy? God, I can't wait to have that girl again.

Shit. *Now is not the time, Little Rad. We have important things to do, like win this race so I can claim my prize and my girl.*

Speaking of…

I grin, rounding another turn and climbing the last rocky hill. Every bone in my body jostles at the dangerously high speed I'm rolling with. Pushing it faster and harder than before, I make it to the top, overlooking the trees and people waiting along the rocky dirt road. As soon as I come down the hill, there she is with a grin a mile wide, jumping up and down with excitement at the bottom of the valley. Cal grins down at her like the love-sick dope he is and hoots when I pass with his fist into the air, cheering me on. After so many months of moping around and feeling guilty, I finally see Callum's joy return. And it's all thanks to the bouncing Central girl beside him.

When I cross the finish line—first as always—I turn circles with my bike, kicking up the dust around the losers, finally trickling in.

"Holy shit!" my pretty girl says when she walks forward with a smile. God damn. That tight, lacy, black top I had her wear makes her boobs jiggle with every step. The stark image of my face, motorboating her titties, comes to mind, and I know what I'm doing tonight.

That and teaching Cal a little thing or two in the bedroom. Tonight, I'll cook dinner on the grill like a sophisticated gentleman and then motorboat my girl. Hashtag—goals. Hashtag—adulting.

"You were amazing!" she shrieks again, jumping up and down with a beautiful smile.

My pride blooms even bigger at her compliment, and I grin, pulling her close once she's in grabbing distance. If I had my way, I'd ride off into the sunset with her clasped behind me, holding my waist tight. But I rarely get my way, so holding her against my body is as good as it will get.

"I had a good luck charm here today," I say, throwing my helmet off and into Callum's unsuspecting arms. He grunts, narrowing his eyes at me with a shake of his head, securing the helmet on the bars of my bike. "It was all you, Pretty Girl. Oh, and the panties I stole from your drawer this morning. I'll keep them forever in your honor," I chuckle, tapping my pocket where a black, lacy thong sits like a good luck charm.

"He's never lost. Don't let him fool you with those pant-panties," Callum says, turning beat red at the prospect of her panties being in my pocket.

Her brows furrow. "You actually stole my panties, you psycho?" She gapes at me, staring at the bulge in my pocket, which I'd love to say is little Rad happy to see her.

You know, I've tried for years to get Callum in on my shenanigans and to loosen up. But the man is like a brick wall and never wants to play. Such a pity before, but now seeing him with our girl, well—things are changing in Callum's world. Actually, in our world. I know Kieran is fully invested in this River thing, and now we are, too. The only person sitting on the bench is Asher. He'll continue to fight with himself until he gives in and sinks his teeth into our girl. And boy, I can't wait for that day. Not only will he loosen up and get the large stick out of his ass, but he'll also finally get laid.

Callum is finally opening his horizons and seeing how easy it is to talk to her. When I walked into River's bedroom this morning after breaking in through her sliding glass door—which reminds me, I need to punish her for leaving her door unlocked. A wicked grin splits my lips. I guess that's what my handcuffs are for.

Anywho, the image of them snuggled so closely and the peace on his face I hadn't seen in over a year was heart-stopping. So, I took a picture. And backed it up several times. If they ever get ahold of it, they'll castrate me. She more than him. But I like my family jewels and would prefer them intact. I've seen what she can do with a knife, and I'm good.

"Once again, you're unbeatable," comes a deep voice behind me, causing River to stiffen against my body.

No, damn it, she was just warm and pliable against me. Now she's as stiff as a board, glaring at Van with so much hate. Finally, she relaxes in my hold, rolling her eyes toward the sky in annoyance at his presence.

Van eyes River like a prize he wants to claim, but too bad for him. She's fucking mine. Stupid, jealous idiot. It's like if he can't have River to himself, then no one can. But I have news for him.

I almost forgot old Donnie Boy started coming down to the track after he had to dump his Central girl into the gutter. Too bad for him. I scooped her right up, and now she's mine and onto bigger—yeah, bigger —and better dicks. Except we have much nicer personalities, too. We're the whole damn package, and Donnie is the trash panda begging for scraps.

"Ah, Donnie Boy," I greet with a smile, pulling a resistant River further into my side.

I frown when she's still stiff, barely breathing in this toxic idiot's presence. Don't resist my love, Pretty Girl. Go with the flow. I'll never let this idiot touch you ever again or hurt you.

"Fancy seeing you here." I grin again, tilting my head when his jealous eyes turn to River, who frowns at him with unease.

His eyes light up, jealousy taking him over. If he were a monster, he'd turn green with envy, snatch her out of my arms, and carry her to his kingdom. I'd be the gallant knight with sword in hand, ready to defend my girlfriend's honor.

"Rivey," he whispers, furrowing his brows. "You're here?" His voice dips low in warning, like he's secretly trying to tell her something.

"Yes, my girlfriend is here. With me," I say, goading him with a friendly grin.

His eyes widen a smidge, and his head jerks back. Hook, line, and sinker, fucker.

Keeping my hands on her waist, I squeeze her into me, loving how her body feels against mine. God, I can't get enough of her. I'd eat her… WAIT… I will eat her all up. But later. Maybe I'll tie Van down and force him to watch as he kicks and screams, and I give River the best orgasm ever.

I love the way Van's jaw ticks when he glares at her in disappointment and shakes his head.

"How much of a wager did you put on this one?" I ask, once again, poking the Van bear for my entertainment.

His jaw ticks, telling me all I need to know. He's squandering away what his daddy paid him to step away from River and stay in college. I bet he never told River a thing. I wonder how he did it? Did he just walk away from the precious jewel in my arms like she was nothing more than toilet paper? I bet he did.

His nostrils flare, and I want to cackle at his stupid fucking face. "Callum," he greets, ignoring me entirely while still watching River with an interested eye.

"Van," Callum says in a deep voice, inclining his head in greeting, taking a step closer to River. The back of his fingers lightly skims against hers, drawing her into him.

"Congrats on the win. I guess I'll see you at the neighborhood cookout next week," Van says, thinning his lips. His beady, evil eyes fall on Callum and River's pinkies hooking together.

I grin triumphantly when he balls up his fists. I live to piss this juvenile prick off. Nothing grinds my gears more than some idiot laying down and doing what their mommy and daddy told them to do. You know what mine told me to do? They told me no tattoos and piercings, and the moment I turned into an adult, the band was done. Fat chance is what I told them. No one takes away my band. They're more family to me than the people who raised me.

In turn, they raised their haughty eyebrows at me like I was still their sweet little Rad. The son who didn't move a toe out of line. Little did they know I had plans for freedom. The night of my eighteenth birthday, Cal brought me to his tattoo guy and helped me celebrate with the musical notes on my chest.

"I'm home!" The door slams behind me, louder than necessary, announcing my arrival.

"It's ten-thirty!" my mother hisses, drying her hands on a towel in the kitchen.

"It's Friday," I retort without an ounce of emotion and grab a drink from the refrigerator.

The cold liquid slides down my throat, giving me the necessary courage. Throughout the entirety of my tattoo, regret sat in the back of my mind. My father's words constantly played on a loop as I lay there, suffering through the pain of the needle. But it was what I wanted. I've been subjected to my father's iron fist for so long. He may not have ever hit me, but I was done being subjected to something I didn't quite believe.

Locking everything inside, I turn to face the man of the house. Wrinkles mar his older-looking face, tinting with disapproval. His dark eyes, similar to mine, rove over my neck, covered in protective plastic, and his entire body locks up.

You know, I could have gone the safe route and gotten music notes behind my ears or hell on my ass. My parents wouldn't have seen those. At least, not right away. But why go small when you can go big and all the way? For years, my parents have warned me time and time again that every inch of my body is God's temple. Every scar or scratch, they'd tsk me into being ashamed of falling off my bike or breaking my damn arm.

"Your body's a temple, Ashton. Treat it like one. No tattoos or piercings are allowed under our roof." Yeah, right. Okay. Sure.

"What did you do?" he shouts, inching closer with a snarl lining his wrinkly face.

I hold my breath in my lungs when he inches down, eyeing my tattoo closely.

"Ashton!" my mother yelps, coming to inspect my newest piece. "What have you done?"

I shrug. "What I wanted to do," I say in a low, warning voice. "This is my body; I wanted something to represent myself through."

It's the only piece of me I have. My parents have restricted every ounce of everything I've ever taken an interest in. Video games, TV, and even the band—limiting my time with each. They've thrown them to the wayside when it became too much. Hell, I couldn't even watch The Wizard movie I wanted to when I was twelve because of magic. Their entire logic makes my eyes roll into the back of my head.

With this tattoo, I took back a little piece of what made me, me.

"What you wanted to do? Do you know how expensive that is to get removed?" my father spits, standing straight.

"I'm not getting it removed," I tell him simply, staring straight into the abyss of his darkening eyes.

"Then you're not staying here," my father spits, crossing his arms over his chest and lifting his chin.

"Ashton," my mother begs my father with pleading eyes. "He's only eighteen. You can't just kick him out." She swallows hard when his burning gaze turns to her, and she shakes her head. I swear I've never seen my mother cry, but in this instant, tears stream down her cheeks. But she should have seen this rebellion from a mile away.

"Get out of my house until that abomination is peeled from your skin," my father says, waltzing toward the front door and throwing it open.

"Call me," my mother whispers, kissing me on the cheek. "Don't hesitate." I nod when I only want to scoff at her hypocritical face. How can a woman stand by while her husband throws out their only son?

As the door slams behind me and all the lights disappear from the house, I realize how fucking alone I am. It isn't until Callum's mom steps out from the shadows and offers me her hand.

"Callum may have spilled what you two have been up to today," she whispers, leading me across the street toward their house.

I swallow hard, on the verge of tears when she pulls me into the lively house and sets me down on the couch.

"You have a home here for as long as you need, Rad. Okay?" I nod with gratitude, washing away the tears from my cheeks.

"Thank you," I whisper, receiving the tall glass of water she hands me. Silently, I promise myself that I will never let another person stifle my wants and needs. I will never live under a cloud of bullshit.

I swallow hard, coming out of the memory with a shaky breath. There's nothing like winning a race and immediately being thrown into the wolf's den. My parents and I aren't exactly on speaking terms, especially my father. Occasionally, I talk to my mom and update her on my life. But for the most part, they're living their life, and I'm living mine. I guess that's why Callum was so surprised when I called my mom asking for any home nurses in the area.

"The cookout?" Callum groans quietly, shaking his head. "I hate that tradition."

Yeah, me too, buddy. It's the one day a year our parents all get together with mimosas, margaritas, and catered barbeque ribs, all in the name of neighborhood unity. We're forced to stand in the scorching sun, watching as they gossip and flitter around while stuffing our faces with the catered food that they were too lazy to make themselves. Fucking Gloria and Nigel Montgomery and their ridiculous traditions of unity. Unity, my ass. They want to wave their money around for the world to see in the form of social events and rub their neighbor's noses in it.

"Me too," Van grumbles. "But they make us go."

Van is so fucking hopeless. I snicker when I lean down, plant a kiss right on River's lips, and overtake her in front of him, shoving my tongue down her throat. He curses under his breath, huffing and puffing. There's nothing this idiot can do to stop this from happening. Nope.

Instead, he walks away with his pride bruised and his dick hard—hopefully. I want him to drown in the misery River has felt all this time; we'll build her back up and take her away from this place.

Her breaths heave frantically, and her hand swats at my chest over and over like she wants me to stop shoving my tongue down her throat. I pull back, squeezing my eyes shut as I catch my breath. Her mouth tastes as good as I remember, and I want to live inside it for eternity.

"That was my prize," I murmur, nudging my nose against hers, fluttering my eyes open, and staring into the abyss of her green eyes. "Think we have some time to play before practice?" I wiggle my brows at Callum, who turns beat red, averting his eyes to the fallen sticks around us.

"It's only three," he murmurs, looking at his phone. "They don't get out of class for a few more hours."

Right. Kieran and Asher were forced into university after high school. So, while they are suffering while getting their degrees, Callum and I make the cash for our band. One day, we'll save enough and hightail it out of here. But first, we need to secure as much as we can. With their college degrees in hand, we'll safely be on our way to the top, far away from here.

"All right, Pretty Girl. We'll take you back to our house and handcuff you to the bed. It's about time Callum learned a little something about cunnilingus." I grin, rolling my extra-long tongue out, creating waves with it.

Her eyes widen at the length, and she nearly chokes, staring at it when I scoop her up and force her legs around my waist. Digging my fingers into her pert ass, I grin, mounting my bike with her wrapped around me. Those delectable fingernails dig into the back of my neck, breaking through the skin.

Trembling, her eyes dart around as she pales.

"Rad," she hisses, staring frantically into my eyes.

Furrowing my brows, my heart rate doubles at the sight of her distress. Yeah, I'm not fond of that at all. I want to ease her tension, not cause it.

"You good?" I ask Callum, and he nods with a roll of his eyes.

"I'll see you at the house," he confirms, waltzing into the woods with his hands in his pockets.

Before he passes a large tree, he stares back at us with longing. A small smile touches his lips, and then he's gone—lost to the trees surrounding us.

"I gotta get my prize, and then… it's tongue town for you, Pretty Girl. I'm going to suck your clit so hard you're going to cum in my mouth," I murmur in her ear, starting up the bike. "I can't wait to taste you."

She shivers against me and shakes her head. "Rad, I've never been on a bike."

Anxiety sparks in her voice when her worried eyes find mine again. A drum pounds in my ears and my brows furrow as a deep-seated need to keep her safe overtakes me. I tighten my grip on her waist and kiss her cheek, lingering longer than necessary. She shudders against me, clinging tighter to my body.

"You'll never have to worry with me, Pretty Girl. I'll fight off the monsters and keep your brains in your head," I murmur, shoving the helmet over her head.

She grunts when I fasten the strap under her chin and wiggle the helmet to ensure it's secured properly. Like her, I'd rather she not get injured on our ride home through the woods.

She side-eyes me and probably frowns under the helmet. "I'd appreciate it if my brains didn't hit the pavement," she says in a shaky voice, looking toward the ground.

"Have no fear. Your Rad boyfriend is here," I whisper, starting the loud bike as the sound fills the woods, and she scoots closer to my front.

People wave and cheer as we slowly make our way through the small crowd, lingering against trees and discreetly drinking out of flasks. Down in Raccoon Run, no one seems to follow the rules. It's the one place we can disappear and hide from expectations. We drink, have races, party, and have a fun time.

"Good race, bro."

I grin, stopping in front of my most trusted track manager—Reese. We met him a few years back in school. He's always been a financial god and a trustworthy individual—well, for a drug dealer. Now, he helps around the track, taking bets and selling what he wants. You'd never guess his parents lived in Lakeview, and he did, too. For a time, that is. Then he found his crowd in Central City and moved there to continue growing his empire.

"Thanks, man," I say, taking the plastic bag filled with a mixture of crisp and crinkled bills. AKA—my winnings for being the badass I am. "How much?" I ask, cocking a brow when he grins.

"Eight hundred," he says, side-eyeing the surrounding people, and I nod. We exchange a few more words before he returns to handing out more winnings to the people who put their money on the safest bet—me.

"All right, Pretty Girl. Let's go to my house," I say, revving up the engine again and kicking off with a cackle.

I peek behind me, meeting Van's steel gaze, and flick dirt in his stupid face, laughing with glee when he sputters and bends at the waist. Asshat. You can stare at me like you want to kill me all you want, but it's not going to happen. River will never be yours again.

River is mine.

Okay, fine. She's ours. I mean, I've never had to share before. But what can I say? I'm a marvelous and caring lover who enjoys sharing. Just this once.

After a five-minute drive through the woods using my trails, I pull up to my backdoor with a grin. Looking down at my girl, I smile; she lights up my whole damn life. Not once did she try to jump off the bike or yell at me or smack me again. Instead, she pulled herself closer and closer to me, pushing her center against my raging hard-on.

I set both feet on the ground, balancing the bike and shutting it off. I rub my hands up and down her back, slowly working toward the helmet, weighing her down. She huffs when I gently pull it off her head and hang the strap on the bar where it sways in the light summer wind.

"If you enjoyed that ride, I'll give you an even better one in the next twenty minutes," I say, grinning with a wink.

"I did not enjoy the ride," she huffs, running a hand through her wild long strands and blowing some out of her face.

Moving some hairs from her face, I stare down at her again. I'm so fucking smitten with this damn girl, and my damn heart flutters out of control. Even when she gives me the stank eye, probably plotting my death.

"How about another one? Maybe on my bed as we roll around on eight hundred bucks?" Her pretty, pouting lips pop open, and her green eyes bounce to mine in shock. I grin more, holding up the plastic bag I had shoved in my pocket. Her eyes dance across the multiple crinkled bills. "After we pour this on the sheets, I'm going to lay you down," I rasp, nipping at her jawline.

Her breaths pick up, her chest heaving against mine. The feel of her fingernails ripping into my flesh has me grinding myself against her center, begging to rip through her shorts and fuck her until she says my name.

"And then what?" she whispers when my tongue swirls down her neck, and I suck her flesh between my teeth.

She groans, letting my hand wander between our bodies to the soaked, promised land I can't wait to live in. Do you think she'd let me sleep with my cock buried inside her—hard or not? I shiver at the thought, moving her tiny shorts and panties aside with my fingers.

"You good, Pretty Girl? Can I stick my fingers in your pussy and make you come on my bike?"

What I don't tell her is I want her to christen my winning bike with her pussy juices so I can continue to win fat stacks of cash to fuck her on.

Shit. My dick rages inside my jeans, begging to punch through and fuck her right here. But If I fuck her first, I can't show our precious Callum how to use his tongue correctly. Soon, he'll be an expert. First, though, I need to prime her and get her juices flowing, so he has a juicy fruit to sink his teeth into.

"Yes," she moans as I shove my fingers inside her, basking in the feel of her contracting inner walls seizing around my fingers.

"Good girl," I whisper, slowly pumping my fingers in and out. "You're so goddamn wet, Pretty Girl. Did you really not like the ride? Was it the vibrations that got you going?" I murmur, nipping at her neck again and leaving my marks behind on her flesh.

Mine. Fucking mine.

"Shut. Up," she gasps, hiding her face in the crook of my neck. "Harder, Rad."

Well, she doesn't have to tell me twice. Grunting, I pick up the pace, enjoying my name on her lips. Her moans ring in my ears like music until she cries out into my neck, squeezing around my fingers as she comes so hard her damn body trembles.

"You are fucking exceptional," I whisper, kissing her cheek.

Her warm breath brushes across my skin when she pulls back, staring at me with glossed-over green eyes—a small smile tugs at her lips when she looks my face over. Dare I say, she seems impressed and likes what she sees.

"You're not too bad yourself," she murmurs in a daze, leaning her forehead against mine.

Her breath picks up again when I wiggle my fingers, still nestled inside her. I contemplate leaving them inside her but decide against it. Bringing my soaked fingers to my mouth, I suck them in. Her taste explodes on my tongue. And yup. I'm keeping her forever. There's no doubt about that. I'll lock her on my bed or tie her up in my closet.

"God, you taste so damn good. I want to put this in a jar and keep it forever and…" River puts a hand over my mouth with a shake of her head.

"You're really disgusting sometimes, but I'll forgive you just this once because you gave me an orgasm," she huffs, but my damn pride blooms, and I lick her hand.

"The best one ever, right?" I say with a grin, lifting her off the bike and setting her on her wobbly feet. I jump off, kicking the kickstand down so the bike rests. "Now, let's throw some cash around and teach Callum a thing or two."

"Teach him?" She raises a skeptical brow but still follows me through the back sliding glass door into the spotless kitchen—my domestic work of art. "What would we teach him?" Her skeptical voice echoes through the room, turning to me, awaiting an answer.

"Well, definitely not science or math, Pretty Girl. I'm talking…" I stick out my long tongue again, loving the way her eyes dilate at the sight, and wiggle it around. "Butt stuff, pussy stuff, tongue stuff… Any type of stuff, really." I shrug, walking further into the house with wild ideas running through my mind.

Ideas like River sprawled out with her pussy in the air and my mouth on it while he fucks her mouth, and then we take turns fucking her until my cock can sleep inside her. Shit. I discreetly adjust my cock inside my pants, watching her from the corner of my eyes.

Her nose wrinkles. "Butt stuff? Really? What are you, an alien?" Her eyes roll toward the ceiling.

"I could dress up as one if you wanted! I could paint my skin blue and probe you all night long." My grin spreads when she shoots me a scathing look, shaking her head. "Well, in that case, welcome to Casa Callum and Rad," I offer, spreading my arms wide and highlighting the beautiful house we own together.

"You two?" she asks, running a finger over the countertops. "You weren't kidding about your domestic duties, were you?"

"I am the man of this house," I proclaim with a grin, pulling my pants up further on my hips.

"Second man," Callum mutters, moseying into the kitchen with his hands in his pockets. The telltale sign that he's nervous as fuck, having a chick in the house. But not just any chick, our River.

His eyes light up when she turns toward him and grins, offering him a little wave.

"Did you like your ride?" he asks quietly, never lifting his head. His eyes drift over the floor, studying the damn tile like it's more interesting than the beautiful girl standing before us.

She side-eyes me, mischief sparkling in the depths of her green eyes, and shrugs. "Meh, it was okay." I nearly sputter at her but decide to bite my tongue.

He smiles softly, finally lifting his eyes and meeting hers. Hearts explode over his head at the sight of her. "So, you hung-hungry?" he asks, taking a deep breath. I've never seen him so damn flustered before, let alone talk to a girl.

She shrugs again, once again looking around our place. "I could eat…" she trails off, looking off toward the small living room. "This place is nice," she murmurs, offering him a warm smile. "How did you two?" I jerk my gaze to Callum, who looks off toward the small living room again, getting lost in his head.

"After my parents kicked me out, I came here," I say, fondly looking around. I've only lived here for three years, but this has been more of a home for me than my other one ever was.

The environment my parents cultivated behind their four walls was more than toxic; it was downright deadly. My father, the beloved pastor of the Lutheran church, ruled that house with an iron fist. They placed rules upon rules on me, their only child, for years. No one ever knew the moment he stepped into the church, a firm mask fell into place. He became the man he thought the world wanted to see. Father of the year, if I say so myself. The moment I could escape, I did.

"Why'd they kick you out?" she asks, brows furrowing in concern. Her fingers work up my arm, eventually stopping to massage my shoulder. I lean into her touch, taking comfort in her.

"They're assholes," I say with a big breath. "I got some tats, and they didn't approve, so I moved in here with my boy Callum."

"My parents invited him to stay after they did-did that," Callum whispers, peeking at us. "They were the best. They really liked him."

"How?" River laughs. "Seriously? They liked him?" My mouth opens at her insult, and she giggles, making Callum's face light up.

"Somehow," he quips, "but yeah, they did. He lived here with us when…" My heart falls into my ass when the ghosts of his past, grab hold of him, but before I can do anything, River's on him with a giant hug.

"You don't have to say it," she murmurs into his chest, rubbing her hands up and down his back. Relaxing in her hold, he puts his cheek on the top of her head, sighing with contentment. Every worry leaks out of him with her in his arms.

Shock takes me over at her words. My jaw hits the ground. He fucking told her the tragic story of his parents and sister. Callum doesn't tell anyone what happened, instead keeping it bottled up and reliving it every day in his genius mind. I never thought I'd see the day when he opened up to someone besides us. River's done the fucking unthinkable and grabbed his attention.

He whispers something in her ears until she pulls away, staying at arm's length. His fingers run through her hair, curling it behind her ear. Love emanates from his gray eyes, pouring out to her. It would break his fucking heart if we had to leave her behind in this shit town. And we won't.

River West is ours to keep.

Leaning down, Callum tentatively presses his lips into hers with uncertainty. Tangling her fingers in his blond locks, she holds him there until their tongues dance together, and they're left breathless. Callum groans into her mouth when his shaky hands find her ass, and he squeezes it, pulling her closer.

"All right," I say, wrapping my arms around the both of them as they pull away from each other with swollen lips, eyeing me like I'm up to something. "I'm feeling a little left out of the fun. Let's teach our boy some tongue tricks."

Callum sucks in a breath. A blush takes over his entire head, turning him into a strawberry. I expect River to give me sass, but that cute smile she loves to toss around crosses her lips. She shrugs, getting to her tippy toes. Her soft lips kiss the edge of his, trailing down his neck. He groans, running both hands through her hair and holding her there.

"You-you don't have to," Callum stutters through the tremors shaking his body. "I…" He loses himself in the feel of her fingers roaming over his chest, slowly guiding down to the bulge growing in his jeans. She squeezes him, earning a full-blown moan from him.

That's right, Callum. Let loose. Let our River guide you into a den of sin.

"So, shall we go?" I say, wiggling my eyebrows, and gesture to the bedroom.

"Lead the way," River rasps, holding out her hand.

We stare at Callum, waiting for him to decide. Because ultimately, it's up to him whether he wants to participate.

"You—you'll teach me?" he asks softly, refusing to look at her.

"I'm fine with it," River proclaims with a shrug. "You, him, and me? Hell, yes."

And that's all Callum needs. With as much confidence as he can muster, he grabs her arm and leads her to my bedroom down the hallway. Dare I say there's a little pep in his horny step and pride swelling his chest.

"Well, this should be fun!" I whoop, ripping off my shirt and tossing it on the couch when I pass, heading down the hallway.

"AND EIGHT HUNDRED," RAD SINGSONGS, PLACING THE LAST TWENTY-dollar bill onto the white sheet.

Stepping back, he nods a few times, fixing a few bills until they're straight. His arms are wide, showing off his newest masterpiece with pride, just like he promised—a bed full of money ready to roll around on.

"Was that really necessary? Like… you seriously want to screw on money?" I raise a brow, grasping for his logic, but come back empty-handed.

Rad doesn't seem to have a lot of logic to his actions, but I can't fault him for that. Secretly, I like him just the way he is—weirdo tendencies and all. In my eyes, he will always be the kind-hearted hero who scooped my broken body off the darkened lawn.

He turns his energetic smile toward me and winks. Warmth fills my chest at how he smiles, looking at me like I'm already the light of his life, and he can't wait to get boned on a pile of money.

"You christened my bike. Now, you have to christen my money. For good luck!" he proclaims, tossing a fist in the air and doing an odd dance by twirling in a circle and whooping.

I groan, wrinkling my nose. "You know, that money could have been in some dude's ass last night after he stripped and his sweaty balls got stuck to it," I quip, raising a brow when his face brightens even more, and he laughs.

Looking down at the pile of money, he shrugs, waving my comment off. Sometimes I think the guy needs something to calm him down. But other times, he turns me into a mushy, giggling schoolgirl with his antics. Fuck. What is happening to me? I've kept people at arm's length for years, and these assholes march in like they already own my heart. And I'm giving it to them willingly, without a fight. Here, take my heart into your palms and promise you won't crush it. I can't deny the heart of gold Rad seems to have and his caring yet odd nature. Between saving me and saving my mom, my heart flutters in his presence. Maybe I've spent too

much of my life guarding my heart. For good reason, I suppose. But fuck it if I don't want to give in.

"You've won-won every race for two years in a row," Callum stammers, keeping his wide eyes on the money, refusing to look at either of us.

"Facts!" Rad says, pointing at Callum. "But what's a little extra pussy juice for good luck?"

Callum sputters, turning beet red, and turns away with a huff. Hiding behind his head, he releases a deep, calming breath before turning toward Rad again.

"Ra-Rad, for fuck's sake."

"Come on, man, we've lived together for three years now." Rad's grin grows when he places a hand on Callum's shoulder and leans in. "You should be used to me by now." Rad laughs when Callum shoves him sideways with a grunt, tossing him onto the pile of money.

Rad doesn't seem to mind the assault as he rolls around on top of the money, collecting some bills in his hands and then throwing them above his head. The green bills slowly fall and land on his chest and stomach like snowflakes floating through the winter breeze. His grin never breaks when he rubs it all over his chest with a menacing chuckle, turning all of his attention to me.

Rad may not be as intense as Kieran or even Asher, but the look he levels me with has my heart pounding. All the care and love he can provide shines through, and there's no doubt about how he's feeling.

"Am I sexy like this, Pretty Girl?" he asks, playfully wiggling his brows.

I lick my lips, eyeing his lean body when he props his head on his hand, turning to his side. Something dangerous lurks in the depth of his dark eyes, promising nothing but pleasure in my future.

My eyes trail from the tip of his curly mullet soaked in sweat to the ink blotting his chest and neck. Music notes curl over dark black ink, crawling up his neck and only stopping on the right side near his skull, where more music notes dot his skin. He smiles up at me so brightly it's almost blinding. I suck in a breath, staring intensely at his tattoo, losing myself in the lowest part of my life, brought on by the memory of what I endured.

"Don't," I warn, frantically trying to kick him off. "Please," I whisper, gasping for breath, kicking a foot out and landing my kick somewhere on his body.

What a night to leave my knife behind. From now on, I will carry it everywhere. No exceptions.

"Hey," he whispers softly, running a soft finger down my wet cheeks. His touch momentarily calms my nerves. I heave a breath. "You fell asleep on the way to the hospital. I'm not them, remember? We're at the hospital now." My eyes roam over his concern-filled face when he crouches in the opened passenger's side door. The warm breeze of August swirls around us,

lifting my long brown strands. I shiver as they tickle along my back, and memories of those monsters' hands grabbing and pulling make my stomach turn.

Behind Rad rests the four-story Central City Hospital. Flags wave and lights blink on and off in the night sky filled with sagging clouds thick with moisture. The smell of rain hits my nose, and my chest caves in. Chaos runs free through my mind at the thought of stepping foot in the hospital. Behind those walls rests my salvation—the answer to the pain radiating from between my legs. It throbs and aches with every move of my body.

The softness in Rad's expression makes more tears trail down my cheeks and fall to the leather seats. With a quivering lip, I shake my head.

"I'm sorry," I gasp out. "I..." Without a second thought, he brings me into his arms, holding me close when he stands at full height, closing the door behind us.

For one split second, I panic at his touch. My mind begs me to thrash and save myself, but the adrenaline that once coursed through my veins ebbs away, leaving my muscles tired and my brain in a foggy existence. I sag into him and realize he's holding me tight and secure without really touching me. Not sexually, no. He's touching me protectively like I'm his little injured bird needing rescue.

"If you ever want to name names, I'll kill them for you." His voice wavers for only a second, something arctic taking over like he's plotting my revenge on the walk through the front door. "My name is Ashton Radcliffe," he says in a rare moment of vulnerability, swallowing a large lump in his throat.

If I were in a better state of mind and not slowly drowning in the grief of my rape, I'd have told him I knew who he was, that we go to the same high school and have all year. But he didn't seem to recognize me, and that was fine. I hold my tongue, feeling oddly comfortable in the arms of my savior.

The heat of his gaze staring down at me with curiosity seers through me. He doesn't utter another word until we're standing in front of the emergency room desk, refusing to let my feet hit the floor.

"Can I help you?" The nurse says I'm sure looking us over with an inspecting eye.

"I..." he begins, but his beautiful face twists, and his dark eyes dart to mine for permission.

I swallow all the hurt, aches, and pains, burying them in the pit of my stomach. Tears burn the back of my eyes, and my nose tingles against his shirt. If I could stay covered and protected in his arms, I would.

"I was raped." And those words hit me harder than anything my life has brought me. It's real now. I've said the words, and they carry a heavy weight. The truth of my situation now hangs in the air.

"I found her. We were at a party. They..." He takes a shuddering breath.

"Pretty Girl," Rad whispers, cupping my cheeks, grounding me in the present. "Why're you crying?" Two seconds ago, he was light and happy, rolling on his side in the money he insisted on laying down, and now he's sitting on the edge of the bed with me nestled between his legs. I hover above him, planting my feet on the ground.

Wetness coats my cheeks and chin. Shit. I'm really fucking crying right now. How'd I get so trapped in the past that I didn't realize what was happening?

Seeing his tattoo brought everything I had buried for so long back to the surface. When I opened my eyes after the rape happened, it was the first thing I saw hovering above me. I should have been frightened, but something was soothing in his words and gentle in his touch when he placed his coat around my exposed parts.

"I'd never force you to do anything," he whispers with concern, taking over his tone, "Pretty girl. We can watch a movie. We can…" I lose his voice in the vivid memories of my past. His lips keep moving, but nothing registers in my mind. Nothing but the words he's uttered before flash through my mind.

"You'll never have to worry with me, Pretty Girl. I'll fight off the monsters."

His words hit me hard in the chest, knocking the remaining oxygen from my lungs. My lips pop open, fighting to bring much-needed air into my body. Fighting the memories floating through my mind evades me, and I once again fall into their depths as Rad strokes fingers through my hair and Callum rests at my back. He whispers encouraging words into the nape of my neck, seeming to know exactly where my brain went.

Nervously, I peek around the empty school hallway, standing before Rad's locker. Hearts and other notes decorate the outside.

Every inch of me trembles at the prospect of him catching me standing here with a tiny note clutched in hand—a small message filled with the two names I never wanted to see again.

After returning to school a week ago, their faces were the only thing I saw. When they passed in the halls, they discreetly checked me over—even being as bold as cornering me and reminding me of what they could do as punishment for opening my mouth. Every detail plays like a damn movie.

The police refused to do anything about the situation. Instead, laughing me away after I had given them their names and showed them their faces. My innocence was lost, and it was nothing but a joke. Who wouldn't want to lose their virginity to the star football player? Or two? Even better. Now, I have no other options.

No one else is on my side.

With one last breath, I shove the note through the top holes of his locker, silently begging that he finds it. And then finds them. I don't know what I want to accomplish with this, but I want justice.

"I never told you thank you." My voice breaks in half as my fingers trace over the musical notes on his chest.

"Oh, Little Star," Callum whispers with encouragement, wrapping his arms around me in gentle support. "Tell him." Rad's brows furrow in confusion, darting his eyes between the two of us.

"Thank me?" Rad asks, shaking his head. "Today was…"

"Not for today," I whisper, my voice full of unshed emotions I let no one see. Callum tightens his hold on me, burying his face in my neck and helping me breathe evenly.

"Did you hear?"

"Oh, my God!" Tessa says in a hushed voice, turning toward the front doors with Sara right beside her.

They continue to whisper until Bradley and his best friend Kyler march through the doors with matching black eyes and limps. I hold on to my gasp, watching with wide eyes as they walk by without passing off another threat.

"A long time ago, I slipped two names into your locker, and you…" I roll my lips together as his thumbs brush across my cheeks. "And you…" My heavy tongue refuses to cooperate, but Rad picks up.

"My locker?" He looks down, scrunching his cute button nose. Losing himself in his thoughts, he finally stiffens when realization smacks him. Jerking back, his lips pop open, and he stares at me in disbelief, shaking his head. "We beat the ever-living shit out of those assholes. Kieran, Asher, and me… we cornered them and made them regret what they did to… to… Wait…" More realization swiftly takes over his paling face, and he clasps my cheeks tighter as if I were about to run away from him.

The night of the party, he could have turned the other cheek and walked away, leaving me exposed to the world. He could have had his fun, too, and I would have had no power to stop him. Instead, he cradled me in his arms and took me away from the party like my personal protector.

"You?" he breathes. "No, I would have remembered. I looked everywhere for you." He shakes his head. "I would have recognized you anywhere." But he didn't, because I didn't want him to. That night, he may have been my hero, but I wanted to shrink into the shadows and pretend it didn't happen.

Tears stream down my cheeks when the first cut snips off ten inches of hair, landing in a spiral on the bathroom floor. They used my hair as a weapon to hold me down and inflict pain. Now, I'm ridding myself of the weakness that caused me so much harm. By the time I'm finished, my brown locks lay lifelessly by my jaw, framing my face with uneven strands and imperfections. But I don't give a shit. I raise my chin, eyeing my new stony exterior. No one will ever get something over on me again.

My fingers run through his curly mullet, tracing down his neck and onto his chest. The warmth of his skin bleeds through my fingertips, taking away the darkness of my memories. Terrible things happen to everyone every single day. It's what you do with those dire situations that count. I drowned in my misery for an entire year, blaming myself for everything. If I hadn't done this… If I hadn't done that… But it happened. And it wasn't my fault. Through shitty therapy provided by the reluctant state, I made it through to the other side. I embrace who I am now and who I was. We're one and mentally stronger than before. Sure, I've had my fair share of hurdles, but I always make my way through them.

"I cut my hair after it happened and wore big clothes." I swallow hard, keeping eye contact, but my fingers still wander down his flesh. Callum squeezes my waist in support, holding me as I talk through it.

"Why don't I remember?" he whispers, seeming pained that he can't remember me or my face.

"Because I didn't want you to," I whisper with a break in my voice, cupping his crestfallen cheeks so tinged with hurt his eyes water.

"I went to the police," he says, swallowing his emotions. "They…"

"They laughed me away. How dare I accuse the two starting football players of something so heinous? Their words, not mine." Rad gently wipes the remaining tears from my cheeks with understanding. "I wanted to disappear, Rad. I wanted… To forget about it. They haunted me…"

"And when you saw him at the bar?" he questions, tensing up.

"It was like seeing a ghost from my past, but that's it. Nothing more," I murmur, vividly remembering the terror I felt when Bradley bumped into me that night, shattering glasses from my tray. And then again, down the road where he stood next to another man draped in shadows.

"Oh, Pretty Girl," he urgently whispers, putting his forehead on mine. "You saw him, and then you… God, I didn't force you into anything that night, right? I didn't…" My desperate lips pounce on him, shutting down his train of thought until I pull back breathlessly. Wild, nervous eyes inspect mine.

"I decided a long time ago to take my body back. I didn't want the memory of those assholes holding me back from doing what I wanted. Trauma healing comes in many forms, and I took mine by the horns." I search his eyes, hoping he understands my meaning.

I've never thought twice about the men I sleep with. As long as we're safe and clean, I take what I want and give my body the pleasure it deserves. Some might say it's too much and I shouldn't heal in the arms of another. But what do they know?

Leaning in again, I lay my lips on his, waiting for the moment he gives in. His fingers softly roam, not daring to delve into other places. Tracing softly up my leg, he leaves goosebumps in his wake with the tiny circles he rubs against my skin.

"I'm not a breakable doll," I whisper, nipping at his bottom lip. Securing it between my teeth, I nibble more, forcing a groan from the back of his throat.

"I know you're not, Pretty Girl," he whispers, bravely cupping my ass and squeezing until he pulls me into his lap. "You're the bravest girl I know."

I fall into his kiss, letting him overtake my mouth. My fingers rake through his hair. He touches me everywhere except the places I need him. I pull back, panting when his mouth descends my jaw toward my neck, nipping the whole way.

"I'll leave you two," Callum whispers behind my ear, kissing me one last time.

"Wait," I say through an exhale, my breaths shuddering in my chest when I reach for him, grasping his forearm. Warily, I look at Rad, who stops his kisses on my neck with one last loud pop.

A slight smile picks up the edges of his lips against my flesh. "Yeah, dude. You can see the live show this time. No more hiding behind walls." I roll my eyes, squeezing Callum's arm in reassurance.

"Stay," I murmur, staring into the abyss of his gray eyes, darkening with a maddening lust at the sight of us together.

"Ok-okay," he murmurs, stumbling over his words as a red tint fills his cheeks and stains his neck.

Callum stays close when I remove my grip from his forearm. Licking his lips, his eyes drop to mine, and I seize the moment before he can think anything about it. Gently, I press my lips to his, savoring the shudder that runs through him. His tongue dives into my mouth as Rad's hands wander down my body, pulling at my shirt.

"Pause the tongue town session, and let's get our Pretty Girl naked," Rad murmurs, forcing Callum to break his kiss. Callum pants against me when Rad pulls off my shirt and tosses it aside.

"I'll be over here," he whispers, pointing to the beat-up recliner in the corner.

"Oh, no, you don't. This is a teachable moment, dude. Lay down," Rad says, pointing to the bed.

"But-but, I…" Callum turns such a dark shade of red I almost swear he's going to run away.

"No buts, well, maybe hers," Rad chuckles, and I swat him in the chest. "Just lay down. You want to learn the logistics of fucking? Then you need to be deep in the trenches when I fuck her," Rad says in a no-nonsense tone. "Watch as I fuck our girl and learn a little something."

"It's okay," I say with an encouraging grin, nodding toward the middle of the bed.

Tentatively, he sits on the edge of the bed, keeping his distance, staring with such intensity I swear my skin is about to go up in flames. Every caress of my skin lights me up until I'm completely naked, sitting in Rad's lap. Callum sits back with wide eyes, staring like a deer in headlights. From here, I see the tension lining his face and the enormous bulge pressing against his jeans.

"Touch yourself," I demand softly, aching to see his hand stroke his length.

Callum's Adam's apple bobs with a heavy swallow, and his teeth sink into his lips. Nervousness takes over his trembling fingers when he tries three times to grip the bottom of his black T-shirt. Finally, with one last frustrated huff, he throws his shirt next to him, exposing his beautifully toned chest and stomach. His tattoos come to life with every move he makes. And I want nothing more than to lick every inch of him if he'll let me.

"Pants too, dude. Show our girl your dick," Rad snickers, rubbing up and down my body. "Again," he adds, causing Callum to cover his reddened face with his hands.

With one last curse, Callum slowly undoes his jeans and shoves them down his legs. Sitting back, his long fingers curl over his dick, trying its hardest to come out from his boxers.

"Now sit back and watch the show. If you're lucky, maybe Pretty Girl will let you come all over her titties again." Rad wiggles his brows playfully, turning his attention to me. His large, brown eyes take me in, and it's as if a switch was flipped when his fingers caress my cheeks with deep concern etching across his face.

"You're seriously good with this?" Rad whispers, pressing light kisses on my lips. "We can stop. You just told me a lot of heavy shit, Pretty Girl. And I'm a damn gentleman."

I smirk against his lips, forcing him back into the bed. Money lifts into the air when his back lands against the mattress, and he grins at me, running his hands down my bare sides. His thumbs swipe across my nipples, and shivers roll down my spine, causing goosebumps in their wake. Over and over, he swipes against my sensitive nipples until their painful buds beg for the warmth of his mouth.

"Maybe I don't want a gentleman right now." I cement that fact by leaning down and running my tongue over his hard nipple. His sharp intake of breath eggs me on, and I pull it between my teeth until his moan and whimpers fill the room.

"River," he moans my name, thrusting himself against my center with desperation, seeking friction.

My hand runs down the length of his lean body and over his jeans, still secured around his waist.

"Why aren't you naked?" I whisper, rolling my tongue down his chest and over his abdomen, nibbling near his pants line where his muscles flex and tense from the sensation.

A deep groan vibrates his chest when he lays back, putting his hands under his head. With glazed-over hooded eyes, he watches my every move. Piece by piece, I remove his leftover clothes, tossing them aside with haste. Saliva pools in my mouth when his dick springs free from his boxers, begging me to taste it. Pre-cum drips down the side of his engorged and purple tip, pulsating with need.

Rad moans when my fingers wrap around his shaft, and I pump a few times, marveling at the feel of his smooth, warm skin beneath my touch. Leaning down, I lick the sweet curve of his dick, slightly leaning to the right. Running my tongue from base to tip several times, I lick him like I'm eating my favorite ice cream. Faintly, I taste the vanilla I crave so badly and continue sucking his tip into my mouth and running my tongue along his weeping slit, swallowing his pre-cum. Nothing beats the desperate sounds Rad makes when I take him into the back of my throat and squeeze around him. He writhes beneath me, silently screaming, with his head thrown back and fingers pulling at my loose hair.

"Pretty Girl, I'm desperate," he moans, tossing his head back again and arching his back. His cock throbs in my mouth, on the brink of spewing into my throat. Anticipation settles through me when I use my tongue, swirling around the base. A tight grip grasps my hair, pulling my mouth away. "I need you," he reaffirms, guiding me on top of his body and my legs straddling his hips. "I need to be inside of you now." Rad reaches over to his bedside table, flicking through the contents. Pulling out a condom, he carefully rolls it down his length and grips my waist tightly. "Next time, Pretty girl, I'm going raw. This time, we'll be careful," he murmurs, sucking my nipple into his mouth and swirling the tip of his tongue around my hard bud. "I won't have a barrier between us from this moment on." Something wicked sparks in the depth of his deep brown eyes, sending shivers down my spine when he surges forward and enters me with one thrust. His words ring through my mind on repeat. Raw. Nothing between us. Fuck. My pussy flutters around him, and he groans. "Yeah, Pretty Girl. You like that, don't you? I want my cum dripping out of you and down your legs."

Relief floods through me the moment he thrusts into me over and over. Pleasure sensations roar through me when I lift my hips and slam back down on his length, jamming him further into me. Stars brighten my eyes, and my brain turns to mush.

"I'm on birth control. I have been for years," I gasp out, tossing my head back and letting my hair cascade down my back. The white ceiling comes into view when my eyes flutter open, and I swallow hard.

Memories try to come through, but I force them down. There's no way in hell I'm thinking about that right now. Not when Rad is taking me away from this world thrust by thrust. I swear I see stars when he grunts, pounding into me from underneath. The sweet curve of his dick hits that spot deep inside me perfectly, making me want to let go.

"Thank fuck," Rad gasps, thrusting up into me. "You feel like a goddamn angel wrapped around my cock. I'm going to live in your cunt any time I can," he confesses, groaning when I lift my hips and slam back down.

"You don't feel too bad yourself." That's a lie. He feels fucking amazing. The curve of his dick hits right inside me. I'm two seconds away from orgasming and exploding all over him.

"Well, let me make it feel even better," he grunts, pulling out with a gasp. "On your hands and knees. Maybe we should include our watcher."

My eyes find Callum immediately when I get to my hands and knees. His soft, pink lips part in ecstasy as he pumps his hand up and down his shaft, swiping the pre-cum from his slit for friction.

"Scoot closer, bro," Rad demands, beckoning him with a finger curl.

Callum settles closer, brushing his thigh against my fingers, curling in the sheets. Lust brews deep behind his stormy gray eyes as he watches with an intense stare, taking in every touch Rad places against my flesh.

Rad's hands settle on my hips when he gently reenters me from behind with a long, drawn-out moan.

"Seriously, I'm never leaving. I'll sleep with my dick inside you if I have to," he groans, resting his forehead between my shoulder blades.

Reaching around, his hand grips my breast again, squeezing hard. All the breath leaves my depleted lungs when his hips snap forward harder and harder, driving into me like a man on a mission. Until he stills, laying his front over my back, leaning against me. Soft fingers swirl over my clit, beckoning my orgasm closer to the surface. And then backs off. Repeatedly, he swirls his fingertips over my clit until it's a throbbing mess and backs off.

"Rad, please," I moan, rocking into the sensation threatening to take me over. Every swirl has my eyes rolling into the back of my head and moans spilling out.

"River," he rasps in a deep voice. "You're so fucking beautiful. And you're mine," he grunts the last part quietly, easing into his thrusts again. "Should we invite him to join? I think he wants a repeat. Maybe you should ask him?"

Callum's eyes widen, and ragged breaths spill from his lips when his hand stops pumping his length, and he swallows hard.

"Callum," I moan his name, blindly staring in his direction as my vision blurs.

Callum's movements stop completely, frozen by his name on my lips, and he stares when I wiggle my finger, beckoning him forward more. He stumbles, scooting even closer. A deep red tint takes over his cheeks and neck and spreads on his chest. Lust swims deep in his eyes when he sits on the edge of the bed, staring at Rad and me with a curious but watchful eye. With every drive of Rad's cock forward, Callum watches closely.

"What-what do you want me-me to do?" His beautiful gray eyes dilate when Rad moves his hips, and my eyes roll into the back of my head.

"Whatever you want," I moan breathlessly, digging my fingers into the money and sheets beneath me.

He licks his lips again, staring at mine with raw desire.

"Either kiss her, come on her tits, or let her suck you off, bro," Rad directs, squeezing my tit in his hand, breathing heavily into my neck. "Because I won't last much longer," he whispers, snapping his hips forward several more times, grunting my name.

Callum stays close, dryly stroking himself from base to tip. His eyes never stray from Rad's erratic movements, dilating when Rad picks up the pace, shoving his cock further inside me.

"Rad, stop," I gasp out, and he instantly stops, pulling out.

"Shit, you okay? Sorry! Did I hurt you?" he asks with desperation, grazing his hand up and down my back.

"I'm fine," I insist, looking over my shoulder at his twisted face. "But Callum needs some lube," I say, raising a brow.

Rad's gaze finds Callum's dry hands rubbing his dick raw. A slow smile spreads across Rad's lips, and he nods. "For Callum, of course. Come here," he says to Callum, beckoning him forward.

Callum trembles, crawling to my side, close to where Rad resides. Looking over my shoulder, my gaze connects with his dilated eyes. Nodding, I give him a soft smile when his fingers brush over my ass cheek.

"Right here," Rad says in a soothing tone, taking hold of Callum's wrist and directing him to my dripping pussy before stopping. "Are you good with this? I'm not trying to push, man."

Callum licks his lip, sinking his teeth into his bottom lip. "Yes! Oh-oh, Jesus," Callum groans when he brushes against my pussy lips. "Oh God." His eyes roll back when Rad directs his fingers into me.

I groan when he shoves his long fingers inside me and twists them around, gathering my juices with Rad's. Four fingers from two different hands push the boundaries of my fluttering pussy walls.

"Feel that, man? She fucking loves it. She's going to cum all over them. And then you're going to finish yourself with her cum. Okay?" Rad asks through the fog of my mind, and I hear him moan in the distance.

Fire spreads throughout my limbs, and everything trembles as Rad and Callum pick up their pace, slamming into the depths of my cunt and turning me inside out. A moan lodges in my throat the moment my pussy contracts, and fireworks explode behind my eyes. My pussy clamps down on them, earning more groans from behind me.

"Fuck, River," Rad grunts, stilling inside me.

"Oh, f-fuck," Callum gasps, pulling in and out with urgency, staring at the wetness coating his entire hand with wonder.

"Use it, bro. Slather her pussy juices all over your dick, and then come on her ass while I come in her pussy." Rad doesn't waste a second when he buries himself deep in my cunt and pounds harder than before.

Callum moans, confidently putting the tip of his dick against my ass cheek, pumping as hard as he can. I watch his every move through my limited view of him over my shoulder. His head falls back, and his mouth drops open in ecstasy, lathering his dick with my juices.

"Come for me," I rasp, staring into his gray eyes. "Come, Callum." Heavy breaths pour from his mouth until every muscle in his body locks tight. Deep moans pull from his chest when he sprays his cum all over the flesh of my ass, dripping down my crack and toward Rad's chaotic thrusts and mixes.

Leaning over in desperation, Rad buries his teeth in my shoulder, spilling his seed into the condom with labored breaths and moaning.

"You're goddamn amazing," he murmurs, licking the wound on my shoulder. Rad kisses my shoulder, moving my hair from my neck. "Don't move. I'm staying here," he rasps.

I roll my eyes, wiggling my hips. "You can't seriously stay inside me. We have lives to live."

He snorts. "You underestimate my commitment," he murmurs, gently pulling out with a groan. "But for today, I'll let it go."

For one brief second of silence, Callum's wide eyes stay transfixed on the cum sliding down my flesh, through my crack, and mingling with my juices. I shiver when his finger bravely runs through the line, swirling it into me.

"Come-come on," Callum murmurs, grasping my hand with a blush, pulling himself from the visual. "Let's get cleaned up." I swear he sounds breathless when he helps me off the bed. My legs wobble when I take my first step, but Cal is there to catch me when I tumble.

"I'm going to take that stumble as a win," Rad says with a tired grin, throwing the condom into the trash. Sighing, he throws himself back into the bed with a groan. "Thanks for christening my money, Pretty Girl. You're officially my good luck charm." Warmth fills me when his earnest eyes find mine, and I see nothing but honesty reflecting. For some reason, he honestly believes I'm his good luck charm.

"Any time," I quip, clinging to Callum as he leads us into the oversized bathroom fitted with a large tub, stand-up shower, and a nice-sized closet connected to it.

Leaning down, Callum runs a bath and plugs the drain. He stands, collects the shampoo, conditioner, and body wash, and places them around the edge of the tub with care. His fingers brush through the rapidly rising water, and he nods, approving of the temperature.

"I think it's ready-ready," he says, taking a deep breath when he stands back, gesturing for me to climb in.

He helps me ease my legs over the tall bathtub with gentle hands until the water laps at my calves and feet. I sigh when my feet are enveloped in warmth, tingling my toes and legs. When I turn, Callum watches me with an intense stare, watching my every move as I slowly sit down in the water's warmth.

"Are you coming?" I ask, raising a brow and gesturing to the spot behind me.

His eyes widen for a fraction of a second, and I think he's about to tell me no until he marches forward with determination on his face. Deep down, I think Callum fights with himself and what he wants. Something holds him back from jumping into the fray and getting his too.

Settling behind me, he gently eases my back to his front and carefully wraps his arms around me. Resting his hands on my stomach with trembling fingers, I can tell he's trying not to touch anything he shouldn't.

Resting my head against his shoulder, I savor the warmth and protection he offers me. Callum is a gentle soul, and I never want anyone to take that from him. This world is a cruel, evil mess, and he's the only goodness left to bring me light. Besides the other two, I've seemed to have fallen for them in a short time. Sometimes I can't stop my heart from falling for the wrong people.

"Can I ask you something?" I whisper, running my wet fingers up and down his tense thighs on either side of me. His hardening dick rests at my back, but he makes no move to do anything about it. In fact, I'm sure he's ignoring it.

"Sure-sure," he says, stumbling over his tongue again. "You can ask me anything."

"What holds you back from sex?" Turning, I peek over my shoulder at his red-tinted face. Worry lines the creases in his brows, and he nods like he knows this is coming. "I'm not trying to pry, Cal. You don't have to talk about anything if you don't want to," I murmur with encouragement, turning back to face the wall.

I'd never force him to tell me anything. We all have hidden secrets, guidelines we live by, and boundaries we like to keep. Some people can't stand to be touched because of sensitivities. Some people are saving themselves for the right moment. And some haven't found the perfect person to connect with. Whatever the reason, he's still a virgin. That's up to him.

He leans his forehead against the back of my head, laying a sweet kiss on my hair. His shuddering breath blows across my wet neck as he composes himself to answer. Deep down, I suspect he's again hiding the embarrassment from his face.

"I want it to be right," he murmurs into my hair. "It probably sounds-sounds so stupid, but I want the moment to be something that I'm proud to remember. I…" He stops himself, taking a deep breath. "I never forget a moment."

"Never forget?" I ask, trying to look into the depths of his eyes, but he hides again and nods.

"Every life event. Every day. If you asked me what I did on March fourteenth two years ago, I'd be able to tell you in great detail how my day went," he murmurs, almost ashamed of what his mind can do.

Absentmindedly, I rub my fingers along his, tracing the wrinkles on his knuckles, trying to ease the rising tension. His muscles bunch, and his breaths grow haggard behind me, attempting to hold back all the frustrations that must come with his unique ability.

"So, what did you do on March fourteenth?" I quip with a smile, tugging at the edges of my lips.

Finally, after a few seconds of silence, he snorts, lifting his face from my hair. Those gray eyes connect with mine, filled with relief, spilling everything without saying a word. People must judge him when he confesses what his mind can do, expecting a lot from him. I could never imagine having the ability to remember every moment of my life. Our brains are meant to forget and ease away from painful moments.

He hums under his breath and closes his eyes. I wonder if the memory is right there in reach, and all he has to do is open a file and view it, much like a computer. A slow smile spreads across his lips, indicating it must be a wonderful memory.

"Woke up as usual at seven a.m., had cereal without milk, drank a cold coffee, and then celebrated my little sister Jenny's birthday." His eyes squeeze shut, and he takes a deep breath, reliving the memory vividly.

"And July second?" I ask, raising a brow, secretly knowing the answer.

"Woke up, had cereal with no milk, drank a hot coffee with two packets of sweeteners and a splash of vanilla creamer, and then went to the May Fair event out on route seven. We had one of our first gigs. Kieran stumbled over his words while singing. Rad got so hot and sweated so much that he threw his stick off the stage. My string broke. And Ash's dad scolded him for embarrassing him in public," he rambles in detail about the first day I ever saw them perform on stage, but my brain neglected to remember the chaos of their first performance.

"Ah, I didn't think you guys sounded too bad," I say with a shrug, nestled deeper into his tight embrace.

"You were there?" he asks in a soft voice, leaning his head on the edge of the tub.

"How do you think I knew to email you guys? I mean, you handed me your card," I ask with a laugh. "Although I didn't remember you guys messing up too much, I remember being enamored by you all." Enamored was an understatement. Like before, they drew me in with their magical voices and strumming fingers. They hypnotized me every step of the way, leading to now. Perhaps our unions are inevitable, and fate brought us together.

"It was me, wasn't it, Pretty Girl?" Rad asks, waltzing into the bathroom, still naked and swaying his hips—among other things. He marches toward a door next to the tub, proceeds to pee without shame, and reemerges, washing his hands.

I scoff. "The world doesn't revolve around you, Ashton Radcliffe." He grins, splashing water on my face, causing me to yelp from the sudden warmth.

"Be nice," Callum murmurs, splashing Rad back with warm water.

Rad scowls, pulling back to dry off his face. He rests by the tub for another few minutes and helps Callum wash me. They run shampoo and conditioner through my hair, washing it away. Soon I'm scrubbed clean with Rad's body wash, which he smugly rubs into my skin, promising he'll get me a bottle, so I smell like him at all times. Plus, he swears it'll piss off Kieran to no end.

Soon enough, we're all out of the tub, dried off, and lying covered in Rad's bed. We don't bother to get dressed, instead lying lazily around and cuddling. Callum nestles into my back, draping an arm over my stomach and Rad stays to my front, looking deeply into my eyes.

"Well, how was your day off, Pretty Girl?" he asks, brushing my wet hair behind my ear.

I smile. "It was one of the best days I've had in a long time," I freely admit, letting the happiness settle in my gut.

I'd never tell them I haven't had this much fun in years. I've always had to worry about work and school and never had downtime, never ridden on a bike, gone to the races, or hung out just to hang out. Especially now with my mom, her illness, and her dependency on me. I'll never have another day like today. So, I'll savor it forever.

Rad hums happily under his breath, softly putting his face on my neck. "Just lie here with me. I see the exhaustion in your eyes and the hurt in your bones. Lie here with me and feel my warmth." Rad sucks in a breath, reaching for something on the shelf above my head with urgency. Cranking my neck, I see the moment a dark notebook lands between us. "I need to write this down," he mumbles to himself.

"Lyrics?" I ask, scrunching my nose.

Rad grins, not breaking his concentration by repeating the lines repeatedly.

"Lyrics come from the heart, Pretty Girl. Unexpectedly. Beautiful. Raw. Lyrics appear out of nowhere," he murmurs, scrunching his brows.

A light flickers above us, highlighting Rad like a spotlight when he uncaps a pen with his teeth. Pages ruffle when he turns to a blank page and sighs in relief. Writing this down is the most important thing he's done all day.

A sparkle of excitement lights up his mahogany brown eyes. No one else in the room exists. Not me. Not Callum. These are just the words he casually said. Watching him scribble lyrics down fascinates me. One day they'll be someone's favorite song, sung worldwide, and it all started here in this tiny bedroom.

I take the unexpected chance to take all of him in, in his most vulnerable state. His dark, curly mullet sticks up from our romp in the sheets. His bare shoulders and chest, splattered with his tattoo, are tanned from his time in the sun. Freckles dot the tops of his shoulders and sprinkle down his tanned arms.

"There," he says victoriously, putting the notebook back above our heads and settling in. "Let's nap now," he grumbles with a small yawn.

I nearly jump out of my skin when a piano riff echoes through the room until I realize it's my phone sounding off with a message. I swallow hard at the ominous sound, knowing precisely who's texting me this time.

"Your-your phone," Callum mumbles, blindly reaching behind him and grabbing it on the end table.

"Pretty Girl, that thing is so damn cracked and beat up," Rad says, closing his eyes with a yawn. "We'll get you a new one…" his voice trails off when his hand brushes up and down my thigh, slowly stopping when Rad completely conks out and snores.

"Fat chance," I mumble, unlocking my phone. Peeking behind me, I make sure Callum's face stays buried in my neck, and he slowly drifts off with even breaths.

Swiping on my cracked screen, I bring the message up and wrinkle my nose.

VAN

I need to talk to you.

Why won't you talk to me anymore, Riv?

You're like a stranger.

Please talk to me.

I saw you go to Callum's, Rivey….

I shake my head and silence my phone. I don't need Van in my ear, whispering things I don't want to hear. He broke my heart. He's the one who left me because his parents couldn't stand the fact, I was who I was. And now he's suddenly crawling back on his hands and knees, begging me to talk to him?

Hell no.

Van Drake can drown in the depths of the misery he put me through.

If I never had to step foot into a classroom again, I'd be fucking ecstatic. Why can't I move on with my life without the hassle of a degree in hand? I would have rather gone to trade school and learned to weld. Then, I would have been at work, already making my money. But instead, I'm stuck in a prison of expectations and no way out. Leaning my head back against the side of the Tahoe, I soak in the late summer sun and close my eyes.

"It's important, Kieran!" My mother hisses in my ear the moment Nigel tells us we were attending college right after high school graduation. And given the fact I didn't apply to any sort of college. It meant Nigel stuck his nose in something he shouldn't have. He was probably using the green lining of his wallet to get us into the college of his choosing—sans applications. Standing under the blaring May sun, a warm breeze passes over us. I haven't even taken my robes off. I had no plans to attend regular college. In fact, they knew I wanted to leave. Maybe live on the other side of the country, but they've again tied my hands financially. "This will give you a much better life than I had. Don't dive back into the gutter I got us out of."

"Yeah? By what? Spreading your legs to that monster," I hiss back, earning a sharp slap across the face.

"I will not let you fail. No way, no how. Nigel made us a good life here," she says in a haughty tone, lifting her chin.

I eye every inch of her overly made-up face and scoff, counting the marks lining her cheeks and under her eyes. Deep purple bruises shine under the sun, letting the world know what goes on behind closed doors.

"Yeah? And at what cost, Gloria? So, he can hit you every day? Hit me? And Asher? What about Camilla? What will you do when he lays his hands on my little sister?" I step up to her, towering above her with gritted teeth.

Her face falls, and I know I've hit a nerve, but she backpedals, waving a hand like it's not a big fucking deal that he does what he does. She has no idea I hear the awful words he shouts at her behind the bedroom door. How

can she act like this is all okay? How can she sit there and pretend he's not the bad guy? Fuck. I thought graduating high school would get me the fuck out of here, but now I'm even more stuck than before.

"Don't be so obtuse, Kieran." With that, she spins on her thousand-dollar high heels and struts away toward the man who has become nothing more than a nightmare.

I grit my teeth at the raw memory resurfacing from absolutely nowhere. The last thing I want to think about is the man I'm bound to because my mother purposely got pregnant by him years ago. Through the years, he's molded her into the perfect wife and Camilla into the perfect, dutiful daughter. Asher and I have silently resisted every command he's given at every damn turn. I'll be damned if I become his perfect stepson. And Asher feels the same. That clawing desperation closes my throat when the man in question peeks out the upper-story window, watching us as he always does with a sharp eye. He scowls when Cami bounces on her toes with excitement, staring up at Asher and me like we're saints. Big blue eyes meet mine when she stops in front of us and gives us a toothy grin.

"Cami," I murmur, watching my sister jump excitedly in front of us with a large pink bouncy ball in her hands.

"Kieran. Ash," she says in a small voice, shrinking in on herself when she peeks up at the window looming above us, and suddenly, our warm and happy sister disappears.

"It's okay, Cam," Asher whispers, reaching out and touching her arm. She relaxes at his touch, scrunching her face when she sighs, looking up at the window above us again with apprehension and nodding. "He's in there. We're out here. We'll always protect you, right?" She nods, nibbling on her bottom lip, knowing it's the truth. I'd protect my sister to the ends of the earth, even making sacrifices I shouldn't. Whatever those might be.

"How'd your project go?" I ask, sparking a light in her big blue eyes.

"I turned in my project today at school and got an A-plus!" she says with a beaming grin, pride puffing out her chest.

"Good job! See, you did it all on your own," I say, ruffling her long brown hair until she playfully swats me away with a little grunt.

"Good job, Cam," Asher says with encouragement, squeezing her shoulder.

"Better go play while you can, okay? We'll be back later. You have more homework?" I ask, discreetly watching the old prick glaring down at us. To him, it's like having a good time is a fucking crime, especially on his own lawn.

"Yeah," she says, furrowing her brows. "It's science." Her face scrunches when she says that, but she quickly gets called by one of her neighborhood friends and takes off, leaving us with him and the weight of his intense stare beaming down on us. I swear my skin catches fire when he shifts in the window, putting his hand in his suit pockets.

"Get a life, old man," Asher grunts quietly, leaning against his Tahoe and shaking his head.

"Only a few more months, man," I murmur, clapping him on the shoulder. "We've survived twelve years under his shoe, and we can do it for a few more."

"The moment that letter comes in with our invitation, we're out," Asher grumbles with confidence, swiping a hand down his face.

"Or the moment we get our diplomas, right? We can't put all our hope into that fucking gig. There are how many bands applying for this spot? We have to think about the worst-case scenario," I surmise, turning to Ash, who nods in agreement.

"Either we get the letter, or the moment that fucking diploma touches our hands, we're gone. We need something to fall back on, and that degree is it. We've been saving for years. You, me, Rad, and Callum are out," Asher growls, throwing a hand around in anger as he speaks. "Callum even mentioned selling the house to help pay for our trip to California. And then you and I can work, play in the band, and wait for our break far the fuck away from here," Asher says, rubbing his chin. "So, when his trust ends, we can get out." A small smile takes over his lips. "Then it's just the four of us against the world.

"Hell, we can get out," I murmur, rubbing my hands together. No matter what—we're out of here. The moment my diploma touches my fingertips, we're leaving this place before my father can sink his claws into me.

"Yeah. We'll talk to the guys about that. What do you think they've been up to today?" They've been silent throughout the day.

Rad had a race to raise money for our band fund, and Callum usually looks through venues, contacting managers hoping to play. Obnoxiously, they typically keep us updated throughout the day on their activities. But today? They've been silent as fuck. Which is suspect at best. But I suppose we'll know exactly what they've been up to in twenty minutes.

"Six sharp for dinner! Don't keep your mother waiting!" Nigel yells out the window with a growl. "Not a second later! Don't give me more reason to pull the plug on your little side project. Such a waste of time," he huffs with a snarl, perpetually hating our band with a passion. He thinks it's a waste of time and it'll take us nowhere in life. Just because he had nothing exciting in his life besides work doesn't mean he gets to bash ours.

"Yes, sir," Asher and I say in unison without missing a beat.

We've figured out how to stay under his nasty radar this long. The last thing we need is for him to take away our freedoms. We may be twenty-one and adults, but he's made sure we depend on him every step of the way.

Our vehicles? His. Our phones? His. Our clothes and allowances? His. Our college education? His. His insistence that we do not get jobs—all his.

And we're powerless in all situations. Nigel has us right where he wants us, needy and dependent on his dime. So, when the time comes, and he offers us some big wig job within his company, we'd be dumb not to take it. Well, at least that's what he thinks.

Nigel Montgomery has tainted everything we own, hoping he can twist our arms into running his company alongside him. As much as it pains him to have his sons at the bottom, he knows he can mold us like he has everyone else. The only thing he hasn't accounted for is our waste of time hobby, which has made us our own money this past year. And he can't touch it. Our band is ours: our home, our family. And there's nothing Nigel can do to stop it.

Once we enter the Battle of the Bands and hopefully gain entry, we're gone. We'll buy vehicles under our names and drive to California without a second glance.

Nigel steps away from the window, grumbling loudly about our laziness and being unappreciative of his kindness. In his eyes, we're never enough, and I can't live the rest of my life like that.

"Let's get out of here while we can," Asher mumbles, grabbing me by the shirt. "We'll bring up the competition and what we have to do. More live shows to film, a recording of our music as professional as possible, and a social media presence are what we need. We can't let this shit slip through our fingers, bro. We need this or…" He side-eyes me, swallowing hard. I see the wheels turning in his big ass brain, and I know precisely the subject of his thoughts.

"She doesn't know her family, bro," I murmur, regret seizing my heart. "She can't get us into the KC Club any better than we can waltz in there. The Battle of the Bands is our best hope." I shake my head, remembering the plan Asher came up with, which has blown itself out of the water.

I'm way too deep with her, drowning in my obsession. There's no resurfacing from this as the same man I was before I met River West again. Mine to keep. Mine to hold. Mine forever.

There's no way I'm letting Asher use her to get to her brothers' record company or venue. From my memories, she hasn't had the best relationship with that side of the family. They abandoned her. And I won't force her to see them again.

"It was worth a shot," he grumbles, wiping his face. "You think she would ever reconnect with them?" I shake my head immediately, blowing out a breath.

"I don't know, man…"

Asher stops on the sidewalk a block away from Callum and Rad's house, putting a hand on my chest.

"You've got her in your grip," he says with an odd glint sparking in his eyes, making me frown. "She's your old bestie from the bad side. You've…"

"I'm going to punch that shit out of your head and laugh while you bleed. River West is not a toy to use in some scheme to get to her family. Sure, we thought that before we got to know her, but it ain't fucking happening. She is not someone we fuck over. Ya hear?" I growl, curling my fingers in his shirt to get my point across. "She. Is. Mine. Asher." I punctuate every word by dragging him closer and closer until our noses touch.

But my message doesn't seem to compute in his thick head. His eyes roll toward the sky in exaggeration, and he mutters angrily under his breath.

"Are you sure about that?" he says, cocking an eyebrow at me.

"Yes," I grunt, shoving him away.

His teeth grit again when he finds his footing. "I see how she looks at you and them," he hisses, pointing down the street.

"So?" I gape. "You think I didn't know what I was doing when I let Rad in on our little moment? He's fucking obsessed with her, just like me. And Callum? He's ten seconds away from pouncing on her. Thank God. Besides, that was your whole fucking grand plan, right? Wine and dine her and make her fall for all of us. But maybe she doesn't have to choose in the end. She gets us all. Well, except you." His eyes widen a smidge, but he quickly covers his surprise and hurt. "You could be a little fucking nicer," I quip.

That's right. Asher may seem like he wants nothing to do with her, but he wants her, too. His only complaint is that he can't reel her in with his assholeness, and he has to try. Before with other women, he's just kind of grunted, went along with their plans, and got what he needed. But with River, she's an entirely new breed of woman he's never experienced. But fuck, it's fun to watch him struggle. The way I see it, Asher will flounder for months until he's crawling on his knees and begging for her forgiveness. He'll be so in love with her that he'll insist we take her with us. I can see it now in vivid imagery. Now, we have to get to that point where he digs his head out of his own ass and gets on board with the rest of us.

"Fucking nicer," he mumbles, walking away in disbelief. "I'm fucking nice!" he yells offhandedly in disbelief.

"You're a perpetual grump!" I shout after him, finally catching up and throwing my arm over his shoulders.

"Grump this," he quips, shoving me away with a soft chuckle.

"Just don't be a dick for once, okay? River is cool. River is…" I smile, thinking about the way she feels when I'm nestled deep inside her. And the way she lights up when I walk into a room. God, she's extraordinary, and I never want to let her out of my sight.

Asher grunts in response, rolling his eyes at my expression and digs his keys from his pocket once we reach the bright red front door of Rad and Callum's shared home. It's a quaint ranch-style home nestled on the edge of the neighborhood. Heavy woods surround the backyard and side yards, leading to Central Lake glistening in the evening sun. The house itself is off on its own, giving us the privacy we crave. It's the one place we love to come to when we need to get away. It's our space—our home.

"Let's discuss what we need to do with the Battle of the Bands and how we're going to get there in the first place." Asher shakes his head, shoving the front door open to a quiet house. His nose wrinkles when we step inside, shutting the door behind us.

"Well, they weren't playing Angel Warrior all day," I mutter, noting the dark TV and living room.

On any given day, that's where we find them—curled up on the couch in an intense battle between the angels and demons. They'll yell and fight after a long day of making money any way they know how. Recently, we've gotten income from Rad's dirt bike races and the few gigs we find here and there from our performances. Callum brings money in through stocks, which doesn't give us a lot to go on because he invests it straight from the leftover cash of his trust. The same trust that pays his house bills and gives him a little spending money which has never been enough to get us out of this stupid town and away from Nigel... But we're saving as much as possible and as fast as we can.

"There aren't even dishes in the damn sink," Asher mutters from across the room, looking down at the shiny sink with a wrinkled nose. "His bike is outside." He peeks out the back door window, furrowing his brows.

"Maybe Cal took his car?" I mutter, peeking in the large dining room off the kitchen, and note an empty table still decorated for the last Christmas Callum's parents spent here almost two years ago. A heavy-weight presses on my chest at the sight.

Callum's parents were the best of all of ours. Caring. Kind. Loving. They let us come here and hang out, fed us, and ensured we were okay, never knowing the extent of Nigel's temper against Ash and me, but they could tell we needed a place to hide and regroup. They supplied a sanctuary for us while they were alive, and now, they still are.

When they died, a trust kicked in for Callum, paying his monthly bills and house payment. It provides everything he needs to keep the roof over his head, but nothing more.

It feels like a century ago that they left this world and shattered our reality. At the same time, it feels like only yesterday when we visited Cal in the hospital after the accident. His leg was broken, and his soul was shattered. Somehow, by some miracle, we pieced him back together one day at a time. All of us. Together. Here in this house. It took months to help Callum out of the shadows of his depression. Music has always been our go-to, and his especially. He's poured himself into his bass every day since.

"Fuck. I'll go check the damn boathouse," Asher grunts, pulling the back door open and walking through the woods to the tiny boat house nestled near the lake and dock where Callum's parent's boat still hangs, ready for use.

Fond memories resurrect in my mind. Of all the times spent hiding in the boathouse with a fifth of vodka and a can of coke as a chaser. We've spent our lives down there and grew up together here.

I roll my eyes, walking down the darkened hallway toward Rad's room, keeping my ears open for any noises in the silent rooms. It isn't until I'm right outside the door do I hear two distinct snores echoing through the room—my brows furrow when I push the door open and stop dead.

A grin explodes on my face at the sight before me, and I glue my eyes to her. Even sleeping soundly, she draws me in like a moth to a flame, threatening to burn me alive. Fuck. I'd gladly let her at this point.

There, squished between my two best friends, is the woman I had dreamed about all day. Her chest rises and falls under the thin blanket. My fingers itch to touch her skin and caress what's mine.

"My fucking River Blue," I mumble quietly, walking on my tiptoes toward the bed and hovering above them. "So, this is why you two were finally entertained all day?" I whisper above their heads, watching their every move.

"Yes, now go away," Rad grumbles, pulling River into him. "She's mine now. I live inside her." River doesn't stir when he tucks her head under his chin and soothes back her long brown strands until her peaceful face is all I see. Tiny freckles dot her cheeks, and her pouty lips turn down into a frown—the only sign she's listening.

"Sharing is caring," I murmur, slapping him on the back of the head until he jerks completely awake.

He frowns, finally opening his dark eyes, and glares at me with a venomous stare. A big, toothy smile takes over my face just to piss him off more. Rad is a happy-go-lucky guy, but if you wake him up, he's rather testy and often threatens murder.

"Why?" he groans, holding the back of his head. "I'm telling on you," he whines, shutting his eyes again. "Asher, come collect your brother. He's being a douche again."

"You two are annoying," River rasps in a sleepy voice, snuggling into Rad.

I long to see the warmth of her green eyes staring up at me, but they remain closed. It's only then that I feel a hint of jealousy spear through me. I want her wrapped around me and snuggling into my chest. Not his. Mine.

"They're not in the fucking boathouse!" Asher shouts, slamming through the back door and shutting it with a loud thud. "Where the fuck are they?"

Rolling my eyes, I reach over and flick Callum in the ear. Stormy gray eyes find mine when his body jolts awake, and he looks around with confusion, furrowing his brows.

"Band meeting. We have shit to discuss," I announce, leaning over Rad and kissing River's cheek.

"You all have fun," she mumbles, burying her face deeper into Rad's neck with a whine. "I'll hold down the fort in bed." I snort, pulling the blankets off all of them.

"Why?" Rad whines. "This is the rudest wake-up call in history. Can't we sleep for five more minutes, Dad?"

"No," I chuckle, reaching over him, wrapping my arms around River, and kissing her again.

Fuck. I can't get enough of her soft skin beneath my lips.

"What the?" Asher stops at the threshold, glaring at the four of us in bed. "So, this is what you guys did all day?"

Rad scoffs. "I won eight hundred bucks at the races all because of my good luck charm. Now, get off me," he grunts, shoving me away from the warmth of River, who groans into his pillow. Rad glares at me the entire time he rifles through his closet, throwing on a shirt over his naked body, glaring more when he picks out a long shirt for River and throws it at her when she sits up without shame, catching it and putting it over her head.

"Band meeting," Asher announces in a sharp voice. "We've got some business to discuss." His eyes narrow on River, who wrestles to put on a long shirt she's in, securing it over her ass when she sits on the edge of the bed with a scowl. Blinking wildly, she looks around the room, meeting Asher's eyes.

Callum and Rad reluctantly peel themselves from the bed, knowing Asher means business when he barks orders. Without hesitation, Rad and Callum get dressed, throwing on comfortable clothes.

"Here," Callum mutters, handing River a long pair of sweatpants from his drawer.

She murmurs thanks, pulling them up and securing the pants around her slim waist. Seeing their half-naked bodies and her wearing their clothes sends jealousy through me again.

Fuck.

That should be my shirt and my sweatpants. It should have been my hands all over her. I shake my head, tamping down the green monster threatening to burst through my skin. There's no room for jealousy between us. I haven't asked River to be only mine. Not that I could now. The way Rad grins at her when she tosses her hair into a messy bun and frowns at our existence has his eyes lighting up, and he's as obsessed as I am. His whole face screams joy and happiness, and I couldn't take that away from him. Or Callum. His entire being vibrates and simultaneously bursts with red cheeks. He's absolutely smitten by her. Just like I am.

River isn't just mine, no matter how badly I wish she were. She's ours.

Asher stands rigid in the living room, watching us as we make our way into the room. River shuffles in behind us, mumbling something about coffee and possibly stabbing us.

"I'll get you some," Callum offers, squeezing her hand before heading into the kitchen and heating a cup of coffee. If I asked, he'd tell me to fuck right off and shoo me from the kitchen. But with her? He fucking lights up, pouring the cup.

I smirk when she hums into the warm mug sitting in the middle of the couch. Sighing, she sips her coffee as we all crowd around her, sitting on either side—Rad on her left and me on her right. Callum sits at the other end of the couch, keeping a distance from us. But his eyes don't stray from her for too long.

"Can we do this now?" Asher growls, pulling his phone from his pocket.

"Someone grab the salt and draw a circle around him," River mumbles into her cup, watching Asher with a mischievous spark lighting up her eyes.

His eyes snap in her direction, but he shakes his head, thinking better of saying anything.

"So, what's going on, boss?" Rad asks, sitting back on the couch with a sigh.

"We have an opportunity," I say, taking the reins of the conversation.

"Go on," Callum softly says, rolling his wrist for me to continue.

"West Records is holding the Battle of the Bands at the KC Club," Asher announces, opening a checklist he created on his phone.

The room falls into silence. Even River stiffens between us, eyeing our every move.

"It's an application process, and only five applications will be selected. They invited the rest of the bands to compete. So, it's stiff competition. All we have to do is have certain things checked off, and then we can submit our application through their website," I say, leaning my elbows on my knees.

"We need more live shows," Asher says, staring down at his phone. "We need to record a few songs and have them available on the Dot…"

"Like Sorcha does?" River asks, tilting her head to the side.

Asher's calm eyes find hers, and he nods. "Exactly like she does. We have to figure out how to digitally get our music on there."

"First, we have to figure out how to record the shit," Rad mumbles, running a hand through his hair before dropping his head back. "There aren't many recording studios in a hundred-mile radius, let alone one that'll let us do it for cheap." He shakes his head and worries his lip. "Maybe…"

"Um, Central City Community College has a recording studio. It's part of the music business associates program," River says, looking around the room warily. "I know a guy." My ears instantly perk up at 'know a guy,' and my fingers curl in my lap, more jealousy running through my veins, ready to attack this so-called guy.

"Know a guy?" Rad asks, raising his head to meet her gaze. I snort because he beat me to it. The same jealousy sparks in his eyes, and images of us pounding our fists into the guy I don't even know has a smirk pulling at my lips. Oh yes, we'd pummel him into next week for even thinking about talking to River. Shit. We're hopeless and semi-toxic.

She instantly rolls her eyes and takes a sip of coffee. "Yeah, as in, I know a guy. Like we went to high school with him, and he's the student head of that department right now. Meaning we need that guy to rent time to get to the studio. Meaning, you can't kick his ass or whatever meat-headed ideas you have running through your caveman brains," she says, shaking her head.

"Pretty Girl, I'm offended you would even consider me a meathead. I wasn't…" Rad says with his hand on his chest.

"I see it in your eyes, Assface," she grumbles, shimmying out from between our bodies. I almost don't let her go but grin when she plunks down on Callum's lap, and he engulfs her with his arms. "I'll be with my new favorite over here until you two decide to play nice."

Callum's cheeks turn a deep red, and his eyes widen. "Fav-favorite?" he murmurs through a heavy breath. She grins, nestling further into him.

"Am I going to have to make a rule about no chicks at band meetings?" Asher snarls, gaining all of our attention. "We still have more shit to discuss."

"No, please go ahead, Evil Ash," she says with a smirk, sipping her coffee. "I won't interrupt with my brilliant ideas again."

"Bro!" Rad says, throwing a small couch pillow at Ash. "She just said she could secure us a spot at a legit recording studio. Don't bite the hand that feeds you, dickweed."

"Now say you're sorry," I antagonize, nodding my head at a grinning River, who squirms in Callum's lap.

Asher closes his eyes like an impatient parent and blows out a breath. I know it's taking everything in him to keep his shit together, but it's too much fun fucking with him. He's like a loose cannon. One day, he'll explode, and I can't fucking wait to see it.

With one last deep breath, he refocuses on her with a grateful smile. "Thank you for the suggestion. We'd appreciate it if you could kindly point us in the right direction."

River snorts. "Who knew Evil Ash could be so kind?" she snickers into her coffee but nods. "I'll text Rion today and see when the studio is available. I'll get it all set up and let you know."

Rad jumps in the air and whoops. "You're the best, Pretty Girl."

"What else do we have to do?" I ask.

"Performance videos, social media presence, we need to build up our audience, and maybe get some more venues under our belt." Asher worries his lips, swiping through his phone. "And we have to submit all of this before November 1st. Submissions start on September 1st. So, we don't have very long to get all this done." He gives one last nod before looking at our smiling faces around the room. Even River feels the excitement humming through us.

"It's time to make our dreams happen," Callum says with a grin.

"We're going to be famous!" Rad whoops, throwing his fist in the air, and shakes his ass.

"We're really going to do this," Asher says, letting his excitement come through.

"We are," I agree, rubbing my hands together.

"I can give you the hook up to more venues around Illinois. I've been in contact with people from The Umbrella Club and The Barn." My eyebrows raise to my hairline when she mentions the two best venues around Central City. "Hell, I can get you more gigs at Dead End if you want."

Looking around, I see the awe in everyone's eyes. River may not be able to introduce us to her family like we initially planned—which, in hindsight, was dumb. But she's still our best bet at more gigs at other venues.

"You're like our sugar band manager," Rad quips.

"A sugar band manager? Are you high?" she asks, setting her coffee cup on the end table. "But yeah, I can help you in that area. As long as we have one thing understood," she says sternly, raising a brow.

"Yeah? And what's that?" Asher asks, shoving his phone back into his pocket.

"My father abandoned me years ago. I have no contact with him or my brothers. I can't help you with connections. But..." She bites her lip, looking down at her lap, looking more vulnerable than I've ever seen her in front of us. Sure, as a kid, she spilled her guts and tears, but that was just for me. This is for all of us. She's opening herself up to the room instead of just one person. "But I can help you with this if you want me to."

Callum leans in, whispering in her ear as his hands work up and down her arms.

"Nah, Pretty Girl. We never expected you to do that," Rad whispers, guilt tinging his tone.

"I'm going to pretend you didn't lie to me," River says in a light tone, leaning into Callum. My heart kicks up at her words. Did she know that's why we initially tracked her down at the bar? Shit. I hope not. "Anyway, I'll help you. But when you go, I want to come with you." She rushes her words, nervously licking her lips.

My heart seizes at her confession, and her eyes stay firmly in her lap.

"I want to see California..." She'd never admit she wanted to meet them, but her brothers are there, and we'd be there, too.

"Well, that saves Kieran from having to kidnap you then," Asher says in an oddly vibrant tone. "All right, let's get to work. We got lots of shit to cover before we're ready." Asher claps, marches toward the basement door, and throws it open. "I'll meet you down here," he says one last time before disappearing into the depths of the basement. The sound of his guitar coming to life filters through the house, and one string at a time, he tunes it.

"You heard the man," Rad says with a grin, climbing to his feet. "You coming, Pretty Girl. We can give you your own private concert."

Callum rolls his eyes and kisses her cheek. "He tends to get naked."

"Well, in that case," she says sarcastically, climbing off his lap and plunking down on the couch.

"You'll stay?" I ask as the other two meander toward the door but look back with hopeful looks. Leaning down, I get eye level, staring into the abyss of her moss-green eyes.

Her nose wrinkles, and she nods. "I'm calling my ma and making sure she's okay. Then, I'll text Rion and get you a spot at the studio. But yeah, if everything is fine there, I'll stay," she says, blowing out a breath. "But don't get used to it." A slight grin picks up the edges of her lips, and I laugh.

"River Blue," I murmur, leaning forward and pressing my lips to hers. "Be a good girl and stay here. I'll reward you later." I grin when her cheeks flush, and her eyes dilate wide, letting me know she will enjoy the reward I give her later.

Images of River coming to California with us rush through my mind. Us at the beach. Her at our concerts, egging us on from the sidelines. It's a beautiful image of a beautiful future I can't wait to explore.

As band practice continues, River slowly makes her way down and rests on the ratty old couch in the corner while playing on her phone. We each watch her with different intensity levels, but she seems to bring out the good in us. Our music gets heavier and better. A new song emerges from the flames of our fingers, and we dive into a new chapter of our lives.

One with River in it at our side.

Forever.

River

So, this is what suburban hell feels like. Hot sun. Barbecue roasting. Loud country music. And hoity-toity moms and dads looking down their noses at me when I pass by with a plate full of food in one hand, Kieran's arm around my shoulders, and Rad on my tail as the latter talks a million miles a minute. Sometimes I don't think he takes a breath to speak. Is he even human?

As we pass people, Rad loudly introduces me, without shame, to each and every person and lets them all know I'm his girlfriend. I'm constantly reminding the fucker that we're not in a committed relationship. We're—well, whatever we are. Fuck buddies? Having a fun time? I mean, the way he looks at me gives me butterflies. But still. Do we need an actual label to put on ourselves?

He seems to think so because he's constantly reminding me that we are in a relationship—I just won't admit it. In Rad's mind, we're probably married by now and have two kids and a white picket fence.

It's only been five days since we rolled around on Rad's bed and had some of the best sex of my life. Since then, we've taken advantage of our time together. Any chance I get, I'm at Rad's, watching him and Callum play some game called Angel Warrior while doing my homework. I'm falling into a weird routine with them: they pick me up from home, take me to work, and then take me back. Every step of the way, they're there. Always following me. Their faces are all I see, and I'm beginning to get used to it, halfway expecting them to be there every turn I make. Rad, Callum, or Kieran make an appearance every night outside my sliding glass door, begging to crawl into my bed. Some nights we rest together, but most nights, we have our wicked ways with each other until the sun comes up and I'm exhausted. It's gotten to the point where I rarely lock the door, opting to leave it open for them to slip through.

"I can't believe we're going to be in a recording studio in a month," Kieran murmurs with a grin, squeezing my shoulder with happiness.

Wednesday, the one day a week I make it on campus for classes, I signed the boys up for a recording session after talking to the guy in

charge. Come October first, they'll be nestled away in the recording studio, making their dreams come true. And mine. The more I've thought about it, the more excited I get for the adventure to California with the guys to watch them perform.

Come December, I'll be walking the cold beaches and shivering in the waves. Something I've always dreamed of. You crave change when you've lived almost your whole life in one town surrounded by bean and corn fields with no ocean in sight. I want to breathe in the salty waters and watch as the waves crash down. I want to walk the beaches without any stress.

And maybe… just maybe, I'll find my father and brothers, too. It can't hurt, right? They may have forgotten about me for the past nineteen years, but I haven't forgotten them, even after all the rejected letters I received. It's a tough pill to swallow, but I'll know for sure when I meet them face to face.

"Yeah, and my only reward for being such a big help is these ribs and wings," I quip with a grin, nudging playfully into Kieran's ribs as he chuckles at me.

My mouth waters at the sight of the delicious barbecue ribs and wings filling up my plate, and on cue, my stomach erupts with growls begging for the food. I haven't had anything this good since my ma took me out for my birthday to the local buffet, where I ate anything and everything I wanted. And now is no exception. No matter the judgy eyes following me around and watching my every move. What do they think? That I'll steal their TVs while they're outside or something? Sheesh. They need to cool their jets. I'm no thief. I work for everything in my life. Just because I come from the other side of town means nothing. So, they can shove their judgmental glares and whispers up their tight assholes and go back to minding their own business. I've got food to demolish. Finally, we make it to a picnic table set up in the middle of the cul-de-sac, fit with a white tablecloth, salt, pepper, and even a fancy napkin holder set up in the middle.

The warm breeze blows through my hair as I watch the cookout in full swing and marvel at their dedication. They've literally blocked off the entrance to their block with police barricades and a sign that says, road closed to traffic. How they pulled that off, I'll never know.

People meander around, carrying plates. Their gossiping whispers and wandering eyes pierce through me, but I don't give a shit. I'm eating home-made ribs dripping with barbecue. And I'm in heaven. Screw their mean glares and noses in the air.

"K!" I raise a brow when a cute little girl throws her arms around Kieran, hugging him tightly and nearly knocking him over.

A marvelous smile lights up his face, chasing away any ounce of dark-ness bringing him down when he happily chuckles at her antics. He doesn't hesitate, pulling her into his lap and wrapping his arms around her little body. When she pulls back, a huge grin lifts her lips.

"I didn't know if you'd make it," she says in a small voice, her big, blue eyes dancing around the cookout. "I thought maybe…"

"Nah! We made it, Cam," he murmurs, straightening out her perfectly curled brown locks. "Cam, I want you to meet my girlfriend, River." My heart pounds double time, nearly melting, when she turns to me and politely offers me her little hand. "River, this is my little sister, Camilla."

"Nice to meet you," she whispers, biting her lip when we firmly shake hands.

"Nice to meet you, too," I say with my heart in my throat, watching the two of them interact with each other in such a loving way. With every word Camilla says with excitement, Kieran leans in and listens attentively. He doesn't take his eyes off her until she skips away when her mother calls Camilla over to her.

"She seems sweet," I mutter through another bite of food, nearly coming from the glorious taste hitting my buds. I swear, if the boys tasted half as good as these barbecue ribs and wings, I'd never leave them alone.

"She is," Kieran mumbles, rubbing his chin as something odd sparks across his pensive face. Something darker brews between Kieran and his parents, judging by how his eyes narrow in on the man moving toward Camilla and her mother.

"You having fun yet, Pretty Girl?" Rad asks with a grin, putting an arm around my shoulders when he settles into the seat next to me with a big plate of food.

"You kidnapped me on my day off. I'm just here for the food," I groan, ripping a bite off the ribs like a damn animal.

So. Damn. Good. Fuck what I thought about these assholes before. They can cook. Well, the people they hired can cook, that is. They've been milling around, filling the pots with more food in their white chef outfits. I swear I've seen the guy on TV somewhere. Probably one of those barbecue competition shows. Because damn, this is tasty food!

So, they get a River-approved gold star. Only for the cooking, though. Their hospitality is lacking in several departments.

"Kidnapped you?" Kieran says with a raised brow. "You willingly got in the car." I glare at him when he grins more, tilting his head to watch me savagely bite into another wing.

"Yeah, Assface…"

"Oh, we're back to Assface now?" he quips, biting his bottom lip. I swear his eyes light up, giving me his undivided attention.

I frown. "Yeah, Assface. As I was saying. You tricked me into your vehicle by using him." Callum stiffens when I point to him. He sits across the table with a blush so deep sweat drips from his brows.

"I-I…it was them," Callum says with an accusing glare, shaking his head.

Poor Callum. They sent him into my room as I laid in bed watching the damn ClockTok app on the new phone Kieran insisted I have. I put up a good fight, but at the end of the day, it was a gift—an expensive gift, but one, nonetheless.

"Your new phone," Kieran says with a smug grin, puffing out his chest when I take the device from his hand and shove it back.

"I'm not a charity case," I snap, tossing the phone back at him from the backseat of the Tahoe and nearly laugh when it bounces off his big head and lands on the floorboard of the driver's seat.

"I never said you were a charity case, River Blue," he grumbles, picking the phone off the floor and wiping it on the tight black shirt stretching across his defined pecs. "But Callum doesn't use it anymore. It's collecting dust. And your fingers are fucking bleeding from swiping." I frown, looking at my fingertips.

"Do not," I say, shaking my head. "My phone does just fine. Seriously."

"Seriously, nothing, Pretty Girl. Take the phone! You'll need it anyway. I started a group chat." To prove his point, Rad sends eggplant emojis on repeat at least fifty times.

"Could you not?" Asher snaps, turning in the passenger's seat with a scowl, glaring at Rad. "Last time, you bombarded my phone with pictures of your dick. And they don't make water hot enough to get those images out." He fake shivers and shakes his head with disgust.

I snort at Rad's fallen face until he snatches my broken phone out of my hands and tosses it to Kieran. Traitor!

"You're supposed to be on my side!" I hiss, slapping his chest, but he catches my hands.

"I'm always on your side, Pretty Girl. That's why I want you to have this phone," he mumbles, leaning in so fast and shoving his tongue down my throat as a distraction. I moan into his mouth, pulling him harder against me, and DISTRACTION! Rad snorts, grinning at me when I pull back, all flushed with puffy lips. "Teamwork, bro," he says, high-fiving Kieran, who turns to me with a smug, victorious look.

A smug look I wish I could punch from his face. Do you think he'll miss his nose when I push it through his skull for being such a prick? No? Okay, then. Worth a shot. I grit my teeth.

"It wasn't a request. It's a gift that you're keeping," Kieran demands as he tears my broken phone apart, digs out the damn SIM card, and places it in the other.

"Don't fight it, Pretty Girl. It's either that or he spanks you," Rad says, wiggling his brows. "Although, I'm down for the spanking." I shiver at the image in my mind of pink butt cheeks and the burn it leaves behind.

"Or me," Asher says in a low voice that turns my insides into knots.

I swallow hard, catching the slow smile spreading across Asher's lips. If there's one thing I can say for the guy, he'd be an excellent hate fuck. Like, pound me into oblivion, hate fuck. He'd be good at it, too. Too bad he's an asshole and not touching me with a twenty-foot pole. Yet.

"Mmhmm," Asher hums, snatching the new working phone from Kieran's hand. "Now, be a good little brat and use this phone."

"Jesus," Rad murmurs, adjusting himself. "You gonna spank her? Or should I? Bend over my knee, Pretty Girl," he says jokingly, tapping his lap.

"Like fuck," I quip, snatching the phone out of his hands. "Thanks for the phone," I murmur, looking over the sleek screen and four camera lenses in the back. "I guess." I shrug, shoving it into my pocket with a calm demeanor.

But I'm anything but calm. No one has bought me anything like this before. I've paid for everything out of my own pocket. Van didn't even buy me flowers or chocolates. The only thing Van brought me was heartache. And yet, these four guys have already come to my house, set up a home nurse for my ailing mother, slept with me every night, taken my mind off my shitty circumstances, and got me a new phone. It's a longer list than anyone has ever done.

Later that night, Callum snuck back through my sliding glass door, stripped to his boxers, and held me all night. My new phone played soft melodies, and we drifted to sleep in each other's arms. He seems to be sleeping better since he started crawling into my bed and rarely wears his earbuds anymore.

When Callum walked through my sliding glass door with an innocent grin, I instantly lit up. I was still in my pajamas when he innocently convinced me to get dressed in shorts and a T-shirt because we had somewhere to go. I thought we were going to hang out. They had other plans. So, here we are at the Lakeview neighborhood cookout, eating everything under the sun.

"Now, now," Kieran says, shoving another barbecue wing into my fingers. "He did good. He got you here so we could show you off."

"Show me off," I scoff, ripping into another wing and moaning at the taste in my mouth.

"Right," Rad rasps, staring straight at my mouth as I bite into another wing like he's hypnotized by the way I eat. "You just keep eating, Pretty Girl. I'll hide this boner somehow. Unless you want to sit on my lap and talk about the first thing that pops up." He doesn't take his eyes off me even when I set the cleaned bone on my paper plate. "Then we could play just the tip. Or hide the hotdog. Or maybe…" He wiggles his brows, letting that charismatic smile fall across his lips.

"Mmmm, maybe," I moan into my fingers as I suck them one by one, getting the remnants of the sweet barbecue sauce off my fingers. Seriously. How do they get this shit so sweet but tangy? I could drink a gallon of this stuff or bathe in a pool full of it.

"For fucks sake, Little Brat," Asher huffs, yanking my fingers from my mouth and holding my wrist hostage in his tight grip. He shakes his head, lust swimming in the depths of his hazel eyes. I suck in a breath when he leans closer, a breath away from kissing me, and mumbles, "This is a family event."

A protective growl vibrates through his throat when he gestures to the older males standing around and staring in my direction. Some of them shift away, hiding their interest. And by interest, I mean their old man dicks standing at attention for the first time since Reagan was president. Perverts. Talk about losing my appetite.

I snort, shrugging. "Better watch out, Asher. I might just become your new mommy," I quip, digging into the remaining ribs on my plate with zest.

"I need a drink," he hisses, adjusting himself with a grunt. Narrowing his eyes at me, he stares at me like I might do something else wrong. Asher huffs, trying to cover his boner.

Me? Do something bad? I would never march over to the grill and demand more ribs or cause a scene if I don't get any.

Asher leans closer than before, brushing his lips against my cheek. My breath leaves my body entirely at the sparks flying from his touch, heating my entire being.

"You're trouble with a capital T, Little Brat. Be a good girl and stop licking your goddamn fingers in front of them. You really want to give them something to jack off to tonight?"

My nose wrinkles, and I cut my eyes to the old men standing in a circle across the party. Some of them look this way but suddenly stop when they realize I'm watching. Asher's breath brushes against my cheek when he chuckles.

"Will you?" I ask suddenly, jerking my face to his and nearly kissing him.

He swallows hard, his eyes dilating. "That drink," he barks, marching away.

"Yeah! That's right, get your drink. By the time you get back, I'll be…" A hand covers my mouth, settling their warm body beside me, chuckling.

"I wouldn't finish that sentence," Kieran says with a grin, shaking his head. "Asher will blow a gasket, and he really will bend you over his knee."

"That's hot," Rad groans, running a hand down his face. "We gotta stop being so sexy out in the open. My dick…" he trails off, shaking his head.

"Ashton Radcliffe!" Bellows an angry woman from across the cul-de-sac. "Come here this instant!" Her demands echo through the neighborhood, turning everyone's attention this way for one brief second.

"That's one way to make a boner disappear. Thanks, Mother," he mumbles, pushing up from the seat with a frown. "Fuck my life, man," Rad hisses, running a hand through his hair. "I'll be back. And don't you dare move."

"Aye, aye, Ashton," I say, saluting him as he walks away. Only looking back once with a storm brewing in his eyes, promising me of the things to come later.

"For someone who didn't want to come, you're enjoying yourself," Kieran says with a grin, watching as I gobble down my last rib.

"Well, you should have started with 'the food is top-notch, River.' Then I wouldn't have put up such a fight." I chew through the pieces of meat, reveling in the melt-in-your-mouth deliciousness on my tongue.

Screw sex, bands, rock and roll, and anything else in between; I'd die in the depth of these barbecue ribs any day just to get another taste. Shit. When I reach down to grab another, all I get is a cleaned-off bone.

"I need more," I hum, nodding to my plate. If I'm going to be here for free food, I might as well stuff myself until I want to puke. They invited me, so I'm taking advantage. Besides, he wants to show me off, right? Well, take that, Kieran Knight.

Kieran cracks a grin. "I'm going to remember this moment forever." He barks out a laugh and straightens his spine. His smile melts away into a grimace until he's standing behind me and places a firm hand on my shoulder. "Go get your ribs and whatever else you need. Apparently, our parents are having a tizzy fit."

"A tizzy? Over what?" I ask, looking around the party, taking it in. And what I see sends my heart into a frenzy. Of course.

Like every other parent on this side of the green grass, they're concerned about their boys hanging around a Central girl. Oh, right, that's me. The Central girl, who they think is too stupid to make any good decisions and will convince their sons she needs a baby or will rob them blind. I'm just here for the food, and well, their dicks are nice, too. But no babies for me, thanks. I have life aspirations that don't include children until I'm at least thirty.

"Got it," I mumble into my empty plate when Kieran gets up and waltzes toward the woman glaring daggers at him.

Her face wrinkles when Kieran approaches with his hands in his pocket, murmuring a few things to him and shaking her head in disappointment. If they only knew I wouldn't be here unless these assfaces had dragged me here kicking and screaming. It was a kidnapping. Whatever. Nothing I can drown my sorrows in more food.

"I'll be back," I tell Callum, pointing toward the food.

"You-you want me to come with you? I don't have parents to disap-point," he says, cracking a smile when I snort.

"Nah. I got this. You stay here."

I march my happy ass toward the long row of potluck food. The entire neighborhood chipped in, bringing a slew of homemade sides that would make Martha Stewart jealous. Chicken and noodles, with those thick noodles, mashed potatoes, beef and noodles, pulled pork with barbecue sauce, and finally, the glorious barbecue ribs stacked high. I nearly come when more gets added to the platter, fresh, hot, and ready for my mouth. I'm practically drooling by the time I grab a clean plate and pile it high with ribs, adding mashed potatoes and even a little potato salad because nothing says hello Midwest, like cold potato salad on a hot day or any kind of cold salad, for that matter.

"I know what you're up to." A menacing voice says from beside me, breaking me from my rambling potato thoughts.

I clutch my plate, and my heart races in my chest. Shit. I almost dropped my food at the sound of his deep voice. And that's a goddamn tragedy. There are hungry people all over this city who'd die to get a taste of these ribs and the seven different types of cold ass salad that doesn't involve lettuce.

"Wow, you caught me. I'm just grabbing a bite to eat," I say, my voice dripping with heavy amounts of sarcasm. There's no way I'd show this man any amount of respect.

Every time I'm face to face with this pain in my ass, he's nothing but a walking, talking dickhead. I cock my head, imagining his bald head into the shape of a dick, and wouldn't you know, he's not as intimidating.

He snarls at me, lifting his upper lip. "First, you poison my son, Van, with your filth, and now those four? You're really moving through them, aren't you?" Disgust fills every molecule when he steps up to me, letting me feel every inch of his over-inflated body.

Reading between the lines, I see exactly what he's throwing down. Whore. Slut. Trash. Yeah, I've heard it all. But screw him and all these people who look at where I come from instead of looking into my heart. I know exactly who I am and where I come from. The fucked-up thing is, if I had even some of my dad's money, I'd be richer than all of them. How ironic is that?

Wrinkling my nose, I pick up my plate and take a big bite of my rib. "It's funny you think that," I say with a shrug, moving to walk past him, but he grabs my arm with lightning speed, squeezing tight.

I narrow my eyes at the fat fingers holding me captive. I could tell a cop when he leaves bruises, but big and round Judge Drake is just that—a goddamn judge. No one would believe the poor Central girl over the reigning judge of Central County. Besides, I've been down this road before with the police. They laughed at me then, and they'd laugh at me now.

"I don't think so. I know so. We all know how you tramp Central girls work. Trap a nice, hardworking Lakeview boy, and then you have a cushy future." His teeth grind back and forth when he speaks. I'm surprised he doesn't break a tooth.

I nod, taking another bite of my rib without care, working around the hand holding me hostage.

"You know, I shouldn't explain anything to you because, in your mind, I'm nothing more than this idea you have. But let me clarify it for you, Judge Drake." Van's father's eyebrows raise when I use his formal term with venom. "I work two jobs, more than your precious little angel Van ever has. I go to community college to better my future. I literally don't give a flying fuck about anyone on this side of town. I want to get out of this place. Now, let go of me." I bite into my rib again when his fat fingers finally peel away from my arm, and he wipes them on his pants like I have a disease on my skin.

What a twatwaffle.

"Don't think their parents will sit back and let them continue this little pipe dream of theirs, which doesn't include you. Go back to the hole you crawled out of and leave this side of town," he growls his entire sentence, shaking his head in disgust. "I'll make sure they know all about you." At that moment, I see the first glimmer of a wicked plan developing in his pea-sized brain.

"River," Callum says in a tight voice, coming to my side and placing an arm around my shoulder. "You okay?" he murmurs, staring daggers at the Judge, lifting his chin.

"We were just chatting," Judge Drake says with a crude smile. "I'd watch yourself if I were you, son. She'll bring you nothing but a damn headache."

Callum cocks his head to the side. "I happen to like my headache," he says confidently, squeezing my shoulder. "Come on, let's go sit." I nod in confirmation as we take a few steps from the stupid judge and stop in front of the large trash can.

Great. Just what I need, pissed-off parents coming after me for no reason. I sigh, looking down at my delicious plate of food, and grieve with a broken heart that splits in half and cries. Lead sits in the pits of my stomach, threatening to send my already delicious ribs back up. I have a feeling they won't taste as orgasmic the second time around. There's no way I'll be able to inhale this food like I wanted to after all his words sink in. I'm only human, after all, and sometimes the words people throw at me do stick. I'm not worthless or whatever because of where I come from. I'm trying my best, but no one will ever see it from this side of town. They only see a Central girl clinging to their kids with stars in her eyes.

With a heavy heart, I mean seriously, my heart hurts when I toss my full plate in the garbage, thinking about all the hungry souls out in the world begging for a full plate of food just like that—what a waste. But I can't imagine biting into that food without it tasting like ash in my mouth. Grabbing a few napkins, I wipe all the sauce from my sticky fingers and mourn the loss of the delicious food staring back at me.

I shove my hands into my shorts pocket and peek around the party again with Callum at my side. The parents mingle, drinking their martinis and whatever fruity shit they have in their glasses. Judge Drake stands close to Kieran's mom and another man I haven't seen before, discussing something. Or someone.

"How-how about a walk?" Callum suggests, nodding his head toward the sidewalk.

I wrinkle my nose, flipping them off from my pocket, as we start walking through the party. Looking around, I don't see the others who dragged me here anywhere. How can they abandon me in the depths of Hell like this?

"You're still my favorite," I mumble, leaning my head on his shoulder for support.

"I won't-won't tell them," he whispers, kissing my hair with such love my heart pumps double time.

"Good, because they're seriously trailing behind," I grumble when we make our journey up the sidewalk away from prying eyes.

A soft chuckle vibrates through his chest when he kisses my head again and hums. Every day I swear he breaks out of his shell more and more. We haven't done more than kiss—oh, and what we did in bed with Rad. Callum's taking things at his pace, doing what he needs to do, and I'm waiting on him. Whatever my sweet Callum needs, he'll get.

"Can I ask you something?" Peering beneath my lashes, I glance up at Callum, who shrugs.

"Sure," he says through a breath, furrowing his brows.

"Your house," I mumble as our walk slows. "I…" Callum's lips pull up into a tight smile, and he shifts uncomfortably to my side, nervously peering around the neighborhood. "No. You don't have to talk about it. I'm just nosy," I say, playing it off with a laugh.

"What do you want to know?" he asks in a deep voice, slowing our steps to a stop at the edge of the party madness as we overlook everyone milling around with plates of food in one hand and an alcoholic beverage in the other.

"How?" I ask, nibbling my bottom lip. "It's just you and Rad with no jobs and no school. You guys play in a band and barely make enough to get out of here. So, um… how?" I ramble, spitting out my question as fast as possible.

He nods, eyes falling to the large crack in the road's asphalt and studying it intently. For several long seconds, he doesn't say a word. I'm almost to the point of apologizing again and dropping my nosy question, but then he speaks, stunning me into silence.

"When my family died, they left all their bank accounts, life insurance, and assets in a trust with their lawyer," he heaves a trembling breath, finally peering at me with bloodshot eyes. "It pays my monthly bills and leaves me with a little spending money to get by, but nothing substantial. At the end of December, the trust will be completely signed over to me, and I'll be free to do what I want. My parents wanted me to go to college and get a degree. So, they stipulated that if they passed before I was a certain age, I'd have to hang onto the house for that long. I don't-don't think they realized it would be like living in a tomb," he wheezes the last words, clamping his eyes shut.

I swallow hard, pulling his face down into my neck, letting him cling to me for dear life. His fingers dig into my ribs as he pulls in deep breaths of oxygen. "I'm sorry," I whisper, running my fingers through his blond locks and twirling them in my fingers. "I didn't mean to upset you like this."

"It's okay, Little Star," he mutters into my flesh. "I rarely-rarely talk about them anymore. Sometimes, I need to let this out, and I'm… I'm glad you asked. I want to tell you everything," he whispers, lifting his face from my neck. Staring deep into my eyes, I see all the vulnerabilities swimming in the depths of his gray eyes as they soften more. "Once I can leave, have access to their money, and sell the house, we'll have enough to invest more into the band. I-I don't know what our plans are. But you'll come with us, anyway. Right?" he whispers the last part, making my heart fall into my churning stomach.

"More than anything," I reply without thinking about the future's implications or consequences. I'm living in the present, and I can't think of what will happen come December when they walk away and live their dreams. Will I go? Or will I stay home with my ill mother? Only time will tell.

out of view from the party, and we settle ourselves in the grass between the two big houses. Callum's brows furrow when he looks at me and leans in, kissing my cheek.

"I gotta-gotta…" His lips roll together when he stands, gesturing to his house down the block. Swallowing hard, his face flushes. "Go to the bathroom," he mumbles with embarrassment, shoving his hands in his pockets. "You want to come with or…."

I smile at him and shake my head. "I'll stay here and away from the predators," I say, pointing in the party's direction.

He nods. "Stay and be safe. He… he looked at you with so much hate. I kind of wanted-wanted to punch him." I smile even wider at the imagery of his fist hitting Judge Drake's face.

"Don't mess up your hands," I say, shaking my head.

Callum nervously waves as he jogs toward his house with urgency, leaving me to fend for myself. I pull out my new phone, enjoying the privacy the homes provide for me, and scroll SpaceFace aimlessly, looking for anything to entertain me while I wait for the assfaces—totally renaming their band that whenever they win the Battle of the Bands—who left me here to fend for myself. Seriously? How can they just walk away with their heads hung low and their puppy tails tucked, leaving me up against the damn lions circling me. My stomach churns with the similarities between them and Van. I mean, Van never would have brought me here in the first place, but still. He left me because his mean daddy said so. Oh well, I'm better off without him.

"River."

I sigh to myself, leaning my head back against the cool side of the house. Speak of the devil. It's like I summoned him to join me in my hiding place. I squint, looking up toward the towering figure looming above me.

"Van," I say in an equally ominous voice, shoving my phone into my pocket. To equal the playing field, I jump to my feet and wipe away the

grass clippings from my ass. "What brings you to my little oasis?" I ask with scathing sarcasm dripping from my tongue.

He rolls his eyes toward the sky, shaking his head like he can't with me. "I saw you got cornered by my dad, and I wanted to make sure you were okay." He swipes his foot along the manicured grass, looking at me coyly through his eyelashes.

Fucking boys and their beautiful eyelashes. How'd they get so damn blessed? And me. I have to apply fakes to achieve what they get just by waking up and greeting the sun.

I scoff. "Okay? No, I'm not. Your dad made me lose my appetite." I shake my head in disgust, mourning the food I had to throw away.

Ugh. The feeling of his slimy fingers wrapped around my arm lingers on my flesh, and I want to hurl. No one should touch anyone without permission.

He snorts. "Sorry about him. He was just surprised to see you here. Me too, actually." He shrugs nonchalantly, but I know Van better than he thinks I do. He's fishing for answers from me in his usual way.

"Oh, yeah? Surprised to see me? I'm always at these barbecues. What're you talking about?" I quip, earning myself a scoff of disbelief.

"Why're you here, Rivey?" he asks, narrowing his eyes, using the nickname I never wanted to hear from his lips again. It's the one he used to seduce me into the backseat of his car and the one he moaned when he thrust into me.

"I'm here for the food," I snark, rocking on my toes. I mean, it's not a lie. "Delicious, by the way." I point fingers guns in his direction, earning another scowl. I live to piss this guy off.

"No," he grits out, stepping up to me, effectively entering my personal space. "You're here with them. Aren't you?" His brows furrow like he's constipated, and I almost suggest adding some prune juice to his diet. But I bite my tongue because he knows the answer. He apparently watched me go to Callum's a few days ago.

I frown. "And what if I am? What is it to you?" I bite back, putting my hand on my hip.

Here we go. Another lecture from someone I don't want a lesson from. I trust only five people in this world enough to listen to their lectures, and it doesn't include this assclown.

"I thought I warned you away from them, Rivey. Seriously! What are you doing with them? They're users. They only want you for one thing," he growls, caging me in against the house. His eyes dilate when he presses his entire body against mine, relaxing into me. My whole body stiffens beneath his chest, and the worst thoughts roar through my mind. We're alone, and he's a lot stronger than me. Plus, the wild look in his eye doesn't promise a happy ending. I swear my throat closes, and my heart pounds in my ears when he leans down, getting into my face. "They are going to use you and then throw you away. Mark my damn words," he hisses between his teeth.

"What? Like you did?" I seethe, clenching my teeth.

I cock my head, running my fingers over the wooden grip of my special knife in my pocket. Since my rape, I've never left without it. It has protected me on many occasions. And right now? Yeah, I'm half tempted to sink it deep into his balls and watch him scream in agony and rue the day he ever warned me and tried to run my life.

If Van thinks he can corner me like this and put his face directly into mine, then he's way too fucking comfortable with me. Like everyone else, he deeply underestimates me, thinking he can pin me against the wall and tell me what I can and can't do or who I can fuck. He's way out of line, and I'm about to show him the error of his ways.

"You didn't like it when I called you daddy when we screwed. So, what makes you think you can act like my daddy now?" I seethe, fitting my closed knife against his balls. In one flick, I could have him flayed open and begging for the hospital. "You have some balls on you, Van. I'll give you that. But you're about to lose them for overstepping if you're not careful. We've established that I'm a big girl and don't need my ex-boyfriend to protect me anymore. So, what will it be? Balls? No balls? Your choice. With the flick of my damn wrist, I could relieve you of them." His Adam's apple bobs when his eyes dart down to my fingers wrapped around the handle of my knife. I swear all the blood rushes to his face, and he shakes his head.

"Rivey," he grumbles, hanging his head in defeat, and takes one step back. "You'll thank me one day for giving you...."

"The fuck you think you're doing?" A low, menacing voice comes from beside us with such possession, I swear my nipples pebble under my shirt, showing their approval.

In the blink of an eye, Van is pushed off of me and stumbles backward with a stunned expression lining his face. Kieran charges him again with flaring nostrils and tight fists like a damn wild bull on the loose.

"Kieran," I say in a deep voice, scanning his face and trying to stop it. "He's not worth it." His eyes flick to the knife in my hand, hanging loosely without the blade protruding.

"You felt threatened," he hisses, nodding toward the knife. "What the fuck were you saying to her, Donny boy?" he asks, flexing his fists. "You looked like you were getting fucking cozy with my girlfriend."

"Again, with the girlfriend remarks!" I hiss, tossing my hands up in exasperation.

It's like they think if they keep saying it over and over again that I'll finally believe it. But there's no way I'm their anything. Nothing but a good time and.... whatever else I have to convince myself of.

Kieran shifts his weight from foot to foot, cracking his knuckles like a crazy man hell-bent on defending my honor. Great. He's going to kick Van's ass. Not that Van doesn't deserve a good-ass whooping, but still. At a family cookout where their parents already hate me. It's not what I need right now. What I need is a stack of ribs, a damn strawberry milkshake, and no damn drama. Is that too much to ask for?

"Kieran," I warn with a growl, stepping toward him.

"What's it to you, Knight? Huh? Her pussy that good that you're going to punch me in the face?" Redness takes over Van's face when he steps up to Kieran, facing off with him with a snarl.

I frown. "Leave my pussy out of this. You know what? You're all jackasses." I throw my hands in the air when Kieran grabs him by the collar and holds him close. Idiots. They're all fucking idiots. I shake my head, stuffing my knife back into my pocket. They can keep their balls and have fun beating the snot out of each other.

"Nah. You're just a jealous asshole," Kieran spits through gritted teeth. "It tears you apart that the girl you're in love with is on my dick, not yours. But that's your fault, isn't it, Drake?" Kieran cocks his head as Van seethes in his grip, shaking with anger. His eyes cut to mine, and I fucking sigh at the situation. Who knew my Knight would argue and defend my pussy against my stupid ex-boyfriend who broke my heart. It'd be romantic if he weren't being such a dick.

"You shouldn't have her," Van grits out, shoving against Kieran, and knocks them both to the ground. Van lands on top of Kieran and raises his fist, letting it dangle.

"God damn it!" I hiss, marching toward them and grabbing his hand. "This isn't cute, romantic, or whatever the hell you two think you're fighting over. This is fucking barbaric. Get. Off. Of. Him." I grunt, trying to pull Van's lean body off Kieran, but he doesn't budge. He stays on top of Kieran, glaring down at the smirking asshole beneath him who eggs him on with a sparkle in his eyes.

"Do it, Van," Kieran says in a low, gruff voice. "Punch me like you want to."

"You're not helping, Assface," I huff, trying to pull Van's hand back, but it backfires when I stumble over my feet and land hard on my ass. As soon as my hand releases from his fist, he throws it into the side of Kieran's laughing face.

"Oh God, yes," Kieran shouts when Van whales on him repeatedly, pounding his fist into his face until blood spurts out of his nose. He laughs, thrashes around, and soaks up the pain every fist inflicts.

"Van, you asshole!" I hiss, getting into the mix and launching myself at my stupid ex, who couldn't leave it alone.

"What the hell?" Rad's voice rings through the fray of fists, and he forces Van off and helps my aching body off the ground. "Dude, seriously?" he asks Kieran, who jumps to his feet, wiping the blood from under his nose. He loosens his neck and grins with bloody teeth in Van's direction.

"Feel better?" Kieran asks in a condescending tone and cocks his head.

"Loads," Van grits out, popping his knuckles.

"Go the fuck back home, Van," Asher demands, strolling between the houses with so much fucking confidence it chokes the air. "You've said your peace. Now get the fuck out. She doesn't want you. We don't want you. Run along." He flicks his wrist with an arrogant attitude.

"I'm just trying to keep you safe, Rivey," Van says, cutting his eyes to me. "They're going to hurt you." I swear his eyes mist over when he looks at me, pleading with me to heed his words.

"Just like you did?" I say, letting all my vulnerabilities shine through.

His lips roll together, and his eyes drop, dripping in shame. "Yeah," he mumbles. "But I'd never make that mistake again." He shakes his head, snapping back when a new voice comes toward us.

"Van, baby! What are you doing?"

I jerk my head when a beautiful brunette strolls up with her hand on her chest and shock on her face. But that's not what draws me in. Nope. It's the giant diamond glistening on her left hand—an engagement ring. Correction, a massive engagement ring. Jesus. That has to cost more than my yearly salary. "Did you.... did you fight?" She takes his hand, examining the blood on his fist, and then looks at Kieran's face. "Oh, no," she gasps.

"Heya, Whitley," Rad greets, tipping his head in her direction with a small, knowing smirk.

"Rad," she greets with a frown, taking the crowd in until she gets to me. Her face hardens, and her ice-blue eyes cut to Van, where guilt is written all over his face.

"I see," she huffs and turns to walk away.

"Whitley, wait!" he shouts, running until he catches up to her. "It's not what it looks like, I promise."

"And her?" She points her manicured nail directly at me.

I groan, running a hand down my face. Jesus. I just need one day when I'm not put in this kind of situation. Just one! That's all I'm asking for.

"It's nothing." His words would have cut like a knife a few months ago and bled me dry, but today I'm thankful I can smile in his direction and not feel a damn thing. Thanks for that, Van. You've been a real treat. But I've moved on to bigger and better things.

"Don't worry!" I shout, waving my arm at her. "He was only warning me away from their dicks! Not his!" She gasps, slapping Van across the face, and takes off with choked sobs.

Am I an asshole? Sure. But I won't let anyone spread lies about me right to my face. If I didn't mean a damn thing to him, then he would have let me go completely. He's just mad I won't let him sneak into the record store office with me anymore. I'd say he's pussy deprived. But that would be a lie. He's obviously been hiding a girlfriend—no, scratch that—a fiancé away. The question is, when did he start dating her? And was it while we were screwing around? If there's one thing I don't stand for, it's fucking cheating.

"Oh, Pretty Girl." Rad barks a laugh, wrapping his arm around my shoulders and turning my face toward his. "Don't listen to him, okay?" he asks, wrapping his fingers around my jaw and directing my mouth to his.

"Get off me, you sweaty asshole," I grunt, pushing his body away. He cackles as he stumbles, only righting himself when he bumps into the side of the house.

"He's such a fucking dick," Kieran explodes, grinding his teeth.

"Takes one to know one," Callum offers with a grunt, strolling towards us with his hands in his pocket. "You-you okay?" he asks, coming to my side and taking my cheeks in his palms. With worried eyes, he looks me over and nods, kissing my forehead.

"I'm fine," I mumble, leaning into his embrace even though I'm anything but fine.

"Fuck sakes," Asher mutters, running a hand down his face, shaking his head. "I'm going to kill that guy." Yeah, me too, pal.

"Welcome to the shit show," Rad says with a grimace, looking me over too. "Where every year our neighborhood cookout turns into a Real Housewives drama."

I wrinkle my nose. "You've watched Real Housewives?" I ask, raising a brow and bursting out laughing when his cheeks turn pink.

"*Real Housewives. Laguna Beach. The Hills.* Any old-school reality drama you can think of, Rad loved to indulge in," Asher says dryly with an eye roll.

"Dick," Rad mutters, swiping a hand through his mullet.

"Well, listen. As much as I've so loved being forced to live through this hell, I'd appreciate it if someone could take me home. I have homework, and some of us have to get up and go to a job in the morning," I say with a pointed look.

"Grab your things, Pretty Girl," Rad says with a pout, nodding toward his house, reminding me I left my backpack at their house because I was under the impression, we were doing our usual couch dates. "I'll take you home," he says through a defeated sigh, clinging to me like he doesn't want to let me go.

Before we can manage a step, Asher huffs, crossing his arms over his chest. "Little Brat will have to wait. My father has requested our musical presence," he says through gritted teeth.

"What?" Callum murmurs, knitting his brows together when Asher heaves a breath.

"Musical presence?" I snort, nearly jerking back when his heated gaze finds mine, overflowing with a wave of fiery anger he can't seem to contain.

"He wants us to play?" Callum asks, cocking his head to the side, inspecting Asher's agitated state.

"He never wants us to play," Kieran confesses, scrunching his face. "Why?" His Adam's apple bobs when he swallows hard, looking intently at Asher, studying his reaction.

"Yeah…" Asher says with confusion, shaking his head. "Fuck. I don't know. It's weird… The entire party wants to hear us." He shrugs, moving a hand through his hair.

"You'll stay?" Callum murmurs in my ear when we meander back into the house, standing an inch apart in the living room.

"Sure," I say, offering him a tight smile, despite wanting to run as far away as I can from Van and his weird, psycho bullshit.

With a few more murmured words, I sit my stuff down and help the boys move their equipment to the center of the cul-de-sac, prepping for their impromptu performance for the entire neighborhood crowding around. The crowd's drunk voices rise into whistles and hollers the moment Asher hits the first note of the evening.

Leaning forward, I put my elbows on my knees, gripping my phone. Heart after heart floats up the screen, accompanied by comments of praise and admiration. My breaths shudder in my chest, ballooning with elation and pride.

Wow! Following you guys now!

You guys sound amazing!

Holy hell! They're hot as hell!

Wow! @whisperedwordsband! Who are you? You sound so good!

Fan for life!

My eyes widen as I scroll through the comments, and I flush. If this is what even a sliver of fame feels like, then I'm fucking blown away. All these people are lining up to get a piece of us and begging for more videos and performances. Some are local people. But most are scattered across the country and overseas.

Holy shit.

The list goes on with more intrusive questions just as our newest video hits one-million views on ClockTok. Disbelief slams through me as the numbers climb and climb with each passing second. We'll be internet sensations before the night is through, and everyone will shout our names. Now, we need to deliver more performances to the masses before we fade into obscurity before the competition.

It's hard to believe that just yesterday, my father forced us to play an impromptu concert for the neighborhood. Begrudgingly, of course. Never in a million years would he actually want us to live out our little fantasy, as he calls it. But when the public wants something, my father will deliver.

My father's talk from yesterday rattles in my mind when he pulled me away from the cookout and threw me into his office with such force I landed on my ass with a grunt. The pain seared up my tailbone, letting me know the kind of mood he was in.

"Stay away from the trash, son. You're a fucking embarrassment," my *father hisses, sending a fist into my gut as we stand in his brightly lit office.*

All the breath leaves my body when I double over, counting to ten.

Desperation to remove myself from here clamps my tongue down. I refuse to say a goddamn thing and inflict more pain on my body when I could simply shut my mouth and walk away. One day, I won't have to endure his angry fists—but that day is not today.

"Stand up straight," he barks, grabbing me by the collar and yanking me up despite the pain of his blow, knotting my stomach.

My lips pop open when he releases me and leans against his mahogany desk in a relaxed pose. River teases me that a demon resides in my body, but the actual devil stands before me with black eyes, a cruel smile, and a wicked right hook.

"Enlighten me on why the trash is eating my food. Judge Drake seems to think she's nothing but a whore, luring you in for money," he says in a smooth voice, straightening his ten thousand dollar suit he insisted on wearing to the catered cookout. "And we all know what happens when a whore lures a man of our status in with her pussy." He raises a brow, alluding to the woman he married and now loathes.

My father may be a good business owner, making more money than anyone in a ten-mile radius. But as a father? He's shit. It's no wonder my mother buried her anguish in a needle and slowly poisoned her veins to leave his tight grip. Some days, I wish I could do the same. Financially, though? I'm stuck, rooted in the spot with nowhere to run.

"She's not luring us in for money," I say in a small voice, locking my hands together in front of me. I keep my eyes down low and my body locked tight. The last thing I want to do is provoke the devil even more, but I have to tell him something believable. "We're the ones using her."

She may not be after our money, but there's something about River West that makes me want to either fuck her or run her off. She's dangerous for us; I don't know to what extent. Something is nagging in the back of my mind warning me to watch my back and my boys. They're my family, and I'll be damned if one chick swoops in and ruins what my family has built for the past five years.

My father scoffs, checking his watch. "Right. Using her?" Great. He wants me to elaborate more than I fucking should.

I clear my throat. "River is Corbin West's daughter. He owns…" Ding. Ding. Ding. For once in my short life, I've uttered the correct words he wants to hear. His eyes light up and widen, and his body puffs up with pride.

"I know who he is and what he owns," my father barks in a deep voice. Bravely, I meet his eyes. His lips purse, and he nods, something churning in his mind. "That man is worth more than this entire neighborhood combined and more than Montgomery, Inc." He opens his lips to possibly say more but rethinks it when he shakes his head, redirecting the conversation. "The neighbor, Susie, specifically requested you boys to put on a show for the

neighborhood. She says you sound really good for a waste of time and would like a live concert."

"A show?" I ask, my heart pounding against my chest at the prospect of playing in front of the crowd.

"Get your fucking guitars and shit and bring it out. You and the boys are performing tonight." He steps forward, towering over me with a twisted face. "Don't fuck this up and embarrass the family, Asher. Make it good."

"Of course, sir," I say quickly, taking a step toward the door, aching to escape the oppressive atmosphere putting pressure on my chest.

"Impress me, boy," he mutters from his desk. "Prove to me it's not a waste of time." My eyes widen when I leave the office and head out the door, trailing Kieran and Rad just as he pushes Van off River.

That conversation was all the permission I needed. I felt lighter than I had in days, elated at the opportunity to impress my overbearing and relentless father. If I showed him what we could do, even for a night, we'd have a better shot at making it all real.

That night, we blew everyone away with our raw talent, drawing praise from the drunk housewives and stuffy old men. My fucking father even nodded in my direction with a sense of pride swallowing him. He didn't utter another word to me that night, instead locking himself away in his office. Even Gloria stood stupefied by the closed door and retreated somewhere in the house. For one night, the man who always disapproved of our actions left us alone.

Turning my attention back to the screen, I smile. There we are with the sun on our backs, barely beaming down. Dusk settles in, leaving nothing but a pink sky as our backdrop.

Kieran leads us into the beginning of our set list, starting with *Midnight*. His voice rings through the microphone, and his piercing eyes follow the camera as it moves in front of him, getting a close-up. The smirk that lights up his face and the sparkle in his eyes makes my heart drop into my stomach. As she moves, his eyes follow like a predator watching his prey, ready to pounce.

River leans the camera over Kieran's shoulder, capturing Rad's intense grin. His arms pound the sticks into the snares several times before crashing them into the cymbals and back down to the rest of the kit. Rad's tongue pokes out from between his lips, and a look of concentration crosses his face. But when his eyes find River standing before him with the camera, he brightens completely and watches her as she backs away, turning to Callum and then me. Throughout the rest of the performance, their eyes follow her every move, never straying from her presence.

"Dude! It's fucking amazing!" Rad whoops, slumping down on the couch beside me with a dopey grin. Bringing a beer to his lips, he takes a long swig and then sighs when he pulls it back.

"One million views and counting," I gape, shaking my head in disbelief. Who knew this many people would want to see us perform?

Jesus. Images of our future shine brighter and brighter in my mind, and genuine excitement starts to settle in—us on the big stage with big lights shining down on us as the crowd chants our name over and over. People fall to their knees to get a taste of the music we've bled for. Staring straight ahead, I get lost in the fantasy that could one day be our reality. To leave this place and never see my father again lifts a massive amount of pressure off my chest. I've always ached to see the rest of the world from a tour bus, and the closer we get to making our dreams come true, the lighter I feel.

My only worry… My only concern holding me back is our little sister, Camilla. Her little face pops into my mind twisting in grief as our father strikes me down to the ground, raining blow after blow after he had a rough night of drinking, forcing her to see the consequences of my actions. Forcing her to see what her life will be like if she doesn't bend to my father's every whim and desire. She's seen it a million times—his fists hitting us and tearing us down. For every punishment we receive, she's there to witness our downfall with tears in her eyes and a distraught expression.

If I leave her behind, what will happen? Will he threaten her with a sharp tongue and swift fists? Her cries from over the weekend plague my nightmares. Camilla shouldn't have to go through what we do—ever. Somehow, I need to get Camilla and Gloria away from my father for good. But how? I have no idea.

I swallow hard, returning to the murmured conversation going on around me between the guys, snapping me back to the present instead of sucking me into the past. The boys mill around Callum and Rad's house— our home base.

"She did good, yeah?" Kieran asks with pride, referring to the camera woman in charge of filming our entire show.

"Little Brat," I murmur, motioning for her to come to me with the curl of my finger.

As the drunken crowd of suburban moms moves closer, creating a circle around our setup like sharks circling blood in the ocean, they still. Their glazed-over eyes light up when Kieran tunes his guitar, quietly listening for the right notes. It's like they're hoping to relieve their shitty teenage years with booze, bands, and... Yeah, I'm not finishing that disgusting thought. Even Gloria straightens her spine in the crowd with a glass of red wine perched in her hand, quietly assessing the band. We've never played for anyone in this neighborhood, instead hiding in our home base's basement, trying to conceal our sound.

Per her usual, River raises a defiant brow a few steps away, refusing to budge until I'm huffing mad. And fucking hard. One day, I'd love to pound the attitude out of her ass until she's panting and begging me to stop the punishment, which I wouldn't. My little whore would tremble before me after coming so many times… I… Shit. Why does she take my mind there?

No one gets a rise out of me like this. Not even Rad, who tries his hardest. The longer I'm around River, the more I want to bend to her every whim and then bend her to mine. Something deep, dark, and dangerous hides in River. Calling me to release whatever it is. A wildness she never sets free. The tears she refuses to shed. I want to be the one to tame her and then hold her, letting her know everything will be okay. A sliver of darkness filled with unresolved trauma rests behind the spark in her eyes, hidden from the world but not hidden from me. I see behind the tough mask she presents to the world, and one day, I'll pull it off. I close my eyes, groaning at the serious hold she has on us. It's borderline dangerous.

Knocking the dick-hardening thoughts from my mind before I mount her in front of everyone, I watch as she places her hands on her hips. Then, and only then, does her magical grin spread across her luscious lips, making me wish my lips were on hers. Fuck me.

"Yes, Evil Ash?" she asks in a sarcastic tone, batting her lashes playfully at me, hoping to get a reaction.

I lick my lips, wanting to confront her about that stupid nickname. But I think better of it and huff.

"Take your phone from your pocket and record us."

It's not a question. It's a demand for her to comply. If there's one thing about my little brat, she loves to poke the bear—aka—me. Brats like River need swift direction, not options. Her lips pop open, exposing the argument on the tip of her tongue. I roll my eyes.

"Please, River," I bark, placating her with the niceness everyone else offers her. Kieran always says I'm a perpetual grump, which must be true, judging by how she stiffens.

"Did that hurt?" she quips, digging her brand-new phone from her pocket.

"No," I growl, clenching my teeth. Here she goes again, winding me tighter than I was before. One day, I'll fucking explode and grab her by the hair. But that's not today. Not when the crowd closes in even closer than before.

She shrugs, clicks a few things on her phone, and nods. "All right. This will be good for your ClockTok account."

"We don't have a ClockTok account," I deadpan with a grimace, thinking about the ridiculous video-sharing app everyone obsesses over.

"You do now, boss man," she says with a grin, shoving the stupid phone in my face.

My teeth clench when a picture of the four of us pops up in the little window, accompanied by the username: whisperedwordsband and a little bio about who we are and where we're from. There's even a link to all our social media profiles—the same profiles we barely use—at the top. Fuck.

"You've thought of everything, haven't you?" I ask, blinking at her. Who knew a Central girl could be so damn useful with these sorts of things.

"Sometimes, I think you underestimate my abilities. It's kind of offensive, Evil Ash. Now, play your little show, and I'll capture it all." She grins one last time, stepping back and settling herself next to Gloria.

I swallow hard, watching Gloria lean in, whisper something into River's ear, and back away. Their faces give nothing away, but I know something out of left field was said when River's lip curls, and she shakes it off. Something to ask her later when we're alone, and I can force the words from her lips.

FUCK!

I blow out my breath, running a hand down my face when Kieran walks by, swiping the phone from my hand as he passes by. "Jesus. There are like forty thousand comments!"

"It's about how hot we are, isn't it? Cuz we're fucking smoking!" Rad explains with an even bigger grin.

"Nigel gave me permission to do that," I say in a monotone voice, keeping my eyes forward, refusing to meet his bewildered expression.

Kieran chokes on his drink, snapping his head at me. "He what?"

"He said impress me," I blurt, running a hand down my face.

What I don't say is, judging by the non-existent interaction we had with him last night, that I succeeded in impressing him.

"Impress him?" Kieran mumbles with confusion.

I shrug. "No idea. But he seems semi-on board. So, we can head to the competition without issue whenever the time comes."

Without issue would be a dream come true. But I'm a realist. At the drop of a dime, my father could change his mind. Not that he has any real say. If I want to leave this place with my life intact, we need to be smart about it.

Kieran snorts, knowing exactly what's going through my mind. "Right," he mutters, throwing my phone back to me.

"Looks like we need Pretty Girl to get us more shows so we can keep feeding the fans," Rad says with a lazy grin, putting a joint between his lips and lighting it. "Speaking of. How was she today?" he asks Callum, who turns a deep shade of red.

"Fine," he mumbles, settling back on the couch.

"Just fine?" Kieran asks with an ounce of protectiveness leaking into his tone.

Callum snorts and rolls his eyes. "She wasn't expecting me. I had to force her into my car, and even then…"

"She bitched the whole way?" I gripe, earning a smack to the back of my head.

"Bitch and her do not belong in the same sentence. Have some respect," Rad says with a frown as I nurse the pulsating pain in the back of my head.

"She was fine," Callum continues with a stronger voice. "I took her home, and we hung out with her mom for a little while. Then, I took her to the bar for work."

"She works too goddamn hard," Kieran mumbles in awe.

I couldn't agree more. River works herself to the bone day in and day out, looking increasingly more exhausted as the days go on. Sprinkle school she's putting herself through without help from anyone around her, and she's killing herself for a better future. Seeing such a young person balance so many things in life is odd. Not only does she work two jobs, but she goes to school and somehow cares for her mother in the process. My heart aches at how much she does for everyone else but never seems to take time for herself. River really does deserve better than four assholes who started by using her for her last name and wanting a better future for themselves. Fuck. How did we get down this fucked up rabbit hole? Guilt gnaws away at my insides, churning my stomach.

"Does she have a car?" I ask, looking around the room as they shake their heads.

"If she had a car, then we wouldn't be able to drive her around or force her to come over," Rad gripes like a psychopath.

"Not when we're around," Kieran says in agreement. "If she has one, we can fix it as slowly as possible."

Callum snorts. "I'll keep taking her anywhere she wants to go," he mumbles with satisfaction, pride puffing out his chest.

I shake my head at their obsessive tendencies. Jesus. I may have rogue thoughts about fucking her into oblivion, but I'm no caveman.

"Then she doesn't walk alone anymore," I declare, earning nods of approval.

"We're her road to safety!" Rad whoops, throwing his fist in the air.

I sigh when our phones ding, indicating the only other person in our group chat needs us. Anticipation roars through my veins when I dig my phone out of my pocket. My heart rate skyrockets when the words flash across the screen, and I jump to my feet like the others.

RIVER

Fuck. I need your help. Can you meet me at the bar?

RAD

What is it? That fucker again? I'll rip the skin from his dick, fry it, and shove it down his throat.

I throw him a look, eyeing the cold fury passing over his face. There's something there he hasn't told us. Sure, Bradley is the biggest waste of space in the universe. But Rad's expression says there's more to River's story that we don't know about. Kieran may not have caught on, but I sure have.

RIVER

> Wow, ever the romantic. But no… I… you know what?
> Never mind. I can handle this.

KIERAN

> Nice try, River Blue. But we're already in the car and on
> our way. We'll meet you there in twenty minutes.

She thought she could dismiss us with a few words. Yeah, that shit doesn't fly. Before we know it, we're in the damn car, flying down the streets of Central City until we pull into the parking lot behind the raging bar. Music spills from every orifice, and people stumble on the sidewalk.

THE WORST THINGS IN LIFE COME IN FOURS. MORE SPECIFICALLY, THE FOUR bumbling idiots I texted out of desperation. Commit me now because I don't know what ran through my mind when I pressed send. Too bad I can't take it back. I'd give anything to have a time machine. Then I could go back in time, smack myself over the head, and throw my phone. It's too late now, though. Here they are, pushing into the bar like wild animals stampeding over anyone who gets in their way.

"Bitch, you've got them wrapped around your finger," Ode leans in awe, watching intently as they stumble through the door with feral looks. "They look like they're about to rip this place apart for you. My god…" She whistles under her breath, looking at them with disbelief and fanning her face with a nearby menu.

I sigh, watching Kieran stomp his way through the rowdy crowd with a stone-cold expression. I swear everyone jumps out of his way when his eyes look around the room for the threat.

Said problem lurks in a booth at the back of the bar, hiding in the shadows, watching our every move when Kieran locks eyes with him and growls, planting his feet. Rad pushes through people with a grin, setting his sights on me.

"There she is," Rad proclaims with glee, breaking through the rising tension.

Coming around the bar, he wraps his arms securely around me and squeezes me into his chest. The scent of his body wash filters through my nose, and subconsciously, I know I'm safe. Every ounce of tension melts away when I breathe in his scent and bask in the warmth of his hug.

"Here I am," I mumble into his chest, gripping the back of his shirt and keeping him there within my reach.

Ashton Radcliffe may be outspoken and unable to hold his tongue, but he was my hero once. My knight in shining armor continues to protect me from the dangers threatening me.

Tipping my head back, I gaze into his sparkling brown eyes, tinted with concern. With a content sigh, I press my lips to his, savoring the flavor of

his tongue dancing with mine. He groans into my mouth, pushing me back into the bar. Warm hands encase my jaw, holding me firmly in place.

"Is that what you needed?" Rad asks breathlessly when he pulls back, cocking his head and examining my flushed face until I nod. "Good," he murmurs, rubbing his hands over my shoulders, relaxing me even more.

His dark eyes search the bar with predatory intent, finally landing back on me with a frown. "Why is Van here? Fuck. I thought maybe that other fucker had shown up again to harass you." Worry lines crease on his face when he looks at me for confirmation.

"No," I murmur, running a thumb over his cheek. "He hasn't been back since you kicked him out. And hell, that was the first time I had ever seen him here."

Lakeview residents rarely show up to Dead End unless they're desperate. They've got fancier, nicer bars on their side of town without the crime rates surrounding it. Besides, Van has never come here before. Hell, he practically refused to come and meet me on this side of town unless it was at the record store. So, to see him out of his usual territory has me on edge.

"Why the fuck is he here?" Kieran questions with a growl, curling his fingers into a fist. Glancing at Van again, he frowns more, baring his teeth at the threat. Van, in return, lifts his beer and salutes the guys tauntingly. "I'll kill him," he mutters, tightening his stance and squaring his shoulders. "I'll fucking murder him if he fucked with you. Did he do anything to you? Talk to you? Touch you?" A wild shift happens in his eyes as his voice raises with every word he speaks, pulling back his lips into a snarl.

"Is this why-why you texted?" Callum asks, blinking rapidly.

Stepping forward with a hardened face, which is so unlike himself, he looks over his shoulder. Every inch of his body tenses up, pulling his shoulders into his ears when his eyes find Van and his friend lounging in a booth, drinking their beers. Callum sighs, slumping into the bar stool. Shaking his head, he runs a hand down his face in frustration.

I nibble my lip and nod, not willing to admit he's shaken me up as much as he has. It seems like everywhere I go, Van's face pops up. The cookout. The record store. Just last night, after Callum had settled into bed with me, I swear I heard someone outside my sliding glass door rustling the leaves and tapping on the windows. I thought maybe it was Rad coming for a visit. Through the darkness, I couldn't make out any shapes lurking outside, but I felt it. The eyes searched me out in the night, sending goosebumps down my arms and raising the hairs on the back of my neck. The only way I could shake off the feeling was by snuggling into Callum more and ignoring it until I fell fast asleep. In Callum's arms, I felt more protected than ever.

"Is he bothering you?" Asher asks, settling across from us on a bar stool with a deadly expression tightening his beautiful face. If he weren't such an assface, he'd be handsome as hell.

"No, and yes," I sigh, shaking my head. "I don't know, I felt… Fuck, he makes me feel uneasy, okay?" I spit out, rushing my words together. My stomach turns at my admission, and my eyes fall to the floor, avoiding their stares.

Rad picks up my chin with two fingers, forcing me to face the twinkle in his eyes. "We got you, Pretty Girl, okay? That's what boyfriends are for. And lucky for you, you have four."

"You are not my boyfriends. How does that even work?" I say, shaking my chin from his hold. "There's four of you and only…"

"Three holes? Yeah, we've discussed that. But you have hands, too. It's like a fivesome for all, and we're all satisfied." Rad grins, pride puffing out his chest.

"That makes no sense, jackass," Kieran quips, shoving Rad to the side. "And you are our girlfriend. You have no choices in this discussion."

I frown. "Again, with the demands, Assface. I am my own fucking woman. I swear to God, you're asking for a dick punch tonight."

"The good kind?" Rad asks, wiggling his brows, and then his face falls at our sour expressions. "Okay, so not the good kind?" he questions again with furrowed brows.

Asher huffs. "There is literally no such thing as a good dick punch, idiot. For fuck's sake," he grumbles, running a hand through his hair. "I'm surrounded by idiots every day," he mutters, along with several more unintelligible words.

"I take offense to that," Rad says with mock hurt, rearing back.

"Shut up," Callum grumbles with a snort, effectively shutting Rad up, who still grins like an idiot.

"Anyway, we'll stand guard, Little Brat," Asher says with a shrug, sitting back on the stool. Looking over his shoulder, his eyes connect with Van's in a challenge like a dog staring down a perpetrator ready to bite.

"We got you, Pretty Girl," Rad says with conviction, turning around and grabbing three beers from the fridge, opening them, and handing them out to the boys. "Now, can you make me a Pina Colada? I'm aching for some sweetness, which I'll get from you later, but I need liquid sweetness," he says, punctuating his words with a butt slap and grab.

"Sure, just help yourself," I quip, throwing my arms in the air and promptly shoving my new bodyguards out from behind the bar before they destroy something—like my sanity.

"I got it," Ode says with a sigh, mixing his drink for him and bringing it back. Rad grins when she sets it down in front of him and hums when he takes a sip. "So, are you boys stepping up and protecting my girl here?" she asks with a grin, throwing her arm over my shoulders and squeezing me into her side. Leaning her head on mine, she sighs.

"Anything for her," Kieran proclaims with a slight smirk, bringing his beer to his lips.

I flush, sweat breaking out on every inch of me. No matter how often they tell me they're my boyfriends or get that funny, protective look in their eyes, I have a hard time thinking they'll stick around. Every important male in my life has walked away without looking back. So, what makes them so different? They can have my body over and over again. But my heart is a different story.

"These ones?" Ode whispers directly in my ear like she's seen inside my brain and knows exactly what I'm thinking. "These are the good ones. That one over there? He's bad news. Should we kick him out?"

My eyes stray to the man himself, sitting back in the booth, discreetly watching me with interest. Should I kick him back to his side of town? Probably. But he hasn't done anything to warrant these feelings tumbling inside me. There's just something about him blaring warning signals in my mind.

"He's been steadily buying beers for himself and his friend for the past two hours. He's not really doing anything wrong," I murmur nervously, twiddling my damn thumbs.

"You say the word, and we'll destroy his existence," Asher says in a— fuck with me and find out—tone, pulling my eyes to his. "No one fucks with what is ours." He raises a brow, daring me to argue.

Fuck with what's ours? This again? I swear to God I'm going to wake up with a tattoo on my forehead that says Property of Whispered Words, and then I'm going to start throwing hands and breaking balls. Sinking my teeth into my tongue, armed with a retort, I sigh, deciding better of it. They came all this way to help me, and I should be grateful they dropped everything—which I am. So damn thankful they dropped everything to be with me. But sometimes, when they chip away at my independence, I want to bite their heads off. Is it irrational? Fuck yes. But I'm a strong, independent woman who just happened to need her men to fight her battles.

"I'll keep that in mind. Thank you," I say, blowing out a breath and earning a satisfied smirk from the jerk in question.

"Looks like your little stalker needs a refill. I got them," Ode says with reassurance, clapping me on the shoulder. "I'll be back."

"You're not allowed to go over there," Kieran demands with narrowed eyes, following Ode's every move as she speaks with Van, who smiles up at her, lazily swirling his finger over the edge of the glass beer bottle.

I blink a few times, staring at him. "Did he just say that?" I ask Callum, who nervously grins at me and nods in confirmation, scooting back in his seat. "Look, I'm grateful as hell you guys came, but you can't put me in a damn corner. I have no intention of walking over there. But you can't tell me what to do." I raise a brow when Kieran whips his head toward me and gapes in surprise.

"What the fuck?" he growls, discreetly moving his free hand over his dick for protection. "Then don't make me tie you to the damn bar because I will," he growls, shifting in his seat. "And then throw him out with the trash."

"Sounds like a plan, Big Guy. I like the part where we throw him out with the trash," I quip, rolling my eyes. "But the controlling part? I'm a big girl." Leaning forward, I snarl in his face. "Don't tell me what to do. Got it?"

"If you're such a big girl, Little Brat, you wouldn't have texted us to come here and save the day," Asher snarks, raising a brow and sipping his beer when I whip my snarling face toward him.

"Not-not helping," Callum warns with a shake of his head.

"I am a big girl. But I don't need someone telling me what I can and can't do. You're not my daddy," I growl, inching closer to Asher, who grins wider.

"Yeah? And who says I'm not?" he huskily asks, knocking me back to my feet. I swear my face heats ten million degrees, and then he fucking winks at me. "Call me daddy, Little Brat, and see what happens." His reply is laced in a threatening manner, but an edge sits in his words, warning me that if I do, in fact, call him daddy, he'll explode. Most likely in his damn pants.

"Now, what about the tying down part? I've got rope at home. We could…" I grunt, putting my hand over Rad's mouth until he's grinning behind it.

"Leave it," I grumble with a shake of my head, pulling my hand back and wiping it down my jeans.

A pounding headache knocks on my skull, begging for entry. Ugh. Could this night get any worse than it already is?

"Incoming alert," Ode hisses, hurriedly coming toward me and nodding toward Van leaning against the bar, watching me with a mask of indifference lining his face. In reality, he's anything but. His beady, dark eyes catalog the guys' interactions with me, down to the wink Asher sends me again.

I spoke too soon.

Awesome. Here we go. Just what I needed. Kieran growls, aching to jump to his feet. Release the damn psychos. Next time I'll rethink this whole River needs help scenario and maybe do it all myself. Who needs overbearing boyfriends, anyhow? Wait! Not fucking boyfriends. Just boys I fuck on multiple occasions and spend lots of time with when I'm off work.

"You're our girlfriend, whether you like it or not."

Shit. I think I am. And it's totally against my will. When the fuck did this happen? And why the fuck am I halfway okay with it? Not that I'd ever admit that to them. That'd give them way too much satisfaction.

I lick my lips, locking eyes with each of the boys for good measure, letting them know who the boss of the situation is. Always look the bulls in the eyes to show dominance. Or maybe not. Kieran huffs, flaring his nostrils, attempting to get up. Asher rolls his eyes, clamping a hand down on Kieran's shoulder as he struggles.

"For the love of God, don't fucking move. I'll take care of this," I hiss under my breath, running my fingers across my throat threateningly because I will cut them if they move an inch. That's not a threat. That's a goddamn promise.

"Is this foreplay?" Rad asks, leaning on the bar and winks. "Do the sexy thing with my throat again. I love it when you suffocate me with your pussy!" he says louder than necessary, leaning over to glare at Van standing ten feet away. Heat envelops my whole body when I bury my face in my hands with a groan.

Van's entire body locks up, and his fingers curl into tight fists on the bar top. Clueing me into how much Rad's words affected him. But that's the only indication he heard Rad's words.

"Go before you unleash the beast," Rad murmurs, narrowing his eyes at Van like he wants to slap him upside the head.

Me too, pal. Me friggin, too.

"Van," I say, raising a brow. "How can I help you?"

Van bites his lip, looking around the bar. "So, this is the other place you work?" His fingers drum along the top of the bar with impatience as he peers around, finally looking at the four idiots who glare daggers at him.

I scoff. "Yeah, the whole time we dated, you knew exactly where I worked and never visited. What is up with that?" Not that I'm bitter or anything, but still. He can't just waltz into my place of business months after we broke up and expect me to fall back into his arms.

He frowns, scrunching up his face. "I was always busy. You know that." He waves a hand, once again staring in their direction, just asking for a damn beat down.

"Busy, right," I mumble, rubbing my temple in irritation. I've been working all day, plus school, and I don't have time for Van Drake's shit tonight.

"So, you're really hanging out with them?" Van asks, leaning against the bar and tilting his head. "Like for real?"

"I don't have the mental capacity to deal with your shit tonight, Van. Yes. I like them. Are they assfaces? Absolutely! But I enjoy their company. Get that through your thick skull," I say with a groan.

"I'm just... I'm just looking out for you, River. I'm trying to keep you safe. I don't trust them." He shakes his head, running a hand down his face. "I'm just..." I hold up my hand, meeting his desperate eyes.

"Once again, thanks for your concern. But you have to let it go, Van. Like... are you following me to work? Watching me? You're becoming kind of stalkerish."

He rolls his eyes. "Right, me looking out for you is stalkerish? One day, Rivey. You'll see, and then you'll thank me for it. Until then, I'll be around," he says with one last long look and then walks out the front door with a huff.

"So, fucking weird," I mumble as Ode comes to my side and shakes her head.

"What the hell is up with that?"

"No friggin idea. He's been acting weird since I started hanging with them," I say, jabbing a thumb over my shoulder, aiming at the boys.

"Well, you might want to get back. Booker is here and talking their ear off. He's probably asking them if they're treating you right and wrapping it before they tap it. Then he'll go into the whole spiel about you being the daughter he never wanted, and if they hurt you, he'll castrate them and mount their dicks on the wall," Ode snickers when my face falls, and I swivel around to face the horror show.

Somehow in the past two minutes, the owner of Dead End has snuck in without being detected, setting his sights on Whispered Words. I watch in horror, my jaw falling open as they listen to Booker intently, nodding their heads to whatever he's saying. No fear crosses their faces. Instead, they smile and high-five each other with excitement.

"Hey, Booker," I say with a slight wave, interrupting their chatter.

Booker's dark eyes meet mine in amusement, nodding in greeting.

"Hey, kid," he says in a gruff voice, running a hand through his long dark hair and pulling it over his shoulder. "I was talking to the band that packed the place a few weeks ago." Something evil sparks in his eyes, and my stomach drops.

"He says we were good, Pretty Girl," Rad says with a grin, easing some of my tension.

My cheeks flare red when Booker raises a knowing brow. "They were pretty good," Booker reaffirms with a nod. "That's why I just offered them the Celebration stage in a month."

My eyes widen at his offer. Not just any band gets to represent Dead End at the Celebration Street Festival. That stage is usually reserved for bigger names, drawing the crowd to our tiny little section of the festival. We have a tent, a stage, beer, and lots of food to sell to the thousands of people walking the streets and enjoying the festivities.

But we're not the only attraction drawing people in. Food vendors from around the country, musicians, crafts, the carnival, and so much more line the ten-block downtown area for one weekend a year. It's our biggest investment and the biggest moneymaker. It's make it or break it. So, seeing Booker invite Whispered Words to our little corner of the world is shocking.

My eyes widen. "The celebration?" I question through a breath, confirming I heard him correctly. "Wait! What happened to Break? I thought the times were full?"

"Break took off to New York," Booker says, scratching his scruffy chin and pulling at his beard.

"So, now we're going to fill their shoes!" Rad throws his fist in the air with excitement. "We'll be high on the stage in front of thousands of people!"

"Calm your tits," Asher grumbles, pulling Rad down. This evening, Asher has been nothing more than a glorified babysitter. "Excuse my friend, sir. We appreciate this opportunity. We've gone to the Celebration street fair every year."

"We always wished someone would take a chance on us. So, thank you," Kieran adds with an earnest grin, saluting Booker with his beer.

"Well, I saw your video on ClockTok. It seems to be doing very well. Besides, River has been gushing about you guys for months now. She's been so excited to have you guys perform. I haven't heard the end of it." Ope, yup. There it is. That's why he couldn't stop smirking at me, letting me know he was up to something.

My entire body becomes a cooked tomato, heating my flesh with embarrassment. I give Booker the stink eye, and he chuckles, tapping the bar top a few times.

"The gig will pay. We'll give you twenty-five percent of our earnings that day. My advice would be to start letting everyone know where you'll be now. There are no tickets necessary and no charges. Unless they want to buy food, and that's where your money comes in. Most bands that come through have merchandise they sell: T-shirts, mugs, and EPs. But that's up to you, boys. If you have any other questions before the festival, River can fill you in." Shaking their hands one last time, Booker smirks when he walks by me. "They're better than the last one. All of them, though?"

"Jesus fuck," I mutter, meeting his stare. "What the hell did you guys discuss in the two friggin minutes I was gone?" I hiss through clenched teeth.

"Enough," he mutters with a fake shiver of disgust. "Now, you'll be in charge of their appearance on our stage. I'll handle the food and the booze. Come October tenth, they're your complete responsibility. It'll give you a little taste of what band management is like." He smirks, patting me on the shoulder before walking away toward his office with his hands in his pocket. He greets a few patrons here and there, shaking their hands, and finally disappears.

"So," Asher begins, tapping the bar. "Looks like we've got a lot to plan before that show."

For the rest of the evening, and every night after for the next three weeks—they come to the bar and plan out their set lists, hyping the future performance. Throughout the nights, they drink, eat, plan, and—my favorite—send Van the stink eye.

If I thought Van had gotten the message before, I shouldn't have. Every night he sits in the same booth with a different friend, drinking while keeping an eye on me. And every night, the boys escort me out, drive me home, and Callum or Rad—or both—stay with me. Somehow, they feel the anxiety crawling under my skin and soothe me by never leaving my side. I'm still a strong, independent woman, and I happen to have four very protective bodyguards. The more I get used to their barbaric ways, the more my walls come down.

"HOLY SHIT! I CAN'T BELIEVE THREE-HUNDRED AND SIXTY-THOUSAND people like us enough to follow us," Rad gapes, marveling at his phone from my right.

Swiping up, he clicks through all the stitched and duetted videos of their performances. A pang of jealousy hits me square in the chest as these beautiful women grace the screen with their reactions, going on and on about how charming the guys are and what they want to do with them.

I cringe. God, they're gorgeous girls. What will happen when Whispered Words are famous? And I'm me? Shit. I can't think like that. They're mine for now—in the present. But who knows what the future holds?

"FlashGram, too," I say, tapping the screen a few times until it pops up. "It's almost the same amount. You guys need more pics," I murmur, scrolling through the hot action takes I took over the weekend at Dead End. Nothing beats standing on the bar and snapping pictures as they perform. It gives me the best height advantage and the best snapshots.

"Jesus," Callum murmurs from my left, wrapping his arm around my shoulders and tucking my head under his chin. Shivers roll through me from the proximity of our bodies. Day after day, Callum gets increasingly comfortable in my presence, always finding ways to hold my hand or touch my body. One day, I'll corrupt this boy into doing the one thing I know he wants. "I can't believe it," he says in awe, with his eyes glued to the screen.

"Well, believe it," Asher says with a cocky grin, startling us from our huddle. "Whispered Words is taking over the damn world one stage at a time." Asher tips his head back, admiring the back of the main stage we're nestled behind, concealing us from the growing crowd beyond. The largest grin I've ever seen slithers across his lips. And this time, it's not so damn scary.

Joy lights up his face, chasing away the massive amounts of shadows plaguing him. I don't know what Asher's home life is like, but every time he holds his guitar and strums the strings, he's a different man—a lighter man. Music seems to have the same calming effect on Asher as it does me, and it draws me in.

"And it's all because of you, River Blue," Kieran says, stalking toward me with predatory intent. Warm hands grip my cheeks, tearing me from Rad and Callum's grip as his lips graze mine, entirely devouring me in a matter of minutes.

Jesus. I'm panting by the time he lets me come up for air. Oh, and soaked, too. I swear my shorts are sticking to my damn vagina. But maybe that was his plan. By the look crossing his smug as fuck face, I'd say he did what he set out to do—claim me and make me horny.

"I didn't do much," I breathlessly say, panting to regain my breaths against his lips, melting into his grip.

"Don't sell yourself short, Little Brat. You're the reason we have videos on ClockTok. The only reason we were able to record our EP last week. Our downloads on The Dot are through the damn roof. And now, here we are," he says, spreading his arms out, aiming his chest toward the large stage looming before us.

"Let's start unloading," Kieran says, nodding his head toward the Tahoe parked a few feet away and dropping his hold on me.

I wrinkle my nose, ten seconds away from asking him to unload in me instead. With a few choice words inside my head, and a lengthy lecture from myself, I think better of it. They have so much to do before their performance in two hours. And Asher would throw a fit. I'm going to Rad and Callum's after the show, anyway. Speaking of...

ME

Ma. You doing good?

MOTHER

Just peachy, kiddo. Korrine brought me a nice dinner. I'm feeling a lot better.

ME

Glad to hear! I probably won't be home tonight. The bar is closed, but I have lots of work to do at the Celebration.

MOTHER

I figured. You've been a busy girl lately. Keep up the good work. Don't worry about me.

I snort. Right. Don't worry about her. That's all I do. If it wasn't for the nurse and Korrine sharing the responsibility of caring for her, I'd be drowning in it all.

Looking back, I take in the boys who have clawed their way into my heart as they huddle around the Tahoe and slowly unload their gear.

Thankfully, the street festival workers let us drive it back here and back it up to the stage. Or we'd have had to walk a mile through the enormous crowds and back for more. Asher and Kieran pop the doors on the Tahoe and begin unloading it.

A blush takes over my cheeks, and I look away, focusing on the flapping curtain dangling backstage. In two hours, Whispered Words will put on the show of a lifetime for a roaring crowd of eager fans who came from across the country to see them. Since their ClockTok fame, their fan base has grown exponentially.

My heart skips a beat, anticipation shooting through me. Every time I see them perform; it never ceases to amaze me. Their music. Them. It all clicks in my soul like this entire thing we're doing is meant to be, and fate brought us together like this.

Over the past three weeks, their social media presence has blown through the damn roof. Like an elevator exploding through the ceiling and flying into space, type of boom. The boys have recorded their EP at the school, uploaded their music to The Dot, and successfully invested in merch. All in a short period. It's like all they needed was for me to light a fire under their ass and get them going with these goals. My chest puffs with pride watching my little worker bees make their dreams come true. I'd say I'm a proud mama, but that would be awkward. I'm the proud woman, standing on the sidelines, watching as their empire grows with every song they sing.

"Jesus, it's hotter than Satan's asshole out here," Rad gripes, tugging at the collar of his new shirt. I'm sure he can't wait to tear it off. "I'm sweating like a whore in church," he whines more, puffing out his bottom lip like a damn child.

"You are a whore in church," I mutter playfully. "But the shirts, huh?" I ask with a grin, slapping his hand away and plucking his lip.

He groans, catching my wrist. "Yeah. They're cool, Pretty Girl. All fancy with our band name on it, but I'm so restricted." Rad leans in closer to my ear. "It feels like a damn lake in my pants. My balls are so sweaty, babe," he pouts, begging me with his eyes to give him permission to strip them off and air out his dangly bits.

"Keep your pants on, Cowboy. You can't scare away the crowd. You can air those out later tonight, in private," I say, smoothing out his shirt that sticks to his skin. His lips pop open in retort, but he's cut off.

"The sun will set soon, and it'll cool down when it does," Asher grunts, rolling his amp down the ramp attached to the back of Kieran's SUV. "Please keep your dick in your pants." He scowls in Rad's direction. "We're in public," he mutters the last part with a headshake. "And there might be children present. The last thing you need is a trip to jail."

Rad recoils at the thought of jail but continues his rant anyway. "But it's hot now. Can't I strip?" Rad whines, pulling at the ends of his shirt, attempting to take it off.

"You heard Evil Ash. There's definitely a no stripping rule on stage," I say, fixing his shirt and earning a scoff. "But I do have an idea."

Rad's eyes widen when I whip out my knife and flick it open, exposing the sharp blade gleaming in the sun.

"Pretty Girl," he says with apprehension. "I might be into a little stabby-stabby in the sack, but uh…" he trails off when I pull the sleeves away from his skin and yelps when the blade tears through the fabric, eliminating the sleeve. I swear his body sags in relief when the slight breeze blows through, cooling him off. "Ah, finally. Fuck. I think I love you, Pretty Girl. Will you marry me?" he asks breathlessly as I do the other sleeve and even cut down the sides to expose his ribs.

"Evil Ash?" Asher huffs, amusement pulling the edge of his lips. "We'll discuss that later." I roll my eyes at his attempt to discipline me.

We definitely won't be discussing that later. What is he going to do? Spank me? Bend me over his knee and tell me I've been a bad River? I shiver. Okay, so it doesn't sound like a bad idea to me. He seems like the— take control in the bedroom—type. I'm down for that only if he's ready to take on a brat.

Over the last three weeks, Asher and I have grown a little closer. We aren't besties by any means, and sometimes I want to smash his skull in the doorway, but we're getting there. Just recently, we've gotten into this push-and-pull sort of relationship mixed with heavy amounts of sexual tension. One day, Asher will blow his lid and take me like I know he wants to. So, I'll keep pressing his buttons and getting on his last nerve.

"Fine." Rad frowns, looking up at the back of the stage, losing his pout.

A closed, dark curtain cuts off the audience's view, separating us from the growing crowd beyond. Our stage is nestled in the back of Central Park, situated just past the large fountain, and facing a blocked-off street. Several businesses line the road, towering above us. People drunkenly walk the streets, free to roam without worrying about traffic. It's street festivals like this that I live for. The atmosphere, people, and smells of food—make it perfect.

People hoot and holler as they roam the blocked-off streets of the Celebration. Police barricades sit at the end of every downtown road, forcing traffic to avoid this area. Not like they'd get through the crowds or people, anyway.

The Central Fall Celebration started over fifty years ago. Street vendors who offer food, wood carvings, toys, and anything you can imagine line the streets. Bands play on five different stages, placed around a ten-block radius. It's practically a holiday for the people of Central City. A time to let loose, drink, eat, and socialize with everyone in their path. It's the only time both sides of the city come together and celebrate as one unit, bringing in the new season with a bang.

"Sounds like-like a lot of people are here already," Callum mumbles, hanging tight to his bass case with wide eyes, white-knuckling it. A large lump bobs in his throat when he swallows hard, frantically looking around.

"It's your fans. You go on in two hours, but everyone is already lining up at the front of the stage." I peek between the curtains. "Yup, there's already two or three rows of people."

Even Tessa and Sara sit front and center as usual with their tits pushed up to their chins and fake smiles on their faces. A gaggle of girls surrounds them, moving their arms excitedly around, anticipating the boys getting on stage. Great. Just who I want to deal with all night. The boys have already dismissed them repeatedly, and I'm not sure how they're not getting the hint. Maybe I need to jump one of the boys on stage and claim what's mine for them to get the message to fuck off.

Asher's grin grows when he stops beside me, peeking out. "Fucking hell," he mumbles in awe. "You got us somewhere, Little Brat." Color me shocked when he places a hand on my shoulder and squeezes. Dare I say he's happy and proud? "This is the best thing anyone's ever helped us accomplish."

Meeting his eyes, I offer him a soft smile and tap his hand resting on my shoulder.

Something odd happens inside my body when his praise hits my ears. I stand taller. My chin juts out, and my heart pounds with excitement. If Asher happens to call me good girl, I might drop to my damn knees and suck his soul from his dick.

"You almost sound proud of me, Evil Ash," I quip, swallowing the odd feeling bursting inside me. "Is Daddy proud?" I bat my eyelashes, poking the rigid bear.

Ash's eyes widen, and a little red tint takes over his cheeks as he sputters, collecting his breaths. His eyes slide to mine with a knowing look, most likely remembering the words he spoke a few weeks ago.

"For fuck's sake, Little Brat," he gasps, tightening his grip on my shoulder. "You remember what I said, right? What happens when you call me daddy?" he murmurs, inching his face close to mine.

Asher looms over me, bringing our bodies closer and closer together until my back hits a wood support, and he cages me in, examining my eyes. I don't know what he sees behind them, but he grins, exposing all his teeth.

"I am very fucking proud. Maybe you'll get a reward later," Asher murmurs, inching closer until his soft lips land on my cheek, awakening the butterflies in my stomach. "But stop calling me daddy," he says against my flesh, verbally pleading with me. "Or you won't like the consequences." Shivers roll through me when he pushes away and walks toward the SUV.

"Okay, Daddy," I taunt, watching as he halts his steps before making a mad dash away.

"You've gotta stop winding him up, River Blue. Especially before a performance," Kieran chuckles, wrapping a sweaty arm around my shoulders.

"Um, what's the fun in that?" I laugh, shrugging off his heavy arm. "You boys have two hours until the show. It gives you time for sound check and all that fun stuff."

"And you?" Callum asks in a small voice, making his way onto the back of the stage with his bass. Standing high above me, he tilts his head and examines me. "You're staying, right-right?" Big puppy dog eyes greet me when I look up at him, drenched in the shadows of the stage.

Offering Callum a soft smile, I nod. "Of course. I'll be out there setting this up. Let's see how much your fans love you," I say, picking up a box full of shirts.

He grunts, setting down his bass, and jumps off the stage. Landing with a soft thud, he yanks the box from my hand. As we walk from behind the stage, we finally catch a glimpse of the full view of the crowd lining up to see them.

"That has-has to be the biggest crowd we'll ever play for." Callum shudders, placing the box on a table set up to the right of the stage. He swallows hard, surveying the crowd with awe, and reaches for my hand, squeezing tight.

"You'll do amazing," I whisper, squeezing his hand back.

His cheeks darken at my compliment, and he nods. "Thanks, River," he murmurs, kissing my cheek.

"No problem. Now, go get ready. You have a raging crowd of four hundred people to impress. And hopefully, sell lots of merch," I say, nodding toward the box full of their new merchandise.

I shoo Callum away with a grin, watching his retreating form. He only looks back once, reddening at the sight of me, and offers me a little wave.

So, as the boys do their thing backstage, getting their equipment set up, I do my thing at their new merch table, setting everything up.

After planning a design and chatting with the printer, we got shirts, pins, and postcards with their band name for a reasonable price. Everything's coming together for them in the past three weeks since they sat down and got to business. It's the first time I've seen them hunker down and put effort into their future as a band. Sure, they've played at a few venues but never invested in themselves.

Scooting the long plastic table next to the stage, I set out their merch. A few people meander over, looking over the shirts, and buy a few before the boys go on stage, explaining they can't wait to see the show. As two hours tick by, I hear the boys' hushed conversation behind the curtain protecting them from view. If I leaned back far enough, I'd have a clear shot of them murmuring in each other's ears and braiding their hair.

"Telling secrets?" I quip, pulling a piece of the curtain back to reveal the boys standing in a circle. I lean my elbows on the stage that comes up to my chest and raise a brow.

"You're nosy," Asher deadpans, grabbing the curtain from my hand.

"Back to your table, Little Brat." I snort when he pulls the curtain closed, blocking my view of them.

"Secrets don't make friends!" I shout, taking a few steps back to my table and plopping down on the lawn chair I thankfully remembered to pack.

My eyes roam the ever-growing crowd, mesmerized by the mass of people forming around our small area. Every year we invite popular bands to this stage, and every year they draw sizeable crowds. But nothing like this. This crowd is massive, swaying together in anticipation.

As my eyes look over the rest of the crowd, I groan at the sight of my high school enemies. Fuck. A few girls around Tessa and Sara stare in my direction with narrowed eyes before leaning in to whisper to one another. God, it's like we're back in high school. Hello, bitches—we're adults now.

Each and every one of those girls was a dick to everyone else, especially me. Their fucking plaything for two years. And now, it seems I'm their target—once again. Yippee. Little do they know; I won't roll over and be a good puppy anymore. I have more bite than bark. The sooner they realize that the better. Because if they keep coming after me, I'm going to rip their annoying faces off.

The curtain behind me draws again, revealing a smiling Rad, glowing with pre-concert jitters. I swear he's the damn sun beaming down, and I'm the little planet, soaking it in. Crooking a finger, he pulls me toward the stage with one finger flick. I raise a brow, leaning against the wooden structure, staring into the abyss of his dark eyes that twinkle in the dwindling sunlight.

"Pretty Girl. I've got a new shirt for you," Rad says, trying and failing to hold back his grin while holding up a dark shirt that says: Property of Whispered Words.

I blink rapidly, taking in the meaning of the words scrawled across the black shirt waving in the warm breeze. Once it settles in, I narrow my eyes at the possessive fools standing above me on stage.

"Really? You want me to wear a shirt like that?" I raise a brow when Rad looks at the crowd mixed with women and men. Without hesitation, he nods with enthusiasm—or maybe it's possession hiding behind his intentions.

"Uh, huh. Yup! Now, put it on," Rad demands, holding it in front of my face with expectation. "Put it on, beautiful! I want to see our band name stamped over your pretty titties for the entire world."

"It's to keep the other vultures away," Asher says with a noncommittal shrug. "They'll know who you belong to."

"Wear it to work, too," Kieran adds, placing his guitar strap over his shoulders and settling it across his body. His fingers tweak the strings a few times, tuning it by ear.

"Then everyone will know not to talk to you," Rad adds, freeing his grin.

"No talking to other boys," Kieran barks with possession, curling his lip back, and eyeing all the people wandering the streets with drinks in their hands. Slowly, his eyes move over the crowd.

I blink. "Excuse me? Did I hear what I think I heard?" I huff, putting my hands on my hips. There's no way in hell they can tell me who I can and cannot talk to. No fucking way.

"He's right, Pretty Girl—no more boys. There are four of us. How many more dicks do you need? None. That's the answer," Rad says, shaking his head. "Don't let them look at you. Here, put this damn thing on." Rad grunts, forcing the Whispered Words shirt over my head, no matter how hard I struggle against him. Kieran chips in, jumping down from the stage after setting his guitar down, forcing my arms through the sleeves, and chuckles when I curse at them, threatening their lives.

"What the fuck, Rad?" I hiss, pushing him away as he cackles, falling onto his ass. Placing his hands on his knees, he grins more, eyeing the words across my tits.

"Perfect. Property of... It has a nice ring to it, doesn't it, K?" Pride puffs Rad's chest out, and he grins with satisfaction.

Kieran tilts his head when I cross my arms, giving him my meanest scowl. "Yup. Property of Whispered Words. Find a marker, and we'll print our names on her tits. Then no one will talk to her," he grunts, looking out at the crowd again from behind me.

"If you bring a marker anywhere near this, I'll bite off your fingers," I growl, poking Kieran in his chest. "Don't you have shit to do?" I point toward the stage, shooing them again with my hands.

"Be a good girl," Kieran whispers in my ear and kisses my cheek, letting the warmth of his lips linger for longer than necessary.

"Always am," I murmur through a chill spreading down my body, creating goosebumps. I swear, when his lips touch my skin, my resolve drains down the toilet.

"We'll see," he says, swiping his thumb lovingly across my cheek. Affection lights up his eyes, and a soft smile pulls at his lips.

"Let's go, Lover Boy!" Asher barks, waving his hand.

Kieran nods, hopping back onto the stage and grabbing his gear. Together they stand like a wall, taking deep, soothing breaths.

"Whispered Words! Whispered Words!" The crowd chants over and over with excitement, holding their brightly lit phones in the air like lighters.

"You hear that, boys?" I shout over the crowd, leaning my elbows on the tall stage. "They're calling for you!"

I grin when the curtain swings open, and they wave to the crowd with bright smiles—swaggering further on stage, oozing confidence from every inch. They captivate the crowd, drawing them in with their grins and waves.

"Kiss for luck, Pretty Girl?" Rad says, flopping to his belly on stage. Leaning close, he takes my mouth with his, dirtily shoving his tongue in and out. I moan when his hands roam through my hair, pulling me closer.

At this point, he could pull me on stage and fuck me in front of the crowd right now, and I'd say yes, please. It'd definitely show those bitches who they belonged to. The thrill of their eyes on me sends shivers up my spine, and my pussy clenches, ready to take it further. That is, until a certain asshole lightly kicks Rad in the ribs and clears his throat.

"Come on, bro. You're humping the damn stage. Save it for later," Asher grumbles with a shake of his head.

"After this, I'm going to fuck you, and you're going to take it," Rad pants, raising his brow until I nod. "Good girl." I shiver when he says those words and watch in awe when he wanders away, setting himself behind his drums set with a relaxed grin.

Asher watches me from his side of the stage, staring with interest at my heaving chest and flushed face.

"Are you ready for the carnival after this, Little Brat?" he asks, looking off in the distance at the enormous Ferris wheel lighting up the now dark-ened sky with its red, blues, and yellows.

"The carnival?" I gaze over at the carnival rides in full swing.

Asher smirks, tilting his head at me. "Oh, yes. The carnival. We'll let loose after this. Besides, I have plans for you," he rasps, eyeing me up and down.

"Plans? Wait! What plans?" I blanch, hoping he has time to elaborate or fucking tell me something. Instead, he grins, moving a few feet forward, giving me his back. Strumming a loud tune over the speakers as he tunes his guitar, drowning out my shouts.

The crowd cheers when Kieran smiles at them from the microphone and then, turning, winks at me like a cocky bastard.

"Hello, Central City!" Kieran's raspy voice bellows through the speak-ers, echoing through what seems like the entire town.

The crowd reacts immediately, jumping in place and cheering as loud as they can. A smile forms on my lips when he grins at the sea of people looking up at him like he's a God. Shit. I'm probably looking at him the same way.

"We love you, Kieran!" Tessa and Sara shout, holding up a poster with all their names and hearts surrounding them.

I roll my eyes as they jump up and down, jiggling their tits in an effort to get Kieran's attention and call his name with a girly shriek. Thank God they're keeping those puppies under wraps. They could poke someone's eyes out.

A weird pinch of jealousy roars through me when he looks at them.

Fucking looks at them and grins when he reads the poster, giving them the thumbs up. That's my thumb. Keep it to yourself, assface. Narrowing my eyes, I glue my gaze to his and thankfully; the assface doesn't drop his eyes to their pointy tits, still freeballing in the night air.

"Put away your goddamn titties!" I shout, cupping my hands over my lips to amplify my voice.

Ignoring my demand, they continue to swoon and scream more, inciting weird feelings brewing in the depths of my green monster. I want to rip their hair out and knock their perfect teeth in with one punch and laugh as they scatter on the ground. My fists curl, envisioning tying them to a pole deep in the woods, slathering them in honey, and watching as bears rip them to shreds as they beg for their lives. Try clutching your pearls with no fingers, toes, or body. Fuck.

Jesus. Deep breaths, River. You damn psycho. Stop plotting their deaths and focus on the music, for shit's sake. Music is what you live and breathe. Not violence against two stuck-up Lakeview girls who don't have a chance with the boys rocking out on stage.

My mouth pops open, watching Kieran work the tiny stage with grace and familiarity. Walking back and forth with a goofy grin, he lays down the first note, inciting the crowd more. They yell and scream, the louder the music gets until all the boys join in and open with their first song. I watch them with matched possession. The thought of other girls touching them makes me stabby. I grip my knife, toying with the handle in my shorts pocket, running my thumb over the words printed across it—River Blue. Touch them and die might be my new mantra.

I rub my temple. What the hell am I thinking?

Peeking down at the shirt stretching over my tits, I scoff. Fuck. I'm in this constant war with myself, my mind going to battle with itself repeatedly. Letting go of my reservations is more complicated than I ever thought. Visions of Van and what his stupid ass did to me burn bright. A constant reminder of what could happen if this goes to shit. But taking a deep breath, I shake it off. This is now. I'm having fun. I'm falling hard. And in the end, if I get fucked over. It'll be my fault. For now, I'm along for the ride. I have to keep telling myself that the further they drag me into their wicked web.

The music blares through the speakers again, garnering more attention from the late-night crowd enjoying the festival. Person after person loiters with beers in their hands and smiles on their faces, momentarily stopping to catch the free show. Their heads bob, and their swaying bodies move with the tune echoing through the night air. Every hand shoots in the air for what seems like miles, waving around with pure joy. For one singular moment, we live in musical harmony.

Kieran's raspy voice blasts through the microphone again and straight through my damn soul, lifting me to a higher plane. Music always calms the storm brewing in my mind and eases my pain. Music erases everything on my plate and sets me free. It sounds silly. But music has always been my escape from the life I've lived.

"Ahem, bitch," a very unpleasant voice says, knocking me out of my reprieve.

Fuck my life. Is this how Tessa greets everyone, or is this just reserved for me? Probably just for me. Seeing as she looks down her nose at me for the millionth time.

I plaster on a fake smile and shove my tits out. Let's see how much she likes my personalized Whispered Words shirt.

"How can I help you?" My sugary sweet voice gives me cavities. I'd slam her face into this table a few times if it were up to me. Maybe knock some sense into her stupid skull. They don't want you. I am theirs.

She scans my shirt, narrowing her eyes. "We want some shirts," she says, pointing to mine. "Something like that."

I grin more, widening my arms to the shirts folded on the table in front of me. "Sorry, this is an exclusive shirt for their girlfriend." I freeze, dropping my arms. I probably looked as shocked as her pinched face.

Heat envelops my neck, creeping onto my face. I wholeheartedly blame my damn jealousy for my decisions. That bitch is going to get me into trouble. But damn, the look on Tessa's face is worth the fallout. Whatever. I'll roll with it. Yeah, their girlfriend. All four of them belong to me. If they're going to put their claim on me, then I'll return the favor. Maybe I can stamp my name on their dicks.

"You're joking, right?" She throws her head back and laughs in my face. "Like they'd ever choose a piece of Central trash like you. You've got to be kidding me." She slaps Sara on the shoulder in laughter, and her friend joins in, screeching along and ruining the damn music.

I blow out a breath and cross my arms, deciding not to push it. "These are your only options. Not this. This is mine, and so are they."

Welp. So much for dropping it. It looks like I'm officially about to throw my hat into the ring. Only I'll win, not them. I'm always up for crushing my competition. I'm competitive like that.

"You've got to be joking," Tessa snarls, pounding a fist on the table. "Not you," she scoffs, looking me up and down.

Leaning forward, I get right in her face with a bright, knowing grin. She doesn't know I hang around them every day. Or that they're my stalkers, watching my every move. They join me at work—both places. Play at my bar and drink my drinks while laughing with me. I said Tessa was my competition before, but the reality is, she's nothing. I've already crossed the finish line and won while she's in last place, slowly jogging toward the yellow tape. She doesn't know it yet.

"Does this face look like it's joking?" I grin cockily, tilting my head. Sometimes antagonizing the girl who made high school hell is fun. "Back off, Tessa. Buy a shirt or don't. But you're holding up the line." I gesture to the four people behind her, sending her scathing looks for taking so much damn time.

"Just two shirts, smalls," Sara says in a hurry, placating her fuming friend.

I nod and hand them two black shirts with the Whispered Words printed across the chest.

"That'll be fifty," I say, putting them into a black bag and setting it on the table.

Sara grumbles about the price, digging through her purse. Tessa snatches the bag with a haughty attitude and growls at me, exposing her teeth. Down, girl. I'll put you in the pound.

"Let them have their fun with your diseased ass. But they'll come running back to us, and I can guarantee that," Tessa hisses, stomping away with her friend in tow.

"Sure," I mumble sarcastically, helping the other customers with their purchase and the next after that.

The show continues for another thirty minutes without any incidents. When the line for merch lulls, I grab my phone, record their performance, and take several stills for their FlashGram. There's nothing more intoxicating than a sweaty rock star holding their gear on stage, rocking out to the beautiful music they created.

"This last song goes out to a very special girl," Kieran says, side-eyeing me from the side of the stage with a knowing grin. "We have a new song for you all! It's called: The Roaring River."

When the new tune comes through the speakers, I sputter, choking on my spit, and he growls my name into the microphone. Finally, after a solid minute of choking on my tongue, I catch my breath and record the song's chorus. Every word makes my cheeks heat, and butterflies blossom in my stomach. When I peer over at Tessa, her lips set into a straight line, and she frowns in my direction.

"I won," I mouth to her and then flip her off for good measure.

Take that. You mean girl.

As the music dies, the boys wave their goodbyes at the edge of the stage. Large, beaming grins adorn their faces when the crowd goes nuts, cheering them on with hoots and hollers. Watching from the sidelines, I smile as they jump up and down with their hands in the air. Their music hums through my veins long after the last note. My fingers tap along my bare leg as the beat pounds in my head, never forgotten. Their lyrics will hide in my mind for years to come, even if they fizzle out—highly doubtful at this point. In my mind, we're already in California, celebrating the win of the Battle of the Bands. Whispered Words isn't meant for the small stage. They're meant for the entire world to hear.

"We want more! We want more! We want more!" the crowd chants, pumping their fists in the air.

Kieran's gaze finds mine immediately. With a nod, he grins more and turns back to the crowd.

"One more!" His voice reverberates through the screaming crowd as they jump for joy.

Standing back, I dig my phone out of my pocket and hold it up for the last time tonight. Kieran gives me the thumbs up, belting out the first line of their encore song. This time when I press record, I test out the live function on ClockTok, hoping to give their other fans a fiery treat of sweaty man meat performing on stage. And boy, their comments don't disappoint.

So, fucking hot!

I want to lick the sweat from his nipple!

That one makes me snort and shake my head. No one's licking that man's or any of these men's nipples—but me.

Wow! They sound so good! They aren't signed?

Holy shit, when can I see them in concert? Are you guys coming to Texas?

Come overseas!

Kieran girl for life!

I'd give my left tit for Rad!

Me too, sister. Me too.

Asher looks hot!

Callum's so cute!

Flashes of their future fame fly through my mind in rapid succession. I realize then Whispered Words would be famous enough one day to have gaggles of girls following their every move, hoping for a piece of their pie if I left for California and stayed with them. Is this what it will be like? Will I have to swim through an ocean of horny women begging for a piece of what's mine? Fuck. Why are my thoughts suddenly coming to this futuristic planning of bashing in groupies' faces? *Focus on the present, River! And stay in it.*

"All right, Central City!" Kieran's breathless voice booms through the speakers, quieting down the rambunctious crowd, growing drunker and drunker by the minute. "You guys have been great! Thanks for having us! Check-in with us on FlashGram and ClockTok to stay updated on our performances. We'll see you at Dead End on Halloween. Details are on our sites." He grins, placing the mic back on its stand, waving one last time as I turn off the recording.

Rad doesn't waste a minute rushing off stage, whipping his shirt off with an excited whoop. His bare chest glistens with sweat, reflecting off the dull streetlights. It drips down his beautiful abs, forcing my eyes to watch the descent, momentarily stunned by the sight. Shit. They have to stop pulling me in with their bodies, music, and souls. Or I'm a damned goner, for sure. I can keep telling myself over and over that this isn't going anywhere, that this is in the present. But the more I think about it, the more the future calls. Is it so wrong to want to spend years with them instead of months?

"Pretty Girl!" he shouts, charging toward me at full speed with mischief glistening in his eyes.

I grunt when he slams into me, knocking me off my feet. He chuckles when he lifts me into his arms, and his fingertips dig into my ass cheeks until my legs wrap around his waist and my arms around his neck.

"Oh my God, you're so sweaty!" I shriek through laughter, beating a hand into his bare shoulders with fake disgust. I swear every inch of my shirt soaks with his sweat and sticks to my flesh. "Gross!" I shriek when he spins me in circles, roaring with laughter.

Like a child free of worry, he throws his head back, looking up at the sky while clinging to me. These simple moments of pure ecstasy pull me in and keep me in their grasp. When I'm with them—all of them—I'm not River West, the overworked bar manager. I'm just River West—theirs. Carefree from the music infecting my soul, I join him, letting my head fall back and howl at the damn moon.

The full moon shines down on us like a spotlight, aided by the sparkling stars twinkling above in the cloudless sky. A cool breeze blows through my clothes, soothing the nasty sweat from my skin.

"Did we blow your panties off?" Rad rasps, leaning in until his nose touches mine when he stops spinning. "Did we rock that shit hard? Cuz, I think we did."

His hardened dick presses into my center to prove his point, swiveling around my already-damp panties. The faint memory of his promise an hour before shines like a neon sign in the forefront of my mind. I grind against him, forcing a gasp from his lips, slowly turning into a soft moan.

I grin, rubbing my nose against his, and let everything go. Our lips graze on a soft kiss, and I hum, gliding my tongue along his sealed lips until he lets me in again. I throw caution to the wind, give in to the nagging feeling slowly taking over, and take what I want. I want him again. Over and over. I want him to lay me down and fuck me behind the curtain where anyone can hear my moans but never get a peek.

"Yes. You rocked it," I whisper against his lips, nibbling them.

"Good. Now we can go to the carnival," he insists, carrying me toward Kieran, Callum, and Asher, crowded backstage.

"The carnival?" I whisper. "Why not behind the stage?" Rad immediately stops, inspecting my eyes. "You could take me against the stage. I could…" Rad growls, shoving his long tongue down my throat again. I moan into his mouth until he pulls away, shaking his head with regret.

"I have an idea for that. You want to ride me? Let's ride some rides first." His eyes sparkle with some knowing look, and he grins, tucking my loose hair behind my ear.

"Don't keep me waiting for too long," I whisper, lust dripping from every word, practically moaning into his ear.

"Oh, I won't," he says, walking forward again with me in his arms. "Pretty Girl says we rocked her panties off!" Rad whoops, throwing a fist in the air.

"Of course we did," Asher says in his usual pompous tone, leaving no room for argument. "We were amazing." His chest puffs out, and his nose raises—cocky shit.

I snort. "Humble much?" Rad drops me to my feet but keeps an arm around my shoulders and me close. Fingers dive into my back pockets, roughly squeezing my ass.

Asher rolls his eyes, drying off his forehead with a white towel. "Always," he says with a tiny smirk, pulling at his lips, which drops the moment his eyes lock on the advancing figure, beelining it toward the boys.

"Oh, my God!" Tessa screeches from nowhere. Seriously, how does she keep finding us? Like, can't she go away?

I mentally groan at her screechy voice as she rounds the backstage area and lunges at Kieran. He grunts, reluctantly catching her when she latches on like the little leech she is. I could have sworn I told her I won. Hell, they even made a song about me and not her. Granted, it was called Roaring

River—so not sexy. But still. Get your pink press on nails out of my man's neck and get a move on to someone who wants you.

"What the hell?" he asks, pushing her away and keeping her at arm's length.

"You were so amazing!" she coos again, side-eyeing me with victory. I'm not sure what kind of victory she's feeling, but more power to her.

"Uh, thanks," he says, scratching the back of his neck and looking at me for help.

"I even bought your shirt!" she shrieks again with a grin.

Where the fuck is her handler? Paging annoying Sara, come collect your friend before I pummel her face with my fist. Repeatedly. No one will recognize her when I'm done rearranging her features.

"Pretty Girl," Rad whispers breathily, running his lips up my jawline. "If you beat her ass, I'll pound your ass so hard you'll forget your name. Whattya say?" My breaths quicken when he sucks my earlobe between his teeth, and a soft moan falls from my throat. Well then, in that case. It's time for an ass beating so I can get my ass pounding.

"That's it!" I say, pushing forward and away from his horny ass. "Scoot. You're making the band uncomfortable." I wave a hand, stepping between Kieran and Tessa with force.

"Um, maybe you're the one making them uncomfortable, bitch. They happen to like me," Tessa scoffs at me, crossing her arms with a haughty look.

"Are you sure about that?" Asher asks in a sharp tone. If it were a whip, he'd have left a mark.

Her mouth drops open in defeat, looking at each of the guys for confirmation.

"Tess, you're a nice girl. We had our fun, remember?" My stomach drops when Kieran says that, and my face falls. They fucked before? Why does that make my green-eyed monster growl even more?

"It was fun," she says, batting her eyelashes. "But I was hoping for a little more. I'm throwing a party tonight at my apartment. All the party favors will be available. You know, for old time's sake," she giggles.

I narrow my eyes at Kieran, who scoffs.

"We've got plans, but thanks," Kieran says, pulling my back to his front. "And it doesn't include you."

Hurt glistens in Tessa's eyes, and she gives a pitiful nod. "I'll see you around then. But if you ever get tired of the trash, come to the queen," she snarls, tossing her hair over her shoulder, and giving me one last scathing look.

Who's the trash here? Because it's definitely not me. I'm the mother fucking queen, and it's about damn time someone knocked her off her high horse. I volunteer as the damn tribute because this bitch is two seconds away from meeting the special piece in my pocket.

"No. You won't see them around. Take your stuck-up ass and scoot. I won, remember? And if I ever catch you sniffing around like the desperate poodle you are, I will cut you. They. Are. Mine." I don't know what happens, but something possessive takes over my tongue, and I'm just a passenger on this crazy train ride called: stamping my name on their asses.

By the time her stunned face recovers from my verbal lashing, she's huffing and puffing like she might blow my house away. *Down, big bad bitchy wolf. There's nothing here for you.*

"You heard her," Asher reaffirms with a growl, stepping between us. "Go home." With a flick of his wrist, Tessa stumbles with a crestfallen face and tears in her pitiful eyes.

When Tessa disappears into the shadows, a boohooing mess, Asher turns to me with a grin exploding across his lips. The boys exchange a suspicious look, and with one nod, suddenly the walls close, and four bodies press on either side of me, creating a circle around me. I'm at the center of their attention and panting with need.

"It's about damn time you know your place," Kieran says, moving my hair over my shoulder. "You're the fucking queen of Whispered Words, understand? And next time, knock her teeth loose," he chuckles, kissing the side of my lips.

Callum's face blooms red, and he shyly takes my hand, squeezing our fingers together. "You're-you're the queen, Little Star." His eyes drop to the pavement, fluttering, his long lashes fanning his cheek.

"Now, let's pack up our shit, and then let's go take a ride," Asher smirks knowingly, cocking his head. "You'd like a ride or four, right, Little Brat?"

Heat envelops every inch of my body when he licks his lips and nods in the carnival's direction to our right. Laughs and screams come from the area. The hairs on the back of my neck stand on end when I try to wrap my brain around what he's saying.

"Um, this isn't exactly the kind of ride I expected," I say, looking out through the large cage of the Ferris wheel resting high in the sky above the town.

The cage encompasses the whole cabin, enclosing all of us in the six-seater ride. Usually, I'd enjoy the carnival rides, but the first thing Rad insisted on was this Ferris wheel. It soars above the city, boasting an enormous height, claiming to ride higher than normal carnival Ferris wheels. Lights flicker in the distance from the towns around us when we finally reach the top. The other carnival-goers' distant sounds echo through the metal cage coming from below. From here, they're tiny ants marching along the darkened ground and barely visible from here.

Abruptly, we stop at the tippy top, leaving us with a breathtaking view of our broken city. I see the darkened outlines of houses, tall businesses, and the tops of trees for miles. The cool October wind whips through the cage, blowing my long strands as I sit nestled between Kieran and Callum on a bench-like seat.

"You're-you're shivering," Callum murmurs, pulling me into him. His fingers run up and down my arms, alleviating the goosebumps spreading across my flesh.

"I have an idea," Asher says with a smirk, taking me in snuggling up to Callum.

I raise my brow. "Oh, yeah? Like maybe getting off this ride?" I quip, and he grins more, shrugging.

"Or you could be a good little brat and strip every piece of clothing off your body and then hand them over." As he delivers the words, the phrase *the woman was too stunned to speak* bounces around inside my head.

As I stare into the hazel-eyed devil's eyes, my entire body locks up, pressed between Callum and Kieran. That familiar tug in my gut heats at the mere look he sends my way. Adding insult to injury, he drags his tongue along his bottom lip, wetting it, so it's glistening under the Ferris wheel lights. And I melt. I fucking melt under his scrutiny, and that's just bullshit. He gave me a simple demand, and here I am, lusting over one little tongue flick.

More vicious shivers run through me, despite not feeling an ounce of cold. Because, yeah—it's not because of that. Every inch of my body heats, and I swear my heartbeat plays a symphony in my ears. Just from Asher's words. Fuck. Me. I'm sick, and the only ailment to relieve my sickness is the four dicks searing me with expectation.

So, I play dumb.

"What?" I barely comprehended the demand he gave me. Blinking, my lips pop open when he does that sexy guy thing and leans his elbows on his widely spread knees. His thumb caresses his pointed chin, and he smirks again, watching my reactions like a hawk. Asher Montgomery knows precisely what he's doing when he leans forward, cocking a brow.

"You heard me, Little Brat. There's a reason we're stopped at the top of the world. Now, strip," he demands again, roaming his hungry eyes all over my body, taking in my heaving chest and trembling fingers.

"Why… Why should I listen to you?" I ask breathlessly, shaking my head.

There's no way in hell I *should* listen to a word he says. Sure, he's calmed his Assface ways down these past three weeks since we started planning. Dare I say he's been cordial? But he's still Asher Montgomery—

assface extraordinaire—Evil Ash—the boogeyman in my closet, taunting me with his devilish, warm hazel eyes, lighting me up from the inside out.

Fire ignites everywhere when he looks me up and down, his want desperately showing to the world. My weak heart pounds against my ribs, echoing in my damn ears at that one simple look, begging me to defy his demands.

For him, I am a brat—his little brat, more specifically. Asher has this way about him that draws this need to rebel out of me without even trying. I can't help but fight the feelings brewing inside me, especially when he drives me fucking insane.

This push and pull between us has me on the edge of craving his demands. I want to fall to my knees and bend to his will. With resistance, of course. That's how our relationship has worked so far. He pushes. I pull. Somewhere along the way, we've gotten into this tension-filled relationship, and one of us is about to crack.

Asher cracks his knuckles and shrugs.

Rad grins, getting to his knees in the cramped space. "Fuck Asher. Take off your clothes for me—for them," he says, nodding to Callum and Kieran pressing in on either side of me.

Crawling in my direction on the hard metal floor, Rad finally stops right before me with desire dilating his pupils, making them as dark as shadows. My breath halts in my damn chest when his warm hands spread my legs open. Soft fingers inch up my exposed thighs, drawing circles against my flesh.

"You can't be serious. We're on the Ferris wheel. There are other people," I gasp when the palm of his hand grinds against my teased center, still excited from all the stolen moments before and after the show.

Despite the growing desire flaming to life in my abdomen at the potential eyes watching us, I still have reservations about dropping my pants in public. Anyone could see what we're about to do.

"Did you see other people?" Asher lazily asks, leaning back on the bench opposite us with his legs still spread apart.

I frown, looking below at the empty carts rattling in the wind with no people in sight on the ride. The only voices for miles away are the people walking below, oblivious to what's about to happen. If I let it, that is.

"Um, well—no," I stammer, shaking my head. "There's no way." I throw my head back when Rad's fingers dive into my pussy unexpectedly from the sides of my shorts and he pulls my panties to the side, completely exposing me to him.

"I knew you'd be wet for this, Pretty Girl," he whispers, licking up my thigh. His fingers mercilessly dive in and out of my pussy, scissoring when his fingers bottom out.

I cry out, reaching for Kieran's and Callum's hands and squeezing hard. "Holy fuck," I pant, arching my back and begging for more.

Everything ceases to exist at the moment when my eyes roll into the back of my head. Teetering on the edge of an orgasm, Rad pulls back completely, purposely leaving me a wet and needy mess.

"Ashton," I whisper his full name, making him moan.

"Take your damn clothes off, Little Brat," Asher barks in a voice dripping with desire. "There's no one else on this fucking ride. Rad slipped the guy fifty bucks to leave us up here for thirty minutes. So, what are you going to do to pass the time?" he growls, leaning his elbows on his knees.

His hazel eyes eat me alive when I stare him down. Even when I lift my shirts over my head and toss them to him, I keep eye contact.

"Lean forward," Kieran demands, undoing my bra and bringing it down my arms when I do so.

The cool metal of the ride bites into my skin when I lean back, gasping for air. My breasts rise and fall rapidly, begging for their lips to attach around my puckered nipples.

"Good girl," Ash purrs, studying my breasts in the pale moonlight mixed with the beautiful red and blues illuminated by the Ferris wheel, bouncing off my flesh.

"Now take off your shorts and hand your panties over," Asher demands, holding out a hand and curling his fingers. His jaw clenches when I don't immediately bend over and do as he asks.

"Make me," I grit my teeth, snarling in his direction. If he wants my damn panties, he can come take them off with his fucking teeth.

"Asher has officially entered the ring," Rad whispers with a grin, eyeing Asher as he falls to his knees in the confined space and crawls to me with determination.

Raising a brow, he silently questions me again with every slide in my direction. I sit firm. Our cart sways as he inches closer and closer, finally settling in front of me. His lip peels back when he leans closer, a breath away from my lips.

"Be a good little brat and take your panties off for me," he whispers with demand, wrapping his long fingers around my throat. My breath shudders when he takes control, tightening his hold around my throat and squeezing until my heartbeat pounds against his palm.

"Take them off, and I'll let them fuck you," he whispers an inch from my lips, teasing me with the tip of his tongue.

"Make. Me," I hiss in defiance, begging Asher to yank down my shorts and panties and hate fuck me into oblivion.

Having Asher Montgomery on his knees, staring lustful hate vehemently into my eyes, should scare the panties directly off me. Instead, empowerment fills me, and my courage grows. No matter what happens, he will work for this pussy after everything he's ever said to me.

"Oh, Pretty Girl. You're asking for it," Rad chuckles, drawing circles on my inner thigh.

"Take off her damn shorts and then her panties," Asher demands Rad, never taking his eyes off mine. He holds me with his stare, a cocky smirk pulling the edge of his lips.

"As you wish," Rad hums, not waiting for my approval.

When Rad works my shorts and panties down my legs, I don't fight him. Even when I'm bare for the world to see and the chilly breeze puckers my nipples, I don't swat him away as I should because I want this. I want to be at their mercy under Asher's intense stare. I want them to fuck me in this stupid metal cart high above the city with only the wind as our witness.

With a grin, Rad hands Asher my panties without hesitation.

"Look at me," Asher whispers, a breath away from my lips again.

Bringing my thong to his nose, he inhales deeply and shuts his eyes with a groan of approval. The noises he makes go straight to my dripping pussy, convulsing around nothing.

"You are wet for us, aren't you? Do you want them to fuck you, Little Brat? Do you want their cocks so deep inside you that you feel them for the next few days?" Asher whispers, loosening his grip on my throat.

Straightening my thong until the moist material glistens in the lights, Asher runs the length of his tongue along the fabric with a guttural groan, reveling in my arousal.

"Now," he rasps with dilated eyes. Undoing his pants, he settles himself on the bench across from us. "I want you to fuck them," he demands once again, bringing his massive dick out through the fly of his jeans. He moans, wrapping my panties around his aching cock, and slowly strokes himself. Never taking his eyes off me as he does. Up and down my panties go, gliding over his hardened dick.

"Do you do this often?" I rasp, looking between the four of them with wonder.

"What's that?" Kieran groans, sucking on my neck. His fingers roam, squeezing my tit and pinching my nipple.

"Sharing like this," I moan, leaning my head back and falling into the pleasurable sensations taking over my body.

Silence fills the caged car. Nothing but my heavy breaths fill the air. I peek an eye open, greeted by their heat-filled gazes when they look at one another and shake their heads.

"I'm not in the habit of sharing what's mine," Asher says with finality, a growl brewing in the back of his throat as he strokes himself with my panties again, picking up speed. "But for you? For them? It seems to be a packaged deal."

"Only twice before," Rad whispers, sucking my nipple into his mouth. "With you. Kieran and Callum. Those were the only times."

My breaths shudder again, and I loudly cry out. My voice echoes through the cage, and I'm sure if there were other people here, they'd know exactly what we were up to in this isolated cage—raised high in the sky with no soul in sight.

"Turn around," Rad says, twirling his finger. "Put your ass in the air and let me finally fuck my pussy raw." Possession seizes his voice, knocking it into a low growl.

I moan when I lean down, putting my elbows on the bench and my knees on the floor. Rad runs a finger down my spine and spreads my cheeks, blowing his warm breath down my crack. Digging his fingers into my hips, he lines himself up, dragging himself through my arousal dripping out of my cunt.

"You remember what I said before, right, Pretty Girl? There will never be a barrier between us ever again. There hasn't been for three weeks, and now is no exception," he rasps, collecting my hair into his fist, and pulling my back against his chest. "You're the only one I've gone raw with," he breathes into my neck. "The only one I want to feel pulsating around my bare cock."

"Yes," I moan my approval, giving a firm nod.

I cry out when he plows into me and stills, reveling in my clenching cunt. My orgasm sits on the cusp of bursting, aching for him to continue his thrusts and bring me to oblivion.

"Jesus," he rasps, breathing heavily into my neck. "Your pussy feels like a fucking vise around my cock. You're going to milk every damn ounce of my cum. You got that? I'm going to spill so hard," he moans, burying his face in my neck, pounding into me harder and harder until he slows again.

"Callum," Kieran calls to his stunned friend, rubbing his fingers along my chin. Drawing my eyes up to his, he gives me a soft smile.

"Yeah-yeah?" Callum rasps, squeezing his dick through his jeans with stiff movements. He stares at me in awe, watching my tits bounce when Rad picks up his pace again.

"Are you ready to take Callum's cock in your mouth, Pretty Girl?" Rad whispers in my ear, slowing his thrusts and stills again. He groans when I squeeze around him, giving him my answer.

"Do you want that?" I ask through heavy breaths, licking my lips.

Through my lashes, I gaze up at Callum with want, begging to feel his warmth slide down my throat and coat it. We've kissed, touched, and held hands, but he's never alluded to being ready for more. Hiding away, he usually sits on the sidelines in wait, stroking himself and watching with rapt attention as Rad or Kieran fuck me into oblivion. Only the one time he stepped up to the plate and came on my ass. Tonight, though, feels different from those occasions. I feel it in my bones tonight that Callum's ready to advance to the next base and take what he wants.

Callum's eyes widen, taking a heavy breath. "Only if you want to," he whispers, squeezing his dick again through his jeans and moaning at the simplest sensation.

My pussy flutters at the sound of his deep moan, and I lick my lips, eager for a taste.

"Oh, yeah. I definitely think she wants to," Rad strains, pulling my elbows off the bench.

"Scoot over, Callum," Asher barks out his desperate demand, lending Callum the extra push he needs. "Pull your dick out and get it wet in her mouth." Callum swallows hard, fumbling to get his dick out of his jeans. When he scoots over, he looks down at me with excitement, lust, and a hint of fear. "Good. Now, rub the tip along her lips. Ah," Asher grunts through his directions, breathing heavily and slowing his pace. Leaning back, Ash stops his strokes and stares at the ceiling with glazed-over eyes.

Licking my lips, I look up at Callum. "It's okay," I whisper. "I want to suck you off," I whisper, putting my hands on his knees, gently squeezing.

He shakes his head, a pink tint taking over his cheeks. "I've never…" He closes his eyes in shame and takes a deep breath. "When it happens, I'll remember it forever. I didn't want it to be just anyone," he whispers, trailing a shaky finger down my jaw and tracing over my popped-open lips. "But if I have to relive this moment over and over for the next one hundred years, I want it to be you."

A drum plays in my chest when he grabs his dick and gently strokes his girth. No one says a word when I lean forward and let him use me how he wants. If his memory doesn't let him forget, I'll make this the most incredible experience of his life. There will be no doubt that this will be the moment running through his mind in ten years when he pops a chub randomly in public and curses my name.

"River, fuck," he hisses when I scrape my teeth lightly over his tip and take him all the way in until my cheeks hollow out, and he lets out a deep, drawn-out moan.

Taking a deep breath, I shove him further until he feels the contractions of my throat and moans, grabbing my hair. My pussy clenches, convincing Rad to continue his thrusts with new abandon, slamming our hips together.

Fingers twirl around my clit, calling my orgasm, and bringing me back to the edge of the cliff. I moan around Callum's dick, earning a pleasing groan in return. His hips lift off the bench, shoving himself down my throat even more until he stills, reveling in my contracting throat. Every muscle in his body tightens, and his fingers grab my hair like a handlebar, slamming into my face until he cries out, arching his back, and finally, his salty come splashes down my throat.

Callum's eyes widen when he pulls his semi-hard dick from my mouth with a lazy grin, leaving him in a blissful state. His fingers retrace my lips, gliding over the warmth of his come spread across my glistening lips.

"You missed some," he whispers, gently shoving his thumb in my mouth. My tongue swirls around his thumb, sucking the spilled come from his flesh and swallowing it down without complaint.

"Such a good girl," Asher groans, throwing his head back with several labored breaths falling between his parted lips. White sticky come spills from the tip of his dick, jutting directly into my thong, encasing his length. His heavy breath fills the cart, and another look of contentment passes over his face. "Fuck, River," he mumbles through heavy breaths, staring at the ceiling of the cart with glazed-over eyes.

"My turn," Rad says, ramming into me so hard I double over, coming all over his cock. "Fuck," he shouts, digging his teeth into my shoulder and coming deep inside me with a shout. "You feel that, Pretty Girl?" he whispers in my ear as his fingers roam over my naked body. Squeezing my breast, he groans, slowly pulling out. "That's what marks you as mine. No matter how far you get, I'll always find you." It's a promise, not a threat, weaved in his possessive tone.

I shiver when Rad's come drips down my thighs, sticking to my flesh. As the cool breeze blows through the cart, a shiver works through me. And the moment my eyes connect with the mismatched gaze looking down at me, my pussy clenches again.

Kieran softly moans, stroking his thick length. With one silent demand and finger curl, I crawl toward him on my hands and knees, stopping when I'm directly between his sprawled open legs. Biting into his lip, he moans when I place my hand over his, adding more pressure around his thick cock. Moans spill from his throat when I lean forward, licking his shaft toward his weeping tip. I groan when the taste of his pre-cum lands on my tongue, making my pussy ache even more.

Without wasting a second, Kieran pulls me off the ground and settles me in his lap until I'm straddling him with my knees, biting into the cool metal. His lips savagely attack mine in such a heated kiss my damn toes curl, and I grind against his hard dick.

"I couldn't wait for a second longer, but we're going to have to hurry," he rasps, gripping my hips with bruising force. "Can I fuck you raw?" he whispers, moving his tip over my sensitive clit in heavy circles, sending goosebumps down my flesh. Every part of me shivers as he plays with me how he wants.

"Yes," I gasp out in desperation, sinking onto him until he's nestled deep inside my cunt.

"You feel so damn good," he whispers before plunging his tongue back into my mouth, desperately dancing with mine until we're out of breath.

Working him up and down, I moan when his fingers twirl around my clit, bringing another orgasm slamming right through me, and I clamp down on him.

"Watching you with my friends was torture. I kept thinking that it should be all me. But feeling Rad's cum dripping from you and knowing mine will be there too has me on edge. I'm going to come now," he moans, slamming his hips up into mine until his warmth fills me.

Slumping against his shoulder, I try to regain my breath just as the Ferris wheel slowly comes back to life, and we're jerked forward from the force.

"Time to get dressed," Rad whispers, helping me dismount Kieran, who tucks himself back into his jeans.

"H-here," Callum says gently, coming before me with my bra in his hands. Working the straps up my arms, he clasps the back of my bra together, only fumbling a little and gently kissing my shoulder. Rad hands me the Property of Whispered Words shirt and helps me put it over my head. He clings tight to my original shirt, clasping it.

"We're almost to the bottom," Ash says in a lazy tone, standing beside me. He grins, holding up my come-filled panties, dripping with his essence onto the floor between us. "Now, for being such a damn brat, you're going to put this back on. You're going to wear it home and remember what happens when you disobey me. Next time, I'll bend you over my knee, spank your ass raw, and then fuck your tight hole." Asher leaves no room for argument, cocking his brow and watching the delighted twitches erupting across my face.

Jesus. Everything clenches, including my offended asshole. No one has touched it in a long time, especially not this dick. But I bite my tongue for once, reaching for the soaked thong, and put it on. His warm come sticks to my tiny hairs and my lower lips, mixing with his friends' come as it drips from my sopping pussy. It's like they've marked me and ruined me for everyone else. As the ride comes to a halt, I slip my flip-flops back on and turn toward the door, waiting for it to unlock.

The man operating the Ferris wheel turns bright red the moment our eyes meet, letting me know we had an audience of one. Despite being up so high, my loud moans must have traveled down here. Thankfully, no one else was in line after us.

Rad wraps an arm around my shoulders as Callum takes my hand, interlocking our fingers together.

"Thanks for the ride, man," Rad says, digging a wad of cash from his pockets. The man doesn't utter a word when we awkwardly walk away with looks of utter satisfaction lining our faces.

Other carnival goers roam the area with drinks in their hands. Since the sun went down, the children left, and the adults stayed to play. But they don't pay us any mind, not knowing what we did in that unsuspecting Ferris wheel cart.

I groan with the wetness pooling more in my panties. With every miserable step, their combined cum leaks from me, running down my legs.

"You wanna go home, Pretty Girl? Or come over?" Rad asks, kissing my cheek when we get to the SUV still parked near the stage.

I contemplate my life in a matter of three seconds. Ma is probably sleeping and doing okay, and I don't have any other obligations in the morning, making my decision ten times easier.

"Take me back to your place," I squeal when Rad picks me up, throws me in the backseat, and climbs on top of me. Looking up, Callum grins, lifting my head so it's on his thigh. His fingers run through my messy strands as he looks out the window, not once reaching to put his earbuds in.

"I'm still running down your leg, aren't I?" He grins with satisfaction, running his fingers over my soaked thighs, and smearing the leaking come sticking to my flesh. "Lick it," he says, rubbing his wet fingers along my lips until I open wide and suck all their essence off his fingers.

"Jesus," Asher curses, swerving the SUV.

"Eyes on the road, dickbag," Rad grumbles, sucking on my neck.

"Can't you fucking wait? Why does this have to happen in my car? And when do I get my turn?" Asher gripes, choking the steering wheel.

Rad grins, biting my neck and sucking my flesh between his teeth. "The Ferris wheel was just the beginning," he whispers, loudly popping off my neck. "There's more in store for you back at the house. You ready, Pretty Girl? We're going to fuck you all night long."

Staring into his eyes, I see the promise nestled deep; all I can do is nod.

"Rock my world, Ashton," I whisper, earning a groan and an eager tongue down my throat.

"I SEE YOU'RE FINALLY PUTTING YOUR MANAGERIAL SKILLS TO GOOD USE," Ode says with a grin. Nodding toward the new girl sitting tall at the front door, taking over my old job.

I lean against the bar, watching from behind as the chaos unfolds around us. People pile in, storming the tiny stage in massive waves. Unfamiliar faces. Old faces. People from every walk of life. Just to get a glimpse of Whispered Words. Their excited energy pours through the venue, infecting everyone—including me. Searching the crowd, I furrow my brows, not spotting my stalker, who's been here every night for the past month, watching me. Whatever, so long, Van. I hope never to see your face ever again.

I blow out a breath, focusing on the new girl at the door instead of the fire hazards piling into the already-packed bar.

"Well, Booker gave me the okay to hire someone. He said I couldn't do my job if I sat up front taking tickets. So, he said I should take in Tammy and let her do it." I shrug, watching the new girl with admiration.

"She's good people," Leon remarks, cutting through the bar with a large plate of delicious-smelling nachos.

My mouth waters as the sharp scent of spicy cheese hits my nose, inhaling deeper, wishing the nachos were already resting in my gut. Fuck. When was the last time I ate? Breakfast? Shit. I didn't have time for dinner today after Callum dropped me off at my apartment after work. I knew tonight was going to be big. And if I admitted to working a little harder on my makeup and picking out the perfect pair of shorts, you'd call me desperate. Some days I miss having my car at my fingertips and caring for my own damn self. But having the boys driving me around like a princess? Yeah, I kind of like spending so much time with them in a confined space.

"I think I'm in love with you," I say with a grin when he sets the nachos down in front of me with a wink.

"Oh, you wish, baby girl," he quips, kissing my cheek with a laugh. I'm too desperate to eat to bat him away like I should.

I snort, digging into the delicious, melted cheese and chips, moaning

into it when it hits my taste buds. "You're too damn good to me," I groan, shoving more food into my mouth.

"Now, that's something we can both agree on," Marcus, the bartender, says from my side, sliding two beers to grabby patrons waiting at the bar.

"Shush," Leon mutters, shoving Marcus as he returns to the kitchen with a laugh.

"Oh, Pretty Girl. You've got a lil something," Rad says with a smirk, pointing to my chin. With my tongue, I try clearing off the remnants of the cheese but fail. Rad grins more, leaning over to run his tongue up my chin and over my parted lips. "Yummy nachos," he says with a wink, pushing his tongue into my mouth. I groan, holding his face to mine until he pulls back, panting and wide-eyed.

"Fucking gross," Asher grumbles, shaking his head at our antics.

"Yo, barkeep!" Rad barks out with a laugh, slamming his hand on the counter.

Marcus sighs, meandering over with a frown. Leaning against the bar, he shakes his head. "Listen, kid. How many times do I have to tell you? I'm not the barkeep," he grumbles, cocking his head to the side.

"Meh," Rad says, waving a hand. "Can you get me…"

"Just four beers," Asher commands through gritted teeth. "You don't need that fruity shit when we're about to perform." He stares daggers at Rad, who puffs out his bottom lip and pouts. "It'll upset your damn stomach. I don't need a barf-fest repeat of last year." I wrinkle my nose at the reference, not wanting to ask what the barf-fest involved.

"You really need to get laid, man. You're getting way too stuck up for your own good. Pretty Girl, why don't you tell him?" Rad wiggles his brows when I shove another cheese-filled chip into my mouth.

"Nope. Not touching that subject," I say through my mouthful of food, tasting the lie on the tip of my tongue instead of the spicy nacho cheese.

Asher raises a brow at me like he's pried my brain open, reading my every thought. If he did, he'd see the images of our night together on the Ferris wheel running through my mind.

"I got off just fine into your panties," Asher says in a deep voice, stopping the cheese-soak chip from entering my mouth. Color me shocked and awed because I swear to hell he's flirting with me, which is confirmed when he moves my hand toward his mouth and eats the chip in my hand, moaning at the taste.

"Yeah, so fucking good. Maybe I'll get some later," he says, wrapping his mouth around my fingers. My body stiffens when the tip of his tongue roams the length of my fingers, sucking it into his mouth. Over and over, he swirls his tongue, sucking all the cheese and salt from my flesh. With a pop, he frees my hand and grins at me, only offering me one small wink in return for my stunned expression.

Fuck. Me.

My cheeks heat when his gaze stares right through my damn soul, and I swear, if they didn't have to go on stage, I'd slather cheese on my lady bits and have him lick his way to the center. How many licks does it take for the Asher to get to the center of the kitty cat? We'll never know because just as I'm about to entertain his panty comment with a quick retort about coming somewhere else besides fabric, we're interrupted by the she-devil I swore I told off.

"Oh my god, Asher Montgomery!" Comes a shrill familiar voice from the depths of the large crowd. My skin immediately crawls, and my stomach sours. Great, there goes my damn nachos. Another meal ruined by some stuck-up jerk. I set my chip down like it offended me and pout.

"Yay! Tiny Tots Tessa," Rad mumbles, running a hand down his face with irritation. "I bet she'd volunteer as tribute." All the air leaves Rad's lungs when Ash's elbow meets his gut, and he huffs. "Not cool, bro. You almost hit the little dangling Rads."

"I'd rather you bite off my dick and then feed it to me after you grill it like sausage than ever dip my dick into that," he grits out, standing rigidly when she approaches with a big smile. "I'd fuck Little Brat for forty-eight hours straight on Viagra, chance chafing and dick pains than ever fuck that," he grunts, sending shivers down my spine.

A sparkle twinkles in his eye when I shiver at the thought of a sexathon with him for hours. Oh, hell. Asher must be growing on me. Or I'm just horny. When I turn to Rad, he's grinning like crazy in my direction with a dreamy look on his face.

"I think we're going to have to put her on the no-fly list," I grumble, earning a smirk from Asher, who snorts.

It's like the night of the celebration never happened, and she's back to looking at Asher like he's her future baby daddy. Fat chance, Blondie. Maybe I'll have to remind her who these boys are dicking down these days. It's definitely not her.

Tessa's long blonde hair is thrown into a pretty bun on the top of her head. And this time, she forgot the pearls at home, replacing them with a small black choker hugging her throat. Well, hey. She's at least trying to fit in with the crowd with attire this time, sporting her new Whispered Words shirt and distressed jeans.

"Asher! I can't wait to see you play tonight!" she says with enthusiasm, bouncing on her toes. "Any new songs yet? My mom said you were going to the Battle of the Bands! You're going to be famous!" With every word Tessa shrieks, the further Asher pulls himself away from her. He visibly cringes when she winds her arm through his, leaning her head against his arm with hearts in her eyes.

My fists curl at his visible discomfort. You know, strange men make my skin crawl with anxiety in situations such as this. Whenever they touch without permission and take, take, take. So, what's so different about a woman making a man uncomfortable? The band has repeatedly told her to fuck off and leave them be and that they aren't interested. Yet, Tessa doesn't get the hint and keeps coming around like a desperate hussy looking for dick any way she can.

"We have a rad-diculous new song called, Fuck You," Rad deadpans, taking a long sip of his beer to cover up his disgust. His dark eyes lock on me when I raise a brow, and he shrugs in response.

Tessa beams, looking smugly at me. "Oh, my god. We can't wait to hear it! You guys are so good!"

Ugh. Sometimes I wish I had a remote so I could mute people. Like, click—you're muted now, bitch. Then she'd flap her gums, and no one would hear the shit she spews.

"Yeah," Asher says through a tight smile, trying to pry her hand off him. "I can't either. Are you ready?" he begs Rad with furrowed brows, stepping away from the harasser. Tessa swoons, staring at his tall form with hearts in her eyes.

"Fuck off, now," I snarl in Tessa's direction, watching with glee when she rears back with disgust.

For some reason, Tessa doesn't utter a word when the boys wave good-bye, heading for the stage. Instead, she watches them like a fucking predator about to pounce on her prey.

"See ya backstage, Pretty Girl!" Rad hollers as the crowd swallows them whole, and they disappear behind the tall bodies of their fans.

"Are you guys doing anything after? We're having a party!" Tessa screams after them as they walk away, completely ignoring her stupid ass.

She stares after them with such hope. Lust practically pools around her. But I have news for her. They're mine. And the sooner she gets it through her thick, bitchy skull—the better we'll all be. Maybe I should kick her out and never let her come back. Hmm. Manager status does have its perks.

"I'm getting the impression they aren't fond of her," Ode stage-whispers into my ear, loud enough for the perky blonde to hear.

Tessa turns on her toes with a frown, marching up to the bar. Her scathing eyes rake up and down my body, giving me her best stink eye.

"I need four mojitos right now." The venom in her voice makes me want to take her into the alleyway and let my fists have their way with her face. Or maybe I could grab our trusty baseball bat from behind the bar and shove it down her throat…

Nah. She's not worth it. She's a try-hard, trying to get into the good graces of the boys who I have no doubt will be famous in a year. I can't wait to sink my toes into the sands of the beach and wallow in the sun. Ah. Never in a million years did I think I'd be doing something like this. Helping them and potentially meeting some of my family. Not that I'm holding any expectations on that end, but still. I'm allowed to dream of a future that might not be...

"Of course," Marcus replies in a deep, professional voice, turning to mix the drinks even though he's muttering under his breath about her attitude.

"So, what exactly do you do around here?" Tessa asks me haughtily, lifting her nose in the air.

I blow out a breath. Sheesh. People don't have enough respect to read the word Manager on my tit. It's big and bold in red letters, but no one seems to notice. So, I point to the word with a raised brow, laying it all out for her.

"I run the show." Simple but effective.

Her perfectly sculpted eyebrows pop up, and she rolls her eyes with disgust. Lifting her lip, she leans against the bar getting as close to my face as possible. If I were anywhere else, she and I would have major problems.

"By the way, Central Trash. I see how you look at them," she says, pointing to the empty stage. "And I just wanted to warn you; they're mine," she snarls the word mine possessively.

I nod with a smirk. She could piss on them, and they still wouldn't be hers.

"Sure, Tess. Whatever you say," I hum when Marcus slides over her drinks more forcefully than necessary, spilling liquid over the rims of the glasses. "But I swear we had this discussion already. Do my words go in one ear and out the other? Have you choked on too much cock to understand? Has it damaged your hearing? Let me repeat myself. They're mine. You'll find yourself missing fingers if you lay your hands on what's mine again." I raise a brow when her eyes go wide, and she sputters.

"You're… you're threatening me! Did you hear?" No one pays her a lick of attention, and she huffs, turning on her heel.

"Unclench that jaw, bestie," Ode snickers, pinching my cheek and pulling me out of my thoughts.

"Ode," I groan, swatting her away.

"Don't worry, baby girl," Leon says from my side, watching Tessa make her way back through the crowd. She bounces off a few people giving them the stink eye and yells something in their faces. "Guys like that don't want a girl like that. That's who their parents wish they had. Hell, I bet all their parents want some stuck-up rich bitch for a daughter-in-law. But those Lakeview boys always have a weakness for one thing," he says, side-eyeing me with a smirk.

"Yeah? And what's that? Oh, genius," I snark back when he laughs.

"The magical Central pussy." He cackles when I slug him in the arm with a heavy punch.

"You're such a dick," I grumble as the lights dim and the crowd lets out a collective whoop of excitement.

More people pack the place than ever before. Even Sorcha's concert didn't garner this much attention. All my hard work from their social media platforms has finally paid off, and we're about to reap what we've sowed all the way to California.

"I have one!" Leon shouts, grabbing his crotch. Leon ducks his head when I try to swing on him again and cackles when I miss. "Now, Miss Manager! I'll go back to the kitchen. No need to resort to violence." A large grin takes over when I narrow my eyes at him.

"Oh, I'll resort to violence, dickhead. Back to work!" I bark out my demand, sending him a wink in return.

Once Leon disappears into the kitchen with a playful grin, I turn back to the men of the hour.

"You have it so damn bad," Ode remarks, leaning against the bar.

"Don't you have work, too?" I grumble when she bursts out laughing, shoving me to the side.

"Nah, bitch. I'm friends with the manager. Didn't you know? She needs my moral support right now," she says with a grin, leaning closer. "How fast are you falling?" Her eyebrows wiggle out of control until I flick them, and she laughs again.

"It's bad, Ode," I groan, rubbing my forehead. "How can this happen again? And not just one… fuck."

"Oh my god, you love all of them? Even the dickhead on guitar?" she says, pointing directly at Asher, who raises a brow at her from the stage like he heard every word. With the chants of the raging crowd and whoops or excitement ringing through the place, there's no way.

"Jesus. Didn't your mama ever tell you it's rude to point?" I gasp, pulling her arm down to her side.

"She did, multiple times. But I'm a rebel." Ode grins more, if that's even possible, and fully faces me. "All four of them, huh? Their dicks that good that they're about to lock down my bestie who swore off love?"

"What can I say? I'm a fucking sucker for musicians. My heart…"

"And pussy," she snickers, interrupting me.

"As I was saying. My heart just can't stay away. I don't know what it is. They're protective, gentle, and they're… fucking hot, and hell, dynamite in the sheets. And fuck. I'm so fucked, Odes. Pull me away from them," I groan, covering my heated face, and the memories of our illicit moments run like a runaway train through my mind.

"Riv. Not everyone is Van. He was a dickless fuck who ran away like a puppy. But these guys? They took you to their neighborhood. Girl, you practically met their families. They're not him and not embarrassed by you. Hell, they stalk you everywhere. If anyone is pathetic, it's them," Ode says, wrapping a supportive arm around my shoulders.

"But what if…"

"No fucking what ifs. Give it a chance and let yourself like them. Fuck them. Do whatever the hell you want to with them. I kinda like 'em, babe. Plus, if they break your heart? I'll hunt them down, and they'll face the wrath of Ode Mills." Her nose wrinkles when she gives a convincing nod.

My heart races in my chest at the prospect of letting all my reservations go. Everything Ode said is precisely what I am afraid of. What if they fucked me over? Shit. My head pounds with an oncoming headache from all my chaotic thoughts. I've given so much to them already.

"Don't stress yourself too much," Ode says into my ear over the sound of the first notes bleeding through the speakers.

"You don't know me very well then," I grumble back, looking at the sweaty boys jumping on stage.

Kieran's sultry voice rasps through the microphone again, belting out a new song. I take out my phone, finding this the perfect moment to show-case their talents. Once Kieran hits the chorus, I jump onto the bar and press record. Kieran smiles at me from the stage, locking his eyes on the camera when the music ends.

"Thank you, Central City. You're fucking great. If you didn't know, we are Whispered Words. You can find us on ClockTok and FlashGram. Join us at whisperedwordsband," he says through a smirk, winking at the camera, capturing them.

I give him the thumbs up when I jump down and immediately lean against the bar watching with admiration.

"They have you doing their bitch work now?" Ode asks, placing drinks on the bar for three patrons.

I snort. "I'm helping them film performances and shit. I told you they're trying to apply to the Battle of the Bands." I give her a pointed look when she raises a skeptical brow.

Speaking of, that's something we'll be doing this week. They only have two more weeks to submit their application before the website won't take them anymore, and they want everything to be perfect—including their social media numbers.

Within a few clicks, I upload their video to ClockTok and watch the notifications from the thousands of followers pour in. I swear, a month ago, no one around the world knew who they were. Now they're getting tens of thousands of likes and comments, begging for more covers and original songs. Oh, and nude photos. Crazy fangirls.

"Yeah, and they promised to take you…" she trails off with a pointed look in my direction.

I shrug. "Maybe they will. Maybe they won't. Gotta film this one, too," I say, quickly jumping on the bar again and away from my nosy BFF.

"You can't avoid me forever, bitch," she cackles, leaning over to take someone's drink order.

"Yes, yes, I can," I murmur, standing high above the crowd. Tonight, they stand shoulder to shoulder, squished together like sardines.

Rad grins at me when he throws this shirt off and tosses it onto the stage. I smirk when he winks at me, wiping away the sweat from his brow. I'm sure if he had it his way, he'd be naked by now instead of in his jeans. Judging by the thirsty shrieks from the front of the stage, I'd say his fangirls wish for it, too. Too bad, suckers, that's mine later. Every girl in the crowd shrieks when Rad flexes his pecs and bangs on the drums with more force than necessary, putting on a show for the crowd.

"Hey there!" a deep voice says from below me, tapping my ankle with his calloused finger.

I frown. "Yeah?" I ask, stepping back and jumping down behind the bar. "Can I help you with something?" I ask, leaning over to hear him over the loud music.

He grins wide, exposing his yellowing teeth. With a nod, he taps the bar, leaning in closer. His crystal blue eyes check every inch of me that he can see. Disgust eats away at my flesh, but I hold my composure. I'm professional and all, even when I want to shrink away.

Alarm bells activate in my mind, blaring a siren to run away, and I'm suddenly very aware of everything around me. But just because the pretty boy with yellow teeth gives me the damn willies doesn't mean he's going to harm me. But my momma always told me to trust my gut, and that's exactly what I'm going to do.

"Give me two beers and your number," he says when another equally intimidating man walks up beside him. They both stare down at me with a grin.

"Beer, sure. My number, hell no," I spit, trying to hold my damn tongue, but she always has a mind of her own.

The man turns up the charm, brightening his smile. "Come on, beautiful. A nice bartender like you could use a little something like me," he says in a gravelly tone, which I'm sure most girls fall to their knees for.

"Sorry, buddy. I'm not interested. But here's your beer. That'll be twelve ninety-nine," I say, holding my hand out after setting down his beers.

"Come on," his buddy says, grabbing my wrist tightly.

"There is no come on about this," I say through clenched teeth, trying to reign in my anger. "But if you don't let my hand go, we'll have some serious problems." I raise a brow when he sneers at my words and tightens his grip on me, attempting to pull me closer.

"Whatcha gonna do?" he teases, trying to pull at me again.

"This," I hiss, whipping out my knife and flicking it open in one move. The man's eyes widen when I hold the tip against his precious fingers, dreaming of cutting them off one by one.

"Get your hands the fuck off her," Kieran's deep, growly voice comes through the microphone, sending chills down my spine.

Every eye in the bar swings in my direction, widening at the sight of my knife digging into grabby-man's fingers. At the sound of Kieran's second growl, every man in the bar takes their hands off whatever woman they showed up with. Screams erupt for the asshole to take his hands off me, and some even attempt to take him away from the bar, but it does nothing but encourage him to cling to me harder. He sneers in my direction, not deterred by Bert screaming from the front door, unable to make it through the crowd standing shoulder to shoulder, watching the entire situation unfold.

"I'm coming!" Bert growls over the roar of the crowd.

"Don't worry!" I shout to Bert, who grunts his disapproval at my nonchalant attitude. Bringing my attention back to the man of the hour, I focus on the digit suffering beneath my blade. "I can cut your fingers off one by one." I'm challenging him. Would I cut off his fingers for funsies? Uh, yeah. Just for the simple fact, he's touching me. Fuck the cops. This is self-defense. He won't let go and keeps leering at me like I'm his favorite Sunday brunch. I'm no biscuit and gravy meal, pal. So, fuck off.

He smirks again until I dig the tip further into his finger, drawing blood and watching with glee as it pools on the wooden bar top. Movement catches my attention out of the corner of my eye, and I smirk as two over-bearing figures come into view with deep scowls and clenched fists. My heart gallops in my chest as they inch closer and closer, pushing through the crowd of people and shoving them aside with a possessive vibe wafting off every inch of them.

"You bitch," he hisses, but before he gets a chance to do anything else, he's yanked back by the very possessive assholes I've come to enjoy.

"I believe she said no fucking touchy," Asher growls, pulling the scum-bags' face into his. "You tell him no, Little Brat?" Holy hotness, Batman. Asher looks at me with a kindling fire sparkling in his eyes, ready to pummel this douche into the ground.

I say, bury him.

"Definitely said don't fucking touch me," I hiss, climbing over the bar and grabbing our beat-up wooden baseball bat for more protection. I can't go around stabbing everyone who touches me, but a friendly knock to the teeth will help.

"Sometimes guys like this just need a little reminder." Before my eyes, my panties melt when Asher connects his forehead to the yellow-toothed offender and knocks him back a step.

Asher grins, rubbing his forehead as his opponent stumbles around. Fuck! As hot as this is, I can't let them fight in my damn bar.

"Back off," I say, putting a hand on Asher's chest, forcing him to stand still.

"This is where you say thank you, Asher," he snaps, staring daggers at me with a heaving chest. His wild eyes glare at the offenders with pure hate, and he's ready to lunge at them again to finish the job.

"Asher, Daddy," I murmur half-jokingly, running my fingers down his jaw and drawing his attention to me. "I appreciate what you did." I swallow hard when his fingers wrap around my wrist, holding my fingers against his jaw. "They scared the shit out of me," I breathe my confession with careful words. "So, thank you." Every ounce of vulnerability leaks from my voice, and he nods. "But I can't let you fight in here." No matter how hot it was. I swear those images will bleed into my dreams forever. The way his forehead smashed into that fucker's face, knocking him back.

"I told you, Little Brat. No one touches what's ours." He gives me a firm nod, squeezing my wrist with reassurance. "Whoever you need me to beat, I'll fucking end them."

Be still my beating heart.

"You good?" Kieran asks through several heaved breaths, peering around the circle that formed around us.

"I'm fine. Let me deal with these idiots," I grumble, nodding at the idiots squaring up for another fight. "All right, boys. Because that's what you are. You're not fucking men. Men don't touch things they're not supposed to. Now, get the fuck out. You're not welcome here ever again." I raise a brow when they square up again, eyeing the bat in my hand with a cocky expression until it falls.

"I got 'em, Riv. We'll take their picture and everything," Bert wheezes out of breath, finally making it to the bar after it's all said and done. Sometimes, I wonder why I still keep him around. Fuckery keeps happening on his watch when he's nowhere to be found. Maybe the bar needs more changes than I initially thought.

"Thank fuck." Once Bert has the two troublemakers kicked to the curb, the boys jump back up on stage but keep their eyes on me, and they continue their set list with more enthusiasm than before.

Leaning on the bar, I eye the boys on stage, rocking the shit out of the crowd. A strange feeling settles over me, thinking back to the two dumb fucks from earlier who were escorted out and thrown on the street. Something about them has anxiety rolling up my arms and prickling my skin. It's like they had a mission marching here to touch and egg me on. There was something dead in their beady eyes, like they never took no for an answer.

As time passes, I make my rounds through the bar, ensuring everything runs smoothly. The rest of the crowd remains respectful, albeit fucking messy, but still. They rock out to the hour-long set, chanting the guys' names and going ballistic when they offer the crowd an encore.

"Thank you, Dead End! It's been fucking great!" Kieran shouts into the microphone breathlessly, trying to catch his breath. Running a hand over his forehead, he swipes the sweat away and smiles at the cheering crowd. "We'll see you next time!" The boys each stand at the edge of the stage, taking their last bow. Reaching down, they shake their fans' hands before waving and disappearing backstage to cool down before they pack everything away.

"Another good show, bossy lady," Ode says over the loud chatter of the crowd, slowly making their way toward the door. Only a few will stay and continue to drink.

"Once everyone's out, I'm going to clean up and take the trash out," I say, squeezing her shoulder.

"Isn't that what we're for?" she shouts back, handing another patron a drink, and then closes their tab.

"Pfft. Bitch," I scoff with a wave. "I may be the manager, but I'll still get dirty." I wink, heading to a supply closet next to my back office and grabbing a trash bag.

As soon as I hit the main floor, I begin cleaning up. Candy wrappers, beer cans and bottles, old receipts, and even old food sticks to the floor. Ugh. Animals! There's a trash can at every friggin corner, and they decide to leave their shit on the ground.

"Ode!" I shout, tying up the heavy trash bag and throwing it over my shoulder with a grunt. Shit. I swear there are a few cement blocks in here. "I'm taking this out!" Ode gives me the thumbs up as I make my way out the backdoor and into the cool air.

I take a deep breath, relieved the staleness of the bar no longer infiltrates my nose. Replaced by the fresh, night air blowing through the abandoned alleyway. An eerie feeling churns in my gut as I approach the dumpster, stopping me in my tracks.

Flipping open the lid, I peer over my shoulders and shake my head. This alleyway at one in the morning had always been a little creepy. Not to mention the attacks that have happened on this side of town. I've always been cautious, hence the knife in my pocket, but tonight it feels like eyes are burning right through me.

Once the heavy bag is deposited into the dumpster, I turn on my heel, ready to get back inside. The guys promised me a ride home after a long day of working, and I can't wait to settle into bed. Lately, Rad and Callum have been stopping by for sleepovers or vice versa. Kieran and Ash hang out but never stay over. They've alluded to family issues but have never gotten specific about why they can't stay over. Often, I find myself squished between their bodies in a warm cocoon of comfort. Something that should cause concern, but doesn't anymore, because I'm free to do what I want with who I wish to and…

Pain erupts in my skull the moment something heavy knocks into me and sends me to my hands and knees, scraping along the pavement. All the air in my lungs blows out into the asphalt, and I'm left gasping for breath. My fingers dig into the ground, desperate to move and stand, but moving seems impossible. The world around me spins endlessly, and I'm pushed belly first onto the road, scraping every inch of my legs and arms when I skid forward.

"I don't think so," the menacing voice from my nightmare's growls, placing his heavy foot between my shoulder blades. "I've got a job to do," he says with a laugh, gripping me by my hair. "I won't find this hard at all. I'm not one to hit it twice, but you were so damn pretty and tight the first time. Why not?" His low chuckle does little to settle my damn nerves.

No. Not again. Not him. What in the ever-living fuck is he talking about? God. My heart races out of my chest, spearing through my damn ribs. I kick my leg out and, by God's grace, land a strike to his knee. He grunts, gripping my hair tighter than before until my eyes burn and tears run down my cheeks. Popping happens in my neck when he yanks it backward, forcing a cry from my lips.

My lips pop open, pleading for help when he turns me over on my back, yanking the strands of my hair between his fingers. Pain encases my entire body like a fire scorching my skin, from the scrapes burning on my exposed legs to my fingers clawing at his arms.

"Scream all you want," he murmurs. "I kind of like it."

The world blurs before me, and I shake my head. Fuck. I must stay coherent, or I'll never make it through again. I have to stay the fuck awake and acknowledge the fact my biggest monster holds me captive in the isolated alleyway behind the bar.

"Fuck you, Bradley," I slur, spitting in his face. Or what I hope is his face. All I see are wiggly lines and weaving colors splashing the world.

By the force of the first blow to my face, my glob of spit must have hit its mark. The next impact reigns down on my face in a fury of fists, crunching my nose and cheekbones. Static takes over my ears when he finally stops his violent assault, leaving me a groaning, pleading mess.

Pain is the only thing radiating through my body, pulsating pain through every inch of my muscles. No matter how hard I try to move my arms and legs, they don't cooperate, leaving me at his mercy. At fucking Bradley's mercy—the last place I want to be. The last time I was, he took my innocence and fucking ran with it.

Time ticks by slowly as I lie there, feeling his hands in places they shouldn't be. He murmurs words in my ear, but I can't fucking hear him over the beating of my broken heart. The entire world fades into the shadows as I fumble for the weapon nestled deep in my pocket, the one I don't leave home without—because of this man. The one time I didn't have it with me, this happened, and I won't let it happen again. I'll die before I let him get what he wants.

"Hey! What the fuck are you doing?!" someone—a familiar resounding voice—shouts, and his footsteps clomp forward loudly as if he is running.

My eyes stay closed, and my body is too spent to move as he remains on top of me, taking his damn time to get what he wants. Thank God my shorts are still on, and he hasn't started doing what I know he wants to do.

"The hell do you want?" Bradley spits, easing off of me, but doesn't fully get up. By the sound of the crunching beside me, he sits his ass on the pavement.

"What the hell?" the voice fills with panic, and a hand touches my warm forehead. "She's bleeding!" he hisses, rubbing a finger down my jaw. "You weren't…"

"Weren't what? You fucking…" I flinch, drowning out the words when the fingers run over my nose, and I cry out from the pain filling every inch of my fucking body.

I'm so fucking tired of everyone thinking they can take whatever the hell they want from me. I've fought too hard for far too long to carve my way into this world. I won't let some pissant fuckboy take what he wants again and again.

I'm fucking done. So, I do the only thing I can.

Flicking open my knife, I wildly stab wherever I can reach, basking in the roar of agony right before my entire world shuts down and I fall deep into the shadows of my mind.

you asked me what, though. I have no fucking clue. An urgent alarm desperately claws at the back of my mind, nagging at me. For some fucking reason, and I can't put my finger on it. Everyone I love sits before me, de-stressing after our third show in a row. River has put us through the fucking ringer, with gigs almost every night this week, exhausting us to the max. But it's so damn worth it. Our rock star dreams rest at the tips of our fingers, finally in grasp.

"That show was badass!" Rad says with a grin, guzzling down a bottle of water twenty minutes after the performance.

Sweat pours from every inch of his glistening body, dripping off the long ends of his mullet. He groans, standing in front of the oscillating fan, opening the fly of his jeans.

"For the love of God, please keep your dick in your pants," I groan with exhaustion, leaning against the wall for support.

"The little Rads are hot as hell! I have swamp dick—Swamp. Dick, Asher. They're basically cooking in my jeans. My chestnuts are roasting! So, unless I want cooked swimmers, I need to cool them off," Rad scoffs at me, pulling his jeans and boxers down, exposing himself for the fucking world to see. "Ah, that's the stuff right there," he mumbles, wiggling his ass around and allowing the air to flow to his fucking flapping dick blowing in the breeze.

"Your ass is disgusting," Kieran barks, slapping a hand across his butt cheek, rippling the skin, and leaving an angry red welt behind on his pasty skin.

"Oh, baby! Do it again!" Rad howls, locking his hands behind his head. "Ah, this is freedom," he groans with relief, arching his back.

"How the hell did we get to this?" I mumble, closing my eyes, so I don't have to stare at his dimply ass while sliding down the wall. I swear the dude can't keep his pants on to save his life. Every chance he gets, he drops trou and lets his dick fly free. Must be nice to have no restraints. But someone has to keep him in line.

We've been dead on our feet since we walked backstage into the dark-ened space dedicated to the talent. It's small, shabby, and fucking gross. Shifting my weight, my nose wrinkles when my pants stick to the floor. Don't they ever clean this place? Shit. Images of River frantically cleaning every inch of this place, runs through my mind. Hell, she probably hasn't been back here to clean, because she's working her life away and killing herself here.

Taking a deep breath, I revel in the surrounding nothingness—no noises, shouting crowd, and most importantly, no groupies shoving their titties in our faces. This moment of silence gives us time to unwind after such a killer performance. All these gigs are starting to wear us down, but we don't have time to stop. We're persevering and fucking rocking this shit before we hit enter and submit our talent for the most prestigious record company in the US. In the future, this could be our life. Performance after performance. City after fucking city on a tour bus filled with Rad's naked ass. Okay, maybe not that. Shivers of disgust roll through me, envisioning him running naked everywhere. And now I need bleach for my brain.

"If I never have to see your dick again, it'd be a good day," Callum murmurs, tossing his head back and sighing with a grin.

"Agreed," Kieran snaps, running a towel over his face and neck, soaking up the sweat dripping down his skin, grinding his teeth. He closes his eyes, taking several deep breaths, trying to reign in his after-perfor-mance anger. I swear it's what got us into this whole debacle, anyway.

If he hadn't banged River, well—we wouldn't be here or on our way to California. Sure, we could have gotten someone else to record our videos or gotten us more gigs. River's been a saint through this whole thing—a dangerous saint, leading us down a path we can't come back from. Doubt seeps into my mind, infecting my runaway thoughts with insidious ideas. Some days I wonder if we're taking the right road with her. Looking around the room, I gaze at the faces of my brothers'. Happiness radiates from every inch of them. But is it from our performance? Or the woman who supplied us with this opportunity? Because of her, we're here. One question repeats in my mind over and over again. Do we actually want to bring her to California? Since River came into the picture, our band dynamic has drastically changed. But for the good? Or bad? How much more damage can she inflict before we implode and throw our dreams away?

Internally, I groan, running a hand down my face. River brings nothing but a whirl of confusion, storming inside me and pulling me in different directions. She's this… annoying gnat, yet beautiful little brat who I want to choke… with my cock so she can't utter another witty remark. She's… getting way too into our heads—especially mine.

The crowd beyond the black curtain's loud chatter slowly fades away into nothing but crickets. Looking at my phone, I note it's almost closing time. Just on cue, the bubbly little bartender's voice rings through the system, telling everyone to get the fuck out, and they comply. Soon, we're left in comfortable silence. But in the quiet, something still nags the back of my mind, and looking around, I notice the missing piece who trails after us like a desperate groupie—River.

"I swear to God, bitch, if you're back here sucking dick," shouts Ode, the bubbly bartender, right before she rips open the curtain and sticks her head in with a frown. "Well, not sucking dick," she says, shaking her head. "But someone certainly has their hairy ass out," she quips, looking the room over. "You four seen your girlfriend?" she asks, raising a brow.

Rad grins, pulling up his boxers and pants and turning around. "I'm glad someone else finally admits that she's my girlfriend!" he says with way too much enthusiasm. "But wait. Where is River?" he asks, making my fucking heart skip a beat.

Something is wrong… Something is off, and it smacks me in the damn face. River isn't here to annoy me.

"That's what I'm fucking asking. Come out, come out wherever you are, bitch!" she yells jokingly, but I see the worry sitting behind her dark eyes as they crinkle when she doesn't get an answer. Her fingers tighten into fists as her eyes flash around the room, and she huffs. "I haven't seen her since she took the trash out. I swore I saw her come back in…" she trails off, looking toward the single window blocked out by a blackout curtain, only letting a sliver of light come through the split down the middle.

"What do you mean she went outside at one in the fucking morning to dump the trash?" Kieran barks, jumping to his fucking feet like a mad dog with his nostrils flaring as he marches toward her. The only thing stopping him is my hand on his heaving chest.

"Cool your shit," I hiss through clenched teeth, side-eyeing him. "You're in—fuck shit up and ask questions later—mode right now."

"I said what I said. River is a big girl despite you treating her like a fucking baby. She did what she always does every night. You'd all probably shit your pants if you knew she's walked home at three in the morning more times than I can count. You all know better than I do. That woman does whatever the fuck she wants to and…" Ode pales when a light flashes between the sliver of the curtain, lighting the room up in reds and blues. "What the fuck!" She shrieks with urgency, marching toward the side door, and slams out of it with a cry.

Kieran doesn't waste a single moment stomping out the door after her. It isn't until I hear the roar of his anger do I pile out the door with Callum and Rad on my tail. Only, we don't make it too far and come to an abrupt stop, freezing on the spot. Every muscle in my body locks tight. My eyes dart around, taking in the scene with a critical eye.

Numerous police officers stalk the alleyway with their heads down, moving up and down with critical eyes. One points to the ground, shaking his head as they follow the trail. On further inspection, my breath leaves my lungs and I'm left gasping for oxygen. Two officers walk along a dark red trail of blood leading out of the alley and onto the street. And that's where I see him, cowering in the shadows with a pale face and vacant expression—fucking Donavan Drake.

"What the fuck?" I murmur with outrage, watching with wide, horrified eyes as the scene gets worse and worse by the second.

"Oh-oh no," Callum cries out in a quivering voice. Covering his mouth, Callum frantically shakes his head and forces his eyes closed—removing himself from the situation mentally.

"It'll be okay, Cal," Rad murmurs through a crack in his voice with the reassurance I'm sure he doesn't feel. Slowly, he rubs circles on Callum's back in a soothing manner, whispering barely audible words, hoping to soothe his grief.

Turning Callum, so his back is to the scene, Rad consoles him through his anguish. With shaky hands, Callum rips his earbuds from his pocket and forces them in his ears, shaking in Rad's embrace. With every fiber of his being, I know he wants to run to her and ensure her safety. He wants to hold her against his chest and heal her wounds. But he also doesn't want to remember the scene. He doesn't want it seared into his memory, where he can recall it for eternity—the blood, the fucking carnage of it all.

My aching heart fucking sinks into my gut, swallowed by the churning acid threatening to obliterate it into pieces. EMTs surround her body. Her fucking body! Frantically checking her pulse and noting the injuries with two police officers who take notes.

Deep red dripping blood catches my eye first, splattered like fucking spaghetti sauce on the white walls. There it is all around her unmoving body laid out on the pavement. And on her face. Her fucking hands gleam in it. Bright red scratches split the skin of her shins and knees, working toward her thighs where her goddamn shorts button was popped open, exposing the front of her panties. My stomach churns more, burning the back of my throat with bile, when the police officers finally notice it too.

If someone touched her, I'll fucking bury them so deep no one will find the evidence.

"You son of a bitch!" Kieran wails before I even think about catching him by the shirt and stopping him from drowning in his emotions and acting without thinking. All the pent-up, after-performance rage rushes through his system and infects him with violence.

I'm a frozen mass of hysterics when Kieran slams his vicious fist straight into Van's face over and over again, knocking them to the ground in front of two police officers, watching their every move. Great. This is just fucking great. The last thing we need is that idiot getting into trouble or worse, arrested.

"It wasn't me!" Van cries, trying to heave a fist into the side of Kieran's face, but fails. Kieran is way too gone, sinking into the abyss of his blacked-out anger like it's overpowered and taken him over. "It wasn't me! I found her!" Van wails, catching Kieran in the side of the jaw and knocking him on the ground.

"Stand down!" Someone shouts in Kieran's direction, but he doesn't pay them any attention.

Kieran grunts, rolling onto the pavement with a snarl and jumping to his feet. He's like a fucking lion with a blood scent stalking toward Van, who jumps to his shaky as fuck feet, staring at Kieran like he's finally gotten the idea of who he's up against. A fucking animal is who. And if I don't jump in and save his stupid ass, he'll be dead before the cops can subdue my foolish brother.

"Kieran!" I bark, running toward him at full speed, slamming into him. My finger curls in his shirt, forcefully turning him until I back him up against the brick wall. "Knock it the fuck off! They're going to take you to fucking jail for suspicion and fucking assault!" I growl through clenched teeth, shaking him.

Too fucking late.

He barks out a humorless laugh, glaring in Van's direction as the cop approaches slowly with his hand on his gun, hanging from his hip.

"Stand down," he barks again, putting a placating hand out, trying to ease the tension between Kieran and Van. "I need you to turn around and face the wall. I'm detaining you." There's no room for arguments in his voice, glaring at us.

Another officer approaches Van and his fucked up and bleeding face with apprehension, checking over his wounds with a careful eye. His hand rests on his hip, shifting away from Van with heavy suspicions. Leaning in, he nods when Van speaks, making me wonder what words he's poisoning the police with. Van points our way, shaking his head and dropping his arm when the officer narrows his eyes at us. More words are exchanged, and the officer begins documenting every word Van says and hands him a card. Most likely, telling him to call if he thinks of anything else.

"Son," the officer barks again. "Turn and face the wall," he growls, stepping even closer to Kieran, ready to pounce on him if he doesn't comply with his words.

"Turn around, you fucking idiot," I hiss, putting my forehead against his. "We'll find out what the fuck happened. But now you've truly outdone yourself. I'll get to the bottom of why the fuck Van's here."

"Go with her," he pleads, slightly slumping against the wall. Tears burn the back of his eyes, glazing them over when River's unmoving body is loaded onto the stretcher and is strapped down for safe travels.

Turmoil takes over my foggy brain, watching as her limp body jostles with their movements as they guide the stretcher toward the open ambulance. People shout, and noise fills the alleyway, but my thumping heart blocks it out. My fingers curl into fists, wanting to march over and ease River's pain. She doesn't have to shout or scream or even be conscious for me to see the bleeding wounds marking up her face.

Kieran's fingers curl again, watching with an intense glare when the ambulance takes off with none of us inside. When she wakes up from the slumber some asshole put her into, she'll be alone in the hospital, wondering what the hell happened and why she's there, of all places. And then to realize someone knocked her around and tried to get into her fucking panties when she wasn't awake. FUCK! Every molecule in my body wants to hitch a ride with the ambulance, hold her hand, and fucking comfort her until she wakes up in my arms.

Huffing several breaths to calm myself down, I eye Van, who's suspect as fuck. Not for a second do I believe that stalking mother fucker had nothing to do with this. He was here. But why? All night I watched the crowd for signs of that slimy snake and came up empty-handed. He's there every fucking night. So, what was that dickhead up to? And why did he show up in the same place River was hurt? Yeah, this place stinks of his doing, and I'm going to find out every fucking thing I can.

"Get on the ground," the same officer repeats with patience, eyeing Kieran with a commanding eye.

From here, I can tell he doesn't want to throw Kieran down to the ground himself, but whatever Van told them has him on edge. His fingers squeeze his gun at his hip again, anxious to pull it out and light my brother up. But he holds back, possibly knowing who we belong to—Nigel Montgomery. Sure, to the naked eye, my stupid brother pounced on Van unprovoked. In their eyes only. To me, my brother pounced on him to get even for fucking with River for so damn long. And he deserved every hit in the face. Plus, so much fucking more. No matter the consequences, I'll sort this out entire fucking situation.

"Do what they fucking say. We don't need Nigel finding out about your fuck up!" I growl, throwing Kieran into the wall and watching helplessly as they cuff his hands behind his back, hauling him between two police officers.

"You see anything?" Another officer approaches with apprehension, staring between me and Callum and Rad, who huddle close with fear crossing their faces.

"No. Where are they taking her?" Rad rasps with tears streaming down his pale cheeks. "She's our girlfriend. We had just walked out here when we saw the lights. Her friend said she had just taken out the trash." He shakes his head, sniffling.

"We didn't see anything. As my friend said, we ran out here when we saw the lights. We were playing in Dead End for over an hour," I say with a sharp nod, refusing to admit anything about my stupid brother and his moronic anger issues.

"And your friend?" the officer asks, pointing to Kieran, who begrudgingly lowers his head and climbs into the back of the cop's car without fanfare.

I scrub a hand down my face. "An overprotective boyfriend with a chip on his damn shoulder," I gripe, trying as best as I can to say my words carefully. The last thing I need to do is implicate that asshole into anything further.

The cop nods, turning and radioing the information we relayed, and begins writing our names and checking out our fists for confirmation we had no part in the attack. After he's done a thorough job of talking to us and gathering information, he finally cracks where they're taking River.

"They're taking her to Central Memorial Hospital," he says as he shoves his notebook into his pocket.

"Any news on her condition?" I ask, but he shakes his head with regret brimming in his eyes.

"Alive and unconscious. That's all I can say," the cop says, waltzing away from us and observing the scene with the three other officers standing in a semi-circle around the blood-soaked pavement, talking in low tones.

"Take me to the hospital with you," Ode says, popping out of nowhere with tears flowing from her eyes. "TAKE ME!" she shouts through her emotions, earning a side hug from Rad. He whispers something in her ear, and her shoulders sag.

"Let's go," I grumble with a sigh, worrying about the girl floating in an ambulance toward the hospital and the man in the back of a cop car for finally beating the tar out of Van—the stupid idiot who can't seem to let go.

"You two go to the damn hospital and monitor River. I have to bail out my stupid brother," I say through gritted teeth. "Take me home first? Gotta grab the damn Tahoe."

"Take some of our saved band money if you have to," Rad says, leading Ode into the backseat of the Tahoe and shutting the door. "It's in the house." I nod, remembering the place where we hid all our savings.

"Yeah," I gripe, jumping into the passenger's seat. "I'll do that."

The entire ride home, listening to Ode cry in the backseat, the scene plays over and over in my head. We went from zero to a million in five seconds flat. Now, I have a brother who sits in jail. Another brother who won't listen to our words without music in his ears and tears in his eyes. Another brother who, as we speak, cries hysterically as he steers the car along the road, heading to the hospital. And at the center of it all, a broken girl who they've all fallen head over heels in love with—me included.

Fuck.

TODAY HAS BEEN A SHIT SHOW OF EPIC PROPORTIONS ON SO MANY LEVELS. The weight of everything that's happened in the span of twenty-four hours barrels down on me, sitting heavily on my chest and shoulders. Leaning back, I rest my head against the cold, textured wall, drawing in air. It's all I can do to ground myself and stay in the moment. If I don't, her lifeless body, covered in blood spatters, comes back to mind and tortures me all over again.

Seeing River bruised up like that, has me twisted into knots and so goddamn conflicted. Half of me wants to scoop her up, fix her, and soothe her discomfort. The other half of me wants to keep her at arm's length to protect the band in case it all goes sideways like today. One horrific injury has them clawing at the walls like feral animals.

The large waiting room in the emergency department of Central Memorial Hospital is stifling. Rogue coughs from others waiting float through the air, mixed with whimpers and complaints. Jesus. My skin crawls with the onslaught of germs crawling all over the place. I'd rather lick the urinal at Dead End than sit in this germ-infested cesspool.

Fuck. I need fresh air. But I can't leave Kieran. He's on the brink of losing his mind, and I need to catch him when he falls. As cliche as it sounds, I'll always catch my brother when he falls with open arms—any of them. They're my family, and I'd give my life for them and risk it all.

My eyes narrow when police officers waltz into the emergency department with their heads held high, flashing their badges. My eyes follow their every move, wondering what they're doing. If they're here to interrogate River, they have another thing coming.

"We got a call on a stabbing victim," one of them says in a faint voice, but it carries through the room.

The nurse behind the desk clicks her nails against the keyboard of her computer and nods.

"Oh, yes. The patient is in room 30B, but be advised, he's very combative. It's superficial, but whoever did it to him accomplished whatever they

needed." Her voice trails off when she leads the officers down the long hallway and beeps them into the official emergency department.

I rub my chin, watching through the doors for any sign of River. Secretly, I hope she comes marching through those doors with a grin, telling us it was all a joke, and we can all go home. It's wishful thinking on my part to hope she wasn't injured so badly. So, I'll support the band and make sure my Little Brat pulls through.

By the time Kieran and I showed up to the waiting room, Ode had gone back with River, apparently claiming she was her sister. Leaving us out here waiting and waiting with no updates, which is all fine and dandy if Kieran, Rad, and Callum weren't falling apart at the fucking seams.

Kieran leans his elbows on his knees, cradling his face in his hands, constantly fidgeting. He hasn't uttered a word since we left the police station. And I haven't either.

All this consuming rage builds inside me like a fucking storm. Here I am, deathly afraid Kieran's about to burst when I'm the one on edge. Someone put their fucking hands on my Little Brat for no good reason, and someone is going to die with my hands wrapped around their throat.

Van may have been present after the fact, bent over her after the assault, but I have doubts it was him in the back of my mind. Was he involved? Possibly. Maybe? Who the hell knows?

Speaking of… My eyes narrow into slits when I gaze at the suspect sitting as far as humanly possible from Kieran, holding an ice pack on his face with a grimace. Every few seconds, his eyes stray this way with fear tinting them.

Good.

He should be fucking afraid of what Kieran will do if he keeps sniffing around what he's marked as his. Van had his chance, and he blew it. It's pathetic as fuck when grown men can't take no for an answer.

Time and time again, River has blown him off, telling him no. So, why he's here, sitting in the waiting room, still blows my fucking mind. The audacity this asshole has to cling on like a leech dangling from my ass cheek baffles my too-tired brain.

I close my eyes and heave a breath. This has been the longest night and earliest morning yet, but there's still more to come. Kieran and I may be over eighteen and adults, but we didn't check in or make it home last night. Sure, Nigel allows—and I use that word loosely—us to play gigs until three a.m., staying out to fulfill our hobby. But make no mistake, there will be hell to pay when we finally crawl home.

NIGEL

We'll have a very long discussion when you two get home.

I roll my lips together, reading the text message repeatedly. He sent it six hours ago when I walked Kieran from the police station. My stomach rolls and knots all at once. Kieran and I are up shit creek without a paddle the moment we walk through the threshold of our front door.

"I'm here for Kieran Knight," I say with no emotion, grinding my damn teeth at the plated window protecting the front desk.

The woman behind it peers up, doing a once over, and nods. "Ah, yes," she mumbles, typing a few things into the computer. "You're in luck. He should be right out." She nods toward a set of double doors secured by a lock mechanism.

"Out?" I question with skepticism. I didn't expect this fight to be easy. Hell, I half expected Kieran to rot away for a few days until the judge came in and charged him with assault and set his damn bond.

"Yes, Mr. Montgomery," she says with a knowing look. My stomach sinks into my ass at the sound of my name, meaning only one thing. "It seems you have friends in high places." My fucking father. He always gets his way. Wonderful.

I hope Kieran likes the backyard because that's where we'll spend an eternity buried under the dirt with the worms and bugs.

"Mm, thanks," I mutter, curling my fists at my side, waiting on the edge of my seat until my stupid brother smacks through the doors with a growl. He doesn't utter a word when he marches out the front door with me on his tail and still doesn't when we pull into the hospital parking lot.

"Why the fuck is he sitting there?"

Great. After six hours of silent brooding, here comes the bull at a full charge. I take a breath, preparing for the utter shit show that's inevitably about to go down.

"He's just fucking staring at us like he didn't do this." Kieran narrows his eyes again and clenches his fingers into fists around the ice, numbing his pain.

"Maybe he didn't," I remark quietly, earning the full brunt of Kieran's ire.

"You don't think he did? He was right fucking there, Asher!" he hisses so loudly that his voice bounces off the tall ceilings. "He did it! And I'm going to bury him for it." A tick forms in his jaw when he whips his head, holding Van's gaze.

Yup. Shit show.

I shrug, closing my eyes. "Don't jump to so many conclusions," I say through a yawn, sinking further into my chair. Maybe if I fall asleep, this will all be a distant dream.

"You're just… you're just going to let him get away with it?" Kieran growls, I'm sure, throwing spittle everywhere with each word.

I sigh. "You've already been arrested once and released. Do you want to chance it again? It's called silent planning, Kieran," I mutter through the thick fog clouding my mind. If I don't get some sleep soon, my head will explode from the headache working its way up my neck and into the back of my skull. "Maybe you should learn the skill." He huffs at me, throwing himself back into the chair.

"Asher, man." I sigh again, peeking an eye open, revealing Rad's concerned and fallen expression. It twists, contorting his face into an anguish-filled feature. "You gotta do something. He won't take them out. He's losing his shit. I don't know what to do. He hasn't been this bad since-since, Jenny," Rad murmurs the last part, hiccupping at the thought of Callum's little sister and everything he went through concerning the plane crash. "He's in love with her, man. We gotta…"

Holding up a hand, I stop him in his tracks. The sad truth is they're all in love with her. They may not admit it yet, but they're head over heels, stupidly in love, leading us down dangerous roads of sabotage. I won't let my best friend suffer in silence by drowning out the world and ignoring everyone around him.

Climbing to my feet, I make my way to Callum's silent bubble with purpose. His head rests back against the wall with his eyes closed and his hands buried deep in his pockets, slouching in his chair.

Settling beside him, I lightly nudge him with my shoulder until he peeks an eye open. An array of emotions filter through his gray eyes when his broken gaze meets mine. A tiny twitch forms at the edge of his lip, letting me know the man doesn't want to speak about the situation. He'd rather lose himself in the loud music thumping through his earbuds than face reality. I tap my ear until he huffs, yanking out his earbud.

"What's up?" he murmurs in a soft voice, thick with emotions. His eyes drop to the ground, taking in the disgusting tile pattern.

"I should ask you the same. What's going through your mind, Callum?"

He meets my eye at the sound of his name, quickly locking away any emotions he feels. Usually, Callum is an easy book to read. For me, anyway. Every emotion inside him slides across his face like an open book. Today he's a blank canvas, not giving any hints as to why he's isolated himself. Given the circumstances, I understand why.

"It's all I see," he mutters, fidgeting with his earbuds between his fingers.

"What is?"

Even though I know the answer, I still ask. It's the only way to break Callum out of his rut, by forcing him to utter the dreaded words. He's not alone, though. The second my eyes fall shut, she's all I see. All broken, bruised, bloodied, lying on the cold, dark pavement forever haunts my nightmares. But for him, he'll literally never forget.

He shakes his head, and his face contorts into deep hurt. "Her just lying there," he whispers as tears fall down his cheeks. "I can't get that image out of here," he cries out, thumping his fist into his head several times. "I can't make it stop, Asher." My heart fucking breaks for my friend, shattering into pieces at the emotions rolling through him.

"Think of happier times, man," I murmur, rubbing a hand down his back and soothing his pain. "Think of the time we had on the Ferris wheel. Or the amazing show she helped us put on last night. Think of anything else." Images of River's broad smile and snarky attitude come to mind, and my shoulders sag at the memories in tune with his.

"Those were good times," he whispers with a nod. The more I rub his back, the calmer he becomes, and soon, all his anxiety leaves. Sure, the image will live inside him forever. There's nothing I can do about that. But for now, I can ease his worries.

"Yeah, because you finally got your dick sucked by a gorgeous chick," Rad quips, coming to rest beside him. "Let those be the images you think about forever. You gotta block that depressing shit out."

"I'm going to fucking kill him," Kieran growls, jumping to his feet.

Under normal circumstances, I'd tell his ass to sit down and take a chill pill. But Kieran's emotions are in the driver's seat, controlling his actions. There's no stopping him from doing stupid shit like marching toward Van like he's about to chew him up and spit him out. Only this time, Kieran won't leave any bones behind.

"Fuck sake," I grumble, jumping up to catch him by the scruff of his shirt and haul him back. "We're in public. Unless you want Nigel to beat your ass even worse," I mumble the last part, earning a scowl. "I'll make him leave," I say, silently pleading with the idiot to sit down.

"Fine. I can't look at his stupid face anymore," he grumbles, turning on his toes and plopping back down in the chair with a grunt. Running a hand over his face, he closes his eyes and hopefully counts to ten.

I shove my hands in my pockets and walk toward Van, sitting a good thirty feet away with an ice pack resting against his swollen face. If one good thing came out of this situation, it's the bruising on Van's pathetic face.

"My suggestion would be to leave," I say, sitting beside him. "Unless you want my idiot brother to rip your face off. Again," I huff, rolling my eyes. "Look at him; he wants to march over and put his fist through your teeth." A chuckle works its way up my throat when Van stiffens, clearly threatened by the big dummy death-glaring in his direction.

That's right, Van. Be deeply afraid of him. He's had years and years of pent-up aggression. And he'd be excited to use it on you.

"I'm waiting to hear how she's doing," Van stubbornly grumbles, crossing his arms over his chest.

"I'm curious," I say, slumping down into the seat. Running my fingertips along my chin, I pop my eyebrow when I pique his interest. "How would Whitley feel about you being here, waiting for River to get released?"

"What the hell does it matter to you, man?" he asks through gritted teeth. "Why're you so damn hellbent on telling her anything? She has nothing to do with any of this. River is my…"

"I'm just saying," I say, waving a hand lazily. "One of these days, your fiancée will catch on." I shrug, climbing to my feet and letting my implication hit its mark. "Besides, I can text you when she gets out and is healthy."

"You would, wouldn't you?" he growls, shifting the ice on his face to scowl at me. "You'd really send that email and let her know…" He swallows hard, shaking his head.

"What? That you used to fuck River behind her back at the record store? Or that you're stalking her now? Or that you really had something to do with all this?" I wave a finger, smirking when he gets paler and paler with every word I speak, eventually turning green. "There's plenty I can do. Now or later, that's your choice," I say with a shrug, waltzing back toward Kieran and plopping down next to him. He raises a brow at me, practically begging with his eyes about what I said.

Satisfaction spears through me when Van grabs his shit and stomps out of the emergency department. Seconds later, his engine roars to life, reverberating through the lofty room. Finally, I settle back in my chair, letting my eyes fall shut. Maybe now I can get some rest. All the children are snug in their chairs without worry.

"Finally," Kieran shouts, jumping to his feet.

My damn body bounces out of the chair on instinct with a pounding heart. Swallowing hard, I blow out a breath as Ode emerges from behind the locked ER doors.

"Nice to see you, too," Ode quips with a tired groan. Bags sit under her red, puffy eyes, letting me know she hasn't slept a wink.

"How is she?" Rad asks, out of breath, rushing Ode with urgency, furrowing his brows.

Ode sighs, running her fingers over her forehead. "She's finally awake and talking to the doctors and cops. It's fuzzy for her, but she's doing okay. They're going to run tests and shit. Doc thinks she has a concussion and abrasions from the attack. So, she's fortunate it wasn't worse. But we'll see after the MRI."

"Jesus-Jesus," Callum mutters with a quivering chin, pulling his fist to his mouth.

"She's a tough cookie," Ode says, clapping him on the shoulder and gently squeezing. "Believe me, and she's already bossing around the doctors and demanding to leave. Don't worry too much about her, okay? I'd say you should probably go, but then I'd probably be talking to brick walls," she huffs.

"Yeah, we're not going anywhere until I know my pretty girl is feeling okay."

"Can we see her?" Kieran asks with hope.

Ode wrinkles her nose. "I think like one at a friggin time. Whoa, dude!" she hisses, turning on her toes when Kieran pushes past without care and marches back into the ER, disappearing behind the doors.

I roll my eyes. "Friggin idiot," I mumble through a tired sigh.

"I'm next," Rad says, rubbing his hands together. "My pretty girl needs a nice massage and a dose of penis-cyclin."

"You'll only hurt her," Callum grumbles, slapping him on the back of his head.

"By the way," Ode says with furrowed brows. "Did you guys know that Bradley from high school came in with a stab wound?"

"He what?" Rad yelps, and his body stiffens, fury taking over his face.

Yeah, there's something up with him and Bradley. Every time that fucker enters a room, he tenses. And those cops before, they were here for him. Who the hell finally stabbed that dick? My entire body locks up, drowning out the noises around me.

Bradley Bradford is officially on my shit list. A stab wound? That's awfully fucking coincidental. Images of River's fingers dripping with blood run through my mind, and before I know what I'm doing, I'm marching down the hallway without a clue as to where I'm going. Kieran grumbles something behind a curtain before I throw it open, revealing River nestled against his chest. His arms lock around her protectively, gently running his fingers through her long, ratted strands.

Looking around, I pull the curtain back behind me, huffing when the rest of the idiots pile into the room and hover around a broken-looking River. Tears threaten to burn the back of my eyes as I take her in, noting the black and blue bruises lining her face. The three of us stand there with gaping mouths as she untucks herself from Kieran's grasp and refuses to look in our direction. Keeping her eye downcast, she summons Ode to the edge of the bed.

"Leave," River rasps, taking Ode's shaking hand. "Get some sleep, please." Exhaustion pulls at her tiny voice, tugging at my fucking black heartstrings. She sounds like she's fighting a battle she won't win—like she's already given in to the pain, and defeat has taken over. But that's not the River I know. The girl I know fights tooth and nail through anything and with anybody. Fuck.

Ode's face falls, but she squeezes River's hand. "Fine, I'll leave y'all to it. Bitch, I love you. But don't you ever pull that shit again." Leaning down, she plants a soft kiss on River's cheek, lingering long enough to whisper something, and pulls back with a stern look. "I'll check in with your momma, too. And you four," she says with a demanding tone, putting a hand on her hip. "You fuck with River. You fuck with me. Got it?"

We all nod in unison. Not daring to toe an inch out of line while she death glares at us with mama bear vibes emanating from her. The fierce expression doesn't leave until we're protectively cupping our balls and shivering from her threat, and with one last look, she waves, walking out the door with apprehension.

Once Ode clears the room, Rad wraps his arms around River, smothering her with light kisses.

"I'm fine," she groans, trying to weakly shove him off.

"No, Pretty Girl. You're not," he murmurs lovingly, moving a piece of her hair out of her face. "Bradley did this, didn't he? Did he…?"

River visibly cringes at his words, recoiling into Kieran's chest and hiding her face from us. The world blurs around me, mixing into a multitude of colors, and my heart fucking drops out of my fucking body. Ice runs through my veins, raising the tiny hairs on the back of my neck. Grabbing my skull with force, I massage my temples until the pain subsides into a dull ache. It all makes fucking sense now. Every goddamn piece of the puzzle clicks into place, and murder vibrates through me.

"You stabbed him?" I blurt breathlessly as piles of information storm through my mind like wildfire blowing through. "He did it?" I accuse now, narrowing my eyes and taking in her reaction.

"You what?" Kieran asks in a deadly voice, looking down at her with fear twisting his expression. His eyes widen, and he tugs her impossibly closer, with emotions pulling him in every direction. By the time we make it home, he will be so rung out. "He what?" he murmurs in disbelief.

River hides her face in his chest, taking several deep breaths before she collects herself and speaks.

"Please, let it go," she murmurs in a broken voice. "Please, just let go. I don't want to talk about it right now." No. It seems she doesn't want to talk about it ever again. So, it's time to force the words from her tongue so we can cut Bradley open and feed him to the vultures.

"River," I bark, marching to her side. Leaning over Kieran, I gently grab her chin and force her to stare at me. So many emotions rest in her moss-green eyes. It's hard to tell how she's feeling. Fear. Anguish. Pain. Resentment. It's all wrapped into one. "He'll get what's coming to him, Little Brat. Don't even worry about it," I promise through a growl, envisioning his death by my hands.

"Don't worry about it?" she whispers as fat tears drop onto her cheeks, sending searing pain through my chest at the sight of her pain. "I have to worry about it. I have to make sure he gets punished for his crimes! He got away with it once, and I won't stand back and let him harm any more women." Her body trembles in Kieran's embrace, and the room falls silent.

I don't miss her words. Or how she said them. All the answers reside there and understanding pushes through me. River was the girl Bradley bragged about for months on end. Only, she wasn't a willing participant like he eluded her to be.

"Got away with it once?" Kieran asks, furrowing his brow. "What?" River's face pales when the realization hits Kieran hard, and a gasp forces its way through his parted lips. "No," he murmurs, running a thumb gently across her cheeks and jolts, eyes bulging. I swear he stops breathing, and his head shakes in denial. "The fucking beating we gave him over the girl you found? No!" His fingers flex, engorging the veins lining his forearms.

Grabbing his arm, River shakes her head with a pained expression. "It was a long time ago. I don't want to talk about it. I just want to move forward. I want Bradley to get what's coming to him."

She rolls her lips together, sadness glazing over her eyes. Something about the situation sends shame through her; it's even more apparent when she closes her eyes. Kieran swallows hard, rubbing the back of his neck. Anguish takes over his expression when he kisses her cheek, murmuring words I can't hear.

"More than a stabbing, Little Brat?" I quip, finally earning a soft smile that doesn't quite reach her eyes.

"Jail time. Anything to make sure he doesn't hurt anyone else," she whispers in complete and utter defeat—something I've never seen from her.

Sitting back, River stays snuggled in Kieran's arms, soaking up his support. "We'll get you a wonderful lawyer. We'll help with whatever you need," Kieran promises, kissing her forehead with a feather-light kiss.

"Everything we have, we'll give you," Callum promises, leaning over to kiss her head.

"I'll bury him in acid and laugh as his bones disintegrate," Rad mumbles, kissing her temple.

A million thoughts rush through me when we leave River lying in the hospital. After sitting there all day and through nine p.m., they kicked us out, stating they admitted her until they got her results back. Our visit was over, but our night had only just begun.

Tension rises in my chest when we pull into the house's driveway, looming in front of us.

"It was nice knowing you," Kieran mumbles, hanging his head with a heavy sigh.

"I can't believe you got arrested," I say, sitting back in my seat and huffing a breath.

Over her—the girl we need in our corner. Over the entire situation—is what I want to say. Every inch of Kieran vibrates with a restless rage begging to come back out. So, I zip my lips and inspect the situation one more time. Another time and place, I'd let him pummel Van into oblivion. Not now. Not on the heels of his arrest.

Getting arrested is the least of our worries at the moment. Kieran didn't just get himself thrown into jail; he got the both of us thrown into the lion's den, covered in blood and defenseless. Now it's time to face the devil himself.

Raising a brow, I stare at the dark, empty office window my father always peers out of and note the darkened room and closed blinds. In fact, the entire house swims in darkness, ready to swallow us whole. Somewhere in the depths of hell, our demon waits to attack us when we least expect it.

"Where is he?" I murmur, peering at every window, half expecting the damn boogeyman to pop out and attack.

My skin tingles in anticipation of the night ahead. We've been out for twenty-four hours and haven't reached out. We may be twenty-one and old enough to hold our own, but in his eyes, we are children he's successfully controlled.

"I don't care as long as he's not lying in wait, ready to attack us," Kieran says, frowning up at the window when we exit the car. "Again," he murmurs, shivering at the memory of Nigel popping out and taking us by surprise. He lives to make our lives miserable.

Looking around, I take stock of everything around us. Empty driveway. Empty street. The only logical explanation is his vehicle is in the garage, or he's not here. I peek in the garage window, only to find Gloria's BMW. Relief slams into me, and for the first time today, I feel like I can breathe, and the heavy pressure lifts. Not that my father won't punish us when he returns, but we have a reprieve from his cruelty. For now, at least. That's all I can ask for after a long day of waiting.

"He's not here," I rejoice confidently, leading the way and quietly entering through the front door. Silence clings to every inch of the space, and peace washes over me for once in my damn life.

"Maybe we got away with it," Kieran says with false hope.

"Don't hold your breath. Now, I'm going to bed," I say, not waiting for his response, and quietly enter my bedroom at the top of the stairs.

Darkness greets me like an old friend, enveloping me in a warm hug. Once again, something eerie crashes over me, and my hairs stand on end. A lone figure hovers in the shadows, looking out my window.

"It's that girl, isn't it?" Gloria asks in a haughty tone, turning toward me. No expression breaks through the darkness concealing her face. "That bitch from Central City? The same one Kieran obsessed over as a kid." She scoffs at that, coming toward me. "My advice?"

"Sure," I say, committing to a non-answer with a shrug.

"Leave her as far behind as possible. Those Central girls will only bring you one of two things: disease or pregnancy," she hisses in disgust. "She'll only bring you boys down. You're destined for greatness."

"Greatness, huh?" I rub my chin, milling over her words.

A normal child would preen under her confidence and praise with a grin. But I refuse. Gloria may seem like she's looking out for our best interest, but by the devious gleam in her eyes, she's up to something. I'm not sure what. What could she gain from this conversation?

"You boys have talent, and the word on the street is you are applying to a big competition?" She raises a brow, stepping more into the light of the moon beaming through the windowpanes. "Something in, say… California?"

I raise a brow, my heart secretly thumping against my ribs. If it's out in the open that we may go to California, my father might screw it all up by lifting his finger. It's bad enough we're financially strapped to him with our cars and phones, but he could take them away with the snap of his fingers. There's nothing more heart-stopping than realizing we're dangling a treat in front of his face to hurt us with more.

"I can make sure he doesn't have a clue," she sniffs, sticking her nose in the air.

"And what do you want in return, Gloria? You can't be doing this out of the kindness of your heart. So, tell me what you're willing to do and what you want in return." I lift a brow when her shoulders push back, and she turns on the lamp next to my bed, revealing the black and blue bruises lining her face. I'd gasp if I were surprised by the marks on her body, but I'm not. Figures Nigel would work out his frustrations on her.

"I'm your reminder, Asher," she says, cringing when she runs a finger down her bruised cheek. "When you're not here, he does this. And I'm tired of being a punching bag." She waves her hand, showing the damage on her face and further down her body.

"Fair enough," I say, looking her up and down as she clings to the silk robe encasing her body.

"You want the money to go? You want the car to get you there without issues? Do you want your father not to know anything about it? I can help, but I have stipulations," she says, straightening more with a cringe.

"Enlighten me, Gloria. How would my father not know about the missing money or the Tahoe? How do you intend to get away with any of that when you're just as stuck? Hmm?" I raise my brow, trying to keep the condescending tone from leaking through. If I remain pessimistic about the situation, I can't get my hopes up on making our great escape. Nothing will stop us. Not even Nigel Montgomery.

You know, all I wanted was my bed and a nice long sleep without this bullshit floating around in my mind. A clean cut from my father's grasp is all I've begged for, for years now. But every day gets worse and worse, and his control tightens on our reigns. Some would scoff at our age and tell us to leave without notice, but they don't have a fucking clue what this life is like. Having someone hovering above you and micromanaging your every financial move is more complex than they could imagine. Add in fists and shouting matches—yeah, it's heaven. Nigel controls every aspect of our life. So, even at twenty-one, we're stuck in his grasp until we can slowly ease our way out.

For once in Gloria's pathetic life, she looks stricken when she scrunches her bruised nose. "It's my money," she says in a soft voice. "It's all I have, but I could help you get there and set up. Any extras will help."

My brows fly into my hairline, and my lips pop open. Hers? My father doesn't allow us to have our means, keeping us tightly wound around his grubby finger.

"Why?" I ask, crossing my arms. "What's stopping you from taking Camilla and running with what you have?" Leaning against the wooden door frame, I sigh, watching the indecisive cross her face. If she had money, then she could flee without a glance back.

"It has to be you. Once you're out, I can get out," she whispers with glossy eyes. "I have something to take care of before I can leave. Besides, he'd hunt me down and drag me back, kicking and screaming. Think of Camilla. What would he do to her? He'd take custody and bury me so deep in court fees I'd never come up for air. I'd end up like your mother." A cold slap in the face would have been better than hearing my past on her lips. For once, Gloria is right. She'd end up at the wrong end of a needle and buried so deep her secrets would never resurface—like my mother. Longing hits me out of nowhere, but I swallow it down. I don't have the time or energy to relive my tragic past with the cravings for my mother.

"And what's that?" I ask, clearing my throat and shaking away the thoughts in my head.

"Do you want the deal or not?" she huffs with obvious annoyance.

"Maybe," I say with a nonchalant shrug. "If you keep your mouth shut about it."

Gloria's lips thin, and she nods. "I have two stipulations."

Of course, she does; Gloria can't do anything as simple as turning the other cheek when we need her to. Keeping my father's nose out of my business is priority number one. Especially when it concerns the Battle of the Bands—the one thing we need. He gave us one year to sow our wild oats with the damn band, and I'm making the best of it without his interference. There's no stopping us now.

"What are they?" I ask, holding back a yawn.

"When you win the Battle of the Bands, help me leave," she says, looking directly into my eyes.

"If we win. There's a whole competition. It's us against fifteen bands, and it's not a guarantee." I shake my head, running a hand through my hair. "And where'd you like to go, Gloria?" I ask, seriously wondering where this woman would want to go.

"Anywhere but here," she says with a shaky nod. "Far away from him…" She swallows hard at that admission, but good for her. "You'll win. You guys have to win. Second stipulation…"

"Go on," I say, waving a hand.

"The Central Girl stays here," she says, firmly pointing a finger down. "I know you've offered to take her with you, but she belongs where she is. Not out there."

I snort. "Right. Try prying her out of your son's hands." Or mine. She's valuable to us, especially in East Point, California. If she doesn't go, then we might not have a chance of winning. There's no way... I shake my head, rubbing my chin.

"Think it over, Asher. Watch the way she's wearing each of you down. Soon, she'll split you all up, and Whispered Words won't be a thing anymore. In less than a year, you'll be suited up under your father's thumb. All because you couldn't leave one girl where she belongs. You're going to be famous. Do you want some lost, stray skank following you around?"

Fuck! My eye twitches. Hook. Line. And sinker. An ache forms in my chest as she hits every point of my worries in the head. She raises her brow, reaching for the handle until I grab her wrist.

"How much money are you offering to get us away from here?" I growl through gritted teeth.

She smiles at me like the snake she is, winding her tail around me and squeezing me until I give in to her every whim. "I have five thousand. It's good enough to get you there, help you get established, and then once you win, you'll have so much more than that. Plus, whatever you've been saving over the years."

"Are you spying on us, Gloria? And how do you know what the prize is?" I ask, raising a brow.

"You should be more careful with your internet searches," she says with a cluck of her tongue. "Just think it over. Watch the girl. See how easily she gets what she wants. Central girls are all the same," she says with a shake of her head.

"Like you?" I mutter when she walks out and shuts the door behind her.

EVERY PIECE OF FUCKING SKIN ATTACHED TO MY BONES PULSATES WITH MY heartbeat, burning from the dark bruises dotting my body and face. Flashbacks from my night of terror overwhelm me as I lie awake in the early morning. Bright sunlight beams in from the fucked-up curtains I told Rad to secure the night before.

Clamping my aching eyes shut, I try to block out the horrors following my every step. The phantom feel of Bradley's fists driving into my face over and over again sends my heart pounding against my ribs. Oxygen seems to thin, evading my lungs. Warmth presses into each side of me, like most days and nights now, bringing me back from the brink of my waking nightmare.

Squished between Rad and Callum in my bed, their presence doesn't drive the memories of my attack any further away, but they help to keep me grounded here on earth. I would have sent them home the first night and suffered in silence if it wasn't for their insistence. And I'd rather suffer between their bodies than between my cold sheets. Their presence keeps the monster in my mind at bay, but the memory of my attack will live forever.

Groaning, I try flipping to my other side. A giant hand wraps around my waist, holding me down. Even when he's snoring, Rad's handsy as hell and pulling me into him like I'm his precious possession. Next thing I know, he'll have his tongue down my throat while experiencing some sort of sex dream, and then… A flush of warmth spreads straight to my pussy at the thought. Shit. I need to get laid soon. They've each treated me like a little porcelain doll since I came home, and it's driving me bonkers. I may be broken, but I'm damn horny.

The tip of his nose drags across my neck, murmuring sleepy gibberish. The tone of his deep voice sounds so damn happy and raspy. His hands wander across my stomach, peeling up my sleep shirt and rubbing circles across my belly. *Lower. Go lower,* I mentally chant, feeling empty when his hand stills and a snore escapes him. From the moment I got home from the

hospital, Rad's been clingier than ever, following my every move and watching me every chance he gets.

"I'll be okay," I murmur, grimacing when I lie in my cold sheets for the first time since getting home. A headache forms in the back of my skull, pounding until I squeeze my eyes shut.

"It almost happened again. On my watch, Pretty Girl." Deep anguish leaks into his low voice, and his eyes fill with tears. "I can't ever let that happen again," he mumbles, kissing my cheek and silently promising protection.

With major reluctance, I peel myself away from Rad and climb over Callum, missing their warmth. Silently, I giggle, forcing my hand over my mouth when they scoot together, filling the space. Rad's hand lands on Callum's hip, squeezing until Callum groans, wrinkling his nose. Rad's hand turns circles over Callum's hip until it freezes, and another snore fills the room.

I shake my head, running a hand over my forehead, and wince when the blinding pain hits me again, whitening my vision. It's been a whole week since the attack and five days since they let me out of the hospital. There, they determined my injuries weren't life-threatening, but they wanted to keep me on stronger pain meds through the IV. So, I sat with four vigilant guys, watching my every move.

"Go. Home," I groan when Kieran lies in the hospital bed next to me. "I'm getting out tomorrow."

Please let me breathe, you overbearing oaf.

"I'll stay the night, Pretty Girl. Your momma wanted hourly updates!" Rad chirps, sitting on the small couch next to Callum in my assigned hospital room, staring down at their phones. "Besides, Angel Warrior has a mobile app now. We have plenty to do. Die demon!" he hisses, smacking his phone screen with his thumb several times.

"I got 'em," Callum murmurs, poking his tongue out in concentration. "Onto the pearly gates."

"Hells yes, die, you dirty demons! We're headed to Heaven's light. Shit, look. Someone else is here, too." Rad leans in further, squinting his eyes. "Looks like it's just you, me, and this SGW2100. Fighting the good fight. Yessss!" Rad cries out in victory, high-fiving Callum. "And high five to you, too, internet dude."

I blow out a breath, blocking out their over-joyous celebration. "Didn't you hear what I said?" I groan, snuggling into Kieran more despite my protests of wanting to be left alone.

I need peace and quiet, something I don't get when they're around. But yet, they're a comfort I can't explain. It's a weird twist of fate to want peace, but they're the peace I need.

Leaning into Kieran, I sigh with exhaustion. It's only three p.m., but the urge to close my eyes and sleep the day away settles in. Probably thanks to my pain meds.

"Close your eyes, River Blue. We've got you, baby," Kieran murmurs, kissing my hair with a sigh. "They've taken Bradley to the station. That asshole isn't getting out any time soon." Finally, that prick is going to pay for his crimes. Knowing my luck, though, they'll come after me for injuring him. Worth it.

"They kept my knife," I grumble, closing my eyes and relaxing into him more.

"I'll get it back for you, Little Brat. It seems you need to protect yourself more these days. Always looking for trouble." I don't bother giving him an appropriate answer. I lift my middle finger in the air, earning a scoffed "rude" remark and then a deep, rumbling chuckle.

Looking at Callum and Rad snuggled together in my bed makes a smile cross my lips. They're so damn cute together, and I can't help but snap a picture for blackmail later. But right now? I need pain meds like my life depends on them. Every step toward the living room jostles my face, and my nerves light up with pain like a damn Christmas tree.

"Hey, Ma," I murmur, heading to the kitchen for a glass of water.

I need pain meds, food, sex, and sleep, in that order.

"Baby," she says softly, slowly climbing to her feet with a grunt, grabbing her walker beside her, and balancing herself. Standing straight, she puts weight on her booted foot, only wincing once.

"You're getting around better," I say with a small smile, gulping water. "But wait. Why're you dressed?" I ask, taking in the loose jeans and white blouse, even her shoe that is slipped on.

She flashes me a beaming smile, slowly sliding forward. "It's a good day. Korrine and I are going out for lunch after she takes me to my doctor's appointment. They're going to see how my ankle is healing, and I think I'm getting a bladder infection," she says, making her way toward me. "How are you feeling? My poor baby," she mumbles, running a trembling finger along my jawline. "I can't believe someone did this to you." She shakes her head. "I always knew Booker's place was dangerous."

I take a deep breath, ignoring her last comment. As a whole, Central City is rough, but we've always made it. Booker's place is definitely not in the best area, but it's what I've had to do to contribute to our financial situation. If it weren't for me, we would have frozen over many winters and not had the extra cash for food.

"I'm okay. It hurts, but I'll survive," I say, blowing her off with a shrug, causing her to drop a hand with a frown.

"You're not working, right?" she asks, raising a brow as a knock sounds on the door, followed by Korrine's voice.

"I'm here for ya, Stella. Car is warming up," she shouts through the door.

"Gimme just a sec!" Ma shouts with a head shake.

I snort into my glass of water, swallowing more and soothing the constant burning in my throat. "No. Booker informed me I'm off for a month until my face heals."

Internally, I groan at the sedentary life I'll be living. Sure, I'll still have schoolwork and online classes to attend, but I'm sitting still without my work. And that's not me. I've held a job since I was fifteen, and to do nothing is messing me up. Fuck. At least I'll have Whispered Words to keep me company and busy with their schedule coming up. They'll press submit on their application tonight, and then we'll cross our fingers.

"Good," she says, kissing my cheek. "Those boys still here?" My face heats when a knowing grin plasters on her face. "They're sweet. I like them. But now, I have to go, baby. Be good today, okay?" she mumbles, kissing my cheek.

Opening the door for her, I put my hand on her forearm and help her get over the lip of the door frame.

"Bye! Be good," I say, waving them off as they head to Korrine's bright red Lincoln and take off down the road.

Blowing out my breath, I head back into the bedroom, stopping short.

"What the hell are you doing?" I ask, wrinkling my nose.

I half expected the idiots to be asleep still, not rifling through my panty drawer.

"Listen, Pretty Girl! I woke up stroking Callum's…"

"Rad," Callum hisses, shaking his head with red tinting his cheeks and over the bridge of his nose. He quickly covers his face with his hands and groans.

"His leg! His damn leg! But it should have been you, Pretty Girl. Then I felt hair where hair shouldn't have been, and I freaked. I might have smacked him…"

"In my-my dick." Callum frowns, holding a hand over his boxers. "You punched my dick."

"But it was a sexy dick punch, right?" Rad beams, looking between the two of our fallen faces. "Right. There's no such thing as a sexy dick punch." He shrugs, continuing to paw through my damn panty drawer like it's normal.

"What exactly are you doing?" I ask again, earning a wave in my direction. "The fuck?" I sigh, pinching the bridge of my nose despite the pain.

Humming a wild tune under his breath, he finally finds a tiny pink thong and holds it up in the air in victory.

"Ah, look! Your panties are Simba, Pretty Girl. Welcome to the winning circle of life! You're going to win me a race." He bobs his head, shoving the tiny panties into his pocket, and shuts the drawer with a thud.

Standing before me, Rad buttons the top of his distressed jeans and grins more, taking me in with lustful eyes. I groan, shaking my head, too damn tired to deal with his crazy ass. By the gleaming look on his face and his delicious shirtless chest, I know exactly where he's headed.

"You've got a race?" I surmise, stepping up to Callum, who rests on the edge of my bed in his cute Batman boxers. His golden skin glows in the late morning sun beaming through the opened curtains.

"Your-your pills," he says, opening his hand and revealing two tiny pills. One is for pain, and the other is a preventative antibiotic in case of infection.

"Thank you." Throwing my head back, I wash the pills with the rest of the cold water and hum as they go down my throat. In thirty minutes or less, the pain will evaporate, and I'll be free for another four hours.

"Yes, Pretty Girl! It's a huge race. Some fools from up north are coming down and entering the race. Can you believe it? Someone thinks they can beat the speedy Rad," he scoffs, rolling his eyes and thumping his chest. "But I'm the best, baby! No losing for me. And now that I have your pretty girl panties in my pocket, I'm sure going to cross that finish line a thousand dollars richer." He nods a few times, so damn sure of himself.

"The horror," I mumble, groaning when I climb back into bed and cover my face with my hands. I don't want to see the sun or the outside for another five days.

Rad huffs and heavy footsteps march toward the bed with intent.

"Pretty Girl, you can't just lie in bed for the next month. You have to get up and do things," Rad mumbles, kneeling at the side of the bed. "Don't waste away," he mumbles, kissing my cheek when I sigh. "Come play with me?" he asks with a hopeful expression, giving me his best puppy dog eyes and puffing out his lip.

"Not today," I whisper, leaning into his fingers as they stroke through my hair and disappointment pulls at his face.

The fact is, I'd rather hide away in my damn apartment than show my broken face to the world. Not until it heals. The moment they showed up and barged into my hospital room, I wanted to hide and not let them see me. Somehow, they've peeled back every layer protecting me, getting right down to my vulnerabilities. They see the real me hiding behind my snark and knife—the real River. A cold sweat covers my skin at the realization, and I blow out a breath.

"I-I know," Callum says, scooping me into the side of his body, infecting me with his warmth. Snuggling deeper into him, I sigh, basking in his comfort and letting everything else disappear.

"Kieran and Asher will be off house arrest soon," Rad says with a determined look, clenching his fist.

"Why haven't they ever moved in with you?" I ask, peeking an eye open, feeling something open up in the pit of my stomach.

They both avoid my eyes, staring at the comforter, the floor, and each other's eyes with an intense stare. Shaking their heads in unison, they blow it off. But I know something is up with Asher's dad. I remember him from years ago. The man who marched through the complex in a tight suit, sticking his nose in the air. Once he made it to Gloria's apartment, he'd promptly kick Kieran out, sometimes without shoes. Then, we'd meet on the hill and bask in each other's company.

"Their-their father's the biggest dick around," Callum mutters, burying his nose in my neck and hiding the guilt crossing his face.

"They'll be out tomorrow. Thank God. One bark from Asher, and you'll be out of bed before he can slap you with his dick."

I wrinkle my nose. "They're twenty-one… why're they still listening to him? Like they're grounded? That's stupid." Swallowing hard, I wonder how hard life is for them. If they can't leave, he has some sort of hold on the boys, keeping them there. But how? And why?

Rad's lips turn down, and his face softens. "I know, Pretty Girl. It's hard to understand. Believe me. We've tried to get them to move in and say screw school and go all in for the band…" He shakes his head, running a hand through his unruly mullet. "They just can't, babe. They… he's…"

"He's holding something over them and-and I don't know what he does to them, but I don't think it's good. Not with Nigel Montgomery hanging around," Callum mumbles with sadness, tinting his tone.

"Does he?" I ask, swallowing my words before they can even leave my tongue.

"They don't say," Rad says, picking at the comforter and scrunching his face. "But we do what we can. However, we know how," he mumbles, swallowing thickly.

"Okay," I whisper, unconvinced of their words. Someone has to be able to get them out if they're in a bad situation.

Clearing his throat, Rad straightens up and takes my hands. "Well, Pretty Girl. You're staying here with Callum today. Make sure you corrupt him a little," Rad says with a wink, kissing my cheek one last time before jumping to his feet.

"No shirt?" I ask when he pulls his sneakers on and shrugs off my comment.

"No shirt, panties in my pocket. This is all I need for good luck," Rad says, jumping to his feet. "I'll see you later!"

And with that, Rad marches out the sliding glass door toward the parking lot. A loud rumble sounds as his dirt bike sparks to life and reverberates through the walls, making my brows dip. Did he seriously bring that here and leave it outside? He's lucky the thing is still there.

"Looks like it's just me and you, hot stuff," I mumble, turning in his arms to look up at his beautiful face.

His gray eyes cloud over with some emotion when his hand brushes back the hair from my face and tucks it behind my ears.

"Looks-looks like it," he breathes, roaming his eyes down the dark bruises on my cheeks. "How's it feeling now, Little Star?"

The first night after my attack, Callum pulled into himself more, relying on his earbuds to guide him through the trauma. My heart broke for him when he broke down with tears in his eyes, telling me he could barely look at me.

"It's not-not because of your looks," he sniffles, wiping away the tears on his cheeks. "I just... I can't look at you and see the mess he left-left after hurting you so badly. If I have to remember those bruises for the rest of my life, I'll hunt him down and kill-kill him," he breathlessly proclaims, growing increasingly agitated by the second.

Gripping his hand tightly, I lean my head on his shoulder, keeping my eyes down. "I know," I mutter, emotions digging their dirty claws into my throat. "I'm sor-"

"Don't you dare," he hisses, pushing his fingers through my hair and bringing his face to mine. Stormy gray eyes blaze into mine, and he shakes his head, lightly pressing his lips into mine. "Don't ever be sorry, Little Star. Not now. Not ever."

As the bruises darkened and then moved into the healing stage, he managed to look at me for more than a split second. I don't blame him for his caution. Callum has to take care of his needs in any way he knows, and I respect that.

Placing my hand on his, I intertwine our fingers together. "So much better now. I think the medicine is finally kicking in," I hum, finally feeling the relief run through my veins and take away the bits of pain left over. Thank God for pain meds, or I'd have rolled over and died from the pounding taking over my nerves.

"Good," he whispers, examining me again until his eyes fall to my lips. "Can I kiss you, Little Star? I've been aching to put my lips on yours," he whispers an inch from my lips.

I nod, sighing into the soft kiss. Whenever his lips touch mine, it's like coming home, and the sun shines through, warming my entire being. Bravely, his tongue brushes along the seam of my lips, begging for entry with a small, desperate moan.

Our tongues twist together in a slow dance, tasting each other and taking our time. Callum molds his body to mine, becoming more frantic when his fingers clasp my hair, forcing my lips harder against his with urgency.

Pain spreads through my face from my injuries, but I don't dare stop him when he's gracefully taking what he wants for the first time in his life. It feels too damn good to stop, and I want this. I want to give Callum the damn world.

A deep groan vibrates through his chest when his trembling fingers clasp around my breast and squeezes tight through my long shirt.

"Do what you want to," I murmur against his lips when he kisses down my neck, softly avoiding the bruises and wounds.

Sucking my skin between his teeth, he leaves his marks behind, stoking the fire brewing under my skin. My back arches, pressing my breasts into his hand, and I moan when he tweaks my nipple between his fingers. My pussy suddenly flutters, begging for him—all of him.

"Finger me, Callum," I breathe with desperation, arching my back and begging him to do me in when his hand slowly moves south. "I need you," I gasp out when he rolls his hardness into me, pushing it right into my aching center.

"I-I—" His breath shudders when I take his wrist and force his fingers on my upper thigh, letting him rest until he's ready to go up to my weeping pussy, begging for his long fingers to plunge in and make me cum.

His warm breaths blow across my hair, picking up speed. His hardness presses through his boxers, poking me in the belly and twitching against me.

"Just like that," I gasp, guiding his fingers in tiny circles over my aching clit. "Tiny-tiny circles," I moan, bringing his lips back down to mine with desperation, thrusting his tongue into my mouth and confidently overtaking every inch of me.

"And-and this?" he whispers with uncertainty, furrowing his brows.

"God, yes!" I shout when his fingers tentatively slip inside me.

Callum's gaze spears through me, taking in every facial twitch and moan. Slowly, he glides them in and out, taking his time and savoring every moment.

I nod with encouragement, biting my bottom lip, trying to keep my moans at bay. Silent screams force my mouth wide open, and my back bows when he scissors his fingers, hitting all the right spots inside me. Bright lights blossom behind my eyelids, with my orgasm on the brink of exploding through.

"Fuck yes, Callum," I cry when stars burst behind my eyes, and my pussy clamps down on his fingers, holding him there. My hips roll with tiny thrusts, begging for more as my orgasm slowly ebbs away, leaving every inch of my flesh tingling with pleasure.

My eyes pop open when Callum shifts beside me. His dilated eyes, thick with lust, meet mine. Heavy pants heave his glistening chest, vibrating with moans when he pulls his fingers out. I cannot look away when he brings them to his mouth and thoroughly licks them clean with a loud, pussy-fluttering groan, satisfied with the taste.

With trepidation and shaking limbs, Callum cradles the back of my head, turning me to my back with such devotion I nearly burst into tears. The moment the weight of his body presses down on me, hazy memories resurface from the brutal attack I endured at the hands of some grabby asshole. Clamping my eyes shut, I take a deep breath as he settles his chest against mine.

"Little Star," he whispers with urgency, nudging his nose against mine. "Tell me you're okay. I can…" he trails off when my fingers dig into his shoulders, holding him there and not letting him go.

The warmth of his skin grounds me back to the moment, zapping me from the alleyway my mind drifted to. It's bad enough that the monster had restarted the nightmares from when I was fifteen, but now when Callum trusts me the most with intimacy, that bastard is interfering too much.

"I'm fine," I say, peeling my eyes open, getting lost in the vastness of his irises, staring back at me with concern.

"I don't…"

"I'm fine, Callum. This is the first time we've… And the first time someone has touched me since the attack. I'm just tamping down the bullshit panic rising, okay? But I want this… Whatever we're going to do," I whisper, running my fingers through his shaggy blond locks.

His breaths pick up, leaning into my touch, and his tense muscles relax. For a solid minute, we lie together—skin to skin, soaking in each other's presence.

"I-I want inside of you," he whispers with a crack in his voice.

Redness blooms over his cheeks, and his eyes shut tight when he rests his forehead against mine.

"Is that what you want?" I whisper, pressing my lips against his until he nods. "You're ready?" I ask, searching the lust-filled storm brewing in his gray eyes.

"I want to fuck you, Little Star. I want this memory to live with me for the rest of my life. I want to see this… your face when you come… and remember the feel of your pussy wrapped around my dick. It's you, River. I've been waiting for you," he says with such conviction I can't turn him away.

All the panic I felt before vanishes when I look into his hungry eyes, begging for a taste of me. It's him and me. River and Callum. Our time to show what we mean to each other.

"Then fuck me, Callum," I practically beg, staring into his eyes and pleading with him to take the ache from between my legs. His entire body shivers, and he closes his eyes. "It's just you and me, Callum," I whisper with encouragement. "Just us. This is our moment. If you want…"

"You and me, Little Star. I don't know… know how long I'll last," he whispers, swallowing hard.

"That's okay. We have plenty more opportunities, okay?"

He nods, and a small smile breaks out. Kissing my lips one last time, he pulls back, dragging his fingers down my bare legs. He hooks the edge of my panties and brings them down my legs and over my feet. In stunned awe, he stares at my glistening pussy with rapt attention. Spreading my legs further, he licks his lips like he's hypnotized by the heat blossoming between my legs.

Swallowing hard, I see the nerves roaring through him when he carefully removes his boxers and tosses them aside, leaving him bare to me. And what a beautiful sight it is. His long and thick dick stands at attention, red and purple, with desperation for me. Pre-cum glistens in the sunlight when it twitches and leaks down his reddened tip and twitching length.

"Why don't you lie down?" I ask, patting the spot beside me on the bed.

"O-okay," he gasps, settling down on the bed.

His fingers fidget in the sheet, twisting it until he's gripping it hard with white knuckles. He blinks rapidly up at me when I step back, lifting my sleep shirt over my head and tossing it aside, standing naked before him at the end of the bed.

Goosebumps erupt, puckering my skin when he gazes at me in wonder, like I'm the most perfect woman in the world, taking every inch of my body. His lips pop open in awe, and his irises disappear beneath the blackness of his dilated eyes. My heart beats double time when I step forward, running my fingers through the blond hairs lining his muscular thighs. Every inch my fingers move up his leg and over his abdomen, he groans softly, arching his back to receive my touch.

Callum may have seen me naked before, but this time is entirely different. I'm all his—all he can focus on. There's no one else in the room to eat up his time but me. The way his eyes eat me alive as I hover above him has my breath catching in my throat. Anticipation trembles his fingers when he curls them in the sheets, desperate to reach for me but not daring to make a move. Not yet at least.

This moment is for him and only him. Our time together. A special occasion we'll covet for the rest of our lives—him more than me. The trust he's putting in me to give him that memorable first time brings butterflies to my belly. Almost as if it were my first time, too.

Heavy breaths heave his chest, and he nibbles into his bottom lip, locking his gaze on my puckered nipples, begging for his warm mouth.

"You're okay with this, right? You're really ready?" I ask with furrowed brows, climbing onto the bottom of the bed and resting on my knees.

Hesitation slams into me, and I can't help but wonder if I'm the one to do this for him. But all that soon disappears with his following words, knocking me into action.

"River, please," he begs, moving his shaky fingers up and down his hardened and angry shaft, rubbing his thumb over his weeping slit, spreading around his pre-cum.

Moving up his body slowly, I trail my finger up his thigh, lightly coated in blond hairs, and swirl them around. I smirk when his hips jump, begging for friction, and he groans. Gently, I move his hand away from his twitching cock and place it at his side. Immediately, he twists the sheet again for leverage.

"Please, River," he pleads as I blow a breath over his length, loving the groaned response he gives me.

Wetness explodes in my pussy as I blow again, and his head turns from side to side.

"How bad do you want it, Callum?" I ask huskily, running the flat part of my tongue up his length and circling his tip.

"Please-please, River!" he cries out, thrusting his fingers into my hair and pulling me up to his mouth until his lips attack mine. He groans when I straddle his lap, grinding myself against his hardening dick. "I need you. I'm ready, Little Star. Please! Please fuck me. I've dreamed-dreamed of this moment for months. Since the moment I saw you... I knew. I want to remember this until the day I die. I'm yours, Little Star," he breathes his confession against my lips, grunting when I take him in my hands and line him up. "I'm yours," he breathes again, barely above a whisper, staring deep into my eyes.

"You're good with no condoms?" I ask with hesitation, eyeing him as he nods without hesitation.

"Yes, Little Star. I want you raw. I want to feel the flutters of your pussy when I finally settle inside you. Please, do it now. I'm so desperate —" His entire body locks up, and his fingers dig into my hip when I push him inside, and he gasps. "Oh, fuck," he moans wide-eyed, staying rigid until I sink down on him, taking him in all the way.

With approval, my pussy rejoices and flutters around him, basking in the thickness of his cock, stretching me.

"How does it feel?" I rasp through a moan when I lift my hips slowly and slam back down onto him, grinding my pelvis against his until he's crying out.

"Like I'm meant to be here. Like I'm finally home," he moans, and his eyes roll into the back of his head. "You're going to be my most cherished memory, Little Star. This moment... will—ah!" He moans as his entire body locks up, and his dick pulsates inside me repeatedly, spilling himself into me and coating my walls.

"That good, Big Guy?" I murmur breathlessly, resting my chin on his heaving chest. His fingers work through my crazy hair, and his cheeks turn red again.

Closing his eyes, his breaths shudder. "I-I thought... I could hold off-off. I thought-thought I could last. But-but." I follow the movement of his tongue when it darts out, and he licks his lips. Redness tints his cheeks, and he clamps his eyes shut, huffing an annoyed breath at himself.

"It's okay. We have plenty of time to do that again..."

"And again, and again?" he asks with a slight grin, opening his eyes to take me in again.

"However, many times you want," I say with a snort, kissing his chest. "Was it good?" I murmur, kissing my way up his flesh and pressing a kiss to the edge of his lips and down his neck, sucking his skin between my teeth.

"More than good. I don't-don't want to move. Stay here," he whispers, burying his face in my neck and forcing my hips to sink on his hardened cock again, grinding my hips back and forth.

"Again?" I ask with amusement, and he nods, thrusting up with a deep groan.

My lips pop open as the pleasure soars through my veins, and a fire erupts in my belly.

"I want—" Callum's breaths shudder, falling into moans.

"Tell me what you want, Callum. Don't be afraid now," I murmur, kissing his lips again, growing more frantic until our tongues dance, and he cradles the back of my head.

"I want on top. Turn over?" he hesitantly asks, searching my eyes, and I nod, placing myself flat against him.

"Turn us over, Big Guy," I murmur, almost giggling when he turns us over clumsily and his elbow rams into my boob. I yelp, laughing when a look of horror crosses his beautiful face. His eyes frantically check me over, looking for spilled blood or instant bruises.

"Sorry-sorry," he whispers, peppering kisses all over my face and chin and down to my breasts. "I didn't mean to hurt you."

"It's okay," I whisper, moving his blond locks from his eyes. "Now, fuck me again, Callum. Fuck me until you can't anymore," I moan when he thrusts himself into me with a loud groan, knocking the headboard against the wall.

Sorry, Ode. Now's a bad time to be my neighbor, I think when he does it again and again, plowing into me at a rapid pace. I move my legs, wrapping them entirely around his waist until my heels dig into his flexing ass muscles, begging him to go deeper.

"God, you're doing amazing, Callum. Just like that!" I moan, arching my back when a searing fire brews in my lower abdomen, flaring heat through my limbs and down to my curling toes.

"Come," he grunts with force, demanding me. "Come around my dick, River. Please. I want to feel you flutter around me, Little Star."

As soon as the words leave his mouth, my fingers twist around my clit, and I come with an explosion around Callum's cock, screaming my pleasures for the world to hear.

Callum's body stills again, and his muscles lock up, spilling into me a second time with a loud, drawn-out, satisfied moan. Staying nestled deep inside me, Callum leans down and presses his lips into mine, hovering there.

"I never want to leave," he admits, kissing my cheek. "Should-should I get a washcloth?" Looking down, he groans when he pulls out, spilling our mess onto the sheets. His eyes lock on the come dripping out of me, and his teeth sink into his bottom lip, mentally absorbing the scene and taking it all in.

I snort. "I don't think it matters now. Let's rest?" I ask when he falls to my side and pulls my naked body into his again.

"Of course, Little Star." He gently runs his fingers up and down my lower back when I pull my comforter up to our chins, heaving a sigh. "Thank you," he whispers when my eyes flutter shut. "For making this-this so special."

"Don't thank me," I mumble sleepily through a yawn. "You were amazing. But I need to pee," I grumble, not wanting to move from the cocoon of warmth. Exhaustion sweeps in, threatening to take me under.

"Your wish-wish is my demand," he says, pulling the blanket back from our naked bodies, scooping me into his arms, and taking us to the bathroom.

Gently, he lowers me to my feet and gets a washrag from the edge of the sink. Without a thought, I do my business and flush.

"Spread," Callum demands, gesturing to my legs until I spread them out. I shiver when the warm water hits my sore pussy, and he cleans me up before taking me back to bed.

As the clock strikes noon, we snuggle together and fall asleep in each other's arms under the warmth of my comforter and our combined mess beneath us.

"What the hell! I leave for three hours, and you two bump uglies without me? Without. Me?" Rad shouts, jolting my body from a glorious deep sleep.

"Dude," Callum curses, throwing a pillow in Rad's direction.

"It smells like *bu-dussy* in here," he says, waving a hand in front of his nose and taking a deep breath. "You finally corrupted my boy, didn't you? How was it, Cal? Her pussy is the chef's kiss of all pussy." Rad obnoxiously brings his fingers to his mouth and kisses them.

"Dude," Callum whines, pinching the bridge of his nose.

"Tell me! Tell me!" Rad chants, charging forward until he's at the end of the bed and crawling over our bodies. He grins, lifting the blanket. "You two are naked under here. Oh man, my boy finally lost his V-card!" He whoops, shaking the entire bed. "This is the best day ever!" he proclaims. "We should celebrate." He grins more, with dirt gleaming between his teeth.

"Celebrate?" I question, rearing back when he leans in and presses his lips into mine.

"We're going to hit submit tonight and finally enter the Battle of the Bands on the damn wire, too. Shit, we only got twelve more hours until it's closed! Also, I won my race, Kieran and Asher are free from jail, and Callum jammed his dick in the best cock socket in town. I'd say today is a damn victory! Besides, my pretty, Pretty Girl. Your face is more beautiful than ever," he says with a grin, hovering above me.

I blow out a breath at his long-winded answer. "Your point?" I ask, raising a brow. "And seriously? Cock socket? What the hell? It's a vagina. Say it with me now…" I grumble when he covers my mouth and shakes his head.

"Listen, Pretty Girl… Pack your panties, pills, and nothing else, because we're going to the Ozarks!" he shouts, pulling out a set of keys from his pocket.

"The Ozarks?" Callum asks, raising his brow. "The lake my parents used to drag me to in Missouri?"

"That's the one," Rad says, wiggling his brows. "Not only did I win the race, but I convinced Reese to give me his vacation house for seven days. Imagine the possibilities! Far from town, in a secluded cabin by the lake. It's prime, pound town territory. Now, let's go!" he shouts, jumping off the bed.

I look over at Callum and smirk when he shrugs. "Looks like we're going to the Ozarks, Little Star," he says with a grin.

"To the Ozarks, we go," I murmur, leaning in to kiss his lips.

"All right, clothes on! We've got shit to do. Up! Up!" Rad shouts, pulling back the blanket from our bodies. "Ohhh, on second thought. I've gotta eat dinner first," he says with a grin, shoving my legs apart and burying his face in my pussy until I'm a moaning mess, writhing beneath his wicked tongue.

"Uh," I stammer, pulling my poor excuse for a coat closer to my body as the crisp November wind whips through the thin material. "You said cabin." My teeth chatter when the wind picks up, and I curse my lack of good winter wear. Frowning, I look down at my phone and sigh. "And I have no phone signal."

"Nope!" Rad says with a satisfied grin, rocking on his toes in his T-shirt and shorts. "We're out in the middle of nowhere! There's not a single neighbor for ten miles. Isn't it glorious?" Rad grins more, tossing his phone into the Tahoe and shutting it inside.

I swear, I don't know what it is about these Midwestern boys and their shorts in the middle of November, but they're all the damn same. I had a thirty-minute conversation with him about why he shouldn't wear his socks and sandals. He argued with me every step of the way until he huffed, shoving his feet into sneakers.

"You-you definitely said cabin," Callum mutters, putting an arm over my shoulders, and rubbing a hand up and down my arm.

"This is a fucking castle, Rad," Asher says, staring up at the curious-looking structure with furrowed brows. Skepticism lines his face, and he shakes his head. "Not a cabin. We're at the right place, right? You didn't Rad this up and write down the wrong house numbers?"

Kieran snorts. "We're about to walk into someone's family home as they get busy on a Sunday night." Shaking his head, he runs a hand down his face and steps toward me until he's at my back and invading my space.

"Yes! You guys are such buzzkills. We're at the right place, damn it!" Rad grumbles, cursing under his breath. "My track manager loaned me this place for a week. Here…" Poking out his tongue, he digs through his pocket and pulls out a sheet of paper. "Right here! Here's the address, and right there," he says, pointing to the fucking castle with large numbers printed on the front. "It matches. So, we're staying at a castle. And boy, do I have plans to defile every inch of it." Wiggling his brows, he cockily smirks at me.

"Who builds a castle on the lake in the middle of Missouri?" Kieran

murmurs, laying his chin on my head from behind me with a sigh, staring up at the massive fortress with the beautiful lake as the backdrop.

The autumn sun beams down on the crystal lake, reflecting off the turbulent white waves rolling along the surface. A boat in the dock near the water sways on its lift, far above the waters. My nose wrinkles. It's too damn cold to be at a lake house, let alone loitering outside for an obscene amount of time.

"Who cares. It's cold as hell," I grumble through a sharp shiver. "Let's go. I'm freezing my nonexistent dick off."

Asher snorts at my comment and shakes his head. "She has a point," he grunts, tightening his sweatshirt around him.

Rad snorts. "What're you guys complaining for? It's beautiful out!"

"Says the idiot in shorts." Callum scowls, pulling me further into him, letting me eat up his warmth like a greedy girl.

The large castle-like structure looms above us in white brick, and millions—okay, that's an exaggeration—of windows line the structure. A round turret hangs off the front of the house with large, reddish-colored vines creeping up the side.

In unison, we finally head to the front door, fighting against the wind as it whips around me, knocking my long strands in front of my face. I huff a breath, scowling at Rad when he looks at his keys with furrowed brows. With so much damn relief that we'll be in heat soon, Rad turns the key, and we walk inside, greeted by the warmth of the house.

"Ah," I grunt, shaking my hands out and basking in the glorious warmth of the gigantic lake-side castle. "Glorious heat!" I moan, wanting to hug the damn furnace and never leave.

"Fuck. Next time, let's make this a summer trip," Asher gripes, waltzing toward the thermostat and turning it up even more.

He rubs his arms as he looks around, gazing up at the tall ceiling and skylights blasting sunlight into the large living room with an enormous chandelier glistening in the sun, creating small diamonds on the wall.

"So, this is how the over-privileged live," I murmur, running a finger over the marble countertops of the oversized kitchen, inspecting the beautiful brand-new appliances.

Peering around, I see no dust on any countertops or cabinets. The fridge is smudge-free, and even the sink is perfectly polished. It's like a damn show house you see on TV where the wealthy live, and I've only dreamed of staying in. Today, though, it seems my dreams are finally coming true. The kitchen is as big as my apartment and fit for a chef.

"So many places to fuck you against," Rad quips, kissing my temple affectionately. "But first, we need lots of grub and lube to get through this beautiful week of fornication."

I roll my eyes at his stupid words and wander around the large living room, running my fingers over the turquoise leather couches and oversized chair.

"We're off for the food and sex toys. Be naked when we get back, and we'll get the orgy started ASAP. Ouch!" Rad grunts when Callum knocks him on the back of the head with a smirk.

"Shut up," Callum says through a small laugh.

"I'm serious," Rad says, pointing a finger right at me. "This," he says, waving his finger now, "is a group dynamic. We're all boning. Asher needs to let loose and discover how beautiful your…" Rad's brows furrow when Asher covers his mouth with a grunt.

"Food. Now," Asher demands, sending the two on their way.

As soon as they leave, I meander to the back wall, wholly made up of windows overlooking the lake. If it were warmer, I'd demand we strip down naked and jump into the water for hours of swimming.

"There's a hot tub," I say, pushing my nose against the glass door, eyeing the massive hot tub sitting on the deck outside.

"Getting naked outside in the freezing cold sounds like a dream," Asher grunts sarcastically. Walking forward, he side-eyes me until stopping in front of the glass.

For several minutes we stand in silence, taking in the beauty of our new home for the week. Asher nibbles his lip, shoving his hands into his jean's pockets. Clearing his throat, he scoots closer until we're shoulder to shoulder. Something sparks between our connection and heat encompasses my face.

Looking up into his gorgeous hazel eyes, something about him strikes me as different. His shoulders sag lower—almost in relief. His hard-as-stone face softens, letting his genuine emotions peek through the dark veil.

"How're you feeling, Little Brat?" he asks with a hint of concern, searching the yellowing bruises on my face with twisting anguish.

"Concerned about me, Evil Ash?" I jokingly say, shoving my shoulder lightly into his until he smiles. "But I'm fine," I say, shrugging it off.

I'm still on my pain meds and only have one day left of the antibiotics, so I'm looking forward to finishing it all. The tiny pills are a constant reminder of my attack. Each and every time I swallow them down, the memories replay on repeat. Once the bruises fade and the pain meds are gone, it'll be like it never happened. Only it did happen. But from my experience, I've learned how to heal and slowly move on. Not entirely, but I'll get there knowing this won't break me.

"Fuck it. I got you something," he says quickly, shaking his head.

My heart pounds against my ribs when he removes his hand from his pocket and holds it out. The room spins, and my heart leaps from my chest. Sitting in the middle of his palm is my most prized possession that the cops refused to give back to me. I fought and fought with them, telling them I needed it to protect myself, but it was evidence of a crime, and they could not hand it over until all the proceedings were finished.

And now, here it sits right before my eyes, shiny and looking brand new. Last I saw, dark, red blood stained every inch from stabbing stupid Bradley.

Tears prickle at the backs of my eyes. "Asher." My voice comes out rough, clogged with so many emotions.

The tip of my nose burns, and my eyes cloud over as I stroke the name carved into the knife, I've held dear for more than ten years. It's my life-saver, the one thing that saved me when a maniac thought he could take what he wanted, sending him right into the arms of the cops. There was no denying what he had done to me this time. They couldn't push it under the rug and laugh me away. This time, they listened to every word I had to say, wrote it down, and took me seriously. So seriously, Bradley sits behind bars with no bail available to get him out. After he recovered from his stab wound, that is.

"Don't even mention it, Little Brat," he says, clearing his throat and keeping his eyes on the turbulent waters in front of us.

"Thank you," I murmur, leaning up to kiss his cheek and linger, basking in the feel of his skin beneath my lips. He stiffens, taking a deep breath. "This is the nicest thing anyone has done for me in a long time. How?"

Taking my chin between his thumb and index finger, he backs me against the windows, pressing his entire body into mine, letting me feel the planes on every inch of him. Standing tall above me, he pauses and takes in the length of my body in with one swoop. I swallow hard, staring into the abyss of his turbulent eyes filled with deep longing.

My breath shudders when his hip presses into mine. Chest to chest, we breathe each other's air, practically gasping for it. For one split second, thoughts of Asher giving in to the desperate craving surrounding us for months. It chokes me when I breathe. And he's the oxygen I ache for. Dangling like a sweet treat in front of my face, it rests there like a temptation out of grasp and forbidden from touching. The closest we've dared was the night on the Ferris wheel. That dark scene plays on a shrine in the back of my mind. Whenever my fingers slip beneath my panties, it's their faces watching me work my clit in circles.

"I have my ways," he murmurs in a low, raspy voice, keeping the details locked tight behind his luscious lips. Leaning in a little, he's a breath away from me—a millimeter from pressing his lips into mine. "Make it up to me later, Little Brat. You can even call me daddy." The last words leave his wicked tongue on nothing but a murmur, barely audible against my flesh. It's a promise, sealed with a tiny peck on my cheek.

Fuck. I swallow the moan lodged in the back of my throat. Every inch of me throbs, aching for this man who's mercilessly flirted with me the more time has passed. Shivers roll through me when the faintest kiss presses to the edge of my mouth, and my eyes flutter shut on instinct, leaning into the feel of him. As quickly as the warmth of his kiss presses against me, his body vanishes, replaced by the frigid planes of the window pressing into my back.

"What the hell?" I groan out of frustration, curling my fingers into a fist.

Kieran's chuckle comes from somewhere beside me, and my body sags, letting all the frustrations go. "Oh, River Blue. We've got plans for you this week."

Promises. Promises. The whole way down here, Rad went on and on about his plans for me this week.

"Oh, Pretty Girl," Rad whispers directly in my ear, wrapping his fingers around my throat. "I'm going to fuck you within an inch of your life. I'm going to flood your pussy with so much come, and you'll feel me leaking out of you for a week." My breath hitches when he grins, kissing my cheek and tightening his grip. "Yeah, I thought you might like that. We're going to have so much fun this weekend," he murmurs in a deep, husky voice thick with lust.

Rad wasn't the only one to whisper sweet nothings into my ear, working me up and letting me flatline in the land of almost orgasming. Over and over, they teased and primed me for this exact moment to finally let me detonate. I knew every whispered word they promised would eventually come true—well, later. Asher had zero plans to help the ache between my legs right now.

"What the hell was that?" I whisper through my frustrations, searching for Asher amongst the shadows of the house.

If his touch hadn't seared into my skin five seconds ago, branding me with his fingertips, I would have sworn he was a ghost passing by.

"Don't mind him. He's fighting a lot of feelings right now," Kieran whispers, taking me into the warmth of his arms, and resting his cheek on my head with a satisfied sigh.

"Fighting what?" I murmur, placing my ear against his heartbeat and basking in the familiarity of it.

"Everything about you. You scare him. This band is the only thing he has, and here you are, bringing us happily to our knees. He's afraid to fall. He's afraid you'll tear us apart," Kieran murmurs, leaning into me more. "But don't worry, River Blue. Asher's coming around, and once he does, you'll be all he thinks about and obsesses over. I can see it now." A grin tips up the edges of his lips, and he nods with certainty that it will all play out how he says.

But half of me disagrees as a lump forms in my throat at Kieran's nonchalant confession. *He's afraid you'll tear us apart.* Tear them apart? Whispered Words? They're tighter than any family I've ever witnessed.

There's no way little old me would come close to being a threat. The boys are more than a band; they're a damn family unit. Has my presence disrupted that in any way? Am I doing more harm than good by being so close to each of them?

"That's stupid," I murmur, shaking my head. "I don't plan on breaking anyone up."

"I know, River Blue. But he's always cautious and calculating our next moves. You're a move he didn't anticipate," he says, kissing my temple.

"But you actively set out to meet me, right?" Kieran blanches at my question and stiffens with me in his arms, giving away his true intentions.

Blowing out a breath. "Truth?" he questions, and I nod. "We wanted to meet you because of who your dad was, but I didn't expect it to be you. You were a surprise, River Blue. The truth is, I'd track you down, again and again, to be with you. No matter what."

Kieran's confession doesn't surprise me in the least. But my heart does sting. What would have happened if I hadn't been his River Blue and was just some rando they intended on using? Would they have taken it this far and brought me here for a weekend of fun? Doubt creeps in where it shouldn't, filtering through the sliced-open cracks of my heart. In the back of my mind, I've always had my guard up around them and lived in the present. But sometimes, it does nag and tugs at me, making me re-examine every interaction.

The number of times people have come into the record shop claiming to be my brothers and wanting to talk to me is astronomical. They waltz in with a chip on their shoulder and a smarmy smile and run out like their asses are on fire, with fear lining their faces.

Let's say these persistent ass people don't like meeting the end of my knife when I whip it out and tell them to kick rocks. They'll hesitate. They'll beg, flashing me megawatt grins. Pfft. Like that shit will convince me. In the end, I shoo them out with a knife shake and a cackle. Never seeing their scammy faces ever again. Seriously, who is afraid of a five-foot-five girl holding a knife? Apparently, those jokers. But good thing.

People hear the West name and go bonkers with greed, wanting to meet with my sperm donor in person. For some reason, they always think I'm that person. Sure, I am a West, but I'm not connected to shit. My brothers, possibly sisters, and father—are strangers to me. One day though, I'll waltz into their operations and introduce myself after I've lifted myself out of poverty and have made it as some big-wig manager. Then they'll see and regret the day they blew off River West.

I always wanted to distance myself from my family and run from the West namesake. But family is everything. I couldn't have gotten through the last few days or weeks without my mom, Ode, and her family—hell, even the boys. Helping the guys has shown me that music lives and runs in my veins. I've nailed many of the challenges a business career could throw at me.

Managing a music venue—check. Building a band's social profiles—check. Managing a band—check.

"Well, now we're hopefully going to California," I say, leaning back to look at him, dreaming of our future at the tips of our fingers, ready for grasping.

Well, maybe. They may have submitted their application to the Battle of the Bands, but it still has to be reviewed and announced, which should be coming up in the next week or two. For now, we sit on the edges of our seats in anticipation of what will come.

"We're definitely going. There's no question about it," Kieran proclaims. "They're going to beat down our doors to get a piece of us." I snort at his confidence but revel in it, too. Whispered Words is good—well —more than fucking good. They're unique and saturated in raw talent that the world will eat up and take hostage. I can only imagine what people across the globe will think when their ears feast on Whisper Words' tunes.

"Will you go anyway?" I ask, biting my bottom lip. The question has been on the tip of my tongue for weeks. And why wouldn't they? They're free to live their dreams and leave this hellhole, even if I'm not a part of the equation.

His palms lightly encase my cheeks, holding me still as his mismatched eyes examine the sadness taking over my face. The thought of separating from them sends pain across my chest. Rubber bands constrict around my lungs, and panic soon settles into my soul. Never in my life did I think I'd want to depend on anyone again; yet, I am right back down the love… rabbit hole. The same damn place I refused to return to after Van obliterated my trust and crushed my cracked heart into pieces. It took me months to get over the sudden breakup. I mean, obviously. I still let that bastard slither between my legs when I was supposed to be working.

The front door bursts open with a loud bang reverberating off the tall, vaulted ceilings, and Rad and Callum's loud laughter and chatter fill the space. Noisy plastic bags rustle in their hands, but I can't drag my eyes away from Kieran as he stands tall. Those mismatched eyes take all of me in. From the tips of my toes to my heaving chest and finally gaze longingly into my eyes.

"We'll wait for you, River Blue, to finish whatever you have to do at home. You're in school and…"

"Fuck no," I say, swallowing the pain of my words. "You guys have to take the opportunity now. You can't wait." I shake my head in his grip, refusing to believe they'd wait around for me when something so spectacular has been laid before them. As much as I want them by my side, I can't destroy their dreams.

"That's right, we will, Pretty Girl! You're our girlfriend." My lips pop open to refute his proclamation, but I hold my tongue. That fact is, I am their damn girlfriend by now—all of them—even the evil one who refuses to show me how he feels. Wrinkling my nose, I glare at a grinning Rad, who zeros in on my unsaid realization with a knowing look.

"Fuck yes! You finally get it, don't you? We'll wait for you if you can't make it to California. Maybe we'll try the Chicago circuit. They're always looking for new talent, and it's only two hours away," Rad says with a grin, grunting when he sets the groceries down on the kitchen counters.

"We'll-we'll wait for you," Callum says with conviction, setting more bags down and rifles through them.

Finally, Asher comes into view, frowning at the island in front of the groceries, lost in thought. A crinkle takes over his forehead, and the color slowly drains from his face. His eyes shift between the boys and finally land on me, where something odd sparks but extinguishes just as quickly.

"You guys can't give up your dreams because of me. I can finish school anywhere," I say with a shrug. "It's basically all online, anyways." At least, that's what I planned to do on our trip. All my professors agreed to send me online material to complete while I was gone.

"But your mom," Rad says with a frown, running a hand across his neck. "You'd leave her?"

The realization smacks me square in the face, and my stomach sinks into the depths of my churning stomach. Could I leave my mother, who is so ill amid a flare-up that she's barely functioning? Could I leave her while she's hobbling around on her broken ankle with no income? Shit. Sweat breaks out on my brow as the worry slams into me and knocks the breaths from my lungs.

"I don't know," I say, swallowing the cold, hard truth.

"Don't you dare worry about me, River. My health is on the rise. My medicine is getting squared away, and I can move more. Enjoy this tiny vacation, okay? You're nineteen. You shouldn't have to worry about your mother," she says, cradling my face with a sad smile.

"But, Ma. I'll be away in another state for like a week. I can't just…"

"You can and you will. This is my illness to carry. Besides, the nurse is coming over again to help me get around and help with showers and meds. Even she says I'm on my way to coming out of this flare-up." She cringes when she holds a hand to her side and shakes her head. "It's just a pesky bladder infection. I've got antibiotics to help and all the pain meds I need. I have a neighbor and a nurse on speed dial. Please, be a kid for once," she pleads with me, and my eyes well up, burning with unshed tears.

"Okay," I say as a tear slips down my cheek.

The responsibility I hold for my mother sits heavily on my chest. Her well-being is something that goes through my mind on several occasions. All I can think about when I'm away is, is she okay? Did she fall? Can she walk without feeling dizzy and make it to the bathroom, okay? Can she get to the store? So many damn worries rest on my shoulders when I'm running around working two jobs and trying to balance it with some fun with Whispered Words.

"Go have fun. Don't worry about me. Come back refreshed and renewed." Her smile lights up the room, and she looks healthier than ever when she kisses my cheek and returns to her recliner. That night we had dinner together in front of the television, watching some murder mystery she loves. We laugh for the first time in a long time together and enjoy each other's company.

"Enough of that," Asher barks, raising a brow when he pulls out an entire bottle of fancy tequila, staring at it. A wrinkle forms on his brow, and he scoffs. "Seriously? We send you for food, and you come back with seven bottles of tequila?" he asks with a grunt, pulling out multiple bottles of booze and setting them down on the countertop.

"Tequila makes her panties drop," Rad says with a scoff, taking the bottle from him and cradling it in his arms like a baby. "And the lube makes the booty pop," he says, nodding to the large bottle of lube Asher places on the counter with twisted lips.

"Pretty sure you don't need tequila to make Little Brat's panties drop. She does that all on her own," he quips with a cocky smirk. "But the booty pop? Well, we can make that happen tonight." He shrugs when I blanch, and my butt cheeks instinctively clench together at his unsaid promise.

"I think I need to sleep with a salt circle around me tonight," I grumble, flipping him off. A glorious smile spreads across Asher's lips when he barks out a laugh, grabs the bottle of booze, uncaps it, and gulps down a few swigs.

"Ah, the return of Evil Ash!" Rad proclaims, thumping Asher on the back several times until he chokes and rights himself, swiping a hand across his wet lips. Asher promptly shoves him away with a grunt, cursing him under his breath.

"All right," Callum says, stepping up to the bags. "Let's grill some steaks, drink some tequila, and maybe utilize the hot tub?" At that, his eyes turn to me, and I grin.

"Sounds like a good plan," I say as we get to work seasoning the steaks.

We drink mixed drinks and watch a few movies for the rest of the night. Once we're good and sloshed, we head out to the hot tub and take advantage of the warm bubbles and jetted sides.

The same happens every night we're locked away in this glorious house. We even convince Rad to skinny-dip in the freezing lake on a dare. Let's say little Rad didn't fare well when he jumped out of the water and ran for the house, screaming bloody murder. We laughed our asses off that night, getting sloppy drunk, and fucking on almost every surface of the house.

WHEN RAD SAID HE WANTED TO DEFILE IT, HE MEANT IT. THE COUCH. THE kitchen. Every bed in the house. Against the railing and on the stairs. Up against the fridge and in the shower. No surface went untouched as we went rounds and rounds every night since we'd stepped foot into the castle house of fucking.

The only person who didn't take the bait was Asher. It's been six nights of him on the sidelines with those hazel eyes flaring with lust as the guys take turns railing me over and over again. I was the fruit for the taking right in reach, but he never caved. He sat in the corner of the room, stroking himself to oblivion, coming hard with my silent name on his lips. But there's always something holding him back from taking what he wants—me.

So, tonight is our last night at the house, and I promised myself I'd seduce the ever-living fuck out of the man standing on the sidelines. Operation get Asher to fuck me is in full effect, and boy, is he taking the bait at every turn. The more alcohol he drinks, the fierier the looks he tosses in my direction, heating my entire being. Asher rests on the edge with his toes testing the waters. But what will it take for him to dive headfirst and take the leap? Only time will tell, but I'll try my hardest to convince him.

"Who's ready for the hot tub? One last time?" Rad asks, looking around the eight-seater, oak dining room table with massive, hopeful eyes. Without answering, he throws his shirt off and tosses it aside, revealing his gorgeous, tattooed chest and slim waist. "We'll all go naked this time. No more boxers or hiding your heinie! Time to let it all hang out." He emphasizes his words by wiggling his hips and brows simultaneously, giving me a slow, seductive smirk.

Asher drunkenly frowns, takes a swig of the last bottle of straight tequila, and shakes his head. "I'm not getting naked with you," he scoffs, wrinkling his nose.

"Aw! Come on, man! Live a little. Those who get naked together get pussy together! You need to loosen up and get some," Rad whines, leaning his elbows on the table and puffing out his bottom lip.

I snort into my now empty glass and set it down. "Maybe I don't want to get naked with you either," I quip, raising a brow when Asher's gaze sears through me, and I fucking melt under his stare, heating me from one to a boiling one hundred. My face flushes when I reach for the bottle of tequila and take a large gulp, hating the burn running down my throat.

"Why wouldn't you, Little Brat?" Asher asks, furrowing his brows. "Stand up," he gestures calmly, waving his wrist.

I cross my arms over my chest, running my tongue along my bottom lip. "Why?" I ask in defiance, earning a chuckle from Kieran.

"I'll get the hot tub going. Then, we're getting naked," Kieran says, giving Asher a pointed stare before walking out of the room toward the hot tub resting on the deck outside in the frigid air.

"Stand up," Asher directs, leisurely taking a drink and gulping it down. His red-glazed eyes stare holes through me, lighting me on fire without saying more words. "And come here," he demands with a feral growl, pointing to the table in front of him.

Every part of me throbs and rejoices all at once. We've walked on thin ice around each other, suffocating in the tension growing thick in the air for days. And now, my brain chants a tune of "fucking finally!" No matter how often I told myself I'd never touch Asher's psycho ass with a ten-foot pole. Well, call me a liar all you want, but I'm about to get dicked down and hate fucked within an inch of my life. It's all that rests in the back of his dilated hazel eyes, promising me a multitude of things with one glance.

Rad chuckles, rubbing his hands together. "Oh, finally! Asher, my man!" Rad whoops, sitting back in his seat with wide eyes like he's about to watch the best movie of his life.

"Not another word," Asher demands, pointing in Rad and Callum's direction, and they nod, zipping their lips like good little boys. "Little Brat. You have three seconds to crawl to me. I won't tell you again."

"And if I don't?" I ask, getting to my feet on the other side of the table and placing my palms against the cold wood. My palms are slick with sweat, and my heart pounds a crazy beat inside my chest when his eyes narrow at my reaction.

"Then you won't sit right for a week." He stares with no emotion, drumming his long fingers against the tabletop. "Come here," he rasps, desperation leaking into his tone. "I want my fucking dessert."

Shivers roll through me at the slightly drunken state he's in. I've never seen any sort of desperation come through, but now he acts like he wants me badly and can't stand to stay away. Maybe it's the booze. Perhaps it's the distance from Central City, but I'm giving in—all in. We're doing this no matter the consequences. No matter how hard he'll hate himself and me tomorrow morning when he rolls out of bed, realizing what he's done. The moment we get home, he can return to the same dickbag I've come to love and hate and keep his distance. He can return to the jerk bag, who watches from the shadows while stroking himself until he's exploding all over his fist. But tonight? Tonight, is our time to explore each other's bodies and say fuck the consequences of our tryst.

Without a second thought and fanfare from the silent audience of two, Callum and Rad, who watch with rapt attention, I climb onto the large wooden table. It squeaks beneath my pressure as I hesitantly crawl across the smooth surface, digging into my knees. Inch by inch, I come closer and closer to Asher, who stares at me with hooded eyes, zoning in on my low-cut shirt, exposing my black, lacy bra, and swaying tits. Heavy breaths heave his sculpted chest, and with every slide of my knees, my heart works double time, pumping against my ribs. The tip of his tongue darts out, running the length of his bottom lip. His heavy eyes drag from my fingers, curling into the table, slowly dragging up my bare arms to my wide eyes staring down at him.

"Now what?" I ask breathlessly, an inch in front of his blank face, begging for the direction to fall from his lips. Leaning in, I test the waters, running the tip of my nose against his.

His eyes darken when my nose brushes against his, and his breath shudders, affected by me. Little by little, Asher is losing the tight grip of control he's held tightly to for the past few months. For some reason, I'm here for it. Eager to see his breaking point. How far can I push Asher until he's choking me with his cock as punishment? Fuck. The imagery alone makes my pussy flutter around air, begging for him to fill me.

I'm living for today and today only. No regrets. No holding back. I'm taking what I want by the balls and seizing the day.

His eyes fall to my lips, and he licks his without thinking, forcing me to back up an inch. "Take your fucking clothes off," he demands, resting his elbows on the table with anticipation sparking in his eyes. Nervously, he shifts, adjusting himself in the chair, but keeps those steely eyes locked on me.

His voice brooks no arguments, snapping like a whip at my resolve. I don't argue this time—well, maybe just a little. Something about Asher brings out my inner brat, desperate to poke and prod the beast until he snaps and takes what he wants. Mischief dances in my eyes, and a smirk plays on my lips when his gaze heats me to the core. The look he gives me lets me know I am the main course, and he's hungry to devour me.

I cock my head and lean back, resting on my knees. My arms float above me in a warm sensual dance of seduction. Digging my knees into the smooth, wooden table and creasing my flesh, I raise and slowly rake my fingertips up and down my arms keeping it teasingly slow. Asher's eyes darken, taking in every movement I make as I sway him with a slow strip tease.

My skin puckers with goosebumps when I lift my shirt over my head, twirling it a few times, throwing it in Asher's unamused face. Tossing it aside with a flick of his wrist, he sits back and watches me without speaking. Everything heats under the intensity of his stare, bursting every inch of me into heated flames. Without warning, I'm aching for his touch to soothe the pressure building under my flesh.

"Everything," he rasps with urgency, grabbing the bottle of tequila. Mesmerized, I watch in fascination as his Adam's apple bobs with every gulp he takes, hypnotizing me until, piece by piece, my clothes are gone and thrown in Rad's direction.

"I'll keep these for luck," Rad murmurs, burying his nose into the fabric of my panties and groaning. "She's so fucking wet already," he rasps in a low, gravelly voice, unbuckling his pants with no shame and strips until he's completely naked. His moans rumble through the room as his hand works up and down his shaft, using my panties for friction. "You do what you want; I'm going to stroke one out to her bouncing tits."

"Eyes on me, Little Brat," Asher says, beckoning me with a finger until he's sitting back in the chair with a bottle of tequila in his hand, commanding the scene like a king. "Callum," he says with authority. "I need salt and a lime," he demands again, climbing to his feet and towering above me. His calloused fingers run the length of my jaw, standing silently before me without muttering a word or new demand. It's there, resting in the back of his dark hazel eyes—the promise of what's to come.

My head spins when he barks those orders, and Callum pushes from the chair, stumbling over his feet a few times before disappearing into the kitchen. Drawers slam, and cabinets open and close before he reappears with a flushed face. He nibbles his lips, nervously looking anywhere but me, when he sets the chunky, wooden chopping board on the table beside us, along with a sharp knife and the glass saltshaker.

"Mmm," Asher hums, picking up the salt and shaking it. "Hold out your wrist," he mumbles, grabbing my wrist when I don't do it fast enough and yanks it forward with force. "Look at me, Little Brat," he says, closing in on me with a deadly expression. "I'm holding on by a fragile string. Please don't test me right now. Okay?" When I nod, he swallows heavily, squeezing my wrist between his large fingers. "Now, hold it here, and don't move."

Through several shaky breaths, I confirm his demand with one nod. Practically trembling under his stern fingers latched around my hand, restraining me from moving. My mind conjures ropes and chains securing me to the bedposts as he takes what he wants and laps away at me with vigor. But I shake those away, returning to the present when he methodically touches my wrist with soft, feather-like strokes, gaining my attention. Turning my arm over slowly, he exposes the inside of my wrist and deposits several shakes of salt on my flesh, falling like snow, and covering my skin in tiny white specks.

His darkened hazel eyes snap to mine, holding me captive in his desire-filled gaze. Tingling sensations of pleasure flood my body like a fire igniting under my skin.

"Hold it," Asher orders me, taking his hand from my wrist. "And don't lose a single grain of salt. If you do, you'll regret ever defying me. I'll bend you over my knee and paddle your ass until it's red and blistered." He quirks a brow, eyeing the multitude of white specks on my wrist, and steps beside me, beginning the process of cutting limes into several bite-sized pieces—perfect for sucking.

"Okay," I say through a shaky breath, counting down the seconds until his tongue brushes over my flesh.

Heat overtakes me like a damn fever as I strain to keep my arm straight out in front of me. Too damn scared to lose a single grain to the floor. A thrill shoots through me at the thought of his punishment if I did happen to lose one, but my ass wants to be pounded into next week. Sooner rather than later. So, I stay as still as possible, closing my eyes and counting down each shink of the knife severing through the limes.

One. Steady your fucking arm. Two. Shit! Don't fucking move. I breathe, counting the knife's third, fourth, and fifth clink against the wooden cutter until a deafening silence fills the room. My eyes flutter open, focusing on the man in front of me, looking as wild and dangerous as ever.

"Open," Asher murmurs, holding the lime to my lips and placing it peel first between my teeth, so the juicy fruit sits on the outside. "Good little brats get rewards," he whispers against my cheek, and I whimper around the lime, begging for more contact. "Now, I'm going to lick, drink, and suck—in that order. Don't move a muscle, baby."

I swear his eyes dilate to blackness when the warmth of his tongue glides across my wrist, licking up every speck of salt. Scooping up the bottle of tequila, he gulps down a few drinks until he's swiping the extra droplets from his lips. Lurching forward, he desperately crashes his lips down on mine, sucking the lime between my teeth and holding me still between his palms on my cheeks. Stepping back, his chest heaves up and down quickly when he spits the lime out onto the ground with a feral growl.

"Lie down," he demands in a gravelly voice, pointing to the table. "And spread your legs like a good girl." My lips pop open in retort, but before I can speak, his fingers wrap around my throat, and he drags me closer until we're nose to nose as he lightly squeezes, knocking the air from my lungs. Silently, I beg for oxygen beneath his cruel fingers, but none comes, heating my face. "Don't fight this," he pleads in a breathless whisper, brushing a stray strand of hair from my moistened face. "I've held back for so long. And now I want what I want, liquid courage and all."

I swallow his moan when his lips attack mine, swirling his tequila-soaked tongue with mine in a dance of domination. He takes me completely. Body. Mind. Soul. With one kiss and I'm a goner, bending to his demented will and happily doing it without a fuss.

"Holy shit," Rad whispers in a throaty tone somewhere in the dining room.

"Down," Asher demands, loosening his grip on my throat, but he doesn't completely let go until I'm laid on my back. Shivers break out when my heated back comes into contact with the cold surface, and a gasp escapes me as the overwhelming sensations expand through my body.

Asher spreads my legs wide, placing my feet on the edge, showing off my glistening pussy, as he drags my ass off the edge table. Now, I am open and exposed to the last man I ever thought I'd let touch me. But this has been building and building for months.

"We're doing this again. All of us," he says, adjusting the growing want bulging from his pants with a low groan.

"Lick, drink, suck?" Rad asks with a grin, climbing on the table and hovering above my face. His dick throbs right above my line of vision, thick with pre-cum, red and angry, almost poking me in the damn ear. "Come on, bro! You're missing out on the best tequila shots!" he shouts, looking in the direction of the living room.

Kieran stops short, wiping his hands down his jeans when he waltzes back into the house. Bewilderment widens those beautiful, mismatched eyes as he takes in the scene before him: me, laid out on the table with my feet propped up on the table edge and my pussy dangling, ready for the taking. Swallowing hard, he takes a side, staring at Asher with a twisted expression.

"The game?" Kieran asks, tilting his head to the side as Asher takes another few gulps of tequila straight from the bottle.

"Tequila shots. Drop the salt anywhere you want to lick. Take a shot, and then get the lime from her mouth, pussy, or wherever you want. But right now, this pussy is mine," Asher says with determination as a cold-like sensation enters my aching and swollen pussy, doing little to alleviate the pulsating between my legs.

I swallow down the gasp stuck in my throat. Anticipation fries my damn nerves, and my fingers tremble against the wooden tabletop, waiting for the first stroke of someone's tongue. Or fuck, anything! They all hover above me, standing motionless, forming a circle around my naked body like I'm some sort of sacrifice.

Moving as one, they pass the saltshaker around the circle, depositing heavy amounts all over certain parts of my body. From my stiff and aching nipples to my belly button and the spot right above my pussy, they all pick a place, admiring it from above with heated eyes. Cocking his head to the side, Asher grins, rubbing his fingers up and down my thigh.

"Who is in the salt circle now, Little Brat?" He quirks a brow and then nods, beginning their synchronized torture with the flick of their tongues in unison.

I moan when they lick the salt simultaneously, and the warmth of their tongues overtakes me. Uncontrollable gasps spill from my throat when Asher pours his tequila shot over my clit, and through my pussy, letting it flow straight into his mouth and drenching me completely.

My eyes roll back into my head when his manic tongue darts into my pussy over and over, vibrating his moans against me as he sucks the lime into his mouth and spits it out onto the floor before diving back in for more. His tongue thrashes against my clit as his long fingers enter my pussy, wildly thrusting in and out, moving my body against the table. Fire spreads through every limb deep in my gut until I'm on the brink of exploding. A mouth comes down on mine, moaning into me as my back arches off the damn table in preparation for the best orgasm I'm ever going to experience in my damn life.

My fingers urgently dig into someone's hair until I'm exploding around Asher's fingers, eagerly thrusting in and out of my pussy. On a loud cry, filling the space with my raspy moans and begging for more, I come. And I come hard. Harder than fucking hard. Shit. I think I meet Jesus behind the stars dancing in my eyesight.

"Jesus!" Rad whimpers.

Yeah. Met him. I groan and babble through my thick tongue when Rad leans down, gently kissing my cheek with a grin widening his face until he steps back. In fact, they all step back, giving me and the man of the hour the space we need to consummate our union.

Locking eyes with Asher, I see my life flash before my eyes. There's a promise hiding in the depth of his glazed-over hazel eyes, and I don't know if I'll survive to tell the tale of our adventures. Death by dick—is what the headlines will say when they tell the story of how Asher Montgomery royally dicked me down and fucked me to death. Dig my grave now because there's no coming back from this moment.

"Turn over, Little Brat," Asher says, heaving a breath.

Keeping those perceptive eyes searing into mine, he takes every inch of clothing off and tosses them aside. I see him in all his naked glory for the first time since getting to know him. Lean muscle lines his arms, accented by the thick blue veins protruding from his flesh—has me panting like a pathetic bitch in heat. All I can imagine is running the length of my tongue over his skin and tasting him for the first time. My eyes fall toward his thick and hairy legs, working up over his dick, standing at attention and leading to a fit stomach without defined abs. Darting my tongue out, I lick my lips, imagining how he'll taste in my mouth when he coats my throat.

"Please," he rasps until I comply and turn over with my ass in the air, presenting my aching pussy to him.

I yelp when he grabs my ankles and shoves my feet flat onto the ground. With force, he places my palms on the table, and I give into him, letting him take what he wants and how he wants. I'm all fucking his right now. No interference from me or the other three, who look on in fascination. My pussy flutters with excitement at his take-charge attitude, and my mind goes blank, leaning into him to make the decisions.

"Don't move your hands," he whispers against my neck, carefully wrapping his fingers around my throat. "I'm going to fuck you now, okay?"

For a moment, it's just us in the room; the others slink into the shadows and cease to exist.

"Yes, please, Asher," I moan, crying out when his thick dick roars into my pussy without warning.

Asher grunts as he pounds into me, mercilessly pushing the table with our force and digging my hips into the edge with every frantic thrust of his hips.

"This has been building for days. I won't last long, so come for me, Little Brat. Come all over my cock and show me how much you love it when I fuck you hard enough to leave bruises," he groans, gripping my throat harder until my lips pop open in a silent, breathless scream.

My head swims in a mess of emotions as my orgasm plows through me with such force everything turns white behind my eyes, and I leave this earth once again. At this rate, I'll have to fuck Asher's evil ass to get these fantastic orgasms I'm sure I'll be hooked on for the rest of my damn life. His body stills, and he spills everything inside me in one long, drawn-out groan resembling my name in hushed whispers.

Breathlessly, Asher pulls out, briefly kissing my cheek. "Good girl," he praises between breaths. "Now, let the others enjoy our pussy." I shiver when he pulls away, moving to the chair across from my face, and sits back with his hands behind his head. "I'll give you one hour, and then, I'm taking you again," he commands me again with a cocky smirk, looking lighter than before. Reaching down, he takes his dick, stroking himself as he lazily watches from the sidelines.

Rad leans forward without hesitation and takes my mouth with his, pulling back. "We've done some group stuff, Pretty Girl. But have you ever been fucked in the ass?"

I swallow thickly and blanch at his crass words. It's the one sexual experience I've only been brave enough to do a handful of times with reluctance. It didn't hurt, but it wasn't with people I felt I could trust. But with my boys, I have faith in every molecule in their bodies, and I know they'd never hurt me on purpose or make it too painful. So, with those words running through my mind like a warning, I give in to them.

"I haven't done it in a while. It's only been a few times," I whisper, licking my lips.

"First time with us. We'll make it hot as fuck, Pretty Girl," Rad says with a smirk, looking deep into my eyes when I nod in confirmation, and my heart skips a fucking beat. Holy hell, I'm going to let one of them stick their big fat cocks into my asshole while the other fucks my pussy. Shivers roll through me at the thought, and excitement thrums through my veins with anticipation.

"It'll burn a little at first, Little Brat. But once you're nice and stretched out, taking two at a time will be easier. Kieran, stretch her asshole out." My eyebrows raise into my hairline when Kieran nods without putting up a fight and marches toward me with determination.

Fingertips run down my spine, sending goosebumps everywhere as I lean on the table where Asher left me, not daring to move an inch. I swallow hard, focusing on the compassion in Rad's eyes when Kieran runs his fingers over my ass and dives them deep into my come-filled pussy.

"I'll make it feel so good, River Blue, okay?" he murmurs, and I nod in confirmation, desperately aching for them both.

"Scoot her back," Rad says, waving a hand.

Kieran steps back with me in his arms several steps until Rad can fit in between us and the table. A devilish smirk crosses his face when he drops to his knees, still stroking himself with my panties. Looking up at me, he grins more, with purpose settling across his face.

"I'm going to eat you until you come at least two times on my tongue. I don't even care about Asher's come dripping out of you." Rad runs a finger up my calf, catching it in his hand and heaving it over his shoulder, moaning when he runs his nose through my folds, bumping into Kieran's fingers as he stills. "God, Pretty Girl. You smell like sex on a stick." The tip of his tongue barely brushes my bundle of nerves, and I cry out through the overstimulation. My skin crawls with the need to run away, but they both hold me captive in their arms, tightening their grips.

Kieran curls his fingers inside me, slowly working them in and out at a torturous pace. My head falls back onto his shoulder, moaning loudly at the onslaught of sensations pounding through my entire body. My nerves are on fire again, ready to combust, and the moment Rad's tongue turns circles around my clit, I'm prepared to detonate.

"That's my River Blue," he whispers huskily against my neck. "Come for us again, baby. Come on my fingers and Rad's tongue."

Crying out, my head moves back and forth as another orgasm presses through, squeezing the life out of Kieran's fingers. My body sags in Kieran's arms, utterly fucking spent. Can I go on? I hope fucking so. I have three more boyfriends to fuck before the night is through. And then again in a few hours. I'm living life to the fullest at this moment before we have to go back to reality—something I almost don't want to do. If I could stay in a fairytale land with endless orgasms and four men at my disposal, I would.

"Now, River Blue. You'll feel a lot of pressure, and I want you to relax. Focus on Callum." My eyes flutter open as Rad backs away, stroking himself with no restraint. Callum comes into view with his shirt off and his boxers hiding the massive stiffy tenting them.

"Cal," I murmur, trying to relax as much as possible when Kieran removes his fingers from my soaking pussy and glides them through my crack.

"That's a good girl," Asher reaffirms from across the table, watching them work me over. Standing, he marches around the table, grabs the large bottle of lube, and pumps a few streams in my crack. "Now let my brother fuck your ass," he murmurs, kissing my cheek. His eyes never stray from Kieran's finger, working into me, slowly opening me up.

Callum's fingers brush against my jaw, leaning in slowly and kissing me. His tongue mixes with mine, engulfing me in him as Kieran slowly parts my ass and pushes in one finger, knuckle deep.

"So, fucking beautifully done," Kieran rasps in my ear, working his second finger through the burning ring of muscles. "Relax, River Blue. That's it," he breathes heavily, working on a third and fourth finger until I'm completely open and relaxed.

"Not-not too bad?" Callum asks, furrowing his brows when my eyes roll into the back of my head, and I gasp for air, clinging to Callum. He groans when my fingernails dig into his arm, and I swear to fuck, another orgasm sits at the brink of it all, and I don't know if I can fucking come again without becoming a noodle in their arms.

"More," I moan, earning a chuckle from Asher.

"I'd say it's time to lube up your prick and fuck her with it. Callum," Asher says, gaining the trembling man's attention away from me. "What do you want to do? Take her pussy while Kieran takes the back?"

Callum swallows nervously, looking between the two of us. Eventually, his eyes drop toward my pussy as Kieran pushes his lubed-up dick into my ass an inch at a time, slightly bending me over.

"Doing good," he gasps, sinking all the way in. "We'll take our time, baby. I don't want to hurt you, okay?" I nod several times, catching my breath as he remains still.

"Kieran, how about you sit on the edge of the table? Callum wants to tag in," Asher says with a vicious grin across his lips.

Kieran doesn't waste a moment, wrapping an arm around my waist. With ease and precision, Kieran rests his ass on the table, carefully rearranging us, so I'm spread wide, ready for Callum.

"Jesus," I shout, throwing my head back onto his shoulder.

"Pretty Girl. Are you okay?" Rad asks with concern, brushing a finger down my tightened face.

When I peek an eye open, I'm greeted by his dark eyes and him resting on the table beside us.

"Too full," I say, blowing out a breath.

Asher scoffs, walking around the table and into my eyesight. Leaning against the wall, he crosses his arms over his chest and smirks. "You can take it, Little Brat. Spread your legs and let Callum in," Asher demands with a cock of his head. He watches for several minutes until my pinched face relaxes, and I nod, permitting Asher to spread my legs slowly like before. "You're being such a good Little Brat," he murmurs, fixing my legs, so they're spread wide open. "You know... You know we would never hurt you, right?" His brows furrow, and he squeezes my knee.

"Thanks, Evil Ash," I whisper, snorting when he kisses my cheek affectionately.

"Good girl. Now, Callum, it's your time to shine," he says, stepping back so Callum can take his place.

Callum steps between my spread legs with trepidation and takes it all in with a heated gaze. No doubt, memorizing this moment as a shrine in his head for years to come.

"You're good?" he asks, gently pulling his boxers down and kicking them to the side. I nod, breathlessly unable to answer as the tip of his dick slowly works into my pussy, and he grunts. "Oh, f-f-f-uck," he mutters, leaning his forehead against mine. "You feel exceptional, Little Star."

"Aw, my little Callum is all grown up. But now, you gotta get a move on, man. My dick has an appointment with her mouth in five seconds," Rad grumbles, standing tall on the table, stroking himself while patiently waiting for Callum to pull away from my face.

Callum grumbles under his breath, pressing one last kiss to my lips. Pulling back, he snaps his hips forward, sending lightning bolts throughout my body. I silently scream through the sensation, but as soon as my mouth pops open, Rad seizes the opportunity and acts as my gag before any noise can push through my lips.

"Jesus fucking hell," Kieran curses, barely moving beneath me. "This... this is something that... fuck," he grunts, holding my hips with bruising force until he's burying his face in my neck, thrusting up into me.

"Jesus. I don't know how long I can last," Callum mutters, moving in unison with Kieran and Rad.

"Don't hold back, boys. We have all night to tie her up and come in her, on her, and everywhere," Asher rasps from somewhere in front of us, sounding like a ghost in the shadows, enjoying his view.

Callum's the first to go, frozen in time as his mouth hangs open and his thrusts stop, depositing his come deep inside me and mixing with Asher's, painting my fluttering pussy walls.

"Shit," he murmurs, kissing my cheek and pulling out. Slowly, he stumbles back, plopping into a chair with a dazed look on his face.

"And just like that, one down, two to go," Rad grunts, working his dick in and out of my lips at a steady pace.

"Fuck this. I gotta move better than this, man," Kieran grunts, wrapping his arms around my body. Rad's dick is forced from my mouth as Kieran leans my front side over the edge of the table again and pounds into me repeatedly. "Fuck yes," he grunts one last time, pulling out until the heat of his cum spreads all over my ass cheeks.

"Move, dickhead. It's my turn now," Rad proclaims, practically jumping down from the table and pushing Kieran out of the way. "You're mine now, Pretty Girl," he whispers, swiping my hair over my shoulder and kissing my flesh. "You're still good?" he murmurs, teasing his tip through my folds until I nod. "Good girl," he says, groaning when he entirely pushes inside and gently thrusts in and out, savoring the feel of me around him.

"I can't," I whine in a tired voice when his fingers circle my clit, eliciting more moans from my throat. "I can't, Ashton," I groan a protest when he presses harder, quickening his thrusts.

"One last time, Pretty Girl. Come on my cock, and then I won't make you come anymore," he grunts, pounding his hips into mine and filling the house with the sound of smacking flesh.

Without warning, another orgasm barrels through me, tightening around Rad's dick until he comes on a grunt and stills behind me.

"You did so damn good, Pretty Girl. I think I might live in your pussy forever," he murmurs in a tired voice, kissing my shoulder one last time before pulling out and stumbling over his feet. Groaning, he dramatically lies on the ground, putting his arm over his eyes. "Wake me when we fuck again," he quips through a heavy breath.

"All right," Asher says.

"Who is ready for round two?" His deep voice sounds from right behind me, his fingers moving through the come dripping out of my pussy and running down my leg. "You're leaving some behind," he tsks while clucking his tongue, gathering it all up on his finger, and shoving it back inside.

"Looks like someone needs to be the plug." And with that, Asher enters my pussy once again with a groan, not giving me time to recuperate.

But there are no complaints from me when we start another round of—Fuck River silly until she can't walk anymore—my favorite type of game.

After another round, I'm lying dead on the table, looking up at the tall ceilings and examining the peculiar-looking chandelier. My heartbeat pounds in my ears as a body crawls over mine and settles against me.

"Good, Pretty Girl?" Rad asks, moving some of my sweaty hair from my forehead.

"Dead," I mumble, closing my eyes.

"Aw, Pretty Girl. We killed you, didn't we? Next time we'll…"

"Next time?" I grumble, swatting him away from me as he laughs.

"Uh, duh. You don't just live through one five way and think that's the end. This is just the beginning of our gang bangs, baby," he quips, kissing my cheek with a chuckle.

Footsteps sound beside us as Rad's ripped away, and a familiar face hovers above mine with flushed cheeks and a grin.

"How about we get cleaned up in the hot tub? It should be nice and ready by now. Shit, it's been three hours," Kieran says, scooping me up from the table and holding me in his arms.

"Don't let me drown," I say through a yawn, leaning my head on his sweaty chest, completely relaxing into him.

I hum when the five of us sink into the heated water of the hot tub and look up at the stars shining down, accompanied by the bright moonlight. No streetlights or other neighbors interrupt our serenity as we relax together until it is time to crawl into the large king-sized bed, we all manage to squeeze into—one last time.

The following day we eat a quick breakfast, hit the showers, and make sure the house is spotless for the owners when they return next. The last thing I wanted them to see was the ass impressions we left on the dining room table they eat meals on. What a shock that would be.

"So," I say as we pack up the Tahoe and stare back at the castle, we're about to leave behind forever. "Thanks for this week."

Rad smirks, swooping in to cover me in kisses. "You needed it, Pretty Girl. And so did we."

"It was nice-nice to get away," Callum murmurs, kissing my cheek. "Nice to spend time with you."

"And in you!" Rad whoops with a grin, pulling me by the front of my shirt. I swat him away with a roll of my eyes. "So, do you understand now?" Rad asks, twisting me until my back hits the cold metal of the vehicle.

"Understand what?" I ask, raising a brow.

"That you're ours. Forever. There's no getting away from us now." He grins, not giving me a moment to argue when his lips descend on mine, and his tongue eats my answer.

"Exclusively ours," Kieran reiterates, shutting the back hutch after putting our bags inside.

"Exclusive, huh? When did that happen?" I quip as Kieran rounds on me, shoving Rad out of the way.

"Dude!" Rad gripes, stumbling sideways.

Grasping my chin, he growls, baring his teeth. "Don't play with me, River Blue," he says in a low, no-nonsense voice like a possessive idiot.

I snort. "I guess I'll have to let my other boyfriends down easy." I roll my eyes when they all tense and grunt, ready to shout their outrages.

Asher rolls his eyes, forcefully removing the big lug's body from draping over mine. "She gets it. You pissed on her enough. Let's go." Asher drags me around the car by my arm and throws open the passenger's side door. Without a word, he grabs me by the hips and puts me in the seat, only pausing to put my seatbelt on.

"Let's go home," Asher grumbles, jumping into the third-row seats and lounging with his eyes closed. "Don't kill us with your driving," he quips with an easygoing grin.

Rad snorts. "You're the asshole who gets us stuck in ditches and mud puddles. K at least drives like an adult."

Asher frowns as Kieran pulls out of the drive and heads down the miles-long curvy road with one destination in mind—home.

"I'm not that bad," Asher grumbles, throwing an arm over his eyes.

"Worse than bad," Callum quips with a twinkle in his eye, ducking as Asher's hand wildly swings for him and misses. "You always stop in the middle of the road! Remember that squirrel you hit? Or the mailbox? Or the… Ah!"

"Shut it," Asher playfully barks, leaning over the bench and taking Callum's head hostage with an evil grin. "What should I do to your lover boy, Little Brat?" he asks with a big wolfy grin, squeezing his arm around Callum's throat with a laugh.

"Asshole!" Callum grunts, trying to shove him off.

My heart squeezes in my chest at the lightness surrounding Asher like a halo draping over him. This whole vacation, he's held back, and then yesterday, something burst through, and he allowed himself to let go of whatever was holding him on the sidelines, introducing the real Asher. The one who had been shoved down into the pit of his misery. The man who brightly smiles at me now as if the sun reflects off him, producing a halo hanging over his head.

"Nothing," I say, turning to watch as he knocks Callum's head to the side with a slight shove and snorts at me.

For the rest of the six-hour trip, we joke, nap, and stop for snacks until we're back in Central City as dinner hits residents' tables.

"Home sweet misery," Asher grumbles, sitting up with the same frown he's always worn, scowling at the world as it passes. "Take us home. I'm sure the devil will want us there ASAP," he grumbles, swiping a hand down his sleepy face.

"We'll take you home, Pretty Girl!" Rad says as we pull into Callum and Rad's driveway.

"Thanks for this," I say, leaning over and kissing Kieran on the cheek. "I'll see you later?"

His lips roll together, and he nods, bringing his lips to mine.

"Definitely," he murmurs, kissing me again before letting me go on my way, and I step out into the fading sunshine with a groan.

Asher hops out of the back, stretching his arms above his head and exposing his stomach. I bite my lip, imagining the delicious things he did to me yesterday against the table, getting lost in my thoughts. Before I climb into Callum's car, Asher grabs me by the arm, pulling me into him.

Wrapping his arms around me, Asher secures my head against his chest without saying a word. My heart squeezes when he hugs me tighter. It's like something sits on his tongue, ready to be said, but he kisses my head and lets me get in the vehicle. Even as we pull away from Callum's house and they get into the Tahoe, I feel him. His stare. His hug. Something shifts, turning sideways inside me. What was that all about?

Rad rambles away from the front seat on our way back to the center of Central City, pulling into the parking lot of my apartment building. I stiffen when chaos unfolds in front of me. People sit outside on their porches, and some wander around the crowded parking lot, watching the spectacle playing out.

My eyes widen when an ambulance, a fire truck, and police vehicles surround the parking spot located in front of my apartment. My. Apartment.

With shaky hands, I get my phone from my pocket, scrolling through the multitude of missed messages and calls I received in the last thirty minutes. Bile burns in the back of my throat.

"What the hell?" Rad asks, throwing the passenger door open and opening mine. "Is that?"

My heart sinks into my ass when Ma's body is wheeled out of the apartment on a stretcher. A paramedic straddles her, pushing into her chest repeatedly as someone holds a bag to her mouth, pumping air into her lungs.

"River!" I turn toward a teary-eyed Ode, covering her mouth with her hand.

"What the hell happened?" I ask in a raspy voice, not processing the scene before my eyes.

"We don't know yet, baby," Korrine says, swallowing hard as I lean into her open arms. Her hug settles the anguish beating down on me and the guilt crushing my heart. "We checked on her last night, and she said she had the flu and wanted to be left alone. I went over about an hour ago, and she was barely responsive." Tears stream down Korrine's face when she pulls away, patting my cheeks with affection. "Follow the ambulance to Central Memorial," she says, nodding as they close the doors and take off out of the apartment complex parking lot at a high rate of speed.

Rad immediately jumps into action, holding me in his arms, and guides me back to the car.

"Let's go to the hospital, Pretty Girl. We'll see what's going on," he says in a small voice.

"Okay," I say, climbing back into the car, and we head to the hospital, following behind the ambulance.

 Glaring up at my father's office window, he shakes his head and shrugs at me. Maybe that's a good sign that the old bastard is finally loosening the leash of our collars. Pfft. Fat fucking chance. Nigel Montgomery has a knack for being in control. If it isn't his idea, then it's not possible.

Kieran doesn't wait for me, opting to head into the house with his head hung low and his hands in his jeans.

The weekend plays on repeat in my mind. I promised myself the moment we left Central City that I would let whatever happens—happen. It didn't take a genius to know what we would do to pass the time the moment we stepped into a secluded lake house.

My time with River was highly eye-opening and fucking hot. Being deep inside her pussy and feeling the effect I had on her—twice over was invigorating. Swallowing hard, I squeeze my eyes shut, willing my damn dick to go back down before I step out and deal with my father. Oh, yeah. That did it.

Just as my hand attempts to open the door, my phone vibrates in my pocket repeatedly. Scrunching my brows, I dig it out of my pocket. Who the hell calls people these days? Especially so late in the evening? Scammers, that's who. Shit. Looking at the number on the screen, it screams scam call. Out of the area, area code. Long number. I roll my eyes, expecting a robot when I answer the phone.

"Yeah?" I ask, blowing out a breath. "Listen, if this is a robot scammer..."

A chuckle greets my ears. "Uh, nah, Man. Not a scammer, I promise. You'll want to hear this. Is this, by chance, Asher Montgomery, Ashton Radcliffe, Kieran Knight, or Callum Rose? This was the phone number we had on the application for the submission."

Number on the submission? Jesus. Fuck. My fingers tighten around the phone in fear of dropping it as my palms dampen. My heart beats out of my damn chest and falls onto the dash. All the blood in my body swishes in my ears, almost drowning out the voice on the other end.

"Uh, yeah. This is Asher," I say, swallowing hard.

My back stiffens at attention when I take the phone off my ear and stare at the number again. Only this time, the location of the call sits under the number—East Point Bluff, California. California. Fucking, California. Gasping for breath, I bring the phone back to my ear just in time.

"Fucking awesome, man. I was looking at your submission again for the thousandth time, and I'm blown away. Do you know how many applications we've gone through trying to find such a unique sound? Thousands. And you guys are fucking it," he says with so much excitement that goosebumps break out my arms.

My entire body locks up. Butterflies blossom in my churning gut, threatening to send my dinner up. Is this happening? Is this a fucking joke at my expense? Deep breaths, Asher. Deep fucking breaths.

"You… you what? Wait? Is this…"

"Hey, man, I'm Seger West. I'm calling on behalf of West Records. We are pouring through the submissions this week, and I gotta say, Whispered Words has the shit we're looking for. Fuck. You guys were…"

"Not professional, dude. You can't say fuck to potential winners. You'll scare them away with your Seger attitude," another voice says in the background with a scoff.

"Fuck off, Elf Ears," Seger grumbles, returning to the phone. "Sorry, man. My brother is…"

"Husband-in-law! I swear you're ashamed of me. It's been how many years now?"

"Shut the fuck up, Elf Ears!" another person growls in the background. "He's in the middle of a phone call. You're worse than Dash when he wants a fucking cookie. Jesus. I have enough kids to wrangle. I don't need you, too."

Seger sighs heavily, muttering a few colorful words into the phone, and everything dies down behind him.

"Jesus. Sorry. My brothers are helping me with this whole event," Seger says through a tired breath. "Anyway, you'll get something in the mail with a formal invitation today. We've overnighted everything. But we just wanted to talk to the guys behind the music. Your fans are incredible, too, and your sound… I can't wait to hear you live," he gushes in a low voice.

"Holy… fuck," I gasp out. "You're serious? You're fucking serious! We got… we got in? We fucking made it?" I ramble into the phone as my thoughts catch up to the situation.

"Yeah, man. You guys are the shit! Once you read the letter, it'll have all the information you need. We'll see you guys in a few weeks!"

"Holy shit. Thanks, man! Thanks for taking a chance on us! Wait till I tell the guys they'll be…" I trail off as haunting words play on repeat in my mind.

"We'll wait for you, River!"
"We can play in Chicago! No problem!"
"There will be a next time."

After exchanging goodbyes, I hang up the phone, slowly dropping it into my lap. Slumping in the seat, I lick my lips. How the fuck am I going to get them to California if they're more concerned with staying with River than playing in the band. This is our fucking band—our only chance to make it in the big leagues. Tours. Buses. Recording studios. Screaming fans. They're all within grasp, handed to us on a silver platter for the taking. And here they are, convinced they'd wait for her.

Like fuck.

I will not let my brothers wake up regretting their life choices one day. No matter the consequences. No matter how much I'll hate myself and drown in my guilt, we're going to California. No. Matter. What. With or without River West.

CALLUM

River's mom is in the hospital. Something happened last night.

RAD

She's super sick, man, and River... she's...

CALLUM

She's not okay. I can't get her to... move or speak. She's just....

RAD

Catatonic.

I take a few breaths, swallowing down the panic rising inside me. Despite the win we just achieved, nothing but desperation claws through me, threatening to pull me under the waves of anxiety. If River's mom is sick, how the hell am I going to convince them to go to California with me? They'll insist on staying behind and caring for her even more than they already do. Fuck. Listen, I'm not a cold-hearted bastard, but we've had our sights set on this goal for years now. I can't idly sit back and let our plans derail off the tracks. If there's one person who can keep these fuckers' eyes on the prize, it's me.

Whatever it takes.

ME

Fuck, man. Tell Little Brat I'm sorry. We'll be there soon.

Kieran frantically knocks on my window with concern etched on his face. Rolling it down, all the energy rushes from me, and my head swims in a fog of confusion. It's on the tip of my tongue to sing our win and confess everything. Something holds me back, though, keeping my lips sealed. For some reason, I need time to think about everything. River. The competition. And our promise to her.

"I'm going to meet them at the hospital. Wanna go?" he asks with his brows furrowed. His fingers fidget in the open window, drumming against the car's interior.

I shake my head. "I'll meet up with you in a bit. I'll grab whatever River needs. Just text me, okay?"

"You good?" Kieran asks, looking me up and down. "You look like you're up to something." His nose scrunches. "Or about to shit your pants." I blanch at his words, shoving my hand into his chest and pushing him away. He smirks, swatting at me when he rights himself.

"I'm fine, asshole. Just go away. I'll be by in a bit. I'll unpack and shit." I pinch the bridge of my nose.

"Fine, shitbag," he grunts, shoving off my Tahoe and climbing into his own. He glares at me with suspicion when he pulls out of the driveway and peels out of the neighborhood.

My eyes gaze up at the large, intimidating house full of an array of monsters ready to attack. Whether they're manipulative gold diggers or the devil himself, they reside here in a seemingly ordinary neighborhood. With trepidation, I climb out of the car and head into the pits of Hell with my head held high. Finally, hope shines somewhere in the back of my darkened mind, slowly coming out of the box I shoved it into years ago. It fills me to the brim with anticipation and so much goddamn hope I could vomit. This is fucking it. We're achieving what we set out to do. We fucking got in! We did it! Now, all we have to do is blow the rest of the competition away and leave no doubt in the West brothers' minds that we're the best.

When the front door closes behind me, I'm greeted by a smug-looking Gloria bustling around the kitchen. With practiced grace, she sets a few sets of papers on the countertop, grinning as she reads the words. Eyeing her face, I note the lack of bruising and swelling, meaning my father must be far away on his so-called business trips.

"It seems we have a score to settle," she says, sitting on the edge of the stool in front of the paper, tapping them with her nail.

"How so?" I raise a brow, strolling through the living room with my hands in my pockets.

A million thoughts race through my mind as I settle across from her, crossing my legs. A bored look crosses my face when she grins more, tapping her nails against the papers on the counter. Thick silence encases the room, doing little to rile me up. Her beady blue eyes glare at me when I huff, rolling my eyes.

"Speak, for God's sake, Gloria. Spit it out already," I growl, reaching the thin end of my patience.

My fingers curl and uncurl on the countertop, waiting for her to finally open her mouth and reveal whatever bullshit she has up her sleeve. But my patience wears thin when her eyes widen, and her lips flap like a fucking fish out of water.

The stool squeaks against the linoleum floor when I abruptly stand, digging my phone from my pocket. I don't have time for her shit, especially not today. Not after this weekend. And not after that phone call I received. I need to plot this entire thing and expertly move the pieces on my board before I make any moves.

"This is yours," she says, gesturing to the paperwork on the counter.

I grunt, walking back and sitting down. She swallows hard when I scowl in her direction, making the poor woman flinch. If I were nicer, I would hold back the anger brewing slowly inside me, but I can't seem to help it around her.

"What is it?" I ask, putting a hand out, and thankfully, she gives it to me.

"It's everything you need for the competition," she says, sitting back and folding her arms across her chest in victory. "Remember our deal?"

I raise a brow, flipping through the pages.

Congratulations on your win! The West brothers have officially chosen you and hand-picked you to participate. Please read the rules below...

The contest will be held at the KC Club in East Point Bluff, California, on December 15th of this year. All chosen participants will receive a call directly from the showrunners, confirming their win. All selected participants must RSVP within seventy-two hours by texting 555-425-1933 with their answers. All chosen participants must arrive on December 14th for registration.

"Seems you only have two weeks to make it out there," Gloria says, staring down at her manicured nails with a smirk.

"Seems that way," I huff, continuing to read the stipulations and rules. Fuck. I need Callum to read these over, so we don't miss a damn thing. The last thing we need is to forget a damn rule.

"Which means," she says in her snobby voice. "You only have a week to get everything in order."

My heart pumps double time at all the shit we have to do to get to the damn contest before it starts. Packing. Getting money. The car. Fuck. Getting the guys on board and...

"Here's the five grand," she says, waving around an envelope full of cash. "And my word that your father hasn't found out. In fact, he'll be on a business trip for the next week or so." She lifts her chin, looking smug as hell. But I'm too concerned with the amount of shit I have to do to pay her any mind. She can jump off a cliff for all I care.

"Great," I say, collecting the paper and shoveling it back into the envelope they came in. "You know it's a crime to rifle through other people's mail." Looking over my shoulder, I look at her, and she shrugs, holding onto the cash with a firm grip.

"Callum asked me to look for the mail," she sniffs. "You have been away for a week."

Every possible outcome runs through my mind.

"Remember, though," Gloria says, climbing to her feet and brushing her hands down her pants. "The other part of our deal. I'll give you the extra funds if you…"

"Yeah. Don't worry. I won't forget about you and Camilla." I shake my head. I can only imagine how insufferable my father will be when his two main punching bags disappear from the situation.

"And?" She raises her brow, coming to stand in front of me.

"Would you spit it out? I don't have time for this."

"The girl stays here. No matter what. She'll ruin everything we've set out to do."

"We've? You mean the band?" She swallows hard and waves her hand.

"Of course, your band," she scoffs.

I wipe every emotion from my face and nod. No matter how much I want to fight it, Gloria's right. The guys are ready to hand over the keys and fucking stay here in Central City, where we'll never go anywhere. We'll never get our band off the ground if we stay for River.

Gloria's grin grows a mile, and she bounces on her toes. "If you want my advice," she says, leaning in as I scowl. I don't want anything from her. I want to lie down and collect myself. Maybe take a hot shower and leave the memory of River down the drain, which is impossible to do. "A little birdy told me you'll want to speak with Donavan Drake. He might have a few ideas on how to rid yourselves of the trash. Pictures included." She taps my cheek condescendingly and waltzes away with a victorious pep in her step.

God. Burn my eyes out now. Please take me away from this miserable place.

Although, I don't blame her for wanting to take my sister and run for the hills. My father is less than desirable. She has an ass-backward way of doing things. I sigh, rub the headache away from my forehead, and pull out my phone. My plate fills higher and higher with bullshit, but I know the remedy to alleviate it.

As I step into my bathroom and set my phone on the counter, I take a long look in the mirror. My tired, hazel eyes stare back at me, bloodshot and guilt-ridden. My messy blond hair sticks on end as the room fills with steam, slowly erasing the face in front of me.

Every choice I've made has been for the band—my family. The boys who have grown to be my brothers in the shit storm called life. Whatever I do with this information will affect us, even River. She won't go unscathed.

It may break her heart for a week or two, but she's resilient and one tough chick. She'll move on to some other poor schmuck, and then, we'll be a distant, painful memory. That's all the motivation I need to contact the last person I ever thought I'd want to speak with.

ME

We need to talk.

Staring at the blank screen, I shake my head and jump into the shower. Memories of our weekend flash through my mind as my fingers work through my hair, massaging my roots. My eyes squeeze shut, and I groan at the images sitting behind my eyes. River's naked form sprawled out and ready for the taking. River panting and moaning as we fuck her against the dining room table. The taste of her flesh as I licked the salt off and forced my tongue down her throat. My fingers tightly wrapped around her throat, squeezing until she silently begged for breath. My dick impaling her over and over until she screamed my name. Fuck. My dick gets hard as the heat pounds against my back and neck, washing away the world pressing down on me. I stare at my traitorous dick. It was one weekend of fun, and that's it. I made myself a promise and let go, embracing what I had wanted since the Ferris wheel. Her. The whole package. And now that I had her, I had to let go and let her essence wash down the drain with every ounce of guilt pressing down on me.

Once I'm out of the shower and running the soft towel across my skin, clarity hits me smack in the head. I know exactly what I have to do to get us through this and onto California without the distraction. Now, all I have to do is set it all up.

ME

How's Little Brat?

Walking into my room, I get dressed in jeans, a shirt, and a sweatshirt.

KIERAN

.... Meet us in the ER.

RAD

Can't say it through text, bro. But it isn't good and...

My heart sinks. They said her mom was taken by ambulance and sick, but did she succumb to whatever was ailing her? Jesus. That would complicate everything times ten. But whatever the issue, I'll push forward with all my might and get what we need. It's for the better of the band... my family.

The smell of cheap, burned coffee fills my nose when I round the corner, greeting the solemn faces of Callum and Rad, resting in the uncomfortable-looking ER waiting room. Tears stain their cheeks, and a deep-red tint fills their glazed eyes.

The whole drive to the hospital had my thoughts in a tailspin of worry, guilt, and trying to convince myself I was doing the right thing. I am, right? Am I doing the best thing I can for the guys? For the fucking band? I'm the one looking out for them. They don't know what the fuck they want right now. Well, except for a win at the Battle of the Bands. One day, I'll be able to reflect on this and not drown in the misery I've created for myself.

"What's going on?" I ask, coming to a halt right in front of them.

My brows furrow when Rad shakes his head with tears streaming down his cheeks, and his bottom lip quivers with anguish resting in the depths of his dark eyes. Instantly my heart drops, and the worst possible outcome runs through my mind. What the fuck happened? My gaze drifts to Callum, burrowing into the stiff seat with white earbuds resting in his ears as he drowns out the rest of the world, covering his eyes with his hands. The old Callum, the one so stuck inside his head with the awful memories of his past, slowly emerges, taking away the blossoming butterfly Callum had become. My jaw clenches. She may have brought him out of his shell, breathing life into his lungs with her wild ways, but she's the cause of all the heartache on his fallen face. If it weren't for her, then we'd all be peachy. But she's come in and fucked us all up. This is just the cherry on fucking top.

"It's bad, bro," Rad whispers through an array of emotions clogging his throat.

"What is it?" I ask through the tension rising in my chest, beating down on me.

"They tried so fucking hard," Rad says, wiping away the tears. "Her mom is gone," he mumbles, gripping his hair tightly. "She fucking… she fucking died because we took River away from here. They said something about an infection in her blood."

"No," I bark, plopping down next to him and gripping his shoulder. "This is no one's fault. If she was sick, this was meant to happen." I give him a sharp nod when he slumps in the seat with a twisting expression. More tears escape down his cheeks, and he sniffles.

"Where is River?"

Rad's lips roll together, and his brows furrow. "Talking to the funeral home people. Some pastor came by and prayed with us, but uh, they needed to know where to take the body in the morning." He shakes his head in disbelief. "How did this happen, man? I don't understand. Stella was a good woman she…" he chokes on his words, bringing a fist to his mouth, stopping his words.

Knots form in my gut, memories of death smothering me. Stella, River's mom, is no longer with us. Unlike my mother, it wasn't by her own hands. It was something her body did to her and let her suffer. My heart mourns with River, who's probably so distraught she doesn't know what to do with herself. And I feel for her. I've been through it before at a younger age. No one prepares you for life without the woman who brought you into this world. She's supposed to live for an eternity by your side, helping you as all mothers should. But now, River won't have that opportunity.

"It happens to the best of people," I murmur, eyeing Callum as he heaves a shuddering breath. The storm hiding in the back of his blank eyes startles me into putting my hand on his shoulder and gently squeezing. Looking at me, he shakes his head, breaking our eye contact. Slowly, the old closed-off Callum takes the reins and refuses to meet my eye, staring at the floor instead.

"Where was her nurse?" Rad sniffles. "Where was anyone?"

"Her symptoms were like the flu," Kieran says, stumbling into the seat beside me. "They said she would have been feverish, puking, and feeling sick. The neighbor checked in on her and gave her Tylenol but didn't recognize the symptoms for what they were." Grabbing his long, dark locks, misery takes over his twisted expression.

"How's Pretty Girl?" Rad asks, jumping to his feet. "We need to be with her."

"She asked me to leave," Kieran grumbles, lips twisting into furry. "She's hiding in her fucking grief and pushing me away."

"Maybe we should give her some space," I say, folding my hands in my lap. "She doesn't…"

"Like fuck, bro. Respectfully, of course. River pushes us away when she doesn't want us to see her vulnerabilities," Rad snaps, getting in my face. "I won't be dragged away when she needs us."

I sigh, nodding. I knew it would not be easy to convince them that we needed to give her some space and talk sense into them.

"She wants to be alone." We all jump when her best friend Ode marches out of the emergency room doors with a grim expression, shaking her head. Her heated, dark eyes lock on us, and she sighs, hurt, making her face fall. "She even kicked me out," she mutters, putting a hand on her forehead. "My mom is going to take her home. We need to give her a day or two to process, alone. That's how she handles shit. It's stupid, but that's the River West way."

"Let's regroup at Callum's," I suggest, getting to my feet. "Make her think we've given her space."

Looking around, I see the war brewing in their minds. They don't want to, but they know we need to. River will push and push until we're so far away we'll never get back. And somehow, this works into my plan to pull them as far apart from her as I can. Pain tightens my chest at the thought of abandoning her like my father did to me the moment my mother took things into her own hands and ended her existence. Unlike me at the time of my mother's death, River has a family with Ode and Korrine. They'll guide her through this rough time with love and compassion.

River doesn't need us. Not now.

"Fine," Kieran barks with a frown, pushing past me with a rough shoulder check. "Let's go to Callum's and work out a plan. But after tomorrow, I'm not leaving her alone. Do you fucking understand? I'm here for her. No matter what."

Fury blazes to life, lighting up his haunting mismatched eyes, giving me all the confirmation I need. He's too deep, and it's time to pull the plug.

"Men," Ode mutters under her breath, rolling her eyes. "Could one of you run me home, please?" she asks, eyeing each of us with raised brows.

"I will," I say with a sharp nod, gesturing for her to follow. The more distance I can put between the guys and River's apartment, the better. "I'll meet you back at the house," I confirm before they do something stupid like camp out at the hospital all night or try to break into her apartment again.

"I'm going to bake her a pie," Rad murmurs, putting his love into his food. "And fried chicken, potatoes, and corn." Listing off more food, he rambles on until he's settled into his car and starts it, cutting him off. I wave each of them off and take Ode home without a word.

"Thanks," she says, climbing out. "And uh, you know. I don't usually say this shit, but you guys have turned River around. She's been in this funk for years, working her ass off. And then you guys come into her life, and I've never seen her smile more. You guys don't know what a gift you've been to her. She's my best friend; all I want for her is the best. So, uh, thanks," she says with a grimace, shutting the door before I can speak.

She won't be as accommodating when I have the courage to answer the text message awaiting me. It came through at the hospital, discreetly vibrating in my pocket, but I refused to answer when so many people were around. Indecision pushes at my mind, and guilt pushes down on me like a heavy weight on my shoulders. Now is the time to embrace River and take her with us; let her grieve in our arms as we make our dreams come true. Not run away and do it all ourselves. But what other choice do I have? They're eating out of the palm of her hand, bending over backward to make her happy. What about us? Me? Our dreams? That's what it all boils down to—our future. We can't sit around here forever waiting for River to decide what she wants to do with her life. We need to act now while the iron is hot, and our talent is what they're looking for—not three years from now when she graduates.

Leaning over, I catch my reflection in the mirror and quickly look away. I do what I have to do to ensure our future stays on track.

Their words from our trip play in my mind, making the decision easier.

"We'll wait for you."

"We'll wait for you…"

"We'll stay if you can't go…"

Instead of going to California, they'd rather risk our careers and stay with River. Sweet, sweet fucking River. The girl we sought out to help us get to this point. And now, everything is one big fucking mess. They're damn near in love with her and ready to propose a fucking five-way marriage.

I heave a breath, glaring at the ceiling. Without overthinking my actions anymore, I grab my phone and look at the screen, swallowing the heavy lump in my throat. One message rests unread from an hour ago that I haven't bothered to answer. Or fucking look. If the guys knew what I was up to, they'd fucking murder me on the spot.

ME

I need to talk to you.

VAN

Why?

ME

You want your girl back, right?

Don't get shy about it now.

We all know who you want.

Silence rests in the night air around me when I pull the Tahoe out of the parking lot of River's apartment complex and drive toward home. Looking down, I spy his response and risk texting and driving.

VAN

We can talk. When?

ME

Now. I'll be there in twenty.

Nerves eat away at me the closer I get to my damnation. There's no going back. The moment I open my mouth, I can't take it back.

As I get closer to my destination, the world passes by in a blur. I'm so lost in my guilt that I don't register when I pull up in front of Van's house, or he gets into the passenger's side, slamming the door hard.

"What do you mean to get your girl back?" he asks with slight desperation ringing in his voice.

Fuck. This might be easier than I initially thought. From what I have planned, Van will be an intricate part I can't afford to lose.

"Exactly what I said," I grumble, throwing the car into park and keeping in the shadows. Callum's house may be a block away, but there's no way they'll see me from here. "So, do you want her eating out of the palm of your hand again? Or what?" Disgust burrows in my gut at my own damn words. What in the fuck am I doing? I close my eyes. It's what I have to do. But fuck. River's mom just died. She's in goddamn grieving, and here I am, plotting behind her back.

Images of River float through my mind. Me behind her, pounding her hips against the table. Her moans will forever live on a shrine in the back of my mind. Nothing will erase them. Not even the hate she'll feel for me, in the end, could erase our intricate past. But as far as I'm concerned, in another week, we'll never hear from her again. We'll be too far away in California, living our dream. And she'll be here, living hers.

"What's in it for you?" Van rightfully asks with suspicion.

"Her away from them. Us in California. Take your pick." I shrug, watching the shadows dance along his face as he processes my words.

"You got in?" he asks in disbelief, with his jaw hanging open. "Holy hell."

"Now, imagine once we leave. Her mom just died. Who do you think River will come running back to?" I lift a brow when something dark sparkles in his eyes, and he nods.

"Oh shit," he breathes, eyes widening at my words. "She's dead? Now she's more vulnerable. Perfect," he mumbles more to himself than me, rubbing his palms together. "She's always been mine." A certain amount of possession rests in his tone, enough to raise the tiny hairs on my arm in alert.

Right. Always been his? Isn't that a load of shit? My heart squeezes. Fuck. What am I doing? I'm handing River over to a fucking psychopath. Not that she'd ever waltz back into his life, anyway. But that's the grand illusion of it all. River will never want Van. Not again. Ever. She'll always pine for the boys who walked away if I can get this plan to work. If I… I take a deep breath, already regretting this conversation. What the fuck am I doing?

How's that saying go? If you love something enough, you should let it go, and if it genuinely loves you, it'll come back. That's laughable at best. Once we escape and the boys forget about her, we'll never see her face again. And that's what I'm forcefully doing. I'm peeling their fingers from around the butterfly, setting us free and letting our band escape.

My heart pounds as I stare out the front windshield, noting the frigid wind knocking against the windows. Little white flakes float down from the sky, melting on my windshield when they hit, leaving tiny wet droplets behind.

"So, you didn't come talk to me without reason. What is it?" he finally asks, focusing entirely on me.

"You have something I need." Something crucial to pry their fingers away from River and something that will knock them back and down a peg or two and reevaluate their relationship with her. They wanted her exclusively, with no extra boyfriends in the background. With a sigh, I feel the enormity of my words.

He snorts. "Something you need? And what could that be? You've been pricks to me since you all started seeing her and stealing her away from me." He shakes his head. "So, why should I even help you?"

"Because I know what you did," I say, side-eyeing him when he stiffens, and his expression hardens.

"You don't know shit about me," he growls through clenched teeth. "Are we done?"

"I find it funny the one night you're not stalking River through the bar is the same night she gets laid out and almost taken advantage of. Or is that just a coincidence?" I raise a brow when he pales, unable to keep his shame off his face, but quickly hides it behind his rolling eyes and twisting lips. "I'm sure the cops would love to hear the tidbit about you organizing the entire thing so you could feel like some sort of disgusting hero," I huff, feeling revulsion slither through my veins like a thick sludge weighing me down, hoping what I'm saying isn't true. But the fact is Van's a slimy piece of shit who is desperate enough to pull something as disgusting as this off.

"You… What the hell do you want?" he asks, swallowing his nerves without refuting my claims against him. My damn heart sinks at the realization of what he's done, but I shake it off and push forward with my stupid plan, even when my stomach rolls and vomit creeps up my throat.

"A little birdy told me you have some videos. Videos, I don't want to know how you obtained pictures. You. River. I need them." My eyes burn into him as he wilts under the pressure and slumps.

"Why?"

"I should ask the same. Does River know you filmed your sex life with her?" I seal my lips shut, holding back the vomit threatening to break through. If there's one thing in my life I'll regret forever, it's this. I am stooping so damn low to obtain the ultimate dream that I'm disgusted at my actions. "Send them to me, and all will be forgotten. By next week, we'll be forgotten. River will run to you, and all will be normal."

We sit silently for another moment, and Van nods, getting his phone out. "Sure," he says, scanning through his phone, clicking a few pictures, and then hitting send. "What're you using them for?" He asks when my phone vibrates, but I refuse to look at the multiple videos and photos he sent.

"Be available tomorrow," I say, narrowing my eyes at him. "Your girl might need some dinner at her place to make her feel better." Every word I speak feels like ash on my tongue, turning bitter and chalky.

I fucking hate myself.

"Sure," he mumbles, getting out of the car with crinkled brows. He doesn't look back at me when he goes inside, and I don't look at him.

This is a means to an end. A way to live our dream, and that's it.

A plan formulates in my mind as I drive back to Callum's, and we regroup, coming up with a solid idea on how to get us the fuck out of here and keep River here. Now all I have to do is break my best friends' hearts.

Numbness fills every molecule in my body. The past day's events play like a movie that happened to someone else. Not me. Never me. There's no way I went from the best fucking vacation to this dismal existence bathed in loneliness.

Emptiness surrounds me—a nothingness sinking deep into my bones. The world around me keeps moving and has been for the past two days. Leaving me here, in the home I once shared with my mother. She's the same woman who suffered while I was away, having the time of my life and insisting to the neighbor that she was okay—insisting to her nurse that she didn't need her on those days and let her have a few days off. Why did my mom do this? Why would she leave me when I needed her in my life? Things were going to look up for us in the future. So, why did she leave me now?

Sitting on the edge of my bed, I stare out into the dark abyss. Shadows dance along the sliding glass door, but no one enters through hellbent on getting me out of bed. Their voices play in the back of my mind like ghosts whispering in my ear, trying to pry me out of bed. But I'm a frozen mass, unable to motivate myself. It's been like this for days. Me, myself, and I— planning a funeral. Something I never thought I'd have to do. I mean, who the fuck does that? Who plans a funeral for their mother at nineteen? Fuck. Why? Why did this happen?

Why did she leave me?

Of course, my neighbors, Odette, Leon, and Korrine, stopped by and ensured I was okay by feeding me dinner and keeping me company—until I shooed them away. But the boys? It's like the moment I told them to leave me alone in the ER, they listened. Half of me is pissed off and conflicted because I wanted the solitude to process the immeasurable amount of grief pressing down on me. The other half wants them by my side, hugging me and telling me everything will be okay. I'll be okay, right? Everything will work out, right? But fuck. Why aren't they here? Where the fuck have they been while I've been drowning in grief and unable to find a life raft to pull me ashore? Don't they understand I didn't *really* want them to leave me

alone? They were supposed to fight me tooth and nail, hovering above me until I gave in. But they… They left me when I needed them, and I only have myself to blame.

My body desperately craves Callum in my bed, snuggling with me until I fall asleep with peaceful dreams. Or Rad taking me on his dirt bike through the light snow dusting the ground, erasing the depression darkening my mind. I want Kieran to hold me and tell me I'll be okay with his possessive nature and nurturing me until I'm well again. And Asher, I'd let him fuck me out of my grief, bringing me to so many damn orgasms I forget why my world is unraveling.

I sigh, massaging my temples. I never thought loneliness would settle so deep inside me, overshadowing my damn life. With a sigh, I head to the kitchen and grab a glass of water. No matter what happens in my life, I must press forward and continue with my goals. And the first step is getting out of bed.

ME

Hey, uh… you guys want to hang out?

I tap my nails on the counter, watching the screen with a sharp eye. I scroll, looking at the two other unanswered messages I'd sent last night, asking if they'd want to come to see me and maybe watch a damn movie. Yet, I was ghosted.

A deep ache forms in my gut, turning it into knots as I over-analyze their shifty ways. Maybe they're playing a gig somewhere, leaving me alone to pick up the pieces, which I'm barely doing. One false move and my reality will shatter, and I'll be no more than a pile of broken edges on the floor.

Tomorrow my mother's funeral will kick off at noon at the Central Funeral Home. A part of me is ready to continue with this life and move on as quickly as possible. I'll miss the hell out of my mom, but everything happened so fast. It hasn't set in yet that she's truly gone. It's only been two days, but it feels like she's at the grocery store and will march through the front door with a grin at any time. Nothing feels real right now.

When I walk past her recliner, my stomach churns at the misery she must have felt lying there and slowly dying all by herself. I stop beside it, running a finger over the worn material, reveling in the feel of the rough fabric against my fingertips. Why didn't she call for help? Why didn't she ask someone to take her to the hospital before it was too late? Or had she just given up on life?

So many questions run through my mind with little indication of the answers. The only person who could give me clues has been shoved into a large box destined for the ground tomorrow.

My heart jumps through my chest when a knock sounds at the front door, alerting me to unexpected company. For the most part, everyone has respected the space I requested—almost too much. Ugh. My head swims in confusion. I want people here, but I don't want people here. I want to wallow in my own misery, yet I want people here to guide me through it. I'm so damn conflicted with what I want; it makes my fingers curl into fists, ready to punch my frustrations away.

"Van?" I blanch when I open my front door, greeted by a sheepish-looking Van holding out a food container.

"I-I heard about your mom, Rivey," he mutters, rubbing the back of his neck. "I know you've always lived alone with her, so I wanted to stop by and see if you were okay. Also, I wanted to drop off some food." Licking his lips, he hands it over, and the most delicious smell wafts from the lid, making my stomach grumble loud enough for him to pop a smile. "You always did have a hard time taking care of yourself," he rumbles, pushing past me and waltzing into my apartment like he's been here before.

I frown at his chastising words, momentarily stunned at his actions. How dare he march into my home and scold me on how I take care of myself. I mean, sure. I haven't technically eaten all day. Eating when you're stuck at home with nowhere to go and numbing pain gnawing at your insides makes it challenging to crave food. It's the last thing on your mind.

"Um, thanks for the food," I say, shutting the front door and locking it before facing him. "I appreciate the concern. But, uh—what're you doing here? You've never come here before." Placing the food on the kitchen counter, I peel open the lid. My mouth waters at the sight of the freshly baked meatloaf, mashed potatoes, and a side of corn, and a small biscuit with melted butter rests on top of it all, and my brows furrow. "Did you…?"

Van grins with pride, leaning against the counter next to me, and nods. "Yeah. I made it just for you, Rivey. I thought you would need comfort food." He shrugs, looking smugly satisfied with himself, and my hackles rise.

I've pushed this asshole away for months now, and suddenly, he's standing in my kitchen like I'm his number one concern. He's the one who dumped me and pushed me away. Usually, he's watching from the shadows, stalking my every move. Now, he's in the home he swore he wouldn't be caught dead in. This is the same douchecanoe who used to fuck me in his car and then drop me off a block from home because he was too scared to be here.

"Thanks," I say with apprehension, grabbing a fork and tentatively taking a bite of the delicious, mashed potatoes smothered in gravy. I'm so fucked if this is laced with poison, and Van's sole purpose is to kidnap me because it's so damn good, it melts on my tongue—poison be damned, I grab more. "This is delicious. Exactly what I needed," I mumble through my bite, shoveling more food into my mouth with a hum of satisfaction. Maybe this is one more step in the right direction to getting myself out of this dark, miserable state I've put myself in for the last two days.

Van's eyes track around the apartment, taking every dismal detail in with the scrunch of his judgmental nose. "So, this is where you live?" he asks, coming to stand beside me, knocking his shoulder into mine. "It's not too scary here," he says with another unsettling, cocky grin.

"Um, thanks," I say, pushing the half-eaten food away. "Is this all you came by for?" I ask, gesturing to the food as I put the lid back on and hand it back to him. "I mean, I appreciate it. But I'm kind of busy..." Busy getting the fuck away from this intruding asshole. Where's Odette when I need her to barge in with a bat and whack this chucklehead all the way back to his car and send him back to Lakeview?

My hairs stand on end when he pushes the Tupperware back into my hands, shaking his head. "Just keep it. You can wash it and give it back to me." Give it back to him? That means he wants me to see him again or bring it by.

"I don't have a car, remember? I can't bring it back. So here, take it back now, and I appreciate it, Van. Seriously, this was so nice of you, but I need to get back to funeral planning," I mumble, shoving the plastic back into his stomach until he grips it.

"Shit!" he yelps when the lid blows open, spilling the contents of the container onto his white shirt, staining it brown.

"I'm so sorry," I say, grabbing a paper towel, wiping it off the floor, and handing him one for his shirt.

Shaking his head, he cringes. "It's okay," he says with a pained expression; grabbing the back of his shirt, he takes it off and shrugs. "It's no biggie. Do you have a washer here? Can you put it in there?" Van slowly leans down, pinning my back against the kitchen cabinet like a predator swooping in for its kill.

I jerk back, trying to keep him as far away from me as possible. My skin crawls at the sadistic look crossing his face that he's hiding behind a sympathetic expression. Van has always had his claws in me by following me around and luring me out of my pants. But not this time.

"Maybe you should leave," I say through a heavy breath, keeping my eyes on the predator in front of me. I swear if I blink, he'll keep getting closer until he swallows me whole.

"Rivey, I can't leave now," he says, furrowing his brows. "You're hurting," he murmurs, running a finger down my cheek, and I flinch away. Hurt sears into his face, but he shakes it off, looking at me with pity. "Your mom just died. You can't stay here all by yourself."

"I can. I'm fine." I put my hands up, resting them on his chest and attempting to push him away.

I'd be much better if he stopped looking at me like I was a broken doll needing healing. He's not the one I want. I want the boys who hold my heart in their hands, the ones I didn't even mean to fall in love with. That's how it happens, though, right? We fall for those bad boys we swear off, knowing they're tinged in poison, ready to infect us with their wicked ways.

"No. You can't! You need someone, and obviously, those idiots who've been following you around like puppies aren't around. Where are they, Rivey?" he asks, leaning in closer to look me in the eyes. "Where are they now?"

"I… I…" I roll my lips together because I have no idea. It's like they're avoiding me for some reason, but I can't think of why. Did I do something to piss them off? I mean, I told them to leave me be, but I didn't actually think they would for this long.

"I tried to tell you," Van murmurs, pinching my chin. "They're users, Riv. You know they made it into Battle of the Bands, right?"

"Wait, what?" I ask, sucking in a breath. "No, they would have… they would have told me…"

Wouldn't they have? Wouldn't I have been the first person they told? They promised they'd take me. They promised me a lot of shit. And now they've gotten what they wanted from me. Closing my eyes, I take a deep breath. I'm a fucking adult, and I'll talk to them about it after everything settles down.

My heart skips a beat when Van's brown eyes lock on something behind us, and he growls. Before I have time to analyze what's happening, he leans in, putting his lips on mine with vigor. From the moment our lips touch, my stomach turns, wanting to vomit right into his mouth. Maybe that'd get him to back off and stop touching me like he owns me.

Letting out a shriek into his probing mouth, I jam my fist into his side several times without results. Jamming his tongue onto my mouth, he plasters himself against me, holding me hostage with his unwanted kiss. A sharp pain pierces my lip when he bites down, splitting my flesh. An angry moan bubbles up from my throat when he licks at the spot and returns to forcing his tongue into my mouth. I couldn't fucking move if I wanted to. Shit. With his hands in my hair and body pressed into mine, I'm at his mercy until he pulls away, panting for air with a flushed look.

"I've missed you so damn much," he says louder than necessary. "You're so damn perfect for me, Riv. I knew you'd finally choose me over them."

I grunt, trying to squirm out of his grip, but he holds me tighter. A devious grin spreads across his lips, sending chills down my spine. Before me, Van changes into some sort of frightening monster, clinging to me harder than before. A low, menacing chuckle explodes from his vibrating chest, and glee lights up the darkened shadows on his face, making him out to be the true villain he is.

Fear slithers through my veins at what he's capable of. Here I am in my own home, backed into a corner, forced to make out with the man who apparently has a hard time hearing no. Over and over again, I've asked him to fuck off, and repeatedly, he hasn't listened.

"You don't have to pretend you don't like it, Rivey. I know you do." With every word he speaks, his voice gets louder and louder, making my ears ring from the volume of his deep voice.

"I really don't," I grunt, attempting to push him away, but my hands become trapped between our bodies.

Every attempt to turn my head behind me is blocked by his massive hands gripping my hair with bruising force. Panic creeps up my spine, clawing at me to run the fuck away. From deep within, I find the strength to push Van off me and kick him straight in the dick. His brown eyes widen in terror, and he grunts, holding a hand to his balls, and sinks to his knees with a crazed expression. Betrayal flashes through his eyes when he groans, trying to ride out the discomfort of my kick on the ground.

It seems Van needs another—fuck around and find out—type of lesson because verbalizing my discomfort doesn't seem to register with him. So, without uttering a word, I grunt, pulling my fist back and heaving it straight into his face.

The burning, crunching pain hits my fist first as I shake it out in the air, wishing I could punch him again. Basking in the glory of his blood splattering against my fist, I heave a breath, trying to wash away the unwanted touch of Van as I make my getaway. How could someone so close to me force themselves on me like that? Again? How many times will it take for men to understand the word no?

My heart pounds in my chest at the phantom feel of him pushing against me, and I shake it off, running toward my bedroom. I slam the door shut, locking the damn knob, and turn toward my sliding glass door. Freedom is within my grasp until I stop dead, freezing in place.

My heart shatters when Callum stands outside the sliding glass door, shaking his head in disbelief. Tears run down his face in rapid succession, falling to the floor, agony twists his face when he wipes away the tears, and his jaw tightens as I've never seen before.

"You-you kissed him? So-so, it's true?" His face twists more, pain tearing through him and, in turn, splitting me open with his visual anguish.

"What? What's true? Callum," I say, reaching for him. "Listen…"

"Goodbye, River," he rasps through thick emotions in a low voice, sending shivers down my spine. The final nail in the coffin has sealed my fate.

"No, wait!" I shout with desperation cracking my voice when he walks as fast as he can down the sidewalk and fucking disappears into the night, not bothering to let me explain anything to him. I could chase him all night, and he'd still turn his back on me.

How could he walk away without letting me explain anything? How could he not see that Van had assaulted me in the kitchen? Pulling out my phone and texting the group, I don't waste a moment.

ME

I know what you think you saw…

Please talk to me.

He KISSED me… He did it against my will! I said no! I punched him for fuck's sake.

I didn't want it.

Please… can someone talk to me?

Why're you all ignoring me?

"River," Van murmurs through the door, lightly knocking against the wood.

"Go away!" I cry out, trying to hold the emotions clogging my throat. "You fucking psychopath! No means no, asshole!" I hiss, sucking in oxygen.

"Look, I'm sorry. I… I still love you, Rivey. I can't help it. I won't leave until I know you're okay," he says with concern, tapping on the door again.

"I'll be okay when you fucking leave!" I shout through shuddering breaths, feeling the warmth of my tears spreading down my cheeks as my heart breaks into a million pieces.

"Fine," he says softly, "but I'll be a phone call away when you need me. I'll always be there for you, Rivey. Whether you like it or not."

Crawling into my cold bed, I silence my sniffles with my comforter until the sound of my front door slams shut, leaving me with only the tumultuous thoughts wreaking havoc inside my brain. Here I am, once again alone like I always thought I'd be on the night before my mother's funeral.

I stare at my phone for hours, counting the minutes until the sun rises, and I heave myself out of bed. The same numbness sets in like before. This time, it wraps me in its arms like a hug that I embrace, carrying with me all day.

I expect to see the guys coming to pay their respects throughout the funeral, but they never show—not even a quick pop-in to say goodbye. Unlike them, Van dares to show his face, filled with massive amounts of sympathy. He even drops flowers at my front door with a note apologizing for his actions and asking me to call him. My heart sinks when the funeral wraps up, and I'm left with one last pitying look from a pastor I've never met before going home.

That night, I settle into my cold bed by myself. The loneliness presses in on me from all sides, squeezing my chest. Usually, Callum is here by now, kicking off his shoes and climbing into bed with me. Sometimes with Rad in tow. It's been three miserable nights without them. Longing sets in, making me reach for my phone again.

For the thousandth time, I check my messages and sigh. They've all been sent, but the boys have not seen or acknowledged them. What the fuck is going on? They can't seriously think I'd ever kiss Van voluntarily or enjoy it. They've seen how many times I've refused his advancements. There's something more going on than meets the eye, but I don't have the energy to inspect it.

My eyes refuse to shut as the painful memories of the last few days play through my head. The look Callum gave me when he shook his head full of disappointment and took off will haunt me for the rest of my life.

And they got into the Battle of the Bands and didn't bother to tell the one person who rooted for them since the beginning—me.

"AND YOU HAVEN'T HEARD FROM THEM?" ODE ASKS, BITING THE EDGE OF her nail with suspicion.

Her eyes follow me through the entire disgusting bathroom of the bar I'm pacing through. Watching as I slowly spiral into the dark abyss of bullshit that my life keeps serving up to me on a pretty plate of fuckery. "Like, they just dropped off the edge of the earth?" Her shrill voice echoes throughout the bar bathroom, bouncing off the tiled walls.

I shrug, continuing my pacing in the small space of the bathroom.

"No. Not a fucking word," I seethe, anger brewing like a firestorm under my skin. If I get my damn hands on them again, I'll wring their necks and make them wish they had died a slow death. "I've fucking called and texted, and it always goes unanswered." Every goddamn day. Every hour. I'm desperate to get their attention or make them talk to me. Fucking cowards!

My fists curl at my sides, desperate to lash out and punch the damn wall, but I stop myself. Taking a breath, I waltz back over to Ode and shake my head.

"How the fuck does this happen, Ode?" Tears burn down my cheeks in a fury, glaring at the three innocent pregnancy tests lining the shitty countertop, all coming up positive.

Positive! How could my uterus betray me like this? I'm on birth control to prevent this kind of thing from happening! Millions of women pray for this tiny miracle every day, and I've been handed one without trying. How the hell is that fair? Especially when I'm not sure if I can handle this right now. A baby? Me? Not without a support system. And seeing as Odette and her family are the only people I have left; my options are limited. God. A hammer pounds in my skull, filling my ears with the sound of my beating heart. Panic swarms through my entire system, threatening to send me spiraling down the damn drain if I don't get ahold of myself and process what the fuck is going on.

Ode's eyes turn sympathetic when she pulls me into her arms. "Fuck them," she murmurs. "You don't need them. I'll be your baby daddy. I'll be

a better daddy than them, anyway." I snort into her shoulder, cursing the fucking idiots who put me in this position. "But to answer your question. You usually get a little P in the V action, and then... bam! Baby batter makes tiny humans," she says with a sly grin, grunting when I smack her on the arm. "Ouch, bitch. I was just trying to make you laugh. No need for all that violence," she huffs, rubbing her arm with fake outrage.

If it weren't for Odette and her constant support, I would have curled up in a little ball on my bedroom floor, unmoving for days. Hot tears burn behind my eyes from the anger boiling deep under the surface, mixing with resentment. December 15th came and went without a word from the guys. The day we would have gone to the Battle of the Bands. My California dream sizzles into smoldering ashes right before my eyes. Not only did the guys stop texting and calling me weeks ago, but they also blocked me from every form of social media they had and changed their passwords and usernames so I couldn't access them like I had before.

So, my nosy ass looked it up, and wouldn't you know, they were as gorgeous as ever rocking out on the big stage at The KC Club. The crowd had roared with delight, throwing their hands in the air and waving them around at the sultry sound. Much like I had before, standing in awe before the Gods on stage. Then reality crashed, and I closed out the video, refusing to see if they won. And you know, I don't give a shit. Not at all. They can win or lose or walk off a cliff for all I care. Shit.

Where was I during their performance, you ask? Wallowing in my fucking grief all by my damn self. Stuck in my lonely apartment with no one at my side—my mom six feet deep, my boyfriends MIA, and my best friend on the fringes. My only reprieve has been coming to both jobs and making up my homework. I had a lot of shit to make up after getting beat up and then processing the fact my mom keeled over and left me with all this shit. But you know what? I've tried over and over to get into contact with these ghosting dickbags, and they've never responded. I could send an SOS, and they'd wave a hand and let me die.

One day, Odette drove me to Callum and Rad's place with little success. No answer. Empty house. It's like they never even existed. Maybe I made them up, and my boyfriends were figments of my imagination, and now I'm slowly going mad.

"Babe," Ode says, squeezing my shoulder. "You're going to have to go find them. Or something. I mean, they'll have to know, right? You can't just... have their kid and keep it a secret. Jesus. *Their* kid, Riv. Who is the father?" Her eyes widen as mine narrow into slits, and she grins. "Sorry, I'm just trying to lighten the dismal as fuck mood."

"Odette, you bitch," I say as a slight smile pulls at my lips. I might as well let a little humor crack through the bullshit of my life to keep me above water.

"I'm just saying! Four baby daddy possibilities!" she quips, shaking her head. "But seriously, you have to let them know."

I blow out a breath. "I know," I mumble, putting a hand on my flat stomach, trying to imagine the watermelon I will have in a few short months.

Images of my future with a baby flash through my mind as I pace in front of Odette. She sighs, leaning against the counter and watching me work everything out.

"You have options, you know. We'd never judge you for your decisions. Just saying, babe," Ode says with a sad grin.

"I know," I sigh, groaning when I put my forehead on the wet counter and groan more. "Fuck. This is bullshit! They fucking left me for weeks now! And they did this to me? Fucking Castle house on the lake…"

"Fucking sounds about right. Isn't that all you did on your little getaway? You were the main course, and they were the…"

"Please don't even finish that sentence, Ode," I mumble, trying to keep the pressure building in my brain at bay.

"Right. We're very pissed off at them," she mumbles with a defeated sigh. "Extremely pissed off at them." Ode's eyes fill with tears, and she sniffles. "I thought they were so good to you. And here they went and…"

"Acted like every other Lakeview guy on the planet. Who would have predicted that River West would get screwed the fuck over by four fuck boys? They succeeded, didn't they?" Tears fall freely from my eyes again, my fingers digging into my palm. "They fucking told me they got close to me for my name, and what did I do? I got fucking knocked up by them. I let them in, Ode. I fucking…" My entire body trembles with rage, hurt, and disappointment. But mainly, my fucking heart shatters to the floor. "I fucking loved them," I whisper through my quivering lips and shake my head when Ode tries to wrap an arm around me.

"I know you did. And I swear the way they looked at you… I thought they loved you, too. I don't understand. How could they walk away without talking to you first?" she asks, running a hand over her forehead.

"Because they didn't want to," I say with resignation. "Maybe that was their plan all along." And I was too blind, once again, to fucking see what was going on in front of me.

And that's the gist of it all. Callum saw something, misunderstood it, and fucking walked away with a trampled heart before hearing what I had to say. It's like that shitty misunderstanding trope everyone loves to hate in movies and books. None of this would have happened if they had just talked it over like adults. The drama would cease to exist, and they'd come back with open arms and tell me they were sorry. But this isn't a book or a movie, this is real life, and somewhere along the way, it all got twisted into this entire situation. And it's entirely Van's fault. I'm going to castrate him beyond belief for kissing me. Then, I'm going to throw his body to the damn pigs and cackle as they eat through his bones and make him disappear entirely. Ah, that would be the dream. I'm no murderer—but I'll get my revenge if I ever see his face again. Lately, he's been in the damn wind, only texting me instead of showing his face, mentioning something about being in Europe for some damn internship I don't care about. I know I'll see him eventually. He's like a damn pest, always turning up.

"You need to go demand answers," Odette says, pursing her lips. "You need to knock on their doors, punch their faces, and force them to listen to you!" she harps on, raising her fist in the air. Next, she'll get the pitchforks and fire, and we'll storm their castle.

"Already tried that, remember? They weren't home. Hell, maybe they stayed in California," I say with a defeated shrug. Throwing my head back, I stare at the ceiling, letting more frustrated tears fall.

Odette doesn't say a word. Silence falls between us until I stare at her guilt-ridden face, and she huffs. "They won." Those two words punch me in the fucking gut, and all the air leaves my system.

The groupie part of me is fucking ecstatic they're living their dreams. But the baby momma part of me wants to yank their balls through their throats and dig their graves with my bare hands.

"Of course they did," I huff, throwing my hands in the air. "They fucking won. They're living their best life and shit... here I am. I'm knocked up and fucking fuming..."

"Direct that anger at them, babe. Take my car and go and confront someone. Maybe Kieran's mom? Ask her and see what she says. Oh shit, don't give me that look. I'm just saying," she says, placatingly holding her hands in the air.

"Every single person in that neighborhood hates my guts," I grumble, butterflies making my stomach swoop. "But fuck it. Someone has answers for me."

Ode hands her keys to me and pats my back. I shove all the pregnancy tests into my jeans pocket and quietly walk out of the bathroom and into my office, grabbing my coat.

"I'll hold down the fort here, okay? It's too early for a big crowd. So, we'll be good. Now, go get them bitch!" she shouts with encouragement, shooing my broken-hearted ass away.

I bet ten bucks she's tired of watching me pace and angrily cry out my frustrations. Ode won't admit it, but she wants me to handle this before I work myself up to stab someone. Again.

"So inspiring," I grumble, waltzing out the side door toward the parking lot, pulling my coat tighter around my body.

Chilly air smacks me in the face as a few snowflakes float from the heavy clouds from above. Shaking off the shivers, I gasp for breath. If I thought Illinois summers were awful, meet Winter, her ugly, cold bitch of a sister, delivering several inches of snow today.

I shake my head, walking past my poor Bessy, and stop dead. Last time I checked, my poor Bes was covered in a thin layer of dust, yet she sits here, cleaned up, and… What the hell? My brows furrow at the small white note tucked beneath the windshield wiper, soaked from the weather. Picking it up, I carefully open it and nearly drop it on the ground.

"Stop fucking walking."

That's it. That's all it says. Clear and decisive, yet unclear about who it's from. Shivers roll down my spine when I dig my keys out and hop into my unlocked car. Every piece of trash is cleaned up—because I'm messy, so sue me—and the inside is wiped down. The smell of cleaning products wafts through the air. The hairs on the back of my neck stand on end when I put my key into the ignition. Holding my breath, I turn the key, and Bessy starts without a damn fight. Quickly, I press the buttons to heat instead of air conditioning, remembering the last time I drove Bessy was at the beginning of August. Now, here in December, I've finally gotten her going again. Well, someone did, at least. This time, I won't question this gift from God. Instead, I'll take Bessy out on her maiden voyage and hopefully find some answers.

The whole drive across town, my nerves flared to life again, slickening my cold palms. As I drive through the neighborhood entrance, I stare at the sign welcoming me to Lakeview Division. I raise my middle finger and salute the neighborhood the entire time I drive down the main road, turning off toward Callum's house.

To my surprise, two vehicles sit in his driveway and have been since the snow started twenty minutes ago. Thankfully, it's not coming down as hard when I stomp out of my car and walk onto the porch. Anger fuels my every move, and my heart pounds at the prospect of seeing them again. Maybe they're inside, or perhaps they're gone. Either way, I'm letting someone know I'm pregnant and moving on with my life—with or without them. I love them with my entire heart. More than I ever thought I could. They swooped in and stole every piece of me without even trying. I could repeatedly tell myself that I wouldn't give them my heart or love or hold tight to my reservations. But the reality is I'm a sucker for love, and they pulled me into their orbit. But I can move on and restart. I'll get over them… well, eventually.

As I raise my hand to knock on the door, it opens. An embarrassing yelp leaves my lips when I jump back, and a tall, blonde woman carrying folders against her chest stumbles out.

"Sorry," I say, shaking my head.

"Oh, that's all right," she says, wrinkling her nose like she has a bad taste in her mouth. Hell, maybe she swallowed a lemon the way her face morphs, and then she shakes it off. "Well, Gloria," she says, turning toward another woman I recognize standing in the doorway. "I had better get going. I'll get this listing up ASAP. Tell Callum that it'll fetch a good price." She offers Gloria a tight smile, side-eyeing me when she walks back to her fancy car and gets in with a huff, slamming the door.

I swallow hard at the implications of her words and stare at the ground. Callum is selling his house after all this time, completely wiping away the memory of his family. I don't blame him for wanting to get rid of this place and start somewhere new. His family meant so much to him. But his place was a tomb filled with the ghosts of his past, constantly haunting him at every turn.

"Well, well, well," Gloria practically sings with glee, looking down at me with a smirk. "I was wondering when you'd show up. They don't have any money for you. So, you can go back to the slum you belong in," Gloria sneers, sticking her nose in the air and waving her hand.

I try as hard as I can to hold back the eye roll, but it slips through, making her scoff again.

"I was wondering if I could speak to them?" I ask with so much hope I'm practically puking it out of every orifice on my body. I shove my hands into my coat pocket when her assessing eyes stare me up and down.

"Why don't you come in," she says, sweeping a hand, gesturing for me to follow her through the front door.

Suddenly, I feel like I'm walking into a giant trap, and my face is about to be on the back of milk cartons everywhere. With words like 'Local Central City girl has gone missing after attempting to speak to her baby daddies and hasn't been heard from since December.' Shit. Ash may have plotted my demise from the moment he laid eyes on me, and now it's all coming to fruition. They planned to use me and then dump my body in the backwoods. I shake my head, tossing away the crazy thoughts going through my overactive mind.

I reluctantly follow Gloria through the front door, instantly relaxing in the heat pouring through the vents. Looking around, my heart sinks into my ass, and more tears burn the backs of my eyes. Where the couch and big screen TV once sat is empty, void of any furniture and life. Everything within the home is gone, except for the woman staring at me with a victorious smile.

"As you can see, they ran from you, Central girl. They don't want you anymore. They're onto bigger and better things," she says with glee, practically having an orgasm at the fact I'm here and they're...

"They're still in California?" I ask, raising a brow, knowing in my heart what the answer is.

Keep your shit together—no falling apart now.

Fuck. Every fear I had conjured over the past three weeks is coming true in vivid detail. They're gone. They left me here. And they don't fucking care about me like I thought they did. Was everything a fabrication for their benefit? Were all the things they said big, fat lies to capture my heart in their grasps and fucking crush it after they left? Who the hell does that? I don't give a shit if they thought they saw something that wasn't true. In my heart, I know Van kissed me against my will, and Callum saw it without waiting for an explanation. It's like they saw what they wanted to see and didn't hang around for an answer.

"Well, they did win the entire competition and got offered a record deal, not to mention the million dollars sitting pretty in their bank account, which you'll have no part of. I won't have you ruining their lives," she says, turning her nose up again.

What is with this lady and her prejudice about where I come from? Didn't she do the same thing and bag some rich guy who wasn't who she thought he was? She's really projecting herself onto me, and it's really beginning to piss me the fuck off.

"Well, I need to speak to them. It's pretty important," I grumble, hating to admit I need them right now. All I want to do is fall into their arms but also punch their noses into their faces. Is that too much to ask?

"No," she says, shrugging and giving me the stink eye. "There's no way…"

"I'm pregnant, lady," I say through clenched teeth. "And I'd appreciate speaking to the boys responsible. You know, all of them. So, can I please talk to them or what?" Okay, so that wasn't as polite as I had intended it to be. But my bullshit meter is flying through the damn red on dangerous levels, and I'm about to explode if I don't get any answers quickly.

Her face pales when her arms fall to her sides, and she shakes her head. "No… You can't be…"

"Yeah, I can be. Not that I did it on purpose. So, can I talk to them? They won't answer my calls," I say in a small voice, trying to reel back in all the rage brewing beneath my flesh. If Gloria isn't careful, I'll turn green, hulk out in Callum's empty living room, and destroy everything.

Gloria fumbles with the phone in her pocket, turning a sick shade of green. I take it back; maybe she'll be the one to turn green instead of me. Hers, of course, will be from sickness instead of burning rage. Or perhaps I spoke too soon. Her blue eyes meet mine in a frenzy when she brings the phone up to her ear and holds up a finger.

"I'll contact them. They blocked your number for a reason," she snaps, turning her back to me, and waltzes into the kitchen.

Against my better judgment, I stand in the middle of the room, taking it all in. They blocked my number? That explains the lack of phone calls and texts. They must have done it the moment Callum returned with evidence of my infidelity—or lack thereof. At this point, I'd rather pounce on Gloria, drag the phone away from her ear, and give those assfaces a piece of my mind, but I refrain. I have manners—sometimes.

"Yes, she says she's pregnant and would like to speak to you," she murmurs into the phone, side-eyeing me as I stare daggers through her skull. "Of course," she says with a few head nods and then hangs up the phone, placing it in her pocket. Gloria sighs, reaches into her purse, sits on the empty countertop, and pulls out a little black book that I instantly recognize.

It's a fucking checkbook. Anyone could see that from a mile away. But why the fuck… Every part of me slumps when she grabs her pen and writes something quickly before tearing it out.

"Here," she says, waving it in the air until I snatch it from her hand. "The boys send their regards but want nothing to do with you or it. Kieran says to go ahead and get rid of it," she sniffs, putting her nose in the air again. "Something about Van being the real daddy?" she asks, raising a haughty brow. A victorious smile spreads across her face, and she nods. "That's probably right. They caught you red-handed slutting around, didn't they?"

"Slutting around?" I gape, rearing back. "Wow. For a grown woman, you sure speak like a catty teenager. Just wow, Gloria. Thanks for the check, but you can shove it up your tight ass and maybe knock something loose, like that haughty attitude you parade around with. Have a good life, bitch," I hiss, staring at the amount on the check and laughing. "Seriously? Nine hundred bucks for what? An abortion? Get fucked," I say, tearing it into pieces and throwing it like confetti around me. "Although, you probably don't care right now. Someday you'll see this child and want to be in their life, and I'll tell you the same thing. Get. Fucked."

Redness coats her cheeks when she vibrates with the same rage fueling my words. With stiff movements, she reaches into her purse again and slams down four separate envelopes with another grin.

"These are for you then," she says, tapping each envelope with her long nails. "They wanted to ensure you didn't follow them out there and ruin their lives again. So, here are your restraining orders forbidding you from ever contacting them again. No calls. No texts. No social media messages. The moment you do, they'll report you to the authorities. They will be famous, and they don't need the trash of their past slipping through the cracks. It also notes that you're not allowed to mention them on any form of social media and slander their name. Your hands are officially tied, Miss West." Her smug look makes my head rear back.

Anger builds more, and tears fall down my cheeks at her words. Restraining orders? Christ on a cracker, they've lost their fucking minds. But fine. Fine! If that's how they want to fucking play it, then so be it. I'll work my ass off for the rest of my life to forget about them and the fucked-up games they played with my heart. My only hang-up is the constant reminder they left me with. The one they want nothing to do with. Whatever. Odette and I will give this baby as much love as they need without the help of the four idiots who helped create him or her. They can brainwash themselves for as long as they want with whatever lies they want to.

I know the truth.

And one day, they will too.

The hot July sun beams down when I step out of Bessy, groaning when I can stretch my legs. Sweat sticks to every damn inch of my skin, slowly dripping down my back. I swear, it's only nine in the morning, and the sun is already trying to roast me like a Thanksgiving turkey. Shit. Turkey sounds delicious.

And now, not only am I starving for the thousandth time in the two hours I've been awake, but every bone in my body aches. Seriously, it was only a ten-minute drive to the local grocery store, but it was still Hell on earth for my hips and legs. My least favorite activity these days is walking or any form of exercise. Minus sex, now that'd be a pleasant activity. Except no one wants to bang a broken-hearted, pregnant girl. So, here I am, seven months along and hornier than I've ever been in my life and fucking lonely. Where's the good dick when you need it?

Normal women glow at this point in the pregnancy, raving about how their morning sickness has gone away and their acne has cleared. I call bullshit. I love this child with every fiber of my being, but I wish it were two months from now and she was here. Despite the circumstances and the lack of money, I'm over the moon to bring her into this world with me. It's just her and me against the entire world. As she ages, I plan to tell her about those assfaces who tucked tail to live their rock star dreams and left us here. All positive, of course. I don't want her to go a day without knowing who helped create her.

"If you could stop kicking my bladder, that'd be great," I mumble, rubbing a hand over my large stomach as she kicks me again. "Or not," I quip, reaching into my backseat with a grin. "Just you and me, Lyric," I say in a soothing voice, grabbing the grocery bags and hauling them into my hands. With a grunt, I shut the door and head up the back staircase of the record store to the apartment above it.

Seven months ago, my landlord informed me that I had to leave because my mom and I were in government-placed housing. We moved in

there when I was a kid, and before my mom died, she had never added me to the lease. So, needless to say, I had to leave on a thirty-day notice, pregnant, grieving, and completely fucked up from the betrayal from the boys. Booker, bless his fucking heart, let me take over the abandoned apartment over the record store. I swear, when I'm a badass band manager, I'm buying him both businesses and a brand-new car for all the support he's given me over the years. The plus side? Van has no idea where I live and can't snoop around, knocking on my doors every hour of the day, begging me to let him in.

My new apartment is a small one-bedroom, maybe, eight hundred square feet of living space. But it's home now—a place to lay my head and a place for me to bring baby Lyric home when the time comes. It's mine for now until I get through school and work.

One day, I'll have more than an apartment above the record store. One day, I won't depend on the government to help me buy food and provide for my medical needs. But that's not today. Today, I'm still growing into the woman I'll be in a few years and taking what I can get to survive.

Checking my phone, I note the time and curse. Quickly, I put my groceries away and head down to the record store to open with my laptop in tow.

For the past few months, I've been going through non-stop classes, getting closer and closer to my degree. Thankfully, the community college offers summer courses as a way to guarantee degrees at a faster pace. The faster I get this, the better off I'll be. And maybe, sometime in the future, I can get my bachelor's and expand my business degree in music.

Finally, I sit after hours of grocery shopping, walking, and moving around. Relief slams into my damn throbbing feet when I prop them up on the counter and pop in my one working earbud, groaning at the weight off my damn toes. God. Whoever said pregnancy was magical was a big, fat liar. Listen, I'll love this child until I die, but if I ever have to go through this again—I might pluck the child out too early and call it a day.

As I settle in and sign into school, the professor begins speaking in a monotone voice. One day someone will let this man know his class is boring and he should lighten up a little bit.

I internally groan when the bell above the door rings, announcing the arrival of… Fuckity, fuck…

"Van," I say through gritted teeth when he waltzes in with a grin, coming straight to the counter.

He cocks his head, taking me in when he leans on the counter, and his eyes widen. "I didn't believe the rumors, but here you are. And you're…"

"Very pregnant," I grit out, narrowing my eyes at his smug face when he whistles. "What the hell do you want, Van?" I say, pinching the bridge of my nose in exasperation.

I haven't seen this fool since the night he kissed me. So, to see him now up close and personal reminds me of the promise I made myself about castrating him and selling him as pig food.

"Just came by to see how you were doing," he says, grinning and looking me over. "How've you been? I've been away for a while." Genuine concern fills his eyes, but I don't fall into his manipulative trap like I used to.

"Oh, just peachy. Living the good life," I quip, dripping with so much sarcasm we're practically swimming in it.

"Rivey," he says in a low, pained voice. "I just… I just came by to see how you were coping with everything. And I wanted to tell you that I never took the money my dad offered me over you. I only broke up with you to go to college and get my degree. Not like them," he murmurs, shaking his head. "I would never take money over you. In fact, I've been away making a better future for us." I blink rapidly when he emphasizes the word *us*, and I wrinkle my nose.

"Like them? For us?" I indulge him just this once, hanging on to his words and ignoring my professor yapping in my ear.

Like I give a shit if Van took the money over being with me. That ship sailed a long time ago. Besides, that's all on him and his problem—not mine. He can do what he wants. And by the crease in his forehead, I'm not giving him the reaction he wanted.

"Yeah. I… listen, I wasn't supposed to say anything, but Kieran was bragging about the massive check his mom gave him to leave you," he says, watching my unmoving face. "And I would never do that. I went to Europe on my dad's dime for an internship, and now I have every arsenal in my pocket for us to have a better future. You, me, and the baby."

Even when it feels like a knife stabs through my fucking heart at the sound of his name. Kieran. The name I've refused to utter for months now. It feels like ash on my tongue the more my brain repeats it. Asher. Kieran. Callum. Rad. Shit. My stomach rolls, knotting around the memories we've shared.

Taking a deep breath, I shove that shit down as far as it'll go and lock them away. I'll remember them for Lyric and tell her every story I know, but I won't let Van barge into my place of employment and undo seven crucial months of mending my heart back together. Thanks to pregnancy hormones, it took many nights of crying myself to sleep and cursing their names for my heart to heal finally.

"He said that if they left you here, she'd pay for their trip to California and help their living situation and everything. I can't believe they took the money over you." Shaking his head, he runs a hand over the back of his neck, dropping his eyes to the floor with shame.

"Nice story," I say with a shrug, busting through my bullshit meter for the day. "They did what they did. That's fine. They can live their dreams in

California without me, regardless if they took a paycheck over a human being or two." My nose wrinkles when I rub my grumbling stomach.

I see red when I roll my eyes, huffing at his mere existence. I'm holding back the angry tears welling in my eyes. Again, thanks to my pregnancy hormones throwing my body into some whacky ass emotions, I cry at every tiny inconvenience. Anger rises to the surface at the thought of those jackasses taking a big, fat check instead of hanging around. If I hazard a guess, I bet Gloria suggested the restraining orders, too. Among whatever else she thought of. Whatever. That's in the past, and this is the present.

Leaning forward with desperation, Van attempts to grab my hand. "I can take care of you, Rivey. I can... I have money. You'll have a good place to live, and we could be together. Half the town thinks it's my kid, anyway. I want... I want that," he murmurs, pleading with his eyes.

I blink a few times, letting his words register in my mind. For the first time, I'm seeing the true psycho he is. Like, really? He wants to take care of me after he stalked me and watched me for months when the guys were here. Even after the unwanted kiss and the groping. I knew he was a little unhinged in the head, but this takes the fucking cake. If I didn't know any better, I'd say he had something to do with this entire situation. Minus the pregnancy, of course. His tiny flesh flute didn't come anywhere near me. Thank God.

"Your kid?" I yelp, kicking my damn brain into gear.

"Yeah, I mean. They saw us at your house, babe. They know..." He waves a wrist, alluding to the horizontal tango we most definitely didn't do that night.

I grind my teeth and curl my fingers into fists. If I let my hands have free reign of the situation, I'll stab him in the throat. And there's no way I can go to prison now at seven months pregnant.

"You mean the kiss you forced on me. Or the way you cornered me in the kitchen? Or showing up uninvited? I could go on and on, but my answer would always be the same. Get fucked, Van. This isn't your kid. I'm not yours. And I'd really like to stab you right now." My eyes narrow when he swallows hard and takes a step back. Wise man, he's not underestimating me for once, probably because he's seen what my little knife can do and wants nothing to do with it.

"Jesus," he yelps, putting his hand in the air and staring at the knife in my hand.

Oh. Would you look at that? How'd that get there? I could really poke someone's eyes out with this, preferably Van's.

"I won't ask again. Please leave. I'm really, really not in the mood for people right now, and you're no exception." I shake my knife, making him lose all the color in his face.

"Fine. My offer still stands, even if you want to stab me. Shit," he says, bolting out the door like his ass is on fire.

Fuck. Finally, I can relax and pay attention to class. Maybe in five minutes, I'll head up to my apartment and grab the chocolate chip cookie cake I snagged at the grocery shop for cheap. It may expire tomorrow, but it sure as hell won't last that long in my home. Those things are my damn kryptonite right now. Take away the cookie cakes, and you might as well take away my life. Oh, and milkshakes. God. I can't shake this sweet tooth plaguing my every waking moment. It's no wonder I've already gained thirty pounds and am still growing. But fuck it, I'm building a tiny human one day at a time. I'll happily eat my weight in food.

Movement outside the store makes a grumble work up my throat. Great. Two guys linger outside, scrunching their stupid noses at the neighborhood. Narrowing my eyes, I watch the tattooed one secure his phone in front of his jeans, almost on instinct. I snort. That won't do anything around here, but I'm not breathing a word of that. They're already trembling in their designer shoes, giving their fancy schmancy lifestyle away. Looking them up and down, I furrow my brows. They may not be from around Central City, but they're not from Lakeview either. These identical guys stick out like a sore thumb. A hint of familiarity slaps me in the face the longer I stare at them standing outside the window.

The door overhead finally rings, indicating they've entered and are ready to browse or stare at me in awe. I feign ignorance like I wasn't watching their every move.

"Welcome to Dead Records. If you need anything, my name is River. Just let me know," I say through a heavy, tired sigh, suddenly feeling the exhaustion weighing me down.

Now that I'm seated and staring at the shocked faces of the guys in front of me, I need a damn nap, which won't come anytime soon. Not only do I have to deal with customers, orders, and pregnancy, but I have to get through my classes.

"You're River Blue West?" one guy asks overly seriously, making my eyes snap to his similar moss-green eyes.

Whoever gave me that name should be shot—AKA—my father. It's bad enough that the entirety of the West clan is named after our father's favorite bands. But to give me the middle name too? Sucks.

I frown, scrunching my nose with suspicion and taking out my earbud. I don't know who these fuckers are, but I'm too tired and pregnant to deal with bullshit.

"Whoever you are," I say, cocking my head to the side and examining them with a calculating eye. "I'm not interested. You assholes keep coming to me thinking I can get you whatever you think, but that's not how it works. I am a West. One of over a dozen, and I'm not the West that can get you fucking famous." I shake my head, trying to set my earbud back in my ear to listen to my professor's rambling, but I stall when the colder-looking twin opens his mouth.

"I'm Zeppelin, and this is Seger. We're—"

"My fucking brothers. Yup! I've heard that one before," I say with real-ization, narrowing my eyes and scoffing, waving a hand. "It's funny. Last I checked, my billionaire brothers were living it up in California and signing douchebags like Whispered Words to their label and not coming to bumb-fuck nowhere, Illinois. It's almost laughable. You scammers will do anything to get a buck. But newsflash, dickweeds—I'm as broke as an unfunny joke," I grumble, scrunching my nose again as the other idiot bends at the waist, barking out a sharp laugh.

"You're definitely a fucking West. Shit." He breaks out in a deep laugh, putting his hands on his knees, and wheezing.

I scowl. It really wasn't that damn funny.

"You done?" I ask, raising a brow at his antics. I swear he turns blue from all the laughter squeaking through his nose.

"Here, here, fuck," he wheezes again, digging into his wallet and throwing his license at me. On instinct, I catch it with ease from my seated position. My brows immediately furrow at the name, looking back at me.

"Jesus," I mutter inaudibly. My fingers tremble around his driver's license, and the realization of who they are smacks me in the chest like a runaway train, knocking the breath from my lungs.

"See? I'm Seger fucking West. The real fucking deal." Turning to his twin who can only be Zeppelin fucking West with a gigantic grin and murmur, he says, "I think she and Kace would get along fucking fine."

Zepp side-eyes Seger with a snort, steps up to the counter, and flips open his wallet. Everything inside me goes numb and haywire at the same damn time. My jaw drops open, and their shit falls to the counter with a loud thud.

"The fuck are you doing here? Listen, the shit I said about Dad, I..." I ramble through terror until Seger holds up a hand, stopping my words.

"Dad was the biggest fucking cock on the planet when he was alive..." he says with a cringe, running a hand across his neck.

"We're not here to discuss a dead man's shortcomings. We're here to discuss your inheritance," Zepp says, gaining my complete and utter attention.

I swallow the hard lump forming in my overly sensitive throat and shake my head. Rage once again boils in the pit of my stomach. How could a man who gave me life walk away without contributing anything and have his two favorite sons show up and tell me there's money? Nope. Even if I need it more than anything right now, I still have my morals.

"I don't want his fucking money. I don't want anything from the piece of shit. He kicked Ma and me out without anything but the clothes on our backs. Ma dragged us back here, and we've lived on food stamps and the medical card for fucking years. I don't need a damn dime from Corbin

West," I hiss, jumping to my feet, which is a damn miracle these days. "I've done fucking fine without him."

My teeth grit when pity takes over Seger's eyes as they fall on my giant stomach protruding from my long band shirt. I frown when he doesn't take his eyes off it, staring like he's never seen something like it before

"What? You've never seen a pregnant woman before?" I chide, narrowing my eyes at him.

He snorts playfully, running a hand down his face. "Sure, I have. It's just fucking uncanny. You're as far along as our wife. Twenty-eight weeks, right?" He looks at me as my hand flies to my stomach and my nose scrunches.

"Um, yeah," I say quieter before nibbling on my lip when he nods.

"Do you have time for lunch?" Zepp asks, gesturing toward a diner across the street.

I lick my lips, envisioning a delicious burger and strawberry milkshake, as a loud rumble erupts from my stomach. I could have denied lunch because of a lack of funds. My stomach, on the other hand, had other plans and outed me for the starving woman I am.

"Now that you know we're your brothers, we have some shit we'd like to discuss with you. And I think you may want to hear it," Seger says with a little too much enthusiasm, licking his lips.

When I finally meet his eyes, indecision weighs heavily on my mind. They showed me their licenses with their names on them. So, I shouldn't be afraid. But something holds me rooted to the spot. Every person I've ever trusted has left me dangling over the cliff with no way back up. Who is to say they're different? Are they lying to gain something from me? Is there an inheritance to receive? I blow out a breath, weighing my damn options. It isn't until Zeppelin speaks that I finally decide to say fuck it.

"Let's get some burgers, fries, and hell—a milkshake. We do have things to discuss with you—important things," Zepp tacks on with a convincing voice.

I lick my lips again and finally sigh. "Fine. Class was fucking boring today, anyway. Who cares about the history of business bullshit? Take me to lunch, but don't expect me to take a damn handout," I gripe, shutting my computer down and closing it. Quickly, I pick up a small backpack-style purse and fling it over my shoulder before grabbing a set of keys off the counter.

Whatever this lunch leads to, I'll listen. But I won't make any promises, especially regarding the people in my family.

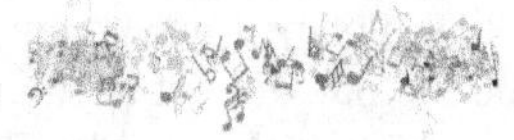

"Hold the Weiner," I say, putting a finger in the air. My entire body trembles with my mouth hanging open. Did they say what I think they said? There's no way in hell. This can't be right. "Twenty million dollars? Shut the front door," I gasp, slumping on the bench as the waitress drops off my delicious strawberry milkshake and mounds of food. I've been starving all day, holding out for the food I got from the store. But when we came in, they said to order whatever I wanted. And who am I to deny that? "I just… I can't… he just…" I stutter, shoving a handful of fries into my mouth, and moan at the greasy, salty taste slithering across my desperate taste buds. God, this is even better than sex.

"Twenty million is just the tip of the iceberg, River. More will be deposited, according to our father's lawyer. He left money for each of you…"

"Each of us?" I ask, taking a swig of my milkshake. "You've met…"

"All fucking fourteen of the West children, yeah. We've been down that road, and you, dear sister, are the last damn one," Seger mumbles, shoving his cheeseburger into his mouth with the same zest as me. Maybe we're more alike than I thought. "Fuck. Nothing beats a quaint little diner's burger," he moans around his food, taking another bite.

"Animal," Zepp grumbles, taking a small bite of his burger.

Every muscle in my body locks up at the sultry sound blasting through the speakers. Looking around, every patron stops what they're doing to marvel at the song playing overhead with smiles. Seger bobs his head with a grin, closing his eyes and taking the tune in, seeming pleased with himself.

My milkshake turns to ash on my tongue, and heavy lead is in my twisting stomach. I've avoided everything Whispered Words from the moment they walked away without another word. I've avoided anything online mentioning their newly found success and articles interviewing them for various reasons. If I hazard a guess, I'd say they're taking over the world one song at a time.

"Is this?" Zepp asks, tilting his head.

"Fucking right it is. They're hella fucking talented, and I can't believe they came out of nowhere," Seger says with a grin, turning to look at me.

His face falls at the sight of what I'm sure is my pale face. Moisture beads above my lip as a heat of rage boils my blood, and my fists clench under the table.

Angry tears pool in my eyes, and my breath shudders in my chest. Of all the songs I could have heard today, why did it have to be theirs? And why did it have to be Roaring River? Like, do they seriously sing that still? Why couldn't they have lost and gotten what they deserved? To rot in the depths of hell. I swear to God, one day, I will enact my revenge on the boys who stole my heart, crushed it, and then abandoned me when I needed them most.

"Whispered Words," I mutter with my lips twisting into an angry scowl.

"Uh, yeah. That's them. They won the Battle of the Bands seven months ago and have taken the world by storm. They're absolutely…"

"Absolute fuck heads," I hiss, clenching my teeth and unleashing my anger.

Seger holds up a hand. "Um… I feel like I'm missing something," he mutters, side-eyeing his brother with confusion.

Licking my lips, an ingenious idea pops into my mind, easing some of the rage boiling over. I swear the moment my body decided to create a tiny human, my emotions ran rampant. So, with that thought, I'll use all my energy and become what I've always wanted to become—a band manager. And who better to give me a chance than the brothers I happened to meet?

"I'll sign the papers for the money," I say, taking a deep breath, but steely determination settles on my shoulders.

"Okay, cool," Zepp says, reaching down for the manilla envelope and placing it on the table.

"On one stipulation," I grind out, looking over the papers with so many zeros I nearly faint on the spot.

"What's that?" Seger asks.

"I want a job at West Records. I want to intern. I want to become a band manager," I say, nodding vigorously as I look over the papers again. "I have experience managing bands from the area. So, in return, I'll sign the papers if you give me a job. I'll move out to California and start as soon as possible."

Whatever it fucking takes. I'll start at the bottom again and work my way up. I'm not entitled enough to think they'd hand me a corner office and say, "have at it." No. I want to learn and dive deep into the music industry. So, when my chance comes, and I come face to face with the dickless wonders who left me, I'll be in charge.

"I… Umm…" Seger looks at Zepp, who scratches his chin.

"To become a manager is a hefty undertaking. You'd have to intern at the bottom and get a feel for it. A bachelor's in music management is a necessity at West Records. We want the best of the best, but you're family. And if you want a job…"

"I'll start at the bottom. I'll sort fucking mail. I want this…" I say again with a snarl, taking another gulp of milkshake to calm myself down.

"But why? You could take your inheritance and never work another day in your life. Why would you want to?"

I rub my stomach, caressing the tiny human inside who depends on me and only me to provide for her. Looking out the window, heavy memories plague my mind. The laughs. The love. The fucking heartbreak. Everything I've endured over the past year sits on my shoulders daily. And I'm tired of it. I want a fresh start in the industry I've been dreaming about.

"I'm getting my business degree right now and working through summer programs to obtain it ASAP. I can change my major to music business. I'll put in the work. Anything to make those assholes pay for what they did to me." I frown slightly, shaking myself out of my haunting thoughts. I don't need to think of Callum's innocent smile or Rad's contagious laugh. I have to focus on what's suitable for Lyric and me.

"Who?" Zepp asks, furrowing his brows.

"They promised they'd take me with them. They promised… they loved me." A slight hiccup escapes from my trembling lips, but I look away, refusing to let them see me break. I've cried enough, and today, that stops. "They promised me everything, and I believed every lie they told." I swallow hard, vigorously wiping away the tears falling down my cheeks. "They left me, and they left her," I whisper, pointing to my belly.

Seger blows out a breath, filled with so much fucking confusion, and I have to bite my cheek to stop smiling. "Who?" he grumbles, shaking his head.

I stare out the window again, letting the emotions take hold. "Whispered Words promised me the world, and then they turned their back on me."

"They… They what?" Seger asks, curling his fists on the table.

"Not now," Zepp grumbles, putting a hand on his shoulder and squeezing. "We have watchers." With that, Zepp nods for us to follow him as he pays the bill.

The warm sun greets us when we step out of the diner, and I sigh, clutching the envelope tightly to my chest.

"They did this to you?" Seger immediately asks, pointing angrily to my stomach.

"Well, I was an active participant in the endeavor," I quip with a snort when he pales, looking away. "But yeah, this is one of theirs."

"I'll kill them," he murmurs, clenching his fists.

"No need," I say with a shrug, looking off into the distance. "I'll do it." Once I get my hands on them, I'll make them wish they never attempted to use me.

"Okay. You have a job, then," Zepp says, stroking his chin.

My heart soars with excitement, and I grin. "Thank you! Seriously, it's been my damn dream job to do this."

"Paid internship. We'll have you start in the office, delivering mail. Once you've had the baby and come back, we can start getting you more acclimated. And once you have your degree…"

"I'm working on it and have been for a year. I'm on track to get my associates in December through the quick pace program." Tears form in my eyes, and I sniffle. "Thank you for tracking me down and giving me this. I don't want his money, but…" I shake my head, roll my lips together and gather my emotions.

"By the looks of it, you need it. We had no idea that he saved it for you all these years. So, take the money and come start your new life in East Point Bluff with us," Zeppelin says, putting a hand on my shoulder and squeezing.

"I'll need maybe two weeks to get everything squared away here," I say, meeting Zepp's eyes, and he nods.

"Of course," he says with a slight grin. "I have a good feeling about you, River."

I snort, wiping away the stupid hormonal tears dripping out of my eyes. "Thanks for taking a chance on me."

"Eh, what's a long, lost, forgotten family for? We couldn't help you when we were kids, but we sure as fuck can help you now. Pack your bags, little sister. We're going to California."

California. All my dreams are coming true in the blink of an eye.

"To California," I mumble with an excited grin.

"But first, maybe sign the papers, and we can get all this wired into a secure bank account for you. That'll help with the move…"

And so much more than they even knew. That night, my brothers left on a private jet, needing to get back to their pregnant wife, leaving me to stew in my newly found fortune.

The next day, as soon as the money was within my grasp, I did what I always wanted to do. I paid off Booker's mortgage, the loan on the bar, and the record store. The man who took so many chances on me now lives a debt-free life and can focus on the greater things. Every cent of Korrine's, Odette's, and Leon's debt was erased with the money I paid for them to move into a beautiful new house with zero bills. From here on out, I'll pay their monthly expenses and let them live the life they deserve. They've been through everything with me and have been by my side for all of it, never turning their backs.

Over the next two weeks, I helped Booker rent the apartment above the record store to a new worker down on her luck. She was a great fit and took over my position. Leon managed to snag the manager title at the bar and quickly took over my duties easily.

Finally, the day came when I have to say my goodbyes. Odette cries the entire time we say our goodbyes in the empty airplane hangar, hugging for what seems like an eternity. My rock. My best fucking friend. And I was about to say goodbye to it all. Well, not goodbye, goodbye. But I hadn't lived more than ten feet away from her for the last twelve years, and now, I was headed to a different coast by myself.

"I'll call every day," I murmur, hugging her tight.

"And my niece!" she wails, sprinkling her tears on my shoulder. "I'll miss her birth…"

"I'll fly you out. I want you there if you want to be," I say with emotions clogging my throat.

Odette chuckles, pulling back to cup my face. "You're a rich bitch now. I'll fly you out?" She snorts when I crack a smile.

"You're my sister," I murmur, patting her hand. "I'll miss the hell out of you," I grunt when she throws her arms around me again.

"You make them pay," she sniffles on my shoulder. "Make them regret ever fucking around with you, okay?"

"Believe me, Ode. By the time I'm done with Whispered Words, they won't know their ass from their elbows. Anyway, I know how. I'll fucking destroy them," I vow, formulating the long game I'll have to play to get at them.

By now, they're living their rock star dreams under the spotlight with their adoring fans at their feet. But my time will come, and they'll be under my heel, and I'll squish them like the little bugs they are.

"You ready?" Zepp asks, nodding toward the private fucking jet they brought to pick me up in.

"Yeah," I say, wiping my tears. "It's time for me to go," I whisper, squeezing Ode's hand one last time before getting on the jet. "Thanks for coming and getting me. The stupid airlines wouldn't let me travel," I grumble, putting my seatbelt over my belly.

"What's ours is yours now," Seger says, shrugging when he gets comfortable.

"So, are you ever going to tell us exactly what this band did to you?" Zepp asks, sitting back as the plane moves down the runway.

I shrug, staring out the window. "One day," I murmur, watching as the cornfields stretch in for miles and miles, and I settle back in my seat.

Five Years Later

"Hey! I'm on my way, I swear," I breathe into the phone, shoving my foot into my heel, instantly regretting the uncomfortable shoe.

But you know what? These heels make my legs and ass look amazing. And I'm all for feeling a little more confident in my skin these days. Ever since my baby girl graced me with her sassy appearance, my body has massively changed from the nineteen-year-old girl I was before. I'm a full woman now, blessed with wider hips, stretch marks, and a baby pooch that will never leave, no matter how many sit-ups I do. Whatever. I'm still me and damn proud of who I am.

"Uh-huh," Seger snorts into the phone. "Just, uh, meet us in the main office, okay? We have something we want to talk to you about." I raise a brow at his serious tone and peek out the window to the mansion across the street, biting my bottom lip.

"Is this about Break?" I ask, cocking my head. "They did it to themselves. They signed the pledge contract, and they blew it." I gave them many chances to clean themselves up from the booze, parties, drugs, and debauchery. They promised me in a contract that this was their last chance, and they blew it out of the water last night.

My eyes track the twenty movers across the street in fascination as they start tugging out Break's equipment, clothes, dishes, and whatever else they moved into the Band House with. The band shamefully watches with their heads hung low, berating Aiden, their lead singer, for his lack of self-control.

Shaking my head, I recall the surprise visit I paid the band last night at their first concert after moving into the Band House across from me. Call me their babysitter or the new manager, but most people call me The Fixer these days. Give me any band, and within six months, they're either making hits again or hitting the road with their tails tucked. Hence Break, hitting the damn road after breaking their contract with me and West Records.

I knew they were done when I walked into Aiden's backstage green-room and witnessed him snorting drugs out of some groupie's asshole and then fucking her into oblivion. Nothing says tear up my contract more than breaking the rules within the first month of said contract being signed. So, after Aiden finished his little show with a shout, I let him know they were over by clapping my hands from the chair I sat in, watching as he fucked himself and his band over—literally.

Seger snorts again, bringing me back into the conversation. "Yes and no, you fucking ball buster. Shit. I can't believe that dumbass fucked his whole future up after signing a contract saying he'd give up the drugs, chicks, and improve his music," Seger growls, most likely ready to punch something or someone.

"Ballbuster? I resent that, asshole. I'm just doing my job, bro. You know, the fixer?" I roll my eyes, searching the kitchen for my missing tiny human. "Fuck, it's quiet in my house. Listen, we'll be there in about an..."

"An hour?" Seger quips at my lateness.

Shit. I never used to be late until I had my baby girl, Lyric. Now, I'm a perpetual hot mess, constantly late to everything–even work. Zepp says I'd be late for my funeral, and yeah, I think he's right.

"No! Not an hour. I have to find Ly, and then we'll be there! She's excited to see Maggie again and have a sleepover. So, she should stop hiding now!" I shout louder than necessary, greeted by crickets.

Great. She's probably slathering lipstick all over her face and giving herself a mustard face mask. Again.

"Yeah, see you at nine. Drive safe and all that fucking good stuff," Seger says as we say our goodbyes, leaving me with a wary feeling bubbling in my gut, feeling an awful lot like suspicion. My brothers don't call me into their office very often. Usually, it's to talk to me about a band or assign me to another group.

"Lyric!" I shout for what seems like the millionth time this morning from the kitchen, tapping my heel with impatience.

I sigh, walking into the family room, and heading toward the little girl standing in front of the large screen TV with her head cocked to the side. Fuck. My heart sinks when one of the men who haunt my nightmares walks across the screen, bombarded by paparazzi.

Her long black locks hang past her shoulders, brushed straight, and her little nose scrunches in disappointment.

"Why is Daddy leaving another hotel with another lady?" she asks with a heavy sigh, turning to look at me with disappointment ringing in her beautiful, mismatched eyes. Big, blue eyes stare up at me, making my heart sink into my ass. A deep brown streak takes up a portion of her right eye, similar to the man currently on the screen.

It's a kick in the gut to stare at this little human who baked in my belly for nine months and shot out of my vagina with no help from him—them—

but turns into an exact replica of the man waltzing around on the celebrity gossip channel with another woman under his arm.

Huge sunglasses sit on Kieran's face, and a grim expression crosses his lips when he holds up a hand and tells the cameras to fuck off. He's been out of my life for five years and hasn't changed much in the looks department. He's still as delicious as he was years ago with those muscles and dark hair. But fuck. Loathing builds inside me as I stare at the same man who denied my child and walked out of my life without a second glance.

"Mommy. Why? This is…" She scrunches her brows, looking down at her fingers as she counts down the number of women, he's been spotted within the past two weeks. "The fourth one. Daddy is a ho."

I choke on my spit, grabbing my throat, wheezing as she stares up at me, blinking like she didn't say the funniest thing on the planet.

"Ly, where the hell did you hear the word ho? You know what? Never mind. Yeah, your daddy is a ho, but that's okay. That's the lifestyle he wanted, right?" I raise a brow when she shrugs, turning to look at him with sadness.

Every other kid in her preschool class has a daddy, everyone but Lyric. She has her four uncles who have managed to step up and wheedle their way into our hearts. But to Lyric, it's not the same. She wants him—them —in her life. And I can only hold out for so long before she gets some stupid idea about running away at midnight.

I've never lied to Lyric and never sugar-coated our situation. One day I knew she'd ask who her father was. So, I gave her the best possible solution—Whispered Words. They helped create her, but only one sperm won the frantic, impossible race. Sometimes though, when I watch her, I think their sperm merged into one massive bundle of cells and created my beautiful Lyric.

Sometimes my heart hurts when she laughs just like Rad or uses her brain just like Callum. The looks she gives me when she's upset were plucked straight from Asher's mean-ass scowl. And her attitude? Straight from the man who helped create her.

"We gotta get to mommy's work," I say, quickly shutting off the TV and grabbing her hand. Looking down at those gorgeous, mismatched eyes, I sigh, tucking a strand behind her ear. "I know this is weird and hard to know who they are, but…"

Lyric bites her lip, seeming more grown up than any four-year-old I've ever known. "It's okay, Mommy," she mutters, looking to the ground with resignation.

"Are you ready to go to Aunt Kaycee's house?" I ask, accomplishing what I set out to do. Long forgotten is her sperm donor's face on TV. Instead, she beams, jumping on her toes with excitement, filling the house with her squeals.

"Yes!" she squeaks, grinning up at me. "Me and Maggie have lots of stuffs to do. I need to grab Barbie!" Lyric takes off through the living room, down the hall, and into her bedroom on the first floor. "Got her!" she says, marching down the stairs with a bag, Barbie, and a smile.

"Let's go," I say, guiding her into my SUV, strapping her into her seat, and kissing her cheek. "It's you and me against the world, baby." Looking into her big, blue, mismatched eyes and running my fingers over her plump cheeks with a sigh. The love I've never felt slams into me every time I look into her little eyes.

She's mine. Always and forever.

"Okay, I'm here! And…" Slamming into Zepp and Seger's office, I hold a hand to my chest, begging for air.

"You're two minutes late," Zepp quips from the corner of the large room with a drink in his hand, swirling the ice cubes. "And did you run?" His brows raise when I flip him off.

Righting myself, I waltz into the office and heave myself into a leather chair across from Seger.

I scrunch my nose. "Sorry. Traffic sucks, and Ly was a little trouble this morning," I grumble, running a hand through my hair. "She flipped on that stupid celebrity gossip channel again and saw Kieran parading himself around with some new chick." Rolling my eyes, I huff out my frustrations.

"Fucking prick," Seger gripes from behind the large desk and blows out a nervous breath. "You fucking tell her. I'm not telling her." He waves his hand, fear washing over his expression.

Zepp's expression falls, and a slight paleness takes over his face when he nods, straightening his spine.

"What?" I ask, looking between the two of them. Fuck. My heart falls when they nod to each other, doing that weird twin talk without saying a word. "Whatever it is, tell me."

Zepp grumbles under his breath and sets his drink down. "You have a meeting right now. Follow me," he says, waving for me to follow and giving me his back.

I've gotten to know my brothers more than I would have thought possible over the past five years. We're best friends, something I never thought I'd have the chance to say. For years I resented them, unknowing what they were going through with their stepmom and our ailing father. Zepp and Seger are the best damn family I could ever ask for. Even when Ode comes to visit, which isn't as often as I'd like with her two kids and everything, they accept us with open arms. So, I can always tell when they're walking me into the lion's den and offering me up on a silver platter.

"If you fucking murder us, remember we have four innocent kids at home who would miss their daddies," Seger says, holding his hands up placatingly.

"I'm sure Chase and Carter could pick up the pieces after I dig your graves. Are you ever going to explain why I'm going to murder you?" I ask, raising a brow as we walk out of the office and head toward the conference room. "A new band?" I ask, tilting my head.

"You are the fixer, sis. And this fucking band needs your help. They're falling apart at the fucking seams. And you, dear, beautiful sister, are the only one who can help them," Seger says with a grin, buttering me up with his words.

Opening the back door, they lead me to the two-way mirror over-looking the conference room from a discreet position.

My heart drops, momentarily stopping inside my chest. I immediately shake my head, slowly backing away as my skin crawls in disgust. "No. No, absolutely not. Fire me for all I care. I won't fucking do it," I rasp through the emotions bubbling in my throat after years of repressing them into the deep, dark abyss of my mind.

I can't. I can't fucking look through that piece of glass without tears burning the back of my eyes. I knew one day I'd run into them. I work for the company they signed with, but I've carefully avoided them for five years at every turn, until now. Here they are after all these years, ready for the damn taking. I promised myself five years ago I'd do everything in my power to bring them down piece by piece. But I've grown up since then, loving every aspect of my job and what it brings. I've met so many bands and helped them achieve their wildest dreams by picking them up by their bootstraps and forcing them to mend whatever is bringing their potential down. My heart pulls in every different direction. My stomach churns with heavy waves of bile climbing my throat. Lyric flashes through my mind with her curious, puppy dog eyes begging for scraps of knowledge on her fathers.

Fuck.

I can't face them.

"Wait!" Zepp pleads, grabbing me by the shoulders and halting my retreat. "I know that this is…not what you ever wanted..." Panic spears through his eyes, and he heaves a breath. "They're failing right now, Riv. They're going to implode within five months." He swallows hard when I narrow my assessing eyes. "They need you, the fixer of West Records."

"Or they're going to fucking dive off a cliff and never work in this industry ever again. It's either you fix them, or they're done," Seger pipes up, crossing his arms over his chest.

Swallowing hard, I turn on my heel, glaring through the two-way mirror. My heart pumps against my chest at the sight of them sitting around the conference table with their noses in their phones, barely paying attention to one another.

"You want me to fix them?" I rasp, looking between the boys, taking in their appearances.

"Take them under your wing. Have them sign the six-month contract and move them into the Band House. Repair whatever the hell is tearing them apart," Seger says, standing beside me with furrowed brows.

"But I…" Bringing my fist to my lips, I conceal the quiver taking over my bottom lip.

"You're their only hope, River," Zepp says, putting an arm around my shoulders and pulling me affectionately into his side. "They'll be done for after this."

"You can fucking do this. Think of Ly. Wouldn't she want to know her fathers are successful? Wouldn't she be happy to know the piece of shit is off the gossip station?" Seger raises a brow, crossing his arms over his chest, knowing he's right.

"That's low," I growl, flicking the tip of his nose.

"Ow," he gasps, rubbing the spot I hit. "Rude as fuck," he mutters, turning his attention back to the boys sitting silently around the table.

Their eyes avoid each other's, and their bodies stiffen when Rad shifts in his chair, giving a bored yawn.

"They hate each other," I mutter, intently watching their every move. "They…" Fuck. My brothers are right. "Give me their files," I groan with reluctance.

Seger grins, shoving every file on the band into my hands. "That's everything. Their numbers. Their profiles. Everything you need to light a fire under their fucking asses and get them back on track."

I sigh, flipping through the pages quickly and slamming them shut. A devious smile falls across my lips the more I watch them. At the lowest point in my life, they left me with nothing, depriving me of the partners I needed the most. They intentionally left without the knowledge that they could have cleared my name. If only they had understood. If only they had come back and talked it over like adults. Fire brews in my gut. My face hardens, and a new resolve festers in the depths of my mind. I hate them for what they did. But if this is my destiny, then so be it. Maybe they'll survive the boot camp I put them through. Or perhaps, I'll discard them within the first month of our contract. If they sign it, that is.

"Fine. I'll do it. But don't expect me to be nice or understanding. They may have been something to me at one point in my life. But not now. They'll have to work hard. No passes. And definitely no Lyric." I raise a brow when my brothers nod in agreement. "I'll have the movers on standby to collect their shit," I mumble, sending out an email to the company we always use in cases like this.

"Riv, they'll have to meet her at some point. You can't hide her forever.

One look at her and him," Zepp says, gesturing to Kieran as he leans back in the chair, stretching his arms over his head. "They'll know."

"A problem for another day," I gripe, waving my hand. "Now, I'll go work my magic." Nerves eat away at me with every step I take in their direction.

Five years ago, Callum saw something he misinterpreted into something more. His tear-filled expression haunts every aspect of my life. For years, I wished I could go back in time and redo that entire thing, starting with not allowing Van into my apartment. Now, I'm faced with the four assholes who served me with multiple restraining orders in Illinois and told me they wanted nothing to do with our child. Thankfully, my beautifully brilliant sister-in-law investigated it a year ago and confirmed it expired within the first year.

"Get it, sis," Seger mutters, pumping a fist as I turn the knob on the back door and heave a breath.

"If this is a bloodbath, I'm claiming insanity and blaming you two," I quip, narrowing my eyes at my brothers.

"Fucking worth it," Seger says, barking out a laugh. "I'll get the fucking popcorn while you obliterate them into submission." Promptly, I flip him off, trying to shake the terror from my trembling fingers.

In two point five seconds, I'll be face to face with the assholes who broke my heart. And I'm supposed to guide them into a better future, eliminating any sort of distraction.

Fat chance.

As my heels click against the hardwood floors of the conference room, my heart beats double time. I'm breathing the same air as them again and standing before the four assholes still glaring down at their phones. They don't even have enough respect to look up and watch the person entering the room with a fire under her ass and revenge bleeding through her veins.

Once I step up to the long conference table, I set the files down lightly on the gleaming wood and take stock of the men around me. A smirk pulls at my lips as I gain their attention one by one, reveling in the paleness that takes over their faces.

"Hello, boys, my name is River West, and I'm your new band manager. Congratulations," I say, cocking my head when various emotions cross their pale faces.

Yeah. Revenge will be delightful, slow, and painful. Whispered Words will one-hundred percent get everything that's coming to them—all in due time.

"How about we get started?" I hum.

Sweet Strings
ALY BECK

"Hello, boys, my name is River West, and I'm your new band manager. Congratulations," I say, cocking my head.

My heart pounds against my ribs. Pain encases my chest, tightening like rubber bands and constricting my air. Every ounce of oxygen stalls in my lungs until I blow out a calming breath, forcing myself to stay in the present—with them—the boys who broke my heart five years ago.

Who knew staring into the eyes of the four exes who screwed you over five years ago after they ran away would be so fucking nerve-wracking. I should despise them. Hate their fucking existence. I should want to see their careers spiral down a dark hole and hit rock bottom as I laugh maniacally at their demise.

Instead, with as much confidence as I can muster, I utter the fourteen words that will forever change our lives and throw us down a wicked path of devastating revelations and wreckage we may not come back from.

Varying degrees of emotions cross their pale faces, sending victorious goosebumps down my spine. Their utter fear empowers me to sweep my gaze around the room.

Callum blinks rapidly like a flickering mirage stands confidently in front of him. And he has yet to believe I'm actually here in person.

My eyes move with ease to Rad, who stares at me with those big, brown puppy dog eyes I used to get lost in for hours and hours on end. Quickly, though, he turns away to study the conference table, avoiding any more eye contact.

Kieran's face twitches in disbelief, and his jaw pops open. A reddish tint takes over his flesh, starting on his neck, and slowly seeps color onto his cheeks. Sooner rather than later, I see an outburst in our future.

And Asher. My breath catches in my chest, stopping me cold. Never in my life did I think I'd see the day Asher Montgomery would freeze in place with horror lining his face.

An array of feelings slams through me. Fear. Sadness. Utter betrayal. Wide, unblinking eyes look up at me in horror, and disbelief pulls their muscles rigid in their chairs. One by one, the realization of what's

happening slams into their chests, and they're nothing but frozen men with gazes glued to me—the star of the damn show.

Something deep inside me bubbles with excitement, yet the fear and utter devastation they left behind reside there, too. Reminding me of what happened when I ran to their doorstep with pregnancy tests in my back pocket, begging to see them. I vividly remember Gloria, Kieran's sadistic mother, answering the door and throwing me a life-changing grenade of knowledge. Kieran, Rad, Callum, and Asher were gone—vanished into thin air without a goodbye or explanation. The most devastating part of it all was the way they left without a word, leaving our child and me in the dust with nothing more than a restraining order forbidding me from speaking with them.

And they knew. They acknowledged the existence of Lyric by having Gloria toss me a check, advising me to 'get rid of it' and stating they didn't want her. They denied my daughter having fathers. Sure, she knows them by name and calls them daddy by choice, but she'll never have the chance to know them in person unless they step up to the plate. But that's only if I let them. They can hurt me all they want, but I'll be fucked if I let them hurt her, too.

Somewhere in my mind, a little voice begs for revenge against the men who callously threw us away like yesterday's stale bread. Like we had meant nothing to them—like I wasn't someone important to them. Like I hadn't had an instrumental impact on their ability to even enter the Battle of the Bands competition—let alone win it.

Oh, how the tables have turned in my favor. No longer am I the scared girl with a baby in her belly and vengeance on her mind. I'm a woman, a mother, and I'll fucking get what I'm owed. Professionally, of course. I can't simply destroy these men without consequence. This job, my daughter, and this entire record company are my life force that kept me going when I thought my world had fallen apart. I wouldn't have made it this far without the loving support of my brothers, Seger and Zepp, and their family. They've taken me in and given me everything I've ever dreamed of and accepted me as one of their own.

These men are at the root of it all, and karma is quite the bitch when she wants to take back what is owed. Whispered Words will 100 percent get everything that's coming to them—all in due time, of course. Whether by me or by the universe—Karma is on her way to lay claim.

"How about we get started?" I hum, letting the shocked silence embrace me in a warm hug and revel in their awkward expressions.

"What-what are you doing here?" Asher utters through his shocked expression, gripping his chair so hard, I swear he'd choke it if it were breathing. "Why are you here?" he mumbles again, shaking his head.

I'm the ghost of your fucked up past coming back to haunt you—is what I desperately want to say, but I bite my tongue. I'm a goddamn professional. I won't let Whispered Words screw up my career. Besides, Zepp and Seger are watching my every move from behind the damn glass.

"So nice of you to ask, Mr. Montgomery," I say as politely as I can and add, "I'm working." Shrugging, I set the thick folder my brothers gave me on the conference table and spread their paperwork out for further examination.

Clearing my throat, I drag myself out of my thoughts and focus on the plans before me.

On the outside, I'm completely unaffected by their presence with the right kind of professional smile and squared shoulders. But on the inside, that's a completely different story. I can act as tough as the next person. But a tornado unleashes my emotions, sending mixed signals throughout my trembling body.

"Working?" Kieran asks in a deep voice. "There's no way," he says in a cold tone, tinged with disbelief. "You can't work here! What the fuck?" he growls, narrowing his eyes at me with suspicion.

"There is a way," I retort with no emotion, thumbing through a few more pages, finally finding the numbers I should have been able to study yesterday. You know if my stupid brothers hadn't sprung this on me ten minutes ago. Right, that reminds me. Murder is definitely still on the table. I wonder how my sister-in-law, Kaycee, will take the news when her twin husbands disappear off the face of the planet.

"Relax," Rad says in a bored tone, forcing himself to stare at the phone clutched in his white-knuckled grip.

"You fucking relax, dickhead," Kieran snaps. "This can't be possible."

"Believe it or not, but I'm standing right here," I say, still staring at the messy, down-turned numbers lining the page with a crease forming in my brow.

Fuck. This is worse than I thought.

When my brothers, Zepp and Seger, hired me, I never imagined it would lead to this. I completed my college education, garnered a degree in music business, and set out to make waves within the company with my ideas. The Fixer. I'm the person West Records turns to when a band is on their last leg and needs intervention before they're expelled from their contracts and kicked out on their asses. We give them a chance at redemption to show us they can still perform and bring in money again. Or else, they're out.

Over the past three years, since I took on this position, I've seen countless bands. Some work hard and regain their contracts, going out to make a new name for themselves. Others, well, they snort coke out of groupies' assholes and ruin their careers. *Looking at you, Break.* Idiots.

This time, though, it's them—Whispered Words. The four men I tried my hardest to forget, which is hard when one of their mini-mes calls me mom. My heart jumps, pounding against my ribs in a rhythmic drumbeat.

Lyric. My daughter. His child. My eyes glide across Kieran's twisted-up face, reddened by boiling anger that's simmering beneath the surface of his skin. His mismatched eyes, so similar to the little girl who holds my entire heart now, burn into me with hate so visceral a shiver runs down my spine.

Letting out a low whistle, I shake my head with disappointment. How could a band at the top of their game for years suddenly fall so fast and hard?

"Your numbers," I say, scrunching my nose.

"What numbers?" Asher asks cautiously, losing his breath when my gaze slams into his watery, hazel eyes filled to the brim with worry and concern.

"I'm so glad you asked," I reply in a professional tone, sliding the paper in front of his face. His brows furrow when his eyes gaze over the page. "It's your performance numbers. The amount you're bringing in through ticket sales, online sales, and everything in between. It's the numbers we evaluate every year to see if our investment is still paying off. And by the looks of it, Whispered Words is on their last leg," I say, pacing back and forth at the head of the table. What they can't see are my hands clasped firmly behind my back, trying to keep the shaking away from their eyes.

"Last-last leg?" Callum breathes, finally speaking up after staying silent for so long. The room falls away when his eyes finally connect with mine. A dark bruise rests beneath his eye, blackening his skin. Quickly, his eyes dart to the table once again, sinking his teeth into his bottom lip and losing himself in the pattern of the table.

My heart hammers in my chest, nearly knocking me back into the past. Callum. Sweet, lovable, caring Callum has marks on his flesh. But from what? Who could have caused him so much damage? And what the hell has changed? It's only been a few years. The last thing I could ever do was picture Callum putting his fists into the air and fighting with someone.

How much has each of them changed?

"I think you're lying," Kieran says, jumping to his feet and readying himself for a fight. "This is a fucking joke. There's no way some Central girl could be working here. Let alone be our new band manager. This is bullshit!" Kieran explodes, slamming a hand down onto the wooden table. Everyone flinches away from his outburst, watching his contorted face twist with hate.

Ouch. Is that really what he thinks about me? A painful pang spears through my heart. My eyes barely recognize the boy who held my hands under the stars and told me I'd be okay. Who is this man standing before me? Has this ruined him? And why the fuck does Kieran hate me so much?

"Well, you should know that you're here because West Records has placed your contract on probation." I raise a brow when Rad's face crumples, and his dark eyes glare down at the table, refusing to meet mine.

Tension laces every inch of his muscles, locking him in place, which gives me a chance to give him a once-over. Ashton Radcliffe may look the same as he did back in Central City with his dark and curly mullet and his lanky physique, but there are crucial differences shining through, hardening his closed-off exterior.

"This isn't a joke. Believe me; I wouldn't be here if it was some big ruse. You're stuck with me. Like it or not." I shrug again, taking a huge breath to relieve myself of the hurt brewing beneath the surface.

Anger vibrates through the entire room, setting my teeth on edge. Never in my life have I been met with such hostility, but I guess there's a first time for everything. But what the hell do they have to be so hostile for? They left me. They left her. Not the other way around. I'm the one who should hate their guts. I mean, don't get me wrong, I fucking do. But my professional duty binds me to their cause.

"What the hell is that supposed to mean? Probation? We haven't done anything wrong. This is bullshit," Kieran growls, slamming his fist into the table again. His hulking body heaves with every breath he takes, and those mismatched eyes glare at me head-on, ready to take me down.

"Well, that's why we're having this meeting, Mr. Knight," I say, tilting my head. "We're here to discuss your future."

Kieran's fiery eyes slam into my gaze, hardening the longer he stares, filling to the brim with hate and unsaid wrath ready to unleash on me. My breath leaves me, and my head spins until I collect myself and my heart off the floor.

His stare is a stark reminder of the little girl just a floor above us, patiently waiting for her Aunt Kaycee to collect her for a sleepover. It's the reminder that he left her. They left her knowingly, refusing to listen to me. They gave up their responsibility with the flick of their wrist and signatures across restraining orders.

Fuck them.

"We have no future here with you. I'll speak to my agent about this. There's no way in fucking hell I'm working with you," Kieran barks, twisting on his heels and stomping away.

Oh, cue the dramatics from the biggest dickhead around. Of course, he'd stomp and throw a fit at the sight of me. Idiot. *Deep breaths, River. You have to reel them back in.* Kieran always did have a flare for the dramatics, but this is pushing it too far. He's running away like the big fucking coward he is instead of facing me. Sounds way too familiar for my liking. I'd rather him go back to the boy who strummed his guitar on the hill behind our apartment complex, singing songs he envisioned during school. Instead of that man, the one I fell in love with twice, I'm left with the angry shell walking away from me.

"Fucking Kieran," Asher growls, climbing to his feet with determination. "You can't fucking walk away. Not because it's her." His eyes follow Kieran's slow, angry retreat, almost afraid to take his eyes off him.

My eyes narrow at the emphasis on the word her. Again. If they say it one more time like I'm not standing in front of them, I'll lose my shit. Seriously, though. Who, me? Little ole River West? The girl you dumped so fast after witnessing Van Drake, my stupid ex, forcefully kiss me without permission in my kitchen as I nursed my grief alone. Alone! They left me at my own mother's funeral without so much as a "sorry for your loss, Riv." Anger simmers beneath the surface of my skin, bubbling and aching for me to act on it at the harsh reminder of their betrayal. My mind begs me to lash out and put them in their place, but I bury that piece of me. I'm not here to talk about the past. I'm here to discuss the future of their band. Nothing more. Nothing less.

As Kieran drifts farther away from the group of men staring at him with wide eyes, I slip back into my professional persona. With one last deep breath, I become River West—The Fixer. Not River West—The Broken-hearted.

"I can do whatever I want. I can't be in the same room as her," Kieran growls, picking up his pace toward the French doors on the opposite side of the room.

My edges harden at the word *her* again and how it's implied. Maybe I should remind them of who they're fucking with. I discreetly rub the handle of my old knife nestled in the pocket of my dress pants. Images of Kieran behind the counter at the old record store I worked at come to mind. I smirk. This time Kieran wouldn't get a boner when I sit the edge of my knife near his dick, which I'll promptly cut off if he keeps up this defiant rock star bullshit attitude. He's on thin ice, growing thinner. Soon, he'll drown at my hands.

Asher looks at me and back at Kieran with wide eyes, expectantly waiting for him to come back to his seat like a good boy. But if there's anything I know about Kieran, he's not a very good boy.

Every step Kieran takes is a step closer to him forfeiting their contract. I could let him go and walk out into the hall and wipe my hands clean of them and never look back. I could laugh as they realized they'd fucked themselves over by not staying in the same room as me. No more concerts. No more fangirls willing to suck their mediocre dicks on their tour bus. And no more West Records. Bye, bye Whispered Words. You can return to Central City and explain to your mommy why you're back penniless and contract-less.

Inwardly, I groan, staring at the ceiling and counting backward. I'm better than that. I'm more professional than that petty behavior. Plus, my brothers would never let that fly. For some fucked up reason, despite knowing exactly what they did to me, they like their music.

The moment Kieran's hand touches the handle, I sigh. My responsibilities nag at me to do the right thing, just this once, and I comply.

"Mr. Knight, you should know the moment you step out of this meeting, you void not only your contract with West Records but all their contracts as well," I say in a smooth voice, crossing my arms over my chest and surveying the room.

Someone grumbles. Another gasps. And Asher, the once smug bastard, fucking begs—much to my delight. There once was a prideful man named Asher, who never got on his knees to beg another human being for anything. And yet, here he is, about to drop down and save face. I shouldn't have a giggle bursting up my throat or joy humming through my body at the stark difference.

But I do.

"Kieran, you have to give this a chance. It's a second opportunity for us to continue with our dream," Asher pleads with desperation, falling back into his chair with a desperate huff, never taking his pleading eyes off Kieran's retreating form.

"Bro, you can't walk out." Rad finally slides his gaze to me, quickly darting away with a twist of his lips and a shake of his head. His brows furrow, almost in confusion or maybe pain, but he shakes it off, running a hand through his curly mullet. I can't believe he's kept it after all these years.

"I can do whatever the fuck I please," Kieran sneers, twisting away from the door. "You can't be our band manager. You don't fucking belong here. You belong in the gutter like the rest of Central City. Is this a fucking joke?" Kieran barks out, throwing his arms all around like a child.

"Oh, ouch. Awesome," I mutter with so much sarcasm I swear one of them chokes on my tone. So much for biting my tongue. *Must. Remain. Professional, River.* Ugh. As much as I want to bash my fist into his dick and make him drop to his knees, begging for mercy, I don't.

"You can't be," he hisses again like a hysterical child, readying himself to drop to the floor and throw a full-blown fit.

You'd think our daughter Lyric was in front of me, throwing herself around and screaming at the top of her lungs because I refused to let her eat unicorn ice cream for dinner—cue the eye roll. Somehow, my four-year-old manages to regain control of her emotions better than this full-grown man. Pathetic.

Cracking my neck, I straighten my posture and ready myself to face the bull. There's no doubt in my mind that he'll fight this every part of the way. And I say, bring it on, Kieran Knight.

"I am your new manager. That's something you'll have to get over right here and right now. I am in charge of you, officially, this time. You fuck with me. I fuck with your career. Do we have an understanding?" I ask with an even tone, trying not to let my boiling anger get the best of me. "This is a professional environment. We will not disrespect each other. The past stays in the past. This is the present. I will not be disrespected again. Got it?" I ask, narrowing my eyes on each of them as they nod in unison, still giving me the stink eye. Reaching into the paperwork, I pull out a thick copy of their contract with West Records and throw it down the table. "If you want to read for yourself, it's on page fifty-seven, subsection B. It'll lay out everything you need to know when dealing with me and the professional services I offer at West Records."

Kieran grunts, shoving the paperwork at Callum, who sits rigidly in his seat, clinging to the armrests of his chair.

"You read it," Kieran barks out his order, pointing at the stack of papers.

Callum doesn't flinch when he reaches for the contract and flips through the pages, using his photographic memory, no doubt. "Fine," he mutters, stopping on my part of the contract, and he nods. "It's-it's all right here," he says, heaving his breath while pointing at it.

A pang pierces through my chest. The old Callum was doing so well and coming into himself. Now, it seems like he's reverted back to the stuttering, shy man I helped come out of his shell.

Those beautiful, gray eyes spare me one glance, and my heart thunders. Despair rests deep in his gaze when he flicks his eyes up and down my body. A familiar redness tints his cheeks until his gaze hardens again. Every ounce of life spirals out of his eyes, leaving me with his blank stare. My lips pop open when I zone in and really examine the faint remnants of black surrounding his slightly swollen eye, and then he turns away.

"How?" Asher mutters in a shaky voice, rubbing circles over his ghostly white temple, bringing me back to the conversation.

"I still don't fucking believe it," Kieran growls, throwing himself back into his chair. His fists clench when he leans forward, placing his elbows on the table.

Ignoring their questioning glares, I pull out another copy of their contract, flip it open to the page marked by Zepp, and scan the words.

"Well, believe it. As a matter of fact, don't forget it. I've been doing this for three years now, and this is how it will go. There are moving vans on their way to all your residences right now." I raise a brow when Kieran glowers at me with an unrelenting stare, but I shake him off. Nothing he can do will deter me from doing my job. "You're to pack whatever you want to take with you on a six-month vacation."

"Six months?" Rad gasps with wide eyes, finally looking up at me again. My heart pounds as memories of him and I on his dirt bike come back to mind but quickly dissipate. I don't have time to rehash memories that bring me nothing but pain. The quicker they get this done, the quicker we can move on with our lives.

"You'll never have to worry with me, Pretty Girl. I'll fight off the

monsters and keep your brain in your head," he murmurs, shoving the helmet over my head with force and buckling it under my chin.

I shake myself out of that stupid, childish memory. I did have to worry about him. He loved me with his entire soul and pursued me the hardest. Only to drop me for whatever reason. Was it the Van kiss? Or did they decide they'd gotten their use out of me with Battle of the Bands? I did my job. They just didn't hold up their end of the bargain.

"You can't be serious," Kieran shouts. "I can't leave my place! That's mine. There's no way—"

"It says it in the contract," Callum cuts in with a quiet but authoritative voice.

"Why the fuck didn't we read that better?" Kieran grumbles, pinching the bridge of his nose. "Why didn't you?" He glowers at Callum, who reads through the contract again, shaking his head.

Clearly, their friendship is falling to pieces. Judging by their cutting glances at each other and snarky attitudes, they can't wait to leave each other's presence. The Kieran I knew before was never *this* cruel to anyone. Sure, he had an attitude problem. But this? This seems like more.

"Yes. You owe West Records six months of total dedication. You've had time to sow your wild rock star oats, and now you need to prove that our investment was worth it. Six months at the Band House. Six months of practice, therapy, and rebuilding yourselves up. Six months of being mine." An ominous grin spreads across my face, making each of their expressions drop. "And if you fail, you can say goodbye to your contracts and hello to unemployment. No other record company will dare to sign you after you leave us. They'll all know you failed my program because I'll make sure of it. The choice is yours. Music or nothing. At any time during this process, you're free to leave. But your contract will be void. Oh, and I'm the ultimate judge. So, piss me off again, and you're done." I hold Kieran's stare when his gaze hardens again. But for the first time since stepping foot in this room, he bites his tongue.

Good boy.

One point River. Zero for the boys.

"What the fuck did we sign up for?" Rad asks, swallowing hard, apprehension crossing his face.

"Bullshit, that's what," Kieran so helpfully adds with a huff.

"Glad we have that settled. Moving vans are at all your places now. I suggest grabbing everything you'll need for the next six months. Your new home will be furnished, and a recording studio will be in the basement. I expect all your instruments to be there. We'll start practice at 8:45 a.m. Monday morning."

"Eight AM?" Kieran shrieks again with wide eyes. "What the fuck?"

"I'm well aware of your extracurricular activities, Mr. Knight, which include not waking up until two in the afternoon, but this is rock star boot camp. Welcome to your new hell," I say, gathering my papers into the folder and nodding at each of them. "You're dismissed. A limo will pick you up at your respective homes, and they will escort you to the Band House. There we will have another meeting of expectations, rules, and another six-month contract for you to sign."

Each of them nods, looking more confused as I step away from the table, clinging to the file folders resting against my chest. It's the only thing grounding me. I hold my breath the entire way through the back doors, only releasing my breath when they close behind me and block me from the boys I once loved.

My brothers rest on the loveseat near the wall, cautiously eyeing me as I rigidly stand there. Everything inside me wants to crumple into a ball and not exist for a day just from seeing them. I'm all for putting on a brave face, but right now, tears burn the back of my eyes. Once upon a time, they meant the world to me. Apparently, I meant nothing. An ache forms in my chest as I collect myself, swallowing the hurt and betrayal.

"You did good," Seger sings his praises, rising from his seat. Having observed the entire encounter through the two-way mirror, he probably watched me like a hawk.

Immediately, he engulfs me in his arms, holding my shuddering body. "So fucking good, River. You're going to knock them into shape; I can see it now. We know your history with them, but you've got this."

I give myself a moment to break down. And then, I back away, lifting my chin at their praises.

"Very impressive," Zepp says, nodding his head as he approaches me. Placing a hand on my shoulder, he gently squeezes, taking me out of my momentary freak out that I'll save for later. "We believe in you, River. We would never have made you do this if we didn't think you could handle it."

"This feels like a shitty test," I grumble through a quivering lip, recalling the ugly name the band used. Central Trash. It fucking hurts to be reminded of where I came from. But then again, it proves how far I've come from the girl stumbling through life.

"You're a fucking rock," Seger adds, sidling up to me on the other side. "No one in this fucking place can do better than you. We know you'll be able to help them turn their fucking life around." He raises a sharp brow, emphasizing his belief in me.

A belief I don't feel.

I came into that room with revenge bleeding through my veins, begging for vengeance against the men who fucking ruined me. And now, I have to face them daily, organizing their lives and hoping they don't wreck me all over again.

We all flinch away from the two-way mirror, watching in horror as Kieran practically destroys the conference room with his anger.

Instead of running in there to stop him, Seger chuckles. "Ah, that one will be the fucking worst to tame."

"You've got this," Zepp mumbles with reassurance. "We'll give you a raise after this."

"Much deserved," I quip, shaking my head when Kieran storms away.

"Miss West!" Kat, my assistant, comes rushing in with a grim expression on her lips.

"Kat, call me River. Miss sounds way too damn formal," I grumble, noting the pale expression she's wearing.

"River," she murmurs softly, leaning in. "It happened again." My heart fucking drops into my ass, and I numbly nod.

"Um, thanks for that… I'll deal with it." Something seriously has to give. First them, now this shit. How much more can I suffer through in one day? Ugh.

"Okay. I need to…" She motions out the door, and I dismiss her with a wave of my hand.

"Is she doing okay?" Zepp asks, watching her retreating form.

"As good as she'll get," I say with a shrug. "Still needs some improvements, but she'll get there."

"There you fuckers are!" Chase chides, walking into the tiny room with his arm around their wife, Kaycee. Her brows dip as she looks me over, examining my ruffled expression. But before she can speak, Chase interrupts with his usual cheerful disposition, dipped with concern. "What did you do to Little West?" Chase asks with a frown, eyeing my face and heaving chest.

"Not now," Seger gripes, running a hand down his face. "We'll explain later."

Waving a hand, I shake off the doom sitting on my shoulders and plaster on my best fake smile. "Nothing. I'm fine. Just a hard job ahead." Hard is the understatement of the fucking century. "I'll run and get Lyric from the daycare and meet you in the lobby?" Kaycee nods, brows furrowing like she wants to ask what's wrong, but decides against it.

"Okay," she says with a tight smile. As I walk past her, she grabs my elbow and stops me. "Something is off. We'll talk about this later, right? Maybe a girl's night?" She examines my face when I nod, promising to fill her in later over a glass of wine. Scratch that; make it four glasses.

With that, still clutching their files to my chest, I make my way through the large skyscraper and head to the daycare to get Lyric the hell out of this building without being noticed.

My heart drops into my ass when the ghost of my fucked up past strolls into the room with her head held high and stops right before us. *What the hell is she doing here? In our domain?*

Determination lines her sharp face, not giving any indication our presence affects her. No heavy breaths. No tears. There's nothing hiding behind the face of the girl I purposely screwed over and forced my best friends to leave behind.

Shit.

Pain spreads across my chest as the repressed memories I locked away long ago flood back into my mind, released from the confined space I shoved them into. Everything about River I've blocked and purposefully forgot about her. Our time together. The moments I spent between her luscious legs and shared with my bandmates. She went so far to help us get here, and then, I shit all over her existence. Imploding everything she'd built by one single lie I had orchestrated.

How has she been? Why is she here? How bad did I fucking break her with my betrayal because I was so damn desperate to get away?

Familiar pangs of guilt churn in my gut, and burning bile rises in my throat. I've avoided everything River West for the past five years. I never sought her out.

Out of sight. Out of mind.

Besides, there was no trace of her anywhere, with all her social media accounts shut down after we left. For me, it was a godsend. I didn't have to look at my mistake head-on and acknowledge the fact I fucked up. My refusal to think about her had me locking my memories away behind several heavy doors in my mind. My survival on this planet relies on her nonexistence. And today, I'm coming face to face with the karma I deserve by seeing her again.

Goddamn. What did I fucking do? Sometimes I don't understand myself. But if there's one thing for certain, it's that I'm not worthy to be in her presence. Kick my ass and lock me away, it's the least I fucking deserve for the vile actions I perpetrated against her.

Eyeing her up and down and taking in her appearance is its own form of torture. My heart pounds double time. My fingers fucking tremble around the arms of the chair. Staring at her is like looking too hard at the sun, and I'm bound to be burned. Not that I don't fucking deserve it. I deserve every ounce of ire this woman has, even if she doesn't know what I did. No one does except Gloria. Not a soul. Not even the men around me. I intended to purge my sins and confess them when we were famous, and she was long gone, but the words never left my tongue. I couldn't—wouldn't. We were good for so long, and then, we weren't.

River's long, brown hair remains the same as it always had, hanging past her shoulders. Only now, it seems smoother and more professional, framing the edges of her filled-out face. No longer does she look like the poor girl from Central City, barely eating and running herself ragged. She's filled out and looks healthier than I've ever seen her. More defined curves fill out the professional black pantsuit, highlighting just how much she's grown up.

Something beneath the surface of her calls to me again, much like it used to. River is a siren standing in a room full of sailors, begging them to come to her. Her aura hasn't changed one bit. I shift in my seat, determined to, once again, not heed her call.

"Hello, boys. My name is River West, and I'm your new band manager. Congratulations," she says, cocking her head.

I swallow the lump in my throat when all the oxygen leaves and suffocates me. Her voice drifts through the room with authority. Together, Callum, Kieran, Rad, and I sit like statues waiting for her to speak again. Every agonizing minute she stands there in silence, watching us with an eagle eye, is torture.

Her inspecting moss-green eyes take in the changes each of us has experienced in the past few years of a harsh rock star lifestyle. We're rougher. Maybe edgier from our time in the spotlight, entertaining millions, but yet, slightly more damaged than before. I always thought if I removed myself from the beast roaming the halls of my home, I'd heal the demons darkening my soul inside me. Boy, how wrong I was.

A new demon followed me around, relentlessly taunting me. Guilt. Over the years, I've tried to lock everything away in a small box and forget my transgressions. Who could forget, though? I never realized what I had, until it was gone. It was too late. Now, everywhere I look, my stomach turns, and bile rises at the simplest of reminders.

The longer she stares, waiting for us to acknowledge her, I swear fucking sweat breaks out across my flesh. Instinctively, I reach for the package of antacids in my pocket and toss one in my mouth, discreetly chewing the chalky substance to settle the nausea swarming in my gut.

The more I look at her, the more I see the ghosts of what I left behind.

Flashes of our intertwined past roar through my mind, leading to the worst decision I've ever made. Her name sits in the back of my mind, chanting like a prayer, patiently waiting for me to acknowledge the peak of our downfall. The person who cleverly built us up and helped us to succeed by granting us the golden ticket, only for us to turn our backs on her and leave her in the dust like she never meant a damn thing to us all. And that's the core of it all. I was young, stupid, and demented enough to think I could erase her from our lives without repercussions. But if there's anything I know about karma, she always comes back to bite you in the ass and take back what you put out into the world.

"How about we get started?" River hums with more confidence, not bothering to look up at us again.

"What-what are you doing here?" I swear I utter it without permission. "Why are you here?" I mumble again, trying to shake the specter from my vision.

"So nice of you to ask, Mr. Montgomery," she says in a polite yet professional tone.

The mere mention of my name sends shivers down my spine and goosebumps down my legs. Fuck. No, she can't affect me like this again. I can't let River work her way under my skin as she did before. I resisted so well back then, but with my guilt currently eating me alive, I don't think I can ignore the call she gives out.

"I'm working." Shrugging, she spreads massive amounts of paperwork out on the table. Her eyes look through the pages, humming under her breath until she comes to one that shocks her into silence.

Kieran says something snarky. Rad retorts. The entire room moves on without my conscious mind present. The only thing I can focus on is the past, instead of the present or future—where my mind should stay firmly planted. She mentions numbers, and I respond, staring at the dismal view of our existence at West Records. We're fucked. Kieran keeps babbling on, but I tune out his shitty attitude. The only reason he acts this way is because I'm a fucking tool and made him think she betrayed us.

Since then, I've lost touch with him. Hell—even myself. We aren't the same people we were rocking out in Callum's basement with stars in our eyes. We've changed. And we've ripped apart at the seams. I locked myself into music, focusing on the words and melodies. I tore myself away from the guys, promising myself I'd come clean. But I never did. In turn, they've collected their own vices, leading them away from the once tight-knit, brotherly bond we had.

My fingers white-knuckle around the armrests, hoping to choke the mirage standing before me from my vision. I blink hard, wishing her away. Many times before, my guilt chased me down with a vengeance. From the woman standing in the crowd of our performance to another walking down the sidewalk—she haunted every waking moment of my life, reminding me of the bullshit I pulled.

River tilts her head, looking us over with such confidence my heart aches in my chest. I swear someone utters a question of what she's doing here, and why the fuck is she standing in West Records, but I don't hear it. I hear nothing but the past calling back to me, forcing me to recall the bullshit I put her and my brothers through.

It's the one thing that keeps me staring at the ceiling night after night, until my eyes are bloodshot and burning. It's the rumbling in my stomach when I can't keep the acid from burning me from within. It's the itchy skin, pulling taut over my bones, and the patches of eczema reddening my damn flesh. An itch I can't fucking scratch because my guilt manifests in unpredictable ways.

It's consuming me whole. Before I know it, I'll be nothing but hollow bones wandering this earth.

Fuck. My gut churns, praying the constant loop of my nightmare rolling around in my brain will leave me for good. Sometimes I wonder if this is how Callum feels, reliving everything in vivid detail with his photographic memory. Sinking further into the darkness of my wicked mind, the memories of the only girl I've thought about since the moment I put my stupid-as-hell plan into motion comes back to haunt me, seizing the breath in my lungs.

"She's been cheating on us," I growl, tossing down my phone as the video on my screen plays at full volume, filling the room with her illicit hook-up with Donavan Drake, the thorn in our side—but my secret ally.

The lie rests like sour milk on my tongue, begging me to break free and tell the truth. I suck in a breath. Am I doing the right thing for us? Am I doing the right thing for River? Would she be better off without us? Probably. We'll do nothing but drag her down into our brand of fucked up bullshit if we stay. But this? Is this too much? Taking it too fucking far?

Quickly, I avert my eyes at the image of River climbing on Van's lap and his low voice murmuring dirty words. Or it would be dirty words. God, he fucking sucks at everything he does. I fucking hate his face. My only hope is we never have to see his stupid ass again. From here on out, River is only his and... My eyes squeeze shut as Callum cries out in anguish. My heart fucking breaks as they grasp what I've laid down in front of them.

"No-no!" Callum sobs out, jumping to his shaky feet, nearly falling over. Fat tears well in his eyes, and he shakes his head, gripping the ends of his hair tightly in his fist. "That-that can't be true! That can't be her," he says, swallowing the lump in his throat. "That..." he trails off, covering his mouth with his fist, trying to hold back the rampant emotions surging inside of him.

"I've tried to tell you. Something was off," I say, running a hand down my face like I'm exasperated with the entire situation. "That's why we needed to stay away." I swallow the lie over and over. If I do, maybe they'll

plant themselves inside my brain and sprout like it's the truth. Then, I might believe the words coming from my mouth.

"No," Callum says with conviction, shaking his head. "That can't be true. She'd never do that to me...or us," he whispers, letting the tears fall down his pale cheeks. Callum shoves past me, bumping my shoulder angrily with his, pacing near the front door of the home we've all made our own. I squeeze my eyes shut and grab my phone, mentally fighting with myself on the rights and wrongs of this entire scene.

I have to do this. We have to go to the Battle of the Bands without her. If she comes, they'll never get over her and move on with their dreams. If she can't go, then we'll never have the opportunity to leave this town. We'll live in this hellhole for the rest of our lives, wondering what our future would have been like if we had gone to California. And I can't let that happen to them. This is all for their own fucking good. In five years, they'll thank me for the sacrifice I made for them.

With my mental pep talk fizzling out into reason, I turn my back on my friends, as I've already done. I type out a single message to my stupid fucking ally and hit send. There's no going back now. Even as an elephant sits on my chest and compresses my breaths. Sweat forms on my brow when I return to the anger-filled conversation happening around me.

ME

Go.

He doesn't utter a word back, but I know he's seen it and is all too eager to get to the girl he's obsessively had his eyes on like a fucking stalker. Heavy iron sits in the pits of my stomach as I continue to tune out the mess I've created. My brows furrow as it all smacks me in the face at once. Van is a fucking stalker. We've had to fight him off her in more ways than one. And yet, I've fed the lamb to the mighty lion. Just like that. Gloria's words about talking to him come back to mind. How the hell did she know what kind of videos he had? Burning bile singes up my esophagus, begging to expel through my tightly held lips.

What the fuck have I done? I'm doing what's right. Shut the fuck up, mind! I'm putting this whole thing into motion. Fuck the consequences. Fuck everything else! We need this. This is our time to shine, and we can't let some Central City girl hold us back any longer.

"Where are you going?" Rad rasps, interrupting the guilty thoughts rushing through my mind and dragging me back to the conversation at hand. Holding back his emotions as he stands, Rad blankly stares, giving nothing away.

"To see for myself," Callum growls, clenching his fists. "You can't just believe some video. He could...could be fucking her over. Again." With those parting words, Callum shoves out the front door with a bang. The

rumble of his car fills the air, followed by screeching tires, and then he's gone.

It's not him fucking her over—it's me. I'm the one doing this to us. But it's for the damn best. It's for the damn best! My chest heaves.

If I don't get them away from her, then we'll never leave. I'll be stuck with Nigel and his fists for the rest of my life. Our dreams won't mean anything if I'm six feet deep at the hands of my father. And I can't let that fucking happen. This is for the best. For all of us. We'll be happier in a few years. And I'll be fucking free.

"I can't believe it," Kieran says with a stunned expression, running a hand down his face. "This is fucking unbelievable." His face pinches when he looks up at me for confirmation, and I nod. "But fucking why? I don't understand why she'd go back to him so easily. There's no way, man. She wouldn't go back to him like that. There has to be something going on that we don't know. Maybe he's blackmailing her," he grunts again, pulling at his hair. "I should go with Callum. I should…" He shakes his head, pacing the small living room with a pinched face.

"Fuck," I grunt in false anger. "How'd we let it get this fucking far? Huh? This was supposed to be simple! We weren't supposed to actually fall for her. How could you assholes let this happen? See what she did! I've been telling you for weeks that River has been up to something when she lets Van come into the record store. There's more to their relationship than she lets on," I growl, trying to weave more lies into the equation. Truth is, I've been doing this for the past few days, trying to implant false information into their brains. So, when it came time for this whole thing to go off, it'd be easier to make them believe.

"This was all your fucking idea!" Kieran shouts unexpectedly, with harsh emotions warring on his face. He's torn between not wanting to believe what I've laid out and firmly believing what I've shown him. And the latter is obviously winning when, within three steps, he's in my face and fisting my T-shirt. Kieran teeters on the edge of being a loose cannon and is minutes away from slamming his fist into my face. It wouldn't be the first time, and it won't be the last. When they find out what I've done, they'll kill me. "You made us… I'm going to fucking murder Van for this."

"I didn't make you do shit," I grunt, pressing my nose against his. "You all fucking agreed to this plan. Remember what we did it for? We wanted her for West Records and look at what we have now."

"But we didn't need her," Rad whispers, running his hand through his mullet. "We just…"

He fell in love; that's what he did. Head over heels with his ass in the air, his heart in his hand, and blood on his sleeves. They fucking love her, and I'm…fucking destroying them. I'm dismantling their love for her brick by brick; they never saw it coming. Day by day, since we've separated from her, I've been planting things in their heads. Hint by hint, I've been forcing them to conclude that this is what she did to us—betrayed us in the worst possible way. And this video? This is the nail in the coffin for our relationship.

No matter how badly I want to pull back and prevent this from happening, I can't stop myself. It's a necessary evil in my plan for our future. One day, when this comes out, I hope they can all forgive me for what I've taken away from the five of us. I'll get on my knees and fucking beg for their forgiveness. But for now, I must keep pushing through before it's too late. We have one week to get to California for the competition, and I need their heads in the game. Not on her. Not on their hopeless love. Us—the band— Whispered Words.

"And see where it got us?" I snark, knowing the quicker we move on, the faster we can get out of here and never have to think about this godforsaken town again. Goodbye Gloria, Goodbye fucking Nigel. And Goodbye River—may your life be what you always wanted it to be.

My chest squeezes when Kieran's expression falls, hurt lining every inch of him. "I just don't fucking understand, man," he growls, squeezing his eyes shut. "I need to fucking see for myself. I need to fucking talk to her and square this away. This can't be the fucking end." His fingers squeeze into fists, glaring at the front door.

Rad plops down onto the couch again, gripping the roots of his hair, muttering words I can't understand. "She wouldn't go back to Van," he says, scrunching his crumpled face and shaking his head with disbelief. "She wanted nothing to do with him. He's a stalker. Why the hell would she sleep with him behind our backs?" he asks, trying to rationalize the situation. "I'm with Cal. We need to talk to her and figure this out. There's something so fishy about this. We need…"

"It's all true," Callum says through heavy breaths, shuffling in through the front door. Deep, soul-crushing despair paints his long expression with tears staining his reddened cheeks, and his gray eyes darken in anguish.

"What's true?" Rad asks, lifting his head to meet Callum's eyes.

"Van was there," Callum mumbles through quivering lips. "He fucking kissed her. Before I left, I saw it. I…I saw it. They were there together. He brought her dinner, and then they fucking kissed. I couldn't-couldn't stay after he leaned in. How could she?" he gasps out, clutching his chest as mine tightens, feeling his misery from where I stand. Reaching into the depths of his pocket, he pulls out his phone, displaying one picture of Van shoving his tongue down River's throat.

Kieran leans forward with a scowl, taking the phone from Callum's hand. Without a word, he throws it back into Callum's hands and storms out of the house without a glance back, going to do whatever it is he's doing.

My dinner threatens to come up my throat and out my mouth for everyone to see. From where Callum stood, she looked so willing and compliant to Van's advances. That's all it takes for them to never question the accusation again. It is the nail in the coffin and all the motivation they need to pack their bags and turn their middle fingers up to the city we are leaving behind. There's no going back now. I've set everything in motion to get us to the Battle of the Bands without a distraction. Without the woman who helped get us there.

So, why do I feel like the human equivalent of a pile of shit in the front yard on a rainy day? This is my shining moment. The point I'd hoped to get to when I discovered that they'd stay behind and live normal lives for her. Only it's not.

By the time we made it to California and won, I knew I had made the biggest mistake of my life, leaving her behind. A wide crevice developed behind my ribs. Nothing in this world could fill it besides her. The love I gave her, without knowing it, shattered the moment we left town, leaving my insides a mess. I prided myself on not developing feelings and keeping my distance, but I was not only a liar to my best friends, but to myself. After our departure, something fundamental changed within the guys and in me. Almost as if they developed the same black mass inside them that ate away at everything it could get its hands on. We were never the same as we were in the small town of Central City, where we became famous.

Monumentally, I fucked up the best thing in our lives with one single lie that blew everything away. That tiny white lie was only the beginning of our story. Staring at River now has more thoughts and plans formulating in the back of my mind. I epically fucked up their lives by tearing them apart in the worst way possible. Maybe now that River is in front of us, I can fix this all. Maybe, just maybe, I can weave our lives together again and confess my bloody sins.

Even if they hate me—they'll still have her.

"You're dismissed. A limo will pick you up at your respective homes, and they will escort you to the Band House. There we will have another meeting of expectations, rules, and another six-month contract for you to sign," River declares, turning her back on us with her head held high.

My heart sputters, threatening to pop out of my chest. Until she slips from sight out the back door, leaving the four of us to wallow in the anger brewing like a dangerous storm around us.

"Well, this has been entertaining. Said no one ever," Rad snarks, lazily climbing to his feet. With ease, he grabs his motorcycle helmet from below the table and cradles it under his arm. "Apparently, I have a house to pack up. See you nut jerkers later." Pulling his phone from his pocket, he stares at it as he walks out of the room without a backward glance.

Since we settled in East Point, he's had this unaffected air about him. Almost as if River was just a blip on his radar and nothing more than some floozy, he messed around with on the Ferris wheel. Not the love of his life.

The thing about Rad is, he's put a mask on since the moment we left Central City. And now, he never lowers it and lets us see the pain he's hiding away from us.

The walls press around me. Over and over, I've lived with the damage I inflicted on four other human beings due to my selfishness. I, alone, crushed the love from Rad's veins the moment I pointed my fingers at her with my cheating allegations. More guilt builds in my chest, crushing me where I sit rigidly in my chair, basking in the silence of the other two who stay in their seats.

"Does this not bother him?" Kieran asks with a deep scowl, watching as he disappears through the door leisurely. "We left for a fucking reason. We…" Kieran grunts, jumping to his feet and throwing the chair across the room until it bounces off the wall with a thud. We don't even blink at his outburst. Kieran's been nothing but fumes, waiting for the match to strike. And here it is…

"We left because she…she…fuck!" he shouts, pounding a fist into the

edge of the table. Releasing a pained grunt, he stands tall, gathering his emotions. Emptiness fills his blueish eyes, and he shakes his head. "I'm out," he says, clearing his throat and taking off out the door at a quick pace.

This is going to go swimmingly. The four of us, stuck in a house together. Throw in the girl they think cheated on them in the worst betrayal ever. What was past me thinking?

Pinching the bridge of my nose, I huff and climb to my feet. "You coming?" I ask Callum, who sits ramrod straight in his chair, most likely reliving the worst night of his life on repeat.

I swear I've never seen a man go from one extreme to another. From full of love and life, to an empty, speechless shell of a man. River's ghost may have haunted me from the moment we leapt on stage at The KC Club and swept the competition, but the remnants of what I did stood right before me, slowly falling apart at the seams.

All of this is my fucked-up masterpiece of manipulation. I took good men and molded them into angry beings. I robbed them. I fucking robbed her of our promise. God. If I could create a time machine, I'd go and change the past. We may have our freedom and money, but at what cost? I take a deep, painful breath, begging the oxygen to fill my glass-coated lungs and squeeze my eyes shut.

Callum solemnly nods, slowly rising to his feet with the contract we signed years before clutched tightly in his hands. Slowly, he makes his way out of the room with his head hanging low, leaving me here in the silence of the conference room to suffer in the hell of my own doing.

Tears burn the back of my eyes as I stare at the tile ceiling with self-deprecating thoughts swirling a million miles a minute. I take a few moments to gather myself and push the looming guilt to the bottomless pit of my soul.

As I walk out the door, shoving my hands into my jeans and balling them, massive amounts of guilt swim in my gut, churning until bile hits the back of my throat. My only sensible solution after all these years is to set the truth free. I squeeze my eyes shut, assaulted by another memory lurking in the shadows and ready to strike.

"Are we ready for this?" I ask, flexing my fingers around the steering wheel of my Tahoe, eagerly awaiting the moment we leave Central City behind.

"Fuck this town," Kieran grunts, shoving his middle finger into the air. "Fuck her," he mutters with venom lacing his tone. Nothing but hurt sits on his twisted-up face. Proving to me that pushing River away was the best option for us. Eventually, I'll have my brother back. Eventually, I'll have my best friends back.

"Yeah, let's roll," Rad grumbles with less enthusiasm, staring out the window with a blank expression, losing all the spark he once held. Hell,

he's barely blinked since the night they discovered what River's been up to. Or, what they think she's up to.

Peering at Callum through the rearview mirror, I note the nod he gives me. Not bothering to say a word. Since he's come back from watching Van kiss River, he's spoken less than usual. Nearly turning mute in our presence. If I can get them out of this River funk and into our bright future, we could turn ourselves around.

I swallow thickly and pull out of the driveway, driving us toward our new destination—East Point Bluff, California. Where dreams come true. My mind endlessly wrestles with me on the rights and wrongs of this entire situation.

"Let's start a new chapter in our life," I say with confidence I don't exactly feel.

The more distance we put between River and us, the more my heart aches in my chest, cracking from the wool I pulled over my friends' eyes. Even though it's for the best. It's necessary. It needed to be done. Right? I had to do it. She would have just slowed us down. They would have turned away from our mission—the Battle of the Bands.

"Fuck," I gasp out, clutching my chest as the pain engulfs me once again from the inside out, hollowing me further and opening the dark pit of despair inside me.

The world tilts when I collapse against the wall, holding my face in my hands. No matter how hard I tried to tell myself it was the right thing to do, I knew in my heart I had thoroughly fucked up and made a sticky fucking mess of the whole thing. I took each of their trust and crushed it in my hand. And for what? This? We're fucking miserable together. Sure, we're still making music, but apparently, we're on our last leg. It's only been five years. And our career is already in the damn toilet. Worst of all, we haven't been brothers since we stepped foot in California, because we left our glue back in Central City.

And it's all my fault.

They weren't the only ones who fell for River's whims and free spirit— I did too. I held off for so long, the fear of getting close holding me back. Once I got my hooks in her, it was hard to release her from my grasp. It tore me apart to run to Van Drake. It still tears me apart that I climbed into that vehicle and planned the ultimate betrayal against her with a damn predator. But I did what I did because I thought it was what was best for the band. For what I thought was for our own good. Selfishly, I erased her from existence and ran away like a pussy.

"Fuck," I mumble, digging my palms into my eyelids, pushing away the pain of my past.

Silent, pent-up tears stream down my face at the reality of it all. In a few hours, the four of us will be locked in a house together for six months. I've held this secret for way too long, and it's time I come clean. And maybe we can get back to the people we were before I ruined everything. It's like fate came and slapped me on the head. And…

"You're crying," says a little voice from in front of me, getting a front-row seat to my breakdown.

Sucking in a breath, my whole-body jolts, and I'm knocked out of my spiral. My gaze snaps forward, locking on a little girl standing before me. Her tiny dark brows furrow, and a frown pulls at her lips. Discreetly, I wipe away the tears streaming down my cheek and shake my head. Looking up and down the long, empty hallways, a lone thought filters through my mind. Where the hell are her parents?

I swallow hard when she gasps, looking me up and down. A tiny smile lights up her little face, and she taps my shoulder, gently squeezing in a comforting manner. "It'll be okay, Daddy." She pats me again and leans her tiny head on my shoulder with a dramatic sigh. "No tears," she coos, gently squeezing again, sighing contentedly on my shoulder.

I lick my lips, sitting rigidly beneath her grasp. "Uh, kid," I say, clearing my throat and feeling an odd heat billowing up my neck. She has to be wrong. There's no way I could be anyone's daddy. I haven't touched a woman since… River. That night at the castle house on the lake was the last night I ever sunk my dick into someone.

"I'm not…" I swallow my tongue when she raises her head, looking directly into my eyes. She smiles again, taking in my face as I take in hers. My breath leaves, and confusion swirls in my mind at the familiarity. It's like looking at a small River with darker hair and… "Your eyes," I mumble, unable to look away from the blue, mismatched eyes much like… like… Kieran's. They're so damn rare to have; I've only ever seen one person with them.

Long, dark hair hangs over her shoulders, nearly down to the middle of her back, her mismatched eyes take me in, and her cherub face fills with light and love. Gently, she clings to a small white rabbit held against her chest.

"Bunny makes me feel better when I'm sad. Here," she says, thrusting the tiny stuffed animal into my hand. "Now you'll be okay," she says with truth behind her words.

I scrunch my brows, staring down at the poor ripped rabbit, filled with light food stains and a ripped ear.

"Aunt Ode gave her to me," she says, fiddling with the little ribbon secured around the intact ear. "She came out to see me. Do you know her, Daddy?"

I'm completely frozen, staring at this child. I shake my head, lifting a hand to touch her cheek almost out of instinct when a piece of her hair falls in front of her face. It's odd to look into the eyes of a stranger and find comfort in the loving gaze she sends me. Like she knows me somehow. Like I should know her.

"What's your name?" I ask cautiously, removing the piece of hair from her face. Her expression crumples from the beautiful smile she once held, and her brows furrow.

"You don't know my name?" she whispers in a heartbroken tone, pulling at my heartstrings.

"I'm sorry, kiddo," I whisper, shaking my head. "Where are your parents? Are they around here somewhere?"

She sucks in a breath, heavily fidgeting with her bunny until she snatches it out of my hand. "It's okay," she whispers. "Mommy said…"

"Lyric!" I drop my hand the moment a frantic voice echoes from down the hall. I swallow hard as River comes hauling ass in our direction with determination taking over her expression. And then she stops right beside us, silently shaking her head. Every ounce of color drains from her face when she sees my tear-stained face standing so close to…

"You," I whisper, furrowing my brows, watching intently as she collapses to her knees and pulls the little girl away, shaking her head frantically.

"Lyric, I've told you before. You can't go wandering off on your own, okay? Even here." River's voice evens out into a soothing one, something my mother used to coo at me when she tucked me in at night and told me she loved me.

"I love you so much, my Asher," my mother's soothing voice echoes in my mind. Her hazel eyes stare down at me filled with so much love, I beg her to lie beside me. "Just for tonight," she murmurs, kissing my hair as her warm arms envelop me in a hug. "Stay my little Asher Bear forever," she whispers one last time before my eyes flutter shut, and my chest feels whole.

"Mommy," she whines, pointing a finger in my direction and making my body lock up. Lyric's lip puffs out in a pout with puppy dog eyes that could give Rad a run for his money. "He doesn't know my name," she says with more sadness, breaking my fucking heart. "It's Lyric," she says through a pout, eyes threatening to spill tiny teardrops.

"I know," River soothes, side-eyeing me with apprehension, but shakes me off. "Aunt Kaycee is waiting for you," she says in her mom voice again, successfully steering the conversation away from her child and me.

Her fucking child. Jesus. My heart gallops so damn fast in my chest that I swear it's going to finally take the leap and kill me. River has a kid. When the hell did that happen? Fuck. I run a hand through my hair, gripping the roots. She has a kid who has mismatched eyes and…

Every ounce of oxygen expels from my lungs. The entire world tilts on its axis and stops turning. Little pieces click together without her having to say a word. I snap my gaze to River, who swallows hard in my presence and silently shakes her head. Long gone is the woman who confidently walked into the conference room with her head held high. In her place is a woman scared shitless that I'm here in front of her daughter.

"And Maggie!" Lyric squeals with excitement, tightening her tiny fists, seeming to forget my mistake.

"And Maggie," River confirms, shaking off my presence and taking the little girl's hand in hers. With one last look in my direction, River drags the girl away from me with worry lining her face.

"Bye, Daddy," Lyric says, waving with her bunny in her hand and a bright smile on her face, reminding me so much of the woman holding onto her for dear life.

"Bye, Lyric," I rasp, waving back as a multitude of emotions roar through my body.

"Mommy! Daddy said my name!" she squeals, breaking away from her mother's grip and charges me with a grin. Her tiny body slams into mine, still seated on the ground. Her tiny arms wrap around my neck, and she nuzzles her face into my neck. "I knew you'd remember me, Daddy," she whispers into my flesh. "Please, don't forget me again." My heart fucking cracks inside my chest and splinters into pieces. I don't know what River has told her. Hell, I don't know how the fuck this happened, but I'll get to the bottom of it.

"Lyric, babe. We have to get you downstairs. Maggie is waiting," River's voice cracks when she says those words, slowly peeling Lyric off me.

"Bye, Daddy! See you tomorrow!" she says in a cheerful tone, waving to me one last time until they disappear around the corner and out of view.

"See you tomorrow," I whisper a promise I can't keep to no one but the empty hall.

I sit there for another five minutes, staring at the same spot they disappeared through. Rampant thoughts roll through my mind at hyper-speed, sending my heart into a damn frenzy. She called me Daddy. Daddy. Me? Fuck. I bring a hand up to my mouth, contemplating throwing up the acid still burning holes through my esophagus. This is my fault. Every ounce of this situation is on my shoulders. More tension mounts inside me, wreaking havoc. A pounding headache hammers through my skull, pressing me down onto the floor. The weight of the fucking world rests on me because I did this.

I'm to fucking blame. The guys have no clue River had a baby. Fuck. I didn't know! And here she is, this beautiful little creature calling me daddy and begging me to never forget her. Goddamn. Kieran is going to break my face open when he finds out.

And I'll deserve it.

I rub my eyes and lean my head against the wall. Fuck. I have so much to do, but I can't seem to get myself to move from this spot. Just as I'm about to rise from my spot, a figure comes marching down the hall with gritted teeth and balled-up fists.

"Why're you still here?" River asks with suspicion when she walks by, only stopping right beside me. "Shouldn't you be packing? I'm sure you have a lot of stuff to do." She raises a pointed brow, taking out a key from her pocket. Like a silent invitation, she opens the door I'm beside and walks in. It isn't until I climb to my feet do I read the plaque outside the door.

'River West–Manager–Fixer'

God damn. She really went and made something of herself, like she had always hoped. All her hard work and determination have paid off. How many days and nights did she work herself to the bone to achieve her dreams?

My heartbeat roars in my throat when I step into her office and stop short in the middle. River's brow furrows as she leans over her desk, running her finger over a piece of paper. She swallows hard, turning to another page.

"You had a baby?" I question through a rasp, startling her from her stupor.

"Great deduction skills, Asher. You're a regular detective," she bites back. "You're as smart as I remember. How long did it take you to remember her?" She scoffs, tossing whatever she was looking at back into a large envelope with her name on it. But I note the tremble in her fingers and the shiver that runs down her spine. Quickly, she picks up her phone and types out a message with pursed lips, not letting me see her emotions. Paleness erases all the color from her face, and she mutters a name under her breath, shaking her head. "Fucking, Kat."

"Remember?" I ask, furrowing my brows. "What the hell are you talking about?" I ask, rolling my shoulders back.

She rolls her eyes and sets her phone back in a large purse. "Don't you have more important things to do? Like pack and get your ass in the limo?" Cocking her head to the side, her green eyes narrow at me as she waits for my answer.

"Yeah, I have important fucking things to do. But you had a baby, and you're evading the question, Little Brat. Is it his?" I ask, crossing my arms over my chest and matching her aggression. Her nickname feels foreign on my tongue, but yet, oh, so right. I don't know what it is about River West, but she brings this side out of me. This demanding prick that begs to put her on a string and force her to my will.

"It's none of your business now. And my name is River, River West to you," she says with a simple head shake and collects her purse. "Now, get out of my office. I have a meeting," she demands, pointing toward the open door and shooing me away.

"No," I say, grabbing her arm and halting her retreat. "Is that little girl my brother's?" I whisper, looking deep into her wide, moss-green eyes. "Tell me."

"Why the fuck do you care now?" she grunts with emotions bubbling through her words, tinged with hurt and so much rage, it punches me in the gut. With defiance, she pulls her arm out of my grip and rights herself. "Five years of knowledge that, yeah, I kept our fucking kid. But why now? Why care now, Asher?" she growls, taking a step back, but keeps her eyes on me. "Explain it to me because I'd love to hear the words come out of your mouth."

My throat constricts at her tiny admission, and I press forward, pushing through the confusion. "You seem to be under the impression that I know what you're talking about. I didn't know you had a kid, let alone Kieran's baby. If we'd known…" I stop myself, running a hand through my hair and gripping the ends.

God fucking damnit! Guilt tears me in two, bringing fresh tears burning in my eyes. My stomach churns more, and I barely suppress the dry heave constricting my throat.

What? Would we have turned around? Giving up our dreams? Shit. Does Kieran know? Fuck. My heart sinks. Did he throw them away because of me? Did I… I heave a breath, tamping down the panic swelling like a surging storm in my chest. I did. I fucking destroyed a family. We could have had something wonderful, and I fucked it all up by being an asshole with my one little lie.

Not only did I fuck over River and my bandmates, but I fucked over his kid—our kid. Jesus, she called me daddy.

Time stands still around me as this pinnacle moment smacks me over the head, forcing me to see every mistake I've made flash before my eyes. We have a daughter. With River. Our time is running on fumes. I need to sew these wounds shut and fix our issues. For Lyric. For us. For River. I've been complicit in this for far too long and sitting back without opening my mouth. It's time to set everything in motion and bring our family back together. It's time I make this up to everyone.

She blinks a few times, staring at me, and shakes her head. "Out," she barks with much less fire in her voice, and her shoulders slump.

With reluctance, I follow her out, staying close as she locks the door and watching her every move.

"River?" I ask when she turns to walk away without glancing in my direction.

"What?" she asks in a sharp voice, stopping in the middle of the hall.

"Why did she call me daddy?" I ask, furrowing my brows. She's clearly not my blood, but I'd love her just the same, even if she wasn't.

My heart pounds when her shoulders rise and fall with her heavy breaths. Without turning to look at me, she utters words I never thought I'd hear.

"Despite you assfaces deciding to ditch me for no reason or letting me explain. Even after the restraining orders and the fucking check I tore up, I wanted Lyric to know where she came from. She knows exactly who each of you is." She shakes her head and turns on her heels, glaring at me when my mouth hangs open in shock at the tears rolling down her cheeks. So much hurt sits behind those beautiful eyes. My damn mouth goes dry.

"My mother never gave me the chance to know my dad. But don't mistake her calling you daddy as a chance for you all to swoop in and play fathers of the year. I won't let Lyric get hurt like you hurt me. Because you all discarded us like trash, and I won't let you do that again. Not to her. She deserves better. *I* deserve better than some fuck boy rock stars who break their promises." River's eyes screw shut as she heaves a breath, collecting herself before she speaks again. When her mouth opens, every ounce of hurt and emotions wipes from her tone as she says her next words, "Now, go get your shit and go to the band house. Or your contract will be voided immediately." Wiping the tears from her face and with one last huff, River marches away, leaving me in a confused-filled fog that threatens to send me on my ass.

The world spins as I move down the hall, attempting to find the exit and get the hell out of this place. River's words live rent-free in my mind when I finally stumble to my car. Resting my head against the headrest, my thoughts continue to swirl. But there's one thing she said that stands out and makes me question everything from before.

What fucking restraining orders? What fucking check? What the fuck is she talking about?

ME

Anything? Can we get out of it?

CONSTANCE

Short answer? No.

I GRIT MY TEETH, MY FINGERS TIGHTENING AROUND MY CELL PHONE. Anger storms through my body, tensing every inch of me. But that's nothing new.

ME

No?

CONSTANCE

It's in the contract, K. Nothing you can do about it unless you walk.

ME

Any other offers?

I drum my fingers on my thigh, nervously bouncing my leg. All we need is another offer, and we can flip West Records the finger and walk. We don't need them. We don't need her.

CONSTANCE

I'll keep my eyes open. But right now? No. Good luck.
Stay nice.

"Fuck," I mumble, pinching the bridge of my nose, eager to lash out at the gym and relieve myself of all this anger festering inside me. It's the only thing that chases any sort of feelings away. I can't afford to feel around her.

"Didn't go well?" Rad asks, staring down at his phone with longing in his dark eyes.

The edge of his finger runs over the picture he doesn't think I know about. The one he stares at day in and day out like a hurt puppy dog,

waiting for his master to come back and claim him. It's never escaped me that he's still madly in love with her, even after what she did.

Rad sighs heavily, biting into his bottom lip as we pull up to Callum's condo. The limo comes to a complete stop, idling on the curb as we wait a solid three minutes for him to appear. Callum's bulky form comes into view with his hands tucked in his pockets. A large, black hoodie swallows his body whole, and the hood covers his eyes. The moment he flips it down, I know the evidence will be on his face in the form of blackened bruises and swollen flesh.

Callum doesn't utter a word as he shuffles into the limo and finds a seat next to Rad, not bothering to meet our curious gazes. Leaning back, he rests his head and closes his eyes, tuning us completely out with his earbuds snug in his ears. Like so many years before, Callum only speaks when spoken to, but worse. He only opens his mouth if it pertains to the band, and that's it.

Lead fills my stomach at the onslaught of memories banging around inside my head. Five years ago, something fundamental fucked us all up. We've thrived in our own ways. Some more than others, finding hobbies to take our wandering minds off the woman who crushed us with one single action. We don't speak her name. Or mention our past in passing. Together, we've avoided the topic altogether and moved forward. Well, mostly. Sometimes the ghost of my past comes back to haunt me, pulling me into unwanted memories.

Marching through the parking lot of River's apartment building, I tightly ball my hands into fists. Rage consumes every molecule in my body when I see the familiar red Mustang parked right in front of River's apartment. I stand, frozen next to it, when the front door of River's apartment slams open, and out walks Van with a victorious grin spreading across his face. His shirt hangs over his arm, and he whistles gleefully under his breath.

"You fucking her?" I accuse, stepping out of the shadows with a scowl and folding my arms over my chest.

Seeing the picture Callum had taken didn't satisfy my curiosity one bit. I had to see for myself. River and I have way too much history for me to just walk away without investigating what the fuck is going on. But now, the scale is sliding in an unfavorable direction, leading me to believe that everything is true.

"For a few months," Van says with a cocky grin, pulling his shirt over his head.

My fists clench at my side, and before I know what the fuck I'm doing, I grab Van by his arm and throw him against the side of his car. "You've been fucking her for months?" I hiss, getting right in his face.

"Yeah, bro. Aren't you happy I told you? God, she was going to let you all think you were hers when she's fucking half the town," he sneers,

pushing his forehead against mine. Without a thought, I throw my fist into his temple, crumpling him to the ground, and taking my frustrations out on his curled-up body.

As the memory ebbs away, I come back to the reality of it all. I never made it inside to talk to River after witnessing Van walking from her apartment. For the next few days, I snuck away from the guys and watched him come and go from the parking lot, convincing me that the truth was right in front of my eyes the entire time. She cheated and felt nothing for us.

"We're stuck," I say, sucking in a ragged breath. "My agent says it's in the contract that we have to put up with this for the full six months, unless we get another deal from somewhere else."

"Somewhere else?" Rad asks, raising his brows. He heaves a sigh, shoving his phone into his pocket. "Like that'll happen."

"Like where?" Callum mutters, peeking an eye open.

"EJ Records across town has always been interested," I say confidently as the car takes off across town toward Asher's massive house on the damn beach.

I squeeze my eyes shut when visions of River walking into the conference room fill my mind and refuse to let go. For five years, I've wiped her existence from everything. I pretend she never existed. I pretend she never shattered my heart into a million pieces. But she always seems to show her face in my nightmares. Now, she's here in the flesh, ready to haunt me more.

And it pisses me off more than anything. How can she walk around like nothing happened between us? What we had was more special than anything. And she gave it away for a good fuck in the back of a Mustang.

A picture of Van and River in her kitchen. Kissing. His fucking lips are on hers. Her lips on his.

I see red. My mind goes haywire. Accusations sit on the tip of my tongue. Anger rises in my chest and crushes my ribs, ripping my heart from inside me. Opening a deep, dark pit of nothing in my chest. Numbness prickles at my mind and tingles down my limbs.

And then I feel...nothing.

A part of me wished what Asher had said wasn't fucking true, and that it was all some sick joke on us. It was a video; it could have been staged. Some last blaze of glory for Van to try and win her back without us in the picture. I was prepared to march to her apartment and spank the truth from her ass. Then Callum came and set me straight with his picture.

There it was in bright colors. The truth I've been dreading with a sickening knot in my stomach since Asher opened his mouth.

How had I fallen so hard again? With her? Only to have to force myself to put one foot in front of the other and leave her behind, forgetting she ever existed.

I used to think my heart only beat for her, but now it beats for no one.

Not even me. I'm a broken man without my River Blue. Or not mine. Was she ever? Was it all fun and games? Did I not make myself clear who owned every inch of her?

Apparently not. Because Donovan Drake swooped in and stole her back like he had planned. Maybe we were just a way to pass the time, and we were never exclusive. Whatever it was, I'm done, but not before I find out for myself. Without a word or a glance back, I throw open the front door and storm away, hellbent on finding the truth for myself.

I blow out a breath, shaking the stupid memories out of my mind just in time to retrieve a pale-looking Asher. Something plagues him when he settles in his seat beside me, fiddling with a key between his fingers. Nervously, he darts his eyes around the car and swallows hard, before looking out the window again. It's always the same with him. Since we moved here, he's been sketchy as hell. Always locking himself in his room, unless it has to do with the band. Then he'll come out and play with us. He's always so quiet and so damn reserved. It drives me fucking nuts to see him act so differently from the guy I used to know.

He hasn't been the same since River.

"What is wrong with you?" I mutter, wrinkling my nose.

I've never seen my perfectly put-together stepbrother—or I guess not anymore—lose his shit like this. Sweat beads on his forehead, and he heaves another breath.

"Nothing," he murmurs so quietly, gazing out the window as we take off down the road with all of us settling in.

"Anyone know where this mysterious band house is?" Rad asks in a lazy tone, keeping his eyes trained out the window at the blurring colors passing by.

Rad may seem like the same old goofy dude, but he's not. He's thrown himself into music, girls, booze, and parties. All to forget her. She who shall not be named. The one who ruined us all with her selfish ways. And that idiot? Yeah, he still pines for her every night.

Sometimes I think River West was our one true love. Something we'll never find again.

"I'll find it," Callum says, pulling out our contract from some mysterious place in his hoodie. Flipping through a few pages with trembling fingers, he points to a spot on the page. "Number Four, Lyric Lane, is the official address listed in the paper."

Rad snorts. "Lyric Lane? Sounds made up."

Asher's breath beside me shudders in his chest, and he shakes his head, drawing my attention to him again. He's acting fucking weird. I've never seen someone who is all business all the time, so fucking rattled by this situation. I run a hand down my face and shake my head.

"Don't let her get to you," I offer, sitting back and getting comfortable. "We'll get out of this. I'll never let River rule my life ever again."

Asher swallows hard, snapping his hazel eyes at me. Licking his lips, he looks at the other two and leans into my personal bubble.

"You know River had a kid?" he asks in a soft voice, trying not to draw attention to the other two.

I snort. "Of course. Gloria called me," I spit, rolling my eyes. "I've known for the past five years." My heart beats heavily against my ribs at the thought of her having a kid. *His* kid. After all that time together, she still went back to him before we even left and opened her legs.

"You knew?" Asher asks with furrowed brows, and his face twists in disbelief. "You knew about her? And you've never..."

I scoff. "Why the fuck would I care?" I wave a hand. "River can do whatever she wants. She's not my concern. Not anymore." A pain stabs my chest, tightening like rubber bands constricting my breath. Even after all these years.

I loved her once. Hell, more than once. She was my best friend. I really fucking loved her, to the point I would have jumped off a cliff for her without a second thought. Until that night when I watched with my own eyes as she jumped into that psycho's lap and fucked his brains out, and then Callum's proof was all I needed. We used her at first, hoping to get by on her name to get here. Then, somehow under our noses, she used us right back, faking Van's stalker interest in her. Using us to defend her honor and all that shit. It's the only explanation I've come up with after all this time.

"River has a kid?" Rad asks, the conversation piquing his interest. Leaning forward, he rests his elbows on his knees, staring between the two of us. "Since when?" His face twists, and more betrayal spears through his dark eyes.

"Five years," I say with a shrug, focusing outside the window.

Rad gives a brief whimper, letting me know he's still affected by her presence, too. I wasn't the only one hopelessly in love with her. We all were. And she fucking decimated our hearts. Even after all these years and the betrayal of a lifetime, we're hopeless.

The conversation ceases, and only our breathing can be heard through the large cabin as we sit in the first conversation we've really had in a long ass time. It's hard to remember when it happened, but at some point, we fell apart. Right about the time Asher started retreating into himself and avoiding us at all costs was about the time Callum did the same. He barely speaks these days. Hell, he barely looks at us. And Rad...the poor, poor guy hasn't lost himself in enough pussy to get over her yet. It'll happen eventually, but I'm sure with her being our new boss, it won't help one bit. One day, I'll help him get over her and bring the rest of them back on board. Our band hasn't felt like a family for years, but they're the only ones I have. If I don't have this band, then I don't have shit.

Iron gates come into view with a large metal 'W' lining the entirety of the ornate metal. A guard shack, complete with a guard, who pokes his head out from the little window with an inspecting eye. His words to our driver are murmured through the separating glass, and his voice barely registers.

"A guard?" Rad raises his brows, eyeing the thin man nestled inside his office, complete with a small TV visible to us. A large badge displaying the name of 'D&D Security' clings to the upper arm of the dark blue uniform.

"What the hell does she need a guard for?" I snark as the gate opens wide, allowing us entry to the long, winding driveway. "Spoiled ass princess," I mutter, sulking as I eye the guard who is already sitting back in his chair with a drink in hand, lazily scrolling through his phone—some guard he is.

As we make our way down the drive, a bright blue street sign confirms what I already guessed. We're on Lyric Lane, heading to the house that will be our home for the next six months of hell.

Anticipation buzzes across my skin as we keep going, not seeing a home in sight. Grassy lands surround us, and to our right, a long beach with white-tipped waves greets my eyes. Jesus. West Records really went all out for this. We're secluded. Maybe fifteen minutes from West Records offices.

I can still hear Gloria's smug voice over the phone as she relayed the information on River's little secret. Like I cared at that point. Still don't. River can live the life she deserves far the fuck away from me. All I want is to fix the band. Not that we need it. We sold out shows last year. We packed the stadiums. Maybe we've had some mishaps and exposure to our mistakes, but we've always pushed through.

The limo comes to a stop in the short driveway of a simple two-story white mansion. There's nothing particularly special about it. But what catches my eye when we pile out is the matching house across the street with an SUV in the driveway. The license plate reads RWest.

"Whoa, dude," Rad says, turning in circles, admiring the luxurious view around us. "This is… Wow," he settles on, looking around both properties in awe.

I sigh when my phone buzzes. Pulling it out of my pocket, I frown when her name flashes across the screen. Everything in me tenses, and I shake my head. Of course, she'd ask this today.

GLORIA

I need some more money.

"Hello, boys," comes a sultry voice from the garage as the door lifts, revealing River in a tight red dress with matching come-fuck-me heels. A scowl forms at the idea of her outfit change, going from completely professional to this. This… God. Even if I hate her, she's fucking beautiful. "Welcome to your new home. If you'll follow me, we have some rules to discuss."

I swallow hard when her moss-green eyes connect with mine, and she tilts her head. Immediately, I look away, hiding the sadness resting in my soul every time I look in her direction, and snarl instead. If I can't show the fucking hurt bleeding my heart dry, then I'll turn to the rage I've felt since the moment I realized it was all true and punish the woman who crumbled my heart into a million pieces.

My heart can't take another round with River West again.

What the fuck does he mean he didn't know?

Tears cascade down my cheeks at an unstoppable rate when I finally park in my driveway. Bone-crushing emotions surge through my body as his words repeat in my mind. Deep anguish grabs hold, sinking its claws deep into me, letting everything I've held in over the last five years out. Even if I wanted to stop the waterworks, I couldn't. Not now. Placing my forehead against the steering wheel of my SUV, I allow myself a moment to grieve the fathers Lyric could have had.

Thankfully, Lyric is with her cousin tonight, because I don't think I could hold it together with her here asking me questions like she did before. So, for now, I cry for all the things they missed out on and the family they could have had. I cry so I won't cry when I pick Lyric up and bring her home. That's the thing about moms, we put on a brave face even when we're drowning in misery.

The late-night feedings, diaper changes, and the quality time getting to know the men who could have raised her alongside me. Only, they didn't. They walked out without a goodbye, leaving me to do it all by myself because it inconvenienced their chance at a better life. But what about mine? Where would I have been if Seger and Zepp hadn't tracked me down and handed me more money than I knew what to do with?

Confusion swims in my foggy brain, making a groan escape my lips. Asher's words reverberate in my mind, ping-ponging over and over again.

He acted like he didn't have a clue Lyric existed, and he should have known. Shouldn't he? Shouldn't they all? I shake my head, second-guessing everything that happened. Gloria called them right in front of me. I heard her from the vacant living room of Callum's old house. So, why did he act like he'd seen a ghost? Why was it such a damn shock that she was with me?

The way he gazed at Lyric with tears in his eyes and held her in his

arms when she hugged him broke me in half. I will forever tattoo the scene in my thoughts. Through my efforts, Lyric holds strong feelings for each of these men after years of seeing their pictures and asking me about them.

What was I supposed to tell her? That they refused to acknowledge her? That she was a mess up, and they didn't want her? Fuck no. I did what any good mom would do; I let her know them through photographs and music, letting her sing their songs at the top of her lungs. No matter how hard it hurt at the time. I told her stories of our times together and the adventures we had as a unit. Then came the ending of our union. It's something I've kept hidden from her small ears. There's no way I can break her heart like they broke mine. So, for her sake, I keep them on a shrine for her to worship.

"But where?" Lyric's little lip pouts as she holds up a picture of Kieran, Asher, Callum, and Rad from some red-carpet event this past weekend on her tablet. Her big eyes zone in on their fancy suits and smiles on their faces.

"Ly," I murmur, curling a piece of her dark hair behind her ears. "Sometimes parents aren't ready to be parents. And your daddies weren't ready to be that just yet." It's all I can manage to say to my broken-hearted daughter, who will never understand the magnitude of the betrayal that sits heavy on my heart.

"Do they not like me? I'll be better! I won't hit cousin Rome anymore. I promise. Just call all my daddies and tell them. I be good," she says in a hurried tone, tinted with emotions.

Her big, mismatched eyes well up with tears and spill over onto her reddening cheeks, ripping my heart from my damn chest and splintering it into a million pieces. Sometimes I think I'm doing the wrong thing by telling her where she came from. I'm leaving her with these high expectations of four daddies who can't be with her yet. Lord knows our relationship was unconventional. But I'm thankful everyday Lyric has Kaycee, Seger, Zeppelin, Chase, and Carter to round out her yearning for her fathers.

I have to remind myself every day when the guilt slams into me that I wasn't the one who walked away. They were. She'll know their lives and faces like the back of her hand if I can help it. And one day, when she's old enough to understand, I'll explain it all to her the best I can.

"I'm sorry, Ly," I gasp out, pulling her into my arms. Rocking her back and forth, I kiss the top of her head, holding my tears at bay. "They'll come back when they're ready, I promise." And maybe I shouldn't have promised her something so massive and life changing. I assumed one day, they'd come knocking and admit their mistakes, wanting to be present in her life. After five years, I'd given up hope for Lyric to ever know them.

"Maybe he didn't know," Odette, my best friend from Central City, says through the speakers of my SUV. Breaking me from my morbid thoughts. Because why cry by yourself when you can call your best friend and cry with her?

"But she-who-shall-not-be-named called them. Right in front of me, Ode," I sigh, rubbing a hand down my face. "I watched her do it. I heard the conversation. They knew. Or, one of them knew and didn't tell the others. Fuck. My head hurts. I'm so confused. Why is this happening right now?"

Ode snorts through the phone. "Did she? Seriously, Riv. That crazy bitch had it out for you the whole time you were with them. You have no idea what happened, girl. She could have pulled a fast one or something. The only way you'll find out is if you ask them. And I know, I know, that's the last conversation you want to have. I think you all need to hash this all out, once and for all, before you murder them, or Ly apparently tackles them and loves them to death."

I snort, pinching the bridge of my nose. "Yeah, yeah. I know you're right. I'll talk to them at some point."

Whenever that is. How the hell do I sit down and say, *"Heya, assfaces, we need to discuss our child. And oh, why the hell did you leave so quickly?"* It's one of those scenarios I've envisioned many times in the shower. You know, the anxiety-filled fake conversations that happen only inside of your head as you shampoo your hair and mock fight with people. Yeah, that type of situation, and it always goes one way—them laughing at me and me punching their nuts.

"And Jesus, I can't believe your brothers pulled that shit. Want me to kick their asses? I'm not above hopping on a plane and laying the smack down," Ode quips, lightening the mood instantly.

"Please," I grumble, wiping the tears from my face. "I need someone to help me dig their graves."

"Oh, we're hiding bodies now, babe? I'm on my way," she snickers. "I'm always here for you, Riv. But…"

"But?" I question, leaning back in my seat with a huff.

"But I think you're entitled to some answers. They owe you a hell of a lot of words," she encourages. "You know I've never felt right after they left. Something stunk really fucking bad. And the way Gloria did you dirty with those restraining orders. I don't know; it didn't settle right with me." I envision her shaking her head in disbelief and running her fingers through her wild curls.

Longing hits me square in the chest. Years ago, I could walk to Ode's apartment to visit with her, Leon, and their mom, Korrine. Now, she's halfway across the country running my former bar, Dead End, with Leon and raising a family with her boyfriend Ricky.

"I miss you," I confess with a groan.

"Miss you, too. We need to vacation, or hell, you could come home. Mama is…" She sucks in a breath, stopping her emotions.

"Worse?" I whisper, feeling my heart sink.

"The chemo is kicking her ass. You know Mama, though, she's fighting tooth and nail," she says in a soft voice. "She misses you, too, Riv. Say you'll come home soon?"

"Yeah. I think I will soon." No matter what, my chosen family has always come first. Korrine helped to raise me. Ode was my sister. And Leon was my annoying brother. They've always shown up for me. So, I do the same for them. They were my damn rock when Ly was brewing. They helped me with everything I could have needed. And the moment I came into the money my father left me, I took care of them right back.

Now I'm stuck helping the guys get their dream back on track. The same dream that left me and my growing belly behind in another state. What does our future hold? Will we butt heads the entire time they're under my orders or will they get over themselves and forge ahead?

Ode is right, though; they owe me some answers, and I'm going to get them one way or another. I deserve that after so long. First, I have to get through this first meeting with them at the house and not stomp their balls with my heels.

"Now tits up, bitch. Go show those boys who is really in charge. Show them no mercy!" she says through a chuckle, making me smile.

"Fuck, Ode. I have to face them again," I groan, leaning my head back into the chair.

"How long?" she asks.

"Maybe an hour until they get here with all their shit."

"Good! Now, push your tits out and put on your best outfit and heels. Demand the damn room. Show them what they walked out on, babe."

I blow out a breath, staring at my tear-stained cheeks, and nod. "You think it'll be cruel if I give them a 10:00 p.m. curfew every night?" I ask, wiping under my eyes and removing the wetness from my flesh.

She snorts. "Hell no. Leash them to that damn house. Show them how a big girl gets petty revenge."

"Petty revenge?" I ask with a laugh. "I don't know about that..." I trail off.

"Think about it. Talk to them, get a little closure, and revenge, and move on. It's time to stop letting Whispered Words rule your life. Now, go get them bitch. You got this. And text me after."

"Bye, love you!" I chirp, hang up the phone, and head into my house.

Maybe it is time for a little petty revenge, right? It can't hurt. So, with that in mind, I open my laptop and start typing the new contract they'll have to abide by for the next six months.

I puff out my cheeks and release the air through my parted lips, hoping Ode's words of wisdom are just that—words of wisdom. I need all the damn encouragement I can get to not storm away from these assfaces and continue my life. Screw them. Screw our future talk. But, ugh. I can't. This is my livelihood, and I won't have them ruining the steps I've taken to get my life back. Plus, Lyric would be disappointed.

So, after refreshing my makeup following my woe-is-me pity party, I decided that taking a sliver of revenge was in order, thanks to Ode's wise words. I may be unable to buzz their body hair while they sleep and laugh as they look in the mirror with no eyebrows, but I thought of a creative way to get back at the assfaces taking residency across the street from me. So, after finagling my curves into a smoking hot red dress, I apply a little makeup, including deep-red lipstick. What? I want them to know what the hell they walked away from and what they'll never have again.

After sending Ode a picture, she assured me it would do the trick and have them drooling within two seconds. I quickly put on a pair of slightly unprofessional six-inch heels and made my way to the band house to greet my new neighbors with a smile.

The moment I walked in and showed them to the dining room table was fucking priceless. Their faces tightened, and lust swam in their eyes. For a fleeting moment, at least. Until they all averted their gazes, sat in their seats, and awaited my direction. But who says I can't saunter through the damn house, swaying my hips and making them regret every minute of walking out on me without a goodbye.

So, here I stand nervously in the kitchen, tapping my damn toes, anxiously waiting for them to finish the read-through of their final contract. The one they must sign before they settle into this place, and I take total control of their lives. My mind screams *run, bitch, go back home,* but my body remains rooted where it needs to be. Who knew being in their pres-

ence for only a few hours would have my skin fucking crawling with the need to run and hide like a coward. Did I ever want to face them again? Nope. Not a chance. But here I am, facing the bulls head-on.

My eyes drift toward the dining room, where all four of them sit quietly, discussing the paperwork I handed them an hour ago with civility. Well, kind of. The occasional huff, scowl, or grunt comes from their direction, letting me know how delighted they are to be here, too. Thankfully, I haven't been verbally attacked in the last hour. I'd call that an improvement. So far, so good. I guess.

Only the tiniest spark of tension hangs in the air like a persistent rain cloud between the five of us. It's so small I barely notice the divide. All bets are off when I step into the room, and by the down-turned look on their faces, they're getting a glimpse of my fun stipulations. But what can I say? I typed these rules up an hour before they showed their faces. So, I had plenty of time to set the boundaries they must adhere to without question because I'm the damn boss this time.

I glance at my phone, hoping for a text back about the package I received this morning, but get nothing in return. I shrug it off. Sometimes my other best friend Olivia is prompt with her responses. Sometimes, she's chasing her three-year-old son around the house while wrangling her five husbands. Other times she's hard at work as an agent at Veritas. She's a ridiculously busy woman. So, it's a toss-up on what she's doing.

I take a deep breath and reign in the antsy feeling crawling over my flesh. Leaving my phone on the counter, I head into the open-concept dining room. Bright afternoon sunlight streams in through the floor-to-ceiling windows from the spacious living room and bounces off the dark wood floors adorned with the most comfortable couches and recliners money could buy. Three years ago, I invested my own money into this home across from mine, hoping to make something of my new position— my damn dream job. My brothers agreed without protest, letting me take the lead on my newest project. And since then, I've blossomed into this, restoring one band at a time to its former glory.

Kieran snorts in anger, flipping through the pages of rules. "Seriously? We're not babies," he complains with a shake of his head. "We're grown damn men. If I want to stay out all night, then I fucking will. I don't need to be here twenty-four seven."

Heat spears up my neck and onto my cheeks, as my rage builds. I'm getting sick and tired of his mouth running, and I've only been in his presence for a few hours. Whatever is going on between us, we're going to have to solve them, just like Ode suggested. Before I do something stupid like explode or stab them.

Maybe this is all a sick and twisted test from my brothers, so they can watch me squirm and laugh at me as I stumble my way through this.

Sounds like them. Those assholes. Usually, this is easy. The bands respect me the moment we meet, eager to build themselves up again and follow my lead. Instead of respect from Whispered Words, I'm getting verbally abused by four whiny babies stuck in the past. *You are, too, idiot.* I huff at my inner voice and shoo it away. I'm not as stuck as they are. I've moved on with my life and made something of myself. I have a kid, a house, and a damn beach all to myself. It's everything I've ever dreamed of. So why do I feel like a piece of me is still missing?

Taking a deep breath, I soothe my rage monster. "Absolutely," I say with a shrug, slowly pacing the space around the table. "Go ahead. You're free to do whatever you want to do. Go gallivant in front of the cameras again with your arm around a different chick every day. See what West Records does. See what *I* do," I say, crossing my arms over my chest, begging him to test me and my thin patience.

"You sound jealous, River Blue," he goads, spitting the name like poison. Slowly, he climbs to his feet, ready for a fight. "Is that it? Did it tear you apart to see me on TV?"

No, but it killed your daughter, you buffoon.

I'm tempted to shout in his face. But for the sake of my profession, I sink my teeth into my tongue and quickly stop my burning retort. If he wanted to be in her life, then he'd make it happen. So far, he hasn't stepped up to the plate like a man. He hasn't even asked about her or seemed to care that she exists, which is going to make our conversation in the future all the more difficult. He's either in or he's out, and that's the end of story. Whoever else wants to step up; I won't stop them. Lyric wants a daddy—more specifically, these four idiots. I'm not about to deny her a relationship with them if she wants it, even if it kills me a little on the inside.

I raise my brow. My heart pounds against my ribs when I lock my challenging gaze with his. *Bring it on, Kieran.* I can go as many rounds as you want, but I will always come out on top.

"Jealous?" I ask, seething on the inside, but soothing out the rasp of emotion in my voice. "Not by a mile. It's the rules, Mr. Knight. Every band that's lived under this roof has had these rules." My index finger pokes into the wood of the table, stabbing it with every word. I swallow the lie, expertly perfecting my indifferent mask as if this doesn't affect me.

"Leave her alone," Asher pipes up, shaking his head at Kieran, and signs his contract without question. "Just sign the damn papers."

Sure, every band has rules, but never ones like this. Am I a fucking professional? Yes. Am I keeping Whispered Words on a shorter leash? Also, yes. So, sue me if I want to enact a little petty revenge for leaving Lyric behind. I can't cut off all their hair and then glue it to their balls as a form of retribution without blinking. So, I do the next best thing and professionally tie them to this house after 10:00 p.m. It's genius if you ask me.

"Bro, sit down. Sign the papers," Rad grumbles, grasping Kieran's forearm and setting him back in his seat with a reluctant huff. Picking up his pen like a good boy, Kieran flips to the last page and signs his name in messy cursive, pouting the entire time.

I bite the inside of my cheek when he grumpily throws the pen down and crosses his arms, glaring out the windows, refusing to look in my direction.

Callum's head stays down, studying the rules one at a time, memorizing them at a glance with his photographic memory. It's always stunned me to know he can replay anything at will in full detail. In the past, the memories from his parents and sister's death held him by the throat and didn't let him go. I wonder how moving out here has helped him cope and grieve properly, or is he still stuck in the same damn relentless loop? Does he think about the kiss Van forced on me when he stood in my kitchen and watched it happen?

"A 10:00 p.m. curfew? No parties? No alcohol? And no guests?" he murmurs, running his finger over the words with furrowed brows. "Band practice every Monday through Friday at 8:45 a.m. Weekly shows at undisclosed locations. IE; The KC Club South, The KC Club Shores, and River's Run, on Saturday evenings. A once-a-week group therapy session." Swallowing hard, his gray eyes meet mine with confusion.

"Whoa. Therapy?" Rad asks, holding my stare, and I shrug. "Pretty Girl, I don't need therapy. I'm as right as rain," he says with a lop-sided grin, brushing off his shoulders like this is nothing more than a little stop before he returns to his fame.

My breath hitches at the nickname, and my lungs squeeze in my chest. Seeing the same old, carefree Rad from five years ago sitting before me liquifies my insides. A multitude of memories hit me square in the chest, reminding me of our adventures together. From the man who insisted I was his girlfriend when I wasn't to the man whose eyes drop to the table, filling with sadness. Rad refuses to look at me again like I broke his damn heart, and maybe in his mind, I did. But that's on him. If only they had come to me and let me explain what happened, we wouldn't be in this damn mess.

"Right. No matter how right you feel, it's required of all bands that stay in this house." I give a sharp nod. "This isn't a negotiation," I say with authority, reminding them I'm the one in charge here. Not them. The sooner they realize they're stuck, the sooner we can move on to fixing their career and getting them the hell out of my house.

"I can't fucking believe it," Kieran murmurs once again, letting his attitude out to play. Still glaring out the window, he rubs a hand down his face.

"Well, believe it. That's why you're here. This is a unique opportunity for each of you. So, don't blow it. No matter our past, you have a better future. And whether you or I like it or not, this is happening," I say in a calm tone, clasping my hands in front of my body. "Does anyone else have a problem with that?" I ask, staring around the table at each of them shaking their heads. All except shithead Kieran, who glares at me with a scrunched-up face filled with more rage than before.

"Unless we get a better offer," Kieran mutters more to himself than anyone.

I really shouldn't punch him, should I? You think one knock to his stubborn as hell head would do the trick? I'd love to find out.

"Sure, go ahead and try."

I know my fucking worth and what I bring to the bands. So do other record labels out there. Try and see where you get, you insufferable dickhead.

Collecting the contracts from each of them as they sign, I place them into a folder to file later.

"Your belongings should be here at any moment. Please unload your possessions into one of the rooms you select upstairs. There is storage in the attached garage for vehicles and such. I will allow you all to get settled in for the rest of the weekend and explore your new house. There's a home gym in the basement with anything you may need. There's also a recording studio down there for when inspiration strikes." My eyes scan the boys, as they sit attentively, listening to my speech.

"Remember, we will start band practices on Monday with no exceptions. Same time, same place, in the practice room. Every amenity possible is here that you could need. Per the rules, you're permitted to leave the property to get groceries or some fresh air. But please remember, you represent West Records and always have. Your public image is also important." My eyes zero in on Kieran when he scoffs, muttering under his breath again like a petulant child.

"Also, under no circumstances are you allowed to visit the house across the street without warning. That's my home. So, no unannounced visits. The moment you step foot inside, your contract is terminated unless you are given permission to do so. If you need me, my direct phone number is on the fridge. I am your contact for anything you may need now. I am your boss. This house—this opportunity is your last chance with West Records. If you fail, there is no more. Are we clear?" I scan the guys again when they each nod their heads in reluctant agreement, not wanting to accept the fact that I'm now in charge of their every move.

"Good. I'll return with copies of your signed contracts on Monday. I'll also put a copy of your new schedule on the fridge for practices, therapy sessions, and your performances." I give them all a tight smile, deciding this is as best as any time to walk out the front door and let them unload their things. The next six months will test them and me beyond belief.

The moment I step into my house, I release my frantic breath. Fuck. That was worse than I thought, but I survived the ordeal unscathed. Besides a few snarky comments here and there, they all seem to be settling with the fact I am momentarily back in their lives as their damn boss.

My phone buzzes in my pocket, alerting me that my other best friend, Olivia, has texted. It's useful that my friend has connections to higher powers and is a badass agent with Veritas–the government agency resembling the FBI, only more secretive and illusive.

OLIVIA

Sorry, Riv. Busy day on the home front. Just saw your message. Is it the same content as before? Anything new?

ME

It's okay. And yeah…same shit… Same flowers… Somehow it ended up on my desk.

OLIVIA

Really? Your desk? Did Kat leave it there?

That reminds me. My assistant and I need to have a very serious discussion again about the packages I receive from the obsessed psychopath who loves to watch my every step. Hell, she even scheduled the installation of my home security system and cameras when I felt threatened enough. She should know this is serious and not something to mess around with. Yet, she leaves the reminders of his obsession on my desk.

ME

Yeah. Going to talk to her. Want me to pass it on to Carter?

OLIVIA

Yeah. I'll get it from him tomorrow. So sorry, Riv. We'll get them, I promise.

ME

It's escalating, Liv… I'm starting to freak out… What if this gets worse? Effects Ly?

OLIVIA

Don't. Not now. Let Veritas handle it, ok? We got this. We got you guys. We'll always protect you.

ME

Ok. Thanks, Liv.

I blow out a breath and close my eyes. The moment I saw that package on my desk with my name scribbled in perfect cursive and a million stamps placed on the corners, my heart sank. For a brief moment, I hoped they had forgotten me and moved on to something else productive. But they didn't. They never do.

The package is a silent reminder that they're still there after three years of anonymous harassment, watching my every move from afar with a camera in their hand. I've been down this road before. We've looked for suspects left and right. Hell, they even looked into Van as a safety measure, given his previous stalking ways.

"You're positive it's not him?" I mumble, tracing the picture my stalker sent me. It's nothing but my grinning face, roasting in the sun. Lyric had a dance recital that day, near the lake on an outside stage. It could have been anyone.

Olivia runs a hand down the left side of her face, drawing my attention to the faint scars lining her flesh. I can't imagine going through what she did when she was a teenager. She rarely talks about the trauma of the fire or losing her three best friends.

"Yes. We've looked into Donavan Drake several times. He's been overseas with the production company he works for, for several months now. There's no way he could follow you around and be halfway across the world."

My only saving graces are Liv and Veritas having my back, or I'd be up shits creek without a paddle. A hopeless feeling envelops me, not knowing what to do about this stupid stalker. When will it end? It's been three miserable years of watching my back, and now I have to worry about Ly, too. I'm tired of looking over my shoulder and making sure whoever they are isn't there lurking in the shadows.

I rub circles over my temple, trying to settle my rampant heartbeat. It pounds in my ear, taking over everything around me. It isn't until a distinct rumble coming down the drive, vibrating my entire house, brings me back to reality. As four moving vans park on the curb and open their back doors. Peeking out my window, I raise a brow when Rad wheels out his old dirt bike and places it in the garage.

I'd recognize that bike from a mile away. It's his winning bike, the one he raced around Raccoon Run, and the same one he finger-banged me on before spreading me over his winning eight-hundred bucks. *Fuck.* I close my eyes, trying to erase those happy memories from my brain permanently. Seeing them again awakens something odd inside of me. Something I never thought I'd have to face again. Maybe they're my nightmares, or maybe they're here to set things right.

Back then, when we first met, we were thrown together in a whirlwind and fell hard for each other. We were simplistic kids with enormous dreams, just trying to find ourselves. Then it all went to shit, which is something I won't let go of easily. They used me, intentionally, and admitted it. They invited me along on a trip they never intended to take me on and then left like I meant nothing after witnessing something they didn't fully understand. Forgiveness is not in my vocabulary at this moment in time; maybe, if they make it up to me somehow, but I highly doubt that.

I've moved on with my life with Lyric by my side. I don't need them anymore.

"See you, assmunchers, later. I'm going for a ride," I grumble, running a hand through my hair, trying to distract myself from her—River. The woman I fell head over heels in love with. Only to have my heart ripped violently out of my chest and spit on. "Fuck," I mumble, squeezing my eyes shut as the pain of her betrayal sears through me again. Stopping before the garage door that connects to the house, I recover my breath and sigh. I have got to get a handle on my fucking self. I'm being ridiculous. I can't fall apart because she's back in the picture. Not now. I've fought too damn hard to get back to the easy-going, carefree guy everyone loves to see. No matter the dark cloud floating over my head whenever I'm alone.

Once upon a time, she was my pretty girl. The most beautiful woman in the world. And I called her mine. All mine. And well, theirs, too, I guess. I thought she felt a semblance of what I felt for her. Love. Adoration. Major attraction. God damn, the sex was off-the-charts hot, too. Even thinking about spreading her ass out on a pile of money makes little Rad perk up. Even now, after all this time, she's still on a shrine in the back of my head with candles and a curtain concealing her memory. If only I could contain it from ever spilling out into my waking thoughts. Then I might be okay.

I guess I was mistaken about us, though. She managed to jump into Van's arms again, like the moments we had meant nothing to her. She threw out the Ferris wheel ride, the way she built our band, and the fucking dining room table incident like they didn't play on repeat in her mind, too. Because fuck, even through my hate, I fuck my hand to the memories of River's cries at the top of the Ferris wheel. *Fuck.* Not only am I sad, but now I'm saluting in my damn pants.

Hell, maybe I pushed my pretty girl too much and way too fast. I did kind of stalk her and put a flag in her ass, claiming her as my girlfriend. She had no choice. So, that's on me, I guess. She didn't want me the way I desperately wanted her. She didn't want any of us.

I huff a breath when the familiar burn behind my eyes threatens to spill tears again. I'm so damn tired of crying myself to sleep. It's been fucking years. Why can't my heart move on?

"You're going for a ride?" Callum asks in a soft voice, placing a hand on my shoulder. I grunt, shrugging his hand off, and nod, clutching my keys.

"Yeah, man. I gotta clear my mind," I mumble, wiping away the tears leaking out.

Stupid tears; I don't need you right now. Never again. I'm tired of crying over her; she's not worth it. She broke my heart once; I won't let her trample it again. Lesson fucking learned. Not even those sexy as fuck six-inch heels that accentuated her long, lean legs under that come-fuck-me-dress she wore over here for our meeting can win me over. God. She's amazing. I love her. But I fucking hate her. And what's wrong with me? My heart tears into two different pieces, going in two separate directions.

When I turn to look up at Callum, my brows furrow, there's a hint of something brewing in the back of his determined gray eyes, and suspicion hits me hard in the chest. That fucker is up to something.

"You're not thinking about going tonight, are you?" When he darts his eyes away toward the ground, I get my answer. "Bro, we can't leave, remember? Not even for that."

His jaw clenches tight, and he nods. "Thanks for the reminder, Dad," he grumbles, working his jaw back and forth, biting back all the rage consuming him.

I swear, my brother Callum hasn't been the same man since he witnessed River kissing Van. It's like the sweet piece that made him, him—was left behind in Central City and with her. She stole that from him. He had just started opening up and becoming the person he wanted to be, and now, he has effectively shut down completely.

"Sorry, Man. I didn't make the rules. Take it up with her," I say, throwing an arm out toward River's house, which sits just across the street from us.

Thankfully, she hasn't shown her face today, giving us the weekend to move in and settle into our gigantic new home. I'd rather not face my past head-on. Until Monday morning, of course, when she'll meet us for our very first band practice under her new rules. Shit. I feel like I'm back under my strict parents' control. The ones who forbade me from getting tattoos and staying out past ten. Now here I am, twenty-seven, and on full lock-down enforced by my ex. Life is fucking weird.

"Look, I know it's Saturday, and I know that's what you do, but I can't lose this contract." If I don't have music, I don't know what I have.

Emptiness? More time to focus on my heartbreak? I'll self-destruct in no time. Even if we haven't been the same since we got signed, I never want to lose my grip on what makes me whole. Music. The tunes. The way I smash my sticks into the drums. It helps me to remember I'm alive, and if that's gone, what will I do?

Kieran snorts, walking past with a piece of pepperoni pizza hanging from his mouth. "Sneak out. No one will know," he says nonchalantly like he doesn't even fucking care we're in this predicament because of him.

He's why Whispered Words is failing, and it hasn't gone unnoticed by Callum either. Sometimes I wonder what life would have been like if we had never met River. We wouldn't be here, that's for sure. But we'd still be brothers and damn happy about it, too, unlike now, where we can barely be in the same house without bickering or wanting to throw punches. Or, in Callum's case, beating the shit out of Kieran every chance he gets. Been there. Done that. Cleaned up enough of their blood to last a damn lifetime.

"Why? So, you can move on without us?" Callum asks in a low, deadly voice, cracking his knuckles.

Kieran grunts, tearing into his pizza again. "Going to kick my ass again? Hmm?" He raises a haughty brow, practically begging Callum to punch him in the face. I'm rooting for that. Maybe it'll knock him back a peg or two and pull his ego out of his ass. Stupid fucker.

"No fighting. You're an asshole. Go eat your damn pizza and leave them alone," Asher gripes, walking past with a plate of pizza. He shakes his head when Kieran narrows his eyes at him, grinding his teeth. "Just shut the fuck up. We're here to stay. Get over it," Asher says, softening his voice. "This is our last opportunity. If we don't take this seriously, then we can kiss our music career goodbye."

"Not if I can fucking help it. I've got my agent on the lookout for better contacts. Away from that lying, cheating, manipulative…"

"Don't be so insulting," Callum grumbles, cutting Kieran's words off.

"Right, because you still love her?" Kieran asks, stepping into Callum's face. "How can you love someone who went behind your back and kissed and fucked and cuddled another man? Why?" Kieran growls every word, pressing his nose into Callum's as they face off.

"I don't," Callum growls back, pressing further into Kieran.

"Right," Kieran scoffs like he isn't still pining for his childhood best friend.

"Fuck off," I say, laying a hand on Kieran's chest and pushing him away from Callum's rage-filled body. "Go eat. Leave him be," I growl, narrowing my eyes at Kieran, who smiles through the whole damn altercation like he has since we left Central City. River did a number on his ass, and I can't wait until someone fucks him up and straightens out his attitude problem. Fuck. My fingers curl. A man can dream, right? But could I forgive River for what she did? I don't fucking know.

Once Kieran saunters away and shuts himself in his upstairs bedroom with the slam of his door, I can finally breathe. Turning to Callum, I put a hand on his shoulder and level him with my best serious stare. "Don't get caught, okay?" I mumble, squeezing his shoulder, and he nods. I know he needs this more than anything, especially after the two days we've had under River's rule. But fuck me if he gets caught sneaking out. "Be discreet or some shit. There's a guard, remember?"

"I never do," he mutters, pushing my hand off his shoulder, and heads into the basement, where the gym punching bag calls his name as he prepares for what the night has in store for him.

Tension rises through my body, locking my muscles in a tight grip. Now more than ever, I need to hop on my old bike and ride until I can't feel this black hole swirling inside me and swallowing my insides. I swear, she decimated me—all of us. They may not admit it, but I know it's true. Callum resorted to violence to take his ache away. Kieran's attitude needs a good fucking punch, and if he didn't have such a talented voice, I'd sock him one. And Asher? He's completely flipped from the man I knew in Central City. Sure, he's still domineering and anal, but for someone who didn't even like River as he claimed, he's been a wreck ever since, mostly keeping to himself. The same vibe we had on stage has not carried over since we left Central City. It's like all drive, passion, and love stayed behind. Now, we're a shell of who we once were.

I walk out into the garage and run my fingers over the worn paint of my beloved bike; I couldn't leave it behind. We only made it back to Central City once after winning the Battle of the Bands, and this is what I brought back with me before the real work began. I knew I'd always need it, no matter how much money I made and how many new bikes I could afford. This one holds a special place in my heart for various reasons. Not only did it help me win multiple times on the racetrack, but it's where she sat with me and helped me christen it for good luck. God. I'm so hopelessly fucking in love with her still.

Fuck! How? Why does my heart continue to squeeze like it's been put in a vise, draining it dry?

Even after the heartbreak and all the shit she did to us, I can't help myself but to think of her and feel flutters. Stupid heart. Stupid fucking dick. Why can't I work her out of my system? She cheated on you with that scumbag! And then, when I'm almost to the point of getting over her, she shows up in a short, come-fuck-me dress, begging me to tear it up to her hips and fucking punish her for breaking my goddamn heart. I squeeze my eyes shut and take a deep breath.

The video of her and Van screwing lingers in my memories in the background. As always. Yes, I absolutely will always love River West. But fuck. My heart cracks into tiny pieces again. Usually, I take that emotion-filled feeling inside me and utilize it the best way I know how—beating the shit out of my drums. I can never seem to shake her, though. She's a ghost living rent-free in my mind whenever I close my eyes. And it's very fucking irritating not being able to let go and long for someone who was a passing phase in my life and fucked us over so hard.

Rifling through a tall box situated near my bike, I throw on my helmet for safety and ignore the burner phone vibrating in my pocket. At least I made one good decision since I got famous, never giving out my real phone number to groupies.

Since there's nothing other than the sandy beach on her side of the road and a mile-long driveway down to the gate, I'll have to stay on the pavement or take a joyride through our grass lawn. I smirk, imagining her yelling at me for being so damn loud and tearing up her grass. I'd love to get her all fired up and witness it once again.

Once I'm seated on my bike, the entire world disappears. It's nothing but me, the wind in my mullet—or my helmet since I'm a responsible guy—and the long road ahead of me. I rev my engine and book it down the light-up drive, going full speed until the gate comes into view, forcing me to stop suddenly. With heavy breaths, I can't help but to let my head fall back and laugh to myself. Shit. This is what I needed to let loose.

Adrenaline pours through my veins, breaking a grin across my face. Happiness and relief I haven't felt in days lifts me to the clouds like a damn drug keeping me in its grip. Thank fuck. I revel in the heady feeling when I race up the drive again, jostling over rogue rocks and tiny bumps in the road. I whoop, returning to the road's end nestled between each house, and my heart soars with excitement and pure fucking joy.

"Rad!" I whip my head toward the figure standing at the edge of her grass, clutching a large sweater around herself. Hell, even dressed down in her starlight pajama bottoms, a messy bun, no makeup, and a scowl—she's still hot as fuck. It's too bad she went and broke my damn heart.

"Can't hear you, Pretty Girl!" I yell, cranking up my engine again as I sit and watch her with amusement. A smirk pulls the edges of my lips when she narrows her eyes, sparkling in the bright moonlight. Yes, Pretty Girl. Give me all your anger, baby.

"It's nine-thirty at night, Ashton!" she barks, stomping toward me with determination.

"I still have thirty minutes, Mommy!" I shout again, revving it until she's standing right beside me and clasping my wrist.

"Yeah. You still have thirty minutes until you're grounded," she quips, shaking her head. Running her fingers over her bun, she finally meets my eyes when I throw my helmet off and give her my best grin.

"Then give me thirty more minutes to blow off some steam. Unless you want to help with that, Pretty Girl?" She sucks in a breath, and her eyes dilate before she shakes herself out of it.

Huh, she's still horny for the Rad Ride. I'll store that in the back of my mind for later, whenever I need it. Like tonight, when Mr. Fist meets Mr. Dick, and they come together with Mrs. Strawberry lube. It's a fantastic union, and she'll be the center of my fantasy.

"Not happening, assface," she says, glaring at me when I shrug.

"Had to try. If I can't have booze or girls over at your other mansion, you're all that's left." I cock my head, letting my hurtful words dig deep into her heart like her actions did mine. Would I invite other girls over? Fuck no I wouldn't.

Instantly, I know I've landed my mark when her face hardens, and she steps back. "Listen, my kid is asleep on the couch. Can you at least wait until tomorrow? She isn't feeling the best," she says softly, avoiding my eyes.

My brows furrow. Right, the kid she had after we left. Who more than likely belongs to Van's dumbass. Why couldn't she have been mine? Why couldn't my swimmers have won the damn race and given me my mullet baby? I clench my jaw and slam my helmet back on my head.

"No can do, Pretty Girl. Now, if you'll excuse me," I grunt, revving the engine and taking off.

Or I would have if a little dark figure didn't run right in front of me, screaming at the top of her lungs and stopping in front of my accelerating bike. I grunt, overcorrecting myself, and narrowly miss her by a fucking millimeter. My heart pounds when my bike wobbles, jostling my entire body until it tips over. I go fucking down onto the road. Hard as fuck. All the breath leaves my lungs as I'm dragged an inch, but it's enough to inflict some damage. My back scrapes against the pavement as my bike dies and flies somewhere in the middle of the road.

My breaths come in short pants as I stare at the twinkling stars mocking my luck. My entire body heats as pain envelops me, and I groan, thankful for the helmet protecting my damn head from scrambled brains.

"DADDY!" A LITTLE FRANTIC VOICE YELLS ABOVE ME, DRAWING MY EYES to her. "He's dead!" she dramatically cries, laying her head on my chest. "No, wait! His heart is still here," she says softly, wrapping her little arms around me and squeezing with all her might. "You'll be okay, Daddy, I promise."

"Daddy?" I groan, trying to regain my breath as her words register in my mind.

Daddy? Who the hell is she calling daddy? I'm no one's daddy. I mean, Pretty Girl could call me that as I spank her ass. But, no. Fuck. She wouldn't.

"Lyric," River says softly, but I hear the concern laced there when she pulls her child off my chest. Grunting, I reach up and tear off my helmet, throwing it to the side. Fuck. My head pounds. "Hey, Rad. You okay?" she asks, gently running a finger down my cheek. Slowly her fingertips run down my chest, poking through a new hole produced by the fall in my shirt. I hiss, trying to slap her hand away, but my body doesn't cooperate with me. "You took a hell of a spill."

"Yeah," I groan, sitting up and taking stock of my injuries. "I'm good." The world spins in an array of colors when I go to stand, stumbling into River as she catches me and wraps her arm around me. Her fingers dig into my side as we take a few unsteady steps, wobbling on my jelly legs. She grunts, continuing to hold me up. "Fuck," I hiss, trying to regain myself and pull away from her. She smells too damn good and fits too perfectly to my side. I can't fall down this River rabbit hole again, because I know where it leads—to heartbreak.

See? My fucking head is all over the damn place.

"Yeah, I don't think so," she murmurs with a resigned sigh. "Come on, let me check you over before you go to sleep. Can't have the talent dying before you even get started."

"I'm fine, Pretty Girl," I murmur, leaning into the warmth of her side.

A pounding headache roars through my brain as she drags me through

the front door of her house and settles me into a chair situated in her spacious living room. I squeeze my eyes shut, pinching the bridge of my nose, pleading for the room to stop spinning before I puke. Fuck. My stomach churns, and a knot forms in my stomach when the sweet scent of River's body wash hits my nose.

"You got some hellacious scratches, Rad," River murmurs, poking at my aching back. I flinch away from her touch, and she sighs. "Want me to clean the wounds?" I nod without thinking, giving her permission.

"I got bandages!" says the little voice again from in front of me. "Mommy, I'll help," she says in a serious voice filled with determination. "Daddy needs them all over."

"Ly, you and I need to have another discussion about running in front of cars and wandering off. You can help, but we'll discuss this more later," River sighs, tugging at the back of my shirt and lifting it to expose my back. "Do you want me to help?" she asks me cautiously in a soft voice.

"Uh, yeah. Thanks," I murmur, secretly loving the way her fingers feel as they ghost over my aching flesh as she pulls my shirt over my head and places it over the arm of the chair.

I hope she sees the pain I etched into my back via lyrics and musical sheets. I hope she sees the agony I've lived in for the past five years inked into my flesh in the form of skulls, knives, and anguish.

"Barbie or fishes?" the little voice asks until I peel my aching eyes open and focus on the little beauty standing before me.

The world ceases to fucking turn, skidding to a halt as my eyes widen. My body weaves back and forth. I suck in much-needed oxygen, trying to clear my vision. Rubbing my eyes, I finally focus on the little River standing before me with her dark hair bordering between brown and jet black. She gives me a toothy grin, holding up two boxes of Band-Aids with colors swirling through them, obviously made for children. I blink a few times, staring into her eyes that look an awful lot like someone else's who lives across the street.

"River," I say in a low voice, leaning forward. My lips pop open in surprise. "Either I have a concussion, Pretty Girl. Or I'm staring into the eyes of…" I whip my head to her as she stands beside the chair, shaking her head with tight lips. I go to stand, but River pushes my shoulder down and frowns.

"I'll get the alcohol," she murmurs, stepping out of the room, muttering something about a fifth of vodka and needing something to drink.

I turn my attention back to the little girl standing in front of me and really take her in, feeling my chest cave in.

"You want fish, Daddy?" she asks, holding the box up. "You have a boo-boo right here," she says, roughly poking her finger onto the spot on my forehead. "There's blood," she says with a frown, holding her little finger right in front of my eyes. "See?" she asks until I wrap my fingers around her wrist and inspect the small dot of blood soaking into her fingerprint.

"Fishes are fine," I mumble, blinking rapidly at her as she pulls out a small Band-Aid, poking her tongue out until she's huffing, trying to peel it open. "Here," I say, taking the tiny piece from her and peeling back the paper. Her unmistakable mismatched eyes search my face, looking for more injuries. "What's your name?" I whisper in awe of the little girl roughly sticking a Band-Aid on my forehead.

She frowns, pouting out her bottom lip. "You don't know my name, either?"

"I'm sorry, Little Pretty Girl," I whisper, shaking my aching head. "I hurt my head. I can't remember right now. I totally know." I try to give her my best smile, but she sighs, staring down at the ground. Her entire demeanor falls, and her shoulders sag in defeat.

"Mommy said my daddies weren't ready to be daddies. But you don't even know my name," she murmurs, sniffling a little. "You don't remember me. You don't love me."

Jesus Christ. Talk about someone reaching in and tearing your heart out. Only she's itty bitty and holds my beating heart in her hand with just those simple words. My face falls as I try to recall if she's said her name, but my goddamn brain rattles in my head. God. I haven't taken a spill like that in years.

Reaching forward, I put my hands on her shoulders, forcing her eyes to meet mine. I swallow hard, staring into the eyes of my former best friend, and my stomach falls out of my ass.

"Your eyes," I murmur in amazement. "You have such beautiful eyes." The same brown spot located on the same side as Kieran's twinkles back at me.

"It's Lyric," River says, coming back into the room with cotton balls and a bottle of alcohol. "And I didn't know it could be hereditary. Apparently, genetics are a hell of a thing."

My fingers tremble on her tiny shoulders, slightly shaking her. That's all the damn confirmation I need to send my heart into a flutter. Question after question runs through my mind. Like how? Why didn't she tell us? Fuck. What the hell happened after we left?

River had a kid—that I knew of as of yesterday, at least. But she had our kid—Kieran's kid—and no one knew. Fuck. Fucking Kieran. That dog dick. His words from yesterday echo in my rattling mind, and I groan. I'm too injured to think this damn hard about anything. He knew. And he doesn't give a shit about her.

I curl my fingers into fists and grind my teeth. Not only from the pain of the alcohol on my back but from Kieran's betrayal, too. Even if River fucked us over, he has a living, breathing human with his DNA walking around, and he discarded her existence. For what? Fame? Fortune? The band?

"Lyric," I confirm, turning back to the little girl, slowly wiping away the fat tears dripping down her cheeks. "Hi, Lyric. I'm Rad."

Her little eyes narrow at me. "I know. You're my daddy. Mommy said," she says in a small voice, waving a hand at River, who stiffens beside me.

"Why don't you give Daddy a little slack, Ly? He hit his head, remember? Always remember to wear a helmet. How about you cover his boo-boos in those bandages and make him feel better." A sly smirk tugs at the corner of her lips as the scent of rubbing alcohol fills the air. "Might hurt a bit," she murmurs before placing the cold as fuck alcohol on my stinging wound, which I don't think she minds doing one bit. In fact, I hear a sadistic laugh from under her breath every time she cleans a wound.

I hiss through my clenched teeth, making Lyric smile as she pulls out a wad of bandages, and I know by the determined look in her eyes she's about to punish me for not knowing her name by placing those brightly colored bandages filled with images of ocean life to my skin.

"So, Lyric," I start, grunting when she climbs onto my lap and starts placing Band-Aids on certain spots on my jaw, cheek, and chest. "How old are you?"

"I'm four. Mrs. Harper is my teacher; she's not very nice. Apple says she's only mean 'cuz she had to poop." I snort at her story, cracking a smile as she continues rambling and placing three more Band-Aids on my face.

"Lyric," River chastises, shaking her head with a laugh.

"Go on, Little Pretty Girl. Tell me all about Mrs. Harper and how mean she is," I indulge her, fighting through the pain of River dotting my wounds with more alcohol.

"I'm in preschool," Lyric says, poking her tongue out again when she sticks a Band-Aid right over my pierced nipple. Her nose crinkles. "Are you a robot?" she asks, touching it through the bandage with a scrunched-up face.

I chuckle. "Nah, Little Pretty Girl. It's a piercing. Like this one," I say, pointing to the septum piercing I've had for years. "And a few more." Like hell am I telling a four-year-old there's metal in places she's not allowed to see below the belt. Only her mother would get that honor. If that ever happened again, that is.

Her little eyes light up, tearing the shadows away from my heart. If this is what happiness is, then I never want to leave. No matter what River did, this tiny human calls me daddy, and that's all that matters to me.

"Mommy, I want my booby pierced, too. Just like Daddy," Lyric says, causing River to choke on her own spit. I bite the inside of my cheek, trying to cover the smile begging to emerge. This kid is something else.

"Jesus, Ly. No booby piercings for you. Where did you even hear that word?" She shakes her head, and a red tint spreads across her cheeks. "You have got to stop watching TV," she murmurs to herself.

Lyric shrugs, looking over my face and chest with satisfaction. "All done!" she beams, wrapping her arms around me. Gently, she squeezes herself against me and pulls back, cupping my cheeks. "All better, Daddy," she murmurs with furrowed brows. "Will you come see me again?" She blinks a few times.

"As long as your mom says it's okay," I whisper, pushing a few strands of her hair out of her face, and she lights up. "I'm right across the street now."

"And my other daddies?" she whispers.

"All there," I breathe without thinking about my words.

"Okay, Ly. I'm sorry. But it's your bedtime. It's ten-fifteen, and you, my love, need your beauty rest." River offers her a hand, and she quickly takes it.

"I'll see you tomorrow, Daddy," she says with the biggest, heart-melting grin as they disappear behind the wall separating the living room from the rest of the house.

"See you," I whisper, clamping my eyes shut, letting everything I've learned in the past forty-five minutes really sink in. I have so many questions for River and so few answers to go on.

My head still pounds when I stand from the chair, checking out the pictures lining the bookshelf near the fireplace across the room. Young River with baby Lyric in her arms, nestled in a hospital bed. Wet tears line River's cheeks, but her smile lights up the damn picture.

"It was right after she was born," River says, standing stiffly beside me. "I was two weeks overdue, and she refused to come. Longest day of my life," she says, blowing out a breath. "Nine pounds, three ounces, and twenty-one inches long."

"She's amazing, Pretty Girl," I rasp, trying to keep the brewing questions at bay when she sighs.

"She's something else. She's special," she says, side-eyeing me with glossy eyes. "Just don't make promises you don't intend to keep. She's four. She won't understand when you walk away."

"Whoa. Wait. Walk away? That's awfully presumptuous of you," I say, curling my hands into fists at her accusations.

She shrugs, wiping her face, and turns to leave the room. But I'm hot on her trail, shoving her gently against the wall. Her jaw tightens when I cage her in, trapping her body against mine. Fuck. The warmth of her breath feathers across my cheeks, and her heaving chest bumps into mine. Do not pop a chubby. And do not—Shit, I looked at her tits in her tiny sleep shirt. I shouldn't have done that. I shake my head and tame the wild little Rad and reel myself in before I end up poking her in the stomach. Yeah, she'd chop little Rad off before she ever let that happen again. I happen to like my damn disco stick intact, thank you very much.

"Why didn't you tell us?" I ask, scrunching up my nose, refusing to acknowledge the burn tingling the tip. "Pretty Girl, we would have come back no matter what. I just…"

Every muscle in River's body freezes. Squeezing her eyes shut, she blows out several controlled breaths until two small tears fall from her eyes, cascading down her reddened cheeks. Her fingers curl into fists, and her entire face scrunches angrily.

"You don't still have a knife buried in your pajama pants, do you?" I quip, watching her hands like a hawk, so she doesn't hold my balls hostage with her little knife. The River from before would most definitely kick my ass and stab me sideways with no regret.

She lets out a cruel laugh and shakes her head. "If I had my knife, you'd know," she says, taking another ragged breath.

Well, thank fuck for that. I don't need any more holes than I have in my body.

"It was two weeks after my mom died," she confesses with stirring emotions, choking me up as much as her. With tear-filled eyes, she glares directly at me with a hardening stare. "Two fucking weeks, Rad. Two weeks of silence. Two weeks of being thrown away like I was trash. If you had known, you'd have come back? Yeah right. You know what I did? I ran to Cal's to tell you all that I had found out. I just wanted to talk to you and resolve whatever happened. But you were gone, and Gloria called you. And you fucking rejected my child. You said it was probably Van's. And then…"

"Back up," I say, holding up a finger and jumping headfirst into the past when we left Central City. Every word River spits in my face, my heart breaks a little bit more. "You said Gloria called us? When? She never called us or told us anything. As far as I know…" My brows furrow, thinking back to the time we left and the time we got here and won our music contract. She didn't bother to call Kieran until after, and it was only to let him know about his stepdad. And that was a doozy of a call. Besides, he would have mentioned it to us, right? Fuck.

"She did it right in front of me. She said…" River closes her eyes, reliving the moment over again as if it's dragging her under and drowning her. Pure emotions reach out from her soul when she opens her eyes, and the tears fall, squeezing my damn heart. No matter what happened between us, this moment broke her for eternity. "You guys didn't want Lyric. And then she handed me four restraining orders, Ashton. So, what am I supposed to believe? Huh?"

I cringe at the sound of my first name, reeling back. Ashton. She only calls me Ashton when she's upset with me or fucking me. But this time around, she's pissed as hell. I'd rather get back to Rad.

Wait a minute… My lips pop open. "Restraining orders?" I question, furrowing my brows. My damn churning stomach drops. "What the hell is happening?" I groan, rubbing my fingers over my forehead as my headache continues to rattle around in my brain, putting pressure behind my damn eyes. Maybe I have a concussion after all. Is this shit even happening right now? Or am I hallucinating? Shit. I know I'm not. She's breathing heavily against me, crying out in frustration I don't understand. But I want to. Something about what she says doesn't sit right with me. There are things not adding up. I'll get to the bottom of it.

Just as I'm about to grill my Pretty Girl like a damn delicious steak and hash this out, the loud rumbling of a familiar motorcycle echoes from outside, rattling the windows. My heart drops.

"Fucking Cal," I hiss, hanging my head at his totally discreet retreat. If he wanted to get out of here unnoticed, then he failed…miserably. So, fucking miserably I'm now missing the opportunity to have an important discussion.

"What the hell was that?" River asks, stiffening where she stands. Her eyes whip to mine and harden when I give her my best innocent smile, which isn't very innocent looking. "Rad," she barks with authority, pushing me back without a fight, and heads toward the window, peering through the blinds. "Is that Cal? Where is he going?" she asks as his lone headlight lights up her house and takes off down the mile-long road, where he'll use his code to leave the premises. If he was trying to be sneaky about leaving, he fucking failed spectacularly. "Ashton," she holds out my name like a damn song, and I lose all control of myself.

Blowing out a breath, I sigh. "He's gone to fight."

Her eyes widen, blinking several times. "I'm sorry. You said fight?" she asks skeptically. "Like…" She holds up her fists in a mock fight until I nod. "Why?"

"Why do you think?" I asked as softly as I can. "You broke us. When he saw…" I shake my head. "It's not my place to tell his story."

She snorts a humorless laugh. "Right. When I kissed Van and he saw? Maybe he should have been there ten minutes earlier when that fuck nugget pushed his way into my house. Didn't you idiots ever think, I don't know, to try and communicate with me about it? That asshole forced himself on me in my kitchen. Forced. Himself." She punctuates every word with venom, punching the organ in my chest and pounding wildly.

I swallow hard, memories of her history prickling my mind. That stupid, wild party and the unpleasant night River and I shared. The moment I picked her broken body off the hard ground and put her in my car after her assault, and carried her into the hospital, always stayed with me. She was so small, so fucking broken then.

"What?" I ask, scrunching my brows. "He forced you? He…" He fucking took what he wanted, and she didn't have a say in it.

"We'll talk about this later," she says, pulling out her phone and calling someone.

"Later?" I ask, stiffening. I want to continue this conversation, but fuck, if she thinks… "No. Fuck Cal. I want to talk about this right now, Pretty Girl," I plead, cradling her jaw in my palm, trying to learn more about that night and about the entire situation.

"Yeah, later. You're taking me to wherever Callum has run off to if you want to keep your contract." She raises her brow and steps away from me, while bringing her phone to her ear and sighing. "I never thought I'd ever say this, but I need your help. Can you come over? Mhmm," she mumbles and hangs up. "Let me put some clothes on, and then we'll leave."

Fuck. Fuck. Fuck. Not only did I find out a whole stack of shit I had no clue about, but now I was about to take River into a fighting den full of angry assholes looking for a fight or pussy. Shit. I may not know all the information about what happened that night, and I'm getting the sneaking suspicion that someone is lying. And that someone is not her. But who?

A soft knock lands on the front door as River races down the hall, shoving her foot into a pair of worn sneakers. My eyes light up at the tight band shirt clinging to her chest and hugging her curvy sides. Tight jeans cling to her legs and fuck. If I could shape-shift into fabric, I'd be the denim between her thick thighs. Shit. Discreetly, I fix my dick who has a mind of his own. Asshole. That's three times now he's tried to show himself. But I guess when he smells the sweet pussy of his girl, he gets a little too excited.

"Hey, thanks for coming over," she says in a soft voice, ushering someone in.

"Ash," I say, stiffening when he meets my eyes.

"Your bike's in the middle of the road," he says, disregarding my greeting and avoiding my eyes. Bastard! He knew! He fucking knew! That's why he said that shit to Kieran. Mother fucker.

"Yeah, I almost ran my kid over and had to bail," I murmur, rubbing my chin. "You know, don't you?"

"I know," he says slowly, confirming.

"Only since yesterday. It's amazing. So many people know. Now, you," River demands, pointing a finger in my direction. "Take me to Cal. And you babysit, please. She's sleeping soundly down the hall. She shouldn't wake up. Just please don't snoop," she says, folding her hands together, and he nods.

"Anything for her," he says in a low voice full of emotion. Swallowing hard, he continues to avoid my gaze.

"Perfect. Thanks. Now, Let's roll." She waves a hand, begging me to follow her out the front door, and I do once I grab my torn-up shirt.

"We'll talk about it later," Asher murmurs as I pass, staring straight into my eyes.

"Somethings not right, man," I say softly, watching the shadows outside swallow River until she jumps into her SUV.

"Yeah," he says, looking away. "You're right. It's not."

Callum

Her smile hangs in my memories like a memorial of something I once had—my Little Star. The girl who brought out the best in me, helped to build me up, and then let me crash and burn in the worst possible way. I rub my chest over the masterpiece plastered on my skin in her honor.

Her lies eat away at my every waking thought, drowning me in the pain of her betrayal, even after so many years. No amount of distance eases the pain of watching your life fall apart at the seams.

Low music hums in my ears through my earbuds, low enough to be aware of my surroundings. Music eases some of the pain tearing through my chest. I focus on the words wrapping around my brain and unclench my fists, preparing myself.

My second reprieve stands opposite me behind the cage of the octagon, staring daggers in my direction. With a menacing smile and a scar running the length of his left cheek, he should send shivers of apprehension down my spine. But I wave it off, focusing on the screaming and heavy drums in my ears easing my soul. If he wants to fuck me up, then I'll serve myself up on a platter for the taking. Knock me around. Bash my fucking skull in. It's what I crave when I step into the cage—anything to momentarily numb the memories trying their hardest to resurface. I eye him again as a small man whispers to him, standing on a stool to reach my opponent's impressive six-foot-seven height.

"He's going to annihilate you, man." I peer over at the fight coordinator, Ruthless, as he likes to be called, nervously biting his bottom lip with a frown. Worry sits behind his dark gaze, and he shakes his head, running a hand through his dark locks and grunts.

He's an intimidating man himself, running this entire operation with his brothers. Standing at six-five, with his body covered in tattoos and a part of an underground gang, he should frighten me, too. Hell, there are a lot of things that should scare me. Not him, though. He's as harmless as an annoying gnat fluttering around. However, he's rarely on edge like now, bouncing on his toes and forming fists. He shakes his head.

"Seriously, Cal. You need to rethink this entire thing. He's going to

bash your damn skull in," Ruthless grunts with irritation, glaring at me. What does he care? I'll make him money tonight by taking a few punches. "Not to mention he fights fucking dirty. I better not have to scrape your brains off the damn mats after he razor blades you."

"That's what I'm hoping for," I mutter, pulling my arm across my chest and stretching out. Ruthless continues his spiel on how I'm about to die and that he's not responsible for burying my body or carrying me out of here when The Beast tears me a new asshole and takes my heart.

"You have a damn death wish every time you come in here," he huffs, pushing away from me with a frown deepening the wrinkles on his fore-head. "Just be careful. And watch the damn Beast's moves," he hisses out a warning with finality, nodding toward the tall asshole across from me, jabbing his hands out an excessive amount of times.

The crowd wanders into the old bleachers on either side of the gym we're currently taking residence in. An old panther's logo, peeling from the walls, stares back at me with its mouth wide open, and the words East Point Prep splattered above it. I've never asked Ruthless how he came upon this empty campus. Years before, it was a prestigious prep school, then turned into a public school. Somewhere along the way, it was aban-doned for good and left to rot.

I've never inquired on how he uses this without getting caught, despite the parking lot full of cars. Somehow, we're never interrupted by law enforcement, and I'm forever grateful for the reprieve from real life. This is my haven. It's where I go when my head fills with too many memories that my brain refuses to erase and knocks them into a black box.

The rising voices of the crowd crescendo through the vaulted space, infiltrating my ears over my soft music, which is another nuisance. I close my eyes and take several deep breaths, calming myself down and drowning out their cheers and taunts by tuning into the heavy melody playing through my earbuds.

My mind drifts to a faraway time, when I was nestled in the arms of the girl, I thought I loved—my Little Star. Even now, butterflies flutter in my stomach, heightening my nerves. That woman opened me up on so many levels, bringing out the confidence I shut away.

Fuck. I take several deep breaths, focusing on the smile she'd give me out of the corner of my eye, giving me tingling skin and tied tongues every time. Or the way we laid so many nights under the artificial stars placed above her bed. The memory of sneaking in through her unlocked sliding glass door, slipping beneath her sheets, and holding her tight, always rests just within reach in my mind. There's something so precious about River West and what we shared for all those months until the rug was pulled from beneath my feet.

Ultimately, in the end, she ruined it by turning her back on us and sneaking around. So, we did the same when we left without a goodbye.

Some days, I wish I had that closure to grasp instead of wondering how she took it or how she was. No matter how badly she tore my heart in two, she's always with me.

My breath shudders when another unwanted memory resurfaces in the forefront of my mind. I stand rigidly as it flashes like a movie flickering to life, unable to stop it as it advances on me like a waking nightmare. Only this time, I don't try to tune it out. Instead, I keep it close and let the rage, pain, and heartbreak overtake me as fuel for the deadly fight I'm about to endure.

Van growls, locking his eyes on me when I emerge from the shadows of the hallway of River's apartment. My brows furrow when he pushes her up against the kitchen counter, slamming his lips into hers. Taking a step back, I shake my head, swallowing the bile rising in my throat. Out of instinct, I take my phone out and snap a picture of her infidelity. I may remember every detail of this moment, but my brothers need proof to move on. If they didn't believe it before, they will now, just like me. There was no way I believed anything that came out of Asher's mouth. He was never ready for her, always standing on the sidelines like an observer.

"She's been cheating on us." Ash's voice echoes in my mind as I witness the deepening of the kiss and the unmistakable sound of her pleasure. "Cheating." Again, it plays, forever haunting me as I retreat from the situation with haste and don't look back.

The world sits on my shoulders when I throw open the sliding glass door, and I halt my exit, listening to the muted conversation down the hall. It's barely a whisper in the wind, and I'm unable to make out what they're saying.

Every inch of me splits into two at the heartbreak soaring from her betrayal. Fat tears track down my cheeks, but I quickly wipe them away. She doesn't deserve my tears. Or my heart. Or anything that has to do with us. She took our love and crushed it in her palm, easily throwing us to the side for Van fucking Drake.

"Callum." My name is a plea on her lips as she reaches for me, begging me to stay and saying more words I can't understand over the roaring emotions turning inside me.

"Goodbye, River," I mutter, giving her one last tear-filled look as I retreat and memorize her horror-stricken face.

She mutters more words, calling me back into her apartment. But the loud pounding of my heart drowns out her voice until I've made it to my car and hop in. For several minutes I stare through the front windshield and collect myself, turning every ounce of feelings I have off.

For the first time in years, I felt alive in the arms of the woman I grew to love. She brought me out of my shell and helped me face the world. I gave her my first, and I gave her my last. No longer will I allow women in my bed to manipulate or use me. My only future is the one in the limelight, playing my bass and living out my dreams, trying my damnedest to forget River West ever happened.

A drum pounds in my chest again as I revel in the anger her memory stirs and savor it for later. Never will I forget the kiss she shared with Van in her kitchen as I watched from the shadows. His shirt was off. His filthy hands were all over her. She didn't protest when he leaned in and kissed her lips. That's all it took for me to turn my back on her and walk out the door. Yet, here she is again in the flesh as our new band manager, living directly across the street from us, sent straight from the devil himself to torture our already fractured band. She'd never know it, but she's the reason we're four separate people who happen to play music together instead of one brain creating masterpieces.

She's also the reason I'm here tonight, eager to have my memories erased. One kick and punch at a time if that's what it takes.

Blood pumps through my veins as my steady heart speeds up, thumping against my ribs, while adrenaline pours through me. Steadying my movements, I watch my opponent's every move, memorizing his strike and speed. In the back of my mind, I catalog them, storing them for later when we square off. So I can use it against him. No one here knows my superpower. They'd never suspect I use the very thing I'm aching to be relieved of to become the champion.

I blow out a ragged breath, bringing my shirt over my head, and lay it on the stool beside me. Finally, I take out my earbuds, letting the full effect of the audience overtake me. I continue stretching out, getting everything limber for the chaotic fight I'm about to jump into.

As the minutes tick by and Ruthless calls our names at the center of the beat-up octagon, all my thoughts leave, finally giving me the blank thoughts I've longed for since yesterday when I came face to face with my most bothersome nightmare.

I shake out my limbs and stretch my neck from side to side, forgetting everything. Inside the cage, there's no past, present, or fucking future. It's only my opponent and me. My fists against his. His kicks against mine.

The crowd grows louder as bets are placed around us when the bell rings, and we descend on one another. The Beast smirks in my direction, lazily making his way toward the center of the ring, where I wait for him to advance, and we tap fists as a sign of respect.

Rolling my shoulders back, I take the first hit to my right temple, and then the predicted uppercut knocks me back a few steps, knocking the air from my lungs. Swerving right, I barely miss his next throw and regain my stance with a sadistic grin.

A small cut opens on my forehead, trickling warm blood down my cheek, dripping to the mats below. I grin more in his direction when he advances with a frustrated growl again, with a cockiness dictating his every move. He's so damn confident he's about to take me down, but I have more tricks up my sleeve.

Stepping to my left, I throw up my arms and block his next hit, thudding against my flesh. A chuckle bubbles up from my throat when I leap back, putting my fists to my side.

"That's all you got?" I ask with a light tone, smiling more when his nostrils flare. Like a bull running at full speed, he advances toward me in a fury of fists and kicks my thighs as his answer.

Around and around, we go trading punches and kicks. With a grunt, my foot lands in the middle of his abdomen, knocking him back a few staggering steps. Exhaustion sweeps through his fallen expression as he stumbles into the cage, bouncing off it with a huff. With one final growl, he advances on me, pummeling me with a fury of fists against my skull and jaw. Black dots spot my vision until adrenaline blasts through my veins one last time, and I knock him back with one single blow to the head.

Victory rings through the crowd, howling my name so loudly the walls shake and clap with enthusiasm. I grin, raising my tired arms in the air, as The Beast lies flat on his back with his arms curling in the air, looking lifeless with his eyes closed. Bruises line his body and face, swelling from the intensity of my hits, and peace washes over me.

"Rock Star! Rock Star!" they chant over and over as Ruthless grips my bloodied hand in the air, waving it around in victory.

"You fucking did it," he mutters with an impressed grin.

I snort. "And you doubted me?" I raise a brow, gazing through the crowd, memorizing all the usual fans heading toward the betting desk to cash in on their winnings. All thanks to me.

My mind melts into static with no visions of my memories coming to the surface. This is the moment I live for. The minute I stand in victory with my arm raised and my emotions buried so damn deep, even my photographic memory can't touch them and torture me.

Standing on my throne above the rowdy crowd, I gaze around, taking everyone's faces. My eyes grow wide, and my entire body stiffens when a pair of familiar green eyes stare back at me with her arms crossed and her brow raised.

"Fuck," I mutter as Ruthless lets my arm go and pats me on the back in congratulations.

"Your cut is at the booth or…"

"Donate it to the usual charity," I say, unable to break my gaze.

Satisfaction roars through me when her eyes wander down my bare chest and widen at the art adorning my flesh. All the air leaves my lungs when she stiffens, eyes locking on the intricate tattoos carved into the skin over my heart. Her jaw falls, and her brows furrow with confusion. It's a special piece I knew she wouldn't miss once her eyes locked on it. If only I had wanted her to see it yet.

"You got it," Ruthless says, stepping to the side of the ring and demanding one of the workers clear the blood off the ground and get ready for the next fight.

My heart pounds when Rad tenses beside her, discreetly shaking his head at me. Guilt swims across his features, and he swipes a hand down his face, shrugging over the situation like he had no choice but to come here with her.

I know the moment I walk over there; my ass will be facing the music. My fate—our fate—lies in her hands. But it was all worth it. The sneaking out. The fight. Even if it means our music career is completely over. It was a good fucking ride. Maybe I'm ready for it to be over because you never really know what you have until it's yanked from your grasp.

I long for the brothers I had before. The ones who looked after me and never turned their backs on me. I long for the basement concerts. Something that was just for us. Sure, I love the stage and more than appreciate my fans. I wish I had more time to live for myself and enjoy the music again. An ache forms in my chest, longing to turn back the clock to a simpler time.

My mind turns off momentarily, letting me forget the persistent memories knocking around in my head. For one fleeting moment, I had peace. And now, I'm about to shatter it with the reality of what I've done.

I take one last long sweep of the crowd, finally breaking River's stand-off. The usual suspects dot the crowd, talking with their buddies and drinking beers with smiles. In the corner of the room, I take stock of a large man near the bleachers, huddling with three other men. Something in the back of my mind tells me to pay attention to this moment because, in these parts, they're strangers.

"They newcomers?" I ask Ruthless, nodding to the men in question, and he nods.

"Friends of The Beast," he says with a shrug. "Been here a few times before." I rub my chin at the new information and purse my lips. "That one is Adrian something or other," he says pointing to a larger man, scowling at his friends. "Then there's Kaleb, Derek, and Greg."

I narrow my eyes when the large man, Adrian, leans down, having a heated discussion with a shorter man dressed in black, hiding his face from view under a ball cap. Shaking my head, I shrug off the odd feeling building in my chest in a warning. Whatever they're discussing sends Adrian on his way with a scowl. By the way, his head soars above the crowd; he's a few inches taller than the Beast I destroyed. Speaking of...

I peer back at the giant still laid out in the octagon, mumbling to the shorter man who was with him until they hoist him up and cart him off the mats.

Collecting my shirt and earbuds from the stool where I left them, I take a few steps toward River and Rad, standing in the back of the crowd, just as the big man knocks into both of them, flinging River to the ground. My damn heart jumps out of my chest, and my jaw clenches. She shrieks angrily, her entire body disappearing from view.

My lip raises in disgust when he looms over them, poking a finger into Rad's chest. With every poke the big man gives, Rad's face tightens, and his nostrils flare as he goes toe to toe with him and doesn't back down. Fuck. I have to get over there and help him, despite our differences these days. He's still my oldest friend, no matter the weird tension we've felt lately between the band. We've never been the same since we left Central City. Or since River West.

I curl my fists, laying my shirt over my bare shoulder, and beeline it toward Rad, whose reddened face gives away his rising rage. He's two seconds away from snapping on the man, just like I am.

"Watch yourself," I grunt, getting into Adrian's face and bumping his shoulder as he continues leering down at River, sprawled out on the sticky floor.

"You watch yourself. You think just because you won against him, you could win against me?" he growls, grinding his teeth together.

He inches his face toward mine, snarling as he takes me in. I roll my eyes at his attempt to rile me up and shove a hand into his chest, knocking him back a step.

"Shut up and leave," I say, folding my arms across my bare, sweaty chest. "Or you'll have the same fate."

Blinking a few times in my direction, he chuckles at me. A smirk lifts at the edge of his lips when he peers down at River again, letting his eyes roam the entirety of her body. A deep growl works its way up my throat at his apparent interest, and I step up again, forcing him to look at me. Not her. No one looks at her like that.

He smirks at me and waves a hand like I'm not worth the effort. "Sure, I will," he chuckles without another word and leaves the building without fanfare.

"Fuck's sake," River grumbles, slapping Rad's awaiting hand away, climbing to her feet.

Rad frowns, bringing his hand to his chest. "Rude," he grumbles, shaking it out.

River's nose wrinkles as she brushes the dirt from her jeans and rights herself. "What an asshole," she huffs angrily, watching where he disappeared. Turning her gaze to mine, she raises an expectant brow. "So, fighting. Huh?"

I blow out a breath, running a hand down my face. How the hell do I explain this to her and keep our contract intact? I might not want this anymore, but Kieran's sanity depends on this damn gig. If he doesn't have music in his life, I don't know what he'll do. And the other two haven't said they're ready for a change. Not that we fucking talk anymore, but still.

"Um, yeah-yeah," I stammer softly, getting lost in the expanse of her green eyes that soften at my voice. "Better than drugs," I mutter as dread fills my system.

That was a different time when my open wounds still bled from the lies, and I took things into my own hands to forget the misdeeds of the woman I loved. The poison was too accessible, and we had too much money at our fingertips. Only, it didn't work. It never took the pain locked in my damn bones away. It didn't even numb the ache in my chest and left me craving more. After days of detox, I sought other forms of relief. Then came fighting. One knock to the skull, and all the pain hidden inside my body disappeared into thin air, and sweet oblivion took hold, letting me forget my misery.

Blowing out a breath, she shakes her head almost in disappointment at me. "Okay, well. Obviously, we need to have a little chat. So, let's roll," she says, waving a hand and taking off toward the door without another word or looking back.

"Sorry, man," Rad murmurs, standing close to me as we follow her through the exit and step out into the warm air. "But you weren't exactly discreet with your escape. Next time, roll your bike to the damn gate or something." He side-eyes me with disappointment.

I shrug, poking at a children's bandage plastered to the side of his face. "Why are you wearing so many?" I grunt, pulling my shirt over my head and situating it against my sticky skin.

He rubs the back of his neck, looking at River, who walks ahead of us and then back to me with apprehension.

"I, uh, fell off my bike, and her kid patched me up," he says softly, keeping his voice low.

I snort. "With fifty bandages? Damn. You hurt?"

"So, you don't know either, do you?" he whispers with discretion, stopping our retreat by curling his fingers into the front of my shirt and bringing us chest to chest. His dark eyes widen with desperation.

"Know what?" I ask, trying to pull away from him, but he clings on.

"You should see her, dude." His whisper comes out with strain, holding back tears and swallowing the emotions. Shaking his head, he swallows hard. "She's the spitting image of him." His lips roll together, and he shakes his head. "Do you ever feel that something isn't right about how we left and what happened? Like something feels so fucking off right now. Have you ever felt that way? Like everything was set up just a little too easily?"

"What are you talking about? Who is she? And who's the spitting image of who?" I ask through my confusion. My heart falls into my ass as the past rushes forward at his words. He had the video. I had the picture. It was as clear as day as to what happened. She cheated. We left. End of fucking story.

"Lyric," he mumbles, wincing when River calls our names from the parking lot and puts her hands on her hips. "River's daughter. Kieran's daughter. *Our* daughter." The way he says our gives me pause.

My entire body locks up. "What?" My breath leaves my lungs as my mind reels. "Kieran's? Ours?" What the hell is he saying?

"Yeah," he whispers, letting me go and heading down the path toward the darkened parking lot.

"What the hell are you talking about?" I hiss, stomping after him and grabbing his shoulder, stopping him again. My brows furrow. "What do you mean Kieran's kid and her kid? Our kid? She...." I stop dead, reliving that night over and fucking over, like so many times before. It never leaves, especially since she walked back into my life a day ago. Maybe I missed something. Perhaps my damn emotions ruled my decisions that night. But fuck. I trust Asher with my entire life. So, would he lie to us?

"She called me daddy, dude. She..." He shakes his head again, wiping a hand down his face looking more heartbroken than I've ever seen him. "River and I talked. But I think you need to talk to her, too. Especially about what you saw, bro. I think..." He shakes his head wearily. "I don't know what to fucking think anymore." With that, he walks away with his head hung low.

What the hell was going on? I shake my head, trotting after him at a quick pace, meeting them at River's SUV.

"Fuck," she grumbles under her breath, patting her pockets. "Did I bring my phone?" she asks Rad, who shrugs in response. She blows out a frustrated breath. "Monday morning, we'll talk about this, okay?" she says, cocking her head to the side when I nod.

"Yeah, okay," I mutter, shoving my hands into my pocket.

"So, you're not kicking us out yet, Pretty Girl?" Rad asks with an easy grin, rubbing his hands together.

"Your contract is safe for another day. Believe me. You're not the only idiots to try and press my buttons. But next time, let's have a discussion before we sneak out. I know you guys had lives before I became your warden. At least you didn't snort coke out of some groupie's ass," she mutters the last part with a wrinkle of her nose.

"What?" Rad chokes, bending at the waist.

"Out-out of the ass?" I ask, clearing my throat and trying not to laugh.

She snorts. "Oh, long story. Can I trust you'll be a good boy and go back to the band house? I don't need to follow you around and document your activities for the label?"

"Scouts honor, Pretty Girl. He'll head straight home," he says, giving me the stink eye.

"Yes-yes. Straight home, boss," I say with a smirk lifting the edge of my lips.

"Fine," she says with a heavy sigh. "Let's go."

I stand back as River starts the car, and Rad pops into the passenger's seat with an animated smile. There's something there with him as he leans closer to her and whispers something. She shakes her head with a small smile before taking off down the highway.

I meander toward my bike and pop my helmet on, starting my Harley. The loud, echoing boom from my exhaust bounces off the abandoned administration buildings of the old prep school. Ruthless once told me why this place shut down so many years ago and why so many people from East Point Bluff refuse to step foot here or pretend this place doesn't exist. It chills my blood to know such a powerful and murderous cult walked the same streets I do now.

Taking off down the highway, everything hits me at once. Rad's words. The fight. My memories. Most importantly, Kieran's daughter. His comments from the limo fester under my skin, and my teeth grind.

If he fucking knew about River's daughter, why hasn't he said anything? Why hasn't he stepped up and taken responsibility for her? Fuck. My brain screams at me as I travel along the highway and finally make my way to the gates separating our new home from the outside world.

"Daddy," a small voice rings out through the darkness of my mind, rousing me back to the land of the living.

I groan, wiping the damn drool from my lips, getting my bearings. Where the hell am I? I swipe my palms along the textured surface of the chair I'm resting in, bringing back the memories of River's frantic call from earlier, asking me to babysit so she could chase Cal. Wherever the hell he goes at night when he thinks no one else is listening. And I fell asleep.

My brows raise, and I peel my eyes open, staring into the eyes of my tear-stained daughter. Daughter. Shit. I don't think I'll ever get used to that. I adjust myself in the recliner I'm sitting in and sit forward.

"Daddy," she whines again, pulling on my shirt with a little grunt, waking me up completely.

"Lyric," I rasp, quickly clearing my throat when she snuggles her bunny close to her chest and sniffles. "Are you okay?"

"Mommy is gone. Other Daddy is gone. You're here," she says tiredly, rubbing at her eyes with a frown. "Why?" she asks in a small voice, eyeing me up and down.

"I said I'd see you tomorrow, right?" I ask with a soft smile. "Here I am."

"Okay," she says without question, climbing into my lap with the most trusting grin. With a heavy, sleep-filled sigh, she snuggles into my chest. I wrap my arms tightly around her, securing her to me.

"Why're you awake?" Running my fingers through her long dark locks, I pull them from her cherub face and marvel at her familiar features. Up close and personal like this really brings out her mix of features. Kieran's nose and eyes. River's bone structure. Tiny freckles.

"A dream," she sniffles, wiping her nose across my shirt, leaving a snot trail behind.

In normal circumstances, I'd be repulsed by the snot shining on my dark shirt. But this isn't a normal circumstance. This is a little soul who calls me Daddy. And I robbed her of the experience of having us in her life

because of my desperation to leave town. I owe her so much more than snot on my shirt and cuddles after a bad dream.

Guilt presses down on my chest, stealing my oxygen until I take a huge, relieving breath.

"What kind of dream?" I ask, running my fingers soothingly through her hair, hoping to ease the little trembles rumbling through her body.

"Mean monsters outside my window," she mumbles with a sniffle. Her bright, mismatched eyes search my face as it softens for her. "Tap. Tap. Tap," she mumbles, moving her little finger along with the words.

"I won't let the monsters get you, Little One. Ever. None of your daddies will allow that," I murmur soothingly, as her eyes flutter, and her long lashes brush against her cheeks.

Her body wiggles a few more times as her whimpers die down, and she relaxes in my arms. It dawns on me that she trusts me, feeling safe in my presence. After a few minutes, her soft baby snores fill the room as she clings to my shirt. "I'll never let anything bad happen to you ever again," I mutter, studying her face again, getting lost in the soft glow of her skin.

How can I already love such a small human after only a few days of knowing she exists? It shouldn't be possible. But fuck, since the moment she uttered daddy, I was a goner. Lost to the way she held me close and asked me never to forget her again. My emotions have been haywire and spiraling since that moment. Lyric may not biologically be mine, but I'm here for this. I want this. Need this. Need her. She's a piece of me I never expected to find, and now that I have, I can't give it up.

Since River walked into that conference room, I've been biting my tongue. On the one hand, the guys deserve to know the truth about our departure. They've earned the right to know why I did what I did—what I had to do for us to get us here. Back then, it all made sense. All the pressure that was on my shoulders forced my hand. But that was me then, and this is me now, looking back and realizing I was an absolute idiot. Since coming into the spotlight, I've been forced to grow up.

On the other hand, I'm being a selfish fucking prick. If I confess my deceitful sins to the boys on why we had to leave and why I told so many goddamn lies to get us here, then I'll lose everything. The band. Lyric. Hell, even River. My life would implode, and I'd be left to pick up the pieces by myself. There's no way they'll stand beside me after I tell them.

Fuck. The indecision wars in my mind, giving me a damn pounding headache.

I stiffen when the front door bursts open in a flurry of movement. Shielding the little girl in my arms from any harm, my eyes widen as Callum races through with wide eyes and a heaving chest, followed by Rad sheepishly entering the front door with a frown.

"Bro," Rad says, tapping Callum's chest and nodding toward Lyric, situated snuggly in my lap. Callum's face softens at the sight of her dark hair and tiny snores.

"Shut up," I growl, nodding toward Lyric sound asleep on my lap. "She's asleep."

"You assfaces are not supposed to be in my damn house. You keep pushing my damn buttons," River grumbles in a sharp tone, marching into the house and shutting the door. "Has anyone seen my damn phone?" Quickly she checks her pockets and looks around the room with a frown and shakes her head, worry lines creasing her forehead. Her nose wrinkles taking in the bundle in my arms and sighs. "What happened?" she asks, eyeing the position I've found myself in.

"Monsters outside her window," I mumble, clutching her to my chest, rising with a groan. I didn't hold her for that long, but my muscles protest from the stiff position and my refusal to move an inch while she was in my arms.

River blows out a breath, running a hand down her face. "Yeah, that's been happening a lot lately."

"Is it not normal, Pretty Girl?" Rad asks, stepping forward with a grin and staring down at Lyric's sleeping face.

"Oh shit," Callum mutters in the background, stumbling over his feet to get closer.

"Told you," Rad mutters smugly.

"Want me to take her back to bed?" I ask River, who reluctantly nods and leads me down the long hallway of her one-story home toward the bedroom at the far end.

Footfalls softly sound behind us as all four of us step into the purple princess room. Fairy lights decorate the edges of the ceiling, hanging down the walls like rainfall, illuminating the medium-sized bedroom. Clothes, toys, and even snack wrappers line the floor, causing River to frown.

Gently, I place her in the middle of the bed, covering her with the plush comforter designed with princesses and crowns. Perfect for our little girl. Running a finger down her cheek, I bask in the tiny sleepy smile she gives me.

"Night, Daddies. You come tomorrow?" she asks in a little voice, melting my fucking heart all over again. Jesus. All she has to do is call my name, and I'm already wrapped around her tiny little finger. I'll do anything for her, and I don't think I'm the only one.

"Yes, Little One," I murmur.

"Yes, Little Pretty Girl," Rad says at that exact same time with enthusiasm and a grin.

"Yes-yes," Callum stammers in awe, stepping forward and meeting her barely open eyes. She grins at him and yawns.

"Other Daddy," she murmurs, looking up at him and examining his face. "You came, too," she says in tired awe, staring up at Callum with stars in her eyes.

"I did," he manages to whisper, staring directly into her eyes. I see the moment everything truly clicks for him, and he shudders. I'm sure Rad opened his big mouth and told Callum everything.

"Okay. Night, Ly. Sorry, Mommy had to run an errand. Now all your daddies are going to leave. But you'll no doubt see them again," she says with a pointed stare in our direction, silently ushering us out of her house where we're not supposed to be in the first place.

Rad snorts at her sarcastic remark but doesn't utter a word when she shoots daggers in his direction. As quietly as we can, we shuffle through the bedroom door, shutting it behind us. On silent feet, we follow River out to the living room, standing awkwardly in a spaced-out circle, with her putting more distance between us. Looking around the room, she awkwardly shifts from foot to foot and heaves a sigh.

"Um, thanks for the last-minute, late-night babysitting," River mumbles with a cringe. If I could see the inner workings of her mind right now, I'd be able to hear the warring thoughts displaying on her transparent face. "I appreciate it," she says again with a tight smile, standing rigidly in the awkward silence surrounding the four of us.

"It's no problem. I wasn't doing anything, anyway," I say with a shrug.

To be honest, I liked getting to spend a little time with Lyric. Even if it was for a short time. There are still so many questions sitting on the tip of my tongue that I need the answers to. And there's only one woman who can offer those up—Gloria. I'm sure she'll be eager to see my face at her front door this week when I make time to visit her in her penthouse apartment. Courtesy of Kieran's bank account, but that's a whole other story.

River's body turns rigid when Callum looms over her with furrowed brows, staring with confusion. Her eyes avert to the wall behind my head, avoiding his questioning stare at all costs.

"I'm confused," Callum mutters, rubbing a finger along his forehead. "You-you had a baby? She's—" He halts his words and shakes his head. "When?"

River pinches the bridge of her nose in agitation. "Let me guess; you weren't informed, either?" she asks in a low, emotion-filled voice, still refusing to look in Callum's direction.

"None of us were, Pretty Girl. Well…" Kieran. That's what he wants to say.

Maybe that asshole knew and decided he didn't want to tell us because of our new gig. He didn't want to jeopardize our future like I didn't want to either. But she's a child, and she needs us to be in her life. How could he make that decision without telling us, too? It affects us all. *Hypocrite,* my subconscious shouts at me as a familiar burning pain tightens my chest and trickles up my throat. Reaching into my pocket, I grab my antacids and pop two into my mouth. The relief isn't instant when I chew them up, but at least it'll tamp down the pain for a few more hours.

"No. I wasn't aware you had a baby. Let alone… She called me other daddy," he whispers, heaving a frantic breath. "You told her that…"

"I wasn't going to hide where she came from," River cries out in frustration, taking another step back from us and shaking her head. "She knows all about the four of you. For five years, I've been under the impression that you all denied her and didn't want her. You all walked away from me. You didn't say goodbye. You ignored my fucking texts! And then Gloria said you wanted nothing to do with her. I don't fucking know what the hell to think right now." Confusion swims through River's eyes, and her brows dip, creasing her forehead. Moisture pools in her eyes, most likely from frustration and rage. It's on the tip of my tongue to tell them that they'd been tricked into leaving, but I hold my tongue like a coward.

"Gloria?" Callum asks us softly, furrowing his brows again. "What did she do?" Fuck. What didn't she do? She had her hands in our doomed relationship before we even left.

River's jaw works back and forth, and her fingers curl into fists, whitening her knuckles from the pressure. "Listen, it's late. Could you all go? I really don't want to talk about this right now. I shouldn't have to defend myself any more than I have. It's you all who owe me an explanation. I'll see you all on Monday, okay?" River stands firmly where she is, watching wearily as we all nod in agreement.

"Sure thing, Pretty Girl," Rad says softly. "But this isn't over. You know that, right? We'll talk more." He raises a brow when her eyes narrow into slits, and I know a snarky reply sits on the edge of her tongue, ready to tell us all off if I don't get everyone out of here.

"Let's go," I say, grabbing his shoulder and pulling him out of the house as Callum follows slowly behind us with his hands in his pockets.

The moment we're outside, the warm summer air smacks us in the face. I take a breath, listening to the hypnotic sound of the ocean waves crashing against the shore behind River's house. Oh, how I ache to run down the beach, exerting myself into forgetting my sins.

"Fuck," Rad grumbles, picking up his discarded dirt bike from the middle of the road, looking it over under the streetlights shining down on us as brightly as the sun.

"Looks fucked," Callum says, stopping beside me as Rad looks it over.

"No shit, Einstein," Rad grumbles with a frown. "Old reliable has finally met his match," Rad pouts, running his finger over the deep scratches in the metal. "And all it took was one little girl to bring her down. I could have squished her." He touches the side of his face covered in brightly covered bandages and sighs.

"What the hell is going on?" Callum finally asks, shaking his head with frustration. "What was she saying about Gloria?"

"Don't forget the restraining orders on top of that," I grumble, rubbing my chin, still perplexed by that statement.

"That's what she told me, too! She fucking said Gloria handed her four restraining orders," Rad growls, wiping the beads of sweat from his forehead as he lifts his bike off the ground.

"With our signatures on it," I point out.

Callum's gray eyes bug out of his head. "Restraining orders?" he asks, looking to Rad for confirmation. "What the hell? We didn't do that."

"I told you. Something fucking stinks like a dirty coochie fish on the beach." Rad scrunches up his face, grunting when he tries to roll his dirt bike forward.

"But she-she kissed Van," Callum's voice dips low with accusation and hurt, shaking his head in denial. "I saw it with my own two eyes. Right after you showed us the-the video."

My stomach churns at the thought of the video, starring River and Van from when they were together. It was my only tool at the time to convince them we needed to leave without her. I was so convinced she'd drag us down. Now, look at her. She runs the damn show. If only I'd given her the chance.

"Did she? Or did he force her to?" Rad shouts out in frustration, wheeling around and letting his bike drop again. "Because, according to her, he forced himself on her, and you just stood by and took a fucking picture," he growls with flaring nostrils. "And then you walked away, leaving her there with him. Fuck! We all walked the fuck away because of you!" Rad barks, slamming his foot into the dented rims of his turned-over bike. Over and over again, he slams down on the metal, ruining it further. Only stopping when he's sweaty and breathing heavily from the exertion. "Why didn't we talk to her first?" he growls, advancing on Callum with malicious intent, curling his fingers into fists. This is one fight Rad would not win. Callum stiffens, tensing his body and waiting for impact.

"Whoa," I say, jumping between them and putting a hand on Rad's chest. His heart accelerates against my palm when he heaves a breath. "Fighting gets us nowhere," I say, pushing him back a step.

"Well, I want some fucking answers!" Rad shouts through the anguish, pushing me away and nearly knocking me off my feet. "I just want to know why I left the love of my fucking life. What the hell is real?" His chest heaves beneath my palm until he steps back, shaking his head.

"We'll figure it out." My voice trembles as I speak, knowing the truth of the situation already. Although, there seem to be certain factors I never planned that were put into play.

"Where'd you get the videos from?" Callum asks, spearing me with his knowing gaze. I swallow hard and blow out a breath.

"Van sent them to me," I say, rubbing the back of my neck, actively avoiding their stares.

"Out of the blue?" Callum asks again, scrunching his eyebrows.

"Yeah. Out of the blue." I shrug, crossing my arms so they can't see the tremble of my fingers.

"No idea what prompted it?" Callum asks again with more suspicion.

"No, man. I just assumed he wanted to rub it in my face that he was banging her behind our backs. You know how he was back then. He was fucking obsessed with her and following her around everywhere," I huff, throwing my arms around. "I thought I was doing the right thing!" I shout, pulling at the ends of my hair. "I thought…"

I thought I really was doing what was best for us. She was a distraction. Someone they were willing to stay behind for.

Rad frowns, staring at me. "I get it, man. I guess. But looking back now, I don't think we did the right thing." He swallows hard, staring off at the dark house a few feet away from us, housing the girl we intentionally left behind. "We should have talked to her and heard what she had to say. Like now. But…"

"She probably won't talk to us about it anymore," Callum mumbles, rubbing his chin.

"I don't think we did, either," I sigh, biting into my bottom lip as the guilt tears another piece of my soul into the void of no return. I rub my hand across my aching chest, praying the acid doesn't bubble up my throat as punishment.

One day soon, I'll tell them. I just want more time with Lyric before I'm thrown to the side for my atrocious actions. But I don't blame them. They'll never forgive me. River will never forgive me. If I have to sit on the sidelines and watch them happy together, that's a sacrifice I'm willing to make. I just need a few more happy memories to cling onto when I'm tossed to the side and forgotten about.

Callum stops, cocking his head to the side. "Did you hear that?" he asks with furrowed brows, looking into the dark shadows surrounding River's house.

"Hear what?" Rad grunts, picking up his discarded dirt bike.

Callum's face twists, and he shakes his head. "I thought I heard a click or tap or something."

"All I hear is the ocean waves," I offer, looking toward her house with a twist in my gut.

"The monsters coming for you, Cally boy?" Rad taunts, heaving his messed-up bike forward on its damaged wheels.

"Fuck off," Cal grunts, shoving at Rad's shoulders.

"What are we going to do about Kieran?" The three of us halt outside the open garage, listening to the silent house. All the windows appear black, hopefully meaning his grumpy ass went to bed.

"You think he knows? Like for real knows?" Callum asks, licking his lips. A deadly expression captures his face, brewing a fire behind his eyes.

Rad's teeth grind when he throws his bike into the garage without care and growls. "I'll fucking murder him," he grunts, kicking the bike one more time. "If he knew…"

"Doesn't seem like him, though." I shake my head. "If Gloria could concoct restraining orders, then who's to say she told him the truth?" I raise a brow when Rad and Cal exchange a look, and they sigh.

"What do we do then?" Rad asks, shoving his hands in his pockets.

"We don't say anything yet. The ball is in River's court."

"Fine," Rad agrees. "But if all this turns out to be bullshit, I'm reclaiming what's mine," he says, pointing a finger toward her dark house. "And that's a fucking promise." With that, Rad walks away, sauntering into the house without another word.

"What do you think?" I ask Callum, who narrows his eyes at me suspiciously.

"I don't know yet, but I'll find out." With those foreboding words, he turns his back on me, leaving me to stew in my own fucked up mess I made, now with more complications.

THE TALL BUILDINGS OF EAST POINT SURROUND ME, SHINING IN THE BRIGHT morning sunlight. I squint my eyes, taking a deep breath as I psych myself up for my rendezvous with the devil herself. Who knows if I'll make it out alive to tell the damn tale.

All around me, people bustle by, entering the high-end stores lining the area with bright smiles on their faces and exiting with an armful of bags, giggling about their purchases. Speaking of…two stores down, two brunettes dressed to the nines in expensive clothes and jewelry stop abruptly on the sidewalk with shock splayed on their faces.

"Oh, my God," one woman squeals ten yards away. Her big eyes widen, and her jaw drops, staring at me with awe like I'm a fucking rare God standing before them. "That's Asher Montgomery from Whispered Words!" she hisses with excitement to her friend beside her while jumping in place.

"Oh, my God! It is!" her friend shouts, promptly covering her mouth in embarrassment as high-pitched giggles escape from behind her hand. A pinkish tint takes over her cheeks as she stares in my direction with wide eyes.

"I heard they were living closer now." The first girl says in what she thinks is a whisper, but her voice carries loudly to my ears. Quickly, I hold in the cringe, making me want to melt away from the situation.

Inwardly, I groan, loathing this evil side of fame. For one split second years ago, I adored the attention and fucking ate it up with a spoon. I fucking encouraged it with a sick grin, craving the attention of the crowds coming to see us. It took me a long time to realize that no one wanted to know the real me. They didn't want to sit down and have an easy conversation. They wanted my fucking dick. Not conversation. Maybe a baby to claim what's mine. The fans want the man I portray on stage with the cocky smirk and sexy swagger. They want Asher Montgomery, the guitar player of Whispered Words. And that's a straight punch to the gut because the Asher on stage and the Asher walking the streets are two very different people.

This is all part of the gig. I know it is. But it's fucking annoying that I can't walk out of the house without someone approaching me for pictures and autographs. Some people—no matter their gender—offer themselves up to me on a silver platter. Years ago, I was tempted by their sexy curves and golden smiles. Tempted, being the key word. I've kept my dick firmly in my pants since the night I fucked River on that dining room table and came happily in her eager cunt. Believe me, that moment repeatedly sits on a high pedestal in the back of my head. Especially when the loneliness I've imposed on myself crushes my soul one squeeze at a time. My heart has only beat for one annoying Little Brat, even after all these years. It'll never change. No matter how much she loathes us. My heart is hers and has been for the past few years. My guilt has sat with me for too long to settle down, let alone bone another chick.

Politely, I wave as the fans drag their phones out and snap several pictures of me standing before my self-inflicted doom. I try to plaster on a fake smile and greet them with the kindness I don't currently feel.

"Can we take some selfies?" one girl asks, dragging her friend by the hand and stopping before me. She grins when I nod, and we take several selfies together, huddling in a tight hug. Our smiles light up the photos, despite the annoyance I feel.

"Make sure you tag me on FlashGram," I say as she squeals again, nodding in agreement, and they walk away without another word.

I blow out a breath, swiping a hand down my face, trying to forget the dread building like a damn storm coming. Lead sits heavy in the pit of my churning stomach when I take a step forward, continuing to tell myself this is a good idea. Yeah, a really good fucking idea to come here. I hang my head, peering around again and avoiding the issue at hand. A war is about to begin in the confines of this apartment building.

There's absolutely nothing cheerful about the situation I'm walking into. My stomach turns as I walk through the belly of the beast, waving hello to the front desk clerk, and then enter the large elevator. When I hit the top floor button, my fingers tremble from the uncontainable anger rising through my body.

As the elevator whirrs to life, my mind drifts to River's statements about the restraining orders and abortion check she tore to pieces. Oh, how I wish I were a fly on the wall when River told Gloria to fuck off.

The more I think about the shit Gloria pulled, the more my rage consumes me. Sure, I played an equal part in River's demise, but I never barred her from speaking to us permanently. I never told her to get rid of our kid. I just…did something almost equally as wrong. I grip my hair at the mounting frustration and heave a breath.

"Get a hold of yourself," I mutter, squeezing my eyes shut. "Fuck," I grunt, lightly tapping my forehead against the mirrored wall.

As the doors slowly slide open, I step out into the luxurious hallway illuminated by the sun leaking through the tall windows. Opulence decorates every inch of the space. From the beautiful chandelier to the gorgeous paintings lining the walls to the expensive luxury apartment I'm about to walk into—number forty-seven—on the top floor of the largest, most expensive apartment complex in East Point. Only the best for dear old Gloria—she can't seem to hold down a job or take care of her child. Since my father met his fate and got carted off to prison, Kieran's mother has been our problem. Five years of hell in her presence, why not another minute?

I raise a hesitant fist to the inconspicuous white door, halting mid-knock. Do I really want to look into the eyes of the woman who ruined my life without a second thought? No. I'd rather avoid Gloria as I've successfully done for years. Our only interactions are at Christmas when we return to see Camilla and dote on her as she deserves. But Fuck. This is something unavoidable. It's the only way I'll get to the bottom of everything, and then I can start repairing it one piece at a time.

Annoyance rises inside me as I pound my fist into the door with much more force than necessary, gleefully watching the hinges shake. On the other side, tiny footfalls flitter through the air, and the door swings open, revealing Gloria still in her red silk pajamas and glazed-over eyes.

"Asher, what brings you here?" Gloria's face scrunches as her eyes rake up and down my body with a disapproving frown. "I wasn't expecting you today." Gloria tilts her head, and a look of concern crosses her twisted-up face.

"We need to talk," I demand, pushing into her apartment and whirling around. I cross my arms over my chest, glaring in her direction as she softly closes the door.

"Talk? Sure, why don't you just come on in," Gloria snaps, furiously storming toward the large kitchen. "Could I interest you in a drink, Asher?"

I run a hand down my face in exasperation and nod. "Sure, a drink would be nice." And make it fucking stiff—is what I want to say, but I hold my tongue as she flitters into the kitchen, humming angrily about uninvited guests.

"So, what brings you to my neighborhood? I barely see you boys, and we live in the same damn town," she says with disdain, entering the elegant living room with two coffee cups. I raise a brow, noting the steam wafting from one cup as she gently hands it to me, and the familiar smell of coffee hits my senses, perking me up. Sitting beside me, she cocks her head to the side. "How's the band going? Any new tours ahead of you?" She sniffs her cup with satisfaction and takes a gulp, only slightly grimacing when she pulls back.

Of course, she wants to know about any new tours to line her own damn pockets. She's been bleeding Kieran dry since he's struck it rich, and she loves her walking, talking, piggy bank.

"So, have you heard from my father?" I know the answer as soon as it leaves my lips. Gloria scoffs, taking a sip of her drink, gearing up to defend herself for her actions. But fuck that, I let my tongue take the lead—consequences be damned. "That's right, you don't really talk to him after you sent his ass to federal prison, do you?" Not that I fucking care his ass is in prison. I'm glad he's behind bars where he can't hurt another soul on the outside. He's where he belongs, and now, we can protect ourselves and Cami from his wrath.

She blinks several times, and I know I've hit the mark on the head. "Well, I had to do what I had to do," she retorts quickly without missing a beat. "What was I supposed to do when the FBI showed up on my doorstep with evidence? Turn them away? Go to prison with him? I think not." She sniffs haughty, sticking her nose in the air. "I turned him in like he deserved. It was a win-win for all of us."

"It might have been a good place for you," I mutter under my breath, earning a death glare. Perhaps she's not too drunk yet and still has her wits about her. I need to hold my damn tongue until I can get more information out of her.

"You'll do well to remember who helped bring you to where you are now. If it wasn't for my contribution and the car I allowed you to take, you'd be no one," she says, tossing her hair over her shoulder and lifting her chin. "If it wasn't for me, then you'd be in prison yourself, and I'd still be stuck in that loathsome little city. This is where we belong, Asher. You'll do good to remember what we deserve." What we deserve? Is the alcohol making her dumber as we speak? What the hell kind of high horse shit is she on? "So, who cares if your father is spending the rest of his life in prison for embezzling everything? I sure don't."

"Of course, you fucking don't." I grind out. "Nothing has changed for you. We still pay your way." Because of our little sister Cami and that's it.

"If you're going to continue to insult me, then I'm going to insist you leave. Is this really what you wanted to talk about?" she growls as multiple veins pop in her forehead and her face flushes.

"No, that's not what I wanted to talk to you about," I say, running a hand through my hair. "Since we're bringing up the past, let's have a little discussion."

"Oh?" she questions with a frown, probably seeing her future being ripped away.

"Yeah, Whispered Words is officially on probation. Apparently, our sales have been down, and now they're trying to fix us, or we're fired." I blink a few times as her expression falls, and deep worry takes over her sadistic eyes, which widen in horror at our new reality.

"What do you mean your sales are down?" she snarls in my direction, acting like it's all my fault we aren't performing well.

She wouldn't be wrong, though. We've sucked it up this past year, unable to mesh any fucking more. It was only a matter of time before someone pulled the plug. At least this way, we're getting a second chance. Her body sits rigidly next to me, fury blazing through her veins.

"Just what I said," I say through gritted teeth, glaring in her direction. "Our sales are down, and now we have a new band manager. Can you guess who that is?" My fists clench in my lap when she sneers at me.

"No, I don't know who it could be. Why would I know?" she asks with innocence, moving her body away from mine. She takes a small sip of what I can only guess is alcohol in her coffee cup, and I sigh.

"Because you spend enough of Kieran's money, I figure you'd know all our business," I snark, gnashing my teeth together.

Get your shit together and stop letting her stupid face get to you. Fuck. I take a deep, relieving breath to blow the frustration away. There's nothing that gets my blood boiling more than Gloria Montgomery.

I know why Kieran and I decided to move Gloria closer. I only wish we didn't have to. Her broke ass should have stayed in Central City. Back on the poor side, where she came from. Maybe a little humbling could do her some good.

But we did it for our teenage sister, Camilla. She means the absolute world to us, and we wanted to protect her from Gloria's manipulative ways. Luckily, she got away from my father's abuse before it was too late. But Gloria is a whole other story. So, with strong suggestion, our little sister now attends the new East Point Prep a few miles away on the edge of town, safely tucked away in her dorm room. Far the fuck away from the toxicity, sucking the life away from this apartment. When we aren't on tour, we make sure to take Cami out for lunch and catch up on how middle school is going.

"If you just came here to insult me, you can leave," she says, sticking her nose in the air. Her finger points toward the door, and by the look in her eyes, she's shutting down fast.

"River West is our new manager." There. I said it. Let the fucking pin drop.

Gloria's face falls, and her hand comes up to her heart. Slumping back onto the couch, she vigorously shakes her head in disbelief. "But-but, we got rid of her. There's no way that slutty little Central girl is your new manager. She must have slept her way to the top, like every other girl from that side of town. There's absolutely no way. You have got to be joking," she scoffs, leaning down to take a massive gulp from her coffee cup.

Funny. That's precisely what Gloria did to snag my father as her prize. She slept around and climbed her way to the top, one man at a time, until she locked down the wealthiest man she could with a baby, and he couldn't deny it. And yet, here she is comparing River, who worked two fucking jobs and went to college all by herself with no help. Oh, the irony of it all.

"Yeah, and she's had some pretty interesting things to say about you and what happened after we left," I say, raising my eyebrows when her face pales, and she purses her lips, looking far from innocent. In fact, as the statement settles, the shock evaporates, and she smirks with victory. No doubt reliving the moment she permanently booted River from our existence.

Imagine what could have happened if River had been able to call us and explain her pregnancy. No matter how angry they were at her, they would have wanted to know Lyric. Something I'll forever feel guilty about. Fuck. The burning in my chest rises again, sending the nasty taste of acid up my throat and onto my tongue. I rub a hand over my burning heart, wishing the pain would stop before an ulcer forms.

"And by the way, River isn't just some Central girl. River is worth way more than you'll ever be. And I can't believe I let you talk me into doing what I did," I retort without thinking, letting my brewing emotions take the damn lead. Thankfully, I keep the essential part of the equation to myself. For now, at least. She doesn't deserve to know she has a grandchild who will never know who she is.

"Oh please, don't tell me I didn't do the right thing. That Central slut was going to ruin your lives. And you boys were just going to stand back and let it happen. Not on my watch! I had to do something to get her out of the way completely. Even after she told me that little lie about her being pregnant, all she was ever after was your money. She was so damn desperate, too," she says with a roll of her eyes, dramatically huffing.

I study every freckle on Gloria's offended face. True evil lies behind her eyes. She may not look like somebody that could take you down, but in her own unique way, she can. Every emotion hits me at once, amplifying the guilt closing my throat. Gloria unabashedly used me. She took my feelings, my anger, my desperation and put them in the palm of her hand, effortlessly using them against me with her sly, perfectly placed words.

I pull at the collar of my designer shirt and swallow hard. I swear my heart pounds in my ears, drowning out everything else. Gloria expertly manipulated me into doing what she wanted. With her twisted words and helping hand, she got exactly what she desired—getting rid of River. For good. The money she offered me and the promise to keep my father out of it had me where she wanted me, on my knees and begging for more.

Slowly, I get to my feet and chug the rest of the warm coffee she brought me, grimacing at the bitter taste on my tongue. As I contemplate my next moves, I look around, taking in the grand elegance of the home we've provided her with.

Gloria has everything from professional paintings hanging on the wall to the tiny one-of-a-kind designer statue sitting in the corner. And now, her end is near. I will never let another human being manipulate me the way she did.

My gut churns and bile rises at the entire situation. "So, after you manipulated me into this with the promise of money and my father out of the picture, while the boys and I were away and we won, you swooped in and ensured that River would never be able to talk to us again. Did you really think we would never find out about the restraining orders? Or the check you gave her?" My voice rises with every word, making her cringe back.

"Why do you care what some Central girl has to say? So what if I gave her four restraining orders? Judge Drake had no qualms about helping me secure your future and Van's," she says with a wave of her hand like it means absolutely nothing that she ruined not only River's life but Lyric's. "Besides, look at you now. You guys are the biggest rock stars around. What is she going to do?"

"River is in charge of our contract, Gloria. If we fuck up, then River sends us on our way. Our contract will be void. No more money. No more rock star status." I shake my head, running a hand through my hair in frustration. Tightly, I grip the longer ends, basking in the release of my festering temper. Talking to Gloria is like talking to a four-year-old who doesn't understand the word no. Hell, Lyric understands better than this grown woman, and I've only had brief conversations with her.

I slam my cup down with more force than necessary, praying a crack forms. Glaring down, I take in every inch of Gloria's pathetic form. What a conniving, money-hungry woman she's become. If only she'd known what an exceptional little girl Lyric would become.

"And you're wrong, by the way. River wasn't lying about the baby. Congratulations, Grandma," I say just as I maneuver through the front door, slamming it in her shocked face before she can utter a single word.

Racing down the hallway toward the elevator, I press the bottom floor button and slump against the mirrors as every inch of my flesh tingles and trembles with the exhaustion sweeping through me. So, it's all true. Everything River has been adamant about. Gloria served River with actual restraining orders, signed by a real sneaky judge, hellbent on getting everyone away from River and isolating her. I may have driven the guys out, but Gloria put the nail in the coffin. No wonder I never found River online whenever I snooped. She'd either erased herself off social media or blocked us long ago.

As I make my way out of the building, I clutch my chest and let the entirety of the situation crash down on me. I made the most monumental mistake of my life. Not only did it affect me, but it affects five other people. Old Asher was selfish, stuck up, and a manipulative asshole, and I let Gloria rule over me, bending my will for a few thousand dollars. She dangled my little sister's safety in front of my eyes like a carrot on a string, playing with my need to protect her. I knew it was the only way to drag them to safety, away from my controlling and abusive father. So, I did what

I did to protect the people around me. When the only thing that my heart truly wanted was the girl I left behind on purpose.

Leaning against the sleek high-rise, I take several deep breaths and process the conversation I just had. Nothing prepares you for walking into the lion's den, and that's what I just did. As I search the distance and all the stores surrounding me, filled to the brim with shoppers and happy mothers and daughters and sons, a familiar person catches my eye across the street, coming out of the phone store with a perplexed look adorning her cute face. In a split-second decision, I make my way across the street and loom over her small frame as she stares down at a new phone in her hand. Before I open my mouth, I take the time to examine the woman River has become. And boy, do I like what I see.

"NEW PHONE?" I ASK IN A LOW VOICE, HOVERING OVER RIVER AS SHE stands on the sidewalk, oblivious to her surroundings.

Her brown hair sways with the light breeze brushing down her back. I swallow thickly when her scent envelops me, knocking me back a step and straight into forbidden memories that tickle at the back of my mind—reminding me of the times we shared. Now it feels like a lifetime ago. Seeing River and being around her takes me back to the simpler times when all I had were dreams and aspirations and my girl at my side. Even if we fought like cats and dogs, I'd take that feeling of playing at Dead End and watching her over the fame and fortune I betrayed her for.

"Jesus!" River yelps, jerking her body back from mine with a slight screech. Several shoppers walking past stare intently in our direction with curious eyes, startled by the noises coming from her.

Her expression morphs into a deadly scowl aimed in my direction as the fright wears off. From one scathing look, my balls shrivel, and I swear a fire starts breaking out across my flesh, causing me to pull at the collar of my shirt.

She huffs, putting a hand over her heart, and mutters words I can't quite understand. "You can't just sneak up on people like that, Asher," she barks, heaving a breath. "It's rude."

"Sorry," I say, putting my hands up placatingly. My teeth sink into the side of my cheek, concealing the small smile trying to pull at my lips. "I didn't mean to scare you. I was just in town and saw you over here. Thought I'd come over and say hi." She blinks at me a few times as my words register, deepening the wrinkle on her forehead.

Jesus Christ. What the hell has gotten into me? I'm suddenly transported back to when I was a teenage boy, nervously talking to the first girl I ever laid eyes on. Nerves bristle under my skin. My palms friggin sweat so much, I'm wiping them down my jeans.

River rolls her eyes and sidesteps me, moving along the sidewalk slowly. "Why exactly are you following me?" she asks, shoving her new phone into her pocket.

Good fucking question. Why am I following her down the sidewalk when my car rests a block away from here? Why not just turn on my heel and walk in the opposite direction? The short of it is, I can't. There's a pull between River and me, begging me to tag along as she actively avoids looking at me. Perhaps my crushing guilt pushes me to fix things, or maybe, I genuinely miss her—my Little Brat.

"It's a nice day for a walk." I shrug, shoving my hands into my pockets, and fiddle with the lone key poking into my finger.

The sun's heat blasts down on us as we walk side by side toward the middle of the square that makes up the center of downtown East Point Bluff. Several restaurants feature outside dining, where guests drink their coffees and enjoy a spread of breakfast items while chatting with their loved ones.

"I guess," she says, unconvinced, peering around at the other people walking past on the semi-crowded sidewalk.

All trepidation leaves her face, falling to the wayside when we step into the square and stop directly in front of an unfamiliar shop bustling with noisy customers.

The glorious scent of rich coffee wafts through the air, perking up my senses. The absolute shit Gloria offered me stains my taste buds with its awful flavor, making me eager to wash it away. Not to mention, it did nothing to perk me up.

"Want some?" I ask, gesturing behind us as she looks around at the other shops around the square, still avoiding my gaze.

The remnants of the heated conversation between Rad, Callum, and River hang heavily in the air. Every muscle in River's body seems to tighten with my suggestion, and her mossy green eyes find mine. Apprehension rests behind her gaze as she silently questions whether she should take me up on my offer. "Maybe a muffin, too?" My stomach rumbles at the thought of stuffing my face with sugar. I couldn't touch food this morning without my stomach tightening into knots, but now that the conversation is over—all bets are off.

Her eyebrows furrow as she looks between the shop and me again. "This is really fucking suspicious, Evil Ash," she says, pursing her lips while looking me over for ill intent. I'm unsure what is going through her mind, but it seems to be racing. My breath hitches in the back of my throat at the sound of my old nickname leaving her lush lips. Once again, bringing back the raging memories of our long, complicated past. "As long as you're buying," she says with a slight shrug, throwing open the front door.

I snort when she rushes into the shop without ensuring I am following, seeming so confident that I will be by her side and buy her the things she demands. Something so simple and small settles inside of me being this close to her again. River West has this aura about her that drags you in like a moth to the flame, and I can't seem to help myself. No matter how badly this turns out, the moment River finds out my role in the entire situation, she won't want anything to do with me. I will take my time and truly show River how sorry I am even before I confess my sins.

The smell of delicious coffee permeates the air as I slowly stroll behind her. Radiant energy cascades from her as she smiles at the people around her, pulling them into her happy little bubble. River waves to a few people around the shop, only stopping once to say hello to an elderly gentleman who greets her like she is family. She smirks back at me the moment we head toward the counter, making butterflies burst in my damn belly. The moment the barista's beady eyes set on her; I swear his entire face lights up like fireworks exploding.

"River!" he happily shouts, smiling as we make our approach together. An eerie feeling settles in my gut when his eyes roam her body, greedily taking her in. A deep red blush takes over his neck and cheeks when she smiles at him again in greeting. Something odd bubbles inside me, and on instinct, my fists curl at my side, ready to bash his way too happy face into a pulp. There's just something about him that doesn't settle right with me. "Same thing today?"

"Hey, Nathan. Same coffee. Same breakfast muffin. But this guy is paying for everything. And also, whatever he wants," she says with a sly smirk, patting me on the chest. The moment she indicates she's with me, the barista cuts his gaze to me, giving me a withering look.

"Sure," Nathan says tightly, dropping an octave and oozing with disapproval. "What can I get you?" His teeth grit, popping a muscle in his jaw. I would never notice the slight hostility dripping from him if I wasn't such an observant person. But there it is in his unwavering stare.

It's pathetic at best, but I offer him my friendly smile. "Thanks for asking," I say, looking at his name tag and leveling him with a condescending smile. "Nathan. I'd love your best Peppermint White Chocolate Mocha and a chocolate muffin." Discreetly, I scratch my nose to hide the grin tugging at my lips when he scowls. Begrudgingly, he puts in the order, pressing his lips into a tight line.

In some sick and twisted fate, an intense possessive feeling washes over me when he side-eyes River with a romantic interest. To her credit, she stands utterly oblivious to his affections, without an ounce of interest. Instead, her eyes lock on her new phone as she types something out quickly.

"Your name?" he asks as I give it to him, and he writes it down. "Okay, that'll be thirty-four, ninety-nine," he says, reclaiming his smile when I pull out my wallet and hand him a fifty.

"Keep the change."

I want to tell him that she is way out of his league and that he should set his sights on somebody more his speed. River West would chew him up and spit him out in two seconds flat. Believe me, I know. As I waltz to River's side, I make a show of it, leaning in a little closer than necessary. My shoulders brush hers, and surprisingly she leans into my side without conscious thought.

Nathan's hands curl into fists on the counter until he sharply turns away, mumbling under his breath. If I were a betting man, I'd say he's 100 percent going to spit in my drink as revenge.

"So, you never found your old one?" I ask, peeking over her shoulder as she signs into her cloud, sets up her new device, and gets back all her old pictures, messages, and everything in between.

"You're very nosy this morning," she grumbles, shoving her phone into her pocket again and hiding it from view.

"Just observant," I mumble, staring deep into her gorgeous eyes that further pull me into her. I don't know how I ever thought I'd get away from River and feel complete. The black hole that once swallowed my selfish heart slowly closes the more I'm in her presence.

She rolls her eyes. "I don't know where it went. I think I lost it at that fighting ring." Blowing out an angry breath, she crosses her arms in aggravation. "How long has he been doing that?" She quirks a brow as her eyes silently beg for answers.

"Right," I say, stroking my chin.

Callum's fights. The one he runs to whenever things get too tough, instead of opening up and confiding in the people who have always been his family. Well, until he was scarred for life, witnessing Van shove his tongue down the love of his life's throat. Fuck. No wonder we are falling apart at the damn seams. We can't even confide in each other anymore. All we do is argue, and it fucking shows in our performances. There's so much tension between us I have a hard time understanding where it came from. But the moment that thought enters my mind, I stare at why we fell apart. Years ago, I thought River would be the cause of our demise. I swore up and down that she would be the reason Whispered Words would never make it. And it doesn't hurt to admit I was so fucking wrong.

"Um, a few years," I say, clearing my throat. I can't pinpoint when Callum started sneaking away and returning with bruises and broken ribs. All I knew was that he came back lighter and full of life. If only for a few days, that is. Somehow, he managed to get on stage with a smile and makeup covering his wounds.

"River!" shouts Nathan, standing behind the counter with her drink proudly lifted into the air. "And Asser," he says with a tiny smirk pulling at his lips, slamming my plastic cup onto the counter, causing it to spill.

Huffing, I grab our two drinks and muffins from Nathan, who again gives me a nasty look when I bat River's hand away as she tries to take her drink. Without handing them over, I secure a booth, hellbent on getting her to sit with me. I know the second I give her a chance, she'll scurry away with her free meal, and I can't let that happen. Making amends starts now, and I'll throw everything in my arsenal to earn her forgiveness.

"But why?" she asks, snatching up her large blueberry muffin and coffee from my side of the table. Studying the blueberries adorning her muffin, she nibbles her bottom lip with contemplation. "Doesn't seem like his style," she adds, biting into her muffin with a happy groan.

"No, it doesn't, but it seems to ground him. I guess," I say with uncertainty.

The reality is Callum erected thick walls the moment we left Central City. The entire three-day drive from Illinois to California was painfully silent on his end. So much so that you wouldn't even know he was there. He barely uttered his food orders, let alone let us in to witness how deeply he was hurting. Hell, he still is. Callum has never divulged why he fights on Saturday nights, letting guys bash their fists into his skull, but I have a sneaking suspicion it all loops back to River. All our failures and our successes have always been because of that girl. And here we are again, in an endless circle of leaving and finding each other.

Her eyes meet mine as she sips her coffee. "Grounds him? He snuck out, endangering your contract, and you have no idea why he did it?" She raises a knowing brow. "What the hell happened to Whispered Words, Asher?"

You. That's what happened to us. Everything about you is embedded in our souls. Apparently, we're unable to function properly without you in our lives. But I don't say that. Instead, I smother my words by taking a hot sip of my coffee, risking the damn spit that might be in there.

A deep sigh rocks through me, letting my eyes roam out the windows, taking in the bright sun beaming down on the people outside and continuing their shopping. "A lot of shit happened to us. Fame and fortune." I shake my head, losing myself in the memories of our past.

"Where the hell is Callum?" I bark, pacing the backstage area with my hands gripping my hair. All the control I've carefully crafted over the past few months slips between my fingers like fucking sand and blows in the damn wind.

Kieran sits back, watching me with a calculating eye. "Where the hell do you think he is?"

"I don't fucking know, but we go on in less than an hour. He wasn't here for sound check and isn't here now. Rad, where is he?" I growl, stomping up to Rad, who twirls his drumsticks between his fingers and shrugs.

"Bro, I'm not his keeper. He'll be here," Rad says with indifference, frowning as he taps out a beat on his knee.

"Find him!" I bark again, pulling at the collar of Rad's shirt, bringing him to his feet.

"Get the fuck off me, Asher," Rad hisses, pressing his nose into mine as violence storms through his eyes. "Do you want to know where the fuck he

is? He's trying to drown away her memory. Something I wish I could fucking do, too. One day I'll forget, but you know he won't. Ever. What he saw... What we all saw from that fucking video will live in his genius head forever. Give him some slack. And get the fuck off me."

"He's here," Kieran says lazily, pointing to the door blankly. The light disappeared from his eyes when we left Central City, changing his entire demeanor for the worst.

Silently, Kieran has been falling apart behind closed doors, growing angrier and angrier by the damn day since we left Central City a few months ago and started this gig. For now, we're playing at smaller venues and trying to expand our fanbase. We're in the studio during the day, recording our first album with approved songs from our old playlist and new ones we've been forced to write. Every piece of this career is worth it, but slowly it's breaking us apart. Sometimes I wonder what would have happened if River had been with us all along.

Fuck. The familiar guilt swims through my veins, crushing through my chest again. Someday soon, this feeling will leave, and I'll be able to forget about River West and what I did to make her go away. I had to do what I had to do to manage to get us here. No matter the sacrifices I cut off. First, I must keep the damn band together before we implode. I can practically taste success on my tongue because we're just getting started.

"Callum." All the breath leaves my lungs at the sight of him slumping against the door frame of our green room. Heavy bags plump out the flesh beneath his eyes. "You look like you've been run over by a fucking truck," I say with horror, marching forward and getting in his face. "Where the hell have you been? And... Have you showered?" I sniff the air, catching the hint of body odor and heavy amounts of alcohol.

"Fuck off," he grunts, pushing past me and plopping on the couch next to Kieran. "I'm doing just fine." A whimsical smile falls over his lips when he leans his head back and shuts his eyes. "So, damn good."

Kieran raises a brow, examining Callum's face. "Yeah, he's high as a damn kite right now." Shaking his head, he leans back and pinches the bridge of his nose.

"High?!" I shout, throwing my arms out. "What the fuck, dude!"

"Chillax, Ash. You're giving me a damn headache with all your anal bullshit. Dude, take a shower and wash the stink from your ass. We're on in like thirty minutes," Rad says, shoving Callum off the couch as he stumbles toward an adjoining bathroom, catching himself on the door. Turning to look at us through hazy eyes, he nods in agreement and promptly slams the door in our faces. The moment a wall separates us from view, the sounds of his retches and gags, followed by vomit hitting the toilet, fill the air. I cringe with my stomach turning and try to tune out the disgusting sounds from the bathroom. There's no way in hell that we can continue like this and stay together. Something has to give...

"What the fuck?" I hiss, continuing my frantic pacing in front of the guys.

"He's just trying to forget," Kieran pipes up again with an indifferent shrug, staring down at his phone. "Leave him alone. Get the stick out of your prude ass."

I blink a few times, listening to the shower turn on and sigh in relief. Soon we'll be out on stage, and nothing will take away from that, not even Callum's newfound drug addiction, which he'll hopefully leave behind very soon.

I shake myself out of the memory drowning me. It took Callum twenty minutes to shower, which gave us enough time to find him some clean clothes. Our show went without a hitch, despite Callum's head not being in a suitable space. As soon as the show ended, he disappeared into the night again, only coming back the following day with a black eye and renewed life flashing in his eyes. That night, he promised us he'd leave the drugs behind. And he did. He was somehow giving it up without a fight. Only his new drug was the fight nights he found through the grapevine and aligned himself with some mafia family taking residence at an old, abandoned prep school.

"And you?" River asks, narrowing her eyes, taking the last piece of her muffin. "You're nothing like the Evil Ash I knew back in Central City. You seem…" She taps her chin several times, trying to find the word she's looking for. "More settled. Not as uptight as you used to be. Did you finally pull that stick out of your asshole? What changed in your world? Did you finally drop the demon?" Her eyes memorize my passive face, finally meeting my stare, and she smirks. Quickly, she turns away and licks her lips. A red tint explodes across her cheeks as she sits up straight.

I smirk at her outburst, noting how uncomfortable her posture seems, and sip my coffee. "Times change," I say with a shrug. "People change." I hum, take a bite of my muffin, and sip my coffee.

The moment I left my hometown, everything lifted from my shoulders. My father was no longer on my back to join his company. In fact, he was no longer in my life. After finding our way to East Point Bluff, I severed ties entirely with the man. The only time I ever heard about him was the news when the bars slammed on his face, and he was sentenced to prison for his crimes, leading to a whole new crock of bullshit. The only feeling that followed me from home was the constant guilt, crushing my soul for manipulating the girl sitting in front of me. Nothing prepares you for that when you decide to betray someone.

"But do they, really?" she questions, sitting back and folding her arms.

Licking my lips, I distract myself by pulling apart my muffin and shoving it in my mouth. "Sometimes," I say, staring out the window. For good or bad, people change every day, and I happen to be one of them.

"Why did you leave?" she exclaims, adjusting herself in her chair with a grimace.

I raise a brow at her, staring off at the apartment complex in the distance. Why did we leave? Because I felt like we had to.

"You see that apartment building over there?" I ask, pointing out the window toward Gloria's home.

River huffs. "You know what? Forget it. I've explained a lot of shit to you assfaces over the last few days, explaining myself over Lyric. But you assholes can't even answer one question I have." Slamming down her cup, she moves to get up, but I catch her by the wrist. When my flesh touches hers, a fire ignites beneath my skin, and electricity darts up my arms. Taking a deep breath, I ground myself.

"Gloria lives in that apartment complex." Her expression falls, and a paleness washes across her face. "That's why I was downtown before I saw you. I had questions for her myself."

She swallows hard, settling back in the chair. "What did that conniving bitch have to say for herself?" River asks, a flame burning bright in her eyes, ready to burn the world at her feet. That's the River I remember. The girl who took no one's shit, especially mine.

"Well, you have the conniving part right. I went to have a friendly discussion with her. After what you said to me in the hallway, I had a lot of questions I needed answers to." River blinks rapidly, grinding her teeth so hard a vein protrudes from her neck. With a wave of her hand, she silently encourages me to keep going. I sigh, running a hand across the back of my neck. "We didn't sign restraining orders, River," I say in a low tone, reaching across the table and chancing my fingers when I brush against hers. She doesn't pull away from my soft touch, but I can tell she wants to back away and put as much distance between us as possible.

"You didn't?" she asks, pursing her lips and keeping her emotions locked tight behind the fire in her eyes.

"She admitted to getting Van's dad to sign the papers without our signatures," I say, gripping her hand in mine. "Believe me. We didn't leave on those terms. We…"

"Then why the fuck did you?" Pulling her hand from mine, she shakes her head and abruptly stands from her chair. "One day, you guys were my fucking world, and then the next, you left me a grieving mess and deserted me like I meant nothing. Did I not deserve a text or a phone call that you were leaving without me? You promised me that we would go together. I played my part, Asher. Why didn't you? Huh?" Every word she speaks slowly gets louder and louder until the eyes of the other customers fall on our little spat.

River's chest heaves as her fists curl at her sides. She's kept this in for so long that I can tell it's worn her down, and she cannot gain the answers she needs. And it's all my fucking fault. I need to piece us all back together. It's my responsibility now. Whatever happens to us in the future, I will make this better. Even if I have to sit on the sidelines and watch my best friends be happy, this is what I deserve.

"I'll tell you everything if you sit," I murmur, pointing to the chair, and silently I beg her to follow my direction.

With a huff, she sits on the edge of her seat, preparing to dart off if I don't give her the answers she wants. I swear my heart skips a beat, and my tongue sticks to the top of my mouth. I could tell her nothing but the truth. I know that. I could get on my knees, beg for forgiveness, and explain my role in everything. But in the back of my head, I know the consequences if I lay the reality out for her. Lyric's sweet face pops into my mind, calling me daddy with a grin lighting up her tiny face. My conscience yells at me to confess and reveal my bad decisions, but my mouth works faster than my guilty conscience, covering my damn tracks.

"A few weeks before we left, you asked for space after what happened to your mom. It was hell being away from you when you were hurting so bad. Kieran was clawing at the walls to get back to you and take you in his damn arms. But—uh—someone sent my phone a video of you and—um —" I blow out a breath, working myself up to say what I need to say. My fingers fiddle on the table, twiddling my damn thumbs.

"Spit it out, Asher. I'm getting pretty pissed off," she snaps, running her tongue across her teeth.

"Someone sent me a video of you and Van screwing around in the back seat of his Mustang." River stops moving. Hell, I swear she stops breathing at my confession and narrows her eyes. "It came with a text that you'd been screwing him behind our backs just after we'd gone exclusive with you. And…"

"So, let me get this right," she says with a thunderous expression clouding her face. "You all got a video of me and Van doing the nasty. The same Van who had stalked me for months and never really stopped until I left. The same fuckin Donavan Drake who broke my heart as a teen because his mommy and daddy fucking hated my guts. And your first thought was, yeah, that's what River would do when she wasn't with us?"

I swallow hard, feeling the hints of her anger squeezing around me. It's so palpable in the air everyone within a five-foot radius moves away from the hurricane building inside her.

I lick my lips, lying through my fucking teeth. "Callum saw you," I say, trying to clear my throat. "He…"

"Ah, yeah. That's the proof you need then, huh?" she asks with her face twisting in anger. The vein in her forehead expands, and a redness encases her entire face. "He waltzes in uninvited, just like fucking Van did. Then Van forcefully shoved his tongue down my throat, and you know what? Fuck. You. All. We were adults. Do you know what adults do? They have conversations. They communicate with each other instead of leaving without a goodbye." Promptly, River stands, slamming her chair back, and looms over the table with ragged breaths. "Let me make this very clear: Van and I were done, and so are we. Have a good fucking day, Asher. I'll see you at band practice tomorrow. Prepare yourselves," she growls an ominous warning, stomping away and rushing through the door without a backward glance.

"Fuck," I mutter, staring out the window until she gets into her vehicle. That's not how I wanted this conversation to go at all. Fuckity. Fuck. Actually, I don't know what I expected from her. I knew she'd be upset to find out why we left.

Movement whirls around me, dragging me back into the restaurant. Several pairs of eyes glare daggers in my direction, including the scowling older man who shakes his head in disgust. Feeling the awkwardness crashing down on me, I throw my barely-drank coffee and half-eaten muffin into the trash and walk out the door with my head hung low. I have a lot of shit to talk to the guys about if they'll fucking listen. I need to make this better without revealing the absolute truth. There will be a time and a place for me to tell them what happened, but I need to tell them what I discussed with Gloria. Fuck. I rub a hand across my tightening chest, crumbling under the vise, viciously squeezing it.

As I walk out the door, I reach into my pocket and pop two more antacids to tamp down the rising heartburn, eating away at my insides.

Accidentally, might I add. The little bastard followed me from point A to point B, trailing after me like a lost puppy dog. I couldn't shake him off. So, I made him buy me breakfast. I was starving, and he was offering. So, I took the opportunity to drag information out of him.

Something tells me Evil Ash had more to say but wasn't willing to give it all up.

Olivia chokes on her glass of wine. "What?" she croaks, wiping her mouth.

"I had coffee—"

"No, I got that part. I'm just…surprised, is all. Asher Montgomery? Really??" She gives me that—you're not falling for his shit again, are you?—look.

Kaycee watches me with an intense stare and nods after soaking in the information. "Was he informative?" she asks, cocking her head to the side.

"Very," I croak, forcing myself to gulp down the rest of my white wine.

"Do tell," Olivia says, grinning wide.

I sigh, explaining how I stormed out of the shop after learning about the video someone sent him, causing them to leave. Not to mention the whole, they had no idea about the restraining orders thing.

A shiver of disgust rolls through me, imagining why Van decided to do that and then sharing it with everyone. Was he really that obsessed with me? He was the one who broke it off with me because of his parents. Yet, he kept trophies on his phone like a creep.

"Also, apparently, Kieran's bitch mom lives right here in town," I groan, refilling my glass. If I had known that, I would have been more cautious walking around.

Thank God for my bestie's sober husbands. Or I'd be sleeping on this uncomfortable couch and have a headache in the morning before facing the guys.

Tomorrow is the day. The day I face these assfaces with confidence and determination. It's up to them now whether they succeed or crash and burn.

Kaycee wrinkles her nose. "I can drain her bank account if you want. Or hack into her FlashGram." Kaycee shrugs when I snort. "We can set her house on fire. I have connections." She wiggles her brows playfully until I'm bending at the waist with laughter.

"I'll pretend I didn't hear that," Olivia murmurs into her glass, slightly cringing at the mention of fire but plays it off by laughing at Kaycee's dedication.

I'll mention that to her later. Fire makes her uneasy. I don't blame her though. After what happened when she was a teenager, she's overcome a lot. But to be locked in a house while bleeding out and then having to fight her way through a blaze? Yeah. It was brutal for her. So, even at the slightest hint of fire, she cowers away. Yet, she's a badass Veritas agent, fighting the good fight and taking bad guys down without fear.

Trauma is a hell of a thing.

"I'm just saying I can help," Kaycee says, taking another sip.

"I'll remember that," I groan, rubbing at my forehead. "Is this reality?" I murmur, looking at my best friends. "How am I going to survive this?"

"Because you're a strong, independent woman who don't need no man!" Olivia shouts, shoving her glass into the air.

"She's right. You're you. Strong, sassy, and you don't take any shit. I could have used you as my bestie in high school," Kaycee says, blowing out a breath.

"Pfft. You did fine on your own," Seger says, sauntering into the room with a grin. "When you hacked into that bitch Hadley's FlashGram, that was a fucking riot."

Kaycee's grin lights up her face when she stares at him with dopey eyes. "I guess," she says with a shrug.

"So, fucking modest, Angel," Seger coos, kissing the tip of her nose.

"Yuck! Gross!" I playfully say, throwing a couch pillow at Seger's head.

"Umph," he grunts, tossing it back with a frown. "Rude." I grin in return as he grabs a magazine off the table and whacks me in the head.

"Asshole!" I laugh, clutching my head.

"I love ya, Sis. But I think we would have murdered each other back in the day." He grins, kissing Kaycee one last time before disappearing out the door, humming under his breath. Probably heading upstairs to continue watching Lyric, and the rest of his children–Maggie, Axel, Dash, and Roman.

"Back to this topic," Olivia chides, tapping on the table. "What the fuck is happening with you right now? Them?"

"Absolutely nothing. I'm their boss. That's it." I feel Olivia's eyes on me as I guzzle more wine and ignore her snort.

"Sure. That's it."

"They fucked me over, Liv. Like…so fucking bad. I can't fall into that trap again."

As I empty my glass, I finally feel the effects of the wine swimming through my veins. Instead of stopping like I should, I pour another glass, clinging to it like a lifeline.

"You don't feel anything for them?" Kaycee asks.

"Hate. Disgust. Wanna punch them in the dicks. Does that answer your question?" I ask with my brow rising high.

Liar! I may hate their guts and hope they rot in the desert. But dear God, they're fine as hell. Hot. Fucking smoking. I'll never understand why I'm being punished so much with their chiseled rock star looks.

Couldn't they be, I dunno—less attractive? Mouth-watering, assfaces.

They're like my damn wine, getting finer with age. I may despise their asses, but I have fucking eyes. I see the way their clothes fit snugly against their bodies, emphasizing their goodies. And I do mean goodies. Asher's ass alone is biteable…pinchable. I could bounce a quarter off it.

Jesus, what's wrong with me?

It's the damn wine, that's it. Nothing more.

Colors swirl before my eyes, blending in a rainbow. Fuck. When did the room start spinning? I squeeze my eyes shut, groaning at the sensation.

"Shit. I think the wine's kicked in," I snort, covering my mouth. "Fuck."

"Why? Because you're thinking about them naked now?" Olivia quips, drunkenly poking me with her index finger. "They were hot back in the day, weren't they?"

"No, not naked!" I hiss, swatting her away. "Okay, fine! They're hot as hell."

"No takesy backsies!" Olivia sings, taking another swig of wine with a grin.

"But they're not forgiven," I mumble, taking another sip. "Not one bit. I loathe them. They're dirty little brats." I pout.

"Absolutely not," Kaycee agrees with glossy eyes. "This is really good, by the way. I think we need more. They were so mean to you. How can you look them in the eyes? Do you look at their dicks? Dickmatized, am I right?" We cackle together.

"Dickmatized!" Olivia shouts, folding in half with a cackle. "Seriously, though? It's because she's braver than anyone I know," Olivia says with a grin, recuperating from her laughter by wiping her eyes and taking a breath. "Who else could face their exes like a professional?"

Professional, my ass. I want to drown them. And get dicked down. And… I should never drink wine again when I'm conflicted.

"Speaking of… Have you found any more information about my little stalker yet?"

Good! Change the subject. No more thinking about their cocks and… I wrinkle my nose, glaring at the wine.

"Sorry, babes. We looked into it and kept the pictures as evidence. But per his usual, he didn't leave any fingerprints behind. He's like a damn ghost."

"No one can be that good," Kaycee says.

"And you're like 100 percent sure it's not Donavon Drake?" My heart pounds the second I utter that stupid name. That scumbag doesn't deserve an ounce of my time or space in my brain.

"Still in Europe working with his company. He only has a few ties to East Point. A cousin and aunt live in town, but that's it. He hasn't been here for over ten years. He's out."

Fuck. It'd be easy if it were him. I'd at least have a clue as to why he was stalking me. With a stranger, though? I'm drowning in anxiety.

"And you've checked into Nathan down at the coffee shop? He's gotten extra clingy these days." I shiver at the thought of his eyes following me around the damn cafe every morning when I show up. If their coffee wasn't the best in town, I'd go somewhere else. But nothing beats the smooth taste of theirs.

"Nope. As far as we can tell, he's not it. Doesn't own any sort of digital camera and we checked through his photos on all devices. We've looked through his apartment and his background. We even followed him for a few weeks to make sure. There's nothing tying him to you or the stalking. He may be a little creepy, but he's innocent."

"Who the fuck could it be?" I grumble, massaging my temple.

"I don't know, Riv. But we'll get him. The good news is he hasn't escalated into something more yet."

"Yeah, just pictures of me and Lyric. He isn't hiding in my house or anything," I groan, throwing myself back into the couch.

"And it's still nothing digital?" An odd sparkle forms in Kaycee's eyes at the prospect of hacking.

She's the best in the nation. On par with her husband, Carter. If she weren't a stay-at-home mom with her other husband, Chase, she'd have joined Veritas, too. Olivia has been gunning for her to be on her team since they met in high school when Olivia saved Kaycee and the guys from some weird cult. Something they rarely talk about.

"No," Olivia snorts. "You'd have to be on my team to join the hunt." She smirks when Kaycee huffs.

"Can't leave the boys at home just yet. Maybe Carter will let me sneak a peek," she blurts, quickly taking a sip of her wine.

"He does, doesn't he?" Olivia laughs, shaking her head. "I should have known he'd never come up with half the stuff he does."

Kaycee snorts. "I am the brains of the operation."

I cackle when a grin explodes across her face. I don't know how I ever lived my life without these girls. Since I came here and this whole thing started, they've been Team River. We've had so many of these nights where the kids play, and we drink while the guys cook and babysit us.

After an hour more of laughing, Chase offers to drive me home as Seger follows with my car and Lyric in tow.

Tomorrow is the first day of the rest of my whole damn life. And even though I'm all wined up, my bravery is dwindling.

IT ALL STARTED THIS MORNING AS I PULLED OUT OF THE DRIVEWAY WITH Lyric in the back seat, chatting away as we began our adventure to school. It was at that moment, as I exited the gate and waved to the guard, that Asher emerged on the side of the road. Sweat dripped from every inch of his body as he huffed and puffed, bending at the waist to catch his breath. The moment our eyes connected; a flush worked its way up my neck.

Memories of our night on the dining room table emerge from the darkness, taking hold. The ghost of his dirty mouth wrapping around my clit has my damn pussy throbbing. Having these sorts of thoughts about any of them is just bad for my health. Back then, I went into our relationship with sex on my mind. They were a good time, and then, it all got real for me. Way too real.

Then they vanished like the dickless pricks they are. If history has taught me anything, it's that no matter what these boys say, I should stay the fuck away and keep my pussy, heart, and ass to myself. I groan, thinking back to when I was forced to halt our drive so my beautiful daughter could lure her daddy into the car with one simple smile.

"Mommy, stop!" Lyric screeches from the backseat, sending my heart into a damn frenzy.

Slamming on the brakes, I whip my head in her direction as she rolls down her window with a happy squeak. Fuck. I forgot about the damn window locks again. I grit my teeth when she grins in Asher's direction, who falls for her trap. Peering into the car with a smirk, he leans his bulging forearms through the open window.

"Daddy! I'm going to school!" Lyric says with a toothy smile, peering up at Asher as he pokes his head in and places a quick kiss on her forehead. Lyric's tiny hand immediately reaches for him, squeezing his arm with excitement. "Can you come with me? Please?" she asks with the biggest, roundest, and most pleading eyes I've ever seen. Puppy dog eyes, be damned. Lyric wins every damn time. It's so hard to tell her no, but I've had some practice. Asher? Not so much.

"Ly, Daddy probably doesn't have time," I say softly. Immediately, her face falls, and her grin disappears, replaced by a pout.

"Please, Mommy? I want all my daddies to see my school," she says in a little, pleading voice on the verge of begging.

Asher chuckles, turning his gaze to my narrowed eyes. "Well, Little One. That's up to your momma."

"Please, Mommy! Please! I want Daddy to see my school and meet my friends!" she insists again, folding her hands together until I'm huffing and unlocking the door.

"Sure," I say, smiling at her while dying a little on the inside.

The door slams with a thud, and Asher's half-naked body rests against my leather seat. His manly musk fills the air.

"Daddy, I can't wait for you to meet my friends! There's Maggie and Kaitlyn and Dorothy and Connor."

"Connor?" Asher's head whips toward her, and she freezes, pursing her lips.

"Yeah, my boyfriend, Connor. He says..." Asher cuts her off, putting a hand in the air.

"My daughter has a boyfriend?" he asks in a low voice, raising his eyebrows at me.

I huff, pushing the accelerator. "It seems to be that way," I say with a shrug.

"He's nice, Daddy. He got me a flower!" she says happily, blabbering on more about school and her friends.

As soon as Lyric jumps out of the car in the pickup line, Asher's gaze turns to me in all his half-naked glory.

"Expect me tomorrow," he says with a smirk. "I can even buy you some of your favorite coffee from your favorite barista."

"Don't hold your breath," I grumble, pulling out of the line with one last wave to Lyric as she holds her teacher's hand.

I glare in the direction of the house across the street as if it's the cause of all my problems. Because, well—it is. They are, I should say. They're sick, evil bastards who marched their way back into my life and give me so many damn emotions. I'm trying my hardest to be patient as they meet Lyric and bond with her. Lyric deserves to know who helped create her, even if they are jackasses.

Heaving a sigh, I grab the copies of the contract I promised them and make my way across the street, dragging my feet. Today's the day the boys find out what exactly I have in store for them. Our time together won't be fucking daisies. Happy Monday, boys. Your nightmare is about to walk through the door.

As I smooth out my form-fitting black lace tank top and pull my hip-hugging jeans up, I brace myself for the real test. For the last few days, we've danced around each other. They've tested the boundaries of the contract like I knew they would. Now the real work begins. Much like a sergeant, I'm about to tear them down to bare bones and build them back into the rock stars they were before. It'll be hard and somewhat complicated, but I believe they can do it. If they put their heads down, get to work, and obey my commands, we won't have a problem.

Like that's going to fucking happen.

With one last look around the scenery, I let the ocean waves take me over and calm everything inside of me. Without knocking, I use my key and enter the silent band house. Nothing stirs around me as I walk on light feet through the abandoned living room filled with the sunlight beaming in from the tall windows. My eyes narrow when I walk down the stairs into the basement. There by his lonesome, Callum sits on the couch with his bass in hand, listening closely as he tunes it.

His gray eyes widen, taking all of me in as a familiar blush pinkens his cheeks.

"I take it everyone else is still sleeping," I question, raising a brow.

Callum clears his throat giving me a stiff nod. "Yeah-yeah." He swallows the lump in his throat, quickly averting his gaze toward the ground. "I haven't heard a peep from them this morning," he says softly, reminding me of the boy I knew before.

"And you didn't wake them?" I ask, raising a brow.

"They-they're adults," he murmurs again, still refusing to look at me.

Pulling my phone out of my back pocket, I check the time, noting that it's 8:45 a.m. on the damn dot. Late bastards wasting my time. It seems that they're still trying to push my buttons and their boundaries. I guess it's time to show them who the boss really is.

"Don't worry. I'll take care of them." A small smile pulls at the edge of my lips when Callum's gaze snaps to mine, and he stiffens with momentary fear.

"What are you going to do, Little Star?" he breathes, turning slightly.

Every so often, when their little nicknames break through, my heart cracks a little more than before. Like the duct tape and pins keeping me together are fraying at the edges. It knocks me back in step, transporting me to the past when I was on top of the world in their arms. I may not have been in the best financial state, and I may not have had the best home life, but I had them. I had those nicknames. I was alive and full of energy, ready to conquer the world. Now I don't. I let the name slide this time because the way Callum looks at me now makes fire erupt under my flesh.

Clearing my throat, I straighten my posture and turn on my heel with determination. Looking over my shoulder, I gaze at him, sitting there fiddling with his bass guitar. The most mischievous grin spreads across my lips as my brain cooks up genius ideas for waking two sleeping idiots.

"They're late. I'll do what any good boss does," I say without context and make my way up the stairs. Half of me expects Callum to follow me.

And the other half of me is thankful that he didn't because he'd try to talk me out of it.

Standing by the stairwell, I peer up where the bedrooms are, listening closely for any sounds of movement. When no one makes a move, I start the first action of my plan at the kitchen sink and fill a bucket with ice-cold water. As it fills to the brim, I grab a handful of ice cubes and toss them on top. For good measure, of course. With the bucket in hand, I make my way up the stairs just as Ash emerges from the steamy bathroom with a white towel wrapped around his toned waist.

Jesus fucking Christ in a hand-basket. Don't look at the damn V near his waist. Fuck. I pretend I'm looking anywhere but his toned body as I stand before him. If he sees me checking him out, he doesn't utter a word.

His jaw drops when he sees me carrying a heavy bucket, and he shakes his head. "River," he says, drawing out my name with suspicion. "What are you doing?"

I shrug. "Last Friday, I told you guys my expectations. At 8:45 a.m. on Monday, you were all to report to the basement for your first band practice under my rule. And now three of you are late," I say, holding up my phone and showing him the time that says 8:50 a.m. "Is that water? And ice?"

"Seems pretty self-explanatory to me," I say with nonchalance, side-stepping him as he watches me closely.

A distinct chuckle greets my ears when I look back at him and his reddened face. "Let me get dressed, and I'll be down there in a second," he says, holding a fist over his mouth to cover the laughs. "I don't want to be up here for this. Especially Kieran. He's going to hate you."

"That won't change anything," I mutter, hobbling with the bucket another step. "You're safe then. This will make them think twice about sleeping when they should get to work like Callum." I give him a pointed stare as he wanders toward his bedroom, watching my every move, and goes inside. As the door shuts, I stand, debating which door to choose. Rad or Kieran? Who deserves this more? Without a second thought, I veer to the right, opening the first closed door.

As I step through the door, I nearly screech.

"Jesus Christ," I say, covering my eyes and blocking the view of Rad's naked ass in the middle of the bed, sprawled out like a starfish.

He doesn't stir at the sound of my voice or when I walk in further with the sloshing bucket of water and set it down. As he softly snores, I take the time to examine the man that once held my heart.

A deep, burning blush creeps up my neck, covering my cheeks when I walk around the bed and fold my arms over my chest, examining the naked man before me. New tattoos adorn his entire body, from head to toe, leaving little naked flesh. Even his bubble butt has ink covering it. Shit.

"Rad," I whisper, shoving my foot into his butt cheek and rattling him around.

And nothing. He doesn't respond when I do it again, shaking him even harder. Instead, a loud snore escapes him, along with several mumbles telling me to fuck off.

I roll my eyes toward the ceiling in agitation. Okay, I tried to be nice. If he won't respond to his name, then I'll give him something to respond to.

"Okay, you asked for it," I say, heaving the bucket of water into my arms and dangling it above his naked body. With a grunt, I pour the frigid liquid right onto his bare ass, earning a startled yelp as his entire body soaks up the liquid.

"What the fuck!" he screeches, twisting and sitting in the middle of the sopping-wet bed.

With wide eyes, he looks around the room and finally settles his narrowed gaze on me.

"Pretty Girl, what the hell are you doing?" he asks through several heaving breaths. His long fingers search the sheets, scowling when they come back wet and dripping. "Did you pour water on me?" he asks incredulously.

I smother the snicker trying to escape from my lips when he stares up at me in utter disbelief. Regaining my control, I nod. "Yeah, I just poured a bucket of water and ice on you."

"Not just on me, Pretty Girl. You poured it on my ass," he says as his voice escalates around the room. "My precious bum! God, that shit was cold! I think little Rad went into hiding! Pretty Girl, that was not cool!" He squawks every word, growing louder and louder by the second.

"It's Monday morning, Rad." I raise a knowing brow when he shrugs and tosses his arms in the air with subdued anger.

"Yeah, happy Monday, Pretty Girl," he says, narrowing his eyes at me with a mischievous glance bolting through his dark eyes.

Keeping my eyes locked on him and refusing to look down at his utterly nude body. I smother another laugh.

"Yes, happy Monday indeed. It's now 8:55 a.m., Rad," I say, holding up my phone so he can examine the time. "What is supposed to happen at 8:45 a.m.?" I purse my lips when he shrugs in response and suddenly stills.

Before I can even think, move, or protect myself, Rad wraps his arms around my waist at lightning speed and throws me in the middle of the bed. I screech when he throws his body over mine, and the wet blankets over us with a grin, soaking us both to the bone with cold as fuck water.

"Is it bed wrestling time?" he says, pushing his body onto mine and holding me down as I wiggle, trying to get away.

"Rad, get off of me," I grunt, struggling beneath him as he laughs.

"No can do, Pretty Girl," Rad says with a gigantic grin, mocking me as I struggle.

I try with all my might to remove my hands from between our bodies, only stopping my struggle when the stark realization hits me square in the chest. Oh god. Something hard and heavy rests against my thigh, jumping every time I fucking move. Swallow me up, world, and take me away! An unwanted blush heats my face when I lock eyes with Rad, who wiggles his brows.

"I swear to God, if that's your dick on my leg, I'm going to slaughter you," I growl through gritted teeth. Rad's face lights up even more when he stares down at me with satisfaction.

"Now you're speaking my language! He's just trying to find his home, Pretty Girl. You hear that, boy? We're almost to where we belong. It's like somewhere over the rainbow, but my pot of gold is your pussy." If I could cover his mouth, I'd slap my palm across his lips. But alas, I'm still stuck and forced to listen to him.

"No, I swear! If your dick gets any closer to me, I will chop it off. You asked me if I still carried my knife. Well, it's still in my damn pocket. Ashton, if you don't get off me, there will be blood," I say, making him laugh. His nose nestles into the crook of my neck, with a happy sigh rocking through him. Every muscle in his body relaxes, and for a few golden seconds, he doesn't utter a word.

"I'm sorry, Pretty Girl." Rad doesn't move when my body stiffens. Oxygen evacuates my lungs, leaving my head a muddled mess.

"You're sorry for what? For dragging me into this wet bed or putting your dick on my leg?" I whisper, with my heart pounding against my chest. I swear it's about to come through my ribs and fall out onto the floor when his glossy eyes find mine.

Rad swallows hard, gracefully moving my hair from my face. He examines me with concentration, taking in every aspect of my features. Silently, he shakes his head.

"For all of it, Pretty Girl. For years, I thought the worst about you. I thought you fucking broke my heart. I've been a different man since we left Central City. I've become someone I'd never wanted to become. But seeing you and Lyric, I see that I missed out. I missed out, Pretty Girl, because I didn't talk to you before I left. So, you ask why I'm sorry? I'm sorry because I was a jackass. No matter what actually happened, even if you did..." He sucks in a breath, closes his eyes, and regains himself as a tear leaks down his cheek. "River, I believe you."

I reel back as if I've been slapped. Just two days ago, he sang a different tune. And now...

"You believe me?" I ask through a shuddering breath, swallowing the emotions drifting up my constricted throat.

Rad slowly nods in confirmation, leaning closer and hovering his face above mine. If he moves another inch, his lips will press into mine, and I don't know how well I'll be able to stop him. Thankfully, he doesn't. He lingers there, examining my eyes as they wildly take him in.

"Yes, I believe you. I just have to figure out what the hell actually happened. Something fucking stinks." He shakes his head in aggravation but doesn't make a move to get off me.

Raw emotions splinter inside of me, cracking open old wounds I thought had festered closed many years before. Seeing Rad and hearing all the feelings behind his words does something to my insides. I've erected walls for so long, trying to keep the pain of what they did to me at bay, that it feels strange to let the dam break. But it doesn't mean anything that he is sorry now.

"You're sorry now?" I whisper through trembling lips, trying to keep my emotions on the inside. I don't have time or the energy to dissect our relationship or lack thereof.

Rad nods again, shakily running his fingers through my hair. If he doesn't stop touching me, I will lose all of my composure. If there's one person who can break down the walls I've put in place, it would be him.

"I'm so sorry that I ever doubted you. I was in love with you, River. I wanted so many things with you, and I fucking blew it because I took Asher's word for it. Now I see that not only should I have talked to you first. That I shouldn't have listened to him. But Callum, when he came back from your apartment, he looked so devastated and… I'm sorry, Pretty Girl."

"I believe that you are, Rad." I swallow my tongue when he looks at me again with raw emotions emanating from him. You can practically taste it in the air.

I don't know what happened. Why the hell is he all of a sudden sorry? Was it our talk from last night that resonated with him, and he finally listened to me? Whatever the case, I feel in my soul that he truly is sorry for what happened back then. It just doesn't make up for what they did. No matter if they didn't sign the restraining orders or if they didn't know about Lyric. They walked away. Endpoint.

"You never signed a restraining order?" I ask, swallowing hard.

"Fuck no. We were hurt, but not that hurt. We would never have done that. How can I make this up to you, Pretty Girl?" he asks with pleading eyes. "How can I show you or tell you that I'm sorry? That I believe every word you said." Rad's grip tightens on me as he lays his forehead against mine and closes his eyes with a deep, heavy sigh. "I lost you once because of my stupidity, but I will make up for it with every fiber of my soul."

With a labored breath, I turn my head forcefully, trying to remove his grip from mine. The warmth of his body wraps me in a hug, and something screams in the back of my mind for me to stay there, stay under him and enjoy his presence. But the hurt I feel bubbling up and wanting to come out in tears has me retreating inside myself. As I stare at the plain white wall, with my ex-lover on top of me, begging me to forgive him for his indiscretions, I shake my head.

"It's too late, Rad," I say in a shaky voice, barely above a whisper.

"There's nothing you could do now to make up for what you did. The only reason you will ever stay in my life is because of Lyric. She needs her fathers, and that's all you'll ever be. I don't forgive you," I whisper, holding in the hurt I feel with every word I say. It's not that I don't believe them. I do. I believe every word I say. "You hurt me too badly."

Our relationship isn't fixable. Asher, Rad, Callum, and Kieran will only be her four fathers. We will co-parent, and we will coexist together for the next six months for the sake of their jobs, but I will never put my heart on the line ever again and have them eviscerate it by walking away. If they did it once, what's stopping them from doing it again?

"I understand, Pretty Girl. But you think I'm going to give up because you said that it will never happen again? Seriously, you don't remember who I am. At all. I am Ashton Radcliffe the Third. And I go after what I want. I will make this up to you. I will follow you to the ends of the earth on my hands and knees and bleed for you until you're back in my arms just like this. Mark my words. One day soon, you, my Pretty Girl, will be mine again. Oh, and also scream my name. But we'll get to the sexy stuff once I prove myself." With reluctance, Rad peels himself off my body and sits back on his heels. With a grin, he lets his naked body hang out without shame.

I groan, covering my eyes and removing myself from the wet sheets. What a bad fucking idea water was. Next time, I'll get more creative with cymbals or something loud and disruptive.

Somehow after our conversation, I feel a little lighter, knowing that Rad believes me. Something in my gut tells me that they were lied to. They had no knowledge of Lyric like that bitch had said. They seemed highly offended when I mentioned restraining orders. Rad is right, something does fucking stink about the situation. But until I know the whole truth, I can't make any sort of judgment.

"Oh, come on, Pretty Girl. You act like you've never seen it before. Just wait. One day soon, when you forgive me, I will make up for everything; you'll be down for the Rad ride." He wiggles his brows with an adorable grin plastered on his face.

"Nope. Never going to happen, Rad," I say, groaning when I stand up on jelly legs, feeling miserable in the wet clothes. "You might want to change your sheets and let your mattress air out." I wave a hand in his direction, only earning myself a chuckle. I feel his eyes burning into me when I turn my back, and his fingers brush across my shoulders, removing the hair from my neck.

"Oh yeah, Pretty Girl. I'll definitely have to air out this mattress. I need to get it ready for all the nasty stuff we're going to do on it. Just you wait," he says, placing a soft kiss on my shoulder and then slowly backing away.

"Oh God, get dressed," I groan again.

"I meant what I said," he says, rifling around in a drawer somewhere in the room. Grunting, the sound of elastic snapping against skin and clothes rustling offers me a reprieve from his naked flesh. Turning, I stare at him as he pulls his tight-fitting black band shirt over his head and grins. "I will fight for you every step of the way." I raise a brow when he wraps his arms around me like he has the damn authority to do so. "Bring on the fight," he whispers, slapping my ass, and then walks away.

"What the hell, Rad!" I yelp, rubbing a hand over my butt cheek. "I am your boss!" I hiss, smacking his shoulder when we exit the room.

"Yes, bossy lady. You sure are. And you're my girlfriend. That ass is mine and…"

"I forgot how annoying you were. Now, go! All of you!" My voice carries through the room, finally getting another response as another door opens.

Kieran steps out with a scowl. "The fuck you wet for?" he grumbles, running a hand through his dark hair.

I blow out a breath, getting ready to open my mouth.

"She was in my bed, that's why!" Rad shouts, quickly moving down the stairs and onto the main floor. Turning slowly from the bottom, he gives me a megawatt grin, seeming happier than he's ever been in my presence since we reunited.

"Rad," I growl in warning, earning a chuckle before he disappears, running downstairs.

"Why're you here?" Kieran grunts. "And already in his bed?" He raises a stupid judgmental eyebrow, looking me up and down with a wrinkled nose. *Prick.*

"Did no one else remember that Monday, mandatory band practice begins? Was I talking to brick walls?" I ask, crossing my arms over my wet shirt.

"Right," he grunts, shoving away and waltzing down the stairs. "You should know your shirt is see-through," he quips, showing his humor for the first time in my presence.

"I swear by the time this six months is up, I'm going to murder them," I mutter to myself just as their practice starts without me and I head home with the intention of changing out of my wet clothes.

As I re-enter the house with fresh clothes, my phone buzzes, lighting up with one of my other best friends' names. Rocco.

ROCCO

Sushi date? *Winky face*

ME

Sure, and stop winking at me.

ROCCO

Haha. *Wink*

ME

Remind me to slap you when I see you.

ROCCO

How about Cherry Blossoms? Saturday night?

ME

Sounds good.

ROCCO

Wear something sexy...

ME

You are impossible...I swear.

ROCCO

That I am, babe...but I can't wait to hear about this mysterious band you've gotten yourself assigned to. *Winky face*

ME

I hate you. Goodbye...

I scowl, discreetly peeking out the blinds with narrowed eyes. There, beneath the streetlights, in River's driveway is a loaded-up, flashy, black sports car. In my girl's driveway, which definitely isn't mine. I fucking wish; it looks sick as hell. But still! Not! Mine!

About ten minutes ago, the loud exhaust of an accelerating vehicle plowing down the driveway caught my attention, dragging me to this spying chair and magically splitting the blinds for me to watch. With a rapidly beating heart, I focused my gaze on a tall man with dark hair and a fancy suit walking straight into River's house without knocking. A man! In her house! That isn't me!

Jealousy rages through my system at the thought of another man not currently in this house laying a finger on her. River West is mine to win back. Not Mr. Fancy Pants, who better keep his hands firmly to himself. I nibble my bottom lip, watching with rapt attention for any movement outside the house.

A few nights ago, after kicking the shit out of my bike and clearing my head, a light bulb went off inside my brain. An important, life-altering decision came to me like a damn epiphany. Within two seconds of my ah-ha moment, I erased the past with a flick of a switch and decided to bury everything that happened. There is no past between us; there is only the future. That I will absolutely be in.

After our short, intense talk and seeing the raw emotions simmering behind her gorgeous eyes, I knew everything she said held nothing but the truth. Sure, a few more incidents need to be investigated. But I'm all in again.

And if I'm being real, I never really got over her. I'm ready to prove that I'm up to the task of being her boyfriend. More importantly, I'm ready to be a father to the little girl who bandaged my face and made me feel something for the first time in years. Everything seems so damn clear to me now. My Pretty Girl belongs to me. Not Mr. Tall, Dark, and Sexy in a suit with a fancy-ass car.

"What are you doing?" Callum asks, plopping down next to me on the couch. Looking me over with a curious gaze, he raises a brow.

I grit my teeth, glaring out the window. "There's a car in River's driveway," I grumble, wildly gesturing.

"A car?" Callum asks with suspicion, peeking out the blinds. "Who is it?" he asks, nearly growling at the thought. That only fuels me further, making a grin spread across my face.

"You care, don't you?" I ask, studying the darkening of his face when his eyes meet mine. The little shit doesn't have to say anything. For the first time in a long time, I see his transparent feelings shining through. "Callum likes River. Callum wants to FUUUCK her," I sing-song mockingly, earning a slap to the back of my head. "Ouch, Fuckface. That's not very nice." Rubbing the back of my head, I shake off his attack and continue my ninja spying.

He grunts his answer, huffing as he peeks out. "Who is that?" Callum questions with suspicion, eyeing the man who has the audacity to have his arm around River's shoulder.

God damn. My heart drops when she smiles up at him, laughing at whatever he says. It lights up her gorgeous face, highlighting her flawless look. A beautiful teal dress clings to her body, letting the world—me and Callum—see her shapely form. She's definitely not the same girl from Central City. Half of me bets my daughter is the reason she's filled out after all these years. God damn. I bite my damn fist. No matter how big or small or tall or short River West is, she'll always be beautiful. Even with a top knot on her head and mismatched pajamas.

"No idea," I mumble, tracking their movements as he opens the passenger-side door for her. Briefly, she stalls, staring up at him and running a hand down his chest. "Whoever he is, I'm going to bury him." My heart accelerates when they get into the car together, and I jump from the couch, attempting to walk away. Callum catches my arm, studying my face with concern.

"Where are you going?" he asks softly yet demanding me to answer him. Ah, there he is—the Callum I grew up with. Finally, he's coming back, and so am I. Call us the comeback kings of East Point. It's time to reclaim our girl and reclaim ourselves—and cum on her back, of course. It's the greatest comeback of all time!

"To follow them, duh. I thought that was obvious. Grab your cape and black hood; we're going stalking, Cally boy." I grin at his unwavering frown as he stares at me for a few more seconds until the sound of the stupid flashy car roars to life, and he lets me go with a resigned sigh.

"Okay," he says reluctantly, digging into his pocket and pulling out his keys. "But you're riding bitch," he snickers when my face falls.

I purse my lips. "Asshole. Ash has a car we could steal," I mutter, crossing my arms over my chest. "He wouldn't fucking mind."

Since the day we moved in here, we've been cooped up. Well, some of us have. I brought my damn dirt bike but no other forms of transportation like an idiot. The guys, on the other hand, brought their vehicles and stored them in the garage—genius assholes.

"Ride bitch or don't, but I'm following to see. You can sneak up the stairs, steal Ash's keys, and then try to keep up. But they'll be long gone by then." Fuck. Fuckity, shit balls. I hate his stupid logical side.

I scowl even more, huffing at his words. "Fucking fine," I grumble, shoving my feet into my sneakers as he does the same. "But if I get a boner, it's from the vibrations. Not you."

Callum stiffens, stopping dead at the doorway to the garage. "Really? That's the first thing that pops into your head?" Pops up, hell yes, it will.

"Vibrations, dude! It's like…" He holds up his hand, cutting me off.

"I don't want to hear about the vibrations, Rad. Keep those thoughts to yourself. And your fucking dick. If I feel anything stiff behind me…"

"What are you going to do?" I goad, grinning when we walk into the garage. "Stroke me? Cuz yeah, I might like that, baby," I quip, earning a gut punch that knocks the air from my lungs. "Fine, fuck. No need to get violent," I wheeze, bending at the waist. "Your punch is wicked good."

"Get on," Callum demands, patting the seat behind him as he settles his helmet on his head and hands me mine. "They haven't left yet, but they will soon." He raises a brow as the idling car outside starts revving in the driveway. "Now or never," he says, hitting the button to the garage as the car's loud exhaust echoes as they drive off down the long, winding driveway.

"This never gets out," I grumble, straddling the bike. "Like ever." Callum snorts in response, shaking his head.

"Hands on my waist," he says, as the garage door lifts, and he revs the engine, taking off at full speed toward the closing gate.

"Fuuuck!" I shout into the air, clutching Callum's waist with my tight grip. The wind whips around us when he accelerates more, narrowly making it through the closing gate until we're free and on the road. In the distance, I swear I hear River's guard yelling at us to stop or go get the girl. I'll pretend it's the latter, because that's what I'm about to do. Go get the damn girl.

"There they are!" I shout, pointing to the stupid car ahead. "Follow that car!" Shit, I've always wanted to say that.

A sense of joy spears through me for the first time in years; I finally feel fucking alive. No more drowning myself in groupies. No more chasing a high that never fucking came. This entire time, I needed River. I needed her back in my damn arms. This go-around, no matter what, I'm not letting her go. Ever. I'll beg and plead and suck her clit until she forgives me again.

"It's a restaurant," Callum grumbles, bringing the bike to a halt in an alleyway next to the fancy-looking eatery.

"Fucker took my girl out on a date," I huff, jumping off the bike, watching like a hawk as he opens the door for her, and she snorts at him, looking up at him with those big eyes of hers. She is probably batting her eyelashes and flirting and shit. Fuck. I grunt, removing my helmet and smoothing down my curls.

"Your girl?" Callum asks, shoving his helmet off and setting it on the bike with a grunt.

"Yeah. My girl." I shrug, peeking through the big picture window, spying on them through the glass. "Fuck. He's wining and dining her and pulling out all the stops. Look at that shit! I bet it costs thousands of dollars. Shit. He's hot. So, fucking hot, and I'm…" I frown, looking down at my torn jeans and my damn cut-off shirt that splits over my ribs, showing off my tattoos. "Different," I mumble, folding my arms over my chest.

Years ago, she loved this version of me. Watching her now, it seems her tastes have changed from broody, quirky rock stars to stuffy, suit-loving douchebags.

"What's going on?" Callum asks gruffly, running a hand through his blond curls. "Your girl?" His face twists in confusion, and a pained expression takes over. "But she…" My gaze snaps to him, recognizing the war he's fighting inside his mind. Because I was there, too. Fighting with myself on the rights and wrongs of what happened. There's so much we don't know the truth about. But you know what they say? The truth always has a way of coming to light. Sooner or later, we'll fully understand what happened.

"Cal, bro." I lay a hand on his shoulder, squeezing tight.

"How can you… I don't understand," he mutters, squeezing his eyes shut. Pain flashes across his face in waves until he's sucking in breaths. "She kissed him, and then that video—" I squeeze again, forcing his gaze to meet mine. "I saw it all, Rad. How can you—" He swallows hard, unable to finish his sentence without letting his feelings known.

"We don't have the whole story, man. I feel it right here," I say, pounding my fist into my aching chest. "Look past the hurt and the damn pain from losing her. Use logic, Cal. River West was so annoyed by Van. Why would she go back to him? Why would she willingly get in his backseat again? Why would she willingly kiss him? Tell me because right now, nothing makes sense."

Callum runs a hand down his face in contemplation, staring off into the distance. From here, I visibly see the memories working through his mind, and he shakes his head. "She wouldn't," he murmurs, collapsing back with realization. "She called us for help when he stalked her at the bar. I remember the weariness in her eyes every time he was around. She never asked for help and did with us," he whispers with a cloudy look fogging his eyes. "She trusted us," he finally surmises exactly what I've been saying. I vigorously nod, noting the moment my dear Callum gets on board with my plan.

"You see it, don't you? Yes! Now, all I have to do is figure out what the hell else happened. We know Ash got the video from Van. For whatever reason. Then he was there at the damn apartment when you showed. But why?" I pace the small length in front of us, wracking my damn brain about the entire situation. By the end of it, my brain aches from trying to figure it out. "Why the hell was he there? It's like someone told him to go or something. But how fucked up would that be?"

"It's odd," Callum agrees, scratching at his chin. "I still don't under-stand. Why would he be at her apartment? I thought he was there like it was a regular thing," he murmurs, blowing out his cheeks and releasing the air. "He was so damn comfortable there."

My pacing takes me back and forth, finally delivering me to my intended target. Stumbling over my feet, I right myself just in time to see my worst fears coming true. God damn it! I can't be too late! She can't get involved with him. She's mine! Unless we become brothers in the dick brigade for River. Now, that could work. But I'm not sure how I feel about another dick when there are four of us. If the others jump on board, that is.

"Motherfucker!" I hiss, peeking through the window, eyeing my damn mission. "He's holding her damn hand from across the table!" I frown, stepping back and checking my reflection in the glass. "I look okay?"

Callum blinks at me several times. "What the hell are you about to do?" His muscles turn rigid, and he cocks his head. "Rad."

"I'm going in there, of course," I say, waving a hand in the direction of the restaurant where my girl sits with another fucking man. "Duh! We didn't stalk her all the way downtown to a fancy restaurant to not interrupt her date." I narrow my eyes looking around the area, noting how empty the streets seem on a Saturday night. "I can't go in there empty-handed, though," I grumble, stepping out of the random alleyway and taking in the shops around me. "Ah-ha! I'll be right back!" I shout, taking off down the road at a full sprint, slamming into the flower shop as Callum shouts my name.

 acquired gift in my hands, smiling at Callum's bored expression.

"Okay," I say, breathlessly fanning my face with my free hand. Jesus. I haven't run in years, and I guess it shows. "Now, I'm not empty-handed."

"Rad," he says sternly, stiffening my spine.

"What?"

"You can't just march into the restaurant, hand her a bouquet of tulips, and expect her to forgive you."

Ah, Callum, the cricket on my shoulder whispering logic into my ear. Always full of reason and concern, guiding me on the right path. But not today. I don't need the right path this Saturday evening. No. I need River, a thorough discussion of forgiveness, and her pussy in my mouth. Yeah, everything in that order, too.

"Sorry, bro," I say, clapping him on the shoulder. "There's nothing stopping me from marching in there and winning her back one flower at a time." Callum's face drops in defeat, and his eyes roll toward the star-filled sky with a loud, long-drawn-out groan.

"Christ," Callum curses, knowing he's lost this battle with me. "If you piss her off, it's all on you. Then you can tell the other two why she's making our lives a living hell." He gives me a pointed look, leaning against his bike with interest. He can pretend all day long that he doesn't want me to do this, but I can see it in his eyes. Excitement sparks there for the first time in years.

"You don't want to join?" I wiggle my brows, earning a scoff in return.

"She'll bury us alive. Better you than me," he grumbles, pulling his phone from his pocket.

"I'll be back soon," I say with a confident grin. I straighten out my shirt, double-checking the tulips in my hands and counting all twelve of the pink and white blossoms beaming under the streetlamp above. "Please, let this work," I softly beg, staring at the bright orbs twinkling in the darkened sky above me. It's all I have right now.

Something deep festers inside me, guiding me through the ornate doors

of the restaurant with the name Cherry Blossom hovering above the entrance in golden letters. The intense need to sit beside River and soak her presence in has me bursting into the eatery like a bat out of hell.

I heave a breath, glimpsing the intricate decorations adorning the walls. The light atmosphere envelops me in a hug, pushing away the urgency I had waltzing in. Soft music filled with harps and violins floats through the air.

"Sir." I raise a brow, turning to stare at the man beside me with his nose in the air. Wrinkles drag down his cheeks and forehead as he scowls, raking his gaze over my attire, and he scoffs. "You do not meet our dress code. I'm going to have to ask you to leave," he says, pointing toward the door with a haughty attitude I don't quite like.

"Nah, that's okay," I say with a grin, digging into my pockets. "I can't leave yet, bro. I have a girl to win back. You see her over there?" I ask, pointing toward the back of the crowded space where she sits with Mr. Handsy, snacking on delicious-looking sushi. When he should want to snack on my delicious Pretty Girl, looking like a full damn meal in her dress.

God damn. Up close and personal, she looks hotter than from across the street. Back in Central City, my girl would never be caught dead in a tight-fitting dress. Not to mention the makeup. But I guess she has that privilege now that she works for her brothers and has created this entire empire. My Pretty Girl sure has made something phenomenal out of herself, and I couldn't be more damn proud of her. I'll show her in the upcoming weeks that I'm all into this repair and refresh service she's offering. And other things if she wants.

"A tragedy," he mutters under his breath, following my finger. "But you're still not appropriately dressed. Our attire requires suit jackets and closed-toe shoes."

I huff, digging into my back pocket and pulling out my wallet. "I'll pay you five-hundred bucks to turn the other cheek," I say, waving the green under his greedy little nose. Instantly he perks up, watching the money like a pocket watch in front of his face. Yes, doorman, get hypnotized by the green in front of your face. Let me in! I want to beg and plead, but I know in this town money talks.

He peers around at the rest of the crowd, snatching the money from my fingers. "Then, Welcome, Mister…"

"Ashton Radcliffe the Third, my guy," I say, patting his shoulder with an eager clap. "Now, if you don't mind, I'm on a mission to get my girl back." I saunter away without a backward glance, darting toward the quaint little table located in the back. The further I walk through the tables and booths, the dimmer the lights become, and I squint until I get to my destination.

My fingers turn white around the stems of the bouquet when the fucker my girl is with raises his gaze to mine. A cocky smile pulls at his lips when we lock stares, and I'm eager to punch the sureness from his damn body—over and over. He hasn't faced the mighty Rad rage yet, but he's about to meet the bull if he doesn't stop touching my girl. With more confidence than I feel, I wink at him, nodding in greeting.

"I believe you're in my seat," I say, pointing in his direction.

Mr. Tall, Dark, and Handsome has the audacity to laugh at me, waving a hand to the unoccupied chair next to River. Even better. I don't need to sit across from her and play footsie; I need to be beside her, luring her in with my manly musk.

Shit. Discreetly, I sniff myself and recoil. If I had more time to get ready for this stalking adventure, I would have prepared a little better. Earlier, I pounded the drums to beat my damn frustrations away. And unfortunately, it shows with the stench coming from beneath my armpits. No wonder Mr. Doorman didn't want to let me in. I'm ripe as hell.

"Take a seat," he says in a smooth voice full of generosity.

"No! What the fuck!" River hisses at the same time, glaring in the direction of her date. Ha. If he's not careful, I really am going to win her over and steal her away from him. But only after she stabs him in the dick to assert her dominance.

"For you, Pretty Girl," I beam, presenting her with the vibrant tulips, even bowing a little to prove to my queen that she's important.

"Wow! What a gentleman," the man says, folding his hands under his chin with stars in his eyes, watching closely as I take a seat. "So, you must be one of the exes I've heard so many wonderful things about."

"Rocco, I swear to God," River mumbles, taking the flowers with a tight smile and setting them beside her on the table.

"Well, I suppose that's me. Just depends on what you've heard about me. Charming, irresistible…"

"Annoying," River gripes, slapping her palm across my lips. "What exactly are you doing here, Rad?" She raises a brow when I grin beneath her hand, basking in the feel of her flesh against mine. "This is a private dinner. No one invited you." Her glare intensifies tenfold, lighting me from the inside out. Holy hell. I forgot how damn sexy her glares were. I'm going to—fuck, too late. *Not now, Little Rad,* I grumble to myself.

"Fascinating. I'm Rocco, by the way. It's wonderful to meet you." Reaching across the table, we clasp hands and shake in greeting. Rocco's dark, devilish eyes twinkle in the low light with mischief when we separate, and he places his chin in his hand.

"Ashton Radcliffe," I say through the gag over my mouth, grinning wildly when River huffs and pulls her hand away, wiping it on a napkin to remove my spit. "Great to meet you too. So, are you two…" Holding out the last word, I point between the two of them. A stark ray of hope flashes inside me when Rocco chuckles, turning a shade of red.

"Will you excuse us?" River asks sharply, jumping to her feet.

"By all means," I say with a cocky grin, sitting back and expecting him to take the hint and leave the table.

"Idiot," River mumbles.

"Oh God," I yelp when her thin fingers grab the top of my ear and yank me out of my chair. "Pretty Girl," I groan, grabbing hold of her wrist and trying to yank her hand from me.

"Excuse us, Rocco. I need to square some things away with Rad here before we finish our dinner," she says in a sickeningly sweet tone, yanking me forward.

"Take your time, Doll! We've got all night," he calls, waving us along.

"Pretty Girl, I swear!" I groan, hunching over as she drags me through the restaurant with no shame and throws me outside.

"You swear what? Rad!" she shouts, throwing her arms all around.

"I just…"

"You just what?" she shouts, pointing a manicured nail straight into my chest. "What the hell are you doing here? I don't—" Her eyes lock on someone behind me, and she groans. "You, too?"

"In my defense, he-he dragged me into this," Callum stutters, shoving his hands in his pockets.

"Liar," I hiss in his direction between clenched teeth. "Don't let him lie to you, Pretty Girl. He came all on his own with little to no convincing." I raise a brow when Callum flips me off with a grunt, kicking a foot at the ground.

River pinches the bridge of her nose, stepping back from us. "Just explain this to me. Why are you two here?"

"Ask him," Callum says softly, eyeing River with hooded eyes. He watches her every damn move, just like I thought he would.

"Ashton," she hisses my full name, making my heart leap from my chest when she glares at me again.

"Well, fuck! Pretty Girl. I saw that man at your house, and you look like that," I say, waving a hand up and down her body.

"Like what?" she asks through gritted teeth. "And having a man at my house is none of your damn business! None of my life is your fucking business!" she shouts angrily, turning redder and redder by the second. "You lost that right when you left."

Swallowing hard, I take in the rage she exudes. My damn heart hurts when she looks between the two of us. This is not how I saw this going. I guess I should have expected it, though. We're not exactly on good terms right now. I have a lot of making up to do before she'll jump into my arms again.

"I'm sorry, Pretty Girl," I say softly. "I…"

"Just because you're fucking sorry doesn't mean you have the right to follow me out. This is my private time. I've lived without you assfaces for years now. Do you think I'm just going to open my arms and invite you back in?" she asks with moisture blooming in her eyes.

"No." I shake my head. "That's not what I expected at all," I say seriously, taking a step forward. Gripping River's chin between my thumb and forefinger, I force her to stare into my earnest eyes and really see what I'm saying. "I am sorry. I will prove to you how sorry I am over and over again. I will be your damn tail, following you on all your dates and outings. I'm sorry. I'm sorry. I'm so fucking sorry, River. That I left you. That I left our fucking baby. That you had to do all this yourself." Tears burn the back of my eyes when she stares up at me with those wide, moss-green eyes filled to the brim with much-deserved anger. "I'll never give up on you," I whisper. "Not again."

River pulls back, anger twisting her face. "Just leave me alone. I'm your damn boss. Not your girlfriend. Not your romantic interest," she chokes, bringing a fist to her lips. "I'm going back inside and…"

"Here you go, Doll," Rocco says, emerging from the door with a grim expression. Handing her a Styrofoam box, he kisses the top of her head with affection, keeping his eyes firmly locked on us. "We'll postpone this to another time." Looking between me and Cal he frowns, shaking his head. "Take care of my girl, yeah?" He raises his brow, taking a step away. "Call me later." With one last wave, Rocco disappears into the shadows, leaving the three of us.

"Wait!" River shouts, turning on her heel and groaning when Rocco's sports car speeds down the road, leaving her behind. "Well, there goes my ride. And my phone. And my damn purse. This is just great!" she shouts in frustration, clutching the take-home box.

"Who is h-he, Little Star?" Callum asks softly, bringing her attention back to him. Almost.

Her eyes fall to the ground, and she shakes her head, refusing to look at him. There's something so broken between them, worse than all of us. She can't even stand to be alone with or look at him.

"Come on, Pretty Girl! Spill the beans. Is that your boyfriend, too? Are we adding him to the firehose brigade? There's always more room for cocks, I guess. Is he nice? Is he hung…"

"He's not my fucking boyfriend, you assface!" she shouts, her voice echoing off the surrounding buildings and filling the air with her rage. "Do you think I've had a fucking second to have any sort of relationship these past few years?" Her gorgeous chest heaves when she covers her mouth with her fingers and shakes her head like she didn't mean to yell that. "You think I had any time to date while finishing college, raising a baby, being an intern, and then running my own department?" Pain encases my chest when the first tear falls, and she growls out with frustration, curling her fingers. "I barely had time to think, let alone chase dick."

"We're-we're sorry," Callum whispers, stepping toward her with a twisted-up expression, dripping with the grief I feel pouring through me.

We weren't there for her. At all. We fucking abandoned her when she needed us most. Not only did she soar through the clouds, she fucking flew higher than the sun and achieved her goals. Just like we did ours. But the worst part about it is we didn't do it together like we had planned. We promised to bring her with us and help her start a new life with us out here. We failed her. Miserably.

"You're sorry?" River asks, shaking her head.

"Yeah, I'm sorry, Pretty Girl. We both are. Aren't we, Callum?" My eyes snap in his direction, catching the emotions building in his gray eyes.

"Yeah-yeah, I am sorry. I've regretted a lot of things in my life, Little Star. But there's one scene that plays in my mind over and over again, riddled with regret. It's the night I came to your apartment and saw him there with you. I couldn't hear anything that was said. But I watched him kiss you. And I ran. I ran so far away that I tried to force the memory of you out of my mind." Callum runs a hand down his face and shakes his head. Grief flashes across his face at the woman that he lost in a moment of fear and misunderstanding. "I've never been able to admit to anyone that I regretted running. I didn't really know what was going on, and it kills me that I never stopped to really think about what was happening right in front of me." Callum's breath shutters in his chest. Quickly, he averts his eyes from her as she silently stands on the sidewalk, clenching and unclenching her fists. "But I see the mistake I made now. If I had just stopped and not let my emotions take over and thought logically about what was happening, I wouldn't have left."

I can't tell if the tears falling down River's face are from anger or sadness. Her body doesn't move, standing stock still watching as Callum continues to war with himself.

Angrily running her tongue over her top teeth, she shakes her head. "Why? Why the fuck are you guys doing this to me now?" River's eyes look between the two of us, searching our faces for the truth that she's heard from us in the past few days. I'm not sure what she sees when she looks at us, but I hope she sees that there's nothing but honesty behind our eyes.

"Because it's time that we set everything straight," I say, stepping forward again and putting my palm on her cheek. Whether she wants to admit it or not, her entire body shudders when our flesh meets. "I think it's time all of us sat down and talked. You know we didn't sign the restraining orders. We had no idea about Lyric. It's time, River. For our future. Whether we return to what we were before and start fresh. Or whether it's too late to fix what we broke. We need to have a discussion and figure out what happened and why it happened the way it did."

Once again, those big green eyes look up at me with continuous amounts of moisture pooling in them and running down her cheeks. I can't tell what's going through my Pretty Girl's head, but I know at some point I'm going to get an ear full. My heart pounds when she gives me a tight smile, stepping back from my embrace.

"Okay," she says with a resigned sigh. "But not tonight. I know we have a lot to talk about. I'm so fucking angry at you guys. But I deserve an explanation from all four of you. For now, can someone take me home?"

"Yeah, Little Star. I'll take you home," Callum says, waving a hand for River to follow him.

"Hey, wait! You're my ride," I say, sprinting after them as Callum hands River my helmet.

A smile blossoms across my face when she stares down at the helmet like it's the bane of her existence. Her nose crinkles, and she shakes her head.

"There's no way in hell you're getting me on this deathtrap." She shakes her head when I advance on her, pulling the helmet from her hands and plopping it over her head, nestling the straps under her chin. Ah, just like old times. "Rad," she warns with a growl, reaching to take the helmet off again.

My fingers wrap around her wrist, stopping her from removing it. "No, Pretty Girl. Do you remember what I said before?" She shakes her head, frowning at me. "It was when you were about to get on my dirt bike. Do you remember that? You didn't want to because you thought I was going to drop you. Callum's got you, babe."

"I won't let-let anything happen to you, Little Star." He eyes her up and down, taking in her trembling fingers and flaring nostrils.

"I swear to God, Callum. If I die on the back of this moving deathtrap, I will come back to haunt you," River says through clenched teeth, glaring down at his motorcycle.

For the first time in a long time, a genuine smile crosses Callum's lips. It's like a breath of fresh air fills his lungs, and he can breathe for the first time in forever.

"Don't worry, Pretty Girl. He's got you. You just have to hang on tight," I say, patting the back seat as Callum climbs on and scoots forward.

River stares down at the empty seat contemplating her options. Moving from foot to foot, she shakes her head and backs away.

I snort at her discomfort. Putting my hands on her hips, I suck in a breath. The feel of her warmth beneath me does funny things to my insides, and butterflies take flight in my stomach. Gently, I help River straddle the bike, biting my lip when her dress rides up her delicious thighs.

"I swear I'm flashing the entire world right now," she grumbles to herself, pulling her tiny dress down. Gently, she places her hands on Callum's shoulders with trembling fingers. "I should've just called a ride."

"Now, now, Pretty Girl. You're going to fall off if you keep your hands on his shoulders. Right here," I say, pointing to Callum's waist, noticing his shoulders bunch when I drag her hands around him and secure them at his front, forcing her chest against his back. "There! Now, you won't fall off. Just stay like that and lean into my boy Callum. And you'll be as good as new."

"You-you ready?" Callum asks, peeking behind him as River tightens her hold on him and nervously nods.

"Hold on to your ass, Pretty Girl. He's about to take off." And with that, Callum and my Pretty Girl ride off into the moonlight, slowly making their way downtown and out toward the mansions we live in.

Shoving my hands into my pockets, I begin the long trek back to the band house. Sure, I could walk a few blocks and make it to my normal house, grab my keys, and drive my car back there. But I decide a nice, long, relaxing walk could do me some good. Besides, it gives Callum time to get over his fear and talk to River a little bit more. Because I have a feeling that in the next week or so, change is on the horizon.

"KNIGHT!" RIVER'S SMALL VOICE PULLS ME OUT OF MY REPRIEVE AS SHE runs over to me with her arms spread wide.

A small laugh escapes me when she bounds into me, knocking me over into the grass, flat on my back.

"What's up, Blue?" I chuckle, righting us, so we're sitting side-by-side on the hill behind our apartment building.

Something about these stolen moments with my Blue cements my need for her. Nothing on this planet will ever compare to our rendezvous. Not my guitar. Or my favorite chocolate bar. This is it for me; I feel it in my bones.

She giggles, staring at the guitar beside me, and shrugs. "I just missed you today. Where were you?"

Kicked out. My mom didn't want me anywhere near the apartment today but didn't have enough sense to get me on the bus for school. Or even dress me properly before she gave me the boot. In only a T-shirt and jeans, the only other things I had time to grab when she yanked me by my shirt collar were my guitar and a pair of socks. My stomach rumbles violently from missing not only breakfast but lunch. Hours ago, I ventured back to my apartment door and knocked, hoping my mother would at least have enough sense to feed me, but she didn't. That man answered the door with his shirt off and a scowl, telling me to get lost. I'm sure I'll hear about my indiscretions later.

"I missed you, too, Blue. Mom has someone important over. She says he might be my new dad soon." I shrug, hoping it's not true. He may have gifted me a guitar, but I see how he looks at me with disdain.

"You won't leave me, will you?" she asks with a quivering lip. Tears pool in her big, green eyes, and I swear my heart breaks from one look.

"Never," I murmur, picking up my guitar. "Want to hear my new song?" I ask, strumming the strings and humming under my breath.

"Yes!" she shrieks with excitement. "Play me a song, Knight."

I grunt, slamming my fists into the hanging bag over and over until my raw knuckles bleed. Red pours down my arms in tiny droplets, but I don't

fucking stop. I revel in the pain, washing away the happy memories pouring through the black box I locked them in. My only happy times as a kid were with River on that hill and my guitar on my knee. I didn't know how to play, but the internet was a hell of a teacher. Slowly but surely, I figured it out and played River song after song. Then we left Central City for greener pastures with the man who not only ruined and controlled my life but my mother's, too. Sometimes I wonder why the fuck she jumped into bed with him and stole my fucking life from me.

Fuck. Her. Fuck River. Fuck. This. Fuck. Everything.

Why did it have to be her? Why? It could have been anyone else on the West's payroll, but it just had to be River fucking West. The once love of my damn life, and now…

I shake my head, dispelling the tumultuous thoughts banging around in my mind. The need to walk away from this entire situation sits heavy on my chest as I continue to pound into the bag with all my might, forcing myself to fucking forget everything—even how to breathe.

When I stop my frantic jabs, black spots dance in my vision, numbing the rage and pain eating away at me. Leaning my forehead against the bag, I suck in oxygen, refueling my body until the world returns to focus. Slumping down onto the mat, I lay on my back, staring at the tall ceiling.

Whoever built this house knew exactly what they were doing. A full-sized gym with every piece of equipment possible surrounds me. And in the next room, a full-blown recording studio taunts me, begging me to create new music, and digitally immortalize it for the world to hear. If fucking only.

Not only does my dick refuse to work around other chicks, the moment River numbed my heart—the music fucking died inside me. Like she sucked the spark from my damn soul and stole that shit from me. I curl my aching fingers into fists and snarl at the fucking ceiling for the millionth time in the past week. A helpless feeling of being stuck in the damn mud, unable to take control of my destiny, creeps up my spine.

I huff, turning to my side and forcing myself to stand on my jelly legs. Looking at my smartwatch, I stop the timer at precisely two hours. Blowing out a breath, I bask in the momentary reprieve this session has given me. My mind quiets for one bliss-filled moment, and serenity runs through my veins. Right now, it's as if I never laid eyes on River West and had my soul stomped out, only to return to her years later and have to follow her orders.

"Fuck," I grumble, stumbling toward the white towels dangling from a rack attached to the wall.

Wiping the sweat from my face, I smack my lips, desperately seeking the water I forgot to grab before disappearing. Every inch of me aches deliciously as I trudge up the steps into the brightly lit kitchen heated with the sun's rays. It's like walking out of my damn casket and into the real world.

When I entered the basement two hours ago, the sun hadn't even peeked over the horizon. And now, the new day is here—Sunday. A day of nothing but working out and taking it easy before the reality of our new week begins, band practices, and our early morning therapy sessions.

Over the past few days, the guys have already started to fall into her bullshit. Again. They're falling into her fucking honey trap and gravitating toward everything she says, like lost little puppy dogs with big heart eyes. It fucking disgusts me. How can they do that? After everything that she put us through.

Fuck. Despite the grueling work out this morning, my head is still a damn mess. Sure, I momentarily distracted myself from the bullshit happening. But the pain never truly leaves. Every time she walks into the house, she rips open another scab and exposes my wounds.

This entire situation has been one fucked up, long nightmare, and there's no way out. Believe me, I've checked every day. My agent has been searching this entire week, hoping to bring me good updates about another prospect. But nothing has come of it. According to her, I should stick to my contract, even though we could void it by walking out and starting somewhere new.

Stick it out? Yeah right. She has no idea what I'm up against. When I walked away, I walked the fuck away. Endpoint. Nothing was going to bring me back to the woman who crushed my heart in the palm of her hand. So, thanks, cruel world, for plopping me smack dab in the middle of this shipwreck with no lifeboat in sight. I'm fucking drowning in rage, pain, and the constant memories holding me captive. One day, I'll be able to break the surface and breathe again.

Nothing in this world could make me forgive River West for what she did. That fucking video lives in the deep confines of my head, reminding me to never again fuck around with relationships. Women, yes. Well, fuck —kind of. If my dick would fucking cooperate. It's like he's holding out on me for someone I refuse to let him have. Fuck him.

My fingers curl into fists when I step further into the kitchen and rest my head against the cool metal of the fridge. I heave a breath, trying to shove down the emotions River always brings up. I've locked that shit up for so many years with success. Now, here it is again, trying to ooze out of me. I would rather swallow my emotions and let the numbness take me over than feel what I felt for her.

Taking a deep breath, I ground myself to the now. Fuck my brain. Fuck my thoughts. As I listen to the sounds around me, I note the others must still be asleep. Like hell do they get up early and fight invisible demons at the gym like me. Not that I get up fucking early. Ever. But today was different. A calling clawed through my ribs and pulled me toward the gym so early in the goddamn morning.

Thud. Thud.

My face scrunches when a small scratching sound comes from some-where in the house, followed by a small, strangled cry.

"What the hell?" I mutter, pushing off the fridge and looking around for the source of the sound. "Better not be a goddamn rat," I grumble, cautiously walking toward the sound.

The more I walk away from the kitchen, the louder it gets, seeming to come from the large living room.

"Help!" a little voice calls, making my heart slam in my fucking chest. "Please, Daddies!" It comes again through sobs.

That's when I realize it isn't scratching coming from anywhere. It's light pounding coming from the front door.

A million thoughts race through my mind when I march toward the front door, catching more words from the tiny voice on the other side.

"Help! Mommy is dead!" The tiny voice cracks with emotions, snif-fling behind the front door. "Daddy!" the voice calls frantically, sounding more urgent than before. The pounding continuously beats against the wood until I'm standing right in front of it with my brows furrowed in confusion.

Daddy? There's no one's dad here. Unless one of these idiots knocked up some chick and decided not to tell anyone. Fuck. What a dick move that'd be. I don't care who the chick is. I'd never abandon my child like my dad left me high and dry.

"Fuck," I shake my head, throwing the door open, and freeze at the sight of her.

A beautiful little girl with fat tears rolling down her cheeks and a white bunny clutched to her chest shivers outside my front door. Her eyes screwed shut as she sniffles on her bunny's head.

"Hey, little girl. Are you okay?" My hoarse voice falls from my lips in a soothing tone, grabbing her attention.

I swear all the oxygen in my lungs ceases to exist when she looks up at me, cries even harder, and launches herself at me. Her little face buries into my thighs as she sobs harder, clinging to me for dear life.

Panic ensues inside me. What the hell do I do? If this were my little sister, I'd scoop her up and soothe all her pain. But I don't have a fucking clue who this is or why she's at my damn door. Almost instinctively, my protective side roars to the surface, and I run my fingers through her long, dark locks in a soothing manner, getting snagged on the knots.

"Hey, little girl? Are you okay?" My voice softens as I crouch down, pulling her from my leg and cupping her cheeks in my palms. "What's going on?" I ask again, earning a small hiccup in return.

"My mommy. She-she, I-I can't get her to move. My mommy is dead," she wails again, squeezing her eyes shut and trembling beneath my hands.

My heart skips a beat as I take her in, noting the similarities between her and River. Fuck. Her long, dark hair with tiny freckles on the bridge of her nose. Little pajamas hang loosely around her body; hell, she's not even wearing shoes. But where else could she be from? We all know River has a kid, but I never expected to see her standing shoeless outside my front door with tears falling from her eyes.

"Your mommy is River?" I ask as my eyes roam over her face, memorizing the shape of her nose and the pout of her quivering lips.

Time stands still when River's daughter blinks open her moisture-filled eyes, hiccuping in my grip. Oxygen evades me. My fucking head spins. Something primal and deep inside me snaps into place when her eyes connect with mine, full of terror and sadness. She quivers in my grip, nodding vigorously in confirmation.

More tears stream out of her identical mismatched eyes, falling down her small chin and dripping on me. Her wetness coats my flesh as those big, hurt eyes flash with disappointment, taking in every inch of me, too. Dipping down my chest and arms, she silently notes the tattoos etched into my flesh. She doesn't spare a second, gripping my wrist and trying to yank me across the street.

But I'm too stunned to move. Her tiny words don't register in my damn walnut brain as I process the fucking situation. River had a baby four years ago. She wasn't Van's like Gloria had claimed. This beautiful little girl standing before me is one hundred percent my flesh and blood.

This little girl isn't just a spitting image of River. She has my fucking eyes. My. Fucking. Eyes. Something my goddamn dad passed down to me before he bailed to pursue music. How fucking ironic. There's no goddamn way that's some sort of coincidence. You don't just show up with these eyes and not have similar DNA. It's an anomaly. Yet, here she is, looking at me.

There's no goddamn way.

This can't be fucking happening right now.

No.

A tidal wave of guilt crashes over my head, pulling me into the depths of the turbulent waves. My muscles jump under my skin, begging me to make a move. An itchiness spreads across my flesh, stretching too damn thin. I run a hand through my hair, digging into my scalp as the memories of my father resurface.

"Where's Daddy?" I whisper, staring out the window of our home. Longing clings to every inch of me. He's been gone for way too long. He said he had to work. And the sun is down.

Mother scoffs, gripping a beer bottle. "He's never coming back," she mutters coldly, staring at the wall with glossy eyes.

He's never fucking coming back. Is that how my little girl felt? Does that run through her mind, too? Late at night as she stares at the white ceiling with hope dwindling day by day that she'll ever see her father again. If he'll ever walk through the door with a smile, saying he was joking about leaving? That he'd never do that to his family and perpetuate the hurt?

I abandoned my child like my father did to me.

I fucking did that!

Holy fucking shit. The walls close in on me. Oxygen refuses to refill my empty lungs. When did the air become so damn thick?

Fuck! When–

"Daddy," she whispers with urgency, knocking me out of my own damning thoughts. "I think my mommy is dead," she says more calmly now, tugging at my wrist again with all her strength. "Please," she begs, yanking again until I'm on my stumbling feet and dumbly following her out onto the step.

"Wait," I struggle to say through the tightening of my throat. "Fuck," I rasp, collapsing to my knees again. My limbs tingle like damn Jell-O has replaced my bones, sending me spiraling to the ground. "You're…" I jerk my hand from her grasp, blindly gripping her cherub cheeks. Moisture burns behind my eyes when I really look her over again. "Mine," I mutter with a heavy tongue. She's too young to confirm or deny my ramblings. It's something I'll have to discuss with the fucking corpse she keeps talking about. Fuck! River.

"Daddy," she wails again, tugging at my arm. I shake my head, trying to knock the fog from my brain, processing all her words.

"Hey, whoa. Lyric!" Rad says, breathlessly running through the open front door with a pale face, falling to his knees beside me. "What are you doing here, Little Pretty Girl? And why are you crying? Did big, mean Kieran make you cry?" Rad asks with a low tone, tinged with unveiled anger.

I swallow hard, watching helplessly as she runs into his arms. Burying her face into the crook of his neck, she cries harder, taking comfort in him. Jealousy rushes through me. I clench my damn jaw, wishing I was the warmth that brought her salvation. Instead of him.

"What did you do?" he hisses, narrowing his eyes at me with such venom I have to shove away all the damn hurt and anger.

Mostly, it's the questions resting on the tip of my numb tongue that beg to come out. I swallow them all, ready to unleash them at the right time. Not now. Not when River is possibly in danger. Adrenaline spikes in my system. I push to my feet, glaring down at him as I march away with determination leading the way.

"What the fuck are you talking about? I didn't do anything. She was pounding on our door…" I shout over my shoulder and curl my fists at my side. "Doesn't fucking matter. Something is wrong with River."

"Fuck!" Rad huffs, climbing to his feet with her in his arms still. "What's wrong with your mommy, Little Pretty Girl?" he huffs, hoisting her further up his body as we quickly walk toward the house that now seems like a damn mile away.

Oh, how I ache to comfort her like a father should and make all the pain leave her. From here on out, I'll give her anything she desires. I'll never be my fucking father, sending a few post cards here and there. But he never really fucking cared. He rode off into the sunset with his guitar strapped to his back and a dream on his mind.

Sounds so damn familiar. God.

"My mommy is dead!" she sniffs again, shaking her head with a renewed sense of sadness clinging to her voice.

"Dead? Tell me what's going on, Little Pretty Girl. Tell daddy what is going on," he says, emphasizing daddy and glaring at me like I have any idea what's happening.

I cock my head to the side when he says the word daddy. Daddy? What in the ever-living fuck is going on in this house? Why is he daddy? My face twists into an unmasked expression, flushing the color from my face.

Something in my spooked expression must give me away as Rad soothes the little girl, pumping his skinny legs harder toward River's house.

Turning his gaze to me, he cocks his head to the side and gives me a tight grin. "Welcome aboard, Daddy Kieran. Fucking finally. Now, apparently, River is dying, so we should probably go save her," Rad says with urgency, waving me along as I blindly follow right behind him, staring at the little girl in his arms with longing.

It's ridiculous to feel so much toward someone I met two seconds ago on my front step. But it's all there. A ball of feelings formed in my tight chest and squeezed out my breath. So many fucking questions beg to unleash as a sliver of denial hits me square in my stomach.

"Rad, what the hell is going on? Why does she… Who is her…" My heavy tongue is barely able to work as we slam through River's unlocked front door, loudly entering the pristine home. "Tell me what I'm thinking isn't the truth. Tell me that this is..." Because if it's true. Then I'm a piece of fucking shit. I walked out. I left her.

Without ever knowing she existed.

Rad turns sharply on his heel in the middle of the living room with a scowl. The little girl clutches tighter to him, whimpering like she's known him for years. Has he? Fuck. My heart pounds like a drum against my ribs as so many thoughts go through my mind. I knew River had a fucking kid. I knew because of Gloria… Gloria fucking knew and fucked up my entire life. She fucking…

I grip my hair tightly, pulling at the roots. My brain goes in a thousand different directions, leading me back to the same damn conclusion; Gloria somehow lied to me and led me astray. She used my vulnerability against me when I was at my lowest and manipulated me into thinking that, for some reason, River's baby was Van's. Shit. The phone call I received so many years ago plays in my mind on a constant loop.

The beautiful scenery of the large bluffs overlooking the blue ocean, my phone vibrates on my side table. I groan when it displays the name of the last person I ever wanted to speak to again. It's bad enough that growing up she was the world's worst mother, but the second the boys and I won, she called me and begged me for some money. With reluctance, I answer the phone, inwardly groaning at the lecture I'm sure I'm about to receive.

"Hello?"

"Kieran, so lovely to hear your voice again," Gloria sings through the phone with a cheerful hint to her tone.

"Sure, I guess. What's going on?" I ask, getting straight to the damn point.

"Well, I'm fine! Thanks for asking. Everything is settling so well since you boys left. Nigel has been on a business trip for the past week, and it's been so quiet around here. I've missed you so," she says through a wistful sigh. I'm sure not missing my ass at all.

"That's good to hear," I grunt, plopping down on the edge of my new king-sized bed. "So, why the call? It's been a few weeks."

"Well," she huffs out a laugh. "You'll never guess who got herself knocked up!"

"Hopefully not you," I grunt, cringing at the thought.

"Heavens, no! A few days ago, I got a little visit from someone you used to know. You know, that cheating whore you ran from."

I physically recoil from the phone, almost throwing it across the room. My mouth instantly dries as my gut tightens at the news.

"She-she…"

"Yes. She came sniffing around looking for you boys, claiming she was pregnant by one of you. Don't worry, though. I got her to confess it's Van's. Can you believe that? She tried to pin it on you four! What a lying slut she is." Gloria rambles on and on about River until I clear my throat.

"So, she's pregnant by Van?" I ask hoarsely, squeezing my eyes shut. It's bad enough she fucked him behind our backs. But this? Getting pregnant by the dickhead is the ultimate fuck you to us.

"Yes," Gloria sniffs. "It appears so." She talks more, but her words move like sludge through my ears, drowning out her annoying voice.

"Okay, bye," I mumble, not bothering to listen to her goodbye.

Through my stunned daze, my phone slips from my fingers, landing with a thud on the ground. Whatever effect the shocking news has on me knocks me out of my stupor. Uncontrollable rage storms through my system, turning my vision a dark shade of red. My nostrils flare as everything Gloria said settles heavily on my chest, caving it in. Through my fit of anger, I march toward my old guitar leaning against the wall—the same one I wooed River with so many years before. Everything blurs around me. Sound stops. My feelings cease to exist.

Before I know what's happening, my long fingers wrap around the long end of my guitar. The only sound that fills the room besides my pounding heart is splintering wood crashing against the hardwood floors. Over and fucking over, I smash it to pieces, basking in the destruction of my once precious guitar.

I stand tall with a heaving chest, keeping the news of River's pregnancy to myself. No one marches into my room to check on me because the distance between my brothers and I have hit a fever pitch for the past few weeks. A black void has split between us, making us strangers more than brothers. Callum barely talks. Rad is chasing anything with an ass. And Asher has folded in on himself, remaining quiet and calm—nothing like the man I knew two months ago. But I know something is distracting him into silence. I've never seen him like this before.

At that moment, I vow to myself never to fall into the grips of another woman and let her ruin them or me ever again. Pussy, sure. But a full-blown relationship? Fuck that. The last one I had exploded in my face.

I swallow hard, shoving that awful memory into the back of my mind, bringing me back to the situation at hand. River is off somewhere dying, and I've come face to face with our daughter, the little girl who magically resembles us.

A perfect damn mix.

Fucking hell, this can't be real. Is this real? Is this little person with my eyes really standing before me? My heart thumps wildly against my damn ribs.

"This is River's daughter, Lyric." A pained expression crosses Rad's face as he looks down at her and shakes his head. "And by the look on your face, you've already guessed that. You're pale, Bro. Are you finally figuring out that you're a damn dad? That you purposefully… That you goddamn… Fuck." Shaking his head, Rad squeezes his eyes shut. Anger swims across his down-turned features until he blows a breath and smothers it away. "We'll have to talk about this later, so we're not in front of little ears."

"But you swears a lot, Daddy," she murmurs through a sniffle, wiping her nose along Rad's shirt.

Rad stiffens. "Fuck! I mean. You're right, Little Pretty Girl. I'm sorry." She nods, sniffling again.

His words crash into me like a wave, taking me under. Momentarily, it's hard to suck in oxygen, and my lips pop open. Over and over, his words repeatedly play until they finally fucking stick in my brain. I'm a fucking father. A dad. Shit. The walls close around me as my panic rises and sweat glistens over my flesh. My chest fucking tightens like thick rubber bands constricting the oxygen from my body, and I'm only saved by the heady amounts of adrenaline shooting through my system. Deep breaths, idiot. I can't freak out now. There's too much going on to fall down the rabbit hole of realizations. Wiping a hand down my face, I erase everything going haywire in my body and numb it. The time for panic is later, not now.

Kieran

"Lyric," I say softly, running a hand through her hair again. "Where is your mommy? And what's wrong with her?"

Lyric sniffles, finally lifting her head from Rad's neck. Her big, mismatched eyes look directly into mine, and she sniffles again, silently pointing down the hall with a hiccup.

"She's dead in the bathroom," she says through a quivering lip and clings tighter to Rad for protection.

"You watch the kid, and I'll go see what's wrong," I say with apprehension, taking a step toward the hallway. "We'll make sure your mommy is okay. Okay?" I swallow hard when she meets my eyes again, and I swear it's like looking in the mirror. A million questions run through my mind when she nods in agreement, still clinging tight to Rad, who soothes a hand down her back and murmurs soft words in her ear. Protectively he stands taller, watching as I exit.

I have a kid, is the only thought that runs through my mind as I make my way down the silent hallway. I perk my ears up, listening for any sound, but nothing comes to me. On quiet steps, I continue down the never-ending hallway and stop at the end as light catches my attention, leading me to a gigantic main bedroom.

A fully made king-sized bed sits in the expansive room, with a glittery purse thrown on the comforter. Everything around me is in pristine condition. No dust. Not even a scrap of clothing on the ground. I walk further into the room and turn to my left, where the light shines on the semi-closed door. I hold my breath as I slowly push the door open, and my heart speeds out of control. When Lyric said her mom was dead, I didn't expect to actually find an unmoved body.

"Shit," I grunt, marching into the bathroom with determination. "River?" Gently I move my fingers through her hair, guiding it off her pale-looking face. Gently I press my fingers into the side of her neck, noting that she still has a heartbeat. Thank fuck. The stench of stomach acid and vomit fills the room. My stomach turns at the putrid smell. God, it reeks

like fucking death walked into this bathroom and grabbed River before running away.

River's upper body clings to the porcelain God as she sleeps, pressing her cheek on the open toilet seat. How uncomfortable. But it was probably the only way to simultaneously get some rest and vomit. I cringe at the thought, crouching in front of her and running my finger over her heat-filled cheek.

"River?" I ask again, trying not to shake her.

"Fuck off," she mutters but doesn't move to make me fuck off. In fact, she doesn't move a muscle at all.

I smirk, almost chuckling to myself as the memories once again assault my mind. It's so like River to act like this even when I'm trying to help in such a dire situation.

"Sorry, River Blue, but I can't fuck off. A child was knocking at my door this morning. And I think you and I have some things to discuss." Emotions creep into my voice, taking them hostage and effectively choking me up. Tears burn behind my eyes as new feelings spill through me in her presence. Sure, I'm still pissed the fuck off at her. She cheated on us like we were nothing. But this? This is a child, and I'm sensible enough to realize there's more to this story than just black and white. There's a gray area that needs to be discussed.

River's eyes pop wide and frantic, refocusing on me as I crouch beside her. Her brows furrow with confusion as she takes me and the bathroom in. At that moment, I hear the distinct gurgle of her stomach as panic swallows her, and she heaves over the toilet.

"Oh God," she groans as she spills the contents of her stomach into the toilet. "It won't stop," she heaves again, spitting more chunks into the water.

My goddamn stomach turns at her noises, desperate to empty, too. But I hold it back, turning my head to give her some privacy. Like a gentleman, I grip back her hair despite the growing, conflicting feelings rising inside me. Just an hour ago, I beat the shit out of my hanging bag to her memory. Now here I am, holding back her hair as she's helplessly getting sick.

"I think I have food poisoning," she grumbles, squeezing her eyes shut. "Stupid sushi. Never again." A shiver runs down her spine, eliciting goosebumps when she sets back, heaving a few breaths. Blindly, she feels for the toilet paper, tears off a piece, and wipes her mouth.

"Well, whatever it is, you're definitely sick. And apparently, dying," I grunt, loosening my fingers from her hair as she settles her cheek against the rim of the toilet again. Exhaustion pulls at her features, and she huffs at me.

"Dying?" she grumbles, licking her chapped lips. "Why would I be dying?" she asks softly, flinching away from my touch when I remove some fallen hair strands from her face.

She watches me with suspicion when I plant my ass beside her. My eyes wander across her familiar yet grown-up features. She's still the same girl I knew back in Central City, yet not.

"Is she mine?" My tongue dries out as I wait on pins and needles for her answer. Even though, in my heart, I already know the damn truth.

The realization of having a kid and not knowing she existed breaks me in half. I promised myself a long time ago that if I ever had a child, I would never do to my child what my father did to me. He took off and never looked back. He made something of himself. He may not have been famous, but he took off for greener pastures and left my mother and me all alone. What kind of man does that? How can a man do that?

"Can we talk about this later when I'm not on my deathbed?" River rasps, squeezing her eyes shut with a pained expression crossing her features.

Although it's the last thing I want to do right now, I give River the reprieve she needs. "Yeah, but we will talk about this. And the fact that Rad knew…"

"Yeah," she says, heaving a breath and blowing it out between her lips.

Nervously, I rub my neck. "Do you need any water? I need to fill Rad in on what's happening."

River peeks an eye open, staring at me like I've grown a second head. "Um, sure. I don't think I've moved for at least six hours. Thanks," she says with reluctance, watching my every move like I might poison her water.

"Okay, no problem. I'll get you some water, and… I'll be right back, stay here," I grunt, stumbling my way to my feet, nearly falling over. A tight smile crosses my lips when I give her a little wave before exiting the bathroom.

The awkwardness of the situation presses down on me and doesn't leave until I walk out of the bathroom and down the hall. Running a hand through my hair, I halt in the living room doorway. My brows pull together at the sight of Asher, Callum, and Rad surrounding Lyric and cooing soft words into her ear. There's a familiarity between them that pulls at my damn heartstrings, tugging me in so many damn directions. She's mine. Yet, I don't have that connection with her.

"Is she okay?" Rad asks, jumping to his feet with concern etched onto his face.

My eyes stare from him and Lyric to the rest of the guys sitting there, staring up at me with wide eyes. "Um, yeah, I think she has food poisoning. She's stuck on the toilet and doesn't look very good," I say, scratching at the back of my neck. "But she's definitely not dying," I say confidently, locking eyes with Lyric, who sags with relief in Callum's lap.

"My mommy is going to be okay?" she asks with a quivering lip—

more moisture pools in her eyes, threatening to cascade down her cheeks again.

"Yeah," I say, clearing my throat, not sounding as reassuring as I wanted. "She's going to be okay."

"Yeah, Little Pretty Girl. We'll make sure that your mommy is all better. Sounds like she's just got the flu," Rad says, narrowing his eyes at me. What the hell did I do? Shit. I'm trying to make a difference.

Without another word, I walk into the kitchen and search through the cupboards for a glass with Ash on my ass.

"You good?" Asher asks with reluctance, rubbing his fingers over his stubbly jaw.

I grunt, grab a glass from the last cupboard, and slam it down onto the counter. "Define good," I hiss through gritted teeth, filling up the glass. "How long?" Asher's eyes fall to the ground, and he shakes his head.

"I only found out about a week ago." He doesn't elaborate more, but it pisses me off. Rage boils through my veins, and my fists clench at my sides.

"And you didn't fucking tell me?" Stalking up to him, I grab him by the shirt and pull his face into mine, letting him see all the emotions bursting through the surface. "I have a fucking kid, Asher. And you didn't think to tell me that you met her and that she existed?"

"You said you knew," Asher says, aggressively growling in my face, pushing his forehead into mine. "I asked you if you knew River had a kid. And you said you fucking knew. How long, Kieran? How fucking long did you know?" he grunts back, pressing his face harder into mine.

I blink several times, going over our conversation in the limo. Yeah, I did know she had a kid. Gloria told me that she did, and she also fucking lied through the damn phone.

I grunt, pushing Asher away from me, and pace around the kitchen with my hands clenching at my sides. "Gloria called me. We had just moved into our first apartment together. She told me that River had come to her and told her that she was pregnant with Van's baby." I stare at Asher as the news computes in his mind, and he shakes his head.

"So, you had nothing to do with the restraining orders either?" Rad asks, strolling into the kitchen and giving me the death glare.

I recoil as if I was slapped, and my lips popped open. "Restraining orders? What the hell are you talking about?"

"No, I think that was all Gloria's doing," Asher surmises, darting his eyes around the room and avoiding our curious stares.

Confusion swirls around me as I fall back into the countertop. "Somebody better fucking explain what is going on. Before I lose my shit."

"I think that's a better conversation between you and River," Callum mutters, shuffling into the kitchen and shaking his head.

My eyes drop to Lyric clinging to his hand as her wide eyes take every inch of me in, sizing me up. I swallow the hard lump forming in my throat. She's a fucking mini version of River mixed with my features, too.

In my heart, I know there's no denying who she belongs to. You take one look at her and you know without a doubt, without getting a DNA test, that she belongs to me. And because we walked away, we never got the chance to know her. I never got the chance to watch her walk or talk or crawl. Fuck.

"I'm going to take care of River," I say softly, peering into Lyric's eyes. "I'm going to take care of your mommy until she feels better, okay? And then maybe we can hang out?" I question, raising a brow when she slowly nods in agreement.

My heart seizes in my chest when she pulls away from Callum and slams into me, hugging my thigh. Her strong little grip clings on as she takes several deep breaths and finally peers up at me.

"Thank you, Daddy," she says in a raspy, overused voice.

"You're welcome," I say, as a burning heat rises behind my eyes. My fingers trail through her long dark locks, trying to soothe the worry.

"Yeah, Little Pretty Girl. Why don't we get you dressed and have a fun daddy's day," he says with uncertainty, looking down at her like she's the fucking sun in his sky.

Looking around the room, I examine all their varying expressions. From the looks of it, they've all known for a period of time and haven't said a word to me.

An off-feeling of understanding presses down on me. I fucking get why they didn't talk to me about it, but it still fucking sucks. I was so bitter in the limo when Asher asked.

It fucking hurt so goddamn bad that she would go behind our backs not only sleep with Van but have his baby, too.

Gloria picked on me when my nerves were raw as hell and dropped the news on me at my lowest. Her mothering skills were weak at best, and I don't know why the hell I took her word for it back then.

Rad scoops Lyric into his arms, navigating toward her room like he's tucked her in a million times before. Within ten minutes, Lyric is dressed in a mismatched outfit and a worried expression lining her face.

"My mommy will be okay, right?" she asks in a quiet voice when I crouch in front of her. The back of my fingers brush against her plump cheeks, and I nod.

"Don't worry, Little Blue. I won't let anything happen to your mommy today." And that's a fucking promise. River has to feel better so the five of us can sit down and have a lengthy discussion.

As if my words erase the worry sitting on her shoulders, she gives me a toothy grin. She's melting my fucking heart without doing anything at all. The need to not only protect her but heal her wounds has my fatherly instincts on overdrive. Without another word being said, she wraps her arms around my neck and squeezes me while kissing my cheek.

"Thank you, Daddy."

Those words. They stay in my mind long after they take Lyric across the street and do God knows what with her. Our house isn't exactly childproof.

I silently chastise myself. Grabbing the forgotten glass of water, I silently walk back into the bathroom where I had left River minutes before. River has barely moved from her spot. Except now she leans against the wall with her eyes squeezed shut and her knees at her chest, sucking in air.

"Sorry," I mutter gently, sitting beside her and handing her the glass of water. "I met Lyric. Don't worry about her, though. The guys took her across the street." Her breaths shutter in her chest as she gives a slow nod. Taking the glass of water, she gulps down a few mouthfuls and takes a deep breath.

"Let me guess; you didn't know either." She doesn't bother opening her eyes, instead squeezing them tighter. She grimaces, rubbing a hand across her stomach.

"If I would've known, I wouldn't have stayed away. Even if I fucking despised you for what you did… I would never stay away from my baby." My sentence starts out strong but dissipates by the end, coming out as a breathy whisper.

River doesn't react like I thought she would. I expected a scoff or some form of disagreement, but she simply lays her head against the wall.

"Yeah, I'm getting the distinct hint that nothing I believed is real," she grumbles, finishing off the water in three long swallows.

"Gloria told me that you had a baby. But she said it wasn't mine or the guys; she told me it was Van's."

Running a hand down my face, I relive all the situations that long ago I shoved into a little black box of forgotten memories. From the moment we left Central City to the day we got to East Point. It all comes back like a tornado, wreaking havoc on my emotions.

"And you believed her," she says defiantly, with anger rising in tinging her voice. If this conversation keeps progressing, we are going to have an all-out brawl of words we can't take back.

"Not now. Let's do this when you're feeling better; then you can bust my lip. Right now, you're sick as shit. And you need to rest before we can hash this shit out." As much as I want to continue the conversation and get to the bottom of what the hell happened, I know my words are true. I want her to get better, and I want to figure this out.

"Fine," she says through a breath. "I'm going to bed. You can go home," she says, trying to get to her feet. River stumbles around a little bit before catching herself against my body. Fuck. The feel of her pressing against me messes with my damn head. Fire brews beneath my skin. Her touch is so right. Yet so wrong at the same time.

"Yeah, I'm not going anywhere. You've been here for six-plus hours. You need help. And that's what I'm going to do. Once you're better, we are all going to sit down and have a nice long conversation." The familiar glare I grew to love years ago stares back at me in defiance.

"You really don't have to stay. I'm a big girl, and I can take care of myself. I didn't ask you to come over here…"

"This isn't a discussion, River Blue." She scowls at me even more, angrily snarling at the nickname I refuse to let go of. "This is me doing what I said I'm going to do. You are going to bed, and I'm going to get you more water. Then when you're feeling a little better, I'll get you some crackers. I'm not leaving until you feel better."

River doesn't say anything else, leading me back to her bedroom. Plopping onto her mattress, her fingers run the length of her forehead, and she groans, refusing to meet my eye.

Today is the day everything changes for us.

EVERYTHING HURTS, AND I'M SLOWLY DYING FROM CRAMPS AND CONSTANT nausea, turning my damn stomach. I groan when my phone goes off at my bedside, vibrating incessantly until I put it up and view the messages I sent Rocco a few hours before, informing him of my delicate situation. Of course, the bastard retorts with this…

ROCCO

I'd ask if you were pregnant…

You're not, are you?

Is one of them there now? Beside you?

Are you the cheese in the ham and turkey sandwich yet?

The cheese in between the many layers of lasagna?

ME

*middle finger emoji** I'd actually have to have time to fuck to achieve that. I blame you and the sushi.

And no. I'm still a single Pringle with no dick on the horizon.

Now stfu…

ROCCO

Do you need anything, Doll? Christian is making his famous chicken noodle soup right now… *wink*

ME

Consider me interested…

ROCCO

Figured. He says…feel better, babe. I'll be there soon, then. Please don't go into the light…it's not your time yet.

ME

Sometimes I wonder why you're my other bestie…

ROCCO

Because I bring you soup and quick wit...

ME

And poisonous sushi...

ROCCO

Debatable. Just make sure your baby daddies don't murder me. I like my life, and that mullet one at dinner wanted to pin my dick to the wall. Not in a fun way, either.

I snort, rolling my eyes.

ME

They'll behave... They're at home anyway.

ROCCO

Like you can control four dickish rock stars...

ME

Stfu...and bring me soup.

ROCCO

So demanding and bossy...

I groan, forcing myself into the seated position. A rock band plays off-tune inside my head, pounding repeatedly. Peeking an eye open, I stare at the tall glass of water and the note sitting next to it.

River Blue—
I went home to eat. Drink the water. I'll be back soon. Don't fucking move.
Knight.

"What the fuck?" I hiss, rereading the note. Just a few days ago, he was being an unbearable ass. Now he's leaving me a concerned message demanding I drink water. What in the ever-loving fuck is happening right now? Shit.

I met Lyric. His words ring through my head. That's right. In my haze of sickness, he met his daughter. Shitballs. No wonder he's trying to butter me up. Pinching the bridge of my nose, I head into the bathroom and wash the sickness from my body under a steaming hot shower. By the time I'm out and dressed in my comfy leggings and oversized shirt, I meet Rocco at the front door and lead him into the kitchen where he bustles around like a concerned mother.

"There's my sickly Doll," he greets me with a smile, kissing my forehead. "Christian sends his regards but refuses to step foot in here while you're contagious."

I frown. "I don't have the damn plague. Your husband is ridiculous."

He shrugs, waving his hand. "You know him. He'll give you all the soup you want, but don't you dare invite him to the germs."

"Well, thanks for the soup," I say, making grabby hands at the container he's holding.

Flicking my forehead, he takes the precious container away with a villainous cackle. *Prick.* Marching into the kitchen, he riffles through my cabinets until he finds a large bowl and pours it in.

"Sit," he demands, waving at the stool by the marble-topped island.

"I'm not a dog, you asshole," I grunt, sitting in the chair with a huff. Rocco, ever the smartass, opens his lips to retort, but I stare at him, forcing his mouth shut.

"Fine. I want to make sure my bestie is feeling loads better. Now, eat the soup and spill the tea," he says with a grin, setting the large, steaming bowl of chicken noodle soup in front of my face.

Taking in a large breath, I catalog the delicious scents wafting from the bowl and test how far I can push my stomach. It gurgles as I slurp the first spoonful of broth, protesting until the heat hits. I haven't gotten sick since Kieran held my hair back and embarrassingly watched me puke my soul out.

God. What a fucking day. I'd been over the toilet for what felt like twenty-four hours, puking out the sushi from the night before. Every damn minute, I heaved until I had nothing left. Eventually, I fell asleep with my cheek plastered against the toilet seat. Only waking when Kieran gently nudged me and talked me out of my sick-induced slumber. My cheeks heat at the memory. The last thing I ever wanted was for one of them to see me in such a vulnerable position ever again.

Then I learned sweet Lyric thought I was fucking dead and introduced herself to Kieran, blabbering about my sickly status. Granted, I didn't tell her I was keeled over by the toilet. She just happened to find me, and I wouldn't wake up.

By the way Kieran talked, he had no fucking clue she was his. Or that she existed at all. Heartbreak rested behind his eyes, and my fucking heart tore in two. It was at that moment I knew that, for some reason, Gloria had lied to me about everything when I made my way to Callum's house. I don't understand why she would. Wouldn't she want her potential granddaughter in her life? Not that I'd want her to be, anyway. She was—and probably still is—a big fucking bitch.

"They'll leave you one day, Central Slut," she leans in, whispering into my ear with a tone of pure evil. "I won't let you drag them down into the depths of poverty. They're better than you and better than this town. One

day they'll be fucking stars, and you'll be here. Where you belong." My jaw ticks from the back of the crowd, gathered to watch as Whispered Words plays for the entire cookout, they drug me to. Not only have I had to deal with my stupid, stalker ex, but now I must deal with Gloria sputtering abuse in my ear.

I catch Asher's eye as he watches us closely, no doubt wanting to know what she said. Too bad I never gave him the satisfaction of knowing what she had to say.

I guess that evil cunt kept her promise, after all. My stomach turns again. Not from the food this time. It's her words playing on repeat like a damn nightmare. I never honestly thought she'd be so damn vindictive enough to pull something so cruel. Apparently, I was wrong.

My fucking head hurts thinking about my current predicament. Constantly warring with my damn self on the rights and wrongs of the situation. I'm still deeply hurt, and that won't change. More than deeply, I'm fucking shattered with deep crevices splitting further inside me the more I'm around them, held together by fucking super glue for the past five years. At the slightest inconvenience, I'll completely crumble. Fuck. I'm ready to move on and heal from my trauma. But I know I won't. Not until I've hashed it out with them—really hash it out. It might be through strong words. I'll have to step out of my boss shoes and into the hurt River shoes and get to the nitty-gritty of what went wrong and why they left.

I take a tentative bite, groaning as the mild flavors hit my desperate tongue. "Tell Christian never to stop cooking," I hum, slowly slurping the broth.

"He wouldn't dream of it," he says with a snort. "So, tell me about these baby daddies you suddenly have hanging around. How's life, Doll?" He raises a brow, ignoring the twisting expression crossing my face.

"There's nothing to tell, Roc." I shove a spoonful of soup into my mouth, distracting myself from the question. I've gone down this spiraling road before. "They're there, and I'm here. I'm their boss, and they're my— the band I'm taking care of. End of story."

"That's why you're avoiding the conversation altogether. Discussions are a healthy part of life. Now, tell me all about them. Have they apologized? Have you found out new information? How is my godchild holding up now that her four daddies are in her life? Spill." His tone accepts no arguments as he glares at me. I nibble on my bottom lip when he raises a brow. "You are afraid," he states, eyeing my face. "Why?" Reaching across the table, he gently squeezes my hand.

Rocco has been my best friend for four years now. Hell, he's one of my damn pillars to lean on. Greater than any partner in the world. We met on the set of a music video I was helping with, and he was the actor they had hired. From there, we hit it off. At one time, I thought he might be interested in me and pursued it. After a fun night, we discovered we were good friends. Several months later, he found this amazing chef named Christian and married his soulmate. Granted, their relationship started off rocky with several toxic breakups, and then, Rocco pulled his head out of his ass.

"It's annoying how well you can read me." Slurping more soup into my mouth, I completely avoid his gaze.

"Like an open book, Doll," he huffs. "It's quite annoying that prying you open is so hard. We've been friends for years. You'd think you'd trust me by opening up and telling me how you're feeling. I know you're strong, but trust me, you'll feel better when you talk about it." He squeezes my hand in support.

I blow out a breath, stabilizing the nerves eating away at my insides. Sometimes it's frightening how well he knows me and can easily peel my layers open one by one. Staring into his dark eyes settles the wrath and pain stirring in me. Sometimes I swear Rocco is my friendship soulmate. The one truly meant for me, but not romantically. And throw in Kaycee, Olivia, and Ode to form my perfect circle of friends. I couldn't live without them. They're all my family in their own way, building me up and supporting me through this whole mess I call life—the after Whispered Words fiasco.

"What if they leave again?" The words leave my lips, barely in a whisper. All the fear swirls like a damn tornado inside me, spiraling my damn mind in so many directions my breath stalls. "They're rock stars. What if this is all a passing phase to them?" I swallow the lump in my throat and ignore the burning behind my eyes. "If they walk away, Roc. If they decide this is too much for them and bail on her. She won't survive. Lyric will burn down the fucking world to get to them now. She's had a taste of their fatherly love. I can't protect her from them like I protect myself." Everything in the room spins from my revelations, and my fingers clutch the edge of the countertop.

"The way I see it, Doll. You're going to have to make a big decision. They're in her life now. You told me over dinner that they didn't know about her or the blasted restraining orders. It seems they were in the dark for a lot of it. Did they leave you? Yes. They knowingly walked away without a goodbye and blocked you. What was the true reason? Only they know. Now, it's up to you whether or not you'll ever truly trust them again. From what I saw of Mullet when he showed up to our dinner, there was a lot of determination and love behind his mischievous eyes." I stiffen at his words, snapping my gaze to him. There's no way in hell he had an ounce of love for me.

"Love?" I scrunch my nose. "There's no way…"

"I'm a love-sick fool, Doll. Christian and I didn't have the greatest start. But I knew when he walked away and right back into my life that the look he gave me when we finally reconnected was a look of admiration. I worked every step of the way to amend my wrongdoings. That look Mullet gave you was the same one Christian gave me. They're not giving up on you. They obviously want to be in Lyric's life. Isn't that what you've always hoped for?"

I nod, nibbling my damn lip again as a headache pounds against my damn skull.

It's all I've ever dreamed of since the moment she was born. It's why I educated her on who they were and familiarized her with them. There's never been a second in her life that she didn't know who helped create her.

My father's existence was hidden from me for so long. My mother refused to talk about him until I snooped, finding more information when I was little. That's when I started writing to him every day, professing my innocent love, and begging him to come back, hence where all my daddy issues stem from.

"I don't trust them. At all. They're going to break her baby heart, and she can't… I can't…" I suck in a breath, squeezing my eyes shut as moisture burns, begging to unleash down my cheeks.

She can't take a first-round heartbreak. Like I can't take another round of them breaking my heart.

Warm, strong arms wrap around me, pulling me into his chest. He kisses my temple like the loving best friend he is. With a deep sigh, Rocco lays it all out for me.

"No one's asking you to fall head over heels for them again. I mean, you could, but it's not a requirement. Feel them out. Get to know them as adults. You're wiser—Co-parent with them. Let them fully into her life. Let them help you through the overzealous schedule you've created for yourself. Now is the time to stop depending on your brothers and start leaning on the men who seem to want to step up," he whispers with sincerity, holding me close to his chest. Comfort surrounds me at the sound of his beating heart thumping a lullaby in my ear.

"I hate you," I mutter through the bubbling emotions tightening my throat.

A deep chuckle vibrates against my arm, and he kisses my temple again. "You love it when I make sense."

"I do. But goddamn, Roc. I'm going to fall apart. They…they broke my heart once, and I…" Haven't let anyone in since *them*. They were my forever, and then my forever ran away and became my never again, leaving me behind.

I've only hooked up with maybe a handful of men since they left and never let anyone in. I haven't dated. I haven't opened the protective cage I had put my heart in for some time. Fuck. And now my child is involved.

Sure, I've versed her with everything I know about the boys. But this is real now. They're here, live and in person. No longer pictures in an album marked: *Daddies*. They're a fixture in her life. She won't forget about them overnight. She'll want more until they're tucking her into bed and staying under our roof. Lyric is persistent as fuck, just like her damn fathers. There's no moving forward without them.

"I'm not telling you to jump into bed with them. Although maybe four dicks would really do you some good. Umph," he grunts when my elbow lands in his gut.

"And we were having such a special moment," I grumble, biting my lip to hide my smile.

"I'll say one last thing. Take it day by day. Don't roll over and forgive them. Make them beg. Make them get on their damn knees and earn your trust back. Let them see Lyric and prove themselves to her and to you. I don't know them very well. In fact, I'd rather rip their testicles out for what they did to you. But I have a feeling there's a lot you don't know. And neither do they. One day at a time, okay?" He raises a brow, pining me with a stern look. "Promise me you'll repair your heart and fix their wrongdoings. No matter what."

"Fine, Dad," I grumble, relaxing when he hugs me again, pulling me into his chest and kissing my head.

"So, do they know about your special visitor?" he asks, squeezing me one last time before stepping back.

"God no," I say, taking another bite. "I'll cross that bridge when…"

"When he kidnaps you, Doll? He's getting brazen. Pictures of Lyric at school." Rocco frowns, concern twisting his features. "I worry about you and her being all on your own out here. First, it's pictures, and then—"

I hold up my hand, shaking my head. "Olivia has it covered. Carter has his eye on things, too. I have security cameras everywhere around here, plus the security company who provides my guards and everything. No one is getting into this house or onto this property without them or me knowing."

He rolls his eyes. "Katrina likes to keep me updated; you know?" I swallow hard. Ugh. My PA Kat and her big ass mouth. Thankfully, she's the best PA I've had in a few years, keeping my office in order when I'm away healing bands. We're not close like some would think, but I know we care about each other in a professional and personal way. The way her eyes tear up whenever my packages come, lets me know she's feeling it, too.

"What happened to boss-personal assistant confidentiality," I grumble, shoving the bowl away and rubbing my temples.

"When it comes to you and me, it doesn't exist. She's extremely worried, too. Your stalker is dangerous. No matter if he's laid low for three years. That's three years of watching you and taking pictures." He shakes his head. "Be extremely careful."

"I know. I will. We've talked about this a million times before," I say, blowing a breath.

The only thing my stalker has done is send me pictures of myself from a distance. No notes. No trying to get at me or kidnap me. I'm worried, yes. But they seem to be resigned to the sidelines and watching from afar.

"Fine. So, is your assistant Kitty Kat single yet?" Rocco grins, leaning his chin on his hand.

"You're despicable," I mumble. "You've both been captivated since meeting her six months ago. Too bad she's still in a relationship with Trevor," I say, sticking my tongue out at him.

He shrugs. "We'll be here when they break up," he says confidently, staring wistfully at the wall. "There's just something about her that connects the three of us. She seems to complete our void—our perfect third. But alas, my elusive Kitty Kat hasn't realized it yet," he pouts, sticking his bottom lip out.

"One day," I say, plucking his lip with a soft laugh. "Thanks, Roc. I'm feeling so much better now."

"You still look like shit," he quips, flicking my forehead again.

"Dick," I huff, sitting straight up as a loud knock sounds at the front door before it flies open.

Almost in slow motion, we turn our attention to the wide-open front door where four rock stars with angry scowls stare at Rocco with untamed jealousy roaring through their systems. Lyric grins in her mismatched outfit, staring up at Rocco with stars in her eyes.

This should be good. Especially when she runs toward him with her arms opened wide, waiting for a hug.

"What the hell is he doing here?" Rad growls, pointing directly at Rocco, who holds his hands up in a placating manner and steps back.

Great. This will be fun.

A Few Hours Earlier

"You went out for lunch and brought back that?" Asher's brows furrow as I set the large bag on the counter of our kitchen at the band house, along with the food bags and drinks.

I grunt in response. The tension between the four of us stifles the damn house with its thick fog. It's the giant elephant in the room we've avoided for hours now. The only entity able to break through the thick cloud currently sits on Callum's lap, asking a fresh round of unrelenting questions about his tattoos. The ones she can see crawling up his arms, on his fingers, and wrapping around his neck, she pokes at them.

Ink has been his therapy over the past few years. Rarely does he talk about the miserable night between River and Van, instead throwing himself into complicated riffs on the bass and under the tiny needle. Or in the fight ring, where he risks his life every Saturday, getting the shit knocked out of him.

He and I aren't so different. While I take out my haunted past on the swinging bag until I can't feel anything anymore, he pounds flesh until her memory is beaten away.

Out of the corner of my eye, I watch her with rapt attention, soaking in the presence of this tiny being I helped create. Me. I did that. With the help of River, of course. Somehow, someway, we brought this life into the world. Only I wasn't a part of it. Not entirely. Not at the beginning. I was away living what I thought was my dream. Instead of taking care of the one responsibility unknowingly thrust upon me. Watching her now, I note her familiarity with each of us. Openly calling us daddy and laughing at whatever we say. There's always a smile for us when we talk and a hug when she needs it.

Fuck.

A sharp, painful ache pounds in my chest, desperate to drag all the answers out of this tiny being. River never hid us from Lyric. So, why weren't we allowed to know she existed? The familiar rage I've come to

know spikes in my veins like an old familiar friend, but I swallow it down. Now is not the time to lose my shit like I want to. Like I always do.

"That's something we need to talk to River about," Asher informs me when I stomp my way through the house, shouting my anger until the walls bleed and break. After I had left River in her bed, softly snoring her sickness away. The compulsion to beat the answers out of the three men I considered my brothers drove me through the door with a scowl.

"Yeah, bro. We don't have all the answers either. We only found out, too." Rad grimaces as he speaks, rubbing a finger over a scratch on his cheek.

"You need to cool down." Callum gives me a knowing look, discreetly cracking his scarred knuckles in my direction.

Deep down, I know he's eager to pop me in the fucking nose again as retribution for my damn attitude—like always. We've been at each other's throats for years since we left the woman across the street behind. Now, it's hitting a fever pitch. If I don't go, I'll wreck whatever semblance of a relationship we have left and bury it in a grave so deep, it'll never have a fucking chance to resurface and renew.

So, I did. I grabbed my keys and split for fresh air, which led me to the children's store. A place I never thought I'd step foot in. I wandered around the deserted aisles with my head in the damn clouds, wondering what the hell was happening and how it happened without my knowledge. How could I not have known? How could she not have reached out and told me? She knew. She fucking knew what my dad did to me... What her dad did to her. So, why did she fucking keep this secret from me like I wouldn't fucking care?

"My dad disappeared, too," I mumble, laying back on the grass and staring at the stars.

"We're bastards," Blue mutters with a pout, looking over at me when I burst out laughing.

"Bastards under the moon," I say through a sad smile, keeping the pain of his absence to myself.

"Dear man in the moon," she says, turning on her back and clasping our hands together in the grass for support. "Will we ever meet our fathers again?" I bite my tongue. She may. I'll never find mine. He's long gone, dust in the wind.

I thought my life was spiraling out of control when River walked into the conference room with her head held high. Then came her announcement. Our band manager. Meaning she'd be in our lives for the next six months without pause. We'd see the ghost we'd left behind daily until our contract said otherwise, haunting us for eternity. Well, okay—six months. But six months can change everything. Six months can become a lifetime.

Now this bombshell.

My daughter. A whole fucking, walking, talking child that I didn't have a clue about knocked on our door and called me daddy. *Daddy*. Somehow, she knows who I am, but I don't know who she is. Not yet. I will, though. I will not be Dennis Knight, the man who ran away. I will be Kieran Knight, the best fucking father she's ever seen. No matter the sacrifices I make to ensure my child is cared for. Gloria was a shit excuse for a mom time and time again. The moment my father walked out, so did she. I was never a human being to her. I was just…nothing.

But Lyric is vibrant and full of life and love. Everything inside me melts, thinking about the amazing mother River has become. Lyric is living proof of the love and support she's given her.

I shove all those thoughts away, interrupted by the voice beside me.

"Is that a—" Rad stops dead, glancing at my purchase. A tight smile pulls at his tight lips as he approaches the counter, locking eyes on the tiny brunette pushing her way through.

"Daddy!" My heart fucking stops when she hugs my leg, tugging at my shirt to get a peek at the new gadget I impulse-bought.

"Little Blue," I breathe, hauling her into my arms and securing her to my body. It's so right. I feel it in my fucking bones. She's mine.

"Is it mine?" she asks, curiously looking at the large bag and poking it with her finger. Those eyes find me again, filled with hope; I can only nod. It hasn't even been five hours, and I'm wrapped around her little finger. Forever in her debt and destined to carry out every request she throws my way.

"All yours," I reply in a gravelly voice, thick with emotions.

Every minute I'm in her presence, a rightness clicks inside me. Like I was meant to do this or be here in her company, River promised we'd sit down and talk this over because the number of questions I have could fill up an entire twenty-four-hour period.

Lyric's entire face lights up when I completely unwrap the cotton candy machine, and she squeals with delight, clapping her hands.

"Cotton candy!" she shouts again with a grin. "Can we do it now?" she asks, looking around the room at the four of us with those big, puppy dog eyes she's somehow perfected.

"Of course," I mutter, furrowing my brows as I stare at the box, perplexed by the damn instructions. "But after you eat your burger." With eagerness, she shoves her burger into her mouth and quickly eats her fries without argument.

Like a real family, we all gather around the kitchen island, inhaling our food in silence, keeping our eyes on the ringmaster—Lyric. She's the only reason we're able to stand being in the same room as each other. It's been years since we've stood side by side without arguing or shouting. Somewhere along the way, my best friends became strangers. Now, it's time to mend our bond. For River and Lyric—the two most important women.

After we've discarded our food bags, we once again settle around the island with our hearts in our throats.

"Let's do this, Little Pretty Girl," Rad says, tearing open the box and setting it up on the countertop. "What flavor should we try first? Cherry? Pink Vanilla? Grape? Blueberry?" With each flavor he reads off, he grabs the bottles from the box and sets them down.

"Blueberry," she says in awe, watching as Callum reads over the instructions and starts setting up the pink machine.

After ten minutes, we manage to wrap the blueberry cotton candy around the tube and grin when Lyric devours it with happy hums of approval. My heart swells ten times bigger at her satisfaction. Her simple happiness is better than fucking music and my guitar. It soars beyond the feeling I get when I'm front and center on the stage, with the spotlights blaring down on my sweat-soaked face with millions of fans chanting my name. Lyric encapsulates that mood just by the smile on her face and the tiny laugh from her throat. She takes away the stress on my shoulders, replacing it with pure joy. I'll hold onto this feeling for the rest of my life.

"What the fuck," Rad hisses, straightening to his full height as the rumble of a loud car roars down the driveway. "It's him!" Rad hisses, widening his eyes. "Dude!" he shouts, marching toward the window. Throwing open the blinds, he watches with rapt attention. "Mr. Sexy-In-Tight-Jeans is sauntering into her house. Again!" I shake my head at his antics but slowly move toward the window when Lyric hustles over, planting herself in his lap.

"Uncle Rocco," Lyric says, taking a big bite of her cotton candy and staring out the window.

We each peer down at her and then at each other with our brows raised into our hairlines. Rocco? Why do I suddenly feel like a protective monster ready to tear his head off?

"Just your uncle?" Rad asks, swiping some of her hair back from her face. "He's not another daddy, is he?" His brows furrow when she giggles. "Better not be," he mumbles through gritted teeth. I swear he mutters no more dicks under his breath. I haven't seen Rad this pumped up for something since—well—River. I swallow hard as his eyes lock on the house across the street with interest.

Are we really heading down this road again?

"Just Uncle Rocco." She shrugs, leaning her head on Rad's shoulder. "Not my daddy."

I'm not the only one she's got in her grasp. They all look at Lyric the same way, like she's the sun in the sky, shining on their day and warming their hearts. Adding my—our—daughter to the equation brings hope to our situation. Finally, something positive rests on the horizon for Whispered Words. Not just for us as a band; it's for us as a whole. Rad. Callum. Asher. Kieran.

"Uncle?" I ask curiously, raising a brow.

"That fuc–uh, that big tool took River on a date Saturday!" he grits out in a quiet voice, with anger lacing his tone. A possessive light streaks in his eyes. My damn face twists.

"And you?" I question, keeping it as vague as possible.

"Jesus," Callum mumbles, pinching the bridge of his nose. "Stalked her to the restaurant and made his presence known."

Asher and I blink at Rad like he's lost his goddamn mind. Again. He's pulled some stunts in the past. But this? My heart fucking twists at the implications. When Rad wants something, he goes after it in full force without looking back. He's really doing this again without knowing the whole picture. How can he do that?

"Shh, little ears." Rad points down to Lyric in his lap, greedily sucking in the cotton candy as a bluish tint stains her lips and chin, leaving the evidence of her sweet treat behind.

"Avoiding the conversation," Asher notes, crossing his arms over his chest with a huff.

"Does Uncle Rocco spend the night with your mommy?" Rad questions in a gentle tone, brushing her long strands of hair away from the sticky mess.

Lyric snorts, eating the last of her cotton candy. Handing Rad the spit-soaked tube, she nods. "Only when they drink too much grown-up juice." Rad stiffens, narrowing his eyes out the window.

"Time to go," he says, heaving Lyric into his arms. She giggles when he twists her around and puts her on his back. Her tiny arms wrap around his neck, and her legs secure around his middle.

"Go?" I ask with a grimace.

"Are you seriously going to…" I blink several times, talking to Rad's back when he turns, and fucking walks out.

"Yeah, he's gone," Callum grumbles, marching after him out the front door with determination, ready to catch the blazing idiot.

"What the fuck?" My eyes connect with Asher's. He shrugs, grimacing.

"You assholes coming?" Rad shouts from outside, seeming so far away. "We've got some investigating to do!"

"Guess we should?" I ask, motioning toward the door.

Asher and I walk side-by-side, catching up to Rad and Callum in the middle of the road between our houses.

"Anything to stop this train wreck," Asher mumbles, swiping a hand down his face.

Before I can stop anything from happening, Rad practically breaks down River's front door, taking a step inside.

"What the hell is he doing here?" Rad growls, pointing directly at the mysterious man who has sleepovers with River. Innocently, he holds his hands up in a placating manner and steps back.

"Fancy seeing you here, Mullet," the man says with a cocky grin, laughing under his breath when Rad growls in his direction.

"Uncle Rocco!" Lyric squeals, jumping down off Rad's back. Running full force, she jumps into Rocco's arms, wrapping her arms around his neck.

"My monster godchild," he rumbles, squeezing her tight with love. He kisses the side of her temple, eyeing us with an inspecting glare. I recognize the protectiveness he exudes, filling the room with his warning. *Don't fuck with his girls.* "Did you have a good time with your fathers? Oh, what's that?" he questions with a smile, swiping at the blue on her lips.

"Cotton candy," she mumbles shyly with glee.

"Cotton candy?" River questions, weakly raising a brow.

My gaze wanders to her, inspecting the paleness spreading across her flesh. Those moss-green eyes glaze over with sickness, begging her to return to bed and rest some more. Her entire body sags with exhaustion when she rubs her fingers across her forehead.

"She only had one," I amend with a tight smile. "I bought it…"

"You bought it?"

I shrug, rubbing the back of my neck. "Wasn't planned, but we didn't have anything else. She ate lunch before it."

River purses her lips, sighing heavily. "Did you have fun, Ly?" she asks, running a finger down Lyric's leg, getting her attention.

"So much!" she grins, climbing from Rocco's embrace. "We ate cotton candy and hamburgers. Daddy Callum showed me his art. Daddy Rad said bad words." She wrinkles her nose.

I snort when Rad turns beet red and throws his hands up. "Sorry, Little Pretty Girl. Not used to such tiny ears being around all the time." He winks at her, earning a smile.

"Well. It was very nice to meet you, gentlemen. I expect my girls to be in good hands if I take off and return to my husband," Rocco says, scooping up a large, empty container and his car keys. His eyes bounce around to our faces until we're nodding in understanding. He's laid it out clearly to us; he's not a threat to whatever the fuck this is now. "Good. I shall take my leave. Get well, Doll. And remember what I said." He raises a brow, earning the stink eye from River. I can't help the smile that pulls at my lips at her defiance.

"Thanks for the soup. Kiss Christian for me," she mutters when he kisses her temple, much to the unhappy sounds escaping Rad's throat like a possessive idiot.

"You've got it, Doll." Coming to stand right before us, he reaches a hand out and clasps my hand in a gentle handshake. Peering over his shoulder, he confirms River is locked in a deep conversation about cotton candy with Lyric before he speaks next. "It's been a long road for them. You understand? She's endured a lot. My unsolicited advice?" He eyes my face and the other guys who crowd in, reluctantly listening to this strange man in River's house. "Listen to her. Breathe her damn words. Reevaluate whatever is going through each of your minds. Have an open heart. And if this isn't something for you, walk away and never look back. Disappear into the fucking darkness. Go back to where you fucking came from. Once you fully commit to them—to Lyric. There's no walking away. Fix what you broke or forever leave it in shambles so they can repair themselves." He raises a poetic brow, taking his hand back.

We don't say a word when he slips between us. Or when he starts up his car and drives away slowly, leaving us with his parting words.

Fix what you broke.

Determination lifts me in its grasp, choking me without a single thought of leaving this. Lyric is my daughter. My flesh and fucking blood, hidden from me. River was once my best friend—the love of my life. Every action from the past comes back, forcing me to relive our memories in vivid color. My River Blue isn't the same girl I left in Central City. There's an edge to her now. Because we broke her. We walked the fuck away without ever knowing the truth. God. How could I have been so damn stupid to just leave her without uttering a word? I'm confident now that the truth will come to light. It always does. No matter what happened in the past, River is ours now.

Lyric is ours.

"LAY YOUR HEAD DOWN, PRETTY GIRL," RAD DEMANDS, RUNNING HIS hands through River's hair. To her credit, she mumbles her disagreement as he forces her head into his lap.

"Rad," she hisses, squeezing her eyes shut, looking white as a ghost.

"You're making it worse," Callum grumbles, swatting him in the back of the head. Rad shoots him a cutting glare. "You good?" he asks softly, looking down at her where she begrudgingly rests her head on Rad's thighs.

Shaking my head, I rest on the couch opposite them. Nerves prickle beneath my skin. This is our moment. The desperate need for answers hangs in the back of my mind, nagging me to figure it out. We all crowd around her living room, waiting with bated breath for the conversation we've been anticipating.

"I'm fine. I guess," she mumbles, situating herself on the couch better as Callum sits beside her feet. Swallowing hard, he glances up and down her body with a concerned look. His fingers twitch, but he stops himself from touching her.

"It'll be okay, Pretty Girl. We'll care for you and Lyric while you're not feeling good. Do you need any more soup? Crackers? 7-Up? Or—" Rad frowns when she blindly puts her hand over his mouth, effectively shutting him up. Thank God. He babbles when he's fucking nervous, and right now, his voice grates on my nerves.

"I'm fine," she reiterates with a sigh, forcing herself out of Rad's lap. Running a hand through her matted brown locks, she wearily looks around the room, taking the three of us in. "Thanks for today," she mutters. "I appreciate you guys jumping up and helping me with Lyric."

"She came to our door," I say gruffly, taking a deep breath.

All the frustrations boil to the surface after being swallowed for so long. It's getting harder and harder not to show my frustrations physically.

She grimaces. "She knew where you lived."

"And who we are," I grunt, jumping. My fingers grip the roots of my

hair as I pace back and forth opposite them. Don't freak the fuck out on her now. You can't be an asshole when you need to stay calm.

"Dude," Rad warns, standing up from the couch with a frown.

"Don't dude me. My daughter knew exactly who I was, but I didn't know about her. I didn't even know she fucking existed," I say in a low voice, gritting my teeth through every word.

The last thing I want to do is rile Lyric up as Asher reads to her just down the hallway, preparing her for bed—something I should have done every night for the last four years of her life. I've missed so much of her growing up, and I don't want to waste another minute without knowing it all.

"We don't have to do this right now. River is sick," Callum says, shaking his head. "We can do this when you feel better," he says, looking directly into River's eyes.

"No," she says, swallowing hard. "Let it all out," she says, waving a hand in my direction.

"Why did she know who we are?" I ask, stopping and towering above her. "Why, River Blue?" All the rage turns to desperation, leaking into my tone. It catches in my tightening throat.

"Because, even after you left, I wanted her to know where she came from. Even after you denied her and…"

"Denied her?" I gape, leaning over her body and forcing her head against the couch. Our eyes lock in an intense battle. "You know me better than that. Or at least you did. I'd never in my fucking life deny my child. Ever," I growl, curling my fists at my side.

River sighs with exhaustion, closing her eyes. The selfless part of me wants to walk away and let her rest more. She's been ill all night and day. But the answers I've been desperate for since the first knock have me prodding further. There's an incessant need gnawing at the back of my mind, desperately searching for an answer.

"That's what we tried to tell her." Rad grimaces in pain, shaking his head. "Tell him, Pretty Girl. Tell him the whole story. Please."

She cracks an eye open, promptly rolling it in his direction. "The whole story?" she rasps. Her jaw tightens, pulling the rest of her face into a tense expression. "Where to begin? Like the fact I ran to Callum's house, only to be greeted by your mother." I tense, jerking back like I've been slapped, but she continues. "You can be pissed off at me all you want, but I've already told the other three the entire story. You knocked me up over the dining room table on our little vacation. Not only did you ghost me after my mom fucking died, but you also left me. You fucking— You fucking promised me that you'd take me with you. That—" Her eyes squeeze shut, holding back the emotions boiling to the surface. Anger roars through her system, twisting her expression until she uses all her strength and climbs to her feet. Her painted red nail pokes into my heaving chest. "You assfaces left me when I needed you the fucking most. My mom died, and where were you? Winning Battle of the fucking Bands. I mean, fucking good for you," she grits out with a bitter laugh. "Good for you for living your dream. But what about me? What about what I needed? You left me like I was nothing more than trash on the curb."

"What the fuck about my mother?" I ask, gripping her finger in my fist, squeezing it gently so she can't back away from me.

"Oh, that bitch," River snaps, trying to yank her hand away from me. "I drove to Callum's with this fucking secret. I needed you—all of you," she cries out, trying harder this time. I eye Rad and Callum as they move to her sides, wrapping their arms around her until she stops fighting me. Angry tears pour down her face, and she shakes her head. "I was pregnant, and all I got were restraining orders and a nice check to 'get rid of the problem.'"

"What?" I breathe, shaking my head. No. No. No. That's not what I would ever fucking want. How could Gloria do all that shit behind my back and not fucking tell me?

"She called you right in front of me. Called you by name. Said you didn't want the baby. You said it was probably Van's," she says through gritted teeth as a fire erupts behind her heated eyes. "Said you wanted me to get rid of it! How could you?" she breathes the last part, staring daggers in my direction.

"I didn't." Words fucking fail me as I stare at the hurt encasing her every movement. "I didn't fucking know, River. I swear to all fucking things holy that I had no clue Lyric existed. Gloria didn't fucking call me. Not then. No, she called me weeks later and told me about you. But she-she said it was Van's baby and that you… That you…." I suck in a breath as the world I've built around me deteriorates. The thick lies that built me crumble in the burning flames of truth, turning to white ash.

"But you still left," she whispers so lightly I have to strain to listen. "You still fucking left me. You left her. You didn't even come and talk to me. You didn't even check on me to see how I was doing." River shakes her head again, shrugging all of us off of her. With a deep breath, she stops a few feet away from us. Her glossy moss-green eyes drag up and down our stunned expressions. "How could you? You were my best friend. You left me once, and I thought maybe it wouldn't happen again. But you left me."

"But Van?" My heart pounds when her face morphs into disgust. "That video. That kiss Callum caught on camera. You-you—" I trail off, losing myself in past events that have haunted me.

"Right. You're convinced I cheated on you. Is that why you turned your back on me?" She crosses her arms across her chest. "Is that really what you believe? I don't know why in the fuck—"

"It was me." The world ceases to turn as those three guilt-ridden words wrap around the four of us arguing in the living room, cutting off our voices.

I blink several times as his words sit heavily on my chest. Turning to Asher, who stands stoically across the room with tears flowing down his pale cheeks, I shake my head.

Asher's been through hell in his life. I've watched Nigel beat the fuck out of him, throw him across the room, and stomp on his ribs. All the while, Asher never made a sound. Tears never came. Not even as an adult. Asher's a fortress, holding his emotions prisoner in those walls.

So, to see the tears welling up and falling down his cheeks like rain cascading down the windows has me flinching back.

"What do you mean?" Every muscle in my body tightens at his words.

"What was you?" Rad asks tersely, balling his hands into white-knuckled fists.

"What the fu-fuck did you do?" Callum shouts brokenly, staring at Asher with wide eyes. He shakes his head several times, stumbling back onto the couch with a ghostly expression like he's figured it out. It only takes a second for reality to take hold of Callum. He stands on silent feet, cracking his knuckles. A deadly expression thunders across his face, and he snarls in Asher's direction with such malice my balls shrivel. "You fucking asshole!" Callum growls through clenched teeth.

"It was me. I did it. I…" He heaves a breath.

"What do you mean?" River asks, taking a tentative step toward him, cautiously approaching like he's a wild animal about to bolt. "You did it? What did you—" her words trail off, staring at him in disbelief.

Wiping a hand down his face, he pushes all the tears dripping down his cheeks away. "River didn't cheat on you. She never touched Van. Even when you went to find her," he says, throwing an arm in Callum's direction.

"What in the ever-living fuck are you talking about?" Rad shouts through clenched teeth.

"You were all so content with staying behind!" he sputters, stumbling back into the wall. Through vigorous head shakes, he finally settles his eyes on the ceiling. "That night at the castle house on the damn lake, you told her you'd stay behind for her. You said you'd drop the Battle of the Bands until she could come with—" His lip trembles until he covers it with his hand. "I couldn't let that happen. This was our destiny, and I was afraid."

"No, you fucking didn't," Rad says through a shallow breath, disbelief pulling his lips open.

"Looking back, it's the stupidest fucking thing I've ever done. And I'm so damn sorry! But I was so goddamn desperate to get away from my father and live our dream. I couldn't stay in Central City. This was it —my only chance. You remember what he was like, right?" Asher's chest heaves when his sorrow-filled eyes connect with mine, but thankfully, he doesn't go into full detail about our abuse at the hands of his father.

"Of fucking course, I remember how he was. But that… That doesn't fucking…"

"What the hell is going on right now?" River mutters, looking around the room, slightly shaking her head. "What exactly are you trying to say?"

"Explain!" I bark, taking a step forward with urgency, slamming into the front of his body. "Explain every fucking thing you did!" My fingers curl on the front of his shirt, pulling him forward so he can't lie to my damn face. "What. Did. You. Do?" I growl, pushing my face into his. "Asher!" I shout again.

"I set it up!" he gasps out, slamming his eyes shut. "The videos were old. River didn't sleep with Van. He sent them to me because I asked him to. I had to convince you guys—" He doesn't get to utter another word when my fist slams straight into the side of his head, knocking him back from me, but I cling on by the scruff of his shirt, keeping him within striking distance.

"You what?" River breathes, going completely still. Her mouth falls open, eyeing Asher as he sways on his feet. If it's humanly possible, all the color drains from her body. A twisted look of betrayal and horror takes over her features, and she shakes her head. "Why would you ask him to send you old sex tapes that I didn't even know existed?" River's words stammer together. Sharp shivers run through her body until she's trembling uncontrollably. Her knees knock together, and her breaths saw in and out of her flaring nostrils.

"Pretty Girl," Rad rushes to her side, throwing an arm over her shoulders. "I got you," he whispers, holding her tightly to his side and kissing her head tenderly.

"Here," Callum grunts through his anger, handing Rad a blanket to drape over her shoulders. Quickly, he drops a kiss on her temple, freezing there for a millisecond before his eyes flash to Asher.

A ringing forms in my ears, cutting off the noise around me. Asher set it all up. He led us to believe a big fucking lie. One that's destroyed every piece of not only us as people but the goddamn band. My gut lurches, threatening to spill my damn dinner. Colors blur around me. Everything swerves out of fucking focus.

"What was real? Was anything you said that night real? Did—" A knot forms in my stomach. "We left her for no reason?" My tongue dries up, sticking to the roof of my mouth. "We left River… My daughter… We left everything…"

My face falls at the realization. All the fucking hate in my heart for the woman I loved was false. I was misled into believing all these radical bullshit lies. I've treated her like utter shit since we reconnected because I was under the assumption she cheated on me and fucking deceived me when the snake in the grass was my own damn brother.

"You fucking snake," I hiss, stumbling back.

"How could you?" Callum says, breaking the silence with a low growl. "We fucking loved her, and you knew it! You fucking knew how we felt, and you…you took that from us!" Callum's fingers ball into fists, and his body vibrates with pent-up anger. "How could you fucking do that to us?" He shudders, stomping forward. Before I can stop him, his fist connects with Asher's nose once and then his ribs. Blood spurts from his face, dribbling down his lips and chin. The more hits that come his way, the less he blocks and takes the pain. "We lost five years with River and our daughter. All her firsts! All her…everything!! Because of you," he grunts, slamming his fist into his cheek and knocking him to the side. "We lost the most precious gift on the planet."

"Stop," I grunt, pulling Cal back before he fucking kills the little snake. Not that I don't want to obliterate him. He deserves every fucking piece of pain doled out to him in retribution.

"I'm sorry," Asher wheezes, clutching his side. His eyes squeeze shut, leaning against the wall for support. "I thought…I was doing the right thing. I thought I was saving us," he says, taking painful puffs of oxygen.

"Saving us?" Rad rasps through his emotions, still clutching River as her eyes glaze over. "How would you be saving us?"

Asher blinks several times through the pain ricocheting through his body. Good. He fucking deserves it. Fucking deserves the pain and resentment and fucking hate we feel.

"I was so fucking stupid," he gasps out, cringing from the pain when he tries to straighten out his spine. "And selfish. I know I was. I've been carrying this around for years, and it's been killing me."

"That doesn't fucking absolve you of your goddamn crimes," Callum growls, tracing the carnage he left behind with his fierce eyes.

"I can't believe you," I say, shaking my head. "You're a fucking manipulative dickbag!"

"What about the restraining orders?" Rad asks, pulling River's trembling body into his.

"That wasn't me," Asher whimpers, grimacing when he tries to reposition himself. "That was all Gloria."

"Gloria?"

"She started it," he whispers with a voice filled with shame and regret. "She came to me and offered me money. She even told me about Van and the tapes. She…she told me everything."

"Money?" Callum growls.

"How much was your betrayal worth?" I shout, filling the room with my voice.

"Keep it down," Rad chastises, nodding toward the wall separating us from our sleeping daughter.

"How much?" I growl, lowering my voice. No matter how angry I am, I don't want to startle the little girl sleeping just down the hall.

"It wasn't just the money," he wheezes. "It was a way to get us away from Nigel. Away from that fucking house!" he grits out like that justifies his actions.

"How much fucking money did you take to pull your betrayal off?" Callum grits out, flexing his fingers again.

"Five grand and a promise to keep Nigel out of it." His eyes squeeze shut again, sucking in air. "And a promise to leave her behind," he whispers so softly I almost miss the implication.

"You fucking weasel!" I bark, stomping toward him and taking him by the shirt again. "You made a goddamn deal with the devil and lied to us about everything!" My fist tightens again, ready for another round of bashing the asshole who lied.

"Stop," River says, clearing her throat. We all watch as she slowly walks forward, eyeing Asher with apprehension. Standing before him, her lips curl. "Did you send Van to my apartment?" she whispers, almost in shock.

"Yes. I knew they'd go to you, so I had to have a backup plan to leave. I—" Asher's face jerks to the side when River slaps him across the face, leaving behind her handprint.

"River Blue," I whisper, pulling her trembling body into mine. From behind, Callum touches her shoulder with reassurance. A worried look twists his face as he stares at the girl he once deeply loved, so much so that he trusted her with his virginity.

She shakes her head against my chest, burying her face in my shirt before pulling away with flaring nostrils. Anger rests behind her glossy moss-green eyes, ready to burn down the world.

"How could you?" she accuses sharply, balling her fingers into a fist. "How fucking dare you do that to me and send him to my fucking apartment." She shakes her head in disgust, curling her lip back.

"You'll never know how fucking sorry I am," he gasps again. "I was a stupid fucking idiot. Please believe me when I say I'm so fucking sorry. I know—" He cuts off, bending out the waist and crying out in pain. "I know I fucked up so fucking hard." Tears roll down his cheeks in rapid succession. Whether it's from the pain or the deep regret, I don't fucking care. He took everything from us when he went behind our backs and fucked us over. "Please," he whispers, looking at River. "Please don't take her away from me."

"How fucking dare you!" I growl, making a move toward him again.

"Stop," River says, putting a shaking hand on my chest, which I promptly grasp. "No more violence. Not here. Not when she could walk out of here and see this. I'd like you all to leave now."

"Don't fucking come to the band house," Callum growls. "I'll bury you," he promises, curling his lips back and baring his teeth before stomping off and slamming through the front door. Two seconds later, his bike roars to life, accelerating toward the gate.

"Fuck," Rad mumbles, pinching his nose. "He'll be at Ruthless's fucking ring in two seconds." His eyes whip to Asher, who collapses to the floor and leans against the wall. "I love you, Pretty Girl. I've never loved someone as much as I love you. No matter the pain I felt when I thought… thought you hurt me. I'm sorry. I know I've said it before, but I am," Rad mumbles without a second thought, leaning down to kiss her cheek. She startles at his confession but relaxes in his touch. Good. That's a good fucking sign for us. We can make it up to her one day at a time. "I'll leave and take him with me. Call us if you need anything, okay? You're still sick as fuck." He kisses her temple again, reluctantly peeling himself away. As he passes me, he grabs my arm and jerks me back.

"You get the fuck out of here," I spit, trying to advance on Asher.

"I'll take care of it," River says, holding my arm. "Give me some space, okay? I'll see you guys tomorrow for your band practice. We still need to keep up with it."

"Not with him!" I grunt, cupping the side of her face. Searching her eyes, I swallow hard. "I'm sorry, River Blue. I'm so fucking sorry I didn't try hard enough to get to you. I'm so sorry I didn't talk to you. I'm so fucking sorry I walked away. Again. That's on me. Every fucking mistake I made that led here is my fault. But I promise that every day from here on out, I'll be here. For you. And for her. I want to get the chance to be a real dad and someone worthy of you," I whisper through the burning lump in my throat. Leaning forward, I press my lips to her cheek, savoring the feel of her skin beneath mine. She's still as soft and beautiful as I remember. "I'll work my ass off to prove to you that I'm your Knight again."

With those parting words, I let Rad drag me out of the house. Leaving River with my stupid, broken ex-brother. My heart aches from his confession. Rage. Fucking betrayal. Every emotion rushes through me. How fucking could he? He took our blind trust in him and used it against us.

As I lie in bed that night, sleeplessly staring at the ceiling, I make a vow. A vow to be the man I promised River I would be years ago—her worthy Knight.

PRESSING MY FIST TO MY LIPS, I COVER UP THE PAIN-FILLED WHIMPERS trying to escape. Leaning my head back against the wall I'm slumped against, I squeeze my eyes shut. The truth finally set me fucking free from the lies I cultivated so damn easily. The guilt that gnawed at me for the past five years ebbs away—no longer sitting heavy on my chest, aching to spill the beans. The burn still sears through me, but it's muted slightly, over-turned by the new demand to make the situation right. Driving me to jump head-first into the churning ocean of my betrayal and mend what the fuck I broke. For the first time in years, I can breathe fresh oxygen. Metaphori-cally, of course.

Pain ricochets through my whole damn body, bouncing around every place; Callum and Kieran's fists pounded into me. Rightfully so. Every punch they rained down on me was penance for my unforgivable sin—my betrayal of the only family I could ever count on.

I'm such a worthless asshole, undeserving of so many things.

I groan, sitting perfectly still inside River's house. At any moment, I know she will kick me to the damn curb. As I deserve, I know that. Who would have sympathy for the likes of me? A traitorous dickbag who couldn't handle a woman coming between his other band members. Defi-nitely not her. Not that I blame her one bit.

But where the hell do I go? I could go back to my townhouse on the other side of the city and sit in my damn misery by my lonesome, letting it swallow me whole. If it comes down to it, that's my only option. Kieran, Callum, and Rad would obliterate me before they let me back in that house. Fuck.

"Here." Peeking an eye open, I stare at the blurry slender hand in front of my face, blinking until it's entirely in focus. "Let's get you on the couch," she says softly, wiggling her fingers. Pain still fills her eyes from my confession, but she's extending a small olive branch despite it all.

"Why?" I grunt, shifting on the floor. "I can leave."

"You could. Or you could take my hand," River snarks, wiggling her

fingers again. "It's not that hard, Evil Ash," she murmurs my old nickname with a pained expression.

"Thank you," I mutter, reluctantly grasping her hand and letting her pull me to my aching feet. Violent pain shudders through my body when I stumble up, gasping for air. "Shit," I wheeze again, clutching my ribs with urgency. With every move I make, my ribs splinter like they're about to break and spear me in the lungs. River has the patience of a saint as she slowly leads me to the couch and helps me sit on the edge.

"Let me get you some ice," she says through a heavy sigh, retreating quickly into the kitchen. Coming back, she gently lays a soft ice pack on my swelling eye and hands me two pain pills with a bottle of water.

"Thanks," I rasp. "But I don't understand why you're taking care of me. I expected—" Rage. Hate. Heated words. Anything but the pity in her eyes. Fuck. I want her anger or fists or anything but her kindness because I don't deserve an ounce of understanding.

"For me to kick you out in this state? You look like shit." She raises a brow, settling on an ottoman across from me, leaning her elbows on her knees. Her eyes track my movements as I settle on the couch, trying to get comfortable and not hurt my ribs more.

"After what I did—" I trail off, averting my eyes to my lap in shame. "Why're you helping me now? I screwed you over so fucking royally." Deep remorse once again turns my stomach into knots.

"Yeah, you did," she agrees, running a hand down her face. "You really went behind my back and used my obsessive ex against me. He forced himself on me, Asher. Van marched into my kitchen and took what he wanted."

"Fuck," I heave, squeezing my eyes shut. My stomach rolls at the idea of him waltzing into her house and doing that. She didn't deserve that shit. Not again. "I'm so fucking sorry he did that. I'm sorry I went to him and trusted him to help me." If I could build a time machine, I'd go back in time and kick myself in the balls.

River gives me a blank look, blinking several times. "You forced them to walk away from me." Pain laces every inch of her words like that was the worse offense. Dropping her head back, she stares at the ceiling and releases a breath. "But I can't believe I'm fucking saying this—I get it. I don't know what the hell your home life was like—"

"You see this right here?" I ask, cutting her sentence off and pulling up my pant leg. Drawing her eyes to the thin surgery scar on my ankle, she nods, inspecting it as my finger rubs up and down the raised skin. I take a deep breath, losing myself in the awful memory of my father's rage.

"Stay down there until you learn your lesson!" Tears prickle at my eyes, staring up the long, dark staircase at my father's massive figure. Agony spears through my twisted ankle, instantly ballooning out. "Worth-

less," he snarls, shutting the basement door behind him, leaving me with only my pain, tormented thoughts, and pure darkness.

Goosebumps prickle at my skin. My heart rate accelerates and sweat glistens on my skin from the vivid video-like memory roaring through my mind. Swallowing hard, I shove it all down, trying to forget. What my father put me through was nothing a child should have endured. Yet, I did —we did. Kieran and I have been on the battlefield together, forging our bond through our hellacious trauma. It's why we worked so damn hard to keep him away from Cami. Even if it meant more punches and punishment, she was safe.

"My father had this insane rule of being seen—not heard. I was seven and dropped a glass while trying to get some milk—" My breath shudders, jumping back in time to when I was a scared seven-year-old kid with wide eyes, looking down at the remnants of my glass shattered on the ground. "All I wanted was a little drink before I went to bed, but he heard. Stormed out of his office with this rage-filled face. He scooped me up, yelling profanities in my face, and then—" I swallow hard, squeezing my eyes shut. A slight tremble takes over my fingers, still mindlessly tracing over my scar. "He opened the basement door and threw me down the stairs. I hit every fucking step on the way down and finally landed at the bottom with a twisted foot. The agony was so fucking real. My foot was on fire, and then…he just shut the door and told me I could come out when I learned how to be quiet."

"Jesus fucking Christ," River mumbles, turning a sickly green. My stomach bottoms out when sorrow shines in her wide eyes.

"Yeah," I say, clearing my throat. "I'm not telling you that for any sort of pity. I just want to help you understand why I was so fucking desperate to leave Central City." I lick my lips, taking a big breath. "I passed out on the ground, only waking when he forced me to my damn good foot. He yanked me up the stairs and told my nanny to take me to the hospital. He couldn't be bothered to care for me. After explaining that I had accidentally fallen down the stairs, I had to go to surgery. That hospital was my only reprieve from him. My father was a sick son of a bitch. He took his anger out on Kieran and me for years. He was going to make us follow in his footsteps." I shake my head again, groaning at the pain. "So, he gave our band a year to make it…and I was so fucking determined to get away. I wasn't going to let anything get in my damn way… Not even you," I whisper the last part, firmly shutting my eyes as the tears burn.

"So, that's why you hated me so much," she murmurs, breaking me out of my self-deprecating fog. "I was in your way of getting out of there."

I bark out a humorless laugh, shaking my aching head. "Quite the opposite, Little Brat," I rumble through the pain, cringing when my laugh sends pain through my ribs.

"So you didn't hate me?" she asks, raising a skeptical brow.

"It took me way too long to realize how I felt about you." Biting into my bottom lip, my body sags with the realization I've kept under wraps for so long. "I craved you just as much as the other three. But I fucking fought it. I fought everything about you because you scared me. No one in the history of the damn world, except my mom, had ever made me feel the way you did. So, I did what any asshole would do. I tucked my tail and ran the fuck away."

"But you still…" she trails off, shaking her head.

"Yeah, I still did. My fear led me down that road to do what I did. I was so desperate and scared that I let it get to me. I destroyed something so fucking beautiful because I was a selfish fucking bastard."

River blinks at me a few times, processing my words as silence engulfs us. "You can stay here tonight," she says, getting up and walking toward the freezer again. "Here, take another ice pack so your face doesn't swell too much."

"But why?" I whisper, holding tight to her wrist as she sets the new pack on my eye. "I don't understand."

She gives me a tight smile, takes her hand back, and sighs. "I'm not your karma, Asher. You have to face down what you've done. Do I forgive you for breaking my trust and putting a dangerous guy in my path? No. Not by a long shot. You'll have to earn that. Somehow… But it's not me you have to get the most forgiveness from. It's them. They were your family—your brothers. But by the look on your face, you already know that. You've probably tortured yourself. Honestly, I don't understand how you've lived with yourself." She shakes her head, crossing her arms over her chest.

I snort. "Not very well. Sleepless nights. The heartburn. My fucking guilt ate away at every inch of me and having to face the guys I deceived so cruelly… Yeah, I fucking hate myself for what I did."

"It's a start," she says with a small shrug, taking a few steps away but stopping abruptly in the doorway. "It's for Lyric." Her tiny voice carries through the room, leaving a crater in my chest. "You're staying because she knows who you are, and I can't drag my kid away from her daddy. She already loves you, and I won't destroy that love by forcing you to leave."

"Thank you," I breathe in relief. "I know I'm a big fucking disappointment, but I want to…I want to be there for her for everything. Now that I know… River, thank you for giving me a chance to prove myself to her."

She nods a few times. "Just don't break her heart like you broke mine," she whispers, leaving the living room altogether.

"I won't," I vow to no one, sinking further into the couch and trying to get comfortable despite the pain pulsating through my body.

From this day forward, I'll be the best version of myself for Lyric. For a chance to fix things with River and the guys. I'll never keep another secret again.

For a chance to prove I'm not the Asher Montgomery from five years ago. No more lies. No more secrets.

Just me.

The following morning, I startle awake at the sound of a sweet little voice in my ear. Her little fingers sweep down my broken face, tracing what I can only assume are bruises darkening my skin.

"Daddy. Oh, no," Lyrics mumbles softly, laying her head on my aching chest. "What happened? Did you get beat up?" her little voice shakes when I finally crack my eyes open and run a hand through her hair.

The darkness of the room greets me with the first hints of the sun rising in the sky. A heavy sigh rocks through me when I look at the clock on the wall, noting it's only six-thirty in the morning. Fuck. Way too damn early to be awake.

"I'm okay," I mumble, bracing her head against my chest in a soft hug. "Why're you up so early?" She hums in response to my question.

"But you're hurt," she mumbles through a crack in her voice. "You got a bruise right here," she says, poking my face and making me flinch away from her touch.

"I do," I say through a breathy laugh. "But I'll be okay," I whisper, kissing her head. Bringing myself into the seated position, I pull her into my lap, wrapping my arms around her. Despite the pain spearing through me, I settle her securely against me until she hugs me back with a relaxed sigh.

"What happened to you, Daddy?" she asks, blinking up at me.

"Just grown-up stuff. It's nothing, Little One," I say with a tight smile. "How are you this morning? Did you have good dreams?" She grins big and nods in response.

"I dreamed of pancakes. Daddy, I want pancakes," she whispers, batting her eyelashes at me. Well, who can deny those puppy dog eyes?

A laugh spills from my lips, and I nod. "Of course. Should we look? See if we have anything to make pancakes?" She beams, jumps off my lap, and drags me into the spacious kitchen.

"Here!" She points to an upper cabinet storing the pancake mix and grins when I pull it down with a pained groan.

"All right let's get to work," I say, smiling down at her beaming face.

Over the next thirty minutes, Lyric helps me mix the batter and oil the pan. She giggles with me, getting the mix all over her face and fingers. Our pancakes morph into weirdly shaped blobs rather than round.

"Taste good?" I ask when we sit together at the island on stools with plates in front of us.

"The bestest," she says, shoving a big piece of pancake into her mouth, sticky syrup hanging from her chin and sticking to her fingers.

"Well, looks like you made a big breakfast," River says, eyeing Lyric affectionately. A smile grows across her lips when she kisses Lyric's head as she walks by.

"Me and Daddy made yummy pancakes!" She giggles around another bite, humming with satisfaction.

Whenever she says Daddy to me, I swear joyous butterflies burst in my damn soul. A smile creeps across my lips when Lyric side-eyes me with a giddy giggle, tearing into another misshapen pancake.

"There's plenty more," I softly say, nodding toward the plate on the stove filled to the brim with pancakes.

River's brows rise as she pulls a plate and coffee cup from the cupboard. "I didn't know you could cook," she says, plopping a few on her plate and pouring some syrup.

I shrug. "I learned to do a lot of things myself as a kid. My father went through a lot of nannies and eventually left me to my own devices at eight. Well, until Gloria came into the picture with Kieran." I swallow hard, finding relief flooding me as all the pent-up childhood memories flood out my mouth unbidden.

"Ly, I think it's about time for you to wash your hands and get dressed for school," River says, scoping up Lyric's empty plate.

"I'm sick," Lyric says, frowning when her mom takes her plate away and sets it in the sink.

River snorts. "I don't think so, missy. Up. Dressed. School. We have ten minutes." She raises a brow when Lyric stubbornly crosses her arms over her chest and pouts with a little huff of annoyance.

"But I want to stay with Daddy," she grumbles, stomping her feet.

"Better get to it, Little One. Daddy will be around later, okay?" I say, ruffling her ratty dark locks, earning a huff.

"It's a never-ending cycle," River sighs, watching Lyric's retreating back as she scurries down the hall and slams her bedroom door shut with a heavy thud.

"Does she fight it every day?" I grunt, grabbing my plate. Stiffly, I shuffle to the sink and clean our plates off.

"Since the day she started preschool. I've asked her why she dislikes going, but she says she's bored and the youngest one there. I just hope it's nothing like bullying or anything else. She seems happy in the classroom. At least that's what her teacher says. I don't know." She shakes her head, heaving a frustrated sigh. "So, every day, we have this argument," she hums softly, looking toward the hallways as little steps come our way.

"Ready!" Lyric announces through a big grin, marching into the living room ten minutes later, wearing a little frilly blue dress, leggings, and flat black shoes with bows on them. Her once ratty hair is brushed out, and her face is clean of the evidence of our sticky breakfast.

I can't help but smile at her when she proudly beams up at me.

"You look beautiful," I say with pride.

"Thanks, Daddy!" she says, throwing her arms around my waist. "Are you coming to take me to school today?" she asks, batting those damn eyelashes again, wrapping me further around her damn finger. My eyes flick to River, and she nods without reluctance. "Let's get you to school," I whisper, bending and kissing her cheek, reveling in her tightening hug and happy squeal of delight.

I swallow hard when she lets go and takes off, grabbing her backpack and slinging it over her shoulder. Without waiting for us, she marches out the front door toward River's SUV in the driveway.

"Thanks for letting me tag along," I say, clearing my throat as we step out into the warm morning sunlight beaming down on us. Momentarily, I lift my face toward the sun, soaking in the day's warmth and basking in its refreshing glory. Today is a new damn day, and I am a new man.

After locking her front door, River turns to me, shrugging. "I told you I won't keep her away from you. You're her father as much as the other three are." Her brows furrow when she digs into her pocket and brings her phone out. Tapping a few times, she opens something, and her body freezes. A slight tremble takes over her hands as she scrolls up on her phone and leans in with a horrified look crossing her face. A ghostly white complexion drains the color from her face, and her eyes widen almost in fear as her eyes rapidly move across the screen.

"What's wrong?" I ask sharply, stepping closer and putting a hand on her stiff shoulder. "River?" Gently, I squeeze, coaxing her out of whatever trance she had been put in.

Her eyes widen when she takes me in, realizing she's been stuck on the porch for a solid minute. With a head shake, she brushes off my touch with a tense smile.

"N-nothing," she stammers, unsteadily taking off toward the vehicle. "I'm fine."

I furrow my brows when she shakily gets into the driver's seat, heaving a few breaths until I follow and get into the car. Yeah, fucking right. It's not nothing. Something spooked her, and I'm determined to find the cause. Whether she likes it or not.

As we drive toward the school, worry eats away at me. River doesn't say a word about what happened. She talks back to Lyric, who excitedly chatters away about anything and everything she can think of, avoiding my quizzical gaze. After about ten minutes, we arrive at Lyric's school and drop her off at the drop-off line. As Lyric exits the car, she grins at me through the window, waving as her teacher takes her hand. I watch with rapt attention when she stands in line by the school door, chatting with a little boy.

"Who is that?" I mumble, pointing to the little boy, throwing his arm around Lyric's shoulders with a grin. He lights up at the sight of her.

River snorts. "That would be her boyfriend. Oh, and that one, too. It seems she's collecting boys."

"Wait! What?" I hiss, staring at the two boys walking Lyric into the building with grins on their faces. "No fucking way," I grunt, attempting to open the door. "River." I narrow my eyes at her, but she scoffs, driving off.

"Nope. Leave her alone. She'll grow out of it. Besides, you'd be a hypocrite." I frown, sit back in the seat, and stare out the window as the horizon blurs by.

"I guess," I murmur, sucking in a breath as I look at the time. "So, will you tell me what freaked you out back home?" I ask, raising a brow when she drives up her long driveway and parks in front of the band house.

"No," is her simple answer as the locks disengage, and she stares over at me expectantly. "It's time to face the music," she says, waving toward the house. "I have an errand to run. I'll be a little late."

"Does it have to do with the text, email, or whatever you got?" Stalling. I'm fucking stalling before I have to walk into that house and face the men I betrayed, too. River may go easy on me because I'm one of the fathers of her child, but they won't fucking care. They'll beat my fucking ass again. Not that I don't deserve it.

Her lips roll in. "Yes," she says reluctantly. "I need to go take care of it. But you all have band practice in an hour. So, might as well tear off that Band-Aid."

I snort, staring up at the looming structure with apprehension. "Yeah. Like a Band-Aid," I mutter, nervously biting into my lip. "If I'm not here when you return, they've buried me somewhere or set me on fire. It's up to them, really," I quip, fighting through the nerves that are begging me to run the fuck away again.

But that's not me anymore. I don't run from the problems I created. I go at them headfirst, even if I'm about to die. Nothing but the truth moving forward.

"I'll make sure your obituary says something about how bullheaded and brave you are," she jokes with an edge to her voice.

"You sure you're—"

"You're stalling, Evil Ash. Get it over with or walk away. Talk to them. Do something other than avoiding the problem. If you leave this house by the time I return, I'll assume it was too much, and Whispered Words will be done with West Records. It's up to you to mend the brotherhood you snapped into pieces." Every word she speaks lights a fire under my ass, motivating me to walk up those stairs and face the guys who hate me more than anything now.

"You're right. Thanks," I say softly, opening the door and stepping out. "But whatever is bothering you, you know we'll help. We're here for you. Even after all this time."

"Thanks." She nods a few times and finally takes off, leaving my traitorous ass in the middle of the driveway.

"Well, well, well. Look what the cat dragged in. A lying, manipulative piece of shit," Kieran says from the porch, sipping a piping hot coffee.

I brace myself for the abuse from my brother and nod. "You're right," I say, lifting my chin. "But if I leave now, she's promised to rip up our contract. Either I'm here as a band member, or we're done as a band forever."

Kieran sits back in a patio chair, taking another sip, contemplating my words. "Don't expect those bruises to fade any time soon."

"Fine." I shrug, ready to take my punishments like a damn man.

"Good," Kieran says through a sadistic grin, standing from his chair. "Watch your back, Asher. You have no friends in this house anymore."

"Just got them this morning." The chilling memory of the email coming through burned into my brain the moment I received them on the porch. It was on the tip of my tongue to tell Asher what was going on, but I knew I had to get to Olivia and Carter at Veritas first. They're my contacts with this whole situation.

"This is nuts," Olivia mumbles in disbelief. "You can't trace it?" She eyes Carter as he grunts, sitting behind his mahogany desk at the Veritas Headquarters, tapping away on his computer.

"No," he growls, scowling at the computer screen. "I don't know why it's doing this shit. It's fucking—"

"What?" Olivia asks, bending over to look at the screen. My heart drops when her eyes widen, but she shakes it off. Olivia can fool many people with her blasé attitude, but she can't fool me. I know her too well to see when she's internally freaking out. Even when her eyes dart to mine, and she locks her feelings up behind a tall brick wall—I know when she's scared. And right now, she's fucking terrified. It sends shivers down my spine and tightens my muscles.

"What? Am I in serious danger?" I ask in a low voice, nervously bouncing my leg.

"Don't fucking panic," Carter grunts, shoving Olivia from the screen.

"Yeah, that's what you tell a victim of stalking," she huffs, rolling her eyes. "Don't panic," she mocks his deep voice with a roll of her eyes.

Carter side-eyes her with an arctic glare, gritting his teeth so hard the veins in his jaw pop out. She doesn't seem to notice, though, probably used to his attitude since they've worked side-by-side for years. Olivia continues pacing the room without a retort, muttering about what an idiot Carter is.

"As I was saying," Carter grumbles, running a hand down his drooping face.

"Then what is it?" I interrupt in a panic, feeling like my heart is about to explode out of my chest.

Carter sighs, running a hand down his face. "Listen, Little West. We were able to trace the email."

"That's good news, right?" I ask with hope filling me.

"In normal circumstances, yes. But it's tracing back to your phone like it's coming directly from it. Like you sent it, and that's not fucking possible." Carter's eyes fill with sympathy, taking me back to the first time I got several Polaroids sent directly to my brothers at West Records. Carter came immediately, taking them from me to examine every inch of them for a clue. One he never found. Whoever they are, they've taken great care in keeping themselves hidden from detection—up until now, though.

"That doesn't make any sense," I breathe, feeling the walls closing in on me from all sides, ready to smother the breaths from my lungs. "There's no way that it could be coming from my phone. I didn't send it to myself." How could they— "Holy mother of fucking shit."

"What?" Olivia asks, crossing her arms.

"My phone… I just… I lost it and had to replace it. You don't think?" I stare at her with my mouth hanging open and thoughts swiftly moving through my brain at hyper speed.

Someone stole my fucking phone and used it against me. If they knew how to get into it, then they probably got into my security app, gained access to my cameras, and even worse—they came to my fucking sanctuary.

So, who the fuck did it? And why? I don't understand this person's obsession with me. I'm no one—just a woman trying to live her life to the fullest and raise my daughter right. It's insane to think someone would follow me, taking my picture from the shadows.

"You mean to fucking tell me you lost your goddamn phone? You have a stalker out there watching every move you make, and you just—"

"Shut the fuck up, Carter," Olivia growls, staring at him like he's the devil's spawn.

But his words. He's fucking right. I've been so naive in thinking my stalker would forever hold back and be happy taking pictures of me for the rest of my life. Stupid fucking idiot. I've watched that show where he follows the girl around, watching from the street through her windows. Jesus, if I end up in a plexiglass room—I'm murdering everyone.

"Listen, they've obviously spoofed your location and your new phone's IP address. We don't know how they're doing it, but we'll find out." Olivia's eyes shine with determination when she finally halts her pacing and slams a hand down onto the desk. "I swear, River. We will find out who has been doing this to you and throw their asses in jail."

I rub a finger over my temple, soothing the headache pounding in my skull. "But why now? It's never escalated like this. It's always been photographs of us in the mail. So, what has changed?" I can't for the life of me figure out what the hell has changed, bringing my stalker out of the woodwork.

"We're not for sure, but we have a theory," Olivia gripes, balling her fingers into a fist. "It seems whoever your stalker is, doesn't like the fact the guys are back in your life. Look at the x's over their faces. It's a clear sign they want them gone and away from you."

"Fuck," I mutter, swallowing the lump forming in my throat.

"Sorry, Little West. I'm keeping a close eye on it. Nothing is going to fucking happen to you. You fucking understand that?" Carter asks through gritted teeth, slowly rising to his feet. He looms over my seated body with a protective spark lighting in his eyes. "Keep vigilant. Lock your doors and keep your cameras on. Don't answer the door for strangers. How's your security holding up? I obviously need to have a fucking talk with the guards stationed at your house." He raises a brow, giving me a no-nonsense look.

I snort. "Yes, Dad. I still have my guard at the gate. I have video surveillance on the inside and outside of my house." I've done everything imaginable to protect Lyric and myself from harm, including building my house with a gate and off the beaten path. Fuck. "But…do you think it's going to get worse?" A thick knot of nerves twists in my stomach when they silently communicate with their eyes.

Finally, Olivia heaves a big breath and shrugs. "This isn't our area of expertise. But from what we've studied, stalkers never just disappear. We can only assume it's going to get worse, River."

"But you fucking have us, Little West. Veritas, your damn brothers, and even those assholes won't let anything happen to you. You've taken every precaution necessary to maintain your safety and Lyric's," Carter adamantly vows. "Besides, when you look over your shoulder now, you'll have a friend every step of the goddamn way. There's no way I'm letting you walk out of this room without a discreet security detail."

"I…"

"You will take my fucking gift, and you will like it. Tom will follow you everywhere. You won't even know he's fucking there half the time. Get the fuck over it. We're here to protect you and my little niece. I actually like your fucking faces. So…" he trails off after growling his words and clenches his fists.

"Okay," I say in agreement.

Olivia rests her hand on my shoulder, squeezing softly. Her comforting gesture does little to calm my rampant nerves running amok inside me. But it's nice knowing I have more people in my corner as this escalates.

"We got you, girl. You are being monitored. You are protected every step of the way; we will find this bastard and throw him in jail once and for all."

"I know you guys do. I appreciate all the help you've given me. Since this started three years ago, it's been hell. Never knowing who it is or if they're watching my every move. I'm just trying to live my damn life." I run my fingers over the crease of my forehead, worry gnawing at the back of my mind, trying to find solutions. "I just want to feel safe," I whisper, desperately seeking a life without the constant threat lurking behind me.

"We're on this twenty-four-seven. We won't rest until this stops. I fucking promise. Besides, your brothers will have my damn balls if I don't figure this out soon," he groans, glaring up at the ceiling.

"You're going to have to tell them," Olivia mutters, twisting her face when I give her the stink eye. "Don't give me that look. They're your neighbors. Your baby daddies, as you've so eloquently put it. She's in danger, too. They deserve to know what's going on."

"You're such a bitch sometimes," I quip with a huff, knowing she's right. It's wrong to keep them in the dark about my stalker, who is apparently stepping up their damn game and directly threatening them. But God, I can only imagine how that conversation will go. Cue the freaking out and demanding me to stick like glue to their sides, especially after our conversation yesterday. Dread fills every molecule inside me. This will fucking suck, but Lyric's safety is my number one priority.

Olivia laughs, settling in a chair beside me. Throwing an arm over my shoulders, she forcefully brings me closer to her as the chair digs into my side. "That's not the first or last time you've called me that."

"Definitely not the last." A grin breaks free for the first time in an hour, and I sigh. "Okay, well, I have to make sure my band is still alive," I mutter, wrinkling my nose at the prospect of entering the tension-filled band house. My imagination has run wild all morning since I dropped Asher off in the driveway. Will I find blood stains? More bruises? A repaired band? Yeah, that last one isn't possible right now. I'll have to give them more time and way more therapy to work through the betrayal that happened. Good thing it starts this week. Even I haven't forgiven any of them yet.

"Afraid they'll tear each other apart after Asher's confession?" Olivia asks, raising a brow in my direction.

After our enormous discussion last night, Olivia was the first person I called when I snuggled into bed. Talking to the guys about everything that happened opened ancient wounds, bringing more tears to my eyes. If it weren't for her, or the other three I call my best friends, I would have cried myself to sleep. Instead, I chatted with her, Ode, then Kaycee, while texting Rocco and snuggled with Lyric after tossing and turning.

"Want me to pound his face in, Little West? I could use an extra punching bag." What I would call a sadistic grin lights up his face at the prospect of beating Asher up.

"Jesus. Calm down, Killer. His ass whooping yesterday was punishment enough," I say, standing from my chair. "Now, I have to figure out how to get them past this. If they ever want to become a band again."

I shake my head, wracking my damn brain on how I can help them move on from Asher's deceit. Not that it's going to happen easily. Hell, the only reason I didn't kick him to the curb was for Lyric. She's attached to each of them uniquely, and I can't break that bond or her little heart.

Carter deflates and mutters under his breath, finding his way back to his seat. With a grunt, he sits back down and rubs his chin. "Don't be a stranger. If you need a boy band to disappear without alerting the feds, I'm your guy."

Olivia scoffs, throwing a pen in his direction. "We are the feds, you asshole."

"Exactly. We won't be alerted," he quips, chuckling when she throws another pen at him.

"All right. Thanks, guys, for the help. If I get anything else, I'll let you know." Waving goodbye, I stroll out of Veritas' headquarters, making my way across town, hopefully walking into a band practice with little to no blood.

Out of the corner of my eye, I watch with fascination as Asher heaves his guitar strap over his shoulder, gritting his teeth through the pain radiating from the wounds I caused him yesterday when we finally found out the truth of our situation.

Violence never used to be the answer to all my frustrations—music was. My bass was my relief. A way to step out of this world, dive straight into the music, to forget I'm a human walking this earth. Forgetting all the pain life has brought me at every damn step. When I lose myself in the music, I'm no longer Callum Rose—airplane crash survivor. I'm simply the bass player, strumming along to the beat of our creations—a no one with nothing stirring inside me but a constant heartbeat.

When I witnessed Van kissing River and what I thought was her reciprocating, I lost that special piece of me to the noise of the world. I let it take me over, becoming a no one without an escape. Every note and string reminded me of her. My River. My Little Star. Her smile. Her laugh. The ghost of my past constantly followed me, threatening to jump out at every corner. Much like my parents, she was dead to me. She may have had a heartbeat pumping blood through her veins, but she was as good as gone.

To push her existence out of my mind, I injected poison into my veins, falling victim to its intoxicating addiction. Once again, I found something to lose myself in for hours at a time, floating above the noisy world. It fogged my mind, subduing my wayward emotions threatening to spill out of me. With every hit I took, the more the edge seemed to loom in the distance, getting closer and closer until the drugs didn't do it for me anymore. I felt more, no matter the amount I took. It was either take more and fuck myself up badly or find something new to take my pain away.

Stumbling across the cage boss, Ruthless, in that empty alleyway outside some random bar was the best mistake I ever made.

"Yo, you're going to fuck up your fists if you keep trying to break the brick," the random voice rings in my ears as I grunt, pummeling my flesh into the scratchy brick, breaking my skin. Blood pours from my wounds,

leaving my mark behind on the unforgiving surface. "I said fucking stop," he growls, pulling my fists away from the wall and forcing my back against it. "You wanna fight, Killer? You want to pound into something that will give back as good as you give?"

"Let me the fuck go," I snarl, trying to yank my wrists back.

His grip tightens until I'm stuck between his broad body and the brick behind my back. A large, raised scar runs the distance of the left side of his face, from his forehead, down his eye and cheek, and finally stops before his collarbone.

"Get yourself together. You want to make some money, Killer? Prove to the world you aren't some junky rock star looking for his next damn fix? Hmm?" He raises a brow, pushing off me when my body slumps against the wall.

"You don't know me," I grunt, pulling my shoulders back and squaring my chest. "You don't—"

"Callum Rose. Whispered Words. Rock star extraordinaire," he snorts. "You almost fell off the fucking stage last night in front of thousands. Yeah, I know exactly who you are." He rolls his dark eyes, pulling a cigarette pack from his back pocket. "Listen, I could use a real fighter like you in my octagon. Not only would your pretty boy face bring in a crowd, but by the looks of your punches, you need the damn release. Are you interested?" Fire illuminates his face as the end of his cigarette blossoms red, and smoke pours from between his lips.

"Sounds tempting." Staring down at the wounds coating my knuckles, I swallow hard. All I wanted was another fix to try and take away the pain rotting my fucking insides and poisoning me day by day. But nothing is working like it should right now.

"Yeah, how's your fucking head right now after beating that wall?" My muscles tense at his question, but it's then I realize...

"I don't feel a single thing," I mumble in awe, breathing fresh oxygen for the first time in months instead of drowning in my own damn sorrow and darkness.

"Yeah. Here's the deal. You ditch the fucking drugs, and then you come to me. I'll set you up with as many damn fights as long as you're healthy. You'll bring more people to the show, and my place will bring you relief."

"Who the fuck are you?" I ask when he hands me a card with an address close to the edge of town on the bluffs.

"They call me Ruthless," he says with a shrug, taking a step back. "See, now we know each other. Come to that address when you're feeling frisky. You scratch my back, and I'll scratch yours." The mystery man marches down the alley and disappears into the darkness, leaving me with a spark of hope.

Fighting became my damn religion, blackening everything and dulling my pain. Pounding flesh became my drug of choice. Spilling blood became my addiction, relieving all the pain festering in the depths of my soul, rotting me from the inside out. For thirty minutes at a time, I was no one— a blank space, circling opponents with one mission in mind—causing pain.

The daily cravings grew less for drugs, going completely extinct without trying. Soon, my mouth watered for the opportunity to jump into the octagon. In a sick way, it knocked her memories away and blanked out my damn mind from the useless noise around me. After pummeling Asher's face, I went to the ring and took on two more opponents, winning each round within five minutes until I wore myself out. Absentmindedly, I rub along the bruise forming under my right eye, reveling in the slight tinge of pain.

Seeing Asher black and blue for his crimes leaves me with a mixed bag of emotions. On one hand, I feel victorious for my swift retribution. Asher got what he deserved and much more. On the other hand, my stomach churns at the thought of what I've become due to my unswallowable pain —a violent monster addicted to cruel bloodshed. The old Callum would vomit at the thought of what I let consume me.

Asher slightly shakes his head, twisting his expression. "I don't know. She didn't exactly say," he mutters, darting his eyes across our faces, scrutinizing our expressions.

Kieran scoffs, hastily marching toward Asher and baring his teeth like a rabid dog on the damn hunt. My body stiffens when Kieran pushes at Asher's shoulder, knocking him back an agonizing step and causing him to cry out in pain. His body pitches forward, slumping over his guitar hanging from his body.

"Fucking hell," he wheezes, taking deep breaths.

"Jesus," Rad groans, rubbing his forehead. "Didn't we just discuss that violence wasn't the answer? Drag your balls across his face or something. Let him smell like cottage cheese dick for a few days. Lesson learned."

I snort at his reasoning. Pure fucking Rad. Pure fucking stupid. There's no getting over what he did or leaving it alone. Asher deserves multiple punishments.

"You'd seriously just forgive him? Just like that?" Kieran snaps, curling his fingers into Asher's shirt and bringing him close again. Asher frowns but doesn't fight him off, letting him growl in his face. "After he fucked not only us but River over?"

"You think I'd let it slide?" Rad asks through clenched teeth, slamming his drumsticks down on his stool. "He deliberately fucked us all in the ass with no lube and a spiked fucking dick. There's no way in hell I'd forgive him with the clap of my ass cheeks." Rad takes a deep breath, pinching the bridge of his nose. "But we have shit to do. Instruments to play. And a lucky lady to get back into our good graces."

"Her good graces? You think she's going to forgive us?" Kieran asks, dropping Asher back to his feet, forgetting his rage.

"Pfft. I'm not giving her a choice," Rad quips, waving a hand. "Ask Cal about my date." He beams with pride, puffing out his stupid chest.

"Your date?" I scoff. "More like a third wheel no one invited along." I'd never tell Rad how invigorating it was to spy on her while she dined with Rocco. The way her body fit into the dress she wore nearly gave my attraction to her away, even if I was still in denial about it all. Rad was right about everything that night when he slapped his chest and told me nothing felt right.

"That offends me! I bought her flowers—"

"And then she pulled you out of the restaurant by your ear and rode home with me." My eyebrows raise when he frowns, turns his back to me, and mutters to himself.

The warmth of her arms ghosts around my middle, pulling herself closer to me. Discreetly, I hide the heat traveling up my neck and face as I remember how she felt against my back. Like she was meant to be there— like she was mine again. But will she ever be that girl for me again? The one I look for in a crowded room? The girl who holds my aching heart in the palms of her hands? Fuck. Maybe I never belonged to anyone else. I sure haven't touched another woman since her—my one and only.

"Anyway, it was a good date," he quips, twirling his sticks between his fingers. "And I can't wait to do it all over again. It's all about the actions, boys. Do you want River again? You gotta show my Pretty Girl how much you want her. Tell her sorry all you want, but she won't buy it." Rad's smile fades into nothing, swallowed by a darkness clouding his face, plopping on his stool. "Believe me, I tried."

"You tried?" Kieran asks, rubbing his chin. "Even before this asshole admitted to what he did?"

Rad shrugs, twirling his sticks again. "I can't fight this feeling, bro. I almost forgot what I was fighting for. And what I'm fighting for is my lady. All of her. My daughter…"

"Mine," Kieran growls, clenching his fists.

"Lyric is all of ours, you tithead. She doesn't just call you daddy. River made sure Lyric knew who we were."

"But why?" I croak, hanging my head in shame. I've missed everything in Lyric's life.

"I don't know," Rad murmurs. "She knew whose kid she was biologically. Yet, she still introduced Lyric to our faces as her damn fathers."

Silence fills the space. Our thoughts consume each of us with the possibilities of what we missed and what the future holds. At least, that's where my mind travels to. Lyric. Our child. She calls us daddy, looking at us with wide, loving eyes like we didn't put her mother through hell by walking away with our tails tucked. Looking back, I wish I had done so many things differently.

Our story isn't written in pencil. We can't erase the things we've done with a few swipes and move on like nothing ever happened. We'll continue our broken tale on damaged paper riddled with marks and scars, filled with old wounds and betrayals.

Every foundation starts somewhere—built on shifting rocks and unsteady ground. We won't move on until we've patched up our past, talked through our failures, and begin to rebuild on—sturdier terrain.

"Because of her dad," Asher rasps, clearing his throat as he leans against the wall in defeat.

"What?" Kieran snaps again, turning his furious focus on Asher again.

Asher rolls his eyes. "She told me that her mother never let her know her father. So, she gave Lyric a chance to get to know us. We are her fathers." He hesitates another moment, sucking in a breath. "We can't break Lyric's heart. She comes first through everything."

"No. I don't fucking plan on being without my daughter for another damn moment. I won't break her fucking heart, but you're pretty damn good at manipulating and breaking hearts. Aren't you? Fucking prick. Stay away from her." Kieran narrows his eyes at Asher, who doesn't move. But I see it in his determined gaze. There's no way in fucking hell he will back off from knowing Lyric. Somehow, he's known her the longest.

"No," I say, squeezing my eyes shut. "River told Lyric we were her fathers for a reason. Lyric expects all of us to be in her life."

"Fuck! Even him?" Kieran grunts, pacing the length of the practice room, pulling at the ends of his dark locks.

"Even him, asshole," Rad grumbles, shaking his head. "I know he royally fucked us over, but Lyric is four, bro. She wouldn't understand why he stopped showing up."

"It would break her heart," Asher whispers, licking his lips. "And mine."

"Then we need to make a pact," I say, turning to look at each of them, letting them see the seriousness of my expression.

"What kind of pact?" My eyes drag to Asher's ghostly pale face as he slumps to the floor, cradling his guitar to his chest.

"For our daughter," Rad agrees without a second thought.

"It's for Lyric. Right here. Right now. We promise each other that no matter what shit happened in the past, we don't show it in front of Lyric. She's our priority, but so is River."

Wild plans of groveling run through my mind. I'll get on my knees for hours on end until she looks me in the eyes and tells me she forgives me for my misdeeds. I failed River in so many fucking ways, and it eats away at me. I'm the reason we fucking left. I confirmed what I saw. Hell, I took a picture of his lips on hers. I'm the reason we all got into that SUV and drove away with nothing more than bitterness and our thoughts guiding us into the future.

And I'll never forgive myself for what I did.

"We will not be my fucking parents," Rad proclaims. "Fuck them."

Though he doesn't show it often, his parents' neglect wears him down, even after years of being out of their grasp. Sure, they fed him, housed him, and clothed him. But their cold stares and constant need to control his every move drove him away from them in the form of rebellion. It's something they've never forgiven him for. As for Rad, he'll never forget their words, actions, and the catalyst of it all—when they kicked him out.

Pain envelops my heart. My parents were fucking saints through everything, taking in Rad when he needed someone most. They nurtured us with love and support, letting us explore our passion for music and never tearing it down like Rad's parents insisted. I was the lucky one. The others didn't fare well in the parents' department and look at where it got us. Deep down, it isn't that big of a surprise that Asher let his desperation drag him down the road of betrayal in hopes of leaving his father's grasp.

"Hell no," Kieran agrees, stopping right before all of us. "Fuck our piece of shit parents."

"Lyric comes first," Asher agrees from the ground, staring up at the ceiling with a pained expression.

Kieran blows out a breath, and his face falls. "We'll be the parents we never had." Running a hand down his face, he turns his icy stare in Asher's direction. "But you stay the fuck away from River. No canoodling or trying to prove yourself. Your story with River is fucking done."

Asher lets out a humorless laugh. "You think she'd have me after what I did? I know it doesn't mean shit, but I am sorry. I was a—"

"Selfish fucking prick?" Rad quips without an ounce of humor lining his tone.

"That," Asher agrees, pointing a finger toward Rad. "More than a fucking prick. Listen, we can disagree as much as we want…" he trails off, taking a deep breath. "But if we want this to work, we need to work together to achieve this band shit…and with Lyric." He swallows hard. "I'll be the best dad I can be. I won't interfere with anything. But I will continue to make it up to River in any way I know how so she sees how fucking sorry I am. I just—"

"I get it," I say, surprising myself with my admission. He may be a prick, but I can see it in the desperate expression he's sending our way. He needs Lyric in his life as much as she needs him. He loves her and has a strong connection with her in just a short time. "Lyric is all of ours. River has made that clear."

Kieran silently broods, deep in thought, rubbing a hand over his jaw. "Fine," he concedes with a nod. "We do this together. Even if I can't stand to be in the same fucking room as you. We do this band shit, go to the therapy she insists on, and try our fucking best. At the end of the day, we step up and help with Lyric. Whatever River needs, we need to be available for her. We need—"

"To let her know how sorry we are," I say softly, earning a nod of appreciation from Kieran.

"Yes," he whispers, taking a deep breath and swallowing the emotions I know he's feeling.

"Here, here!" Rad shouts, tapping out a light rhythm on the snare drum, adding a few light crashes of the cymbals. "Here's to our new future, bros!" he shouts before jumping into our first song, sounding more confident and crisper than he has in months.

We'll make it through no matter the heartache or the trials before us. One day at a time. One steppingstone at a time. The boys and I have been through hell, but now it's time for us to pull our heads out of our asses, swallow our hurt and rage, and let River know we're here for good.

There's no getting rid of us.

THE SUN BEAMS WARMTH ACROSS MY FACE AND BARE CHEST WHEN I STEP out the front door of the band house into the fresh early evening air. Every ounce of tension from our two-hour band practice, and the rest of the day's tension with the new therapist melts away with the sun's unforgiving rays, evaporating into dust.

Finally, I can breathe. My jaw loosens, and my muscles sag.

After practice, the boys and I decided to cool off in our respective rooms. Alone. Hours of side-eyeing, snarking, and undermining each other had put a real damper on our attitudes. We set our egos aside for River and Lyric and did what we had to do until it became too much to handle. Without a word, we trudged to our rooms, shut the doors, and fucking locked them, trying to catch our breaths.

Or, we tried to, at least. Nothing says piling on more stress like an unexpected knock on your front door. Five minutes. That's all the reprieve I got. I barely sat on the edge of my bed, running a hand down my face when it happened.

Knock. Knock. Knock. *Who knew something so simple could echo through an entire house, pulling us from our rooms? It was comical, really. Each of us stuck our heads out our doors with frowns, looking at one another like they were the culprits.*

"Who the hell is it?" Rad grumbles, wiping the sweat from his wrinkled forehead sans pants and shirt, barely fitting into his tiny briefs.

"No one should be here..." my words trail off as we step into the kitchen, eyeing each other with suspicion, ready to tear each other's heads off.

"It's the therapist," Asher declares with his know-it-all attitude, shoving his chin in the air. I don't miss the wicked wince he gives when he pulls a piece of paper off the fridge, reading the words. Hobbling toward us, he grunts when he holds it up for all of us to see. "River left this here for us. It's our schedule."

Right. Although we've seen her a few times without a schedule, it's time for more structure.

Kieran snatches the paper from Asher's hand and turns his back to him. "Lucy Steadman Ph.D.—noon on Mondays and Fridays," he says, looking over the paper.

"Ah, man, I don't want to talk to some stranger about my damn problems again. It was already awkward the first time," Rad grumbles as the hand pounds against the front door again.

"Remember the pact," I say, raising a brow when he puffs out his bottom lip. "We promised."

"Fuck, I know. All in. All for our girls. I'll tell this lady everything on my mind. But fuck—" His cheeks turn red, and he looks away, avoiding our stares. "I'm just scared to do it, I guess." He shrugs nonchalantly, but I note the tension lining his shoulders and the clench of his teeth.

Truth be told, I'm scared shitless to unleash my past on a stranger. Digging up old wounds won't be easy. Reliving my nightmares repeatedly and telling them to some woman with a certificate makes my stomach turn. I want to fucking vomit at the thought. Hell, my doctors tried this after my family's untimely death. They swore up and down it'd help me cope with the ghosts haunting my dreams. Back then, I refused. But I'll do it for the brighter future ahead of us.

"For the pact," I say, staring between Asher, Rad, and Kieran, standing a distance apart from each other. They each nod in confirmation before I open the door and let Lucy in to evaluate us one by one.

Over the next few hours, she takes each of us aside in a private office off the living room, effortlessly discussing our lives. The conversation between her and me flows easily. An odd sense of familiarity sparks between us, and I find myself revealing more about myself than I have for anyone.

The only thing that fuels my eagerness to spill my demons is the two girls across the street.

The road separating our house from River's burns beneath my bare feet as I make my way across the street toward the soft sound of the waves crashing against the beach. Briefly, a few days ago, I caught a glimpse of the paradise River has built for herself.

Something I know she's always wanted.

"I want to bury my feet in the sand and stand on the beach when we get to California," she confesses, burying her face in my neck. My arms tighten around her, pulling her body against mine. As we lie side by side on her bed under the glowing stars glued to her ceiling, filling the small space with neon light. "I'd live by the water if I got the chance."

"Anything for you, Little Star," I murmur, running my fingers through her long strands.

The blue sky, mixing with fluffy white clouds, looms above me as I draw in the fresh salt-scented air. Waves crash against the beach like a steady chorus. Peace washes over me—consuming me for the first time today. The hot sand cushions my feet as I make my way down the small hill, only stopping when a small voice calls out to me from a distance.

"Daddy!"

My body stiffens when her little voice carries from the water's edge. Small hands wave frantically in my direction, drawing my eyes to her. Not that you could miss her. A bright, neon green bathing suit covers her tiny body like the stars in her mother's old bedroom.

"Daddy! You're here!"

Sand kicks up behind her tiny feet as she rushes toward me with a massive grin on her reddened face. With her arms wide open, she slams into my legs, hugging me tight.

"Lyric," I breathe, momentarily stunned when her head tips back, and she looks up at me with down-turned lips.

"Daddy," she whines with a wobbly lip, examining every inch of my face and chest. "You've got a boo-boo just like Daddy Asher." My heart sinks when the waterworks start, breaking it into tiny pieces. Dropping to my knees, I quickly wipe away the fat tears falling down her cheeks, desperate to eliminate the sadness. "Why are you hurt?" she sniffles, tracing the bruises under my right eye with her little finger.

Panic grips me tight in a vise, squeezing my chest. My daughter is crying. Fuck, and I'm the cause of all her pain. How do I explain to a four-year-old that I intentionally let another man put his fists into my face?

Frantically, my eyes dart around the beach, catching a glimpse of River sitting on a towel in a red one-piece suit. Those long, filled-out legs stretch before her, soaking up the heated evening sun. A slight breeze blows her long strands back past her shoulders as my eyes eat away at her appearance, taking in every ounce of the woman I once thought was mine forever.

Lava pools in my belly, reactivating the attraction and pulling me to River. No matter how angry I was at her. Or how betrayed I felt. Her flawless beauty always draws me like a moth to a flame, searing me. Last time, I burned to ash. This time, after learning the truth, I sink fully into the flames of my doom. Or resurrection. However, this turns out. One day I'll prove to River how fucking sorry I am that I walked away without talking to her. How fucking stupid could I have been? The guilt of my ignorance will haunt me for the rest of my fucking life.

Swallowing hard, I avert my eyes when fiery heat envelops my cheeks. Those laser moss-green eyes latch onto our movements, slightly narrowing in on my hands, combing through Lyric's wet strands as I attempt to soothe the hurt bubbling out of her eyes. I breathe when she tips her head in my direction, not uttering a word about my perusal of her body. Thank fuck.

"I'm okay, Ladybug." Her face softens when I speak. "It was just an accident, but I'm okay now. You don't have to cry for me," I whisper, catching her tears as they fall out of her eyes. "So, what are you doing on the beach today?" I ask, trying to divert the conversation to something better than the bruises lining my flesh.

"Sandcastle," she whispers, pointing toward where she was sitting. Sure enough, a few small buckets, shovels, and a mound of sand sit, waiting for her to continue.

"Does it have a moat?"

Lyric immediately grabs my hand and yanks me toward the direction of the sandcastle.

"It can!" she squeals, pulling me forward.

"Give me just a second, okay? Let me ask your mommy if this is okay, all right?" Lyric's eyes whip to River and then back to me as she nods.

"Okay. I can't wait to build the biggest castle with you, Daddy!" she shrieks with a grin, wrapping her arms around my neck again. "I can't wait," she whispers, kissing my bruised cheek with so much love I choke on it.

Climbing to my feet, I watch with stars in my eyes as she runs back to her creation near the water. Plopping down in the sand, she grins up at me as she fills a bucket, continuing to build up the castle.

"Hey," I say, clearing my throat and dropping beside River.

"Hi," she says softly, keeping her eyes on Lyric, who dances at the water's edge with a grin.

"I–I didn't know you guys would be here. I-um just wanted to take a swim and walk. But—"

River snorts, waving a hand. "Thanks for asking permission. You're more than allowed to hang out with her." Her eyes cut to mine from beneath her lashes. My breath catches when she examines the tattoos lining my chest. More specifically, the one for her.

Ask me. Ask me about it, Little Star. Please.

Before she can utter a word, she rips her gaze away from the art etched into my flesh.

"Oh-oh, okay," I stammer, reverting back to the mess I was when I first encountered River.

I'd like to think I've grown these past five years. Nerves no longer prickle at my skin when I'm in front of a crowd on stage, and meeting new people is a breeze. I'm no longer stumbling over my own two feet.

There's something about River that makes my heart skip a damn beat and weighs down my tongue as if concrete encases it. She drives me back to the nervous boy I used to be. And a part of me clings to the old Callum resurfacing because that's the man I want to be. Should be.

For her. For Lyric.

"Thanks. I'd really like that," I say, clearing my throat.

"Daddy! Come on! Our castle needs lots of work!" Lyric shouts over the roar of the waves and light breeze blowing through the little paradise.

A small smile pulls at the edge of River's lips. "You'd better get going. She's a very persistent little girl."

I snort. "I've noticed," I quip, locking my eyes on the little girl excitedly jumping up and down in the sand, waving me over.

"Cal," River whispers, resting a hand on my arm, stopping me from getting up.

My heart beats double time when the warmth of her hand seeps into my flesh, stopping my movements. Shit. The world swims in front of my eyes, swirling together in a mass of colors. My body weaves. All from one simple, electrifying touch. And I think I might pass out.

Swallowing the lump in my throat, I stare at where we're connected and get myself under control. "Y-yeah?" I croak when she gently squeezes my arm.

"Lyric likes to come out here every day after school. It's the first thing she does when she throws her backpack in her room, she gets her suit on and plays in the waves and sand. Sometimes she likes to swim, but most times, she likes to sit right there and watch the waves or build a castle." She squeezes one last time and drops her hand from my arm.

Immediately, I miss the way her hand felt on my skin. My vision clears, and my head returns to its usual messy self.

"Thank you," I whisper, earning a nod in return.

"I'm not here to keep her from you. You know that, right?" She swallows hard, gazing at the blue horizon where the sea meets the skyline in the distance. Away from me and the noise bubbling in my throat.

"I-I don't believe you'd keep her from us. That isn't like you." I shake my head, rolling my lips together as the anger from Asher's betrayal stabs me in the back once again.

There are some wounds you never heal from. They cut deep—to the bone—flaying your soul open. This is one of them. Sure, it may superficially mend back together out of necessity, but deep down, the pain, anger, and pent-up rage will always be in the background, reminding me of what he did. There's no getting away from Asher now. We're in too deep unless we tuck tail and leave the band and go our separate ways.

After today's session with Lucy, I'm thinking we might make it out of this alive. If we band together and really sink into our feelings, we'll get through this and make it to the other side. We may have bruises and scrapes, but we'll heal. Once and for all.

"That was Asher and Gloria's fault that we've been apart for so long," I say, watching Lyric closely as she dips her bucket into the water. "I'm just sorry I missed so much," I whisper longingly, staring at the daughter whose childhood I missed out on. But no more.

Callum is here to stay. To make memories full of laughter and love. I'll be here until the end. No matter what.

Happiness fills every molecule of my body. I'm floating above the damn clouds with a smile etched onto my face. A deep laugh vibrates through my chest when I throw Lyric's squirming body over my shoulder, much to her protests. Her loud giggles fill the dusky air as she pounds a fist into my back, begging me to release her.

"Daddy!" Lyric laughs, hitting me a few times. "Put me down! I need to pick up my buckets!" she squeals again, stopping me in my tracks. "Pleaseeeee!" she begs again until I bring her face right in front of mine.

Her freckles pop over the bridge of her nose, dusting lightly over her sun-kissed cheeks. Her toothy grin lights up my damn life as she examines my face. No longer pouting over the dark bruises.

My blood may not run through her veins, but that's the thing about family, isn't it? You're not always born together. You're brought together by circumstances out of your control, crashing into each other much like the waves of the sea. Lyric crashed into our lives like a tiny hurricane. She's shaking the foundation of everything we've known and believed, and I, for one, am ecstatic to have this little human in my life.

"Okay. But I'll give you two seconds, and then we'll race to the house. Your mom looks like she's about to come and get you." I raise a brow when Lyric wiggles out of my arms and dashes off to get her things. With another loud giggle, she races past me, clinging to her buckets.

River stands on her back porch, leaning against the railing and watching Lyric with a smile that lights up her face. A red towel sits snug around River's body, warming her as the sun slowly sinks in the sky, turning it a bright hue of pink.

"Straight to the shower, you sand monster," River says through a big grin, lightly smacking Lyric on the butt.

"But, Mommy! Daddy…" Lyric points to me with a pout, waving her arms all around. "Can he read to me tonight? I wants Daddy to read to me!" she says again, folding her hands together and silently begging her mom.

River looks at me with uncertainty but nods. "If that's what Daddy wants to do."

Butterflies burst in my stomach, and I nod before I can even think about another response. "Of course, I'll read to you."

One of the happiest memories is when my mom and dad would lay on either side of me and take turns reading lines from all my favorite books. Their voices changed with each new character, and they'd stay there until my eyes fluttered shut. I never thought I'd get to experience that warm feeling again. Only this time, I'll be reading from the book and watching as she falls asleep with my heart in my throat.

"Now, off to the shower! Then we'll have some sandwiches," River says again, shooing Lyric toward the bathroom down the hall until she marches into the bathroom, slamming it shut. "And don't slam the door," River mutters too late.

"Little-Little Star."

I swallow hard when she connects her gaze with mine. Reaching out, I bravely wrap my fingers around her wrist, holding her hostage. Please don't walk away from me now. A familiar feeling bursts inside me as I look deep into her eyes. It's something I haven't felt since I walked away from her. Electricity bristles. My hair stands on end. And a deep, gut-wrenching ache forms, begging me never to let go of her.

"She's amazing. I'm sorry I wasn't here, but thank you for allowing me to be here now. I—" I roll my lips together as the heat behind my eyes intensifies. Guilt tears through me like it has since I found out the truth from Asher's lips. We left because of what I saw. I sealed our separation with a picture, not bothering to ask questions or dig further.

River swallows hard, shaking off my grip. "Well, as long as you're here now."

Not fucking good enough.

"So, she's always known about us?" I ask, stuffing my hands into the pockets of my swim shorts to keep from touching her again—the only thing I want to do right now. Well, beyond a simple touch.

Licking her lips, River nods. "Eventually, Lyric would know where she came from and who her father was. In the beginning, I wasn't positive about who she belonged to. Then she opened her eyes… And I… Couldn't deny her the reality of our situation. So, I did the next best thing. I told her the truth. And wouldn't you know it? She latched on."

"She didn't know about…what happened and why we were apart?"

"No. And she won't either," she says. "I will not break my daughter's heart, nor will you. She's—" She takes a deep breath, rubbing her temples. "Lyric is finally at peace. It's like she needed to touch you all. Don't ruin her peace." Her eyes plead with me until I nod at her request.

"I'd never do that to her. It's only been a short time, but I already love her," I admit quietly as my cheeks heat.

"Come here," River says, waving a hand for me to follow as the sound of water slapping into the tub suddenly turns off. "Here," River says, taking a large photo album off a bookshelf and handing it to me.

My eyes bug out as I flip through the pictures. Page by page, River has organized everything into neat little sections. From her first birthday to her forth. And every holiday in between. Glorious snapshots of Lyric as a baby, learning to crawl and taking her first bites of ravioli. Her red-stained face smiles up at the camera from her highchair with the remnants of her meal squished before her. Mischief lives in those mismatched eyes—much like now.

Without the perseverance to hold them back any longer, I unleash my emotions. Tears stream down my cheeks. Embarrassing sobs choke my throat. Fuck. I'm a goddamn mess at the sight of my baby girl, who grew up without me. I cry from the anger of missing out, for walking away, and for everything in between. I let it out into the world, letting River see and feel how fucking sorry and fucked up I am over this.

"She was a good baby," River murmurs, turning the page and running her manicured finger over a picture of Lyric's toothless grin, staring up at the camera with cake all over her face. "That was her first birthday. It was our first month in this house." Her eyes dart around the living room, stopping near the entrance of the open-concept kitchen.

"And I missed it all. Fuck," I heave a breath, losing my grip as the photo album thunks to the ground. "River," I breathe, turning to her as she tilts her head, not giving me an ounce of emotion.

She's a goddamn wall of nothing, staring at me and refusing to open up. One day I'll peel back those layers of forgiveness. But for now, I know I have my work cut out for me. We all do.

"I truly am sorry you missed it all, Cal. She would have loved for you to be here this whole time. But the important part is, you're here now. Make the most of it while you can."

I nod, wiping away the remnants of my emotions off my cheeks. "I will," I proclaim, holding her gaze with mine. God, I could get lost in the depths of her eyes and swim in her damn soul. "For you, too," I whisper, drifting a finger across her silken cheek.

The warmth of her skin sends goosebumps pimple down my arms. Tiny hairs stand on end. Electricity runs between us in an undeniable force, pulling me into her. My lips tingle, begging to kiss the last pair I ever touched with my own.

"Words don't mean much, Little Star. Not with you. I could look you in the eyes and promise you a million and one things. But they're just words —empty promises. From here on out, I will prove who I am and what you mean to me. We may have had time apart, but we're grown up now. No longer the kids running around Central City. You've changed. I've changed. Some for the worst. Some for the better," I whisper, rubbing my thumb against her cheek. Her brows wrinkle as she takes in my words, but I'm not done yet. "I deeply apologize for walking away from you. The moment I saw Van kiss you, I should have known better. Asher had just dismantled my entire world with those fake videos, and then when I saw what I did, I ran without even questioning it. That's on me. I was an idiot… probably still am. Every day and night, I'll show up here and be present. That's my promise to you, Little Star. Because the way I see it now, you're my whole damn galaxy, and I can't stand to be away from you and her any longer."

River shudders as I breathlessly finish my speech, getting lost in her presence. Clarity has completely taken hold. I was an idiot for ever thinking River would turn her back on us. River was better than that—still is. I'm not fucking worthy of her.

River sniffles, slightly leaning into my hand. "She's going to want you to stop doing that," she whispers, running the tip of her finger over the bruises on my face. "She thought you were hurt, and it upset her. She will know something is wrong if you keep showing up with those bruises." She licks her lips before dropping her hand. My body misses her touch when she steps away from my hand.

"Okay," I agree, nodding. "I won't fight anymore." Music will be what I live and breathe from this moment forward. I'll pour my damn soul straight into my bass. For them.

"Why did you?" she blurts before she can stop herself, widening her eyes. "It just…doesn't seem like you, Callum. You were so peaceful and quiet." Still am. Only around you, though.

I shrug. "It was better than the drugs," I whisper through a crack in my voice. "Truth?" She nods, eager to hear my response. "It was the only thing that could knock the joyous memories of you out of my head. For just a second, I wasn't drowning in my misery. I—" I blow out a breath, preparing myself for the conversation ahead of me. "I loved you a lot, Little Star. So much so that I didn't realize how I truly felt until you were gone. But I failed you in so many ways. Will you take this healing journey with me?" I ask, licking my lips. "I want to mend us."

"And what if I… I can't?" she questions, taking another step back. "You did fail me…you all did. You walked away from us. What would have happened if I hadn't made it here? Would I still be in Central City with Ly alone?" She crosses her arms over her chest. "I want to heal, too," she finally whispers, squeezing her eyes shut. "But just give me time, okay? Be present. And I'll—"

"You don't owe me anything," I mutter, stepping forward and taking her into my arms. Stiffly, she rests her forehead against my chest as I soak in her presence. "One day at a time, Little Star. Okay?"

"One day at a time," she whispers with confirmation, and I know that's as good as it's going to get right now. River isn't mine or ours. Not yet. But we'll get there. I know we'll all prove to her that we're serious about this.

My eyes fall shut when the warmth of her fingers glides over my bare chest with curiosity. She doesn't step out of my arms, which I'm thankful for. I want to revel in her body heat for a moment longer until we're pulled apart.

"These weren't here before," she barely whispers, tracing the shapes repeatedly.

"They weren't."

Lifting her head, her red-rimmed eyes lock on mine. "They're over your heart, Cal."

I lick my lips. "That they are." My breaths pass over her face, traveling down her neck. The persistent urge to hold her tongue hostage with mine gnaws at my brain. Not the right time, damnit.

"You got neon stars over your heart," she whispers with an edge, emotions creeping in and ruffling her hardened, emotionless exterior.

I see you, Little Star.

"Truth?" She nods, eagerly awaiting my answer. "I may have wanted to erase the memories from my mind, but there was one place I felt whole." Without a thought, my fingers capture hers over my heart and rest them there. "It was with you, under the neon stars illuminating your bedroom as we lay together, hidden away in your space."

"Oh, Cal," she murmurs, choking out my name like a sin. Her fist clutches near her mouth when she takes a step away from me, refusing herself the comfort of my arms.

Fuck.

"Just remember, I'm not going anywhere," I whisper, stepping up to her again and invading her space. "Ever again. If there's one promise you should take to heart. It's this one."

The old Callum would cower away from her—hide his face from the world. But the new Callum craves her with every ounce of his being like a damn drug or fighting. My body jolts when a little person stares at us from a few feet away, sleepily rubbing at her eyes. Deep blue star pajamas line her frame. Long dark strands of wet hair drip on the hardwood as she eyes the two of us with suspicion.

"Daddy, will you read to me now?" Lyric yawns, stretching her tiny arms above her head.

"I'll get some sandwiches ready," River murmurs, scurrying as far away from me as she can.

You can run, and you can hide, Little Star, but we'll bulldoze through the thick walls you've erected around us. All in due time, of course. Mending our broken relationship and betrayal comes first.

"Of course. What are we reading tonight?" Lyric grins, suddenly looking more awake than she had ten seconds ago, watching me with the biggest eyes I've ever seen. Excitement thrums through her veins when she bounces on her toes.

"Well, it's about this girl who gets picked to compete in this crazy ring. She has a bow and arrow and two boyfriends. Like me!" She giggles when I stiffen, side-eyeing River, who shrugs from the kitchen and hides her smile. Somehow, I feel like I'm missing something vital. "Come on! Come on! I'm ready!"

My brows furrow. "What kind of book is she reading?" I hiss in her direction.

River snorts, patting me on the shoulder. "You'll see," is all she says before she kisses Lyric's head and walks away, leaving me with an eager four-year-old who promptly grabs my hand and yanks me down the hall to her room.

"Your room is so pretty," I awkwardly say, rubbing at my bare chest. Thankfully, my swim trunks have dried since we were outside, but I still feel the sand shifting in places it shouldn't be.

"Mommy helped me pick out all the purple. I'm afraid of the dark, Daddy," she murmurs, climbing into her bed and patting the place beside her.

"Is that why you have a lot of lights shining down on you?" I question as she snuggles into my side, looking up at me with those big, blue eyes.

"Mhmm. There's a ghost in here," she whispers with a slight hint of fear jumping into her tone. Her eyes dart toward the window above her bed, and she shudders.

"Ghosts? Well, I'm here now, Ladybug. Let's scare them away." She nods in agreement, handing over a large, used book with a bookmark in the middle.

"She marched forward with her bow at the ready, aiming to take down the enemy," I say in a deep voice, only raising it when the character speaks her line. "You will step away from her before I put this through your hands and mince your fingers for dinner." Jesus. What is my child reading before bedtime? Looking down, Lyric looks up at me expectantly, silently egging me on to continue. And so, I do. River meanders in, leaves sandwiches in the middle of the bed, and walks out before I can say a word.

Over the next hour, I lay beside my daughter, nibbling sandwiches and reading about a strong, independent woman who kicks ass and takes names like nobody's business. Also, she shows great interest in the two leading male characters. Many times, I turn to the blurb on the back, making sure I'm not about to read some crazy romance story to my four-year-old. As the clock ticks by, my eyes grow heavy until the thick book lands on my chest, and the world around me is darkness as my eyes close.

"Night, Daddy," she whispers, snuggling further into my side.

"Night, Ladybug," I murmur, falling victim to the perfect night's sleep.

I think my girlfriend is slowly trying to murder me. Not with a knife or poison. Nope! She's slowly draining me dry, and I don't know if I can make it any longer. And not the good kind of draining me either. I mean, she can drain my dick as much as she wants. If I had the energy for it, that is. I'm like a damn sack of potatoes heaving myself into bed each weekend.

It's been two goddamn weeks of this. I think I'll put an obituary in the paper and just announce my death ahead of time.

Here lies Rad. Gone too soon at the hands of his Pretty Girl, who over-worked him night after night on stage.

When River said we'd have to perform every Saturday per our contract, I didn't think it'd be like this. Hashtag–Radisdead. Hashtag–some-onesaveme.

It's all for the pact. Every one of her demands, we follow like good little boys. Now, if she'd only throw me a bone and reward me for my good behavior.

"Should I cut off my balls and put them in River's purse now or later? I can't decide," I wheeze, lying flat on the ground, soaking up the cold tiles. It's like running ice cubes all over my flesh, and it's refreshing as fuck.

Kieran grunts in agreement or disagreement; I can't fucking tell. Splashing water on his red face, he sits back on the leather couch, shaking his head. "I don't know, but I think she's trying to kill us."

"More like punish us," Callum murmurs with a pained groan, resting on the leather couch beside Kieran with ease.

"Why are your clothes off?" Kieran asks, raising a brow like he hasn't known me since middle school.

Hello, being naked is like my damn calling card. Naked Rad has a ring to it, right? I can't help myself. The moment I get on stage and the suffo-cating heat hits me, I need to take everything off. Fuck clothes. I'd rather live in a community where clothes were banished. Welcome to the Radali-cious Naked Compound. Population: 5. Just me, the guys, and my Pretty Girl… And shit…we can't be naked all the time. Oh, the sacrifices we

make for our Little Pretty Girl and future babies. Because yeah, the second I get back inside of my woman, that's all I want. Little me's. Little them's. Another little her. God. My dick springs to life at the thought, which is terrible, because I'm barely dressed. Not like they haven't seen my dick flag fly.

"It's hot as fuck. Fuck pants. Fuck shirts and socks. You're lucky I still have my boxers on." I lift my middle finger into the air, saluting the boys in more than one way. Oops. "If she keeps this up, she might," I grunt, searching for a fan. "You guys see a fan anywhere? I need cool air on my dick like yesterday."

If I don't cool my nuts off soon, they will pop right off in protest and wander away, taking my dick with them. I swear they're boiling inside my damn boxers.

"Do you think this is payback?" Callum murmurs, wiping the sweat from his face.

Kieran snorts. "It's not like she can avoid us or get some sort of revenge for what we did." His eyes cut to Asher sitting across the room under the ceiling fan. He hasn't moved an inch since we got off stage and hasn't spoken.

He's retreating inside himself again like he did when we came to California. Back then, he focused on the music to escape her memory. And now, he's doing the same and withering away right before our eyes. He may be an asshole, but it hurts to see him so beat down all the time. The good news is he's moved back into his room at the band house. Since the moment we made the pact two weeks ago, we've been civil with him. We've had to be. He's important to Lyric, and River to an extent. I will not jeopardize my future with my girls. Not one bit. So, If I have to be the nice guy, then I'll be the nice guy. Besides, between therapy and group sessions, we're really starting to hash some shit out and get back to the family we used to be.

Kieran's rage has settled to nothing. He's giving it his all and smiling more, especially when it comes to Lyric. Callum stopped fighting cold turkey and hasn't had a bruise in two whole weeks. It's odd to see him without the discoloration on his face or body, but I'm glad he stopped.

More often than not these days, Callum sneaks out around three and comes back at six covered in sand, with a goofy smile lighting up his face. I was starting to worry about my damn brother all the time. I knew one day I'd find him dead in an alleyway after mouthing off to some asshole on the street. Thankfully, it never happened. So, I can rest easy now.

"At least you bitches just get to sway and look pretty. I'm pounding my shit into the drums as hard as I can. God, I think I'm fucking dying." I wave my hand in front of my face, trying to get cool air across my overheated skin. What I wouldn't give for one of those glorious ice baths.

Ahh, yeah. Dip my nuts into the ice until they're scurrying back inside me instead of trying to melt off. A guy can dream.

I love my Pretty Girl. I really fucking do. With my whole goddamn heart and body, I also know what she's up to. She doesn't think I do. Probably doesn't think I'm as quick as I am. But I know she's trying to get us back into shape. I'm an intelligent guy when I want to be.

But something has to give. It's been like this since everything came to a head, and we made our pact to not fuck anything else up.

And this last stint of torture has been three long ass days.

Yesterday, we were kidnapped and taken to a county fair four hours away. Don't get me wrong, being on stage again felt glorious. It's been months since we've been on tour and getting back up there playing our music in sync was fucking beautiful. Sure, we've played a few shows per the rules of our contract with River. But it wasn't like this. This is fucking brutal.

Then, after our orgasmic performance. Because yeah, I may have cum a little during because I knew my Pretty Girl was right in my sights, watching my every move. I could have used Little Rad as a fucking drumstick. Scratch that. That wouldn't have felt very good unless it was a pussy drum attached to my girl.

Then after that performance, we were ushered home to the band house, where she ripped each of our testicles off and made a damn necklace. With pride, too. Her smile may have lit up the room, but it put the fear of God in our souls. I mean, she's hot with nuts all around her face. Or nuts on her face. But not at that moment. Abso-fucking-lutely not.

"I want you boys to look this over," she says, handing Kieran a piece of paper.

"What is it?" Kieran asks, taking the paper from her outstretched hand. As his eyes gaze at the report, they widen in surprise. His body stiffens, and he sucks in a breath.

"This is a list of everything I noticed that could be improved during your shows. I want you guys to look over this carefully. This will help you be aware of what I'm looking at and what you can adjust. This is your homework for tonight. We have two more shows tomorrow."

"Two?" I choke on my water, letting it dribble down my chin. "Tomorrow?" I squeak pathetically, clinging to the couch. Please don't let it be true. I don't know If I can survive another two rounds of performances.

"Two," she says, giving me that oh-so-pleased smile she's perfected lately.

Evil Pretty Girl is hot as fuck, but goddamn, I need a break. My body might give out on me if I have to drum again.

Yup. This is fucking torture. It's our goddamn penance for being little shits and walking away from her instead of being big boys and having a conversation. Oh, if I could go back in time and pull my dick up—we'd all be in a better place. Maybe we wouldn't be rock stars in the prime of our lives. But nowadays, that doesn't seem as important as River and Lyric.

"There's like twenty things here, River Blue. Were we really that bad?" Kieran asks, rubbing a tired hand down his weary face.

"Not terrible. But not good either."

Well, ouch. Spank my ass and call me Ashton because this woman is bending us over and telling us exactly how it is. Add in a spiky cactus up our asses without the necessary lube. I shudder. Damn, my butthole puckers at the stern look she gives each of us. Would she be offended if I called her Mommy and sucked her tit? Probably. Then we'd be in even more trouble, and she'd probably add another thousand shows to torture us with.

"When I watched you guys before you played as one, you moved around and commanded the stage, forcing everyone to have their eyes on you. You were electric, enthralling, and now, you're like watching paint dry. You're as stiff as boards up there, eyeing each other like you're ready to pounce and rip your heads off. You don't smile anymore; you don't even act like you like music. So, I'm curious, do you guys still enjoy playing, or is this a chore?"

Talk about a slap in the dick. She accused us—Whispered Words—of not enjoying our passion. The audacity! But wait, do we enjoy our passion anymore? Reaching deep inside myself, I try to pull out the magical feeling. Shit. It doesn't come. Where's the giddiness and eagerness I always felt before shows? It's…empty. The well is dry. I frown, staring around the room at the other guys, oblivious to the pain ricocheting through me.

"Just think about it. I'll see you in the morning. We have a show at noon and a show at the KC Club in the evening. Get some rest, boys," she coos, strolling out of the room, sashaying that curvy ass that I want to paint red with my palm. But I'm a good boy. I stay planted in my seat, blinking rapidly, and trying to digest what the fuck just happened. Also, I'm too tired to fucking move.

"Did that just really happen?" I frown, saying my thoughts aloud.

"Yeah," Kieran grunts, staring over the paper. "Looks like we have fucking homework."

"For the pact," Callum murmurs, leaning over to peek at the paper.

"For the pact," I reluctantly say.

I'd much rather sleep it off in my bed than look over my critique. *All for the Pretty Girl*, I repeat in my head, cringing at her words.

"For the pact," Asher agrees.

When River leaves us sitting in our self-deprecating juices, we discuss how we want to move forward with this. We have to prove to my Pretty Girl that this is it for us, we want this, and there's no other way around it. Music is our damn lives. Always has been and always will be. Maybe.

"So, I had an idea."

All our eyes turn to Ash, who grabs his guitar, strumming a few chords. His brows furrow as a soft melody picks up. Over and over, he plays it until it sounds like a solid chorus.

"What is it?" Kieran asks, jumping to his feet. Never taking his gaze off Asher, who closes his eyes and sways with the tune.

"We haven't written in forever," Asher says with a hint of sadness. "Let's build off this. It came to me last night in the shower, and it's been stuck in my head ever since. I want to do something for Ly." A deep, red blush takes over his cheeks when he looks around the room at our eager faces.

"A song for Ly?" Callum asks, rubbing his chin and nodding. "Fuck yeah."

"That would be a perfect way to show our girl how serious we are!" I whoop, jumping to my feet.

"Lyrics come from the heart," Callum murmurs, scrunching his brows.

"Wait, what?" I ask with a renewed energy taking me over.

"You said it once when we were in bed with River. Lyrics came to you, and you said…"

"Lyrics come from the heart and out of nowhere. They're unexpected…" Callum trails off with his eyes widening. "You don't think she…"

My heart beats double time. "That she named Lyric that because she was unexpected?" I will not cry in front of the guys. I will absolutely bawl into my pillow tonight. No tears here. Nope.

It isn't until that night, when I'm staring up at the ceiling do I let my tears fall. If what Cal remembers is correct, he's usually spot on and all. Hello, photographic memory. Then my girl named my baby girl after something I said. One day, I'll bring it up to her. For now, I'll savor it in the palm of my hand and keep the knowledge to myself.

"Yo dummy, are you putting a fan on your shit?" Kieran grunts, throwing a water bottle at me and knocking me out of my thoughts.

I furrow my brows, realizing I'm dangling a massive box fan above my junk. On fucking high. Huh. No wonder I'm starting to cool off. But also, there are enormous fan blades inches from my crotch. Geez, that was close. I could have cut the boys.

"Yeah," I murmur, setting the fan beside me so it still blows the cool air across my flesh. "I think this is a punishment." Definitely a way to get back at us for being dicks. Rightfully so. We were major fuckers.

Here I thought we were on the right track to forgiveness. Maybe we aren't doing enough to prove ourselves. Shit. We need to step up our game and get it together.

We've already been on a date. Well, I mean, I joined her and Rocco again because you can't get rid of me. I'm Rad, the never-ending rash that sticks to you even when you put ointment on me. Can't get rid of me! At least she didn't kick me out this time. I was allowed to sit at the table and eat my Italian food like a good boy.

Take that, Pretty Girl. I'll never give up until you're completely mine.

Like an angel in six-inch red heels, River burst through the backstage door with an adorning smile.

"Did we do good, Pretty Girl?" I ask, lifting my head off the cold ground and giving her my best puppy dog eyes.

"Color me impressed, boys," she says, giving us a little clap. "You put in the work out there. I felt more included in the performance. Kieran, your voice was on point. Rad, your drumming and smiling brought the crowd out. Asher and Callum, you guys did good, too."

I beam under her compliment, peeling myself off the sticky tile floor. "Thanks, Pretty Girl. We're always here to impress." I grin when she snorts.

"Right. Well, you might want to put your clothes on. You have a line of rabid fans begging for autographs and pictures."

"We don't really do autographs," Kieran grumbles with displeasure.

"Oh, but now you do, Knight. I expect you by the bar in five minutes! Look alive, boys!" she shouts, clapping her hands again.

"This is a goddamn test," I hiss, finding my pants crumpled in the corner. "Avoid the titties and ass signatures as much as fucking possible! No flesh." I grumble in disgust when my wet T-shirt sticks to every inch of my upper body. Usually, I waltz out of here half-naked, not caring who sees me nude. Not now! My Pretty Girl is watching our every move. I will not fuck this up.

My body is River's fucking temple. She's the only one who can worship me now: no more ogling eyes or touchy hands from fans. I am a one-woman man. Forever. No matter what.

"She wants to watch us with the fans," Callum surmises, rubbing his chin.

"You think she's trying to see how we handle the girls?" Asher asks with uncertainty.

"My bet? Yeah, she fucking does." Kieran smirks when he stands, running his hands down his ripped jeans. "Our girl is secretly jealous. So, let's show her we can be as professional as her. We sign autographs but stay close to her."

Ohhh, I like secretly jealous Pretty Girl. She gets all stabby and punchy. It makes my dick hard just thinking about it.

"Let's do this. Operation prove ourselves commences," I say, throwing a fist into the air with a whoop.

"Have a good night, boys," I say, sauntering out of the band house at midnight with my head held high.

Three days of running them through the wringer has every muscle in my body wound tighter than a damn spring. Ready to unload.

Three days of watching their asses sway on stage.

Sexy, stupid bastards. Why do they have to look so damn good and delicious in their natural habitat?

Three days of watching the sweat drip down their bare chests as they move with grins on their faces. Three goddamn miserable days of watching girls flock to their sides, pawing at them, and helplessly watching as I kept my shit together with gritted teeth and fake smiles.

Now, I'm free from them for a few days. I don't know why I thought this torture would be good for them. They flew through my rigorous training exercise with ease.

Bastards.

Sure, the first concert was like watching a cactus soak in the sun. They were stiff pricks, avoiding eye contact with each other, including the roaring crowd. After that, they took my critical notes and ran with them like wild animals. Everything I laid down, they took it like champs.

I had to get creative by torturing their asses somehow and enact a little revenge of my own. I can't exactly burn the house down with them inside to get some retribution, so… I may have overextended their abilities on stage.

Just a little. Three shows in a thirty-hour period isn't too horrible. They survived. Maybe on fumes.

Okay, maybe it was just a little too much.

So, fucking sue me.

If I had it my way, I would have shoved them on a boat, duct taped and unconscious, and driven them out to sea. Sleep with the fishes now, boys.

Fuck. Not really. I couldn't do that. They've been—

Great.

So, fucking wonderful with Ly. They've been here for me, too. Every

step of the way. They aren't fighting me on the demands I'm putting them through.

Asher makes her fucking breakfast every morning and brings it over. Even though looking at him simultaneously breaks my heart and hardens it. He's still so bruised from their punches. And so damn subdued and polite.

It's hard to hate a man who isn't the same person he was years before when he pulled this stunt. He may wear the same face, but the demon that once sat on his shoulders disappeared the moment he confessed. Maybe my exorcisms really worked.

See? So damn conflicted.

Callum reads her bedtime stories, and sometimes Rad joins in for comedic relief.

Kieran spends as much time as possible with her on the beach with his guitar in his hand and her on his lap, teaching her the notes.

They've been fucking great. It both pleases the piss out of me and irritates me to no end.

Why couldn't they be bastards so I could continue to hate them?

But no. That's not what I want either.

Goddamn, my head aches with all the different opinions rattling through my head. I try to remember what Rocco and I talked about when he dropped soup off a few weeks ago and live by that mantra. I can't fault these men for trying their hardest. Even when they fucked up in the worst possible way.

Take it day by day. Don't roll over and forgive them. Make them beg. Make them get on their damn knees and earn your trust back. Let them see Lyric and prove themselves to her and to you.

And I've done that. I haven't rolled over. Or forgiven them. It may be on the horizon. Sometime in the close future. But not yet. They still deserve more shit from me.

I slam through the front door of the band house and beeline it toward the beach behind my home. Nothing says refreshing like yelling at the ocean at midnight until your throat is raspy and your emotions are spent. It's the remedy to my problems. For now, at least.

As soon as the warm night air hits my skin, everything crumbles. My facade. My walls. My fucking hormones. I'm in shambles. Reeling from the effects of being in their presence. How can four men wreck me so damn hard without even trying to?

Who said being a badass HBIC was easy? Commanding Whispered Words on what to do while performing on stage is hard as fuck. I'm feeling the after-effects of watching them for hours.

Vivid memories of their hands running down their bare chests as they whipped their shirts off and tossed them in my direction. Always at me. Never the screaming girls. Whether I was standing just off stage or in the front row, they made sure their shirts were mine. Sweat-soaked and all.

God fucking damn it. My head spins, weaving a mess of webs in my mind. Should I jump in headfirst, or should I just let them be fathers? It rattles around in my messed-up brain, pushing me further down the rabbit hole.

My broken heart is slowly stitching together piece by piece. They're the menders of my soul. How fucking ironic, huh? The men who broke it are now fixing it with the little things. It's always the fucking little things.

We've talked. Cried. Yelled. Argued. Raised our voices. Every bit of healing conversation has been present. The sorrys and stepping up are all there. They're taking therapy extra seriously, too, which surprised the hell out of me. I never expected the guys to willingly talk to a stranger. I knew it would benefit them, especially after learning about their upbringing. Hell, Asher even goes into her office an additional time each week, and Kieran tags along.

Yet, I remember the way I felt when they walked away. They fucking eviscerated me. My heart literally shattered in my chest, turning into tiny fragments of what I once was and numbing me for so long. I tried every day to forget their existence. Whispered Words, who? But it never worked. Every time I felt Lyric kick inside me, I was reminded of who helped put her there. And the moment I finally saw her eyes, I fucking broke in half.

Three of them had no clue what trap they were falling into. Only one knew the truth this whole time. He's the man suffering the most with the remnants of his bruises and the alienation.

He's also trying, too.

How can I be so damn conflicted on something so simple? Do I trust them again, or do I take my chances? Do I drown them in the sea, or keep them afloat?

"Fuckkkkkkkkk!" I shout into the night sky as I stand at the edge of the sea. "Give me a damn sign. Give me something!" I roar at the sparkling stars. They give nothing back. "I just don't know what to do or how to feel —" I trail off, sinking my teeth into my lip. "I just want to know what to do with the future."

Stepping forward, I sigh when the cool water soaks through my shoes. Shivers burst up my spine the moment the water retreats and then splashes me again.

My head falls back, and I groan, counting the dots in the sky.

It's times like these that I'm thankful for my family. They may have come later in life, but I feel more loved and adored than I did throughout my entire childhood.

Kaycee let Lyric come over for a three-day sleepover so I could take care of business with the boys. Not only did it give me free time to reflect on all this bullshit, but I didn't have to worry about Ly. She's safe with her cousins, aunt, and uncles.

And I'm here. Horny and miserable. How could my life get any worse?

Looking out into the soft waves of the dark ocean, I take a deep breath. I've got this. Tits up and all that good badass girl shit. I'll navigate through these muddy waters as best I can. After I change my now wet shoes and pants, that is. As therapeutic as screaming at the sky was, it doesn't solve a damn thing.

I huff, walking up the beach toward my house, getting sand in and on my damn shoes. With a grunt, I toss them on the back porch with a mental note to clean them later.

After securing my home and taking a hot shower, I grab a tall glass of white wine, open my window, and stand in the middle of my bed naked.

The beautiful sound of the waves crashing against the sand filters through my room, relaxing every inch of my body.

The soft, warm breeze brushes against my bare skin as I close the curtains and secure the wedge so no one can push the window open further. You know, like my stalker who looms in the back of my mind. Always there. Every step I take, I swear he's behind me, watching my every move and taking pictures. I shudder at the thought but try not to let him rule my life. I'm vigilant with everything I do. House alarm. Locking my doors. Having a guard at the end of the drive. I know he's been in here before, invading my damn privacy. But I won't allow some pussy coward, who hangs in the shadows, to steal my peace from me. This is my home. My haven.

I nibble my lip. At some point, I'm going to have to clue the guys in on what's been happening to me. I have a stalker. He takes pictures of me. Follows me around like a lost puppy dog but never shows his damn face. Fuck. How can I tell them? Do I sit them down for a meeting and casually throw it out there? No. I can't. It'll change everything once they find out. They'll look at me differently and… I'm not ready for that.

I groan at the pent-up tension coiling in the pit of my stomach, begging me to unleash the feeling. My thighs tighten, and my breaths pick up as I imagine laying back in bed and relieving myself to the images of the boys across the street.

I chug the last of my wine, setting the glass down on my end table. Plopping on my bed, I reach over and open the drawer beside me with a grin. Oh yes, this will do.

"There you are," I murmur, pulling my rose-shaped vibrator out. Energy hums through me, prepping my body for the orgasm I'm about to bless it with. "I've missed you," I murmur, aching to kiss it in relief.

Lying back on the bed, I settle myself on my pillows with a loud sigh. The cool sheets encase me in their grasp as my eyes flutter shut.

My imagination ignites into naughty fantasies as the little rose rapidly thumps against my aching clit, begging for sweet relief. Bring on the orgasm that's been building for the past three days.

Fire roars through my veins as images pour through my mind at a rapid pace. A moan slips from my lips as I reach down and plunge my fingers into my pussy, pumping them in and out.

The vibrations around my clit send liquid lust straight through me. My back bows when my head falls back into the pillow. Moan after moan fills the room, and I'm panting, mentally begging for the real thing. Loud, thumping footfalls stop me in my tracks just outside my window. My heart plummets into my ass. My worst fears are coming true. Visions of my stalker standing outside my window, listening to me getting myself off have me recoiling. Until I hear my stalker's voice just outside my window…

"Shh, fuckers. Did you hear that?"

Relief slams through me as I hold my breath at the sound of Rad's voice. It's so close. Like he's whispering dirty words straight into my ear. Shit! My pussy flutters around my fingers. A moan bubbles up my throat. My teeth sink into my bottom lip, suppressing the noise when my fingers curl inside myself.

"It sounded like screaming," Kieran remarks.

"I'm sure it was an animal," Callum murmurs.

"Now, shut the fuck up. We're going for a swim, and that's it," Kieran urges them on with his commanding voice.

"Fucking finally. You think my Pretty Girl is still awake?" No! I'm not awake. Don't you fucking dare, Ashton.

"All the lights are off. What are you doing?" Callum grumbles as footsteps approach near the window above my head.

If he peeks in, he's going to get a full view of my fingers in my cunt and my vibe against my clit.

"Don't you fucking look in the window, you creep. She'd remove your balls and feed them to you."

Well, he's not wrong.

Time to have a little fun with those assholes who drive me insane. Time for another goddamn punishment.

A thrill shoots through me, tingling through my limbs as my orgasm builds. Something about them being outside my window, able to hear what's going on, heightens my desire.

"Fuck," I moan as loud as I can, gasping for breath.

"Don't cum yet, Pretty Girl," he wheezes outside the window. "Don't do it. Wait for me!"

"But I'm so close," I grit out. "And this is my damn show. I do what I want. You don't get to cum."

"Jesus fucking Christ. Tell me she's not…" A rustling happens, and I grin when I feel his gaze wandering over my naked body sprawled out on the bed. "Yup. She is."

"What?" Callum asks with desperation.

More rustling happens until they're all standing in my window, watching me as I'm about to unravel.

I huff when Kieran groans beside Rad in the window. But I refuse to look at them.

"Shut up and watch. No coming," I demand, working my fingers harder inside myself. "Fuck," I moan in a raspy voice, throwing my head back. My heart thumps wildly in my chest.

"This is torture," Rad groans.

Yeah, that's the point. It's what I want. They deserve to suffer after teasing me for so many days.

"You're going to cum, River Blue. Cum right now!" Kieran demands, growling through the screen with such force I fucking combust.

His voice carries me through the most explosive orgasm I've felt in years. It's like I needed them to bear witness to my final crumble.

Blowing out a breath, I throw my rose back into her drawer. I'll just clean her later. "Okay, boys. Go home," I say, making a shooing motion with my hand.

"Go?" Rad all but shouts in hysterics. "My dick is currently saluting and applauding your performance. I can't leave. He needs to show you how much he loved it!"

I snort, staring up at the window with no shame. Thank God for liquid courage. I may regret this in the morning. Or not. I got a damn orgasm and showed these assfaces that I don't need no man to get me off. It'd be nice, don't get me wrong. But that's not the point I'm trying to prove. I could have walked into Rad's room, demanded he strips, and then went to pound town. But I didn't. I did it all on my own.

"Go stroke your dick to the memory of me, assfaces. Because this is all you're getting," I say, throwing a long T-shirt on, covering my naked body.

"Little Star," Callum mumbles through the screen with desperation in his eyes.

"Sorry, boys. I'm all relaxed and sleepy now. Have a good night!" I say, jumping up onto the middle of my bed, bringing me face to face with my peeping toms.

"Fine," Kieran grumbles, glaring at me with lust filling his eyes.

"See you later, Pretty Girl! I'll think of you as I'm stroking my cock in the shower and cum with your name on my lips."

I shudder at the imagery, eliciting a grin from Rad.

As soon as they're walking away, I shut my window and curtains with a sense of pride puffing out my chest.

They can look all they want. But I won't let them touch me until they've proven themselves more.

I grin more when my phone buzzes. Swiping it off my end table, I swipe it open and fucking freeze.

UNKNOWN NUMBER

I heard what you did.

You're more beautiful than I remember. Next time you'll
cum with my name on your lips—Not theirs.

You're MINE, goddamn it!!

It's about time you realized it.

My breaths heave when I forward the messages to Olivia and Carter,
who get back to me right away.

OLIVIA

I'm on it, babe. Don't worry.

CARTER

Get the fuck over here…

NOTHING SAYS GET THE FUCK OUT OF YOUR HOUSE FASTER THAN A TEXT letting you know your stalker heard every single fucking thing you did in your bedroom.

Everything.

The moans. The buzzing. My fucking pleasure.

He stole it from me by listening through my own camera system. The very same security that's in place to keep me safe.

Fuck.

I heave a shuddering sigh, staring up at the white ceiling above me. One that isn't my own. After getting that bullshit text, I threw on some pants and scurried to my brothers' house with fear running rampant through my damn veins. I didn't even grab a fucking bra in my panic. Let alone underwear.

My first thought was seeking sanctuary with Carter. He's Veritas, after all.

I didn't have time for anything. My mind went into overdrive, shoving me out the door before I had time to process what the hell happened. He heard me. He listened in on my most intimate moment. It was different when the boys watched me through the window. I wanted them to see what they had missed out on. But this stalker? He can fuck right off.

My privacy is officially blown. According to Carter, who collected my messy ass at the front door last night, he's escalated everything in terms of my safety.

"I'll fucking figure this out. Understand? Don't you fucking fret over this shit. That's what me and Liv are for. Now, go the fuck to bed and stop freaking out. I'm going to tap into your camera and track down every goddamn IP address attached to your files. I'll track that bitch. He can't hide from me."

I swallow hard when my phone buzzes on the nightstand next to me. Flashes of the messages my stalker sent me race through my mind.

Is it him again? Is he somehow watching my every move?

My eyes dart around the room. No. There are no cameras in here. I'm secure. This entire mansion is behind a thick fence and beefed-up security. After their scare with the crazy cult years ago, they've never let their guard down. It's half the reason Carter went into Veritas.

Fuck. My stomach somersaults, and my adrenaline spikes. It's not him…

ASHER

I'm bringing breakfast for Lyric. Hope that's okay?

If not…it's okay…just wanted to see her this morning before school…

I can stop by…say hi, and then leave…

Fuck, I sound like a stalker…

Stalker. I squeeze my eyes shut, blowing out a big breath. He doesn't know what he's saying. They don't even know I've been dealing with this for so damn long. When will I tell them? When it escalates too much? My skin crawls, begging me to scratch through it and relieve the persistent itch just out of reach.

What the fuck am I supposed to say? Stay the fuck away? You ruined my damn life? Fuck you, Asher Montgomery? I should say all those things and more. But I can't. Asher isn't stepping into my life for me. He's here for Ly and genuinely putting forth the effort like a good father should.

I'm so damn torn. He's the cause of all my problems. The man who put everything in motion. I hate him. But yet, I don't. Not really. Why can't I? Because I get it. His reasoning, that is. But it doesn't excuse his behavior. Not one bit.

They left me behind because he was a coward. And now, he's putting forth actual effort toward forgiveness.

My damn head throbs as I make my way out of the bedroom. Coffee, small whispers, and food greet my senses. Coffee. I need all the damn coffee in the world to make it through today like nothing happened last night. Or maybe it's time to reveal to the boys what's been going on. It's not just my safety that's at stake. It's Ly's and theirs, too. That maniac has only ramped up since they've come into the picture. Who knows what he'll do to them?

Fuckkk. My head pounds even harder. Why is being an adult so damn hard?

ME

Breakfast is fine. But we aren't home right now… Maybe in an hour? We can meet you there.

ASHER

> An hour is perfect…gives me time to make some stops…
> And coffee? Your usual?

My cheeks heat. Fuck. He'd really go to creepy Nathan, the ever-smiling barista with a knack for staring at me with lust-filled eyes, all for my perfect cup of coffee?

ME

> If you insist.

Like fuck am I going to stop him. If this is Asher's way of buttering me up in hopes of a sliver of forgiveness. Then so be it. But let it be known; I'm not persuaded by coffee, enticing words, or damn tattoos… Nope. I need something concrete to cling to before I even think about forgiving them for their transgressions. If I ever do.

ASHER

> Are…you guys okay?

I lick my lips, silently going through the list of shit they did to me and convincing myself that I shouldn't fall for their traps again. Nope. Never will I jump headfirst into the deep end named Whispered Words. Not gonna happen.

Liar.

ME

> I've been better…

Looks like we're having a talk later, after all. Fuck being an adult.

Huffing a breath, I waltz down the stairs and into the sparse kitchen filled to the brim with children and half-naked men.

"Oh God, my eyes," I hiss, playfully covering them as Kaycee snickers in her seat. "Put some clothes on!"

"Shut it," Seger quips, rubbing at his stomach when I finally open my eyes. "You're in our domain. And in this house, we don't wear shirts."

This isn't the first or last time I've seen my brothers and their husband-in-laws—as Chase makes me say—half naked. It's always in the morning when I've stayed over after drinking just a little too much wine on girls' nights. Sometimes, like before, they happily drive me home. Or Liv and I crash in the bedroom upstairs.

"Good morning to you, too." Chase grins as he flips over a pancake, humming a tune. His shaggy blond hair flaps around as he dances along to the music playing on his phone. "Want some pancakes?"

"They're pretty good," Zepp says, taking a large bite.

"See! I told you I could cook, Grumpy," Chase gripes, glaring at Carter, who scoffs in his direction, not even bothering to make a response.

"Morning. I need lots of coffee, and then Ly and I have to head home…" I trail off at the thought of going home. Dread builds in the pits of my stomach. Home. Am I safe there anymore? Will the same thing keep happening until this asshole has enough and takes me as his own? Shit. I suck in a breath and squeeze my eyes shut. This is the second meltdown I've had this morning. Understandably so. I guess. Fuck. I need to pull myself together, so Ly doesn't sense anything really being wrong.

"Ah, you're getting pancakes from the douchebags living across the street, aren't you?" Seger asks, settling on a stool with a plate loaded with food in front of him. "I'm shocked you haven't murdered them yet."

I wrinkle my nose, falling down the rabbit hole of what-ifs and my family's safety. "They're being punished," I grumble, swallowing the razor blades in my throat.

Carter's eyes dart to mine with suspicion. He nods his head to the side, clearing his throat. "A word?"

I nod, licking my lips, following behind. As I pass Kaycee, she gently hands me a piping hot cup of coffee without a word. Bless her soul.

"You look like you're fucking terrified," Carter remarks, eyeing me as he leans against the wall. He crosses his arms over his chest.

"You think, Sherlock?" I grumble, taking a sip of my coffee.

Ah, the sweet nectar of the Gods. It'll perk me right out of this shitty funk. Soon, I'll be ready to face my stalker head-on. Just give me thirty minutes and more coffee.

"I'll forgive you for that. I was just stating the fucking obvious. You're terrified to go home."

"As I should be, right? That asshole listened to me…me…" I trail off, my cheeks heating.

"Oh, well, that ought to be fucking good. Want to enlighten me on what you were doing?" He grins wide with a mischievous glint sparking in his eyes.

"Fuck off. Nope. No way." I'm definitely not telling him I was getting myself off as my former boyfriends watched and listened, begging to come inside.

"On a serious note, Little West. We've been working all night to secure your camera system. No one else can view it. We scoured the damn server looking for whoever was in there too and booted them. Unfortunately, we couldn't track them to their location. Only the security company you hired. But we were able to make sure no one else but Veritas has access now."

I swallow hard. Someone was using my cameras to look at me. Hear me. Fucking watched me. And my child. My poor fucking baby has had someone's strange eyes set on her. My stomach drops. How could someone do that? Who even knows how? This is absolutely ridiculous. Our safety is my number one priority. I'm just so damn fed up with watching my back and over my shoulder. I want my safe space back.

"Thanks for looking out for us. Um… Is it safe to go back home?" Despite the intrusion, I want to sink into my bed and never get up. That place was built just for me and Ly. It's my damn sanctuary. I won't allow some desperate asshole to take over my life.

"You're good to go home. Just know, I'll be keeping an eye on you. So, keep your clothes on." He raises a brow, smirking when I flip him off.

"You're an asshole. I don't know how my angel sister-in-law puts up with you," I scoff, faking my anger as he laughs.

"She tamed me," he whispers with affection, eyeing the space near the entrance of the kitchen where Kaycee walks around, kissing her children on the head and handing them their breakfast.

"Okay, well… I'll be heading out then. Anything else I need to know?"

"Keep vigilant. Carry your damn knife… Or that gun Liv gave you a year ago for protection. You remember how to shoot it, don't you?"

"Yes. She forces me to go to the range at least once a month. I'll never forget how to shoot," I grumble into my coffee, taking another long swig.

"I know you don't like it. But knowing how to point, aim, and shoot will be useful if you're ever in a situation with that deranged fuckhead. Got it?" His tone brokers no room for argument. Much like a damn dad's voice.

"Yeah. Yeah. I'll dig it out from my closet and—"

"Load it, River. Load it the fuck up. Put the safety on and put it beside your fucking girly toys in your drawer. Have it available. If he was watching through the fucking cameras… What's stopping him from jumping through your windows? Set your fucking alarm. Load your gun and protect yourself," he growls, inching closer to me. A tic forms in his jaw as his eyes assess the fear on my face and paling skin. Blowing out a breath, he wipes a hand down his face. "I'm not trying to fucking scare you. I'm trying to make you understand. Right now, you're safe. We're doing everything in our power to prevent this from escalating. I have some agents surveying your property and watching for anything serious."

"Okay," I say, swallowing hard again. "Thanks, Carter."

"You're in safe hands, Little West. You just gotta take the fucking precautions yourself, too. That's all."

With that, I finish my coffee slowly, preparing myself for the inevitable. My skin crawls when Ly and I climb into my car. As I buckle her in, I kiss her cheek as she waves to all her cousins, watching us go.

"Are you ready to go home? Your Daddy Asher promised breakfast again." My voice croaks at the word home, but I shake it off. Carter assured me we were safe. There are agents wandering around my property. And Asher is going to meet us there.

We're in good damn hands. I just can't shake this nagging feeling something is about to pop up and throw me off my axis.

Lyric grins. Everything about her lights the fuck up at the mention of them bringing her breakfast.

"Pancakes?" she whispers with big, pleading eyes. She had a few an hour ago, but my child is always down to eat.

I shrug, watching the light in her eyes sparkle brighter. My heart pounds. This is so damn new for us. Slick sweat coats my palms as I slide into the driver's seat, giving one last wave to my family. All the shitty what-ifs bounce around my skull like an unpleasant smell. What if they leave again? What if they break her heart? Or yours?

No.

Scratch that last one. River's barely mended heart is currently locked beneath thick steel and razor blades. It's impenetrable. Maybe bulletproof. More importantly, Whispered Words proof. They can show up as dads. That's it. Nothing less. Nothing more.

Keep telling yourself that.

"He didn't specify," I murmur, driving away from the only family that has ever given a shit about me.

It's odd. Years ago, I hated Seger and Zeppelin for what they had. Dad's love. His money. Everything under the sun while I barely survived on food stamps, two jobs, and a dream. It wasn't until they came to me that I understood what they didn't have either. They may have had a swimming pool with a cave and waterfall, money galore, and twenty cars, but they didn't have love either. They only had each other. Well, and Kaycee, Chase, and Carter, too. They made their own family. Just like I did.

Not until we formed our own bond. I mean, the twenty-million dollars helped out a lot. But money can only buy so many things.

"I hope it's pancakes! Or French toast!" She giggles behind her hands, watching out the window as we drive past all the familiar spots on our way home.

"I should have named you Maple," I quip when she wiggles in her seat with an excited giggle.

No one should be this cheerful in the morning. I need to siphon off some of her energy.

"I like syrup, Mommy," she murmurs, plastering her little face against the glass, leaving marks behind as we pull through the gate of our driveway.

My eyes pass over the guard, sitting at attention in the hut. He eyes me with concern but waves me on. From the looks of it, he's on high alert after last night's incident. I'm sure Carter and his crew filled him in on what fuckery could be on the horizon.

As I pull into the driveway, my brows furrow. There, standing with a tray of coffee in his hand and a large plastic bag, is Asher. His back is turned to me as he stares off toward the house.

"Weird," I mumble, throwing the car into park and turning to look at Lyric, who is scrambling to undo her seat belt. I jump when Asher's worried expression peers through the window as he taps. "What's up?" I ask, raising a brow when I roll the window down.

His eyes dart to Ly in the backseat. "Um, could I talk to you outside? Leave her in here," he whispers.

"Ly, stay here for a second. Daddy needs a word. Okay?" I raise a brow when she crosses her arms and throws herself back into her booster seat.

"Fine," she grumbles dramatically.

"What's wrong?" I ask, stepping out of the car after rolling up the window so Lyric can't spy on us like she loves to do. Sometimes I think my kid is way too observant for her own damn good.

"I don't want to freak you out—"

"You're already freaking me out." My heart pounds out of control when he swallows hard, looking over his shoulder.

"There's a package for you on the porch. And it's—covered in what looks like blood."

I blink rapidly. My breath catches in my damn throat, closing in on me.

"What?" I croak.

"Let's just go through the back and go inside, okay? Then we can look at it. I just want to make sure Ly doesn't see it." I nod without thinking, letting Evil Ash take control of the situation.

My mind doesn't allow me to peek at the porch when he ushers us in through the back sliding glass door.

Once we're inside, he sets the coffee and food down on the counter, spreading it out as a distraction, and puts it onto plates.

"You did bring pancakes, Daddy! I love them!" Lyric squeals in delight as she shoves a piece of sausage link, smothered in syrup, into her mouth with a hum of delight.

"Let me look, okay?" His hand clamps down on my shoulder, drawing my attention to his deeply concerned hazel eyes.

Like hell. "I'm coming with you," I say, lifting my chin. If this is something my stalker did, then I'm going to face it head-on. Fuck his games.

"Your hard-headedness hasn't changed a fucking bit," he grumbles, shaking his head. "Let's look then."

I quickly type out a text to Carter as we walk through the house. My heartbeat echoes in my ears as we slowly make our way toward the front door.

ME

I got a package this morning… It's on my porch…

CARTER

What the hell? Don't touch it! I'll be over soon! Fucking incompetent agents…

Asher puts a hand across my chest when he swings the door open and nearly gags, stumbling back.

"Don't fucking look…"

Again. Like fuck.

I peek over his shoulder, almost wishing I hadn't. My heart sinks into my ass. All the blood runs from my face as I stare, transfixed by the red mess on my porch. Blood. It's fucking blood. Pooling. Dripping. Smeared over every surface of the concrete, staining it. It wasn't just a box like we thought from the driveway. It's a plethora of pictures and crushed fucking flowers.

Mine.

It says mine amongst the carnage. Photos scattered around of my face. My naked body. My privacy soiled. Fucking again! It's bad enough he heard me through my cameras last night, but this seals the fucking deal.

"Lyric, I want you to look at me right now!" Asher demands, turning around at the sound of her frantic screams coming from right behind us.

Lyric shivers. I'm fucking glued to the ground, listening to my child's cries of horror.

"What the hell?" Callum's voice booms through the house, knocking me out of my stupor. He collects Lyric into his arms, bringing her face against his bare chest. Her sobs echo through the living room.

Where the fuck did he come from? A breeze wafts through the house, coming from the sliding glass doors we came through. Eyeing Callum, he's in his running shorts, dripping sweat from head to toe, panting like he just ran a mile. Fuck.

Asher invades my home with his authority, quickly shutting the fucking door in our faces. Fuck. Blood. It seeps into my mind. It's everywhere all at once.

"It's okay," Asher murmurs, pulling me against his chest. His warm embrace soothes the ache pulling at my lungs. "I have you, River. Okay?" His deep voice rattles through my brain, dragging me from the deep fog surrounding my stupor.

"Little Star?" Callum whispers, putting a hand on my shoulder, gently squeezing until my mind flips back online.

"I have to see it again," I murmur, reluctantly pushing away from Asher. Why did he have to feel so damn good in a moment of crisis?

I shake my head, barely opening the front door again. Photos. Blood. Mine. My eyes dart around the disgusting display.

"You need to come to River's now. Wake up Rad, and get your asses… This isn't for me. This is for River. Something… You're a real dick right now, which I'll let slide. Fucking idiot."

They say when someone dies, you grieve in steps. Denial. Bargaining. Depression. In my case, no one has died. Not yet, at least. But I'm jumping from completely shocked to straight-up rage. It boils through my veins like lava bubbling, ready to spew. I'm so fucking tired of letting this asshole run in the shadows. It's time to bring him out into the sunlight and let him burn.

"The audacity of this motherfucker," I hiss, slamming the door shut. My teeth grind to dust as I march through the house with purpose, only stopping when the incessant sound of my phone dinging nonstop hits my ears.

"What the hell is happening? What's that shit?" Kieran's deep, confused voice travels down the hall, rising above the sound of my phone, getting louder and louder as I step into my room.

"Pretty Girl." Warm arms wrap around me, pulling my back into his chest.

"I need to call Olivia," I mutter, reaching for my phone.

CARTER

I'm on the way… Stay the fuck put.

"What's happening?" Rad murmurs, looking over my shoulder. His entire body stiffens against mine, pulling me impossibly closer.

As I look down at my phone, several more messages come through, displaying the same thing the bloody carnage from outside does.

You're mine.
YOU'RE MINE!
You're mine, River West.
No one else's.
Make them leave.
Or I will!

"Jesus fucking Christ," Rad murmurs, holding my shivering body.

"Olivia," I croak into the phone, ignoring the constant messages coming through.

"You never call me…" she trails off in a soft voice.

"My stalker left me some presents. More than pictures…more than…" My voice croaks to a dead stop when the images return, running through my brain at top speed.

"Fucking stalker?" Asher hisses from behind us. He blinks several times, processing my words, and scowls when I turn my back to him and shake Rad's embrace off.

"There are more pictures...and blood, lots of blood." I swallow hard as the images flashes behind my eyelids in rapid-fire succession. "Lots of fucking blood," I murmur again, squeezing my eyes shut. Red. It's everywhere. Infecting me. Invading my damn senses.

"Hold the fuck up, River. You said blood? Are you—" she trails off, emotions building in her always professional tone.

"Not hurt. It's on the porch with some questionable pictures. Every few seconds, I'm getting messages. It's—"

"Escalated to the point of no return. Get the fuck out of that house. Don't touch anything. Get to your boy toys' house and—"

"I'm fucking here!" Carter growls, slamming through the front door with gritted teeth.

"Oh good, he's there," Olivia says, blowing out a breath. "Get. Out. Riv. Leave." She grunts as the sound of fabric rustles. "I'm on my way. Go across the damn street. Protect yourself and my godchild!" I blow out a breath when Olivia hangs up on me, and I stare at the lit-up screen.

"Do what she fucking says," Carter grunts, pacing the tiny space of my living room, looking around at every little corner. "We'll have a lot to discuss."

When I turn around, a wall of men greets me with frowns. Callum clings to Lyric, who's still in his arms, holding onto him as she sniffles.

"Seems like we have a few things to talk about," Kieran growls, crossing his arms.

Fuck. Yeah. Seems like we do.

"How long?" Kieran demands in a low voice, snuggling Lyric close to his chest as we all sit in the tension-filled band house. Far the fuck away from the blood bath currently being investigated.

There, nestled in his lap, is my quiet daughter, sucking her thumb for reassurance. Her other hand clings to Asher's with a death grip. He swallows hard, stiffly sitting shoulder-to-shoulder with Kieran. Unease pulls at his muscles, nestled so close to the same man who vowed to put his fists through his ribs not long ago. For Lyric's sake, he doesn't move an inch.

"Yeah, River. Inform them," Olivia barks, ping-ponging in front of me at a quick pace.

Back and forth she goes, nibbling on her thumbnail like her nerves are eating her alive. She will cut into the wood with her sharp heels if she keeps up the intense pace she's set for herself.

I narrow my eyes at her when she huffs. "Three years," I breathe, nervously running a hand through my hair, not bothering to say anything else.

Blood drips in the back of my mind, spelling out the dreaded word. *Mine.* My head spins, and colors swirl together. Shutting my eyes tight, I breathe through the panic running rampant. When did this sicko go from taking simple pictures of our outings to this? Spying on me inside my home —my fucking sanctuary—as I undress and go about my life. Vomit soars up my esophagus, ready to spew at the mere thought of what they've seen through their camera lens. Everything. That's what.

"Three. Years?" Kieran growls quietly, keeping his anger at bay.

Barely. Kieran's like an unstable volcano, ready to spew his lava everywhere when the pressure gets too much. If we're not careful, we'll all burn under his intensity. Hell, I could probably stick nickels in his flaring nostrils right now. One false move, and we're all dead. Me, especially.

I sigh. The jig is up, and I'm backed into a corner. The last thing I wanted to speak of or acknowledge was the man following me around like a lunatic. "Yes. Three years of having some stranger following me and taking pictures. It's never been an issue—"

"Don't let her play it off as nothing. He takes fucking pictures of her and Lyric. Up until recently, that's all it's been. Then you chuckleheads came into the picture, pissing the little bastard off. Hence the cow blood on the porch," Carter's gruff voice echoes through the house with authority. Plopping down, he yanks his laptop open and taps a few keys.

"What the hell, Pretty Girl?" Sitting beside me, Rad pulls my hand into his, gently squeezing. "I know we're not in a good place or haven't spoken, but your life is in danger. How could you not tell us? You could have come to us, no matter what." Hurt lines his expression more than the concern etching into his face.

"I'm sorry. I—" I swallow my words. I shouldn't have to apologize. They're the ones that walked away. Not me.

What the hell can I say? *Sorry for not telling you right away that some creep has been following me around. Sorry you weren't here for the past three years to know what was happening. Let's not pretend we're some happy family now. Because of Asher, we were separated and could have done nothing about it.*

"Whoever the fuck this is has a knack for computers. Your cameras have been compromised. Inside and fucking out. Fucking manipulated, too. This fucker took out footage and replaced it with a damn loop," Carter grumbles, staring at the screen with his lips peeled back.

"So, whoever it is—"

"Made themselves fucking invisible." My face falls at his words. "But don't fucking worry, Little West. I'm not the owner and operator of CC Tech for nothing."

"Plus, a Veritas consultant," Olivia adds, snapping her fingers.

My muscles tense at his words. Concealed. Undetectable. Fucking invisible like always, hiding in the damn shadows. Fucking coward! How someone could walk onto my damn property with a security guard and cameras and not get caught is a goddamn mystery. It's like they knew exactly what they were doing and planned it all out.

I've ignored their presence for years, refusing to look over my shoulders. Like hell, would I allow them to see the fear in my eyes. Or the shudder of my nerves when the wind blew just right, and I felt eyes searing through my flesh.

I'm not a raging idiot. I knew they were hiding in the distance with a camera attached to their hands, probably jacking their tiny penis to my image. Denial is a hell of a drug to suffocate yourself in. It convinced me many times that I was okay and that they wouldn't harm us. Until the pictures arrived more frequently. And now this.

"What are we going to do?" Rad asks, squeezing my hand again, comforting me in unexpected ways.

We. Not you. Or her. He's including himself, maybe all of them, into this equation. Something stupid flutters in my chest. Maybe it's the hope of reconciliation. Or perhaps it's the same foolish organ that got me into this situation in the first place.

"Run and fucking hide," Carter suggests without peering at us. A permanent scowl etched onto his face, but I'm used to it by now. He only smiles for violence and my sister-in-law, Kaycee.

Olivia side-eyes him. "Thanks for being subtle like we discussed." He waves a hand, ignoring her presence altogether.

"What do you mean?" Don't say it. Don't fucking say the most rational thing that's about to fall out of your mouth. Please don't. I'm not prepared for this.

"River," she says sincerely, dropping into a chair across from me. "You're more than my friend, babe. I love you and Lyric. I want to protect you both more than I have in the past. It's never been this bad."

"I know." Razor blades slide down my throat at her implication. My mind whirls in so many different directions. I swear I'm giving myself whiplash.

"Then don't hate me when I suggest our safe house in Maine. It's the farthest place away from here. Away from that asshole who won't leave you alone."

Fuck me running, sideways, and up the damn stairs. Maine? Shit. My heart crashes into the waves of my volatile stomach. It's either fly across the country or die at the hands of my crazy stalker. And I like my damn life.

"In the meantime, I'll scour this footage and unscramble what this dickhead did. I'll find this bastard if it's the last thing I do, Little West."

"Maine?" I ask, shaking my head. "I can't go to Maine. Liv, I have a life here… I can't run just because of some weirdo. I'm braver than that."

Fingers squeeze mine in support as my mind jumps off a damn cliff into the what ifs. My calendar flies by in my swirling mind reminding me of my obligations coming in the next few months. The boys need me. They have gigs to rock and mental hurdles to overcome.

"I'm sorry, Riv. I can't give you a choice in this. At midnight we're extracting you. Whether you like it or not, babe. This is for your safety and hers. This is non-negotiable." She rubs a finger along her forehead, nervously watching my blank reaction. "You trusted me with your safety three years ago when Carter introduced us. And I'm saying all of this for your damn safety."

"It'll be for the best, Pretty Girl," Rad whispers with an aching sadness squeezing his voice, running a finger along my chin, and bringing my gaze to his. "I don't know much about the situation. But we need you safe."

"You'll be safe. That's the only thing that matters," Callum says, sidling up to my other side. "You two are too important to lose." He swallows hard, keeping his eyes locked on mine.

"Why Maine?" I mutter.

"It's on the other side of this place. So far away that your little stalker will have no way of getting to you," Olivia says, raising a sharp brow. "We've been trying to nail this fucker for years. Now, we'll finally have the opportunity."

"What are you going to do?" An evil glint appears in Olivia's eyes, cluing me into her nefarious plans in my absence.

"Whatever we need to do to bring this fucker down."

"What she means is, we'll camp out on your property. Get a little look alike to parade around and act like you while you're away. We'll get this asshole," Carter says, shaking his head. "I'm going to have to take this shit back to the lab and let them work on it." Snapping the laptop shut, he throws it to the side with a worried expression.

"What about—"

"Shh," Olivia interrupts, shoving a finger over my lips. "Think of this as a much-needed vacation. How long has it been since you could not focus on work and live your life to the fullest? Nope, don't answer that. You'll tell me you don't have time, that you're building your damn empire."

"I love you, but I hate you sometimes," I mumble through her finger secured over my lips.

"I'd say pack a bag, but you're under house arrest until we leave tonight. No stepping outside. No going home. You get the picture. There's a team discreetly at your house right now cataloging the weird mess left for you."

"You mean the naked pictures they took of her?" Kieran asks, putting his large mitt over Lyric's ear.

Olivia's lips roll in, and she nods. "Looks like whoever they are, they've been busy."

Carter sighs, rubbing his forehead. "I know how they did that."

"How?" I ask, swallowing hard.

Do I want to know the answer? How they've been getting pictures without my consent and looking at me in my most private moments. No. I'd rather stay ignorant. That's bliss, after all. But I give in like a curious cat for my sanity's sake and the urge to protect my daughter from everything harmful. She doesn't have a clue that a psycho lives on the fringes of our life, snapping photographs of our every move.

Carter locks his gaze on mine, licking his lips like he's nervous for once in his grumpy life. "Not only did they manipulate your cameras, Little West. They hacked into them. They've been fucking watching your every move. Inside and out. Wherever you have a camera, they've been following. Creepy fuckers," he grumbles the last part with a grimace. "Thankfully, you don't have cameras here to compromise us further."

"No, but I have security measures that obviously meant nothing. Fuck. Where was the guard? They're on twenty-four-hour duty." There are four of them for various shifts. Someone should have seen something odd and flagged it for the police to check up on.

Years before, when I got my first piece of mail from my stalker, I invested in a security firm. From there, they sent four guards who watched my place day and night. My cameras also came from them with a live stream sent directly to their database where someone watches for anything suspicious. Window alarms, door alarms, and anything in between secures my home.

"He was there all night. We checked with him. Carter even gave him his scary look, almost making him piss himself. It'd be funny—" Olivia trails off with a huff, and another worried look crosses her face.

Carter chuckles. "Yeah, he was there all night. Believe me. He wasn't lying. Says he didn't hear or see a damn thing. I also checked with your security people, who gave the same answer. Useless fucks if you ask me."

"Great. What good is a security guard if he doesn't see anything?" I shake my head, looking toward the front door as it quietly opens, and Olivia's long-time partner saunters in with a grin.

"Oh, River. You really got yourself into a pickle now, didn't you?" Jordy remarks, twirling his keys in his hand.

"Nice to see you, too," I quip to the Veritas agent I've gotten to know over the past few years.

By looking at his grinning face and easy facade, you'd think he'd be easy to read. He's not. Over the years since he and Olivia took over the Veritas, he's perfected his calm demeanor, even when raging on the inside. With his small-town hunk looks—curly blond hair, boy next door face, and sparkling blue eyes—you'd never guess that he's a full-blown killing machine, taking down the enemy without blinking. Yeah, I'm always happy to have him on my side. He'd put my stalker down in a nanosecond. If we could catch the fucker first.

"Maine is out," Jordy grimaces when Olivia shoots him a look, and he shrugs. "Don't give me that look, *Espie.* There was a storm, and it disabled the house, making it unsecure. You need a new plan."

"How many times do I have to remind you it's Olivia," she growls, narrowing her eyes at his full-blown grin. He shrugs, twirling his keys again, loving the way he's egging her on.

For a time in Olivia's weird and complicated life, she went by another name in the field. It was the name her uncle gave her after the murder of her parents and sister. Or so she thought. As I said, her history is complex and hurts my brain. Since reuniting with her old friends and discovering who murdered her parents, she's returned to her birth name—Olivia.

"We need something now. Everywhere else is occupied." She waves a hand in Jordy's direction.

"I can hide her in my basement," Jordy jokes, grunting when Olivia pushes him away. "Cool your tits, Liv. Sheesh," he grumbles, stumbling over his feet. "Anywhere is better than here. I can hear Riv's phone from a mile away." His nose wrinkles in disgust, staring at the object lighting up on the table in front of us.

He's not wrong. Message after message. Email after fucking email, lighting my phone up like a damned Christmas tree. My stomach twists into a million knots. Whoever is stalking me has finally snapped into a miserable person, hellbent on making my life hell on earth. As long as I'm around my phone witnessing their increasingly aggressive messages, I'll never sleep. Or eat. Or function, for that matter.

"I might have somewhere we can all lay low." Every eye in the room snaps toward Callum as he rises from beside me. Uncertainty twists his face, but he continues before anyone can say anything. "I have a house in a small town. I have a security system and privacy fences. It's completely secure in the middle of nowhere."

"So was this compound River has built up for herself," Jordy remarks, lifting a brow. "You sure some Podunk house will facilitate River and Lyric, and nothing will happen to them? Are you confident?"

Callum stiffens, crossing his arms over his chest. "Yes. It's secure. I built it myself with my fame in mind. It's completely secure. No one knows it's there."

"Where is it?" Olivia asks, slapping a hand over Jordy's mouth. You'd think they were in some ill-fated relationship by the insane chemistry they exude. I told her as much one drunken night, and she laughed. They're friends—nothing more and nothing less. Besides, Jordy has somehow fallen in with my long-lost sister Zandt's grasp. But she's a whole other story. "I need more information before I send my best friend to some ill-equipped house in the middle of nowhere."

He nods, side-eyeing me. "It's in Central City, Illinois. Besides, who said River and Lyric were going by themselves?"

Olivia blinks at him, releasing her hand from Jordy's mouth. "You're willing to go with them? Keep them safe? That's a big task for little boys." Oh, ouch. The boys physically recoil from her remark, tightening their expressions.

"There's no willing about it," Rad pipes up, rubbing his hands together.

"We'll go with them," Asher says for the first time, still clinging to Lyric's hand, despite her tiny snores filling the room as she lies on Kieran's chest.

A satisfied sigh rocks through Asher as his weightless gaze locks on the beauty clinging to his hand. A sparkle flashes in his eyes, relaxing his body on the couch. Asher looks at peace for the first time since our big blowout, where secrets filled the room and choked us. His eyes stare down at her with admiration, filling the holes once left in my soul. How he looks at her is how he looked at me once upon a time when he didn't know I was looking.

"We'll never leave them alone again." His words pierce the room with authority, leaving no room for arguments.

Olivia nods, biting back the grin of *I told you so.* "Good! This is good! The six of you will be extracted from here at midnight. I'll have a local team prepare your house. You say it's secure? Let's go over some details."

And that they do. Thoroughly.

As they make plans, I make my own. Calling the important people in my life about where I'll be, knowing they won't tell a soul. My brothers freak the fuck out. But they knew something was up when Carter took off and came here after I got my package.

"Hey, Kat," I say, pacing around the kitchen as Asher watches me with a close eye.

"Miss West," she says with a surprised tone. "Is something the matter?"

I swallow hard, rubbing my forehead. "Hey, yeah. I'm going to be out of town for a little while. My stalker paid my house a visit last night, and I need to go into hiding, basically. It's for my safety and Ly's."

"Oh my god! Your stalker? Where are you going?" she asks with concern, breathing heavily into the phone. Soft murmurs come from the other end from a low, deep voice, and my brows raise.

"Uh, Central City. Back to my home. We've got a secured house there." I won't tell her anything else when someone is obviously sitting close to her.

"Got it! I'll keep everything running smoothly in the department. Is there a way for me to get ahold of you? Or should I go through the bosses?"

"My brothers, yeah. Just talk to them about anything you need. I'll be unreachable for however long this takes. Thanks, Kat."

We say our goodbyes and hang up. Worry slams through me at what we're about to do.

The day goes by in a blur as they hash out the details of our extraction and new living situation. After hours of research and ground teams inspecting Callum's house, they clear it for our use.

Under the camouflage of night, Olivia disappears across the street, sneaking around and gathering Lyric and me some essentials for the trip and subsequent never-ending vacation. Only coming back when several bags are filled with our clothes and other items, we may need for weeks to come.

How long would I be away? From my job? From my damn home? Olivia wouldn't give me a direct answer, simply shrugging and telling me to enjoy the dick I was about to receive.

If I wasn't so panicked, I might have killed her. Dick is so not happening.

"I know none of this is glamorous. But if they've hacked into your camera system, they're probably tracking your phone somehow. So, we'll keep that here. We're going to use it to our advantage if they are. We'll start by trying to lure them out and grab them when we can." Her eyes dart to the floor, and she worries her lip.

"I trust you, Liv. You've kept me functioning and safe these last three years. You'll get him. Just...keep me updated or something?" She nods, curling my fingers around the new cell phone, before going to each of the guys and retrieving theirs.

"Sorry, boys, it's a safety precaution." Without a fight, the boys turn in their phones. "Also, Riv. I'll let Rocco know what's up."

"Thank you. He'll worry," I mumble, chewing on my bottom lip.

Before we know it, we're loaded into a blacked-out SUV at midnight and escorted to a private airfield on Veritas' property.

Kieran carries a sleeping Lyric onto the plane, sitting her beside him and buckling her in. He smiles at me, informing me he has her, and urges me to get some rest.

Fat chance.

Murmurs vibrate around me in muted conversations. Some snores ring out. But not mine. I'm left begging for sleep and staring out the darkened window, wondering how my life ended up like this.

Away we go, back to the city that started it all. Our beginning. Our love. Our brutal fucking ending.

For so long, I've held onto this grudge, letting it infect me with the need for revenge. Suddenly, I'm not feeling so vengeful. Day by day, though, they're breaking down the walls I've put in place.

Forgiveness is on the horizon, but there's still so much work to be done to earn my trust and prove their loyalty.

Do you ever feel like you're falling down the deep, dark rabbit hole of déjà vu? One second, your life is going according to plan. Work. Kiddo in school. And a nameless band across the street eager to improve under your direction.

The next? There's a stalker on your ass, and you're being whisked away on a not-so-vacation with the four guys you'd rather bury in the sand than spend more quality time with.

Liar!

I frown at my thoughts. Shut it, brain. There's no room for your intrusive thoughts right now. We have more important things to worry about. Like stalkers, security, and whether or not I can fucking sleep tonight.

Besides, if these men want to make up for what they did to me as boys, then bring it on. I'm all for their redemption if they're eager to prove themselves to not only me but Lyric. They can fall to their knees, beg for mercy, crawl over glass shards, and scrape their knees. There's so much they can do to make me truly believe they're sorry for their actions.

Speaking of, they've already achieved step number one…

"Daddy! This is so cool." Lyric's voice echoes through the fucking mansion on a hill smack dab in the middle of a field on the outskirts of Central City near their old stomping grounds—Lakeview.

From my spot on the driveway, I can see nothing outside the tall fence protecting the property all the way around, with cameras sitting everywhere. Callum wasn't kidding when he said this place was a fortress.

The only question that remains is why? Why Central City again? Didn't they run away from this place with the intention of never returning?

It's fitting, though, sitting here in the familiar early September heat, sweating my ass off and wishing for the AC. Only this time, I don't have to walk a mile to work or worry about my computer taking a shit on me for class. My only obstacles are four men, a stalker, and a child to protect.

"Are you coming, Pretty Girl?" Rad's hand slides to my lower back, fitting there as he waits patiently.

His brows dip when I nod, looking around the semi-familiar space.

"Yeah," I say, clearing my throat through the mess of emotions bubbling to the surface.

"Okay, now that everyone is here," Jordy says with a pleased grin, clapping his hands. "Let's go over some rules and whatnot."

I plop on the oversized couch in the spacious, modern living room, sinking into the fabric. Rad does the same, staying insanely close to me. Since this morning, he's refused to leave my side, plastering himself to me. His fingers seek mine, and I let him grip my hand in his without protest. If he asked, I'd deny the immediate ease wrapping around my soul like a blanket on a cold winter's night. Finally, I can breathe. If even for a moment.

"All righty. Callum, I'm impressed. A few of our Illinois agents looked this place over from top to bottom, and I gotta say, bro, it's like you were expecting this. No one could trace this back to you, even if they tried. You don't have any stalking tendencies to confess to, do you?" Jordy raises a playful brow, grinning at Callum, who stiffens on my other side.

"No." He blanches.

"Glad we have that settled. There are cameras everywhere, which we've commandeered to our feeds. I'd highly suggest not strutting around naked outside because I'll see what you're packing. Speaking of the outdoors, do that as little as possible. Consider yourselves under house arrest. No sunlight. No midnight ice cream runs."

"No ice cream?" Lyric pouts, climbing into Asher's lap.

Jordy snorts. "That's where I come in, Ly. You tell Mommy to text me, and Uncle Jordy will bring you all the ice cream you need. Only if you stay inside, capiche?"

"Okay," she says, settling back onto Asher, who wraps an arm around her and whispers something in her ear, causing her to grin. My heart melts when she lays her head on his shoulder and sags with relief in his arms.

"A house phone has been placed in the kitchen, and you also have the flip phone in River's possession. That's your tool to the outside world. If you need anything, give me a ring. Food. Toilet paper. Hell, I'll even buy you some micro condoms." He snorts at his own joke, earning glares from the rest of the guys.

"Tool," Rad mutters under his breath, bringing Jordy's grin back in full force.

"Anywho, I'll be here in ten seconds flat. You're completely secure in this giant-ass house in the middle of nowhere."

"You'll keep me updated, right? If you catch him or whatever?" I question timidly, picking at my nails.

"Every step of the way, River. Liv is working hard at your property, trying to lure that asshole out. We checked and double-checked during extraction; whoever they are, they weren't aware you left. Leave this to us. We've got you." He seems so damn earnest when he breaks through his grinning exterior, leaving me feeling settled and secure. "Now, any questions?" he asks, studying each of us as we shake our heads. "Then I bid you good day. Take care of yourselves. Call if you need me. Yaddy…Yaddy… ya. Oh, and set the goddamn alarm!" He rolls his wrist as he exits, lightly shutting the front door and leaving the six of us in a chilling silence.

"So," Kieran mutters, looking around as he stands from the couch. "When did you build this?"

"And why all the crazy ass security, man? This seems over the fucking top," Rad adds.

My eyes snap to Callum, watching intently as he shrugs. "A few years ago. I wanted somewhere to go, and no one would bother me. Especially our fans. You-you know how they can get," he whispers, rubbing his neck.

"This is where you used to disappear to, huh?" Rad asks.

A red tint envelops Callum's cheeks. "Yeah. Whenever I needed to get away, it was like a paradise. No one knows about it. I like to come and see my parents and Jenny."

Ah. That makes sense. He's never really come to terms with the death of his entire family after that crazy plane crash. I don't blame him. I've missed the hell out of my mom since I've been away. Once a week, I visited her grave before I left, leaving her flowers and mementos.

"We literally had the ocean in our backyard, bro. What happened to surfing? The sunshine?" Rad quips.

"Surfing wasn't for me. No coordination on the board," Callum mutters, rising to his feet and setting the alarm through the panel near the front door. When the alarm system rings out that we're protected from danger, I lean back further, closing my eyes.

Sleep was not my friend last night. Not that I could have gotten a wink on the stuffy plane filled with all my ex-boyfriends and worry that my stalker was in the cargo hold, ready to murder me.

It baffles me that one person would follow me around for so long. I'm not that exciting of an individual. Hell, the first two years I lived in East Point, I did nothing but mom, work, and run all over the place. My schedule only settled down when I walked across CaliState's stage with my diploma in hand, if you call my schedule slowing down. Ah, the simple days.

Now, here I am, smack dab in the middle of some shitty joke with no punchline. One girl walks into a house she can't leave with four men who used to put their dicks in her… What could go wrong? Everything, that's what. Fuck. What am I doing? Why did I decide to do this?

Because you sort of had to—yeah, that, I guess. For Lyric. For our safety. Besides, they weren't too keen on walking away from us and letting us go at this alone, which shows how determined they are to earn my forgiveness and make amends.

It's more than absolution, though. I see it in their movements and possessive gazes. Since we cleared the air and freed our sins, their motivations have been strictly pure. No malice or manipulation—they're sincerely trying to prove themselves to Lyric and me.

"You're tired," Callum murmurs from my left, somehow getting there without me noticing. Trembling fingers shift the hair from my face, tucking it behind my ears.

God, his touch does something funny to my insides. All gentle and so full of care. It's a stark difference from the man in the octagon, beating the shit out of his opponent. I shiver at the thought. Memories of his bloodbath come forward. I'd never tell him how much I enjoyed silently cheering him on as he bashed the other guy's brains in.

"Mhmm," I mutter, heaving a breath.

"I can show you to a room," Callum whispers.

"I have a better idea," I say, peeking open an eye. A loopy grin spreads across my face. "Got any wine?" Because God knows I need some wine to settle my nerves and get through this undetermined number of days stuck in this house with an eager four-year-old and four men who look at me like I'm the light of their life.

"Now you're talking, Pretty Girl. How about some tequila shots off…"

"What's tequila?" Rad stops dead, snapping his mouth shut when Lyric cocks her head with curiosity, awaiting his answer.

"Grown-up juice," Asher says, hiding his smile when she pouts.

"But I want the tequilas. And shots! Shots! Shots!" she shouts, pumping her arm in the air.

"Be better," Kieran rumbles protectively, narrowing his eyes at Rad. "You can't say that shit around kids."

"Shit. Shit. Shit," Ly murmurs.

"Ly," I grumble. "You know that's a grown-up word. Save it until you're eighteen." She pouts more, crossing her arms over her chest.

"Sorry," Rad mutters, putting his hands in the air in defeat, looking guilty as hell.

"Ly, where did you learn to say shots, shots, shots?" I groan, lazily looking her over as she pouts more.

She shrugs. "TV."

"What kind of TV do you watch?" Lyric grins at Kieran when he asks the question that opens Pandora's box of questions.

Lyric's brows furrow. "I saw you on TV, Daddy," she says with furrowed brows. "You won't be a ho anymore, will you?"

"A… A ho?" Rad cackles, falling back into the couch and clutching his stomach.

"What the hell, River Blue?" Kieran hisses when I snort. "What have you been letting her watch?"

I wave a hand, sinking my teeth into my cheek. "Nope! Nu-huh! This is your bed; you lie in it." A laugh bursts from my lips, unable to hold it back any longer.

"Daddy, I saw you with…" Lyric stops abruptly, counting on all ten of her fingers, muttering numbers to herself. "A hundred girls on TV. Did you kiss them? Maggie says that makes you a ho, cuz it was lots of girls." She cocks her head again when Kieran's eyes bug out of his head.

"I am not a ho! And for God's sake, Little Blue. Stop saying ho!" he sputters, standing from his spot. "River! Tell our child I'm not a goddamn ho."

"Your daddy is a ho," Rad sputters, singsonging, unable to contain himself again. "God, Little Pretty Girl. I'm going to bottle you up and keep you forever!" he howls.

"You were in front of the camera a lot with the ladies," I cackle, feeling the effects of my lack of sleep. "She just happened to see you in the aftermath."

Kieran blinks several times at me and huffs, stomping toward me. Standing tall in front of my seated position, he hovers above me, bringing his face to mine. All the laughter leaves me breathless, staring into the intense eyes of the boy I once loved.

"You wanna know something, River Blue?" he whispers, getting in my face.

"Sure." My breath hitches when he inches closer, brushing his cheek against mine.

I shudder when the tip of his tongue brushes against my ear, removing any trace of oxygen from my body. My eyes squeeze shut, and my long-forgotten vagina wets her lips in greeting. Oh, what I wouldn't give to get dicked down. In better circumstances, of course. But fuck. I'm too muddled and exhausted to have any sort of rational thoughts. If I'm not careful, I'll ride them like a cowboy screaming Yeehaw. Yeah, I need wine and a long nap resembling a coma.

"I couldn't get it up." Nothing more. Nothing less. Just a goddamn cocky look with redness spreading over his cheeks.

"What?" I squeak when he chuckles in my ear.

"Did you watch it with her as I walked outside the hotels with my arm around a woman?" I nod. "Mmmm. My dick doesn't like to work for anyone but you. Even when I hated you, he knew the truth. I have over twenty NDAs signed and locked away with their signatures stating they'll never talk about my lack of performance. Couldn't get it up because it wasn't the pussy I needed," he whispers, brushing his lips against my cheek for longer than necessary. "Unlike now," he growls against my flesh, fighting off a groan. "Thicker than steel in my jeans."

"Jesus," I croak, pushing at his chest until he stumbles away with lust dripping from his stare.

Don't look. Don't fucking look. Shit! My eyes dart to his dick straining in his jeans until he discreetly turns his back to Lyric and walks toward the kitchen. Not before sending me a smirk over his shoulder, knowing exactly what he fucking did to me.

"Oh, yeah. This will be the best damn vacation of our lives," Rad whoops. "Now, how about that wine, Cally Boy? I know you have a basement in this monstrosity."

Callum's grin lights up the room. "Yeah. There's, um, a wine cellar and a practice room."

Rad lights up. "Tell me you didn't. Tell meeeee!" he says, slapping his knees.

"It's all downstairs," Callum says through a breath. "Every piece we used to play on before we moved."

"Yes! You saved it all!" Rad whoops. "Come on, Little Pretty Girl! It's time Daddy Rad teaches you how to beat the drums!" Rad grins, holding out his hand. Lyric grins, jumping from Asher's lap and taking it. "Let's go have some fun," he says with a manic grin, leading her to the stairs and disappearing to the basement.

"What kind of wine do you want, Little Star? White? Red?" Callum's body heat pours through my side when he shifts closer.

"Bubbly?"

"Bubbly it is. Anything you want, it's there. I've been collecting them for years. Pink Moscato?" I nod immediately, licking my lips.

"You're the best."

"I'll keep proving it to you every day," he whispers, eyeing my lips until he shakes his head. "I'll be right back."

"How about food?" Asher asks softly from the opposite sofa, staring at me hopefully. I nod in agreement, refusing to move from my spot as the sound of uneven drumbeats and soft laughter echoes up from the basement.

"It's fully stocked," Kieran says, rubbing his hand along his neck.

Asher nods, climbing to his feet. "I'll see what we got, and then we can decide?" Nervously he stands before me, and I nod.

"I'll—uh, help," Kieran mutters, following Asher out of the room.

As everyone leaves the room, my eyes slowly fall shut, succumbing to the much-needed rest I've been craving. The last thing that goes through my mind when the noises around me cease to exist is...

This is what life would have been like if they had been there from the beginning. One to watch her. Two to cook. And one to gather the necessary wine.

THE FIRST THING I NOTICE WHEN MY MIND COMES BACK TO THE LAND OF the living is… I'm not on the couch anymore. A softness cradles every inch of my body like a floating cloud. The only thing missing is the blissful winds cooling me as I slumber.

The second thing I notice is the burning heat searing through two sides of my body. Front and back. Oh, and the hands in places they shouldn't be, petting my skin in soft circles.

My eyes fly open, greeting the dark world. Only the outline of one mullet-headed, determined man snuggling his face into my neck greets my waking mind.

"What the hell?" I croak, trying to remove Rad's face from burrowing further into the crook of my neck.

"Brings back memories, doesn't it, Pretty Girl? You, me, and Callum snuggled close." His warm breath brushes against my neck, sending delightful shivers. "I didn't even have to sneak into your room this time."

But also…what the fuck?

"Rad," I grumble, trying to bring my hands to his chest.

Instead, the stupid covers hold me hostage, tying them together. Not that I'm complaining. Every girl deserves a little nookie. Right? It's scientifically proven that sex reduces stress. Orgasms bring relief and chase everything else away. Am I convincing myself that what I'm doing is okay? Yeah, probably. I've avoided these feelings with them for days now. And suddenly, I'm falling headfirst into them without stopping myself.

Besides, I don't have the heart to move. For some fucked up reason, my body sags into them. My comfort. My damn home between their bodies. Memories float to the surface of our time together beneath the sheets of my bed in my old bedroom.

"Don't sweat it, Pretty Girl. It's early. We don't have shit to do. Rest with us," he mumbles convincingly, holding me closer. "Just stay here in our arms for a little while."

I sigh. Defeat washes over me. Not that I fought to remove their hands from wandering over my bare…

"Rad! Where are my pants?" I hiss, wiggling my bare toes. "And socks? Shoes?" I swear, before I came in here, I had all the necessary clothes covering my body. And now? Poof! They're missing.

"You, uh…kicked everything off when we helped you to bed," Callum rasps, resting his large, lethal hand on my barely covered ass under the damn blankets. "We tried to stop you, but you told us…"

"You're a bunch of assfaces. Let me get naked for you and rub my titties all over you," Rad mocks with a high-pitched voice, chuckling through the entire sentence.

"Something like that," Callum mutters with a huff.

"I did not." My cheeks heat at the thought. Why the fuck can't I remember? I didn't even drink the wine. Did I?

"You didn't even stay awake for the pork chops Asher cooked. That asshole is getting more and more domestic. Lyric tore into the meat like a rabid dog," Rad chuckles, silently reminiscing about the dinner I missed.

My heart sinks. I left her without a second thought, falling asleep the moment I sat on the couch. Granted, it was a long ass night of hopping on a plane and making it to Illinois so damn early. Then, the trip to Callum's house took hours from the nearest airport. By the time we settled in, it was evening. Guilt churns through me. How could I do that to her? She's probably frightened by the sudden change and not to mention the damn blood that was on our porch. Whenever I close my eyes, the evil word—mine—shines bright red behind my eyelids, haunting me. I can only imagine what it's doing to my four-year-old.

"She was brutal," Callum murmurs. "I think she almost bit Kieran's finger off." A deep, vibrating laugh rattles through my back. Callum takes several deep breaths, burying his nose in the depths of my hair. A deep, relaxed sigh rocks through him when he finally settles against me.

"Where is she? I didn't… God, I'm a terrible mother," I mumble, squeezing my eyes shut and making a move to peel myself away from them. Heavy hands hold me down, refusing my efforts to escape.

I've been so damn consumed with everything happening that I haven't checked in with Ly again to make sure she's okay. She sat between Rad and Kieran throughout the plane ride, entertaining them with her wild stories. She seemed okay—happy, even.

"She's fine, Little Star."

"You're not a terrible mother, Pretty Girl. I'm fucking positive you're the best I've ever seen. You raised a spectacular human being." Taking a deep breath, Rad brushes his lips against my neck without hesitation.

Fuck. Fire devours my insides. My teeth sink into my tongue, refusing to let the moan billow from behind my lips. If he keeps that up, I'm a goner, falling deeper and deeper into them. And it's always them, isn't it? Rad and Callum together have this way of unraveling every inch of me until I'm theirs.

"Thank you for being there for her. You're a goddamn amazing mom, and I feel so fucking honored you included me in the dad category," Rad murmurs, kissing up my neck.

And wouldn't you know, my traitorous body melts under his touch. My neck elongates, allowing him access. And that damn moan I hid softly leaks out, filling the room.

"I-I never wanted her to feel like she didn't have a father..." My breath shudders in my chest. "Fuck," I moan when Callum swivels his hips. A hard, long object pokes my ass, and his sexy-as-sin, low moans fill my ears. One after the other, igniting my entire body into an inferno of need.

"You say the word, Pretty Girl, and I'll oh-so-reluctantly stop kissing you. But I've been dreaming of this for weeks."

I could stop this.

I could tell them I hated them for their actions and that I would never forgive them. Ever. There is no way in hell I'll ever be intimate with them again, not after what they did to me. Not to mention Lyric. They left us— walked the fuck away without a backward glance.

After all that, I shouldn't give in to my wild whims. My mind screams at me to get up and walk away. To keep my interactions with them purely professional and not dip my toes in the same waters that fucked me over years before.

But when have I ever listened to reason? Especially when my body demands their hands glide over my flesh at an infuriatingly slow rate.

I fucking need this release. I'm no longer interested in holding a grudge against men who are proving themselves over and over again. Consequences be damned. Asher betrayed us. Yes. It happened. He fucked up. Majorly. But from what I can see, he's stepping up and taking charge of his mistakes by paying for them. He's there for Ly. They all are. They're finally the fathers I've dreamed of since I pushed Lyric from my body, hoping they'd return to my side.

And here they are.

"Don't you dare stop," I moan, leaning into Callum's embrace and aching for the friction.

"Your wish is my command, Pretty Girl."

"We'll take this slow, Little Star."

"Just like old times." I don't need my eyes to hear the grin of excitement on Rad's face. "Lift her leg, Cally Boy. Teamwork makes the dream work," he chuckles, kissing down my jaw until his tongue invades my mouth and takes me prisoner.

Thick fingers wrap around my throat from behind, holding me still as Rad takes everything he's been craving. My soul. My damn breath. My every fucking thing escapes me. Becoming Rad's—theirs.

Every inch of me vibrates. The fire-hot need presses down on me, suffocating me in the incessant tingling, begging to break free. It's been so damn long since someone else has touched me. I'm practically coming when his fingers brush against my stomach, slowly falling to the elastic of my panties.

"Fuck, Pretty Girl," Rad groans when his fingers disappear beneath my panties, gliding through my wet folds. "You're so wet for us," he whimpers, thrusting two fingers inside.

The world disappears, falling away into nothing but the pumping of Rad's fingers going in and out of me. I think I meet God himself when I float into the clouds of pleasure I haven't felt in so damn long. Fuck. White bursts behind my eyes like fireworks blasting off and taking over my damn vision. Explosive moans leak from my throat, resembling their names, when my orgasm finally hits its peak and throws me over the damn edge.

"Oh, Little Star," Callum groans in my ear, stopping his movements and stiffening behind me. One long, drawn-out moan breaks me from my fog. "You made me cum in my damn pants," he murmurs into my neck. A breath shudders through me, and heat forms over my cheeks.

"That was hot as fuck," Rad groans, flopping on his back and admiring his glistening fingers in the pale moonlight slipping through the blinds. "Eyes on me, Pretty Girl," he whispers, releasing his dick from his boxers. When the hell did all his clothes come off, too? "Watch as I cum to the memory of you."

My eyes lock on how he thrusts into his hand, using my cum on his fingers to coat himself. His eyes roll into the back of his head as large streams of cum jet from his dick, landing on his stomach, painting his flesh with his own release.

"Holy fucking hell," Rad heaves.

Those large, brown eyes gaze straight into my soul. Satisfaction sparkles through him, and he grins, leaning over and gently placing his lips on mine. Instantly my eyes close, losing myself in the softness of his mouth and the warmth of his probing tongue.

"Oh, Pretty Girl," he whispers, running his lips down my jaw, only stopping when his face snuggles into the crook of my neck. "You're my home. My everything. I'm going nowhere. I'm stuck on you like my cum has dried and glued us together." He sighs like his words are the epitome of a romantic gesture.

But so, so Rad.

"Never again will we leave your side, Little Star," Callum whispers, shifting slightly behind me. "You can push us away. Light us on fire. Yell at us… But we'll always come back for more. We're in this together from now on. And so fucking sorry for letting Asher talk us into leaving."

"Or believing anything he had to fucking say," Rad gripes with a huff. "I can't believe he fooled us for so long."

I suck in a breath, basking in the moment of declarations. Words are cheap. Meaningless, even. But their actions. They've been proving themselves to me. Callum offered this house as a refuge, and they followed me here. They're protecting us from the person stalking my every move. The guys are just more than empty words and promises.

Their grips tighten on me as they pledge their futures. Promising me things they've broken before. *We'll never leave you behind. We'll take you to California with us.* I've heard that one before. Am I crazy to believe them this time around? Have they changed their ways? So many possibilities run through my mind now that I'm post-climax. They could leave again. They're in a band, after all. What happens in six months when they kick this program's ass and go on tour? I'll be here. Ly will be here.

Fuck. Stay in the present. Yeah, that's what got you here in the first place.

"Don't answer," Callum whispers, running a hand over the curve of my bare ass, letting it rest. "You have every right to overthink this and question our motives."

"I'd marry you tomorrow, Pretty Girl. I'd give you the Radcliffe name in a heartbeat. But it's not up to us. It's up to you. We're all trying here. Even that dickbag Asher. I see it in the way he looks at you and Ly. We're all here for you."

Pfft. River Radcliffe, my ass. This is my damn show. "If anything, you're taking my name. We'll be the West family," I murmur with a grin.

"Mr. Ashton West." He nods a few times, scratching his chin. "Hell yeah, Pretty Girl! I'll take your last name. Fuck my parents and fuck the asshole I was named after. I'm Ashton West from now on. I'll make it official, too."

"Take all the time you need. We still have a lot more to prove to you that you're our end game…"

"You always were, and we were dumb fucking idiots," Rad grumbles, kissing my cheek before he pulls away. Cradling my face in his palm, a slight grin tugs at his lips. "Mrs. Radcliffe has a nice ring to it. Doesn't it? You like it, don't you, Pretty Girl?" His brows wiggle when I whack him in the chest and snort. Those big, expressive eyes of his cloud over with worry as his easy-going expression falls away.

"What's wrong?" Worry takes hold as the serious expression my funny guy usually wears disappears.

He blows out a breath. "If anyone's the ho, it's me, Pretty Girl. I…" He shakes his head, cursing under his breath. "I didn't wait for you like all the others. I…" I place my hand on him, resting it there until he continues. "After we left, a hole opened in my damn chest. There was nothing I could give anyone else except music. No one owned my heart like you did—still do. It was always with you, sitting in your palm. But I… I slept with a few girls here and there. It was never anything serious. I just drowned myself in their existence to rid the pain of what I thought happened."

"We were apart," I whisper, squeezing his hand. "I never would have expected you to." Who would? This is reality. They thought I betrayed them. So, why not enjoy themselves? Move on. As much as it pains me to think of them with other women, they were free of me. Not tied down.

"I know. We were done. Broken and over. But, Pretty Girl. I've felt so damn guilty since we came back together. And since… You didn't with Van. And I…" he trails off again with a heavy sigh. His shoulders slump, and defeat crosses his expression.

"You think I was celibate the entire five years?" I raise a brow when his gaze whips to mine in alarm.

"Of course not," he says, scrunching his face. "Although that's a punch to the damn heart. You and other guys? Fuck. But no, I can't judge you. We were apart…"

"And now we're together." It slips before I can think about the implications of my words.

Together. As in, we're in a relationship. Maybe? No. Ugh. I swallow the razor blades in my throat. There's no time to take back the words now out in the open. Free for their interpretation. Only a few weeks ago, the truth came out about Asher's betrayal. And now, a deep need plows through me. It's more than sexual. It's the connection I've always had with each of them. I want this. Despite everything I went through. I deserve to be happy, right? And so does Ly. Why should I hold back from them when they show me daily how much they care and want to make amends?

Rad blinks at me several times before a sly grin explodes. "I knew you'd come around to being my girlfriend. It was only a matter of time!" he chuckles, resting his head on the pillow.

"Slowly," I whisper with apprehension.

"You're still hurt," Callum says in a soothing voice.

"One day at a time, Pretty Girl," he murmurs, brushing his lips against mine. "But I'll still call you my girlfriend." He snickers when I roll my eyes.

"How about you?" I ask, looking over my shoulder. "Any dirty deets in the sheets?"

If the darkness hadn't covered Callum's face, I'm sure I'd see the redness seeping up his neck.

"You were my first and my last," he murmurs, squeezing my ass with his large palm.

"Well, Jesus, Cal. Way to make me look horrible. Kieran can't get lil Kier to work in the presence of another woman. You haven't touched anyone but our girl. And Asher…well, I don't know about that dickbag… Pretty sure he locked himself up and threw away the key. The only thing that bastard was interested in was music…" he trails off, scrunching his face. "Then there's me, Ashton, the asshole man-whore."

I snort. "You're not a man-whore. Shush," I murmur, feeling the ache of exhaustion pull at my limbs. A tingling starts at my toes, slowly working its way up both legs until I'm on the verge of sleeping again. "You're just fine."

"Night, Pretty Girl. We'll be here when your eyes open." Rad's lips rest on my forehead.

"Night, Little Star. We'll watch over you," Callum murmurs, brushing his lips against my nape.

"Night," I mutter through a heavy tongue, falling into a dreamless slumber.

 something happened between the three of them. Something monumental. Something I want. Fuck.

"You're grinning," I grumble, side-eyeing Rad.

Rad rifles through the fridge with nothing but his boxers on, shaking his ass as he walks. He softly hums a tune under his breath, brimming with joy.

And it makes me fucking sick. My stomach turns at his happy movements. What did he get to do with her? Why is he so goddamn happy? And why wasn't it me?

"I don't kiss and tell," he replies, sticking his head in the fridge. He grins more when he pulls out the coffee creamer and goes to the Keurig. "You have to make your own way."

Running a hand down my face, I blow out a long breath. My own way? How can I show River how sorry I am? Dates? Food? Music? Shit. I've got nothing brewing in my idiotic brain but jealousy and wanting to wring Rad's neck.

"You, too?" I raise a brow when Callum snorts, hiding his blush from me.

Prick.

"Actions, not words," Rad says, plopping beside me with a steamy cup of coffee. "Lots and lots of action." He wiggles his brows, slumping back into the seat.

"A child lives here, too. Don't you think wearing some pants and a shirt would be smart?" I ask, flicking the metal pierced through his nipple.

"Fucker," he yelps, backing away from me and holding his nipple, giving me a hate-filled look. "How dare you touch my mighty nipple with your fat fingers. Asshole."

"Your mighty nipple?" Callum scoffs, sitting opposite of us on the fluffy loveseat.

"Leave Stanley alone," Rad gripes, rubbing at the metal speared through his nipple and…

"Please don't tell me you named your nipple."

Rad scoffs at my words, continuing his soothing circles. He acts like I cut it off with a knife. I fucking could if he wanted me to. Maybe then he'd shut up. Great. Now, he's pouting at me and sipping his coffee like a baby.

Sometimes it's hard to believe that there was an open rift between the four of us, threatening to swallow everything we'd worked so hard for. Since Asher's admission, the tension has settled. We've drifted into a neutral area where we all have an understanding. Everything we do is for them—Lyric and River. Whether we hate each other or don't get along, we try. For them.

"Doesn't everyone? This is poor Stanley, who is now red and irritated. No thanks to you," he says, throwing nasty looks my way.

"For fuck's sake," I grumble, shaking my head.

"I'm curious what the other one is called," Callum says, further provoking his stupidity with a smirk.

"Don't rile him up." I side-eye Cal, who shrugs, sipping more of his coffee.

"Well, this is Stanley, and this is Shirley. They're married."

"Nipples can't marry, asshat," I gripe, throwing my arms in the air. "This is the weirdest shit I've ever been a part of."

"You pretend like you haven't known me since middle school, K. It's rude as hell. Leave S and S alone." Rad rolls his eyes in complete seriousness.

What ring of hell do I live in?

God, sometimes Rad drives me up a wall. But he's been my brother for far longer than I can remember. He was the first person to pull me into his orbit in middle school. The first person to make me laugh after falling into my miserable life with Nigel and Gloria.

Sure, he annoys the hell out of me. Sometimes. Other times I want to punch him in the face. Or hug him. The thing about Rad is, even when we were falling apart at the seams, I still loved him like a brother. I don't know how I could have gotten through life without his crazy ass.

River's bootcamp has shown us what we had lost. Why did I fight everything so hard? She's always been the answer both personally and professionally. Here in Central City, she helped us build our band and brand, and now we are back, and she's doing the exact same thing. It's not social media and recording our EP this time, it's family and brotherhood.

"He's got a point," Callum quips.

My eyes snag in the doorway where a very disheveled Lyric stands, yawning. Her tiny fists rub at her eyes as she stands in a long white t-shirt I recognize as Asher's. Her dark locks stick up in every direction as she squints, looking around the room.

My heart aches when my green monster reactivates. Last night, after River passed out from exhaustion, we tended to Lyric. Together we ate dinner, watched a little TV, and hung out. It felt nice having all four of us in the same room without fighting one another. And Lyric, of course.

Am I still pissed as fuck at Asher for what he did? Uh, fuck yeah. He can swallow glass for how he manipulated us into leaving. But for Lyric's sake, I'm trying to keep an open mind and swallow my anger as best as possible. What would she think if her dads always fought in front of her? How could we protect them both if we weren't in sync? Besides, the longer I'm around him, the less rage I feel. Asher did a fucked-up thing, but I'm slowly forgiving him for what he did. Because I get it. To an extent, I understand his reasoning. Albeit fucked up, I get it.

Besides, last night when Lyric was sleepy, she curled up in Asher's lap and begged him to snuggle her in bed and read a story. So, I compromised, even when we locked eyes, and he asked permission with his dopey stare.

Something has changed in Asher in the past few weeks, and it seems to be for the fucking better. He's rounding out, seeming less stressed. It makes sense with the massive secret he was holding in for so long. I'd never admit it to Asher, but seeing the man he should have been peeking out after hiding for so long is nice. For so long, we were under his father's iron fist, facing his wrath daily. We were in survival mode. Now, we're not. Especially him.

"Daddies," she says softly, shuffling her feet as she approaches.

"Sleep well, Little Blue?" I rasp, reaching for her the moment she's within grabbing distance. I drag her onto my lap and place my arms securely around her, wanting to keep her there forever.

"Daddy snores," she mumbles, rubbing her face along my shirt. Her tiny body sags into mine with relief.

I marvel at her when I brush my fingers through her hair. A sense of peace washes through me with her in my presence. This is all I've needed these past few years. I've been angrily stumbling along in life, blindly feeling for my next move. She was it all along. Her and River. The beacons I've begged for, dragging me out of the miserable fog I was in. Finally, the veil has been lifted. I'm seeing clearly for the first time.

"Sorry, Little One," Asher rasps, smoothing down his hair as he walks into the living room, awkwardly looking around. "But you weren't too innocent yourself. You kick like a donkey. Did you have dreams?"

I try to hold in my snort, but it doesn't work when she frowns at me and gasps. "I do not kick! I sleep like a log, ask Mommy. That's what she says." She pouts a little, crossing her arms. "No dreams. Not like at home when the ghosts tap on my windows." My brows raise at her admission.

"The ghosts tap?" I ask carefully, and she nods, blowing out a breath.

Asher shakes his head, rubbing at the bruises lining his ribs with a wince. "You're a little ninja when you sleep, Little One," he says, giving her a genuine smile as she stares up at him with a grin.

"You hungry?" he asks her until she nods.

"I want ice cream!" This time she directs those big, mismatched eyes in my direction, batting her eyelashes.

"No ice cream," I mutter. "That's not breakfast."

"How about some pancakes? I think I saw some ingredients in there." Lyric immediately perks up, nodding with excitement. "Okay. Pancakes it is. Um, anyone else?" Asher asks, clearing his throat as he looks around the room, rubbing the back of his neck.

"Make a stack, but serve me coffee first," River grumbles, stumbling into the room, squinting her eyes. "When did the sun get so damn bright?" With a sigh, she sits down next to Rad and me, closing her eyes with a groan. "Fuck morning," she grumbles again, slumping into the couch.

"My sentiments exactly, Pretty Girl. Fuck today. Let's just go back to bed." Leaning in, he brushes his lips against her cheek. "So, I can lick you all over. Again." He grins when my brows raise into my hairline.

"Coffee first, licking later," she mumbles, blindly taking a coffee cup from Asher, smirking at her words. "You're my savior, Asher. Today, at least." His entire face lights up, displaying how fucking pleased he is with himself.

My heart pounds at her words. Him? Her fucking savior? He's the reason we left. It's all his goddamn fault. Everything is. Has she already forgotten in the midst of the chaos? Fuck. I glare at him, telling him with my eyes to back the fuck up. He has no claims over her right now. If he wants her, he'll have to beg for her. Just like I'm going to do. At some point, when I figure out how.

"Daddy," Lyric murmurs, looking up at me with a frown. "Your face is tight."

Right. I can't be hostile—the pact. We're in this together and getting along for the girls, especially for Lyric. She can't see the four guys she calls daddy arguing or hating each other. So, I suck up my pride and relax my facial expressions, letting all my rage go.

"I'm fine," I say soothingly, rubbing a hand down her back.

"I call dibs on coffee tomorrow," Rad declares, eyeing everyone around the room. "Then we can let the licking commence." He cracks a grin until my fist meets his gut.

"Little ears," I growl, nodding toward Lyric, who frowns as I put my hands over her ears.

"Dude!" he wheezes, clutching his stomach with a frown.

"Are they little?" Lyric asks earnestly, pouting a lip.

"He means your daddy is saying grown-up things around you, Ly. And he doesn't want Daddy Rad to say anything bad." River sips her coffee, humming under her breath. "Your ears are perfect for your noggin."

"Oh," Lyric says, removing her hand. "Okay."

"Sorry, Little Pretty Girl. I've got to get better at not saying naughty things," he says, touching the end of her nose with a grin. "Will you forgive me?"

She taps her chin like she's thinking about it, letting a little grin slip through. "Maybe. I like ice cream," she says, shrugging.

River snorts. "She also drives a hard bargain. Good luck."

"Well played," I murmur in her ear as she giggles, looking at me with the hope I'll give in and give her the ice cream she's been craving.

River shifts in her seat, heaving a breath. "Despite where we are, I'd like to resume with band practices and my procedures."

"I want to watch daddies play!" Lyric shouts with wide eyes. "Can I?"

My heart swells. "Of course." I grin when she excitedly claps her hands.

"Oh good! You're all dressed!" We all jerk toward the front door as it's thrown open, and the alarm blares through the house.

Seemingly on instinct, Callum rushes to his feet in a flash, squaring up in front of Jordy, who is grinning like an idiot in the face of danger. I've seen what Callum can do with his fists. He's a goddamn deadly weapon these days.

"Aw, how cute, Fighter," Jordy quips, tapping Callum's shoulder condescendingly. "But you can put your dukes away and shut off that alarm." He shoos Callum away with the flick of his wrist.

"Jordy, be nice," River chastises him, narrowing her eyes with familiarity. My spine stiffens at their camaraderie. What does she have with him? Have they known each other for long?

"Me? Not nice? I'm always a joy." I snort at his words, earning a stare. "Anywho, got some updates, Dollface. But first," he grins, holding up a pink tablet.

"My tablet!" Lyric shrieks, abandoning me for the piece of technology and snatching it out of Jordy's hands. "Thank you, Uncle J." She grins up at him as he pats her head.

"No problem, kiddo. Now, do Uncle J a solid and go rest in your bed and watch some TV. I even have your favorite all geared up and ready for you. I need to have a big discussion with your parents—all of them." His eyes roam around the room when he says those words.

"Okay," Lyric says without a fight, skipping off into one of the back bedrooms and disappearing from view.

"All right, kiddies. Time for a discussion. And uh, pants are mandatory," he says, gesturing to Rad, who still only has his boxers on.

"Pants lovers," he grumbles, disappearing into the hall and returning with sweatpants as we approach the kitchen island.

"What's going on?" River asks with a pinched expression. "You've got that serious constipated look about you." I don't see it, but she obviously knows him better than I do.

Fuck.

I wonder if they've ever slept together or…

"Right. It is serious," Jordy sighs, bringing out another tablet. "The lab worked all night unscrambling the mess your little stalker made with the cameras. We were able to scrub some manipulation away and get a visual of the asshole who painted your porch in real blood," he says, cringing when he clicks a few times and stares at the screen. "Cow's blood, before you all ask."

"Do you know who it was?" Asher asks, leaning against the cabinet near the stove as the pancakes he promised to cook are on the griddle.

Jordy's eyes drift to Asher with a grim expression pulling at his features. "We got a look, but it's not perfect…"

"Can I see?" River asks as Jordy turns the screen toward her. "No… I… How?" she stutters through her words. A despondent look takes over her face, glazing over her eyes. Like she's losing herself in the abyss of no return.

"Pretty Girl. It's okay. We got you both. Okay?" Rad mumbles, wrapping an arm around her shoulders. Her nose scrunches when he forces her head to lean against his, but she doesn't push him away.

It's progress.

"Sorry, Dollface. I know it's fucked up to think that someone was lurking around outside your house. Here, I have the footage," he says grimly. "It's not perfect. There's still some static over the picture, and it jumps with lines. But It's the best we could do."

"Okay," River says, clearing her throat.

Jordy sets the tablet out on a stand and presses play. Collectively we hold our breath as someone walks onto the distorted video, huddling near the front door with supplies in his hands. He keeps his ball cap pulled low over his eyes, hiding his face from the cameras.

As he maneuvers around the porch, he carefully lays out the scandalous photos. Vomit rests in my throat as my eyes flick to a paling River, frozen as she watches. If I could scoop her up and protect her from everything, I would. But this seems to be the one thing I can't handle here. Except by being here in this house and ensuring no one but this asshole agent enters.

"Wait." Callum reaches for the tablet with urgency, holding it close to his face. "I know this guy," he says, pointing to the larger-statured man, positioning photos on the porch and throwing blood from a bucket everywhere.

He snarls, looking around River's property in the dead of night. Only illuminated by the night vision, highlighting his pockmarked face.

"Seriously, Genius?" Jordy quips in awe with wide eyes.

Callum glares in his direction but nods. "I remember his face. He's the one who knocked River down at the fights," he says, elbowing Rad, who stares at the screen, blinking rapidly. "He came every weekend with a group, always in the shadows. Ruthless told me once his name was Adrian Spencer." His brows furrow.

"Holy hell. That's the giant who looked like he would eat us for dinner. And not in a sexy way, either," Rad says.

"I remember that," River grumbles. "Knocked me right on my ass, and then I lost my phone that night. You almost got into a fight with him."

"Wait," Jordy says, holding up a finger. "You lost a phone? Liv never tells me anything."

"Yeah. I don't know where it went, but it disappeared after he knocked me over."

"It's possible he stole it. In my book, there's no such thing as coincidences. I'll relay this back to Liv and see what she says," Jordy says, clicking on the screen a few times and then turning it around. "Adrian Spencer. He's been nothing but trouble in the East Point underground for a few years." He shakes his head, scrolling through the contents. "Burglary, arson…looks like anything his boss tells him to do, he does."

"Who does he work for? You said his boss, so he must work for someone?" I question, tapping my finger along the marble countertop.

"You'd be correct," Jordy says, rolling his lips together. "Adrian is the muscle in the local gang we've been keeping an eye on."

"Why is he stalking me?" River whispers with a horrified expression.

"That we don't know. Liv and the gang back home are searching for him to question him as we speak." Reaching over, Jordy puts a protective hand on River's, earning several threatening growls. Jordy smirks, tapping her arm. "It'll be okay. You know we're the best, and we finally have some answers. Your safety is number one. But you still can't leave this place, and we're keeping you under lock and key. Just in case this person was hired for this. We don't have definitive answers. So, stay vigilant."

"Thank you, Jordy," she says through a breath.

"Also, you dickheads should know I have my own girl. River's great and all, but I like her sister more." He winks in our direction and steps away, tucking the iPad into a sleeve. "We'll be in touch." Saluting us with two fingers, he makes his way to the door. Before I can even think about it, I follow him out into the warm September day.

"Hey, man," I say. "Could I…um...ask you a favor?" I rub a hand over the back of my neck as nerves take over me.

"What's up?" he asks, folding his arms over his chest.

"I want to do something special for River and kind of…make amends and shit for…"

"Walking away? Leaving her with a baby? I know all the deets, douche. You're lucky I'm a professional." With a frown, he brings his fingers to his ear and scoffs. "According to Agent Asshole in my ear, I am not being professional. Yeah, yeah, shut it…" He shakes his head, blowing out a breath. "What do you need?"

Anger heats my face. Who is he to judge what we did? It wasn't our fault we were misled by our damn brother. "Listen, I know we fucked up, but there were other things happening that made it happen..."

"Like your brother, the pancake-maker, manipulating you all into thinking she cheated?"

"How the hell do you know so much about our lives?" I growl, growing tired of his cocky smirk.

He shrugs. "Hello, I'm a super-secret agent in a company that doesn't exist on paper. I know things. Lots of things. So, what do you want?"

"Okay, so..." And I tell him every detail of the date I've had brewing in my mind since we stepped back into Central City.

MOISTURE LEAKS FROM EVERY SURFACE OF MY BODY, POURING LIKE A damn waterfall. It stains my pits, and slickness coats my palms, making it hard to hold the flower in my damn hand. I bounce on my toes on the concrete patio just outside the back sliding glass doors leading to the beautiful backyard.

Calm down, dickbag. It's just a date. With a beautiful girl. You used to be in love with her and fucking tore her heart out. Shit. That's not the pep talk I needed to have with myself.

Tonight is the night I prove myself worthy to River with no expectations.

Noise from beneath me echoes through the glass doors, making me smile. Ever so slightly, my nerves die off when pride puffs out my chest.

First, it's the random banging of Rad's drums. Then comes the loud screeches of Asher's guitar. Finally, like music to my ears, Lyric's loud screech through the speakers fills the house, followed by deep laughs and applause.

I blow out a breath. This is it—the moment I've been planning for the past few days with the help of Jordy. When I mentioned my idea, he seemed impressed. Well, kind of. I'm unsure how to make that man believe I'm sorry for what I did.

"It's a fucking start, dickbag. I'll see what the team and I can come up with. But my advice?" He raises his brow.

"Yeah?" I reluctantly ask, anticipating his wicked words.

"Don't fuck it up again, fuck boy. River West doesn't need you. She's only letting you close because Lyric means everything to her. You walk away again for any reason. I'll cut your dick and balls off myself and feed it to you." I swallow hard at the disturbing imagery.

"No dick-cutting necessary. We fucked up. I fucked up. I want to make it up to her."

"Might work," Jordy says with a shrug. *"Now, if you're done planning your romantic date. I have a stalker to catch, so we can all go home."*

For a split second, I thought he would blow me off and not pull

through. But this morning, he discreetly showed up when River was in the shower and threw boxes filled with my requests at me.

"Good luck. You'll fucking need it," Jordy mumbles, *silently slipping out the door.*

"What's that?" Asher asks, stirring something in a skillet on the stove. Lyric rests on the stool with her nose in her tablet, laughing at a random video, patiently waiting for Asher's promised lunch.

"I'm taking River out on a date," I say, clearing my throat from the emotions trying to bubble up.

He nods. "I bet that will be fun." His eyes drift to Lyric, who is so lost in her tablet that she doesn't realize I'm standing beside her with four large boxes in my hands. "I'll watch her so you guys can have some privacy. Any time you guys want a date."

I blink several times when he shrugs, returning to cooking. "That's—uh, great, man. Thanks."

"I won't interfere," he says softly, not bothering to look at me. "I don't fucking deserve her, anyway."

No, you don't—is what I want to say, but I bite my tongue. Asher is already hurting so much, and I can see that now. Hell, he's been hurting for years, and I never bothered to pay attention. Was it his fault he was in this mess? Yes. We all fuck up, though, don't we? We all make major mistakes when it comes to the people we love. Not once has he stuck his nose in the air and denied the facts since he spilled the secret. I'm still fucking pissed at him. A little sliver of that anger will probably permanently hide away inside me.

But I want to let go. For my fucking sanity.

Therapy has helped so damn much to come to terms with what happened. Without that, I wouldn't be here with a clearer mind. Asher and I have talked it through in the presence of the therapist, and she's helped us really talk everything out. Every mistake. Every word said. We've discussed it at great length. Slowly but surely, we're getting through this as a team again. A family unit. Our next session, though. I want to talk to him about what he thinks he deserves versus what he actually deserves. He'll live with these mistakes for the rest of his life, but he shouldn't keep punishing himself. The way he is with Ly proves to me he loves River more than anything, too. His actions speak volumes. And it's time they get recognized.

So, now I wait for the woman of the hour on pins and needles, nervously pacing. I pull at my collar, marveling at the suit Jordy picked up for me. Somehow, it fit me perfectly from neck to ankles. I'm almost afraid to ask how he managed to get my measurements and make this happen.

The stars above twinkle on the warm September night, overlooking the beautiful setup on the back porch. For one night only, I'll have River all to myself. Uninterrupted. Mine. And no one else's.

And I can't fucking wait.

"River Blue," I whisper, stopping her as everyone drifts to the kitchen for the meal Asher and Rad made together.

"Kieran," she says playfully, raising a brow.

"I, umm…" My tongue sticks to the roof of my mouth. Fuck. Nerves eat away at me. Why am I having such a hard time asking her? This should be simple.

River, go out with me. River, forgive me for being a dumbass.

"You're sweating," Rad quips as he passes by with a steamy plate of food, grinning as Lyric follows, begging for the meal. "At the table, Little Pretty Girl. I'll cut up your steak as your Daddy Kieran tries to woo your mommy."

River's gaze whips to mine. "Woo me?" she asks, wrinkling her nose.

Rad smirks in victory. "Do it," he mouths.

"Will you go out on a date with me?" I ask, clearing my throat. Silently, I flip Rad off. The bastard. He's still smirking as he cuts Lyric's steak into pieces. Leaning in, he whispers something into Lyric's ear that makes her spine snap straight.

"Do it, Mommy," she says, batting her eyelashes. "Daddy wants to eat you."

"With you!" Rad laughs.

"Daddy wants to eat with you." Lyric nods, shoving a small piece of steak into her mouth.

"Please?"

River's eyebrows raise. "Where?"

"I have a plan."

"He has a plan!" Rad announces over-dramatically, throwing his arms around. "You think it's a good one?" He leans into Lyric as she nods, chewing on her food.

"Daddy always has good plans," she says confidently, lifting her chin.

I snort, the tightness in my chest loosening when River smirks.

"Sure." She shrugs, looking me over. "But you had better show me a good time, Knight."

Knight.

Her Knight.

Relief flies through me at the sound of that simple nickname. Something I've longed to hear for years, even through my hatred.

A grin breaks free as I cup her jaw in my palm. "I got it all covered. Tomorrow night, outside on the patio. Under the stars. Just you and me." She shudders from my intensity and nods.

"If you say so."

"Well, well, Mr. Knight. You clean up well," she quips from behind me.

Fuck! When the hell did she make it out here? I didn't even hear the sliding glass door open or close. My heart leaps out of my chest at her sudden appearance.

Almost in slow motion, I turn to face her. My eyes bulge out of my head at the sight of her standing before me in the most beautiful outfit I've ever seen her in.

"Holy fucking fuck," I mutter, taking her in with heat filling my cheeks and blood rushing to inappropriate areas, especially for a first do-over date.

"Did Jordy have anything to do with this?" she asks, gesturing to the long evening gown dragging along the concrete. Its deep red color accentuates the blood-red lipstick lining her lips, making her look red-carpet-ready as opposed to having a meal under the sparkling night sky.

Fuck. Her lips. I wish I could claim them with my own and make her mine again. Or with my dick. No. Not that. Shit. I have to stop thinking with my cock. It's too damn soon to expect any sort of physical relationship with her. I want to prove myself to her every step of the way and make up for all the wrongdoings from our past. Including the temper tantrums I pulled at the sight of her in the conference room.

"You look beautiful," I breathe, marveling at her in awe as she rolls her eyes.

"So, this is your idea?" she asks, pointing to the fairy lights sparkling along the pergola extending over the concrete patio.

My cheeks heat. "I...yeah. I wanted to have some time with you," I murmur with uncertainty. "Alone time, away from the other guys."

"And the dress and tux?" I shiver when her eyes trail up and down my body, taking in the dark suit with a red bowtie to match.

"All Jordy's idea," I mumble, blushing more under her scrutiny. "Um, I've got a table set up over here," I say, stumbling over my words. "Oh, and I got this for you." Without stumbling, I hand her the single red rose with my heart in my throat. That beautiful smile crosses her lips when she brings it to her nose and inhales.

"It's beautiful," she murmurs with a twinkle in her eyes, looking me over again. Taking her hand, I lead her toward the table and stop before it. "Kieran," she whispers, running a finger over the white tablecloth, only stopping at the dozen roses acting as the centerpiece. "Your doing?" she asks, leaning in to smell the rest of the flowers from the two-dozen-piece bouquet.

When Jordy said he'd lend a hand and get me everything I needed, he didn't skimp a dime.

"Yes. That I take credit for," I say confidently this time, erasing every ounce of nerves shaking my body. "They're for you," I murmur, taking another rose and placing it in her hands, careful so the thorns don't puncture her skin. "You're so strong, River Blue. You always have been. With everything life has handed you, you've always come out on the other side stronger. So, here's a flower as beautiful and as fierce as you. You're a damn rock." My eyes mist over when she shudders, staring down at the flower with an unreadable expression. I'd like to think she's taking my words to heart. Because every ounce of what I've said is true. She's the only person I've ever known who walks through life with her head held high, even when shit hits the fan.

"Well, it's beautiful," she murmurs, staring intently at the flowers. "Thank you, Knight." My heart catches in my throat at the name she used to call me under the stars at our old apartment building.

"Here," I say, stumbling around her chair and pulling it out. "Please sit. I have dinner ready for us. And some bubbly wine." I grin when she arches her brow but sits in the chair.

We're not the only people who have changed since we left this place. Before, River was the skinny girl in short shorts, tight shirts, and beat-up sneakers. Now, she's an elegant lady wrapped in satin, creating her brand in the music business world.

I'm honestly surprised I never knew what she had been up to. Perhaps I was so blinded by the need to collapse into music and forget about what happened that I didn't even try.

River has been in front of me the entire time, and I'm only now seeing her.

I swallow hard when I pour her a tall glass of wine, not stopping until it's at the brim.

"Trying to get me drunk?" she asks, leaning in to take a sip. Her eyes follow me as I bring over a deep aluminum tray filled with the best foods in town.

"Will it work?" I quip, setting the tray between our two plates, grinning when she snorts.

"Maybe." A crooked grin greets me when she takes a large swig, humming under her breath. Once she sets the half-empty glass down, she stares at the covered food tray with big eyes. "What's that?"

A deep chuckle vibrates through my chest as I sit opposite her and pour my glass of bubbly pink wine. "Do you remember that barbecue you came to?"

"You mean that awful one you kidnapped me to?"

"We did not kidnap you," I laugh, shaking my head. "We said there'd be food, and you practically climbed me!" I chuckle when her face falls.

"You literally met me at school, put me over your shoulder, and manhandled me into the back of your vehicle. Say it with me, Knight. Kidnapping. You assfaces wouldn't take no for an answer. I had no choice in the matter."

I grin at her. "I like that," I whisper, reaching over and brushing my fingers against hers.

"Like what?" she murmurs, staring at my fingers rubbing over hers.

"How you still call me Knight..." I trail off, clutching her hand. "Thanks for giving me a chance again, River Blue. I know I have a lot to make up for, and one dinner isn't going to cut it. I just—" I suck in a breath when she squeezes my fingers in understanding.

"But you're trying," she says, nodding. "It won't be easy. You know? You were the world's biggest brat a few weeks ago."

I cringe. "Sorry. God. That was the fucking anger talking. I've bottled it up for so damn long and put it into my music that I… I went off the rails. I'm sorry I ruined our first meeting. But I'm more sorry that I walked away in the first place. I should have known Asher was full of shit." I shake my head, running my free hand down my face. "I was the biggest, most gullible dumbass ever, River Blue. Will you ever find it in your heart to forgive me?" My eyes fall to the table when she squeezes my hand again.

"Maybe. But first, you have to show me what's under the lid. It smells familiar…and delicious," she murmurs, pulling me from the morbid thoughts of no forgiveness overtaking me.

I was wracking my brain for days on how I could show my River Blue how much I cherished her, especially within the confines of this house. I couldn't take her out without risking her safety. And I'd never fucking do that.

Then it hit me as I laid in bed, staring up at the ceiling. The moment I fell in love with her the second time. Our neighborhood barbecue. The time we forced her to come with us and endure our families, all in the name of unity.

It was the way she didn't give a fuck half the people there were looking at her like she had grown a second head. She ate, laughed, and was fucking merry, surrounded by us. That moment in our history will forever live in the back of my mind as the moment River Blue became the one. With everything that's happened in the past few days, I wanted to give her the comfort of something she loved. I wanted to relive that moment with her. Just the two of us.

"Right," I say with a shuddering breath. "Right. It's, um… Well. You remember the cookout."

"I do," she confirms, watching me with big eyes. Reaching over, I peel off the aluminum lid and reveal the goodies I ordered just for her. Or, well —Jordy ordered and delivered them thirty minutes ago, so it was still nice and hot.

"I remember you liked the barbecue we had. The ribs, especially. They had it catered from a small restaurant in town. And I thought maybe we could enjoy them again. Together."

Her fucking eyes light up when the ribs and chicken wings appear with steam rolling off them and dancing in the air. Immediately the smell of sweet barbecue hits my senses and my damn stomach gurgles. But I'm more focused on her reaction to care about my body right now.

Her tongue pokes out, licking her lips. "Dear God, Kieran," she murmurs, reaching in and taking a gigantic bite of ribs. "They're even better than I fucking remember. Oh. My. God," she hums, closing her eyes. "I think I've died and gone to heaven. You know, this is what I craved when I was pregnant with Ly. All she wanted was ribs, mashed potatoes, and some thick chicken and noodles. I went by Loretta's and got it a few times. But fuck—" she trails off, finishing the piece of meat and setting the bone down on her plate.

"Was it an easy pregnancy?" I breathe. Pain envelops my heart at the thought of pregnant River being all alone without me—us.

Who took care of her? Who helped her get to the doctor… Shit! She had no fucking car to get back and forth. How in the hell did she manage before her brothers found her and brought her to California? Guilt eats away at me more, chewing on my insides and swirling them. I wasn't there to protect her from anything. After everything that happened in the alleyway when she was attacked by that fucking dickbag Bradley. And now this with her stalker.

I'm here now. That's what matters. I'll protect her and Lyric to the ends of the world.

She shrugs. "It was. Everything went great. She was huge, though. Nine friggin pounds and some change. It took me so many hours to push her out," she whispers, tilting her head to the side. "But she was the happiest baby I ever met and came right at the end of September."

September? Hell, that's this month. "When is her birthday?" I ask, swallowing hard as another exciting scheme forms in my mind. Only this time, I'll bring the guys in on my plans and not leave them out.

"September 29th," she says, ripping into another piece of meat.

Duly fucking noted. I won't miss another birthday. I've missed four already, and we'll make sure turning five is epic.

"I'm sorry I wasn't there to hold your hand or cut the cord. Or do any of the things I would have done if I had known, River Blue." I shake my head as the shame of my actions consumes me once again. It pulls me deep into the raging waters of guilt, swallowing me whole. I'm drowning in the shame of what I did. I won't resurface until I've made every ounce of my wrongdoings up to her. "What Gloria did…is unforgivable. When we return to East Point, I will speak with her."

River drops the next piece of bone on her plate, not stopping when she shoves more meat into her mouth. God, why is she so fucking hot when she eats and gets barbecue all over her lips and cheeks? I'm memorized when she tears into more meat, humming.

"Don't let her near me," River says, wrinkling her nose. "I have some not so fucking nice words for her. In fact, she and I have a lot of shit to discuss. Do you think she'd screech if I put my fist through her nose?"

Yeah, she'd scream a lot. Probably call the cops, too. But it'd be so fucking worth seeing her fall on her ass, getting what she deserved.

"That can be arranged. Do you want to tell her off? I'll let you come with me when I do the same. There's no excuse for what the bitch did and took away from me." I blow out a breath.

After learning everything Asher did to get us to abandon River, I have no doubts Gloria planted the seeds. Her role in the entire plot was way too evident after I sat down and stewed on the information. My mother may act like a stuck-up suburban mom, but she's no dummy. Not at all. She's the key to this entire situation. If it wasn't for her meddling and dangling money in front of Asher's desperate face, this wouldn't have happened. She's the reason we left River. She's the devil in disguise, using people however she wants. And that person she molded like clay was Asher. She took his desperation and used it against him. Fuck. It's her goddamn fault. I shake my head at myself. I've been so blinded by my rage toward Asher, that I didn't stop to think about the situation as a whole.

But that stops now.

My next move is removing Gloria from the cushy apartment she's been gifted by Asher and me. She doesn't deserve to have a nice place to stay when she took my fucking kid from me before I even had a chance to know her.

And then, I'm going to look Asher in the eyes and forgive him.

"Deal," she says, biting into a chicken wing and groaning. "Seriously, Knight. This is the best thing ever. I swear I've died, gone to heaven, and now I have an endless supply of delicious barbecue to hold me over. This is better than sex."

I blanch. "Better than sex?" I gasp in mock horror, earning a toothy grin.

She shrugs. "Maybe," is all she says as she continues to devour our dinner and finishes off her glass of wine. "So, you really couldn't get your dick to work around other girls?"

Just as I'm about to swallow my bite of ribs, I choke on my food at the sound of her words. "Fuck. River Blue, you can't ask that shit when I'm eating," I hack, coughing into my hand. Taking a big gulp of wine, I settle back into my seat. She patiently waits with an expectant look that says: well, do tell.

I lick my lips. "Fine. If you need to know. Yeah, I couldn't get him to pop up. And believe me. I had plenty of opportunities to do so." I shake my head. "He just…wouldn't rise to the occasion." Unlike now, where he's fully rising to the occasion. Awake and alert all because of her in that red dress with those pleading eyes and luscious lips. Even the barbecue sauce makes her the most beautiful woman on the planet. No wonder my cock never cooperated with me. He knew where his home was this entire time. And dummy me didn't.

"So sad for you," she snickers at my pain, taking a small bite of mashed potatoes.

I groan at her comment, washing my hands on the little wipes provided by the restaurant, making sure the sauce is completely off my skin.

"Yeah, yeah. It was a terrible time for me." I shake my head. "I thought I lost the woman I loved." That makes her eyes snap to mine, and the smile fades away into sadness. "I'm ashamed of how our past is tainted with so much fucked up shit. But I did—do—love you, River Blue. I'm sorry I wasn't there for your pregnancy or her birth. Fuck, do I wish I could have seen her. She's the most amazing little human I've ever encountered. I don't know how I won the lottery with her but thank you. Fuck, thank you."

Without warning, she jumps up and plants her barbecue lips on mine, sealing the rest of my words in my throat. The slightest hint of our dinner invades my mouth when she pokes her tongue between my lips, forcing her way in. Fuck I don't even care what she tastes like. It's goddamn heaven to me. I groan into her mouth, plunging my tongue against hers in a slow dance of passion.

"River Blue," I groan, pulling her into my lap. My fingers weave through her long locks, holding her against me. "What was that for?" I examine her darkening eyes, filling to the brim with lust.

Biting into her bottom lip, she squeezes her eyes shut. "I'm sorry you weren't there, either. I promise I kept you alive in Lyric's eyes. That's why she knows who you all are. I never wanted to keep her from you. I just thought—"

"I know," I whisper, pressing my lips against her cheek.

I groan when she shifts in my lap, stiffening in my grip. Her moss-green eyes fly open, connecting with mine in question. I can't help the sly smirk pulling at my lips. Well, until she shifts again, forcing another groan.

"You don't seem to have a problem getting it up now," she whispers, leaning in to press her lips against mine.

My cheeks fill with warmth when she shifts again. The friction between us sends heat straight to my pulsating dick, begging to thrust deep inside her until she's moaning my name for the world to hear. If she's not fucking careful, I'll cum in my pants or take her right here against the table.

As much as I want to fuck her into oblivion and regain my Blue, I lean away, stopping her movements.

"Fuck," I grunt, gripping her waist. "If you keep that up, I won't be able to contain myself." Besides, I have more plans than this. I need to keep my wits about me instead of letting my dick take the lead.

She chuckles, swiveling her hips again. "No," she whispers, leaning in and resting her lips against my cheek. "I won't stop. And you won't cum in your pants like an inexperienced assface. Hold your cum, Kieran." Fuck. Fuck. Shit!

No! I can't do it. I'll explode before she even has the chance to swivel her hips again.

"Can't," I gasp when my eyes roll into the back of my head. "River Blue," I groan when she picks up speed and swivels her hips more. "I have more planned." I grunt in relief when she stops. Lifting her head, she gazes into my eyes with a mischievous look, having no intention of stopping this madness.

"More planned?" she hums, resting her forehead against my shoulder.

"Yeah," I grunt, lifting her into my arms as I stand. "As much as I wanted to continue that, I have more to show you."

Kieran

"Kieran," she mutters when I take a few steps into the night, letting the stars shine above us. There's a hint of storm on the horizon, but that only reminds me of the woman sitting next to me.

"River Blue," I hum in return, settling us onto a blanket in the grass and holding her close. "I dreamed of you for five years. I was so mad at you. So fucking hurt that—" I shake my head. "That doesn't matter anymore. I want to restart with you, Blue." I swallow hard, looking directly at her. "I want to make up for my absence. Be there for you and Lyric. Can we restart?"

"One day at a time?" she breathes, brushing her lips against the edge of mine. My fingers work through her hair, massaging her scalp.

"Yeah, Blue. One day at a time," I whisper, kissing her lips. I pull back. "But I have something I want to sing to you. Just a little something that came to me on the plane."

River's smile lights up my entire being when she flashes it my way with enthusiasm.

"Okay."

"Okay," I retort, gently setting her beside me.

I lay my acoustic guitar, which was set up beside the blanket, over my lap, strumming a few notes, letting them infect me with their melody. It's been a long time since I picked up my guitar and felt inspired to write. For years it's been someone else handling all our music. Sure, we performed it with ease, but we were never the ones to write it. Not after we came to East Point.

This is different. River's different. Fuck. Everything is so different now, and I fucking love it.

As I strum and sing the rough words, she sways in tune. Those big moss-green eyes fill with happiness and disbelief.

"I never knew heartbreak until I walked away," I sing softly, strumming lightly. "So, broken. Empty. Unloved. Second chances come and go. Third chances take your breath away. I'm on my third opportunity to make you mine. And I'll continue to show you all my pieces. Mend me, baby. Make

our puzzle one. No longer broken. I'm filled with third chances and love. Mend me, baby."

"Oh, Kieran," she mumbles with tears in her eyes. Gently she clasps my cheeks and pulls me down on top of her. I grunt, discarding the guitar to the side.

"You were my first heartbreak and my second. But never again will I walk away. Ever. You're my forever girl," I murmur in between manic kisses. "My fucking forever."

"You're a jackass," she whispers, laughing when I pull away.

"That's rude, Blue." I raise a brow, staring down at her heaving chest and marveling at her breasts, begging to spill out and have my mouth on them. "God, I missed you."

"Me or them?" she quips, gesturing to her tits as I run my fingers lightly over the swell. Goosebumps rise on her flesh as I trace my fingers between them, reveling in the plush, smooth skin beneath my fingertips.

"Both," I say, grinning up at her when she groans, rolling her eyes.

I swallow hard, aching to sink my teeth into her. My brain screams at me to lift her dress and expose every inch I want to ravage with my tongue and dick. I'm practically drooling when I throw caution to the wind and get the first taste of my girl.

Leaning down, I run my tongue over her neck, nibbling her flesh between my teeth. Her soft moans fill the night air. Bravely, I run my hand over her breast, pulling the material down inch by inch until both pop from the confines of her tight dress. Fuck. They're more fucking gorgeous than I remember. Bigger than I remember.

As my eyes eagerly take in her form, I marvel at the white scars stretching across her flesh, softly kissing every inch of them. These marks represent the human life she grew in her body. I'll worship every inch of her stretch marks. I'll show my devotion on my knees until she understands that I'm in love with whatever body she has.

"You're more beautiful than you were the day I met you," I whisper, running my tongue over her erect nipple and softly blowing on it, causing shivers to run through her body under my touch.

"When did you become such a sweet talker?" she murmurs, running her fingers roughly through my hair. I chuckle, sucking her nipple into my mouth again until she rolls her hips against mine. "Oh fuck, Knight," she moans, holding my face against her tit.

"Never," I quip, tugging on it with my teeth.

River's breaths shudder in her chest, rapidly moving with her breasts until it pops out of my mouth, giving me a chance to take in her flushed expression. Lust drips from every ounce of her body, calling to me like a siren at sea. I ache to do so many bad things to her, but I intend to hold myself back.

For now, at least. Not until she's ready for my cock. And me.

Once I thrust myself deep inside her and paint her with my cum, there's no going back.

"Are you wet for me, Blue?" I murmur against her glistening nipple, running my tongue along the hardened flesh.

Pre-cum drips from my dick, soaking my boxers when I tweak her between my fingers, collecting my saliva on my fingertips. Repeatedly, I twist it between my fingers as she squirms beneath me, breathily panting.

"Maybe," she moans when I tug it a little too hard, and her body fucking stiffens beneath me.

"Let's see." Her moans are music to my ears, filling me with every ounce of her pleasure.

My balls throb with need, begging for more friction. My damn brain begs to fuck her right here and now. How I ache to feel her wrapped around my cock. God, fucking damnit. Years of not being able to cum in the presence of a woman has royally fucked my brain into a scramble.

Stay focused, dickbag.

My fingers slowly drift up her bare leg from underneath her dress. Swirling around her bent knee and onto her silky thigh, basking in the feel of her under my fingertips, once again. Anticipation for what's about to come holds my oxygen captive inside my chest. "Fuck. I can't wait to worship every inch of your body. You're a goddamn queen, River Blue. I'll kneel for you every chance I get," I murmur. Pulling her silky panties to the side, I work my fingers up and down her slit until I'm thrusting them home with a loud groan escaping my lips.

"Jesus," she moans, throwing her head back into the blanket.

"No," I rumble, slowly pumping my fingers into her wetness, basking in the sounds she makes as she arches her back into my touch. "Knight. Call me Knight, River Blue."

"Knight," she gasps again on the cusp of letting go.

My fingers pump harder until she clamps down on them and pulls them further into herself, spreading her cum all over my fingers. Her moans break through the night air, letting the world know…she's mine. Fucking mine! Never again will I walk away from her. Or leave her side. Or do anything to jeopardize the best fucking thing I've ever had.

River West carved her name in my heart when I was seven, claiming ownership over my being. I just never realized it until now. I am hers. Forever and always. No matter what happened in the past. Or what our future holds, she's mine. Until the day comes, and I take my last breath, and my heart stops pumping; she's mine.

"Good girl," I murmur, diving my tongue into her mouth, twisting with hers. She pants when I pull back, looking up at me with lust-filled eyes.

"And what about you?" she asks, cocking a brow.

I snort. "I'll fuck my hand until I'm worthy of your pussy." River flushes further, licking her lips. "Until then, we'll meet your needs. Then, when you're ready, I'll get on my knees and wait for you."

Always.

"You'll wait for me?"

"We tore you apart when we left. It's only been a few weeks. We can't just jump in with both feet and expect not to fall. Starting over, remember?" She nods a few times, staring up at the stars above. Heaving a sigh, she runs her fingers through my hair as I fall to the side of her and fix her dress, so she's no longer exposed to the elements.

"This was amazing," she whispers. "Thank you for tonight. For the barbecue and the song. It reminded me of all the times we sat on the hill and just…were."

"Those were the simpler days," I mumble, resting my head on the blanket, continuing to stare at the rise and fall of her chest and the peace washing over her expression.

"We were just kids trying to make it through."

"I'm sorry about your mom," I murmur, resting my hand on her stomach. "I'm sorry I wasn't there at the funeral."

"It was beautiful. She would have loved all the people coming to see her," she whispers, sadness clutching her voice.

"I'm sure she would have, River Blue," I murmur, sweeping my fingers through her long brown strands. "She would have greeted each of them with a smile."

Stella was never as terrible as my mother, but she still had her faults. As a kid, River often met me in the dead of night to listen to me learn songs on the guitar behind our worn-out apartment building. Her biggest fault was ignoring River when she needed her most, and that's where I came in. Well, until my mother married a psychopath. Then we moved far away, forcing me to leave my girl behind. Somehow Nigel's crazy ass made me forget all about her. For her protection, of course.

I swallow hard when lightning illuminates the sky, highlighting the darkening clouds closing in on us from a distance.

"Looks like rain, Knight," she mumbles tiredly, gluing her eyes to the incoming storm.

"Maybe we should head inside."

"Okay," she murmurs as we slowly rise to our feet.

Tiny droplets pelt our skin as we gather our things. The wind howls all around us, blowing our hair in different directions. At the last second, before we're safely nestled in Callum's secret house, River captures my lips one last time, silently thanking me with one last heated kiss. In our finest clothes, the rain beats down on us, soaking us to the bone. The only warmth we feel is the heat between the two of us. She presses into me, shivering when I wrap my hands in her wet strands, holding her there. I never want this moment to cease. I'm never letting her go. When we finally pull back breathlessly examining each other, I notice the flowers floating in tiny puddles all around us, surrounding us in their beauty. It's a picture from a magazine, something perfect to forever remember.

Lyric may be the hurricane that stormed into my life. But River is the tornado swirling around me, sucking up my feelings and love.

"Thank you," she whispers, taking my hand as we enter through the back sliding glass door into the warmth of Callum's house.

It blows my mind that the man ran away to Central City so many times and never told us. Granted, we weren't exactly on speaking terms for the past few years. I can look back now and realize that it was, in part, due to my anger and all the tension bubbling between us that drove a wedge in our friendship. We were so damn close at one time, but now, we're slowly rebuilding ourselves, too.

We stop dead in the living room, dropping the wet blanket and supplies near the backdoor. River smiles at the sight in front of us, fondly looking Asher over as he clings to Lyric's sleeping body on his lap. Together, they're in dreamland with their eyes closed and breaths even.

"Will you stay with me tonight?" I whisper, catching her arm before she scoops Lyric up and settles her down.

River bites her lip, staring between us, and nods. "Yeah. She'll probably want in on the snuggles, though." She grins, pointing to Lyric, who still hasn't stirred.

"You take her and get settled. I'm in the back bedroom." Thankfully, the bedroom had a big enough bed for us to share.

When I promised River about waiting for her, I meant it. It might be a year from now until she can fully forgive us, or it could be tomorrow. No matter the wait, I'm here for them. I may not have done the manipulating myself, but I was compliant in leaving her alone.

As only a mother could, River lifts Lyric into her arms without waking her. She sends me a soft smile and leaves the room.

"Good date?" Asher rasps, peeking an eye open.

"Good date," I confirm with a nod, eyeing the multitude of healing bruises lining his chest and ribs.

Some are tinged green, and some are already yellowing and entering the healing stage. Finally, Guilt slams into me. He may have fucked up so royally and deserved our fists, but violence, to me, is never the answer—unless genuinely called for. Like that time Van and I had a discussion with our fists. The fucker deserved it. But Asher? He's my brother. We've been through a war together on the home front, fighting Nigel off and taking his blows. We've been through so much together. He's more family than I ever had. And Gloria fucking ruined that by pitting us against each other. She just had to stick her nose in something that was none of her business and contort the situation in her favor. She knew what she was doing every step of the way, and that includes playing Asher like a lost little puppet.

"Sorry about your face, bro," I say, running a hand through my wet strands. "I shouldn't have hit you like that. It was just... I couldn't stop the feelings."

Asher's brows raise. "No need to be sorry. I needed it."

"Nah, man. You fucked up. Like so thoroughly fucked up. But we all did, too. You may have led us to leave and manipulated us into believing lies, but Gloria was the man behind the mask. It's her fault, too." I shake my head, hammering the point home that Asher alone isn't at fault. This wasn't totally his doing. "She did this to us. But I want to put it behind us. For them. For us. For everything. What do you say? Can we move past this together?"

Asher blinks several times when I reach a hand out, wiggling my fingers. Hesitantly, he grabs on, and I pull him to his feet, shaking his hand. He swallows hard, shame tightening his face.

"Thanks," he croaks. "I don't really deserve it."

"Yes, you do," I say without hesitation. "But you did what you did. And I get it after thinking about everything that happened. This isn't solely on you, Ash. You were fucking used." It's true. I get why he was so damn desperate to leave. I was, too. But not at the expense of River. That's the part that fucks me up the most. That we left River without even knowing about Lyric.

"If we would have stayed, we would have been stuck with Nigel and then...probably gone to jail with him." Yeah, he would have lifted us in his company to the highest regard and then sent us to the slammer in his stead after all that shit the FBI found out. I'm thankful we skipped town. "I was desperate and obviously not thinking." His eyes fall to the floor, and he heaves a breath. "I'll say I'm sorry a million times."

"I get it. Fuck, do I get it. I didn't really want to stay behind. I just wanted to be with her. Imagine where our life would have been..." I trail off as several scenes rush through my mind. Lyric being born. Hell, River confiding in us that she was pregnant. The baby shower. Moving her in with us at Callum's because that's where we would have been despite Nigel's iron fist. So many possibilities. And yet, here we are.

"We would have survived," Asher says, squeezing my hand.

"Like we always did, brother," I murmur, squeezing back.

Finally, our hands drop to our sides.

"I bet Callum has some cream for those bruises somewhere in this place. It will help take some of the pain away if you still have any."

He shrugs, rubbing the back of his neck.

I know what he's thinking by the sadness clouding his eyes. He doesn't want it. He wants to suffer because he wants the remnants of what we did to him to remind him every day that he fucked up.

"Don't worry about it," he says, waving a hand. "Have a good night. I'm heading back to bed."

"Thanks for taking such good care of Ly," I say, catching him before he leaves the room. "You're not a bad guy, Asher. You just made a shit decision."

He gives a humorless laugh. "Yeah. I am a bad guy, though. That's the problem."

"But you wouldn't do it again, right?"

His shoulders stiffen, and he shakes his head. "Fuck no. Never again." He scratches his neck. "I've felt empty as fuck, and I finally feel full again just being around them. Being with Ly and having her call me daddy. It's bringing me back from the grave I put myself into." He heaves a breath as his watery eyes meet mine.

"You and me both. I love ya, Ash. I know we still have a lot to work out," I say, giving him a respectful nod and heading to my bedroom.

When I enter, I stop dead at the dress pooled on the ground and River sitting on the edge of the bed in my oversized T-shirt. How the fuck am I supposed to keep my hands to myself all night long?

My heart fills with so much love when I change into my sweats and climb into bed. Lyric's sleeping form rests between us, snoring.

"Should I tell her she snores, too?" I murmur, marveling at her little face.

River snorts, snuggling close to Ly. "She'll fight you tooth and nail," she murmurs, giggling. "Like father, like daughter." I swear my chest puffs out a million times more at the thought of Lyric gaining my stubborn streak.

"Night, River Blue."

"Night, Knight," she whispers with a whimsical smile crossing her lips. "See you in the morning."

WHAT THE HELL IS GOING ON WITH ME? I PROMISED I WOULDN'T CAVE, BUT goddamn, I'm falling into the darkness with only them as my guides. Again! It's so easy falling back into their arms. It's like time never slipped away from us.

Even as I sit in the basement, remarkably similar to Callum's old house, watching the boys jam out with smiles on their faces. For the first damn time, joy ignites in them. Completely different from a few weeks ago.

Lyric dances before me, lip-syncing the lyrics to the song she's memorized from years before.

"Again!" she yelps, stomping impatiently, staring at me until I relent.

The last thing I want to do is subject myself to Kieran's sultry voice. But I can't deny those big, weeping eyes staring daggers into me.

"If you say please," I murmur, hovering my finger above the first song of their new album.

"Pwease, Mommy. I want to listen to daddies sing!" Yup. I'm whipped despite hating the voices blasting through the speakers of our home.

"Okay, one more time." Let the record show it wasn't one more time. It was twelve more times that day and beyond. Every day from then on out, Lyric demanded Whispered Words on repeat. I tuned it out as best I could, but you can only do it for so long.

"Hold on," Kieran says, raising a hand. The loud music dies down as the guys watch him with curious gazes. "Come here, Little Blue," he says with a grin, curling a finger in her direction. She doesn't hesitate a second, barreling into Kieran's legs with a squeal. "I see you're singing. Do you know all the words to this one?"

"Every song, Daddy," she says with a huge grin and a clap. Kieran quirks a brow in my direction. I nod, biting the inside of my cheek. No way in hell am I admitting our spawn forced me to listen to them every damn day until I fell asleep to their voices rattling inside my brain. Nope. Not gonna happen. "I listened to them every day!" she whispers directly into the microphone, letting everyone hear our dirty little secret.

My cheeks heat when all their eyes fall on me. Can the ground please

swallow me up, I'll never hear the end of this shit. Not until I'm six feet deep with flowers blooming above my decaying body.

"Every day?" Rad grins, wiping the sweat from his forehead.

Fucker.

"Every day!" she squeals in confirmation when Kieran hands her the microphone.

Rad smirks in my direction. "I see you, Pretty Girl," he quips, settling back on his stool.

"Why don't you help us practice then, Little Blue? Sing with me?" He questions with pride, lighting up his eyes at the prospect of singing with his daughter.

Lyric frantically nods, screeching joyfully when Kieran pulls her into his arms.

"This one's for you," he says in a low voice, locking eyes with me, sending shivers down my spine at the intensity of his gaze. Fuck me. It's the same look he gave me last night when he rested above me, with his fingers settled deep inside my aching core. My pussy clenches at the memory. I'm such a fucking goner. I need Ode's advice before I jump in headfirst and drown in them. "How about River's song? Rushing River?"

Double fuck.

Rad snorts, whooping. "Let's do this! Get ready, Pretty Girl. I'm about to serenade your panties off."

"Panties?!" Lyric giggles into the microphone, making everyone else chuckle.

"Cal?" Kieran asks, locking eyes with the silent bassist.

A grin tugs at Cal's lip, lighting up his face. "It's been a while," he says, plucking two strings on his bass.

"Ash?" Kieran asks with a broken voice, catching the guitarist off guard.

Licking his lips, Ash gives an unsure nod. "Yeah, man. River's song."

And with that, Lyric belts out the song she shouldn't know. The song they only played at the Battle of the Bands winning celebration and recorded for their demo became a short-lived radio hit. The song they swore—because I happened to catch an interview—that they'd never publicly play again. I heard it everywhere I went. It followed me like their betrayal clung on. The day I had lunch with Seger and Zeppelin at that shitty diner, this song buried knives in my back, forcing me to relive what they did to me. Over and fucking over. And for some strange reason, my fucking daughter loved the shit out of it, making me suffer further.

Here it is again. The words are the same. About a roaring River, breaking through and making a life for themself. It's about strength and perseverance. Before, Kieran snarled every word until he refused to play it again. Now, their tone is different. Happier. Joyful. Full of life. And dare I say, love.

Their smiles light up the room when Lyric perfectly duets Kieran, matching his pitch changes. Sometimes she goes higher. Occasionally she dips lower. Together, they're creating an out-of-this-world sound. Almost like this is their destiny, like they belong together.

"Holy fucking shit!" Rad shouts, jumping from his stool. "Little Pretty Girl, you've got some pipes on you!" Kissing her hair, she giggles at his words, thanking him with a big hug.

"You sounded amazing, Little One," Asher marvels, staring at her with stars in his eyes.

"So damn good. Shall we go again?" Kieran asks, earning a yes from her.

"Again!" she screams like she used to, begging to continue.

I watch in awe for the next several hours as my daughter commands the makeshift stage. She prances around with the microphone, throwing out some ballet moves. She screams. She wails. And dear God, she sings, carrying the tune like a damn pro.

"When did that happen?" Kieran asks, sitting beside me on the couch after calling it quits for the night when Lyric showed signs of slowing down.

Do not look at his shirtless chest. Or his tight jeans. In fact, don't look at any fucking thing regarding him, or you'll jump his bones. There's a child in the room, for God's sake.

He guzzles a water bottle in two seconds flat before wiping his mouth after he's done. Why something so simple sends shivers directly to my pussy, has me questioning my sanity. I've gone without sex for so long without a thought. Now my body has reawakened, begging for more orgasms. Stupid body. It's been two nights of orgasms, and suddenly, I want more.

I swallow hard, averting my eyes to my sleeping child snuggled beside me after too much activity. And stealthily avoid the half-naked man. If I don't look at him, he'll disappear, right? Before I do something stupid.

"When did what happen?" I ask, clearing my damn throat from all the lustful thoughts trying to break free and fulfill my damn fantasies.

Make it more obvious, would ya?

They're already starting to cloud my thoughts with their manly scents, heated touches, and sinful looks. My stalker better be behind bars before long, or I'll lose myself to them. Again. God, they're like a fucking drug I can't escape, infecting me with their beings.

I'm so fucking screwed, aren't I?

I want to take it glacially slow and build something meaningful. Before I stupidly jump into the sack with them like I did before. Sure, sex sounds so wonderful now, but I want to be sure they're in it for the long haul.

"Her singing."

With so much affection, Kieran stares at Lyric, too, gazing at her sleeping form. She doesn't move an inch when my fingers touch her tiny, red ears—barely stirring when my fingers weave through her hair and straighten it out.

"She's a natural talent," I murmur.

"Good news, everyone!" Jordy shouts from the basement stairs with a grin, throwing his arms out wide.

Dressed in his usual black attire with guns hanging off holsters, he strolls in like he owns the place. Typical fucking Jordy. A cocky smirk plays on his lips until he's at the center of the room. Everyone eyes him when he untucks a file folder from beneath his arms and takes us in.

"How do you keep sneaking into my house?" Callum asks with a tic forming in his jaw. Agitation sparkles in his eyes like he's ten seconds away from laying Jordy out flat. A fact I don't doubt when he puts his bass down and cracks his knuckles.

"Special agent, duh," he quips, affectionately eyeing Lyric as she rests beside me.

"What's up, Professor?" I say jokingly, making him snort. "Anything good?"

Jordy nods, tapping the file folder and handing it to me with a grim expression. "Adrian was caught last night," he says as I flip open to a picture of a messy apartment littered with trash and debris. How anyone lived there is beyond me. Dirt and grime make up the walls and the furniture.

"Is he in jail?" Kieran asks, straightening his spine.

"Better," Jordy says, helping me flip to another page. "Adrian was such a pussy about getting caught that he ended everything before we could question him." He rolls his lips together. "Sorry, we didn't get you any clear answers, Riv." Shaking his head, he points to the report, stating Adrian shot himself in bed. "But it's over, at least."

"No notes or anything?"

Jordy snorts, scratching the back of his head. "We're still investigating his apartment. But we found your old phone, a camera, and a shit ton of pictures of you. From errr…your house, the beach, and anywhere this sick fuck could get into. Basically, it's all pointing to this asshole 100 percent."

My damn heart drops. Right. That asshole had access to my house. "Fuck. He saved them from my house?"

Jordy squats down, making eye contact with me, and gives me a reassuring look. "From what we could tell from your old phone, he was able to gain access to your cameras." I blanch, bringing a hand to my chest, trying to calm my rapidly beating heart. Another hand grasps mine, squeezing in support as I get the full picture of my stalker's activities.

"You'll let me know if you find a connection? I don't understand why someone I don't even know would follow me around."

It's always blown my fucking mind that someone would want to follow me around. I'm so damn dull and do the same shit every day. Go to work. Take care of Ly. The list goes on and on. I'm never in the same spot for too long and always taking care of others. So, why in the hell would some asshole want pictures of my boring life? I'll never fucking understand.

"Always, Dollface. I'll keep you updated on anything new. So far, all we have is what we've investigated. Stalkers tend to latch on to a person who fits an idea rather than the person themselves. Our running theory after checking into his background is Adrian had an ex who passed four years ago, who was around your age, build, and height. So, we think somewhere along the way, the two of you crossed paths, and he latched on to you. And as soon as these assholes came into the picture, something flipped in him. Maybe it was meeting you again in real life at the fight, but we're not totally sure. But we're pretty damn confident he's our guy." He claps his hands with confidence, shutting the door on my entire stalker situation.

I should feel relieved that this whole thing is over, and I can rest easy now, but something nags at the back of my mind. From here on out, I'll be looking over my shoulder. No matter what.

"Liv will keep you updated, too. Since she's your go to and all. Which is hurtful by the way. I thought we were pretty tight. She'll be thrilled to have you under her nose again. She's been a damn beast since she sent you away." He scrunches his nose. "Please come home soon," he quips, flicking my nose like the annoying gnat he is.

Fucker.

"Bastard," I grunt as the others tense at his actions. Gently, I run my fingers over the soreness on my nose.

"When can we?" Rad asks, running a towel through his sweaty mullet.

"Whenever you want," Jordy says. "We see zero threats from here on out. All of our intel suggests it was him, and with the evidence…Liv has officially declared you free to leave your sex house."

"What's a sex house?" Lyric asks in a tired rasp, scratching at her eyes.

"It's how your little brother or sister gets produced," Jordy says, earning a glare from me and everyone else in the room.

Oh hell no. I've had an IUD secured for four years now. Since the moment Ly blessed me with her presence, I wasn't taking any chances.

"Not cool, asshole," Rad mutters, shaking his head.

"Brother? Sister?" she squeals, sitting up with big eyes, looking at all of us with hope. It's the one thing she's begged me for since she was three —siblings.

"Maybe one day, Little Pretty Girl," Rad says, giving her a lopsided grin and winking in my direction.

"Nope!" I croak, turning to Ly. "They're using adult words again. Something you shouldn't repeat." She blinks several times at me and nods.

"Okay," she says with a shrug.

"Okay, here are all your phones," Jordy says, reaching into his pocket and pulling out four phones. "Both of yours are still in evidence."

I cringe. "Will you keep it forever?"

"Believe me. There's nothing on there you want right now." Jordy shakes his head, giving me a look. "All right, kiddies, especially you," he says, grinning at Lyric. "We're leaving our post. You're free to leave. Our private jet is waiting for you all to decide. So, call me! I've put my number in each of your phones. I know we have this intense bond now," he quips, walking backward and pointing finger guns in our direction.

"Bye, Uncle J!" Lyric waves as he disappears up the stairs and presumably leaves the house.

"We'll get you a new phone," Kieran says, squeezing my hand.

I snort. "I can buy my own these days."

Memories of the phone they gave me run through my mind on repeat. They had been so thoughtful when they did it, and it helped so much to finally have a working phone that didn't abruptly end calls or have a cracked screen.

"I know," Kieran smirks, looking down at his phone and scrolling through his messages. Without warning, the joyous look he has falls away into annoyance. "Fuck," he grunts, scrolling through message after message.

"Everything okay?"

Kieran sighs, showing me his screen. "It's never-ending."

GLORIA

I need money....

I'm almost out of coffee, Kieran!

Kieran! Where are you?

Kieran! Please!

KIERAN!

Kieran rubs his temple with a pained expression. "I've been paying her way," he mutters. "I was trying to look out for my sister, and I had to take care of her. But if I would have known what she pulled, she never would have been given a penthouse and princess treatment," he growls through clenched teeth, glaring a hole through the floor.

I pat his arm. "You didn't know. Plus, she's your mom."

"A mom who went behind my back and filed a restraining order without my knowledge. She knew what she was doing. Now, I just have to figure out how to punish her," he says, squeezing his fingers into fists.

"I'll help," Rad says with fire in his eyes. "You're not the only one she fucked over with her scheme. I'll put a boot in her stuck-up ass and throw her out onto the streets. Where she belongs."

"I helped you get her into the mess. I'll help you evict her," Asher says, sitting on the edge of a chair with his brows furrowed.

"Okay," Kieran says with a nod. "You can all help. But we'll have to come up with a plan."

GLORIA

You know what? I just found some. I'll talk to you later, K.
:)

His nose wrinkles at her message before he darkens his screen and shoves it into his pocket.

"I'll deal with her later," he grumbles, putting his hand on my knee.

We sit and talk for a few more hours, reminding me of the old times when we hung out at Callum's and did exactly this. We don't discuss anything important. But they make me laugh more times than I can count.

And that night, when I slip into bed, two more bodies follow, helping me drift off to dreamland. Getting the best night's sleep I've had in ages. The overwhelming feeling of rightness settles over me. No matter my reservations, they will always have a piece of my damn heart.

They're my damn kryptonite.

"Night, Pretty Girl."

"Night, Little Star."

"Night," I sigh, snuggled between them without any mom guilt, knowing Ly is safely tucked away in a bed down the hall.

The moment we came upstairs, Lyric clung to Kieran and asked him to read her a bedtime story and stayed with him for the rest of the night.

you. It twists my stomach into knots. Everywhere I look, memories sink their claws deep into my psyche. In the front seat of Callum's modest SUV, I twiddle my thumbs as the world flashes by. Discreetly, I peek at Lyric, sitting the same way in her booster seat, which Jordy procured before he left. Her tiny blue eyes take in the colors flashing by with interest.

"Are you going to be okay?" Asher asks from the driver's seat, nervously shifting.

"I'll be fine. Thanks for driving me here." Not exactly sure why he thought he needed to be my chauffeur, but I'm not complaining. I'm in no mood to drive across town by myself. My head is in the clouds and stuffed full of cotton balls. After everything I've endured with the shock of my stalker and my forced visit here—I'm exhausted.

I'm so fucking tired of fighting myself on what is right and what's wrong. I'm so fucking tired of fighting these feelings festering inside and begging to reemerge. Hopefully, my talk with Ode will wield some insight into what I should do. She was always the one to give me a little nudge here and there.

"No problem," he says softly. "They were your family, too." Understanding oozes from his eyes when he sends me a smile, lighting up his face. The bruises continue to disappear, especially since Callum handed him a tiny bottle of cream and instructed him to use it.

I side-eye Ash as we travel through the center of Central City—the heart of my hometown. Down these streets is where I walked daily to and from work, heaving a heavy backpack with determination forcing me forward. This place molded me into the woman I am. Breathing the same air I left is so fucking surreal. I've intended to return for years, promising Ode I'd come to visit her and the family but work always held me back.

As we pass the old record store I once worked at, I smile. Every once in a while, Booker texts me updates on his life. After I paid off all his bills, including his loans, he could relax instead of drowning in debt. He was always the father I never had, taking me under his wing and providing me

with jobs. I worked my ass off for him to prove to the world I could succeed. And in turn, he always believed in me. No matter what.

Before I know it, I'm pointing Asher in the right direction, down a long, winding path toward the beautiful farmhouse in the middle of three acres of grassland. Corn and bean fields lie around the edges, cutting the property off from the rest of the world. Giving the seclusion, they always dreamed about.

"Where would you live if you could ever get away?" I ask, sipping Korrine's sweet tea at her dining room table after a long school day.

Korrine smiles, stirring the pot soup she started for dinner. "Long time ago, baby, my mama and papa had a beautiful farmhouse out on Route 36. It was two stories, surrounded by fields. The best sound was the cicadas as the sun set and painted the sky pink." A nostalgic look overtakes her.

"What happened to it?"

"My brother inherited the property and tore it down. It was unlivable," she says sadly, looking at the murky soup on the stove. "One day, I'd love to relive that. Sitting on the porch, drinking my sun tea without a care in the world. But that's just a dream some old woman thought up."

"This place is huge," Asher mumbles as he pulls the car to a stop near the side of the house.

I grin, pride puffing my chest. As the house was being built under the constant supervision of a contractor, Ode sent me daily pictures.

"It was her dream house. Thanks for coming with me. This might be—"

He snorts. "A little awkward? I'm about to face the wrath of your best friend. All deserved, I suppose." His hazel eyes look upward, cataloging every inch of the house with a grin. "It's beautiful."

"You'll live," I say, patting his thigh without thinking.

The instant my hand comes into contact with him, a buzz zings through my arm, and heat forms on my cheeks. I clear my throat, turning away from his curious gaze. Oh, and I also removed my hand. As quickly as fucking possible before I do something stupid. Like squeeze it. Or lick it or something. God, I need more sleep.

I clear my throat, refusing to look at the man I know is staring at me in question. Not falling into that trap again. No way in fucking hell.

"Ly, are you ready to see Aunt Ode again?" I ask, turning to my quiet child, who hasn't spoken since we got into the vehicle. Saying that's odd is an understatement. Lyric must be feeling the same effects I am.

"Yes," she says with a grin. "Is Daddy meeting Aunt Ode?"

Asher's eyes dart to Ly through the rearview mirror, and he grins. "Yes," he answers, not bothering to explain he met her years before at the bar, knowing exactly who he is facing in about two seconds.

We all pile out, Ly a little more enthusiastically than Asher, who hangs back a step with his hands in his pockets. Now and again, his eyes drift back to the car, probably contemplating driving away and leaving us here, so he doesn't get his ass handed to him. Once Ode sees Asher, she will lose her damn mind and probably try to beat his ass with a broom. It wouldn't be the first or last time she's pulled something like that.

God, I love my best friend.

"My, my… Do my eyes deceive me?" A single rocking chair squeaks against the wooden wrap-around porch, swaying as the owner slowly rocks herself.

Her smile immediately greets me when she comes into view, and I halt as the nostalgia hits me square in the chest. Immediate longing to have her motherly arms wrapped around me has me itching to run up the stairs and bury my face in her neck.

Pure joy soars through me at the sound of her voice. I've missed hearing it in person after all these years. It may not be as strong as it was when I was a kid, but she's still the same Mama Korrine. The woman who helped raise me when my Ma worked overnight. Her home became my home. She was my unofficial second mother, and I couldn't have asked for anyone better.

"Grandma!" Ly squeals, breaking away from us with excitement.

"Ly, careful!" I warn as she charges up the porch stairs and throws herself into Korrine's awaiting arms.

My breath hitches. Korrine has been through the wringer with her cancer treatments but always seems to come out on top. So far, she's had several rounds with success. But by the look in her weary eyes and shaking hands, it's wearing her down to the bone.

"Oh, my baby," she coos, kissing the top of her hair and squeezing her arms around her. Gingerly, she pulls Ly into her lap. "Now, let me get a good look at you." A warm smile crosses her face when her dark eyes take Lyric's features in. "My, how you've grown. I think you got more freckles than before."

"Mommy says it's angel kisses, and Grammy Stella is sending me loves." Lyric's grin expands as she explains, tracing her fingers over the freckles continually popping up over the bridge of her nose and cheeks.

"I think your mama is right. Grammy Stella has lots of love to give you from Heaven," Korrine says, booping a trembling finger on her nose. "Now, are you gonna stand there all day? Or are you going to come and give me some sugar? I've missed you both so much," Korrine rasps, waving a hand in my direction.

I don't need any further instructions. I march up the stairs with burning tears and settle my weary bones in her embrace, letting her warmth envelop me and soaking in the motherly hug she always gives me. It's one of those hugs you don't realize you've missed until your mother is gone. No one prepares you for the mediocre hugs that can't even compare to the last one you gave to your mother. Ever. But

Korrine's do. And today of all days, after finally becoming free, I needed this.

"We've missed you too," I whisper, kissing her cheek and sniffling.

"No crying now," she murmurs, brushing my tears away with the pad of her thumb. "Hmmm. And who is this?" She gestures to Asher as he stands at the bottom of the stairs, scratching his neck.

"That's my daddy, Grandma! Or…one of them. I've gots four. And they're so cool." Korrine's brows raise, but she doesn't utter a word as Lyric recounts her mini vacation trapped in the house with all of them and what we've been doing.

"Well, don't be shy, Boy. Come on up and introduce yourself. I don't believe we've had the privilege of meeting." Korrine's tone leaves no room for arguments, coming out stronger than I've heard her in months through our many phone calls.

"I'm Asher," he says softly, extending his hand as he sways in front of us with a look of pure terror.

Huh. Who knew? The way to scare these boys straight was in front of me all along. Now, I need to get the rest of them out here because Asher's so pale; he looks like he's about to shit his pants.

"One of them?" she asks, taking his hand in a firm grip.

"Yes?" he questions, gazing at me with wide eyes.

Internally I laugh at his pain, biting the inside of my cheek when his terror turns into slight trembles.

"Yes," I say, clearing my throat.

Korrine purses her lips. "Nice to finally have you on board."

"Mama! Who are you talking—" Ode, my best fucking friend, stops at the threshold of the front door, turning pale when she looks me over.

More tears burn the back of my eyes at the sight of her with her mouth agape and her body frozen in the doorway. My heart pounds wildly in my chest. A sense of home settles deep in my soul, unlocking all the turmoil I've faced in the years, months, and weeks leading up to this.

I'm finally where I need to be. If only for a little while.

Her dark eyes widen, and she drops the glass in her hand. It shatters against the wood, hurling glass everywhere. "Either I'm too sleep-deprived from that baby trying to eat every piece of lint off the floor or—"

I wrinkle my nose. "I'm really here."

"You dirty bitch!" she squeals, running toward me. Her arms fly around me as we laugh, hugging each other. "God damnit, River West. You bitch," she cries into my shoulder, snotting everywhere. But I don't give a shit. "If I had known you were coming, I would have laid out the red carpet."

"No, you wouldn't have," I choke, clutching her tight.

"You're right!" she cries, sniffling on my shoulder. "But I would have at least cleaned my house. Alma and Anni have flipped my damn house upside down." Sniffling, she pulls away, clapping a hand on my cheek.

"But I've missed you and—" Her brows furrow. "What are you doing here? Last time we talked to you—" Her eyes widen on Asher, who awkwardly stands beside Korrine, softly talking to her and Lyric.

"Um, yeah," I say, clearing my throat.

"Yo, Ricky!" she shouts her husband's name. "Grab the gun. We've got a snake to fill with pellets!"

"Um, maybe I should just wait in the car," Asher says, gesturing toward the SUV with horror lining his face. If he thought meeting Korrine was terrible, he's now facing the wrath of my best friend, who openly glares at him with hostility.

"Oh, no, you won't. You and I are going to enjoy some sweet tea on the porch." I suppress my snort when Korrine gives him a *I'm not taking no for an answer* look.

"Oh, shit. She's breaking out the sweet tea," Ode hisses, pulling on my arm. "We better get before she breaks out the vanilla wafers and wants to have the sex talk again." Ode snickers under her breath when Korrine side-eyes us with a knowing smirk.

Yeah. I don't want to have that talk again.

"Y'all go inside. Asher and I will sit out here and enjoy the sun and conversation." Asher's eyes scream for help, silently begging me not to leave him in the clutches of Korrine.

"Okay. Have fun," I snort when Asher swallows hard, sitting beside Korrine in a second rocking chair.

"All right, you're coming with me. We've got lots of tea to devour ourselves." Ode grins at me, pulling me along. "Come inside, Lyric, my love! Alma would love to play!"

"Okay, Auntie Ode," she says, hopping off Korrine's lap and running inside without looking back.

"Is he going to be okay?" I murmur as she pulls me through the large living room littered with toys. The TV screams, but not over the squeals of Lyric and Alma, Ode's three-year-old daughter and Ly's long-distance best friend, hugging amid chaos.

"Bitch, please. Mama is going to eat him alive. Maybe he'll be a changed man by the time she's done with him. Converted and everything," she snorts, plopping my ass in front of the dining room table. "Now, how about some drinks?" she asks, setting down a large bottle of tequila in front of me.

"Ew. Why tequila? And it's only like eleven."

"Pfft. Bitch, this is the only alcohol that makes you talk. And it's five o'clock somewhere. Now, explain why douchebag number one is sitting on my porch like a domesticated dog," she says, pouring a tall shot of tequila.

"No lime? Salt?"

"No fucking lime for you, Missy. Take your shot and tell your bestie everything," she demands, pointing to the shot with her brow raised.

"Fine," I grimace, tossing back the shot. "Jesus," I croak through the burning sensation tingling down my throat.

"Out with it!" Ode says, pouring another shot. "I need all the dirty deets."

So, I tell her everything that's happened since we last spoke on the phone, starting with the fights, the revelations, and everything in between. I've texted her updates here and there in our daily messages but being in her presence hits differently.

"I just…don't know how I feel about it, Ode. I'm so fucking conflicted about everything," I murmur at the last of it, drowning myself in another shot of tequila.

"Wow," Ode says, drinking a shot, too.

"Yeah…"

"So, they volunteered to follow you here to protect you and Lyric. They've stepped up."

"Massively. Asher makes her breakfast every morning, even before all this. He wants to be her father. Rad's teaching her the drums. Callum tries to read to her every night. And Kieran is bonding with her like he never left her side. They're all trying as dads and—" I look out the window, examining the bright blue, cloudless sky as I gather my thoughts.

"And with you?" she asks, pouring two more shots for each of us.

I lick my lips. "That's the part that scares me, Ode. What if…"

"What if they break your heart? What if they walk away? What if… What if…" she trails off, shaking her head. "I saw how much it broke your heart when they fucked you over like that. Seeing you so damn sad and mad at the entire world broke my heart, too. You were ready to burn their entire existence down. But hearing that bitch Gloria was the one who did most of it." She grimaces as she downs another shot, sticking her tongue out and making a face when she sets the glass down.

"But Asher orchestrated it with her help. He made this entire thing happen."

"Yeah? And what's he doing now, bitch? He's sitting on the porch with Mama, probably getting ripped into through polite words. He drove you here?"

"He insisted."

Ode nods wistfully, taking another shot. "This could be the tequila fogging my thinking skills. When I saw him outside my house, I wanted to slice his balls open and shove them up his ass. The fucker deserved it. But the way I see it and from what you've told me, they're trying. With you. With her. With every fucking thing. Three of them walked away because they thought you broke their heart. One walked away because his fucking dreams depended on it. They were fucking idiots. So fucking stupid. God! Who put these men on this earth?" she slurs, covering her mouth.

"Way beyond idiots," I snort, taking a deep breath after I force another burning shot down my gullet. "Am I fucking crazy for even contemplating this?"

"Were you contemplating it when Kieran's fingers were in your–" I grunt, slamming a hand over her mouth.

"You get awfully vulgar when you've had tequila." She grins behind my hand, licking my palm.

"Well, I'm just saying… What's the worst that could happen?"

I blow out a breath. "They could leave us again. They are in a band. What happens when they go on tours? They'll leave for months at a time. What about Ly? How the hell is this all going to work out into a happy ending, Ode?"

"No one knows, babe. That's the beauty of life. You don't know the ending. Remember before? You thought you were going to travel the world with them. Maybe you were presented with this second chance for a reason." She shrugs, putting the lid back onto the now half-empty bottle of tequila, and hiccups. "No more day drinking for us, bitch." She giggles, thrusting a finger into the air as a lightbulb illuminates above her head like it always does before she has a brilliant idea. "Okay, so hear me out. I've got two ideas. You have enough money. Why don't you go on tour with them? Be their HBIC all over the world or some shit?" she asks like it's that fucking simple to drop my day job and go off with them on tour.

"I may have the money, but I like my job. And Ly loves her school… We could survive tours, right? We could—" Ode gives me an all-knowing smile.

"You have your answer. You didn't need me and the tequila to decide you wanted them. For some reason, they're your ones. You're meant to fucking be. You just had to go through some trials to get here."

I nibble my bottom lip. "Maybe you're right… But what is your second idea?" I ask, putting my elbows on the table as Lyric, Alma, and baby Anni toddle through the kitchen, singing at the top of their lungs.

"Okay, so… Here's my idea…" Ode says, spilling her idea with a grin on her face. Butterflies burst in my gut, and I nod in agreement. "Come to Dead End tonight with the boys and have them put on a show. You know, like old times. God, it would be great!"

"Holy shit. That's brilliant," I giggle, taking another sip of my shot, much to Ode's raised brows. She'd rather I knock it back, but my head is already swimming in an ocean of tequila. "I'll make a big announcement on their socials later and get the biggest crowd we can. No cover charge or anything. I'll pay for it all."

"Well, then there you go." Ode grins, pouring us one last shot. "To Whispered Words!" she says, slamming her glass into mine before we empty them down our throats.

GAZING AT THE GRASSY FIELDS SURROUNDING THE FARMHOUSE, I contemplate my life choices. Korrine hasn't said a word since the girls excused themselves and went inside to catch up. I had no idea our visit would entail this, or I would have tucked tail and stayed with the guys.

"You know, I've always been curious. Which one of you fixed River's car after you left?"

My eyes whip to her in surprise, widening as she softly smiles. Somehow, I think she knew the answer before she even asked.

"Did she take it?" I ask, hoping River took the much-needed gift without protest. Knowing her, she scowled and cursed at whoever fixed the car but eventually took it because she knew she needed a vehicle to get her around without us there.

The moment we left; the guilt started scorching me from the inside out. The flames of my stomach were impossible to douse. Any remedy to tamp down my heartburn never worked until the antacids. Now, I eat them like candy, popping them six to eight times a day, trying to find some damn relief. Or I did. Since I confessed my wrongdoings, my stomach has been less volatile, ridding me of the constant acid reflux. And to me, that's a win. It still aches here and there as I swim through unfamiliar waters with River, working to earn her forgiveness. But the pain is worth it in the end.

"All the time," Korrine chuckles, pouring us a glass of ice-cold sweet tea.

"Good," I say, lifting the glass to my lips and taking a big swig. The wonderful blend of sweetness fills my taste buds, and I hum in appreciation. If there's one thing I can say about Korrine, she makes a mean glass of tea.

"Boy, you didn't answer my question," she says sharply, again gaining my attention. "Which one of you gentlemen fixed River's car?"

"I did," I murmur in confirmation, letting the comfortable silence envelop us.

The warm September breeze blows through the porch, bringing a

sweet, familiar laugh on its tails. Hearing a hint of happiness sputtering out of River brings a smile to my face and joy to my galloping heart.

Through the open window, Odette and River softly discuss our entire situation. In explicit detail, too. I side-eye Korrine, who nods with a knowing grin and doesn't say another word. It's as if she planned all this.

I sigh, sitting back in the rocking chair and letting its soft sways lull me into a once joyful memory, now tainted by every action I took to get us there.

"And the winner is," Seger says into the microphone, standing tall on stage with all the hopefuls clumping together behind him. The crowd beyond extends for miles, staying silent in anticipation humming through the entire venue. The spotlights above dance across everyone's heads in a multitude of colors, counting down until Seger opens his mouth once again. "Whispered Words!" he shouts, turning to look at us as pinks, blues, and reds dance across us.

"Holy Fuck!" Rad shouts, jumping up and down. His fists pump the air before he turns to us and pulls us into a massive group hug.

"We fucking did it!" I shout with a laugh, hugging everyone tight. Pride spears through me at how fucking far we've come since Callum's basement. If it wasn't for our dedication and... My face falls a mile when a second thought roars in my mind.

We were Whispered Words before we met River. We did fine obtaining gigs and getting there. But we were a different Whispered Words after we met her. She changed our entire life... And she's nowhere to be found to enjoy this win with us.

"Congrats, guys!" Seger says through the microphone again and slaps each of us on the shoulder in congratulation.

We won. We fucking won the Battle of the Bands! My heart pounds against my chest as the words ring through my mind repeatedly. We're a signed fucking band! No more scrounging or praying for a better future. We've done it.

"Holy fucking shit!" Kieran roars out over the crowd's rampant cheering. "We fucking did it!"

We fucking did it...

My brothers and I look around, sweaty and smiling, staring at the adoring crowd as they cheer so loud it sounds like the roof is about to collapse. Not only did we receive the gold microphone as a trophy. We also received a one-million-dollar paycheck and a giant ass record deal.

This can't be fucking real. I pinch myself with a shuddering breath. Nope. I'm not fucking dreaming.

Our dreams are finally coming to life after so fucking long of hoping and praying for a break.

The work will be hard. So fucking hard. This is what we've always wanted. Right? This is everything we've worked for. Everything we've talked about in Callum's basement with stars in our eyes and determination in our guts. It's fucking everything...

So why do I feel so goddamn empty?

As we walk off the stage, shaking hands with everybody who came out to see the contest, something breaks inside me. With desperation, I look around with longing deep in my soul, hoping to see the familiar girl with moss-green eyes smiling in our direction. I ache to see her pushing through the crowd with excitement thrumming through her veins, shouting congratulations in our faces. She'd jump in my arms, wrap her gorgeous, long legs around my torso and fervently kiss my lips. Without hesitation, she'd jump to Callum, Rad, and then Kieran, pouncing on them happily.

My heart cracks when we finally walk into the night air, whooping and hollering—all but me. I hang back as they jump up and down around our SUV, cackling and singing our praises. They don't notice when I shove my hands in my jeans and slowly walk away from the commotion. They don't see me when I slump against the club, crying out in frustration. Or the tears glistening down my cheeks under the glow of the light post. No. They don't seem to notice anything but our win.

"I'm so fucking sorry, Little Brat," I mumble with a quivering voice. Leaning my head against the scratchy brick, I glare at the twinkling stars, not drowned out by the city's lights. "I'm so fucking sorry I ran away from you." There's nothing I can do about it now. I'll keep pushing forward with her on my mind. I'll never forget what I did, the sacrifices I made to get us away from Nigel and Gloria.

As the guys continue their loud celebration across the parking lot, my mind wanders, concocting wild ideas to ease the shame of what I've done. As the night goes on and the celebration gets bigger, I realize there is something I can do for River to ease the pain of our departure.

"Yeah, it's stuck in the parking lot of the Dead End bar in Central City," I say, silently pacing my room at 8:00 a.m. the following day. The boys are still sound asleep after a wild night out, drinking anything they could get their hands on. So, as soon as they passed out, I researched the best shops in Central Illinois hoping to get River's car in.

"Yeah, sure, Asher. I can pick that up today. If you want me to take it to the shop?" he questions gruffly through the phone.

"Uh...yeah, Man, just to fix whatever is wrong with it. Just send me the bill or whatever you need me to do." I rub my temples as a headache forms, pounding against my skull.

Fuck. I didn't even drink that much last night. Not with the way I felt. I couldn't touch more than two drinks without wanting to throw up.

"No problem, man. I'll get it taken care of and send you updates. Anything else?" he asks as I plop into bed and lay back, staring at the dull white ceiling.

"Fix it. Clean it. And then send me everything. But make sure you put it back where you got it from; I'll be in town in about a week to pay."

"Sounds good. I'll see you when you get into town."

"I just wanted her to have a way to get around," I say softly, chuckling when I remember the note I left on her windshield.

Stop fucking walking.

As I stand in the empty parking lot of Dead End at 3:00 a.m., an emptiness engulfs my entire being. My stomach churns, sending acid up my throat as I set the note beneath the windshield of her car. I don't have a clue when she'll come back to it or even see this, but it'll give me plenty of time to sneak away without being noticed. I swallow hard, staring at the piece of shit she drives around. If I was a better man, I would buy her something new so she's able to get to work and school without worry.

But I'm not a better man. I'm the piece of shit under her shoe. So, this is the best I can fucking do for now. Maybe in the future, when we're in a better place as a band, I'll tell them what happened.

"Mmm. She used it, too. Every day until her brothers came into her life. You fixed it up real good, son." Reaching over, she lays a weary hand on my arm, gently squeezing. "You did a damn good thing for her."

I scoff, shaking my head. "I would have been a better man if I could have just let things be and let her come. If I hadn't meddled in our relationship and—"

"Now, now," Korrine chastises, squeezing my arm again before pulling away. "How many years have you put yourself through the wringer?" She raises a brow when I blow out a breath, willing the stupid tears to melt away.

"Since the moment I left," I mumble.

"And she knows it?" she asks as we both take sips of tea. "You've explained and said your sorrys?"

"Of course." I set my glass back down on the tiny table between us, staring at the miles of nothing again, getting lost in the blissful breeze and the sounds of insects. "I'll say I'm sorry forever until I'm blue in the damn face and have bruises on my knees. Even if she forgives me, I'll remember what I did and how it affected everyone. I don't expect anyone in this situation to forgive me, though. I know I wouldn't."

"There's a blessing with forgiveness. Humans never forget what happened but find it in their hearts to forgive, anyway. Some way, somehow, it happens. Not many people know, not even my own children, but the love of my life left me after one year of marriage. Said he couldn't do it anymore and disappeared for a week."

"Why?" I ask, swallowing hard.

"Who knew with that man? We were young and in love, moving through this world at warp speed." She shakes her head.

"He came back?"

"On his hands and knees, begging me to forgive him for being the biggest dummy in history." She sniffles a little, folding her hands on her lap. "He just needed to sow his wild oats one last time before settling down. The week he came back, well... Leon came nine months later. It wasn't as blissful as a marriage like Hallmark would lead you to believe, but we managed. We loved hard. Played hard. Life is full of ups and downs, betrayals, and misfortune. But as long as you keep getting back on your feet and showing that woman how much you care. Then you're on the right path, Asher Montgomery."

I swallow my tears. "Thank you," I murmur as the quiet envelops us again. The only sounds are nature, and the girls getting louder and louder with their conversation through the open window.

My heart beats double time when River's voice floats through the air again, confiding in Ode about her concerns about the future, but the one line filled with so much despair has my breaths coming in short pants and sweat breaking across my skin.

"They could leave us again. They are in a band. What happens when they go on tours? They'll leave for months at a time. What about Ly? How the hell is this all going to work out into a happy ending, Ode?"

"So, now you know what you have to do," Korrine says cryptically, staring at the leaves ruffling in the wind. "Make it happen, or all your pain and suffering will be for nothing. You'll lose her again, before you have a chance to keep her." With that, she gets up from her rocking chair on unsteady legs and enters the house, leaving me to stew in my thoughts.

Yeah. I know exactly what I need to do so River never has to worry about if we're leaving or staying.

I'll make the ultimate sacrifice for her and Lyric. And hopefully, the others will, too.

I'M NEVER DRINKING FUCKING TEQUILA IN THE MIDDLE OF THE DAY. EVER again. Even if Ode convinces me, it's a good idea. It's not. Or maybe it was.

Talking to Ode is like walking through the front door of my house. She's warm and inviting and always knows the right thing to say. I'm still surprised she gave me the green light to follow my weary heart into the ultimate make-or-break situation.

I'm so tired of fighting with myself. With the thoughts rumbling in the back of my mind, screaming at me to fall into their familiar arms. They're my home, too. For some strange, out-of-this-world reason, my heart aches for them.

I take a deep breath, grounding myself in the present. Forgiveness is my new state of mind. The mantra I'm going to live and die by when I sit the boys down tonight and tell them all is forgiven in my eyes. Peace washes through me, relaxing every muscle in my body. Just at the simple thought of no longer holding the hostility inside my warring mind.

My burning anger sizzles into ashes. And it's gone…

Korrine and Ode lean against the white railing of the wrap-around porch. Asher, bless his heart, stands beneath them on the ground with his back to me. The women nod a few times as he shoves his hands into his pockets. His shoulders deflate.

I yearn to see the expression on his face. *Look at me, damnit.* What is going through your head? I'm so desperate to hear what they're discussing.

"Auntie Ode doesn't like Daddy," Lyric says with a little yawn in the back seat, staring in their direction.

Yeah, because your daddy did some fucked up things in the past. But the past is the past. My forgiveness shouts, reminding me.

"She has her grown-up reasons for it," I say, leaning my head against the cool glass window, letting it soak into my drunk-ass brain.

There's no way I'm getting into this discussion with a four-year-old who repeats everything word for word. If she found out what her daddy did all those years ago, she'd hate him forever. Or be so hurt she wouldn't

know how to act. Ly takes everything to heart, and I can't break hers because of him.

To Lyric, her fathers are the saints on her walls. The music in her speakers. And the blood running through her veins. If I wanted to spoil their image, I would have done it years ago.

Sure, Asher manipulated the situation and fucked us all over, but he's grown up. He's making up for what he did. Owning up to his faults. He's trying to make this right every day. I see it. The guys see it.

"Sorry," Asher says, climbing into the driver's seat out of breath, wearily staring at the two women standing on the porch. "I was discussing a few things with Korrine."

Nothing says suspicious like avoiding eye contact. Even when he starts the car and slowly backs out of their little driveway, he avoids me at all costs.

Ode grins on the steps, shaking her head almost in disbelief. Something odd sparkles in her eyes. Even from here, I can see it. I know when my best friend has something up her sleeve. What the hell is going through her head? She grins more, waving as we ease away down the long lane leading toward the main road.

"What was that about?" Please! Give me something. I need to know what you all discussed, or it will drive me nuts.

Asher shrugs at my question, still not bothering to look in my direction. I narrow my eyes on his guilty behavior. He's suspect as fuck, and I can't put my finger on what he's up to. Maybe it's the tequila taking over my brain, but I kinda want to torture the information out of him.

"It was nothing," he says, giving me a tight smile. "I was just…getting some advice. That's all."

Yeah, because that's not suspicious one-bit, Evil Ash. You can keep your secrets. Best believe, I'll find out soon enough. Ode tells me everything. At least, I think she does. My eyes narrow when I pull out my phone and shoot a quick text, earning only a devil emoji in return.

Traitor.

And I tell her so.

"Right. Advice…" I trail off as we head down the main road toward Central City again. "What exactly did they say to you?"

He shakes his head again, chuckling at my curiosity that will one day get me killed.

"Can I—" Asher hesitates a moment, his lips flapping like a fish out of water. "Um, can I take you to meet someone?" I blink several times through his rushed words, leaving him breathless beside me. "I mean, if you want to. I'd really like to introduce you to someone important to me," he murmurs with uncertainty.

"Meet someone?" I ask, raising a brow of suspicion.

"Yeah. It won't take too long, I wanted to stop by before we left town to say hi to her. I, um, haven't seen her since I left." He swallows hard, with a glossy sheen taking over his hazel eyes. "I want her to meet Lyric," he whispers, sinking his teeth into his bottom lip, stopping the sudden quivering.

"I want to meet her! Who's her?" Lyric chirps, leaning forward, clutching the new white bunny Ode gave her as an early birthday present.

From the once dismal expression to something only the sun could conjure, Asher's entire face lights up with a wide grin, exposing his teeth. For the first time in a long time, I see the delight written in his expression and fluid movements.

Whatever we're about to do, lifts the weight of everything off Asher's shoulders, making him whole.

"First, we need some flowers," he says softly. "Then, we can meet her. I promise."

"Flowers?" she questions, furrowing her brows. "I love flowers," she says, cocking her head with curiosity as the car zooms down the empty road on our way back to the city that made us.

"Flowers," he confirms, pulling off the main road and into a tiny gravel parking lot.

A few older model cars rest around us, unoccupied. One license plate reads—flowers2233, attached to a large van with the Central Florist Shop logo painted on the side with beautifully crafted purple, pink, blue, red, and white flowers decorating the entire van. Even the hubcaps have been touched by the bright and cheery colors.

My head pounds as I rest it against the window, staring at my surroundings. "A florist shop," I surmise, glancing over at Asher, who nods.

"She loved this place." He doesn't take his eyes off the front of the shop, directly in front of us. "Her favorites are in there. Roses," he says cryptically, not bothering to mention the name of the woman we're speaking about, which, again, kills my curiosity.

I'm so damn desperate to understand what's going on, but something about the way Asher peacefully stares at the shop eases all my wonderings.

"You can stay here if you'd like," he murmurs, side-eying me until I nod. This seems like something he needs to do all on his own. "But can I take her to help?"

My heart explodes when he stares at me earnestly until I nod. "Of course. Ly, you want to help Daddy pick out flowers?"

"Yes!" she gasps, hurriedly undoing herself from her booster seat.

"Thank you," he breathes, reaching over to squeeze my hand. "We'll be right back."

"Of course," I murmur, gluing my eyes to his loose movements as he removes himself from the car with a smile pulling at his lips.

Who is this Asher? He's a completely changed man from even a month ago. I'm not complaining one bit. The old Asher was a rigid asshole who put me through the damn ringer with his attitude. This is the same Asher who manipulated everyone around him to achieve his dream and leave his abusive father.

But this new Asher. Dear God… I could see myself falling, madly, deeply, head-over-heels, in love with him.

Something weird happens inside my body, like my ovaries exploding, when he gently helps her out of the car with that grin plastered on his face. Light captures his hazel eyes when he bends down, coming eye level with her. His long fingers run through her hair, tucking it behind her ears with a chuckle as they whisper things to one another.

"Have fun," I rasp, waving my goodbye as they set off on their little adventure.

Butterflies burst in my stomach when he takes her tiny hand in his, swinging their grip back and forth. I touch a hand to my lips, watching Lyric's mouth move a million miles a minute. Every ounce of darkness flees from her face like there isn't a worry in the entire universe. Right now, her world is Asher Montgomery.

Asher's shoulders relax as he clutches her tiny hand, nodding his head to whatever she's saying. He grins more, opens the door for her, and follows her inside. It's like they've had these outings a million times before. This is our new normal.

The moment they disappear, tears burn the back of my eyes. I squeeze them shut, refusing to let any tears fall down my cheeks. Happy or sad. It doesn't matter. Despite the need to purge my emotions, a warmth spreads across my chest. Tingling courses through my veins, and a weightless feeling lifts me.

All I ever wanted was Ly and her dads. Them taking her places. Wanting to be there for her and listen to her when she needs them. She's always wanted them by her side; now, she's getting her wish.

I blow out a breath when they leave the store side by side. Ly clutches two small bouquets of dark pink, light pink, and white flowers—one in each hand and a shit-eating grin taking over her lips. Once again, Asher helps Ly get into her new booster seat, carefully strapping her in with furrowed brows.

"Mommy, I picked out the most beautiful flowers! Here, smell," she squeals, bouncing in her seat before shoving the flowers directly into my face.

I flinch back from the petals hitting me in the face. The wonderful scent of roses hits my nose when I inhale, reminding me of the night I spent with Kieran in the rain with roses floating all around us. "They're beautiful, Ly," I chuckle, lightly shoving them away from my face. "You did a good job, baby."

Setting back in her seat, Asher finally straps her in with success as she babbles until he kisses her forehead. "I love you, Daddy." Her big eyes stare at him like he hung the moon for her.

Yup. There goes my heart. It's a melty puddle in my chest, beating rapidly when he beams.

"I love you too," he murmurs, softly shutting the door.

She preens, pulling the flowers into her nose and taking a big whiff. "Mmm, I think Grandma will like them. Do you think Grandma will like them, Mommy?"

"I'm sure Grandma will," I rasp, side-eyeing Asher again when he settles into the front seat, unable to look at me.

"Flowers for grandma?" I murmur, resting a hand on his forearm and gently squeezing until his eyes snap to mine, dilating the littlest bit from the warm contact. Electricity zaps through my fingertips, running straight to my toes from the slightest touch of his flesh. My hairs stand on end when his eyes fall on our connecting flesh, and he swallows hard.

He shudders at the contact, the briefest hint of a blush pinkening his cheeks. "Flowers for both grandmas," he murmurs. "Our mothers are both at the same cemetery."

The world stops moving. I freeze in place, letting his words knock around inside my brain. My mother. His mother. They're in the same damn place?

"Oh, Asher," I breathe, pressing my fingers to my trembling lips. "The cemetery?" I lamely ask with a rock stuck in my throat.

"We weren't there for you when it happened. I feel—" His grip tightens on the steering wheel as his chest expands. Heavy breaths pour from between his parted lips as his body loosens more. "I feel so fucking responsible for you not having the support you deserved. It was me. I did that. We should have been there for you and held you. Let you cry on our shoulders. Rad could have made some ridiculous apple pie and any comfort food you needed. And…and…we weren't there." Asher blows out a shaky breath. "It may be a little late, but that's what we're doing now."

"Yay! Grandma gets flowers!" Lyric sings, swaying in her seat. "I can't wait to give them to her." She continues babbling, not comprehending what we're about to do.

I've had this talk with her before. She constantly questions where my mommy is and why she's not here. I've explained to her by pointing to the bright orb hanging out in the darkened sky that she's with the man on the moon. She left this world because she was sick, and now she watches us with a smile. Sometimes it's hard to explain to a four-year-old that my mom is never coming back to meet her.

"Jesus Christ," I rasp through the razor blades sitting in my throat every time I swallow.

"That's okay, right?" Asher asks, pulling out of the parking lot with concern twisting his face. "I can just take you back to Cal's, and you can do it privately if you want. Take the flowers and do what you want with them. I'll call the boys and tell them you need this time to yourself."

"Please take me there, Asher," I whisper through the tears heating the backs of my eyes. "I want to do this with you."

And I do. Every molecule in my body settles at the thought of visiting these graves with him.

It's been five years since I faced my mother. The moment they lowered her into the ground was the hardest day of my life. I had my found family with me that day. I cried on their shoulders. But when I went home all by myself with no one to pick up the pieces, I fell hard.

When I was pregnant, I made a vow to visit my mother any chance I could. I'd sit in the sun and talk to her, letting her know about Ly and what was happening. I've celebrated her life from far away for too long. It's time to face her again and tell her everything that's happened while she's been away.

AS WE TRAVEL CLOSER TO THE CEMETERY, I CAN'T LOOK AWAY FROM THE man I once saw as a monster. My enemy. The man who took everything away from me with one little lie. He's no longer the man he once was. Not at all.

My gaze eats him alive, taking in every inch of his profile and memorizing them. My eyes trace the tired lines, old bruises, and scrapes I had missed. A few scars line his cheeks and neck, falling beneath his tight black T-shirt.

Were those there before? From his father? From something else?

"Wow!" Lyric proclaims, knocking me out of my thoughts as we travel beneath the iron banner, welcoming us to the last place I ever thought I'd be.

Central Cemetery hasn't changed much since I was here last. Gray stones peek above the trimmed grass. Bright flowers sit all around in memoriam for loved ones lost. Tall mausoleums with last names carved into stone sit on the horizon in various spots.

"Is this where the dead people are?" Lyric asks, swallowing a lump in her throat. Her curious eyes dart across the stones passing by in slow motion.

"Buried here, yes." I watch her shuddered expression closely as she nods.

"No zombies, Mommy?" she whispers frantically, searching her surroundings. "Daddy Rad and me watched zombies, they eat people's brains."

"Did he?" Asher asks with a disappointed head shake. "Idiot," he murmurs quietly, enough so she doesn't hear.

"We're going to have to give your daddy a parenting class on what four-year-olds should watch," I say, shaking my head in disbelief. One dad always throws on a horror movie for a child who shouldn't be watching it, and that dad is Rad.

"And say," Asher chuckles, unclenching his fists.

My heart pounds when the car stops near the row my mother is buried

in. I eye the names etched into the marble with interest, bouncing from one to the other.

Baker. Jones. Hogan. West. Montgomery.

Right there, under the dirt, rests her corpse. Still dressed in the same outfit Korrine and Ode helped me pick out—a dress she loved to wear in the sunshine. A simple headstone poking out of the ground with her name, date of birth, and inscription indicates where she rests eternally.

Loving mother and friend. Gone too soon.

What an understatement that is. If it weren't for her autoimmune disease, she'd still be around, watching Lyric grow.

It's odd that I vaguely remember the day I stood in the sunshine, watching for the last time as my mother's body rested above ground. Her old and new friends gathered around, taking flowers from a large bouquet on her oak casket. Tears fell. Laughs echoed through the large cemetery in her memory. Some good. Some bad. Everyone remembered my mother in a positive light.

As for me? I was utterly frozen, running my fingers over the smooth wood, begging her to come back for one more day, just for a few more hours. There were so many unsaid words and declarations.

My brain was fogging in chaos, trying to digest what had happened. My mother fucking died. The boys left me without a word or goodbye. And I was carrying their child. To say my thoughts weren't in the present was the understatement of the century.

I was a million miles away, but my feet were still in the same spot.

I knew she was in a better place. Or so they say. Her MS wouldn't bother her anymore. She would be free from the complications of life. But it didn't stop me from aching for one more hug. One more kiss on the temple. One more, 'You did good, Riv.' Just a single chance to tell her that I loved her and wished her well.

Fuck. I miss my mom.

My mother may not have been the best human being on the planet. She worked hard when I was a kid—left me to my own damn devices. But I still loved her. Always will. I reread the names, going down the line until my heart plummets into my ass at the realization.

Baker. Jones. Hogan. West. Montgomery.

I blanch, turning to look at Asher. He stares out my window, locking on the tallest headstone at the end of the row. Shade trees block out the sun, blanketing our moms in beautiful darkness.

"They're…" I swallow hard, shaking my head.

"I can't afford this," I whisper to the funeral home director. *"I can't."*

"You don't need to, Miss West," he says softly, eyes brimming with understanding.

"I don't understand. Why was she brought here? I told them… I…" I

squeeze my eyes shut, leaning back in the chair across from him at his mahogany desk.

"It's all been taken care of. An anonymous donor donated the plot, and the funds have been raised for the funeral. It's just enough," he says, sliding a piece of paper across the desk.

"But why would—"

"It was you, wasn't it?" I whisper with tears streaming down my face. I swear, since I had a child, I have cried like a baby at everything. It doesn't fucking matter the circumstance. "The donated plot? The funds for the funeral?"

"You asked for space, and I used that against you..." he trails off, looking over his shoulder at Ly playing with the flowers and lightly humming.

"Asher," I breathe. The roughness of his fingers beneath mine has me gasping for air when I clutch his hand. "You did all that for me? But why?" Why would he leave me and do something nice for me in return? Why would he do that?

"That was my plot. My father bought it in anticipation of my early demise. I... As much as I wanted to be buried next to my mother for eternity, I wanted to give it to someone who could use it more than me. Someone who deserved it. And that person was Stella. I raised funds for her funeral through Rad's parents. I...went to them for help, and the church stepped up. I just... What I did is inexcusable, and I made it up with everything I did. Your car—"

"Jesus, Asher. My car?" I gasp, clutching my shirt over my chest.

Stop. Fucking. Walking.

I remember the moment I walked outside as the snow started falling. Ode handed me her keys and told me to track down the guys using her vehicle. I had been walking since they fucking left me. Then, out of nowhere, I found my car with a wet note attached under the windshield wipers from an unknown person. I should have fucking known, but I didn't question it. It was a gift from someone anonymous.

And I used it every day after that.

"It never gave me problems after that, Asher. What did you have fixed?" I murmur through more tears, trying to hold them back. My goddamn emotions are everywhere lately. It all has to do with the four men who have, once again, broken down my carefully constructed walls. They're the damn masters of destruction and rebuilding.

Redness takes over his cheeks. "I did what any person would do, Little Brat. I fixed everything so you could have something reliable. And I'm glad I did. If you wouldn't have had that for Lyric..."

"But I did," I whisper. "It was the greatest gift you could have given me while I was pregnant."

"Why don't we take a walk," he whispers, nodding out the window toward the headstones. "Lyric, you want to put those flowers in both your grandmas' vases?" He clutches my hand as he speaks softly to Ly.

"Yes!" she squeals, scrambling to remove herself from her booster seat.

The warm sun heats my skin the moment I step out of the car, helping Lyric jump from the vehicle. She giggles as she clutches the flowers, one bouquet in each hand.

"I can't wait to give these to my grandmas!" Her grin brings more tears to my eyes.

"You understand, don't you, baby? That your grandmas aren't living. That they're somewhere different than Earth?" I ask, crouching down in front of her. "Sometimes humans get sick and only get better when they leave Earth for better places."

Bloated tears gloss Lyric's eyes when she nods in understanding.

"Daddy told me." She sniffles, staring into the bright colors of the flowers. "But Daddy said both grandmas were smiling down from the sky, watching me. So, I wants to talk to them." She gives a firm nod, full of four-year-old determination. "I wants to give them flowers and kiss their stones. Daddy said they'd like that lots."

"They would, baby," I whisper, tucking a piece of her dark locks behind her ear. "They really would." I kiss her forehead before I stand tall.

"Lead the way," I quietly say to Asher, who nods, putting a hand on Ly's shoulder, and leads the way toward the graves we haven't been to in years.

It's funny that Mrs. Montgomery was here as I mourned my mother. How many times did Asher stand in this exact spot with tears in his eyes?

"You can put them in here," Asher murmurs, directing the flowers to the tiny vases connected to the base of each headstone.

"And grandmas will get them where they are?" she asks, kneeling before my mother's grave, clinging to both bouquets.

"Yes, Ly," I softly say, kneeling beside her. "You remember Grandma Stella, right? She was my mommy, and she died when she got really sick. Her body couldn't take it anymore, so she went to meet her maker." I kiss her head when she sniffles again, placing the first flower bundle into the vase.

"What about your mommy?" Lyric looks up at Asher with those big puppy dog eyes as he rests beside her, leaning against his mother's headstone a touch away.

He smiles. "Kathryn Montgomery. She was the best cook," he chuckles, rubbing a hand along his chest. "I got my hair from my mommy, just like you did yours."

Ly wrinkles her nose. "Mommy says I gots daddy's hair," she murmurs, running her hand through her hair.

"Every morning, my mom got up early and made pancakes. Sometimes, I'd sneak in and help. We'd add anything we wanted. Blueberries, chocolate chips, and caramel chips. She loved cooking and playing with me." His eyes drift upwards, examining the fluffy clouds blowing in the wind.

"What happened to your mommy?" Ly whispers, shuffling toward Asher with the flowers outstretched.

Emotions choke my throat at her simple question. She's been desperate to know all about them, and finally, she's getting the answers she's been seeking.

Asher pulls her into his lap, leaning against his mother's headstone together. Running a hand through her long hair, he kisses her cheek.

"My mommy was very sad," he whispers with a tortured expression twisting his face. But he doesn't show it to her. He keeps all his emotions hidden from her inquisitive eyes, except for the tears. "She got very sick, too. For some reason, she left this earth. But I know she loved me."

I'm frozen with a heavy tongue. Unable to utter a word as I watch them together.

"I'll give her flowers now," Ly sniffles again, crawling off his lap and planting herself in the grass. Reaching over, she places the last bouquet into the vase with a tiny smile. "Hope you like your flowers, Grandma," she murmurs, kissing the granite.

"I think she will, Little One," he says, leaning forward to kiss her cheek until she grins.

Warmth fills every molecule in my body as they continue to converse one-on-one. Lyric watches him intently, absorbing every word he utters about his mother and the stories he tells.

The sound of crunching rocks pulls my attention away from them and onto another car stopping behind ours. One by one, the other guys get out with suits plastered to their bodies and flowers in their hands.

My fucking heart stops at the sight of them slowly walking toward us with varying expressions.

"Oh, Pretty Girl," Rad murmurs, sitting beside me in the grass, not bothering to keep his new suit clean from stains. "I'm so sorry you had to come and do this all by yourself. I fucking loved Stella. She was so damn bossy," he tsks the last part jokingly.

His fingers brush against my jaw, sending shivers down my spine. Without hesitation, I brush my lips against his, capturing him in a simple kiss, trying to convey my thanks.

"I think she liked you guys, too. She even called you 'good guys,'" I chuckle, pulling back with admiration in my heart. "Thank you all for being here. This… It means a lot to have you here."

Kieran sighs, sitting on my other side, tossing an arm over my shoulder. The tips of his fingers brush up and down my upper arm, eliciting goose-bumps over every inch of my flesh.

"She was a good lady," Kieran says solemnly, staring at her name etched into the granite with his brows furrowed. "She tried her hardest."

"Yeah," I murmur, leaning my head on his shoulder. "She tried the best she could." And that's all that matters to me. She was there. Sometimes. Whenever she could be, at least. I had a roof over my head, food in my belly, and determination in my veins. If there's anything my mom did for me, it was to prepare me to work hard.

Life isn't roses and rainbows with pretty sparkles. It's muted grays, blacks, and whites with struggles.

"Here, Little Star. These are for you," Callum murmurs, falling to his knees to complete our little circle.

I smile, reaching for the pretty white roses bundled together. Inhaling deeply, I catch their scent and hum.

"Thank you," I whisper into the petals, squeezing my eyes shut.

"I've prepared some words," Rad says, clearing his throat. I peek an eye open when his tongue pokes out as he searches through his suit pockets. "Ah-ha," he murmurs, pulling out a white piece of paper with scribbles. "Pretty Gir… River," he says, choking back tears as he takes my hand. "Stella was the most magnificent woman, besides you, of course."

"And me, Daddy?" Lyric asks with a tiny voice.

"Of course! You, too, Little Pretty Girl. You're the most important girls in my life!" he proclaims with a grin, staring between us. "And I wouldn't give you up for anything."

"Even unicorn ice cream?" Lyric whispers, leaning in. "Cuz I love unicorn ice cream."

"I love it, too," he says, grinning from ear to ear. "But I'd give up everything to be by your side, Little Pretty Girl. And your mommy's, too."

Be still my beating heart.

"I really only knew Stella as a kid," Kieran says, squeezing my shoulder. "If it wasn't for her, I wouldn't have had you. Those days and nights on the hill, strumming my guitar with you at my side. They meant the world to me. Stella worked hard. She was nice as hell, giving the shirt off her back. That one time when she fell and hurt herself in the bathroom, I was so shaken up thinking that she was dead. My heart hurt for her and you," he murmurs, kissing my cheek. "It's a shame that she had to leave this world."

"That shit was scary," Rad murmurs, shaking his head. "I think my heart fell out of my chest when we found you crying at your front door. Stella was so hurt, and I knew I had to call my mom to get her some help."

"You talked to her lately?" I ask, squeezing his hand.

"Nah. Haven't talked in a while. She disapproves of the rock star lifestyle. It is what it is. I don't need a negative Nancy in my life, anyway. Besides, I already have a family."

"You do," I whisper, leaning forward to kiss his lips again. "We're a family," I murmur. He grins against my lips until I'm ripped away by Kieran, who pulls me back into him.

"She knew I snuck into your room every night," Callum murmurs with a hint of a grin, pulling at his lips. "Caught me one night," he chuckles.

"She did?" I ask, raising a brow.

"Yeah," he breathes. "I had to go to the bathroom, and she was out in the hall with her arms crossed. She asked me if I was one of the boys making you happy?"

"What did you say?" I ask, staring into the depths of his gray eyes.

"I said… Yes, but the feeling was mutual. You made me so damn happy. So, she nodded and walked away from me toward the living room."

"She was always really nice to me," Asher mumbles, scratching across his chest. "I don't think I was over there as much as you guys, but she always smiled at me when I was by." He swallows hard, looking deep into my eyes. "I'm so sorry you lost her like you did. Especially after being away with us at the Castle house."

"Castle house? I wanna go to a castle!" Lyric pipes up, reminding us of what happened at that damn house.

Her.

Kieran chuckles. "Maybe we can vacation to an actual castle sometime soon. Okay?"

"Yes, Daddy! I want swords and armor! I want to sleep in a castle like a princess." She grins when he chuckles, ruffling her hair.

"Of course, Little Blue. Anything for you."

"Thanks, guys. For coming here with us and for bringing flowers. It means a lot you're here now," I whisper as more tears well in my eyes.

"We missed it the first time, Pretty Girl. So, here we are now. We wanted to celebrate Stella's life."

"And Katy's," Kieran murmurs, locking eyes with Asher, who stiffens.

"Thanks, man," Asher murmurs, rubbing a hand across his chest. "Means a lot."

"She was your mom, bro. I never knew Katy, but I'm sure she was the bomb," Rad proclaims.

"She made daddy pancakes, too!" Lyric giggles. "Just like daddy makes me." She beams when he grins.

"All right, River Blue. How about we all go out for a nice dinner?" Kieran asks, looking around at the boys, who nod.

"Pizza?" Lyric asks with hope.

"If that's what you want, Little Blue. We can go to Tuscany. They've got it all. Pizza, pasta… Whatever your heart desires."

"Yay! Let's go!" she shouts, jumping up as we all rise. Grabbing hold of Kieran's hand, she drags him back to his car as the others follow.

"Asher," I whisper, clinging to his arm as he stops dead.

"What's up?" he questions, swallowing hard.

"I want you to know something," I whisper, moving into his space. We stand chest to chest. Our breaths hitch together.

"What is it?" he questions with furrowed brows. "Are you okay? Did I cross a line? I didn't mean—" The moment my lips touch his, he shuts up, staring at me with wide eyes until he relaxes. His fingers brush through my hair, desperately holding me close.

"I forgive you," I whisper against his lips. "Don't beat yourself up anymore. What you did is in the past. I'll remember it forever, Evil Ash. I'll remember how it made me feel. But I don't want to hold a grudge against you anymore. What you did sucked, but you're... You're so different, and I forgive you for what you did. I want to move forward with this relationship. You're so important to Ly... And to me." I swallow hard when his grip tightens in my hair, and a whine slips through his lips.

"Oh, Little Brat," he chokes out. "I really don't deserve that, baby," he whispers. "I fucked up so hard. I'm...so fucking sorry for what I did. I don't—"

"You deserve forgiveness, Asher. You did a bad thing. But it doesn't mean you're an evil guy. You were desperate. Your abusive father and stepmother were going to force you into something you didn't want to do. Could you have done it differently and talked to me? Yes. You could have. But, Ash. I'm ready to forgive. I feel it in my heart," I murmur, thumping a fist against my chest. "Are you ready to forgive yourself?" I whisper, putting my palm against his rapidly beating heart.

"Little Brat," he whispers with tears falling down his cheeks. "Yes. If that's what you want, I'm ready to move forward. But just know, I'll forever prove to you that what I did was the biggest mistake of my life," he whispers, cupping my jaw in his palms. "The biggest regret I'll ever have is leaving you behind. It was the dumbest thing anyone ever could have done."

"I believe you," I whisper, wiping away the tears on my cheeks. "Now, let's get some Italian food and continue going forward."

"One day at a time," he whispers, leaning in to brush his lips against mine again in a soft embrace.

"One day at a time," I whisper my declaration when he takes my hand, pulling me toward the cars.

The other three guys watch us with neutral expressions. Their arms are resting across their chest, taking us in as we walk up hand in hand.

"I forgive you all," I say softly. "I don't want this grudge to come between us anymore. I know it's only been a short time. Our time here on Earth is never promised. I don't want to go to sleep anymore with this anger I've held."

"We'll continue to support you both," Callum says, marching to me. "Every day, we'll fight the wrongs we put you through." Without a moment to second guess himself, he pushes his lips onto mine in an eager kiss. He hums, swirling his tongue against mine in desperation. "My first and last," he murmurs when we finally break apart. "My forever."

"We'll always show you, River Blue. We'll be here every day," Kieran chokes out, moving forward to capture my lips with his in a soft, dominating embrace.

"There's no getting rid of us, Pretty Girl. You can put a collar around my neck with your name as my girl. Forever and ever…" He kisses my cheek, grinning when Lyric makes a face.

"Gross," she says, wrinkling her nose.

"All right, how about some pizza?" Kieran asks Lyric, bringing her into his arms.

"Pizza! Pizza! Pizza!" she proclaims loudly, thrusting her tiny fist into the air with a giggle.

"And then after pizza, you're going to spend the night with Alma and Anni," I say, grinning when she whips her gaze toward me.

"Really?" she squeals.

"Really," I confirm with a nod as she wiggles excitedly in Kieran's arms.

"Really?" Rad asks with suspicion, narrowing his eyes.

"Yes. Because your daddies have a show, we'll be out soooo late!" I say, pinching her cheeks.

"What show?" Callum asks, tilting his head to the side as a slow smile spreads across his lips. "We do have the instruments."

"What? Where?" Rad begs, jumping on his toes.

"Where else would we go?" Asher snorts. "We're in Central City. There's only one place with our names carved into it." He smiles, chuckling.

"Fuck yes!" Rad whoops.

"Daddy, I think it's time you owe me money with every bad word you say. That'll be thirty-thousand dollars," Lyric says, holding her hand with an expectant look.

I snort. "Yeah, Daddy. Pay up…"

"But… But… Little Pretty Girl! That's a lot of money."

"Pay up, Daddy." She sticks her nose in the air, wiggling her fingers like he'll pay her right here and now.

"I'll add it to your college fund," he grumbles, high-fiving her hand.

I snort. "Responsible parenting," I commend, earning a grin. "All right, Whispered Words. Let's get some dinner and then—."

"Show time," Rad interrupts with jazz hands.

chanting below the stage. Her hands slap at my shoulders over and over, leaving a slight burn behind her hits.

"Stop," I cackle, lightly pushing her away from my side.

"But bitch!" she hisses, hitting my shoulder. "My bar." She shakes her head in disbelief as her dark eyes continually dart around. I swear tears form in her eyes as she chokes back a small sob.

Dead End is still an active place. It's a bar. People come from all over town to eat Leon's spectacular dishes, drink beer, and talk with friends. Even with my help in getting small bands to play every weekend—because yeah, this is my home. I can't leave them down and out with no options. From afar, no matter where I am, I'll always help out the place that gave me every chance under the sun. Still, they haven't been this packed since Whispered Words left the area.

But here they are in all their glory, slowly setting up their equipment in front of the large, cheering crowd. The volume rises with every person who enters with excitement running through their veins. Nothing beats a free pop-up show with no cover charge. Luckily for Leon and Ode, I'm footing the bill. And I wouldn't have it any other way. Besides, this was all Ode's idea.

"I think we might be over capacity," Ode murmurs in awe.

"You mean my bar," Leon chortles, handing me the biggest plate of chicken nachos I've ever seen.

"Yes...yes, his bar!" I quip, salivating at the plate steaming in front of my face.

"I will snatch those nachos away, you traitor!" Ode quips, coming in for my precious chips slathered in melted queso cheese, calling my damn name.

I haven't eaten since we went to an Italian restaurant a few hours ago. The food was amazing. Like out of this world orgasmic. Especially for Central City. Granted, it was on the edge of town near their old stomping

grounds. People stared and pointed as the boys walked in. And even more when I trailed behind them, scrunching my nose.

I've never been the type of person to care what others think about me. Where the hell would that get me? Nowhere. I am who I am. And my roots started in this very city. I'll always give back to the people and places that raised me from the ashes of my demise.

But Leon's nachos? Nothing beats them. Not even a five-layer lasagna with extra cheese and garlic bread at a snooty five-star restaurant. Especially when he adds creamy cheese on top with shredded bits of cheddar below, leaving it a melting pot of cheese, meat, and lettuce on top. It's his specialty he loves to call…

"You love my cheese-on-cheese!" he says, grinning as he leans against the bar, placing his elbows on the top. "This is so surreal, Riv. You. Them. All here again." He blinks several times, staring up at the now empty stage, devoid of human life. The only sign they were there is the instruments glistening in the blue and yellow spotlights. "They treating you right, baby girl?" he asks, raising a brow.

I shove a chip into my mouth, stuffing my cheeks. Nope. Nu-huh. Don't want to have this conversation again.

"She's afraid they'll leave her again," Ode, the loudest traitor, says. "Which I get, by the way. They were jackasses to the extreme. I still don't want to trust them."

Can't she see I'm stuffing my face and don't want to talk about this again?

"Give her some tequila; she'll spill everything," Ode, my former best friend, says with a menacing grin. I snort when she walks behind the bar, standing beside her brother. Reaching behind her, she grabs the most expensive tequila they have and slams it on the bar.

"Mmhmm," Leon hums, grabbing three shot glasses and filling them with tequila. "Take your shot." Sliding the small shot glass in front of me, he watches intently as I swallow my bite.

"Remind me why I call you family?" I quip, tapping a finger on the tiny glass filled to the brim with the devil's golden liquid.

"You love us," Ode says with a grin, holding up her shot glass. "Let's toast!"

"To my sister from another mister fighting for love and happiness," Leon says, grinning when we clink our glasses together.

"Weak toast," Ode grumbles, bumping her elbow into his ribs.

"It was perfect. Thanks, guys," I laugh, downing my shot.

It's time to let go of everything. My hurt. Anger. Resentment. I wash it away with the burning liquid scorching my throat. This is a new adventure. Our past may guide us into the future. But I'm so tired of looking back and remembering how I felt when they left without a word. I'm ready to forgive and move on.

Reaching across the bar, I grab the bottle of tequila and refill our glasses with a grin.

"Oh, Riv's getting wasted," Ode laughs, grabbing her filled glass again.

"This is to new beginnings. New adventures. The door to the past is closed, and I'm ready to open the new door to my future. Here's to us," I say, clinking my glass against theirs. Tossing my head back, I down the shot again, groaning at the slight burn.

"You got this, baby girl," Leon says, squeezing my hand. "Or I'll hide them in my basement." He grins, staring behind me as the crowd goes wild.

Butterflies fill my stomach when Rad pushes through the crowd. His grin lights up the room as he takes pictures with every person who asks him with joy until he gets to me. Those molten lava eyes catch mine, and he winks. He fucking winks, and my insides melt.

I blame the tequila.

"Is that nachos?" Rad asks, settling next to me on a bar stool with hearts in his eyes. "I love your damn nachos..." he trails off when he reaches for a piece. It's the hand slap heard across the world. Or that's what it seems like when he gasps. "Ouch, Pretty Girl. Sharing is caring!" he shouts with mock horror, putting a hand to his chest. "I swear we've had this discussion before. What's yours is mine, and what's mine is yours." He waggles his brows at the implication.

Where's that tequila? Because at this rate, I'm going to need the entire bottle to make it through tonight without doing something stupid. Like jumping their bones in the bathroom. Or reclaiming my office.

Calm your tits. No boning. Not right now. We're just now working on us and becoming an us again. Sex complicates everything.

Or makes you feel better.

Fuck my life. I blame this entire day on the amber liquid sloshing around in my stomach. It's always the tequila's fault.

"Yeah. It is. But I don't share my cheese-on-cheese nachos. Get your own." I give him my best stink eye, and he grins, rubbing his hands together.

"Yo, barkeep! I want some nachos," he says, playfully pounding a fist onto the counter.

Leon frowns, leaning forward with a sour huff. "I'm not your damn barkeep, Mullet. How many times do I need to tell you that?"

Rad pouts, batting his eyelashes. "My girlfriend is stingy and won't share. Won't you help a guy out and make—"

"An extra-large plate," Kieran says, sauntering up with a hungry look taking over his face. And not for me, either. His eyes fall to my plate, practically salivating over my damn food. "Smells delicious." He grins, swiping a loaded chip from my plate, and throws it into his mouth.

"Thief," I grumble, shoving another piece into my mouth and humming at the spicy nacho taste.

I could live on these damn nachos. All I have to do is pack Leon up—aka kidnap him—and take him with me so he'll make food every day.

"Oh my God, it's Kieran!" someone suspiciously familiar in the crowd shouts.

I stiffen at the sound of her voice. That scratchy, shrilly, annoying voice haunts my damn memories. Oh, snap. It couldn't be. Could it? My eyes dart around, searching for her mop of blonde hair. Several catches my eye, but none resemble her. Yet. If she thinks she has a chance, well, I'll show her my damn territorial side and claw her precious little eyes out.

My hands feel around the pocket of my jeans, and I grin when my knife sits snugly against my thigh. Yeah, come at me, Tessa Boo. I have a three-inch treat in my pocket, ready to drive you away.

Rad blinks several times. A look of horror opens his mouth into the shape of an O. He claps a hand on Kieran's shoulder, chuckling wildly.

"Sounds like you know who from high school…" he trails off, grunting when I suck cheese off my fingertips. "Pretty Girl. If I slather cheese on my cock, would you lick it off slowly?" He groans in a low voice, leaning forward to lick a line of cheese off the corner of my mouth. His moan vibrates against me, going straight to my pussy. Who flutters in anticipation. Fuck me. I need to push him away.

"I bite," I hum with satisfaction when he kisses the same spot again, working his way toward my cheese-lathered lips.

"It's okay, big man," Rad mumbles, adjusting himself. "She doesn't mean it." He taps his dick softly several times like he's petting a dog, giving me a lopsided grin.

"I do mean it," I quip, leaning toward him with my face toward his crotch. "But maybe I could slather him in cheese and—" A large hand slaps across my lips with a grunt.

"Shhh," Kieran grumbles. "Before you awaken more beasts." His eyes trail down his own front with a wicked grin. "I might like that, though," he whispers, flicking his tongue across my ear lobe as shivers roll through my body. "I could lay out as you slather my entire body in cheese and slowly lick it off." He groans, heaving in a breath. "Have I proven myself yet, River Blue? Have I made it clear that I'm the only worthy knight for you? Because I'm getting desperate here," he murmurs against my ear as his warm breaths cascade across my heated flesh.

Fuck. Me. Fuck. Tequila.

"You'll always be my knight," I murmur just loud enough for him to hear. "But getting on your knees for me again wouldn't hurt." I shrug when his eyes dilate.

"Good girl," he whispers, kissing my cheek. "I'll always get on my knees for you. Bloodied and bruised with lust in my eyes. You're my forever girl. I just wish I had realized that years ago." I swallow hard when his lips crash down on mine, shoving his tongue deep into my mouth. I have no choice but to moan into his mouth and pull him closer.

"God damn, that's hot," Rad murmurs, squeezing my knee.

"Don't make me get the damn hose," Leon grumbles. "I will spray you both and throw you outside. No sex in my bar."

I pull away from Kieran breathlessly, looking around. He pulls my head against his chest, cradling me there. Where I'm meant to be. In his arms and surrounded by him.

Kieran and I have always been in the fates. No matter who was there to tear us apart. We'll always find each other again. I feel it in the way my soul calls out to him. The way my heart attempts to push out of my chest when he's nearby.

Fuck. I think I'm in love all over again.

"No sex? You weren't here that night, we—" I slap a hand over Rad's mouth. His laugh vibrates against my skin.

"Unfortunately," Leon mumbles, scrunching up his face. "These walls are thin, is all I'm saying." He eyes each of us before making his way down the bar to help more patrons who wave money in his face.

"Well, duty calls. Love you, bitch. Play good tonight, boys. Maybe I can convince my stingy brother to cough up some extra nachos to go." She winks at us, sauntering away to help her brother man the bar. Along with the other servers meandering about and taking orders.

It's a busy ass night.

"Better cool it," Callum says, leaning in and stealing my food.

"I'm going to stab each of you with a fork," I hiss, missing his hand with my slap. He chuckles, slowly putting the cheese-soaked chip into his mouth.

Eating nachos shouldn't look so damn sexual. But here we are. I'm panting like a bitch in heat at the sight of the gooey cheese rolling over Callum's lips and onto his chin.

Don't lick it off. Don't lick it off. Fuck.

I reach up, rolling my tongue across his chin and onto his lips. He startles, gripping my waist hard.

"Little Star," he murmurs with lust-filled eyes dilating his pupils to the max.

"I dunno, Pretty Girl. I might like that. Or, and hear me out—I could stab you. With my dick. He's incredibly hard right now. You won't make me go on stage like this, will you?" He bats his eyelashes at me with a grin.

"Shut up," Asher laughs, reaching across and grabbing another chip.

"You are a buzzkill!" Rad proclaims, eating a bite of my nachos.

"I guess this is a communal plate," I grumble, taking another bite, no longer fighting their grabby hands.

"We have to fuel up," Kieran says with a smirk, taking another bite.

"We do have a big show ahead of us," Asher surmises, sitting next to Rad.

"The biggest one yet." Callum smiles, kissing me again. "I can't get over this," he murmurs against my lips. My fingers play with the shaggy blond strands at the back of his neck.

"Over what?"

"That I get to kiss you whenever I want now. No more dreaming of having my lips on yours and wondering if it feels the same."

"Well, does it?" I ask, raising a brow.

"Does it what?"

"Feel the same?"

"Better," he whispers, kissing my lips again, lingering for longer than necessary as the world disappears. It's only me and him standing amid the crowded bar. His warm hand wraps around the back of my neck, locking me in his grip. Not that I'd want to escape. "Kissing you is coming home. It's my peace in the darkness of chaos. You ground me and make me better."

"Marry them!" Ode says in passing, passing drinks to the guys.

"I agree, Pretty Girl. Marry us!" Rad waggles his brows.

"Maybe someday," I quip, shoving the last nacho into my mouth.

Fuckers ate all my damn food. I side-eye their oblivious asses with disdain.

"Later," Leon says with a grin, pointing to my plate as he takes it from the bar and hands it to another worker.

"Someday?" Rad asks with wide eyes, sitting rigid in his chair. "I'll ask again tomorrow and the next day and the next day after that. I won't stop begging until you become my wife."

"Our wife," Kieran mutters, reaching for a nacho and sighing. "We ate them all," he grumbles.

"Yeah, you assholes ate all the good nachos. That's grounds for divorce. Now, don't you have a show to do?" I ask, playfully folding my arms across my chest.

A lightness takes me over as we grin at one another. It's as if the past didn't happen. And we're back to where we started, like a full-circle adventure.

We'll build and build until our future is secured on trust and love—a steady foundation.

We'll never be perfect. We'll fight. Shout. And make-up again. For some reason, I can't ever get these four men off my mind.

MY EARS BLEED WITH THE CROWD'S ENTHUSIASTIC SCREAMS AS THE BOYS take the stage.

"Hello, Central City!" Kieran shouts through the microphone, heaving a breath.

I won't mention the way his tight T-shirt clings to his sweaty chest, highlighting his delicious and defined pecs. Or, you know, the way his tight jeans outline the package he's smuggling. Nope. I won't mention it at all. My lips are sealed…

"You want more tequila, horndog?" Ode asks, slapping my shoulder with a giggle, knocking me out of my horny thoughts.

My face heats, creeping down my neck. I'm sure I look like Rudolph, the red-faced whore, by now. I grunt, covering my face with my hands.

Again, I blame the tequila.

"Who are you calling horndog?" I ask, pushing my shot glass toward her as the boys continue speaking to the crowd with excitement.

More screams and shouts, chanting their band name over and over again.

"We're happy to be back where all the magic started!" Rad chimes in, kicking his bass drum with excitement.

"You all are in for a treat tonight. We've been working on some new pieces." Wait, what? I turn on my stool, staring at the man grinning on stage. He sends me a goddamn wink as he saunters around, hyping up the crowd even more. That's the Kieran I remember.

"They have new music?" Ode asks over the shouting.

I shrug. "I—"

"You had no idea," she surmises, pouring me another shot. "Well, here's to bigger and better things from those dick faces." She clinks her glass against mine again.

"Bigger and better," I giggle, letting all my inhibitions go as Kieran belts out the first note of the first song he ever sang under this roof.

Twirling in my chair, nostalgia presses heavily on my chest. The first

time I saw Kieran after high school was on that very stage. He sauntered, eating up the attention of their growing fanbase.

Like now.

He eats it up, smiling at them, soaking up their screams. I swivel my eyes toward the door girl sitting in her seat, staring at the men on stage with raw hunger.

Yeah, they're fucking hot. And fucking mine.

That was the same spot all those years ago. Where I sat and watched with my heart in my throat, begging Kieran to recognize me. Just once. I wanted to hear him call me Blue and kiss me and tell me he missed me.

Dead End is where it all started for us. From the moment I sent that email asking them to play, I sealed my fate. From the frantic fucking against Booker's desk with an audience behind us. To that moment we walked into the Castle house on the lake in Missouri and left changed people, leaving me with a little present I'd come to love. Never regret.

Our story isn't a short book. It's long. Fucking tragic. Filled to the brim with angst and betrayal. It's four hundred thousand words of our start, our middle, our tumultuous end. Bringing us to the unexpected reunion. The tears, shouts, fights, and finally—our new beginning.

We've come full circle.

In the very place that started us. This is the story of Whispered Words and the girl they so desperately loved, forgot, ruined, and pieced back together. Only this time, I'm getting my happy ending.

No matter what.

Fuck. Tequila makes me horny and sappy. I need another goddamn drink before I shed some tears.

"Another," I rasp, turning back to Ode, who grins, watching my misty eyes with fascination.

"You've got it so bad, girl," she says, leaning in so only I can hear her. "Make them make it count this time. If they fuck up…"

"They won't." At least, I hope not.

"No," she says, filling my shot glass. "They wouldn't dare fuck it up again. You know why? Because they've got it bad, too. Even worse than before."

I nod in agreement.

Taking another shot, I watch with hearts in my eyes as they continue their set into two more familiar songs. The crowd waves their hands in the air. Phones come out of pockets, recording their free show. People shout their names individually, gaining their smiles.

Kieran huffs breathlessly into the microphone, wiping the rogue beads of sweat dripping down his forehead.

"Central City! You guys are amazing! You enjoying the show?" he shouts, earning yells of approval. "Good! It's so damn good to be back here!" He grins more, showing off his pearly whites. "You all know this is where we started. Right on this stage."

"Hell yeah!"

"You're amazing, Kieran!" that annoying, familiar voice shouts again. I swear if she shows her tits, the new door girl is going to have to walk her out before I beat her eyeballs in.

"Careful, Green Monster," Leon quips, squeezing my shoulder. "I can kick her out if you want. But this is probably the most exciting thing that's happened to her since she had kids."

I wrinkle my nose, finally glimpsing Tessa in her short shorts and tube top. She looks the exact same as back in the day. Blonde hair. Pearls. Lean body. And a beautiful snarl twisting her face.

"Someone mated with her?" I snort.

"Jesus, how drunk are you?" Ode asks, passing by with drinks in her hands.

"Little," I giggle, holding my fingers together.

"Yeah, she has three little spawns running around. She got married to some old, rich prick four years back," Leon says with a shrug. "Take care of yourself, baby girl. Maybe no more tequila for you."

"Tequila lets my girl live the damn life she's craving. Let her drink more so she can go home and get dicked down in the darkness by four hunky rock stars who look like they want to eat her alive," Ode says, sliding the entire bottle of tequila in my direction. "Have at it, bitch. Drink all the drinks. But don't regret a damn thing in the morning."

"No regrets," I say, lifting the bottle to my mouth and down a mouthful.

"That's my bitch," Ode chortles, running off to more patrons.

"River West!" I startle when the sound of my name rings through the entire fucking bar over the speakers.

Oh, no, he didn't.

"Yeah, you, Pretty Girl," Rad cuts in with a grin, waggling his long finger at me.

"Make way," Callum says softly into the microphone, echoing his timid voice through the bar.

The crowd hushes. Their eyes dart around, searching for the person they're calling. Meanwhile, I'm trying to find a cool new place to hide so they can't find me.

"Come on, River. Don't be shy now," Kieran's deep voice pulls me to my feet.

"Fucking hell," I grumble, thrusting my bottle of tequila into the unsuspecting bartender's hands. "Don't let anyone drink that."

"You're River West," she blanches, looking me up and down with wide eyes. "You're a goddamn legend around here."

Legend. Huh. I kind of like that. I thrust my shoulders back and put my chin in the air. I'd look smooth if I didn't trip over my damn feet two steps away from my stool. The room spins. It's either from the copious amounts of tequila I've been drinking. Or…it's the four heated eyes staring at me from the stage. Incinerate me now. Fuck.

Asher holds up a finger, placing his guitar down. "I got her," he says in a smooth voice, earning a grin from Kieran.

Somewhere along the way, the boys not only mended our relationship, but theirs, too. Maybe it was the extra therapy they've been diving into. Or maybe, they're finally healing something within themselves.

The crowd parts when Asher jumps down, making his way toward me with determination.

"How much tequila have you had, Little Brat?" he murmurs, hoisting me into his arms. My legs instinctively go around his waist, where I tighten them, bringing our centers together.

I squeal, clinging to his neck. "Not enough, Daddy," I whisper, blowing into his ear as he groans.

"I'll spank you if you keep that up. I can't go on stage saluting everyone. They'll know I have it bad for you." I shiver at his words, flicking my tongue against his earlobe.

"And do you have it bad for me?"

"So goddamn bad it fucking hurts. Now, stop squirming and be a good brat so we can play you a new song."

"A new song?" I ask, pulling back to stare into his eyes.

"Just for you," he says with a smile, stopping right before the stage. "Climb onto the stage, baby."

I swallow hard, letting go of my anchor, and drunkenly climb onto the stage. Somehow, I fall over my damn feet, straight into Kieran's waiting arms.

"No more tequila," he huffs at my flushed face, kissing my nose.

"But tequila—" I'm cut off when he places his lips on mine, stopping my words. Pulling back, a sparkle in his eyes has butterflies flapping and taking flight inside my damn stomach.

Hoots and hollers bring me back to the present after the world had completely disappeared. I swear, in this heightened state of drunkenness, their touches are unraveling every thread inside my body. Inch by inch. They'll pull and pull until I'm completely raw and naked before them.

"I want you all to meet someone special to us." Kieran's eyes don't drift from mine when the others close in on us.

Four hands touch my flesh. I'm done for. Absolutely fucking unraveled.

"This is the mother of our child," Rad says with a grin, pulling the microphone in front of his lips. "I know! We're daddies!" he says with a whoop.

"That's where we've been for the past month," Kieran says, putting his fingers beneath my chin. "We made a big mistake five years ago in letting this girl go. Something happened that tore us apart."

"Something that will never happen again," Asher says, kissing my cheek. "Never fucking ever again."

"So, this is our official notice," Rad pipes up. "We're officially off the market."

"And committed to one girl only."

"Two," Rad corrects. "Our woman and our baby girl."

Deceased. I swear to fucking hell. I melt into a tiny tequila puddle right there on stage as they take turns kissing my lips after their very public proclamation. Their PR teams are going to have a fucking fit. My brothers will surely hear about this. Not that they'd care. But everyone in the world will now know, Whispered Words is mine.

And I am theirs.

"Here," Kieran whispers, pointing to a chair Ode drags to the middle of the stage.

"You bitch," I murmur, sitting my ass down. "Were you in on this?"

"What? Operation distract River with tequila so the boys could plan this epic humiliation. Yes, yes, I was," she laughs, sticking her tongue out at me. "Don't worry, though. I did my best friend duties. I've thoroughly threatened their balls. For real, this time. I even gave a demonstration. They turned a pretty shade of green." I snort when she strolls off stage, sneaking looks over her shoulder.

"All right, Central City. We want to play you something new. It's something we've been toying with for the last few weeks of practice."

I blanch. What? They've been writing music right under my nose? And I had no idea. I've been too consumed with my own shit that I didn't notice what they were doing.

"Want to count us in, man?" Kieran asks, looking over his shoulder at Rad, who taps out a softer beat than their normal material.

Asher joins with a quiet, slow guitar riff, reminding me of a lullaby. Callum's bass pipes in a second later with the same laid-back, softer tune.

You burst out of nowhere
Like a hurricane beating down my door.
Your tears.
Your laughs.
They're mine forever more.
There's no looking back, Babe.
Tiny lyrics come from the heart.
Out of nowhere
With no design.
Tiny lyrics seep through our souls.
Ride us a mile high.
The end is nowhere near.
The beginning is somewhere we'll start.

You see, Babe…
There's nothing tearing us apart
With lyrics in our veins.
In our walls.
In our fucking songs.
Lyrics is where we'll stay.
The end is nowhere near.
This is just our beginning.
Becoming crystal clear.

Am I crying? Are those tears pouring down my damn face? No. My damn eyeballs are sweating in front of hundreds of people. Good God. I can't stop them. Callum reaches down, pulling my face into his neck as I sob my fucking heart out.

I fucking hate tequila.

"Fucking hell, Little Star. My goddamn galaxy," he whispers, holding me close to his sweaty as-hell body. "I love you," he murmurs. "To the damn moon and back."

"I love you, too," I sob like an idiot. "But I'm never drinking again." His chuckles vibrate against me as I cling to him.

Kieran stops, breathing heavily into the microphone.

"So?" He eyes the silent crowd as they break out into hysterics, screaming his name. "It's a work in progress. We'll keep you posted on how it's going in the weeks to come when we get back to our roots and start this music thing over."

When I finally lift my head from Callum's neck, he stares into my eyes. Gently, his fingers wipe away the makeup, I'm sure I smeared everywhere from my emotional outburst.

Callum's grin lights up my world. Those gray eyes I could get lost in steal every ounce of oxygen from my lungs.

These boys drown me in the best damn way.

After another round of hot kisses in front of the crowd, I walk off stage, using the back exit to cool down. My thoughts race a million miles a minute as I pace the backstage area, heaving in several breaths.

This is real.

This is fucking happening again. I'm letting them consume every part of me. I'm fucking terrified in the best and worst ways. This could go sour. But as my chest caves in from the chaotic thoughts, I know I'm heading in the right direction with them. More than before. We were right for each other, but the timing was shit. We needed room to grow into the people we are now.

After I gather myself, my feet drag me down the hallway with more tequila on my mind. What? Don't judge me. I know I swore off alcohol before, but I left my bottle half empty in the arms of a bartender. It's calling my name. Especially after that song. Those kisses. Those fucking words Kieran belted out. Jesus, I'm a goner.

As I make my way down the darkened hallway, I grunt, running straight into a damn brick wall. "Jesus, sorry," I grumble, pushing my hair out of my flushed face.

I blink several times. My heart falls into my stomach. And not in the good way.

"Rivey, hey," he says with that same slimy grin plastered on his face. His eyes take me in from head to toe. Somehow, his hands are on my shoulders, steadying me from falling over. Gently, he squeezes, something brightening in his eyes at my proximity. Fuck. Cold shivers break out through me.

"Van?" I question, wrinkling my nose. "I thought you were in Europe or some shit," I blurt.

Alarm bells ring in my head for whatever reason when he shifts, shrugging nonchalantly.

"Mom is sick, so I came home for a visit. I saw a post online that Whispered Words was going to be here, so I thought I'd come to see the show. Didn't expect to see you, Miss California," he says with a big goofy grin, finally letting go of my shoulders when I bat him away.

An uneasy feeling floats around in my sloshing stomach. It's either the booze revolting against my stomach, or it's the creep standing before me.

Not much has changed since I left him all those years ago. Same hair. Same stupid face—as if he could change that. Not to mention that sickening grin I once thought was the best thing on the planet makes my stomach knot. How in the hell did I fall for this jackass when I was a teenager? Was it the thought of dangerous dating?

The last words he ever said to me before he fucked right off have haunted me since the moment he walked out of the record store I used to work at.

"I have every arsenal in my pocket for us to have a better future. You, me, and the baby…"

It's like I'm back in that record store, listening to him tell me all that bullshit about him going to Europe for an internship. And how delusional he was in thinking that Lyric was his.

"I just wanted to say how sorry I was for all the things I said and did. You know, back then," he grimaces, obviously still talking as I silently freak out. What else has he said since I've drunkenly stared at him with a blank look, lost in my thoughts? "I was a real creep, and I…just never got over you, I guess. I saw everything as an opportunity to get the girl I loved back. But I went about it all wrong. Sorry, I was such a fucking chump."

Chump doesn't even begin to describe what I feel for him. "Um… Yeah, sure. Nice to see you, but I've got a date with a bottle," I grumble, shoving past him.

"Nice bumping into you, Rivey," he says in passing, waving as he walks away from me without fanfare.

"So not nice bumping into you," I mutter under my breath, watching his every move. He stands at the back of the crowd with no expression lining his face as the guys continue their performance. He doesn't sway. He doesn't fucking move. He's a goddamn statue. Tension lies in the backs of his beady little eyes, raising the tiny hairs all over my body.

"The fuck is Donavan Drake doing here?" Ode asks in alarm, guiding me to the bar by the elbow.

"Being a creep as usual," I grumble, staring over at the place he stood and startling. "He's gone," I say with a shrug, blowing out a breath.

That was a close one. Shit. That's the last person I ever wanted to come face to face with, especially in this condition. I'm liable to say whatever the hell is on my mind. Like, fuck off, Van. Eat a snake, Van. Or my favorite, drop dead, Van. In fact, I should race over there and say that to him. He distributed our damn sex tape like it was a movie. Fucker.

"I'm going to sue his ass," I mutter under my breath.

"I haven't seen that asshole since he left Central City for work. Wherever that was," she says, shaking her head.

"In Europe, right? Veritas has been tracking his ass since my whole stalker fiasco started."

Her brows furrow. The color slightly drains from her face at the thought of my stalker. Thank fuck, that dickbag is dead and gone. I no longer have to look over my shoulder, wondering if some sicko is taking pictures of my every move.

"Yeah, I think so for the first year or so. Not sure what he did after that, but he got a job with his company. I think he travels or something. Fuck, I don't know. As long as he's not around here," she says with a shrug, handing me my bottle.

"Thanks," I say, taking another swig of the burning tequila, drinking the memory of Van away.

He's here doing his own thing. He can't hurt me anymore. Not when I'm living for the future. Not the stupid past.

Damn the consequences. I'll deal with them later. Naked. And freshly fucked. Because any man who writes a song clearly dedicated to me and their daughter deserves a little love between the sheets. A reward, if you will. And then, I'll get a nice reward.

"IT'S GOING TO RAIN," I WHISPER, STARING OUT THE DARK WINDOW OF OUR SUV, traveling down the road near Callum's home.

It's in the air. The smell of sweet rain floats through the breeze, infiltrating all my senses. My hair stands on end. My aching heart pounds rapidly against my ribs. All in tune with the weather changing at the drop of a hat. My eyes widen in awe as the wicked sky lights up, showing off the darkened clouds miles away, heading straight for us. There's nothing that compares to a Midwest storm on the horizon.

Soon we'll be soaked.

My head leans lazily on Callum's shoulder with his hand clutched tightly in mine. Every so often, he gently squeezes my fingers with his. Three times. Over and over. Conveying a message unlike any other—he loves me.

There's no denying the love we have for each other. All five of us. In some weird and twisted way, we care for and deeply love one another. Like we're meant for each other. No matter what we went through in the past. No matter how long we were apart, basking in our hate for one another.

This was always meant to be.

Some would say, it's way too quick. Way too soon to shout it from the rooftops. I'm so damn tired of living in the past and reliving the hurt I experienced. It changed me for the better. Helped me grow into the woman I am today. I'll never forget the way their betrayal hurt. I'll have my doubts. I'll cry and question them until I'm blue in the face. As long as they're there to ease the pain and constantly reassure me that we'll be okay, then I'll believe them.

But tonight, I want to live. Dance in the icy rain. Forget all my inhibitions for freedom. Freedom from my crippling thoughts of doubt. From the pain. From my stalker. From every little thing bogging me down.

Tonight, I want to fall into the arms of the men redeeming themselves for me. The ones who wrote that song. Who pulled me on stage, kissed the oxygen from my lungs, and told the world I was theirs.

I need this.

Rad's fingers trace up and down my jean-clad leg from my other side, bringing me out of my swirling thoughts. Judging by the trembling of his fingers, he's eager to lock me inside the house. How do I know? As soon as we left Dead End, he told me.

"I want to lock you in Callum's house for a month straight to get reacquainted with every inch of your curves. My tongue will own every piece of flesh... inside and out. I'm serious, Pretty Girl! Don't drunkenly giggle at me. Little Rad is going to punch a hole through my jeans if he doesn't get a taste of his obsession," he murmurs with a soft whine in my ear as we walk out into the night toward the SUV. The boys stand near the trunk, lifting their equipment in and securing it in place.

"Show me how much you missed me," I murmur, kissing his cheek. I saunter off toward the others, who watch me with heated expressions. Even in a T-shirt and jeans, they look at me like I'm completely naked and spread out.

Once again, mother nature shows off, illuminating everything outside in a quick flash. Ten seconds later, thunder rumbles, vibrating the car as we pull into the driveway of Callum's house in the middle of nowhere.

The dark trees swish in the wind, picking up speed ahead of the rain blowing in from the west. Rainy September days always mean the changing of the season is upon Illinois.

Thankfully, we're heading home tomorrow evening. Home. What a strange sentiment. Our home is no longer in this town. Central City is just another city. Another stop along the way. No. Our home is nestled in East Point. Somewhere. They'll still work on themselves in the band house for another five months. And I'll be across the street with Ly. At some point, we'll have to figure out living arrangements. I never intended anyone else but Lyric and I living in my home. It'll burst at the seams with all six of us living there.

The future is unavoidable. Scary, even. Will things stay like this? With each of them looking at me like I'm that plate of nachos? Or will we fall into a weird pattern once the forced proximity implemented on us vanishes? Only time will tell where our adventure truly ends.

I take a deep breath.

Fuck the future. Live in the now.

And right now?

It's just the five of us. Ly is at a sleepover until tomorrow morning.

Stay in the now. It's something I've repeatedly told myself through the years after falling victim to memories assaulting my mind.

Water softly pelts against the glass when Kieran throws the car into park in Callum's driveway, instead of pulling into the two-car garage. The dark house looms before us in all its empty glory.

"We'll load everything in tomorrow," Asher says, looking around the car for approval. "That way our things don't get soaked. It's coming down out there." He eyes the heavy droplets dripping down his window with furrowed brows.

He rubs his chin in that calculating way I'm used to seeing on him. Except now, Asher isn't using it against us to tear us apart. He's using his brain to unite us as one.

"Sounds good," Kieran agrees. "How are you feeling, River Blue?"

How am I feeling? I've drank my weight in tequila. Saw a boy from my past. Had a song dedicated to Lyric and me. Also, I sobbed in front of people. God, how embarrassing. I bet someone filmed it, too. My beautiful, snot-caked, tear-stained face will be on all the gossip sites by tomorrow. I can see it now.

River West fucking an entire band! Love declarations! How long will it last?

So, you know. Just fucking peachy. But instead of telling him the truth of how chaotic my emotions are whirling around inside of me. I simply say the first thing I imagined when the rain started falling from the sky.

"Like a dance in the rain," I say, mesmerized by the brisk rain drenching every inch of the earth outside, puddling on the grass.

The rain comes down so thickly it's like staring through static, unable to see your hand in front of your face.

"Must still be drunk," Kieran quips with a smirk.

Assface.

I wrinkle my nose. "You know what they say about people who assume things…"

"Makes an ass out of you and me," Callum snorts, completing my sentence.

Good boy.

"Exactly. So, no. I'm not drunk. I'm stone-cold sober," I grunt, extracting myself from between Callum and a reluctant, clingy Rad.

"Pretty Girl, come back," Rad whines, reaching for me as I plop on Callum's lap and open the door. "I need to feel your skin against mine." I raise a brow when he folds his hands together pleadingly. He even goes as far as pouting his bottom lip with a soft whine, trying to entice me back into the vehicle and near him.

"Calm down, psycho," Callum murmurs jokingly, intently watching as I waver at the open door. I may be perched on his lap, but he doesn't stop me when I look out into the wet world with wonder.

Little sprinkles mist, wetting my hand as I reach out, letting the cool rain soak my fingertips. Goosebumps rise across my flesh, and shivers run through me at the icy feeling crawling across my skin.

The beautiful sound of the rain pounding into the grass greets my ears like a symphony playing through the speakers, begging me to come and play. I extract myself from the car with a serene smile stretching my lips. Heavy droplets pound against my skull, dropping down my hair and soaking every inch of me. Tentatively, I take a few steps, letting mother nature thoroughly soak through my clothes. Through my joy, I swirl with my arms stretched wide, capturing the moment.

"Little Star. What are you doing?" Callum asks in a raised voice, clutching his seat.

I chuckle, throwing my head back. The bitter rain beats down on my face when I stick my tongue out and collect the drops in my mouth, swallowing mouthfuls of fresh water. This is living. Feeling. This is fucking breathing for the first time in so damn long. There's no work bogging me down. No heartbreak at the corners of my mind, haunting me.

I'm free.

My clothing clings to every inch of me, winding around my flesh like a second skin, stretching too tight and restricting my movements. My chest heaves. My fingers beg to tear into the fabric and remove it from the situation.

"Have you ever danced in the rain, boys?" I ask, lifting my T-shirt over my head with a grin, shivering when the ice-cold water pelts my bra-covered chest.

Water drips down my abdomen, making my stomach suck in from the chill spreading through me. No doubt I'll need a hot, steamy bath with four hunky rock stars after this. Maybe some hot coffee to ward off the chill. And then, a cuddle pile to end the night.

Without hesitation, I do the same with my socks, shoes, and my jeans. Leaving them in a heap in the muddy grass as I take a few steps back in nothing but my bra and thong.

I do a twirl with my arms out wide. This is what true freedom feels like. It's so damn liberating. Here I am in the middle of nowhere, nearly naked, with four sets of eyes glued to my every move. I swear, even through the sheets of rain, I see their eyes dilate with thick amounts of lust.

"I have," Kieran remarks through the commotion.

I stop my spin, grinning at his memory. It's funny how he forgot so much about me and our early childhood. Thanks to Nigel, Asher's father. Yet, in times like this, his memories sneak up on him and slap him upside the head, reminding him of the ghost he left behind in the apartments.

I grin. "It was summertime. A random warm rain had just come through. We were on the hill behind our apartment building. It was either we stay dry…"

"Or my guitar does," he marvels, scratching at his chin with a little chuckle.

"So, we chose your guitar to leave under the secret spot."

"Then you grabbed my hand and led me out into the rain," he says, blinking several times and watching me, curling my fingers in their direction.

"So. What do you say? Do you guys fancy a cold dance in the rain on our last night before we return to East Point?" I ask, moving to the center of the front yard with my arms stretched out wide. Leaning my head back, I take a deep breath.

A drum booms in my chest, knocking against my ribs when they sit in the car, darting their eyes at one another. After a few agonizing seconds, they slowly climb out, shutting the doors behind them with predatory intent in their eyes. One by one, they take their shirts, shoes, and pants off. Together, they collect my clothes and shut them in the SUV.

I suck in a breath at their unholy, ripped bodies on display for me and only me. Oxygen refuses to fill my lungs when they walk in unison toward me. No, not walking. They're stalking toward me with hooded eyes. Each of them looks like they're about to sink their teeth into my flesh and mark me as theirs. Fuck. Maybe that's what I want. You know, a wall of man meat decked out in muscles and tattoos. And they're all fucking mine.

Their feet squish in the grass, squelching with every step they take with vicious smirks lining their lips and eyeing each other when they finally stop before me. All their gazes fall on me, taking me in. Inch by miserable inch, flames lick at my flesh from the intensity of their stares. I no longer feel the icy burn of the rain—just the deep heat blossoming in my guts.

"This is for you, River Blue," Kieran says over the noise. "Everything from here on out is for you. For Lyric."

"We all agree," Asher says, blinking rapidly as raindrops collect on his eyelashes.

"Everything we do is for you, Pretty Girl."

"Never again will you wonder if we're in this," Callum says, licking his lips.

"We're all in, River Blue. And you'll never get rid of us now," he says, discreetly eyeing the other boys. They nod in unison.

The entire world flips on its axis and stops spinning. One by one, they fall to their knees in worship, staring at me with lust dripping from their eyes. More than lust. It's dedication. Once again, they're proving to me that they'll drop everything for me. Even to their knees in a time of uncertainty and chaos.

Fuck. My heart stops working. I'm a dead woman walking as I stare at them.

"What the hell are you doing?" I breathe, putting a hand on my chest.

"Kneeling before our queen," Kieran says, grinning when he sees my expression.

"Long live our queen!" Rad hoots, tossing his fist into the soaked air.

"What the fuck," I mutter. "You guys don't have to do that."

Although I had envisioned it a long time ago—them on their knees, begging me to forgive them for what they did. Only in that scenario, I turned my back on them with a humph. Back then, these boys could have done nothing to earn my forgiveness.

Oh, how the times have changed since they sauntered back into my life with cocky attitudes. They've proven themselves to me over and over again. There's no way I could turn my back on them. Not after everything we've been through.

Our tale is fucked up, but it's the kind of fucked up I never want to give up. No relationship is perfect, and we're the prime example. Not only because there are four of them and one of me, but because of the past.

Callum smiles, shifting his weight. "We told you we'd get on our knees for you." Wait…I don't recall this conversation. How drunk was I before? Shit. Did I demand this of them? "And you said you better, Little Star."

"Facts," Rad agrees with a grin.

Well, shit. Maybe I was drunker than I thought after the show. I slightly recall asking them to kneel in the back room. But that was for a completely different reason.

"This is our devotion," Asher says, clearing his throat. "We know you'll have doubts, Little Brat. We know you'll fall and break and cry. But we'll always be here to pick you up when necessary. We're your nets when you fall."

Be still my beating heart.

I blink several times, letting my stupid tears mix with the rain. "All in?" I croak, watching them as they nod in agreement. "You're seriously just… Wanting to dive back into this? Aren't you scared?"

"Absolutely frightened," Callum says, climbing to his feet. "You're not the only one terrified. I know you remember how it felt to have us leave you. And how it tore you apart to have those restraining orders handed to you. But I remember, too, Little Star. I remember how Van kissed you and how it broke me in two. I know he did it. Not you. You weren't to blame. But I'm working through that. I meant what I said on stage. You're my first and last. My one and only. I'll never look at another woman the way I look at you. My light in the darkness. My bright galaxy in this dismal universe," he mutters, capturing my face between his palms. The warmth of his body soaks through the coldness seeping into my aching bones.

"All in," I confirm, even when my gut squeezes with anxiety.

"All fucking in," Rad says from behind me, putting his warm hands on my hips. "The only Pretty Girl I see."

"Better than your groupies?" I hum in ecstasy when Callum's lips press against the side of my mouth.

"No one compares to you, Pretty Girl. Callum had his fighting. Asher had his music. Kieran had…his anger. I had them to try to forget about you. It never fucking worked. You're my girl. You always have been and always will be. I'm just so fucking sorry I sought—"

"No," I interrupt, turning in Callum's embrace to face Rad. Sadness pulls down his expression, and hurt flies through his dark eyes. "You don't have to be sorry. We were not together. You thought I cheated on you…

That's… It's all in the past, okay? We live for the now." My fingers delicately trace his jawline, holding him in my grasp.

"You're mine," he whispers, devouring my face with his lust-filled eyes, dropping down until they rest on my lips. "I'm going to kiss you now. Then, we're going to take you inside and fuck your brains out. Okay, Pretty Girl?"

"We've been hanging by a thread, River Blue," Kieran murmurs, caressing my cheek.

Shit. When did they all get off their knees and surround me? No matter. My pussy flickers to life at the sound of their promises.

"Is that a promise?" I murmur, darting my eyes to Rad.

His grin lights up the dismal weather, and he snorts. "More than a promise. It's a damn commandment now. Thou shalt pleasure River with tongues, dicks, fingers, and toes."

"Dude, no toes," Callum grumbles, pressing the warmth of his lips against my exposed neck, licking and sucking at the water still falling on us.

"No toes," I say, wrinkling my nose.

"But the commandment says," Rad whines playfully, gripping my chin between his thumb and pointer finger. "And whatever it says, goes."

"I really don't want toes near my—" My eyes widen when Rad cuts me off, thrusting his tongue into my mouth with a groan.

Rad's soft lips envelop mine, marking me as his when his moans vibrate, mixing with my own. You'd never be able to hear it over the roar of the rain still pounding down on us.

The caresses of his tongue glide against mine in a slow, sensual swirl, sending frantic sparks of desire through my body. Everything lights up inside of me, just like the lighting flashing overhead and sending shocks of electricity through every inch of my body. I melt into Rad like putty in his hands. Simultaneously, leaning into Callum at my back.

My breath quickens as the kiss hits an all new height, taking me fucking captive. My heart threatens to leap out of my chest when Callum grinds his hardness against my ass with a groan. His fingers curl around my waist as his warm breath brushes over my flesh. I nearly die when his teeth sink into the sensitive flesh of my neck, and an orgasm sits at the cusp of letting loose. And they've barely touched me.

When Rad pulls back, I chase his lips, eager for more.

"Let's go inside," Rad whispers, tightening his hold on my face. "Let's get you dried off and then wet all over again. I can't wait to show you my new piercings. You're going to love them, Pretty Girl. They're going to hit all the right spots deep inside your pussy." He grins with his eyes darting south, toward his dick straining against his boxers.

Right. His piercings. Something he's hinted at before. But now? I'm about to take the plunge.

"You're wet for us, aren't you, River Blue?" I gasp when Kieran's fingers pull my wet panties aside and thrust inside me. There's no running his fingers through my lips or testing it out. He went straight for the gold. And dear god, I flutter around him, yelling at the rain pounding down on me.

"Dude," Rad says when Kieran thrusts again, chuckling.

"Oh, fuck off," I mumble with a heavy tongue. "I haven't gotten laid in years." Orgasms, sure. But getting dicked down beneath the sheets with an actual man? Nah. I haven't had the time.

"Yeah, let's get her inside," Kieran says, kissing my cheek and removing his fingers. "Eyes on me, River Blue." My world collapses into little pieces when he shoves his fingers into his mouth, licking away my cum from his flesh with a groan. "How I've missed the taste of you." Flicking his tongue out again, he makes sure to swallow every piece of evidence glistening on his fingers. His eyes dilate to almost black. And I swallow hard when my eyes fall on his dick, standing at attention.

I yelp when Callum turns me around, picking me up without effort. His hands grip my ass tightly as he marches toward his clothes and digs out his keys. Before I know it, we're in the safety of his home, but he doesn't stop until he deposits me on his king-sized bed.

"Unfair," Rad grumbles, walking into the room with a frown. "We should have drawn straws."

"That's not how this works," Asher quips, standing against the wall with his eyes eating away at my laid-out form.

Callum tunes them out as he drops his soaked boxers to the ground and kicks them aside. "I can't fucking wait any longer," he mumbles, stroking himself. "Please, Little Star. Please take off everything." Desperation lines his tone when I sit up straight, staring into the depths of his gray eyes.

You could hear a pin drop in Callum's bedroom when I remove my bra, flinging it aside. The cool air blows past my nipples, hardening them under their stares. I'm at the center of their attention.

"Dibs," Rad quips, scooping it up with a grin. If he had pockets, I'm sure he'd stuff it in there and keep it forever. Luckily for him, I have more than two bras these days.

With shaky fingers, I pull my thong down and take a deep breath. I've been naked in front of them before. Years ago. Multiple times. Weeks ago, they looked through my window, watching as I brought myself to completion. I'm not insecure about what pregnancy did to my body. But sometimes, I wonder if they still look at me the same. Or expect the same girl I was back then with the tiny waist, average boobs, and tiny butt.

I'm not as thin as I once was. Curves took over my body when Lyric announced herself to the world, enhancing everything. Those new curves brought on the stretch marks pulling at my breasts, butt, stomach, and on the skin around my knees. I've always felt so comfortable inside my skin. I'm me. No one else. No matter the marks lining my body or where the fat situates itself. I'm still River West. Doubt creeps into the back of my mind when silence echoes loudly through the room. Nothing but our breaths. No one moves a muscle or ruffles fabric. They just…stare with heated gazes, zeroing in on my heaving chest.

"So fucking beautiful," Callum whispers, slowly climbing over the edge of the bed until he's hovering just above me. His gray eyes lock on mine with a slight grin, marveling at the artwork before him. "Every inch

of you deserves to be worshiped. One day, I'll take my time. But I'm aching, Little Star. I need to be inside of you. I can't wait for a second longer," he murmurs, brushing his lips desperately against mine until his tongue plunges into my mouth.

"Please, Cal," I murmur through heavy breaths. "Please, do it." I can't stand it any longer, squirming beneath him and seeking the friction I crave.

"Yes, Little Star," he rumbles with a gasp. His jaw falls open when the tip of his dick slowly stretches me wide open, settling snuggly against my pulsating walls.

I groan, spreading my legs further to accommodate him more, aching to feel him deep inside me. My mind begs him to move faster–go quicker. He's so goddamn thick and throbbing when he bottoms out, groaning with deep satisfaction.

"Even better than I remember," he murmurs breathlessly. "You're so fucking perfect. You're so fucking mine," he murmurs with a strained expression.

"Fuck, Cal," I moan through shuddering breaths. "Please move. Please."

"You never have to beg me, Little Star. Whatever you want, I'll do it," he whispers, pulling back again and slamming his hips into mine. For an eternity, he stays there, soaking up the feel of me wrapped around him. Only to pull out and slam into me again and again.

I cry out, running my nails down his back with a gasp. He fills me up. Every crevice. Every fucking molecule. I'm so fucking full of him that I can't help but moan his name as the blinding white pleasure snaps across my body.

He grunts, slowly working himself in and out of me until his eyes roll into the back of his head. His taut muscles shudder with exertion as he slams home one last time. My pussy flutters again when a set of fingers moves over my throbbing clit, throwing me into orgasm sent straight from the wicked skies above. My toes curl. My heart pounds and breaths rage out of control. Static takes over my hearing, muffling out the breathless words of the men around me.

"Fuck," Callum grunts, stilling as he places his forehead against mine. "Little Star. I'll fight for you to the moon and back. Through the damn galaxy and beyond. I'll love you until my last dying breath."

I brush my lips against his. "I love you, too," I murmur, warmth spreading through my chest.

In a daze, I barely notice the bed dipping beside me. Rad lies against the thick, wooden headboard, lazily stroking his hard, pierced cock. I don't know when he got naked, but I can only imagine it was the moment he walked into this room. My eyes zero in on the shiny metal at the tip of his dick forming a cross through his mushroom tip.

"You on birth control, Pretty Girl?" Rad asks, lounging beside me with his dick in his hand, slowly pumping it up and down. Glistening pre cum falls from his slit as he spreads it around. "It's okay if you're not," he murmurs with a mischievous grin.

I blink several times at his question when it finally penetrates through the fog. Not like birth control did me any good the last time they knocked me up so damn easily. Although I blame the antibiotics. My idiotic doctor didn't warn me about the consequences of fucking while treating potential infections after my attack. Well, lesson fucking learned.

"I'm on birth control. I have an IUD." I raise my brow when he shrugs.

"Get rid of it then, Pretty Girl. You don't need it anymore. All you need is us." He swallows hard, a vulnerability wrinkling his brows. I'm not exactly sure what's going through his mind. I know it's pulling him into the depths of something and killing his mood. Something is bothering him about the whole situation.

Reaching up, I take his free hand into mine, gently squeezing. "Maybe when I marry you," I say, winking.

"Fuck yes. I can't wait to marry you and use my baby batter to knock you up. I missed it the first time around. I won't miss it again."

Ah, okay. There's the reason Rad's looking like someone kicked his dog. It all makes sense. And I get it. They weren't here for the pregnancy. A part of me is thankful that they didn't get to see me in all my pregnant glory. Because, yeah, sometimes pregnancy isn't glorious. For me, at least. But I wouldn't be opposed if they want that in the long run. But for now, I want to get to know them again.

"I wouldn't mind that," Callum murmurs, kissing my cheek. With great reluctance, Callum pulls out of me with a pained expression. "I miss you already," he whispers in my ear, leaving one last kiss on my jaw before climbing to the side of me.

"Sorry, River Blue," Kieran pants, taking Callum's place on top of me as Rad desperately holds my hand. "I can't take another minute without being inside you." He shakes his head, hovering above me. "It'll be quick," he rasps, pulling my left leg over his shoulder. "But I'm so damn desperate for you."

And with that, Kieran enters me hurriedly. Plunging into the depths of my pussy with one thrust and a grunt of satisfaction. His mouth forms an O as his eyes squeeze shut. All movements stop. Nothing but our ragged breaths echo through the room again.

"You feel like heaven," he murmurs, pulling out and pushing back in torturously slow.

The entire room falls away. All the noise. The lights. Even the guys disappear completely. Leaving only Kieran and me staring deep into each other's eyes. He groans, holding still, cradling my face between his palms. "You're my own fucking paradise. I'm never leaving this again. You're stuck with me forever. My Blue. My girl." His breaths quicken when his lips meet mine, solidifying the bond we've always held.

Something deep clicks inside me as our tongues dance together in an unhurried kiss. He takes his time with me. Never going too fast. Or too slow. It's just the right amount. Kieran doesn't show his love through just words. He never has. It's always been the kisses and the fucking. Hell, even the guitar on the hill. He's showing me now how much I mean to him and savoring every moment of our time together.

"Please, please, please," I moan, swirling my fingers over my clit. "Please fuck me, Knight. I need to cum."

Pulling back, he stares into my eyes with heavy breaths. "Is that what you want?" he murmurs until I'm nodding. "Say it for me, River Blue. Tell me what you want me to do."

"Fuck. Me," I growl, curling my toes when he slams his hips into mine, filling the room with the sharp sound of slapping skin. "Oh, Knight," I moan, meeting him thrust for thrust.

"Cum for me, River Blue. Let's do this together. I'm going to paint your pussy with my cum. It's yours. It belongs to you. Just like I do. Now cum!" He grunts, slamming into me and rocking my body with every damn thrust.

White hot static blares behind my closed eyelids as another orgasm rips me in half. My pussy clenches around Kieran's length, eagerly holding him in place as he releases himself inside me with a loud, satisfied moan with my name on his lips.

"Holy hell, River Blue. You're ours forever now," he breathes, slowly lowering my leg to the bed. "Forever and ever," he whispers, kissing my lips. "I don't think I've cum that hard since I bent you over that dining room table."

"I'm boneless," I groan, still squeezing Rad's hand like a lifeline. "I don't think I can move."

Nope. Can't move a muscle. My bones are Jell-O, and my muscles are mashed potatoes. I'm so dead from all this fucking. And I still have two more dicks to include. Whoever said being a part of a why-choose relationship was a good idea? Those women in books can go for hours. Me? I'm dead after two dick downs. How can I handle four again? They'll kill me before I have another orgasm.

God save me.

"You're going to have to, Pretty Girl," Rad says, tugging my hand so my eyes connect with his. "I've got a seat for you. I've saved it for five years now. Hop aboard."

I blink several times as he wipes his mouth with the back of his hand, grinning at my stunned expression.

"You want me to—"

"Yup! Ride my face, Pretty Girl. Straddle my head so I can lick you from clit to ass. I want to taste everything you've done. You. Them. Consider me the clean-up crew." His pupils dilate to almost black at the idea of me smothering him as I ride out another orgasm.

Shit. Another one? Can I even pull another one out of my body? Will this be death by sex? Prepare my casket. I'm about to die a pleased but worn out girl.

"Jesus," Kieran murmurs, slowly pulling out of me with a deep, vibrating groan.

"The clean-up crew, dude?" Asher barks out a soft laugh, shaking his head with a grin from the end of the bed where he watches everything unfold with rapt attention.

"I forgot what this was like," Callum muses softly from beside us with a satisfied expression.

You and me both, buddy.

"Uh, yeah. And you can act as her gag," Rad says, raising a no-nonsense brow in Asher's direction. "It's time to double-team our girl, or she's going to fall asleep with only half the team inside her. Operation Fill River Up is on." He grins, curling a finger in my direction. "Come on, Pretty Girl." I blow out a breath, lazily rolling to my stomach, and crawl toward him with the last of my energy.

Like a hawk zoning in on his prey, he watches me every step of the way.

"You're ridiculous," I grumble with Jell-O for limbs when he pulls me into his lap, grinning maniacally.

"Rad-iculous, you mean," he quips as a suddenly serious expression passes over his face. He shakes his head, gripping my waist tightly. "I've been dreaming of you for years, Pretty Girl. You're the only one who has ever been on my damn mind. I want to savor everything. I want to lick you clean and then make love to you. I've been ready for weeks. Hell, years. I'll tattoo your name across my cock so everyone knows who he rises for. Every inch of you calls to me. Please indulge me," he says, staring straight into my eyes.

"One more orgasm…such a hardship," I quip, grinning when he leans in and takes my lips captive. No, seriously. It's a fucking hardship. My body shakes with every movement I make.

"Good. Now, ride my damn face. Smother me with your pussy until I suffocate and die. In the best damn way. Just make sure my grave says something sexy like… Here lies Rad, who smothered under his girl's pussy and choked on her cum." A dreamy look crosses over his face when he thinks about what will come. You know, me preferably. If I can manage not to fall over.

With a quick peck to my lips, Rad shimmies his way down the bed, leaving me straddling his bare chest. Those pleading brown eyes stare up at me. "Climb on my face," he demands, digging his fingers into my ass cheeks, encouraging me to scoot forward.

"Okay," I say through a heavy breath, slowly making my way up his body until my pussy dangles just above his mouth, filled to the brim with my previous encounters with Kieran and Callum.

Excitement hums through Rad when he looks me up and down. "Sit," he whispers, blowing hot air against my lips and sending shivers down my spine. "Asher, dude. Get over here!" he shouts before shoving his tongue into my pussy and back out.

I cry out, looking for leverage to hang onto and find it when Asher's lean body stands at the edge of the bed. His wide, hazel eyes take us in as my hand clamps down on his, begging for something to grip onto. I throw my head back with a groan, nearly coming when Rad's tongue plunges in and out of me. Back and forth. Up and down. Wetting every inch of me from below. Not a spot goes untouched, driving me fucking wild.

"Little Brat," he murmurs, leaning over and kissing my lips. "You're good with this?" he whispers, holding my face in his palms. I nod, moaning at the sensations working through me. "Good. Now, stroke me, baby," he whispers, guiding my hand to his hard-as-steel dick.

Asher's breaths blow out of control when he thrusts into my hand, twitching wildly in my grasp. "You're hard as hell, Evil Ash," I murmur against his lips. "You like this?" I bravely ask, earning a groaned yes in return. "Good. Fuck my hand, Asher. But don't cum yet. Wait until Rad bends me over and fucks me so I can use you as my gag. I want your cum down my throat, not in my palm. Right?" He nods frantically, slowing his pace.

"Yes, Little Brat," he heaves, sucking my tongue into his mouth and getting lost in the sensation.

I moan into Asher's mouth when Rad's fingers creep up my backside and twirl around my ass. "God, yes!" I shiver as another orgasm peeks around the corner.

Fire licks at every fucking nerve, working its way toward my over-sensitive center. The second Rad's thumb enters my tight ass, I come undone, convulsing another orgasm.

"Holy fucking shit," Rad murmurs from beneath me, lifting me off his face. "That's the hottest thing I've ever tasted and done. You're so fucking amazing, Pretty Girl. Are you ready for the last bit? I'm going to fuck your pussy. Asher's going to cum down your throat. And you're going to like it."

"I sure fucking am," I breathe, pulling my hand away from Asher.

"Get on all fours, Little Brat," Asher demands with a flushed expression creeping up his neck. All his veins protrude beneath his skin, showing me he's holding back.

There's a snark on the tip of my tongue. Naturally, I want to fight back against his demand. Tell him to make me do what he says, but I don't have it in me. I'm horny as hell, ready to take them both. But exhaustion sweeps through me at a demanding rate.

I crawl on my hands and knees to the center of the bed and present myself, sucking in several breaths. Rad's fingertips brush down my spine, tingling as he draws patterns.

"You should see yourself," Rad murmurs, gripping my ass cheeks tightly and pulling them apart to expose me to his gaze. "You're more beautiful than I've ever seen. I'm so madly, deeply in love with you. My chest aches for you. I definitely won't last long, but I want you to know that next time we're chaining you to the bed for a whole night of worship."

"Damn right, we are," Kieran's gruff voice agrees from my other side as he plops down on the bed, leaning on his elbow.

"Hang on, Pretty Girl. This is going to be a bumpy ride," Rad rasps, thrusting deep inside me with one go. "This right here is heaven, boys," he gasps, wildly pumping into me.

"You're good?" Asher asks, clutching my jaw in his hand. I nod, opening my mouth, awaiting the treat I'm about to receive.

"You can finally cum," I murmur, running my tongue over his tip.

"Please, Little Brat."

His gasp echoes through the room when I suck him completely into my mouth, running my tongue over his slit. My cheeks hollow out, swallowing him whole.

"Shit!" Rad pants from behind.

I moan around Asher's length when Rad's hand slaps down on my asscheek, leaving behind a delicious sting.

"You liked that, didn't you, Little Brat?" Asher grunts, breathlessly slamming his hips into my face, using me for his pleasure. His loud moans fill the room when his fingers curl into my hair, holding me in place.

I couldn't answer if I tried.

Rad gently rubs the reddened spot on my ass. Leaning over, his chest presses into my back. As he whispers sweet words into my ear.

"I'm so close, Pretty Girl. You're amazing, you're...mah—" His pace slows until he stills, sinking his teeth into my shoulder. Warm breaths caress my skin when he lays his forehead against my shoulder, panting wildly.

Rad doesn't try to move away, keeping himself buried deep inside me as his cock slowly deflates.

"Never leaving. I'm sleeping with my dick inside you. He's finally home," Rad mutters nonsensically.

"Fuck," Asher pants, throwing his head back when his salty cum jets into my mouth and dribbles down my throat. "Holy hell, Little Brat." Frantically, he pulls out, clasping my jaw between his palms. "You're amazing...I...thank you." Before I can ask him what he's thanking me for, his lips are on mine. Pulling away, raw emotions sparkle in his glossy eyes. I don't know what's going through his head, but something profound rattles around in there.

"Fine, I'll leave," Rad grumbles, pulling himself out of me with a whine.

I fall into the bed face-first with a groan. I'm not as young as I used to be. Even if I'm only twenty-four. Nineteen-year-old River could handle four dicks at a time without blinking an eye. But my body feels like I've been run through the wringer.

"Pretty Girl! Did I kill you with my dick?" Real concern drips from Rad's voice as he moves my hair from my face.

"Yes," I mumble into the comforter. "Just leave me here," I quip when he chuckles.

"How about a hot shower, baby?" Asher whispers from my other side, moving his fingers through my hair. "We'll help."

"You'll help?" I question, raising a brow and turning myself over. Looking up, I watch Asher's soft face when he nods.

"Yeah. We got you into this situation. Now, we'll help you relax afterward."

"Okay, take me to the shower," I say, reaching up like a child until Kieran lifts me off the bed and into his arms.

"We got you, River Blue. We'll clean you up. Have a little snack. And then, we can all go to bed."

After a hot shower, they carry me to the kitchen and make me food. And then, after we've all eaten, they take me back to Callum's bed, where they cuddle me throughout the night.

Just like we used to.

After picking up Ly from her sleepover and saying our goodbyes to Central City the next day, we head home with a new outlook on life. And our relationship.

The trickiest part about our newfound life together will be the reality we're about to step into. They're a band. They'll have to travel at some point. And I still have my work. By tomorrow morning, we'll all be back on track with what our lives used to be, while incorporating our new relationship.

"Coffee," I groan for the thousandth time today. Or it feels like it, at least. I've only been awake for thirty minutes, wrangling Lyric into school mode.

I have to get her back into the swing of things after missing so many days from being away. And let's just say she doesn't want to cooperate.

I swear that's all being an adult consists of. Coffee. Work. Zombie mode. Tired. Hungry. Horny. More coffee to feel human. When will this endless cycle stop?

Right. Never.

"Here," Asher chuckles, handing me a large Styrofoam cup of boiling hot nectar from the Gods. "It's your usual." Pride sparkles in his eyes when he looks away, watching with intent as Lyric approaches with a grin.

"Morning, Daddy," she says, reaching a hand out.

"And what do you want, Little One?" he asks, bending at the waist to meet her sparkling eyes.

Her eyes slip to the white bag on the counter containing the treat she's so desperate for. The one thing Asher brings her every morning. Something delicious. Sweet. And will probably rot her damn teeth out.

"My treat," she whispers, pointing toward the bag like it's a secret tucked away.

"What do you say?" I ask, groaning into my coffee like the addict I am. If it wasn't for the caffeine, I think I'd die a slow and painful death.

"Pwetty, please," she whispers, puffing out her bottom lip. Convincingly, might I add. If he hadn't bought it for her, he'd definitely give it to her now.

"Well, who can resist that," he quips, gliding over to the bag and pulling out her treat. "Come sit so you can eat, and then we'll get you to school."

I grin against the lid of my drink, watching him beneath my lashes. Sometimes, I like to watch as they each interact with her, giving away a little piece of their hearts each time.

Every day they fall a little more in love with her. And she with them. Like they never separated, and they've known each other since the moment she screamed her first breath.

Emotions rise in my throat at the love they've shown her in such a short time. And me, too. Even though we knew each other at different times in our lives, it's like we were never apart. But yet, we were. They're so different from who they were.

"So, I'll bring you some lunch today, okay?"

My eyes zone back in on Asher, who eyes me with a little smirk pulling at his lips. I raise my brows. How long have I been staring at him while biting into the damn lid? Fuck. I pull my drink away and clear my throat.

Apparently, long enough. Ly chomps down on the pink-frosted donut with sparkly sprinkles dotting the concoction, devouring it like a little hungry monster. Leaving the remnants behind around her lips.

"Lunch?"

He grins. "Yeah. I figured I could bring something to you since you're going back to the office today."

My cheeks heat. Why is it so hot when a man insists on feeding me copious amounts of coffee and food? I'm not complaining. Like at all. He can stuff me full with… Well, my mind instantly travels down the deep, dark road of cock and moans, heating my face more.

Apparently, I need to get laid. No matter how hard I tell myself to take it slow, my body has other plans. And well, to hell with it. I've always given my body what it wants.

"Lunch is great," I say with a smile, pretending I'm not thinking about his dick.

Totally not, by the way. Nope. I'm not thinking about the way he gagged me just a few days ago. Or the salty cum that slid down my throat as I swallowed him whole. Nah. Not me.

Fuck. It's only seven or so in the morning, and I'm already horny. It's like their cum was the key to awakening my long-forgotten sex drive hiding inside me. Once they entered me, thrust into me, and came inside me—I was a goner, drowning in them again.

Something I swore I wouldn't do. Just yet. But I'm constantly breaking my promises to myself. Take it slow, I said. But yet, I got dicked down by my four baby daddies in one night.

You see, my body remembers theirs now. Every one of them. And now I'm scared I'm addicted to getting bent over and fucked within an inch of my life. I promised myself I'd take it slow. All in, yes. But I want to get to know them again. And at this rate, I'm only going to be reacquainted with their nether regions.

Shit.

"Great. I can stop by after therapy and practice," he says with ease, leaning over to wipe Lyric's mouth off with a paper towel. "Go wash up for school, or we'll be late."

"I'm sick," she pouts, crossing her messy hands over her chest.

"Lyric," he says in a stern dad voice, even giving her the pointed look that has her turning tail and stomping down the hallway to her room.

I shudder at the strength in his voice. Settle down, you hussy. He's not bossing you around. Not yet, at least. He will, though. I'll bring back the dominant man who made me hold out my wrist with salt lines on it so he could cut limes.

It's time to bring the old Asher out. He's said sorry multiple times and proven himself over and over again. Now, it's time to release the beast simmering under his flesh until he's pounding into me without mercy.

I'm so fucking screwed.

Or want to be.

"My little sister from another—" Seger twists his expression when I walk into his office.

"That saying doesn't work like that," I say, plopping down onto a leather seat across from his desk.

Zepp snorts, sauntering over from his desk on the other side of the room, and lounges beside me in another chair.

"First-day jitters?" he asks, taking a sip of coffee before placing it on a coaster on Seger's desk.

"Weird to be back, but I have to get back into the swing of things. They're handling practice and therapy without my assistance now. So, I figured I'd stop in and see how Kat was handling things here."

I raise a brow when they exchange a look, doing their freaky twin, silent conversation bullshit with their eyebrows.

"Kaycee and I agree that's annoying as fuck, by the way," I say, pointing between the two of them.

Immediately, both of their moss-green eyes lock me in place.

"You're not allowed to be friends with our wife anymore," Seger sniffs, raising his chin in the air.

"All you two do is conspire against us," Zepp says, pointing in my direction.

"She's like my sister. We're allowed to conspire against you. Get over it," I say, sticking my tongue out.

Zepp sighs, running his fingers over his forehead. "Kat called out today."

I stiffen. "Called out?"

"Yeah. You know, used a sick day today and yesterday," Seger quips like the cocky asshole he is.

Such a goddamn know-it-all. I swear I would have put them six feet deep if we had actually grown up together. I mean, I plot their murders every once in a great while when they're being jackasses.

Like today.

I blink several times. Seger puts his feet on his desk as he leans back in his chair. Secretly, I hope he falls backward. I don't want blood. Well, not much. But a nice bruise would suffice to knock the little attitude out of him.

Ah, siblings. They're a joy to have.

Zepp's jaw tics with irritation as he glares at Seger's dirty shoe on his desk. "Act like a civilized adult, you pig," he mutters, swiftly knocking Seger's feet off his desk and jolting him forward.

Seger grunts, placing his palms on his desk to stop himself from smacking the wood. Damn, too bad.

"Back to the matter at hand. Is she really sick? She hasn't called out in all the months she's worked here."

Finally, they each take a deep breath. Sometimes I think they need a vacation away from each other. But being twins and all, they have a weird bond. Not to mention they share a wife.

I shudder. I hate thinking about what they do in the damn dark of their home. Stupid intrusive thoughts.

Zepp grimaces. "She and her weird boyfriend, Trevor, are having some issues. Um, she just needed some time to straighten it out. Mental health days are classed as sick days here, so we just gave her the go-ahead." Oh good, that means there is work on my desk ready to be completed. Thankfully, I won't have to worry about any anonymous notes landing there again.

"Well, okay then. I'll be off to my office for now unless you need something." Peering at both of them, they shrug. "Good. I'm out."

"Good to have you back, my sister, from the same mister! Ha! I nailed it!" Seger's whoops follow me as I make my way down the long hallway toward my office, which sits a little ways from theirs, giving me the much-needed privacy I crave.

Since Whispered Words is only a couple months into my program, there isn't too much work for me to handle at the office. My sole purpose once a band is put in my hands is to mold them back into best-selling artists. But it's nice to be back here in the peace and quiet I've carved out for myself. My office is my place of Zen—a place no one disturbs anymore.

As I shut my office door behind me, I dig my phone out of my purse.

ME

Hey, Kat! Just wanted to make sure you were okay. My brothers said you were feeling a little under the weather.

Listen, I am concerned about her well-being. She may not be a close friend, but I like to think Kat and I are on good terms. She may be my employee, but I like to check in on her.

KAT

Hey:/… I was just having a rough time. Trevor disappeared without saying goodbye, and I didn't know where he went… I was worried until he came back this morning.

Jesus. Who disappears without saying goodbye? I hope he had a damn good reason.

ME

Just checking to see if he is okay.

KAT

He's been better. His mom got sick, so he went to check on her, and his phone broke when he was there. He wasn't able to get another one until today. I'm sorry I couldn't make it today. There's a stack of mail on your desk.

ME

Family comes first, Kat. I'm just glad that you're okay, and he's okay.

KAT

Thanks, Miss West. I appreciate you checking in. Glad you made it back safe and sound, too. It must have been terrifying having a stalker out there.

Yeah. Beyond terrifying. Having some stranger watching your every move is something no one will understand unless they've lived it. If I would have known it was Adrian, a man I had never actually met. Then I would have put a restraining order on him. In some cases, though. That doesn't do shit. They walk right through those restraining orders without a second thought. Not like me. When Gloria handed me those papers I thought were from the boys, I thought why bother?

ME

Call me River. And yeah…it was. Stay safe. I'll check in tomorrow.

Leaning back in my chair, I stare up at the ceiling reveling in the silence around me. It's odd going from having five other people constantly making noise to just myself. Alone. Just me and my rampant thoughts.

The morning goes by in a rush. I slowly catch up on some paperwork I need to sign regarding past bands and even potential new ones. It's odd I never saw Whispered Word's name come across my desk. Yet, here I am as their new manager. I swear, even though my brothers knew about the past, they made this happen.

"Talk to them again. That restraining order is over," Seger huffs from behind his desk, slowly nursing a beer he pulled out of somewhere.

"I don't think I can," I mutter, pinching the bridge of my nose. "They walked away. Remember? They're the ones who signed that restraining order. Not me."

"You ever get a funny feeling about it?" Zepp asks, cocking his head to the side and examining my twisted expression.

"No." Yes. I did. It always made me feel uneasy and off. But who was I to question their signatures on the dotted line? Besides that phone call, too. It was pretty damn convincing.

Well, maybe I should have listened back then. I was so determined that they wanted nothing to do with me that I kept it all together for Lyric. She was my priority. It scared the living hell out of me thinking about dropping her in their laps.

What if they truly didn't want her?

Now I know the entire situation was bullshit. Concocted by some psychopath who hated my guts and twisted Asher into her grips to get what she wanted most. Money.

"Knock, knock."

I nearly pee my pants when I jolt upright, staring at Asher loitering just inside my office door with a grin, shutting it behind him.

"You were deep in concentration," he chuckles, walking toward my desk with a tray consisting of two drinks and a take-out bag from my favorite coffee place. "I got your favorite again. The avocado sandwich I always see you eyeing."

I sweep my papers into a pile on the side of my desk as he sets out our lunch.

"God, Asher. You're a lifesaver," I murmur, biting into my chicken and avocado sandwich.

He chuckles. "Well, I figured you needed to eat, and I just so happened to be getting that anyway." His eyes dart away, refocusing on his sandwich as he takes tentative bites.

"Why're you still holding back?" I ask, setting my food down.

"I'm not," he says, shaking his head.

"You are."

He swallows his bite, chugging his Dr. Pepper. "I'm not meaning to."

His teeth sink nervously into the bottom of his lip when he sets his sandwich down and takes a deep breath. "I—"

"It's okay, Evil Ash," I murmur, reaching across my desk to take his hand.

Squeezing my hand in his seems to bring out his bravery a sliver. His hazel eyes stay glued to the ground when he opens his mouth. "I'm all in, Little Brat. I promise I am. I just… I still feel guilty. It sits so damn heavy on my chest. I know you forgave me."

"Completely. You are 100 percent forgiven. I told you that I'll remember forever what it felt like when you left. But I don't dwell on it. Look at you… The old Asher wouldn't have given me the time of day. Not to bring me lunch, at least. He'd only have wanted to jam his cock down my throat."

I smirk when he chokes on his own drink, turning a bright shade of red like he didn't do that exact thing a few nights ago after dancing in the rain.

"Christ," he croaks, shaking his head. "You can't say shit like that."

All the pent-up horniness from before slams into me as I watch him wipe his mouth. This Asher is much more delectable than the old Asher. But there's still one side I miss more than anything.

"Take me," I say, pushing my chair back and slowly rising to my feet.

"Take you?" he asks, lowering his voice into a smooth rumble.

Yes, you idiot. Take me. Fuck me. Make me cum harder than I've ever cum before.

Those hazel eyes latch onto my movements as I begin to slip my high heels off and kick them under my desk, instantly becoming inches shorter. His gaze doesn't leave my movements even when I start to unbutton my work shirt, leaving it half open and exposing my white silky bra underneath.

"Yeah," I say, shrugging out of my shirt and letting it drop to the ground near my chair. "Fucking take me, Asher. Do what you want to do to me."

His eyes blow wide, darkening with each piece of clothing I remove. Yet, he doesn't utter a command. Simply stares at me like I've grown a third boob he can't wait to devour. Wicked thoughts must travel through his mind when his fingers twitch on top of my desk, desperate to reach out and grab me.

The cool air of the room rushes across my flesh, pebbling goosebumps up and down my body as I remove my pants and toss them across the desk, hitting him in the face.

He jerks back, gripping them in his hands. "Little Brat," he rasps with roaming eyes, staring me up and down as I stand before him in only my bra and underwear. "Fuck, you're so goddamn gorgeous."

"Tell me what to do, Asher." I won't move unless he says so.

I won't cum or moan or curl my toes unless he gives me the go-ahead.

This is me taking back the Asher I once knew and giving him back to the Asher 2.0 sitting across from me. Someone needs to take him by the balls and force him to be the dominating man he once was.

He's no longer allowed to stay on the sidelines and wait his turn. It's time for action.

He blinks several times, rubbing his jaw. "Come here," he says with less confidence than I hoped, but it's a start.

"Yes, Daddy Asher," I murmur, sauntering around the edge of my desk.

God. The full-body shudder that works its way through him at the sound of his old nickname has my pussy weeping with delight. If I thought I was horny this morning, this is nothing compared to that.

It's odd having him at my mercy. Or me being at his mercy, I guess. Trying to be, anyway. It brings me back to the night he laid me out on the dining room table at the Castle House and rocked my goddamn world with his demands. Every word he said, I did. Every command he laid out, I fucking followed.

Today will be no different. Today is the day Asher takes me how he wants me.

Asher doesn't reach out for me when I stand before him in my underwear. His fingers may not caress my flesh just yet, but his eyes absolutely ignite with lust, traveling over every inch of my body with a fine tooth comb.

"Fucking hell. You're going to kill me," he murmurs, finally brushing his fingertips over my abdomen and gliding around my belly button.

"How so?" I whisper, leaning into his warm and inviting touch, still refusing to take the reins on this whole endeavor.

Whatever Asher wants to do, it's up to him.

"You're just so fucking beautiful. Then and now." His fingers trail up to the swell of my breast, gliding over the white stretch marks lining my skin. Abruptly standing, he towers over me, still fixated on running his fingers over my boobs.

"This is your show, Daddy Asher," I murmur, pushing my tits into his hand as he cups it through my bra, running his thumb over my pebbling nipple.

"Hmmm," he hums, leaning forward to bite through my bra.

"Fuck," I hiss at the beautiful sting flaring under the intensity of his teeth.

"My show," he murmurs, running his tongue along my bra until he meets my flesh, traveling up my neck and right below my ear.

I nearly cum when he sucks my skin in between his teeth, nibbling around until my lips meet his.

"I want you to bend over, Little Brat," he breathlessly says against my lips, palming my ass.

Fire brews beneath my skin when he watches my reaction with such intensity I feel like flames are licking every inch of me.

"Yes, Sir," I say with a smirk, growing wetter by the second.

Turning around, I place my palms on my desk. My back arches, and when I look over my shoulder, I nearly combust at the sight of him.

Those hazel eyes gaze directly at my ass, trailing toward the wet spot collecting on my panties. All these pent-up hormones run rampant with need, turning me into a begging mess.

"Please, Asher," I moan, wiggling my ass a little.

"Please, what?" he dares to ask, undoing his belt from his jeans and rolling down his zipper. I watch in fascination as his cock springs free, bulging and twitching with need. "What do you want, My Brat? Do you want me to fill you with this cock? Shove it so far up your dripping pussy that you cum?"

Jesus fuck Christ, I've created a dominating, dirty-talking monster.

One that I like.

If he keeps this up, I'll come before he ever fucks me. Or before we finish our damn lunch.

"Yes, Asher." I swallow hard when one finger trails down my ass cheek, slipping beneath the fabric of my panties. Getting closer and closer to the promised land.

I jolt in surprise when the thin fabric of my panties rips in two. My breaths shudder when he holds them in front of my face, displaying the wet patch on the fabric.

"I have been holding back," he admits, pressing his lips to my bare shoulder, trailing kisses up my neck. "I've been trying to respect what we have now. But you make it so fucking hard to respect you when all I want to do is fuck you like you're my fucking little whore. I want to shove my cock down your throat and watch you swallow. Fuck. I've—"

"Then do it. Fuck me like you hate me. Fuck me like you used to."

"But I never truly hated you," he whispers with desperation as his finger finds my clit, turning light circles. "I never ever hated you. I was so fucking madly in love with you that I hated myself. I loathed what I thought about you. What I did to you. Said to you. You're my goddamn angel, River. My Brat. My baby. My salvation into becoming a better man."

"Fuck," I moan, thrusting back into his pelvis. "Asher," I whine, begging for him to fill me.

"I'm going to fuck you now, River. I won't hold back. But you should hold on. I'm going to shove this into your mouth so your brothers don't come running. The last thing we need is visitors when I'm helping you meet Jesus." I swallow hard when he traces the lace of my white panties along my lips, softly tapping them. "Open up, Little Brat." Without hesitation, my lips part, welcoming the panties into my mouth, muffling anything that comes from my throat. "Good girl. Now, wrap your hands over the edge of the desk." My breaths hitch in my throat when I wrap my hands around the edge of the desk so tight my fingers turn white.

That's the last thing he says before he brushes the tip of his throbbing dick at my entrance and thrusts completely inside me.

"Oh fuck me," Asher murmurs. "Goddamn, you're one hundred percent going to be the death of me, and I'm okay with it. I'll die right here," he grunts, slamming into me several times and knocking my hips into my desk.

Whatever bruises I have later will be something I look back on as the moment Asher took back his control.

I groan around my panties as droplets of drool roll down my chin. It does its job, holding back my loud moans so hopefully my brothers don't fucking hear us. The last thing I need is those two idiots interrupting this much-needed fucking.

Asher's pace picks up, slamming into me relentlessly. Without fucking mercy. My desk squeaks with every move, dragging against the floor, surely giving away what we're doing in here.

"I want you to cum around my cock," he demands breathlessly in my ear.

I nod, leaning into the fire eating away at me, and release my fucking orgasm from the Gods, suffocating his dick as I convulse.

"Fuck me," he says, stiffening and releasing himself inside me with a long, drawn out moan of satisfaction.

My forehead rests against the cool wood of my desk as he hovers behind me, rubbing his hands up and down my body. Small words of affirmations are whispered against my neck as he catches his breath.

"Thank you," he whispers with sincerity. "I knew only you could bring me back to who I was but keep me in check."

Spitting out my panties onto my desk, I desperately suck in air. Asher hurriedly hands me my drink, and I gulp it down with him still nestled inside me.

"No, thank you," I rasp, clutching his hand in mine. "Thank you for letting go. Please, don't hold back again. I need both sides of the Asher coin." I swallow hard when he gently pulls out and spins me around.

His palms cup my cheeks as he leans in, suffocating me with his kiss. His tongue darts into my mouth, twisting with mine as he pushes me against my desk.

"Never again will I hold back, Little Brat. I'll be whatever Asher you want."

"A mix of both," I quip with a smirk. "Now, if you don't mind, I need to get back to work."

"I'll wait," he says with a shrug, kissing me one last time. With ease, he puts himself back in his pants and rights his belt.

"You'll wait?" I ask, heaving a breath.

"Yup," he says with a grin, sitting back in his chair and picking up his sandwich. "But why don't you work like that?" He gestures to my bra and the cum dripping out of my pussy and onto my leg.

I smirk, walk around my desk and plop in my seat. "If you insist."

"Oh," he chuckles. "I do."

Until the end of the day, Asher stays with me. He doesn't say anything as he cleans up our lunch mess. He just rests, watching me wade through the paperwork Kat left me until the clock hits 2:00 p.m., and I've run out of things to do.

IT'S BEEN FOUR DAYS SINCE WE WENT ALL IN, DIVING HEAD-FIRST BACK into this little thing we call a relationship.

Well, not little. This is huge. Monumental. Our girl is finally ours again and within our grasp.

It feels damn good to have her back in my arms.

We've all fallen back into our regular routines. Us, as a band, going to morning practices and therapy sessions.

And River, acting as our manager. The boss in charge.

Since our return, it's been a whirlwind of emotions. For me, I realized what I lost when I left her behind. Her. Lyric. All the love we had together.

Now, it's reignited into something bigger and more beautiful.

This is our new normal. Together. All five of us. Plus, our daughter who hasn't stopped smiling since we sat her down and told her we're together now. And she'll be seeing a lot more of us.

My new normal tonight includes taking my daughter to a book reading of some book she's been desperate for me to read. Later, I'll tuck her into bed and kiss her goodnight. Like I do every night.

This is a dream come true. It's my everything. From the time I was a kid, this is everything I always wanted. Family. A wife. And children.

"What book is this again?" I whisper, frantically darting my eyes around the massive crowd gathering outside the downtown library, chatting before they step inside.

River snorts as we walk through the front entrance. I cringe at the mere size of the people huddling together in small groups. Someone is bound to recognize me. Everywhere I look, unfamiliar faces greet me with big smiles and heated cheeks. Their eyes drift over my face, recognizing me from a mile away—the one downside to being famous. I can't walk into a room, especially in this town, without someone pointing at me. Or wanting an autograph.

"My favorite, Daddy," Lyric replies, tugging at my hand with renewed vigor, grunting at me when I don't move quickly enough.

River chuckles, clutching my other hand as we walk further into the

large East Point library built to impress. Marble floors. Large ceilings. Hell, it even has tall columns holding up the balconies above our heads.

"Oh, my God! It's Callum Rose!" a woman's voice squeals as I pass by a group of girls huddled together near the entrance. "Callum! Can I get your autograph?" Her voice echoes, following me until I stop and turn with a tight smile, greeting the red-faced woman, clutching a pen and notepad to her chest. "Please?" she whispers, flicking her long brown hair over her shoulder.

"Sure," is my clipped response.

I get it. I really do. They see a celebrity they love and automatically want an autograph. Or a picture together. Or to beg one of us to crawl under the sheets for a good time.

Never happened. Not for me, at least.

But today.

I'm here with my family. Ready to enjoy a reading of Lyric's new favorite series. The last thing I want to do is stop hanging out with my family to sign her notebook.

"But, Daddy! We gots to get good seats," Lyric whines beside me, tugging at my hand with impatience.

My eyes dart to Lyric as her bottom lip puffs out. Little tears glisten in her eyes as she watches me grasp the notebook.

"I know, Ladybug. Give me just a second, okay?"

"It'll be ok, Ly," River whispers, taking Lyric's hand from mine and forcing her to face River. "Daddy just has to do this, and then we'll find our seats." Lyric huffs, crossing her arms over her chest.

"So, it's true," the fan sneers in River's direction with disbelief.

I blink several times, watching the woman's face morph from a smile to a deep frown, forming wrinkles on her forehead.

I don't dignify a response to the fan's question. It's none of her business. In fact, it's no one's business. They can be as upset as they want to be. Just like our PR manager was.

They can all shove it up their asses and keep their opinions to themselves. We're happy, and that's all that matters.

"Here," I grunt, handing her back the notebook with my tiny signature decorating the page.

"Thank you so much!" she giggles, running her finger over my writing. Leaning in as if she's about to whisper something, she says, "If you don't feel like sharing anymore, I'm available. Only whores share." The bold fan sniffs, sticking her nose in the air with a tiny smirk like she's won something over on River, who snorts beside me.

"I'll take that," I grunt, ripping the page from her notebook and shoving it in my pocket.

"What?" she gasps with big eyes, reaching out to take the paper from me. "But you…"

"That was before you insulted my girlfriend. In front of my daughter, might I add. It was nice of me to even stop and sign this for you. I'm trying to have a nice night with my family, but I stopped because…"

I don't know why I stopped. I suppose it's instinct now. I hear my name, and I stop for signatures. Not anymore. Not when I'm with my girls. I'm here to protect them from everything. And that includes the disapproving look she's giving us.

"I stopped because I thought it would be nice. This is the love of my life. So, have a good night." I don't bother giving her another look as she stands there, staring at me with wide, unblinking eyes.

She could be crying. Or giving me dirty looks. Maybe she'll stay there all night glued to the spot, thinking about the day she stopped Callum Rose and was an asshole. I don't care anymore. No one insults my Little Star without consequence. No one.

The fallout of our announcement hasn't gone exactly bad. Well, until tonight. I guess.

But not good either.

The press is having a hay day with our unusual relationship. That's what they call it, at least. Haven't they seen a poly relationship before? Apparently, not. They're always snapping pictures anywhere they can find us. If we leave the house anymore. It's only been a few days, but we're the talk of the nation.

River doesn't seem to give a shit as long as Ly is safe from harm. So, whenever we're out, I try to cover Lyric as best I can. She shouldn't have to endure public life at such a young age because of us.

River clings to my side as she reclaims my hand, gently squeezing. "Poor girl," she hums with sarcasm lacing her tone.

I snort. "Right. Poor thing."

River grins, looking at me from beneath her lashes. "Kinda sexy how you stood up for me."

Fuck. My cheeks heat when she nibbles her bottom lip. I swear my stomach bottoms out, swirling into a mass of lust as she bats her eyelashes in my direction. If she's not careful, I'll salute the entire crowd.

"Stop it, Little Star," I whisper, leaning over so my lips brush against her ear, sending a shiver down her spine. "We're in public," I murmur.

"Have you ever…" she trails off, looking around the large library with a mischievous grin. "You know, they'll let all the kids sit in a circle around the narrator. We could sneak away and give the books a show."

Fuck. Me.

"No," I choke out, kissing her cheek. "Stop it." Little fucking tease. She giggles, shrugging.

And to think, Rad begged to come with us. He wanted in on the action of hanging out with Lyric. But I wanted this time to myself. Them to myself. Like the selfish bastard I am. Now, I'm kind of wishing I wasn't so selfish so he could sit with Lyric, and I could fuck River over a stack of books in the hidden part of the library.

Maybe later.

As we walk further through the loitering crowd, people of all ages hang around the large, open reading room, murmuring to each other. Thankfully, no one else notices who I am.

A single chair rests at the front of the room reserved for the children's librarian giving the people of East Point a treat for tonight.

"You sit here, Daddy!" Lyric says, bouncing on her toes and pointing to two chairs sitting side by side. "Mommy here. Daddy here," she demands.

If there's one thing I've come to know about my daughter, it's that she's a bossy little thing. One day she'll grow up to be the leader of something. A business. A CEO. A band. Hell, she could form her own army, and everyone would listen to her. She has that kind of presence.

All I know is I'm nurturing her bossy side and helping her turn it into something powerful.

"And what about Lyric?" River hums, settling into a plastic chair with a grin. Looking up at me, she pats the spot next to her.

I grin when I sit, and Lyric happily climbs into my lap, situating herself so she's staring at the front.

Ah. That's where she wanted to be.

"This is book three, Daddy. It continues where we left off last night," she squeals, clapping her hands with such glee I can't help myself.

Her joy infects me. Fills me up with her laughter and claps. Watching her light up as the librarian comes out with the third installment nestled beneath her arms has my hair standing on end.

This is my time with her. Our love for this simple book about a murderous archer, who protects the people around her as she gallivants trying to find a cure for her mother's mystery illness, has me in a chokehold.

One day they'll make this into a movie, and I'll be the first in line with Lyric to watch as they hopefully don't butcher it.

Lyric softly snores in my lap, never having made it to the small circle of kids gathered around the librarian.

I chuckle, running a finger down her reddened cheek as she lets out another tiny snore in front of the crowded room, intently listening as the story continues.

She barely lasted twenty minutes.

The snores are something she swears she doesn't do. Mostly, she blames me or one of the others for waking her up. Little does my baby know she's the one responsible for all the noise.

"She's out," I murmur into River's hair as she rests her head on my shoulder.

I could get used to this. Every night having them by my side, snuggling me until they each fall asleep.

"Let's roll," she murmurs softly, gesturing toward the exit.

You don't have to tell me twice. If Lyric is out, then I can tuck her into bed. After that, I'm going to tie my Little Star up and fuck her into oblivion.

Those remarks from earlier sit fresh in my mind, creating fiery ideas. Her. Me. My mouth between her legs, licking the repeated orgasms from her slick pussy. Fuck. I shake the thoughts from my head and save them for later.

As quietly as we can, we exit the reading without disturbing Lyric and successfully put her into her booster seat in the back of River's car.

"It must have felt like bedtime," River chuckles, leaning against the passenger's side door with crossed arms, staring up at the stars beaming down on us.

A cold chill flows with the tiny wisps of wind, blowing the leaves on the trees. Goosebumps pucker at River's skin, but she doesn't pay it any mind.

"Must have," I say, softly closing the door after buckling Lyric in.

"Did you see the way that lady looked at me when we walked out?" she asks, licking her lips. "I think your groupies might claw my eyes out and try to steal you from me."

"Fuck them," I murmur, crowding her against the car with a smirk. "You're the only one who matters, Little Star."

"Hmm. Is that so?" she hums with sass, staring straight into my eyes.

"It is."

Before she can blink, I brush my lips against hers, leaning into her. Mine. All fucking mine.

Butterflies swoop in my belly every time I'm around her like it's the first time all over again. Something that will never go away.

Every time I'm in her vicinity, my internal wounds stitch back together even more than before. She's the balm necessary for my healing.

Even when she used to be the reason I fell. Now, she lifts me.

"You and Ly and the guys are the only family I need," I whisper against her lips with a grin. "Should we get home?" A soft moan falls from her lips when my hips brush against hers, letting her know how desperate I am to get her to bed. "Those little comments from earlier really stirred something up," I murmur, kissing her one last time.

Out of the corner of my eye, something flashes in the distance, repeatedly going off. I sigh. There they are again, following our every move.

Even at the library, we're not allowed peace by the paparazzi. They can follow us to the end of the world, though. I'll never stop kissing my girl out in public. This is our life.

"Yeah? And what do you want to do to me?" she rasps, oblivious to the cameras documenting our make out session against her car.

I lick my lips when she challenges me with one look.

"I'll catch you," I whisper directly into her ear. "No matter where you run off to." And that's a goddamn promise. She can run as fast or as far as she wants, but River West will always be caught by me. Or the others.

"Sounds like a fun game," she says with a wink, pushing me away from her playfully. "Take us home now, Cal."

God. I wish she'd say my name like that all the time. All breathy and deep, just begging me to take her right now. If we weren't in public, I'd rail her against the car. Fuck that camera still flashing.

River's brows furrow as alarm widens her eyes, focusing on something behind us. My heart rate kicks into overdrive. Her stalker might be gone, but we've all been on high alert, scanning for any more threats. Who is to say that he was the only one coming after her? He had friends, after all. Three of them, to be exact. What if they're upset that their friend is dead because of River?

Swiveling around, I cover her with my body, facing the person who has somehow snuck up on us.

The man grins, plucking a toothpick from between his teeth. His head nods in greeting as a smirk pulls at his lips.

Fuck. I let out a breath but don't move from in front of River. I'll protect her from anyone. Even if I know who they are.

"Jesus, Ruthless," I shudder, blowing out a breath at my former fight organizer.

"Sorry to interrupt, Kid. Saw you over here with your lady friend and thought I'd stop by and say hello." Ruthless offers us a toothy grin as he holds his hands up in surrender.

"Do you come to the library often?" I quip, shaking off the adrenaline pouring through my veins.

Ruthless snorts, nodding to the little person clinging to his hand. "My kid likes the readings. But something came up." He shrugs. "Haven't seen you around much," he says, twirling the toothpick with his tongue. "The crowds miss you. Want you back." He raises an intimidating brow, prodding me for information.

The moment River told me that Lyric didn't like the marks on my face, I quit. No questions asked. I'd do anything for them. Besides, I couldn't stand to see Lyric cry anymore for me than she had. It broke me to wipe her tears away, knowing I was the reason that I had bruises on my face.

So, much to Ruthless' dismay, I talked to him and let him know I was done. Out. No more.

I know he misses the attention I brought to the ring. The money, too. I was Rock Star. One of his best fighters. And I loved it while I did it. But I'm done with that life now. It's in the past. Just like a slew of other things.

"I've found peace," I say, crossing my arms over my chest. "I don't need to fight anymore."

"Can see that," he says with a shrug. "If you ever change your mind…" he trails off, grinning more at something behind me. "Ah, you're the little lady from the crowd."

River snorts without fear. "Something like that."

"If your man here ever needs to let out some aggression, well. I got him covered," Ruthless's deep voice breaks through the darkness, sending anxious shivers down my spine.

He stares at me like a piece of meat. Like I owe him something. Maybe I do. He saved me from a life of drug consumption. Instead, giving me a way to let it all out in the octagon. I'm forever thankful he stepped in and stopped my self-destruction. But I won't risk making my daughter cry again.

"It was nice seeing you, Ruthless. But I'm out."

His dark eyes assess me, and he nods. "Sure thing, Kid. I'm always around. You know where I'll be."

I nod. "Of course…" I trail off, thinking about the last time I stepped foot into the old school.

I won't. That life is behind me. Just like everything that happened before. It's in the past. The old Callum. I'm new again. With a brand-new outlook on life. I don't need to ram my fists into anyone's skull to feel better. All I need is my girl, my brothers, and my daughter.

End of story.

I nod. "Of course. Thanks for the opportunities, man," I say, holding out my hand.

"You're a good kid," he mumbles, clasping my hand with his, and we shake on it. "Miss seeing you around."

I lick my lips when he walks away, holding tight to his kid. Together, they lean in and have a discussion before disappearing into the parking lot.

"He seems lovely," River quips, watching as he leaves.

"Lovely and him don't mix. He's a solid dude. Good fight coordinator…" And he saved my life. But I won't go into that detail just yet. "How about we get her home?"

River and I get into the car and take a long way home, enjoying the ocean views. Her hand slips into mine over the center console, squeezing as we take several turns, enjoying the silence. And each other's company. Finally, after twenty minutes, we pull into her driveway, and I park the car.

"Want to put her to bed?" she asks, inspecting my face in the shadows of the car.

"I'll put her to bed." A smile grows across my face when I bring our conjoined hands to my lips and lay a gentle kiss along her flesh. "And then I'll put you to bed."

Through the darkness, I only hear a sharp intake of breath before I get out and collect a still-sleeping Lyric. I waste zero time getting this show on the road. My girl needs me. I can practically taste it in the air.

When River unlocks the front door, I follow her all the way back to Lyric's room, where I lay her down on her bed.

"Good night, Ladybug," I murmur, kissing her head as River undoes her shoes.

"Daddy," she says with a groggy voice. "Don't leave." Her tiny hand shoots out with deadly accuracy, grabbing me by the shirt.

"Ly," River sighs, throwing her shoes near her white closet doors.

"It's okay. You go to bed; I'll only be a minute." River raises a brow at my demand, but she does as I say and leaves the room.

"Daddy, the monsters are back," Lyric mumbles, yawning as she snuggles deeper into her bed.

"The monsters?" I question, peeling her fingers away from my shirt. Without a fuss, she lets me pull the purple comforter over her legs and up to her chin.

"Mmhmm. Tap. Tap. Tap," she mumbles as her little eyelashes flutter again.

"I won't let the monsters get you." Leaning forward, I brush another kiss on her cheek.

"Night, Daddy," she mumbles just before the snores start and sleep takes hold.

I could stay like this forever at her bedside. Watching her rest so peacefully is the greatest joy.

But I have other plans to follow through on. In detail. With my tongue. And other things.

On my tippy toes, I sneak out of Lyric's room. Determination takes hold as I march across the hall and walk straight into River's room, stopping dead at the gorgeous sight before me.

My heart rate accelerates, pumping blood straight to my dick and hardening it in an instant. She doesn't have to touch me to have this effect on me.

Fuck. She will be the death of me.

There's my girl lying back on her bed. Completely and utterly fucking naked. Displaying her body for me like a treat I can't wait to savor. Saliva pools in my mouth the moment I visualize my tongue running over every surface of her body, worshiping her like the goddess she is.

My Little Star is mine right now. No one else's. They aren't here to disturb us or join. So, I'll take my time with her. Hours, if I have to.

I lick my lips, reaching behind me, shutting, and locking the door. If

Lyric needs any assistance, she can knock. But hopefully, she's sound asleep and will be for the next few hours.

"I heard you wanted to put me to bed," she says in a sultry voice, running her fingertips over the cool sheets of her bed.

"Oh, do I ever, Little Star. Look at you." My eyes travel up and down her body, memorizing it for later. "You're ready for me," I say, taking a deep breath as heat rushes up my neck. "Are you wet for me already?"

Lust dilates her eyes to saucers. Her labored breath pours from between her parted lips. Just as she slowly trails her fingers down her abdomen with deliberate strokes. Forcing my eyes to watch her every move. Leaning back onto the bed, she peels her legs apart, displaying her wet, pink pussy to me.

"I might be," she says on an exhale, keeping her gaze connected with mine.

I sharply inhale as her fingers slowly spread her lips, and her fingers plunge inside her, moving in and out.

"Oh, yeah, Callum," she moans breathily. "I think I am. Why don't you come over here and find out?"

I don't have to be told twice.

As I march toward her, I throw my shirt on the floor, kick my shoes off, and undo my jeans, taking everything off until I'm throbbing and hard, landing on her bed. A primal feeling to take her rushes through me, begging to be where her fingers move in and out.

I watch with rapt attention, barely daring to breathe as she continues her movements. I'm transfixed. By her motions. By the breathy little sounds coming from her throat and softly filling the room. Everything about her draws me in. And it's worse than before. I want to wrap myself in her and never leave.

I throb against her comforter, not daring to make a move. Her toes curl in the sheets, and her body stiffens until I grab her wrist, stopping her movements. She can't get off unless I'm the one making her cum with my name on her lips.

I ache to bring her pleasure.

"My turn," I whisper, slowly bringing her fingers out of her pussy. I groan when her wetness coats them, and then I lick them, savoring the flavor of my girl on my tongue.

My tongue swirls around her fingers until I let them go, letting her hand drop onto the sheets.

"I'm going to eat my dessert now," I whisper, leaning in closer to her pussy until I'm face-to-face with it. My warm breaths blow over her soaked cunt. "Say my name, Little Star."

My name falls from River's lips over and over when I plunge my tongue deep into her pussy, carving my name into her spasming walls. Fuck. She tastes so goddamn good.

Her back practically arches off the bed when I remove my tongue from her pussy and swirl it wildly around her clit. Over and over again, I make circles and thrust my three fingers deep inside her.

"Callum," she gasps, gripping my hair when she comes around my fingers, squeezing them tight.

"You're more delicious than I remember," I murmur, pressing my lips to her pussy one last time. Slowly, I work my lips up her body until I'm hovering above her, lining my dick up with her pussy. "Sometimes I think you were meant for me."

She smiles, running her fingers through my hair and down my jaw, wiping away the moisture pooling on my chin. In unison, we groan when I slowly enter her.

My eyes roll into the back of my head when her softness wraps around me, squeezing when I bottom out.

"Oh, Little Star," I moan, pulling out and slowly working myself back in. "I'm going to take this slow," I murmur, resting my forehead against hers. "Maybe all night."

She moans, bringing her lips to mine, and thrusts her tongue into my mouth. Intertwining together and slowly dancing. Nothing about our connection is hurried. Minutes pass, and an hour ticks by.

She gets on top, riding me with her head thrown back and her tits bouncing with every thrust. Yet, I hang on. I don't blow my load.

Sweat coats every inch of our flesh when I throw her onto her back again, feeling the familiar tingle working down my spine. My balls tighten when I thrust back inside her, working myself in and out at a steady pace.

River moans, throwing her head back when my fingers brush against her clit, turning heavy circles.

"Cum for me, Little Star," I murmur, sucking her nipple into my mouth until she's squeezing around me and calling out my name. "River," I cry out, stopping my thrusts as I cum deep inside her, coating her spasming walls. "You're the best thing that ever happened to me," I whisper, kissing her lips again. "Twice over. I wouldn't give you up for the world."

She smiles, grabbing my hand when I fall to her side, curling myself around her. "I wouldn't give you up, either. We're meant for this life."

"We are. Now, how about we take a hot shower?" I ask, brushing her hair from her face.

A tired grin pulls at her lips. "Okay," she hums with a yawn.

Over the next hour, I take my time washing her body. When I said I'd worship her like she deserves, I meant it. In and out of the bedroom. She'll never wonder again if we're for real. Or if we love her. We do. I do. She's my forever girl, and I tell her so when we fall asleep on fresh sheets after getting cleaned up.

River falls asleep quickly, cuddling her face into my chest. Through the darkness, I watch her bare chest expand and deflate with her breaths. Some would say it's creepy, but I want to memorize what peace looks like drifting over her face when she's lost in dreamland.

I hold her close when her bedroom door opens, revealing a grinning figure standing in the hall.

"Dude," I mutter, shaking my head when Rad waltzes through the room with slumped shoulders.

"Couldn't sleep," he mutters, taking off his layers of clothes, only leaving his boxers.

"You're lucky we unlocked that door," I say with a pointed look as he slips into bed and curls around the backside of her body with a satisfied sigh.

"Yup. Now, I can sleep," he murmurs, kissing her cheek.

"How the hell did you get in here?" she rasps without opening her eyes.

"I have a key."

That makes her peek open an eye. Turning her head, she looks at him with furrowed brows.

"A key? I never gave you a key."

My gaze snaps to him when he chuckles. "You didn't have to give me a key, Pretty Girl. I always find a way in."

"That's creepy, Rad," she grumbles, shaking her head.

He grins more, curling his hand around her waist. "Nah. Not creepy. It's for your protection. What if you needed me, and I couldn't get in? I couldn't let that happen. So, I stole your key and made myself a copy before you even noticed."

River stiffens. "Yeah. Totally not creepy," she mutters with a sigh.

"Besides, I had a brilliant idea come to me. So, I couldn't sleep either. I missed you today. Cal hogged you, and it made me sad."

"Sharing is caring," I say, flicking his ear.

"When did you become so mean?" he whines, covering his ear.

"What's your idea? I'm awake now," River grumbles into my chest.

"Do you have any plans for our baby girl's birthday? Because I have the best damn idea on the fucking planet." Pride leaks into his tone when he grins so bright it's visible in the darkness of the room. "I'm taking your silence as a go-on moment. How about we rent out the East Point Amusement Park? It has that cute little unicorn section for kids and maybe some roller coasters for us adults. What do you think?"

"Not a bad idea," she says. "But let's smooth over the details later. I'm tired again."

"I HAVE AN IDEA!"

I raise a brow when Rad waltzes into the living room, pointing his finger toward the ceiling.

Great. The brilliant idiot has an idea. Judging by the goofy grin stretching his lips, he thinks it's a good one. I'm going to need a shit load more coffee before this is over. I just fucking know it.

The morning sun blazes in through the windows on our lazy Saturday morning. It's been a week since we returned from Central City, and everything is falling into place after our time together with River.

Like beautiful patches coming together after being blown to bits. We're repairing ourselves one stitch at a time. Not only our relationship with each other, but our relationship with ourselves as individuals.

We came to an agreement with River when we got back about taking things slowly. She's determined to get to know us better again as the men we are now as opposed to who we were back then. AKA—she wants to take things at a glacial pace, which is fine. Totally fine.

Slow and me don't mix anymore. I've had my taste, and now, I need to devour her completely. With all the restraint I have nestled in my body, I'm trying to hold back from tearing every inch of her clothes off whenever she's around.

More than anything, I want to show her I can respect her wishes. And I do. I love that she wants to reacquaint herself with us before we jump into the deep end with each of us. The last thing our new relationship needs is for us to drown before we ever learn to swim together. Despite the paparazzi constantly watching us and photographing our every move, which she doesn't seem to mind, I'm letting my River Blue come to me, like she has the others.

Which immediately took my plans of moving her in with us out the window. If it were up to me, I'd hogtie River and kidnap her, so she'd stay with us twenty-four seven. Her and Ly.

Am I feeling a little territorial about my woman? Yes, yes, I am. I've been away for too long, suffering in an all-consuming rage.

I need her.

She's the light at the end of my darkened tunnel, shining brighter by the day.

"You and great ideas are usually not in the same sentence," Callum quips from the couch, nursing a cup of coffee with one eye open.

Sometimes I wonder how Rad rolls out of bed in the morning with so much pep. It's disgusting.

Rad frowns, stopping short. "I have good ideas. I take offense to that."

I shrug. "Sometimes." More like never.

"Sometimes? Rude," he huffs, plopping down next to me on the couch. "You assholes never change."

"What's your idea?" Asher asks from the recliner, lazily rocking himself.

Rad grins. "I want to throw my Little Pretty Girl a birthday party. She's going to be five soon." His brows furrow, pain twisting his expression.

I know that look. Haunted. Pained. Filled with regret. It's the same one that consumes me every time I think about what we've missed out on.

Instinctively, my eyes dart to Asher, sitting rigidly now. He knows that look, too. It's written on his face. Anguish and utter devastation contort his features, dropping his eyes to the floor where he studies the wood like it's the best thing he's ever seen.

"I'm sorry," Asher says again, licking his lips. "I know we missed a lot of time with her because of me." Guilt drips off every word he utters, thickly laced with a pain I can't even explain. His hand rubs across his chest. No doubt aching from his massive mistake.

I know what he did hurts him, too. It has to. He was an asshole for what happened. But we're moving forward. Together. With the help of therapy and group sessions, we've come to rebuild our relationship as friends. We're a damn brotherhood again. And damn, does it feel good.

"Every birthday. Christmas. Easter. Thanksgiving." Callum murmurs, looking deeply into the swirls of his coffee.

"Every step. Her first words." I shake my head, sinking my teeth into my tongue. "It happened, okay?" My gaze connects with Asher's glossy eyes, and he nods. "You can't take it back. But we're here now. In the present, to be there for Ly. We can talk to the therapist about this more. Okay?"

"Okay." He nods with reluctance, pulling his lips into a tight line.

"So, no more missed birthdays or holidays. We're here for good," Rad says, rubbing his hands together.

"Tell them your idea," Callum huffs, sipping his coffee with a knowing look.

"Four words..." He grins, looking around the room as anticipation builds in the air.

"Go on," I say, rolling my wrist.

"Put us out of our misery," Asher quips with a snort, wiping away the uncomfortable look.

Every so often, I see defeat in his eyes. He's still beating himself up every chance he gets. Even in River's presence, he takes a backseat, offering to care for Ly if we want to go out. Asher did a shitty ass thing when he ripped us apart. But I don't want it to define him anymore.

River forgave him and us. There's no need to keep rehashing what he did. It'd be different if he didn't feel remorse. But he does. He feels it with every step he takes. So, he's off the hook for now.

"East Point Amusement Park." Rad holds his hands out in front of him with a grin. "Huh? What do you think?" His brows waggle with excitement as he looks around the room at our stunned expressions.

I blink several times. "You mean the place off the highway with all the rollercoasters and stuff?"

"Yeah! That's the place." He physically lights up, jumping from his seat to pace the room.

"Why that place?"

East Point Amusement Park is larger than life. Filled to the brim with rollercoasters, arcade games, kiddie rides, special sections, and so much more.

Rad swivels in my direction with a grin. "Because our little girl likes unicorns, and that's the birthplace of her favorite ice cream. Believe me! I researched all night long, looking for the perfect place. Just imagine our baby girl on the unicorn ride holding an ice cream cone and laughing. They even have a whole unicorn adventure inside the park, with kiddie rides, unicorn games, and that damn ice cream. The owner said we could buy out the whole park for a day. Her birthday is next Saturday." He wiggles his brows again, waiting for our excitement to kick up.

"Can confirm. I'm pretty sure he kept River up all night long with his search," Callum says with a groan, finishing off his coffee.

"Well, would you look at that? He does come up with some good ideas," I snark, chuckling when he flips me off.

Poor bastard. He's not sleeping well again. And I know damn well the cause of his ache and the balm to his restlessness—our girl. But apparently, he was with them last night after Cal took Ly to the reading.

"See! I told you! You fuckers didn't believe me." He rolls his eyes in disbelief, shaking his head. "Even my Pretty Girl agrees it's a good idea."

"Book it," I say with a nod. "It can be a big surprise party. We can invite Ly's friends and family."

Excitement thrums through my veins at the prospect of surprising my baby girl with a unicorn-themed party, her favorite ice cream, and plenty of presents. The need to spoil the hell out of my mini-me has me thumbing through my phone on the hunt for the perfect birthday present.

The ultimate unicorn stuffed animal with sparkles and a horn. I grin when it has the option for a voice message. All you have to do is press its hoof, and your voice will come through. And sold.

I furrow my brows when a loud thump comes from the front door, echoing through the house.

"The hell?"

We all look at each other when the sound thumps again, followed by a little voice calling out to her daddies.

My fucking heart drops. Flashbacks of the first time I laid my eyes on Lyric flash through my mind. Her frantic cries. The tears I couldn't wipe away fast enough. Shit.

"River better not be dead again," Rad hisses, running toward the door as we all follow behind with our hearts in our throats.

I grunt when Asher slams into my back as we huddle around the door. Nerves shake my fingers when Rad throws it open, staring down at our little girl.

"Daddies," she says with a big grin, clutching two white bunnies to her chest.

"Little Blue," I say, kneeling down in front of her. "What's wrong?" I frantically check her over, noting the backpack glued to her backside. She smiles so damn wide it's almost blinding.

"Nuffin. I'm staying here tonight. We're having a sleepover! With lots of cotton candy," she says with a shrug, casually pushing me out of the way with her tiny hand. I don't fall on my ass when she shoves by, but I think I could have.

"What the hell?" Rad asks with his eyes glued to the little girl strolling into our house with nothing but a smile, her backpack, and her two stuffed bunnies.

"She wanted a sleepover," River says out of nowhere.

"A sleepover?" Callum blanches.

"Yeah. Good luck!" River says, waving a hand as she turns to leave.

"Whoa! Pretty Girl!" Rad grunts, rushing after her with determination. "What's happening right now?" he asks, clutching her shoulders and stopping her retreat.

"I'll uh…make sure she's settling in okay. Looks like we have a guest for the night." I nod at Asher as he walks away with a grin lining his face. I bet he can't wait to cook and play with her.

Callum sighs. "I'll help him."

"She wanted to stay with you guys," River says, sinking her teeth into her bottom lip. Amusement soars through her sparkling eyes like she finds the prospect of us alone with Ly hysterical.

"Oh, yeah?" Rad asks, lighting up at the idea.

"We don't mind," I say, meandering over to where they're standing at the bottom of our porch. "She's welcome any time. You know we love to spend time with her."

"You could sleep over, too," Rad says in a low voice, smirking when she shudders from his touch.

"That, too," I say, brushing her hair over her shoulder. "You could sneak in after we put her to bed. Then we could play some adult games."

She snorts, batting us away. "Such charmers. Would these adult games include the no pants dance?"

"That could be arranged," Rad says, waggling his eyebrows as he undoes his belt.

"Jesus, keep your pants on," she laughs, shoving him away. "Listen, I couldn't stop her. She just packed a bag and told me she was going. I barely had time to grab shoes when she stormed out the door. For some reason, she was determined to get here. I think—" Her brows furrow. "I think she misses seeing you guys all day, every day."

"We could fix that, River Blue. We could build a big house right over there for the five of us."

I can see it now. Our beautiful forever home rises in the distance with enough room to accommodate all of us, plus more. If we wanted, of course. There's nothing that sounds better than knocking River up ten times more and having kids and pets running around. It's the normal family I've always dreamed of. With an abundance of love pouring through the house to fill the ocean. Our children would never know what it felt like to lie in bed at night, wondering where the next meal or hug would come from.

"Keep dreaming, Romeo," she quips.

I don't miss the way she looks out in the distance to the place I pointed to with dreamy eyes. She's keeping us at arm's length, doing what she needs to do. That's fine. I can tell it's eating her alive not to be by our side. She's aching to fall into our loving arms and ride happily out into the sunset.

"Well, then, Pretty Girl. Enjoy your day all to yourself. Just if you take a hot bath or play with that amazing little rose later, take lots of videos for me. Moan my name a little so I can go to sleep with a smile."

River rolls her eyes, leaning in to kiss his cheek. "Mmmhmm," she hums with mischief.

"Enjoy your day, River Blue. We'll take good care of our baby girl." I kiss her lips before she walks away.

What could go wrong?

"What the hell do we do!?" Rad hisses, panicking as Lyric throws up every fucking thing we've given her tonight.

Cotton candy. Cake. Cookies. Pizza. Shit. We broke our child with junk food.

"Jesus," Callum grunts, pushing a fist to his lips. "Hold her hair or something."

"She's going to need a bath," Asher remarks, standing at the edge of the bathroom with a sickly green tint taking over his complexion, staying as far away from the spewing child as possible.

"My belly hurts," Ly says, sitting near the toilet with her bottom lip puffed out. "Hurts so bad, Daddies."

I turn away, taking a deep breath when she yacks where she sits, spewing chunks of candy, cake, and whatever the hell else Rad engorged her with all down her shirt and onto the floor.

"Oh God, I think I'm going to be sick," Rad groans, clutching his stomach next. "Yeah, I'm going to—" Rad doesn't say another word when he leans over the toilet and empties his stomach into the water.

"Daddy," Ly whines, puking again.

"Jesus Christ, we need an exorcist," Rad moans into the toilet. "Be gone, devils!" he hisses, spitting into the toilet and finally flushing it.

"Fuck," Asher hisses, pressing his hand to his mouth again. "This is like a goddamn puke fest."

"Should we call River?" Callum whispers in hysterics. "We need to call her. She can fix this. Fix this, Kieran!" His wide, gray eyes scan the room frantically, searching for God knows what.

"No!" Rad hisses. "Then she'll never let us have Ly alone again. You won't tell Mommy we fed you too many sweets, will you?" he asks, batting his eyelashes just like she does.

Lyric pouts, rubbing at her stomach. "Nope, Daddy. I won't, I promise —" her little voice trails off when she looks down at her puke-soaked shirt. "Is dirty," she whines, tears coming to her eyes.

First, she has a tummy ache and pukes, and now, she's about to cry about the stains lining her shirt. Not to mention the stomach acid stench wafting from her body.

"Bath time," I say, kneeling in front of Lyric. "Is it okay if Daddy gives you a bath? We can go to the bathroom in my room. I might have some bubbles."

"I uh, have a bath bomb she could use. It's green, though," Asher chimes in, rubbing the back of his neck.

Her entire face lights up, and she nods. "Bath bomb!!" she squeals like she didn't just projectile vomit all over the room.

Little devil.

"Let's take this shirt off first," Asher says, holding his breath as he pulls it over her little head, muttering unintelligible words resembling fuck and shit. "I'll throw this into the wash and grab the green bath bomb. Little One, you have a fun bath, okay? I'll be up there in a sec."

"I guess I'll clean up the mess." Rad's lips turn down as he surveys the vomit chunks on the floor. "I'll just puke my way through it," he whines, covering his mouth.

Lyric nods with excitement, taking my hand in hers. I hold back the hot acid sitting in the back of my throat when she pulls me out of the bathroom, and we make our way upstairs.

"All right, Little Blue. Let's get you into the bath," I grin, starting to fill up the bath with warm water.

"Here," Asher says, peeking into the bathroom and handing me a green-looking ball.

"You use these?" I ask, holding it up in the air to examine it.

"They smell nice," he mumbles, turning beet red, and walks away before I can say anything else.

Within a few minutes, tiny green bubbles appear in the water, getting bigger as the tub fills. After getting Ly undressed and ensuring she's comfortable, I set her in the water and begin washing her face and shoulders with a washcloth.

"Lean your head back," I murmur, finding a large cup.

"Okay," she says, squeezing her eyes shut.

Emotions bubble in my throat as I gently lean her head back and pour the water over her hair.

"Does your belly feel better now, Little Blue?"

"Mmhmm," she hums softly as my fingers work through her hair, lulling her into serenity as I push shampoo through her strands and repeat the process.

"Do you love Mommy?" she asks, wiping her eyes when I'm finally done washing her hair and body.

Sitting back on the floor, my stomach drops at her question. "I do," I whisper, grabbing a towel to wipe her face off. "I've known your mommy since she was your age. We were best friends."

"Then why didn't you want me?" she whispers, squeezing her little eyes shut. Her little lips quiver, and she sniffles, trying hard to hold back her heavy emotions.

"No," I whisper frantically, clutching her little face between my palms. "I always wanted you. I just didn't know about you as I should have." Fuck. My heart pounds in my chest when she sniffles, slicing through my fucking soul. No child should have to feel such deep, earth-shattering emotions. "I've always wanted you, Little Blue. Even if I didn't know about you. I swear, baby girl. I love you."

"I love you, too, Daddy," she whispers, leaning into my touch.

"How about we get you out of there and into some pajamas? Then you can show me what you watch on your tablet," I murmur with a broken heart until she nods.

"Okay, Daddy," she says softly as I grab a towel and help her out.

Once she's wrapped tight in a towel, I set her on my bed and dig out an old Whispered Words shirt. Much to her delight. It's like the entire night didn't happen when she climbs under my sheets after grabbing her tablet.

Selfishly I keep her to myself in my bedroom, lying in bed together under the blankets. Thankfully, the other guys give me that time to cuddle with my baby. Lyric smiles and laughs, like our conversation in the bathroom hadn't shattered her, as we watch her favorite YouTube videos until she falls asleep with her tablet clutched to her chest.

"I'll never let you down again," I murmur into her wet hair, knowing at some point in her life, I'll disappoint her. I'm not perfect. But I'll try to be for her sake. I'll be the best damn father I can be. Unlike mine. He walked away without regretting a damn thing. But that's not me. I walked away, sure. But I didn't know about her.

At some point in the night, I wake up with my brows furrowing in confusion. Last I knew, Lyric was snuggled beside me. Now, a warm body presses against mine, clutching tightly to my side.

My fingers roam the body beside mine, taking in the curvy figure snuggling into my side. Yeah, that's not Lyric anymore. That's my girl. My River Blue. I don't even have to open my eyes. My fingertips are my looking glass, revealing the woman I'm madly in love with. I'm about to open my mouth and ask her what the hell she's doing here, but she beats me to it.

"She woke up and went to sleep with Asher. She's playing musical beds. By morning she'll be right back to where she started," River murmurs against my bare chest.

I blow out a breath, kissing her forehead. "And now, you're here."

"I didn't want to be alone," she whispers, shifting so her eyes connect with mine. Only a sliver of moonlight through the blinds reveals them to me.

"You're never alone when you have us." Gently, I move a piece of hair out of her face, taking in the beauty of my best friend. My girl. My fucking everything lying beside me. "Did something happen?"

Her brows furrow. "It's stupid."

"It's not stupid. Whatever it is. You just had someone following you around for three years. You're on edge being back here."

"The wind was making the branches tap on my windows. I swear... I just felt..."

"It's okay," I murmur, kissing her forehead again. "You're allowed to feel scared, River Blue. We'll always catch you when you fall."

Her fingers trail over my jaw, and she brings her lips to mine, pressing them softly there in an unhurried kiss.

I'll hold her for infinity. Kiss her until the world burns to ashes. I'll never let her go again.

"So, are you excited for Ly's birthday party?" she asks, throwing me to my back with a sneaky grin.

Fuck. My heart pounds against my ribs when she stares at me like I'm the little prey beneath her, and she's the tiger about to rip my throat out.

Her fingers curl around my biceps, holding me in place as she climbs on top of me and straddles my hips.

The second she's settled, my hands descend on her, feeling every inch of her warmth.

"Our baby girl only turns five once. Five is a number important to all of us. We can't rewrite the past, but we're going make this five-year mark count." My fingers curl in her hair, bringing her eager lips to mine.

I groan when my tongue intertwines with hers, dancing slowly together. Her moans vibrate through my damn soul. Even more when she grinds against my hardening dick, waking him up.

"Ride me, River Blue," I groan, licking down her neck. "Put me inside you. I need you right now."

"Beg," she whispers, digging her fingernails into my scalp. "Beg me, Knight." God. Fuck. I could cum right here in my pants if she keeps breathing against my flesh and pulling my hair.

I'm never too proud to beg my girl for what I want. Only for her will I bend the knee. I'm her Knight, after all.

"Please, River. Please ride me. Fuck me. I need you so damn bad right now. I need to be inside you one more time. Pull my hair. Choke me. Fuck me. Please!" I cry out when she claws her fingernails into my scalp again, yanking at my hair. Leaving behind the delicious burn that lights me up from the inside out. My dick throbs harder. My hips push up, begging for friction. "I need you. So fucking desperately."

River's fingers wrap around my length through my sleep pants, slowly stroking up and down.

Now, we're getting somewhere.

"Please," I gasp when she shimmies down my body and pulls me out of my pants and boxers. Her warm tongue glides over my tip, sucking my pre cum from my slit. My hands fly to her hair, holding her in place when she swallows me whole, taking me into the back of her throat. My balls tighten a fraction as heat swarms in my gut. I'm ten seconds away from exploding in her mouth. "If you keep that up, I'm going to cum down your throat," I gasp, yanking her up until she's face to face with me. "Fuck me, River Blue. Fuck me so hard."

She grins, sitting up and taking off her T-shirt and then her bra. I marvel at her fucking beauty. Reaching up, I caress her soft breasts, pinching her nipples between my fingers.

"Fuck," she gasps, thrusting her chest out. I grin as she squirms on top of me.

"Take it all off, Blue." I don't have to tell her twice. In seconds all her clothes are gone, and she's perched on top of me again, sinking down until I'm fully inside her.

"Fucking hell," she rasps, sinking her fingernails into my chest.

Mark me. Use me. Fuck me.

"That's right," I rasp, clutching her hips. "Ride me, River Blue."

River throws her head back with a groan, swiveling her hips several times. With each movement, my dick hits every inch of her pussy. My damn balls tighten embarrassingly early until I'm cumming deep inside her.

"Holy shit," I groan, emptying everything I have deep inside her pussy.

River slumps against my chest, brushing her lips along my flesh. "I think I'm addicted to you," she murmurs, working her way up my neck until her lips caress mine.

"You're not the only one," I whisper, weaving my fingers through her hair. "I'm hopelessly addicted to everything about you. And that'll never change. Ever again. Now, let's go enjoy a hot shower together and get cleaned up."

She grins, slowly rising off me, and stands by the bed. "You better wash me good, Knight."

And I fucking do. At least three more times against the shower wall. Once I had her in my clutches, there was no way I was letting her walk away without walking funny. By the time we're in bed, I hold her close to me, reveling in the feel of her flesh against mine.

"Do you care if I take Ly out for some ice cream tomorrow? Maybe some shopping… I…" My heart breaks when Lyric's questions from earlier ring in my mind. My poor baby has lived her life thinking we didn't want her when the opposite is true. If I had known about her, I would have been there from the second she started growing inside River's womb. Every day I'll live with this ache in my heart that Lyric's first years were taken from me. But I can't live in my past failures. I'll live in the now and make it up to her every second I get.

"Knight," she murmurs, running her fingers over my bare chest. "You don't have to ask. You can take her. She's yours, too."

"Thank you," I breathe, mentally planning out what we're going to do. "Night, River Blue. I fucking love you."

"Love you, too," she whispers before drifting off to sleep in my arms.

"Pick whatever flavor you want."

Lyric's huge, mismatched eyes dart wildly around the tiny ice cream shop with wonder, latching on to the vast display of flavors under the glass container. Pinks. Blues. Hell, there are even sparkles in the damn ice cream. With every color she gazes at, the more excited she becomes, barely containing it as she bounces beside me.

Her tiny hand squeezes mine in excitement.

"Double scoop?" she whispers, staring at me with pleading eyes.

"Triple scoop, if you want."

The worker behind the counter flinches when Lyric's sweet squeal rings through the shop, catching the attention of several parents sitting with their families. Cue the curious whispers starting all around us, saying my name beneath their breaths to their friends, knowing exactly who I am.

"I wants a triple scoop of unicorn sparkle ice cream, pwease," Lyric says with confidence, standing on her tippy toes barely as tall as the counter. Her little eyes watch the redhead with the name tag—Penny—behind the counter, smiling at her.

"Of course. And for you, Sir?" A deep crimson tint takes over Penny's cheeks as she looks me up and down, biting her lip.

Shit. This is the downfall of being famous. I can't even have ice cream with my daughter without eyes watching our every move. The heated stare the worker gives me is nothing new. I'm used to women stopping me for autographs. Or soliciting me for a good time. It comes with the rock star territory. They don't see me as Kieran. They see me as the shirtless guy who walks around on stage doing what he loves. It's tiring.

My need to protect Lyric ramps up tenfold as I survey the room. It's nothing but families, friends, and their children, but you never know who is lurking in the background. Case in point, River, and her damn stalker. Nothing pleases me more than that asshole being off the streets and six feet deep. Now, I feel like I can protect both my girls better. A vow I will never break. They're my number one priority.

"I'll have the same." If my baby girl likes it, then I like it, too. Whatever she wants today is hers.

"Okay! Two triple scoops of sparkly unicorn ice cream coming right up. That'll be… $45.56." I blink several times, computing the amount she fucking said. Is this ice cream made with real gold flakes? What am I missing here? Fuck.

With a grimace, I dig in my pocket, pull out my card, and hand it to Penny as she swipes it. Even though I've got millions in the damn bank from working all these years, spending forty-five bucks on scoops of ice cream makes my stomach drop.

I think it's from all those years of scrounging for food after my dad left. My mother was never stable. Especially the following months after he was gone. We barely survived. Little to no food. Couldn't pay our damn heat bill. Luckily, power companies won't shut off the heat in the winter months due to not paying the bill. But when spring came? Yeah, we were out of luck for a few weeks until the church stepped in and helped us pay. Then came the eviction notice from our rental with thirty days to vacate.

"We'll be homeless," I mumble, staring down at the paper my mother threw at me with disgust.

A cigarette hangs from her mouth as she sits on the sofa, not doing a damn thing to fix it.

"Don't worry; I've got an idea." The smirk that lights up her face when she peels herself off the couch and heads upstairs without another word sends chills down my little body.

I'm way too fucking young to have to understand what's happening. But I know it all too well. Ever since Dennis—since I refuse to call him father— left us without a fucking goodbye, I've had to grow up. I've watched my mom continually dress herself up, bring men over, and then have a few bucks for McDonald's. Then, the process starts over again.

"Make yourself scarce, boy," Gloria says, fluffing up her brown locks. Makeup covers the tired lines and hides all the truths about our situation. "I've got company coming. Then, we'll go out and have some dinner. After that, we'll stop by and talk to the Aid Office. They'll have some sort of housing for us. Especially with this," she says, holding up the eviction notice. I blink several times when she lights up another cigarette and smirks like she's got it all figured out.

Somehow, my mother finagled her way into the government housing apartments after showing them her eviction notice and bank account. After that, we lived there for a few short years. But those short years were the most stable—and I use that loosely—we had ever been. With a roof over our heads and help with food and power, we never lived without the necessities again. Not to mention, moving into those apartments brought me to my best friend. The love of my damn life. Producing this cute little creature watching Penny behind the counter, furrowing her brows.

"I'm so sorry, Mr. Knight," she croaks, turning beet red again. "It says it's declined." Well. That's a first. My heart fucking stops. Declined? How the fuck does a bank account with that much money get rejected? Fuck. Just as it's declined, my phone pings in my pocket as I dig for my wallet again with a sense of dread pulling at my senses.

"Uh, sorry about that. Old card. Just use this one instead." Thankfully, my financial advisor turned me on to having multiple bank accounts as a just in case, spreading my wealth among the five of them.

Penny loses the tint as my second card goes through, and she smiles, handing it back. "If you'd like to pick out a table, we can bring it right out to you," she says, gesturing to the sea of small red and white tables lining the shop.

I nod in thanks, taking Lyric's hand as she searches for the perfect spot to sit.

"Over here, Daddy," she says, yanking my arm toward the corner of the shop where a little red, sparkly tabletop with two matching chairs sitting across from each other rests.

"Perfect spot, Little Blue." I grin when she climbs into her seat, swinging her legs with a pleased grin.

"I love this place, Daddy. Can we come here again? They've gots my favorite ice cream. I love Unicorn Ice Cream." She grins bigger when Penny sets our bowls in front of us with a shy grin, turning her entire face red again.

"I…um… Could I get your autograph?" she asks with a nervous breath. Her eyes dart all around as she scratches the back of her neck. "Whispered Words is my favorite band of all time. And—"

"Sure," I say with a tight smile, trying to remain friendly.

Nothing grinds my gears more than fans interrupting personal time. I get it. They want to meet me. Get my signature. But it's irritating when Lyric sits across from me, watching our every move. I hate taking time away from my daughter. But I also appreciate my fans. I wouldn't be here if they didn't like our music so much. I wouldn't be able to afford the fifty-dollar ice cream my daughter loves so damn much.

"Kieran, thank you so much!" she squeals, pulling a notepad and a black marker out of her pocket. "This means so much to me. You guys are so friggin good!" She's breathless by the time all the words spew from her mouth.

"Thanks! Have you been coming to see us play at The KC Club? We'll be there in two weeks." As she hovers above me, I quickly sign my name, trying to get a move on so others don't catch on that I'm handing out autographs.

River let us off the hook this weekend and next, letting us adjust from our trip back home. Next Saturday, we celebrate Lyric in the best way with tons of sparkly ice cream, her friends from school, and rollercoasters galore. Rad's really gone off the damn deep end with these crazy plans for her. Secretly, I love his enthusiasm. He's prepared to spend an arm and a leg just to get this crazy birthday party off the ground. He had a point, though. We've missed so much; it's time to make up for our absence.

"Yes-yes!" she stammers, taking the notebook back with trembling fingers. "We saw you guys a few weeks ago. You were amazing. Any plans to go back out on tour?"

I swear to fuck. My heart stops beating, ceasing to pump blood through my body. Tour. If we go on tour, we'll have to leave Lyric behind for months at a time. There's no fucking way we could take her and River with us. There wouldn't be time. It's nothing but eating, sleeping, and playing music twenty-four-seven.

Fuck.

"I, umm. We're on a break right now. We're taking some time off from touring. I'm not sure when we will again. But locally, we're playing."

My bright smile is an illusion of the turmoil spreading through me.

How could I have been so damn stupid to think this could all work out? There's no way in hell I can leave my daughter. Not even for music.

Music is the life force keeping me going. Or was it? Maybe Lyric is the only thing I need now to make life worthwhile. Since she entered my life like the little hurricane she is, the weight of everything has lifted off me. Internally, I'm so much happier than I was a year ago on the road in Europe, playing for sold-out shows.

"That's cool! I'm always watching on FlashGram to see your pictures. You guys are so good. Gah! Thank you so much!" she squeals, running her words together as she backs away, grinning.

At least I could make her day with something so simple.

Lyric watches the exchange with inquisitive eyes, watching Penny's every move as she makes her way back behind the counter.

"One day I be famous," she says with a grin, digging into her first mouthful of ice cream.

Famous, my ass—is what I want to say. There's no way in hell my baby girl will live this lifestyle. It's rough being on the road for weeks at a time. It's more than that, though. Drugs run rampant. Fans are fucking crazy. And I don't want her exposed to the wildness of being famous. But I also want to give her a chance to spread her wings and make her dreams come true. I'll do anything for Lyric. Even if it means mentoring her through something as crazy as rock and roll. Or acting. Or modeling. Whatever she wants. She can have.

"What would you want to do?" I ask, tentatively tasting the crazy, sparkly concoction on my spoon. "Well, I'll be damned," I mumble, shoving the strawberry-tasting ice cream into my mouth. "I think you're onto something here, Little Blue. This ice cream is pretty good."

She grins at me, giggling when she shoves another bite into her mouth. "Told ya, Daddy."

While Lyric is distracted with her treat, I pull my phone out of my pocket. Immediately, my heart drops when a notification from my bank card displays on my screen. Fraudulent Charges Detected. Followed by an alert that my card was locked until I called in and spoke to my advisor. Fuck. What the hell? Has someone been using my account to buy things? Why haven't I been getting any sort of alerts on my phone?

Lyric and I fall into an easy conversation as I type out a message to my financial advisor asking about my accounts. Lyric talks on and on, telling me about her all-day preschool and how she's the youngest and smallest but claims to be the smartest. It makes me laugh when she grins, exposing her teeth full of sparkles.

"I'm the smartest in the class, Daddy. That's why I gots to start early this year."

"Oh, yeah?" I grin, setting my chin in my palm, watching with rapt attention as she hums into her ice cream and babbles more. I think I could listen to my baby girl talk all day long and never get bored.

ME

Hey man, My card got declined. I got an alert, too, that there was fraud charges? Just looking in to see what's going on.

TEDDY

Hey, Kieran. Let me take a look.

I tap my nail on the table, waiting patiently for a response from Teddy. It could be something as simple as fraudulent charges or something else.

I furrow my brow when my phone lights up with a call from Teddy. He never calls. It's usually just text messages or face-to-face meetings with this guy. It's fine by me, too. I loathe talking on the phone.

"Hey, Ly. Daddy needs to take this, okay? It's an important call." She nods, digging into more ice cream, and licks her lips.

"Hello?" I ask, leaning back in my chair, keeping a sharp eye on my daughter.

"Hey, Kieran. Sorry for the call. I was just checking over your accounts. And there's a problem."

"What is it?" My heart leaps into my throat at his hesitation. I know I'll still have money in other accounts, but years of living hand-to-mouth have me panicking. I know what it would feel like to wake up with nothing.

"It got declined because there's been a stop put on the card by the bank."

I blink several times, my head fucking spinning.

"I've been out of the city for a while. Why would the bank do that?

And is that because of the fraudulent charges?" I try to get the world to stop spinning as his mouse clicks in the background.

"I'm looking at it right now. It looks like there were hundreds of charges at places around town within the last two weeks." With every word he says, the more strained he becomes.

"What places?" My jaw tics on instinct, no matter how hard I try to hide it. "And why wasn't I notified immediately?"

"Sorry, K. I'm not sure why you weren't notified. I'm looking into this immediately. There's been charges at Riggs. Jenni's Purple and Lace. Blooming Deals. There were more purchases at several clothing shops and even a purchase at the Coach and Prada stores..." he trails off, clicking more. "It looks like the last purchase was made about an hour ago at Florence's, a department store downtown. They tried to spend—" he chokes off, coughing into the phone. "Twenty grand there." Jesus. Fucking. Christ. Twenty grand? At a damn clothing shop? Who the hell has enough balls to not only spend my money but do it in the same town I reside in? Maybe that's why they didn't fucking call?

Either way, I'm fuming. That's my hard-earned money someone is blowing through. They have no right. I stood on stage for hours on end, singing my heart out. Sweating. Fucking losing my personal time. All for my career to pay for the things I need.

"It was just used?" My teeth clench together. "How is that fucking possible? I didn't give anyone access to it."

I had an extra card in my wallet for emergencies. A duplicate card to hand to my fucking mother so she could buy a few groceries. But I always made her give it back to me. Shit... Pulling my wallet out, I check through my cards, and my heart drops. It's gone. Someone used it in town. Someone took my card. Either Gloria stole it from right under my nose, or someone took off with it.

My stomach turns several times when my phone beeps, alerting me to a new call straight from Florence's Department Store.

"Hey, Teddy. I gotta go. Thanks for the information. The store is calling right now. I'm going to head there." We quickly say our goodbyes and hang up in time for me to answer the call from the store.

"Hello?" I ask, still watching Lyric happily eat the rest of her ice cream, oblivious to the murderous feeling churning inside me. She hasn't moved an inch since this whole shit show came to my attention.

"Hi, this is Angie, the store manager down here at Florence's. Am I speaking to a Mister Kieran Knight?"

"Yeah, that's me," I say, stiffening my spine as a wailing echoes through the damn phone.

"I'm calling to inform you that we've detained a Gloria Montgomery for theft of merchandise. She's asked us to call you before the police get here. We were also concerned after confiscating a credit card with your name on it after it came up as stolen. The police have been called."

I swallow hard. My rage swells like a violent storm pounding through me. I curl my fingers into a fist, ready to pummel my hanging bag to let out some of my aggression. But first, I'll have a few words with Gloria before I let them haul her conniving ass away.

Now, I need to focus on keeping this aggression locked inside so Lyric never sees this side of me.

Not only did Gloria steal merchandise from an upscale department store, but she also stole from me. Not only my money but she also robbed me of fatherhood. It's time to let her manipulative ass rot in jail. Because after today? She won't have anyone on her side to bail her out.

"Do you want to stop this? Or—" she trails off over the phone, knowing full well who I am.

Fuck that.

"Keep her there. Tell the cops I want to speak with her before I press charges against her."

"Okay, Sir."

And we hang up.

I heave a breath, running a hand down my face. My mother. Fucking Gloria. She must have done it at some point when she was desperate for my money. It's been like this since we moved her here with us. Constantly texting and calling us, begging for it. The only reason we've put up with her for this long is for our little sister, Cami. We've tried to protect her every step of the way. Including sending her to a private boarding school on the edge of town to get her away from Gloria's shitty parenting. After Asher's father went to prison, everything fell apart for them. We were the only people who picked Gloria up by her arms and coddled her ungrateful ass. It's not like she deserved a penthouse apartment or money from us. She's never been thankful. Always so damn greedy when it comes to what we earned.

She only saw us as dollar signs. Never humans. Never her fucking sons. So once and for all, the time has come to sever ties with the woman who gave me life.

"Lyric," I sigh, reaching across to clutch her little hand as she sets her spoon down. "I need to run an errand. It's right next door…" I hesitate a moment, not really wanting to take Lyric into this hostile situation. I want to protect her from Gloria's manipulating ways. But a part of me wants to show Gloria what she missed out on by sending River away. Not that she would have been a good grandma, anyway.

"Okay," Lyric says with a shrug. "But you didn't eat your ice cream, Daddy." She points to my melted ice cream glittering in the sun shining through the windows.

"We'll come back, and I'll try it again. I liked it, but Daddy has to take care of something important."

She nods, jumps down from the chair, and takes my hand as we walk to the last meeting I'll ever have with my piss-poor excuse for a mother. No… Gloria. She's no one's mother. She's a user. Manipulator. And her reign of terror ends now, including her hold over Camilla, our teenage sister who luckily lives in her own dorm at the local prep school. Our mother has never been there for her. Never protected her from Nigel's fists, like she should have. So, we did the only thing we could do on our end to keep her safe from Gloria's clutches. Since Asher's father went to prison and now, I'm sending my mother's ass there, Camilla will fall into our hands.

ME

We're going to have to enact plan 'Save Camilla'.

AKA beg our lawyers to give us custody of Cami and prove our mother unfit. It shouldn't be too hard, but it'll be a huge leap for us. Another reason going on tour would prove harmful.

ASHER

What? What happened?

ME

Get the lawyers on the phone…Gloria's been stealing money from me… And is getting arrested.

ASHER

Shit. I'll call the lawyer. The school. The landlord of Gloria's apartment…any other place?

ME

Nah, man. Thanks, tho. I gotta take care of this. Can you meet me at Florence's? Apparently, she stole my card… And I've got Ly…

ASHER

Yes. On my way.

NOTHING PREPARES YOU FOR FACING DOWN YOUR OWN FLESH AND BLOOD. Especially when that person is your mother. My life bringer. The one who carefully cooked me in her belly for nine months, shot me out, and then ruined my fucking life.

She's the one individual who is supposed to look after you. Not take advantage of you. Not steal from you—multiple times. Fuck. Her. The only person that matters now is Cami. I'll protect my sister from everything.

"Mr. Knight."

I stop dead in front of the manager's office with a grim expression, clutching tight to Lyric in my arms. Her eyes dart around, soaking in everything happening. Maybe it was a mistake bringing her with me. But I couldn't pass this up and let Gloria go straight to jail without knowing what I have to say.

Gloria and I are about to have a lot of words.

"Yes. I'm Kieran Knight," I say, holding out a hand to the police officer standing guard outside the door. "I was told my mother was here?"

His lips roll tight, and he nods. "Yes. We were told you wanted to speak to her before we took her in. And that you wanted to press charges?"

"I do. For using my credit card without permission. I have the records with my finance guy. He'll be able to prove without a doubt it was her who spent over fifty-K of my money." I seethe on the inside, thinking about all the cash her grubby hands got onto before I was alerted.

"Okay. We've got her for theft of merchandise with a value of over a thousand dollars," the officer says, looking down at his notepad.

"What exactly did Gloria try to steal?" I ask with a tic forming in my jaw again. Shit. Even saying her name now puts a bad taste in my mouth.

"Diamond earrings," he states flatly with thinned lips.

"I'm here," Asher says breathlessly, wiping his hand across his forehead as he jogs toward us.

"Daddy!" Lyric lights up at the sight of Asher, grinning at him over my shoulder where she's snuggly cuddled against my chest.

"Who is that?" the officer asks, eyeing Asher with concern.

"My brother."

At that, the officer drops his shoulders and nods.

Asher grins, stepping right into his element. Being a damn good father. Nothing lights up his face more than baking, cooking, and helping Lyric with whatever she wants.

It's like he's trying to prove the exact same thing I am. We are not our fathers. We take responsibility and love the little human we created. Or I created—but that's semantics. We're all fathers in Lyric's eyes.

"Did you have fun?" Asher asks, cocking his head to the side with a chuckle. "Looks like you ate some sparkly ice cream." Shit. I didn't even think to wipe her face off before we left.

She immediately nods. "Daddy and me had lots of unicorn ice cream. I ate all mines. Daddy only took a few bites." She side-eyes me with so much sass I choke on my spit.

How will I survive raising a tiny little River clone? At this rate, she's going to give me gray hair before I'm thirty. And so will River. Lord. Thankfully, I have the other three guys to balance out the chaos.

"It was good, Little Blue. Daddy just had an important phone call." That's the understatement of the century. Vital. Life changing. All those words ring through my mind.

"Come here, Little One," Asher says, curling his fingers in her direction as she practically climbs over my shoulder and into his embrace.

"I'll—" I stare at the door holding Gloria, whose soft, pitiful voice wheedles through, infiltrating my damn ears and making them ring. She's crying inside, begging someone to believe her that she didn't do this.

"Take your time, man. Are you—" I know what he's asking without uttering a word.

"She stole from me." My lips roll together. "After everything we've done for her. She stole from me, and I can't..." I shake my head. "After what she did to River." My eyes cut to Ly, who listens to our conversation, tilting her head like she's soaking it in for later. "I'm done with her."

God. She's going to tell River everything that happened today. Not that I'd keep anything from her. But I know kids. They're little blabbermouths. So, it looks like I'll be having a good old-fashioned sit down with River about what's to come. Especially with us taking custody of Cami and having her stay with us through the summer and being financially responsible for her, too.

"Okay. We'll be here," he says, kissing Ly's cheek. "Why don't you show me your favorite YouTube videos? You can use my phone."

"Yay!" Ly claps her hands as they walk around the corner and away from me.

"Okay, I'd like to speak to her now." And with that, the officer opens the door to the makeshift hell housing my distraught mother.

"Mr. Knight?" a tall woman with the name tag Angie on it, indicating she's the store manager, asks as I approach.

"Yes, we spoke on the phone," I say, giving her a curt nod.

"Oh, Kieran! Thank God you're here! Tell them…tell them you let me use it! They don't believe me. They-they took your card, and then the police showed up. Tell them, Kieran, that I'd never take something that wasn't mine." Gloria heaves a breath, watching me with tear-filled eyes. Metal handcuffs clink against the table she's tied to every time she tries to reach for me.

"Sorry for the theatrics, Mr. Knight. We were alerted of fraudulent charges through our computer system. But we found this in her purse first." I scowl when Angie holds up a pair of diamond earrings glittering in the low, fluorescent lights of the room. "We watched your mother through the cameras walking around. It was brought to our attention by a few customers that they saw her tossing these into her purse after removing the packaging." She side-eyes Gloria, glaring at her with rage sparking.

Gloria thought she could pull one over on them. And if she couldn't have, she thought I'd talk them out of taking her to jail by paying for the earrings she stole.

No chance in hell.

My jaw tics. "Do you mind if I have a word with her before you take her?"

"Take me? No! Kieran, tell them, sweet boy. I didn't know those earrings were in there! I'm being framed!" she cries out, wrestling with her handcuffs again, trying to scurry away from the situation like the bug she is.

"Absolutely, Sir." Angie spins on her heel and closes the door, leaving Gloria and me alone.

The air shifts as my anger rises, snuffing out the warmth of the room. Cold shivers run down my spine as my fingers curl again at my sides.

"I swear," she breathes with big, pleading eyes filled with tears.

"You swear what? That you didn't take my credit card? That you didn't spend thousands of dollars of my money? Or that you didn't steal those earrings. Tell me which one; I'm dying to find out." I raise a brow, pacing in front of her as she hunches her shoulders, looking as small as possible in my presence.

I'm not buying her sweet little mouse act. She's the fucking snake in the grass. And the orchestrator of my damn demise. Everything Gloria does is for herself. No one else matters in her eyes. We're all pawns in her little game of chess.

Well, not anymore.

Gloria sniffles, rubbing at her nose the best she can. "You gave it to me."

"Enlighten me, Gloria. When did I give you my card?" I cock my head when her bleary eyes meet mine, filling with more moisture.

She's not sad because she thinks she hurt me. There are only tears present because she is upset I found out.

Gloria scoffs, shaking her head in disbelief. "You gave it to me, don't you remember?" Fucking gaslighting bitch.

"Nope," I say with as much indifference as I can.

I learned a long time ago not to give into my emotions around her narcissistic ass.

She rolls her eyes. "Get them to drop the charges. You and I both know you can just pay for those earrings yourself. I didn't take that card. You gave it to me before you disappeared off the face of the earth. It hurt." More tears fall down her cheeks as she looks away, twisting her expression into anguish. "It hurt that you left and didn't even tell me about it. Did you go on another vacation? I could have come, too. You know?"

"Vacation?" I scoff, staring up at the ceiling. After a few big breaths, I look at her pathetic self again.

"Yeah. So, let's just go, Kieran. You know I don't belong in prison."

"See, that's where you're wrong," I say, placing my hands on the table she's attached to. "It is where you belong. I'm tired of bailing your grown ass out of situations you shouldn't have been in the first place."

She blinks several times, turning a beautiful shade of red. "Kieran Knight, you drop these charges against me and pay for those earrings, or I'll... I'll—"

"You'll what? Move away? With what money? And with what freedom? After this, Gloria, I'm going to walk out of this room and forget your existence."

"You'll never see Cami again," she hisses in a rage, pulling at her handcuffs again.

"I think you have that backward. As we speak, Asher and I are gaining custody of Cami. So, it's you who will never see your kids again."

"You can't fucking do this, Kieran!" she cries out, slamming her fists into the table. "I'm your mother!"

"My mother? Were you my mother when you brought strange men to our apartment and kicked me out without shoes on? Were you my mother when you got married and let some man put his hands on me? Leaving bruises and broken ribs? Were you my mother when you fucking offered Asher money to leave the love of my fucking life behind? Which instance were you my goddamn mother?" I heave every word, spitting my rage at the woman throwing a fucking temper tantrum in front of me. My lip curls back when she throws her head back, manically laughing in my face.

"Oh, please." She levels me with a thunderous look, losing all the theatrics from before. "If I hadn't done all those things, then you wouldn't be here. Life is fucking hard, Kieran, and it's even harder when someone leaves you with an ungrateful brat. I did you so many favors in life, including not informing you of River and the bastard child."

Don't hit your fucking mother. Don't fucking throw her into the river down the way and go to jail for murder.

"Bastard child?" I ask with a calm I don't feel. It's nothing but storms and fucking violence brewing inside me.

Gloria scoffs. "It wasn't yours anyway. She was fucking around with that damn Van Drake boy. Probably for the better. He seemed happy to help her raise the baby." My fucking blood boils to a dangerous rate at the sound of his name.

"So, that's why you did it then when you offered Ash the money? And forged restraining orders. So, River couldn't ruin the gravy train of money coming your way?"

"Those restraining orders were nothing. Judge Drake and I concocted that plan, and then he sent Van away so she couldn't poison anyone else with her lies. I also let Asher know about the videos Van had stashed on his phone," she says, rolling her eyes again. "It was easy to put the pieces together and rid you all of the vermin she was. Nothing but a slutty Central girl looking for an easy paycheck."

"That's rich coming from you," I say with a little chuckle. "Is that the whole reason behind it? Because you saw yourself in River and wanted to get her away from me?"

"She was only going to bring you down," she howls. "I knew girls like her."

"You mean girls like you? That's what you did. You sunk your claws into the first man who reeked of money so you could move us to a mansion on the greener side of town. But nothing was greener about that fucking house. You can't sit here and tell me that you enjoyed his fists?"

Her face hardens at the talk of the abuse she endured under Nigel's roof. "It doesn't matter anymore. He's in jail."

"Again, because of you. I'm curious. Did you think all his wealth was going to come to you once they slammed the prison door shut? I bet you never imagined they'd freeze every asset and sell it, did you?"

"It wasn't supposed to go like that," she says through clenched teeth. "All that was supposed to be mine. I…" She rolls her lips together.

"Do tell, Gloria," I say, spreading my arms wide. "There's no one here but me." And the cameras in the corner of the room. It seems my mother has a lot to confess to now that she's caught.

Her back stiffens, and her chest puffs out. "His partner and I had it all planned out. So, we called the feds and set it up so it looked like Nigel was the one skimming money. Once Nigel was out of the picture, we were going to take over and elope. It was all supposed to be mine, but he fuck-ing…he fucking took off too, with the rest of the money. He left me." She sniffles again, heaving an angry breath.

"So, you both set Nigel up to go to prison and then, he fucking left you, too? That's hysterical." I can't help but fucking laugh at Gloria and the shitty life decisions she's made. Now, she'll go to prison for theft and more fraud.

"There's nothing funny about it! He took all the fucking money and left me homeless, hungry, and without a cent to my name! Kieran, he left me like everyone has always left me."

Ah, there it is. Gloria has always looked for love in all the wrong places. Manipulating herself into other people's pockets and circumstances. But the one thing she's always been afraid of is getting left behind.

Seems like her nightmare is about to come true.

"That's when I stepped in, huh? I offered you a cushy life here. All you had to do was sit back and let me take care of Cami. But you couldn't do that, could you? You had to go and fucking ruin it by spending money that wasn't yours. You stole my card. You stole my fucking money. And on top of all that, you stole my life with MY daughter."

Gloria's head snaps up, locking her gaze on me. "Your daughter?"

"If you had managed to do an ounce of research on the girl you were damning to a life without the boys and me, then you'd have found out that River West is Corbin West's daughter. You know, West Records' founder. Then, you'd have known that she received an inheritance. She's also our band manager now. And the baby she had? That was mine. She's four now. Well, five on Saturday."

"What?" she hiccups, staring at me like a deer caught in the headlights.

"So, thanks for all your meddling," I say sarcastically, tossing a hand in her direction. "But, I'm pressing charges now. You stole over fifty-K from my bank account, not to mention the additional twenty you tried to spend here. Don't expect any visits from us while you rot in prison." I stand straight up and waltz toward the door with a light feeling pulling my shoulders out of my ears. "Your lease is gone. Everything in your apartment is ours. You were afraid of people leaving you with nothing. Well, now you really have nothing. I won't bail you out. No one will. Your desperate acts won't work on anyone. Have a good life, Gloria. I hope you fucking rot."

Parting shots fired, I slam open the door with force, nearly knocking it off the hinges, and race out of the room. Once outside the door, I look over my shoulder at the devastation I left behind. There she sits, the woman who thought she had it all, but now, she has nothing. Her vacant eyes stare straight ahead, and she hasn't moved an inch since I walked away.

Good.

"I'm all done here, thanks," I say, giving the officer a tight smile. "Um. Did you happen to get that interview on camera?" I ask, shutting the door behind me. "Because it sounds like Gloria had a few sleazy things up her sleeve."

"Yes, Sir. We'll look into it with the feds and let them know what we caught." The officer extends his hand, and I grab onto it, shaking it with a breath of relief.

"Thanks, Officer. If you need anything else from me, here's my number." Quickly, I jot it down on his notepad and walk away.

I'm sure in the future there will be more I have to do. Maybe go on the stand and tell the court how awful she was. For now, I'm walking away with my head up and my anger gone.

Gloria is in the past.

"Hey, Man," Asher says, standing up from a bench outside. My eyes fall on Lyric as she smiles at his phone, swaying to an upbeat kids' song blasting from the speakers. "Everything good?"

"That was a shit show," I confess, rubbing at my forehead. "She stole earrings, but yet, stole my card, too. She…" Asher clasps my shoulder, gently squeezing in support. "She admitted to fucking everything. She set up your dad to go to prison."

"Good fucking riddance," he mumbles, shaking his head.

"She admitted to what she did to River and… Fuck… I don't know how to feel about this," I whisper, swallowing hard. "She was a horrible fucking mother…"

"But she was still your mother." Asher nods in understanding. "That's how I felt about my dad. I hated him with every fiber of my being. He was an abusive loser. But he was still my dad and… It's confusing."

"It is." I trail off, staring at Lyric, mentally making a vow to never be a bad fucking parent. I'll make mistakes, but I'll own up to them every time.

"We got this, man. Every step of the way. Okay? We'll make sure Cami is ours. We won't have to worry about her getting hurt by Gloria."

"You talked to the lawyer?" He gently squeezes my shoulder again, dropping his hands.

"Yeah. Talked to him earlier about applying for custody. He says we have a really good chance since we're the brothers, and no one else in the family would volunteer. So, we probably won't have a fight on our hands. It helps we're financially secure and can prove we've been taking care of her, anyway."

"Thanks, Asher. I don't think I could have gone through with this… with anyone else."

"What are brothers for?" he asks as a smile pulls at the edge of his lips.

"Brothers," I hum, clapping him on the shoulder. "How about we get this baby home? We've got lots to plan for."

"Plan for?" Lyric asks, staring between us.

"Yup!" I say, picking her up from the bench. "Let's go home."

Together. As a whole fucking family. No more Gloria. No more stalkers. It's just us rebuilding what we had before into something bigger and better.

This is our future.

September 29th. The most special day in history. On this day, five years ago, I was blessed with the most beautiful surprise. My baby girl. The one being who majorly helped me through my depression and rage. It's because of her that I'm living.

Every morning, she brings a smile to my face. Every question she asks or piece of vital information she thinks I need brings joy to my life.

This is where I'm meant to be. Right here. Right now. At Lyric's ultimate unicorn dream.

The boys really came through when they promised they'd rent out the entire East Point Amusement Park. With little to no bribing, they were able to procure it for us at the last minute. Although the bastards refuse to tell me how much it cost them. Stating they were paying for the entire thing, and that I had better just smile and take it like a good girl.

Okay, that last part may have been during one of our few sessions in the bedroom. I may have thrown out the whole going slow thing, because it's not really working out for me. I've never been one to hold myself back from what I want. Or what my body craves.

My heart soars with what they've done for Ly already. And for me. They're proving themselves over and over again. Making me proud to have forgiven them completely and given them a much-needed second chance.

We've been happier than ever, figuring out our new life together. Slowly, of course. I'd never jump into this without caution. Only idiots repeat their mistakes.

Happy children's laughter echoes through the festive air only amping up at the promise of cake amusement park rides later. Family and friends gather around in large circles, catching up with soft drinks in their hands. As the kids play in a circle in front of us with glee.

Nothing beats today.

"You invited your mafia sister?" Rad hisses, not so discreetly staring at my sister, Journey, with wide eyes.

I snort, stepping into his side with a shake of my head. The four of us stand in a little circle on the blacktop, watching the chaos unfold.

The moment my brothers tracked each of us down and handed out our inheritances, we started a family group chat. Some participate fully and others don't bother at all. The ones who do respond to the texts have really become our family through blood and bond.

"She won't hurt you. She's harmless." I shrug, grinning when Rad shudders. From disgust or fear, I'm not sure.

My sister, Journey, may be a little out of her mind sometimes, but she wouldn't start anything here. Not at her niece's birthday party. Who she adores, by the way. Besides, I love Journey. Despite only knowing her for two years, she's become someone I can talk to and depend on.

A sister.

I have my brothers, but she gets me. Like really gets me. I would never tell my guys she threatened to come here and slice their toes off as a threat after she learned about what they did.

"You told me her and her boyfriends—"

"Husbands. They're her husbands." My eyes cut to her three husbands surrounding her like a protective wall, not permitting anyone from getting too close. Especially people they don't know. Liv casually hugs Journey in a tight embrace, rubbing a hand over Journey's engorged belly with a grin. I can't hear what they're saying, but they all seem to be smiling. You'd think three mafia kings wouldn't want a Veritas agent in their midst. And that'd be true if Liv wasn't their cousin.

What a weird West web we've created. It's gotten so big my damn head hurts just thinking about my siblings. All fourteen of them.

"That's Arrow, Jericho, and Shepp. And yeah, they're in some sort of mafia type thing." I shrug; I'm not sure what they actually do. I'd rather stay ignorant if they're committing crimes. Especially if they're sinking people in the river with concrete shoes.

They're family. That's it. They've never threatened us. Seger and Zepp seem to like them, too. So, that's a plus. Even Carter tolerates them to an extent. And he doesn't like anyone except his wife, Kaycee.

I point each of them out to Rad, adding in a little wave when Jericho narrows his eyes at me and then grins, waving back. See? For being the head of a gang, he sure is pleasant and polite. Maybe a little crazy, but that's a whole other book I can't dive into right now. Too much to tell and not enough time to explain the dynamic between my sister and those three. Let's just say they purposefully got her arrested, then bailed her out, and then… Handcuffed her to them so they could keep her forever.

Totally normal stuff. But she's happy. Even when she tells the story, she laughs her ass off.

"I've heard stories from that town…" Rad trails off when Callum snorts.

"Are you afraid of the Briar Cove Devils?" Callum asks in a soft voice, leaning in to kiss my cheek. "They're nice. You should talk to them."

"Yes. Yes, I am. I've heard what they do. They…they…pluck eyeballs, remove fingers, and—"

"Shut up," I mumble. "They're here to enjoy Ly's birthday party. They brought their kid."

I swear Journey hasn't been *not* pregnant since I met her two years ago. Including now. Her guys make a circle around her as she sucks on a large, chocolate ice cream bar like a protective entourage. They watch her every move with love in their eyes. Every once in a while, they gaze at their two-year-old toddling around, following his older cousins—Roman, Axel, and Dash—around with a grin. Ly giggles as the boys chase her, squealing when one of them taps her shoulder. Grabbing her cousin Maggie, she drags her away with a loud yelp as they all continue to run around.

"Miss West!" Kat, my assistant, calls out from behind me, hurrying along at a quick pace.

Turning, I raise my brows as she saunters forward with a grin on her face, holding tight to a large white box filled with Lyric's cake.

Perfect.

It's amazing to see how well she's come into her role as my PA. Not even a few months ago, I wasn't sure if she was going to make it. I'm not sure what happened in her life, but she was a trembling mess. Now, I'm more confident than ever that she's going to continue to help me in my department as the Fixer.

"Kat," I laugh, shaking my head. "Please, I've told you a thousand times to call me River."

She blushes when Rocco saunters up to her side and carefully helps her with the white box filled with Lyric's sparkly unicorn birthday cake.

"Hello, Doll," he says, kissing my cheek. "Mullet. Cal," he says, nodding a greeting.

"Rad. It's Rad. Hell, call me Ashton. But don't disrespect the mullet," Rad quips, fluffing his curly hair in his hands. "The mullet is sacred, dude."

"Sacred in the early 90s, maybe," Callum quips quietly under his breath.

"Heard that!" Rad hisses, lightly shoving Cal as he belts out a laugh while stumbling over his feet.

"I've got the cake," Kat beams, tapping the box. "It's perfect. Just like you ordered. Ly is going to love the unicorns!"

"Thanks so much for picking it up for me," I say with sincerity.

"It was no problem. Now, where do you want me to put it?" Her eyes dart around the enormous amusement park we've rented out. The only people admitted are the ones standing around this large, open courtyard.

The park graciously supplied a few security guards at the gates, turning around customers trying to enter. And keeping us all safe. Not to mention the plethora of Veritas agents wandering around and enjoying the party. They're no doubt packing heat under their shirts just in case anything happens.

Large roller coasters sit off in the distance, darting into the clouds and then plummeting to the earth. But those are off-limits with no attendants running them. The only rides we'll have access to are the small ones for the kids. Unicorn planes, the carousel, the fun house, and a mini-roller coaster make up our little Unicorn hell hole.

I'm not sure what it is about these magical horses with horns on their heads. She loves them, though. More than loves. She's mildly obsessed with them. Even that's putting it lightly. So much so we've had someone redecorate her room with the exact colors and unicorns she wanted as part of her birthday present. The moment she sees it tonight, she's going to flip her lid.

"We have a spot over there," I say, pointing toward a group of picnic tables nestled under a large pavilion.

"Thanks! I'll get it over there. Trevor is in the parking lot, grabbing the cooler of ice cream treats." She shyly grins, looking away at the mention of his name. Her boyfriend. The one we've only heard about and never seen.

My brows raise. They must have made up from the last time he went away without a word.

She's never brought him around. He's always working or busy when he's invited to places. Office Christmas party? He was out of town. New Year's party my brothers threw? Sick. The list goes on.

He's so damn elusive, and we've never even seen his picture. According to Kat, he hates having his photo taken. Seems odd to me in this day and age. Who hates their picture being taken? Or who doesn't have social media?

Joe from *You*, that's who.

"We finally get to meet the ever-elusive Trevor," Rocco quips, with interest flaring in his eyes as he walks in front of us.

"Yes," she blushes, ducking her head and taking off toward the pavilion without another word.

"I didn't think we'd ever get to meet him," I say, watching as she happily sits the cake down.

"Me either. Hopefully, he's a loser," Rocco quips.

"Pfft. With the way she's been getting happier, I think they're getting serious. Back off, Roc." I raise a brow when he pouts.

"Fine," he grumbles, pulling away. "Time to say hello to my Godchild. Oh, Lyric!" he shouts, jumping into the fray of kids and hoisting her into the air. She squeals at his antics, kicking her feet as they spin in a circle.

"I like him," Asher says, cocking his head and watching Rocco play with Lyric.

I snort. "You might be the only one." I point to Callum, Rad, and

Kieran standing side by side with their arms crossed over their chests, watching Rocco's every move.

Fucking cavemen. They should know by now Rocco is nothing more than a very important friend. To me and Lyric. Besides, he's married to Christian and on the prowl for Kat's undying love.

"I need to make you another shirt," Rad grumbles, wrinkling his nose. "Property of Callum, Rad, Asher, and Kieran."

"Good idea," Kieran says with a smirk. "We'll force it over your head any time you leave the house."

"Everyone will always know who you belong to," Rad adds with a grin, high-fiving Kieran over their oh-so-brilliant idea.

I roll my eyes, raising my middle finger to them. "I'm not your damn property. I belong to no one. If anything, you're mine. Maybe I should make you a shirt that says... River's Boys. See how you'd like that."

"You're under the impression that we wouldn't wear a shirt with your face on it," Rad says, raising a brow. "I would, in fact, wear a shirt that says I am your property. In fact..."

Well then. That didn't hit like I thought it would. Who am I kidding? Of course, they'd want a shirt with my name on it. That wasn't a proper threat.

"We'll get them made," Callum snorts, covering his lips with his fist.

"Hell yeah! We'll wear it at our wedding. Speaking of... Will you marry us, Pretty Girl?" he asks, smirking at me.

I huff. It's been like that for the past week or so since we got home. Every morning, I have a text asking if I'll marry them.

"No."

"I'll ask every day until you say yes," he reminds me, kissing my cheek. "I'll wear you down, Pretty Girl. Then you'll be all ours. Forever and ever. I can't wait to stick a ring on that finger." His arm wraps around my shoulder, pulling me further into the side of his body. "Do you think anyone would be offended if I took my shirt off? It's fucking hot."

"Keep your clothes on, Cowboy. This is a children's party."

"Make me those fancy sleeves again, Pretty Girl. Or I'm going to drown in my sweat." Rad pulls his T-shirt away from his body, wafting air on his face. His tongue flops out of his mouth as he huffs. "I don't even care if you cut me with your knife. In fact...cut me a lit—"

"Kids party," I hiss, covering his loud mouth with my hand.

"He's going to start having to pay a fee every time he runs his mouth." Kieran side-eyes him with a smirk.

"Thirty thousand dollars!" Lyric says, passing by, doing a twirl in her pretty, multi-colored unicorn dress. Quickly, she darts off, laughing through a candy sugar high.

Lord help us when we have to tame this baby tonight.

My heart hurts as I watch her carefree smile light up the party. She's five now. Practically a teenager. Just yesterday, I gave birth with my brothers anxiously awaiting her arrival in another room and Kaycee generously holding my hand as I screamed. Even though it made her lightheaded and awkward feeling. She stood by my side, knowing I didn't have anyone else to help ease the pain of having her and losing my boys.

My baby is growing too fast. And there's nothing I can do to stop it.

"Thirty thousand," Callum confirms, holding out his hand expectantly.

Rad licks my palm with a chuckle until I rip it away, wiping my hand down the front of his T-shirt.

"Fine. I'll keep my shirt intact," Rad harrumphs, pouting a little until his eyes fall on my face. "Pretty girl, what's wrong?" he asks, squeezing me tight.

"She's five," I groan, swallowing my emotions. "She's so big."

"She is," Kieran agrees, watching her with a big grin.

"That's a good thing, right? We want Little Pretty Girl to get bigger and grow older." Rad watches my glossy eyes, softening his confused expression. With ease, he pulls me into his side and kisses my temple. "She'll always be our baby."

Oh, swoon. Our baby. Fuck. Don't tear up. Don't show them how messed up your emotions are since having her. I swear I've turned into a pile of gooey feelings, crying at the drop of a hat. Damn hormones.

"I know. It just feels like yesterday that I went to the hospital and had her." I shake my head, reliving the memories again.

"Next time, we'll be there." Kieran's eyes fall to the ground. "I promise."

"Next time?" I ask, scrunching my nose.

"Oh yeah, Pretty Girl! You gave a baby to Kieran. Now the rest of us want a little one. Can you imagine my baby with a mullet? He's getting a mullet." He side-eyes the guys. "Don't laugh at me." I snort when they start to bicker amongst themselves.

"You really want more?" I ask with slight vulnerabilities.

"Thousands." Rad waggles his eyebrows.

"Or four." A slight red tint creeps up Callum's neck and onto his cheeks.

"We'll get to that bridge when it comes. In the meantime, we can practice as much as you want," Asher says with a cocky grin, winking at me.

"We'll enjoy the baby we have now," Kieran adds, grinning when Lyric spins in front of him with a giggle.

"Daddies, I wants to go to the fun house," she says, pointing toward the two-story unicorn house with funny mirrors and bright lights flashing.

"Whoop! Then let's go to the fun house!" Rad scoops Lyric into his arms, chuckling when she giggles more, and we all head off toward the fun house thirty feet away from the courtyard.

"After this, we'll do your cake and ice cream," I say, catching up to her and kissing her cheek.

"Hey, girl! Want me to get that set up?" Olivia asks, running up to my side. "Hey, cutie pie." She pinches Lyric's cheeks, much to her disapproval.

"Hey, Liv," I say, leaning in to hug her with a grin. "That'd be amazing. We're going there, and then we can do the cake."

She agrees, rushing off toward the cake as we leave the area, walking to the fun house.

"Wow, this is bitchin'," Lyric says with a grin, staring up at the house.

"I'm sorry. What did you say?" I huff, raising a brow at my baby girl, who has a knack for saying words she shouldn't.

"Bitchin'. Cousin Roman says it alllllllllll the time." She raises her chin with confidence, huffing at my downturned face.

"Sorry, Little Blue. That's a bad word. You shouldn't say that ever again." Kieran shakes his head, using his best dad voice to get the desired effect. I can tell the moment sadness crosses his face. He regrets being so stern.

Lyric's lip pouts out, and she nods, sniffling. "Okay, Daddy. I'm sorry. But you says it all the time."

I put my hand up to my lips, holding back the laugh that begs to escape. She has them there. They curse all the time without consequence.

"Fuck she's right," Rad groans, quickly covering his lips. "I mean, she's right. No more cussing."

"I can't be mad at that," Kieran whispers in my ear frantically, watching her pouty lip.

"You have to be," I mumble, leaning into his side. "She won't learn unless you correct her bad behavior. You did good." He perks up, kissing me on the cheek when I applaud his effort.

"Let's go," Callum says with his eyes lighting up. "I'm going to take her through," he says excitedly, holding out his hand.

Lyric doesn't waste a moment, grabbing onto his hand and practically dragging him through the entrance of the fun house, which happens to be a rolling, dark tunnel.

I smile when she falls, giggling as the piece continues to slowly roll them. Thankfully, Callum grabs her and drags her through the curtain at the end, and they venture into the unknown.

"Shall we?" Kieran asks, sweeping a hand out with mischief behind his eyes.

"You want to go?"

"Why not, Pretty Girl? Let's go through the fun house and look at ourselves in those ridiculous mirrors. I haven't seen one of these in so damn long."

Without a second thought, Kieran grabs my hand, pulling me forward.

The three of us shake with laughter as we enter the turning tube, losing our balance halfway through.

I fall over my stupid feet, plummeting to the moving ground with a thump.

"Fuck," I grumble, trying to balance myself to stand, but it doesn't work.

And wouldn't you know it? Those assfaces didn't wait for me either. There they are, laughing their heads off at the end of the tunnel, watching as I continually fall.

"Crawl to me, Pretty Girl," Rad quips, wiggling his fingers in my direction as he stands under the black sheet hiding the rest of the attraction.

I grin, shakily moving forward on my hands and knees until Rad's hands grips under my armpits, and he pulls me into the darkened room, only lit by neon LEDs.

"Holy hell," I murmur, leaning my front against Rad's, heaving a breath. "This place is crazy."

Kieran chuckles, kissing my cheek from behind. "Let's keep going."

"Yeah. Let's… But you guys have to catch me," Rad shouts, taking off at warp speed out of the darkened room and through another set of curtains.

I blink through the darkness as Rad's body heat disappears, and he whoops in the distance.

Kieran chuckles, holding me close. "I think he's having more fun than Ly."

I grin. "It's nice to let loose some days and pretend we aren't adults." I lean my head against his shoulder, soaking in the warmth he's offering me in the midst of darkness.

"Should we keep going? You never know what he's going to do."

"Yeah."

Hand in hand, Kieran and I stumble through the dark room, listening to the echoes of giggles from somewhere above us. Callum's deep chuckle, which I would recognize from anywhere, slips through as Lyric screeches with happiness.

"I'm beyond grateful we're a part of her life now," Kieran murmurs, pulling me through the next set of curtains and into a wacky mirrored room looking more like an unsolvable maze.

"Shit. Which way?" I groan, looking back and forth as nothing but mirrors filled with our bodies stare back at us. "And where the hell is Rad?" Who knows where that slippery fucker went off to. Knowing my luck, he's hiding in the shadows, ready to scare the shit out of me.

"I would have reached out," I whisper, twisting my face. "No matter how much I hated you guys, I wouldn't have kept her from you. But the restraining order…and that phone call…I'm sad you missed it all."

"Well, we won't anymore. Okay? We're here."

"Gotcha!" Rad screeches from somewhere, throwing his hands around me and pulling me back into his chest.

"Ashton!" I yell as the warmth of his body encases me, and the smell of his cologne pulls me in.

"God damnit, Rad!" Kieran hisses from somewhere in the distance.

The mirrored maze disappears completely as Rad drags me into a small room, closing the mysterious door behind us.

Stale air smothers me as I look around at the tiny room filled with excess parts and props. I blanch when a clown in the corner catches my attention, forcing my heart out of my damn ribs.

"Heya, Pretty Girl," he murmurs in my ear. "Fancy seeing you here…" he trails off with a menacing chuckle, promising me naughty things in the future. I swear my whole body relaxes the second he spins me around and places his hands on my hips.

His eyes darken further when he looks me up and down, staring at me like a delicious meal he's about to devour. Something I don't doubt. My body vibrates with anticipation. Not only with what we're about to do but with the wrongness of this, too. Here we are at a children's party and funhouse, about to fuck like bunnies.

"Where is here, exactly?"

"Storage closet," he says, grinning as he slowly backs me up against an oversized wooden box until my thighs slam into it. "I needed—" His brows furrow. "I needed some time with you," he whispers, kissing my cheek. "I'm desperate for you, Pretty Girl. So fucking needy."

"You just wanted to take your shirt off," I whisper, running my fingers through his silky mullet, pulling his curls between my fingers.

"Well, it is about to get even hotter," he murmurs, licking at my flesh with a satisfied groan.

"Rad!" Kieran shouts from outside the room, oblivious to where we are. "I swear to fuck, dude!" he grumbles, knocking so hard the walls of the storage closet bow with the force. "I'm going to kick your ass when you're done."

"Or you could join!" Rad shouts with a chuckle, darting his hand underneath my T-shirt.

"He's not invited to this party," I whisper, thrusting my tongue into his mouth.

Our breaths mingle in heavy pants as our tongues collide in a desperate dance of lust. I groan into his mouth, pulling my body even closer to his, feeling every inch of his want.

The warmth of his fingertips pinches my nipple through my bra, causing goosebumps to explode over my flesh. I buck my hips, chasing friction.

"Fuck me, Rad," I groan as his lips travel down my neck. "Make it fast. We gotta make this quick."

"Anything for you, Pretty Girl," he hums against my flesh, reaching down to undo my jeans.

His fingers dive into my denim, underneath my panties, and straight into my throbbing pussy, begging for him to fill it up.

"You're so goddamn wet already," he groans, hastily thrusting his fingers inside of me.

"Yes. Now, fuck me," I beg again, sinking my nails into his neck as I ride out his fingers thrusting roughly inside me.

"As you wish, my queen." Within seconds he removes both our jeans, tossing them to the dusty floor. Another problem for another time. All I care about right now is him taking care of this need brewing deep inside me.

My veins catch fire when he lines himself up with me. Toying with my entrance. The head of his pierced dick moves up and down my slit, teasing me until he's finally had enough.

Our moans fill the air when he enters me in one quick thrust, bouncing my body. My legs wrap around his hips as I lean back on my hands, letting him pound wildly into me.

My breath hitches when his lean fingers wrap around my throat, gently squeezing until my airflow is slightly constricted.

"I fucking love you, Pretty Girl," he moans, leaning in to take my lips hostage with his.

"I love you, too," I wheeze, squeezing my eyes shut.

"Look at me," he groans, forcing my gaze back to him. "That's it, Pretty Girl. I can tell how close you are. Your pussy is squeezing the hell out of me. So, cum with me," he begs, biting into my bottom lip, leaving behind the smallest hint of blood.

"I'm cumming," I cry out as my pussy contracts over his cock, ending his movements with a loud groan, filling the room.

Whoever else is making their way through the funhouse will know exactly what's going on inside this little closet. If they could find it, that is.

I shudder against Rad's hold, coming down from the aftereffects of my orgasm. The whole world tilts as I stare into the darkness of his eyes, reveling in the lust sparking there.

"I'm going to just live in your pussy. Little Rad likes his warm home," he rasps, brushing his lips lightly against mine.

"No," I laugh breathily, slightly shoving at his chest. "That's not going to happen." I groan, leaning into his kiss as he softens inside me.

"I love you, Pretty Girl."

I stare into his dark eyes, memorizing the moment. "I love you, too."

"Come on, asshole!" Kieran bangs against the outside again, still unable to find the door Rad snuck us through.

"Think we should head out?" Rad asks, reluctantly pulling out of me with a groan, pouting as he tucks himself back into his jeans.

"Probably. Ly was eager for her cake." Shit. We fucked inside a fun house while a whole ass party happened outside these walls. I guess that's the perk of having four guys in my life. They pick up the slack with the kiddo while I get boned within an inch of my life.

Well, when I put it that way…

I'm a terrible fucking mother. Guilt slams into me. This was supposed to be a quick, fun family adventure. And I let myself get caught up…

"You're doing something funny with your face, Pretty Girl. The one you do when you're feeling guilty about something," Rad says, bending down to grab my jeans from the floor. When he looks up, his entire face softens. "You're thinking something, aren't you?"

I wrinkle my nose, stepping into my jeans. "I…guess I feel guilty sometimes when I leave her to—" Do things like this. Drink wine with the girls. Go out with Rocco and leave her with Maggie. If it weren't for my brother's insistence I have a social life, I'd be a hermit.

"Pretty Girl," he murmurs, buttoning my jeans and straightening my bra and shirt. "You're an amazing mother. Even if you snuck off to have a one-on-one session with your boyfriend. She's probably having the time of her life. Cal has got her. We've got her. Ly will never wonder if she was loved and cared for. Sometimes moms have to take care of themselves. Or, let their boyfriend take care of them." He winks at me, kissing me one last time. "Now, let's put poor Kieran out of his misery."

I grin, grabbing his hand as he pulls open the door to the mirrored room. Kieran stands beside it with a frown, shaking his head.

"Walls are thin," he grumbles, adjusting himself. "And Liv is looking for you."

"Okay. Let's go cut some cake," I say, leading them out of the fun house.

"Oh, thank fucking God!" Olivia shouts with tears in her eyes, throwing her arms in the air.

"What's wrong?" I ask, searching her concerned face.

She pales. "We can't find Lyric."

"WHAT?" I BREATHE, LOOKING AROUND THE PARK, FRANTICALLY TRYING TO spot Lyric in the people milling around with their kids. "What the hell does that mean?"

Panic doesn't even begin to describe the feelings bubbling to the surface. My fingers tremble, unable to stay still. Possibility after possibility runs through my mind. All ending in the worst-case scenario.

"Deep breaths. We think Lyric just went to play some hide and seek," Olivia says, putting her hands up.

"Whoa. Wait. She was with Cal," Rad says, pulling me into his side and rubbing a hand up and down my upper arm in support. "Don't freak out yet, Pretty Girl. Kids do this all the time."

Freak out? I'm beyond freaking out. My breaths come in short pants. Adrenaline pours through my damn veins until I'm a trembling mess. My daughter is missing, and everyone thinks it's normal. It's not. This party is about her. Making her the center of attention. Something she can't pass up. If Olivia is frantic and pale-faced, then something is truly wrong. You can't convince me otherwise.

"Look at me, Riv. We're at a huge amusement park. She probably wandered off with one of the other kids, and they were playing. Cal turned his back for five seconds to grab a drink for them, and when he turned around, she had taken off. We'll find her." Olivia gives me that Veritas look she loves to give me when she knows she's right. Or wants to prove a damn point. She's awful fucking bossy sometimes.

"I'm so sorry, Little Star," Callum says with tears, looking on the verge of a freakout. "I didn't... I would never..." His gaze falls to the ground. Hiccups fall from his lips as he tries to take deep breaths.

"It's okay. She's probably trying to find her favorite ice cream," I say, squeezing his hand with reassurance. "You didn't do anything wrong. She could have done this with anyone. Even me. She's five. They're slippery at this age." I try to give him my best reassuring smile so he doesn't continue to beat himself up. But it doesn't work. His face falls, and tears slip down his cheeks.

Olivia claps a hand on his shoulder, taking control of the situation before we all start slipping into hysterics.

Ly is probably having fun somewhere with one of her cousins. That's it. She hasn't been kidnapped or abducted by aliens. There's a perfectly rational explanation for this.

"Believe me, that child wanders when she wants to. Something probably caught her eye. Maybe a balloon or a unicorn. We'll all split up and look for her," Olivia demands, looking each of us in the eye. "Calmly and collectively. The partygoers are helping, too. There's no need to freak out yet, okay? Last we saw her, she had come out of the fun house with Cal. They went to the hut, fifty feet away, to grab a drink. No one saw her slip away when Cal put in the order. Remember, she's wearing her unicorn dress. Riv, you've got a picture?" When I nod, she nods back. "Good, send it to all of us. We'll start canvassing the area and trying to find her. Since it's just us in the park, maybe call her name or call out her outfit."

My heart races in my chest when I bring the photo up on my phone and send it to everyone I can think of at the party. Someone will see her. Or find her. They have to. She can't be too far away. It's her damn birthday party.

Right?

"You two, start over there," she says, pointing to me and Asher, who stands rigidly beside Callum with worry in his eyes. "And you two over there, you two over there. Okay? You all have your phones?" Everyone nods in silence as the situation sits heavy on our shoulders. "Good. Please message me. I put my number in each of your phones when I had them on your trip to Central City. And I'll meet you wherever. I will check over by the entrance and canvas, making sure she didn't make a break for it."

My eyes follow her finger, pointing to the right where the unicorn carousel stands still, and the tall roller coasters stand beyond that.

"Okay," I breathe, sucking in air, trying to clear my muddled brain.

"We'll find her, Little Brat. It'll be okay," Asher whispers in my ear, gently taking my hand in his.

Together we walk as a unit, splitting off from the rest of the group as Olivia directs them to different areas to search.

I swallow hard, remembering Lyric's words from this morning.

"Mommy, I can't wait to ride the unicorn ride. The one that spins in circles and has pretty music." I grin as she twirls in her dress, going round and round with a squeal of pure joy.

It was one of the first rides she begged to go on when we stepped foot in the park.

I heave a breath when we all separate. Echoes of Lyric's name being shouted through the park rattles my nerves. This isn't like her. She doesn't wander off. She…

"She's going to be okay," Asher says, clinging to my hand as we walk around the carousel, sitting hauntingly still in the middle of the day.

The sun blares down on us without a cloud in the sky. It's the perfect day to celebrate a birthday. If the birthday girl wasn't missing. How could this happen in such a short period of time? How could she just wander away without anyone noticing? Doesn't this place have cameras? My heart drops more. Desperation claws at me. I need her in my arms.

As we make our way around the ride, the operator casually lounging back in a chair catches my eye.

"Maybe," I mutter, pulling out my phone and bringing up the picture of Lyric from this morning. "Excuse me, Sir. Have you seen this little girl?" I ask the operator as he lounges back in his chair.

A toothpick hangs from his mouth, jolting around when his tongue rolls. He pushes his sunglasses down to the tip of his nose, staring at the picture of Ly in her pink, purple, and sparkly unicorn dress, smiling at the camera.

His brows raise as he checks it over and gives me a sharp nod. My heart leaps out of my chest with hope latching on.

"Yeah. I saw her about five minutes ago. She was walking with some guy in a red zip-up hoodie." He shrugs nonchalantly, pointing in the direction of the rollercoasters.

My heart drops. Red hoodie? Who the fuck was wearing a red hoodie? Everyone I saw was in T-shirts or dresses. It's seventy fucking degrees right now.

So, who the hell has my baby?

"What? What did he look like?" I stumble over my words, begging my heavy tongue to cooperate.

"About this tall," he says, holding his arm up. So not fucking helpful. "Brown hair. That's about it."

My eyes dart around when we take a few steps away from the operator. Someone has her. She could be anywhere. Fuck. With trembling hands, I let Olivia know what I just found out so she can keep an eye out in case anyone wants to leave.

Thoughts scramble in my head. Ly has never taken the hand of a stranger she…

"Up there," Asher rumbles, turning paler than a fucking ghost. His entire body vibrates, pointing toward a giant roller coaster in the distance as he squints against the sun. "She's up there with someone on the boarding platform."

With someone. It repeats in my fucking head. Someone. Not anyone we know. A stranger. I follow his line of sight, gazing at the tall roller coaster in the sky. My daughter sits at the entrance of the tallest ride in the park at the boarding platform. With a stranger holding her hand. High in the sky, barely visible from where we are. The only colors streaking in the wind are the multiple colors of Lyric's unicorn dress. And the dark red hoodie the person wears to conceal themselves from us.

It's her. But who the fuck is he? Who has Ly? It's not anyone in the family. They'd have sent a message.

"Who the fuck is it?" I growl, taking off in the direction of the roller-coaster. Fuck common sense. Fuck it all. My soul calls out to the little being I created, needing her to be with me.

Not him.

"I don't know!" Asher shouts frantically, chasing after me at a quick pace. "I just called Olivia about where we're headed and that we saw her."

"Good!" I shout, running toward the coaster and up the paved slopes carrying me up, up, and into the fucking clouds.

My heart pounds in my ears, drowning out everything as I run behind Asher at full speed. At some point, probably because he's athletic, he passed me, giving me his back and leaving me in the dust with my heaving lungs.

When we finally get to the top of the entrance, I stop dead, slamming into the back of Asher with a quiet umph.

"Shh," he murmurs, looking at me over his shoulder with furrowed brows. I nod shakily, swallowing hard when Lyric's little voice filters through. It takes everything inside me not to jump into action and scoop her up.

"I want my mommy," her little voice sniffles quietly.

"You'll see her again," the unfamiliar man's voice says, carrying through the rock-like surroundings encasing the entrance to the roller coaster currently not running.

It's deep. Gruff, even. No one I recognize from my life. Has some crazed person followed us here? The boy's fan? My brother's fan? Fuck! Another stalker? It can't be mine. He's fucking dead. All the possibilities run through my mind in overdrive.

"I want her," she cries again, yelping when he does something to her.

I tense. Every instinct inside my body screams for me to run in there and save her. I need my goddamn baby to be safe.

"She'll come!" he says in a sharp voice through heavy breaths, causing Lyric to sniffle hysterically again. "She'll come. Now, quiet."

"We need to do this slowly…" Asher's eyes fall on the man with his back to us. His red hoodie clings to his body, and the hood covers his hair.

Asher pulls out his phone and carefully checks his messages, updating Olivia on where we are and that we need help immediately. Also, snapping a picture of him and sending it on. With shaky fingers, Asher connects a call to Olivia and leaves it in his hand, letting Liv hear everything that happens. Hopefully, with her training, she'll record everything for later. In case this all goes sideways. But if the swooping in my stomach is any indication of how this will go, it won't end well.

"This room echoes. You know?" the man in the red hoodie calls out. "I can hear every word you say. It looks like your mommy finally made it," he sing-songs the last part mockingly. "Let's get this party started. I'm tired of waiting."

My heart falls into my ass when he spins around toward us with a black gun nestled in his hand, pointing it toward my baby clutched in his tight, unrelenting grip. Tears work down Lyric's face as she trembles, but she doesn't pull away. Whatever fear she has, she knows she needs to stay still.

The moment my eyes collide with his, I die a little on the inside—those eyes. I know them. I recognize that face. It's someone I saw a week ago at Dead End. Someone I just happened to run into. Maybe it wasn't such a fucking coincidence that he was there.

Donavon fucking Drake. That is the whole reason the boys left. The videos he kept. The way he stalked me back then. My nightmare has followed me here. But why? Why him? And why the fuck now? I already had one stalker. I don't need another psycho in my life. Besides, Olivia checked in on him multiple times, assuring me he was gone. He was in Europe. Away from here. But yet, here he stands with a weapon in his hand, smiling maniacally.

"Rivey, so good to see you again," he coos, tilting his head to the side with a sadistic grin.

My lips pop open, and I shake my head. "Van…" I trail off in horror, shaking my head. "I don't understand…" His grip tightens on Lyric's arm when my eyes dart to my baby in the clutches of madness.

"The one and only…" His eyes immediately dart to Asher, who stays in front of me, protectively covering my body with his. "What the fuck is he doing here?" His teeth grind together as his eyes narrow in on Asher frozen with his hands up. Van wildly waves the gun in his direction. "I told you! You are mine, River West! You both are!" Van shouts erratically, stomping his foot.

I stiffen at his words. "Y-yours?" I stammer.

My heart threatens to punch out of my chest when he throws his head back, laughing like a loon.

"Mine. All mine. You always have been. How do you feel knowing your guy here sold you out? He came to me. Begged ME for those videos…"

"Why did you take videos?" I breathe, stepping around Asher. "Why would you do that? That's gross." I shake my head, begging to keep his attention on me so Lyric and Asher can run away.

Now would be a good time for Olivia or Carter, or fuck, I'll take Jordy, to show their faces with guns blazing and take this asshole down for good.

"Stay back," Asher hisses through his teeth, trying to grab my elbow.

"No more," Van hisses. "You've touched what's mine for far too fucking long!" In the blink of an eye, he raises the gun in Asher's direction, waving it around.

"Whoa!" I shout, stupidly jumping in front of Asher. "Van. What the hell is going on? Explain it to me!" I scream, bringing his attention back to me. "Look at me, Van. Explain what's happening." I lower my voice, trying to sound as calm and collected as possible. Something I don't fucking feel right now. Panic takes me over when he doesn't lower the weapon, leaving it pointed in Asher's direction.

His face hardens—a twitch forms in his right eye, highlighting his loss of composure.

"Oh, right. I'll explain everything to you, Rivey. Just let me touch you. I need to fucking touch you," he pleads with desperation. "Let me feel you, baby."

Fat chance.

"Let Lyric go," I say, motioning toward my baby still in his clutches.

For as long as I live, the haunting expression holding her captive will keep me up at night. Somehow, Lyric has retreated inside herself, no longer blubbering, or trying to pull away. She's a shadow of nothingness. I need to take charge of this situation before she sinks too far into herself and I'm unable to pull her out. My baby doesn't deserve to live through the pain of Van's obsession. I've protected her from this for so long.

"No," Van snarls, baring his teeth. "I let our child go, and you'll take off again and let these assholes raise her. You are both fucking MINE!" His voice echoes off the walls, filling the room with his rage. It's so visceral, the tiny hairs on my arm stand on end.

My breath catches in my chest, refusing to refill my lungs. Our? He's delusional. Concocting this fantasy that Lyric and I are his. His? Really? My mind races out of control. What the fuck do I do here? I'm so out of my goddamn depth. I need to get Lyric away from him. I have to think on my fucking feet to get his hands off of her and onto me.

It's time to save my baby and Asher. No matter the cost.

I inch forward, avoiding Asher's desperate glare to keep me within his reach. His head shakes with limited movements, like he's reading my mind.

"Okay," I say, holding my hands up, placating the asshole. "Let's just talk, Van. Okay? Let's work this out. You can touch me. Just let her go." I swallow razor blades when his eyes light up, traveling up and down my body with intense interest. Disgust fills every molecule of my body when he zones in on my breasts, licking his lips. I shiver, holding back the vomit threatening to spew from my throat.

I can do this. This is for Lyric and her safety. For Asher. For everyone else he wants to injure. I can only hope Olivia gets her ass up here before anything else can go wrong.

"River," Asher begs with choked emotions as I inch closer to Van. Every step I take is a nail in my coffin. "Don't," he pleads, reaching a hand out to pull me back.

But I'm too far gone now. Lyric is the most important thing in my life, and I can't lose her. She's my baby. I'll fight tooth and nail to keep her safe. Even if it means putting my own life on the line. Shoot me. Not them.

"Don't you fucking put your hands on her again! She is not yours! She has never been!" Van cries out, lifting the gun in Asher's direction.

I'd rather endanger my life than have any harm come to Lyric or Asher. It's my job to protect her. My fucking duty as a mother. And I obviously didn't do enough to keep her from his grasp. Somehow, he swooped in when no one was looking and stole her from us.

By why? How? How is he even here?

"What's going on, Van? Why are you doing this? Why are you here?" I whisper, wincing when his angry gaze whips to me and he points the gun right at my heaving chest.

Sweat prickles along my neck the further I walk. With small, measured movements, I inch across the platform until I stand directly before him until the gun pushes into the middle of my chest.

A breath away—within reach.

I turn everything inside of me off, shutting down. If this is my end, then that's it. I've had a good life. Fought the good fight. If it helps Asher and Ly make a break for it, then it was all worth it. They're worth it.

"I had to get your attention somehow. You blocked my calls. I couldn't see you anymore! You wouldn't even talk to me without turning your nose up at me," he growls angrily in my face with a hint of betrayal sparking in his eyes. "So, here I am," he says, lifting his chin in victory.

Every ounce of emotion vanishes from his face when he looks into my eyes. Blank. Dark. Nothingness. Reminding me of his expression at Dead End when I watched him from afar. I try to hold back the flinch when his finger runs down my cheek, caressing me like he used to.

"I've been watching you, Rivey. Protecting you from the shadows. You should thank me for the pictures I took. I had to look at you through your cameras to make sure you didn't do anything stupid."

My lips flap open and closed at his words. My stomach drops at the realization. Sharp memories float through my mind of the stalking I endured at the hands of...

"It was you?"

"Finally, you get it. It was for your own good. I had to keep my girls safe, Rivey. I had to make sure you two were always protected..."

"But Adrian. That... that guy!" My stomach clenches, threatening to spill the treats I had earlier. "He-he..." I stammer, reaching for the words desperate to escape my lips. "No. No. Not you..."

"Killed himself? I know. It was so tragic. But someone had to take the fall. Your little agent friends were getting too close. I had to throw you off the trail. And my poor cousin needed to die." He scrunches his nose at the thought, turning my stomach more. "They took you away from me! You should have stayed in East Point. You should never have run from me! I can't believe you didn't like my gift."

Red blood flashes in my mind. My pictures splayed across my front porch. Dripping. Red. Lyric's screams. It all scrambles in my mind.

"It was always you?"

Hopefully, someone with a gun will get here soon before someone gets hurt. It's the only thing holding me together.

"When they left, he promised me I could have you! He said you'd run right into my arms like they never existed!" His shouts reverberate off the walls again when he yanks the gun from me and points it in Asher's direction with a snarl. "But you didn't. And I was sent the fuck away by my father. An internship. Like I fucking wanted anything to do with my father's career." He rolls his eyes, scoffing at the idea.

"I never promised you anything," Asher says with a fake calm, taking a step forward. His wide, hazel eyes dart to Ly, checking her over as she stands still in Van's grasp. "I never said she'd be yours. I said she might come running to you for support. But that's it." He swallows a lump in his throat, his eyes darting to me as if he's trying to convey a silent message meant for the two of us. "But I know now that I made a mistake that night. I should never have come to you for help." He shakes his head. "I never should have done what I did."

"Shut the fuck up!" Van howls, stiffening his arm. "You're a goddamn liar. You all used River."

"Like you did?" Asher retorts, cocking his head with confidence.

"I didn't use her!" Van shouts manically, waving the gun around. "I didn't do anything! She was mine!"

"Yours?" Asher scoffs, continuing to step even closer to us despite my silent protests.

No. No. Please. Step back. Don't come any closer. I've got this.

"Yes," Van growls, gritting his teeth. "I put my claim on her a long time ago. You had no fucking right to touch what was mine." He shakes his head back and forth, squeezing his eyes shut.

My heart drops into my ass when Asher lurches forward, grabbing Ly by her other arm and yanking her out of Van's death grip. She stumbles forward into Asher's arms with a frantic yelp, knocking her out of her stupor. It's a small reprieve from the craziness going on around us, like time stands still.

"Go," Asher yells. "Get help, baby!" He urges her, throwing her toward the door with tears in his eyes. "Please!" He begs, stepping toward her, frantically hurrying her along and herding her toward the opening.

Tears stream down Lyric's face when she stumbles away from us. Her eyes dart back and forth with uncertainty. Trembles roll through her tiny, frozen body, shaking every inch of her.

"Mommy," she sniffles, taking a step toward me with wide eyes, staring straight at the barrel of the gun, pointing at her tiny chest.

"No!" I shout, gluing my eyes to Van and his movements. Something depraved brews behind his dark eyes as he calculates his next moves. Lyric was his leverage. And now, she's out of his grasp. Will he harm her, too?

"If I can't have her, then no one will," he says, staring directly into my eyes. A void opens in his dark eyes. There are no emotions resting behind them. Just a black hole of nothingness. "No one touches what is mine, again," he says with a deadly calm—the calm before the shit storm about to rain on all of us.

An ache pangs across my chest when he cocks the gun and fucking fires it. No hesitation. No second thoughts. Like this was all a part of his plan. A small smirk pulls at his lips when my body flinches back and my gaze darts to my helpless child, standing stock still.

The bullet careens in Lyric's direction, like a fucking missile aiming straight at her little chest, which heaves out of control as sobs flow from her throat.

I can't fucking move to protect her from harm's way. I can't stop the bullet from speeding toward her little body. Everything is spiraling out of fucking control, and I can't stop any of it from happening.

"No!" I shout as the loud bang reverberates off the stone walls. My fucking ears ring as the noise from the blast blocks everything out. I cry out, covering my ears from the closeness of the sound, deafening everything.

My eyes dart to Lyric, checking her for injuries. I make a move to run to her, despite the gun still hanging in the air, but a strong grip grabs the back of my neck, halting my retreat. Helplessly, I watch from a distance, cataloging her body inch by inch. Her shrill, frantic screams fill the room, penetrating through the static in my ears.

"Go!" Asher shouts, jumping directly in front of her with a fierce expression, pushing her once again and knocking her back.

All the color drains from my face. With an umph, he gasps out, grabbing at his calf. Those wide, hazel eyes connect with mine, darkening as he shouts out in pain, and hops around.

"Again," Van chuckles, pulling the hammer back and firing directly into Asher's thigh.

The blast deafens me further, and I wince, trying to focus on Asher. I pull. I yank. I try to break free. I'm ten seconds away from kneeing Van in the nuts to flee, but he pulls me against him with a satisfied hum.

Asher's eyes widen, rolling into the back of his head when the pain takes him down to his knees.

"I'm sorry," he gasps out, barely audible for me to hear him.

"No!" I grasp Van's forearm, trying to force the gun from his hands. If I could make it fall to the ground then he'd stop shooting Asher, and I could break free.

"Oops," Van grins, firing one more shot into Asher's upper leg.

All the color drains from Asher's face when he falls over onto his back, staring up at the ceiling. He blinks several times, heaving desperate breaths, but the pain is too much. Every tight muscle uncoils in his body, falling limp until he's carried away into unconsciousness. Dark red blood pushes through the fabric of his jeans, staining the fabric at an alarming rate. I don't know much about anatomy, but getting shot isn't good. Even if it's just one leg.

"Asher!" I screech, trying to pull away from Van's embrace again. My foot stomps into his but does nothing to loosen his hold. If anything, he clings on tighter with his painful grip. Digging his fingertips into my neck and holding me hostage.

"Stop fighting me!" he grits out in my ear, pulling me further into him. "You'll never fucking fight me again after all these distractions are out of the way. You're mine. For fucking ever, Rivey."

Sobs wrack through my body as I helplessly watch my entire world fall apart. Tears roll down my cheeks. I can't get away. I can't save anyone in this room.

"Run," I croak out, trying to gain Lyric's attention.

Her saddened gaze locks on Asher lying lifeless on the cold ground with blood trickling out of his leg from the three wounds, no doubt ending his life. He doesn't twitch or fucking react. His chest barely moves with his labored breaths. If we're not careful and don't get the help we need, he'll be fucking dead.

Lyric is frozen, unable to move when she needs to run. Her soft whimpers spear through the room, infiltrating through the static clogging up my ears.

"Daddy!" she cries out, twisting her face in anguish at the sight of him. "Daddy," she whimpers again.

"NO!" Van shouts, huffing against the side of my neck when he raises the gun yet again. "He's not your daddy."

Lyric's eyes dart to mine, gliding over my tear-soaked face and onto Van. Her tiny head shakes at his statement, not understanding him.

"He is my daddy," she says through a quivering lip, standing tall. "And you hurt him." A fierce expression pulls at her face, narrowing her eyes at him. Her tiny fingers form fists at her sides, like she's about to pounce on the asshole behind me.

"Get help," I croak out again through my bubbling emotions. "Ly!" I shout, clinging to Van's forearm and digging my nails into his flesh. He doesn't budge, but the grunt in my ear lets me know I'm inflicting some sort of damage.

"Run!" I shout through my fear, waving a hand at her to get a move on.

If Van has a chance, I'm sure he'll take her out, and I can't fucking witness that and do nothing.

"Mommy!" she quivers with uncertainty, wavering where she stands tall.

"Run, Lyric! Don't look back!" I grunt when Van grabs my hair in his tight grip and abandons my neck. His sickly long fingers weave through my locks, holding me firmly in place. I couldn't move even if I fought again. But it should be me. Not her. I can take this trauma—something she shouldn't have to endure. "Run and get help! Run, baby!" I shout when he lifts the gun again, pointing it right at her stomach.

My skin crawls—my heart races. Stars burst behind my eyes as I gasp for air. The walls close in on me rapidly when his hands land on me.

Lyric's eyes dart between us, frantically taking the picture in. She tries to step toward me. I'm her protector, the person in charge of keeping her safe. She wants to dive into my arms and never let go. But I can't right now. I shake my head as best I can, straining against Van's hold on me.

She needs to run before he does something stupid like hurt her. He could fucking shoot her, and then my life would truly be over. She needs to get the fuck out of here.

"Run, baby! Don't look back at me. Please!"

Get Liv. Get the fuck out of this shit show—is what I want to shout. But I can't give Van any more ammunition. If he knows we have help just steps away, he might do something drastic.

With one last little whine of despair, Lyric runs out of the entrance. My ears ring again, overtaking everything when the gun explodes. My breath hitches when I try to pull away, desperate to chase after her. Or jump in front of the bullet myself. Relentless tears pour down my face when the dust finally settles, and Lyric is nowhere to be found.

A single hole rests in the stone wall with dust billowing from it. She's safe. Lyric is safe, running to get help for Asher. Van can take me. Do whatever he wants to me. As long as Lyric is safe. And Asher gets the ambulance he desperately needs.

My mind swirls as the room softens and all the noises come to a halt. The static in my ears eases away when Van lowers his gun, staring toward the entrance where the bright sun shines through.

Why is this happening?

Van was the one who broke up with me. He sent me away. All because his parents couldn't stand the thought of him being with some Central girl. So, why is he standing here, holding me against my will?

"You see him, Rivey? You see him now?" he asks with a false sense of calm taking over his tone. With the gun in his hand, he grips my chin, forcing my gaze to Asher, lying on the ground with blood dripping like a leaky faucet out of his leg. "He's bleeding and practically begging for his life. How about another shot to make sure he never fucking comes back?" he hisses in my ear, raising the gun again in Asher's direction.

How many more fucking bullets does he have?

His hot breath rolls over my neck as he holds me tight to the front of his body, letting me feel every disgusting inch of him. Spiders crawl under my skin at the nearness to him. My mind begs me to run. Bile rises in my throat. Desperation claws at me.

"Please don't shoot him again, Van. I'll do whatever you want. Please don't hurt anyone else," I beg, with tears pooling in my eyes and rushing down my cheeks. "Van," I plead.

"I love it when you say my name," he whispers, pressing his lips on my hair. "Say you'll be mine forever."

"I'm yours."

For now. A gag sits at the back of my throat when I say those words.

Until I shoot you in the dick for ever laying a hand on Lyric, me, and for shooting Asher three fucking times. If only I had packed my knife. The same one Kieran gave me all those years ago so I could protect myself. But I left it at home, tucked in my dresser drawer with my other weapon. I was stupid to think I'd be safe at my own daughter's birthday party, surrounded by Veritas agents.

"Good. Rivey. This is going so well. It's funny… When you called Kat to let her know you would be in Central City, I was there. Right beside her, listening as you spilled where'd you'd be. I knew I needed to make my moves. And fucking fast. So, here we are, baby," he coos again, dropping his arm to his side, removing the danger to Asher's rapidly deteriorating state.

Everything seizes inside me, and I blanch. "Kat? My PA? Kat?"

"Yeah, baby. That's the girl. Your PA. I'm Trevor. Her boyfriend," he whispers in my ear, forcing me to step back with him into the darkness of the unknown.

I stumble over my feet, unable to fall forward when his grip gets tighter and tighter. My breaths barely have enough room to fill my lungs as the darkening room takes over my vision. How I long for the sunlight gleaming in. How I long to keep my eyes on Asher's unmoving body.

"I've been him for six months. Did you ever wonder why I never showed my face?"

Trevor, Kat's elusive boyfriend. The one she gushed about being in love with. She cried over him when he went away without a word. He never came to our company parties. Never took pictures. He was a fucking ghost in the waiting, preying on an innocent woman. No wonder we never met him and only heard about their time together.

"Why would you do that?" I croak, sucking in harsh breaths. "That doesn't make any sense."

"Kat likes you. She likes to talk about you and what's going on with you. She was my in. I knew where you'd be every fucking day of your life. I had to date her and be with her to get to see you. It was the only way. And God! Sleeping with her, well, it was a way to be closer to you, Rivey. I could close my eyes and imagine it was your face. Your moans. I still have our movies together. I watch them every night before I go to sleep, fucking her… Or fucking my hand to you. It's sad, but I had to get my info from her. After all, being close to her made me close to you. But don't worry, I don't love her like I love you. Poor pathetic bitch she is. I just had to show her a scrap of affection, and she was dripping wet." He tsks at his manipulation, solely putting the blame on poor Kat, who was head over heels in love with this asshole. "Especially today on our daughter's birthday. I wanted to be here to help you celebrate. You'll love the home I have for us. Well, me and you. That's okay, though. We'll have more children. Just you and me. Forever."

The impact of his words settles on my chest, caving it in. Oxygen refuses to enter my fucking lungs, seizing them every time I open my mouth.

"You dated her for the sole purpose of getting to me? You… You stalked me from the beginning?" I stammer, wrapping my brain around the idea that Van had been following me this entire time from afar, waiting in the shadows as he watched our every move. "Wait… Did you even go to Europe?"

Twisting me around, he forces my back into the roughly textured wall. I cry out when my head knocks into the stone, dazing me. Bright stars burst behind my eyelids. A sharp gasp rings out from between my parted lips.

Van cracks a smile, tsking at me in a cruel mockery. "Of course, I went to Europe, Rivey. Where do you think I picked up the cyber skills that allowed me to watch you from anywhere at any time? I was there for three years, eyeing your every move."

"Cyber skills?" I swallow hard at the information flowing from his mouth like a villain revealing all his moves before he executes them. If I'm not careful with this conversation, bad things could continue to happen. I need to keep him talking and make him reveal everything. "What cyber skills?" Please take the bait. Please spill everything.

It's a good thing this cavern echoes because Asher's phone should be picking all this up.

"My favorite was hacking into your camera system, which wasn't that hard, especially since it was my company that protected your precious home. A little slip of the business card to the perfect person had you right where I wanted you. But I couldn't stay away, Rivey. I was tired of watching you on a screen. So, I came back and created Trevor so I could keep a closer eye on you."

"But—I…" I swallow hard, willing my tears to go away. I have to keep him going and admit to everything he's done to orchestrate this entire thing. "I only got the cameras because of the pictures," I murmur with realization as vomit shoots up my throat.

He grins more. "I needed you scared and desperate for protection. Getting your picture wasn't hard, though. It was easy to follow you around and watch you shop or play with our baby girl. It made me want this more," he purrs with victory. "I'm so sorry I frightened you, Rivey. You were just so beautiful. I didn't mean to scare you; I just needed to keep my eyes on you at all times and keep you safe."

My body shudders at the thought of him watching my every move through the cameras in my home. "Why... How?" Fuck, I can't get my damn brain to ask the right questions.

Van's teeth grit when his hand tightens on me. "But then they came back and fucked it all up! They were supposed to stay away. They were supposed to never touch you again. You are mine, River. All fucking mine. You'd never know that I've done so many things for you, Rivey," he whispers, putting his forehead against mine. "I saved you from Bradley's attack at that shitty bar you worked at."

"I saved myself," I say, curling my lip in disgust at the thought of my attack at Dead End, resulting in my hospitalization. "I stabbed that bastard. Not you..." I grunt when his hand slams over my mouth, blocking me from talking properly.

"I was supposed to save you!" he lashes out, spitting in my face with every word. "I was supposed to pull you out of that alleyway and be the fucking hero. Me! Not you," he growls again. "And definitely not fucking them!" The entire darkened chamber he's pulled me into lights up with his voice, echoing for what seems like miles. Only a sliver of light from buzzing bulbs above us illuminates his demented eyes. "I set it all up so I could win you back. But you see how fucking well that worked out?" He rolls his eyes, clenching his teeth so tight, I swear he'll snap them into pieces.

"You?" My muffled voice comes through his hand, widening his smile.

My stomach drops, thinking back to when I took out the trash at Dead End and was attacked from behind by Bradley. My former rapist. My abuser. The man who forced himself on me at the party where I drank too much, and Rad saved me.

"Me," he whispers. "You ever wonder why he was at Dead End that night? Why was I there to stop him? I was the fucking hero. And then that piece of shit Kieran beat my face in." He shakes his head erratically. "I hope he makes an appearance soon so I can give him the same treatment. One bullet for every asshole who has put their hands on you."

My breath hitches.

"You're fucking crazy," I murmur through his hand again. "You can't do this, Van. You can't shoot them. You can't take Lyric or me."

A frantic squeal falls from my lips when he presses the gun to my jaw.

"I don't think you're in any sort of position to make demands. This is how it's going to go. You're going to text your bestie that you're fine. Call off the dogs, Riv. Then, we'll go out of this emergency exit and start our lives together before anyone can come to save you." A sparkle lights up his eyes when his free hand digs into my pocket and pulls out my phone. "Unlock it," he grunts, gesturing to my thumbprint.

"Okay," I say, unlocking my phone with my thumb.

"Text her! They'll be here soon. I'm going to leave them with quite the distraction to stop them from making it here." He grins again when I grab my phone, bringing Olivia's name to the screen.

I stare at it for several long seconds, debating what to say. We don't have a code in place for situations like this. Now, I regret not having something. I can only hope Lyric gets to her quickly before Asher bleeds out.

ME

I'm fine. No rusH. Things are undEr controL... Please.

My heart stops when Van zeroes in on the phone, checking over my message before he allows me to hit send. I know the moment he sees my hidden message when he looks up at me and tightens his grip on his gun. He growls in my face—no doubt about to unleash a massive punishment for even trying to send that message.

"I'm not a fucking idiot, Rivey. I may be a little obsessive, especially when it comes to you. But any idiot would see the message hidden. Help? Is that really what you wanted to say? I have more than a gun in my artillery." My breaths quicken when he drops the gun on the ground with a grin and digs through his pocket—never letting me go. Confidence puffs out his chest like he has this entire thing under control.

My breath stalls when he holds up a small object, reflecting off the soft lights above us.

"Boom," he whispers manically, pressing down on a large red button. In the distance, a loud bang rattles against the walls. My spine stiffens as loud screams happen, and he beams more with pride at whatever the hell he just did. "You remember the night we met, Rivey?" he questions without giving me a chance to answer out loud.

It was a chance encounter at the record store. He came in, like he did often after, to purchase his favorite vinyl. Something he started collecting. One thing led to another, and I ended up ass over elbow in the backseat of his Mustang. The worst mistake of my life was ever entertaining this dickbag and letting him use my body for pleasure. The sex wasn't even that fucking great. But by the way he lights up; he thought I was the best damn thing he ever had. Maybe I was. I mean, he is standing before me with a possessed grin on his face, looking off to the side like the memory of our meeting snapped something inside him.

I stiffen when he drops his nose to the crook of my neck, forcing me still. His disgusting breath rolls over my skin, getting heavier by the second. I quickly ignore the hard piece poking into my abdomen when he inhales again and runs his tongue along my flesh. If I had my knife, I'd cut his boner in two and shove it up his ass where it belongs. But I'm a dumbass and left it.

Fucking bastard. Always taking what the fuck, he wants. If I could move a muscle, I'd knee him in the goddamn dick. Or stab him. I swear the next chance I get; I'm chopping that appendage off so he can never harm another person again.

"You don't have to say anything. I'll remind you of it all," he whispers, flicking his tongue over my ear lobe.

"The sun had just set, blanketing the party in thick darkness, which brought out all the freaks. Everyone was dancing and laughing and drinking their asses off. But they didn't notice the most beautiful piece walking through the party. You were by yourself. All doe-eyed and petrified looking. But goddamn, the way you looked so damn sexy. I knew you were a Central girl the moment you got closer. But you never fucking looked at me. You were watching him and his cronies' taking shots by the pool. I knew Knight from school. Hell, I had a fucking band, too! You never fucking noticed me…"

I soak in his confessions one word at a time, memorizing them for later. The truth is, I noticed him at one point in our lives. That we had fucked around so many times and had been in a relationship with each other. Until his parents intervened, we were a couple. Happy, too. But that's all semantics now. Because they did me a fucking favor by pulling him back.

"So I slipped something special into your drink when you got glass after glass. Nothing bad, just something that'd help you notice me."

The world stops at his confession. It was bad enough he was my stalker for the past three years. But this? He drugged me at a party. All these years I thought it was me who had drank too many glasses of alcohol.

I blanch, shivering at his words. "You did what?" My muffled reply comes out in a squeak.

He grins against my flesh. "Yeah, Rivey. It was me. You thought you drank too much, didn't you? Nah. It was the drugs. Me. All me. I knew how to make you fall to your knees and give me what I wanted. Funny, isn't it? You had no idea who took your V-card. Well, you're looking at him." He grins at that, cocking his head when tears flow freely from my eyes and down my cheeks.

I think I'm going to be fucking sick. Everything in my stomach sloshes, begging to cover his hand with my vomit.

"Why wouldn't you just talk to me?" I whisper, shaking my head as best I can. "I don't…"

"Then, I dragged you to a secluded spot… And well, you see where that goes. When I was finished, I tucked myself back in my pants with the intention of killing those mother fuckers who were waiting in the shadows to get a piece. Fucking Bradley. He had his eyes on you the moment he saw you stumbling around. You were mine to take over and over, and they were going to steal you from me. So, I decided to become the hero… I walked away for five goddamn seconds! They got you, and then Rad swooped in and put you in his car. But I never forgot about you, Sweetness. You were all I craved. So, we met again. This time, I made sure you loved me. And you did, didn't you?"

I swear his monologue goes on and on for five thousand hours. He could probably get off on his own damn voice. But the longer I keep him talking and in one place, the better chance I have at surviving this whole ordeal.

"Why the fuck would you rape me?" I hiss frantically, clawing at his forearm, begging him to release me.

The entire time he's been chatting away, he's held me down. Despite the hand still stalling in his pocket. I'm afraid to know what he has up his sleeve next. It can't be worse than the loaded gun by our side. Can it?

"And that's where my obsession blossomed. The feel of you around my cock. The blood you sacrificed for me, baby. It made me want you over and over again. No matter what."

Gag. Fucking hell.

"And my hatred for them was born. Fuck those assholes." He licks my face again, groaning at the taste of my tears. A deep, hollow chuckle vibrates against my body when he steps back, finally revealing the other part of his plan. In the dim light, he holds up a syringe filled to the brim with a clear liquid. "I had a feeling you wouldn't come willingly, so…" Using his teeth, he uncaps it and plunges it into my fucking neck. The second the liquid enters my bloodstream, my skin fucking boils. Heat spreads through my veins.

I cry out, scratching at him until he's finished. He chuckles, throwing it aside with pride puffing out at his chest. He's so fucking deranged; he thinks he did a good fucking thing.

"Have a good rest," he whispers, grinning as he removes his hand from my mouth, watching his masterpiece fall to pieces.

I suck in a few breaths, trying to stay conscious when he lets me go. He hums to himself, stepping back to observe his handy work with a sparkle in his eyes.

The moment he's off me, I slide down the rock wall with a groan. My head fucking pounds from the impact, and my face fucking burns from the barrel of the gun.

Whatever he gave me has my vision blurring, but not completely. No. I'm still in control of my limbs. For now, at least.

"What did you give me?" I slur, reaching around beside me as he hums again with happiness.

My tongue tingles as I try to lift it to ask the question again, but it doesn't work. My fucking time is running out. Along with the light blinking out around me.

"Just something to make you sleepy. Then I can get you to our home without fanfare. You'll love it!" he shouts, bouncing on his toes with excitement. I tune him out the moment he starts listing the things inside this magical house he built for the two of us.

I suck in oxygen as my vision blurs, producing two Vans prancing around in front of me. My ears start ringing, and numbness takes over my entire body.

I fight against the medicine, continuing to feel around me for the gun he dropped in haste to get the drug from his pocket. He threw it like he wouldn't need it anymore. But I do. I swallow hard, which becomes increasingly challenging as the effects wear on me. But determination spears through me as my numb fingers feel the gun thrown beside me.

With every ounce of energy, I have left, I bring it into my lap to hold it steady. All those times, Olivia took me to the range to perfect my skills in case something like this ever happened finally come to fruition.

My time has fucking come.

Just as the darkness takes over my vision and I'm clinging to consciousness, I use my remaining energy to point the gun in his direction. He doesn't seem to notice. Or maybe I'm too far gone. I grunt, squeezing the trigger, praying to the Gods above that this one shot buys me enough time. One shot fires off before the darkness completely takes over, pulling me under the spell of the drug.

I'm either a kidnapped girl walking, or I shot the man responsible for stalking me for three years.

I guess I'll find out which soon.

River

CONCRETE WEIGHS DOWN EVERY MOLECULE INSIDE ME, REFUSING TO LET ME move an inch. No matter how hard I try, nothing cooperates with me. I'm stuck.

A dense fog swirls deep in my mind, clouding my thoughts and erasing all rationale.

Every ache pulling at my nerves awakens, throbbing into existence the more my mind comes back to the land of the living.

What the fuck happened to me? And why do I feel like I got hit by a damn bus, backed over, and hit fucking again?

A softness encompasses my back like a mattress cocooning my body in a soft embrace.

I grunt, trying to move again. Nothing fucking works. My arms are useless. My legs fucking tingle. Fuck! Sludge moves through my veins toward my frantically beating heart, trying to break through my ribcage.

I have to move, or I'll die here. Wherever that is…

My breath hitches when I'm finally able to lift a finger. Fucking finally! That's one finger of many. Only nine to go. Tingling encompasses every digit, slowly waking up from the deep sleep I was in the more I move.

My breath hitches in my throat again as desperation claws at me to get moving. The faster I'm off this bed, the faster I can skedaddle out of this fucking nightmare I've been put in.

One by one, I'm able to shake off the heavy feeling weighing my limbs down and freely wiggle my fingers and toes. Thankfully, clothes rustle with every move. So, I'm not naked. That's a plus.

I blink several times through the grit crusting over my eyelashes, letting my sight adjust to the absolute darkness before me.

It's nothing but shadows. No lights. No sounds. Desolate. A fucking void of nothing.

Have I died and gone to Hell? God, I hope not.

A chill shudders my body as a cool sweat forms on my palms. Through heavy breaths, I manage to force my body into the seated position at the

edge of the mattress I was left on. Or, I think it's a mattress. If I could fucking see to figure it out, I'd know more.

I groan as the darkness swirls, forcing my eyes to squeeze shut. What in the ever living fuck is happening right now?

My eyes dart around the fucking blackness, trying to latch onto anything I can. A shape. A light of any kind. But there's nothing. It's like I'm lost inside a damp basement that's a maze of corridors.

I inhale, trying to use my other senses to guide me in the right direction. Nothing but a sterile bleach scent filters through my nose. So, a clean basement? That doesn't make any damn sense. Basements are notorious for a mildewy stench. Has someone created this space just for me?

I shake my head, running my numb fingers over my tired face.

Goosebumps erupt over every inch of my body as I ground myself in the heavy darkness blanketing the entire room.

"Hello?" My brows furrow when my voice echoes through the room like a cavernous space lies before me.

Right. This is how every serial killer movie starts. Poor girl left in the basement. Next, a man with a chainsaw will pop out of the wall and grind my body to pieces as I scream. How fucking morbid… I shake those thoughts out of my fucking head. I don't have time to get all mopey about my newfound situation. I have to think and get the hell out of here.

Now, if I could only remember what the fuck happened to get me here, I'd be in a better place.

"Rivey, I knew you'd wake up soon."

My entire body freezes at the sound of his voice. I run a shaky hand over my forehead, wiping the cold sweat breaking out over every inch of my flesh.

"So glad to see you sitting up! We have so much planned today…" His voice echoes again with a manic laugh from somewhere in the distance. Yet, he sounds like he's all around me.

My fingernails dig into the edge of the mattress, grounding me to the spot. How the hell…

How did Van get to me? Where…

Like a whirlwind of memories, it all comes back to me at rapid speed. Nearly knocking me back from my seated position. My lips flop open, gasping for air.

The birthday party.

The needle at the rollercoaster.

The goddamn gunshot…

Asher!

"What did you do?" I shout through my sudden rage, shaking with every move I make.

I jump to my trembling feet, swaying like a tree in the wind. Fuck.

Everything swirls again. I rub my temples, begging for relief from the constant wave of vertigo.

I grunt, stumbling through the darkness with my hand out in front of me. Come on, asshole. Show yourself so I can beat you to a bloody pulp.

My fingers prod my pockets, hoping without fail I brought my knife. Hope blossoms in my chest. Quickly popped by the reminder that I didn't have it with me. Why would I? It was my child's birthday party. I shouldn't have felt unsafe there. Liv was there. Jordy was there. A whole slew of Veritas agents attended as well. Somehow this psycho broke through all the safety precautions we had in place and smashed them to pieces by getting to me.

My brows furrow when his confession rings in my mind. He was Trevor. The elusive boyfriend of my PA. How could we have been so trusting and blind?

"I brought you home!" His voice rings out again from all around me, sounding like an ever-present entity haunting all sides of my life.

"No," I cry out in desperation. "This is not my home! Let me go, Van!" My fingers curl into fists.

Every ounce of fog dissipates into nothing, giving me back my sound mind. Replaced by massive amounts of rage boiling through my system.

I'll fuck him up before he touches me. There's no way I'll let him get his hands on me like he promised. Fuck that. Fuck this. I'm River goddamn West. No one is taking anything from me again. I'll claw his fucking eyes out until he's bleeding on the ground.

"Pretty Girl."

My chest heaves as my eyes dart around the darkened space. Where is he? God, where is he in this darkness? His voice caresses me through the shadows, knocking me back a step. Rad? Is he here to save me from Van's clutches? Or is he a prisoner, too?

Van shot Asher. Will Rad be next?

"Run," I rasp with tears streaming down my cheeks. "Don't come any closer. He's got a gun," I plead, nearly dropping to my knees as they knock together.

"Pretty Girl," he says with a sigh. I swear the faintest touch against my cheek has me jerking back.

My fingers graze against the phantom touch, instantly relaxing me.

"Mine!" Van's voice echoes through the space like a menacing ghost, growling the word. "You're mine! You'll always be mine!" My ears ring at the sound of his frantic shouts.

"No. No. No!" I hiss, covering my ears. "I'm not yours. Let me go!"

"Come on, Pretty Girl!" Rad's voice echoes through my skull with desperation. "You're having a nightmare. You need to wake up. Please wake up. It's been twelve hours already."

Twelve hours? Of what? My unconsciousness? My imprisonment?

I blink several times until a blinding light pierces through the veil of shadows. Squinting against the brightness, I gasp, jolting forward.

My eyes snap open, greeted by the bright lights and a loud beeping sound filling the room. Several articles of clothing rustle beside me, getting closer as I come back online.

"Little Star."

A yelp leaves my throat when I jerk back into a warm embrace. Heavy hands hold me steady, wrapping around my front side. A drum beats in my chest, moving toward my ears and taking over my hearing. My breaths shudder when the unknown hands travel up and down my arm in a soothing manner.

"We got you, Pretty Girl." His voice cracks with emotions, murmuring in my ear.

"Rad," I croak sharply, turning to look over my shoulder.

Warm brown eyes filled to the brim with concern and exhaustion greet my vision.

"Rad," I confirm with a sob, falling apart as he embraces me more. His fingers wipe the rogue tears escaping down my cheeks.

He's here. He's safe. Fuck. I'm safe. There's no longer a stark darkness holding me captive. Just this room. My boys.

"We're so glad you're finally awake, Little Star," Callum says with a quivering voice. His bottom lip trembles when he looks me over, checking for more injuries.

Callum rests in front of me with dark bags blooming under his eyes from lack of sleep. The faintest smile tugs at his lips when his fingertips brush the hair from my face.

"Thank fuck you're finally awake," he whispers with relief sagging his entire body on the bed.

"Awake?" My eyes dart around the room, taking in my surroundings.

"It's okay, Pretty girl. You're safe. You were having a gnarly nightmare," Rad whispers right into my ear. My body trembles from the rumble of his voice, vibrating through my back.

"Nightmare?" I croak, shaking my head.

The never-ending darkness crowds my mind, but I shake it away. I will not be a victim of my fucking memories.

"You were mumbling and twitching in your sleep. It was…" Callum trails off, putting his fist in front of his face.

"Fucking scary as hell. But you're here at the hospital with us. You're safe." Rad softly kisses my hair, squeezing his arms around me as we lie tangled in the hospital bed.

My body jerks when the door to my room swings wide, displaying a new face.

"Oh good! We were beginning to worry about you, Miss West. Your assailant really did a number on you." My muscles stiffen when a woman dressed in all-white scrubs saunters through my room like she owns it.

A mess of brown hair rests on top of her lifted head. A stethoscope rests around her neck, and glasses perch on the end of her nose. A warm smile crosses her lips when she takes the three of us in, easing my initial worry.

"A nightmare," I confirm again, remembering the thick darkness I was just in with Van's menacing voice and… "What about Van? Did they get him? Oh my god…" I trail off as the nurse resets my IV bag and turns off the beeping machine. "My daughter?" I rasp.

The need to see Lyric and make sure she's okay overrides everything. I'm ten seconds away from climbing out of this bed and hightailing it out of this stupid hospital. She's probably freaking out without me. I've been here for God knows how long, and she's been by herself. No. Not alone. She's had the four of them.

The nurse sends me a sympathetic smile, humming under her breath.

"I'll send in the agents stationed outside your door. You should be okay for a while. The doctor wanted to monitor your vitals and make sure you got fluids while the drug was in your system. I suspect he'll want you here for another day to make sure it didn't have any other lasting effects on you." She smiles one last time, squeezing my arm before she walks out the door.

As soon as she exits, Olivia bursts in with a frantic look. Normally, she hides her emotions behind a thick wall of professionalism. Not today. Her eyes glide all over my body, taking me in.

"Bestie," she murmurs, a hint of emotion filtering through her voice.

"Liv. What happened? Where's Ly? Asher? Where's Van? Did he…"

"Don't worry, Dollface. I shot him in the dick," Jordy quips, strolling in casually after Liv with a cocky grin plastered. "Don't give me that disapproving face," he says, pointing at Olivia, who huffs in response.

"He's on Devil Head Island with the rest of the Veritas prisoners. They mended his…" She pauses, twisting her face. "His uh…manhood." She grimaces, pointing between her legs.

"His dick. You can say it. D-I-C-K. Or what's left of it. He'll be permanently limp from now on." He beams with pride, setting his eyes on me. "You missed, by the way. But that's okay. Thankfully, Liv and I stormed the castle before he could drag you away to his lair." He shudders at the thought, looking away with a head shake. "You were a lucky girl, Riv."

"Super fucking lucky," Liv murmurs through a breath.

"What the hell is happening?" I mutter, rubbing my temple. "So, he's gone?"

"In prison for a very long time. The good thing about Veritas is he doesn't need a damn trial. Besides, thanks to Asher's quick thinking, we have his confession on tape. So, Van is there forever."

"With sickening pride, too. Where the fuck did you find this guy, Riv?" Jordy asks, shaking his head.

"He was my ex, but he dumped me," I groan, trying to process what they're saying about him. "So, what is he saying?" I question with curiosity.

Olivia sighs, having a silent conversation with Jordy. Eyebrows raise. Hands move. But their mouths never open.

"I'm assuming everything he told you. From the admittance to what he did to you at that party and to stalking you since that moment ..." Olivia trails off, pinching the bridge of his nose.

Rad stiffens behind me. His breath picks up and heaves at the mention of the party so long ago. Rad, my hero. The man who scooped me up and took me to the hospital after Van and his little friends had their fun.

I squeeze my eyes shut, vomit rushing up my esophagus. Van fucking raped me. He took advantage of me by dumping drugs into my drink and luring me away from the mass of people and witnesses. Then, as a love-sick teenager, I fell under his spell and into his bed. Again. He took advantage of me more than once.

"We went through his house, Riv. It's apparent he's had a thing for you for a long time. Probably has been following you for longer than the three years he let on. We found the pictures, the videos, and everything in between to help him get to you. We also found his security companies shit all over the place, too. The same company in charge of your safety. Over-all, it's another dangerous criminal off the streets. He won't see the light of day for the rest of his life." As Jordy speaks, more anger seeps into his words. A red tint crosses his cheeks, and his muscles turn rigid.

"And Ly? Asher? Are they okay?" My heart pounds against my ribs at the last images I have of them running through a loop in my mind.

Her screams. His anguish. The gunshot. The threats. It's all right there at the forefront of my mind, reminding me I couldn't save anyone. Not even myself.

"Ly's fine. She's snuggled up with Asher right now, Pretty Girl," Rad says reassuringly, running his hands up and down my arms again.

"He got out of surgery hours ago. He's fine. She's fine. Although Ly might be a little shaken up. She hasn't really mentioned it. But Kieran took her to that therapist you have for an emergency appointment to make sure she's okay since you were out for twelve hours, and he said they had a good talk about everything. She wants to continue to see Lyric on a regular basis. Something you might want to keep in mind," Liv says with gentle-ness as she eases forward. "Shoo," she rasps, waving Rad and Callum off me.

"Only this one time," Rad grumbles, kissing my cheek. "We'll snuggle soon. I'll go check on the asshole next door. He's been worried sick about you but couldn't get out of bed."

"See ya soon, Little Star." Callum brushes his lips against mine, finally breaking away and removing himself from my hospital bed.

"I'll beat feet and check on our little captive. I wonder if he had anything else to say. My boys can be so creative with their torture," Jordy says, grinning as he manically rubs his hands together as he, too, exits the room. Leaving me alone with one of my best friends, fighting back tears.

"Oh, girl," Liv murmurs, wrapping her arms around me. "I'm so sorry I couldn't get to you sooner. That asshole blew up my damn car!"

"Fuck, Liv. Your car?" I wheeze, strangled by her tightening hold. I don't even remember hearing an explosion of any sort.

"We thought there was a security breach on the outside. Little did we know it was on the inside." Pulling back, water pools in her dark eyes, slowly falling down her cheeks. "I almost lost you," she hiccups.

"You didn't, though. You got there in time. Right? Everything is so damn hazy. All I remember is him cornering me, and then he injected me..."

"Yeah, just in the nick of time. We found Ash and called an ambulance and reinforcements as your gun went off. We... God, I was so goddamn scared he had shot you. I raced in there with my gun in the air with Jordy right behind me. He hadn't moved you yet. But he was getting ready to take you away. I shot a round in his back, but it didn't stop him. It only made him face us with a gun in his hand. So, Jordy shot him in the dick without hesitation..." She grimaces at the thought.

"He really shot him in the dick?" I ask, trying to hold back the laughter bubbling in my throat. It feels so damn inappropriate to want to laugh, but I can't help it. It bubbles out of both of us as we sit embraced on my bed.

"Yeah. Give Jordy any opportunity to shoot someone where the sun don't shine. He'll do it. We wanted some real answers. The ones we thought died with Adrian... Who happens to be his cousin, somehow." She shakes her head, disappointment pulling her expression down. "I'm so sorry, River. I don't know how he eluded us for so long. All records showed Van Drake was in Europe on business... I'm so fucking sorry we brought you home without further investigation and thinking it was only Adrian. I should have smelled a setup a mile away."

"Don't be sorry. You didn't know. But he was Trevor here, right? He said he was Kat's boyfriend. Jesus, how is Kat?" I swallow the razorblades in my throat, burning with every fucking swallow. This whole situation keeps getting worse and worse by the second.

"Well, she's staying with Rocco right now. Much to his delight. He and Christian are supporting her in any way they know how. She's shaken up. I'd be, too. The man she thought she loved was only using her for you."

I rub my hand along my chest when she pulls away, staring me up and down.

"Well, good. I'm glad she has them. I'll have to check in with her soon and make sure she's okay to come back to work or take some time away from me. God, I'll even give her a raise."

"Well, the good news is the doc should release you soon. You're awake and looking good."

"Is it possible to go see, Asher? Was there much damage to him? I just can't get the image of him lying on the ground with blood pouring out of him out of my fucking mind," I rasp as tears burn the back of my eyes.

"He's fine. They cleaned up the damage from the bullets to his calf and upper thigh and put him in a cast. Thankfully, it didn't do much damage, besides the blood loss, which he's being treated for right now. But other than that, Asher is fine. He's been so worried about you. So, I think a reunion would do him some good. You should see Ly. She hasn't left his side since. She really loves them… I'm so happy you gave them another chance."

"Me too," I murmur.

I SIGH, SITTING AT THE EDGE OF MY BED IN THE BAND HOUSE, RUNNING A hand through my unruly hair. I need a hot shower, food, and this stupid cast off my leg.

Two days. That's how long it's been since I left the hospital in a thick cast and instructions on how to care for my wounds.

For the same amount of time, River has been by my side with concern in her eyes, following me around. Every step of the way, she's helped me cope with this new reality I've found myself in. Sometimes, a little too much.

No one tells you how painful bullet wounds are when they pierce through your skin. They fail to mention the mental decline after someone points a gun in your face and pulls the trigger. Or how vivid the recurring nightmares become. Night after night his evil face flashes through my dreams, jolting me awake. Sweat cakes my skin every time I wake up with wide eyes, frantically searching the room for the cause of it all. It's only then do I have to remind myself that he's in prison and far away from us.

Through my newly found trauma, I've discovered the best coping mechanism for me. Something I never thought I'd enjoy. Or feel relief from. Our therapist.

I had doubts at the beginning when River gave us mandatory sessions. How could I sit in a quiet room and tell a complete stranger about what my father put me through?

That first day, I think I sat in silence for ten minutes. Then, the floodgates opened, and I told her everything. The abuse. The betrayal. My mother's death. It was all out in the open and no longer hidden in the depths of my mind for only me to suffer through.

And wouldn't you know? The relief I felt when she validated everything and helped me learn how to cope with the past was a life changer. Even now, as something sits heavily on my mind, she was the first person I spoke to about it. The therapist smiled at me, letting me know that everything I'm contemplating is good. It's coming from a place of true concern.

She told me she'd help me talk it over with the guys, but I opted to have the discussion myself, without her help.

It's a subject that's been on my mind for some time now and was only cemented further during my hospital stay. After surgery, I stayed for a few extra days, ensuring I was okay. The guys and River stayed by my side every step of the way, especially my Little Brat. She glued herself to me, even then. Refusing to leave when visiting hours were over.

One night, long after the others left, River climbed into my hospital bed where we talked for hours. The future. The past. Everything in between brought us closer together. But there was one sentence that struck me square in the chest.

"You and the guys are doing so well with our training. Before you know it, you'll be back out on tour. After this, of course." River tentatively runs a finger over my cast, slowly working up my leg, and grabs my hand. "You'll be as good as new."

Will I, though? Will I ever become as good as *new in her eyes?*
Fuck.
"What if they leave again? They'll go on tour. What if..."

Her words haunt me, chasing me everywhere I go. The amount of pain and uncertainty that rested in her tone reminds me every day that I gave her that insecurity. It will always be on her shoulder, reminding her of what we did. We left.

And we could do it again.

What if we go on another band tour? Far the fuck away from here. We'd probably go back to Europe or travel through the US for weeks at a time. But it wouldn't be here. Not with her or Ly, where we need to be.

An ache forms in my chest at the thought of leaving them. Years ago, I walked away with no problem. Now? I could never. Not again. They're too damn important to say goodbye to anymore.

Been there. Done that. And have the bruises to prove it.

How can we rebuild our life on the road, anyway?

Answer? We can't. It's impossible. We'll never connect with millions of fans screaming our names when our girls are here. Without us.

Since we left Central City, this exact argument has been in the back of my mind. Every time I think I'm going to bring it up to the guys, I chicken out. I'm afraid of what they'll say. Or how they'll react when I let them know—I'm done.

Anxiety swirls in my stomach. Images of their angry faces pop into my mind. They'll argue. Fight tooth and nail for what we've worked so hard for.

But I won't.

They can find a new guitarist to carry on our legacy. For once, I'll sacrifice my dream to be with River so she can pursue her dream as the Fixer. She's already done so much for herself. Now, it's time for us to step up and be her support system. We can still work as a band, playing local gigs. Hell, we can still have a small-scale contract with West Records. Something that doesn't take us away from this spot we've carved out as our home.

Music has been our life for years now. Even before we moved here. It runs through our veins, feeding us life. It's our escape from reality. A way to glide above our bodies and live in the moment.

Nothing exists when music is involved.

And I'm about to suggest something that throws us off the rails of our future and plummets us into the unknown. A life without music and freedom. A life here. With the girls we've fallen in love with.

If only they'll listen.

After getting dressed the best I can without asking anyone for help, I make my way out of my room and toward the top of the staircase.

I grunt, hobbling down the stairs, carefully maneuvering my crutches. One at a time. Every few steps, my damn leg throbs where the bullets pierced through, and they sewed me back up, fixing the ripped muscles, bones, and ligaments. They promised eight weeks of this cast and then physical therapy to regain my walking.

"You idiot," Rad grunts, coming up to meet me halfway up the stairs. "I told you to yell, and I'd help you." He shakes his head with disapproval, stealing a crutch from me and winding his arm around my shoulders. "Now, lean on me like a good boy."

I sigh, leaning into him for support. A pathetic feeling festers inside of me at the amount of help I need to get around. And shower. That's been the worst. Having to tie a damn black bag around my leg feels so weird and even weirder when River hangs out in the bathroom with me, making sure I don't fall over. I would have, too, the first night.

"Thanks, man," I say, taking my crutch from him as he tsks me like a child.

"Call for help, bro. You got shot. You're in a cast. I can carry you on my back everywhere I go. Don't make me do it," he quips, giving me his best dad look that might work on Lyric.

"I'm fine, seriously. I can do some stuff on my own. I'm a big boy." I roll my eyes when he points to the dining room table, demanding I sit across from Kieran and Cal.

"Bossy, asshole," I grumble, leaning on my crutches as I make my way to the long table.

"Morning, sunshine," Callum quips, leaning his elbow on the table.

I snort, situate myself in a chair, and lean my crutches behind me. "Morning."

Kieran nods in my direction, dropping his eyes to his steamy plate of food. He shifts uncomfortably, drawing my attention to his stiff posture.

I've known the guy for a long time now. So, I can always tell when something is on his mind.

From the kitchen, Rad whistles a little tune, clinking plates and silverware together before emerging again with a plate full of every breakfast food imaginable. Eggs, bacon, hash browns, and even a massive side of biscuits and gravy.

My stomach rumbles when the smell hits my senses, and I swear, I drool a little.

"Breakfast is served," Rad singsongs, waltzing into the dining room with two plates and setting one in front of me. He hums more, wiggling his body as he finds his seat and grins. "God, I love cooking. There's even enough for my Little Pretty Girl before she has to go to school."

"Thanks," I say with appreciation, rubbing my hands together. I raise my brow when I look up from my plate, greeted by two concerned looks from Kieran and Cal.

"I'm fine," I reassure them again, shaking my head when they scoff in unison.

"You say that, but I don't fucking believe it," Kieran grumbles, digging into his food and shoving it into his mouth with a huff.

Rad snorts. "That's because this asshole is never okay. And now, he's been shot, by Donavan fucking Drake. That super bunghole," he grunts, roughly cutting into his biscuits.

"New rule. Never say his name again," Kieran says, shaking his head with disgust. "I'm just...I can't believe that happened," he whispers, keeping his voice low so we don't wake our two guests, still snuggled in bed upstairs.

That's another new development I need to discuss with our girl. River hasn't left our house since this happened. Half of me thinks she's terrified to go home. Totally understandable, too. I wouldn't want to return to the place where my privacy was invaded.

The other half of me thinks she feels guilty for me getting shot. She shouldn't. It's not her fault. I did it to protect Lyric.

We were both at the same place. It could have been her or Ly. So, I'm glad it was me. I took it so they didn't have to.

So, the next time I see River, I'm suggesting the therapist and a good session with her and Lyric. It'll all help us fight through this in the end without losing our minds over it.

The four of us converse softly as we eat our breakfast, trying to stay as quiet as possible. Not only has River basically moved in here, but she hasn't been sleeping. More often than not, she plays bed roulette throughout the night. By morning, she's slept with all four of us and Ly, who also has her own bed here.

The conversation goes on around us as my thoughts bubble to the surface, nagging me to bring it up. Say it already. Tell them how you feel. Express yourself. They're your brothers, they'll understand.

Finally, I set my knife and fork down, staring between the other three stuffing their faces and blowing out a breath.

For the moment, they're happy, conversing about mundane things. The weather. The beach. Simple things. Until I complicate everything.

"I want to quit," I blurt, unable to hold it in any longer.

Shit. I curl my fingers into fists, silently wishing I could run away. But a soothing voice reminds me I'm expressing something important, and I'm allowed to say it.

My heart beats like a drum against my ribs when everything ceases around me. The noise halts. Their bodies stiffen when they exchange curious glances.

"Quit what exactly?" Kieran asks, furrowing his brows.

"Oh boy, I think I know where this is going," Rad murmurs, rubbing at his chin with worry.

"This," I say, gesturing to the house. "This entire thing… I… I want to quit the band. I want to stay here in East Point and be with River." I roll my lips together when Kieran sighs, digging his phone out of his pocket.

"Funny you should say that. I wasn't going to bring this up until later. But you know how Constance was looking into other deals for us when we first saw River? Something that might pay a little more. Well, EJ records sent her an offer this morning for a five-year contract with us. It's worth a hundred mil."

Rad whistles under his breath. "A hundred fucking million? That's like millions more than this contract." His eyes widen in disbelief.

I take his phone, reading the messages she sent him and the email displaying the offer. It's real. We could advance further with our career with another record company. We don't need this gig anymore.

All we have to do is walk away from River again.

I swallow hard, not wanting to hold them back from what they want again.

"What are your thoughts?" I ask, clearing my throat. My eyes fall to my empty plate in shame. I could be dragging them down again instead of lifting them.

"There's no fucking way," Kieran whispers, bringing my eyes back to him. He shakes his head, and his lips twist into agony. "Before all this," he says, waving a hand and gesturing toward the house. "I would have jumped at the opportunity. That's a lot of fuckin money, but…"

"Lyric and River," Callum murmurs. "If we go on tour… How much more are we going to miss? We'll be gone for months at a time, and there's no stopping. They'd have us on the road in a matter of months."

"And my Pretty Girl," Rad says with a sour expression. "I'm never leaving her again. I've been thinking about it for a while now. I love music.

But I don't love it more than my girls," he says, swallowing a large lump in his throat. "They trump everything."

"She sacrificed a lot for us back in the day. She took time out to build us into what we are now. Even now… She's still working her ass off to get us back to our glory days…" I trail off with moisture pooling in my eyes. The fear from before evaporates into thin air.

Kieran's expression softens when he looks me over, giving me a sharp nod of approval.

"I get it," Callum breathes, setting his fork down. With a long look, he takes in all our faces and nods.

"I think it's time we sacrifice something for River," Callum murmurs with the smallest hint of a smile pulling at his lips.

Rad blows out a breath. "You mean, give it all up?" he whispers, blinking rapidly. "Everything?"

Kieran blows out a breath and nods. "Yeah. If we can't be here for them every day, then I don't want to continue on a big scale. We can still play around town and live through our music, but every night we'd get to come home to them. They're our life now."

"We should treat them like it," I say, finishing his sentence. "You guys are sure? We'd be…"

"Throwing it all down the drain. But they're worth it…"

"More than worth it," Rad says, slamming his fist onto the table. "I'm ready to give myself over to my girl!" He grins now, joy lighting up his face. "Maybe now she'll marry us." He waggles his brows playfully, looking around the room.

"Maybe," Callum chuckles with a glint in his eyes, letting me know he agrees with that sentiment.

"All right," I say, feeling the relief of our decision lifting all the weight off my chest.

"It'll be so weird," Kieran says, rubbing a spot on his chest. "Not having the tours or the recording time…"

"We still can. You know? We can rent out a studio and create albums. We just won't put on shows out of town. There are plenty of venues in town we could play at," Callum adds.

"We could have a big ass show every year at the stadium or some shit. Like people will fly from everywhere just to come here and see us. River could be there, and Ly could get on stage with us," Rad says with renewed energy, practically vibrating in his seat.

"This isn't the end of anything. This is a whole new chapter in our band… Our fucking life," Kieran says, heaving a big breath. "Once we talk to her brothers and let them know, we can talk to her about it."

"If she finds out we're doing this now, she'll try to stop us," I say with a sharp nod.

"She wouldn't want us to give up our dreams." Cal says.

"But we've already lived that part of it. Now, it's time to live our River dream and help her raise Ly and be a fucking family," Kieran says.

"Shh," Rad hisses, putting a finger to his lips. "My Little Pretty Girl is stomping down the stairs," he chuckles when the sound of heavy little footsteps stomps our way. "We'll talk after River takes her to school. Maybe go talk to Seger and Zepp?"

We all nod in agreement.

"Slow down," River reprimands in her motherly voice, only earning a giggle in return.

Lyric bursts into the dining room with an enormous grin, running straight toward Kieran.

"Little Blue," he murmurs, pulling her into his lap. "Good morning."

"Morning, Daddies," she chirps, throwing her arms around Kieran's neck.

"Sleep well, Little One?" I ask, grinning when she spins around and nods with an eager smile.

"I love this house," she says, staring at Kieran's plate with big eyes.

"Don't worry, Little Pretty Girl. I got a plate for you," Rad says, jumping up and heading into the kitchen with a bounce in his step. "And you too!" he shouts, pointing at River, who winces from his loud voice.

"Coffee," River mumbles, stumbling into the dining room with a mug in her hand. She groans, taking the first drink with her eyes closed.

As she tilts her head back, I examine the remnants of Van's handy work. A small burn sits on her jaw from the barrel of the gun being pressed into her skin too soon after firing. Bruises sit around her lips from the force of his grip.

Everything in me wishes I could erase all the pain he inflicted on her. Hell, I'd settle for going back in time and taking him out before he got to her or Lyric.

But I can't.

So, I settle for taking her free hand and squeezing.

"Have a good sleep?"

River grins at my question, nodding. "Yes. I slept like a log." Liar. She was up more times than I can count checking on me. Or switching beds, trying to get comfy. The bags under her eyes don't lie. The dimmed light in her eyes doesn't lie.

"Breakfast, my ladies," Rad coos, setting a plate in front of River and a smaller one in front of Lyric.

"Pancakes!" Lyric celebrates with a tiny clap, digging into the food.

"She's going to become a pancake monster," River quips, grabbing a fork and cutting into her breakfast.

"I love pancakes, Mommy," Lyric says through a mouthful of food.

"You sure do," Kieran chuckles, moving her crazy hair out of the way as she eats some more pancakes and sticky syrup, getting it everywhere.

"We're going to have to hose you down before school," Callum chuckles, cutting a piece of pancake for her.

"No school," she pouts, opening her mouth when Cal holds his fork in front of her lips.

"Yes, school," I respond quickly, earning a frown.

I can tell there are more protests on the tip of her tongue, but Cal doesn't give her a chance to speak as he feeds her with a wide smile.

This is how it should have been all along. Us. Our girl. Little Lyric. I like to imagine what it would have been like if we had stayed in Central City. If I had never betrayed River in such a big way.

Baby Lyric would have had four caring dads at her beck and call from the beginning. Night feedings. Diaper changes. Everything that comes with new babies. Kieran and I would have figured out how to handle Nigel and his demands.

It would have worked out. But I guess this is the ultimate journey we had to make. We're fundamentally changed. For better and worse.

"All right, Little Lady. Time to get dressed for school," River says, leaning her cheek on her palm.

"I'm sick," Lyric says with a fake cough, pouting even more.

"Heard that one before, Little Pretty Girl. You're going to have to come up with something better than that," Rad snorts, shaking his head. "There's five of us now."

"Let's not give your momma a hard time today, okay?" I ask, leaning forward and catching her eyes. "Go upstairs, get cleaned up, brush your teeth, and get dressed. I bet your friends have missed you."

She huffs when she jumps down from Kieran's lap and walks up the stairs, stomping the whole way.

"And you want more," River snorts, taking another sip of her coffee.

"It's five adults against babies. We got this, Pretty Girl. Now, go get dressed and take her to school." Rad gets up and kisses her cheek.

"Yes, Sir," she grumbles sarcastically, climbing to her feet and shuffling up the stairs.

"They've agreed to a meeting," Kieran whispers, holding up a text exchange between him, Seger, and Zeppelin West.

"When?"

Kieran licks his lips, looking around between us. "As soon as she leaves. We're going to tell them what we're doing."

Rad grins, rubbing his hands together. "I thought I'd be terrified of this… Losing our music." He shakes his head. "But I'm excited."

As soon as River walks out the door, we pile into my car and take off, about to decimate our careers.

But in the end…

It'll all pay off.

Being scared to enter my own house shouldn't be a thing. Right? Like I shouldn't feel my heart thumping wildly in my neck. Or the anxious swirl in my belly at the thought of walking through my front door.

But yet, here I am, standing in front of my house. By myself, wishing I had someone to hold my hand.

I peek at the quiet band house from over my shoulder. They're in band practice right now, working hard to get back into a routine. At least, that's what they told me they were doing before I left with Ly and dropped her off at school. I could march over there and demand someone help me walk into my house. They'd drop everything to help me. I'm sure of it.

But I won't.

Why? Because I'm a bad bitch who needs to get over the fear coursing through my veins. By myself. Van invaded my privacy here. Multiple times. But he's gone. Locked in prison until his very last breath. There's no way he's getting out now. Jordy made sure of it.

His security firm's equipment is gone from my home, too. Every camera. Every wire. Any trace of him has been erased like he never existed in the first place.

So, why am I so fucking terrified to go inside? He's not here anymore. I am. It's my home, goddamnit. The place I built so Lyric and I could have a paradise of our own on a beach to ourselves. We were safe here. Just us and my security guards. Useless bastards. They're gone, too, replaced by bigger and better people, guarding my driveway and walking the property. Carter gave me my own Veritas agents who will protect me no matter what. Or I'm sure Carter will murder them in their sleep.

So, I should feel safer than before. My stalker is gone. For real, this time. I have better guards. My guys are stuck to me like glue. So, why do I have this constant anxiety running through me, leaving me with sweaty palms and heart palpitations? God, my stomach churns, thinking about all the shit Van put me through, pulling the wool over everyone's eyes.

Van somehow snuck his way onto my property, putting his fingers in situations he shouldn't have. He tortured Ly for months with his constant

tapping on the windows. Mine too. He watched us through the cameras. Probably every fucking day. I shiver, pushing the thoughts of what he did with those videos out of my mind. I have no doubt; he was a very sick man.

I don't know if I can ever live here again without feeling his eyes on me. Or his hand on my mouth. Or his body pressed against mine as he held me captive.

I take a deep breath, grounding myself. I'm free. I can do this. Totally can do this without any help. Fuck.

Looking over my shoulder again, I peek at the band house, which seems eerily quiet from here. Maybe Rad could come over and help? He'd hold my hand and—

No. I can't. I need to face this head-on so I can continue living my life. Van can't dictate my life anymore. I'm done letting him take up space in my brain. He can't scare me anymore.

With trembling hands, I unlock the door and step into the house. I nearly piss myself when the alarm begins to beep at a steady pace, echoing on the walls. Holy shit! My heart nearly leaps out of my damn chest and takes a walk.

Right. Carter added new security for me after dismantling Van's.

After inputting the code and turning it off, I freeze in the living room. My eyes dart around, taking in my familiar surroundings. My home. The place I built as our paradise. I take a deep, calming breath and shake the eerie feeling pushing down on my shoulders.

The feeling of ants marching across my skin starting at my toes makes my skin crawl. It feels odd standing here by myself. My home closes in on me. The walls caving in. I squeeze my eyes shut.

Maybe I should have brought them over. Then I wouldn't feel so alone.

My guys appease me by letting me bed-hop in the middle of the night. Never protesting when I crawl in with one and then leave when I can't get comfortable. Or fall asleep. That's been the hardest part of coping. Every time I close my eyes, his voice rings in my head, and his face appears with that menacing grin.

They know something is wrong, but I just want to go back to normal.

Whatever that is.

I rub a hand up and down my arm, attempting to soothe the swirling nerves taking me over as I walk through the silent house. Nothing has changed. It's all the same as I left it the day we left for Lyric's birthday party.

A deep sigh rocks through me when I plop onto Ly's bed and grab the white bunny she's been asking for. I was too afraid to come here alone and grab it. Just that simple action threw me into a tailspin of panic. And I'm way too hardheaded to admit to the guys that I needed them to help me.

My fingers swipe over the beady little eyes of her white bunny as I contemplate our future. Ly's and mine. Plus, the guys. They're going to graduate from my program with flying colors in a few months. Meaning they're going to leave us again. For months on end. We may still be in a relationship, but they won't physically be here. I know we'll have video chats and text messages. But it won't be the same. I need to be in their arms. And I guess that's what terrifies me. I've fallen down the same deep, dark hole of commitment with them. Last time, they left town without saying goodbye. This time… I don't know. I believe them when they say they're all in, but that nagging voice in the back of my head that's been burned before fucks with me.

I also won't be the person to rip their passion away from them with ultimatums. Rocking out on stage is their fucking dream, something they've wished for since they started in high school.

I also can't do that to myself. Sure, I could go on the road with them and bring Ly. But what kind of life would that be? Becoming a band manager has always been my dream. I shine here and finally feel like I'm doing some good. I thought I'd never achieve it. Not from Central City.

Here I am, doing what I wanted to do. Same goes for them. This has always been something they've wanted. They talked about it from the moment I met them.

We all got out of Central City. Now, I'm afraid of where it's going to lead.

Closing my eyes, I finally settle all the shit going haywire inside me. From the fear of the future to the fear of sitting in my house, I blow it all out. We'll deal with that when the time comes. Maybe we'll strengthen what we have further, and it won't be a problem.

Everything is okay. It will all be fine.

Except…

My head snaps up when what sounds like a dump truck makes its way up the driveway. Gears shift, brakes squeak, and its engine groans when it comes to a complete stop, idling loudly. Low murmurs sound outside as doors slam.

What the fuck? No one else should be here. Unless my new guard let them through.

Clutching Ly's bunny, I rush out of her room and into the kitchen. My heart sputters in my chest at the memories of watching Break leave the band house months ago, listening as their moving trucks pulled into the driveway.

And as I stand in my kitchen, the same spot I was in before, and peek out the window, it's happening all over again.

Moving trucks sit in front of the band house, with twenty or so movers walking straight into the house and grabbing items.

I scramble to grab my phone. There has to be an explanation for this. There's no way they…no. They're practicing. Right?

I bring the screen in front of my eyes, and a call with Seger's name on it is coming through.

"Seger," I say out a breath, unable to take my eyes off the shit happening across the street.

"River," he mocks back in a smooth voice.

"Why…"

"I need you to come to the office. We need to, uh, have a meeting," he says, clearing his throat like uncertainty is rocking through him.

"A meeting?" I ask, swallowing hard. "Wait. Where are Whispered Words, and why are there moving vans outside their house?" Emotions bubble to the surface as I bring a fist to my trembling lips.

Was this all too much? Have they decided that this can't happen anymore? Am I still too much baggage for them?

"Deep breaths," Zepp pipes up in a smooth voice. "Just come down here. Take your time."

"Don't fucking crash on their account," Seger quips playfully, not sounding the least bit worried about what is happening.

"Seriously? That's all you're going to give me? My band is moving out of the house… They…they…"

A sigh rocks through the phone. "I can tell you're overthinking whatever is happening, Riv. Just trust us, okay? And please get down here so they can explain what's happening. You might puncture my lung or something if I tell you. You need to hear everything from them."

"Are they quitting?" I ask, swallowing the thick lump forming in my throat. If they're quitting, then they probably got the offer they were looking for. We pay well, but they're probably due a raise.

"Jesus. Yes. Now, would you get down here so they can explain everything? It's not what it seems," Seger says in what he thinks is a soothing voice.

It's anything but.

Nerves take over when I hang up the phone and make my way to my car. It's not as bad as it seems?

Liar.

"Good, you're here. And shit, you're mad as fuck," Seger whistles, shaking his head.

Well, he's not fucking wrong.

My face tightens as I march through the halls of West Records with murder on my mind. The entire drive here consisted of anxiety and burial plans.

First, my brothers will go. Their wife may miss them, but she's got two more husbands to make up for their loss. RIP, West bros. It was nice knowing you.

Then, it's my turn to murder my baby daddies. All four of them. Whatever they've got up their sleeve is killable. I'll have their graves dug before they can say—River, please don't.

"Yeah! I'm fucking fuming," I grunt, moving past him as he catches my arm, stopping my movements in the middle of the hallway.

His green eyes dart around before he moves in, which is brave on his part. I narrow my eyes, ready to bite his nose off in retaliation.

"Riv," he says, forcing my gaze to his. "Listen to them. Don't just go off, okay?"

Don't go off? No, I'm going to decimate them for leaving my program and walking away. For leaving me. They're supposed to graduate in a few months and live their dream. Now, they're giving it up or going somewhere else.

"In here. You're making a spectacle," Zepp grumbles, nodding us into the small room with the two-way mirror connected to the conference room.

The same damn room I saw them for the first time after five years of being apart. It's like we've jumped in a time machine and traveled back in time to the point at which this all started.

Seger grumbles and curses under his breath, dragging me like a rag doll into the closed-off room. The door softly shuts behind us, leaving us to view the guys sitting around the conference table through the two-way mirror. My heart speeds up. I can't fucking stand to look at them right now. I don't know what scares me more. That they didn't talk to me about this? Or that they're possibly leaving me?

I narrow my eyes. "Why are you so calm? If they quit, that means they're going somewhere else. Doesn't it?"

My eyes drift to them, finally taking in the four men who've come to take over my life. Again. A long time ago, I promised myself I'd never fall into their dirty trap. Or fall in love with them. It's so hard to resist their charms when all these old feelings have resurfaced with a vengeance, begging me to be in their orbit. I wonder if this is how fated mates feel when they finally find that perfect person their soul was made for.

Whispered Words may not be magically mine, but my entire being calls out to them and pulls me into them every time. No matter how angry I am at them, I still see myself with them.

As my eyes scan over the boys, my heart pumps faster, and sweat breaks out across my skin. The last time I viewed them from this angle, they were staring at their phones and barely talking. They fucking hated each other and loathed me even more.

And now?

Kieran smiles at Rad, who softly speaks in his direction, causing Asher to laugh and turn red. Callum leans his elbow on the table with a grin, shaking his head. Whatever they're discussing brings them so much joy.

"Go and talk to them. We'll be right here," Zepp murmurs, gripping my shoulder. "It's nothing bad. In fact, it's something we were expecting."

"Did you guys do this on purpose?" I whisper, looking between the two of them as they once again have a rude, silent conversation.

"No," Seger grumbles. "We'd never purposefully put you through that torture. Scouts honor," he says, holding up two fingers.

"You're not scouts." I roll my eyes, staring at the guys again with longing in my heart.

No wonder they didn't want to help take Ly to school. They were planning… Well, whatever this is.

"I could have been, but dear old dad shoved us into private schools, never giving us a chance to enjoy that kind of shit. Now, get in there before they combust."

"It'll be fine," Zepp says with reassurance, patting my shoulder.

"Fine. But if I have to kill them, you had better protect me with fancy lawyers and shit," I grumble, wrinkling my nose when Seger bursts out laughing.

"Always got your back," he chuckles, opening the door for me, and practically shoves me into the conference room.

I swallow hard when my guys freeze, watching me approach with caution.

"So, you called a meeting?" I ask, crossing my arms over my chest and walking further into the room. "When I left my house, there were moving vans sitting outside."

Rad slaps Kieran on the arm, gesturing for him to speak.

"We got another offer from EJ Records," he says in a deep voice, nearly knocking me off my feet.

An offer? From another company? What in the ever living fuck is happening right now?

"And you accepted?" Anger boils in my gut as his eyes widen, and he takes a step back. His eyes fly to my fingers, curling in my pocket where my knife rests. I'm never leaving without it again. No matter what. Thank God, too. I'm about to put this through each of their eyeballs.

"Fuck. River Blue…" he trails off, swiping a hand down his face. "We didn't accept the offer."

"He told them to shove it up their asses with a smile on his face," Rad snorts with glee, rising to his feet. "All one hundred million, too. That'd hurt." He cringes, shuttering at the thought.

"Is that what you really thought?" Callum asks, cocking his head to the side. I swallow hard when his gray eyes inspect every inch of my body, and he nods in confirmation. "Understandable, Little Star."

"Why else would you be vacating the band house without telling me?

You…" I trail off, wondering what the fuck is going through their heads. If they aren't staying here, then where are they going? They don't have any prospects on the horizon. So, that means… "No," I choke out, shaking my head. "There's no way you're just…"

"We quit," Kieran says, coming to stand in front of me. His fingers brush against my cheeks, and he gives me a small smile. "We quit West Records. We didn't accept that offer. We're done, baby."

"What the hell?" I murmur with a trembling lip. "You can't just walk away from your dream. Guys, this is your fucking passion. You're living something everyone else wants. You're rock stars. You're—"

"Not anymore, Little Star," Callum says with a head shake.

Not an ounce of sadness rests on their faces as they look up at me with soft smiles.

"It was," Asher grunts, getting to his feet with the help of Callum as they situate his crutches.

"We have a lot more dreams, Pretty Girl," Rad says with a shrug.

"But music is your life."

"Was our life," Kieran adds, bringing my gaze to his. "River Blue. This band was our dream for years. Getting here to this place, it was fucking wild. We've soared on stage and sold-out shows. But nothing compares to the little girl that wraps her arms around me and calls me Daddy. That's the real dream with you and her."

"And you, Little Star," Callum murmurs, coming to my other side and moving a piece of hair from my shoulder. "You're the ultimate dream." His face softens when tears burn the back of my eyes.

"No. I can't let you quit because of me," I whisper, sucking in a breath. "You can't—"

"We can," Rad says with a shrug. "Plus, we kind of already did. We've signed the papers giving up our contract."

My eyes cut to the mirror, where I know my brothers are watching. Nosy bastards. They set it up so they could quit, and I'd have no say in the matter. Their death is still on the table. But my guys? Not so much.

"We knew you'd try to stop us if we talked to you about it. We were damn sure that this is what we wanted." Kieran swallows hard, continually tracing the freckles lining my cheeks.

"You'll regret it later," I whisper. "You'll…"

"Nope. No regrets, Pretty Girl. This," he murmurs, pointing between the five of us. "This is our new dream. We're going to build you a house on the beach with enough room for all of us."

"We're going to walk you down the aisle and say I do and make you ours forever," Asher says with glossy eyes.

"I'm going to put so many babies in you—" Rad grunts when Asher punches him in the gut. "Asshole! Why do you keep doing that." He sends Asher a scathing look.

"We're going to take you out to dinner. Make you breakfast in bed. Give you the best orgasms you've ever had," Rad says, wiggling his brows. "We have it all planned out, Pretty Girl. Every day. Just you, Lyric, and us."

"Those, River Blue. Are our dreams. Music will always be here," Kieran says, tapping his chest with his free hand.

"We don't have to go on tour or play for millions of people..." Rad wheezes, trailing off.

"We're right where we want to be. With you and Ly, building our future," Asher says with determination.

"Besides, your brothers offered us jobs," Rad beams, crossing his arms over his chest. "So, you can't say no."

"You're all serious?" I ask in disbelief as tears stream down my face. "You're seriously going to work here?"

"Yes," Kieran chuckles, brushing the tears from my cheeks. "We've lived our dream. You helped us with that, and we appreciate what you did for us. Back then, in Central City, helping us set up for Battle of the Bands. And now, helping us work through our shit. You've done so much for us, and it opened our eyes. We weren't happy because you weren't in our lives. We weren't happy because Whispered Words is nothing without River West."

"We'd give up the world for you, Little Brat," Asher whispers, licking his lips.

"But we're doing this for us, too. We want to be in your lives. We want to help take Ly to school every morning and pick her up in the afternoon. We want to wake up for the night feedings and let you sleep. We want the shitty diapers, long nights, and beautiful sunrises with you," Kieran adds again.

"We want all the things. Firsts, seconds, and lasts," Rad whispers, moving in on me. "We want it all with you at the center of it. You're our number one. You always should have been. Music can take a backseat. Everything else can get fucked. I mean, you can too; we'll help with that. But you're ours. Forever. Whether you like it or not."

I sniffle, leaning into Kieran's touch.

"I can't believe you're giving up everything for me."

"You did it for us," Asher says. "You gave up your whole life because we walked away. You raised our baby into an amazing child. You sacrificed your time and freedom to give yourself the life you deserved all along. Now, we're here to help you keep moving forward. We love you, Little Brat."

I close my eyes when their touches start softly stroking different parts of my body. Arms. Face. Back. Shoulders. They're everywhere, surrounding me, promising to never leave my side.

"I love you, too," I murmur through a ragged breath. "I can't believe it."

"Believe it, Pretty Girl. You'll be seeing our faces every day from now on." He wiggles his brows, forcing a laugh from my throat.

"So, what do you say?" Kieran asks, bringing my attention back to him. "Are you ready to start this new chapter in our lives?"

"Yes." A smile breaks free, stretching across my lips when he leans in and kisses my cheek.

"Good, because I think we would have just kidnapped you, anyway." Kieran shrugs, pulling back.

"I don't doubt it," I say with a laugh, shaking my head. "Well… Looks like I'm free for a day or two. What should we do?"

"Let's go get reacquainted properly," Rad quips, wiggling his brows. "My tongue wants to explore some new places."

I snort when something bangs against the mirror on the opposite side of the room. Serves them right for being nosy assholes.

"All right," I say, holding out my hand for him to take. "Let's go then."

The five of us slowly walk toward the door as a unit, with silence between us. Not the uncomfortable kind, either. It's the satisfied—we finally made it—kind of silence.

It's been five years of pure hell thinking they left without reason, leaving me with our baby and restraining orders. All we needed was time to patch ourselves back together and knit our relationship back to what it was. This time around, we're more cohesive and in better control of our emotions. From this moment on, we'll be a fucking family together. Forever in each other's arms.

"So, how about that wedding proposal?" I ask when we make it out the front door after saying our awkward goodbyes to my brothers.

"Wait, what?" Rad shouts, turning sharply on his heel to face me.

"You heard me," I say, waving a hand in his direction.

He swallows hard, eyeing the other guys, and pats his pockets. "I don't have a ring."

"That never stopped you before," I say, smiling when his face reddens.

"Marry us, Pretty Girl. Please be our wife. Our baby momma. The woman who lets me clean her up when the others are done with her," he asks in a low voice, taking my hand in his as the others gather around us with their hearts in their throats.

"Okay," I say with a grin, squeezing his hand. "I'll marry you all."

"YES!" Rad shouts, throwing his arms around me and lifting me in the air. After several spins, he sets me on my feet and captures my lips with his. "Time to celebrate," he chuckles, dragging me toward my car.

Whispered Words and River West. We started out as something impossible. Five broken people coming together and finding something other people long for. The love was there, but the timing was all wrong.

We spent five years apart from each other, growing into broken adults. We were people who depended on music, work, drugs, fighting, and fucking isolation to get us through the end of the day.

In the end, the five broken pieces patched themselves back together from the inside out and, in turn, connected again. The love is here. The timing is right.

And us?

Well, we're whole.

The Fucking End

Shut the curtain.
Take a bow.
The boys and River are done for now.

"You're going to tell them tonight?" Olivia practically begs, bustling by with bright flowers in her hands. She grins when she sets them on the little table in my master bath.

"Yes. But they won't tell me what we have planned for the honeymoon," I say, wrinkling my nose when Ode brushes bright red blush on my cheek.

"Stop moving, bitch," Ode quips, flicking my nose. "Or I'll miss and poke you in the eye."

"She will, too," Rocco quips, leaning against the bathroom counter, watching intently.

"I will," Ode says, grinning, pointing a makeup brush in his direction.

I side-eye Ode, who grins wider, dipping the brush into the red blush again, preparing to paint my other cheek.

"But definitely tonight?" Kaycee asks, cocking her head to the side and letting her blonde curls fall down her back. "I don't know if I can hold my tongue anymore. This is the hardest secret I've had to keep in a long time." She makes a face, shaking her head. "And I don't keep secrets very well."

"Please tell them before we collectively die of secret-keeping," Rocco groans, shaking his head

I snort, ignoring his whines. "Well, the rest of them," I say with a shrug. "Kieran kinda walked in on me peeing on the stick."

Literally. The man knows no personal space when it comes to me sometimes. There I was, minding my own business and trying to be discreet. Then, walks in Kieran, tossing his shirt off and letting me know he's going to hop into the shower.

"And he's kept it a secret?" Ode snorts, brushing on the red to my cheeks.

I suck in a breath as another round of nausea rolls through my stomach. This has been happening more and more as the weeks have gone on. I

mean, I'm only about seven weeks pregnant, but I found out two weeks ago. Just in time to get this wedding done and start our lives together.

"Like a good boy, yes," I quip, taking a sip of 7-Up. "He's been helping me ever since the morning sickness decided to come along."

He's been the sweetest man since he accidentally walked in on me in the bathroom. Right after I had set the test on the counter.

"Is that?" he whispers, plastering his front to my back. Those mismatched eyes peer down at the test, lighting up when the results finally appear. "You're pregnant," he whispers, wrapping his arms around me. "It finally happened."

I swallow hard, tracing the test with tears in my eyes. "You're only happy because you don't have to wear a condom anymore," I quip, sniffling.

"That too," he murmurs, kissing my cheek. "Oh, River Blue. I can't believe this is finally happening. We're going to be here every step of the way. I can't fucking wait." Emotions bubble in his throat, glazing over his eyes. Silent tears fall down his cheeks, expressing the joy he's feeling. "I'll always regret not being here the first time around," he confesses, rubbing a hand along my flat stomach. "Anything you need, My Blue. I'll be here."

"I want to wait to tell them," I say, catching his gaze in the mirror above the sink we're standing in front of. "Until after the wedding." A slight smirk pulls at the edge of his lip with satisfaction. "It'll be the ultimate surprise."

"So I get to know before those other assholes?" His brows wiggle as his hand glides over my stomach. "I'll keep it a secret for now." He takes a deep breath, brushing his nose against the column of my neck. "They're going to be so fucking excited for this, especially Rad. That fucker's been throwing you in closets every chance he gets."

I snort, closing my eyes and leaning into his touch. "Ever since we decided to start trying, he's been fucking insatiable," I whisper as goosebumps spread across my flesh.

Since we decided three months ago to start trying to expand our family, Rad's been the clingiest. Deep down, I know it's his guilt tearing through him for not being here for Lyric. He's wanted more children since we went all in, and finally, we decided not to wait any longer. We started planning the wedding the moment they picked out a ring and slipped it on my finger.

This is our future, and we're finally settling into our new normal.

"That boy hasn't changed one bit, has he? Loyal as ever," Ode murmurs with sincerity, eyeing my makeup with a satisfied grin. "You're as beautiful as ever, bitch. I can't believe…" She turns away, putting a hand to her lips.

"Don't you start," Olivia sniffles, swiping a hand under her nose. "Every time you start the waterworks, mine starts."

"Nobody start!" Rocco sniffles, wiping under his eyes.

"Can't help it," Ode says through a quivering voice. "I never thought my girl would walk down the aisle after what they did. And now look at her, she's getting four dicks for the price of one," she wails, covering her face with her hands.

"Please don't cry. You'll make me cry, and then my makeup will be ruined for the wedding." Emotions sit in the back of my throat, burning my damn eyes.

"None of that," Ode says, shaking her head and wiping her eyes. "We've got to get you down that aisle and married before they fuck up again."

Olivia snorts. "Oh, they'll fuck up a lot, Riv. But that's the joy of marriage," she says wistfully, looking out the window of the bathroom. She swallows hard, watching the movements of the men outside, working together as they put my flower arch into the sand.

I couldn't have dreamed of a better place to get married than the sands behind my home, under the sparkling stars and moonlight. Even though I was once terrified after Van's invasion to resume living here, I'm not anymore. This is my home. Or will be for the next few months. Just a hundred feet away on two acres of my property, the boys and I are building our dream home. Fit with six bedrooms, four baths, a basement with a recording studio, and room to grow.

As the day progresses and the sun goes down, everyone clears out to get ready for the wedding. Olivia, Kaycee, and Ode get into their dresses for the ceremony. And Rocco leaves to put his suit on.

Our ceremony is simple. Just the five of us standing under the arch. No bridesmaids or groomsmen. We wanted something where people could just come and watch with their families and celebrate with us.

"Love you, Riv. I'm so happy they came around, and you guys were able to fix this," Olivia says, kissing my cheek. "I'm so happy for you." She grins, stepping out of my house, and takes a seat with the audience.

"Show 'em hell, bitch. Don't let those assholes get one over on you," Ode says with a wink, heading out to sit next to Olivia.

"If you ever need assistance. You know who to call," Kaycee says, cocking her head to the side. "But I have a feeling you're used to this."

"Just as used to it as you are, Angel," Seger says, sauntering into the bathroom with a cocky grin. He stops short, throwing his arm over Kaycee's shoulders and nods. "Wow. You clean up good, Sis. They're all ready for you. It's not too late to run, though," he quips, kissing Kaycee's head with affection.

"Like I wanted to run from you?" she asks, raising a brow when his face falls.

"You'd never, Angel…" he trails off, wrinkling his nose. "Would you?"

"She wouldn't," Zepp says, coming to stand beside me. "You look beautiful, Riv. Congrats on the big day."

I sniffle, leaning in to hug him. "Thanks, guys. For being here and for walking me down the aisle."

"What're big brothers for? Besides, Dad isn't here. We're the next best thing," Seger says.

"Well, shall we?" Zepp asks, gesturing toward the back sliding doors.

I nod.

"I'll be out there. You're gorgeous," Kaycee compliments before scurrying off out the door and taking a seat next to Chase and Carter, her other husbands. Leaving me alone with my two brothers, who are about to walk me down the aisle, giving me over to the four men I've loved, hated, and loved again.

"Seriously. It's not too late," Seger murmurs, offering me his elbow.

I snort. "What if I want to marry them? Hmm?" I hum, maneuvering my long, white dress as we take a few steps. It swishes with every movement I make, slightly sparkling under the living room lights.

"We're so happy for you," Zepp says with a grin, reaching for the back sliding glass door, but stops. "And proud, Riv. You've come a long way. You've worked hard. Been an amazing mother…"

"And sister," Seger interrupts. "You're fucking amazing, Riv. And I gotta say, they've really helped you shine these past six months since they quit. They've gone from cocky assholes to fucking amazing dudes."

I smile, peeking out the glass door at the four men who've stolen my heart standing under the flower arch. Tight suits fit against their bodies, showing off their toned muscles.

Since they quit their contract, they've really thrived within the music industry. Rad and Callum have turned into amazing West Records talent scouts, hitting all the small venues in a fifty-mile radius. Callum's eye for stardom and Rad's easy-going personality has drawn in some amazing talent.

Kieran has stepped up as my assistant, since Kat had to take some time off to regain herself emotionally and hasn't been back since. Rocco keeps me updated on her whereabouts and how she's holding up. Day by day, she's healing from the trauma Van put her through.

And Asher? Well, he's anointed himself as a stay-at-home father, soaking up all the love Lyric has to give him while we all work. He takes care of the laundry. Cooks us elaborate dinners, fit with appetizers and desserts. He makes sure all the housework is done and manages Lyric's school pick-up schedule. He's helped Camilla get used to her new life with us and not Gloria. Although, for the most part, she's opted to continue living at the prep school during the school year and will stay with us during the summer.

For the first time in a long time, Asher seems free of everything and is doing what he loves.

"Mommy! I look like a princess!" Lyric's small voice carries through the house as she clutches tight to Rocco's hand.

"You do," I rasp, leaning down to run my fingers through her curly, dark locks. "Are you ready to throw some flowers out?"

Lyric grins, nodding. "I am! Uncle Rocco gots me this basket with pretty red rose petals to throw everywhere!" She squeals, reaching into the basket with a grin. "I'm excited, Mommy. You're going to marry daddies."

"I am," I say with tears burning in my eyes. "Is that okay?"

"Of course," she says, nodding.

"All right, my little doll. How about we start walking down the aisle?" Rocco says, nodding toward the back door with a dopey expression.

"Okay," she says, looking me up and down. "You look like a queen, Mommy." Her grin lights up my fucking world, sending tears down my cheeks.

This is what we needed all fucking along. She needed them. I needed them. And now, we're all coming together as one unit. The guys, me, Lyric, and even their sister Camilla. The girl we adopted after Gloria's ass went straight to prison for her crimes. We're one happy family, just trying to make it day by day.

"Are you ready for this?" Zepp asks, opening the slider all the way.

The cool night air hits my face as we step out onto the back porch. Fairy lights wrap around the wooden structure, illuminating our way toward the small crowd gathered around the flowery archway. The small buzz of conversation halts when our feet hit the sand, and as one, all our friends and family stand from their chairs, watching with eager eyes as Zepp and Seger guide me down the make-shift aisle.

Lyric giggles every time she tosses her red rose petals onto the sand, finally making it up to the arch. Each of the guys kisses her cheek before Rocco guides her to the front row of chairs, sitting next to Christian and Kat. I smile, catching Kat's eyes and she grins, sending me a thumbs up. It's nice to see her out and about after everything that happened six months ago. She's slowly rebuilding herself with the two men surrounding her.

I heave a breath, break eye contact, and focus on my surroundings. Ocean waves act as our symphony in the background when the bride's music starts.

"What?" I murmur, startling when a soft guitar rhythm starts playing through the speaker at the front.

"You're not the only one keeping secrets," Zepp murmurs, raising a brow when I side-eye him.

Kieran's quiet, sultry voice echoes through the quiet crowd. Tears heat behind my eyes, catching on my lashes when his soft, loving words take root in my brain.

Loved you from day one.
Time has been rough.
Broke up.
Repaired.
Now we're one.
The future holds bright
Like a candle steady in the wind
You're the one we want.
Forever.
Always.
Our wife.

"Fuck," I rasp, squeezing my eyes shut in hopes I don't ruin the mascara curling my eyelashes.

I will not fucking cry over a beautiful song they obviously wrote for our wedding day. I will not fucking cry in front of all these people! Fuck it. Who am I kidding? I'm borderline hormonal from the pregnancy, and they wrote me a fucking song. Who does that? The men of my dreams, that's who.

Slowly, we walk through the sand, making our way toward the four men who stare at me with tears in their eyes.

Asher glances away, rubbing away the moisture collecting on his lashes before looking back and smiling at me. He takes in my appearance. Inch by fucking inch, slowly making his way to my gaze. He nods in approval when we finally stop directly in front of them, under the flowery archway.

"I'm the luckiest guy in the world," he rasps, stepping forward with his hand held out.

"Jesus, Pretty Girl," Rad chokes out, covering his quivering lips with his hand. "You look so beautiful. I can't wait to rip that dress in half and then—"

"Don't fucking finish that sentence," Seger grunts, plowing his fist into Rad's stomach.

"Groom!" Rad wheezes, bending at the waist. "You can't punch a groom on his wedding day."

"When you make comments like that about my sister, I do, asshole," Seger grumbles, shaking his head.

I crack a smile when he slowly lifts my hand into Asher's, joining us together as one. Gently, Asher squeezes my fingers in his.

"You take care of my fucking sister, or you four won't have lives to live." He gives them a meaningful look when he steps back, running a finger across his throat for dramatic effect. "Grumpy knows how to dispose of bodies." He tilts his head in Carter's direction.

Carter grins from the audience, throwing an arm over the back of Kaycee's chair, nodding like he knows exactly what Seger is talking about. Casually, he lifts his fingers in a tiny wave, solidifying the threat further.

"Fuck," Callum murmurs, stiffening at the look of pure joy on Carter's face.

"He's going to kill us," Rad hisses, jerking his gaze to me. "Pretty Girl, tell your brothers we're good boys."

I shrug, biting the inside of my cheek to hold my smile. My stomach churns from either the nerves or my morning sickness, coming back with a vengeance. Up until now, Kieran's helped me hide the need to rush to the bathroom and puke my brains out. But nothing will hide it now if I spew all over the beach.

Please don't barf. I suck in a breath, breathing through the torment squeezing my stomach into knots.

"Stop it," I grunt at my brother, shoving him away.

"He will," Rad rasps, rubbing at his abdomen. "I have zero doubts he'll chop us into tiny pieces." He wrinkles his nose when Seger's grin grows, and he nods.

"Just be good," Zepp mutters, kissing my cheek.

Slowly, Asher pulls me forward, helping me maneuver my long dress through the sand.

"You really are gorgeous, Pretty Girl," Rad murmurs, leaning in to kiss my cheek. "This dress is...beautiful." Tears form in his eyes, and he sniffles. "I'm finally marrying my dream girl. My one true love." He cups my cheeks, swiping away the rogue tears dripping down my damn cheeks. Despite my efforts not to cry, it seems impossible at this point. "I knew from the moment I watched Kieran fuck you over that desk that you were the one for me."

"Dude," Kieran grumbles, shaking his head. "We have an audience."

"What?" Rad asks, wrinkling his nose. "It's true! You think we didn't stand there for the full thirty seconds..." Rad grins when Kieran rolls his eyes.

"Was longer than thirty seconds, asshole," Kieran huffs.

"Try three minutes," Callum says, side-eyeing Kieran as he turns beet red.

"I hate you all. I can't believe I'm strapped to you idiots for eternity. You know, River Blue. It's not too late. We can run away together," he says with a sly grin, falling over when Asher pushes him aside.

"I won't let you take my girl," Asher grumbles, straightening out his suit jacket.

"Psst. Get in your spots," Chase, Kaycee's other husband, whispers, pointing to a few spots in the sand. Without a second thought, the five of us take our spots.

Me in the middle with the four of them surrounding me, leaving me in the center of their circle. My stomach swirls again as hot acid leaks up my throat, begging to come out. I take a deep breath, working through the constant nausea. Nervous sweat leaks from every pore.

"Ready, Little West?" he asks with a megawatt grin.

I nod, not daring to speak when he begins the ceremony. The crowd settles into their seats, watching us with rapt attention as Chase belts out the words animatedly.

Kieran squeezes my waist, staring down at me with furrowed brows. "River Blue, you're pale," he whispers right in my ear, not garnering the attention of the rest of the boys.

I shake my head. If I open my mouth, I'll…

"Fuck," I hiss, pushing through the boys, barely making it to a clear spot away from the prying eyes watching our every move.

"I got you," Kieran says, rushing to my side and holding back my hair.

"Well, I was going to say you may kiss the bride, but…" Chase's joking voice trails off as the murmurs start in the crowd.

"I'm okay," I whisper through a ragged breath, holding back the next wave of nausea threatening to pull me under.

"Maybe we should talk to the doctor about those pills?" Kieran says, helping me stand tall. I let out a sigh of relief when he rubs a tissue along my lips and cleans me up.

"Yeah. Might have to. Wait, how'd you know about those?" I whisper, wiping the moisture from my cheeks.

He smiles, fluffing my hair back out. "You mentioned you had to do that with Ly in the beginning. That it had gotten so bad you couldn't go to work or class."

"Pretty Girl, are you okay?" Rad asks with concern, finally making it to my side.

"Are you sick?" Callum asks, turning green when he blinks at the little pile on the sand.

Fuck. I press my lips into a tight line, breathing through the swooping feeling taking over my stomach.

Kieran hums, rubbing a hand over my stomach, which seems to soothe the waves of vomit attempting to come out again.

"Little Star," Callum says with wide eyes, watching Kieran's movements. "Are you…"

I smile, taking his hand in mine and gently placing it on my stomach over the dress. I do the same to Rad and Asher, bringing them in a circle around me again.

"Welcome to fatherhood, boys," I whisper with more damn tears falling down my cheeks.

Rad falls to his knees, pushing everyone away. Gently, he lays a kiss on my stomach, cradling it with his hands.

"I'm going to be the best father I can be, Little Peanut. Just ask your older sister Ly. I swear I owe her two-hundred thousand right now, but fuck, baby. I've longed for you." His dark eyes crawl up my body, meeting my gaze. "Thank you, Pretty Girl. For indulging me any chance you got. I loved helping to create this."

"It's not just possibly yours, dickface. It could be mine, too," Asher says with a grin, kissing my cheek. "Do you need anything, Little Brat?"

"Hmm. No," I murmur, leaning into his kiss.

"It-it could be mine," Callum stammers, staring at my stomach with big eyes. "Holy shit."

Kieran snorts, shoving his hands in his pockets. "Well, it can't be mine…"

"Back door or shut up," Rad quips, jumping to his feet.

"Yeah, that," Kieran cringes, gazing at the crowd watching.

"Do you guys want to continue getting married?" Chase asks, rubbing the back of his neck.

"Yeah," I say, taking their hands and leading them back to our altar. Turning to the crowd, I grin, soaking in their faces. "We're going to have a baby!" I shout, thrusting my fist into the air, laughing as they cheer us on.

"A baby," Rad says, clinging to my hand.

His eyes never leave my stomach, and that includes the entire nine months she cooks to the moment she comes out with rich, dark curly hair and dark eyes.

I guess all those extra moments he shoved me into closets, came to see me at work, and locked me in my bedroom really paid off.

The moment she cried her first breath, Rad scooped her into his arms and proclaimed her as his. And she was. Aria. Our little mischievous one, named for songs and melodies, living up to her father's legend.

Our family grew one by one over the next few years, happening almost right after another. Lyric. Aria. Alana. Maya.

Four girls for four men who helped make me whole.

BONUS CHAPTER

"She's mine. I can feel it..." Rad trails off, rubbing my enlarged stomach with one hand. "So mine," he murmurs in my ear with certainty, pulling my back against his front as we rest on the long sectional couch taking up the living room, cuddled up together.

I relax into him, humming at the light touch of Callum's fingers dancing over my feet. It's the first night in our new house—the one we designed and built together on the same property as my other two houses—the band house and my first home in East Point.

I'm still knuckles deep in my business with West Records. Continuing the tradition of taking bands on the brink of destruction and turning them into gold. Or turds. Their choice, really.

And so are Kieran, Callum, and Rad. We all work together in harmony now. Well, as much as married people can work so close together and then live together. The bickering will never end. But at the end of the day, we're at peace with where our lives are now.

Callum and Rad were hired to scope out talent at local bars, watching for the next big thing. They even help run the yearly Battle of the Bands with Seger and Zeppelin that helped rocket Whispered Words to stardom. My brothers call them the dream team. And they're not wrong about that. They're my dream team, too. Because boy, do those men really know how to work me over together. Phew.

Kieran forced his way into becoming my assistant after what happened with Kat and the way Van used her to stalk me. And I do mean forced. The fucker followed me to work and refused to leave. Even kicking his feet up at my desk with narrowed eyes and harassing anyone who dared to enter my office without permission. It's like I took a bulldog to work and released him on my unsuspecting coworkers. They got used to it. Eventually. God, he even answers my damn phone with a smug, possessive grin, refusing to let anything happen to me. Especially now that I'm pregnant. I

swear he's been foaming at the mouth for the last nine months, growling at anyone who came within one hundred yards of me.

Asher remains at home with Lyric, soaking up being a stay-at-home father. I swear I've never seen anyone so at peace playing carpool with other parents, setting up playdates for Ly, and ensuring her homework is done. Every night, when we all get home from work, dinner is done and on the table. I even caught him wearing an apron once while attempting to make a pie. It burned, by the way. Because while I was jumping his bones in the bedroom and ripping his clothes off, the pie was neglected. Oops.

So, yeah. We've all been committed for nine months with our vows, but I think our future holds something brighter than we ever imagined.

My life has never felt so damn complete.

It's hard to believe how our story started—falling hard and fast until we were decimated at rock bottom. I was alone with Ly for so long. Then, these fuckers burst back into my life like a fucking bomb going off and setting me down a winding, twisted path of rediscovery and love.

Now, here we are.

"There were three other participants," Callum grumbles, digging his thumbs into the bottom of my feet. "She could be mine, too." He levels Rad with a deadly glare. A glare Rad doesn't seem to register when he grins, brushing his comment off.

"Right there," I moan, relaxing further into Rad's hold.

"Just you, me, and Asher pounding the front together and Kieran in the back. No pussy for you." He side-eyes Kieran with a smirk, knowing exactly what our deal was. Kieran flips him off with a huff from the kitchen.

Rad, Asher, and Callum wanted to try for a baby of their own, starting before we got married. We knew we would walk down the aisle¾not that it meant anything more than committing ourselves to each other further—but they still wanted a giant diamond on my finger and a baby of their own in my belly. Kieran already had Lyric. So he either suited up for the occasion or stuck with the back door. He agreed, wanting them to have the opportunity, too. He never complained¾not once.

"Shit. Can you believe we stuffed you full of three dicks at a time, Pretty Girl?" Pride fills his voice with the memories of our time together. "Ah, it was magical." A dreamy look crosses his expression as he loses himself to it.

I shiver, falling into the memories of those moments. Definitely a magical time to be alive. The five of us on the bed. Their dicks were fighting to enter me at the same time. The stretching. The orgasms. Oh, God, the orgasms brought me back to life.

And then knocked me up again.

Good times.

"Besides, my dick is the biggest. Therefore, I win," Rad gloats with a smirk, eyeing the other two over my shoulder.

I snort, leaning back into him without saying a word. I'm not inserting myself into their dick-measuring contest.

Ever.

"You don't have the biggest dick…"

"That's not how that works, dude…"

"Idiot…"

I groan so loudly when Callum hits a small knot in the arch of my foot that I nearly cum from the experience. If that's possible, anyway. For me, though? It probably is. Considering I've been shattering the moment they touch me or enter me. I'll get pregnant a million times over if they promise never to stop this pampering. Or two more times.

That's the deal, anyway.

These idiots somehow managed to convince me they each needed a tiny human. Four in total. And me? Well, I'm the incubator of our creations. Don't get me wrong; I'm over the moon. We've settled into this life as a married five-some with a bundle on the way, raising Lyric and more in the future. I could probably explode from all the happiness.

"Nah. My balls are tingling. It's like they know a little piece of them is right here," Rad hums confidently, rubbing my stomach more vigorously. "Don't you, boys? Yes, you do."

"That's fucking stupid," Kieran quips, walking into the living room with a plate full of Chinese food, shaking his head. "And stop talking to your sack like it's a dog."

The smell of the glorious takeout he handed me hits my senses. My mouth waters. Fuck their argument. I'm starving. But that's life when you're nine months pregnant. Not that I ever go hungry. Nope. My men keep me comfortable, loose, fed, and fully satisfied. Everything I want, they get.

I'm a spoiled-ass princess, and I'll never complain.

Like last night when I was craving ice cream. I mentioned it in passing. Not really thinking about it. And then? Callum jumped on his bike and rode to the store, grabbing me a few pints of my favorite cookie dough ice cream. And when he returned, he fed it to me like I was his princess.

"You'll never have to feed yourself again, Little Star," he murmurs, dangling the spoon over my lips. "Anything you need. We'll provide."

How'd I get so lucky to have them?

I longed for this princess treatment during my first pregnancy with Ly. I begged and pleaded for them to come back and help me but was cut off from the moment I found out about her. I was miserable on my own. Lonely. Cranky. Desperate. Granted, I had Ode and Korrine to help, but they weren't them—the men I needed.

Now, my prayers have been answered. Here, I stare at the piping hot

General's Chicken and shrimp with Crab Rangoon and lots of egg rolls. This is the next best thing since I can't have the sushi I crave.

They spoil me.

"Rude. It is not!" Rad huffs, kissing my head as I lean back against his bare chest. "Tell him, Pretty Girl. It's not dumb. My balls get this tingling feeling deep inside that I'm the one who did this." He rubs my belly again, suddenly stopping. "See, she's kicking! She agrees. Don't you, Extra Pretty girl," he coos over my shoulder, gently kissing my cheek.

"Yum!" I rejoice, sitting up and away from the grabby hands of Rad. I rest against the couch, leaving him to pout beside me. "And she's kicking because I'm finally giving her what she's been craving." All day long, through work and coming home, I've craved delicious Chinese food.

Between the contractions, that is. My eyes linger on each of the guys. I've never seen them so damn happy and carefree. They've finally come into their own despite giving up their dreams.

"We didn't give up our dream, River Blue. We lived it. Breathed it. Everything. But you're more important. Lyric is more important. Being away from you would have been hell."

"So, you'd rather be my assistant?" I ask, nibbling my bottom lip.

Kieran smirks, pulling my front flush against his. "You know how fucking hot it is to watch you put these nitwits in their place? I want to fuck you over the conference table after you've sent them to pack." A shiver runs through me, and I grin when he kisses my lips roughly. "Now, let's show this band who is boss. You. I'm just here to support you and protect you. No one will ever fucking hurt you again." He slaps my ass, grabbing onto it as we peer through the two-way mirror. A position I was in years ago, watching his band with tears in my eyes and fear in my heart.

"I could feed you, Pretty Girl." Rad bats his eyelashes at me. "Let me shove this food or co... Umph! What the hell, Asher, my dude?" Rad groans, rubbing at his shoulder. He plops down beside me and wraps an arm over my shoulders.

"She can feed herself. Can't you, Little Brat?" Asher murmurs, tucking my hair over my shoulders and out of my face.

"I can. Now, shut up. I'm starving," I groan, grabbing the plate from Kieran and digging in.

"I could watch you eat all day long," Rad hums, reaching toward my plate with a grin.

"If you value your fingers, you'll back the fuck up," I say through a mouthful of food.

Why are they always stealing my food? First, it was Leon's nachos back in Central City, and now, Rad can't keep his grubby fingers to himself.

"There's more in the kitchen," Kieran says, slapping Rad on the back of the head with a grunt. "Hands off her food."

"My savior," I murmur, locking my gaze with Kieran's mismatched eyes, loving the heat simmering there.

"Dude!" Rad yelps, jumping to his feet. "Hitting is not nice." He points a finger at each of them, giving them the stink eye before grabbing his own plate of food. The couch dips beside me again as he settles there, shoving food in his mouth.

"Neither is stealing your pregnant wife's food," Asher quips, handing me a napkin with care.

"Facts," I hum, tuning out their fight.

There will never be a time when these guys don't argue. Well, in the bedroom, they're pretty in sync. Especially when I'm the center of attention and horny; I've been that much lately and can't contain myself.

I eye Kieran and sink my teeth into my bottom lip when he catches me.

"Not happening," he quips with a crooked grin. "You're about to pop." Well, he does have a point there. I'm due in one week, but I'm not sure I'll last that long. Not with this one, at least. Ly was two weeks late and made me miserable. This one will definitely make an appearance sooner rather than later.

"Isn't that the best way to promote labor?" Callum asks with heated eyes.

"Hey! I read about that!" Rad grins. "Lyric is with your brothers for the weekend." His hands rub together as his wicked mind comes up with a plan. "I'll grab the handcuffs, lube, and whipped cream."

Mmm. Whipped cream. I lick my lips, making a dirty plan of my own.

"You have that look," Asher comments, taking a bite of his dinner with his brows raised.

"What look, Daddy?" I grin when he chokes.

"For fuck's sake," he grumbles through a cough, chugging his water. "What did I tell you about that fucking word." That he likes it too much, and it gives him an instant boner.

"Don't call me fucking daddy unless I'm balls deep inside you," he growls, gripping my throat against the bathroom wall.

Water drips from our bodies after a quick romp under the hot steam of the shower. Even after getting me all to himself and getting off, he's still hard.

"Why is that?" I ask innocently, batting my eyelashes until his fingers grip me tighter, sending a thrill through me.

He leans his forehead against mine. "Because it does things to me." Bad, bad things he doesn't want to say.

"Whatever you say, Daddy," I quip again, earning a warning glare.

"Warm up the fucking handcuffs. She deserves to be tied to our fucking bed," Asher growls through clenched teeth as he adjusts himself in his jeans.

Yup. There's that instant boner I was talking about. I swear I'd be horny if it weren't for the slight contraction currently trying to rip my insides out, but it passes quickly. Like the rest have today. No biggie. I'll ignore that for now. If I admit I might be a teensy-weensy bit in labor, they'll take my food away from me. And that's a no from me, dog.

"Add in a few spankings for antagonizing you," Kieran quips, shoving the rest of his dinner in his mouth.

I shrug. I don't mind.

"We'll have to be careful," Callum says, eyeing me with worry.

"You can take it, can't you, Little Brat?" Asher says with a smirk, discarding his plate on the end table beside him.

Yes. Yes, I can. I can take anything they have to dish out. The rougher, the better. I open my mouth to agree. Because yeah, I can take their punishments like a champ. Not that they're really punishments. Oh, nooooo, they're tying me up and using me like a fuck doll! What a damn shame. Insert sarcasm.

My stomach cramps. Harder than before, shooting pain straight through my abdomen and stealing my breaths. Damn it, that one really put me in my damn place for the first time today, stopping all my movements. I blow out a breath, running a hand along my hardening stomach, counting the seconds it lasts.

Okay, this one is a lot stronger than the ones before this. Shit. A lot stronger. Like—full-blown labor—intense.

Something on my face must give away my feelings because the room stops. The air thickens with their worry, nearly suffocating me.

"Little Star?" Callum whispers, grabbing the hand on my stomach and replacing it with his. His entire body stiffens. His eyes roam over my tightened expression. "It's happening, isn't it?" he murmurs.

I roll my lips together. Bastard. He's always been too perceptive for his own good. I'm almost sure I have at least twelve more hours before this bundle of joy shoots out of my vagina.

Or not.

That's why I haven't let them know I've been having contractions since I woke up. They were small and nothing to worry about. I even made it through a workday, dropped Ly off with her cousin, visited my brothers for a minute or two, and came home to eat.

Now, I'm not so sure.

"Wait? What's happening?" Rad asks with narrowed eyes.

I breathe, reaching for Rad's hand and holding tight, squeezing with all my might. I swear his bones crackle under the pressure, and he winces but doesn't say another word. The contraction completely wrecks me. Stealing my breath and curling my toes. Until it tapers off into nothing, I fall limp into Callum's side.

"I really don't remember it being this bad."

Well, maybe that's a lie. Having Lyric was hell on earth. The magic of birth was a lie, and then, she was in my arms after two weeks of being late. I forgot about all the pain and suffering I endured to bring her into the world. It was the look on her little face when she was placed into my arms.

Until now. Now, I remember the pain it took to get her out of me.

"Does this mean it's time, Pretty Girl?" Rad leans over, excitement displayed on his face. "Is my baby having a baby? Alert the presses! Grab the bags! Load the fucking car! We're having a damn baby!" Rad shouts, jumping to his feet and pulling at his hair. "What do we do first? Holy shit, why aren't you guys moving?" he shouts, turning in circles and staring at everyone.

Kieran snorts, taking another bite of his food. "How long have the contractions been happening, River Blue?"

Well, hell. He sends me a scathing look like he's peeled back my flesh and knows everything.

"Seriously, Little Brat?" Asher grunts, shaking his head.

"Look at her face." Kieran clicks his tongue, getting to his feet unhurriedly.

Remind me why I got into a relationship with four men. Oh, right. The amazing dick downs. But now isn't the time to think about that.

"Know it all," I grunt, shoving another bite of food in my mouth. If I'm full of food, then their bossy asses can't demand shit out of me.

"Answer the question," Asher demands with a mean ass look. I swear to God, one day, he's going to choke me so hard I pass out. On second thought….

I chew slowly despite four sets of eyes staring daggers into me. "Lyric took hours despite being two weeks late. I swear it was two days of labor."

Maybe that's an exaggeration, but it felt like forever. And I did it mostly on my own. Ode was there by my side through the entire thing. My brothers, too. Hell, Booker even closed Dead End so he could be by the phone to hear the news of Lyric's arrival. I offered to fly him out with Odette and Korrin, but he refused—always such a hard worker and a worry wart, too. So, I wasn't alone when Lyric was born. I had my support system. It just wasn't the support system I was craving. And that's not to say I wasn't grateful for everyone else being there.

But the heart wants what the heart wants, despite the circumstances and betrayals.

"So, all day, huh?" Kieran clicks his tongue at me again and sighs. "All right, boys. Looks like we need to get a fucking move on." he stands, collecting plates—including mine.

"I wasn't done, assface!" I protest, watching as my plate disappears into the kitchen and is placed in the sink. Fuck me. I knew this would happen. The moment these contractions got terrible, I knew they'd steal my precious food away from me. "This will take forever. I need the food as fuel," I whine, puffing out my bottom lip.

"Quite whining," Asher grumbles, getting to his feet. "You're about to push out a human being. The books say you shouldn't eat."

"The books are a fucking lie," I hiss, squeezing my eyes shut.

Yup. More fucking pain. Maybe my plan to hide this until it became real was a bad idea.

"You timing this shit?" Kieran's voice filters through the pain, and I feel him kneel before more. His gentle fingers work up my thighs, working over my muscles until the pain ceases. "You're doing good, River Blue," he whispers, pulling me into him. "Your stomach is like a damn rock."

"Contraction," I breathe out.

"I got it!" Rad wheezes, throwing my packed hospital bags into the middle of the living room before turning around and sprinting up the set of stairs toward the bedrooms. "Getting it all!"

"I texted your brothers. They're keeping Ly for as long as we need." Asher looms above me with furrowed brows, eyeing every twinge of pain. "You're going to be okay, Little Brat," he whispers, leaning over to kiss my hair.

"Okay!" Rad wheezes, entirely out of breath. "Let's go have a baby!"

"She's gorgeous," Rad breathes, peering down at our dark-haired beauty. "And so mine. You can't deny this hair. It comes from the best." He grins, flicking the mullet he refuses to shave off or grow out. It's still as perfect as it was years before. Never changing. Not that I'd want him to change. My Rad can stay the same for eternity, and I'll always love him.

He's right, though. Looking down at her, she's got the same swoops of curls and dark hair. I'm not saying that won't change as she becomes older because it will. I mean, Lyric came out with those beautiful, mismatched eyes and lighter brown hair.

"There were three more participants," Callum grumbles again, running a finger along her chubby cheeks. "Besides, she looks just like River."

His hazy eyes find mine as I lie in the hospital bed, completely worn out. A nap sounds nice right now. The months ahead will be chaotic at best, as I will balance a newborn, Lyric, and all my other responsibilities. It has my head spinning. But I have to remind myself that I'm not alone in caring for her this time. I have her fathers here with me to take on the mental, physical, and emotional tolls it's going to bring.

I'll be okay. We'll be okay.

Kieran snorts from beside me, gently stroking my hair. "He has a point," Kieran snarks, earning the middle finger from Rad.

"My turn," Ash says, holding out his hands. He grins when Rad, ever the stingy father, hands the baby over with a grumble of protest.

A look of awe takes over Ash's features. Tears fill his eyes, eventually running down his cheeks.

Since we've grown up and forgiven each other for the past, we've settled into an almost perfect relationship. Of course, having five people as a unit can get messy. It does, believe me. But we've worked through it, and they've become the best they can be.

"You did so good, Little Brat. She's gorgeous," Ash sniffles, carefully walking toward me with our bundle in his arms. She coos against him, attempting to root around with a few grunts, aching for her first taste of milk.

"I…I'm sorry we missed this with Lyric," Kieran softly says. Shame coats his expression as he watches Ash and our baby, who doesn't have a name yet. "We missed all the firsts, River Blue. Her birth. Birthday. First steps." He chokes up a little, bringing his fist to his lips.

This isn't the first time Kieran has apologized with tears in his eyes about all the things they missed with Lyric. They're making up for it now, though.

"But you were here for this one," I say, gently squeezing his hand. "And you're here now. That's all that matters. Ly loves you guys so much."

"It doesn't feel like enough," he mumbles. "If we had known…if…"

"There's a lot of ifs in there, Rock Star. You didn't know because your mom was a cunt and a half. Everything that happened was her fault."

I'm so glad that dirty, lying bitch is rotting away in prison for all the money she stole from Kieran. Oh, and so much more. Who would have guessed that Gloria was such a thief? I did. But that's beside the point.

"You know that's not true," Asher sniffles, resting on my other side. Gently, he kisses our baby's dark head of hair. "It was me, too." My heart hurts at the guilt clouding his features. He'll forever feel terrible for what he did when he was a desperate kid trying to get away from the abuse of his father.

I know how sorry he is because he's shown me time and time again what I mean to him.

"We've been through this," I say, shaking my weary head.

"Yeah, well, some people don't think we did everything good enough," Rad scoffs. "Can you believe that? We got on our knees for you. We stepped up. Said we were sorry. We showed you through our actions how much you mean to us. And some people, not naming names." Rocco. He means Rocco thinks they didn't grovel enough. "Still, I thought we made it up to you so well. I mean…" He wiggles his brows, earning himself a slap from Callum. "Rude," he mutters.

"The past is in the past, right? We know we're in a good place. You guys more than made it up to me."

"We love you, Little Star," Callum murmurs. "You're the light to our darkness. And you've given us one of the best gifts around."

"I did," Rad quips with a goofy grin, pointing to himself. "I gave you that gift."

"You do realize once we've DNA tested, and it proves you're the father. When we go to do this all over again, you're kicked to condoms and back door only." Kieran raises a brow when Rad's face falls, and his lips pop open.

"That's not fair!" he hisses, shaking his head.

Kieran rolls his eyes. "Play by the rules. I had to."

Rad pouts, crossing his arms over his chest. "Fine! We'll be the condom, backdoor bros from here on out." He rolls his eyes, muttering about how unfair it is under his breath, and then sighs, "Well, maybe we should pick a name."

"Here," Ash says, gently handing me the baby as she begins to cry softly. "I think she's hungry."

Kieran helps me sit up and covers me as I bring my breast out, and she latches on without a fight, perfectly sucking the first streams of milk from me.

"Okay. Did you bring our list of names?" I ask, cradling her head.

Rad nibbles his bottom lip. "I had one come to me that wasn't on the list."

"What is it?" I ask, watching as he nervously twitches, which is beyond his usual. Rad is the most confident guy I know. He's never afraid to spill what's on his mind.

"Lyrics come from the heart, but melodies are all around us. Like air. Like Aria. It means melody and tune." He swallows hard, stepping forward. "I want to name her Aria West. If everyone agrees?"

"Aria," I murmur, running a finger through her dark curls.

I picture her life in the future, full of dark curly hair and big brown eyes. A mini Rad, running around and getting into trouble. Her name being yelled through the large backyard because she's out after the sun has gone down. Her digging through the mud in her clean dress. Her with a mischievous smile on her face after doing something naughty. And it fits. Every fucking piece of it seems to suit her perfectly. Aria West.

"I...I love it," I whisper, unable to hold back the tears in my eyes. Damn you after birth hormones for making me cry at the drop of a hat.

"It's a good name, dude," Cal says, slapping Rad on the back.

"I like it," Kieran and Asher agree with a nod.

"Then it's settled," I say, lifting my gaze from Aria. "Her name is Aria Jenny West." I smile when Cal sucks in a breath, squeezing his eyes shut.

It's a middle name we've talked about for months now. It was a way for him to honor the sister he held while she passed away¾the girl who was robbed of her life by a simple plane malfunction, leaving Cal with no one but his friends for support.

Kieran takes out his phone in a hurry, tapping away at it. A smile crosses his lips when he looks up at me. "Ly's here." Placing his phone in his pocket, he stands from his chair and stretches slightly. "She's going to be a pistol today," he chuckles. Well, he's not wrong there. "I'll be right back. Your brothers are in the parking lot with her. They said they'd visit today, but they have the boys now. Said something about wanting to give us some alone time." He walks out the door and disappears down the hallway.

"She's going to be so excited to meet her finally." Ash smirks.

That's a fact. Ly has been counting down the days until her little sister emerged. Every day, she'd mark it off on the calendar, telling me how excited she was to be a big sister finally. It's like she was made for this role.

Not even five minutes after he left, a squeal happens in the hallway outside the door before it crashes open, and Hurricane Lyric slips through with messy hair and a wide grin.

"Is my baby finally here?" Lyric asks, running into the room with Kieran on her tail. He grins, lifting her into his arms and holding her above the scene. "Mommy," she says, wrinkling her nose. "Why is the baby on your boobie?" I have to let her stop watching TV. She recites whatever she finds. Not to mention the terrible, scary movies Rad seems to love to turn on in her presence.

"We talked about this, Little Pretty Girl. That's where the milk comes from. Remember?" Rad says, hiding his smile behind his hand.

"I knows that," Lyric huffs, looking down at Aria with a grin. Her mismatched eyes light up. "I've got my shirt on, too." She puffs out her chest, displaying a "Finally a Big Sister" shirt Odette made for her just for this occasion.

"It's beautiful," Kieran says, wrangling her in his lap as he sits again. "Now, remember. We have to be extra careful with Aria."

"Aria?" she questions, trying the name for the first time. We decided to keep her name a secret. Or, well—we weren't exactly sure what to name her. "It's pretty. Just like hers. Can I hold her?" She bats her Kieran eyes at me, grinning when I chuckle. "I wants to hold my baby."

I smile. Her baby. That's what she's been calling the little bean named Aria for months now. Since the moment we told her she would be a big sister. I'm sure she won't be so accommodating in a few years when Aria is chewing on her dolls or drooling all over her toys. But for now, Lyric lights up, watching everyone with wide eyes.

"Why don't you sit on the couch over there? Daddy will help you hold her."

Lyric doesn't waste a second, squealing with delight as she scrambles away from Kieran. With hurried feet, she makes it to the couch and plops down. Her arms spread wide, signaling for them to bring Aria to her. Kieran chuckles at her eagerness.

"All right, you think she's ready?" he asks, peering down at Aria, who no longer suckles any milk out. Her lips stopped moving a few minutes ago, and her breaths evened out. She's only been on the outside for a few hours and needs a nap, probably from all the chaos happening around her.

"I think so. You want to burp her before you hand her off?" Asher grins, picking up a burp rag from the small bassinet, nods, and puts it on his shoulder. He gently takes Aria from me and places her over his shoulder as I recover my chest. His hand works softly against her back, patting her until a small burp erupts from her tiny body.

"Daddy, what are you doing?" Lyric asks with impatience, pouting slightly.

"When babies drink, they need help to burp," Callum gently explains, sitting beside Lyric with a soft smile. His fingers move the hairs from her face. "So, Daddy is gently patting Aria's back and helping her get rid of the gas."

"She'll puke on you if he doesn't," Rad chimes in, coming to sit beside my bed.

"Ew," Lyric recoils. "Puke?"

I give her a sleepy grin. "Babies are so much fun, Ly. Your sister is so blessed to have you. But they're so messy." Messy is an understatement; I don't think any of the guys are prepared for it. Poop. Spit up. Peeing while a diaper is off. They're in for a world of hurt when Aria becomes a toddler and refuses to wear a diaper.

Oh, the joys of parenthood.

Asher finally gets another small burp from Aria and then gently hands her to Lyric. "Okay, put your arms like this. And put her head here," he says in a patient voice, moving Lyric so she's properly holding Aria's head. "That's my girl."

"Girls!" Lyric says with a grin, staring down at Aria with heart eyes.

"She's right. They're our girls now," Kieran says, gently squeezing my hand from the other side.

"Knock, knock!" Rocco's voice echoes through the door before he's barreling through it with a grin on his face, peeking through his fingers covering his eyes. "Oh, good. You're decent. I was hoping none of your girly bits were out." His expression softens when he removes his fingers, staring down at my ragged appearance. He's seen worse. "There she is. My tired bestie and her gang."

"Gang?" Rad snorts. "You know, Pretty Boy. Sometimes I wonder about you."

I roll my eyes, too tired for their antics. "Hello to you, too!" I say, waving as his husband Christian and their girl Kat follow him in.

Kat offers me a timid smile, holding a bouquet of beautiful pink flowers. "We got you these," she says softly, placing the vase on my bedside table. "Congratulations," she murmurs so softly I can barely hear her.

Even after her trauma of being with Van, she's still a timid girl. But Rocco blasted his way into her life, taking his husband Christian with him. They've been living as a throuple for a while now. Slowly but surely, I'm seeing the remnants of the Kat that Van left behind when he decimated her trust and put her through Hell. Through West Records, she got an assistant job back with my brothers. They've been easing her back into work. Of course, Rocco told her to stay home. Stay naked. And never leave their apartment. But that's a whole different story I don't even want to think about.

Christian looks around the room with worried eyes, glaring at every surface. He keeps his hands in his pockets and only then offers me a small smile. "I made you some chicken noodle soup whenever you're home."

"Don't let him be so modest, Doll. He made you an entire month's worth of dinner. All your favorites, too." Rocco beams at his husband, who blushes at his words.

"Thank you," I say with a soft smile. "I really appreciate it." And I do. Christian is a chef and lord; I couldn't live without the treats he makes me.

"You made those nachos, right?" Rad perks up, staring at Christian with a hopeful look. "Come on, Chrissy! Tell me..."

"Yes," he clears his throat. "I made you the nachos." His brows furrow with the shyness he always displays, and then he says what I expect him to say. "Please, don't call me Chrissy. We've discussed this." He tries to send Rad a scathing look, but it really doesn't do anything.

Christian is the kindest person you'll ever meet. How he hooked up with Rocco, I'll never know. As Rocco says, he went into Christian's restaurant for dinner and came out with an obsession. It was rocky initially, but they've come forward in their relationship.

Come to think of it, Rocco has always had obsessions. Christian. Kat. Damn, he goes after what he wants, doesn't he?

Rad grins. "Thanks, bro. I'm going to need those nachos to fuel me for what's to come."

Christian blushes again, nodding. "Of course." His dark brown eyes find mine, and he smiles more. "Anything for you guys."

"So, where's my baby?" Rocco asks, looking around the room with a grin.

"Right here!" Lyric says softly. "But shh, Uncle Rocco! She's sleeping." She levels Rocco with a warning stare, making him snicker at her attitude.

She's a very protective girl.

"Well, aren't you doing an amazing job, squirt," Rocco says, standing beside Asher, who offers him the seat next to Lyric. He peers down at them with tears in his eyes.

"She's gorgeous, Doll," he says, his voice cracking with emotions. "You make some pretty babies."

I snort. "I sure do."

"She's mine!" Rad adds on with ownership, leaning back in his chair.

Asher sighs with exhaustion, shaking his head. "Biologically, maybe," he mutters with exhaustion.

"Why don't you go home and get some rest?" I say to him, reaching out and catching his hand in mine.

"Because it's not home without you," he murmurs, leaning down to kiss my hand. "I can't leave you girls here."

Insert swoon. I swear my heart restarts at the sound of his words. Despite our past and everything we've been through with each other, I'll never stop loving each of them. They've given me everything I've been desperate for.

A family.